IN PLAIN SIGHT

ARCANE CASEBOOK 1

DAN WILLIS

Digital Edition – 2018

This novel is a work of fiction. Names, characters, places and incidents are either the product of the author's imagination, or, if real, used fictitiously.

Edited by Stephanie Osborn

Cover by Mihaela Voicu

Published by

Dan Willis
Spanish Fork, Utah.

1

THE JOB

The sign on the frosted glass panel read *Lockerby Investigations* in gold painted letters. The image of a hexagon with an inverted triangle inside it and an inkwell inside that occupied the bottom right corner of the glass, indicating that runewright services were also offered within. Alexander Lockerby turned the handle smartly and walked in. His office occupied a two-room space on the fourth floor of a modest building in Manhattan's mid-ring. Close enough to Empire Tower to have uninterrupted power, but far enough away to keep the rent low. He'd moved into these offices in the spring of 1931 and now, two years later, it felt like home. It wasn't much, but it was his.

Beyond the door with its frosted glass panel was his waiting room, with two sofas, a row of filing cabinets, and a second door marked *Private*. A large window dominated the back wall, illuminating a paper-strewn desk. Atop the desk, long legs crossed and the receiver of a telephone pressed to her ear, was Leslie Tompkins, Alex's secretary.

Leslie was in her early forties but you'd never guess it to look at her. She had long, toned legs, a slim waist, generous bust, and strawberry blonde hair that hung about her shoulders in loose rings. She'd moved to New York from Iowa where she'd been a beauty queen, married a successful salesman, then lost him in the Great War. After that, Leslie's life became a series of jobs that she never held for more than a year. Everywhere she worked, they treated her like an ornament or a wanton. No one could look past her beautiful exterior to see the mind inside.

No one but Alex.

She'd come to work for him two years ago and had absolutely revolutionized his business. People just liked her, and that translated into work. Better still, Leslie was sharp. With a little training, she became a better interrogator than Alex, able to worm information out of virtually anyone over a simple cup of coffee.

"Okay, Dan," she said into the mouthpiece. "I'll send him over as soon as he gets in." She replaced the receiver in the cradle and returned the phone to her desk.

Alex shut the door and Leslie looked up, flashing a million-dollar smile framed by deep red lipstick. She hopped off the desk and stood as Alex approached. Leslie always stood perfectly straight, a result of the beauty queen training, no doubt. With her shoulders back and a pair of high heels, Leslie turned heads wherever she went, and with the top two buttons of her blouse undone, she could make it hard to keep eye contact...if she wanted.

"Detective Pak wants you to look at a body," she said, tearing a paper containing a mid-ring address from a notepad.

Daniel Pak was a detective with the New York Central office of the city Police. Danny and Alex had been friends ever since Alex helped him crack the case that made him a detective. Now Danny brought Alex in as a consultant whenever he could get away with it.

"Well," Alex said, looking at the address. "If Danny wants me to have a look, it must be particularly gruesome. I'll get my kit."

Leslie made a face but didn't move out of his way. "And how did the other case go?" she asked. Her tone clearly indicated that she expected Alex to have a specific answer and that she wouldn't be happy if he didn't.

"You mean the case of the missing wedding ring?" he asked, a disgusted look crawling across his own face. Leslie's face grew cross.

"It's work," she said. "And if we don't get more of it real soon, you're going to have to limit our eating to once a day."

Alex raised an eyebrow.

"It's not that bad, is it?"

"That depends," Leslie said. "Did your Finding Rune work?"

"Nope," Alex admitted. He sat on the desk corner where Leslie had been before and dropped his hat onto the desk. Leslie squeezed her eyes shut and put a hand on her forehead.

"How is that even possible?" she asked, cool anger in her voice. "'Your Finding Rune is better than anyone else's in the city." Her hazel eyes flashed as she locked them on his. "There's nothing lost you can't find with that rune! Hell, if you put your mind to it, you could probably find my virginity."

She took a breath to go on, but Alex put up a hand to silence her.

"The rune didn't work because I didn't have to cast it," he said. Leslie's hand went back to her forehead and she grimaced as if in physical pain.

"What happened?" she said with a sigh.

"When I got there, Mrs. Lola Davis showed me a picture of the missing ring," Alex explained. "Just as I was getting ready to make with the magic, her husband Burt shows up, and he's not happy to see me."

Leslie shook her head.

"Don't tell me," she said. "He lost it in a poker game."

That was why Alex worked so well with Leslie; nothing got by her. If she had any magical talent, Alex figured he'd be working for her, sooner or later. Deep down, he wondered if he wasn't already.

"Close," he said. "When I shook his hand he winced, so I slapped him on the back. You know, friendly like."

"And?" Leslie said, clearly impatient for this story to be over.

"And he damn near passed out. Somebody worked him over good. A pro who knew not to leave bruises on his face or arms."

"What did his wife think happened?"

"He told her he fell down the stairs," Alex said, shrugging. "She bought it, too."

"It was awful nice of those stairs not to mess up his face," Leslie pointed out.

"Give the girl a break," Alex said, offering Leslie a cigarette. "Anyway, I had the story out of Burt in two seconds. He'd been running a tab with his bookie."

"Slow ponies?" Leslie said, taking the cigarette between her ruby lips and lighting it with the touch-tip on the desk.

"Worse. He's a Washington Senators fan."

Leslie dropped the metal match back in the lighter and smirked.

"Ouch," she said. She'd put the match away before Alex could light his own cigarette, so he leaned close and pressed the tip of his cigarette to Leslie's. Her perfume washed over him, lavender and amber oil. He was suddenly very aware of her, and he pulled away. It would have been easy to fall for her, despite her being almost ten years his senior, and that would be bad for business.

"Anyway, Burt hocked the ring to pay off the bookie," Alex finished the story.

"How did the wife take it?" Leslie asked. "More importantly, did you get paid?"

"Wife took it bad," Alex said. "It was her grandmother's ring."

"That bastard." Leslie looked shocked.

"Anyway, he'd cleaned them out, even the cash she had stashed away."

Leslie groaned and put her head in her hand again.

"So no money?" She looked up sharply when Alex crinkled two crisp bills, a twenty and a five, under her nose. "How?" she gasped, snatching the money and holding it up to the light.

"Lola didn't want to stay with her husband anymore, so I took her over to her mother's place. She lives in the inner-ring, right up against the core."

"Ooh," Leslie purred. "Fancy."

"Apparently mother dear had been trying to convince Lola that Burt was a bum for years. She was overjoyed to have her back. Paid my fee and the cab fare."

Leslie smiled and nodded at Alex.

"You did good, kid," she said. "I'm so happy that I'm not even going to ask you where you got the cigarettes."

"Oh, those were Burt's," Alex said with a grin. She took a puff, then held out the cigarette at arm's length.

"Thanks, Burt," she said with mock sincerity. "Now, let's take care of this." Circling the desk, she opened the bottom drawer and pulled out a heavy steel box, dropping it on the table with a clank. The top of the box was plain, with the exception of an engraving depicting an elaborate geometric shape.

"It's me," she said, leaning close to the lid. "Open up."

The rune on the lid glowed with a purple light and an audible click sounded from inside. Alex watched as the rune's light faded. The edges of the engraving were already getting fuzzy and indistinct. Runes were a temporary form of magic, after all. Most disappeared immediately after being used. A talented runewright could make them last longer by using more expensive materials when making the rune, and even engraving it into something. Eventually, though, the rune would lose its magic and disappear, needing to be rewritten by the runewright.

This was what made runewrights the poor cousins of magic. Sorcerers could cast real spells, laying powerful and near-permanent enchantments on whatever they chose. They were rare, of course. Only big cities would have a sorcerer, and most were required by law to serve their governments. America, however, gave sorcerers the same rights as anyone else, so there were more sorcerers in the US than anywhere else. New York had six, each soaring high above the city in their flying castles. If Alex had been born a sorcerer instead of a runewright, he'd never have wanted for cash.

The other branch of magic was alchemy. Alchemists brewed their magic slowly into potions and elixirs. Sorcerers and runewrights mostly dealt with enchantments, making objects magical. Alchemists dealt with people, with their bodies and health. A good alchemist always had work, customers with ready money who needed remedies for everything from gout to baldness. Like runewrights, alchemists kept their recipes secret, passing them from master to apprentice. That meant that some alchemists were quacks and frauds, possessing only a few weak recipes, while others could brew miracle cures in a bottle.

This was the same reason Alex's Finding Rune was so much better than anyone else's. His book of runes had come to him from his father and his grandfather and his great-grandfather. When his father died, Alex's training had been picked up by a British Doctor, Ignatius Bell. Between his family book and the doctor's training, Alex knew some very good runes.

The lid of the strongbox popped open and Leslie inserted the bills in a small stack of cash, in proper numerical order of course. She counted them twice, then made a note of the amount on a pad in the bottom of the box.

"That's rent and my salary for this month," she said with a satisfied grin.

"Wait. What about me?" Alex protested with only the trace of a grin. Leslie picked up the paper that Alex had set aside on her desk and handed it back to him.

"You have a date with the Police and a dead guy. Do a good job and maybe you can buy your own cigarettes."

Alex took the paper and sighed. The police didn't like consultants, and they especially didn't like paying them. They almost never allowed him to cast an expensive rune and he had to give them a hefty discount on his hourly rate if he wanted to work with them at all. Leslie scowled at him when he looked up from the paper, daring him to complain, so he put on a smile.

"It's better than looking for lost wedding rings, I suppose," he said. He turned toward his office, but Leslie put her hand on his shoulder in a firm grip.

"Don't worry, kid," she said, her hard shell melting away into one of her rare, genuine smiles. "We'll catch a break one of these days."

"I know," Alex said, and sighed. "One big case would do it. Get my name in the papers and then real clients would start piling up."

"So many that we'll have to start turning them away," Leslie agreed, her smile somehow managing to show more teeth. Then her face became serious. "It'll happen," she said. "I believe in you."

"Thanks, doll." Alex smiled back at her. "And thanks for keeping this place in the black. Even if it is with lost dog jobs."

Her face slid back into the sardonic smile he knew so well. The mask that hid the real her from the world. "Work is work," she said.

"Work is work," he agreed.

Alex made his way to his office while Leslie returned the strong box to its drawer.

THE INNER OFFICE was just a smaller version of the outer. Alex's desk sat across from the door, facing it, with a large window behind. A row of filing cabinets stood against the right wall, leaving the opposite wall bare, and two overstuffed chairs sat facing the desk. The chalk outline of a door, complete with a keyhole, adorned the blank wall, exactly in the center.

Alex pulled a pasteboard notebook with a red cover from his jacket pocket and began flipping through the pages. The paper was thin and fine, like tissue paper, so he had to be careful. Each page had a rune carefully inscribed on it. Some were simple, only a few lines drawn in pencil. Other were intricate, delicate even, their lines glistening in inks infused with gold, silver, or powdered gemstones. Some had taken Alex a few minutes, while others took days of careful work. All had been infused with magic, waiting patiently for him to release it.

He found the rune he wanted, a triangle with a circle on each point, drawn in silver ink, and tore it from the book. Alex unceremoniously licked the back of the paper and stuck it on the wall in the middle of the chalk door. He touched the paper with the glowing tip of his cigarette and it erupted in flame, vanishing almost instantly. The rune hung in the air, gleaming silver now that the paper was gone, then vanished as well, melting into the wall. As soon as it was gone, a door of polished metal appeared where the chalk outline had been. No hinges were visible, just a brass plate with a keyhole in its exact center.

Alex produced an ornate steel skeleton key from a ring that also held his apartment key and the one to his office. Sliding it in the keyhole, he turned it smartly and pushed the door open. There wasn't anything particularly special beyond Alex's wall, just the neighboring office. But beyond the *door* was a good-sized room with workbenches, cabinets, shelves, and all manner of glassware and equipment. This was Alex's vault, an extra-dimensional workspace he could summon whenever and wherever he needed it. The rune to make a vault wasn't that complex but a runewright could only have one vault at a time. If he made a new one, the old one and all its contents would vanish. Such was the nature of magic.

Alex flipped a switch on the wall and magelights throughout the space warmed up to a bright light.

Leaving the door open, Alex crossed to a large secretary cabinet. He could shut and bar the vault door if he wanted, but if it were locked from the outside, he'd be trapped in the vault forever. Only the runewright who created a vault could open it from the outside.

He pulled the secretary cabinet's foldaway table down, then opened the upper doors. Inside were a row of three leather bags resembling a doctor's valise, and rows and rows of stoppered bottles above them, containing every imaginable substance. Below the bags were pigeon-holes filled with stacks of varying papers, and drawers that held pens and pencils. These were the tools of his trade.

Without a pause, Alex pulled down a battered, brown valise. The top opened down the middle and had a hinge so it would fold out ninety degrees. Under one side, his oculus and breathing mask were held in place by elastic straps. The other side held smaller versions of the stoppered bottles, just not so many. In the bottom of the case were his multi-lamp, pencil box, a tube with a selection of papers, a few other odds and ends, and a Colt 1911 semi-automatic pistol in a shoulder holster. He stripped off his jacket and slung the holster in place, settling the weight of the gun just under his left arm, and checked the magazine.

Full.

He put on his jacket again, making sure it hung so that the bulge underneath his left arm could not be seen, then picked up the bag and exited the vault.

"See ya," he said to Leslie as he put on his hat and headed for the door.

"Try to talk them into letting you use an expensive rune or two," she called after him. "I need a new pair of stockings."

Alex rode the elevator down to the street. A steady rain fell and it seemed dark, even though it was only early afternoon. The glow of neon signs in storefronts cast halos of color through the downpour.

Tearing another page from his rune book, Alex stuck it to the brim of his hat, then lit it with his cigarette. A tingly sensation washed over him from his head to his feet and then he stepped out into the rain. The drops bent and danced as they reached him, moved aside by the magic. The barrier rune would only last an hour, but that was more than enough time for him to catch a cab to the south side mid-ring.

The rings provided power to the entire island of Manhattan, from the south side docks all the way up to the Bronx. The rings were physically centered on Empire Tower, the former Empire State Building. These days Empire Tower held a magical capacitor, created by Andrew Barton, one of New York's resident sorcerers. Once charged, the Tower radiated power over the entire island. Since the Tower was so far south on the island, the field wasn't round, but oval, putting the actual center of the power projection somewhere over Central Park. The farther you were away from the center, the worse your power reception got. This inspired the wealthier of New York's citizens to build luxury buildings all around the Tower in an area known as the Core. Those closest to the Core were in the inner-ring, the high rent district. Mid-ring were businesses and middle-class folk, and everyone else was in the outer-ring.

The south side was actually pretty close to Empire Tower as the crow flew, but since the center was shifted north, the bands were thinner at that end. Most of the harbor and its environs were decidedly outer-ring, but just a few blocks away were nicer, mid-ring apartments.

Alex exited his cab thirty-five minutes later and made his way toward the cluster of police cars parked in front of a neat, three-story brick building. He got a few curious glances when people on the street realized the rain was avoiding him, but he was used to that.

"What do you want?" the officer at the door said in his best "go away" voice. He had a pug nose, close-set eyes and a scar on his cheek that made him look all business. Definitely the right man to put on the door.

"I'm Alex Lockerby," Alex said, handing the officer a business card. "Detective Pak is expecting me."

A surge of emotions warred across the cop's face. He'd seen that Alex was a private investigator from his card, and Pak was the only Japanese on the force. Most Americans didn't think much of Asians, but Pak had proved himself a good detective, and that made him family to the NYPD. Finally the cop decided that his dislike of private dicks and foreigners was less than his respect for his job and fellow officers.

"Third floor on the right," he said, handing back the card. "Room 323."

When Alex reached the room, he knew immediately why Pak had called him. The charred remains of a man lay in a recliner. The easy chair was blackened and burned, revealing the wire frame that supported it, but the walls and floor were fine, apart from some smoke damage. A round side table stood next to the chair containing a pulp novel, an empty shot glass, a pack of cigarettes, and a book of matches.

"Alex," Detective Pak said, noticing his arrival. Danny was about five-foot-ten, three inches shorter than Alex himself, and wore a brown suit with suede patches on the elbows and a gold shield attached to the breast pocket of his suit coat. He had brownish skin, short hair the color of midnight, and dark, almond shaped eyes. An infectious grin spread across his face as he shook Alex's hand. "I'm glad you're here," he said.

"Good to see you too," Alex said, returning the handshake. "I was wondering why you called me," he said, nodding at the charred corpse.

"I know it looks like an open and shut case," Pak said, "but something's wrong."

"I'll say. Whoever this guy was, he was murdered."

2

THE STIFF

Detective Pak opened his mouth and closed it again. "What?" he finally managed. "I just wanted to know why the fire went out?"

"I'd have to look around a bit before I could tell you that." Alex shrugged.

"But you just got here... and you know he was murdered?"

"Of course he does," a new voice interjected. Alex turned to face the sneering face of Lieutenant Francis Callahan. "Lockerby here is always looking to pad out his bill with wild theories and guesswork, that means he'll have to break out his expensive magic."

Callahan was everything an Academy recruitment poster could have wanted — tall, square-jawed, with wavy brown hair, blue eyes, and perfect teeth. Worse than that, he'd made Lieutenant the hard way, by being good at his job. Every cop on the force liked and respected Frank Callahan — and Frank thought Alex was a waste of skin.

"Shouldn't you be out finding someone's dog?" Callahan asked.

Alex felt his face begin to flush and quickly willed that away. Callahan could get under his skin, but only if he let him.

"Of course any client that comes to you has probably lost their marbles," Callahan went on. "So you should probably find those first."

"I don't think you've lost your marbles, Lieutenant," Alex said, smiling warmly. "But since you did hire me, I'll be happy to look for your dog. Assuming he's missing."

A chuckle ran around the room and Danny covered his mouth with his note pad. Callahan's face reddened, but he regained control quickly.

"That wasn't my idea," he said. "You can thank your friend here for that." He thumped Pak on the chest. "But since you are here, what makes you think this is murder, and not another poor shlub who fell asleep while he was smoking?"

Alex turned and pointed to the round table next to the ruins of the chair.

"What's missing?" he asked.

"Decent booze," Callahan said.

"Good literature?" Danny wondered.

"Ashtray," Alex supplied. "There's no ashtray here, and there isn't one in the kitchen either. Not on the table or by the sink."

"So it was in his lap when he burned," Callahan said. "The coroner will find it — eventually."

"How many ashtrays do you have in your house, Lieutenant?"

Callahan nodded, understanding blooming in his eyes.

"Right," he said, then he turned to one of the uniform officers in the room. "Check the bathroom and the bedroom," he said. "Let me know if you find any ashtrays." He turned back to Alex. "Anything else?"

Alex walked over to the round table and picked up the open pack of cigarettes.

"There are three cigarettes missing from this pack," he said. "What do you do with your old pack when you open a new one?"

"Check the trash," Callahan told one of the other officers, then turned back to Alex. "He still could have thrown it away before he got home."

"It's possible." Alex nodded.

"What about the fire?" Danny asked. "It seems to me that it shouldn't have burned out so quickly."

"You'd like it better if it burned down this whole building?" Callahan said with a raised eyebrow. "Seems to me we got lucky."

"Fires from people smoking in bed usually do more damage, Lieutenant." Danny shrugged. "Especially when they char the body like that."

The recliner and a small writing table occupied most of the space to the right of the door. To the left were a couch and two chairs surrounding a coffee table, with a cabinet radio in the corner. The kitchen was just beyond with a sink, counter, and icebox behind a small table and single chair. Alex set down his bag on the coffee table and opened it up.

"If there's anything weird about the fire, I'll know in a minute," he said, taking his oculus out of the bag.

"Not just yet," Callahan said. "I want to make sure there's something here before I put you on the department's dime."

A moment later the officers sent to check for ashtrays and empty cigarette packs reported finding none and Callahan sighed.

"All right, scribbler," he agreed. "Go to work."

Alex strapped his oculus to his head and began adjusting its various lenses. The oculus looked like a short telescope attached to a leather pad that covered Alex's right eye. The tube had several focusing rings running around it, like a camera, and half a dozen colored lenses could be moved in and out of the field of view. All of this made it possible for Alex to see into differing spectrums of light.

None of this was very useful on its own, but with the right light source...

He reached into his bag and pulled out his multi-lamp. This looked like a small, ornate version of the kind of lantern train switchmen used in rail yards. It had an egg-shaped body with four crystal lenses set in it at regular intervals. Three of the crystals were covered with leather caps so the light within could only shine out of the one, uncovered lens.

Opening the front of the lamp revealed a frame with metal clamps affixed to the bottom. Alex selected a burner from the valise with the word *silver* written on it. The burner was basically a reservoir that held a very specific kind of oil, with a wick attached to the top. Clipping it into place in the lamp, he lit the wick with a match and it began to glow with a bright, white light. He felt the runes in the lantern as they activated, like the one on the strongbox in his office.

Alex closed the lamp, adjusted his oculus, then began sweeping the room with the lantern. Silverlight was made by mixing an alchemical compound of colloidal silver with various accelerants and then burning it. The rune-inscribed lens in the lamp focused the light and the ones in the oculus made it visible, revealing the little apartment in black and white, like a photographic negative.

The real magic of Silverlight, was that it revealed otherwise hard to see things, like fingerprints, blood, sweat, and other biological fluids. These lit up like neon when exposed to Silverlight.

Alex swept the lantern over the corpse in the chair. There wasn't much to see since most of the evidence had been burned away, but he liked to be thorough. He shifted his gaze to the floor, then moved around the room, away from the corpse in widening circles. Once he checked the entire room, he moved to the bedroom, then switched the burner in the lamp to Ghostlight. Ghostlight burned a bright green and revealed magical residue and anything supernatural. Finally, Alex put out his lamp and returned it to the case, then stripped off the oculus.

"Well, I know why the fire died out early," he said to Danny. "Whoever killed him used the booze to get the fire going, but didn't use enough. It burned too quickly and the fire didn't have enough heat built up to keep going." Alex stepped over to the recliner and squatted down, pointing at the carpet. "They were messy when they doused him. You can smell some of the alcohol right here."

"Mark that," Callahan said to Danny, who tore a page from his notebook and set it on the rug.

"Then there's some blood spatter here," Alex said, chalking a circle on the floor near the middle of the room.

"Speak English, scribbler," one of the uniforms growled as Alex shooed him away from the spot he was chalking. He had a sour face and the look of a man who'd rather be somewhere else.

Alex rolled his eyes and Danny grinned. Danny had asked this question before and already knew the answer.

"Have you ever seen someone flick a brush full of paint?" Danny asked the officer.

"Sure."

"Well it's like that. When blood falls on something, it forms dots, but when it's thrown, the dots form little streaks."

"So, what does that mean?" the sour-faced officer asked.

"It means," Callahan interjected, "that someone was hit hard enough to bleed, and the blood spattered."

Alex nodded. "My guess? It was whomever was tied to that chair." He indicated the lone chair at the kitchen table. "There are scratches on the floor here," he pointed to the barely distinguishable marks. "They should fit the pattern of the legs."

"So you're thinking Mr. Pemberton here was tied up and beaten before he was set on fire," Danny said.

Alex nodded.

"Or," Callahan said, "he might have cut himself any number of ways and put that chair there to change the light bulb in the ceiling. If you're right, the question is why someone would do this to him?" He turned to one of the uniforms. "What did your canvass turn up on our victim?"

The officer flipped through his book and read. "Jerry Pemberton, age forty-two, lived alone, regular habits."

"Did he smoke?" the Lieutenant asked, looking meaningfully at Alex.

"Don't know," the officer said. "And no one seems to know what he did for a living."

"He was a customs inspector for the port authority," Alex supplied. "He worked in a secure warehouse down at the Aerodrome."

Callahan looked confused and Danny's mouth dropped open like a fish.

"How?" he said. Alex pointed to a wooden plaque hanging above the ruin of the recliner.

"It's an award for ten years of service."

"You sure this guy was roughed up before he was killed?" Callahan's face had gone from mild disgust to intense concentration, and his voice was hard and flat. Alex shrugged.

"Pretty sure, though there is one way to be certain."

"Let me guess, one of your expensive runes?" The Lieutenant's lip curled into a sneer.

Alex flipped through his book and opened it so Callahan could see an immensely complex design, rendered in gold and sparkling red lines. It looked like a stained glass window in a cathedral.

"The red lines are made with powdered rubies," he explained.

"How much?" Callahan asked.

"What does it do?" Danny said at the same time.

"This is a Temporal Restoration Rune," Alex said. "No, it's not like those runes people use to reattach handles to teacups or mend broken mops. This will restore Mr. Pemberton's body to the way it was at the moment he died."

"How much?" Callahan asked again.

Alex looked at him for a long minute before answering, letting the tension build.

"Normally I charge a C-note," he said. Danny whistled and there was a murmur from the assembled officers. "But for you, Lieutenant, I'll cut you a break, sixty."

Callahan's brow wrinkled up as he weighed his options. Alex just watched. His cost to make the Rune was only about thirty-five bucks — powdered ruby was expensive by the pound, but very little was actually required for the rune. Still, it did take several days to create and Leslie had been right, they needed the money.

"Do it," Callahan said at last.

Alex tore the page out of his rune book and stepped up to the blackened corpse. He'd been a private eye long enough to get used to the sight of dead men. That made him wonder just how jaded he'd become.

"I need all you fellas who had lunch in the last hour to leave the room," he said, then turned to Danny. "Be sure to take good notes — this will only last about ten minutes. When you monkey with time there are...repercussions. As soon as the spell breaks, the body will rapidly decompose."

"Why do I have to leave?" one of the uniforms grumbled.

"Because I don't want to have to clean your puke off my jacket," Alex said.

"Is it that bad?" Danny asked.

Alex nodded, then licked the back of the page and stuck it to the dead man's chest — what was left of it. Taking a match from his pocket, he lit it and touched the paper. The rune exploded with light, burning red and gold and white. It pulsed once, then twice, then faster and faster before it detonated into a shower of sparks like a skyrocket. When the embers touched the body, it began to roil and churn.

Alex was tempted to look away at this point — he could take blood and death, but the sight of a dead man's guts wiggling like they were live snakes turned his stomach. He kept his eyes fixed on the corpse, however, knowing that Callahan would never let him live it down if he didn't.

Tissue foamed up and the blackness seemed to contract, leaving pink skin behind. In the head, white blobs became eyes in the skull and teeth leapt up from the ruin of the chair and popped themselves back into the jaw. Muscle and then skin crawled across the face, running like wax until at last the body was whole again.

If whole was the right word.

"Good God," Danny said as the remains of Jerry Pemberton were finally revealed. Deep purple bruises covered most of his body and his eyes were both swollen shut. Whoever had worked him over had given him one hell of a beating.

"Get pictures," Callahan said, breaking the spell that held everyone enthralled. He looked pale; most of them did, but he kept his focus. All business.

Officers moved in with cameras and began snapping away while Danny scribbled as fast as he could on his pad.

While they worked, Alex went over to a little writing table in the back of the room. There were lots of fingerprints on it when he scanned it earlier with the oculus. Without any suspects, fingerprints weren't very useful to the police, but that wasn't what interested him. Inside the desk's single drawer was a blank pad of paper. He hadn't paid much attention to it before, but something about it bothered him. He wanted a closer look.

Taking the pad across to the coffee table, Alex removed a vial of black powder from his kit. He tore a very simple rune out of his book and stuck it to the pad, then carefully poured a few grains of the black powder onto the rune. Striking a match from the book in his pocket, he lit the rune paper and it vanished in a puff that catapulted the black powder up into the air. After a long moment, it began to settle on the notepad, first in random, haphazard dots, but gradually forming lines. In a few seconds the lines revealed the impressions left on the paper from whatever had been written on the missing sheet above. It was a crudely done drawing of a building, showing the points of entry and what looked like locked doors. The words *Secure Area* had been written in a shaky hand on one side.

"Danny," he said, motioning for the detective to join him. "I think I know what this is all about," he said in a low voice. He showed the pad to Danny, and, after a moment, the detective began to nod.

"Lieutenant," he said. "I think Alex has got something here."

Callahan made a noise in his throat that clearly indicated that he doubted that, but crossed to where they stood.

"It looks like someone wanted to rob the customs warehouse," Danny said pointing to the drawing.

"Where'd you get this?" the Lieutenant asked Alex.

"I used a rune to reveal what Pemberton wrote on the page just above this one before it was torn off."

"What makes you think this is the warehouse where he works?" Callahan said. "It could be a map of his mom's kitchen and this is where she hides the brownies."

"Lieutenant!" Danny protested, but Callahan waived him silent.

"I'm not saying you're wrong, but I want to be sure you're right before we go off half-cocked. How do we know Pemberton drew this for the people that killed him?"

"Look at his fingernails," Alex said, walking back over to the body. Three of the nails on his right hand had been torn off. Danny looked confused but Callahan sighed and nodded his head.

"They stopped when he gave them what they wanted," he said. "Otherwise they would have torn off all his fingernails."

"Whoever killed Jerry Pemberton wanted to know how to get into the customs warehouse at the aerodrome," Alex said. "If Pemberton was killed last night, there's a good chance your killers will show up there tonight."

"Unless they've already been and gone," Callahan said.

"No," Danny said, shaking his head. "If they went straight to the warehouse, there wouldn't be any reason to cover up Pemberton's murder. By the time we got here and figured it out, they'd already be gone."

"He's right, Lieutenant," Alex said. "All you have to do is lie in wait and Pemberton's murderers will come straight to you."

"Pretty neat," he said. "All right, finish up here, detective. I'll go over to the precinct and put together a squad to stake out the warehouse." He put on his overcoat and hat and headed for the door. "Nice job, scribbler," he said to Alex. "Maybe you aren't useless after all."

Danny grinned at Alex as the lieutenant left. "I think he's beginning to like you," he said with a smirk.

"As long as he pays me," Alex said with a shrug. He was used to not being liked by cops as well as his fellow runewrights for being a private detective.

"I'll make sure they cut you a check," Danny said. "It'll probably take a couple days though."

"No problem," Alex said. "I know you're good for it."

He felt a magical tremor hit him, just a tiny brush against his senses, but he felt it.

"Are your boys about done with that corpse?" he asked. "Cause your ten minutes are almost up."

"What happens then?"

"It crumbles into dust," Alex said.

Danny made sure the photographers had taken all the pictures they wanted, then had everyone step back. Alex felt the pulses of the decaying magic coming faster and faster until, at last, the earthly remains of Jerry Pemberton disintegrated into a pile of fine, white ash.

"You need me for anything else?" Alex asked, packing away his oculus and the multi-lamp. Danny looked around and shook his head.

"Thanks," he said. "You really helped us out."

"Just keep your head down when they bring these bastards in." Alex patted him on the shoulder. “I wouldn’t put it past them to be packing.”

“I’ll be careful,” he said.

Alex put on his hat and picked up his bag. The pad with the drawing of the warehouse was on the coffee table so he picked it up too.

“Say hi to Amy for me,” he said, passing the notepad to detective Pak. Danny’s face grew stern but he wore a smile with it.

“You stay away from my sister,” he said as Alex stepped out into the hall.

Alex was in such a good mood that he took the stairs rather than taking the self-service elevator. Working with the police could be tense and uncomfortable, but it paid well. Leslie would be thrilled. For the first time in half a year they’d be ahead on the bills instead of desperately behind, racing to catch up. It felt good.

Something bothered him though — a thought in the back of his mind. Something to do with the notepad he handed to Danny. He thought about it for a moment, but it continued to elude him. Shrugging, he decided not to let doubts ruin his good mood, so he pushed the thought from his mind and whistled as he made his way back out onto the rain-swept street.

3

THE MISSIONARY

Alex didn't bother with a barrier rune this time. There was a five-and-dime just across from Pemberton's building and he wanted to tell Leslie the good news. He held his hat down and sprinted across the road.

The rain was coming down harder than he'd thought and he was soaked by the time he reached the store. He muttered a curse and pulled out his rune book before the dampness could soak through his jacket and ruin the pages. They were made of flash paper, the kind bookies used. It was nothing more than paper soaked in sodium nitrate then allowed to dry. The benefits were that if you set the paper on fire it would burn away to ash in less than a second, great for bookies who didn't want to get caught with evidence and runewrights who wanted to create their runes ahead of time and use them later. The downside of flash paper was that it had to be very thin, so when it got wet, it turned into pulp.

Alex stepped inside the store and a bell rang as soon as the door opened. A girl in a floral print blouse, a white apron, and a paper hat leaned on a lunch counter lined with stools. She had brown hair and eyes, with freckles on her nose and a bored expression on her face. She brightened noticeably when Alex came in.

"Really starting to come down out there," she said as Alex brushed the rain from his coat and shook out his hat.

"You said it," he answered with a smile.

The girl reached below the counter and offered him a clean hand towel.

Alex set aside his rune book and wiped his hands until they were completely dry.

"Got a match?" he asked, tearing a moderately complex rune from his book. The girl pulled a box of stick matches from the front pocket of her apron and offered it to Alex. He stuck the rune to his already-wet hat, put the hat on his head, then set it alight. The paper disappeared in a flash and instantly Alex felt the clammy cold of wearing a wet hat disappear.

"Oh!" the girl said, her eyes growing wide.

Steam began to roll off of Alex as the rune's magic dried out his clothes. This was one of his emergency runes, the ones that cost too much to use on a normal day but were worth having if the need arose. One of the few benefits of being a runewright was being able to have runes written in advance, ready when you needed them.

"That's pretty impressive," the girl said. "I wish I'd known you when I got caught in the rain in my silk blouse." She signed. "Now it's all full of water spots. I hate it every time I see it but the thing cost me a week's salary, so I don't have the heart to throw it out."

Alex flipped to the back of his rune book. Here were a few blank pages, ready for whatever he needed. He pulled a pencil from his trouser pocket and drew a square. Flash paper tore easily, so he went slowly and used a pencil with soft lead.

"What's that?" the girl asked.

Alex shushed her and focused on the symbol. Inside the square, he drew a circle, then a magical symbol that looked like a lighthouse being attacked by a steam shovel. As he drew, he felt power being drawn through him from whatever place magic occupied in the universe, through his pencil, and onto the paper.

"There," he said, tearing out the page and handing it to the girl in the paper hat. "Put that on your silk blouse, carefully light just the paper on fire, and it'll be good as new."

The girl's eyes lit up. They were very pretty eyes. "Really?" she said, her voice raising about an octave.

"Cross my heart," Alex said with a smile. She clutched the delicate paper as if it were gold foil, then a sly look came over her.

"Can you make one that'll fix the runs in my stockings?"

"Sure," Alex grinned. "Trade me for some poached eggs on buttered toast?"

"Hard or soft?"

"Soft."

"Deal," she said. She returned his grin.

"I'm Alex," he said sticking out his hand.

"Mary," she said, taking it. "One Adam and Eve on a raft with axle grease coming up."

"You got a phone in here, Mary?" Alex asked as he began drawing another Minor Restoration Rune.

"In back," Mary said, pointing, as she set a pan of water on to boil.

He handed her the rune and made his way to the phone booth. Closing the door, he dropped a nickel in the slot and dialed the number of his office.

"Lockerby Investigations," Leslie's voice came across the line, sounding tinny and flat.

"It's me," Alex said. "I just got done with the police job."

"Any luck?"

"Yeah, they hired me. I even used a Temporal Restoration Rune, but I only charged them sixty for it. Be a doll and get a bill over to Police Headquarters right away, my usual fee plus the rune."

"I'm already writing it up," she said. "Do you have anything else on the docket or are you coming straight back?"

"I thought I'd have lunch first."

"You know it's two-thirty, right?"

"I haven't had lunch," he explained.

"Well," Leslie said, that business tone coming back into her voice. "Father Clementine wants to see you."

Alex swore. "Is his roof leaking again?"

"Yep," Leslie said. "And it's coming down pretty hard here. I didn't want to tell you if you had work to do."

"I always have time for the Father," Alex said, irritation creeping into his voice. "You know that."

"What I know," Leslie replied, her voice going hard as well, "is that you spend a lot of time and resources helping the Father when you should be making money."

"Give it a rest, Leslie," Alex said. "I owe the Father plenty. Call him and tell him I'll be over as soon as I can."

Leslie promised that she would and Alex hung up.

Father Harrison Clementine ran the Brotherhood of Hope Mission out of an old ramshackle church smack in the middle of the west side's outer-ring. In former days it had been a dance hall. Now it was a large open building with a three-story dormitory attached. Alex had spent five years living in that dormitory, between the ages of twelve and seventeen. His father had been a professional runewright, scribbling away minor restoration runes, like the ones Alex had just given to Mary, for a nickel apiece. The Lore Book that he inherited had some good runes in them, but Alex's dad just didn't have the talent to write them. He believed that if he only worked harder and longer than all the other runewrights, scribbling away for nickels, that somehow he wouldn't be dirt poor. The only thing he got from all that scribbling in their cold apartment was pneumonia and an early grave. Alex's mother had split the moment it became clear dad was never going to amount to anything, so that left Alex a twelve-year-old orphan.

Some suit from city hall wanted to put Alex in one of the city's orphanages, but those places were hellholes. Kids as young as toddlers were crammed in with kids all the way up to seventeen, and they all were run by sadists who were in it for their government check. Alex saw enough of that right after his father's death not to want any more. That was where Father Harry came in. Harrison Clementine had been their pastor for years and when Alex's father died, he demanded that Alex be placed in his care at the mission. When the state said that only a licensed orphanage could apply to take Alex, Father Harry got the license. In the end, Father Harry put a roof over Alex's head and food in his belly until Alex was old enough to do it himself. The Father also encouraged Alex to study his dad's Lore Book and learn to write runes.

If it wasn't for the Father, Alex had no idea where he would have ended up, but it probably wouldn't have been anywhere good.

He owed the Father more than he could ever repay, so if Father Harry needed new runes to keep the mission roof from leaking, Alex was happy to do it. Leslie didn't understand, she couldn't understand, and he didn't blame her for that. She was right, helping the Father and his Mission was a drain on the business, but Alex simply didn't care. Family was family, and Father Harry was family.

"Gonna have to take a rain check," he said to Mary as he made his way back to the lunch counter.

"You sure?" she asked, her lips in an adorable pout. "It'll only be another minute and a half." As if to punctuate her words, the toast popped up from the toaster. The aroma of perfectly browned bread made his stomach growl.

He hesitated. Every minute he sat here was another minute water was pouring into the Mission's great hall. On the other hand, it would take him at least thirty minutes to get there on the crawler and anything already wet wasn't going to get any wetter if he took five minutes to eat.

"All right," he said, sitting down. It didn't hurt, of course, that Mary was such agreeable company.

Almost exactly a minute and a half later, she presented him with a plate of perfectly poached eggs on generously buttered toast.

"What did you call these?" he asked through a mouthful.

"That's Adam and Eve on a raft with axle grease," she said with a giggle.

Alex had heard this before, of course; waitresses and cooks in diners were always yelling such unintelligible nonsense around.

"You worked in a diner?"

"I love to cook, so I moved to the big city to try my hand here," she said. Her voice had a lilting, far-away quality to it as she spoke. "Then, when I got here, I found out that being a cook anywhere is a serious boy's club. The only jobs a woman can get cooking is places like this where you have to look good. No one ever wonders what the cook looks like in a diner, or a five-star restaurant for that matter."

"Well, these eggs are perfect," Alex said. He liked them soft, with the yokes hot but runny and the whites cooked hard, something an inexplicable number of cooks couldn't seem to master.

"Thank you, Alex," she said, beaming. When she smiled like that, Mary was really quite attractive.

Alex wolfed down his food and gave Mary a dime tip.

"Are you really a good cook?" he asked. She raised an eyebrow and leaned across the counter at him.

"Come back sometime," she said. "Try me."

Alex pulled out his pocket notepad and scribbled an address on it.

"There's this place a few blocks from the park called *The Lunch Box*," he said, tearing out the paper and handing it to her. "It's a bit of a dog-wagon, but I know the owner. Ask for Max and tell him Alex Lockerby said you need to cook for him. He'll give you a fair shot."

"Hasn't he got a cook?"

"Yeah," he said. "But he stinks. The old cook retired and Max brought this new kid. He's terrible. I hate to eat there anymore."

"Why go?" Mary asked.

"It's the only place near my apartment."

"Thanks, Alex," Mary said, tucking the paper into the pocket of her apron. "Will I see you again?"

"Sure," Alex said. "I expect you to start cooking at my favorite place. You'll see a lot of me then."

"I think I'd like that," Mary said with a very agreeable smile.

Alex doffed his hat, then took out one of Burt's cigarettes and lit it. He tore a Minor Barrier Rune out of his book and cast it on himself.

"See you soon, Mary," he said, then stepped out into the downpour.

THE PROMISE of paying work for the police let Alex justify the taxi ride over to Danny's crime scene, but helping out Father Harry meant taking the crawler. Most big cities had a streetcar service, but New York's was unlike anything in the world. The Crawler was one of J.D. Rockefeller's inventions. Most sorcerers got rich marketing various enchanted materials, like Barton with his power capacitor in the Empire Tower, or

Sorsha Kincaid, the Ice Queen who enchanted the metal disks used to keep iceboxes cold. Rockefeller was a whole different kind of sorcerer; when he put his power to work, he made tens of millions. When he first showed off the crawler, people said he'd finally gone insane.

Alex rounded the corner and made his way down the block to the crawler station. A half-dozen people were crowded under a metal awning that covered a single bench. As Alex approached, they all looked down the block expectantly, so he quickened his pace. The crawler swept into view, two blocks away, but it still made it to the station before Alex. It looked like a normal two-decker streetcar from the wheel carriages up, but it crawled along the ground on dozens of legs made of blue energy. It looked more like a giant, glowing centipede than a streetcar.

The crawler skittered to a stop and Alex jogged the last few feet to board. As he stepped up, he felt his weight cause the streetcar to shift a bit, then its legs adjusted and leveled it. The car was crammed with passengers, all huddling away from the doors to stay out of the wet and cold. Alex's barrier would work for at least another half hour so he sat in one of the front stairwells and watched the city go by. The big advantage of crawlers was that they could go much faster than an electric or cable-driven streetcar, and they rode a lot smoother. They seemed to flow over even the roughest ground as if it were still water. For a dime, it was quite a ride.

ALEX GOT off a few blocks from the Brotherhood of Hope Mission. Crawlers needed reliable power for their energy legs, so they never ventured too far into the outer ring. As he walked, Alex could feel his barrier rune beginning to fade and he quickened his pace. By the time he reached the mission, he was just beginning to get damp.

His knock at the door was answered by an old black nun who looked a hundred if she was a day. Despite her frail appearance, she let out a whoop of joy at the sight of Alex and hugged the stuffing out of him.

"How are you, boy?" she said when he'd finally disentangled himself from her. "Why haven't you been around more lately?"

"I'm sorry, Sister Gwen," he said. Alex blushed and didn't hide it. "Things have been busy at work."

Sister Gwen grunted, a sound that clearly indicated she thought this was a poor excuse.

"I hear the roof is leaking again," he prompted, changing the subject. The old nun nodded and turned away, motioning for him to follow.

"Father Clementine's been expecting you."

She led him down familiar paths, past the dormitories and the kitchen and into the main hall. It was vast and open, like a warehouse, and Alex could see several unbroken streams of water falling down into strategically placed buckets. As he watched, two men in cassocks pulled a full bucket out from under one of the streams while an older man in a simple robe replaced it with an empty one.

"Be careful dumping that," the man in the robe said. "I don't want to have to mop the vestibule again."

Alex gave Sister Gwen a parting hug and stepped up beside the older man. He was tall and worn with a craggy complexion and an enormous nose in the middle of his face. A thick crop of unkempt hair adorned his head, still jet black despite his being at least seventy. His hands were rough, calloused, and big, like boxers' hands. As far as Alex knew, however, those hands had never been used in anger.

"I think two grown men can handle a bucket full of water," Alex said.

"Alex," the big man said, tuning to envelop Alex's right hand in his. "How are you, son?" Before Alex could answer, he went on. "Sorry to bring you down here again, but...well, you see." He waved at the leaks, as if somehow Alex might have missed them.

"No problem, Father," Alex said. "Always happy to help out. In fact, I should have come down sooner to check on the runes."

"You're always welcome, Alex, you know that, but you've got your own life to lead." He put his huge hand on Alex's shoulder.

"Thanks to you," Alex said, and meant it. "Now, do you have those roof tiles I need?"

Father Harry pointed over to a corner of the hall where the roof still seemed to be in good shape. “Brother Thomas has them on a table over by the good light.” He led Alex over to the table that stood under a shaft of bright light. “This corner is closer to Empire Tower,” Father Harry said. “This light never goes out.”

Alex laughed, setting his bag down next to a stack of fired clay roof tiles.

“I remember,” he said. He took a sharp metal stylus and a hard pencil from his bag, then added a jar of grayish paste and a small putty knife.

“I appreciate this, Alex,” Father Harry said. “I hate having to interrupt you at work.”

“It’s really no trouble, Father,” Alex said, tracing a modified Barrier Rune on the first tile. Once he carved it into the tile with the stylus and filled the cut with the wax solution of camphor oil and coal dust, the rune would cause all the nearby tiles to repel the rain.

Father Harry drew up a chair as if he intended to watch. From experience, Alex knew that he really wanted to talk. Alex had only lived here five years, but Father Harry had been like a real dad to him. He’d never admit it, but Alex looked forward to these talks.

“Maybe you should make the cuts deeper this time,” Father Harry said. “So they last longer.”

“You know it doesn’t work that way,” Alex said, smiling at the suggestion. “Runes wear out — that’s just what they do. If you want this roof to not leak permanently, you need to hire a sorcerer ... or a roofer.”

Father Harry chuckled and sighed. “Too expensive. Thank God I’ve got you.”

“You do good work here, Father,” Alex said. “I enjoy helping. After all you did for me, it’s the least I could do. How’s the mission going these days?”

Father Harry’s countenance brightened.

“We’ve got two dozen people living in the guest wing, and we feed over a hundred every night.”

“Sister Morgan still do the cooking?”

“No,” Father Harry said. “She got too old. Asked to be transferred to a convent in Arizona. We've got a whole crop of new Brothers and Sisters now." He looked sad for a moment as the years seemed to weigh on him. "The work goes on, though. There are always the poor and the forgotten to be cared for." His countenance brightened after a moment. "So, how are things with you?"

Alex sighed.

"That bad?" Father Harry said, concern on his face. When Alex just shrugged, he grabbed Alex by the chin and pulled his face around so they were eye to eye. "You listen to me, boy. You're a good detective and a fine runewright, God will give you a break one of these days."

"God sure is taking his time about that," Alex said, trying not to sound resentful.

"In the sweat of thy face shall thou eat bread," Father Harry quoted.

"Genesis, chapter three, verse nineteen," Alex recited. Father Harry had drilled the scriptures into his head while he lived at the mission.

"You know where it's found but you don't know what it means," he said. "God doesn't just give us the things we want, he expects us to work for them. To earn them."

Alex flashed back to the lessons he'd had in this very hall. "The Lord helps those who help themselves," he said.

"So you were listening," Father Harry said, and smiled. "But did you learn the lesson?"

"If I keep working, the good Lord will bless me," Alex said.

"In his good time," the Father said with a compassionate smile and a nod. "We all must be patient."

Alex looked up from his work and met the old man's eyes.

"Thanks, Father," he said. "I've been so busy, I must have forgotten." He meant every word. It was impossible to let the world get the better of you when Father Harry spoke. He carried the light of his faith around like a torch that drove back the darkness. Alex wondered why he didn't come back to the mission more often.

"So," Father Harry said, a sly look crossing his face. "Have you found a nice girl yet?"

"Didn't you just give me a lesson about patience and the Lord's good time?" Alex asked, remembering why he didn't come back very often.

Before the Father could rally, a Sister Alex didn't know came hurrying across the floor.

"Father Clementine," she said. "Sister Catherine can't get the stove lit again."

"Sorry, Alex," Father Harry said, rising to his feet. "Duty calls."

Saved by the bell, Alex thought.

ALEX CONTINUED CASTING runes until the stack of tiles dwindled to nothing. As he finished each one, a Brother in a black cassock would take it up to a walkway that ran around the upper level, fitting it into a slot Alex had cut for them years ago. As each one went into place, the nearby leaks abruptly stopped.

As he worked, a thousand things came back to Alex. The time he scuffed up the floor with a pair of dime store roller skates. Sister Gwen had stayed up all night watching as Alex polished out the marks on his hands and knees. When Father Harry caught him smoking and made him eat the whole pack of cigarettes. He hadn't touched another until he was out on his own. It wasn't the plaza, but there were far worse places to grow up.

Somewhere in the middle of the stack, Father Harry came back and they spent the rest of the time catching up. It was one of the more pleasant evenings Alex had spent in a long time. Eventually, the smell of potato soup began to percolate through the hall. Based on the smell, a local butcher was giving the Mission his fresh scraps to add to the pot. Every little bit helped.

By the time Alex finished casting his runes on the roof tiles, the Brothers and Sisters of the Mission were setting out the evening meal to feed the poor. Alex couldn't see it, but he knew that a line of ragged, downtrodden people had formed in the rain outside.

"Stay and eat with us," Father Harry said, as Alex closed up his runewright kit and pulled on his suit jacket. Alex shook his head.

"Looks like you've got plenty of mouths to feed without mine. Call me when the roof leaks again."

Father Harry put his hand on Alex's shoulder and leaned close, as if he didn't wish to be overheard.

"Can you come back on Saturday?" he asked quietly.

Alex thought about it, then shook his head. Saturdays were busy days in the detective business and he needed to be at the office. "I can't on Saturday, but how about next week? I'll come by and take you to lunch."

Father Harry looked as if he would object, but then nodded.

"That sounds good," he said, shaking Alex's hand. "There's a matter I need to discuss with you. In private."

Alex was about to ask why the Father was acting so secretive, but his hand came away from the handshake with a five spot tucked inside.

"You know I can't accept this," he said, holding the bill up. Father Harry put one of his massive hands over Alex's, closing it around the bill.

"Nonsense," he said. "You really helped us out."

"I can't have you robbing the poor box to pay me," Alex said.

Father Harry didn't loosen his grip.

"I get a stipend from the church," he said. "I put most of it into running this place, but I keep some back for my own use." He looked Alex right in the eye, something he'd done often when Alex was growing up. Father Harry had a way of looking right into your soul with that gaze. "Let me do this," he said. "The laborer is worthy of his hire."

Alex smiled and nodded. For a moment, he was back in the mission school with the other neighborhood kids.

"First Timothy," Alex said. "Chapter five, verse ... twenty?"

"Eighteen," Father Harry corrected. His craggy face wore a look of pride but there was sadness in his eyes.

"I'll come by on Saturday," Alex said. "Around noon." His business would suffer for it, but he didn't care. If the Father needed him, he would be there. It was as simple as that.

"Thank you, Alex," he said. "Now get going. I've got work to do."

Alex cast another Minor Barrier Rune and walked out into the rain, past the line of poor bedraggled men and women waiting for a simple meal. He made a mental note to tell Leslie about his Saturday appointment first thing tomorrow morning. She wouldn't like it, but Alex didn't care. If it hadn't been for Father Harry, he might be standing in that line, soaked to the bone and waiting for the one decent meal he'd have all day.

It was late and Alex felt the strain of the last hours he spent scribing and casting runes. Magic taxed the body and mind as much as any physical work. He lit another of Burt's cigarettes, then turned up his collar and headed for home in the flickering glow of the streetlights.

4

THE MENTOR

Alex caught a westbound crawler, getting off a few blocks short of the park, then took another southbound one until he saw *The Lunch Box*. He thought about stopping in to tell Max, the owner, about Mary, but decided against it. She'd do all right without his help and Max could go on for hours about any subject. All Alex wanted right now was a cold beer and a warm fire.

He lived in a four-story brownstone just six blocks from Central Park. The house belonged to his mentor, a retired British doctor, one Ignatius Bell, late of His Majesty's Navy. Bell had retired to New York to live with his son, Kingsley, who already lived there, but before Ignatius' boat arrived, Kingsley succumbed to pneumonia and died. Bell arrived to nothing more than a grave marker, the brownstone, and enough money to live comfortably for the remaining years of his life.

The British navy used runewrights as their doctors. As Bell put it, *Any fool can shove a healing draught down someone's throat, but only a runewright can cast a Mending Rune and properly fix a broken leg.*

Doctor Bell was full of sayings like that.

After living in New York in his son's home for a few months, Bell decided he needed to pass his Lore on. Kingsley had been a banker and Bell had no other children, so he'd searched for a suitable apprentice.

Eventually he found Alex hawking what simple runes he knew on a street corner. Now Alex lived with Bell and learned from him. It was Bell who convinced Alex to become a detective. *Your skills are too great to peddle Restoration Runes in a shop or Barrier Runes on the street corner when it rains*, he had said. *You've a keen mind, use it.*

Learning the Lore that Bell had collected over the years was hard. Some of his Runes were more complex than anything Alex had ever seen, certainly more than anything in his father's meager Lore Book. As hard as they were, however, Bell's lessons on how to be a detective were worse. He'd started Alex on the stories of Sherlock Holmes, showing him how the skills of observation and deduction could be employed to determine things like motive, and to reconstruct the events of a crime from the evidence left behind.

From fictional crimes, they graduated to real ones. As a Doctor with Rune Lore, Bell had offered his skill to the city medical examiner. Most Doctors these days weren't runewrights, at least in America, so the M.E. was grateful for the help. With access to real cases and real case files, Bell taught Alex how to look for evidence, how to spot errors in witness testimony, and how to use his Lore to find things no cop ever could.

After two grueling years of that, Bell had pronounced Alex ready, and Lockerby Investigations had been born. At first, Bell went with him on every case, watching and correcting when necessary. After a year of that, Bell stopped going along, and only heard a report from Alex each night over dinner. These days Bell hardly asked at all. Instead Alex found himself eager to share the particulars of his cases with the old doctor. Lockerby Investigations had been open five years now, and the nightly report had become a fixed routine.

Alex checked his watch as he mounted the stairs to the door. Bell liked to retire early and it was almost nine. It was possible he'd already gone to bed. Checking his watch served a dual purpose. Powerful runes covered the door to the brownstone. Invisible to the naked eye, Alex could still feel them as he drew closer. Inside his watch, runes etched around the inside of the cover and behind the crystal began to glow. As he touched the door, he felt the magical protections that kept it shut roll away from the presence of the watch. He reached out and opened the door, stepping quickly through, then shut it gently behind him.

He didn't know what runes guarded the door, nor which ones shielded the house itself. Bell cast those and maintained them. They were a part of his Lore Book that he had yet to share with Alex. All Alex really knew about those runes was that the beams in the attic were covered with them, and that without his watch to serve as a key, the wooden front door with its stained glass window would withstand the force of a battering ram.

It gave Alex a chill just thinking about it.

Someday Bell would teach him those runes. That would be an interesting day.

The front door led to an entryway with pegs for hats and coats, an umbrella stand, and a bench with storage for boots and galoshes. An inner glass door separated the entry from the tiny foyer and Alex tried to be quiet as he opened it and stepped inside. The interior of the brownstone had been done over in an art deco style with wainscoting and molding bearing polygonal shapes and angular designs. For a runewright of the geometric style, it was entirely appropriate.

Alex turned right, into the library. An enormous hearth occupied the far wall, with marble columns and a massive cherry-wood mantle. To either side, bookshelves reached up to the fifteen-foot ceiling. The bookcases had been ordered by Kingsley, before his death, and they matched the molding and trim. Now the cases were stuffed with books of all shapes and descriptions. Most were works on medicine and rune lore, but Bell had an entire section dedicated to classical literature, and even a chest where he kept select pulp fiction books that tickled his fancy. The only furniture in the room were two overstuffed arm chairs that faced the fire, each with an ottoman in front of it. A small, round occasional table stood between them, supporting a mahogany cigar box, two ash trays, and a stained glass lamp to provide light for reading after dark.

A modest coal fire had been laid in the iron grate of the hearth, filling the room with invigorating warmth, and pungent cigar smoke swirled around the furthest chair.

"Here you are at last, dear boy," Doctor Ignatius Bell said, shutting the flimsy paperback book he'd been reading. "I was beginning to think I'd have to send out a search party."

Alex laughed and sat down in the chair next to Bell, setting his hat on the ottoman.

"Not to worry, Iggy," Alex said with a grin. "I had to make a stop at the Mission." Alex had dubbed Bell "Iggy" during their first year together and the name just stuck. Bell didn't particularly like it, but he seemed to take it as a sign of affection from Alex, so he tolerated it.

"Yes, your secretary informed me thus when I called."

There was a note of irritation in Iggy's voice and Alex flinched.

"I should have called," he admitted, taking out another of Burt's cigarettes and lighting it. "Did I ruin dinner?"

Ever since Iggy let Alex run his own cases, Alex had been paying rent to bunk at the brownstone. Iggy hadn't insisted, but Alex needed to pay his way. He did, however, let Iggy cook for the both of them. Iggy had learned to cook in the navy and it had become a serious hobby for him ever since.

"I made a quiche," Iggy said, puffing on his cigar. "It was delicate, light as air, and delicious."

"What's a quiche?"

Iggy sighed and put his hand to his forehead as if it suddenly hurt.

"I think your fellow uncultured Americans would call it a bacon pie."

Alex perked up at that. He hadn't eaten anything since the poached eggs Mary cooked him.

"I left you some on the table under a cover," Iggy said.

Alex put his hands on the chair's arms but before he could rise, Iggy spoke again.

"How did it go today?" he said, opening his book again. "It must have gone well if you can afford cigarettes again."

Alex stifled a sigh and leaned back in his chair. Apparently Iggy wanted his pound of flesh for Alex's lack of judgment. The Brits really loved their social rules.

"Funny story about the cigarettes," he said, then launched into a detailed description of his day. For the most part, Iggy just listened quietly, commenting when he wanted clarification on any certain point.

"So," he said when Alex finished. "Father Harry wants to see you in private on Saturday." He puffed his cigar for a moment before adding, "Ominous."

Alex laughed. Father Harry was many things, but mysterious wasn't one of them. The man was an open book.

"He probably just wants me to do some rune work for him and doesn't want to talk about it in front of the sisters. You know what a gossip Sister Gwen is."

Iggy nodded, staring into the fire.

"I'm sure you're right," he said, though he didn't sound convinced. "In any case, I'll wager you're hungry."

Alex stood and picked up his hat.

"Oh, Father Harry even paid me for my work." Alex fished the five-dollar bill out of his pocket and held it up.

"You should probably put that in the safe," Iggy said before returning to his book.

Turning toward the hearth, Alex approached the bookcase on the left. About six feet off the floor, just high enough that Alex had to reach up to get it, stood a thick book bound in green leather. Unlike the other books on the shelf, this one tried very hard not to be noticed. The rune that shielded it was so powerful that it bled over onto the books on either side, a volume of Shakespeare's poetry on the right and a large, thin book bound in red leather on the left.

Alex took down the green book and opened it. The center of each page had been painstakingly cut out with a razor blade, then painted with varnish to make them all one solid piece. From the outside, the book appeared perfectly normal, but once opened, it had a hollow well inside, large enough to hide three of Iggy's pulp novels. Alex withdrew a small stack of cash held together by a paper clip. He added the fiver to it, then retuned the clip and re-shelved the book. This was Alex's emergency stash, money that not even Leslie knew about. Any time he had off-the-books cash, it went into the safe. Iggy said it was an important habit to develop.

Iggy had lived through the big war and several bank runs in his home country. Alex never doubted that the man mistrusted banks. He was also sure that Iggy had his own safe somewhere in the house, under the floorboards in his room, or maybe behind some loose bricks in the basement. It never tempted him. Alex made his own way in the world and he never took what wasn't his just because he could. Still, the idea of it made him want to go looking, just to see if he could find his way through the runes that kept it hidden.

Of course, it was more likely that it was here in the library, in a book or a series of them, just like Alex's.

Always hide things in plain sight, Iggy told him. *No one thinks to look there; they always think you're trying to be clever.*

"Good night, Iggy," Alex said but the doctor had bent over his novel again and seemed oblivious.

Alex ate his bacon pie in the kitchen. For something with a girly name like quiche, it was really quite good. After he finished, he washed his plate, fork, and glass in the sink, then set them aside to dry. He thought about opening his magic vault and replenishing his rune book, but he just didn't have the energy. He was tired. He'd had a full day, but it wasn't full the way he wanted it to be. The police job had started out great, but now Danny and Callahan would lie in wait and catch the murderers red-handed. It was open and shut with nothing more for him to do but pick up his check. Not that he minded that part, but he wanted to feel more useful. He wanted a case that would be hard to solve, one he could make his name with. If Leslie got him one more job finding a lost dog or a cheating husband, he'd pack it in and hawk Barrier Runes on rainy street corners.

Not really, of course, but it had been a long day and Alex wanted to indulge in a few minutes of self-pity.

His room was on the third floor, above Iggy's. It was small and modest with just the bare essentials; a bed, a desk, a wing-back chair, a nightstand, and a dresser. A narrow door led to a tiny bathroom with a toilet, sink, and stand-up shower. A telephone and a bottle of bourbon with a glass stood on the nightstand, and Alex poured himself a slug, then stripped down. He hung up his jacket and threw his trousers over the back of the wing-back chair. His barrier rune only kept falling rain from hitting him. It did nothing about puddles, so his shoes were soaked. He'd have to oil the leather to keep it supple. He poured himself a second slug of the bourbon and set to work.

When he finally got to bed, the clock on the nightstand read eleven twenty-five.

It felt like Alex's head had just hit the pillow when he was startled awake by the telephone. At whatever ungodly hour of the morning it was, the sound grated on his nerves like a rasp. He felt an instant headache form somewhere behind his left eye. Reaching out in the dark he managed to find the phone and fumbled the receiver to his ear.

"Yeah?" he mumbled.

"Alex?" a desperate voice came across the wire. He knew it sounded familiar, someone he knew, but his brain wasn't fully awake yet. It was a woman, he recognized that, and she was just short of hysterical. "Alex!" the voice said again, more urgent than before. "Are you there?"

"Sister Gwen?" he asked, the connections in his mind putting a name to the voice. "What's—"

"You have to come down to the Mission, Alex," Sister Gwen said. Her usually calm voice broke. Alex had never heard her anything but calm and in control, but now she was neither. The relief of reaching him warred with some unknown panic and she sobbed. "You have to come now. Hurry!"

She was weeping and her voice betrayed a fragile state of mind.

"Of course," Alex said, sitting up. "Of course. I'll come down right now."

He hoped this would calm her and she seemed to relax a bit. She drew several ragged breaths and her voice came over the wire in a tense whisper. "They're dead, Alex."

Alex's mind snapped into full wakefulness.

"Who?" he demanded. "Who's dead?"

"Everybody."

5

THE INCIDENT

Alex fumbled at the buttons of his shirt as he jumped down the stairs, two at a time. When he reached the second floor landing, he stopped long enough to tuck in his shirt and buckle his belt, then he headed for the foyer.

"What's going on?" Iggy's voice came out of the darkness at him. It was a little after three in the morning and there weren't any lights burning. Alex could see Iggy's shadow in the open doorway to his bedroom. "Alex," he said again. "What's happened?"

"I don't know," Alex said, heading for the stairs. "Sister Gwen called from the Mission. She said someone's dead. Maybe more than one, she wasn't very specific."

"Call a cab," Iggy said, ducking back into his room. "I'll get my bag and join you."

Alex didn't want to think, he wanted to run, but Iggy's words penetrated the fog of his tired mind. He steadied himself, then walked down the stairs to the kitchen where the downstairs phone was mounted to the wall. He picked up the receiver and gave the operator the number of a cab company. A few moments later, he hung up and headed back up to his room to retrieve his kit.

"They said five minutes," he called as he passed Iggy's room.

Five minutes later Alex and Iggy stood on the sidewalk outside the brownstone, Alex with his kit and Iggy with his medical bag. Ten minutes after that, the cab pulled up in front of the Brotherhood of Hope Mission. It reminded Alex of the scene outside of Jerry Pemberton's apartment, but with more squad cars.

Lots more.

"Steady," Iggy said, putting a restraining hand on Alex's arm. He paid the cabby and the pair of them got out.

"What are you doing here?" the cop at the door asked. Alex recognized him, the scarface cop from Chester Pemberton's building, but he didn't know his name.

"Sister Gwen ... I mean Sister Harris called me," Alex said. "Told me to come right away. She's expecting me."

The cop gave Alex and Iggy the once-over, then made up his mind.

"Wait here," he said. The cop withdrew back to the open doors of the mission and spoke animatedly with someone Alex could not see. After a moment, he waived Alex and Iggy forward.

The foyer of the mission was relatively empty considering the number of patrol cars outside. Black and white tiles covered the floor, giving it the distinct look of a hospital. An oak reception desk, stained black with years of use, stood just inside the door with a long row of pegs for hats and coats on the opposite wall. Next to the pegs were the heavy oak doors that led to the great hall. These were open and a uniformed officer stood by them. The door to the kitchens was just across from the entrance and it stood open as well, but the room beyond looked empty. Lastly, behind the reception desk were the stairs that led up to the dormitories. Two people sat on the stairs — one was a raven-haired policewoman in the blue uniform of an officer, and the other was Sister Gwen.

Alex's breath caught in his throat when he saw her. She had always been old and frail, for as long as he'd known her, but now she seemed to shrink in on herself as if an enormous weight pressed down upon her.

"Alex!" she cried on catching sight of him. She stood and lurched across the entryway to him, throwing herself into his arms. "Oh, Alex, thank God you're here! I don't know what to do." She squeezed Alex around the middle so tightly he had trouble breathing. "What are we going to do?" she whispered. Alex put his hand on her trembling shoulder.

"Sister Gwen?" he said, but the elderly nun just buried her face in his side.

"She's in shock," Iggy said, putting his bag on the reception desk. He pulled a handmade tea packet from a jar in his doctor's bag. "Where's the kitchen?" he asked Alex.

Alex nodded at the open door across the hall.

"Take Sister Gwen in the kitchen and have her sit down," he told the policewoman, handing her the tea packet. "Make her some tea with this and make sure she drinks all of it."

The policewoman nodded and managed to pull Sister Gwen free of Alex.

"Don't worry," Alex told Sister Gwen. "I'll take care of everything. I promise."

Iggy put his hand on Alex's shoulder as the policewoman led Sister Gwen away.

"You want me to have a look first?" he said. Alex shook his head.

"Come on," he said, picking up his bag from where he'd dropped it when Sister Gwen had hugged him. He took a deep breath, then crossed to the open doors of the Great Hall. Inside, a dozen policemen were taking pictures or moving around the floor with notebooks. Two-dozen bodies lay on the floor; some were sprawled as if they'd fallen down, while others were lying in repose, with their hands folded atop their bodies. Still others were up on the long tables that served as a dining area, covered with blankets. A pair of policemen with bandannas tied over their faces were pulling the sprawled corpses from the floor and moving them to a neat line off to one side.

Alex saw people he recognized among the bodies, the Brothers in their black cassocks and the new nuns. The rest were vagrants, mostly men, but a few women, all dressed in shabby, threadbare clothes. At the end of the neat row the policemen had made, lay Father Harry.

Alex's breath seemed to freeze in his lungs and his heart beat wildly. The big man lay on his side with his arm outstretched as if he'd simply gotten tired and laid down on the floor to rest. But he was dead. Alex struggled to believe it. He'd spoken to the man, sat at his side less than twelve hours ago. How could he be dead? How could God have allowed such a saintly man to die?

He felt his right hand clench into a fist and his left squeezed the handle of the old doctor's bag that held his kit. Burning with righteous anger and indignation, Alex started forward into the room.

"That's far enough," a uniformed policeman said, holding out his hand to block Alex's progress.

Alex turned and started to raise his fist, determined to strike the man down for daring to block his path to the Father. Iggy quickly seized Alex's hand and stepped between them.

"The sister called for you and you talked to her, but this is a police matter," the cop continued, seemingly oblivious to Alex's rage. He was short and a little chubby, with plump cheeks and dark eyebrows but his uniform was clean and neatly pressed. This one would be a stickler for the rules.

Alex's mind went instantly to the half dozen runes he could use to render the officious cop inert, but before he could settle on one, Iggy spoke.

"Where is your coroner, young man?" Iggy asked.

"Not here yet," the officer said. Iggy handed him his card.

"I'm Doctor Bell. I consult for the coroner's office. Since he isn't here, I'm offering my services. Who's in charge?"

The chubby policeman scrutinized the card, then nodded toward the back where a group of detectives stood.

"They grabbed whoever they could for this one," he said. "I don't know the Lieutenant in charge, but he's back there."

"Thank you," Bell said, sweeping past the man. "Come along, Alex."

Alex followed along, finally managing to control his anger.

"Thanks," he whispered.

"Think nothing of it," Iggy said "But get hold of yourself for now. There'll be time for grief later."

Alex wasn't sure he agreed with that, but he knew Iggy was right about one thing, if he let his emotions get the better of him now, the cops would throw him out on his ear. As they crossed the hall, Alex noticed the bodies on the floor. Each was pale, with red lesions on their exposed flesh.

"Should we be wearing our masks?" he whispered to Iggy. The old doctor shook his head.

"Whatever killed these people did it in a matter of a few hours," he said. "The police have been here long enough that if it were contagious, they'd already be showing signs."

Alex didn't think that conclusion was wrong, but it felt like they were betting their lives on it. Still, Iggy was almost never wrong.

Almost.

"Who's the Lieutenant?" Iggy asked, as they reached the knot of suit-clad detectives.

"Callahan," Alex said, recognizing the big man. "I thought they'd have you down at the warehouse."

Frank Callahan looked at Alex and a sour look passed his face. "I was," he said. "I was there all damn day and when they finally let me go home, I get sent here. What brings you around?"

"I know...I knew the priest here." Alex turned and nodded toward Father Harry's body. The pain of seeing the great man lying on the floor like yesterday's garbage pierced him again, but much of its power was gone.

"So you're the one the nun called?" he asked.

"Yes," Alex said. "I lived here for five years after my dad died. Father Harry took me in."

Callahan's features softened. "I'm sorry," he said. He opened up a spiral notebook and flipped to a new page. "What did you say the priest's name was?"

"Harrison Arthur Clementine," Alex said.

"The nun said you were here last night," one of the other detectives said. Alex nodded.

"I'm a runewright. I was repairing the runes that keep out the rain. The roof's leaked for years."

"You see anything out of the ordinary?" Callahan asked.

"No. I got here around three and worked till just before eight — that's when they start dinner."

"All right," Callahan said, flipping his notebook closed. "If you think of anything else, call me at the precinct. For now, go home."

"No," Alex growled, his hands balling into fists. "You need my help."

One of the detectives casually slipped his hand inside his jacket, others wore scowls, but Callahan's face remained calm.

"You're too close to this, Lockerby," he said. "You know it and I know it. Now go home."

"He is, indeed, very close to this," Iggy said, stepping up in front of Callahan. "But he's also quite correct, you need his help. His and mine."

"And who are you, Jeeves?" Callahan said, his gruff manner squarely back in place.

"I'm Doctor Ignatius Bell. I'm here to offer my medical services in lieu of your absent coroner."

Callahan turned to one of the other detectives. "When's the coroner supposed to arrive?"

"Just as soon as they sober him up," a sardonic voice replied.

Callahan mulled it over for a long minute, looking back and forth from Iggy to Alex.

"Fine," he said at last. "I want to get home before sun-up."

"I very much doubt that will happen," Iggy said. "You and all your men need to clear this room immediately."

Callahan rolled his eyes and sighed.

"Why?" he asked in a tone of voice that clearly indicated that he didn't want to know. Iggy pointed to one of the corpses, sprawled across a table as if he'd collapsed while eating.

"What do those lesions on his skin look like to you?"

Callahan shrugged and shook his head.

"Boils?"

"It looks like smallpox to me," Iggy said. A murmur swept the assembled detectives.

"Are you saying that smallpox did this?" one of the detectives said.

"I doubt it," Iggy said. "Smallpox takes days to incubate and a week or more to kill. Whatever happened here happened fast. My point is that we don't know what we're dealing with, and until we do, I suggest we limit possible exposure."

"My boys have been in here for almost an hour," Callahan said.

"And they're probably fine, but let's move everyone out of this room until I can run some tests."

"All right," Callahan agreed, then he shouted for everyone to stop what they were doing and go. "Don't be too long, Doc," he said once his men were gone. "I'm sure the Chief has heard about this by now and he's going to want a report...soon."

"We'll be as fast as we can," Iggy said and Callahan withdrew.

"You said you didn't think it's contagious," Alex said once Callahan was out of earshot.

"I just wanted him and his men away from this room," Iggy said. "It's going to be hard enough to figure out what happened here without the police stomping all over everything."

"How do we even begin?" Alex asked, looking around at the room full of corpses.

"Is this everyone from the mission?"

Alex looked around and nodded.

"There are four rooms in the sister's dormitory and four in the brother's. I see three sisters here and three brothers, plus ... plus Father Harry."

"With Sister Gwen outside, that's everyone," Iggy said. "I'll get a photographer and someone to help out from the Lieutenant. Then we'll see if we can identify any of the others."

"I'll see to Father Harry," Alex said, turning.

Iggy reached out and caught him by the arm.

"We don't have much time," he said. "I know it's bloody awful, but we'll have time for grieving later."

"He's on the floor," Alex growled through clenched teeth.

Iggy looked at him steadily. His look was determined, but there was compassion in his eyes.

"You know we have to investigate before we can move him," he said. "The sooner that's done, the sooner we can do right by the Father."

Alex clenched his fists, then closed his eyes and sighed. Iggy was right. The only thing Alex could do for Father Harry was to catch whoever did this. If he wanted to do that, he had to find clues — evidence, and his chance was rapidly slipping away. Callahan and the policemen wouldn't stay out forever. Alex met Iggy's gaze and nodded, stuffing his feelings down deep.

"I'll have a look around with the oculus," Alex said. "Maybe there's something here to be seen by ghostlight."

"You think whatever happened here was magical," Iggy said, nodding his head approvingly. "Good. Once you've done that, go find out what Sister Gwen knows. She'll be calm enough to talk to by then."

Alex set down his kit as Iggy moved off to have a word with Lieutenant Callahan. A moment later, he returned, followed by two officers.

If Iggy was right and whatever had killed Father Harry had done so in just a matter of hours, it had to be magical. Even the black plague took time to kill its victims. With that thought in mind, Alex strapped on his oculus and adjusted the lenses to reveal energy fields. Then he clipped a ghostlight burner into his multi-lamp and lit it.

Ghostly green light filtered out of the lantern's lens, bathing the room in its glow. To normal eyes, it looked dim and indistinct, but through the oculus, the room became flooded with light, and the dark benches and tables stood out in stark contrast. As his eye swept the room, he could see pulses of energy crisscrossing in the open space, like ripples from rocks thrown simultaneously into a pond. The lines bounced off each other and rebounded, forming new patterns.

Alex followed each pulse to its source, but each one ended at one of the stones he'd inscribed with a barrier rune earlier. Each of them was functioning perfectly, radiating out its magic and keeping the rain at bay. Other than that, however, there was no other magic in the room.

What else can kill quickly? Poison?

Alex went back to his kit and took out a ring made of jade. This wasn't the pale green, Asian jade, but rather a dark, forest green stone that came from Alaska, sometimes called nephrite. The stone had runes carved all around its circumference on each side and it hung suspended from a leather cord that had been cut from the belt of a poisoned man.

Taking the purity stone, Alex made his way to the table at the back where the big pot of soup sat. It was mostly empty, meaning that whatever happened here, it hadn't started in earnest until the assembled vagrants had come back for seconds. About an inch remained in the bottom, cold and congealed.

More than enough.

Alex lowered the purity stone into the soup and counted to ten before withdrawing it. If the soup had been poisoned, the ring would have glowed a bright, sickly yellow, but when he pulled it free of the thick mass, it remained deep green.

For good measure, Alex tested all the bowls that still had soup in them. None of them had been poisoned either.

Dejected, Alex cleaned off the purity stone and returned it to his kit. Putting on the oculus once more, he removed the ghostlight burner and replaced it with the silverlight. This time the room lit up and glowed so brightly it took Alex's eye a moment to get used to it. There were handprints, vomit, and urine everywhere. The leaky roof ensured that any old evidence had been washed away, so this was all new.

From the look of it, there had been chaos in the room at some point. Handprints showed where people had crawled and eventually collapsed as they succumbed to the strange illness. It looked like there had been a fight of some kind as Alex found traces of blood on the floor and even a tooth.

The greatest concentration of hand and finger prints were around and on the heavy oak doors that separated the Great Hall from the foyer and the dormitories. From the look of it, the doors had been locked, trapping everyone inside. That didn't make any sense, though. Father Harry carried a key to this door in his pocket. He couldn't have been locked in.

All of this was interesting, but after examining every trace, Alex was no closer to learning what happened than when he started.

Time to talk to Sister Gwen.

He returned his oculus and lamp to his kit and made his way to the kitchen.

"Learn anything?" Callahan asked when he emerged into the foyer.

"Not very much," Alex admitted. "I'm going to talk to Sister Gwen."

Callahan turned and followed him into the kitchen, opening up his notebook. Sister Gwen was sitting at the little table where the brothers and sisters of the mission took their meals, wrapped in a blanket. She still had the mug of tea in her hands and her trembling had subsided.

"Alex," she said when she saw him. "You have to help us." Her voice was distant but firm.

"I will, Sister," he said, sitting down next to her. "Tell me what happened after I left last night."

She took a slow breath and looked up into Alex's eyes. He saw fear there, and pain — two things of which he thought the old nun incapable.

"We just opened the doors for dinner," she said in a small voice. "I get tired helping with the cooking, so Father ... Father Clementine lets me take a nap in my room until nine, when he holds the evening service for the poor. The bells wake me up, but..." Tears welled up in her eyes and she squeezed them shut, sending the water trailing down her cheeks. "But there weren't any bells. I didn't wake up till after two in the morning."

"Then what happened?" Alex coaxed her.

"I went downstairs to make sure the front door was locked, but it was wide open. There wasn't anyone at the desk, so I went to see Father Clementine, but his room was empty. I looked, but no one was in their rooms. I came back down here to check the Great Hall but the doors were locked."

"Is that unusual?" Callahan asked.

"No." Sister Gwen shook her head. "Anyone who needs a place to sleep can stay here, but we lock them in."

"A few years ago, one of the vagrants got up in the middle of the night and attacked a nun," Alex explained. "They lock the doors ever since."

"Since I couldn't find Father Clementine, I went and got the spare key from his office. When I came down and opened the door..." She shook her head as if trying to find the words. "Everyone was in the Great Hall." She looked pleadingly up into Alex's eyes. "They were all dead. " She looked down at the mug in her hands. "All dead."

Alex clenched his fists, feeling the nails digging into his palms. He'd always seen Sister Gwen as a paragon of strength and faith. To see her like this made him want to beat someone soundly.

"I promise you, Sister Gwen," Alex said, managing to hide the rage in his voice. "I'm going to find out what happened here, and if someone did this, I'm going to make them suffer for it."

She looked up at him, her eyes suddenly clear, her old strength suddenly back. "Vengeance is mine, saith the Lord," she said, her voice full of its old power. "If someone did this, you prove it, and you give them to the police, you understand?"

"I do," Alex lied with a nod, and he could feel the weight of the semi-automatic pistol under his jacket. He would find whoever did this, and when he did, he wouldn't bother the police.

He looked up to find Callahan watching him intently. It was obvious from his face that he knew what Alex had been thinking.

"What now?" he said.

"I have to check something," Alex said, more to himself. "Take care of her," he told the policewoman.

Alex left the kitchen and went to the big doors that separated the Great Hall from the foyer. He turned his back to the door and walked across the narrow foyer to the cast iron radiator on the opposite wall. A boiler in the basement heated the building and the radiator. It had been modified to use enchanted boiler stones to heat the water, but the rest of the system still worked normally. Being careful not to burn his hand, Alex felt around under the hot iron fixture, until he found what he sought.

"You find something?" the lieutenant asked.

"Father Harry's key," he said, holding the old-fashioned iron skeleton key up so that Callahan could see it.

"What does that mean?"

"It means I know what happened here, at the end anyway," Alex said, standing. "Now let's see if Doctor Bell can tell us how it began."

6

THE CLIENT

"It's a disease of some kind," Iggy said once Alex and Lieutenant Callahan caught up with him. "It looks like smallpox but it's not. Some of these people look sicker than the others — they have more spots and they're larger, but I can't tell you why."

"What can you tell us?" Callahan said. "At this point I'd take anything."

"It's not magical," Alex said. "And it's not a poison. I checked the soup, the bread, and the water in all the pitchers."

"How is that possible?" Callahan said. "That means these people all came here, contracted some disease no one's ever heard of, and died in a matter of hours?"

Iggy nodded gravely.

"It's time we brought in some professionals," he said to Callahan. "Call over to the University, and wake up whoever you have to. Find out who is running their viral pathology program and get them over here as soon as possible."

"Viral—?" Callahan started, then stopped. "What's that now?"

"It's the study of diseases. Now hurry."

Iggy watched Callahan turn and head off toward a telephone, then turned to Alex.

"Anything else?"

"Father Harry must have realized what was happening." Alex held up the key. "He locked everyone in here, then slid the key under the door."

"He probably stopped whatever this is from killing a lot more people," Iggy said. "I wish I had more data. Who was the first person to be sick? How long did it take for symptoms to show?"

"It took less than an hour for symptoms," Alex said. "Sister Gwen said she didn't wake up till two in the morning because no one rang the bells for the service. The bell rope is in the choir loft, and you can only get there from a stair behind the kitchen. That means the door was locked before nine o'clock."

Iggy began stroking his mustache, something he did when thinking.

"We've got to find out how this plague came to be here," he said. "Is there anyone new to the mission?"

Alex shook his head. "Father Harry said that the Brothers and Sisters were new, except Sister Gwen. But it looked like they'd been here a while at least."

"What about the vagrants?"

"No way to tell," Alex said. "Most are probably regulars but there's bound to be a few new faces."

Alex swept his gaze over the hall. Nothing about the staff stood out and the patrons were all the same with their shabby clothes, unkempt appearance, and worn out shoes.

All except one.

"Hey," Alex said, pointing at a man under a blanket. He had been laid on an out-of-the-way table toward the rear of the hall. When whoever covered him pulled the blanket over his head, they exposed his shoes. His shiny, new-heeled shoes.

"Those aren't the shoes of a vagrant," Iggy said, seeing what Alex meant immediately. Alex nodded.

"That's a man who doesn't belong."

When they reached the table, Iggy pulled the blanket off without hesitation or ceremony. The man beneath it was in his thirties with slicked back hair, a pencil mustache, and a Roman nose. He was dressed in a pair of well-made trousers with a white button-up shirt sans necktie, and his collar was undone.

"Maybe he has an identity card," Alex said, checking the man's pockets. He found them all empty. "No smokes, no coins, no keys," he reported.

"I'm more interested in his condition," Iggy said. "These boils on his skin are bigger than anyone else's, and there are more of them. I think this man was the first person to be sick. He certainly has the worst case."

"So who is he and what was he doing here?" Alex asked.

Iggy shrugged, his hand wandering to his mustache again.

"What does the body tell us?"

Alex felt like he was back in detective school again with professor Bell giving lessons. He ran a practiced eye over the corpse, noting every detail and trying to fit them together into a picture.

"He's well-to-do," Alex began. "His clothes are well made, tailored."

"So he's wealthy?" Iggy prodded.

"No. He's got money, but he's not rich. His shoes have been resoled at least twice and those are new heels."

"Maybe he's thrifty."

Again Alex shook his head. "Wing tips are all the rage with the upper crust these days," he said. "If he traveled in moneyed circles, he'd have a pair."

"What else?"

Alex picked up the man's arm, bending it at the elbow.

"Look at his hands." He indicated a row of calluses along the pads where the fingers joined the hand. "Whatever he does for a living is hard on his hands. I'd say he's some kind of skilled tradesman, a sculptor, or maybe a carpenter."

"Not enough cuts on his hands for a carpenter," Iggy said. "When you work with wood you get splinters. I think you're right about him being well off, though. Whatever he does — did — it provided him a good living."

"That means he doesn't live around here," Alex said. "So what was he doing here?"

"Maybe we're assuming something we shouldn't," Iggy said. "Maybe he's not out of place here. Father Harry got donations from many sources; maybe he's a patron."

"In which case Sister Gwen might know him." Alex turned but stopped. Sister Gwen had seen far more than a saintly old woman should. How could he, in good conscience, subject her to more of this nightmare?

"I'll make sure all the brothers and sisters are covered," Iggy said, reading Alex's hesitation. "As long as they're not visible, she should be strong enough."

"She's strong," Alex said. "I've never met anyone with more grit. It just isn't fair to make her relive what happened when she opened those locked doors."

"She wants to know what happened here as badly as we do," Iggy said, and put his hand on Alex's shoulder. He wasn't wrong, but that didn't make Alex like it any better. He started off toward the kitchen and Iggy left to cover as many bodies as he could.

FIVE MINUTES LATER, Alex led Sister Gwen through the Great Hall's open doors and across the stone floor to the table in the back. Her steps were steady and purposeful, but she clung to Alex's arm like she was walking the edge of a cliff with certain death awaiting a misstep.

"I know him," she said after she'd stared at his face for a few moments. "He'd come in here every Sunday for Mass."

"Do you know his name?" Alex prompted.

"Charles Beaumont," Sister Gwen said. "I remember him because he used to ask Father Clementine to bless him every week."

"How did Mr. Beaumont know the Father?" Iggy asked. Sister Gwen sighed and shook her head.

"I don't know."

"Do you know anything else about him?" Alex asked.

The old nun hesitated as sadness washed across her features. "I probably shouldn't say." She looked up at Alex and her dark eyes bored into him like they had done so many times in his youth.

"It's all right," he said. "We just want to get to the truth. For Father Harry and for you."

She nodded and patted Alex on the cheek with her worn, gnarled hand.

"The Father once told me that Mr. Beaumont was a thief," she said.

Alex hadn't been expecting that. He looked to Callahan, who had just returned, and the big Lieutenant leaned over the dead man.

"Nobody I know," he said. "I'll have the local boys take a look."

"Thank you, Sister Gwen," Alex said, taking her hands in his. He had a momentary flash of all the times she had held his hands and comforted him as a boy. Now it was his turn.

The policewoman led Sister Gwen back out of the Great Hall and a fresh wave of anger washed over Alex as he saw how stooped and tired she looked.

"What now?" he asked, turning back to the body of Charles Beaumont.

"Here," Iggy said, pressing two dollars into his hand.

"What's this for?"

"Cab," Iggy said. "Go home. Get some sleep."

Alex opened his mouth to protest, but Iggy cut him off. "You've done all you can here. I still have to draw blood samples from half a dozen more victims and I need to brief the University people when they get here, otherwise I'd be going with you."

"There must be something else we can try."

"Like what?" Iggy said. "You've been over the whole room with your lantern, twice. You've interviewed the only witness, and now we know the name and possible occupation of the only person in the room who looks like he doesn't belong. And he looks like the first one infected. At least here."

"But—"

"Until something else comes up, we're stuck. Now, you have a business to run, and Leslie will expect you in the office tomorrow bright and early. Go home."

Alex knew he was right, but his mind railed against it anyway. He was a detective, damn it, there ought to be something he could do.

But there wasn't.

"All right," he said, tucking the bills in his pocket. "But if something comes up, you call me."

"Of course, old boy," Iggy said, then pushed Alex toward the door.

As he passed the sheet-draped body of Father Harry, Alex stopped. Iggy had rolled him on his back and composed his hands on his chest before covering him. Reverently, Alex knelt down and pulled the sheet back from the old man's face. It looked exactly as it had the previous afternoon except for a few angry-looking boils. He looked like he was just asleep, calm and peaceful.

But he wasn't.

Alex had faced death before, but never like this. Father Harry hadn't died in his sleep or from some horrible accident. Someone had done this to him. This was murder.

"I'm sorry, Father," Alex said, his voice hoarse and raw. "I should have stayed. I should have been here. Maybe I could have stopped this."

He looked down into the serene face but received no answer.

Alex had been angry before in his life, but what he felt in that moment was a white-hot boiling mass that seemed to crawl out of his chest and down his arms to his fists. Blood oozed from where his nails dug into the heels of his hands.

"I know you wouldn't approve," he whispered. "But I'm going to find whoever did this. And I'm going to make sure they die slowly."

The look on the old man's face didn't change, it couldn't change, but Alex fancied that he saw a bit of disappointment in it now.

The anger that threatened to spontaneously combust inside his ribcage vanished and an unbearable weariness pressed down on Alex.

"Goodbye, Harrison," he said, calling the Father by his proper name for the first and last time. "If I make it to heaven, I'll see you there."

Alex replaced the sheet over Father Harry's face and then strode out into the rain.

THE CAB RIDE home seemed to take a long time. Alex kept reviewing what he'd seen and done at the mission over and over in his mind. Iggy had been right: they'd covered everything they could. The next step would be to figure out where Beaumont lived, what he did for a living — assuming he wasn't a professional thief — and most importantly, where he came from before arriving at the mission.

Try as he might, Alex's exhausted brain simply couldn't figure any way to do that. A man dressed like Beaumont wouldn't be living anywhere near the mission, so where would the police start a canvass? They could have men out for months and not find anything.

He balled up his fists until his knuckles were white, but it didn't help. The only thing left to do was sleep on it and hope his reenergized brain would have better ideas in the morning.

BY THE TIME Alex had showered and dressed the following morning, it was pushing noon. He didn't think he would sleep at all when he got home in the wee small hours, but exhaustion and a few shots of Scotch had worked wonders. His stomach growled as he rode the crawler downtown to his office, but if he stopped for a bite anywhere, it would be lunchtime before he got to work. Leslie was going to have his hide as it was, and she was not a woman to keep waiting any longer than he already had.

When he finally did arrive, he found his secretary sitting behind her desk, buffing her nails with an air of calm detachment. Yelling was to be expected, but when Leslie went quiet, things were really bad.

"Morning," Alex said as if his arrival a mere twenty minutes before noon were completely ordinary.

"And where have you been?"

The tone in her voice could have kept his icebox cold for a month. He was about to answer, but she nodded toward his office.

"You've got a client waiting," she said. "Been here over an hour, insisted she'd wait."

"She?" Alex's face brightened but Leslie fixed him with a deadly stare.

"All I can say is you're damn lucky she didn't leave after twenty minutes. I already lost another client who called in and wanted you to find their missing car. While I waited for you, the police managed to find it."

"Sorry, doll," Alex said. "It was a rough one last night."

Leslie looked like she wanted to make a rude comment, no doubt about his bringing a tramp home and neglecting his business, and by extension, her. Something in his eyes stopped her, and her expression softened.

"We need this one," she said, the fire gone out of her voice. "I don't care if she wants you to follow her cheating husband or find her lost dog, don't blow it."

"I'm all over it, sweetheart," he said. Alex gave her a mock salute and turned to his office.

"You'd better be," Leslie muttered.

Alex resolved to take her somewhere for lunch as a peace offering, assuming he wasn't out looking for a dog.

Beyond the door sat a young woman in a bright blue sundress. She had curly black hair that fell just past her shoulders and large blue eyes that seemed to match her dress. She was pretty with a delicate nose, pink cheeks, and lips that looked like they wanted to pout without actually doing the deed. She had on simple black flats, a wide black belt that circled her narrow waist, and she sat up straight in her chair with her legs demurely crossed.

"Excuse me," Alex said, pulling the door shut behind him. "I was up late working with the police last night. I only just got in."

"Are you Mr. Lockerby?" she asked. Her voice had a slight, lilting drawl in it. Not enough for her to be from the deep South, but maybe Virginia or Maryland.

"I am," Alex said, offering her his hand. If she felt awkward about shaking hands, she didn't show it. "I hope you haven't been waiting too long."

"No," she said, and Alex knew it for the polite lie that it was. "It doesn't matter, Mr. Lockerby—"

"Call me Alex, Miss...?"

"Rockwell, Evelyn Rockwell."

Alex seated himself behind his desk and pulled a notepad and pen from a drawer. “Go on, Miss Rockwell.”

“Evelyn, and I’m in desperate need of your help, Alex,” she said. “You see, my brother is missing and I need you to find him. His name is Thomas Rockwell.”

As she spoke, Alex made notes about her manner and her voice. She was clearly distraught, but there was something she didn’t want to say. He wrote *hiding something* with a question mark after it.

“Thomas disappeared yesterday,” Evelyn went on. “We were supposed to have dinner, but he never came. I just know something bad has happened.” She was trembling now.

“Have you been to the police?” Alex asked, pulling a pair of tumblers and a bottle of bourbon out of his bottom desk drawer. He poured two fingers in one glass and passed it to Evelyn. She accepted the glass and took a sip before shaking her head.

“I had to come to you, only you.”

“Why only me? There are some very good policemen in this town.”

“None of them are runewrights.”

“Why do you need a runewright?”

“Thomas was a runewright,’ Evelyn explained. “He’s been researching something for weeks now.”

“A new rune?”

She shook her head.

“I don’t know. But he’d been withdrawn and moody. I could barely get him to talk to me. Then he called me two days ago. He was happy and excited, like he used to be.”

“That’s when you agreed to meet for dinner?” Alex asked.

“Yes, and then he didn’t come. I waited and waited, and finally I went to his apartment, but he wasn’t there either.”

“Is there somewhere he would go? A friend maybe?”

Evelyn shook her head. Tears were standing out in her eyes now and Alex offered her his handkerchief.

“When I went to his apartment, it was all torn up. Like there had been a fight. I’m so terribly worried, Mr. Lockerby.”

“Alex,” he corrected. “This rune he was working on, do you know what it is?”

"No."

"Does anyone else know about it?"

"I don't know," she said. "All I know is that my brother is missing. Will you find him for me, Alex? Please?"

"Do you have the key to his apartment?" Alex asked.

She reached into her purse and pulled out a small brass key on a ring.

"I charge twenty-five dollars a day, plus expenses," Alex said, accepting the key. "I have a very good finding rune but I'll need to go to his apartment to cast it. I charge ten dollars for the rune."

She reached into her purse again and pulled out several folded bills, peeling one away from the others. "Will one hundred dollars be enough of a retainer?"

"That will be fine." Alex tried not to accept the bill too hastily. "I have a lunch appointment, but as soon as I'm done, I'll go over to your brother's apartment and cast the rune. Is there a phone number where I can reach you?"

She took his pencil and wrote out a phone number and an address in the north side mid-ring.

Alex stood and showed Evelyn out.

"She didn't look happy," Leslie said once they heard the elevator door in the hall close.

"Her brother is missing," Alex said, holding up the c-note. Leslie snatched it and held it up to the light, looking for print errors.

"It's genuine," she said.

"I told her I'd get on it right after lunch," he told her. Leslie fixed a level gaze on him. He shrugged. "I figured I owed you."

Her smile lit up the room and she picked up her handbag.

"None of your crummy dog-wagons," she said, putting on her jacket. "I pick the place."

"Deal."

7

THE BROTHER

It was nearly two o'clock when Alex trudged up in front of a red brick apartment building right against the border between the north side, middle and outer ring. Despite being this close to the low rent district, the building was clean and well maintained, and there wasn't any trash on the sidewalk. The key Evelyn Rockwell had given him had 5C stamped on it and Alex looked up at the five-story building wearily. It was a cinch that a building this far out wouldn't have an elevator.

His lunch with Leslie had gone well; she'd chosen to eat at the *Imperial Table*, a Chinese joint with linen napkins and china plates that were actually from China. Alex used to dislike foreign foods, but living with Iggy had broadened his palate a bit.

He waited until they'd finished their chop suey to tell Leslie about the mission and Father Harry. She hadn't much liked Father Harry, but the news still hit her hard. It's a strange thing how someone you know can be alive one minute and dead the next, but you don't feel it. You don't know until someone tells you, and only then do you understand the things they did that you'll never experience again. Alex found himself talking to Leslie about his youth in the mission and what Father Harry had done for him. With the

Father gone, he wanted someone else to know just how great a man had passed.

Alex pushed thoughts of lunch and of Father Harry out of his mind as he ascended the stairs of Thomas Rockwell's building. There would be time to reminisce later, with a bottle of bourbon.

Preferably two.

The door to Thomas' apartment was shut and locked securely. There weren't any scratches or tool marks that would indicate that the lock had been picked, so Alex inserted the key and turned it. The lock yielded smoothly and he pushed the door open.

Beyond the door was a large room that had once been well appointed. Evelyn had been right, however — the room looked like the scene of a barroom brawl. Furniture had been turned over, lamps smashed, and the contents of every drawer littered the floor.

Someone had been looking for something. Something they wanted very badly.

The fabric covers on the sofa had been slashed open and every pillow was cut. The doors and drawers of a standing secretary cabinet were open and their contents spilled on the floor. Every cupboard in the tiny kitchen stood open, even the door to the range. No stone seemed to have gone unturned.

"All right," he said to the empty room. "Let's get to work."

A sweep with his lantern revealed fingerprints all over, but not as many as he'd expected. Whoever tossed Thomas' place must have worn gloves. He did, however, find an excessive amount of bodily fluids in the bedroom. Thomas might have been a bachelor, but he wasn't spending all his nights alone, that much was clear.

Maybe his exercise partner can tell me what he was working on. On the other hand, if he has a girlfriend, why hasn't she reported him missing?

After the silverlight, Alex used the ghostlight to look for magic. Being that Thomas was a runewright, it wasn't surprising that his apartment lit up like a neon sign. There were protection runes on the door and runes of silence on the walls, ceiling, and floor to keep out noise from his neighbors. A few runes written on flash paper littered the floor, but these were all basic. The interesting runes were written on Thomas Rockwell's kitchen table. A large central rune decorated the tabletop with at least four nodes, and six other runes wound around it. Alex knew most of the runes, but he'd never seen a casting this complex before. The big rune was for concealment — it was almost exactly like the one Alex had put on his book safe in Iggy's library. The others all dealt with either privacy or finding.

Alex took out a pad of paper from his kit and meticulously copied the construct. It looked like something to prevent people spying on Thomas, magically or otherwise.

Something a man working on a revolutionary new rune might do.

Alex wondered why it was so intricate. There were better runes Thomas could have used that would make the construct simpler and more effective. Rune casting was always a balance between simplicity and power. Adding nodes to a central rune could make it more specific and therefore more powerful, but the more complicated a rune got, the more a runewright ran the risk of conflicts and backlash.

Satisfied that no out-of-place magic was operating in Thomas' apartment, Alex packed away the ghostlight burner and turned to the mess on the floor. Clearly whoever got here ahead of him had decided that those things weren't worth keeping, so it was likely they wouldn't be of use to him either. Still, he had to check. Anything he could learn about Thomas' life leading up to his disappearance would help when he cast his own finding rune.

Alex pulled the dining table to the center of the room, then put his multi-lamp on top of it. From his kit, he extracted another burner and clipped it in place, then lit it. He took the covers off the other three faces of the lamp, letting the amberlight inside fill the whole room. Amberlight looked just like its name implied, a ruddy reddish-yellow glow. Everywhere the light touched, rusty-brown shapes began to appear in the air. Iggy called amberlight, *Newton's first law of motion applied to time*. If you shone amberlight on a chair, it would create an image of that chair in the place where it usually stood.

An object under amberlight showed where it was usually at rest.

As the light filtered out of the lantern and filled the room, Alex took a pair of yellow spectacles from his kit and clipped them to his nose. The amberlight after-images snapped into sharp focus, and Alex could see the room as it had been before it had been wrecked. The sofa had stood against the back wall opposite a bookcase that now lay in the center of the room, next to the open secretary cabinet. Alex returned them to their places, allowing the light to shine where they had been. A shower of book images rose up from the floor and flowed up onto the bookcase, each coming to rest where it had been. Several flickered, more indistinct than the others — these were books Thomas moved regularly, and Alex traced each one down where they lay on the floor and set them aside.

Moving around the room, Alex rearranged the furniture and picked up anything that looked important or often used. It took over an hour but when he finally blew out the amberlight burner he had a stack of books, papers, and curios to examine.

An hour later, he had to admit defeat. There was plenty of information on Thomas' activities as a bookkeeper, all of it boring and ordinary, but nothing on his activities as a runewright. The only thing he could find that gave any idea at all about Thomas Rockwell was an old picture of the man himself, standing in front of the doors of Empire Tower. He was a lean and lanky man in his mid-twenties when the photograph was taken, with light hair and a bushy, unkempt mustache. Despite that, Thomas had a debonair air about him; he wore a bowler hat at a jaunty angle and had a genuine, friendly smile. It spoke well of him as a person, but it gave Alex no real insight into the man behind the ratty 'stache.

"Damn it," Alex swore, getting up and pacing the apartment. He wanted more information to use in his finding rune. The more he knew about Thomas and what might have made him disappear, the more powerful his casting would be.

Now he had to do it the old-fashioned way.

Alex went back to Thomas' bedroom and into the bathroom. Despite Thomas' having a regular visitor, there was only one toothbrush. Alex picked it up and started to turn when he caught sight of himself in the mirror over the sink. He remembered seeing fingerprints on the bottom of the mirror when he swept the room with silverlight. Fingerprints on a bathroom mirror weren't exactly uncommon, but only on the bottom?

Alex set down the toothbrush and carefully felt the bottom edge of the glass. Using his fingernail, he was able to pull it away from the wall and swing it upward on a hidden hinge at the top. Behind the mirror was a small space cut out of the wall. Inside were a book bound in blue leather, a gold pocket watch, and a roll of bills with a rubber band around it. Alex took the book and carefully lowered the mirror back down over the secret space. He cursed himself for not looking for this kind of hidey-hole first, but most runewrights would have extra-dimensional vaults. If Thomas had a vault, anything in it would be gone forever.

Alex picked up the toothbrush and went back to the front room. He still needed to cast his finding rune. Without a better connection to Thomas, it wouldn't be very powerful, but he could at least get direction and distance from the toothbrush. The book would give him a better insight into Thomas the runewright, but it would take hours, maybe days of study, and he needed answers now. Evelyn needed them.

Alex set the book aside and removed an inkwell and pen set from his kit. He followed them with a piece of chalk, a vial of green powder, a small leather tool case, and a red beeswax candle. He took off his jacket, picked up the chalk, and drew an octagonal shape on the floor by the table. Around the octagon, at each point, he drew different geometric shapes; circles, triangles, squares, and trapezoids. Once that was done, he took the pen and carefully dipped it in the inkwell. The ink was a solution of several substances, most of them expensive, so he was careful not to spill any. In each of the eight small shapes around the octagon, he drew a rune. The order he wrote them and the shape they occupied were all part of the magic. When he finished, he moved to the center of the octagon and drew an elaborate rune. This was the finding rune base, the rune that tied the whole pattern together. It always reminded Alex of a dragon sitting on a fainting couch.

His writing done, Alex put away the pen and inkwell. He lit the candle, then while it burned, he took out the tool case and vial of green powder. The powder was emerald dust and very expensive, but fortunately Alex needed only the tiniest bit for the finding rune. He took out a metal spatula, that looked for all the world like a miniature shovel, and coaxed a few precious grains of the emerald onto it. Moving with exaggerated care, he tapped the grains off into the still-wet ink of the reclining dragon symbol and the ink promptly turned a deep green. Lastly, Alex took the candle and dripped eight drops of wax on the points of the chalk octagon. When the last drop hit, the entire geometric shape and all its sub-shapes turned red, and the finding rune glowed with power.

Alex put his hand on the rune and felt the power of the universe flow through him. Calling the photograph of Thomas into his mind, Alex spoke.

"I seek to find one Thomas Rockwell," he pronounced in a loud, clear voice. "Bookkeeper and runewright. Brother of Evelyn. I seek him here, in the heart of his domicile. Show him to me."

Usually the incantation that released the rune's magic took longer, but usually Alex had a better idea of who he sought. He'd worked with less, but he didn't like it.

Normally the rune would come back with something almost instantly. It could be a sound or smell, or even just an impression of which direction to seek the target. The better Alex's link to the person or object, the more details he'd receive. Sometimes he could even see them and their surroundings if the bond was strong enough.

This time he felt nothing.

That could only mean one thing. It meant that Thomas was dead.

Alex kept his hand on the rune and reached out with his senses nonetheless. He'd never received a response that took longer than a few seconds, but it didn't hurt to try. After a full minute, he gave up.

"I'm sorry, Evelyn," he said out loud.

Casting a finding rune used a tremendous amount of energy and Alex felt weariness pushing down on him. He dragged himself up into a chair and sat staring at Thomas' little blue book. It had the runewright emblem stamped into the cover and it was stained dark from repeated handling.

Has to be his Lore book, he thought.

If Evelyn was right, something in Thomas' book might have gotten him killed. Alex hadn't been paid to find a killer, but turning the book over to the police would be a waste of time. Only a fellow runewright would know what to look for in a book full of runes.

Alex picked it up and opened it. He smiled as he saw the first, most basic runes in the front. Each page was covered with annotations and drawings. It reminded him very much of his father's lore book that he'd inherited. Flipping through the pages revealed Thomas' training. As the pages progressed, his notes became more specific and more detailed as he learned to draw more utility from a single rune. All of it was familiar to Alex — he had these runes and many more in his own lore book.

When he reached the end, however, everything changed. The last dozen pages were filled with six of the most complex runes Alex had ever seen. One looked very much like his own finding rune, but heavily modified. Another resembled a life rune, magic that would allow a runewright to power his constructs with his own life force. Another looked familiar, but Alex couldn't place it. The other three were alien to him. He'd have to study them intensely to figure out what they were for.

He whistled as he paged back and forth, looking at these last pages. They were orders of magnitude more complex than anything else in Thomas' book. They were certainly something that might have cost him his life. New runes were a rare thing and, depending on what these particular runes did, they could be worth a fortune.

"Well, somebody wanted something here," Alex said, looking down at the mess. It was likely that whoever tossed Thomas' place didn't find what they were looking for. Only a desperate searcher cuts open the couch.

Alex suddenly felt very self-conscious with the book. He'd been in Thomas' apartment for hours. What if a neighbor had been paid to watch it? He could very well find himself running into a welcoming committee out in the hall.

He quickly put away his gear, except for his chalk, and then drew a door on one of the walls. Activating a rune from his book, Alex opened his vault. He placed the book inside along with his kit, then slipped a rune-covered pair of brass knuckles into the outside pocket of his jacket.

It never hurt to be prepared.

Satisfied, Alex closed the door, and scrubbed the chalk outline from the wall with his handkerchief.

He needn't have bothered. No one lurked in the hall or the stairwell waiting to pounce. There wasn't anyone strange at the crawler station either, let alone as a crawler passenger, while Alex rode back to the brownstone.

IT WAS WELL after six when Alex got home, and he wanted nothing more than to tramp upstairs to his bed.

"In here," Iggy's voice came from the kitchen.

Alex sighed and turned away from the stairs and his inviting bedroom. He expected to find Iggy working his culinary magic over a hot stove, but was surprised to see the balding man sitting at the table with nothing but a cup of tea and a lit pipe. He looked old. Alex knew that Iggy was in his seventies, but he'd never seen the man look old. Iggy was usually bursting with energy and enthusiasm for life. Now he appeared drained, hollow even.

"What is it?" Alex asked. "This is about Father Harry, I can see it in your face. What's happened?"

Iggy's brown eyes moved up to meet Alex's.

"Are you sure you want to know?" he asked. "I don't recommend it."

Alex sat down across the table, all traces of his weariness evaporating.

"Tell me." he insisted.

"Doctor Halverson is the man at the University who studies diseases," Iggy began. "I've been up with him since last night at his laboratory. Thanks to those blood samples I collected, Halverson was able to grow samples of the virus and stain them."

"Isn't that a good thing?" Alex asked. "I thought the whole point of staining was that you could see whatever made people sick and then stop it."

"Yes and no, in this case." Iggy nodded. He puffed on his pipe as if searching for the right words to continue. "We got a good look at the little devils, clear as spring well water."

"And?"

"And there's nothing natural about that damn disease," Iggy said, shivering as if taken by a chill. "It's too perfect. It was designed. Engineered by someone."

Alex could feel the blood draining from his face as the implications of that statement took hold of his mind.

"This is terrifying," Iggy said. His pipe had gone out, but he continued to puff at it anyway. "Man shouldn't have this kind of power. I wish I didn't know about it."

"I'm glad you do," Alex said after a long silence.

"What do you mean, boy?" Iggy said, aghast. Alex shrugged.

"Someone has to pay for Father Harry," he said. "Someone has to pay for all the people at the mission." He reached into his coat and pulled his Colt 1911 from its holster, placing it on the table. "I don't know how to kill a virus," he said. "But I know how to kill a man."

8

THE ULTIMATUM

Alex spent most of the night replenishing his rune book, taking apart the hinges that kept it together and replacing the torn out pages with new ones. Work was still the best way he knew to burn through anger, and he was angry. Somewhere in New York lurked the person responsible for the death of Father Harrison Arthur Clementine. The thought made his fingers itch. As soon as the sun was up, he would start chasing down the identity of Charles Beaumont, possible thief. He had no magic to aid him this time, so he'd have to do it the old fashioned way, but someone out there knew something about Beaumont. Sooner or later Alex would find him.

His anger kept him working until well after two in the morning. He hadn't had anything to drink during his long night, so when a pounding in his head woke him less than six hours later, he couldn't figure out what it was. Finally the sound resolved itself into a pounding on the door.

"Wha'sit?" Alex managed as he rolled out of bed onto the floor.

"Are you alive in there?" Iggy's voice came through the door.

Alex didn't reply, dragging himself to his feet instead and shuffling to the door.

"All right," he said, releasing the bolt and pulling the door open. Outside in the hall, Iggy stood dressed in a very British tweed suit with a book under one arm. "What is it?" Alex demanded.

"Cops are here for you," Iggy said, nodding toward the stairs. "They're not very polite, so I left them waiting in the vestibule." His mustache turned up into a grin.

The brownstone's vestibule was a space between the front door and the house proper where visitors could remove their hats and coats in inclement weather. It had a tiled floor with a mosaic of Manhattan Island on the floor. A glass door set into a glass wall were all that separated the vestibule from the house proper, but the runes on the glass made it virtually unbreakable. If Iggy had locked the door before coming up, then no one but he or Alex could unlock it again.

"What do they want?" Alex asked, vigorously rubbing the sleep from his eyes.

"For you to come with them to police headquarters," Iggy said. "They're most insistent. Should I keep them waiting?"

Alex rubbed his face and felt his unshaven scruff. "No," he said. "Tell them I'll be down in a minute."

Iggy shrugged and headed back downstairs at a leisurely pace. Alex grinned at that. He suspected Iggy had been a private detective himself at some point; he certainly had the skills down pat. He also possessed a healthy dislike of run-of-the-mill uniformed policemen.

There wasn't time to shower or shave, so Alex ran a comb through his hair and put on a clean shirt. His shoulder holster hung over the back of his overstuffed chair, but he passed it by. The police seemed upset about something and he had no desire to antagonize them. He did want access to the weapon, so once he was fully dressed, he opened his vault and left it inside.

There were three policemen waiting in the vestibule for Alex. Two were uniformed officers, while the other was a detective Alex didn't know. The uniforms were a mismatched pair, one tall and lanky, the other built like a fireplug. The detective was middle-aged and paunchy with a permanent sneer on his face. All of them seemed sullen and angry. Alex stifled a grin. They'd wanted to roust him out of bed personally and yell at him to hurry up dressing before hauling him off to the station. It was a common enough intimidation tactic, though Alex had no idea why they'd want to use it on him.

"Hello boys," Alex said, unlocking the vestibule and opening the door. "What's the good news?"

One of the uniforms reached out to grab him, but jerked his hand back with a curse when it crossed the threshold of the door. Alex grinned openly this time. He stepped into the vestibule and shut the door behind him. This time the officers each grabbed one of his arms.

"Think you're cute?" the detective sneered.

"My mother always thought so," Alex said. He wasn't sure what this was about, but he wasn't going to let this little puke of a detective think he was in charge. At six foot one, Alex was taller than all of them.

"Well your mother ain't here," the detective said. "Captain Rooney wants a word with you down at Central."

With that he turned and reached out to open the front door, but stopped. He remembered what happened to the squat officer when he'd reached for Alex.

"I'll get it," Alex said, tearing his arm free of the tall officer and opening the door. They needn't have worried. There weren't any runes keeping people from leaving the house, only from entering.

THE OFFICERS BUNDLED Alex in the back of a cruiser with the fireplug on one side and the detective on the other while beanpole drove. The car had an antenna on the roof that collected power from Empire Tower to run its electric motor. The sorcerer William Todd had given the New York police over one hundred of these cars as a goodwill gesture. That, and to annoy Rockefeller, who was trying to make his crawler magic work in smaller vehicles like cars. The two had been feuding for years and the police had benefited from it. Todd had even given the department a small number of experimental flying units he called Floaters, but despite their obvious advantages, they were slow and difficult to maneuver, so the police didn't use them much.

The central station for the Manhattan office of the New York police department was located halfway between Empire Tower and the park. It stood ten stories high and housed most of the Island's officers, detectives, and facilities. The office of Captain Patrick Rooney was on the tenth floor. Rooney was responsible for all the detectives on the island and had a dozen lieutenants under him, each responsible for a section of territory. Unlike Lieutenant Callahan, Rooney had gotten his job the really old-fashioned way — he was the son of a senator. Like most political appointees, Captain Rooney didn't care about the actual police work, so long as nothing made him look bad.

As far as Alex knew, he hadn't done anything high profile enough to get on Rooney's hit list. Still, whatever the Captain wanted to see him about must be bad or he wouldn't have sent his personal goon squad to bring Alex in. They escorted him up to the tenth floor and then to the back of the building where the Captain's office was.

Rooney was a big man with big hands, big feet, a big nose and a big opinion of his own importance. He stood six feet three with broad shoulders, pale skin and red hair that he kept close-cut. When the sneering detective opened the door, Rooney's face was already red as a beet. There were half a dozen people in the room, including Callahan and Danny Pak.

"It's about time," Rooney roared. "What kept you?"

"A septuagenarian doctor," Alex said with a completely straight face.

"Did you search him?" Rooney asked with a gleam in his eye.

The detective patted Alex down and reluctantly reported that he had no weapons. The crestfallen look on Rooney's face gave Alex pause. He hadn't looked around at the others in the room when he'd been brought in, but a quick look told him that they were all trying very hard not to be noticed, even Danny. Whatever got Rooney all steamed up, it was bad.

"So," the Captain said, focusing his attention on Alex. "What do you have to say for yourself?

"Well, I'm a Sagittarius, an above average poker player, and a fine judge of liquor and women."

A chuckle ran around the room and Rooney swelled up like he would burst, then mastered himself and sat down behind his desk.

Whatever he was mad about must be serious for him to exercise such self-control. Alex had probably made it worse with his wisecrack, but at least now he knew the waters in which he was swimming.

"You're a funny man, Lockerby," Rooney said, his voice quiet and even. If anything it was more disturbing than his yelling. "I wonder how funny you'll find it when I charge you with obstruction, interfering with a police investigation, destroying evidence, and anything else I can think of?"

Alex had long ago mastered his poker face, so he just smiled, but his mind reeled at Rooney's declaration. If the Chief could make any of those charges stick, true or not, Alex would lose his investigator's license at best, or at worst, go to jail.

"Now why would you want to charge a nice guy like me with anything like that, Captain?" Alex said. "You know I stay out of your investigations unless you invite me in."

"I never invited you anywhere, you charlatan," Rooney growled, his temper edging back. "That was your friend over there.'" He nodded in Danny's direction. "If he wasn't a damn good detective, he'd be directing traffic by the park right now."

So whatever this was about, Danny had brought Alex into it. The only job they'd done recently was the murdered customs agent, Jerry Pemberton.

"I take it you didn't catch Mr. Pemberton's murderer at the customs warehouse?"

Rooney's fists clenched so tightly that his fingers turned white. He had been enjoying Alex's bewilderment and now his toy had been taken away.

"No, we didn't catch him," Rooney said. "And you knew that all along, didn't you?"

Now Alex really was confused.

"I didn't tell him how to evade your men, Captain," Alex said. "If he got away, I'm sorry, but I had nothing to do with it."

"You knew no one was coming," Rooney roared.

Alex looked at Danny and the detective shrugged and shook his head.

"Don't look at him," Rooney said. "He's in enough trouble because of you. You sent us to that warehouse on a guess and it turned into a wild goose chase. Do you have any idea how much it cost to put men on that building for the last thirty-six hours? I had to get special permission from the Mayor, and the Governor, because foreign governments have shipments in there."

So that was it. Staking out the customs warehouse required the Feds' involvement. Rooney and the Mayor stuck their necks out because catching someone breaking into such a secure and important location would make them look good. When no one came, Rooney had egg on his face.

Damn political appointees.

"Maybe they'll come tonight or tomorrow." Alex said.

Rooney's face screwed itself up into an ugly smile. "Everything in that warehouse has been picked up by the rightful owners," he said. "The entire layout has changed from that drawing Pemberton made. No one's coming."

Alex felt the first pangs of real fear. Rooney's neck was on the block and he was looking hard for a patsy. A smart-mouthed, consulting runewright detective was the perfect target. Still, he wasn't in handcuffs, so Rooney must have something else in mind.

"Get to the bad news," Alex said.

"You really are too smart for your own good, Lockerby," he said. "The bad news is that the Chief of Police wants to see me in his office at ten o'clock, Monday morning. He's given me until then to justify the warehouse stakeout by finding Pemberton's murderer. If I go into that meeting without the guilty party and an ironclad case, I'm giving the Chief you, Lockerby. And not just you," he said, looking at Danny. "Understand?"

Alex understood. He had four days to solve a case where he must have missed something. And, if he failed, he'd take Danny down with him.

"In that case," Alex said, putting his hat back on. "I'd better get to work."

"The rest of you get out, too," Rooney said.

Alex left the office first, but lingered by the elevators. The other detectives and the two officers gave him dirty looks as most of them headed for the stairs, but Callahan marched right for him with Danny Pak in tow.

"We need to talk, Lockerby," he growled under his breath. He pushed the elevator button and a moment later the three of them were descending toward the first floor. As soon as the doors closed, Callahan rounded on Alex.

"I don't know how this case went sideways, scribbler, but you're about to cost me one of my best detectives."

"This isn't Alex's fault, Lieutenant," Danny said.

"It doesn't matter whose fault it is, Detective. The Mayor is howling for someone's head, and if you're not careful, it's going to be yours."

"Relax, Callahan," Alex said with a confidence he didn't feel. "Danny and I will find your killer."

"Who said you get to appropriate my Detective?" Callahan said with a sneer. "You've already done enough damage."

"Danny's head's on the block just like mine, Lieutenant," Alex said. "If you really want to keep him, you'd better give me all the help you can."

Callahan's jaw tightened at that, but he nodded. "Go with Lockerby," he said to Pak as the elevator doors opened.

Danny followed Alex out.

"One more thing, Lieutenant," Alex said, catching the grate as Callahan tried to close it. "Did you ever find out anything about Charles Beaumont?"

"You've already got a case to solve," Callahan said, pulling the grate closed. "No," he said before pulling the lever to ascend. "We've checked pawn shops up and down the east side and no one knows him. It's a dead end. Now get to work."

Alex and Danny watched the elevator rise up out of sight, then turned toward the front doors of the building.

"Where do we start?" Danny asked, following Alex out.

"Breakfast. Your friends dragged me out of my bed this morning."

Alex and Danny took a crawler all the way back to the stop near the brownstone.

"You brought me all the way over here for this?" Danny said when they stopped in front of *The Lunch Box*. "Alex, this place is a dive. Trust me, I'm a cop, I know a dive when I see one."

The diner was made from a converted trolley car that sat on an empty corner just a few blocks from the brownstone. It had been painted red some time ago, but now the paint and the lettering above the door were faded and peeling. Inside, a long counter ran almost the entire length of the building with a row of booths up against the outside wall. Alex slapped Danny on the back and led him inside.

"Trust me," he said. "I hear they just got a really good cook."

Behind the counter sat a bored-looking woman at least fifty years old. Her shirt was stained from years of working the counter and her hair was done up in a messy bun. A faded nameplate pinned to her shirt read *Doris*.

"Hey Sugar," she said in a bored voice when they entered.

"Doris, it's been a while, how's that husband of yours?" Alex asked.

"Still a cheating bastard," Doris reported. "The usual?"

"Did Mary get a job here?" he asked.

"You mean the new cook?" Doris shrugged. "Yeah, she's in back. She does look like your type. You want me to get her?"

"Please," Alex said, then he led Danny down the bar and took a stool near the middle.

"Poached eggs," Mary said, coming out of the back. "Can you believe it? Max gave me the job."

"I'm sure you earned it," Alex said. "This is my best friend, Danny Pak." He pointed to the detective. "This is Mary. She makes a mean poached egg."

Danny's eyes lit up at the sight of Mary, and he stood.

"Charmed," he said, taking her hand.

"What'll you have, handsome?" she asked Danny.

"I hear the poached eggs are good," he said. "I'll have that with some sausage and hash browns."

"Adam and Eve on a log and spike the oval," Mary said. "Got it."

"I just want pancakes," Alex said, not bothering to repress a grin and Danny's reaction. Mary really was quite pretty.

"And one short stack," she said. "By the way, thanks for the rune," she said over her shoulder as she headed back to the kitchen. "My stockings have never been better."

"Hey," Danny said, elbowing Alex. "How come you never give me useful runes?"

"When you get a run in your stockings, let me know," Alex said. Danny laughed but then his face turned serious.

"What are we going to do about Rooney?"

"Is it possible the thieves saw your stake-out and bolted?"

"Not a chance." Danny shook his head.

"Then I must have missed something back at Pemberton's apartment."

"*We* must have."

"I was so sure." Alcx chewed his lip.

"Me too. Why else would Pemberton draw that map of the warehouse? A place where he worked every day."

"Excuse me," a well-dressed businessman at the end of the bar interjected. "Could you pass the ketchup?"

"Sure," Danny said, sliding the bottle down the bar to him.

"Thanks," he said, then poured some on his plate of scrambled eggs.

"Ugh," Alex said suppressing a shudder. He'd seen too many crime scenes to ever use ketchup again. It reminded him too much of... "Blood," he said.

"What about it?" Danny asked, adding milk to the coffee Doris brought them. "Most of it vanished with Pemberton's body."

"Not on the body," Alex said. "On the paper. I'm so stupid! How did I miss that?"

Danny was staring at him, coffee forgotten.

"What blood on the paper?" he asked. "You mean the map? That was clean."

"That's my point," Alex said. "They tore off three of the fingernails on Pemberton's right hand. If he'd drawn that map for them, there'd be blood on the paper, enough to soak through to the second sheet."

"Unless he's left-handed," Danny said. Alex shook his head.

"Remember the body? Pemberton parted his hair on the left. Most people part their hair on the opposite side from their dominant hand."

Danny was nodding now.

"If you're right, Pemberton drew that map before his killer showed up."

"But why?" Alex asked. "You said it yourself, he worked there every day. There's no reason for him to need a map."

"Unless," Danny said with a sly grin. "What if he was the one robbing the warehouse?" Alex gave him a blank look, trying to catch up. "Think about it," Danny continued. "Pemberton knew what was coming in, from where, and when it would be in the warehouse. He was in the perfect position to rob the place."

Alex nodded, thinking it through.

"Probably got tired of putting in all that service just to get a plaque as a thank you."

"All he'd need," Danny said, "is an accomplice. He picks out what to steal, then the accomplice uses the map to break in and make off with the stuff while Pemberton goes somewhere public to establish an alibi."

Alex liked this idea. It explained why Pemberton had drawn a map of his own workplace, and why someone had later beaten the truth out of him.

"So the people that killed him are the ones he robbed," Alex said. "And they stopped tearing off fingernails when he gave up his partner and the loot."

"I like it," Danny said.

"Yes, but our customers don't," Mary said, putting full plates down in front of them. "You've scared off two of them already. If you want to talk shop, lower your voices." Her words were admonishing, but she still wore her charming half smile when she said it.

Danny apologized profusely and promised that they'd be quieter. Alex just smiled.

"So, what do we do now?" Danny asked once Mary had gone.

"Personally, I think you should ask her for her number," Alex said, pouring syrup on his pancakes.

"I mean about Pemberton's killer," Danny said.

"We need to find out who had goods in that warehouse the night before Pemberton was killed."

"Why the night before?"

"Because," Alex said. "Whoever got robbed had to have time to discover the theft and then figure Pemberton was involved. That would put the robbery the night before. You need to ask the customs people for the warehouse manifest for that night."

"Why me?" Danny asked through a mouthful of hash browns.

"Well they're not going to tell me, are they?" Alex said. He finished his pancakes and stood.

"Where are you going?" Danny asked, barely halfway through his breakfast.

"I've got to go give a lovely young woman some bad news."

"Are you finally spoken for?" Danny asked with a smirk.

"No, this is the really bad news." Alex explained about Thomas Rockwell and his sister.

"Oh," Danny said. "Couldn't find him with your fancy rune?"

Alex shook his head and Danny put his hand on Alex's shoulder.

"You know your rune isn't infallible, right?" he said. "The guy might be underground, or magically shielded, or maybe he just left Manhattan. That much flowing water would block even your runes."

"I know," Alex said with a sigh. "But I found a stash behind his bathroom mirror with his Lore book inside right next to a roll of cash. Had to be three hundred."

"So he didn't leave on his own," Danny said, nodding. "He'd never leave those behind. Maybe someone grabbed him?"

"Unlikely," Alex said. "His place was tossed. If whoever did that had my missing man, they'd just beat the location of whatever they were looking for out of him, like Pemberton."

Danny whistled. "Sorry," he said.

"I'll manage," Alex said, putting on his hat. "As soon as you get that manifest, call Leslie and give her the list, then I'll check them out. Once we find out who got robbed, we'll know the identity of our killer."

"It occurs to me that if they killed Pemberton to get their property back, they aren't likely to admit being robbed."

"Don't you worry about that," Alex said. "If they've got something to hide, I'll sniff them out. You just make sure you get that manifest."

"Will do," Danny said, then turned back to his breakfast.

9

THE VISITORS

It was such a nice day that Alex decided he would walk all the way to his office. The fact that when he got there, he needed to tell the lovely and worried Evelyn Rockwell that her brother was, in all likelihood, dead, had nothing to do with it whatever. Danny had been right, of course — there was still a very slim chance that Thomas was alive, but that felt like false hope.

He had to tell Evelyn the truth.

Alex stuck out his arm to hail a cab, but the park was only a block away and that gave him an idea. Right by the entrance to the park stood a public phone booth, so he crossed the street to it and dialed Evelyn's number.

"Hello," she said after four rings.

"Evelyn, this is Alex Lockerby. I have some information about your brother. How soon can you meet me by the carousel in Central Park?"

"Um. About twenty minutes, I guess."

"Fine. I'll wait for you there."

Evelyn promised to hurry and hung up. Alex strolled across the park to where the carousel stood. He bought a bag of hot peanuts from a vendor, then picked a bench a little way away. The ride was noisy enough that anyone walking by wouldn't be able to overhear them.

Alex took out the pack of Bert's cigarettes and checked them. Only five left. With a sigh, he lit one, then amused himself, pitching an occasional peanut to the squirrels while he waited. He had just got down to the bottom of the bag when Evelyn hurried up. She was dressed in a dark green skirt and matching jacket over a white blouse, and her makeup was perfect. She flashed him an earnest smile that made him a little lightheaded.

"I came as soon as I could," she said, sitting down next to him. "What news do you have?"

Alex's good mood evaporated and he wadded up what remained of the bag of nuts.

"I'm sorry, Evelyn," he said in the gentlest voice he could muster. "I believe that Thomas is dead."

He was expecting hysterics, but Evelyn simply pulled an embroidered handkerchief from her clutch and dabbed at her eyes.

"I knew it might be something like that," she said, her voice full of emotion. Alex offered her a precious cigarette from Burt's dwindling pack and she took one. Her hand trembled as she lit it. "Can you tell me what happened?" she asked, her voice weak.

"I don't know," Alex said. "My finding rune couldn't locate him. Now that could just mean that he's left the city. On the other hand, it's clear that someone wanted something from him, that's why they tore up his apartment. I think they were looking for this," he said, taking the blue leather book out of his jacket pocket.

"What's this?" Evelyn asked, taking the book and flipping through its pages.

"This is a runewright's Lore book," Alex explained. "If your brother had gone on the run, he'd have taken this with him."

"I don't understand," Evelyn said, her voice breaking. "Why would anyone kill Thomas for this?"

Alex took the book back and flipped through to the six special runes in the back.

"Have you ever seen anything like these before?" he asked. Evelyn looked at the pages as Alex turned them, then shook her head.

"Is this what Thomas was working on?"

"I think so," Alex said. "These rune constructs are more complex than anything I've ever seen."

"What are they? Are they valuable? Is that why someone wants them? Is that why Thomas..." Her voice trailed off and she suppressed a sob.

"They might be extremely valuable to the right person," he said, and shrugged. "We runewrights usually keep our constructs secret, but Thomas may have discovered something that would be more valuable if he sold it." He paged to the finding rune. "This is the one he spent the most time working on. It's a finding rune. I have one that looks very similar, but I've never seen one laid out this way."

"What was Thomas looking for?"

"I don't know." Alex shook his head.

"What about these others?" she said, flipping the pages. "What are they for? Is it possible they go together?"

Alex furrowed his brow. He hadn't thought of that. He wondered why Evelyn had.

"I just want to know what happened to my brother," she said in response to his questioning look.

Alex pointed to the page where she had turned. "This is some variant of a life rune," he said. "Runewrights power our constructs when we write them. The longer we spend making the rune, the more power it has. With this," he indicated the rune, "we can power our constructs instantly with our own life energy. It can make even a simple rune incredibly powerful. It can also shave years off your life in a matter of seconds."

"Do you do that?" she asked, her eyes full of concern.

"No," he said. "It's extremely dangerous."

"What about this one?" Evelyn said, turning another page.

"I don't know," Alex said, flipping through them. "I've never see that one, or this, or this." He turned to a construct that looked like a roadmap of some crooked European city. "I think this one is a protection rune, but I have no idea what it protects from."

Evelyn stared at the book, turning the pages back and forth until she lowered her head and pushed the cover closed.

"I don't know what any of this means, Alex," she said. "All I know is that my brother is gone, most likely dead."

"I am sorry," Alex said. "If you come with me to my office, I'll refund the rest of your money since I only needed the one day and the finding rune."

"No." She looked up with intensity in her eyes. "I want to know what happened to my brother. I want you to find the person who killed him. If they killed him for these drawings, you need to figure them out, Alex." She shoved the book back into his hands. "You need to find whoever did this and give my brother and me some peace."

Tears were streaming down her face now, ruining her makeup. Alex had an overwhelming urge to put his arm around her and hold her close, to tell her it would be okay.

"You sure you want that?" he said instead. "I might spend a lot of time spinning my wheels and not find anything."

"I've got some money my parents left me," she said. "This is what I want."

Alex couldn't really blame her. Her brother was all the family she had, and someone had taken him away. Just like Father Harry.

"All right," Alex said, looking her square in the eyes. "I'll find out what I can, but no promises."

"That's good enough," Evelyn said.

He waited while she fixed her makeup with the aid of a tiny mirror from her purse, then walked her out of the park to get a cab. He pulled the blue book out of his pocket as she rode away, wondering how he would find out who killed Thomas. Runewrights were secretive about their runes, especially new ones. It was unlikely that Thomas mentioned it casually to a friend.

Maybe he had a partner, someone who worked on developing these constructs with him? But a partner would already know the runes, he wouldn't have to search for them in Thomas' apartment.

Alex shook his head and put the book back in his pocket. He'd have to spend some time studying it later. Right now he had other things to worry about. As soon as Danny got him the warehouse manifest, he'd be traipsing all over town looking for Pemberton's murderer.

Until then, however, he had time to call in a few favors and hopefully find out something about the elusive Charles Beaumont.

He thought about that on the crawler ride to his office. If Sister Gwen had been right that Beaumont was a thief, he couldn't be the kind of penny-ante thief that would sell pocket watches to a hock-shop. His clothes were too good for that. Beaumont was a man of means. Not rich, or maybe rich and frugal, but either way it made him an entirely different class of thief than some pickpocket or street thug. Alex was looking for a man who stole from rich people and that made him either a stockbroker or a cat burglar.

If he actually is a thief.

Alex pushed that thought aside. If Beaumont was a cat burglar, that made him one of the rarest types of thieves. Few people plied that trade — the stakes were too high. Rich people had safes and guard dogs and, on occasion, armed security. Beaumont's thefts might be easy to find, but anything about him personally would be rare as hen's teeth.

He'd look into it, but first he had to see if Danny had any word on the warehouse manifest. As much as Alex wanted to find Beaumont and track Father Harry's killer, his first loyalty had to be to Danny, not to mention keeping himself out of jail.

"Morning, Leslie," he said, entering his office. She sat behind her desk reading the paper. He expected a sardonic comment from her on his lateness but instead her face was serious. She nodded toward the inner office and mouthed the word *Feds*.

Alex groaned. He pulled Thomas' Lore book out of his pocket and placed it on her desk with a nod. She immediately picked it up and put it in her lap.

"Any messages?" Alex said, more loudly than usual.

"Nothing," Leslie said, just as loud. "There are some gentlemen in your office."

"Okay, I'm expecting a call from Danny. Just take a message."

Alex straightened his jacket and took a deep breath. Feds in his office were never a good thing. At best they mucked about with his investigations and at worst they kept trying to put him in jail for getting in their way. Of course they never told him that he'd gotten in their way until after the fact. He plastered a smile on his face and opened the door.

Two men waited for him, and neither of them could rightly be called gentlemen. The elder of the two looked like a G.I. recruitment poster, square jaw, flat nose, blue eyes, and perfectly slicked dark hair. He wore a blue wool suit with a gray vest, and his shoes were well-polished. He sat in one of the chairs in front of Alex's desk with a fedora in his lap that exactly matched his suit and a leather briefcase on the floor by his side.

The younger man stood behind Alex's desk, looking through the appointment book. He was average in height with wavy blond hair and blue eyes in a handsome face. His suit was gray but not so well-tailored. Alex could see the bulge of his pistol under his right arm.

Lefty.

"Something I can help you find?" Alex asked the younger man. He favored Alex with a sneer and moved around to stand behind the dark-haired man.

"Mr. Lockerby," the other man said, standing. "I'm Agent Davis." He stuck out his hand and Alex shook it. "This is my nosy partner, Agent Warner." Alex nodded at the younger man, but didn't offer his hand.

"What can I do for you, Agent Davis?" he said, sitting behind his desk. "May I ask what agency you're actually with?"

Davis reached into his jacket and produced a large wallet containing a badge with the letters FBI clearly printed on it.

"We're here for your help, Mr. Lockerby," Davis said, returning his badge to his pocket. "We need your expertise. One of our investigations came across some rune lore that, well, we've just never seen before. We were hoping you could identify them, maybe tell us if anyone you know uses them?"

"I can take a look, sure," Alex said, shrugging. "But I can't help you with who might use them."

The young Agent curled his lip, but Davis was unfazed.

"I understand your reluctance to involve a fellow runewright in an FBI matter, Mr. Lockerby, but I assure you, this is very serious."

"I didn't say I wouldn't help you, Agent Davis," Alex said. "I said I couldn't. Runewrights are a secretive lot. We don't share our Lore with each other."

Davis seemed to consider that for a moment, then he nodded.

"All right." He reached into the briefcase at his feet and pulled out a manila folder, tossing it onto the desk. "Anything you can tell us about these would be greatly appreciated."

Alex opened the folder and felt his blood freeze. Years of poker had conditioned him to keep emotions off his face so he just stared at the six photographs the folder contained. Each picture was of a complex rune, drawn on a single sheet of plain paper. Alex didn't have to examine them closely — he already knew them. All of them appeared in the last pages of Thomas Rockwell's Lore book. He paged through the pictures slowly, giving himself time to think. Each rune was exactly the same as it appeared in the blue book. There was no way that was a coincidence. What was Thomas mixed up in that brought out the Feds?

"I recognize three of these," he said, being careful not to tell an outright lie. He put down three of the pictures so Davis could see them. "This is some kind of finding rune, this is a heavily modified life rune, and this one is some kind of protection rune. They're more complex than anything I've ever seen before. I'd have to study them to tell you more."

"You sure there's nothing else you can tell us?" Warner said, speaking for the first time. He had a midwestern accent, Iowa or Illinois. Alex smiled.

"I didn't say that. Let's take a closer look." He rose and went to the filing cabinet behind his desk. He pulled out a multi-lamp like the one in his kit and clipped a ghostlight burner into it.

"What's that?" Davis asked, a note of suspicion in his voice.

"Well," Alex said, igniting the burner with the touch tip lighter on his desk. "These are just photographs of runes," he said, indicating the six pictures. "I can't really judge how the magic was laid down without seeing the originals." He pulled a set of mustard-yellow spectacles from a case in the file cabinet and clipped them onto his nose. "This light will let me see if the camera picked up anything." Davis and Warner exchanged nervous glances at that, but Alex continued as if he didn't notice. “It’s a long shot, I know, but I wouldn’t want you boys to think I didn’t do a good job.”

Alex sat back down and held each picture in the light, scrutinizing it as carefully as he dared. The lines that made up the runes had been written in magical ink, so they glowed brightly, but they were the same lines visible under normal light. He hadn’t been lying about this being a long shot; magic auras like the ones these runes possessed required special cameras and special film to capture. Still, it made him look thorough.

As he paged through them, he noticed a small line of script on the bottom right of the pages the runes had been drawn on. Pulling out a magnifier from his desk, he scrutinized each one. All of them seemed to be written in some foreign language until he recognized a number at the end of one line. It was the number seven, but written backwards. The text wasn’t foreign, it had been written on the back side of each page. Whoever drew the runes had made the notes with the same pen and magical ink.

Wasteful.

Reading minuscule text backwards was hard, but after a few minutes of paging back and forth, he got it. Each note said the same thing followed by a page number.

Curiosity piqued, Alex decided to see if he could sneak some more information out of Davis and Warner. He laid the pictures out on his desk, then folded his hands in front of him.

“Agent Davis,” he asked. “What is the Archimedean Monograph?”

Davis about fell out of the chair and Warner looked like he wanted to go for his gun.

“Where did you hear that name?” Davis demanded, his calm, genial voice gone. Alex took off the spectacles and handed them to the FBI man.

“Right here,” he said, pointing to the photograph. He couldn’t see the writing without the spectacles, but Davis could, and he swore.

“How did you know to look for that?” Davis demanded.

“You asked me to,” Alex said, which was absolutely true.

“I don’t know what kind of game you’re playing, scribbler,” Warner began, reaching into his coat. Alex tensed but didn’t drop his smile. He didn't think Warner would shoot him right here in his own office, but the young man looked angry enough not to be rational.

"Warner!" a woman's voice came from beyond the office door. It was cold and harsh and Warner froze with a guilty look on his face. "That will be quite enough," the voice said, and the door opened. Agent Davis had regained his composure and he stood, making the chair available.

"Sorry, ma'am," he said.

Alex didn't know what to expect. From his position behind the desk, he couldn't see the person standing just beyond the door. Then his breath froze in his chest as the most dangerous woman in New York walked into his office.

10

THE SORCERESS

Women tended not to be sorcerers. For whatever cosmic twist of fate, only one in every twenty or so who had the power was female. Suffragettes complained about it endlessly for a while, but since there just wasn't anything anyone could do about it, they eventually gave up. Of the six sorcerers in New York, only one was a woman. Nicknamed the Ice Queen, she made her fortune enchanting metal rods so they would remain bitter cold for over a year. Once these were cut into thin disks and put into iceboxes and room coolers, the Ice Queen made millions.

The Ice Queen's real name was Sorsha Kincaid and, if rumor was to be believed, her personality matched her nickname. Nothing in the Ice Queen's appearance dispelled that rumor when she entered Alex's office. She looked to be in her late twenties, but magic tended to retard aging, and Sorsha had come into her power quite young. Alex had heard that she was closer to forty. She was dressed in a white, button-up blouse with an azure blue vest and dark slacks. Her only concessions to her femininity were her high heels and the design of her vest, which cut under her small breasts, emphasizing them.

If the purpose of Sorsha's clothing was to minimize her sex, it was sorely inadequate. Her face was stunningly beautiful, skin like marble, with high cheekbones, full lips, and eyes of pale blue. They reminded Alex of the way the sun looked, shining through an icicle. Her hair was the palest platinum blonde he'd ever seen, almost white, and it fell down on either side of her face in a short bob. She used makeup to darken her eyebrows, giving her a stern look, and Alex knew it had been done for just such an effect.

Her eyes were hard and fixed on Warner as she entered, and the young man leaned back against the wall as if he wished it would give way and let him escape. She held that gaze for a long moment, then turned to Alex and smiled. The smile was warm enough, but Alex felt a chill go down his back. Sorcerers were immensely powerful and equally dangerous. Most people would take a poke at you if you insulted them, but a sorcerer could turn you into a toad for any perceived offense — and there wasn't much the law would do if you were a nobody. New York was full of nobodies, more than they could ever use, but sorcerers were rare and valuable commodities. Only an especially egregious breach of the law would bring one to account. Alex resolved to choose his words very carefully.

"I must admit, Mr. Lockerby, I'm impressed." Sorsha sat down in the chair in front of his desk and crossed her legs. If she'd been wearing a skirt, that movement would have been quite sensual, but with the Ice Queen, she wore pants and there wasn't any flirting involved. "I had supposed that a runewright who became a private detective must not have been a very good runewright. Seems I was wrong."

Alex inclined his head in her direction. "I appreciate the compliment," he said. "But you still haven't answered my question. What is the Archimedean Monograph?"

The Ice Queen smiled. Her lips were demurely together, but Alex could have sworn he saw teeth.

"I'm afraid that's a government secret, Mr. Lockerby."

"Alex."

"What I need to know, Mr. Lockerby, is what you know about these runes," she indicated the photos on his desk. Alex sat back in his chair.

"I know who these boys are, Miss Kincaid," he said, indicating

Davis and Warner. “But I don’t remember hearing that you joined the FBI.”

Sorsha smiled. Not the cold, mocking smile she’d worn earlier but a warm smile of amusement.

God, she’s gorgeous.

“I help the FBI as a consultant,” she said. “Much the same way as you do the New York police department, though the FBI actually wants my help.”

Alex let the dig go by, but the fact that she knew about his rocky past with the police meant that she’d done some homework about him.

“Now,” she said, getting back to the topic at hand. “Tell me what you know about these pictures. Please,” she added.

“I’ve already told your agents what I know about them, Miss Kincaid,” he said sweeping them back into the manila folder and holding it out to her. “So, if that’s everything...”

“Why were you at Thomas Rockwell’s apartment yesterday?”

Alex smiled. He’d been right to have Leslie hide Thomas’ Lore book.

“So that’s what all this is about,” he said.

Sorsha reached into thin air and pulled a small flip notebook into her hand. It was such a casual display of magic that it appeared ordinary, but Alex couldn’t do anything like that on his best day. He didn’t want to be impressed, but he couldn’t help it. She flipped a few pages and began reading.

“You were seen entering Mr. Rockwell’s building yesterday afternoon around two and you didn’t leave until after five. You appear to have combed through the apartment very thoroughly, despite its being in a disheveled state, and the only thing you removed was Mr. Rockwell’s blue Lore book.”

“I wondered why I kept feeling as though I was being watched,” Alex said. The thought that Sorsha could have been actually watching him while he worked was disturbing. He made a mental note to add a short-term privacy rune to his little book and use it when he did his investigations.

“You’re in a lot of trouble, Mr. Lockerby,” Sorsha said, the cold smile returning to her lovely face. “We’ve got you on breaking and entering and theft. Now I'm perfectly willing to forget that, provided you tell me what brought you to Thomas Rockwell's apartment."

Alex tried to keep the relief off his face. Sorsha Kincaid, New York's most dangerous woman, would have to do better than that if she wanted to put the arm on him. Also, her threats meant that she hadn't been watching him with magic, some Fed had been staking out the building and had seen Alex go in. If she'd been watching him, she'd already know what he was there for. The finding rune was a dead giveaway.

"Someone reported Thomas missing," he said. "They asked me to look into it, find him if I could."

"Why didn't they just go to the police?" Warner asked. Alex laughed.

"The police don't have time to track down missing people unless some crime is involved," he said. "They usually send these exact cases to me."

"Who hired you?" Agent Davis asked. Alex put on his most charming smile.

"Agent Davis," he said, in a wounded voice. "You know I can't divulge the names of my clients. Not without a warrant."

"I can get one in an hour," he said, his tone hard and flat.

"Of course you can," Alex said. "You've got New York's celebrity Sorceress working for you, no judge in the city will turn you down."

"Then why not save us all some trouble and tell us who hired you?" Sorsha asked.

"Some of the people who hire me can't go to the regular police, Miss Kincaid," Alex said, his voice serious.

"Because they're criminals," Warner said with a sneer.

"Sometimes," Alex admitted. "Or they've had bad run-ins with the cops, or they're embarrassed about the reason they're seeing me and don't want it on any official record. Whatever the reason, what do you think would happen to my business if word got out that I gave up a client just because some Feds said pretty please?"

"I don't give a rats ass—"

Sorsha cut Davis off with an upraised hand, then lowered it back to her lap.

"The simple fact is that we have you over a barrel, Mr. Lockerby," she said. "Give us a name or I'll have Agent Warner place you under arrest."

Alex smiled and played his trump card. He tossed the key to Thomas Rockwell's apartment onto his desk.

"What's that supposed to be?" Warner asked, already reaching for his cuffs.

"The key to Rockwell's apartment," he said. "Feel free to check it out. Since you obviously inventoried his apartment before I arrived, you know I didn't get it from there. He gave that key to someone he trusted, and that person gave the key to me when they asked me to find him. So no breaking and entering." Warner's sneer evaporated and it was Alex's turn to smile. "Furthermore, the only person who can complain that I took the Lore book is Thomas Rockwell, and I seriously doubt he'll be pressing charges."

Agent Davis had gone red in the face and Warner had gone absolutely purple. Sorsha just sat with her hands in her lap, glaring at Alex. He wiped the smile from his face. There was no sense in poking a bear.

"Now, I'm perfectly willing to give you whatever help I can with this," he said, pointing to the manila folder. "But I need to know what this is all about first. Those are my terms."

Sorsha leapt to her feet and slammed her hand down on Alex's desk. Instantly a coating of frost spread across the top.

"How dare you dictate terms to me?" she said. Her voice was calm but there was fire behind those pale eyes.

Davis had a look of terror on his face but Warner leered with eager delight. He couldn't wait for the Ice Queen to take this insolent PI apart. Alex pulled his hands off the desk as the frost spread. He hadn't intended to provoke the Sorceress — he hadn't even been pushing hard. Clearly Alex had hit her hot button and now he had to deal with a furious Sorceress.

Goosebumps spread across his arms and his left hand instinctively tapped his right forearm. If things went pear-shaped, his last play was the rune he'd had tattooed there a year ago.

Sorsha saw the move and it seemed to shake her out of her anger.

She pulled her hands off the table, rubbing them together as if they hurt. The frost began to disappear in a cloud of fog.

"Agent Davis, Agent Warner," she said in a trembling voice. "Please wait for me outside."

"But ma'am—" Davis protested.

"Now, please," Sorsha said, now in full control of her voice. "I'll be quite all right, I assure you."

Warner looked disappointed as he shuffled off after Davis and pulled the door closed behind him.

Sorsha sat, slowly, holding Alex's eyes the whole time. Alex didn't know what to make of the Sorceress. She'd been angry enough to freeze him solid a moment ago, but that emotion had passed.

"I'm sorry, Mister...Alex," she said with obvious effort. "You made me lose my temper. Did you do it on purpose? I'd just like to know."

"I didn't think I was pushing that hard," he said, and shrugged. "But I was pushing."

Sorsha closed her eyes and took a deep breath.

"You play dangerous games, Alex. What would have happened if you used your escape rune?"

Now it was Alex's turn to be stunned.

"How did you know about that?" he said, easing his hand away from his right forearm. She fixed him with an amused look and raised one of her darkened eyebrows.

"The FBI consults with me because I know things," she said. "May I see it?"

Alex stood and took off his jacket. He rolled up his sleeve, exposing the intricate tattoo, and held out his arm for Sorsha to see. Escape runes were just what their name implied, last-ditch magic that could transport a runewright out of danger. If they worked. Alex's rune was trapezoidal in shape with four nodes, and each of those nodes had a node of its own. He'd had to touch the tattoo needle the whole time the artist worked, and supply him with component-infused inks he made especially for that purpose. The end result looked like a picture of the view through a kaleidoscope with six colors and multiple, interlocking patterns.

"It's beautiful," Sorsha said, taking his forearm and turning it to get a better look. Despite her icy reputation, Sorsha's hand was warm and soft. Alex almost forgot she was a Sorceress who'd threatened to freeze him to his chair a moment ago.

Almost.

"Where would you have gone if you'd activated it?" she asked.

"It's where we would have gone," Alex said. "Assuming it actually worked, this rune will transport everyone within ten feet to a spot over the north Atlantic about a mile off the coast of Greenland. We'd appear a hundred feet in the air, then the magic would teleport me back to a secure location."

Sorsha's eyebrows rose and she let out a soft whistle.

"I was right to have Davis and Warner leave the room." She released Alex's arm and sat back. "Of course, I'd have been very angry once I teleported home."

Alex put on his most charming smile.

"If you teleported home," he said. "Falling one hundred feet into freezing water is disorienting, and the temperature would send you into shock in under a minute. After four minutes your body shuts down and you drown. The *Titanic* disaster taught us important lessons."

"You are not at all what I expected, Mr. Lockerby." Sorsha looked at him hard, as if trying to look through him. "How did you power it? It must have taken years to prepare."

"It uses a life rune," Alex admitted. "I figure if I ever have to use it, I'd rather part with a year of my life than all of it."

If Sorsha judged him for this line of thought, she gave no indication.

"Perhaps you can be some use to me after all," she said, taking the folder off the desk and pulling out the photographs of the runes. "These runes are pictures of original drawings that came into the possession of the British government during the World War." She began putting the pictures back out on the desk as she spoke. "No one knows where they came from, but they relate to a story about a Lore book called the Archimedean Monograph, supposedly written by Archimedes of Syracuse."

"The guy who ran naked in the streets when his tub overflowed," Alex said. Sorsha smirked.

"Something like that. He was reputed to be a runewright of incredible skill. According to the story, he wrote down his most powerful runes on sheets of vellum. When he died, those runes were passed around among lesser runewrights who didn't know what they had until eventually they came into the possession of Leonardo DaVinci. He collected Archimedes' pages together into a book and began studying them intently. There are supposed to be DaVinci's handwritten notes all through the book."

Alex whistled. Everybody knew DaVinci's work as a runewright; he was one of the great masters. Just to be able to read his notes on Archimedes' runes would be incredible.

"From DaVinci, the book went through the hands of many great runewrights; Rene Descartes, Sir Francis Bacon, Benjamin Franklin and others. Each man added notes to the pages. Somewhere along the way, it began to be called the Archimedean Monograph, and a powerful protection rune was put on the book so that only a worthy runewright would be able to possess it."

Alex had to hold his hands to keep them from shaking. The knowledge in that book could be life-changing. A Lore book that had come down through the greatest minds in history, what secrets would that hold?

"What happened to it?" he asked, a little too eagerly. Sorsha shook her head, her platinum hair flying in front of her eyes.

"No one knows, but many have tried to find it."

Alex picked up the picture of the finding rune.

"Is that what this is?" he asked. "Some kind of treasure map with the book at its end."

"That's what we believe," Sorsha said. "A man named Quinton Sanders believed it, too."

"Who's he?"

"Sanders was a research assistant at the government's runic studies facility," Sorsha said. Alex didn't know that the government even had a research facility for runes. "The facility has an archive with many Lore books in it. During the war, the United States acquired the originals in these pictures from the British Government."

Alex didn't ask if acquired meant stole.

"Since they were supposed to be from the Monograph, the government put their top people to work deciphering the runes. We think we know what most of them are, but all work was stopped in 1926."

"Why?" Alex couldn't imagine being ordered to stop working on something so interesting. Sorsha fixed him with a hard look before responding.

"Because, of the thirteen runewrights they had working on the project, twelve of them went mysteriously missing."

Alex felt a cold chill run down his back that had nothing to do with the Ice Queen.

"So how does Quinton Sanders fit into this story?" he wondered.

"Two months ago, a magical alarm was triggered when someone opened the file on the Monograph. Quinton Sanders was the only person in the office that day who had the proper keys to get into the secure archive."

"Let me guess," Alex said. "He went missing."

Sorsha shook her head. "No, we traced him here, to New York. Since we have pictures of the original pages, I cast a scrying spell to alert me any time any of these runes are cast. So far, this one's been cast twice," she indicated the elaborate finding rune. "I couldn't track the first one, but the second led us to Thomas Rockwell's building."

"And now he's missing," Alex said. "Did Rockwell know Quinton Sanders?"

"Not that we know of," Sorsha said. "That's why we need your help. Clearly Thomas saw the original runes and copied them into his book. We think Quinton is trying to find a runewright with enough skill to help him decipher the finding rune so he can locate the Archimedean Monograph."

"What if the Monograph doesn't exist?" Alex asked.

"That's not a chance the government is willing to take," Sorsha said. "Now I've put my cards on the table, Alex; it's time you did the same. Who is your client?"

Alex hesitated. He didn't want to out Evelyn to the Feds, but he couldn't see how she could be involved. So far nothing he'd discovered pointed to Quinton Sanders or anyone else.

"Rockwell's sister hired me," he said at last. "She was supposed to have dinner with Thomas and he never showed. All she knows is that he kept talking about making some big discovery."

"I need to talk to her."

"Sorry," Alex said. "If I think she can help you, I'll arrange a meeting."

Sorsha glared at him with a look that explained how she got the title Ice Queen.

"I wasn't lying about my reputation," Alex said. "You need to let me handle this. If I run across anything about Quinton Sanders or the Monograph, I'll call you right away."

"Fine," she said, producing a card with her name and number on it from the pocket of her vest. Alex took the card but Sorsha didn't release it. "But I want Thomas Rockwell's rune book," she said. "Right now."

"I can study the runes for you," Alex said, still holding the card. "Maybe give you a clue to what Sanders and Rockwell were up to."

The Ice Queen sighed and for a moment she looked tired. "You seem like a decent person, Mr. Lockerby," she said. "People who investigate these runes are never seen again. You may be irritating and arrogant, but I don't want your death on my conscience." She released the card. "Now, if you don't mind," she said. "I'll take Thomas Rockwell's Lore book."

Alex hesitated. He really didn't want to turn over the book. He'd copied the runes last night of course — it was the first thing he did after getting home with the book, but he promised Evelyn he'd find her brother's killer and he might need Thomas' book to do that. That said, turning over the book looked like the only way to keep Evelyn out of whatever Thomas had gotten himself into. In the end he really didn't have any choice.

He pushed the key on the intercom on his desk. A moment later Leslie answered.

"Would you bring that blue book in here, Miss. Tompkins?"

A moment later, Leslie entered with the book. She handed it to Alex and withdrew. Once the door was shut, Alex offered it to Sorsha.

"I give you the book, you leave my client out of this. Deal?" he said.

"Unless she has information about the Monograph," Sorsha said, taking the book. "Deal."

Alex started to stand, but Sorsha flicked her hand and suddenly he couldn't move. He strained against the invisible bonds, but it was as if he'd been imprisoned in amber like some unfortunate insect. He couldn't move or even blink. Sorsha put the blue book and the folder of pictures into the briefcase Agent Davis left beside the chair, then she stood and walked around the desk.

"If I find out you're hiding something from me," she whispered into Alex's ear, so close he could feel her breath, "I'll make certain you regret it, and I won't bother the FBI about it. Understood?"

Her spell ended and Alex gasped, slumping against his desk. He wanted to say something glib about how she didn't intimidate him, but he was busy suppressing the tremors that threatened to break out all over his body. When he finally mastered himself, he stood and tucked her card into his pocket.

"Understood," he said.

Sorsha favored him with her cold smile, picked up the briefcase, and walked out.

Alex waited until he heard the Sorceress and her FBI escort leave the outer office before he slumped down, into his chair. So far today, a police captain had threatened to put him in jail, and a sorceress had threatened to do worse. And it wasn't even lunch yet.

11

THE LIST

"You seem a little rattled."

Leslie's voice startled Alex and he sat up in his chair. His receptionist stood at the open door to his office holding a cup of coffee in each hand. She stepped to his desk and set one down, then sat down in the chair Sorsha had occupied only moments before.

"Was that...?" Leslie nodded toward the door. Alex opened his bottom desk drawer and pulled out a half-empty bottle of Scotch.

"Yep," he said, pouring some in his coffee. "Irish?" he said, offering the bottle to Leslie. She smiled and shrugged, holding out her cup so he could add some of the amber liquid to it. Leslie sipped at her coffee.

"What did they want, besides that book?"

"It looks like Thomas Rockwell may have been involved in the theft of government secrets," Alex said.

"Must be a big deal if they got the Ice Queen down from her floating castle to chase leads."

"It's powerful magic." Alex nodded. "So powerful everyone who meddles with it disappears without a trace."

"Like Thomas Rockwell." Leslie sipped her coffee. "What are you going to tell the skirt?"

Alex thought about it for a long moment. Sorsha Kincaid was probably right about her thief reaching out to runewrights for help. It was possible that Thomas didn't know where the runes came from, but it was equally possible that he was in on the theft. Either way, it was probably best if Evelyn stopped looking into her brother's disappearance.

"I'll tell her the truth."

"That her brother might be a thief?" Leslie asked with a raised eyebrow. Alex chuckled.

"Well, maybe not that much truth," he said. "I can tell her that her brother got mixed up in something that likely got him killed and that the Feds took his book."

"Think she'll leave it there?"

"I wouldn't," Alex said.

"Neither would I." Leslie stood and headed for the door. "While you were meeting with the frosty blonde, Danny called."

"Does he have that list yet?"

Leslie didn't answer, but returned a moment later with a pad of paper. "The customs people wouldn't give him the names of the foreign governments who use the warehouse, but here's everyone else." She handed Alex the pad.

Alex scanned over the list. There were a dozen companies, everything from a furniture maker to banks to tool & die companies to jewelry stores. All of them were businesses who would have reported a theft to their insurance companies and moved on. Whatever was stolen, it had to be something priceless. One of a kind. That might mean it was smuggled in. Insurance companies didn't pay for their client's smuggling losses, so the owner would have to take steps personally to recover his property.

"So what are you going to do?" Leslie asked, still sipping her coffee.

Alex wanted to follow up on Beaumont. If he really was a high-end thief, he'd have left a trail. A trail that would go colder while Alex chased all over the city trying to find out who killed Jerry Pemberton. He owed it to Father Harry to find out who was responsible for his death, but the more rational part of Alex's brain pointed out that he wouldn't be finding anyone from behind bars. He drained his coffee cup and set it on his desk.

"I'd better get going," he said, tearing off the top sheet from the pad of paper. "It'll take me at least two days to run through all of this and I've only got three. Everything else can wait."

Leslie nodded as if that were the answer she expected.

"Anything you want me to do?"

"Stay by the phone," Alex said, pulling on his jacket. "I may need you. If Evelyn Rockwell calls, put her off. I'll settle things with her when this is all over."

"And if the Ice Queen calls?"

"Take a message."

Alex put on his hat, folded up the list and slipped it into his pocket, then walked out.

He took a crawler to the first address on his list, a company that made grand pianos. They'd been expecting a shipment of ivory to make keys. The owner was genuinely surprised by Alex's presence and his line of questioning. He clearly thought that a Police Consultant was some kind of actual policeman and Alex didn't bother to disabuse him of that notion. Eventually, the owner took Alex into the workshop in back and showed him a bin full of elephant tusks and the craftsmen in the process of cutting and shaping them into the smooth rectangles that would cover piano keys. It was fascinating, but ultimately fruitless. The business owner simply wasn't a good enough liar to be hiding anything. After a wasted hour and a half, Alex thanked the man and left.

Before he caught the next crawler, he stopped at a drug store to call the office. With any luck Leslie would have some news for him.

"Sorry, kid," her voice flowed over the wire to him. "Danny just called to see if you were having any luck. He hasn't found anything."

Alex swore. "If he calls back, tell him I could use some help following up with the list. At the rate I'm going, he's going to be looking for a new job soon."

"When was the last time you ate?" Leslie asked.

"Breakfast with Danny."

"Stop by the Automat and get a sandwich on your way to your next interview," she said. "You're getting grouchy."

Alex was about to tell Leslie where she could stick a sandwich, but that made him see her point. She always looked out for him.

"Thanks, doll," he told her.

ONE CRAWLER RIDE and two Automat ham-and-cheese sandwiches later, Alex stood in front of the Garland Bank, a private bank that lent exclusively to businesses. Once he explained to the manager that someone had been robbed at the customs warehouse and that there was a murder involved, the man couldn't wait to help. He showed Alex the gold bullion that had been brought in, along with his bills of lading, which matched the information on the warehouse manifest exactly. It only took an hour this time, but Alex was able to cross another name off his list.

By the end of the day, Alex felt as if he'd walked all the way from Brooklyn to the south-side waterfront. He'd crossed six more names off his list, but that still left five to go and he wasn't any closer to finding out who killed Jerry Pemberton, or why. His pocket watch told him it was six-thirty. He wanted to stop at the public library and look into Charles Beaumont, alleged thief, but he desperately needed some food and a soft chair. Not necessarily in that order. Between crawler rides, breakfast with Danny, and the Automat, he was down to his last fifteen cents, so he hopped a crawler and headed for the brownstone.

"There you are, my boy," Iggy called when Alex finally staggered in through the vestibule. "I was hoping I hadn't missed a call from you needing me to bail you out."

He found Iggy out behind the kitchen in the attached greenhouse. The brownstone had a very small, walled back yard that opened onto an alley. When Iggy had first moved in, he'd taken up half the space with a glass greenhouse where he grew orchids. Due to the labor-intensive nature of cultivating orchids, Iggy spent many hours a day in his greenhouse. He even had a wicker reading chair in one corner in case he just wanted to enjoy the fruits of his labor.

"Is there anything to eat?" Alex asked, sliding down into one of the carved wooden chairs that surrounded the heavy dining table. Iggy chuckled, pulling the greenhouse's insulated door closed as he exited.

"Is that all I'm good for anymore?" he asked with a grin. "To be your butler and bring you food?"

"Don't forget putting a roof over my head," Alex said. He reached into his pocket for Bert's pack of smokes, but found it empty. He'd smoked the remaining ones during his steeplechase around the city. He wanted to curse, but Iggy didn't allow it in his home, so Alex bit back the profanity and wadded up the empty pack, dropping it on the table.

Iggy removed the crumpled pack and replaced it with a bowl of orange soup. Alex was hungry enough that he didn't ask, he just spooned it into his mouth.

And nearly choked.

"It's cold," he said once he got the first mouthful down.

"In the kitchen, as in the field, one must anticipate one's adversary," Iggy said.

"Meaning?" Alex was too tired for riddles.

"Meaning if you expect your flat mate to be late, prepare something that's meant to be eaten cold. That's gazpacho, you eat it cold."

It took a minute for Alex to process, but then he just shrugged his shoulders and started eating again.

Iggy sat down beside him at the table and let Alex get halfway through the bowl before interrupting. "Since you seem determined to make me ask, how did it go with the police?"

"Captain Rooney stuck his neck out trying to catch the thief at the customs warehouse," Alex said, between spoonfuls of the cold vegetable soup. "Now he needs a scapegoat, and if I don't figure out who killed Jerry Pemberton by Monday morning, he's going to make it me."

"That's dirty pool," Iggy said.

"You said it," Alex agreed, even though he had no idea what Iggy meant. "Worse, he's going to take Danny down with me, so that's priority number one."

Alex then told Iggy about his day, searching for whomever had their goods purloined at the warehouse.

"So far everyone seems to be telling the truth," he said as Iggy set a plate with a slab of cold ham on it in front of him.

"You're sure one of them is guilty?" Iggy asked.

Alex nodded, slicing the meat into bite-sized chunks. "All the government pouches were sealed and accounted for. That just leaves the businesses."

"Well," Iggy said, picking up the newspaper. "It sounds like you had an eventful day."

"That's not the half of it," Alex said, finishing the second bowl and pushing it away. "The Feds came to see me this morning."

Iggy lowered the paper so he could peer over it. "What did you do to draw their attention?"

"Client of mine's brother disappeared," Alex said. "Feds think he was involved in a theft at a government research facility."

"Was he?"

"I don't know," Alex admitted. "He's an accountant by trade and a runewright on the side. Nothing about him says criminal mastermind."

Iggy raised the paper back up and continued reading. Alex stood and picked up his bowl and spoon, intending to take it to the sink.

"Hey Iggy," he said. "You've been around a while. Have you ever heard of something called the Archimedean Monograph?"

Iggy nearly ripped the paper in half as he jerked out of his seat. His eyes were as big as saucers, and the color had drained from his face. He recovered quickly, but Alex had been looking right at him and had seen his reaction.

"I'll take that as a yes," he said, going to the icebox for two cold beers. He opened them with a church key, then put one in front of Iggy, who had retaken his seat, the torn newspaper forgotten in one hand.

"Where did you hear that name?" he asked, his voice nothing more than a whisper.

"From Sorsha Kincaid. She's consulting with the FBI on the theft. Six runes were stolen from the government, and all six are supposed to be from the Monograph. Why don't you start by telling me what it is?"

Iggy put his hand on Alex's, and it was trembling badly.

"No," he said, his voice a gasp. "You can't go looking for it, Alex. You mustn't."

Alex put his other hand atop Iggy's.

"I'm not looking for it, Iggy. I swear. But my client's brother may have had a part in stealing six pages from it that the government had. I need to know what it is, so I can figure out why he disappeared."

Iggy took a shuddering breath and leaned back in his chair.

"All right," he said. He rose and beckoned Alex to follow him. "This is a story that needs a fire, a cigar, and some cognac." He led Alex into the library and opened the liquor cabinet on the back wall. "Make up a good fire, please," he said. "I feel a chill."

Alex poured coal in the grate, then tore out a fire rune from his rune book and lit it over the pile. In a few seconds the coal caught and warmth began to fill the room. Iggy poured a dark brown liquor into two large snifters, then set them in angled holders that tipped them on a forty-five degree angle. Just below the wooden holders were two small tea candles whose flames touched the glass, warming the cognac.

While the candles did their work, Iggy trimmed two cigars and handed one to Alex. Once each man had lit his cigar, they removed the snifters from the warmers and blew out the candles. Alex sipped the cognac and felt a warm glow spread through his body.

"You need to understand something, Alex," Iggy began. "I've only shared this story with one other person in my entire life. There's a reason I don't share it."

"Who did you share it with?"

"My best friend. His name was Felix Tafford."

Alex caught the slight emphasis on the word *was*. "What happened to him?"

"All in good time," Iggy said. "I suppose this story starts when I was in my third year at the University of Edinburgh Medical School. I had it in me to join His Majesty's Navy and become a ship's doctor. For a young man with my background, that was a big step up. Problem was, in order to join the Royal Navy and become an officer, I needed someone to sponsor my commission."

He paused and took a long drink from the snifter, then sat back and puffed on the cigar. To Alex it looked as if the old man were steeling himself for the memories that would come.

"That's where Felix Tafford came in," Iggy continued. "He and I were pals at school, only his father was a Captain of the Line. With his connections, Felix could choose any post he wanted."

"So he used his family connections to get you a commission." Alex guessed. Iggy nodded.

"Just so. The only condition was that I had to meet Felix's father and impress him, something that was rumored to be very difficult. I realized that if I was to have any chance at all, I had to present myself to Captain Tafford in person. So, I left school just as our Christmas holidays were starting and traveled south to the naval station on Gibraltar, where Captain Tafford was stationed. As it turned out, I impressed the Captain quite easily. He had picked up a case of the clap and didn't want that on his service record."

"Or getting back to his wife," Alex said with a grin.

"Precisely," Iggy said with a nod. "I wrote him up a cleansing rune that had him right as rain in a few days and he signed my commission papers right off." Iggy chuckled at the memory, then his face turned serious again.

"I was waiting for my return ship to England when a strange thing happened. A ship was brought into port having been found adrift at sea with no one on board. This was no little sailboat, mind you, but an American brig, just drifting in the north Atlantic. Her stores were intact, so it was no act of piracy, and the ship was in good order, considering that she drifted over a month. The crew was just ... gone."

Alex sipped his cognac as he listened. Iggy's voice was as powerful a weaver of magic as his hands.

"It made all the papers," he said. "It was a sensation. All kinds of theories were offered as to what had happened, but there just weren't enough facts to come to any conclusion. The admiralty put out a call for help to anyone with scientific, magical, or medical knowledge. Captain Tafford recommended me and I found myself on the deck of the *Mary Celeste*. That was her name."

Something stirred in Alex's memory. "Didn't Arthur Conan Doyle write a story about that?" he asked. "You had me read it along with his other works."

"Doyle changed her name to the *Marie Celeste*, but it's the same ship." Iggy nodded. "As I said, everyone had their theories. Anyway, I had just refined my first ghostlight formula, so I searched the ship for any signs of magic."

He paused, staring into the fire, which was burning brightly now, filling the room with a ruddy warmth. Of course, that might also be the cognac.

"I take it you found some," Alex said.

"In the captain's cabin," he said, his expression sad. "I was excited at first. In the middle of the floor, I found the rune. The finding rune."

"The one from the Monograph," Alex said. "The one that's supposed to lead to it."

"Yes." Iggy leaned back in his chair and closed his eyes. "I wish I'd never found it, or that I'd destroyed it, but I was young and ambitious. And foolish. I copied it down for the Admiralty. They were all very excited; my commission was assured. It was only after they left that I saw the shadows."

"Shadows?"

Iggy trembled as if a cold wind had blown across him.

"There were ten crew aboard when the *Mary Celeste* left New York, including the Captain and his wife and daughter. They were all there, in the cabin, or rather what remained of them was. I didn't see them until I was done with the rune. I looked up and there they all were. Ten shadows on the wall, each contorted as if they had been blinded by a bright light. It was all that remained of them when the rune exploded."

Alex had seen runes explode before; they tended to do significant damage to the surfaces they were inscribed on. "How could you have found the rune's residue if it exploded?" he asked. "Wouldn't it have left a hole in the deck?"

"It wasn't a physical explosion," Iggy said. "It was pure magic. It had no effect on the wood of the ship, but it disintegrated the fragile bodies gathered around it. All that was left were their terrified shadows on the wall."

"Did you tell anyone?"

"No one would listen. You see, the captain of the *Mary Celeste* left a Lore book behind that detailed his search for the Monograph. Once the admiralty understood what it was, they wanted the Monograph for England. Unfortunately, many in the admiralty couldn't keep their mouths shut. Stories began to circulate about the Monograph and the rune that would lead the worthy to it. The government hushed it up, of course, but enough people knew that it began to be fashionable for runewrights to search for the book."

"Is that what happened to your friend?"

"I should have destroyed my notes," Iggy said, sadness in his voice. "Eventually I broke the finding rune down into a more basic version."

"That's why I knew what it was," Alex said. "The finding rune you taught me is made from the one in the Monograph."

"Yes. I made the mistake of showing my finding rune to Felix. We had developed many of our runes together and he knew the limit of my abilities. From the moment he saw it, Felix knew I hadn't come up with it on my own. He pestered me until I told him the whole story. From that day on, he was a changed man. He abandoned his commission and chased any mention of the Monograph all over Europe. We lost track of each other, but I heard rumors that Felix found other runes from the Monograph, but never the book itself."

"Is he the one who gave the runes to the British?"

"Probably," Iggy said. "Then one day he called me. Out of the blue. He said he'd figured it out, the finding rune, and that soon the Monograph would be his. He wanted me to come to his house. He wanted to share the book with me."

"Sounds like a good friend."

Iggy nodded and puffed his cigar.

"The best," he agreed.

"Did you go?" Alex asked, afraid he already knew the answer.

"When I got there, Felix was gone." A tear trickled down Iggy's face and into his prodigious mustache. "I wanted to run, to just leave his flat and never return. But I … I had to know. I lit the ghostlight and there, on the wall, was Felix's shadow, arms held over its head as though trying to block out the sun."

Alex stood and poured more cognac into Iggy's empty snifter.

"I'm sorry about your friend," he said.

"It isn't just Felix," Iggy said. "In the years since the rune leaked out, hundreds of runewrights have disappeared, their invisible shadows burned into the walls of their flats and workshops."

Alex remembered what the Sorceress told him.

"Sorsha said the government stopped researching the Monograph because twelve of their brightest minds went missing," he said. "I take it their shadows ended up on walls somewhere too?"

After a long pause Iggy nodded.

"You see why I must insist, Alex," Iggy said, grabbing his wrist. "You must forget about the Archimedean Monograph. Everyone who pursues it thinks they've broken the code and they all end up dead. Promise me." He gripped Alex's arm with more force than Alex would have given him credit for having. "Promise me that you will tear up whatever copies you've made of these runes. Promise me you'll leave it alone."

There was pain in the old man's voice, but more than pain, there was panic. The idea that Alex would pursue the Monograph and its killer finding rune literally terrified Iggy. Alex knelt down by the old man's chair and looked him square in the eyes.

"I promise you, Iggy," he said. "I have no interest in becoming a shadow on the wall. I won't go chasing after this book. Not now, or ever."

Iggy closed his eyes and released Alex's hand. Relief washed over his face and he leaned back in his chair and sighed.

"Good lad," he said, patting Alex's shoulder. "Thank you, Alex."

Alex grinned and helped him up. Iggy had done so much for him, taking him in and training him to be a detective and a powerful runewright. To Alex, Iggy was a second father, well, third after Father Harry.

He really hated lying to the old man.

12

THE JEWELER

Iggy had been so upset by discussion of the Archimedean Monograph that he retired to his bed shortly after he finished his cigar. Alex sat and stared at the fire for a long time after he had gone. Both Iggy and Sorsha seemed to believe that the Monograph was dangerous, perhaps one of the most dangerous bits of rune magic in existence. Alex could see their point, but he also felt drawn to the killer finding rune. He felt certain that if he just took his time, studied it thoroughly, he could crack the code and find the Monograph. He was already beginning to remember some of the flaws in the rune's design.

"I'll bet that's what Quinton Sanderson and Thomas Rockwell thought," he said to the glowing embers of the fire. "Even money says they're both invisible shadows on a wall somewhere."

Sighing with resignation, Alex set the metal ember screen in front of the fire and went upstairs. He had more important things to do than trying to get himself killed over a mythical book that might not even exist. Besides, if he didn't find out who killed Pemberton and why, he would be spending the foreseeable future in prison.

He intended to go straight to bed, but when he reached his room he fished out the brass key to his vault. Sacrificing a page from his rune book, Alex opened the door into his extra-dimensional space. This close to Empire Tower, the magelights in the space winked on and burned brightly, illuminating the gray walls, the workbenches, and the shelves full of ingredient vials. Alex went to an angled drafting table in front of a high stool. He'd gotten this table from a client in trade for his services and it was a much more comfortable position for creating runes and constructs. Switching on the magelight that hung directly above the table, Alex opened a drawer and pulled out a sketch pad of high quality paper. The first six pages of this pad were occupied by the runes he'd copied from Thomas' lore book when he first got it.

One by one, he tore each page free from the pad and stuck them to a cork row on the top of the board with thumbtacks. All except the finding rune. That one he put in the center of the table, holding it down with a round magnet. He sat staring at it for a long time, then took out a legal pad and began filling it with notes. It was well after midnight when he finally went to bed.

HIS ALARM CLOCK jolted him awake at seven and he reluctantly relinquished the warmth of his bed for the chill of his room. He had two days left to find out what had been stolen from the customs warehouse, who had stolen it, and why. The sooner he started, the better. Iggy was still in his room when Alex came downstairs, so he decided to let Mary make him breakfast. After replenishing his pocket money from his safe in the library, he walked the two blocks to the diner.

Word had gotten out about the new cook at *The Lunch Box* and Alex had to wait a few minutes for a seat at the counter. Mary was so busy she didn't have time to talk, so he gave her a wave on his way out.

He caught the crawler across town to his first stop, Anderson Tool and Die, which had received a shipment of machine parts from the French company that manufactured their lathes. It was to be their last shipment, since the owner had found a local company that could manufacture the parts for him. Another dead end.

From there, Alex went to a furniture importer who received several crates full of lacquered furniture from Japan. Next was a glazier who made stained glass windows. He'd received a shipment of pigments used in making the colored glass. Some of the pigments were rare and valuable, but he ordered in advance of his need and had only opened the crate to confirm its contents. Everything was accounted-for.

By four o'clock, Alex still had two names on his list. It was starting to feel like this was a dead end. That didn't bode well for him...or for Danny. If it didn't work out, Alex would have to try something desperate, something that might ruin his friendship with Danny at best...or get him killed at worst.

He pushed that thought from his mind as he entered Van der Waller's Fine Jewelry. As soon as he entered, Alex could tell that this business had seen better days. A long row of glass cases filled one wall, but the rings, bracelets, and necklaces in them were spread out in an attempt to make the space look full. The cases had been polished and scrubbed so there wasn't a fingerprint on them, and the dark green carpet had been vacuumed, but there was no sign anyone had been in today.

"Can I help you?" a short, balding man in a pinstriped suit said, coming in through a curtain that covered the back room. He wore a pleasant smile, but there were dark circles under his eyes. He wasn't sleeping well.

"You the proprietor?" Alex asked.

"James Van der Waller," the man said, sticking out his hand.

Alex shook his hand, noticing the tiny gold and silver filings that clung to the cuff of the man's shirt.

"You do your own work here," Alex said.

"We do, yes," Van der Waller said.

"What's wrong then? Most people like custom rings rather than that pre-pressed stuff."

Van der Waller blushed a bit. "I'm afraid I'm a bit old-fashioned in my tastes. The things I like are just out of fashion," he admitted. Then he seemed to remember himself. "I have hired Melissa Calomey, the famous designer. She's created a whole new line of amazing pieces. I think it will do very well once we get started."

"Well, since you're polishing the settings, I'm guessing you're waiting for the stones."

Van der Waller looked shocked, but his smile returned quickly to his face.

"Yes, I ordered specially-cut stones for the settings, very good."

"Are you making do with the stones you have?" Alex pointed at the display cases. "Is that why you're so low on stock out here?"

"Who are you?" Van der Waller asked, irritation now plain on his face.

"I'm Alex Lockerby. I'm a consultant for the New York Police Department and I'm here to talk about the robbery."

Van der Waller's eyes rolled back in his head and he groaned, then fell face forward onto his immaculately clean carpet. Alex hadn't been expecting that, and he just stood there looking at the unconscious jewelry store owner for a long moment.

"Come on, Mr. Van der Waller," Alex said, rolling the man over and patting his face until his eyes fluttered open. He helped Van der Waller up and steadied him.

"I knew this would happen," he said, his voice faint. "I told them."

"Told who?" Alex pressed.

"My insurance company," Van der Waller said. "They told me not to go to the police. Said they would catch the thief when he tried to fence the stones."

That didn't sound right. "They probably just wanted to stiff you," Alex said. "If they drag your claim out long enough, you won't be able to prove you had anything stolen."

"But I reported the theft to them," Van der Waller said, his face going even more pale.

"And if they lose the paperwork, it's your word against theirs," Alex said. He was sure Van der Waller's panic was real. He'd found the robbery victim, but not the man who beat the truth out of Jerry Pemberton. That was starting to look like Van der Waller's crooked insurance company. After all, if Van der Waller had the stones back, he wouldn't be cannibalizing his own stock to make the new pieces.

"Oh dear God," Van der Waller groaned. "What should I do?"

Alex put his hand on the little man's shoulder to keep him from falling again.

"Don't worry," Alex said. "First, who is your insurance company?"

"Callahan Brothers Property," he said. "And second?"

Alex pulled out his note pad and wrote Danny Pak's name and the number to the homicide division.

"Call this detective and report the theft. Give him all the information you have."

"But what about my insurance?" Van der Waller grabbed Alex's coat, hanging on as if he needed an anchor. "What if they don't pay? I'll be ruined."

"Don't worry," Alex said again, gently extracting himself from Van der Waller's grip. "Once you report the theft, they'll pay your claim or you can take them to court."

Van der Waller sagged against the counter, pulling a handkerchief from his pocket to mop his brow.

"I can't afford a lawyer," he moaned. "Everything I had is tied up in those stones." The man looked like he might faint again.

"I have to go see your insurance company anyway," Alex said. "I'll see what I can do to get them to pay your claim."

"Thank you," he said in a small voice. "If you do that, I'll owe you."

Alex chuckled. "You can thank me with something that isn't selling," he said. Van der Waller straightened up and looked Alex in the eye.

"I will not," he declared. "I'll make sure it's something amazing, from my new line." Van der Waller might not be the heartiest soul around but he had his pride.

"It's a deal," Alex said. "Now where can I find Callahan Brothers Property?"

Van der Waller went in the back, then emerged a moment later with a west side address written on a scrap of paper. Alex took the page and nodded, then Van der Waller stuck out his hand.

"Good luck."

THE CRAWLER STATION was only a block away and there weren't any dime stores or druggists along the way. As soon as he could find a phone, he'd call Danny, have him dig up whatever he could on Callahan

Brothers Property. Maybe there were complaints against them, something he could leverage. He ran for the crawler and caught it just as its myriad of energy legs began to churn, carrying it away. The address Van der Waller had given him was far enough away that his pocket watch told him he'd never make it before they closed. He'd have to go in the morning. That was pushing things, but at least he could spend the rest of the night at the public library.

But first he had to call Danny.

ALEX CALLED from a public booth in the library's foyer.

"I found our victim," Danny's excited voice came over the wire once the call connected.

"Let me guess," Alex cut him off. "Is it a man by the name of James Van der Waller?"

There was a stunned silence, then Danny came back on the line. "How do you do that?" he asked, his voice sullen. Alex related his conversation with Van der Waller and his suspicions about his insurance company.

"You sure Van der Waller's clean?" Danny asked.

"Pretty sure."

"All right. I'll see what I can dig up on Callahan Brothers Property."

"Hey, did you get Mary's number yesterday?" Alex changed the subject.

"No." Danny said. Alex was stunned. Danny had a bit of a rep as a ladies man.

"I thought she was your type," he said. "You know, breathing."

"She's too much my type," Danny said, and laughed. "The kind I could fall for."

"Would that be so bad?" Alex asked. "Not all of us are confirmed bachelors."

"Do you have any idea what my father would do if I brought home a white girl?" Danny asked.

Alex hadn't thought about that. A bachelor he might be, but that didn't mean he didn't like women, and he took them however they came. He'd seen enough guts and brains at murder scenes to know that people were all the same inside so it always surprised him when someone thought what was outside mattered. Still, Alex knew Danny's father, and he was someone you didn't want to disappoint.

"Tough luck," Alex said. "Maybe I'll get her number."

Danny didn't take the bait. "Call me in the morning and I'll give you whatever I find on the insurance company."

Alex promised that he would and hung up.

HE SPENT the rest of the evening at the library poring over old newspapers, looking for any signs of Charles Beaumont. Burglaries were rare. It took him three hours just to find one. In all of the previous year, only six burglaries of rich homes had been reported. Of those, the same man committed at least two of the burglaries, but he was caught and jailed. The other four remained a mystery.

Alex read each article about the four robberies several times and took meticulous notes, but there just weren't any details that stood out in any of the crimes. The homes were in different parts of the city. One victim had paintings taken, another jewelry, yet another antique silverware and vintage wines. The only thing that connected the robberies was the thief's obvious knowledge of high end merchandise. Knowledge that anyone who traveled in those circles would have.

With nothing to connect the robberies, Alex began scanning the police report for each day, hoping to catch a break. He did find a follow-up report on one of the burglaries that he'd missed. It summed up that the police had no suspects and no leads, but took issue with an opinion piece that had been written about the police department's handling of the case. Without any real leads to follow, Alex located the issue with the offending commentary in it and read the short article by an editorial columnist named Walter Nash. In the article, Nash claimed that the police were lax in their pursuit of the obvious suspect in this case, the famous cat burglar known only as the Spook.

Alex had never heard of anyone the police had dubbed the Spook. He soon realized why — Walter Nash had invented the Spook to describe any robbery where the perpetrator got in and out of the dwelling unseen, even the ones where the home's owners were not at home at the time. Alex flipped through the papers reading Nash's weekly columns. It was mostly sensational drivel, but he seemed to pay particular attention to the robberies, detailing the facts and sensationalizing their mythical perpetrator.

Alex wanted to believe that Beaumont was the Spook, but even if he had been, knowing the name a hack reporter gave him wouldn't get Alex any closer to finding the man.

On the other hand, all Alex had to do was follow Nash's columns to learn when a spectacular, unsolved burglary had been committed. That would be a lot faster than going through the papers week by week.

By the time the librarian came by to throw him out, and glare at him for the mess he made, Alex had identified twelve high-end burglaries over the last three years. Each had the same characteristics: the only things taken were valuable and easy to carry, and there was no sign anyone had been in the house.

No wonder Nash dubbed this guy the Spook.

By the time Alex got home, Iggy was already in bed and the house was silent. Alex reviewed his notes at the kitchen table while he ate a hastily constructed liverwurst sandwich. He still didn't have much. Nothing tied Beaumont to the Spook, but he had, at least, found a pattern. That was enough for one night.

Exhausted, he dragged himself to his room and stripped to his boxers. He pulled back the covers to crawl into bed, but a sudden thought made him stop. He picked up his discarded trousers and fished out his vault key. He hadn't given the Archimedean Monograph any thought since last night, but a possible fix for the finding rune had just come to him and it wouldn't hurt to make a few notes.

Just a few.

13

THE DOCTOR

"Well you look like hell," Iggy observed as Alex dragged himself downstairs the next morning. Alex grunted at him and poured himself a large cup of coffee.

"Doctor Halverson called me yesterday," Iggy said.

"Who?"

Iggy sighed and waited for Alex to take a few slugs from his coffee mug. "Doctor Halverson called," he said again.

"Oh. The researcher from the University," Alex said, his sleep-deprived brain finally making the connection.

"He said they've identified three separate strains of the pathogen." Iggy paused as if what he had said were self-evident. When Alex failed to do anything but stare at him blankly, he continued. "It appears the disease gets weaker with every generation."

"So it isn't perfect after all?"

"It's still not natural," Iggy said. "No disease in recorded history is fatal after just two hours."

Alex shrugged. He wanted to do right by Father Harry, but it was Friday and if he didn't talk to James Van der Waller's insurance company today, he'd have to wait till Monday. Since Captain Rooney's meeting with the Chief was at ten o'clock Monday morning, he didn't have that kind of time.

"I've got a full day," he said. "But if Halverson finds anything that can help me track down Charles Beaumont, or whoever's behind this, call Leslie."

Iggy promised that he would, and Alex reached for the phone on the kitchen wall.

"It's about time you called," Danny said once the police operator put the call through to him. "You know we've only got today left to save my job, right?"

"Sorry, Danny," Alex said, feeling like a heel for spending time on the Monograph. "What have you got on Callahan Brothers Property?"

"Not much," Danny said. "A couple of court cases where they were sued for not paying claims, but they won all of those. The rest are cases where they went after people who tried to cheat their clients. It's all pretty regular."

"That's it?" Alex was astounded.

"I asked the boys over in fraud," Danny said. "They said that Callahan Brothers recover stolen property fairly regularly. Much more often than their competitors."

"Like maybe they've got a goon squad who leans on people till they talk?" Alex asked.

"Nobody knows," Danny said. "Or if they do, they aren't talking. I suggest you quit wasting time and get your butt over there and ask them."

"Yes, boss," Alex said and hung up.

THE OFFICES of Callahan Brothers Property were on the top floor of an elegant brick building that had once been an upscale hotel. The lobby alone looked like it had been built by John Astor; it was elegant and stately with marble floors, carved Art Nouveau rails and moldings. The building's elevator had an operator, an elderly gentleman in a red velvet waistcoat who directed the car with smooth efficiency. Callahan Brothers occupied the entire top floor of the building, and the elevator let Alex off right in front of a large desk manned by a receptionist. She was young, maybe nineteen, with plump cheeks and dark hair, which hung around her face in ringlets. Her lips were red and thin, her eyes were blue and there were freckles on her nose.

"Can I help you?" she asked as Alex approached.

"I'm Alex Lockerby. I'm here regarding James Van der Waller's claim," Alex said, handing her his card. "I need to see whoever is handling his case."

The girl's face changed from the pleasant smile to a sour frown as she passed the card back.

"I'm sorry," she said. "We don't discuss matters relating to clients without the client present. I'll have to ask you to leave."

Alex didn't move to take the card.

"Listen sweetheart, if you want me to go, I'll go. But first I suggest you take that card and give it to the man in charge of Van der Waller's claim. It'd be a mistake if you didn't."

The girl's expression wavered between confidence and doubt. In the end doubt won.

"All right," she said, standing up. "Please wait here. I'll be right back."

She stepped around her desk and made her way to a set of elaborate double doors on one side of the foyer. A moment later she was back with a blocky man of medium height. He had a square jaw with close-set eyes and a Roman nose, not at all what Alex pictured when he thought of an insurance agent. He looked more like a bouncer.

Alex kept his smile pasted to his face. If this was an attempt to intimidate him, he intended to show them it failed.

"I'm Arthur Wilks," the blocky man said as the girl took her seat behind the receptionist desk once more. He handed Alex's card back. "I wanted to tell you in person that I have no intention of discussing my clients with you. If you insist on bothering Miss Harding, I'll have to call the police. Now please leave."

Alex took the card and tucked it in his shirt pocket, removing his note pad as he did so. He flipped the top few pages while Wilks glared at him, then started writing. "How do you spell Wilks?" he asked. "I'm sure the police will want to get it right when they arrest you for impeding a police investigation."

Alex expected Wilks to protest but instead, he just glared at Alex for a long moment, then sighed. "All right," he said. "There's no need for that. Follow me."

Wilks turned back toward the double doors. After a moment, Alex followed. He hadn't strapped on his 1911 in a few days and his rune-covered brass knuckles were in his room at the brownstone. It occurred to him that if Wilks wished him ill, he might have a nasty surprise waiting for him behind those doors.

Alex breathed a sigh of relief when the doors led to a wide hallway with offices on either side. Inside each office, well-dressed men and women were busily working, filling out forms or making phone calls. Everyone seemed to be in a hurry. Wilks' office was at the end of one row in the corner, with big windows all around giving him a wonderful view of the city core and Empire Tower. Along the inside walls were dozens of plaques, awards, and framed newspaper clippings. Most dealt with the recovery of missing or stolen property. The blocky man was clearly an important man at Callahan Brothers Property.

"All right," Wilks said once he'd shut his door. "What do you want?"

There was a distinct trace of Brooklyn in his voice that hadn't been there before.

"You used to be on the job," Alex said, seating himself before Wilks' large mahogany desk. Wilks looked startled, then nodded.

"Fifteen years," he said. "How did you know?"

Alex pointed to a framed newspaper article hanging more or less in the center of the wall of awards. Unlike the others, this one was yellow with age.

"The headline says that a police detective was responsible for finding a stolen thoroughbred horse," he said. "Was that when the Callahan Brothers noticed you?"

Wilks raised an eyebrow, then nodded.

"I see you're pretty good yourself," he said. "Now what's all this got to do with James?"

Alex crossed his legs and leaned back, still holding his notepad.

"Why did you tell Mr. Van der Waller not to report his theft to the police?"

Wilks took a deep breath, then pointed to the wall of awards behind Alex. "You see them?" he said. "I got them for recovering property. I was a robbery detective, Mr. Lockerby. And I learned that people who steal things, do it for one of two reasons. Either they want whatever it is for themselves, in which case they have to stash it somewhere. If you look long and hard enough, you usually find it. Or," he continued, "they steal stuff to sell it for money. In that case they have to have someone to sell it to. Now in the case of art, you know, paintings, statues, that kind of thing, sometimes the thief has a buyer lined up before the theft. With loose jewels," he shrugged, "those, they have to fence." He pointed out the window in the general direction of the diamond district. "Sure, there's plenty of guys in the jewelry business who don't really care where their stones come from, as long as the paperwork is right. Provenance, we call it in the trade. Now, since the thief doesn't have any paper trail, he's got to sell the stones to someone who can forge one. That gives the stones provenance."

"Very interesting," Alex said. "But you haven't answered my question."

Wilks smiled. "There's only a handful of fences in the New York area that can move high end stones, and I know them all," he said. "I told James to hold off because I was sure I could get his property back."

"You reached out to these fences and told them to call you if they came across Van der Waller's property?" Alex guessed. "What makes you think they would?"

Wilks laughed an ugly laugh and jerked his thumb at a filing cabinet behind his door.

"I got enough on each of them to put them away for twenty years," he said. "But I'm not a cop anymore. It ain't my job to catch crooks."

"So when you have a case, you lean on your network," Alex said. "The rest of the time you leave them alone. No wonder your record of recovering property is so good."

"I know all the good fences," Wilks said; he smiled and thumped himself on the chest. "And the cops know the rest. If one of my clients has something go missing, I know just who to squeeze."

Alex pictured Jerry Pemberton, beaten and missing fingernails.

"Who did you squeeze about Van der Waller's missing stones?"

"That's a trade secret," Wilks said. "I'm sure a runewright understands that."

Alex did. Wilks didn't have to tell him anything and he had no leverage with the man. As a former cop, he knew that P.I.s had little to no pull with the real police.

"When do you expect to have the stones back?" Alex said. Wilks' grim smile turned sour and he didn't answer.

"What happened to Jerry Pemberton?" Alex asked, quietly.

"Who?" he asked. For the first time, Wilks looked surprised.

"The customs agent who was in on the robbery with the thief. Someone beat his partner's name out of him, then set him on fire."

Wilks' face flushed and he jumped to his feet.

"Get out," he roared. "I don't have to listen to this from you."

Alex didn't move.

"But you will have to listen to the police," he said. "Right now they don't know that you told Van der Waller not to call them. I'm sure they'd find that fact interesting enough to come down here and talk to you."

Wilks turned a greenish color and he sat down.

"I didn't have anything to do with any beating," he said. "I already told you how I work. I don't go after the thieves, I let them come to my contacts."

"Maybe you got tired of waiting."

"I never heard of any Jerry Penballer—"

"Pemberton."

"Whoever," Wilks barked. "I never heard of him, and I certainly didn't kill him."

Alex hated to admit it, but he believed Wilks. Firstly, Wilks would have waited a few days, at least, for his fences to hear something. Killing Pemberton had been an act of desperation, perpetrated by someone motivated to get their hands on the missing stones. Wilks, on the other hand, was like a spider in a web, just waiting for the thieves to come to him.

"All right," Alex said, flipping his notebook closed. "I take it, you haven't heard anything from your people about the stones?"

"No," Wilks said. He opened his desk drawer and pulled out an oblong book, opening the cover and turning it around so Alex could read it. It was a checkbook with a draft written out to James Van der Waller in the amount of one hundred and fifty thousand dollars. It was dated yesterday.

"If I haven't heard anything by the end of today, I'll take this check over to James myself." He fixed Alex with a hard stare. "I may be a bit rough around the edges compared to the rest of the stiffs who work here, but I'm legit." He closed the book and put it away. "Callahan Brothers Property always pay our claims."

Alex stood up, putting his notebook away.

"Good to know," he said. "Thank you for your time."

"I'm sure you can find your way out," Wilks sneered, not rising from his desk.

It was a long elevator ride back to the ground floor. Everything seemed to point to Callahan Brothers, but now Alex wanted them to be his insurance company. Not that Wilks would take his business.

A row of phone booths encased in polished wood lined the wall in the building's elaborate lobby. Alex should have called Danny, but he wasn't ready to admit he had nothing, so he dialed his office number instead. Leslie picked up after the third ring and she sounded harried.

"There you are," she said when she heard his voice. "Everyone's called for you this morning. It's like Grand Central in here."

"What have you got?" Alex sighed.

"Danny called twice wanting to know how you made out at the insurance company. Then Doctor Bell called, said he's over at the University and wanted you to join him. He said to follow the police cars and you'd find him."

That didn't sound good.

"Lastly Miss Rockwell called, wanting to know if you'd made any progress finding out what happened to her brother. She, at least, was polite."

Alex closed his eyes and rubbed the bridge of his nose. "All right," he said. "Sounds like I'd better go see what Iggy wants."

Leslie snorted. She didn't approve of Alex calling a septuagenarian doctor *Iggy*.

"If Danny or Evelyn call back, tell them I'll call them as soon as I can."

Leslie promised that she would and wished him luck.

THE UNIVERSITY WAS SOUTH, past the core, near Washington Square Park. It would take close to half an hour to get there by crawler and he hadn't eaten all day. His stomach growled at him, but Iggy's mention of police cars meant something important was happening. He pushed his hunger aside and headed south.

The campus of New York University covered a few city blocks, but Alex had no trouble figuring out which building he needed to visit. As Iggy had predicted, half a dozen police cruisers were parked along the street beside a four-story building made of yellow brick. All sorts of horrors paraded through his mind as he approached. Maybe Dr. Halverson had accidentally infected someone in the lab and now they were all dead. Maybe Iggy had been there.

No. Leslie had just talked to Iggy, and he told her about the police cars. Alex took a deep breath and tried to focus. What he needed was a sandwich and a cigarette.

When he reached the entrance, there was no uniformed officer there, another good sign, but his gut was telling him something was wrong. It wasn't until he saw the tall, blond man in the gray pinstriped suit loitering in the hall that Alex realized what form the danger had taken. He plastered a smile on his face and kept his pace steady.

"Agent Warner," he said, when he reached the young FBI man. "If you're looking for old books, I hear the University's library has a few."

Warner's eyes narrowed at the sight of Alex.

"Shouldn't you be helping some little girl find her lost balloon?"

Alex chuckled and clapped Warner on the shoulder. "That's what I love about you FBI types," Alex said. "You're all so witty."

Warner snarled and batted Alex's hand away.

"You'd better mind your manners, scribbler," he snarled. "The boss lady may want to handle you with kid gloves, but that doesn't mean I have to."

"I think," a new voice cut in, "that what Agent Warner meant to ask is, what are you doing here, Mr. Lockerby?"

Alex turned to find Agent Davis emerging from a door with the word *Pathology* panted on it.

"I'm here to see Dr. Halverson," Alex said, putting on an easy smile.

Davis's smile looked just as insincere as Alex's. "What business do you have with the Doc?" he asked.

Alex took a deep breath and kept his smile in place. These two were really beginning to get on his nerves, which, when he thought about it, was probably just what they were trying to do. If he gave them any excuse, they'd arrest him and throw him in a holding cell for as long as they could get away with. Some other time it might have been fun to force their hand, but not today.

Too many people were depending on him today.

"Doctor Bell called me," he said. "Asked me to come down right away, so here I am."

"Who's Bell?" Warner asked Davis. The elder FBI man checked his notes.

"The consultant," he said after a moment. The two of them exchanged a long look, then Davis stepped away from the door so Alex could enter.

The room beyond was crammed with lab equipment, work-benches, burners, and beakers of every description — and policemen. Alex saw Lieutenant Callahan standing next to a gray-bearded man with immensely thick spectacles who wore a white lab coat. Alex ventured a guess that he was the famous Dr. Halverson. He seemed to be explaining something highly technical, since Callahan and his detectives kept stopping him every few seconds to write in their notebooks.

"Well, well," a honeyed female voice washed over him. "You do turn up in the strangest places, Mr. Lockerby."

Alex looked toward the back of the room and found Sorsha Kincaid leaning against a lab table with the air of someone who was waiting for something to happen. Unlike when she came to his office, she wore a dress with a white jacket over the top. The dress was pale blue to match her eyes, and it clung to her slender form in a very appealing manner. To Alex's surprise, Iggy stood next to her with a warm smile on his face.

"Why, Miss Kincaid," Alex said, slapping his poker face back in place. "What an unexpected pleasure."

She smiled a warm, genuine smile and shook her head.

"Not for me," she said. "I've been waiting for you for some time. It was very rude of you to keep me waiting."

Alex had no idea what she was talking about and he had to keep reminding himself that the dazzling smile she kept flashing him was probably the one a shark shows just before it makes you its lunch.

"I'm terribly sorry," he said, with a mock bow. "I wasn't aware you were expecting me."

Sorsha turned to Iggy and looped her arm in his. "Doctor Bell here simply wouldn't explain Dr. Halverson's results to me until you got here," she said.

"And I stand by it," Iggy said. "I hate having to explain things more than once."

"You could have just asked Halverson," Alex said. Sorsha frowned.

"No," she said then, replacing the frown with a knowing smile. "I'm afraid that Halverson is far too brilliant to be clearly understood. Whereas Dr. Bell is so very eloquent."

Iggy actually blushed.

"Well now that I'm here," Alex said. "I guess Dr. Bell can explain."

"Not quite yet," Sorsha said. Alex felt the temperature in the room go down several degrees, figuratively at least. "This is the second time this week I find you tangled up in my investigation, Mr. Lockerby. I'd like to know why you are here."

"You think this has something to do with your missing book?" Alex said. He hadn't actually considered that this might be the work of some deranged runewright, but Iggy had said the disease was man-made. Could something in the Archimedean Monograph be that dangerous? Sorsha smiled but her ice blue eyes were hard.

"The incident at the mission was unnatural," she said. "Doesn't that suggest magic to you, Mr. Lockerby?" She tisked at him and Alex caught himself blushing. "I thought you were smarter than that. Now, why are you here?"

"Father Harry was a friend of mine," he said.

"Who?" Sorsha asked. Alex strangled the urge to yell.

"The priest who ran the mission," he said. "I'm here to make sure that the person who killed him," Alex chose his next words carefully, "sees justice."

Sorsha looked at him for a long moment, then shrugged. "All right. But if I find out you've lied to me—"

"I know, I know." Alex held up his hand. "You'll have me drawn and quartered."

"Something like that." A cold, deadly smile crawled up Sorsha's lips.

"If you two are quite finished," Iggy said, exasperation in his voice. He waited until they both turned to him before continuing. "I'm afraid you're wrong about this being magical, Miss Kincaid," he said. "At least not in the way you mean. If this had been some kind of curse or rune, there wouldn't have been trace bacteria in the blood samples."

Sorsha nodded, a look of irritation on her face.

"Magic wouldn't leave normal, biological traces," she agreed. "So what is it then?"

"I think it's some form of Alchemy," Iggy said. "This disease has three distinct stages. The first takes the longest to be fatal. The affected person doesn't even look sick for the first hour. After that, however, they deteriorate rapidly and death occurs about three hours later."

"How do you know this?" Alex asked.

"We've tested it on mice," Iggy said. "Now, the first person sick becomes infectious as soon as they begin to show symptoms, but their bodies are already producing the second type of the infection."

Sorsha's face was a mask of concentration. "So only the first person has the original disease," she said. "The next group gets the second type."

"Just so," Iggy said. "That type is fatal within two hours of being infected."

"What about the third type?" Alex asked.

"People with the second type produce the infection in its third phase," Iggy said. "The third phase is just as deadly as the second, but people with the third type of the illness can't infect anyone else."

"So the first person can infect people," Sorsha said. "And those people can infect others, but after that the disease just stops."

Iggy nodded, then turned to Alex. "Now do you see why I called you down here?"

"No idea," Alex said.

"Think about it," Iggy said. "A disease that only kills for a short time and then stops, leaving no chance of an outbreak. This disease is not some horrible accident or magic gone wrong, it was designed this way. It's a weapon."

14

THE RESTAURATEUR

Alex suppressed a laugh. "That plague at the mission, a weapon? A weapon against what?" he said. "Dinner parties?"

"Yes," Sorsha said. "And any other place where people gather. Office buildings, race tracks, army barracks, Grand Central Station, or a Dodgers game. Whoever made this could target any group of people without risking letting loose a plague. It's a work of genius." She sounded impressed, but Alex detected a tremor of fear in her voice.

Iggy nodded.

"So why is it here?" Alex asked. "Whoever made this thing didn't do it to target a mission full of vagrants."

"It was probably a test," Iggy said.

"Maybe to prove to a buyer that the weapon did what its creator claimed it did," Sorsha said. "Or as a dry run."

"Which would mean," Alex said, "that our mad scientist already has a target in mind?"

"The conference," Sorsha gasped. "There's a conference, Monday, on the European problem. Dignitaries and military leaders will be there from all over the world."

"A conference? What's this conference for?" he asked. Alex hadn't heard about it, but that wasn't surprising; politics in any form bored him.

"Don't you read the news?" Sorsha rolled her eyes.

"Just the funny papers," he said.

"Germany is saber-rattling again," she explained. "Hitler has promised that he has no military intentions, but Europe's worried. This conference is an attempt to get everyone talking." She motioned Agent Davis over to her and began issuing orders to contact Washington and alert them to the threat. When she finished, he scurried off, and she turned back to Iggy.

"This conference is being held in the grand ballroom of the Waldorf Hotel," she said. "Can you give me an idea of how this weapon could be used against the attendees?"

Iggy stroked his mustache for a moment, pondering the matter.

"Well, it's too fragile to remain airborne for any length of time. That means that the disease would have to be spread inside the hotel."

"Why not infect someone before the event?" Alex asked. "Let them carry it inside."

"Too many variables," Sorsha said, shaking her head. "What if the infected person felt sick and went to a doctor, or decided to stop for breakfast? The only way to ensure the weapon hits its target is to release it inside."

Alex hadn't thought of that, but it made sense. Sorsha was pretty good at her consultant job.

"Correct," Iggy confirmed. "Also, whoever is infected first will be someone who will circulate, giving them the best chance to spread the disease — so make it a waiter or a hostess."

"Or security," Sorsha said. "For an event like this, there'll be over a dozen agents. It sounds like the best chance of catching our assassin is when he tries to bring the disease inside." She pulled her notebook out of the air and flipped it open.

"It would be in a flask or vial, sealed with lead," Iggy said. "Not very big, just an ounce or two. He'd have to sprinkle it somewhere the first victim would come in contact with it."

"Like on a towel or in a drink?" Sorsha said.

"Anywhere would do," Iggy said. "Even a doorknob."

Sorsha jotted down Iggy's words. "Good," she said when she finished. "This should help us secure the conference."

"If the conference is even a target," Alex said. Sorsha shrugged.

"You could be right; this might have nothing to do with politics, but I'd rather be safe than sorry."

At that moment, Agent Davis returned and motioned Sorsha over to the door.

"Thank you, Doctor Bell," she said, shaking hands with Iggy, then she gave Alex a frosty look and left.

"I see why you like her," Iggy said, watching the retreating figure of the Sorceress in her form-fitting dress.

"I don't like her," Alex said, watching too. Iggy grinned, and his mustache rose up to meet his nose.

"Sure you don't." Then his face turned serious. "Alex," he said, his voice dropping. "You've got to find out who's behind this. Whatever they're after, they aren't going to stop with the Brotherhood of Hope Mission. More people are going to die."

"I know," Alex said. "If I could just get a line on Charles Beaumont, maybe I could trace him back to where he got infected." Alex recounted to Iggy his efforts to track the elusive burglar. While he spoke, Iggy stroked his mustache, deep in thought.

"So," Iggy said once Alex finished. "If Beaumont was this Spook fellow, he's not just any burglar."

"Not by a long shot," Alex agreed. "He knew exactly what to take; highly valuable, small and light."

"Yes, but he didn't take the kinds of things that would be easy to fence," Iggy said. "You said he took a set of silverware that was once owned by Napoleon, and a painting by Renoir?"

Alex nodded; he'd been through the list of stolen property so many times he knew it by heart.

"What are you getting at, old man?" Alex asked when Iggy didn't immediately respond.

"You can't just sell a Renoir after you steal it," Iggy said. "It's too well known. The only reason to take it is if you're sure you can move it."

"You think Beaumont had a buyer already lined up for the painting? Alex said.

"Not just for the painting," Iggy said. "I'd bet my mustache that he had buyers ready and waiting for everything he stole."

"Sounds reasonable," Alex said. "But how does this help us?"

"A thief, even a high end thief, usually doesn't travel in the kinds of circles where you meet collectors of stolen paintings and hot wine."

"No one likes hot wine," Alex said with a grin. "Least of all a collector."

"My point," Iggy said, ignoring Alex's attempt at humor, "is that rich people aren't likely to know a burglar, so how do they hire one when they want something stolen?"

Alex smiled as the light went on. "They know someone who knows Beaumont," he said. "A neutral third party who serves as the intermediary for larcenous socialites who want to hire a burglar."

"Exactly," Iggy said. "There can't be many people in the city capable of doing that kind of work. It'd have to be someone with serious criminal connections who's also a socialite."

Alex thought about Arthur Wilks and his network of fences, but that wasn't quite right. Whoever Beaumont's fixer was, he was a member of high society, and Alex couldn't imagine anyone on Wilks' list fitting that bill. Besides, there was no way Wilks was going to share any names with a private detective.

Thinking about Wilks reminded Alex of the reason he'd gone to see the insurance agent in the first place. He had half a day left before the weekend, so he needed to find Jerry Pemberton's murderer fast. Still, if Wilks and his network couldn't track down the missing stones, what chance did he have? Whoever had them didn't seem to be in a hurry to sell them, after all.

Or maybe they already had.

What if Pemberton had a buyer already, just like the Spook? Someone who wanted the stones ahead of time and approached Pemberton. Pemberton hires the thief and they do the job.

No, that wouldn't work.

Even with Pemberton's map, the thief would have to get in and out undetected. No mean feat. So it must have been the thief who approached Pemberton. But, how did the thief line up his buyer? He must have used an intermediary, too.

Alex told Iggy his idea, the words spilling out of him in his excitement.

"That would explain a lot," Iggy said, nodding vigorously. "If Pemberton or the mystery thief held out for more money, that would have given the buyer incentive to torture the thief's identity out of Pemberton."

"It also explains why the stones aren't being fenced." Alex said.

"Good work," Iggy said. "I think you're on to something. The question is, how do you find the intermediary?"

Alex had an answer for that, but the thought of it made his stomach turn.

"If you want to find a high class crook," he said, "you ask a high class crook."

TWENTY MINUTES LATER, Alex stood on an inner ring sidewalk a block from the Core. Across the street stood the *Lucky Dragon* restaurant. The *Lucky Dragon* was famous for its dumplings and about as Chinese as Grauman's Chinese Theatre. It was a trendy hot spot for the well-to-do and those who aspired to appear so. It was also a front for the Japanese mafia. Its owner was an older man named Chow Duk Sum. His real name was Shiro Takahashi, an American citizen raised in Brooklyn by Japanese parents.

What only a handful of people in the entire world knew, was that Shiro was also Danny Pak's father.

Danny didn't know that Alex knew about his familial relationships and Alex had never said anything. He'd found out when Iggy was teaching him how to track people through birth records. Alex had used his friend as a test and wound up learning way more than he ever wanted to know. Now he was about to put that knowledge to use in a way that might end his friendship with Danny forever.

It might also get him killed. Alex didn't know much about the Japanese mafia, but if they were anything like the Italian one, just knowing who Chow Duk Sum really was could be enough to earn him a pair of cement shoes.

He took one of his cards out of his pocket, scribbled *This is about Danny* on the back, then crossed the street.

An attractive young hostess in a brightly colored robe greeted him when he entered. Her features were Asian, but her accent was cultured, with a hint of Great Britain.

"I'm sorry," she said, when Alex asked to see the owner. "Mr. Chow is very busy right now. If you're not here to eat, then I'll have to ask you to leave."

Alex handed his card to her, forcing his hand not to shake. "Have someone give him this," he said. "If he still doesn't want to see me, I'll go."

The girl hesitated, then she took the card over to a young Asian man in a silk suit sitting at a table in the corner. After a whispered conversation, she returned, and the young man disappeared into the back. He came back only a moment later.

"Mr. Chow will see you," he said, simply. "Follow me."

He led Alex back, through the kitchen, to a narrow set of stairs that went up to the second floor. At the top, a long hallway ran the length of the building with doors on the left side. The man stopped at the first one and opened it. Alex briefly saw runes glow along the frame. He wasn't familiar with the angular, painted characters of the Kanji style of runes, but he could feel their power as he passed through the door.

The room beyond looked nothing like the somewhat-garishly decorated dining room. It appeared to be right out of the pages of a fashion magazine. Elegant furniture surrounded a low wooden table with Tiffany lamps in the corners.

"Please sit," the young man said, then withdrew, shutting the door behind him. Alex sat on one of the long couches and waited, trying to convince his nervous body not to sweat. He wasn't sure what to expect, but the aging Asian man in a black tuxedo who entered a moment later definitely wasn't it.

Alex stood and bowed to him as he entered.

"Mr. Takahashi, I presume."

The man looked startled, then he bowed in return. He was medium height and slim, with long hair that he tied behind his head in a ponytail. His face was crisscrossed with lines, but his dark eyes were bright. He looked like an older version of Danny.

"I figured I'd be seeing you sooner or later," he said. "You're Daniel's detective friend." He said all this in an easy, conversational manner, then sat across the table on the opposite couch. "You know my real name, so I'm going to assume you know who I am," he said. "That means you understand the predicament you've put me in just by being here."

"I apologize for any inconvenience," Alex said. "I wouldn't have come if it weren't important."

Shiro Takahashi looked him over for a long moment. "Then I guess you'd better tell me why you came."

Alex explained what happened with Jerry Pemberton, the stakeout of the customs warehouse, and how that had made Captain Rooney look bad. While he talked, Shiro simply sat, unmoving, and listened.

"It seems you have gotten Daniel into quite a bit of trouble, Mr. Lockerby," he said once Alex finished. His voice was soft and calm and far more intimidating than if he had shouted. "It took Daniel a long time to convince his fellow officers to take him seriously. Prejudice against Japanese is still strong here." He looked around at the luxurious room. "It took me a long time to carve out a place for myself," he said. "Daniel did it at a much younger age. I'm very proud of him."

"I understand," Alex said.

"Then you will understand that I will take it personally if you cost my son his job."

It was said without anger or malice and Shiro's tone was mild, congenial even, but the threat there sent chills down Alex's back.

"I take it," Shiro went on after a brief pause, "that your presence here means you believe I can help you with your investigation. Unfortunately, I've never heard of Jerry Pemberton."

"Actually, I was hoping you could help me find someone else," Alex said. He explained about the stones not being fenced and his theory that someone had commissioned the theft. "There can't be that many people who can provide this kind of service," Alex finished. "I just need to know who does. If I can find the man who arranged the theft, I can find his client, and that will be the person who murdered Jerry Pemberton."

Shiro steepled his hands under his chin and sat, unmoving for a long moment.

"There is only one man in New York who handles this sort of work," he said. "There are many lesser men, for lesser jobs, of course, but anyone making this kind of arrangement would require ten percent of the job up front. You said the insurance check was for one hundred and fifty large, that would be fifteen thousand down. Only high-end clients can pay that kind of fee, and only one man in New York takes that kind of action. His name is Jeremy Brewer, but everyone just calls him the Broker. You'll find him in a Corc nightclub called *The Emerald Room*. That's where he conducts business."

"Thank you, Mr. Takahashi," Alex said, trying not to stand too quickly, but Shiro waved him back into his seat.

"I've enjoyed our talk, Mr. Lockerby," he said. "You showed both respect and intellect, both in finding me and in knowing what question to ask me."

Alex opened his mouth to respond, but Shiro kept speaking.

"Clearly you are a worthy friend for my son. That said, coming here could expose Daniel, and I won't have that. If you come here again, for any reason other than to eat dumplings, I will take it as a sign of disrespect."

Alex tried to control the shiver that ran across his shoulders but couldn't.

"Furthermore," Shiro said, "the Broker is a dangerous man. He won't give up the information you want without...coercion." Shiro raised his eyes and stared into Alex's. "Under no circumstances is my name, or Daniel's, to come to his attention. Am I clear?"

"Crystal," Alex said. "And thank you."

Shiro leaned forward and picked up a tiny silver bell from the coffee table. He rang it once and the young Asian in the silk suit reappeared.

"Please show our guest out," he said. "And, Mr. Lockerby, good luck."

15

THE WORKSHOP

The crawler flowed over the streets of Manhattan on its energy legs, far faster than any streetcar could move, but it still felt slow to Alex. He had to hurry back to the brownstone and see Iggy. Clubs like *The Emerald Room* wouldn't let ordinary working schlubs in; you had to look the part.

He needed a tuxedo.

The only person he knew who might have one he could borrow was Iggy. The old man was a little shorter and heavier than Alex, but it was his only option.

When he reached the brownstone, Iggy laughed in his face.

"What would I need a tuxedo for?" he said. "What do *you* need it for?"

Alex explained about the Broker and where he could be found.

"So you want a tuxedo so you can what? Kidnap this guy, drag him out the back of a Core nightclub, and then beat the truth out of him somewhere quiet?"

Alex had been so focused on finding a tux that he hadn't actually thought that far ahead. Shiro Takahashi had been right; the Broker wouldn't give up client names without a fight.

"And what are you going to do when you're done?" Iggy went on.

"He'll have seen your face. He won't rest until he's found you and put a bullet in you, so you're going to have to kill him. Is that your plan?"

"What do you want me to do?" Alex yelled, whirling on him. He regretted it instantly, but the stress of the day was getting to him. "I'm sorry—" he began but Iggy put a hand on his shoulder.

"I want you to think," he said. "And I want you to listen."

Alex sighed, his temper back under control, and he nodded.

"All right," Iggy said. "You need to get into that club and find this Broker all without anyone knowing who you are or questioning your right to be there."

"If you're suggesting a disguise rune," Alex said, trying hard not to roll his eyes. "You know those never work, and even when they do, any magic at all disrupts them. I couldn't even ride the crawler while using one."

Iggy did roll his eyes — and shook his head.

"My dear boy," he said in his most professorial tone. "You haven't used one of *my* disguise runes yet. They're as solid as Gibraltar."

Alex's jaw dropped open for a moment, then he snapped it closed so hard his teeth clacked.

"Why didn't you teach me that?" he protested. "Do you know how useful that would have been whenever I was tailing someone, or doing something questionably legal?"

"That's exactly why I didn't teach it to you," Iggy said. "It's so useful, you'd justify using it all the time."

Alex was beginning to see the problem. "How much does it cost to cast?" he asked.

"Forty dollars a rune," Iggy said. "Lots of expensive materials."

Alex whistled. He'd have burned through everything he had in less than a week. He might anyway, if he wanted to get into *The Emerald Room*.

"I figure you'll need four separate runes," Iggy said. "One for your clothes, one for your face, one for your money, and another one for your face when you leave."

"Why don't you do them all in one rune?" Alex asked, doing the math in his head and feeling his wallet groan.

"Illusions work best when you don't ask them to do too much," Iggy said.

"So why do I need a new face when I leave?"

"Because, if you're seen leaving, you don't want anyone to be able to identify you later." He waved a hand at Alex. "Now go away," he said. "It'll take me close to ten hours to do all four castings, so you'll have to go tomorrow night."

"That doesn't leave me much time," Alex pointed out.

"Can't be helped," Iggy said. "On the bright side, it gives you time to figure out how you're going to get the Broker fellow to talk. Now leave me be; I'm going to my workshop and don't wish to be disturbed."

The word *workshop* hit Alex like a runaway cab and he suddenly realized what he'd been missing.

"Thanks Iggy," he yelled as he sprinted down the stairs and out into the street.

EVER SINCE HE'D searched Thomas Rockwell's apartment, something had been bothering him. Runewrights like Iggy and Alex had their workshops inside their vaults, but now that Alex thought about it, Thomas didn't have a vault rune in his lore book. That meant he had to have a workshop in the real world, somewhere he could keep his supplies, write his runes, and research his craft. Runewright work tended to involve toxic and caustic substances, something no landlord would allow in an apartment building, so runewrights usually did their work elsewhere.

All Alex had to do was find where Thomas did his work.

As he rode the crawler south, he wondered what he might find in Thomas' workshop. Would Sorsha's missing rune diagrams be there? Had he found the Archimedean Monograph and fled with it?

More likely the only thing there is Thomas' shadow burned onto a wall.

That thought soured Alex's mood. It was further soured when he exited the crawler a few blocks from Thomas' building. The FBI still had the building under surveillance. He wondered what Sorsha and her goons would do if they heard he was back?

Pushing that thought aside, Alex entered the building and followed the signs downstairs to the basement where he found the apartment of the building superintendent.

"What can I do for ya?" he asked in a brogue that could only have come from Scotland. The super was a short, slight man of about fifty. He had a mop of graying blond hair that looked like it resisted any attempts he might have made to tame it, and bright blue eyes over an infectious smile.

"I'm a private detective." Alex handed the man his card.

The super took out a pair of wire spectacles and scrutinized the card for a moment.

"Now how can I be helping a shamus?" he asked, handing the card back.

"I'm looking into the disappearance of one of your tenants, Thomas Rockwell."

"Thomas is missing?" he said. The super's smile evaporated.

"His sister said he's been gone for almost a week." Alex nodded. "Asked me to help find him."

"That's terrible." The super's voice dropped to a whisper.

"Did you know Thomas well, Mister...?"

"Flynn," he said. "Michael Flynn. And yes, I knew him. He was a simple, kind man, kept his apartment clean, always paid his rent on time. I liked him. He even helped me with the accounts from time to time and didn't ask a penny for it."

"Did you know that Thomas was a runewright?"

"He had a rune that helped with my rheumatism." Michael nodded. "I paid him for those, of course; I don't take charity."

"Do you know where he did his work? He would have had a workshop, probably nearby."

"He had to fix up a rune for me one time," he said, nodding. "He left and came back about an hour later."

A rune to ease pain and improve joint mobility would take about half an hour, more or less. That meant Thomas' workshop was close.

Unless he took a cab.

"Did you notice anything different about Thomas in the last few weeks?"

"Now that you mention it, he did seem a bit different," Michael said, rubbing his stubble covered chin. "Happier maybe? Excited about something. Couldn't tell you what, though."

"Did he have a girlfriend?" Alex asked, remembering the state of Thomas' bedroom under the glow of silverlight. Michael nodded.

"Betty something-or-other. Pretty enough as lasses go," he said. "I only met her once."

"Can you describe her?"

"Oh, a little taller than me, shapely, with long, auburn hair clear down her back. I'm sorry, that's about the best I can do."

Alex thanked him. "Is there anyone in the building Thomas was close to, who might know more about Betty or where Thomas had his workshop?"

Michael stroked his stubble again.

"The old battle-axe in 2F might know."

"She friends with Thomas?"

"No," Michael said with a chuckle. "She's just the type who listens at keyholes, the old busybody. Her name is Hilda Jefferson."

Alex laughed and thanked Michael. As he turned to leave, however, the little man grabbed his wrist.

"Saints be with you, young man," he said, an earnest look on his face. "Bring Thomas home safe if you can."

Alex didn't have the heart to tell the old man that Thomas was probably dead, so he promised that he would do the best he could, and headed back upstairs. He now had a name and description of Thomas' female companion, but he was still no closer to finding the workshop.

The door to Mrs. Jefferson's apartment faced the stairwell and he heard her scurrying back as he approached.

"Mrs. Jefferson," he called, knocking on the door. "Mr. Flynn downstairs said you might be able to help me."

A much slower shuffle approached the door and it opened a crack. A woman's eye appeared, covered by thick glasses that made it look comically large.

"Whatcho want?" she said, her voice like the creaking of a rusty gate.

"You know Thomas Rockwell in 5C?" He asked. "He's missing and I'm trying to find him."

"Don't know you," the woman said, starting to close the door. Alex jammed the toe of his shoe in the jamb to keep the door from closing.

"Please, Mrs. Jefferson," Alex said in a mild voice. "His sister is very worried about him."

"Hah," the old woman cackled. "He's been having a woman up to his apartment lately but if that's his sister, I'm the Queen of Sheba."

"You mean a pretty girl with long, auburn hair?"

"That's her," Mrs. Jefferson said. "Coming and going at all hours of the day and night, whispering her black magic in his ear. She's a bad one, that."

"That's his girlfriend," Alex said. "Name's Becky. Thomas' sister is named Evelyn."

"That's the only girl that visits Thomas," the woman said, though Alex couldn't see how she could know that.

"Did you ever hear Thomas say where he went to work on his runes?"

"No," the old woman said, and laughed. "He never said, but he didn't have to. I saw him out my window."

Of course you did.

"Where did he go?"

"Building across the street," she said. "Next to the five-and-dime there's a door that leads to a stairway. He went up there whenever he left at night."

"Did the auburn-haired girl ever go with him?"

Mrs. Jefferson shook her head. "He always went alone," she said.

Alex stifled a laugh and thanked the old woman. He turned and went down the stairs but Mrs. Jefferson didn't close her door until he was out of sight.

Thank God for nosy neighbors.

If Mrs. Jefferson hadn't gone the extra mile and watched her departing neighbors out the window, Alex would have had to knock on every door in the building in the hopes someone else knew where Thomas went.

He'd gotten lucky.

THE SUN WAS JUST SETTING when he stepped out of Thomas' apartment and into the cool New York night. He wanted to call Iggy, to get an update on the disguise runes, but Iggy was probably working, and even if he was taking a break he'd only yell at Alex for interrupting. On the bright side, he wouldn't yell at Alex for staying out late. That gave him all night to go through Thomas' workshop.

He pulled up his collar against the wind and set off toward the five-and-dime whistling a tune.

"Well you're in a good mood," Evelyn's voice came from behind him. "Did you learn anything?"

Alex turned and found Thomas' sister coming up the sidewalk behind him. Her dark curly hair blew sideways in the wind and she was trying valiantly to keep a broad-brimmed hat on her head. She wore a flowing white blouse with a tight, black skirt that went down to her knees.

"What are you doing here?" Alex asked, delighted to see her.

"Between you and the FBI, Thomas' place is quite a mess," she said. "If he's...if he's really dead, I want to collect his things. You know, family pictures, heirlooms, that sort of thing. It's just junk, really, but it's all I've got left."

Alex felt like a heel. When he didn't speak, Evelyn grinned sadly.

"It's okay," she said. "What are you doing here? Did you find something?"

"I did." Alex turned and pointed to the five-and-dime. "Your brother had his rune workshop in the building next to that store. I'm on my way to see what's there. Maybe I can find out something about his mysterious girlfriend."

"Girlfriend?" Evelyn said, a look of interest crossing her face. "Thomas never said he had a girlfriend."

"Her name's Becky," Alex said. "That's all I know."

"Could she be the reason he's dead?" Evelyn's voice trembled, and Alex put his hand on her shoulder.

"Right now I don't even know her last name," he said. "Let me look around Thomas' workshop and I'll let you know if I find anything."

"No," she said, and shook her head. "I'm coming with you."

Alex thought about what his ghostlight might reveal — Thomas' shadow on the wall. He didn't want to hurt Evelyn any more that she had been. On the other hand, she deserved truth.

"All right," he said. "But I go in first and you don't follow until I call for you."

She folded her arms across her chest and fixed him with a hard stare. When he didn't relent, she said, "All right."

The stairway next to the five-and-dime went up to a long, straight hallway on the second floor of a plain-looking building. Windows filled the left hand wall, showing a view of the five-and-dime's roof and the street beyond. Doors were set along the opposite wall at regular intervals. Only one of them bore the triangle and eyeball symbol of a runewright, right above a sign that advertised office hours from seven to ten PM, Monday, Wednesday, and Thursday.

"It's locked," Evelyn said, trying the door.

Alex had been expecting that, so he pulled his rune book from his jacket pocket and flipped to the back. That was where he kept the rarer, more expensive runes. When he got to a triangular one with what looked like a deformed duck inside, he stopped and tore it out.

"What's that?" Evelyn asked.

"Something I'm not supposed to know," Alex said, licking the paper and sticking it to the doorknob. Lighting a match from the book in his pocket, he touched it to the paper. The rune glowed bright orange as it disappeared in fire and the door lock opened with an audible clack.

"That's amazing," Evelyn said as Alex opened the door. "You must be able to get in anywhere you want."

"Not really," Alex said, tucking his rune book back in his pocket. "That rune costs ten bucks to make. Not to mention that what I just did is breaking and entering."

"Not with me here," Evelyn said. "I'm the owner's sister, after all." She reached over and flicked a switch on the wall, filling the room with light from the magelight crystals hanging on wires from the ceiling. "See," she said. "I'm helping already."

Thomas' workshop was a complete contrast from his apartment; of course, his apartment had been ransacked. The workshop looked like an advertisement for runewright shops. Three workbenches stood in the center of the space; the one on the right had a blotter pad on it. A freestanding set of drawers occupied one side, where pencils and penknives would be kept, with a wire rack on the other, filled with pot after pot of ink. Along the back were two stacks of trays that held paper.

The workbench on the left had a gas canister below it with a long rubber tube that ran up through holes in the tabletop to burners. A maze of glass tubes, distillers, evaporators, and extractors were set up and ready to brew the special inks Thomas used in his work. None of the glass was dirty or smudged.

The middle workbench was completely empty, but based on the scorch marks and scoring on the top, Alex guessed it was where Thomas tested his runes and refined them.

Along the walls stood orderly shelves holding neatly stacked containers, cabinets full of materials, and cases full of books. An industrial sink stuck out from the wall in the back, next to a door that Alex assumed went to a bathroom. In the far corner there was a small workbench up against the wall with a hot plate and a coffee pot on it and a set of cupboards overhead. A comfortable-looking reading chair and lamp stood to one side, with a neatly made bed on the other. Apparently Thomas was prepared if he had to work late. No sense waking Mrs. Jefferson up by coming in after midnight.

Now this is the workshop of a bookkeeper.

"Well, this is it, I guess," Evelyn said. "What are we looking for?"

"First, I need to find what your brother was working on," Alex said, approaching the middle workbench. Set into the bench's top were four brass triangles that pointed out, like the corners of a square. Thomas would slip the corners of his drawing paper under those to keep it in place when he wrote or activated his runes.

Based on the position of the writing equipment on the end desk, Thomas was used to working on the opposite side of the workbench, so Alex circled around. On the back side, a drawer was set just beneath the top. Pulling it open, he found the large square drawing pad that fit the brass holders on the bench top, a box of matches, and a worn and dog-eared notebook.

He set the pad and the notebook on the workbench, then shut the drawer. He wanted to restore the last thing Thomas had drawn, like he'd done with the map in Jerry Pemberton's apartment, but he'd need his kit for that, so he set it aside.

"What's that?" Evelyn asked, peeking around his side to look at the book.

Alex opened it and found page after page of the finding rune from the Archimedean Monograph. Each one was slightly different with copious notes about the things Thomas had tried while attempting to unlock its secrets. Alex turned to the last written page.

"*I've done it*," he read. "*I've finally cracked the damn thing. For a while there, I thought it would drive me mad, but I won. The solution was staring me right in the face the whole time. I knew the rune was written out of phase, but it's also upside down. Once I reversed it, everything made sense. I'm exhausted, so I don't dare try writing it now; I'd probably make a mistake and blow myself up. I'll go home and come back tomorrow. With any luck I'll have the monograph when Becky comes to see me. Won't she be surprised! This is the best day of my life!*"

Alex closed the notebook and set it back down on the workbench.

"Is that it?" Evelyn asked. "What does it mean?"

"It means your brother is dead," Alex said. "I'm sorry."

Evelyn swayed and Alex had to grab her before she fell.

"I'm sorry," she said, clinging to his shirt. Tears were rolling down her cheeks and she rubbed furiously at her eyes, smearing her mascara. "I knew he was gone, I...I just didn't want to believe it."

She stepped away from him, but her knees buckled, and Alex had to grab her again.

"You'd better lie down," he said, leading her over to the neat bed in the corner. Once he had her situated, he went to the cupboard over the sink and searched until he found a clean washrag. After running some cold water on it, he wrung it out and folded it, placing it on Evelyn's forehead.

"Now lie there until you feel better," he said.

She thanked him and he returned to Thomas' notebook. The next time Alex looked up, the clock on the wall told him it was eleven twenty-two. He'd been sitting on the stool behind the workbench reading, re-reading, and re-re-reading Thomas' quest to solve the Archimedean Monograph's finding rune. Alex could see what Thomas had been trying to do and scribbled copious notes under and around the ones Thomas had made. It seemed to Alex that Thomas had been on the right track, but just hadn't possessed the knowledge or skill to fully unscramble the rune.

He checked on Evelyn and found her asleep on the bed. Taking the opportunity of not being watched, Alex chalked a door onto a bare patch of wall and opened his vault. Normally he'd never open his vault in front of someone other than Iggy or Leslie, but he wanted to get his kit and have a more thorough look around Thomas' workshop. An hour later, Alex called it quits.

The lab was just as clean as it appeared in normal light. Silverlight revealed plenty of fingerprints and signs that the workshop was used regularly, but there was no sign of blood, and no indication that anything other than sleeping had ever happened in the bed. Some of the books were more used than others, but none of them contained hidden compartments or scraps of paper.

All was as it should be.

Finally Alex pulled out his ghostlight burner and lit it. He'd been avoiding this moment, but with Evelyn asleep he'd best do it now. The multi-lamp cast its greenish glow around the room until it fell on the back wall. There, reaching out from where Alex stood and running up the wall, was the shadow of a man. It ran over the bookshelf and the little kitchen counter with the hotplate. The form showed a man with his hands thrown up over his face, as if shielding his eyes from a flash bulb he hadn't seen coming.

It was all that remained of Thomas Rockwell.

Alex put his hand on his forehead and pinched it. He'd been without food, liquor, or a cigarette in quite a while and it had given him a pounding headache. The beam of his lantern fell across Evelyn's sleeping form as he lifted it to extinguish the ghostlight burner. She stirred and Alex quickly blew out the flame. The light no longer illuminated her, but he could still see her in his mind. Even disheveled, with her makeup a mess, she was beautiful.

He sighed and returned the gear to his bag. A small wooden box was tucked into one end of the bag and Alex withdrew it, setting it on the workbench quietly. Inside was a flask with a nice single malt scotch that he'd pilfered from Iggy's liquor cabinet. Usually this was his reward for a case solved and a job well done, but in this case, he'd make an exception. Evelyn wanted her brother found, and he'd done that. She wanted to know who killed him, and he knew that now, too. Whoever the mysterious Becky was, she'd brought Thomas the Monograph pages. She set his feet on the path that ultimately lead to his death.

Removing the cup from the top, Alex opened the flask and poured out two fingers of the amber liquid.

Becky had torn Thomas' place apart looking for his notebook. She wanted to see how he'd attempted to solve the rune, maybe use the notes to entice the next patsy she conned into looking for the Monograph. It was the only thing she could have been looking for. Thomas copied the original Monograph pages into his lore book, and they weren't here in the workshop, so Becky must still have them.

"She's miles away by now," he said, draining the tiny tin cup and refilling it from the flask.

"Who?" Evelyn's voice drifted to him out of the semi-darkness. He'd turned off some of the lights when he'd used his lamp in order to see better. Evelyn sat up on the bed and brushed her raven hair out of her face. She looked frightened for a moment, her tired mind not recognizing her surroundings for a moment, then she stood and walked to where Alex sat at the workbench.

"Can I have one of those?" she said, pointing at the tin cup.

Alex nodded and stood, offering her the stool. She sat and he went to the cupboards over the table that had the hot plate, returning a moment later with a glass. He set it next to his tin cup and poured whiskey in both.

Evelyn drained hers in one go, then tapped the glass with her finger. Alex refilled it and she drained it again.

"You're behind," she said, indicating the tin cup. Alex refilled her glass again, then raised his cup.

"To Thomas," he said.

She smiled a grateful smile and they both drank.

"You've been wonderful," she said, putting her glass back, upside-down. "Thank you."

Alex poured himself another whisky and sipped at it, nursing it. "I still haven't found the person responsible for Thomas' death," he said, picking up the notebook. "But this is what she wanted. I might be able to use it as bait to lure her out, but I suspect she's headed for the hills."

"You mean the girlfriend," Evelyn said, and Alex nodded. She looked away. "If she wants the notebook so bad," she said, her voice hard, "I want you to burn it."

"If that's what you want," Alex said, finishing his drink. Evelyn wrapped her arms around herself and shivered.

"I just want all this to be over," she said in a small voice. She wobbled on her feet and Alex put his arm around her waist to steady her. She buried her face in his chest.

She felt good in his arms.

He looked down at her and she raised up, pressing her lips to his. It wasn't a chaste peck or a gesture of gratitude but a fiery, pulsating need. She needed to feel alive, needed to be held. Alex pulled her closer, pressing their bodies together. He didn't know if he'd initiated the kiss or if she'd done it. All he knew was that it felt right and she tasted sweet. A minute later he bent down and picked her up, carrying her toward the bed. He was sure she'd tell him to stop before he reached it, but she didn't.

16

THE BROKER

Iggy was sitting in the kitchen with a coffee cup in one hand and the pot in the other when Alex got home. The old man looked exhausted, but at least he wasn't coming in after sunup smelling of Scotch, silverlight oil, and perfume. When Iggy caught sight of him, he raised an eyebrow.

"And just where have you been?" he said. The eyebrows went up further when Alex got closer. "That's a lovely shade of lipstick on your collar," he added.

Alex said nothing.

"At least you don't smell like a brothel; that's expensive perfume. Did you keep the Sorceress company last night?"

"God, no," Alex said, offended that his friend would even suspect such a thing. Sorsha was beautiful, no question, but she seemed to have a healthy dislike for him. "I don't have a death wish," he declared. "Can you imagine what that woman could do to a man who sent her packing? Or God forbid, broke her heart."

"Planning on sending your companion of last night packing?" Iggy said. "You seem to think that's where all relationships end up."

Alex grimaced. He had his opinions about the entangling proprieties of relationships, and he didn't like Iggy's desire to discuss them.

"Just most," Alex said. "Although I might make an exception for Evelyn."

"The woman with the missing brother?"

Alex nodded.

"She must have made quite an impression on you."

"She did," Alex said. "Now, do you have my runes ready?"

Iggy sighed and rolled his eyes.

"There's nothing better for a man than the companionship of a good woman."

"How about not being thrown in jail where I'll wait to be murdered by Danny's father?"

"That's good, too." Iggy chuckled and shrugged. He reached into his vest pocket and pulled out four folded pieces of flash paper. "I've marked them, so you can't get them mixed up," he said. "Each rune will work for five hours or until you cancel them. Have you figured out how to get the truth out of the Broker?"

"I just need some rope and a couple of pulleys." Alex nodded. "I'll stop at Ralph's place, then I'll be all set."

"Sounds messy," Iggy said, yawning. "I thought you were going to avoid that kind of thing."

"Don't worry," Alex said, and chuckled darkly.

Iggy raised his eyebrows as if weighing whether or not Alex was being straight with him.

"You'll have to tell me about it," he said finally. "I'm spent, I'm off to bed." With that, he rose and went upstairs to his room.

Alex headed up to his room and showered, then changed into some work clothes. He had a pretty good idea how to make Jeremy Brewer, A.K.A. the Broker, talk without having to beat the truth out of him. Such tactics were time-consuming and messy. His idea involved using his vault to transport Mr. Brewer and then to force him to reveal who stole Van der Waller's stones. And, if he had time, he'd ask where Charles Beaumont lived as well. If Beaumont was the Spook, the Broker should know him.

Alex hurried out to a building supply company run by an Italian named Ralph. His parents were *very* proud to be Americans. Alex had helped Ralph uncover a competitor who kept vandalizing his storefront, and now Ralph sold Alex anything he needed at a discount.

An hour later, Alex was back at the brownstone with fifty feet of heavy rope, a sturdy metal chair, two pulleys, and a thick gauge U-bolt. He installed the pulleys and the bolt in his vault in a matter of a few minutes. The walls of the extra-dimensional space were a flat, seamless gray and hard as stone. Since Alex had created the space, however, he could mold it like clay with just his hands. All he had to do was push the pulley's anchor bolts into the material of the wall then let it harden around them. The U-bolt went in just as easily, right beside the door.

That done, he cut a thirty-foot length of rope, looped it through the pulleys on the back wall, and tied the ends to the sides of the metal chair.

"That ought to do it," he said to the empty vault. He pulled his watch from his pocket and found that it wasn't even noon yet. He wouldn't be able to make his appearance at *The Emerald Room* until after seven.

He paced back and forth in his vault for almost a minute before he switched on the light over his work table. Opening his kit, he took out a worn, dog-eared notebook and thumbed through to the last few pages where the handwriting changed from Thomas Rockwell's neat lettering to Alex's more loose script. He scanned through the notes he'd been making last night before Evelyn—

Before Evelyn.

Alex shook his head like a dog.

No time for that.

He pulled out the copy he'd made of the Archimedean Monograph's runes when he first found Thomas' lore book. The original finding rune was very different from the one Thomas had unraveled just before he died. The man had been sure he'd figured it out, sure enough to bet his life on it. Alex had seen right away that the rune was far more complex. Thomas simply didn't have the skill or the training necessary to decode it.

Alex brought out his own notebook and set to work.

Four hours later, he finished deciphering it.

The taxi let Alex off in front of an all-night drug store, three blocks from *The Emerald Room*. He decided to splurge and bought a pack of cigarettes before heading to the phone booth to call Iggy.

"I'm here," he said when Iggy picked up. "If all goes well, I shouldn't be in there for more than half an hour."

"If I don't hear from you in an hour, I'm calling Danny," Iggy said.

"All right," Alex said, checking the time on his watch; it showed a little past eight.

Iggy wished him good luck and hung up. Alex replaced the phone's receiver, but lingered in the booth. He pulled out Iggy's disguise runes and spread them out on the little shelf beneath the phone. Licking the one labeled *Clothes*, he stuck it to his jacket, then lit the paper with a match from his pocket. A tingling sensation ran up his spine and when he looked down, his worn gray suit had been transformed to a lustrous black tuxedo. The ebon pips in his shirt gleamed in the diffused light of the booth and the lapels of the jacket were glossy.

The rune labeled *Face* came next and Alex stuck it to his forehead before setting it alight. He worried that the flame might burn his eyebrows, but the flash paper was consumed so rapidly, he didn't even feel its heat.

Wondering if the rune had done its work, he opened the folding door of the booth and caught his reflection in the glass. Instead of his ordinary, serviceable face he saw an elegant one with high cheekbones, a pencil mustache, and slicked-back hair. He looked like a thinner Clark Gable. He didn't know whether to be flattered or offended. One thing was for sure, no one would recognize him.

The last rune for this part of the plan was labeled *Money*. Alex took a stack of six dollar-sized papers out of his wallet. Three of them had the number one-hundred written on them, two were labeled twenty, and the last had the number five scrawled on it. Alex licked each bill and stuck it to the rune paper, then lit it. When the flash dissipated, the paper looked for all the world like real bills. It wouldn't last, of course, but it would be enough to get him through the evening. He had promised Iggy he wouldn't spend any of it unless absolutely necessary.

He had a feeling that would be a difficult promise to keep.

Transformation complete, Alex checked the rest of his gear. He had two emergency runes in his right jacket pocket along with his rune-covered brass knuckles. The left pocket held the pack of smokes, a book of matches, and a card with the name *Harold Troubridge, Antiquities* printed on it.

He lit a cigarette to calm his nerves, then opened the phone booth and strode back out into the street. This was it. With any luck he was about to learn the name of the man who beat Jerry Pemberton to death. All he had to do was convince a vicious and well-connected criminal to tell him what he wanted to know.

Easy.

Outside the front door of *The Emerald Room* stood a man who had to be six-foot-four. He towered over people in the street and his thick neck seemed to strain the limits of the bow tie he had on. He wore the red jacket of a doorman, but Alex knew him for the bouncer he was. The man's presence made a definite statement — unless you belong here, go away.

Alex took a long drag on his cigarette as he approached. The man mountain gave him an appraising look, up and down, but saw nothing amiss. He turned his attention back to the street as Alex walked right past him. Alex waited until he was inside before exhaling a cloud of white smoke.

The interior of *The Emerald Room* didn't fail to impress. The floors were cherry wood, stained and polished to a red sheen. The walls were papered with a striped pattern, alternating green and white, and the lampshades were Tiffany, all made of green glass. A dance floor occupied the center of the club, with small and medium sized tables arranged around it in a semi-circular pattern. Every row of tables was mounted on a riser, each higher than the last in a stair-step pattern, so they looked down on the dance floor. The far side of the floor was occupied by a long bar made of some dark wood where three bartenders served patrons and the waitresses who took drinks to the semi-circle of tables. An orchestra played a swing tune and the whole club seemed full of the energy of the music. Running around the top of the ceiling were balconies that led to private rooms.

That was where Alex would find Jeremy Brewer, the infamous Broker.

Moving slowly but purposefully, Alex picked his way across the floor to the bar and ordered a drink. He felt the need to hurry but stifled it. Before he could go looking for the Broker, he'd need to do some reconnaissance.

The nearest bartender was a short, pudgy man with an elaborate mustache. He had the kind of face that encouraged men to tell him their troubles. An ideal bartender.

"Can I help you, sir?" the bartender asked with a smile. He had a slightly Midwestern accent along with the kind of physique people got from growing up on a farm.

Alex decided to splurge. He told himself it was to better establish his character, but he knew that the Broker wasn't likely to ask the bartender for a reference.

"Your best single malt, please."

"That would be a Macallan 30-year-old," the bartender said. "Will that do?"

"That sounds acceptable."

"Very good, sir."

A moment later he brought Alex a glass of very smooth whiskey. Alex pulled his fake money from his pocket and peeled off the five spot. When the man returned with his change, Alex tipped him outrageously, then turned and leaned against the bar, surveying the room while he slowly savored his drink.

He wasn't much of a socialite, but he recognized a few Broadway stars and a textile millionaire in the crowd. As his gaze swept the room, he located the stairs going up to the private areas. There was no guard there, but the Broker would surely have someone watching his door.

Regretfully, Alex finished his drink, setting the glass on the bar, and headed back across the floor to where the band leader was conducting a slower number to give the dancers a rest. He got the man's attention, then slipped him a twenty along with a note to play *Tar Paper Stomp*. Alex needed something brassy and loud to cover any noise he might make, since the private rooms had open balconies.

Taking a deep breath, Alex lit another cigarette and climbed up the risers where the tables sat, then up the stairway at the back. A long hall ran along the back of the building with doors set in it where the private rooms were. At the far end was a door marked *Exit* that probably led to the fire stairs. It would also explain how the Broker and his clientele could come and go unseen. Alex knew that while the Broker's clients came in through the front, most of his associates didn't have that kind of clout.

At far end of the hall, nearest to the fire door, a man in a simple black suit stood next to the last door. He had a broad, flat face with a long nose that appeared to have been broken at least once and eyes that looked as if they were always squinting. His hair was slicked back and his shoes were shined, but something about his face told Alex that he was a plain thug. Maybe it was that nose.

"What do you want?" he asked, doing a fairly good job of hiding a Jersey accent.

Alex reached into his shirt pocket and pulled out the card with the name Harold Troubridge on it and held it out. "I'd like to speak with Mr. Brewer," Alex said in his most aristocratic British accent.

The flat-faced man didn't move or accept the card; he just looked Alex up and down, trying to take his measure. "Do you have an appointment?" he asked.

"Unfortunately no," Alex said. "I just arrived in town and I shan't be here long. Please give him my card and tell him I'm here regarding a mutually beneficial arrangement."

The man gave Alex another penetrating look, but Iggy's disguise runes were as solid as he claimed. "Wait here," he said, taking the card.

Down below, the band was striking up In The Mood.

As soon as the guard was gone, Alex took out one of his rune papers and crumpled it up in his left hand, holding it in place with his thumb. He patted the weight of his brass knuckles in his jacket pocket and hoped he wouldn't need them. And if he did need them, that they'd be enough.

When the door opened again, the flat-faced man stepped back, allowing Alex to enter. Inside, dim lamps illuminated two men sitting on velvet-lined couches around a small table. Along the back wall stood a well-stocked liquor cabinet with frosted glass panels and bright brass knobs. Chairs were set up along the balcony side so people could watch the band and the dancers below.

One of the men was large with big shoulders and hard, expressionless eyes. His features were sharp, even his beak-like nose, and he had bushy eyebrows that contrasted with his entirely bald head. He wore a loose white shirt and black trousers with a red silk sash around his waist for a belt. Sitting with his legs crossed and his arms over the back of the couch, he had an air of casual violence about him.

The other man was clad in a red smoking jacket, with a cigar in one hand and a snifter in the other. He had an infectious, crooked smile that showed off perfect, white teeth and his blue eyes were alive with curiosity. This was the man Alex was looking for, the elusive Broker.

"Mr. Troubridge," the man in the smoking jacket said invitingly. "Come in. I do enjoy meeting new people."

Alex relaxed a little, taking his cigarette between his right fingers. This was going better than he'd hoped.

Just as the thought crossed his mind, his arms were seized from behind by the flat-faced man and held tight.

"Of course I prefer to know people before I meet them," the Broker said, putting aside his snifter and standing. "And I don't know you." He came close enough for Alex to smell the Cuban tobacco on his breath and studied Alex's face. "No," he said after a long moment. "I've never seen you before, so how is it you know my name?"

Alex began to turn the smoldering cigarette around in his fingers. He had to move slowly so as not to arouse the suspicions of the flat-faced man. He needed to stall, but only for a minute.

"I heard it from someone who wishes to remain anonymous." Alex said. He didn't even have to lie. Brewer's face grew angry and he nodded to his bald-headed companion.

"Search him," he said. The flat-faced goon pulled Alex's arms in tighter as the big man began patting Alex down.

"What's this?" he asked, pulling the brass knuckles out of Alex's pocket. Alex smiled at him as his cigarette touched the flash paper in his left hand.

"Insurance," he said.

The paper erupted in fire and light, but it didn't stop. The light exploded into the room, flowing like water until it filled every crack. The second Alex felt the paper burn, he'd shut his eyes tight.

It didn't help much.

The light from the flash rune burned brighter than staring at the sun, but only for an instant. He hoped the people in the club below would think the light was just one of the overhead magelights burning out.

The hands holding him let go and the three men not expecting the flash started to swear. When Alex opened his eyes, bright dots swam in his vision, but he had no time to worry about that. Bending over, he picked up the brass knuckles where the bald man had dropped them. Slipping them over his right fingers, he turned to find the flat-faced man and Brewer on the floor; the bald man, however, had pulled a snub-nosed .38 from his waistband. Alex strode over to him and unceremoniously punched him in the arm with the brass knuckles. The runes on the metal flared into sudden life and the man howled in pain, the gun falling from his nerveless fingers.

Alex grinned. The rune was one of his own invention. It delivered a shock that felt like a dozen bee stings and left the area numb.

Without stopping to admire his work, Alex pulled back and slugged the bald man in the gut, sending him down on the floor in a gasping heap. He only had another minute or so before they regained their vision, so he had to work fast. Dropping the brass knuckles in his pocket, he took out the piece of chalk and drew the door to his vault on the wall. Next he stuck the second piece of flash paper in his pocket to the wall and lit it, bringing his vault door from chalk to reality. Taking out his key and opening the door, Alex retrieved the bottle of chloroform and rag he'd left on the table just inside and set to work.

The Broker was shaking his head, trying to clear his vision, when Alex tackled him and jammed the chloroformed rag over his face. Once he stopped struggling, Alex stood and dragged him into the vault where he had a pair of handcuffs ready. The Broker thus secured, Alex closed the vault and the door disappeared, leaving only the chalk outline on the wall.

He turned in time to see the flat-faced man pull a pistol from a holster inside his jacket. It was clear he still couldn't see, but that didn't seem to stop him. He fired three shots before Alex punched him in the face with the brass knuckles. Flat-face went down hard.

"That was close," he said, kicking the gun away from the unconscious man.

"Got you," a snarling voice said, and the bald man drove his fist into Alex's back.

Alex stumbled forward, losing the brass knuckles but catching himself on one of the couches. Turning just in time, he ducked an uppercut that would have laid him out and landed two hits to the bald man's solar plexus. Baldy grunted but didn't give ground, driving his fist into Alex's jaw so hard he knocked out a tooth.

Alex staggered back, but the bald man still couldn't see well and his next punch missed. He lunged forward, trying to tackle Alex to the ground where his lack of vision wouldn't be a hindrance. Bringing up his foot, Alex managed to kick the man away, but both of them went down. As the bald man groped for him, Alex rolled out of his grip, his hand landing on the brass knuckles. He slipped them on and scrambled to his feet, intending to put the big man down for good. When he turned, Alex found that baldy had found a weapon too, the flat-faced man's pistol.

The bald man brought the pistol up and fired. His vision must have gotten better because the bullet hit Alex in the side. Gasping in barely-controlled pain, Alex stepped forward before the other man could fire again and drove the brass knuckles into his jaw so hard he heard it crack.

Finally the bald man went down like a sack of flour. For his part, Alex just stood there gasping, as fire and pain spread through his torso. Grunting, he pressed his hand against his side and it came away soaked in blood.

"Good thing..." he gasped, "I live with a doctor."

17

THE CONNECTION

"Alex?" Iggy's voice came over the phone before Alex could speak.

"Yeah," he said, wheezing like a bellows. "It's me."

"Thank God. I've been worried." The relief in the old man's voice was palpable. Alex imagined he could hear Iggy's muscles relaxing through the phone. "Everything go as planned?"

Alex started to laugh but the wound in his side flared into agony and he groaned.

"Not exactly," he said, his voice a whisper. "One of the Broker's men shot me."

"Where?" Iggy said, a tone of the military doctor snapping instantly into his voice.

"Left side," Alex said. "It's painful to breathe."

"Are you coughing up blood?"

"Don't know; the guy knocked out one of my teeth too."

"Can you get home on your own?" Iggy asked. "I'll need to make sure my alchemical draughts are ready and prepare a restoration rune for your tooth."

"I'll manage," Alex said. "See you soon."

Iggy told him to be careful and hung up. Alex stumbled out of the phone booth, then straightened up and did his best to walk back out of the drug store without attracting attention. He hailed a cab, gave the driver the address of the brownstone, then fumbled with his wallet, pulling out one of the fake twenties.

"Fast as you can," he said, shoving the bill in the driver's hand.

He felt bad, giving the cabbie the funny money, but he didn't have enough real money to cover the fare. He noted the driver's name and promised himself he would make it up to him later. The rest of the cab ride was spent trying not to swear like a sailor every time the cab went over a bump.

"Thanks," he gasped when the cab finally pulled up in front of the brownstone. He got out and staggered up the stairs, hoping he hadn't left too much blood in the poor man's cab.

Iggy opened the door as Alex fumbled for his pocket watch to deactivate the rune barriers. The old man's face was the gray of old newspaper as he ushered Alex inside.

"Kitchen table," he said, lifting Alex under the arm on his good side. As Iggy lifted, Alex's vision seemed to dwindle down to a single point. "Stay with me," Iggy said. "I'm not decrepit yet, but I don't think I can carry you by myself."

In the kitchen, Iggy had pulled all the chairs from their massive table, stacking them against the wall and pulled the table to the middle of the floor. A heavy canvas tarp covered the top along with a stack of clean, white towels. A large pot of water boiled on the stove, its steam rising in a thick mist over the unpleasant-looking handles of metal implements. On the counter next to the stove, a dozen vials with rubber stoppers had been laid out in a neat row, each containing a brightly colored liquid. At the end of the line of vials were three rune papers and a box of wooden matches.

"Looks like you're all ready," Alex said as they crossed the floor.

"Shut up," Iggy said, helping him up onto the heavy wooden table. He carefully peeled Alex out of his ruined suit coat that still looked like a tux jacket. "Get out of your shirt, but don't lie down yet," Iggy said. "I've got to get that tooth growing back first. The rune's only effective if administered within half an hour after losing it."

Alex reached up to unbutton his shirt but stopped as a whole new world of pain washed over him. He could only move his right arm slowly and when he tried to move his left, he nearly blacked out. After a few deep breaths, he tried again, being more careful.

Iggy grabbed the rune paper on the end of the line and rolled it into a small tube. He pinched one end together and twisted it so the paper would not unroll. "Open up," he said as Alex struggled to unbutton his shirt.

"Here I thought the bullet in my side would be first priority," Alex said, grinning through the pain.

"If you were bleeding more, or weren't able to make inane remarks, it would be," Iggy said, retrieving a multi-lamp very similar to Alex's. He lit it, producing a glow of ruddy light, then closed the focusing lens and directed the beam into Alex's mouth. "That hooligan did quite a number on you," Iggy said. "Hold still."

Alex felt the paper jammed painfully into the empty socket where his tooth had been. A second later he heard Iggy strike a match and felt the instantaneous flash of heat given off by the rune paper as it burned. Normal people couldn't feel the magic of an expended rune, but Alex felt it, probing into his upper jaw, burning its way into the roots of the socket where his tooth had been. A moment later he cursed as best he could with his mouth open. A sharp, throbbing pain gripped his jaw like a pair of pliers and wouldn't let go.

"Don't be a child," Iggy said, shining the light into Alex's mouth. "Growing a tooth in a few days' time isn't pleasant, but it's vastly superior to the alternative. Now lie down and let's see to the rest of you."

Alex plucked ineffectually at his shirt, but Iggy produced an angled pair of scissors and simply cut it off him. "Now lie down," he said.

Iggy took half the pile of clean towels and tucked them under Alex's head, then he retrieved the first vial from the end of the line on the counter and pulled out the stopper, breaking the lead seal.

"Drink up," he said, passing it to Alex.

Alex painfully raised the vial to his lips. He had to turn a little on his side so as not to spill the mustard-colored liquid. It tasted vile, as all alchemical potions did, but he choked it down, then lay back down with a groan.

"Now," Iggy said, moving around the table to examine Alex's left side. "Let's have a look at your wound." He touched the jagged hole and Alex flinched. "Easy now," he said. He probed the wound with his fingers and Alex sucked air in a long hiss.

"I'll give you something for the pain," Iggy said.

"No," Alex gasped. "I've got an appointment with the Broker. I can't afford to sleep."

"And I know that," Iggy said, handing him a vial with a liquid somewhere between red and pink. "Bottoms up, lad."

Alex drank that one and immediately felt his hands go numb. The sensation seemed to crawl up his extremities, starting at his fingers and toes and moving inward. In a moment he couldn't feel or move. His brain seemed to go fuzzy as well. He knew that should bother him, that he needed to be alert, but he just didn't seem to care.

Iggy moved in and out of his vision, as he lay looking up at the light fixture on the ceiling. It was old and fancy, like most of the house, made of iron with a complex pattern of vines and ivy clinging to a lattice. The magelights inside were made of some kind of quartz with a yellow tint that always made the kitchen seem sunny, even in the middle of the night.

He saw a flash of light as Iggy used a rune, and then another flash sometime later. Then he felt nothing.

"Rink iss," a voice that sounded remarkably like Iggy's came from somewhere very far away. Suddenly his perspective changed as he was pulled up into a sitting position.

"Drink this," he heard more clearly as the end of a glass vial was shoved into his mouth. Reflexively, Alex gulped down the liquid and the world suddenly came crashing down on him. He doubled over, swearing, as the left side of his body felt like someone was twisting it in a vice.

"Getting shot hurt less than this," he croaked.

Iggy put his hand on Alex's right shoulder and helped to ease him back up.

"Just breathe," he said. "The reason it hurts so much is because the bullet bounced off a rib and hit another. You're very lucky."

"Funny," Alex said, his breathing so shallow that it sounded like a panting dog. "I don't feel lucky."

Iggy laughed. "Give it a few minutes," he said. "And you're lucky because that bullet nicked your spleen. Once I moved it, you started bleeding for real. It was touch and go there for a few minutes."

The pain started to dull and Alex found he could take regular breaths again.

"I guess I am lucky then," he said. "Lucky I know you. Thanks, old man."

Iggy chuckled. "You won't be good as new for a week or two," he said. "But as long as you weren't planning to beat the truth out of the Broker, you should be able to question him just fine." He pressed a rune paper into Alex's hands. "It's the last disguise rune I gave you," he said. "I modified it so you'll look like you did before. Should help with your interrogation. I assume you've got something interesting planned?"

Alex chuckled and instantly regretted it. "You know that pulp book of yours that's just a rip off of *The Pit and the Pendulum*?" he asked Iggy.

"I rather like that book," Iggy said with an indignant look.

"Well it gave me an idea for getting the truth out of the Broker without laying a finger on him."

Iggy's eyebrows rose. "I didn't know you read my books," he said with a thinly veiled look of amusement.

"You said I'd be good as new in a week or two?" Alex said, changing the subject. "Why can't American doctors heal people that fast?"

"Oh, they can," Iggy said with a smile. "If you have the money. I used two major restoration runes on you along with tincture of purity, oil of regrowth, and a tonic of binding. You'd pay two thousand dollars for a doctor to give you that kind of treatment in an American hospital."

"Two..." Alex couldn't even finish naming the amount. "How am I going to pay you back for that?"

"There's no need, lad," he said. Iggy patted him on his good shoulder. "I've had most of that stuff since my navy days. I'm just glad it was still good all these years later." Iggy walked away chuckling.

"You're kidding about that stuff being expired, right?" Alex called after him, but Iggy just kept on going, right up the stairs to his room. Alex thought about going after him and getting a better answer, but one look around the room stopped him. Bloody medical instruments littered the counter by the stove where the still-steaming pot of water sat, cooling. Equally bloody towels littered the tile floor and the canvas on the table was wet with alchemical serums and blood. It had been close to nine when he'd arrived at the brownstone and the clock on the wall now showed just before eleven.

Alex had been on the table for almost two hours. As bad as that was for him, Iggy was in his seventies. The physical and mental strain of saving Alex's life couldn't have been easy to bear.

He slid gingerly down from the table and straightened up. Already the pain in his side was dwindling to a persistent, throbbing ache. Limping to the little table Iggy used to write his correspondence, Alex pulled out a pad of paper and left a note promising to clean up the kitchen as soon as he was done with the Broker. He hoped Iggy wouldn't ignore it and do it himself. Alex owed him big.

With one last look at the kitchen-turned-operating-theater, Alex made his way slowly upstairs and stripped out of the rest of his ruined clothes. On top of everything, he would need a new suit. He only had two and this one was beyond saving.

Iggy had cut Alex's shirt away to work on his side, but his left arm was now bound in a sling. He tried moving his left arm but that caused so much pain he almost blacked out. Working carefully with his right hand, he finally got it off so he could shower, holding his left arm rigid against his chest. Alex knew that the hole where the bullet had entered would be closed by now, so he suspected that showering would be okay. The alchemical potions that closed wounds were relatively cheap.

After a frustrating shower where he had to learn to scrub himself in whole new ways, Alex dressed in his remaining suit and fished his vault key out of his ruined slacks.

"All right, Mr. Brewer," he said, putting on his hat. "It's time you and I had a chat."

Since it was after midnight, he had to walk the painful three blocks to Central Park to get a cab. The cabby wasn't surprised that someone was out at this time of night — it was New York after all — but he did pause for a moment when Alex told him their destination.

"The Brooklyn Bridge?" he said. "You ain't thinking about jumping or anything like that, are ya?"

Alex assured him that he had no such intentions, and then just sat back and enjoyed the ride. The driver let him off right as they reached the bridge and Alex waited for him to be on his way before pulling out his rune book. Alex had crossed the bridge many times and recently he'd seen work scaffolding on one of the pillars in the middle of the span. He walked out over the bridge, along the side of the road until he reached the area, then stepped past the construction barricade and onto the scaffolding.

His heart tried to crawl up into his throat when he looked down. The platform where he stood was only about two feet wide. The moon was up and Alex could see its light reflecting on the rolling water far below.

The scaffolding ran around the tower of brick, out over the water and around the back side. Wooden ladders connected each layer of scaffolding with one above as it went up to whatever the men were working on. Fortunately, Alex didn't care about any of those upper levels — which was good, since he could never have climbed the ladders with his left arm in a sling.

Moving slowly and deliberately, Alex made his way along the scaffold and turned the corner to the outside edge of the pylon, onto the part that faced the river. He inched his way to the center of the big tower of brick, then turned to face the wall. Pulling a piece of chalk from his pocket, Alex chalked the outline of his vault door on the weathered brick. He only drew the door down to a space about a foot up from the scaffolding, but he still had to kneel down to reach it. The shock of his knee hitting the scaffold platform shot up into his shoulder and he gasped in pain, dropping his chalk. It fell, a white streak reflecting the light of a nearly full moon, like a shooting star, before disappearing among the winking reflections of the moon on the water far below.

Saying a silent prayer just in case God did watch over idiots and children, Alex fished a second piece of chalk from his coat and finished the door. He had to hold the rune paper in place to keep the wind from blowing it away, but he got it lit. Finally, with a twist of his key, he swung his vault door open and stepped up and inside. He'd never been so glad to be indoors.

"Who's there?" the belligerent voice of Jeremy Brewer boomed out of the darkness. This far from the core, the magelights in Alex's vault barely glowed enough to be seen in the dark space, but Alex had prepared for that. After all, his vault could be opened anywhere there was a wall.

"Relax, Mr. Brewer," Alex said, affecting the British accent again. "I'll be with you in a trice."

Alex took out his matchbook and lit the oil lamps that hung from fixtures in the walls. As they began to throw their light into the space, they illuminated the Broker. Alex had left him handcuffed to a metal chair with a bag over his head and his legs tied to the legs of the chair.

Once the lamps were lit, Alex was almost ready. Trying not to grunt with the pain of physical exertion, he shoved Brewer's chair over to the door and faced it outward, while Brewer spewed a string of colorful profanities. The chair was attached to the back wall by a rope that ran through the two pulleys he'd installed earlier. Now he tied his second rope to the first, between the pulleys, and pulled it tight through the anchor he'd put in the wall by the door. This created about six inches of play in the rope holding Brewer and the chair. Below the anchor sat a small table with a candle on it and a box of matches.

The stage was set.

"I don't know who you are," the Broker said with a snarl, all pretense of his high society manners gone. "But you'll pay for this. I'll make sure you die spitting blood with my name on your lips."

Alex shoved the chair forward until the ropes stopped it. The front feet of the chair slipped off the edge where the vault door was, and it slammed down hard with the front legs resting on the brick wall outside the door.

"Jesus!" the Broker swore as the chair suddenly pitched forward, "what are you doing?"

Alex stuck the disguise rune to his forehead and lit it with his cigarette. Next, he pulled the bag off the head of Jeremy Brewer and the Broker got his first look at the empty nothing in front of him. He screamed. To his credit, however, he did not lose control of his bodily functions.

"What do you want, you crazy son-of-a-bitch?" he yelled.

"Now, that's what I like to hear," Alex said in his cultured British accent, loosely patterned on Iggy's, of course. He leaned against the wall by the door so that Brewer could see him. "You see, if you'd just taken that attitude back at the club, we could have avoided all this unpleasantness."

He looked up at Alex with a snarl.

"Who told you my name?" he demanded. Alex laughed.

"My employer, who, as I mentioned, wishes to remain anonymous. Privileged information, you understand."

"And what does your employer want?"

"A name."

"Whose?"

"Someone stole a shipment of uncut diamonds out of a customs warehouse at the New York Aerodrome," Alex said. "Now, they've not been offered to the local fences, even the high-class ones, so that means the theft was pre-arranged. By you."

"Well, maybe it was and maybe it wasn't." The Broker chuckled. Alex leaned down, close to Brewer's face.

"You'd better hope it was, for your sake." He nodded toward the open door. Brewer leaned out and looked down at the water far below.

"So if I don't give up a name, you send me to sleep with the fishes, is that it?"

"Exactly that, Mr. Brewer," Alex said.

"So what happens if I tell you?" he asked. "You just going to let me go?"

"You have my word."

"I hope you'll pardon me for being skeptical," Brewer said, his manners returning. "But I've seen your face. If I decided to look for you, there's nowhere in the city you could hide."

"As you may have surmised, I'm from out of town," Alex chuckled. "My employer brought me here to do a job and once it's done, I'll move on. I have no fear of your righteous vengeance, Mr. Brewer, because I will be far beyond your grasp." He paused to take a puff on his cigarette. "Now, the name. If you don't mind."

Naked calculation ran across Brewer's face like tape feeding out of a stock ticker. Alex knew he was weighing everything that was said, judging whether he thought Alex was bluffing. Ultimately, he decided that Alex was.

"Sorry, old man," he said, mimicking Alex's accent. "I'm afraid what you want is a trade secret. Privileged information, you understand."

Alex laughed at the sound of his own words being thrown back at him.

"Yes," he said, walking around behind Brewer, stepping over the ropes that held his chair in place. "I'm a very understanding person. Unfortunately," he added, taking out a match and lighting it, "the laws of thermodynamics are much less understanding. They're downright rigid." He lit the candle on the little table and pushed it under the taut rope, tied to the anchor bolt. Immediately, the rope began to smoke as its trailing fibers were incinerated. "I'm afraid you don't have very long to tell me what I want to know."

"You're bluffing," Brewer said, craning his neck in an effort to see where the rope went.

Alex just smiled and puffed his cigarette while the rope began to burn. Brewer stared at him hard, looking to see if Alex had the eyes of a killer. He didn't believe it.

His tune and his color changed, however, when the first large strand of the twisted rope snapped and he felt his chair tip forward a bit.

"All right," he yelled. "The guys who set up the job had German accents, real heavy."

"Who were they?" Alex pressed as the rope burned.

"I don't know," Brewer said. "They paid in cash, so I didn't ask questions. They didn't even tell me what was in the box they wanted."

Alex ground his teeth. He hadn't foreseen this problem. Still, whoever stole them would have had to deliver them, right?

"Who did the job?" he asked.

"A burglar I work with sometimes, a real pro."

"What's his name? Where can I find him?"

"I don't know his real name," Brewer said as a second strand snapped and the chair dipped some more. "I only know where he lives."

Alex pulled the candle away and blew out the fire on the remaining strand.

"Where?" he said.

"The corner of twenty-eighth and Mercer," Brewer said, his voice still trembling. "That's all I know, I swear."

"What name do you know him by?"

Brewer hesitated. Alex pushed the candle back under the rope and it caught fire instantly.

"What name does he go by?!" Alex yelled.

"Beaumont!" Brewer screamed. "Charles Beaumont!"

The rope snapped and the chair fell forward six inches until the slack was taken up, then it jerked to a stop. By that time, however, Jeremy Brewer had fainted.

18

THE APARTMENT

In the main foyer of Dr. Bell's brownstone stood a grandfather clock made of polished mahogany and burl wood. The face was over-large because it hid a mechanism that told the story of Dickens' *A Christmas Carol* every twelve hours. On the hour of three, a diorama opened showing an intricately painted scene of Scrooge' visit from Marley's ghost. As the quarter hour progressed, the diorama turned to show the ghost of Christmas past. Similar dioramas opened on the sixth, ninth, and twelfth hours with the final scene being Scrooge dining with his nephew's family. On each quarter hour, the clock played the first few bars of *Greensleeves*.

Alex always liked the clock. By the time he trudged wearily back up the steps to the brownstone, the diorama showing Marley's Ghost, with his chains and cash boxes hovering over a terrified Scrooge, had just opened. Alex wanted nothing more than to keep right on going, upstairs to his room where his warm, comfortable bed awaited him, but there was a light still burning in the kitchen. He must have forgotten to switch it off. Thinking of that reminded him of his promise to Iggy, to clean the wreck of their kitchen. He didn't have the strength, he knew he didn't, but maybe he could just tidy up a bit and leave the serious work for tomorrow. He'd need a cup of coffee anyway, several in fact, for his day was far from over. Coffee and tidying could be done while he waited for Danny.

Of course, first he had to call Danny.

The aroma of freshly-brewed coffee washed over him as he passed through the library. When he reached the kitchen, he found it cleaned and scoured, with Iggy sitting at the table. He had a mug of coffee in one hand and a book in the other and dark circles under his eyes.

"You didn't have to do this," Alex said, shuffling to the coffee pot and pouring himself the biggest cup he could find.

"I couldn't sleep with you out there, lad," Iggy said. "I just laid awake for an hour and then I had to get up and do something. At least this gave me something to keep my mind occupied for a time."

Alex downed as much of the hot liquid as he could take in one go, then refilled his cup.

"Well?" Iggy said, closing his book and setting it aside. "Are you going to tell me what happened?"

Alex drank, then poured one more time, before moving to the table next to Iggy and setting his cup down. "Give me a minute first," he said. "I have to make a call." He walked to where the telephone hung on the wall and gave the operator Danny Pak's number. Six rings later, Danny's groggy voice came at him down the wire.

"Yeah?" he said.

"Get your cop suit on," Alex said. "I've got a lead on who killed Jerry Pemberton."

"Alex?" Danny said. "You know I have a gun, right?"

"Wake up!" Alex shouted into the phone. "Get dressed and pick me up at the brownstone. We're going to check out the apartment of the man who stole the gems out of the customs warehouse."

Danny cursed at him. "Fine," he said at last. "I'll be there in half an hour."

"So you know who killed Pemberton?" Iggy said once Alex hung up.

"No," Alex said. "But I know who took the stones from the warehouse. Charles Beaumont."

Iggy cocked his head to the side.

"The man who infected the Brotherhood of Hope Mission?" he asked. Alex nodded.

"I know where he lives now."

"How did you find out?" Iggy asked.

Alex sat down, sipped his coffee, and told Iggy the whole story. The old man laughed when Alex told him about his trick with the ropes. Brewer had never been in any actual danger, of course. The rope Alex burned held about six inches of slack in the actual rope that held Brewer's chair. Once it burned through, the chair dropped the six inches, then stopped. Brewer had believed it though, which was all that mattered.

"I left him, handcuffed to the chair, in the alley behind *The Emerald Room*," Alex said.

The look of amusement on Iggy's face evaporated to be replaced by one of alarm. "But, what if someone finds him?" he said, his voice urgent. "He knows you're going to Beaumont's apartment."

"That's why I'm taking Danny," Alex said. "I'll have him put a squad car on the street while we search the apartment. Since he doesn't know my real face, he'll probably think that the man who handcuffed him to a chair killed Beaumont and now the police are investigating."

"Except you also have your arm in a sling," Iggy said. "A man smart enough to run a criminal matching service for rich bastards might make the connection."

Alex hadn't thought about that, and Iggy had a point. Brewer wasn't going to let this go, that much was for sure. Alex would have to be careful.

"I'll have Danny drop me off behind the building," he said. "I'll just meet him inside."

"Be careful," Iggy said.

"Don't worry," Alex said, standing. He drew a chalk door on the wall for his vault, then opened it. The magelights inside bloomed into intense brightness. He went inside and took down his kit bag. It had been a while since he resupplied it, so he took his time doing that. His 1911 hung in its holster on a peg inside the cabinet where he kept his spare bags. He wouldn't be able to put the holster on with his arm in the sling, so he pulled the pistol from its holster and slipped it inside a hidden pocket in his bag.

He had just finished when Danny rang the bell.

"I'll get it," Iggy said, while Alex closed his vault and scrubbed the chalk off the wall with a damp cloth.

"This had better be worth it," Danny said, once Iggy led him into the kitchen. The detective looked weary and his eyelids were heavy, but his clothes were neat and his hair had been slicked back.

"It will be," Alex said.

"What happened to you?" Danny asked, pointing at Alex's arm in the sling.

"Bad guys," Alex said. He and Danny had long ago established this explanation for things Alex shouldn't tell his police detective friend for fear of putting him in an untenable position.

"Gotcha," Danny said. "Now why did you drag me out of bed at this ungodly hour?"

"Remember the incident at the east side mission? Pemberton's partner was one of the victims."

"The first victim," Iggy added.

It took Danny a moment to connect all the dots, but in his defense, he was not fully awake yet.

"Does that mean that whatever killed all those people could be waiting for us at the thief's apartment?" Danny asked, availing himself of the coffee pot. "I'm not keen on catching whatever they had."

"Shouldn't be a problem," Iggy said. "The disease can't live more than a few minutes outside a sealed container. Or a host," he added.

Danny finished his coffee and Alex picked up his kit, then they both turned for the door.

"I think I can get some sleep now," Iggy said, showing them out. "Once you're done, you need the same. Those ribs won't heal if you keep pushing yourself."

"I promise," Alex said, then followed Danny down the steps to his car.

The apartment building of Charles Beaumont was a well-maintained structure of dull yellow brick right up against the outer border of the middle-ring. Its position ensured it had reliable power and cheap rent. Despite its being in a cheap neighborhood, the building showed no sign of neglect by its landlord. The windows were clean and the entryway swept; even the rear entrance, where the industrial garbage bins sat, was clear of trash.

All that being the case, however, it just didn't seem like the kind of place where a notorious cat burglar would live. Based on Iggy's pulp novels, Alex expected Beaumont to have a permanent room at the Ritz. He should have known better since Beaumont was a Sunday regular at Father Harry's Mass at the Mission. From this apartment, the Mission was only six blocks away. Not close by any means, but not an insurmountable distance either.

Danny called for a squad car to make sure they weren't disturbed inside and it was already out front. He dropped Alex off in back in case the Broker had a man watching the building. Alex hoped the back door wouldn't be locked, but it had one of the new mechanisms that engaged automatically when the door closed. He didn't want to use another expensive unlocking rune, so he waited for Danny to go around to the front, park, and then let him in.

"I'll use a rune to get us into Beaumont's place," Alex said, once they were both inside. Danny snorted and rolled his eyes.

"You're forgetting I'm a police detective. We'll use my key."

Alex followed Danny down to the basement where he pounded on the building superintendent's door until it was opened by a severe-looking woman in a fuzzy pink bathrobe. Her brown hair was done up under a hair net and she wore thick, wire-rimmed glasses. Alex imagined that if she didn't run this building, she would have made an excellent librarian.

"What's the meaning of this?" she demanded in a tone that suggested she was used to being obeyed.

Danny flashed his badge and cited police business, and before Alex could say Jack Robinson, they were up on the fifth floor in front of apartment 57.

"Are you going to arrest Mr. Beaumont?" the woman asked with genuine concern in her voice.

"I'm sorry to tell you this, ma'am," Danny said. "But Mr. Beaumont is dead. His apartment may very well be a crime scene."

"Nonsense," the woman scoffed. "Why I saw Mr. Beaumont a few days ago and he..."

Her voice trailed off as she tried to insert her key in the lock of Beaumont's door. It wouldn't fit and Alex could clearly see why. Someone had forced the lock with what looked like a heavy duty screwdriver.

"Step back," Danny said to the superintendent, pulling his .38 police special from his shoulder holster. He eased the door open, then stepped quickly inside, sweeping the interior of the room with his weapon. The lights were on in the apartment, but only the papers strewn around the floor by the writing desk showed anything amiss. A meal of steak and broccoli with a few potatoes sat, uneaten, on a small, round table in the center of the room. Next to the meal, lay an overturned cup. The chair behind the table lay flat on its back as if whoever occupied it had stood up in a hurry. There were some dirty dishes in the sink and a pot on the stove, but everything else appeared orderly and immaculate. The smell of rancid food permeated the air, a mixture of rotten meat and sour milk.

"Stay here," Danny said to Alex, as he moved toward the bedroom and bathroom beyond it. "No one's here," he announced a moment later when he returned.

Alex set his kit down on the counter next to the stove while Danny thanked the superintendent and shut the door.

"Now what?" he asked when he was sure the woman was gone.

Alex strapped on his oculus and took out his siverlight burner. "Now, you stand there until I can clear you a place to sit." he said. "Before we invite the Captain and Lieutenant Callahan here, we have to be sure we know what happened, so let me work."

Alex went over the tiny living room space at the front of the apartment. Once he'd inspected the couch and the coffee table, he invited Danny to sit.

"I feel pretty useless," Danny said. "Isn't there some way I can help?"

"You are helping," Alex said, examining the table and the uneaten meal. "You're watching my back while I search this place."

Alex examined the residue left behind by whatever liquid had been in the overturned cup. Milk by the smell of it.

"Something's been taken away from here," Alex said, pointing to the table. He took off his oculus and passed it to Danny so he could look. On top of the table, the residue of the milk fluoresced brightly in the silverlight. In the middle of the splash mark, there were three round voids, as if three large glasses had stood there, side by side.

"Did Beaumont move them when he spilled his milk?" Danny asked.

"Too soon to guess," Alex admitted. He took the oculus back and continued searching. He cleared the bedroom and the bathroom next. He found a loose floorboard under which Beaumont had stashed some very fence-able odds and ends, a few jeweled brooches, seven gold pocket watches, five strings of pearls, and a bag full of loose gemstones of all descriptions. The room showed no sign that anyone but Beaumont lived there.

"Okay," he told Danny, coming back into the front room. "I can't see anything suspicious back there. Why don't you search it the old fashioned way while I go over the kitchen?" Danny smiled and moved past him. As Alex turned his attention to the stove, he heard Danny begin going through the drawers and the closet.

After checking every inch of the kitchen, Alex had to admit defeat. Nothing seemed out of place. He moved to the writing desk. It looked like it had been searched, but if so, it was the only thing. Maybe whoever searched it found what they were looking for.

None of the papers seemed important. A few letters, a job offer from someone writing in the kind of code you find in pulp mystery novels. Alex picked up the papers and stacked them on the writing desk. There wasn't anything useful in them, but he couldn't just throw them in the trash.

He paused. In his examination of the kitchen, he hadn't looked at the contents of Charles Beaumont's wastebasket. When he shone the silverlight into the little basket, hundreds of gleaming crystal shards glowed back at him. Someone had thrown away a broken jar, and not just thrown it away, but swept up the pieces too. Alex picked through the can carefully with a pencil, moving the glass shards around until he found what he sought. Reaching in gently, he pulled the round bottom of a glass jar from the wastebasket.

Most glass containers had thick, heavy bottoms, much thicker than the sides, which kept the center of gravity low and helped prevent tipping. When dropped, many would shatter but leave the bottom intact. Alex carried the broken base of the jar over to the table and placed it on one of the voids left in the milk splash. It fit perfectly.

He pulled out his rune book and tore a page containing an expensive restoration rune out of the back. Moving carefully, he placed the broken base of the jar on the counter and positioned the wastebasket on the floor below it. Sticking the rune paper to the base, he lit it and then stood back. The rune pulsed with power, not vanishing like most did. It hovered above the base, trembling and glowing with a violent burgundy light. A rustling sound emerged from the wastebasket and a tiny shard of broken glass leapt up and affixed itself to the broken base. The rustling continued and more and more of the glittering glass shards were pulled up, out of the can and onto the rapidly growing jar. In the burgundy light, it looked like blood dripping in reverse.

After a minute, the rune vanished, and the jar was more or less whole. There were dozens of tiny voids, places where the fragments were too far away from the rune to be drawn back to their original place. Thousands of cracks ran through the jar, making it look like crackle glass, but despite that, the jar was solid.

"Danny," he called, picking up the jar with his handkerchief and placing it on the table. "I think I found one of the missing jars from the table."

"Does it look like it will fit in here?" Danny asked, emerging from the bedroom. He carried a black shipping case a little larger than a standard briefcase. He held it open so Alex could see the padded inside. There were four divots, each big enough for a jar about six inches high and three around. Just like the one Alex had repaired.

"Where did you find that?" Alex asked.

"At the bottom of Beaumont's laundry basket," Danny said. "Though I'm more interested in where it came from." He closed the case and Alex could see several official-looking labels covering its outside.

"That's a standard small shipping case," Alex said, the truth finally dawning on him.

"What does that mean?" Danny asked. Alex grinned at him.

"It means you get to keep your job," he said. "It means we know who murdered Jerry Pemberton, and why."

19

THE MEETING

Alex waited an hour before making the phone calls. Danny called Lieutenant Callahan and Captain Rooney. Based on Danny's reaction, the Captain wasn't happy, but eventually Danny convinced him to come to Beaumont's apartment. Once the police were on their way, Alex called Iggy. He hated waking the old man, but if he was going to save his skin, and Danny's, he might need Iggy's medical knowledge.

"That's wonderful, lad," Iggy said once Alex had told him what they found.

"I know you're tired, but I might need you over here."

"Say nothing of it," he said, yawning. "I'll throw on my clothes and be over as soon as I can."

Alex thanked him and hung up. He wanted to stay on the line. Not because there was more he wanted to say to Iggy, but rather to avoid making the next call on his list. He took out his rune book and opened it to the back cover. Inside the cover was a pocket, sewn into the fabric. Alex kept loose papers there, notes and cards. He pulled out a simple white business card with a name and telephone number printed on it in blue ink. After a long moment, he sighed and dialed the phone.

"Hello?" a weary woman's voice said. "Who is this?"

"Good morning, Sorceress," he said in his most chipper voice.

"Mr. Lockerby," Sorsha said, her voice dropping several degrees. "I trust you have a good reason for disturbing me at this hour."

"You mean other than hearing your sparkling voice?"

There was a long pause and Alex could have sworn he felt the phone's receiver getting cold. He really shouldn't antagonize Sorsha, but she just made it so easy.

"Are you still interested in the disease that killed everyone at the Brotherhood of Hope?" he asked.

"Of course," she said, her voice perking up.

"I can tell you who brought it there, and where it came from."

'Well?" she said after a long moment.

"Not now," Alex said. "Put on your work clothes, grab your FBI lackeys, and meet me."

"If you're wasting my time, scribbler, I'll..."

"No joke, Sorceress," Alex said. "Got a pencil?" He gave her Beaumont's address and hung up.

The first to arrive was Callahan; he came in with two of his detectives and two uniforms whom he left outside the door.

"What's this about, Danny?" he asked, after having a quick look around.

"Give us a few minutes," Danny said. "There's a few more people coming."

Callahan pressed his hand to his forehead. "Please tell me you didn't call the Captain."

"He didn't," Alex lied. "I did."

"Jesus, Lockerby," Callahan swore. "Why don't you just get us all fired?"

"Don't worry, Lieutenant," Alex said. "He'll be smiling from ear to ear when he hears what we have to say."

"You should worry more about whether I'll be smiling," Sorsha said, pushing the door open. Agents Davis and Warner followed in her wake, each looking like they weren't used to being rousted in the early hours of the morning. If getting up early or being rushed out of her boudoir affected Sorsha, it didn't show. Her face was perfect, alabaster skin without a single flaw, as if she'd been carved of marble. The only appearance of makeup were a few precise strokes of eyeliner and bright red lipstick. Alex had heard that the subtler the makeup, the longer it took to apply; if this was what Sorsha could do with just a few minutes, he really wanted to see what she looked like on her way to a party.

Alex introduced Sorsha and the FBI men to Callahan, then directed the Sorceress to the couch to await the rest.

"You do like living dangerously," Callahan said under his breath, once Sorsha had taken a seat.

The next to arrive was Iggy. Sorsha was delighted to see the doctor again and invited him to sit with her on the couch. Last of all was Captain Rooney. He arrived in a rumpled suit with his vest mis-buttoned and his tie showing from under the back of his collar. Callahan and his detectives looked tired, but their clothes were neat and professional, a sign that they were used to going to work whenever the job required it. Rooney, on the other hand, kept banker's hours, and it showed.

He started to shout at Alex, Danny, and Callahan, but stopped when he saw Sorsha.

"I assume," he said in a calmer voice, "that you dragged everyone out of bed for a good reason."

"I did, Captain," Alex said, taking the lead. "You challenged me to find out who killed Jerry Pemberton, and with Detective Pak's help, I have."

"If that's all this is about," Rooney said, his voice dropping low, "I'll have your license pulled so quick."

Alex put his hand on his heart and feigned a wounded expression. "Patience, Captain." He took a step back and addressed the whole room. "I'd like to welcome everyone to the home of Charles Beaumont," he said.

A murmur of recognition flared up briefly, but there were many bewildered looks.

"Before Detective Pak and I get to the reason we called this little clam bake, I need to bring everyone up to speed," Alex added.

Of the people in the room, only he, Danny, Iggy, and Callahan were familiar with both the case of Jerry Pemberton and the incident at the

Brotherhood of Hope Mission. Alex briefly related the facts of each case, then asked for questions.

"How does Charles Beaumont connect to Jerry Pemberton?" Callahan asked.

"Beaumont was Pemberton's partner," Danny said. "The people who killed Pemberton were looking for Beaumont."

"Why?" Rooney growled.

"Because of this," Alex said, holding up the glass container he'd reconstructed. "There were four of these, each full of an alchemical solution that causes the disease that killed Father Harrison Clementine and everyone at the Mission."

"And how do you know this?" Sorsha said.

Alex took out his multi-lamp and snapped the silverlight burner in it. "You'll need to wear this," he said, holding out his oculus to the Sorceress.

She hesitated for a minute, then slipped the strap over her head. Alex lit the lamp and then pointed to the table.

"See here, how three round objects stood here." He put the reconstructed jar on the table.

Sorsha closed her uncovered eye and looked. After a moment, she moved the jar slightly to the left, covering one of the voids.

"What made the circles?" she asked.

"Milk," Danny said, pointing to the empty drinking glass still lying on its side by the plate. "The jars were there when the milk spilled and until after it dried, then someone removed them."

"Who?" Rooney asked. Alex grinned.

"In a moment, Captain."

"I only see three circles," Sorsha said. "You said there were four jars of this plague."

"And I will explain where the fourth one went in just a minute," Alex said, "but first I want Lieutenant Callahan and the Captain to have a look."

Sorsha removed the oculus and handed it to Callahan, who then inspected the table.

"Was there food on the plate when you got here?" he asked.

"Yes," Danny said. "It was pretty rank after five days so we threw it out, but the plate is right where we found it."

Alex was impressed. Not much got by Callahan. From the look the Lieutenant gave him as he passed the oculus to Rooney, he was already thinking along the same lines Alex and Danny had.

"Okay, so what does this tell us?" Rooney asked.

Alex switched out his silverlight burner for a ghostlight one, then adjusted a few of the lenses on the oculus.

"Now take a look at the floor," he said.

Rooney knelt down and scanned the floor on the right side of the table, the same side as the spilled glass of milk.

"Something spilled here too," he said. "It's all over the place, and there's a footprint here," he indicated a spot between the table and the door.

Alex waited for Callahan and Sorsha to take their turn with the oculus.

"Why is this light different?" Sorsha wondered, looking at the table top. "I can't see the milk circles anymore."

"I call it ghostlight," Alex said. "It reveals magical residue."

Sorsha nodded, taking the oculus off and handing it back to Alex.

"So Mr. Beaumont sat here," she indicated the overturned chair. "He put the jars of plague on the table and proceeded to eat dinner. At some point, he knocks one of the jars off the table." She picked up the broken one. "This one. He has quick hands but when he tries to grab it, he knocks over the milk. The jar breaks and Beaumont runs out, trying to escape being infected."

Alex smiled and Danny whistled.

"That's about the way we figure it," Danny said.

"Why would this idiot put jars of plague on his dinner table?" Rooney asked.

"They would have been completely harmless while sealed," Iggy said. "He might have simply wanted to look at them. Many alchemical solutions have interesting color patters and some even glow."

"So why and how did he end up at the Mission?" Callahan asked.

"I can answer that as well," Iggy said. "Sister Jefferson told us that he was always asking Father Clementine for blessings and drinking water from their old well. He thought it had healing properties, or at least he hoped it did."

"It still doesn't explain what any of this has to do with Jerry Pemberton," Callahan said.

"Or where Beaumont got the jars," Sorsha said, setting the restored jar down on the table again.

Alex snapped his fingers, pretending he'd just remembered something.

"That's right," he said. "We forgot to tell them about the shipping case."

Sorsha fixed him with a level gaze and Rooney looked like he might just spontaneously combust. Alex continued as if he hadn't seen either.

"My associate, Detective Pak, during an exhaustive search of this apartment, found this."

Danny held up the shipping case. "It has a receiving stamp on it from the New York Aerodrome."

"Are you saying that Beaumont stole this from the customs warehouse?" Callahan asked. "Then who stole Van der Waller's jewelry?"

"Beaumont," Alex said. "My best guess is that he wanted to keep the theft of the plague a secret for as long as possible, so he grabbed a case with a similar shape and size and substituted it for the one he stole."

"So whoever was supposed to get the plague jars got the diamonds instead? Rooney asked. "Why didn't he report the theft?"

Sorsha smiled and raised an eyebrow.

"Would you report that your jars full of an alchemical plague had been stolen?" she asked.

"Wait," Callahan said. "Aren't things in the customs warehouse supposed to be inspected before they're released? How would they explain these jars? They couldn't let the inspector open one, after all."

"A good question," Sorsha added. "They would have given off a strong magical aura and customs inspectors have detectors for that."

"There's only one way this could have made it into the country," Alex said. "It was part of a diplomatic pouch."

"Anything a foreign government ships to one of their embassies in the U.S. isn't subject to search," Danny said.

"The question remains," Callahan pointed out, "Whose pouch was it?"

"It arrived by airship," Danny said. "I checked the passenger manifest and there were three German citizens on board. No other country with goods in the warehouse had citizens on the airship." He consulted his notepad. "The passengers listed their names as Helge Rothenbaur, Greta Albrecht, and Dietrich Strand."

"Not surprising," Iggy said. "German alchemists are the best in the world. They could have created a disease like the one we saw."

"So," Alex said, "when the Germans discover they have a case full of uncut diamonds instead of their plague, they go looking for it. They beat Beaumont's name out of Pemberton, then come here, breaking the lock on the door to get in."

"But Beaumont isn't here," Sorsha said. "So they take the three unbroken jars and leave."

"Almost," Alex said. "They did stop long enough to pick up the broken glass pieces from this jar," he held up the restored one. "They threw them in the wastebasket." Alex tipped the jar up, revealing fingerprint dust stuck to a large, clear thumbprint on the bottom of the jar. "And one of them was kind enough to leave us his print."

"That could be anyone's," the young Agent Warner piped up.

Alex shrugged.

"Possible," he said. "But the angle is strange unless you're picking up a broken piece. It's likely this is the fingerprint of whoever murdered Mr. Pemberton." Alex handed the jar to Lieutenant Callahan with an exaggerated gesture. "I'll leave the rest to you, Lieutenant," he said.

"That's it?" Rooney asked, shaking his head. "I nearly got my head chewed off getting permission for us to stake out the customs warehouse and now you want me to tell the Chief and the Mayor some cockamamie story about Nazis trying to poison New York?"

"Don't worry, Captain Rooney," Sorsha said, standing. "I shall take care of that. This is a federal matter now. You and your men and your... consultant have done excellent work. I'll make sure the Governor hears about it."

Rooney smiled, ingratiating, but his face had the sickly look of someone who had lost a favorite plaything. “Thank you, Miss Kincaid,” he said, then he turned to Callahan. “Make sure the FBI has everything they need, then wrap it up here.”

Callahan said that he would, and Rooney left without another word.

“Pak,” Callahan said in a loud voice. “This is your crime scene. Make sure everything’s logged and turned over to Miss Kincaid.” He put on his hat and then turned to leave as well. “I’ll make sure your bill gets paid, Lockerby,” he said on the way out.

Danny began giving instructions to the two other detectives while Alex packed up his kit.

“That was a real cute performance,” Agent Warner said, coming up behind him. Alex looked up into his young face. His lip was drawn up in a sneer and his blue eyes were hard. “Thought you’d make the rest of us look like chumps while you suck up to our boss?”

Alex just shrugged.

“I guess I thought that a bunch of Germans running around the city with a plague was something everyone needed to know,” he said. “This was just the easiest way to do it.”

“And to blow your own horn,” Warner said, anger in his voice. “I saw guys like you when I was on the force in Chicago. FBI has a few of them too. It’s never about the job for them, they’ve always got to make a big show. Problem is, while they’re doing their song and dance for the cameras and the brass, the bad guys get away. Sometimes people die.”

Alex straightened up and faced Warner. He was over an inch taller than the young Agent and he stretched himself up to his full height. Something about this was personal for Warner, but Alex had no idea what.

“Don’t worry, Agent Warner,” he said. “I’m not doing this for fame. I’m a P.I. I’m in it for the money.”

For a brief second Warner looked like he might punch him, but he mastered himself and stormed away.

“You look dead on your feet,” Iggy said, stepping up next to him.

Alex nodded. He couldn’t remember the last time he’d slept.

“The Sorceress will take it from here,” Iggy continued. “Let’s go home.”

Alex rubbed his eyes. Now that he'd sounded the alarm bell to the people who needed most to hear it, and saved his and Danny's skins in the process, his job was done.

Wasn't it?

"There's still three Germans running around New York with jars full of death," he said. He indicated the detectives and the FBI with a sweep of his arm. "They needed my help to get this far."

"Do you know anything you haven't told them?" Iggy asked. Alex wearily shook his head.

"No," he confessed.

"Then your part in this little play is done," Iggy said forcefully. "It's time you slept anyway; you're no good to anyone in this condition."

Alex picked up his kit and followed Iggy toward the door, but stopped when Sorsha stepped into his path. She looked at him with her intense eyes, one eyebrow raised.

"That was very good work, Mr. Lockerby," she said.

Alex wasn't sure he'd heard her right, but he smiled and said, "Thanks," all the same.

"I don't give compliments lightly," she said. "Or idly. You should come work for me."

Alex smiled at the thought of being an FBI agent. It would never work out, of course. He cut too many corners and broke too many rules to be a legitimate law officer of any kind.

"If I decide to pack it in, you'll be my first call," he said. "For right now, just find those Germans."

She seemed to have been waiting for a sarcastic answer, and his frankness surprised her. Before she could pursue any more discussion, however, Danny called her away.

Alex didn't remember much about the cab ride home. Outside, the sun was beginning to paint the sky shades of pink and yellow, and the buildings went by in a smoky, gray blur. At some point he collapsed onto his bed, still in his clothes, and fell instantly asleep.

20

THE CONSPIRATOR

Alex's bedroom had a window that faced the street. The brownstone sat on a pleasant lane, lined with birch trees on either side and cobbled with bricks. It ran east and west with Alex's window facing south. When he'd collapsed into bed in the wee hours of the morning, the sun had been rising behind the house. The curtains over the large windows were open and Alex had been in no condition to close them.

Over the course of the day the sun marched its path across the sky and, just after noon, a bright ray crept in through the open curtains and shone on the floor. As the afternoon progressed, the shaft of sun and the bright pool of light crawled slowly, silently across the hardwood floor, then up the side of the bed, and then across the bedspread until it shone on Alex's face.

He grunted, not wanting to return to wakefulness, and rolled over. An hour later, the light shone on his neck and he became too hot for sleep. When he finally sat up and swung his legs down to the floor, the alarm clock on his nightstand read eight forty-five. He picked it up and pressed it to his ear...only to hear silence. He hadn't slept in his bed for over a day before arriving home, and he hadn't thought to wind the clock that morning. It had stopped.

He stood and fished his pocket watch from his pants, then wound and set the alarm clock to four forty-five. Moving slowly, his muscles stiff and his arm still sore, he carefully undressed and hung his only suit on a hanger that then went behind the bathroom door. He took a long shower, letting the hot water steam the kinks out of his body and the wrinkles out of his suit. Danny was safe, and the Sorceress was hot on the trail of the Germans and their plague. He'd handled all that extremely well, he thought, but he didn't feel the satisfaction of a job well done.

Because there was still one thing left to do.

He didn't want to do it, not the way he would have to. But it had to be done, so he dried himself, dressed in his still-damp suit, and went downstairs. A note from Iggy hung on a cork board in the kitchen, saying he'd been called out to consult with Doctor Halverson at the university and didn't know when he'd return. Not trusting his ability to cook anything one-handed, Alex left and walked to *The Lunch Box*.

"Hiya, handsome," Mary said when she saw him come in. It was too early for the dinner rush and only a few customers occupied the booths. Alex sat at the counter. "What happened to you?" she asked, pointing at his arm in the sling.

"I had a disagreement with a taxi," he lied. "Don't worry, though. It's not serious."

He asked Mary how she liked being a full-fledged cook and her face lit up as she told him about her first week at *The Lunch Box*. Alex knew he should hurry, but he just didn't want to. His heart wasn't in it, but he had to know the truth. It was his one great flaw, an inexorable, rigid need to know the truth, and to see justice done.

Mary made him a pastrami sandwich and chattered away while he ate it. As he finished, patrons began to come in, just off work and seeking dinner, sending Mary back to the kitchen. With her gone and his plate clean, Alex had no excuses left.

Despite that, he went to the phone booth outside the diner and called his office.

"Finally," Leslie barked when she heard his voice. "I didn't know if you and Danny were okay, or if I should start scraping up bail money. Why didn't you call me?"

"Sorry, doll," Alex said with a pang of guilt. He didn't like upsetting her. "I hadn't slept in over a day, so once I was done, I went home."

"Did the Captain go for it?" she asked, urgency in her voice. "Are you and Danny safe?"

"Better than that," Alex said. "The feds took over the case and said they'd put in a good word to the Governor about how essential Rooney's help was."

"Thank God," she whispered. "I was worried. So, are we going to get paid now?"

Alex laughed, which made his ribs hurt. "Don't make me laugh," he grunted. "And don't worry. Lieutenant Callahan said he'd get us a check, so we're good."

"I've got some more work lined up," she said. "I can go over it with you tonight if you're coming in."

"No," Alex said. "I've got one more thing to do to wrap up the Thomas Rockwell case."

"You going to give that girl her money back?" Leslie asked, a touch of sadness in her voice. "Or, have you figured out what happened to Thomas?"

"I don't know," Alex said. "I'm going to try something tonight to figure it out. Either way, I'll be done by morning."

"Sounds dangerous." Concern filled her tone again. Alex shrugged, then realized she couldn't see him.

"Could be," he said. "I'll talk to you about it in the morning."

"Be careful," she said.

Alex promised that he would and hung up.

He caught the crawler across town to the five and dime that stood on the opposite side of the street from Thomas Rockwell's apartment. Climbing the stairs to the industrial building, he let himself into the dead man's workshop and marveled again how neat and orderly it was. His eyes did try to avoid the table in the back with the hotplate, where Thomas' shadow lay, permanent yet unseen.

Setting to work, Alex went around the room assembling a long line of jars, pens, and inks onto the center workbench. When all was in readiness, he tore a blank sheet from the large pad in the desk drawer and fitted it into the brass holders. It took him almost an hour to draw the finding rune. He checked and rechecked his notes, forming every line and curve precisely, making sure each one contained the proper inks and additives.

When he had about twenty minutes of work left, he stopped. He'd taken off his jacket, and his shirt was heavy with sweat from the exertion of channeling the power of the universe down into the rune. Patting himself dry with a towel, he went downstairs to the five-and-dime next door. He bought a cheap, brass ring from a case on the counter, then moved to the phone booth in the rear of the store.

"Evelyn," he said once she picked up. "I'm over at Thomas' workshop and I think I've figured out what Thomas was doing. Where he went wrong, I mean." He paused as her breathless voice filled his ear. "No," he said. "I don't mind. Come on over."

She made him promise to wait for her, then hung up.

Alex returned to the workshop and set the brass ring he'd purchased down on the left-hand workbench. He took out his rune book and tore out two pages he'd prepared especially for this evening. Folding the papers into quarters, lengthwise, he wrapped each one around the simple brass band, then lit them. The two runes had been written to join together when cast together and Alex could see their intricate forms wrapping around the band in colorful spirals. After a few seconds, they vanished, leaving the shiny band unadorned.

Satisfied that everything was ready, he slipped the ring on his finger and put away his rune book.

It took Evelyn fifteen minutes to arrive, and when she did, the gray walls of the workshop seemed to brighten with her smile. She wore a simple shirt of deep burgundy that reminded Alex of the glittering shards of the plague jar as they reassembled themselves in the ruddy light of his restoration rune. Her skirt was beige and of the close-fitting pencil style that seemed to flow down from her trim waist, over the swell of her hips and then pull in to a tight circle at her knees. She wore white pumps with a matching cloche hat that let her black hair spill out the back in curls. Her face was tanned and smooth with bluish eye shadow and a dark red lipstick that matched her blouse.

"Alex," she said, breathlessly, hurrying up to him. She threw her arms around him and planted a kiss on his lips. The kiss was hot and fiery, full of passion, and it brought back sweet memories of the night they'd spent in this very room. Alex wanted to dwell on those thoughts, but he pushed them away. There would be time for that later — unless there wasn't.

"I'm sorry to get you out here," he said when they broke apart.

"It's all right," she said, her smile turning sad. "I want to know what Thomas gave his life for. I want to know what he thought was worth that risk. Was it just some old book, or more than that?"

Alex sighed and led her to the workbench where he'd spent the last hour carefully laying out the finding rune.

"I thought this was right," he said, showing it to her. He held up another paper for her inspection. "This is the one Thomas cast," he said, indicating places where it differed from the rune he'd inscribed on the workbench. "He figured out that the original rune was drawn backwards, but he didn't realize that the outer ring of runes isn't aligned properly. See here." He pointed to the inferior runes that ran around the central geometry, a complex dodecahedron.

"So, you figured it out?" Evelyn said, her brows drawn together in concentration.

"I thought so when I called you," Alex said. "But now, I'm not sure. It just feels off to me."

She looked over the two sets of drawings, then looked up with a helpless look on her face.

"What can I do?" she asked. Alex shook his head.

"I'm not sure. I'm going to have to go over this from start to finish. It's going to take hours." He looked at the papers, then back to her. "I'm sorry I brought you out here. You might as well go home. If I figure anything out, I'll call you." She looked disappointed, but then smiled.

"How about I go get us some dinner?"

"No thanks," Alex said. "I actually just ate, and I need to work. I know I can get this if I just spend some more time. The only question is, how much?"

She put her hand on his cheek and he felt the warmth of her fingers.

"You look tired," she said. "Maybe you should give it up...for the night." She didn't look at the neat little bed they had shared together but it was there in the tone of her voice. Alex chuckled.

"Then I definitely wouldn't get anything done," he said. "Go ahead," he said, nodding toward the door. "All you're going to do is distract me."

"All right," she said, taking a step away. "I see you can't be dissuaded." There was a strange note in her voice, but Alex felt a great swell of relief as she started toward the door. He'd pushed her pretty hard but she hadn't done anything...

Evelyn turned after her third step. That particular step had taken her just outside the range of Alex's reach. When she turned, there was a pistol in her hand.

"I'm sorry, Alex," she said, leveling the gun at his chest. "I'm afraid I'm not to be dissuaded either."

Alex put his free hand in the air. "What's this?" he asked even though he already knew.

"You're very eager to get me to leave," she said. "There's nothing wrong with your rune. I think you just decided to cut me out." She waved her gun, motioning Alex to step back, and he did. Once he was away from the table, she looked at his drawings again. "You don't have any doubts," she said. "This rune is perfect."

"So, you're a runewright," Alex said. He'd guessed as much, but it was nice to have his suspicions confirmed.

"Yes," Evelyn said. "I am. I may not have your skill, but I can understand what you've done here. You've finished deciphering it," she indicated his notes. "You just haven't finished writing it." She looked up at him and smiled. "Fortunately, I can."

"So," Alex said. "What now?"

She motioned him over toward the metal bed, though he was sure she didn't have anything so pleasant involved this time.

"Sit," she said, then handed him a pair of handcuffs from her purse.

Alex took the cuffs and looped them around the metal bar that formed the bed's footboard, locking the cuff first onto his bound-up left hand, then carefully onto his right. Once he was secured, Evelyn put the gun against his chest and tugged at the cuffs with her free hand.

"So," Alex said, trying to remain calm. "You must be the person who enticed that government researcher...what was his name?"

"You mean dear Quinton Sanderson?" Evelyn said, slipping her gun back into her purse. "Yes. I got him to steal the original drawings of the Monograph runes. He was very eager to help me once I explained what they were."

"Did you kill him?"

"Of course not," she said, her voice indignant. "He disappeared, just like Thomas."

"So, you're not Thomas' sister either." He thought back to the bed in Thomas' apartment and how obvious it was that he had a lover. Clearly Evelyn had seduced him to get his help. The thought made Alex uncomfortable, especially sitting on the bed where Evelyn had done the same to him.

"No," she said, drawing the stool up to the workbench and leaning over Alex's drawings. "I found Thomas and convinced him to help me find the Monograph after poor Quinton disappeared."

"He didn't disappear," Alex corrected her. "Neither did Thomas. They died trying to find that book."

"And now you have succeeded where they failed," Evelyn said, selecting a pen and an ink pot.

"No," Alex said. "I haven't. If you finish that rune and cast it, you and I will be just as dead as Thomas and Quinton."

She turned and smiled at him.

"Never try to con a con artist," she said. "Even I can see that your construct is finished. It's balanced and elegant, nothing like that convoluted mess it started out as."

She began to draw, filling in the missing parts of the construct, line by line from Alex's notes.

"How is it you even knew about the Archimedean Monograph?" Alex asked after a few minutes passed in silence. "I mean, I can see Quinton stumbling across it in his work, but you didn't work there. If you had, you wouldn't have needed him."

"My mother was one of the original researchers the government had working on the Monograph runes. She used to tell me stories about it as she trained me in her craft. Then, one day, she didn't come home for dinner. My father waited up all night, and in the morning, there were men in suits at our home."

"She'd disappeared," Alex guessed.

"After that, I studied everything she left behind, her notes, her Lore, everything. Of course the government men took most of it, but I saved some. Hid it under the floorboards in my room."

"It wasn't enough, though," Alex observed. 'Was it?"

She stopped her work for a moment and hung her head, the strands of her dark hair obscuring her face. "No," she said. "I tried to get a job at the archives where my mother worked but..."

"But you didn't have your mother's talent," Alex said. "If you did, you would never have needed Thomas to figure out the rune, you could have done it."

"That's why I need the Monograph," she said, her voice full of passion. "Whoever reads it will be the greatest runewright in the world. Can you imagine what secrets it holds, Alex?"

"Maybe it doesn't really exist," Alex said. "Have you thought of that? Maybe that rune is just a trap. A way for some powerful, ancient runewright to kill off his competition."

Evelyn laid aside the pen and stood up; she had finished writing the unscrambled finding rune.

"No," she said. "I haven't considered it. You saw those other runes, how complex they are, so much so that there are still two that the government hasn't been able to identify. Those runes came from somewhere, Alex. The Archimedean Monograph is real and it's time to find it."

She began to clear away the inks and jars from the workbench, leaving only the paper with the rune on it. Alex had no doubt that she'd been able to copy what was left, no matter what her talent.

"I wasn't lying, Evelyn," he said as she worked. "That rune isn't ready. If you activate it, it will kill you, just like Quinton, just like Thomas."

"I don't believe you," she said, taking a match from the box on the table and striking it into flame.

"I knew you were Quinton's partner before I called you over here," he said. "I purposely didn't finish the rune. Believe me when I tell you it won't work."

She dropped the match on the rune paper. Since it wasn't flash paper it didn't catch right away, and the fire spread over it slowly.

"You're lying," Evelyn said as the spell's power began to build. "You couldn't have known about me."

"Thomas' neighbors said he had a girl. One with long auburn hair down her back," Alex said. "It was smart of you to cut it and dye it. I never would have suspected you, but the other night you very agreeably let me take off your clothes and I noticed that you didn't dye all your hair."

Evelyn's look of triumph slipped, and she reflexively looked down. When she looked back up, there was terror in her eyes. She turned to stop the rune, but she was too late. It flashed into existence with a pulse of light brighter and hotter than the sun.

The instant the light flared, the runes on Alex's new brass ring sprang to life. A spherical shield of pure, transparent energy enveloped Alex and inside that, a boiling dark vapor erupted. The rune that made the vapor was called the Rune of Inky Night and no light had ever penetrated it. Alex hoped it would be enough to keep the killing light of the finding rune from reaching him. In the fraction of a second before the runes had activated, the light had touched Alex's exposed skin and he could still feel it burning, like he'd been in the sun too long.

Outside the darkness, Evelyn was screaming. It was not the scream of terror one might expect from someone who has come face to face with their doom, but rather a scream of mortal agony, as her flesh burned in the unforgiving light. Alex wished he'd added a silence rune to the ring as the scream grew higher and higher in pitch. A low, thrumming noise grew along with the screams. After what seemed like an eternity, the scream died down to a gargling gasp...and then nothing. The thrumming went on for another full minute, then it too died away, and the world outside Alex's sphere of midnight fell silent.

Alex took a deep breath and let it out slowly, his hands trembling and making the handcuffs rattle against the metal bed frame. He had been right about Quinton Sanderson's and Thomas Rockwell's accomplice. Evelyn had used them all and she'd paid for her quest for power with her life.

"I'm so sorry, Evelyn," he said, his voice hoarse in the stillness. "I tried to warn you." A single tear rolled down his cheek, but he didn't care. Inside the blackness of the darkness rune, no one could see him.

21

THE SPELL

Sitting hunched over was really beginning to hurt Alex's back. His shield and darkness runes had expended their energy and vanished over an hour ago and now he sat in the empty workshop, handcuffed to a bed. A metal bar curved in a downward facing U shape formed the footboard of the bed. It only rose about four inches above the mattress, forcing Alex to lean over so as not to pull his injured arm against it. He'd tried sitting on the floor, but that twisted his left side even more painfully.

When the FBI came bursting into the workshop with their guns drawn, he almost cheered.

"Agent Davis," he said in his most cheerful voice. "What kept you?"

"It's clear," Davis yelled out into the hall. "No one here but Lockerby."

"Is he alive?" the voice of Sorsha Kincaid drifted in from the hallway.

"Yes," Agent Warner said, his voice thick with disappointment.

The Sorceress came around the corner, and all Alex could do was stare. The previous times he'd seen her, she'd been dressed for her work with the FBI, fashionable certainly, but with the air of a working professional. Tonight, however, Sorsha wore a long, form-fitting black evening dress that clung to her modest curves. The sleeves were transparent and shimmered as she moved, baring her slender, pale arms beneath and ending in what looked like the black cuff from a man's shirt, complete with a large, pearl cufflink. A short, fox-fur stole covered her shoulders and hung down on either side of her slender neck, parting occasionally as she walked to reveal an open collar and a necklace of glossy black pearls against the alabaster of her skin. A close-fitting hat with a white feather and a veil made of the same shimmery stuff as the sleeves completed the outfit.

Wherever Sorsha Kincaid had been summoned from, it was not the kind of party that would have tolerated the likes of Alex. Her dress reminded Alex of some of the women he'd seen in *The Emerald Room*, though Sorsha wore it better. There was something in her slow, confident walk across the workshop floor that gave her elegance, or rather revealed it. The fact that her clothes were fine and that the room was just a simple workshop had no power to add or detract from the Sorceress' inherent grace and femininity.

"I can't say I'm surprised to find you here, Mr. Lockerby," she said, standing over him as Davis and Warner searched the room. She pulled back the veil, revealing her ice blue eyes, and placed a cigarette between her dark red lips.

Absently, Alex noticed that she wore the same burgundy lipstick that Evelyn had worn.

"How goes the hunt for our missing Germans?" he asked as the Sorceress came to a stop, standing over him.

"It's being handled," she replied with a raised eyebrow. "At the moment, however, I'd rather talk about what you are doing here."

Alex smiled his most sincere-looking fake smile. "Why, I'm helping you with your case, my lady," he said in a gallant voice. "Have your boys look in the handbag on the center table," Alex added, nodding at the purse Evelyn had brought with her. "I'm sure they'll find those pesky drawings you've been looking for. Along with a pistol that is not mine," he amended.

Davis and Warner paused in their search and looked at Sorsha. After a moment, she nodded. The FBI men converged on the table as Sorsha searched her own tiny handbag for a matchbook.

"I'd offer you one of mine," Alex said, holding up his right hand as much as he could in the handcuffs. "But, unfortunately..."

"That's all right," Sorsha said, then she bent down and reached into Alex's jacket pocket, extracting a cardboard matchbook.

"They're here, all right," Agent Davis said. "All six originals."

"Now will you uncuff me?" Alex said as Sorsha lit her cigarette.

"Not yet," she said, blowing smoke in his face. "I must confess I'm very curious about how you got those papers, and just who cast the finding rune here tonight. If we dust those originals, will we find your fingerprints, Mr. Lockerby?"

Alex grinned up at her as best his could from his hunched over position. "You won't find my fingerprints," he said. "And I didn't cast the finding rune." He nodded at the handcuffs.

"You could have put those on yourself once you were done," Sorsha said.

Alex smiled wider. "You can tell that I didn't cast that spell because there aren't obfuscation wards and concealment runes on the walls. I knew you were tracking that spell; you told me so yourself. That's how you found Thomas Rockwell in the first place. You didn't know that Quinton Sanderson had a partner and that she came with him to New York. When Thomas cast the finding rune, you tracked it to this neighborhood and then looked for a runewright. That's why you didn't find this workshop. This is where he actually cast the rune."

Sorsha's face carried the look of someone who unknowingly drank sour milk.

"Well," she said. "If you knew I was tracking any casting of that finding rune, why didn't you shield this place? And who cast the rune?"

"I hoped you wouldn't come into it at all," Alex said, and sighed. "But I knew if you felt the rune being cast here, you'd come, and I needed you in case something bad happened."

"What if I hadn't found this workshop for a week?" she asked, arching an eyebrow. Alex chuckled.

"Well, I hoped your aim would be better if you were close to the place it was cast."

"You still haven't told me who did the casting."

"She called herself Evelyn Rockwell," Alex said. "At least to me. She seduced Quinton Sanderson and got him to steal the drawings from the Archimedean Monograph. Then when he disappeared, she moved here and found Thomas Rockwell."

"And then you, when Rockwell disappeared," Sorsha finished, a reproving look on her perfect face. Alex nodded.

"When I put two and two together, I enticed her here. I told her I'd figured it out but I wanted more time. I told her to go home and wait for me to call."

"And," Agent Davis said, stepping up beside Sorsha. He held Alex's bag, casually in his right hand. "If she'd been innocent, she would have gone home."

"That's right," Alex said, his voice suddenly raspy.

"But she wasn't innocent," Sorsha said. "She got the drop on you, locked you to this bed, and finished the rune herself."

"Yes," Alex said.

"What happened to her?"

"Uncuff me," Alex said, "and I'll show you."

Sorsha looked at Davis and nodded toward Alex.

"Before we do that," Davis said with a malicious smile, "you'd better have a look at this." He opened the bag so that Sorsha could look inside. She smiled, showing a row of pearly white teeth any shark would be proud of, offset all the more by her burgundy lipstick.

"My, my," she said reaching into the bag. "What have we here?" When her hand came out, she was holding Alex's rune-covered Colt 1911.

"Nice," Davis said. "I have one just like it, though mine isn't as decorative."

Sorsha turned it over in her hands, scrutinizing the runes on its surface. "There wouldn't be a spell breaker rune on this gun, would there?"

Alex forced himself to relax. He had a permit for the gun, but adding runes to it was questionably legal. If Sorsha wanted to make trouble for him, she could, but not if all she cared about were spell breakers.

Spell breakers were just what they sounded like, runes that reacted with the kinds of magic sorcerers used. The runes weren't too difficult to write and they could disrupt even complex magic, like the crawlers or the capacitors at Empire Tower. As a result, their use was highly illegal. Just possessing one could land a runewright in prison for twenty years.

"Spell breaker runes are illegal," he said with a smile.

"But you do know how to make them," she pressed. Alex shrugged.

"It's in my Lore book," he said. "I've heard you can buy the instructions on the black market for a C-note."

Sorsha regarded him for a long moment, then dropped the pistol back into Alex's bag.

"Unlock him," she said.

Davis's face fell for a moment, but then his smile returned. "Agent Warner went next door to call this in," he said. "He's got my key."

"Oh, for heaven's sake," Sorsha said. She leaned down to the short length of chain that connected the handcuffs. As she did, the fox stole pressed against Alex's face, filling his nostrils with her delicate floral perfume.

Sorsha grasped the chain between her thumb and forefinger. Alex heard a crackling sound as the link turned suddenly white, then, with a gesture of casual ease, the kind one might use to shoo an annoying fly, the Sorceress crushed the frozen link between her fingers.

Trying not to look impressed, Alex sat up straight, his back popping as he stretched it, then he stood.

"You wanted to know where Evelyn went?" he said, holding out his hand so that Agent Davis could hand over his kit. The FBI man reached in and removed the pistol before complying.

Alex took the bag and went to the workbench where the burned remnant of the rune paper still lay. He pulled out his lamp and his ghostlight burner, then shone the green light on the wall. It only took him a few seconds to locate Evelyn's shadow. The shadow was visible under the green light, even without the oculus. She had turned, as if running for the back corner of the room.

The corner where Alex had been.

He chose to believe that in her last desperate moments she had wanted him to save her.

"Is this what happened to everyone who disappeared?" Sorsha asked, her voice husky and low with emotion.

"Yes," Alex said. "If you ask me, this rune is some kind of trap designed to weed out anyone smart enough to be a threat to whoever made it."

Sorsha smiled. "I assure you," she said. "The Monograph is real."

Alex shone his light on Thomas' shadow.

"He believed that too."

At that moment Agent Warner returned.

"The investigators are on the way," he said. "They'll go over this place with a fine-toothed comb."

"Good," Sorsha said. She turned to Agent Davis and nodded toward the door and without a word, he left, taking the young blond Agent Warner with him. Once they were gone, Sorsha fixed Alex with a hard stare.

"How did you know that rune would fail?" she asked.

"Because I didn't finish unraveling it."

"But how do you know?"

"Because I could see that there were parts that weren't aligned yet."

Sorsha smiled. It was not a reassuring look.

"So you admit you could have unraveled it," she said. "Given enough time."

Alex tried to look casual as he shrugged. "Assuming it could be unraveled at all," he said. He didn't want Sorsha telling her government friends that she found a patsy to take another run at the Archimedean Monograph.

Her eyes flashed suddenly, as if lit from inside her skull.

"I think you're lying to me," she said, but her voice was suddenly deep and the sound of it echoed, trailing off after her words until they became lost in a faint blur of noise. At the same time, the room seemed to dissolve around him, colors and shapes blending into a solid plane of gray.

Alex wanted to be alarmed, but felt calm and safe instead. As if this platinum-haired angel in front of him were the person he trusted most in all the world. The person who wanted nothing more than to help him.

Somewhere in the recesses of his mind he knew it was a truth spell. Like spell breakers, truth spells were also illegal, which is why Sorsha had sent the only witnesses out of the room before using it. Now, if Alex tried to make an issue out of it, it would be his word against the word of one of New York's most prominent citizens.

"I have a few questions for you, Alex," Sorsha said, her voice still unnaturally deep and echoing. "Does your version of the finding rune work?"

"No," Alex said, feeling no compunction to lie.

"Did you find the Archimedean Monograph?"

"No," Alex said.

"Are you going to continue to look for the Monograph?"

"No."

She picked up the notebook where Alex had drawn the rune Evelyn used.

"You seem to have this mostly figured out," she said. "Do you think you could finish it?"

"No."

"Why?"

"That rune will never work," he said.

The Sorceress swayed suddenly and leaned against the table. A moment later the room snapped back into focus. Alex shook his head and blinked his eyes a few times to clear them. When he could see properly again, he noticed that Sorsha was breathing hard and sweating through her satin dress. She looked like she'd run a marathon.

"You hexed me," he said. It was not an accusation, just a statement of fact.

"I had to be sure," Sorsha said between gasps. "I'm sorry."

Alex just shrugged. He understood why she had done it.

"If you can just wink your eye and make men tell the truth, why don't you? You don't care about it being illegal, or you wouldn't have used it on me."

"As you can see," she said, her breathing finally returning to normal, "it takes a great deal of focus and effort. Even then, it's not always right. People who know it's coming can sometimes shape their answers in such a way as to speak the truth...but still be deceptive."

"And you figured I was just the kind of dim bulb it would work on?"

"On the contrary," she said. "I knew I would have to surprise you to have any chance of success. You're far too clever for me to have warned you in advance."

"Careful, Sorceress, that sounded dangerously like a compliment."

She blushed. Alex wouldn't have believed it if he hadn't been looking her straight in the face, but her perfect, alabaster cheeks turned a rosy shade of pink.

"The spell has a reverse effect for a few moments," she said. Her face suddenly clouded over, her eyebrows dropping down over her eyes. Clearly she believed she'd revealed too much.

"So if I asked you a question right now, you'd have to answer truthfully?" A broad smile stretched across Alex's face as he tried to think of the single most embarrassing thing he could ask. The look on Sorsha's face, however, told him the moment had passed. Still, he filed that particular bit of information away for later use.

"I'm grateful to you for finding the missing Monograph pages," she said, her voice stiff and formal. She spoke something in that deep, echoing voice and moved her hand down her dress. As her hand moved, the dark perspiration stains vanished, leaving the satin material unmarked and pristine.

"Is there a reward for finding them?" he asked. "Not that your gratitude isn't appreciated."

"I don't know," she said with a shrug. "I'll ask. Now, if you don't mind, a team of FBI investigators will be here soon. I don't want to have to explain your presence to them."

"Can I have my notebook?" he asked.

Sorsha smiled and set the notebook aside on the workbench. "I'm afraid that's evidence now."

Alex collected his kit and his pistol, then made his way downstairs to the five and dime. He called home and Iggy picked up immediately.

"There you are, lad," he said. "I was wondering when you'd be home."

"I don't want to go home," he said.

"Rough evening?"

Evelyn's long, tortured scream still lingered in his mind. Her death had been of her own making, but that didn't make it all right.

"You could say that."

"I'll tell you what," Iggy said with an infectious energy. "How about a picture? There's a Sherlock Holmes one over at Radio City starring Basil Rathbone. What say you meet me there and we'll make an evening of it?"

Alex didn't really feel like another mystery, but Iggy seemed excited. He loved movies, and Sherlock Holmes, so why not?

"Sounds great, Iggy," he said.

"I'm closer than you are," Iggy said. "You hop on the crawler and I'll walk over and meet you there."

"Just take a cab, Iggy," Alex said. This was one of their usual arguments. Iggy simply refused to admit that he was over seventy.

"It's not far," Iggy said. "I like to walk, and I've got plenty of time. It's not like I'm in a hurry."

The words hit Alex like a runaway crawler.

"Iggy?" he said. "Why didn't Charles Beaumont take a cab?"

"What?"

"Charles Beaumont," Alex repeated. "He ran out of his apartment right after that plague jar broke. He must have known what was in it."

There was a long pause, then Iggy answered. "I guess if you want a thief to steal a jar full of plague, you don't want him opening it by accident, so yes, he probably knew."

"So he knew he was sick," Alex said. "So why didn't he take a cab?"

"Who says he didn't?"

"No," Alex said. "If he'd taken a cab, we'd have a dead cabbie and dead fares all over the city."

"You're right," Iggy said, sounding puzzled. "So why didn't he take a cab? He knew he was dying and he believed the water from the Mission could heal him. Why wouldn't he try to get there as fast as possible?"

"Maybe the Mission was his last resort," Alex said. "Maybe he went somewhere else first."

There was a long pause and Alex could almost hear Iggy stroking his mustache.

"If someone asked me to steal a jar full of plague for them," Iggy said slowly, "I might assume they have an antidote."

"It's thin," Alex said.

"And it still doesn't tell us where Beaumont went," Iggy said. "If he went anywhere at all."

"I think we're on to something here," Alex said. "Get a cab—"

"I don't need a cab," Iggy interrupted.

"And meet me at the city morgue," Alex finished.

"Why?"

"We're going to walk a mile in Charles Beaumont's shoes."

22

THE WALK

"Why am I meeting you at the morgue on a Monday night?" Danny Pak asked as Alex arrived in the building's lobby; Alex had called Danny right after he'd hung up with Iggy. "I just got out of trouble that was caused by you. Couldn't this wait a couple of days?"

Alex grinned and slapped Danny on the shoulder.

"Sorry," he said, looking around for Iggy and not finding him. "Let's just say I need you for this one?"

The lobby of the city morgue looked like any office building lobby you might find. There was an aged couch along one wall, surrounded by a few chairs, with a bank of elevators against the back. A reception desk stood opposite the waiting area, manned by a doorman. The only indication that this was not a typical office complex was that the elevator doors were suspiciously large and the man behind the desk wore a police uniform.

Danny rolled his eyes at Alex. "You don't need me," he said. "The coroner likes you better than he likes me. Old coot," he added.

"It doesn't matter if he likes me," Alex said in a low voice. "He's not going to let me take some of Charles Beaumont's property with me no matter how well he likes me."

"Is that what this is about?" Danny said, exasperation in his voice. "First of all, Beaumont didn't have anything on him when we found him. Second, if he had, it would be in a box under Lieutenant Callahan's desk back at the Central Office. Third, there's no way Callahan is going to let you take police evidence, whether I ask him or not."

The door creaked as Iggy pulled it open and entered the building. He wore a tweed suit with a matching flat-cap, and had a pipe clenched in his teeth. Alex nodded to him, then turned back to Danny.

"True," he said. "Beaumont didn't have a pocket watch or a wallet or keys, but even if he had, I don't need any of those."

"Well what do you need?" Danny asked, a note of futility in his voice.

"One of the man's shoes," Iggy piped up.

"Really?" Danny said, his voice drifting from despair to sarcasm.

"Really," Alex confirmed. "And that's why I need you. Beaumont's clothes are still here, and I need you to sign out a shoe for me."

"Do you know how that's going to look if Callahan ever sees the sign-out sheet?" Danny asked.

"He won't have any reason to look at that," Alex said, rubbing his hands together. "Especially if we learn something new about who paid for Beaumont to steal that case. Now come on."

He waved at the officer behind the desk and walked to the elevator with Danny and Iggy in tow.

"Have I ever told you just how much I hate you?" Danny asked as they waited for the car.

TEN MINUTES later they were on their way back up to the main floor with Charles Beaumont's left shoe. It was a quality brand, and the leather was well maintained and supple.

"So how is that going to tell us anything about who hired Beaumont?" Danny asked.

Iggy explained Alex's theory that Beaumont had gone somewhere else before arriving at the Brotherhood of Hope Mission.

"Wouldn't he have infected anyone he'd gone to see?" Danny asked.

"Probably," Alex said.

"Alex, I would know if any more bodies had been found," Danny said. "There weren't any."

"Whoever is behind this might have an antidote," Iggy said. "If they were immune, there wouldn't be any bodies."

"They might not have been home," Alex suggested. "Remember, someone took those jars from Beaumont's place. We assumed it was the same people who killed Jerry Pemberton, but what if it wasn't?"

"Then they would have searched Beaumont's place after killing Pemberton," Danny reminded him. "Since they didn't, we know it was Pemberton's killers who found the jars."

Alex had to concede that Danny was right about that, but he still felt that the secret of where Beaumont had gone when he ran out of his apartment held some truth, some key that would make the whole sordid mess make sense.

"So where are we going?" Danny asked once they all reached the street.

"Beaumont's place," Alex said, spotting Danny's car and heading for it. "We have to go back to where this chain of events started."

Danny shook his head, but followed. Twenty minutes later they were parked on the street outside the modest building that was Charles Beaumont's former residence. The police cars were gone, and no evidence remained on the street of the activity that had taken place the previous morning. Alex led them up to the fifth floor and found a man in a dark suit sitting on a chair in the hallway beside Beaumont's door. Alex shot Danny a meaningful look and the detective stepped up to the fore of their group.

"You with the FBI?" he asked the man who'd been eyeing them since they exited the stairs.

"Beat it, newsie," he growled in a basso voice. "There's nothing to see here."

Danny flashed his detective's badge. "I'm with the police. My friends and I need access to Beaumont's apartment for a few minutes."

The man scrutinized the badge for a minute, then shrugged.

"I can't help you, detective," he said. "I have strict orders not to let anyone in."

"Look, Agent...?"

"Meyers," the man supplied.

"Agent Meyers," Danny continued. "I promise not to touch anything. We just need to look at the table in the middle of the room. I'll take the heat if anyone finds out."

"You don't know what you're saying," Meyers said, and chuckled. "The person who gave me those orders is way above your pay grade."

Alex stepped up.

"About this high," he said, holding up his hand. "Snappy dresser with platinum blond hair down to her shoulders?"

"How did ...?" A look of disbelief crawled inexorably across Agent Meyers face.

"We're acquainted," Alex said. "Look, she already doesn't like me, so if she gets mad, just tell her Alex Lockerby told you it was okay."

"How does that make me look like anything but a dunce?" he asked with a laugh.

"Trust me, young man," Iggy said. "The Sorceress is perfectly willing to believe the worst of my friend here."

"All right," Meyers said, standing up. "I'll let you go in, but I have to watch you the whole time." He took out a key and unlocked the door. "And don't worry about touching anything. That won't be a problem."

He pushed the door open and turned on the light. The apartment was completely bare. Everything from the furniture to the carpets to the coffee pot was gone. The FBI had carted it all away, no doubt to some lab to go over every inch of it.

"Uh-oh," Danny said, stepping in and looking around. "Is this a problem?"

Alex didn't know, and he said so.

"I wanted to use the overturned chair as a starting point for a finding rune," he said.

"If you can use a finding rune to track Beaumont's movements," Danny said, an incredulous look on his face, "why didn't you do that yesterday?"

"The success of a finding rune depends on how much information the caster has," Iggy said in the manner of a university professor lecturing to a class.

"The magic needs something to latch onto," Alex continued. "I knew where Beaumont lived and what he did for a living, but I didn't suspect he'd gone anywhere but the mission. A finding rune wouldn't have shown me anything yesterday."

"So," Danny said. "The fact that you believe he went somewhere is going to make the rune work?"

"No," Alex said, crouching down to stare at the floor. There was a faint outline of chalk where the plague jar's contents had spilled, but the area of floor inside it was scratched and clouded. "We need something that will physically tie Beaumont to wherever he went."

"That's why you needed his shoe," Danny said, putting it together. "Because wherever he went, his shoe was there too."

"Very good, detective," Iggy said. "Now all we have to do is tie that shoe to the place where Beaumont began his journey and the rune should lead us to where he went."

"Didn't you say he started this trip right here in this apartment?" Agent Meyers asked.

"Yes," Alex said, moving a short distance from the chalk outline toward the door. "But the more precisely I can tie the shoe to Beaumont's flight, the more accurately the finding rune can follow his trail."

"So, what are you looking for?" Meyers asked, still standing in the doorway. Danny laughed and stepped forward to a spot about two feet from where Alex was scrutinizing the floor.

"This," he said, pointing to a spot where the finish on the floor was scratched and discolored. "Beaumont stepped in some of the liquid from the jar on his way out the door, remember? It left a footprint here."

"I remember," Alex said, squinting at the spot. "How can you tell it's there?"

"Because it's been sanded," Danny said. "Look at the spot where the jar spilled. The FBI didn't want to risk leaving any residue for future tenants to discover."

"How did I miss that?" Alex wondered, moving over to the spot. "Thanks."

"Why not break out your ghostlight and be sure?" Iggy suggested. Alex showed him a sheepish grin.

"I'm out of fuel for the ghostlight burner," he said. "I used it up on that business with Evelyn Rockwell."

"You didn't tell me what happened with that," Iggy reminded him.

"Later." Alex didn't want to revive those events just now, and he pushed the memory of Evelyn's tortured scream out of his mind.

He took out a piece of chalk and began drawing a complex, geometric figure on the floor. It didn't have to be made of special inks or even particularly straight as it was just a physical link between the rune he'd drawn in his rune book and the floor.

"I think this is going a bit beyond not touching anything," Agent Meyers said, concern in his voice.

"Don't worry," Iggy said, pulling out his folded handkerchief. "We'll clean up after ourselves."

When Alex finished, he dropped the chalk back into his pocket and then tore a finding rune out of his book. Placing the shoe in the exact center of the chalked figure, Alex tucked the rune into the shoe and then lit it. As the paper vanished, the energy of the rune filled his mind.

"Follow the path of Charles Beaumont," he said, willing the magic into form.

A moment later the shoe began to shake. It spun around in a full circle, then snapped to a position with the toe pointing out the still-open door.

"It's found it," Danny said with a grin.

"I'll be," Meyers said, eyebrows flying upward.

Alex picked up the shoe while Danny scrubbed the chalk figure off the floor with Iggy's handkerchief. It tugged in his grip, pulling him inexorably toward the door.

"Thank you, Agent Meyers," he said, leading everyone back out into the hall. "You've been a great help."

Alex followed the pull of the shoe along the hall to the stairs, then down to the street. The shoe led him around the building and into the outer ring, moving between two slum tenements.

"He turned right."

"The mission is to the left," Iggy said. "I guess you were correct."

"Should I get the car?" Danny asked.

"No," Alex said, moving off down the dark street. "It can't have been far or he would never have made it all the way back to the mission."

The tenements gave way to seedy shops, liquor stores, and the kind of nightclubs that were fronts for illegal gambling and prostitution. Alex didn't have to worry about anyone bothering them. The organized criminal element kept the muggers and the bums out and away from their profit-making enterprises. Not to mention that on these kind of streets, people made an effort not to notice who their fellow travelers were.

Beyond the businesses, a row of shabby homes and apartments that were little more than flop houses sprang up. The shoe tugged Alex in the direction of a three-story apartment of the rent-by-the-week variety. It had a glass door that was so encrusted with dirt and grime that the lobby beyond was just a blur of faint light. When Alex pulled open the door, he found the dimness of the light had more to do with the single, naked bulb hanging from a wire than the thickness of the grime on the glass.

A shabbily dressed woman, whose stained blouse was opened low enough to give a good view of her bosom, looked up from a gossip magazine. When she saw Alex, she put on a smile that was more of a leer and leaned forward, showing even more of her breasts.

"What can I do for you, honey?" she said in a voice that indicated renting rooms wasn't the only service she offered.

"You can tell us if anyone's checked out of this dump in the last five days," Danny said, flashing his badge. The woman's face soured and she stood up straight.

"A couple of people," she said with a shrug.

"Upstairs," Alex reported, feeling the tug on the shoe. Danny looked at the woman, holding her eyes for a long moment.

"We're going to go have a look around upstairs," he said. "Do you have a problem with that?"

"Nope." She shrugged.

"We should look at the registration first," Iggy said. The woman laughed.

"The kind of folk who come through here are usually named Smith," she said. "At least the ones that ain't named Jones."

"Don't worry about it," Danny said. "Let's check the room first." He shifted his gaze to the woman, who now wore a look of interest in what they were doing. "You stay here," he said.

The interest faded from her eyes and she picked up her magazine.

The shoe led them up to the second floor, to a room in the back. When they reached it, the shoe turned to point at it. Alex released the spell and the shoe shuddered, the pull from it disappearing. He slipped it into his jacket pocket and left it there, sticking out. His hand was just about to knock when Iggy grabbed his arm.

"You smell that?" he asked.

Alex had been too excited to pay attention, but he was now. A sickly sweet odor was emanating faintly from the door.

"Ugh," Alex said, recoiling. "What is that?"

"Putrefaction," Danny said. "Something or someone is dead in there, and they've been dead a while."

23

THE BOOK

"Could they still be infected?" Alex asked Iggy. Iggy shook his head.

"Not after all this time. Remember the bodies at the Mission."

Alex nodded and took hold of the handle.

"Here goes," he said. The handle turned in his hand and the door opened. A wave of stench washed out into the hall and Alex recoiled, coughing and trying to keep from vomiting. Danny backed down the hallway, gagging. Only Iggy seemed unaffected, but he had taken the precaution of lighting his pipe.

"Dear God," Alex gasped.

"Steady on, lad," Iggy said. "You'll get used to it in a minute or two. In the meantime, however, I'll go in and open a window."

"You all right?" Alex asked Danny, putting his handkerchief over his nose and mouth.

"Yeah," Danny said. He didn't look too bad. "I was on a stake-out down at the docks a couple of years ago. It was about the same."

The two men took a deep breath and entered the apartment. Despite its seedy exterior, the room was neat and clean. There were no dishes in the sink, the ashtrays were mostly empty, and three portmanteau trunks sat in the front room, closed and secured. The only thing amiss were the three bodies.

One lay on the couch, her arms crossed across her chest as if she'd been laid out for burial. A man sat in one of the chairs, a book in his lap as if he'd just fallen asleep. A second man was slumped over the table, a pencil clutched in his lifeless hand. All of them were dressed far too nicely to be staying in this hotel.

Iggy came back into the room from the back; already air was beginning to move through the little space.

"So who are these three?" Danny asked.

Alex bent down and retrieved a book that had fallen to the floor beside the man at the table.

"I think these are our missing Germans," he said, flipping through it. He held it open so Danny and Iggy could see the spidery script. "Anyone read German?"

"I do," Iggy said, taking the book. He squinted at the text, then pulled his reading glasses from his coat pocket. "Give me a minute," he said, running his finger along the text. "It's been a long time."

"If these are the Germans who came over with the plague, they'll have their passports on them," Danny said.

The man at the table had put his coat over the back of his chair before he died, so Alex checked its pockets and withdrew a small, leather-bound black book.

"Dietrich Strand," he read, opening the front cover.

"This one is Greta Albrecht," Danny said after going through the woman's handbag. He pulled out his notebook and consulted it. "That would make this other guy," he indicated the man with the book, "Helge Rothenbaur."

Alex pulled the passport out of the dead man's jacket pocket and opened it. "Sure enough. Helge Rothenbaur," he read. Danny shook his head.

"What are these people doing here?" he said. "Didn't they come to New York on the same airship as the plague jars?"

"Yes they did," Alex said and nodded, "so why steal them once they get into a secure warehouse?"

"They couldn't get to them on the airship," Iggy said. He held up the journal. "Mr. Strand left us his confession. After declaring his love for Greta here," Iggy nodded at the dead woman. "Strand says that the thief—"

"Beaumont," Alex supplied.

Iggy gave him a withering look and Alex clammed up.

"—Beaumont told them to take this room and wait for him."

"He must have used this place to preserve his anonymity," Danny said. "Pretty smart."

"Strand says that Beaumont came here claiming to have broken a jar and demanding an antidote. When he was told there was none, he fled before they could stop him." Iggy looked around at the dead. "There are letters here from each of them to family members and loved ones," he said. "They knew they were infected, that they'd have to stay here until they died."

Alex looked around at the dead and shuddered. When his time came, he didn't want to see it coming.

"Is there anything in there about why they wanted to steal the plague?" Danny asked. "They don't sound like they intended to cause an outbreak."

Iggy paged toward the front of the book. "It says here that these three were part of the team that developed the disease. They were told it was going to speed up disease research, cure things like polio and cancer."

"What happened?" Danny asked.

Iggy paged back and ran his finger down the page until he found what he was looking for. "They overheard the project leader, an Alchemist named Josef Mengele, talking with a government official. Apparently the disease was meant to start a civil war here in America, giving Hitler and the Nazis free rein in Europe."

"How are a couple of jars of a fast-acting plague going to start a civil war?" Alex asked. It didn't make any sense. Worse, it looked like the European conference wasn't the target after all.

"It goes on," Iggy said, scanning the book. "The plague was supposed to be picked up in New York by spies operating in the city and then strike four specific targets."

"Where?" Danny asked. Iggy shook his head and nodded at the dead man with the pencil.

"He didn't know, but he thought it had something to do with New York's sorcerers. Mengele was specific that the plague had to be resistant to magic."

"So no one infected could use spells to purge the infection from their system," Alex said.

"Probably," Iggy agreed.

"It still doesn't explain how four jars of instant plague could start any kind of war," Danny pointed out.

"Four jars," Alex said, the number tickling at something in his brain. There were six sorcerers, not four. He snapped his fingers as everything fell into place in his brain. "Where's the phone?" he asked, looking around.

"There's no phone here," Iggy said. "If there were, these unfortunates could have called for help."

"Why do you need a phone?" Danny asked.

"What would happen if four of New York's sorcerers died from a mysterious magical plague?" he asked.

"Nothing," Danny said. "I mean it would be a disaster for the New York economy, but we'd get through it."

"What if the survivors were John D. Rockefeller and William Todd?" Alex grabbed the detective by the shoulders.

"Who cares who the survivors are?" Danny said.

"Everyone would," Iggy gasped. "Rockefeller and Todd have been feuding for years."

"And Todd is a paranoid hermit," Alex said. "He'd accuse Rockefeller of starting the plague."

Danny began to nod, a look of alarm on his face. "And Rockefeller wouldn't take that lying down. It would start a war between them."

"The New York Six are the most powerful and wealthy sorcerers in the world," Alex pointed out. "With four of them gone, every other sorcerer in America would be lining up to support one faction or the other, hoping to move in once the dust settles. It would destabilize the whole country."

"So, what do we do?" Danny said. "We don't have any proof of this.

You know Captain Rooney isn't going to call anybody about this without ironclad evidence, especially not a sorcerer."

Alex turned and ran out into the hallway. "You call Callahan and get someone over here to take charge of the bodies and the journal," he called as he tore down the stairs.

"Where are you going?" Danny yelled after him.

Alex dashed downstairs and across the lobby, past the reception desk and the woman with the gossip magazine. Laying his good shoulder into the door, he stumbled out into the night, tearing off up the street toward the lights of the nightclubs. They might not serve any useful purpose, but you could always get a cab in front of one. He jumped in the first one he found.

"The Waldorf," he said. "Quickly," he added when the cabbie looked at him incredulously. Not many people went to the Waldorf from this neighborhood.

As the cab pulled away from the curb, Alex opened his kit and dropped Beaumont's shoe inside, exchanging it for his 1911 which he slipped into his jacket pocket. Whoever had the plague jars had four targets, and one of them was Sorsha Kincaid. Thanks to Alex's erroneous assumption that the Germans on the airship were the ones who owned the plague jars, she was right this very minute standing in a hotel ballroom at a conference of boring diplomats.

He might as well have put a bull's-eye on her back.

To keep his mind off how long the cab took to reach the core and the Waldorf hotel, Alex paged through his rune book. He'd used a lot of his powerful runes in the last few days and there were precious little left. After flipping through it twice, he tucked it back in his pocket with a note of disgust. Unless he wanted to fix a run in the Sorceress' stockings, there wasn't much his rune book could contribute.

When the cab finally stopped in front of the Waldorf, Alex shoved all the money he had into the cabbie's hand, hoping it would be enough, and ran to the enormous glass doors. Beyond them, inside the hotel's vestibule, a security station had been set up. All the doors but one were blocked with potted plants, and two policemen stood on either side of the open door. Agent Davis stood in the doorway, clipboard in hand, and he looked up in shock as Alex came tearing through the door.

"Why are you here, Lockerby?" he asked, stepping in front of the open door. Alex stopped short to avoid running into the FBI man.

"Where's Sorsha?" he demanded.

"Miss Kincaid is inside where she belongs," Davis said. "Now why don't you go back where you belong?"

"I need to speak to her! She's in danger."

Agent Davis laughed in his face. "She's in the safest place in the city right now," he said. "Those Germans aren't going to get in here tonight or any other night."

"You're right," Alex agreed. "Because they're dead."

Alex briefly relayed the story of finding the German alchemists and the details they had left behind.

"You have to let me talk to her," he finished.

"Sorsha Kincaid knows how to take care of herself," Agent Davis said.

"She doesn't know this is coming," Alex said. "She has to be warned."

Davis vacillated for a long moment, indecision on his face.

"Fine," he said at last. "She's in the ballroom." He stepped aside and let Alex through. "But don't disturb the other guests."

The ballroom of the Waldorf hotel was massive, three stories high with polished hardwood floors and arcades running along the side walls that housed recessed balconies. Carved columns ran up every wall to large painted cornices, and crystal chandeliers hung everywhere. The thick smoke of a hundred cigarettes hung in the room and a cacophony of voices filled the chamber with the incoherent buzz of conversation.

Alex stood paralyzed for a moment, scanning the crowd, but moments later a head of platinum hair in an A-line cut came into view. The Sorceress had taken off the hat with the veil and now her white-blonde hair shone like a beacon in the dimly lit room.

"Mr. Lockerby," she said with an unamused smile when she caught sight of his approach. She quickly excused herself from the group she'd been conversing with and turned to meet him. "I used to like your penchant for showing up in the most unexpected places," she said. "Now, I'm starting to tire of it."

"Nice to see you too," he said, taking her by the elbow and gently pulling her along in his wake. "We need to talk."

She looked as if she were about to object, but something she saw in his face made her hesitate.

"This way, then," she said, pulling free of his grasp and making her way toward the back of the room where a large stage and podium had been set up. She moved behind the podium and entered a small door so cleverly set into the wall that Alex didn't even see it until Sorsha opened it. Inside the door was a hallway that ran behind the ballroom and enabled the hotel staff to deliver food or move furniture without being seen.

"Now," she said, imperiously. "What is so important?"

"This convention isn't the target for that plague," he said. "You are."

As quickly as he could, Alex recounted the story of finding the dead alchemists, Dietrich Strand's journal, and his theory about how the plague could be used to start a civil war. Sorsha listened quietly with her arms crossed, absently tapping her arm with her fingernail.

"That does make some sense," she grudgingly admitted when Alex had finished.

"The only thing I can't figure is, why haven't they acted yet?" Alex said. "I mean they've had their plague for almost a week now."

"I can answer that," Sorsha said. "As soon as I learned of this alchemical plague, I warned my fellow sorcerers. They've had round-the-clock protection since then. Whoever these agents are, they're going to find it difficult to get up to one of our flying homes and carry out their attack. After all, there are more than policemen guarding those dwellings."

"Policemen?" Alex asked. He'd naturally assumed a sorcerer would have living gargoyles or something like that to protect his house.

"The sorcerers contract with the New York Police for our protection," Sorsha said.

"So what now?" Alex asked. "Whoever has that plague isn't going to stop just because the job is hard."

Sorsha turned and set off at a fast walk, moving along the hallway toward its end.

"I'll need to speak to Captain Rooney," she was saying. "If we organize it right, we might be able to create a weakness the German agents will believe they can exploit."

"You want to set a trap?"

"Yes," Sorsha sighed. "I want to set a trap."

"Then why didn't you just say that?" Alex asked, irritation in his voice.

"Mr. Lockerby," Sorsha fumed. "I hardly need—"

"Sorsha, there you are," a new voice boomed.

Alex's hand dropped into his jacket pocket and curled around the grip of his pistol as he turned. The newcomer was a well-dressed man in an expensive dark suit. He still wore a turned-down fedora, so he'd only just arrived, having not had time to check his hat. He was tall with a mass of close-cut curly hair the same color as copper and bright, intelligent eyes. His smile was crooked and his jaw angled down from his sharp cheekbones to a cleft in his chin.

Alex decided he didn't like the man.

"Director Stevens," Sorsha said, a surprised look on her face. "I didn't expect to see you here tonight."

He took Sorsha's hand and kissed it gently.

"How could I not come when you call for help?" he said, the crooked smile returning to his face. Sorsha, on the other hand looked confused. "Call for help?"

"I know you didn't do that exactly," Stevens said, and laughed. "But I think you were right to request more security. Who's your friend?" he wondered, pointing to Alex.

"Uh," Sorsha said, clearly thrown off balance. "Director Adam Stevens of the FBI's New York field office, this is Alexander Lockerby, Private Investigator."

"The one who found out where the plague came from," Stevens said with raised eyebrows. He stuck out his hand and shook Alex's. "I have to be frank," he said. "I've never had much use for P.I.s, but that was some damn fine work, Mr. Lockerby."

"Thanks," Alex said.

Maybe this guy isn't so bad.

"What did you mean about me requesting additional security here?" Sorsha said. She seemed confused.

"Not here," Stevens said. "For the sorcerers."

"What?" Alex and Sorsha said together. Now Stevens looked confused.

"Agent Warner called a few hours ago," he said. "Told us to round up the agents that you wanted and send them up to flesh out the police details protecting the sorcerers."

"Where are they now?" Sorsha demanded. Steven shrugged.

"I sent them over to Police Headquarters," he said. "They'll catch a floater there to take them up to their posts."

Floaters were basically flying police cars invented by the sorcerer William Todd. They could fly, but they weren't fast, and they could only hold about five people at a time, so the police didn't use them often.

"They're going to need more than one floater," Alex said. "If I were the police dispatcher I'd probably send each group up in their own car."

"Stevens," Sorsha said, her tone one of a general commanding field troops. "Call whoever's in charge at Manhattan Station and tell them to stop those floaters from leaving. All the FBI agents are to be detained and warn the police to be careful; some of them are German spies carrying the three remaining jars of plague."

"You're not serious," Stevens said, but the look on Sorsha's face told him otherwise. "What if the floaters have already left?"

"I'll call the sorcerers," Sorsha said. "They'll be able to capture anyone coming up in a floater as long as they know they're coming. Now go."

Stevens ran off toward the front desk and its telephone but Sorsha just reached into her handbag and pulled out what looked like a makeup mirror in a case. She opened it and set it on the floor facing her. Taking a few steps back, she uttered something in her deep, echo-y voice, and a moment later the image of a man in his late fifties with graying hair and a handlebar mustache appeared, floating above the mirror.

"Sorsha, my darling, you look radiant," the man said in an easy voice. "To what do I owe the great pleasure of this call?"

Sorsha quickly outlined the German plot and its purpose.

"So," the man said, twirling the ends of his mustache. "Hitler thinks he can put one over on us. I'll show that Charlie Chaplin impersonator."

"Focus, Andrew," Sorsha said in a hard voice.

Alex was startled when he heard the name. Andrew Barton, the Lightning Lord, the man who provided power to all of Manhattan.

"Right now," Sorsha was saying, "you are going to pass the word to everyone, and make sure they catch the men in those floaters."

Andrew cupped his hand and a ball of lighting appeared in it. "That won't be a problem, my dear," he said.

"None of that," Sorsha barked at him. "Some of the men in those cars are ordinary policemen. I don't have to remind you what might happen if you kill any of them."

Apparently, Andrew didn't have to be reminded, because he closed his fist and the ball of lightning vanished.

"You take the fun out of everything, my dear," he said with a sigh. "Speaking of which, when are you going to finally come dine with me?"

Sorsha cocked an eyebrow at him. "If I want to be chased around a table by a dirty old man, I'll go to a bawdy house," she said. "Now get the word out before someone gets killed."

She snapped her fingers and the image disappeared.

"I'm guessing," Alex said as the Sorceress bent down to pick up her mirror and fold it into its case, "that since you didn't give any orders for extra FBI personnel, that Agent Warner took it upon himself. How long has he been with you?"

"He's new," Sorsha said, marching off toward the front door. "He and about a dozen other agents arrived in the New York office at the same time."

Alex thought back to his associations with the young, blonde agent. Warner didn't like him, but that was not surprising from an FBI man.

"I don't see him as a Nazi agent," Alex said.

"Let's find him first," Sorsha said. "Then you can ask him. He's working the front door with Agent Davis."

"No, he's not," Alex said, pulling Sorsha to a stop. "When I came in, Davis was there alone. Where else would Warner be?"

Sorsha thought for a moment, then set off toward the elevator. "I have a suite that we've been using as an office," she said.

"Must be nice," Alex said as the elevator operator opened the door for them.

"Penthouse," she said, and the man turned the lever that sent the car rising into the air.

A long minute later they reached the door to the east penthouse room. Alex pulled his pistol from his jacket pocket.

"I have a rune that will unlock the door," he said, before realizing that with his pistol in hand, and his other arm in a sling, he couldn't reach his rune book.

"Never mind that," Sorsha said. "Turn your back."

She didn't wait for him to comply, she simply raised her arms and spoke a word and the door burst as if it had been stuffed with gunpowder. Alex barely averted his face before he was showered in splinters and sawdust.

Sorsha strode into the room as if she had just been announced at Buckingham Palace. Alex followed after her, brushing chips of wood from his suit jacket with his pistol. The room beyond was a parlor, with a sunken area lined with elegant couches and chaise longues. A long bar of some light-colored wood filled one entire wall, and several hallways led out of the room.

Sorsha turned left, so Alex went right. He pulled open the first door he came to and found a bathroom. At the end of the hall was a tiny sunroom with a writing desk, a small couch, and a telephone.

"Sorceress," Alex called, tucking his gun back into his pocket. "I don't think Agent Warner is your Nazi."

"Why not?" Sorsha called from the parlor.

"Because he's dead."

24

THE FALL

Agent Warner lay slumped over the writing desk. Blood and brain matter covered the wall in front of him and he still had a service .38 clutched in his left hand.

"What to do you mean, he's d—" Sorsha came through the door, but at the sight of the corpse, she turned her back. "Dear God," she said, her voice heavy with the effort not to vomit. She took a few deep breaths, then turned back to the grisly scene.

"Did he shoot himself to keep from being caught?" she asked. "How did he know we were on to him?"

"Someone might have called him," Alex said, indicating the phone where it had fallen on the floor, knocked off the table by Warner's falling body. "But I don't think that's it. Especially since he didn't kill himself."

Sorsha looked up at him sharply.

"See how the blood is on the wall in front of him," Alex explained. "He would have had to turn his head and tilt it up before pulling the trigger. That's the kind of position he'd be in if he heard someone behind him and started to turn. If he'd shot himself while sitting normally, the blood should be here," he said, indicating the window on Warner's right side. "Also, that's a lot of blood and brains for a .38.

Looks like a bigger entry hole too. If I had to guess, it was a .45, like the one I carry."

Sorsha raised one of her dark eyebrows.

"Are you trying to make me suspect you?" she asked. Alex shook his head and put his hand on Warner's neck.

"No. This body is still warm," he said. "This happened within the last twenty minutes, and since you and I were together for that time, I couldn't have killed him. We do know someone else though, who uses the same kind of gun I do."

"No." Sorsha shook her head, a pleading, almost desperate look in her eyes. "It's not possible."

Alex pushed on unmercifully.

"Someone else who also had access to your suite."

"He's been part of my team for five years," she said, still not willing to believe it.

"Where is Agent Davis?"

"You said he was at the front door," Sorsha said, her voice distant.

"I'll bet you a steak dinner he isn't there now," Alex said. "In fact, I'll bet as soon as he let me in, he came up here and killed Warner." A disturbing thought occurred to Alex and he stepped around Sorsha and into the hall. "If you're his target, he might still be here."

"No," Sorsha said, confidently. "He knows me better than that. We worked together long enough that he'd know his only chance would be to surprise me."

"So where would he go? He can't do anything to help his confederates aboard the floaters, so what's his play?"

"He's probably fled," Sorsha said. "He'd know that the first thing we'd do is lock down the building."

"I don't think so," Alex said. "If he just wanted to escape, he wouldn't need to kill Warner. He's still in the hotel."

Sorsha cocked her head to the side and her hair fell across half her face. She looked like she was about to disagree with him, but then her head came up, her eyes opened wide, and she gasped. Her hands gripped her gut and she doubled over in pain. Alex grabbed her arm, holding her steady as she swayed.

"What's wrong?"

"He's not in the hotel," she gasped. "He's in my home."

She gasped again, pressing her hand to her stomach and Alex hooked his good arm under hers to keep her upright. Her breathing was coming in ragged gasps and her pale skin took on a yellowish tinge.

"Davis must have had Warner order a floater sent here," Alex said, helping Sorsha back to the parlor and onto a chase longue. "That's why he killed him, to give himself time to get up to your castle undetected."

Sorsha began muttering in that deep, echo-y voice of her spell casting, while rubbing her stomach with her hand. A bright bluish light glowed from under the Sorceress' palm and spread out over her body. After a few seconds, her breathing became regular and her skin tone returned to normal. She opened her eyes and looked up at Alex, standing over her.

"The kind of magic that protects my home is ... intimate," she explained. "It's tied to me."

"What happened?"

"Agent Davis has a spell breaker," she said. "He just used it to break open my front door."

"What does he want in your house?"

"He wants to start a war, remember," she said, standing slowly. "If he drops my house on the city..."

"It would flatten a city block," Alex said.

"More likely two," Sorsha said, her composure fully returned. She spread her arms and shook out her hands like a weight lifter getting ready to set a record. "Now stand back. I'm going to go stop Agent Davis."

Alex stepped close to her, looking her hard in the eyes.

"Not without me, you're not."

"This isn't the time for heroics," Sorsha said, trying and failing to push him out of the way. "I hardly need your help to subdue one intruder in my home."

She raised her hands and Alex grabbed her left wrist.

"Yes, you do," he said. "This isn't some last act of desperation, Sorceress. Think about it. Davis had a floater brought here before I ever showed up. This was his plan all along. He's thought it through.

He knows he might have to face you to succeed. Whatever his plans are, they include taking you down."

Sorsha's face was grim but her cheeks pinked. Clearly she wasn't used to being so completely wrong about someone, or so thoroughly out-maneuvered.

"I bet his plans don't include you," she said with a smile and a nod. "Put your arm around me and hold on."

Alex slipped his right arm around her slim waist and pulled her against him. He was very aware of her, pressing against him, and he pushed the thought from his mind.

Sorsha raised her arms and spoke a long, complicated sentence in her Sorceress' voice. The second the echoes of her words faded away, Alex heard a sound like a thousand nails being scraped across plate glass, and he felt his body being twisted like taffy in a puller. It didn't hurt, but he wanted to vomit. Clinging to the Sorceress, he pressed his face down into her hair. She smelled like strawberries and cream, which he would have found intoxicating at any other moment.

Alex had the distinct impression that he'd been rolled flat in a clothes wringer and slipped under a door. Then, a tremendous light flashed before his eyes and he dropped to his knees on a hard stone surface, still holding on to the Sorceress.

He assumed that she traveled this way all the time, but when he finally looked up, panting and trying not to shake, he found Sorsha leaning against his chest with her eyes shut tight. After a long moment she opened them and gently pushed herself away.

"It will wear off after a moment," she said, slumping down to sit on the stone in her slinky black dress.

Alex put his free hand on his knee to push himself upright, but a wave of nausea gripped him, and he stopped. When his stomach finally stopped vibrating, and his vision cleared, he tried again, levering himself up to a standing position. Once he was stable, he reached down and helped Sorsha to her feet.

They had landed on a stone balcony with a marble railing running around it. A comfortable-looking chaise longue sat under an elegant lamp next to a side table with a book sitting on it. Beyond the chaise stood a set of stained glass doors depicting a woodland scene with trees, shrubs, and wildlife.

"This is my private entrance, Lockerby," Sorsha said, reaching out to open the doors.

If Alex hadn't been looking at her slender hand on the door handle, he would have missed the brief spark of magic that leapt between the two when she turned it.

She pushed the doors open and stepped into a vaulted room with an enormous crystal chandelier hanging from the high ceiling. A large, four-poster bed stood on a raised dais along the right side of the room. Its posts were carved in keeping with the theme of the stained glass, with vines, leaves, and forest creatures spiraling around them, up to the canopy. Around the room stood intricately carved dressing tables, chests of drawers, wardrobes, and even a small breakfast table in a round nook with gigantic windows to let in the light.

As grand as the room was, it appeared to be in a state of disarray. Toiletries on the dressing table were left out, drawers were open in the chests, and a trail of the Sorceress' unmentionables led from the bed to a door Alex could only assume was a bathroom. Alex noted that the pair of lace-trimmed underwear matched the brassiere and the garter belt — all were a light sky blue, like the Sorceress' eyes. He assumed there were matching stockings, but thinking about that was extremely distracting with Sorsha a few feet in front of him. He reached into his coat pocket and took hold of his pistol, focusing his mind on the task at hand.

"This way," Sorsha said, leading the way across her bedroom without comment.

She continued out onto a balcony above a foyer that could have fit Alex's entire office inside it twice. The upper balcony ran around the room in a U shape with carved balusters supporting polished cherry-wood handrails. Thick Persian carpets covered the balcony's hardwood floor, ending in a runner that descended the wide stair, flaring out at the bottom as the staircase did. The main floor was white marble and decorated with furniture from couch chairs to hall trees to elegant tables supporting Asian-looking vases. Only two things looked out of place in this ocean of elegance, the shattered and broken front door, and the figure of a man lying on the cold floor, a large red pool spreading out beneath him.

"Hitchens!" Sorsha screamed, then before Alex could stop her, she hurled herself over the banister. She spread out her arms and uttered a word and her fall arrested just as she reached the floor. She landed on the marble with a sharp clack from her high heels.

Alex tore off along the balcony and around to the stairs. By the time he reached the bottom, Sorsha had the man's head in her lap. He looked to be in his late fifties with gray hair, a salt and pepper mustache, and a weathered face. A large purple bruise had spread across the side of his face and his white waistcoat was dark with blood.

"I'm sorry," he was saying. "He had a spell breaker. When the enchantment on the door broke, it exploded. I tried to stop him but —" The man coughed and blood stained his mustache.

"Don't talk," Sorsha said. "I'm going to get you to the hospital. Where are the cook and the maids?"

"Sent them away in the floater," he gasped.

"You should have gone with them," Sorsha said, stroking his face.

He looked up at her, as if he were about to respond, but there was no life left in his eyes. Sorsha just sat there, weeping openly. Alex reached out and closed the old man's eyes.

"Sorceress," Alex said, trying to rouse her from her grief.

He didn't have to say anything further because at that moment the entire floating castle trembled and shook. Alex stumbled to his feet and put out a hand for Sorsha, pulling the Sorceress up.

"Where are your spells that keep this place flying?" he asked as she stumbled against him.

"In a vault in the basement," she said, pushing herself away from him and starting off toward the back of the grand staircase.

An elaborately carved door with painted panels hid a wrought-iron staircase that spiraled downward into the dark. Sorsha kicked off her high heels, then took the stairs two at a time. As she moved down, lights on the inner pole of the stairway lit up to guide her passage.

Alex plunged after her. At first the spiral stair was encased in a wall of rock all the way around, but after he'd gone down a story or two, the rock fell away and it seemed like the stairway floated over a vast, dark expanse.

When Sorsha hit the bottom, lights bloomed in a cavernous room that turned out to be Sorsha's workshop. Large closed doors occupied one entire side of the room and a massive crane on a metal track sat just inside. Pallets of boxes lined one wall of the room with iron bar stock on the other. A long row of tables ran down the middle of the room with a line of bars, waiting for Sorsha to enchant them.

The Sorceress gave no heed to the workshop, turning and sprinting in her stocking feet to a simple door set in the far wall of stone. Beyond the door, a stone passage ran along straight and then curved to the right. Several doors were set in the wall at various points, but Sorsha ran by them without stopping. At the end of the corridor was a simple, square room with papered walls and walnut wainscoting. On the far wall hung an enormous vault door, at least six feet in diameter and two feet thick. It stood open, revealing a short hallway beyond that led to a wide room. The outer plating on the door had been blasted away and Alex could see the mechanisms that operated the lock.

The sharp sound of a crack, not unlike a gunshot, sounded from inside the vault and the castle shook so hard, Sorsha slipped. She almost fell, grabbing on to Alex's left arm in an effort to stay upright.

Alex gasped and felt the blood drain from his face. His ribs were healing faster than normal thanks to Iggy, but they hadn't healed completely. Pain sprouted from his side and spread through his body, making his fingers and toes tingle. He swore, and Sorsha realized what she had done.

"Sorry," she said, releasing his arm. She moved forward, across the vault threshold. "Stay behind me," she said.

Alex was about to protest, but Sorsha had already moved into the short hallway. Beyond the end of the hall, he could see the intricate patterns of dozens of spells, swirling slowly. Some were blue, while others were purple, green, orange, and occasionally white. Ethereal tendrils of energy emanated from some, reaching out to join them with others, forming a net of pulsing cobwebs overhead, like a dome. The floor was cut into broad steps, like an amphitheater with spells laid out on each level going up.

Sorsha reached the end of the hall, then stepped out into the main chamber. She raised her hands, and power crackled through her fingers.

"Davis," she cried, lowering her hand and sending a bolt of greenish lighting off into the room. A sound like a hammer hitting shatterproof glass rang out and Sorsha raised her hand again. Before she could strike, two shots rang out. Alex saw the first shot hit an invisible shield around the Sorceress and it flashed with light at the impact. The second round hit the shield and shattered it. Alex flung his good arm up over his face and turned away as decaying fragments of the shield hit him. Most just slammed into his suit coat and vanished, but one sliced across his cheek, and he felt blood dripping down his face.

Sorsha cried out and Alex turned back in time to see her fall. He couldn't tell if she'd been hit by the bullet or by shards of the decaying shield, but she clamped her hand to her hip. Another shot rang out as she fell, but it missed its target. Alex darted forward and grabbed Sorsha by the arm, pulling her back into the hallway. He stepped over her and pulled his pistol from his pocket, waiting for Davis to approach.

A booming impact followed by a sizzling sound like a broken electrical cable rang out and the castle shook again.

"Get back," Sorsha gasped, her face a mask of pain.

"You hurt bad?" he asked, still covering the end of the hall. Sorsha forced herself into a sitting position, a grunt of pain escaping her lips.

"I'm not hurt good," she gasped, once she was upright.

"Funny," Alex said. "How bad is it?"

"My shield slowed it down some," she said. "Got me in the hip. Doesn't...doesn't seem too bad. Hurts like crazy, though."

"Stay put then," Alex said, moving to the corner. "Where is he?"

"Don't bother," Sorsha said, her breathing shallow. "He's got some kind of magical shield. A charm of some kind, powerful one too."

"That means it won't last long," Alex said.

The ringing gong sound filled the air again and the castle shook.

"What's he doing?" Alex asked.

"Hitting the central levitation spell with a crowbar," Sorsha said. "Mus...must have a spell breaker rune on it."

"Multiple ones," Alex said with a nod. "Each time he hits a spell, the rune is spent. How much longer can your spell hold up?"

"Don't know." Sorsha shook her head.

Alex took off his hat and laid it on the floor, then inched up to the corner with his weapon at the ready.

"What are you going to do, Alex?" she whispered. "Please tell me you have a plan."

Alex nodded but didn't respond. A moment later the crowbar hit the spell again, ringing like crystal. This time the note wasn't a pure ringing tone like it had been before; this time it sounded flat, sour. The moment the blow was struck, Alex leaned around the corner. Davis stood over a large purple incantation in the center of the room. He held a heavy crowbar of some greenish metal in his right hand with runes of fire running down its length. Alex could see the one on the end unraveling as it was discharged. Davis would only be able to use that spell breaker so long as he had runes to charge it, but with at least four charges left, he was likely to succeed in smashing the levitation spell. Already the spell was spinning slowly, like some immensely tiny galaxy, but with a wobble that made it look sickly.

The floor shook, and Davis held on to the next tiered level. Alex braced himself against the wall and brought his pistol up. Davis's gun was tucked into his holster. He caught sight of Alex just as the room stopped shaking and dropped the spell breaker, going for his gun instead.

Alex fired.

The bullet slammed into the magical shield and it glowed bright yellow for a moment, a perfect sphere around the FBI man.

Alex fired again.

This time, when the sphere glowed, Alex could see cracks spreading out from the point of his bullet's impact. Davis's hand closed around his pistol and he jerked it free.

Alex fired.

Davis's shield shattered with enough force to send the spell breaker spinning away from him and the bullet went through and struck him in the right side of his chest. Alex fired again, and the second bullet caught him in the stomach.

Despite being hit twice, Davis fired back. He wasn't in much of a condition to aim and his shots went wide, but they did force Alex back into the cover of the hall.

"How?" Sorsha asked but Alex just grinned and shrugged. "You lying rat," she grunted a moment later. "You told me there wasn't a spell breaker rune on your gun."

"There isn't," Alex said, picking up his hat. "The runes are on the bullets."

He pushed his hat around the corner and Davis put a hole right through it.

"That's pretty good shooting for a man as badly wounded as you are," Alex called. "You know that belly wound has to be treated soon or you'll die."

"Doesn't matter," Davis gasped.

"Your plan's a bust," Alex said. "Miss Kincaid warned the other sorcerers. They'll be waiting for those spies you sent up to them. No one is going to die. There's not going to be a sorcerer war in America."

"Oh, ye of...little...faith," Davis grunted through the pain.

"Don't pull my leg," Alex said. "If you try crawling over to your spell breaker, I'll have plenty of time to lean out and finish you off. Give up now and I'll see you make it to the hospital alive."

"So your sorcerers can strip my mind of all its secrets?" he said. "No, thank you. Besides, you're wrong about my plans being done for. The spell holding this castle up is unraveling. It is drifting east and south right now."

"Empire Tower," Sorsha gasped.

"That's right, Sorceress," Davis said. "This levitation spell should last long enough for us to reach the core, and then...boom."

"Is he right?" Alex looked at Sorsha.

"Imagine if all the stored energy in Empire Tower were released all at once," she said through clenched teeth. "The impact of my house falling on the tower would shatter the spells that contain its power. The sudden release of all those forces at once would be like the Halifax disaster."

"That left a crater over two miles wide," Alex gasped.

"Think of that, scribbler," Davis said, his voice weak. "Everyone in America will blame that...on the sorcerers. There will be a war, just of a different kind, as you drive your magic wielders out."

Alex ducked his head around the corner and pulled back just as another shot rang out.

"All I have to do...is sit here and wait," Davis said. "I may not have...much time left, but this spell has...even less."

Alex looked back at Sorsha. "He's hiding behind the big purple spell," he said. "If I try to shoot him through it, my spell breakers could destroy it."

"Why doesn't he just shoot it?" Sorsha said. "Doesn't he have a spell breaker rune on his gun?"

"He must have used them up," Alex said. "Remember, runes disappear after they're used."

"I still have enough bullets to keep you at bay," Davis said. "My only regret...is that I shall miss the glorious...rise of the Third Reich."

Alex carefully pulled his left arm out of the sling, then struggled out of his suit jacket. He only had a few runes left in his book and one of them was something he hoped he'd never have to try. He'd give a significant amount of his own skin for a flash rune, but he simply didn't have one, or the three hours and piles of equipment it would take to write one. Even if he had one, there was no guarantee that Sorsha could fix the damaged levitation spell in her condition.

"How on earth are you a Nazi spy, Davis?" Alex asked, gently rolling up his left shirt sleeve.

"I was sent here as a spy during the Great War," he said. "By the time I'd established my cover...the war was over. I was ordered to stay...in case the day came that I was needed."

"What are you doing?" Sorsha whispered as Alex exposed the escape rune tattooed into the flesh of his arm.

Alex winked at her. He wasn't sure himself, and he didn't have time for long explanations.

"Must have been quite a coup when you got into the FBI," he said. Davis chuckled.

"You have no idea how happy my superiors in Berlin were."

Alex paged through his book until he found the rune he sought. It had taken him five hours to write it, mostly with silver ink, and it glowed softly in the dim light.

"My real mission was to bring you back to the Fatherland, Sorsha," Davis said. "What a boon your mind would have been...to the Fuhrer."

"I don't think I would have fit into your new Germany," Sorsha said.

Alex found a blank paper and pulled a pencil from his shirt pocket. Most runes required time and exotic materials to write, but there were a few, like the minor restoration rune he'd drawn so Mary could mend her stockings, that could be done with just a pencil and a few moments. He laid the paper on the stone floor, then leaned over and began drawing a joining rune on the bit of flash paper.

"Of course you would fit in," Davis said. "You are the perfect Aryan."

Sorsha's eyebrows dropped into a scowl. "So was Agent Warner," she shot back. "I saw how much that counted for."

"I am sorry about that," Davis said. "But I couldn't have you discovering my plans...until it was too late for you to stop me."

As if on cue, the castle shook and dipped. It reminded Alex of being on the roller coaster at Coney Island. Sorsha cried out in pain as the castle stopped falling suddenly and her wounded hip slammed into the floor.

"It won't...be long now," Davis said, his voice thick with pain. "You've both been exceptional adversaries. Especially you, scribbler. My only regret is that you didn't find the Archimedean Monograph for me. What a triumph...that would have been."

Alex finished the joining rune, then licked it and stuck it to his arm. He lit a cigarette, then licked the silver rune and stuck it on top of the joining rune. Sorsha reached out and grabbed his leg.

"What are you doing?" she demanded. "I won't leave while we still have a chance to save New York."

A sound like glass breaking inside a bell suddenly filled the vault and the floor dropped out from under them.

"I win," Davis shouted as the castle began to fall.

"Like hell you do," Alex shouted back and touched the cigarette to the flash paper on his arm. Light blazed from the tattoo etched into his flesh and the world suddenly appeared transparent. He could see Davis suspended in the air over the failing levitation spell, and Sorsha clutching at his leg as the castle fell away from under her. Alex reached down and pulled her tightly to him, then everything collapsed inward, and he felt as if his body were made of rubber, being forced through a long tube.

A moment later he felt his body re-expand, but the castle was still falling, and he was falling with it.

25

THE LANDING

The castle fell around Alex and Sorsha. He didn't know how long he had until it ran out of sky, but it couldn't be long.

"What have you done?" Sorsha screamed at him, but her words were cut off by another blinding flash of light.

Alex felt his body going shapeless again, then being rolled and folded in on himself while being pushed through another narrow tube. The sensation went on for what seemed like a long time, until finally he felt himself falling again. He landed heavily on a hard surface and felt the air crushed out of his lungs as Sorsha came down on top of him.

He hoped the scream he heard echoing off the walls was hers and not his, but all he could really be sure of were the purple dots swimming in his vision and incredible pain in his left side.

"What...what have...you done?" Sorsha gasped. Her face flickered in and out of his vision; it was contorted with pain and her mascara was running. "We're still in New York...the castle."

"Is at the bottom of the north Atlantic," Alex managed. "Along with Davis." He felt light-headed, and a pleasant numbness was spreading out from his chest, erasing his pain.

"You couldn't have...have moved my castle a thousand miles," Sorsha said with a groan. "Even I couldn't have done that."

"It's not the distance," Alex said, his voice taking on a dreamy lilt. "It's the mass."

"What the devil is going on here?"

It was Iggy's voice. Alex's enhanced escape spell had dropped them right where it was supposed to, in the library at the brownstone.

"Hi Iggy," Alex said. He was starting to feel drunk.

"A German spy tried..." Sorsha groaned and rolled more onto her side to take the pressure off her hip. "Tried to drop my house on Empire Tower. Alex did something...something to his escape rune. Sent my castle to the coast of Greenland, then brought us...ngg...here."

"Good God," Iggy said, his face going whiter than Sorsha's. "You're shot."

"Hip," Sorsha gasped. "What about him?" She pointed at Alex. Iggy's face grew stern and sour.

"He used his own life energy to power the escape rune. Traded years, probably decades of his life for the power to transport your castle." He leaned down and grabbed Sorsha under her arms and knees. "Brace yourself," he said. "This will hurt."

To her credit, she didn't scream when he picked her up, but from where he lay on the floor, Alex could see her biting her lip so hard that it bled.

"Don't worry, Sorceress," Iggy said. "I'll fix you right up. I'm a doctor, remember?"

"What about Alex?" Sorsha gasped.

"If he still has some life energy left, he'll be all right after a good long nap."

"And if he doesn't?"

"Then the damn fool's nap will be of a more permanent nature."

That sounded ominous, but Alex's mind was drifting now. He couldn't seem to make the words and sounds he was hearing make any sense. The room began to recede, as if he were sinking into the floor, until all that was left was a tiny dot of light far, far away.

Then even that was gone.

A KNOCK at his door woke Alex sometime later. The light of midday streamed through his window, and he winked against its brightness. He wanted to bid whoever had knocked to come in but when he opened his mouth, nothing came out.

Swinging his legs off the side, he tried to stand, but slumped to the floor instead. The door opened and Iggy came in, carrying a glass of water.

"Drink," he said, kneeling down beside Alex and pushing the glass into his hand.

Alex had trouble raising the glass to his lips, and it took him a moment to remember how to drink. During that moment, water spilled down his front.

"How long?" he croaked once he'd got the water down. "How long have I been out?"

"Less than a day," Iggy said. "You and your Sorceress girlfriend dropped in on me last night."

Alex ignored the dig. "How is she?"

"No doubt resting comfortably in her suite at the Waldorf."

Alex shivered, remembering Agent Warner's corpse. There was no way Sorsha would go back there.

"Once I got the bullet out, she started regenerating quickly," Iggy said. He offered Alex his hand and pulled the younger man to his feet.

"Regenerating?"

"Oh, yes," Iggy said. "Why do you think sorcerers age so slowly? Their bodies are constantly regenerating."

"It must not work if they're in lot of pain," Alex mused.

"I imagine they have to be in conscious connection with the source of their magic for it to work," Iggy said. "Miss Kincaid's level of trauma kept her from healing herself until I got the bullet out."

Alex filed that particular bit of information away for a rainy day.

"I'm starved," he said. "Is there any food in the house?"

"A bit of chicken from two nights ago," Iggy said. "I'd make you something, but we don't have too much time. The funeral for Father Clementine and the others from the Mission is this afternoon."

"Right," Alex said, and nodded soberly. "Let me take a shower and we'll go down to *The Lunch Box* on the way. I'll introduce you to Mary."

"I've been there since she started working," Iggy said. "Everyone knows her, including me."

"All right," Alex said, moving toward his little bathroom and its even smaller shower. "Give me a few minutes and I'll meet you downstairs."

"How many minutes have you got left?" Iggy said, his voice quiet.

"What do you mean?" Alex asked, stripping off his shirt.

"You know damn well what I mean!" Iggy shouted, making Alex jump. "The only way you could have transported that sorceress' castle was to power the escape rune with your own life force. So how much did you spend? A decade? Two?"

Alex started to smile, to brush the old man's concerns away, but as he met Iggy's gaze, he saw tears in the old man's eyes.

"Iggy," he said, struggling to explain. "I..."

Iggy sat down on the bed, his eyes staring blankly at the wall. "Do you have any idea what you've done?" he asked, his voice almost gentle. Alex crossed to the bed and knelt down to look him in the face.

"You know what would have happened if that castle had landed anywhere near Empire Tower," he pointed out. The old man was far too smart to have any doubts what the result of that catastrophe would be. "If I'd just used my escape rune, I'd have come right back here in time for an explosion more powerful than any in history to turn this house and you and me, Danny, Leslie, Mary, and everyone else into a fine powder."

Iggy nodded his head, but words seemed to fail him. Alex knew he was living that long moment that Alex had faced in Sorsha's vault. A moment that led to one, and only one, inescapable conclusion.

"Remember what you told me when I asked you why anyone would ever use a life rune?"

Iggy nodded. "I'd rather lose some of my life, than all of it," he quoted himself. Alex smiled at him.

"I don't know how much time I've got left," he said. "But then nobody does really. I could get trampled by a crawler tomorrow. At least, if I do, everyone on that crawler will be alive because Sorsha's castle didn't fall on Empire Tower."

Iggy put his hand on Alex's good shoulder.

"I'm sorry," he said. "You should never have had to be the hero."

"Maybe they'll throw me a parade," Alex chuckled.

"The newspapers are claiming that Miss Kincaid moved her castle out to sea for repairs," Iggy said. "Apparently the government is hushing the whole thing up."

"That's okay." Alex chuckled again and regretted it instantly, as pain blossomed in his mending ribs. "I hate parades."

Alex started to rise, but Iggy held on to his shoulder.

"You're right," he said. "None of us know what time is left to us. In the interest of that sentiment, there are some things I want you to know." He paused and blinked, his eyes bright. "I've always thought of you like a son. The son I never had."

"Iggy, you had a son," Alex pointed out, a little embarrassed. "He paid for this house."

"Don't mistake me," he said. "I loved my son. I couldn't be prouder of him if I tried. But he didn't have the gift. I always wanted a son I could share my trade with. Someone I could teach the things I've learned, the secrets I've discovered. When my son died, I was devastated. No father should ever have to outlive his child. After I came here, I didn't know what to do with myself, but then I found you hawking runes on a street corner. It didn't take long for me to know you were worthy to be my heir."

Alex put his hand on Iggy's shoulder.

"Thank you, Ignatius," he murmured. "That means a lot."

"Don't you see?" Iggy said. "I've already lost one son. How can I bear to lose another?"

Alex stood up and pulled the old man to his feet.

"You haven't lost me yet," he said. "So, if my time is short, let's not waste it. Let's go get something to eat and we'll go see Father Harry off. Then, when we get back here, we can talk about the rest."

Iggy hesitated, then he patted Alex's arm and withdrew downstairs.

Watching him go, Alex felt a pang of guilt. He'd done what had to be done, there was no doubt about that. Hundreds of thousands of people would have died if he hadn't used his escape rune. It had cost him a good chunk of his own life, but he didn't regret that. If he hadn't done it, he would have been dead anyway.

What he regretted, standing alone in his room, was that he had hurt Iggy.

Pushing that thought from his mind, Alex headed for the shower. When he caught sight of himself in the bathroom's tiny mirror, he jumped. His hair had turned entirely white, like new-fallen snow. Whiter even than Sorsha's platinum-blonde hair.

"Well," he said tugging at it. "At least it's still there."

That would definitely take some getting used to.

In the shower, Alex examined the place where his escape rune had been tattooed. Only a fading burn mark was left. He'd wait for it to completely disappear before having it redone. That would give him time to design a new one.

TEN MINUTES LATER, Alex arrived downstairs, shaved and dressed. He'd had the presence of mind to hang on to his suit jacket when Sorsha's castle went down, but his hat had been a loss.

"Here," Iggy said, pulling a slightly old-fashioned fedora from the coat wardrobe by the vestibule.

"Thanks," Alex said, putting it on and turning the brim down in front.

They made their way to *The Lunch Box* and then across town to a cemetery next to a little church on the far side of the Core. Only a few dozen people had turned out for the funeral of a clergyman of no great renown. As the Bishop of the Diocese droned on at the gravesite, Alex wondered if this were the kind of funeral Jesus himself received. It made him smile to think that Father Harry would have liked it. He was a simple man who went about doing what good he could, like his Master before him.

Iggy and Leslie, who had joined them at the cemetery, moved off with the other mourners after the service, but Alex lingered at the gravesite. Father Harry had been a literal father to him when no one else cared. He just wanted to stand before the open grave in the quiet of the little cemetery and pull his scattered memories back into the forefront of his mind. As the years turned back in his head, he fixed the images in his memory, so they would live on in Father Harry's stead.

"How are you holding up?" a frail voice brought him out of his reverie. He turned to find Sister Gwen at his side, and he smiled.

"I'm doing all right," he said, hugging her awkwardly, given his arm was still in the sling. "You?"

She nodded with a wistful smile but then frowned, looking up at him.

"What happened to your hair?" she asked.

"Slight disagreement with a spell."

"It suits you." Sister Gwen said with a determined nod.

"Is the Diocese going to reopen the mission?" Alex asked.

"No," Sister Gwen said in a weary voice. "Too much is gone now. Father Clementine was the heart and soul of that place."

"What will you do?" Alex put his arm around the frail nun and hugged her against his side.

"The Bishop is sending me to a convent in Miami," she said. "I'll be teaching new sisters and helping them learn their duties."

"Sounds like he's looking out for you," Alex said with a grin.

Sister Gwen leaned close and whispered. "I asked him for the post," she said. "I'm getting too old for these New York winters." She hugged him again but didn't let go. "Did you find out who killed Father Clementine?" she asked.

"I did," he said, patting her on the back. "He fell to his death trying to hurt a lot more people."

"Good boy," she said fiercely, then let him go and stepped back. "Well, I've got a bus to catch, Alex. Be good, and God bless you."

Alex promised that he would, and the old nun turned and walked away. "I'll miss you, too," he said after her.

He stood there for a long minute, then finally reached down and picked up a handful of dirt, tossing it onto the simple pine coffin at the bottom of the grave.

"You finished?" Leslie said, walking around the grave to stand beside him. "I didn't want to interrupt."

"I'm done," Alex said, taking her arm and strolling off through the gravestones. "Iggy's waiting for you out front," she said. "So how does it feel?"

"I don't even notice," Alex said, running a self-conscious hand through his white hair.

"Not that." Leslie elbowed him gently. "Solving your first big case."

Alex hadn't really thought about it, but he did save the city. All by himself. Of course no one would ever know what he did, since the government was hushing the whole thing up. Then there was Father Harry, and Evelyn. The price he'd paid solving this case was very high, and that had nothing to do with his lost years.

"Not like I thought it would," he admitted.

"Don't let it throw you, boss," she said, squeezing his arm. "I like the hair; it makes you look distinguished."

Alex laughed at that.

"It'll be easier next time," she said. "You'll see."

Alex failed to see how it could be worse.

"Did you get what I asked for?"

She reached into her handbag and pulled out a folded sheet of paper. "It took me most of yesterday and a good part of this morning to find this," she said. "Can't for the life of me figure out why you want it."

"And yet you seem to be in a very good mood," Alex noted, taking the paper and slipping it into his pocket. "I must send you to the dusty parts of the library more often."

"Don't you dare." Her face soured. "Do you have any idea the kinds of deplorable old letches who inhabit the tables by the card catalog? They practically cheered every time I had to bend over to look in a lower drawer."

"Well, all that attention must have done you good."

"That and the thousand dollar check I found waiting for me at the office."

Alex stopped short.

"A grand?" he asked. "Who'd send us that much dough?"

"Your sorceress friend." Leslie nodded off to the far corner of the cemetery where several people stood for another service. Even at this distance, Alex had no trouble recognizing Sorsha's platinum hair. "The note said it was your reward for finding and returning stolen government documents."

Alex started to smile, but the memory of Evelyn's demise wiped it from his face.

"Be sure to thank her," Leslie said, disentangling her arm from his. "I'm on my way to the bank to put it in the account, then I'm taking the rest of the day off."

Alex winked at her and smiled.

"You deserve it, doll," he said. "Peel off a ten spot and have some fun."

Leslie flashed him her most endearing smile and cocked her head.

"You're the boss," she said and turned away.

Alex turned toward the service at the far end of the cemetery. He stood well back and waited for the minister to leave the little group under the shade of an old oak tree before approaching.

"I didn't expect to see you here," Alex said, stepping up beside her.

Sorsha's eyes and nose were red and her makeup had run down her cheeks. She did not look her usual perfect self. She wore a black mourning dress, a hat with a long black feather in it, and supported herself with a polished cane.

"Mr. Lockerby," she said, quickly wiping her eyes with her handkerchief. "You do turn up in the strangest places."

"The funeral for Father Harry just finished," he said.

"The priest who helped raise you," Sorsha said. She'd done her homework apparently.

"I take it this is the service for your man, Hitchens," Alex said, noting that there wasn't any grave dug, just a headstone. Sorsha nodded.

"He was with me since just after I came into my powers," she said. "He was younger then. I knew him a long time. He was a genuinely good man."

"I'm sorry," Alex said.

"All things end, Alex," she said, though she didn't sound like she wanted to believe it.

"Thank you for the check," he said, after a pause.

"You earned it."

"Where are you staying?" He was just making conversation to fill the awkward silence, but she suddenly turned on him, her face full of anger. She slapped him hard across the face and Alex staggered back.

"What was that?" he demanded.

"Don't you dare ask me that," she hissed, limping up to him. "You dumped my home into the Atlantic. My home! Every precious memory I had, every letter, every memento is at the bottom of the ocean."

Alex held up his good hand to ward off any more blows.

"Might I remind you that I didn't drop your house out of the sky," he said. "I just decided where it would land."

"At no small expense to yourself, I hear," she said, her voice seething.

Alex wasn't sure, but he thought for a moment that this might be the real reason she had slapped him.

"I did what needed to be done," he said.

"Yes," she said, her voice cold. "All hail the savior of New York." Her tone implied mockery, but there was no trace of levity in her eyes.

"That's me," Alex said with exaggerated false modesty.

"And yet only you and I and Doctor Bell will ever know that New York City almost died yesterday."

"I didn't do it for the glory," Alex said.

"I know," she said, then she smiled demurely. "You're in it for the money." Then she stepped forward and kissed him. She pressed against him, holding him by the back of the neck. When she finally let go, her cheeks were flushed and she looked a bit sheepish.

"Sorceress," Alex said, a smile creeping onto his face. "I didn't know—"

She put her finger on his lips to silence him.

"Don't read too much into that," she said. "You saved my life, and the life of everyone in the city. I don't know the exact price you paid, but Doctor Bell seems to think you a great fool, so I can only guess it was high. Decades of your life?"

"Something like that," he said.

The look she gave him swept up from his face to his snowy hair and then back down.

"I don't want to see you again, Alex," she said, her cold, officious voice returning. "Sorcerers live for hundreds of years, but I'm still very young as sorcerers go. I haven't had to watch people I care about die." She nodded toward the stone that marked Hitchens' empty grave. "He's the first."

"And you don't want me to be the second?"

"Something like that," she sent his words back at him. "I wish you well, Alex," she said, then limped away on her cane.

Alex watched her go until she reached the street, stepping into a long, sleek floater. He knew what her request not to see him meant, what feelings she was covering up. He knew all too well, which was why he didn't run after her. She deserved someone who could be there for her. She deserved better than he could offer.

"So long, beautiful," he said as the car lifted up into the air and climbed out of sight.

26

THE MONOGRAPH

The sun was setting by the time Alex and Iggy got home. Neither felt much like eating, and Iggy looked tired and worn.

"Make up a fire," he said. "Then I think we should talk."

"Sounds good," Alex said. He reached for the coal bucket and poured some on the grate.

While Alex worked, Iggy went upstairs. Alex knew from experience that the doc would get out of his suit coat and into his smoking jacket. He lit the fire, then selected a book from the shelf, and sat down in the chair nearest the wall.

It only took Iggy a few minutes to return.

"How about some..." he began, but his face went white when he saw Alex. "No!" he gasped. "You must not read that!"

His voice sounded desperate, like a man facing death while clinging to the last vestiges of life.

Alex sat in the soft, wing-back chair with his legs crossed. A thin book bound in red leather lay open on his lap, illuminated by the light of the table lamp. He had taken it from the space next to the hollowed-out book where he kept his money.

Hiding in plain sight.

"It's a little late for that, Iggy," Alex said, turning a page. "I read this book last week."

"Alex," Iggy told him. "You're not ready."

"For the truth?" Alex said. He reached into his pocket and pulled out the paper Leslie had given him. The culmination of a mission he'd sent her on when he first found the red book. "You know," he said, unfolding it, "I bet you could ask everyone in New York who wrote the Sherlock Holmes books and they'd say Arthur Conan Doyle. Every one of them."

"Alex," Iggy said, imploring him not to go on.

"I bet not a single one of them knows that his real name is Arthur Conan Ignatius Doyle, and that he faked his own death four years ago and came to America."

Iggy sat down in the other chair and just stared at the fire.

"How did you figure it out?" he asked.

"You trained me to be a detective, Iggy. Or should I call you Arthur?"

"Iggy is fine," he said. "You decrypted the finding rune." It wasn't a question, just a simple statement of fact.

"Last Saturday while you were making those disguise runes," Alex said. "You can imagine how surprised I was to discover that the infamous Archimedean Monograph, the book so many people died trying to find, was sitting on our bookshelf right next to my book safe."

Iggy nodded, shaking his head. "Once you knew I had the Monograph, you would have guessed that my name was an alias. Did you search the records of this house's ownership?"

Alex nodded. "You bought the home in your son's name, Kingsley Doyle. It took Leslie a long time, but she finally traced the name to a doctor in the British army. He was killed in the big war. The New York Times printed a story about it because of his famous father. The man who invented Sherlock Holmes."

"You did do the thing properly, didn't you?" Iggy chuckled darkly.

"I also know that Bell is the last name of your favorite professor from medical school, a man you once said was the inspiration for Holmes."

"I was going to tell you," he said. Iggy hung his head and cradled it in his hands.

"When?"

"When I absolutely had to and not a moment before," he said, standing up and pacing to the fire. "You don't know what you've done by reading the Monograph." He paused, looking into the fire. "I wanted to spare you that. For as long as I could, anyway."

Alex closed the book and set it aside on the table. "I get it," he said, standing and moving to the fire. "There are some very dangerous runes in there. Things I don't want to even think about. But you should have trusted me."

Iggy put his hand on Alex's shoulder.

"I do trust you, lad. But you don't understand. Evelyn Rockwell isn't the only person searching for that infernal book. There are others, many others. Most of them are incompetent dreamers, but some are talented — and dangerous. That's why I had to leave my family. That's why I faked my death and came here."

Alex nodded, suddenly understanding. "The story you wrote," he said. "About the *Mary Celeste*."

"I wrote a fictional account of that ship, leaving out the finding rune in the captain's cabin and the shadows on the wall," Iggy said. "I wanted to point people in the wrong direction, erase any connection with the Monograph."

"I take it that didn't work," Alex said. "What happened? Someone find out about your trip to Gibraltar?"

"Probably." Iggy shrugged. "It doesn't really matter. People began writing me, asking me thinly veiled questions about the runes in the Monograph. I never answered any, of course, but that only made them bolder. One night, a few years ago, I received a letter from a friend, begging me to come see him at his home. Luckily, I knew he had gone to the seaside for the winter. I contacted the police, and they caught five runewrights who were lying in wait for me. That was when I knew I had to disappear."

"I don't get it," Alex said. "Why were they so convinced that you had the Monograph?"

"As you've seen, my lore book is full of unique and powerful runes,"

Iggy said. "I developed most of them using concepts from the Monograph." He sighed and looked into the fire. "But mostly it's because of those runes Sorsha was looking for. Your government stole them from mine, but how do you think the Royal Army got them?"

"You gave them to the British? Why?"

"It was after my son died," he said, his voice distant. "I wanted to do whatever I could to end the war. I thought the government runewrights could use those five to help. They already had the finding rune. It didn't matter, though. I was wrong. As soon as they knew the Archimedean Monograph had been found, they wanted the rest. Luckily for me, I had taken the precaution of sending the runes to them anonymously."

"What happened?"

"The military put out bulletins seeking runewrights of exceptional ability. They searched my home, and the homes of others, seeking the Monograph. When the war ended, they officially gave up, but the runewrights on the army payroll had seen enough of what the Monograph had to offer that they couldn't let it go. They formed a secret society to search for it."

"And you already had a target on your back."

"And now, so do you," Iggy said. "Don't you see? Anyone who knows about the Monograph is a target. That's what I wanted to spare you from. Just imagine what would happen if your friend Daniel suspected that you have the book? What if he were to mention those suspicions to his father in casual conversation?"

Alex developed a sudden chill. Danny wouldn't care that Iggy had the Monograph, but his father wouldn't be able to resist it. He'd try to bust down the door to the brownstone and take it.

"And what about Sorsha?" Iggy continued. "Why she'd..." Iggy stopped, a startled expression on his face. He slowly turned to Alex. "You said she used a truth spell on you at Thomas Rockwell's workshop," he said. "That was last night. After you discovered the book. Does she know?"

Alex laughed and shook his head. "You know she doesn't," he said. "You were just about to say what she'd do if she knew the book was here, and you'd have been right."

"Then how...?"

"Truth spells aren't illegal because they work," Alex said. "They're illegal because they're unreliable. Remember the Lindberg case? By the time they got the truth out of the accomplice, the baby was already dead. All you have to do to beat a truth spell is have a better truth to tell."

"I...don't understand," Iggy said. He still had a look of alarm on his face.

"Sorsha asked me if I could finish unraveling the rune Evelyn used," Alex said, ticking it off on his finger. "I designed that rune so that it can't be unraveled, not without going back to the original and starting over. I did that in case it fell into the wrong hands."

"So when you said you couldn't, you were telling the truth," Iggy said. "Just not the whole truth."

"Truth spells compel you to answer," Alex said. "They don't force you to elaborate. Next," he said, ticking off another finger. "Sorsha asked me if I had found the Monograph."

"But you *had* found it."

Alex shook his head with a grin. "No, I just discovered it sitting on our bookshelf. *You* found it. You can only find things that are lost, and a book on a shelf in plain sight isn't lost."

Iggy looked incredulous.

"Isn't that just your interpretation?"

"Of course," Alex said. "But the spell was cast on me; its effect is limited to what I believe."

"Was that it?"

"No, she asked me if I would ever search for the Monograph in the future. I could honestly tell her that I had no intention whatsoever of looking for the Monograph."

Iggy chuckled, but then his face became serious again. "You got lucky," he said. "If she'd asked better questions, I'd have had to disappear again. That's why you need to forget what you've read in that book. If you start adding new and powerful runes to your repertoire, she's going to figure it out. She isn't stupid, you know."

Alex shrugged. Iggy was right, of course. The Monograph was filled with amazing and powerful concepts, but he'd have to keep those out of his professional life.

Well, most of them.

Alex closed the Monograph and held it up.

"There are some very interesting things in here," he said. "I'd love to hear your thoughts on them."

Iggy laughed.

"There are notes in there from DaVinci and Ben Franklin," he said. "I doubt I could add very much."

"Not the way I see it," Alex said. "You took these runes and made them part of your lore book. You had to make them powerful, but not so powerful or complex that people would wonder about their origin. I think you still have a lot to teach me."

"But for how long?" Iggy whispered.

"Does that matter?" Alex said. "I did what you would have done in my shoes, what Sorsha would have done if she could have. Are you going to let that ruin our friendship?"

Iggy straightened up and took a deep breath. "No," he declared at last. "But I'm still angry about the book."

"I'm sorry," Alex said. He didn't know what else to say. He should have realized that Iggy would have a good reason for keeping those things from him. He should have trusted the man.

"I'm sorry too," Iggy said, leaning heavily on the mantle. "The Monograph is a burden I would have spared you, but I am glad that you know the truth."

"What now?" Alex asked after a long moment passed.

Iggy pushed away from the mantle and slipped the Archimedean Monograph back into its place on the bookshelf.

"Now, we carry on as if nothing has changed," he said. "It's our responsibility to keep the book out of the wrong hands."

"But we study it," Alex said. "There's a lot in there I want to know."

"Agreed," Iggy said. "But I decide what we study. You're not ready for all of it yet."

"Agreed," Alex said.

Iggy stuck out his hand and Alex shook it.

"I'm as hungry as a wolf," he said, clearly feeling better than he had in days. "Let's go get something to eat."

Alex put the screen in front of the fire while Iggy changed back into his suit jacket. He didn't feel any different, but he knew the ground had changed under his feet. The hat Iggy had loaned him hung on a peg in the hallway, and he slipped it on over his white hair before stepping outside onto the stoop. In the distance, Empire Tower reached up to the sky, glowing with the energy it contained. Occasionally a bolt of lightning would reach down from above and strike the spire on top.

"Ready?" Iggy asked, stepping out beside him.

Alex nodded, turning the brim down on the hat before following the old man to the sidewalk.

"After dinner we'll look at the Monog—"

"We should probably call it the Textbook when we're out in public," Alex said.

"Good point. Well, when we get back, there are a few interesting things I want to show you in the Textbook."

Iggy's old enthusiasm seemed to be back, and Alex grinned as they made their way to *The Lunch Box*. He didn't know how much of his life he had left, but he had a feeling none of it would be boring.

THE END

A Quick Note

You made it. You got all the way to the end, thanks so much for reading my book. Since you're so awesome, I've got a small request for you — and a free gift. So if you would be so kind, take a moment and head over to Amazon and leave me a quick review. I'd really appreciate it. It doesn't have to be anything fancy, just a quick note saying whether or not you liked the book. As an independent author, it really helps me out.

THANKS SO MUCH.

AS I MENTIONED ABOVE, I've also got a free gift for you, just for being such an awesome reader. You can get the novella *Dead Letter*, the Prequel to this book by going to: www.danwillisauthor.com. It's the story of the case where Alex and Danny met, along with a few other surprises. And, because you're awesome, it's absolutely free. A special thanks for reading *In Plain Sight*.

SO TAKE two minutes and leave me a review, then zip over to danwillisauthor.com and grab your free e-book copy of *Dead Letter*.

ALSO, I love talking to my readers, so please email me at dan@danwillisauthor.com — I read every one. Or join the discussion on the Arcane Casebook Facebook Group.

LOOK FOR *GHOST OF A CHANCE*, the next book in the Arcane Casebook series.

ALSO BY DAN WILLIS

Arcane Casebook Series:

Dead Letter - Prequel

Private Detective Alex Lockerby needs a break and it materializes in the form of an ambitious, up-and-coming beat cop, Danny Pack. Alex and Danny team up to unravel a tale murder, jealousy, and revenge stretching back over 30 years. It's a tale that powerful forces don't want to come to light. Now the cop and the private detective must work fast and watch each other's backs if they hope to catch a killer and live to tell about it.

Dead Letter is the prequel novella to the Arcane Casebook series.

Get Dead Letter Free at www.danwillisauthor.com

Ghost of a Chance - Book 2

When a bizarre string of locked-room murders terrorize New York, the police have no leads, no suspects, and only one place to turn. Now private detective Alex Lockerby will need every magical trick in his book to catch a killer who can walk through walls and leaves no trace. With the Ghost killer seemingly able to murder at will and the tabloids, the public, and Alex's clients demanding results, Alex will need a miracle to keep himself, his clients, and his reputation alive.

Available at Amzazon.com

Dragons of the Confederacy Series:

A steampunk Civil War story with NYT Bestseller, Tracy Hickman

Lincoln's Wizard

Washington has fallen! Legions of 'grays' -- dead soldiers reanimated on the battlefield and pressed back into service of the Southern Cause -- have pushed the lines as far north as the Ohio River. Lincoln has moved the government of the United States to New York City. He needs to stop the juggernaught of the Southern undead 'abominations' or the North will ultimately fall. But Allan Pinkerton, his head of security, has a plan...

Available at Amzazon.com

The Georgia Alchemist

With Air Marshall Sherman's fleet on the run and the Union lines failing, Pinkerton's agents, Hattie Lawton and Braxton Wright make their way into the heart of the south. Pursued by the Confederacy's best agents, time is running out for Hattie and Braxton to locate the man whose twisted genius brings dead soldiers back to fight and find a way to stop the inexorable tide that threatens to engulf the Union.

Forthcoming: 2020

Other books:

The Flux Engine

In a Steampunk Wild West, fifteen-year-old John Porter wants nothing more than to find his missing family. Unfortunately a legendary lawman, a talented thief, and a homicidal madman have other plans, and now John will need his wits, his pistol, and a lot of luck if he's going to survive.

Available at Amzazon.com

ABOUT THE AUTHOR

Dan Willis wrote for the long-running DragonLance series. He is the author of the Arcane Casebook series and the Dragons of the Confederacy series.

For more information:
www.danwillisauthor.com
dan@danwillisauthor.com

facebook.com/danwillisauthor
twitter.com/WDanWillis

PRAISE FOR DAN WILLIS

"Dan Willis is an awesome writer and you should buy this book!"

— Larry Correia, NYT Bestselling Author

Printed in Great Britain
by Amazon

62328031R00163

A NEW ARABIC GRAMMAR

A NEW
ARABIC GRAMMAR
OF THE
WRITTEN LANGUAGE

By J. A. HAYWOOD and
H. M. NAHMAD

LUND HUMPHRIES

Published by
Lund Humphries
Office 3, Book House
261A City Road
London
EC1V 1JX

First Edition 1962
Second Edition 1965
Reprinted 1970, 1976, 1982, 1984
Rreprinted in large-format paperback 1990, 1993, 1995, 1998, 2001, 2003, 2005
Reprinted in Thailand 2009
Reprinted in Singapore 2014
Reprinted in the United Kingdom 2019

ISBN 978 0 85331 585 8

TABLE OF CONTENTS

PREFACE TO SECOND EDITION

The authors are taking advantage of a second edition to incorporate certain amendments, improvements and additions. Care has been taken, however, to include them in such a way that first and second editions can be used side by side. For this reason the more important additions have been printed as a separate Appendix C. It should be stressed that the exercises for translation, which form such an important part of the grammar, are unchanged, except for the correction of a few errors which inevitably crept into the text.

In the Preface to the first edition the authors pointed out that in a major undertaking of this kind they would be more than human if no errors crept in, and they invited suggestions for any future reprints. The authors would like to thank all those who have suggested amendments whether in correspondence, conversation or in learned reviews.

Whilst, as was stressed when the first edition was published, this grammar is intended as a teaching grammar and not as a reference grammar or a 'teach-yourself' work, a key* has been prepared and published separately for the benefit of those students who are using the grammar to learn Arabic without a teacher. This key is suitable for use with either edition of the grammar. The treatment of certain grammatical points in an order which could not be justified logically in a reference grammar is intended to facilitate the use of the grammar in association with courses under qualified teachers of Arabic.

The authors again have to thank the publishers for their co-operation and understanding. It is sad to have to mention the passing of Dr B. Schindler, a distinguished scholar and a fine man, who did so much to shepherd the first edition through the press.

The authors hope that in its modified form this grammar will prove a boon to many students and that it will contribute to the main cause they have in mind, the stimulation of an understanding of and love for Arabic culture.

* J. A. Haywood and H. M. Nahmad, *Key to a New Arabic Grammar of the Written Language*, Lund Humphries, 1964.

PREFACE TO THE FIRST EDITION

The Arabic language has increased in importance since the Second World War. With the attaining of independence by the Arab countries, and the growing importance of the Near East in international affairs, there is a pressing need in the West for people familiar with the language. At the same time, newly-independent countries in Asia and Africa are turning increasingly to the language of their faith – sometimes by way of European text-books.

There is a widespread demand for a new Arabic grammar, even though some praiseworthy efforts have been made recently in both Britain and America. During the last fifty years it is probable that more people have learned Arabic through the Rev. G. W. Thatcher's Grammar than through any other comparable work; but times change, and that work now requires radical revision. The present book, then, is intended to replace Thatcher. It retains all that is still valid in the old work, but recasts the rest to suit modern requirements and the background of the average modern student. In writing it the authors have kept a number of factors in mind.

For instance, the modern student does not have that grasp of grammatical concepts which his parents and grandparents had. This is due partly to the decline of Latin and Greek studies, partly to new methods in modern language teaching. Therefore an attempt has been made to explain grammatical rules in clear and simple language.

There is an increasing demand for modern literary Arabic; but on the other hand there are still many who wish to study classical Arabic, whether to enjoy the literature or to gain a deeper insight into Islamic institutions and history. The authors of this grammar believe that it is possible for one and the same grammar to serve both types of student. They have therefore used both classical and modern Arabic in the illustrative examples, vocabularies, and exercises; at the same time they have tried to indicate which constructions and idioms are obsolete or obsolescent, and which are still widely used. The beginner usually takes some time to master the Arabic script; therefore in the first thirteen chapters all Arabic words have been transliterated according to a simple recognized system.

One of the hardest tasks for the student is to acquire a useful vocabulary speedily. To facilitate this a basic vocabulary of about 4,000 words has been specially selected by the authors from both classical and modern sources. Where rare words are used this is either to illustrate grammatical points, or in actual extracts from literature. Each chapter has its own vocabulary, and there is a consolidated vocabulary at the end of the book. Sentences used to illustrate grammatical points, or in the exercises for translation, have been prepared on the basis of their usefulness in teaching, not for literary merit. On the other hand, there is a substantial Supplement of extracts from literature, both classical and modern, and a few literary extracts have also been used as translation exercises in some of the later chapters.

The beginner does not require a reference grammar which deals exhaustively with each grammatical subject in turn; in fact, to state all the rules at once often confuses and discourages him. Consequently, although within the pages of this book reference is made to all but the very rarest usages, the order in which they occur is often dictated rather by the learner's convenience than by strict logic. Moreover, the space devoted to individual grammatical points varies according to the needs of the average student as observed by the authors in their own teaching. It is hoped that the translation exercises which follow the chapters will be sufficiently comprehensive to meet the needs of both teacher and student.

The compilation of a grammar of this scope is a major undertaking, and the authors would be more than human if no errors crept in; again, there will always be differences of opinion as to the best means of dealing with various points. The authors ask the reader's indulgence for any shortcomings, and would indeed welcome suggestions for any future reprinting.

They are grateful for help received. The publishers deserve thanks and above all Dr B. Schindler, at the request of whom the work was undertaken and who has given us specially valuable advice throughout.

The authors would also like to thank Dr S. M. Saddiq for his assistance in proof reading. Finally Mrs H. M. Nahmad has given invaluable help in preparing the typescript for the printers.

ABBREVIATIONS

a.o. = any one
abbr. = abbreviated
acc(us). = accusative
act. = active
adj. = adjective
adv. = adverb
antiq. = antique, antiquated usage
art. = article

class. = classical
coll. = collective
colloq. = colloquial
comm. = commerce, commercial
conj. = conjunction

d. = dual
dim. = diminutive
dipl. = diplomatic
dip. = diptote

Eg. = Egypt(ian)
elat. = elative
Eur. = Europe(an)

f., fem. = feminine
fig. = figure, figurative
Fr. = French

gen. = genitive
geog. = geographical
gram. = grammar, grammatical

indic. = indicative
imper. = imperative
imperf. = imperfect
intr(ans). = intransitive

juss. = jussive

Leb. = Lebanese
lit. = literal(ly)

m., masc. = masculine
Magh. = Maghribi usage
math. = mathematical
mil. = military
mod. = modern

n. = noun, name
neg. = negative
nom. = nominative

opp. = opposite

part. = participle
partic. = particle
pass. = passive
pl. = plural
pl. pl. = plural of plural
poet. = poetry, poetical
pol. = political
pr. n. = proper noun, name
prep. = preposition
pron. = pronoun

quad. = quadriliteral

relig. = religious

s., sing. = singular
subj. = subjunctive
Syr. = Syria(n)

tr(ans). = transitive
trip. = triptote
Turk. = Turkish

un. = unitary (single)

v. = verb
v.n. = verbal noun
veg. = vegetable
voc. = vocative

CHAPTER ONE

(اَلْبَابُ ٱلْأَوَّلُ Al-bābu l-'awwalu)

The Arabic Language. Orthography. Phonetics. Punctuation

§ 1

THE ARABIC LANGUAGE

Arabic belongs to the Semitic group of languages. Other living languages of this group are Modern Hebrew (as spoken and written in Israel), Amharic, and other spoken languages of Ethiopia, Aramaic dialects current in parts of Syria and Iraq, and Maltese. Among dead languages of this group the most important is Biblical Hebrew; others include Akkadian (Babylonian and Assyrian), Syriac, and Ethiopian.

The characteristic feature of Semitic languages is their basis of consonantal roots, mostly triliteral (three-lettered). Variations in shade of meaning are obtained, first by varying the vowelling of the simple root, and secondly by the addition of prefixes, suffixes, and in-fixes. Thus, from the root *salima*, to be safe (literally, he was safe) we derive *sallama*, to deliver; *aslama*, to submit (also, to turn Muslim); *istalama*, to receive; *istaslama*, to surrender; *salāmun*, peace; *salāmatun*, safety, well-being; and *muslimun*, a Muslim. Word forms derived from the triliteral roots, and retaining the three basic consonants, are associated with meaning patterns. This is a help in the acquisition of vocabulary and partly compensates for difficulties arising from the lack of correlation between Arabic words and European roots.

Arabic is usually classified as (a) Classical Arabic, (b) Modern Literary Arabic, and (c) Modern Spoken or Colloquial Arabic.* Classical Arabic dates from the 6th century

* For further details of (c) see Appendix A.

A.D., if not earlier. It is the language of the Qur'ān and of the great writers and poets such as al-Mutanabbi and Ibn Khaldūn, and others. The modern literary language is exemplified by writers like Ṭāhā Ḥusain and Taufīq al-Ḥakīm, and newspapers and the radio. It varies in idiom and vocabulary from the Classical, but the differences are infinitesimal compared with the changes in the European languages over the same period – e.g. the difference between Chaucer's English and Kipling's. This is because Classical Arabic was hallowed as the vehicle of God's Revelation in the Qur'ān, and was therefore not permitted to change to any marked extent. Consequently, though some usages have become obsolete, the grammar of 6th century Arabic still applies largely to modern written Arabic. This makes it possible to compile a grammar which is suitable as a basis for further study of all written Arabic, whether Classical or Modern. The present grammar has been written with this aim in view.

§ 2

THE ALPHABET

Arabic is written from right to left. The script, which has been adopted and adapted for many languages spoken by Muslim nations, is cursive, and there is no separate printed form of the letters as there is in European languages. Two methods of writing are common: the naskh نَسْخٌ or naskhī نَسْخِيٌّ, normally used in print, and the ruqʿa رُقْعَةٌ.* The beginner is advised to use the naskh as exemplified in this book.

The alphabet (هِجاءٌ hijā') consists of 28 letters (حَرْفٌ ḥarf, pl. حُرُوفٌ ḥurūf) (29 if hamza is counted as a separate letter), which are all consonants; three of them, however, 'alif, wāw, and yā', are also used as long vowels or diphthongs. The following table shows the various forms of the letters. While

* See Mitchell, *Writing Arabic*, Oxford University Press, 1953.

this indicates variant forms according to whether the letter is isolated, initial, medial, or final, it should be noted that in practically every case the letter has a simple basic form. When final, or isolated, however, many letters have a final flourish or hook added to the basic form.

THE ARABIC ALPHABET

Names of the letters	Isolated form	Form when joined to: Preceding letter	Form when joined to: Preceding and Succeeding letters	Form when joined to: Succeeding letter only	Transcription
ألف ʾalif	ا	ـا	—	—	ā
باء bāʾ	ب	ـب	ـبـ	بـ	b
تاء tāʾ	ت	ـت	ـتـ	تـ	t
ثاء thāʾ	ث	ـث	ـثـ	ثـ	th
جيم jīm	ج	ـج	ـجـ	جـ	j
حاء ḥāʾ	ح	ـح	ـحـ	حـ	ḥ
خاء khāʾ	خ	ـخ	ـخـ	خـ	kh
دال dāl	د	ـد	—	—	d
ذال dhāl	ذ	ـذ	—	—	dh
راء rāʾ	ر	ـر	—	—	r
زاي zāy	ز	ـز	—	—	z
سين sīn	س	ـس	ـسـ	سـ	s
شين shīn	ش	ـش	ـشـ	شـ	sh

Names of the letters	Isolated form	Form when joined to: Preceding letter	Preceding and Succeeding letters	Succeeding letter only	Transcription
صَادٌ ṣād	ص	ـص	ـصـ	صـ	ṣ
ضَادٌ ḍād	ض	ـض	ـضـ	ضـ	ḍ
طَاءٌ ṭā'	ط	ـط	ـطـ	طـ	ṭ
ظَاءٌ ẓā'	ظ	ـظ	ـظـ	ظـ	ẓ
عَيْنٌ ع ain	ع	ـع	ـعـ	عـ	ع,ʿ
غَيْنٌ ghain	غ	ـغ	ـغـ	غـ	gh
فَاءٌ fā'	ف	ـف	ـفـ	فـ	f
قَافٌ qāf	ق	ـق	ـقـ	قـ	q
كَافٌ kāf	ك	ـك	ـكـ ـكـ	كـ كـ	k
لَامٌ lām	ل	ـل	ـلـ	لـ	l
مِيمٌ mīm	م	ـم	ـمـ ـمـ	مـ	m
نُونٌ nūn	ن	ـن	ـنـ	نـ	n
هَاءٌ hā'	ه	ـه	ـهـ ـهـ	هـ	h
وَاوٌ wāw	و	ـو	—	—	w (ū, aw, au)
يَاءٌ yā'	ى	ـى	ـيـ	يـ	y (ī, ay, ai)
هَمْزَةٌ hamza	ء	ـأ	ـئـ	ئـ	'
	أَ إِ أُ	ـؤ			

NOTE 1. Care should be taken to distinguish letters which are similar to each other in form. Note especially the following groups of letters which only differ in the diacritical points or dots:

ـبـ ـتـ ـثـ ـنـ ـيـ bā', tā', thā' (and, except when final, nūn and yā')

جـ حـ خـ jīm, ḥā', khā'.

د ذ dāl, dhāl.

ر ز rā', zāy. This pair differ from the preceding pair in (a) having an obtuse angle, and (b) being written mostly below the line. They resemble the wāw in general curve.

ـسـ ـشـ sīn and shīn.

ـصـ ـضـ ṣād and ḍād. (Note that, when initial or medial, a small but distinct inverted "v" follows the loop before the next letter is begun.)

ط ظ ṭā', ẓā'.

ع غ ـعـ ʿain, ghain. Note the flattening in the medial position, ـعـ ـغـ which distinguishes these two letters from the two following ones.

ف ق fā', qāf. See preceding note. Note also that, when final, the qāf has a deep loop going well below the line, while the loop of the fā' is flat.

NOTE 2. When the letter tā' is used as a feminine ending, it is written as a hā', with, however, the two dots of the tā' over it thus: ـة (ة). It is termed tā' marbūṭa تَاءٌ مَرْبُوطَةٌ. This tā' is not pronounced in modern Arabic except when followed by a word beginning with a vowel. In Classical Arabic it was not pronounced "in pause", that is, at the end of a sentence, and became merely the short vowel "a". Consequently, in this book, we speak about "hamza", not "hamzat" or "hamzah".

NOTE 3. In the Maghrib (North-west Africa), fā' is written ڢ and qāf ڧ.

NOTE 4. Sounds not found in Arabic are represented in other languages which have adopted that script, by modifications of the letters – usually by the addition of diacritical points. Such letters may occasionally be met with in Arabic in the transliteration of foreign words. The most common are the following Persian letters: p پ: ch چ: hard g گ. In Egypt and Syria ڤ is sometimes used for v.

NOTE 5. It will be noted that in the table of the alphabet given above the following six letters are shown as capable of being joined to a preceding letter only ا د ذ ر ز و. Under no circumstances can they be joined to a succeeding letter. Sometimes two or more of these letters succeed one another in the same word, as دَارٌ dār, house: in which case all the letters concerned are detached from each other.

NOTE 6. Among the combinations of letters used in Arabic writing are the following (usually referred to as ligatures):

بحـ bā'-ḥā'	حجج ḥā'-jīm-jīm	لحـ lām-ḥā'
بي bā'-yā'	سحـ sīn-ḥā'	لمـ lam-mīm
تحـ tā'-ḥā'	صحـ ṣād-ḥā'	لمحـ lām-mīm-ḥā'
جحـ jīm-ḥā'	عجـ ع ain-jīm	محـ mīm-ḥā'
حجـ ḥā'-jīm	فحـ fā'-ḥā'	حمـ ḥā'-mīm
ني nūn-yā'	في fā'-yā'	يحـ yā'-ḥā'
هم hā'-mīm	يم yā'-mīm	عمـ ع ain-mīm

لا lām-'alif (joined to preceding letter ـلا)

§ 3

PRONUNCIATION OF THE CONSONANTS*

Those wishing to make a detailed study of the phonetics of Arabic, whether Classical or Colloquial, should consult the works mentioned in the bibliography given in Appendix A. The following notes give only practical approximations, to serve the needs of students beginning the study of the written language.

The following letters are pronounced more or less like their English equivalents:

ب bā'=b. ت tā'=t. ج jīm=j (or the *soft g* as in "*gem*"). د dāl=d. ر rā'=r. ز zāy=z. س sīn=s, as in "*sin*". ش shīn= sh as in "*shot*". ف fā'=f. ك kāf=k. ل lām=l. م mīm=m. ن nūn=n. ه hā'=h. *Consonantal* و wāw=w. *Consonantal* ي yā'=y.

Care should be taken to distinguish ث thā', which is the *th* as in "*think*" and

ذ dhāl, which is the *th* as in "*this*".

The hamza, the glottal stop, or spiritus lenis (light breathing) of Greek, may be described in practical terms as the act of breathing which is necessary in English to begin a word with a vowel at the opening of a sentence: as, for example, when one says "*Is* that so?" in reply to a statement. The word "is" would be transliterated into Arabic with an initial

* For more notes on the phonology of Classical Arabic, in amplification of this and the following sections, see Appendix C, §1.

hamza thus إِزْ. In the middle of a word it involves a short pause, such as is occasionally heard in English in words like "co-opt". This pause is often changed to a w in English speech (cowopt), and similar changes take place to the hamza in colloquial Arabic. The hamza is, in fact, rather like a very weak ع ain: hence its shape, which is the top portion of the ع ain in miniature.

For the various ways of writing hamza, see below.

ح ḥā' is a strongly guttural *h* produced by a strong expulsion of air from the chest. It should not be confused with:

خ khā', which is the guttural *ch* as in the Scottish "*loch*" and the German "*Aachen*".

ص ṣād, ض ḍād, ط ṭā', and ظ ẓā', form a group of emphatic sounds corresponding with س s, د d, ت t, and ز z. In pronouncing them, the tongue is pressed against the edge of the upper teeth, and then withdrawn forcefully.

ع ع ain is a very strong guttural produced by compression of the throat and expulsion of breath. This and the four emphatic letters just given are rarely well-pronounced by non-Arabs, and they are best learned from an Arab.

غ ghain is the sound made in gargling, or like the French "r" *grasséyé* with a little more of the *g* in it.

ق qāf is a *k* sound produced from the back of the throat. In modern Arabic in some areas, it is often pronounced as the hard *g* in "*go*", and this was a recognised alternative pronunciation as far back as the 9th century. In the colloquial of Lower Egypt (Cairo Arabic) and certain parts of the Levant, it can be heard as a hamza; but this is inadmissible in correct reading aloud.

§ 4

VOWELS

أَشْكَالٌ 'ashkāl, *pl.* of شَكْلٌ shakl.

There are 6 vowels, 3 short, 3 long; and two diphthongs in Arabic: namely, u, a, i; ū, ā, ī; au (aw) and ai (ay).

While the letters و wāw, ا 'alif, and ى yā' have to do duty as long vowels, short vowels are indicated by signs above or below the consonants carrying them. Unfortunately in most modern written and printed Arabic no vowel signs are given, and the reader has to deduce them.

Short vowels.

a, fatḥa فَتْحَةٌ, is indicated by a small diagonal stroke above the consonant, as دَ da. This vowel is the neutral *a* sound as in "Frenchm*a*n", or like the *u* in "n*u*n". On no account should it be pronounced as the *a* in "m*a*n".

i kasra كَسْرَةٌ, is a similar stroke under the letter, as دِ di. Its approximate sound is the *i* in "d*i*d".

u, ḍamma ضَمَّةٌ, is written like a miniature wāw above the letter, as دُ du. This is pronounced like the *u* in "b*u*ll", not like that in "bun".

The absence of a vowel is indicated by a small circle over the letter, thus ـْ, and is termed sukūn سُكُونٌ, or jazma جَزْمَةٌ, e.g. كُنْ kun. It cannot follow the long vowels, except, rarely, in certain forms from the *doubled verb*, as will be explained later.

The three short vowel signs given above do not really represent all the sounds heard. For example, after the emphatic letters ص, ض, ط, ظ the fatḥa appears to take on something of the *o* sound. For example, ضَرَبَ ḍaraba, he struck, seems to sound like d*o*raba. After the guttural letters, the fatḥa seems to lose its neutrality and have more of the English *a* sound about it, e.g. عَرَبٌ ءarab, Arabs. Again, the fatḥa seems to partake of the nature of the letter *e* when associated with the lām. For example, مَلِكٌ malik (king) sounds like m*e*lik: k كَلْبٌ kalb (dog) sounds like k*e*lb; قَلْبٌ qalb (heart) sounds like q*e*lb.

To lengthen these three short vowels, they are followed by the letters 'alif, yā' and wāw, as in مَالٌ māl, wealth, فِيلٌ fīl, elephant, and حُدُودٌ ḥudūd, frontiers.

There are two diphthongs, ai (ay) as in بَيْتٌ bait (approximately the *i* in s*i*te), house, and au (aw) as in يَوْمٌ yaum (*ow* in h*ow*), day. The previous consonant has fatḥa, and the yā' and wāw must have sukūn. In Classical Arabic, the two component parts of these diphthongs are not thoroughly coalesced. But in modern spoken Arabic this coalescence takes place, and بَيْتٌ and يَوْمٌ may sound like "bēt" and "yōm" (as in *main* and *home* as pronounced in the north of England).

Sometimes a long ā or 'alif at the end of a word, called أَلِفٌ مَقْصُورَةٌ 'alif maqṣūra or shortened 'alif, is written as a yā', as عَلَى ʿalā on, and إِلَى 'ilā to.

§ 5

NUNATION

At the ends of nouns and adjectives, when indefinite, the vowel signs are written double, thus: ـٌ اً ـٍ. This means that they are to be pronounced with a final "n", un, an, in. This is called تَنْوِينٌ tanwīn or nunation, e.g. بَابٌ بَابًا بَابٍ bābun, bāban, bābin, a door. Note that with the fatḥa, the letter 'alif is added. But if the word ends in tā' marbūṭa, the 'alif is not added, as خَلِيفَةً khalīfatan, caliph.

§ 6

DOUBLED LETTERS

A doubled letter is not written twice, unless separated by an intermediate vowel. Instead, the sign ّ (called تَشْدِيدٌ tashdīd

شَدَّة shadda) is written over the letter, e.g. مَرَّ marra, he ssed; قَدِّمْ qaddim, bring (also written قَدِّمْ).

§ 7

HAMZA

The rules for the writing of hamza are complicated, and, in a few instances, alternative usages exist. Consequently, the student will not be burdened with involved rules at this stage. But explanations will be given as required, when words with hamza are introduced. Here, a few guiding points only will be mentioned:

(*a*) Initial hamza is always written on or under ʾalif. e.g. أ ʾa, أُ ʾu, إ ʾi.

(*b*) There is, however, a type of initial hamza called هَمْزَةُ ٱلْوَصْلِ hamzatu l-waṣl, the hamza of connection, written thus ٱ (as opposed to the ordinary هَمْزَةُ ٱلْقَطْعِ hamzatu l-qaṭʿ of (*a*) above). This hamza is only actually pronounced at the beginning of a sentence. At other times, it is merged into the final vowel of the previous word; or if the final letter of the previous word has no vowel, it is given a vowel. The hamzatu l-waṣl occurs in the definite article, أَلْ al, certain nouns such as إِبْن ibnun son, and also in certain verb forms as إِنْكَسَرَ it broke (inkasara).

e.g. أَلْبَيْتُ هُنَاكَ (al-baitu hunāka) the house is there, BUT

وَجَدَ ٱلْبَيْتَ هُنَاكَ (wajada l-baita hunāka) he found the house there.

إِبْنُ ٱلْمَلِكِ حَاضِرٌ (ibnu l-maliki ḥaḍirun) the king's son is present, BUT

وَجَدْتُ ابْنَ الْمَلِكِ (wajadtu bna l-maliki)
I found the king's son.

إِنْكَسَرَ فِنْجَانٌ (inkasara finjānun)
a cup broke, BUT

وَانْكَسَرَ فِنْجَانٌ (wa nkasara finjānun)
and a cup broke.

It should be noted that when a sentence begins with a word with hamzatu l-waṣl, the hamza should, strictly speaking, be written, as أَلْبَيْتُ al-baitu, the house. In practice, however, it is often omitted and the vowel sign only left, thus اَلْبَيْتُ, of which examples are given in the exercises.

(*c*) In the middle of a word hamza may be written over wāw, yā' (without the two dots) or 'alif; and at the end of a word it may also be written on the line, that is, not on a letter but roughly level with the lower part of the other letters of the word concerned. The following are examples with pronunciation. Further explanations will come later in the grammar.

سَأَلَ sa'ala	قَرَأَ qara'a
مَسْأَلَةٌ mas'alatun	وُزَرَاءُ wuzarā'u
بِئْرٌ bi'run	أَسْئِلَةٌ as'ilatun
شَيْءٌ shai'un	يَجِيءُ yajī'u يَجِئْ yaji'
بُؤْسٌ bu'sun	سُئِلَ su'ila
جَرُؤَ jaru'a	ضَوْءٌ ḍau'un

مَجْرُوءٌ majrū'un

§ 8

MADDA

If a hamza with fatḥa is followed by the long vowel, alif, the hamza and fatḥa are dropped in writing, and the long vowel 'alif is written over the 'alif horizontally thus: آ 'ā, for أا. This sign is called مَدَّة madda. This occurs chiefly at the beginning of a word, as آمَنَ 'āmana, he believed. It does, however, occur sometimes in the middle of a word, as قُرْآنٌ qur'ānun, Koran, and رَآهُ ra'āhu, he saw him, for قُرْأانٌ and رَأاهُ.

§ 9

STRESS. THE SYLLABLE

Written Arabic is a language of syllable length, rather than accent or stress. When read aloud all syllables should be given their full length, without slurring any letter, but no effort should be made to emphasise any syllable at the expense of another. The resultant reading may sound as if some syllables are stronger than others, but this will in reality be because of their length.

There are two kinds of syllable, short and long.

(*a*) The short syllable consists of a consonant with a short vowel, like the three syllables in كَتَبَ *ka-ta-ba*, he wrote. In this word the three syllables should be even and equal.

(*b*) The long syllable consists of a vowelled consonant followed by an unvowelled letter. This may be

(i) *Either* a consonant with vowel, followed by a long vowel (which is, in effect, an unvowelled letter), as the first syllable of كَاتَبَ *kā-ta-ba*, he corresponded with, or the second syllable of كَبِيرٌ *ka-bī-run*, big

(ii) *or* a vowelled consonant followed by a truly consonantal second letter with sukūn, as the first syllable of كَلْبُهُ *kal-bu-hu*, his dog.

Thus the word كَتَبْتُمْ *ka-tab-tum*, you (pl.) wrote, is one short syllable followed by two long. كِتَابٌ, *kitābun*, a book, is one short followed by two long.

No syllable can begin with an unvowelled letter: consequently no word may begin with two consonants unless a vowel intervenes. This explains why certain verb forms begin with an extra ʾalif with hamzatu l-waṣl, as اِسْتَلَمَ istalama, he received.

No syllable should close with two unvowelled consonants though this may occur reading aloud in pause, at the end of a sentence. Thus قَلْبٌ qalbun, heart, could be read قَلْبْ *qalb*, without the case-ending, in pause. In certain forms from the doubled verb, however, we do encounter a syllable ending on two unvowelled letters, the first being the long vowel ʾalif, e.g. شَابٌّ *shāb-bun*, a youth.

§ 10

PUNCTUATION

Punctuation was not considered important in early Arabic manuscripts. Even paragraphing was ignored. But the start of a new section was sometimes indicated by putting the heading in a different-coloured ink, e.g. red, instead of black. Again, section headings were sometimes indicated by a line over the words.

E.g. باب الصلاة حدثنى احمد بن حسين . . .

Here باب الصلاة (Chapter of Prayer) is the heading of a new section.

In medieval times, a single point, usually diamond shaped, because of the reed-pen used, came to be employed.

E.g. وَكَانَ صَاحِبَ نَوَادِرَ، وَكَتَبَ كُتُبًا كَثِيرَةً.

Sometimes three inverted commas, thus ،‘، were used.

In modern times, the Arabs have imitated European punctuation, usually – though not always – putting them upside-down.

E.g. ، comma
؛ semi-colon
: colon
. full-stop
« » quotation marks
( ) sometimes replaced by brackets, though this practice is dying out.

؟ or ? question mark.

The exclamation mark and dash are also used.

It is now normal to divide prose passages into paragraphs, as in Europe. Large type is used for headings, and, although italics do not exist, there is a wide variety of ornamental scripts which facilitate clear setting-out.

§ 11

ABBREVIATIONS

A stroke resembling a madda is generally (though not always) put above abbreviations, e.g.. الخ for إلى آخره ʼilā ʼākhirihi "and so forth" (literally "to its end").

The following abbreviations are in common use after the names of certain persons: صلعم = صَلَّى اللهُ عَلَيْهِ وَسَلَّمَ ṣalla llāhu ɛalaihi wasallama "God bless him and give him peace" used after the name of Mohammed.

عم = عَلَيْهِ ٱلسَّلَامُ ɛalaihi s-salāmu "Upon him be peace" used after the names of other prophets.

§ 12

THE ALPHABET AS NUMERALS

This is little used today except for numbering paragraphs, items, etc. in the manner of the English *a*, *b*, *c*, and so on. In this case the order of the letters is that of the old Semitic alphabet. This is called حُرُوفُ ٱلْأَبْجَدِ ḥurūfu l-ʾabjad.

1.	ا	20.	ك	200.	ر
2.	ب	30.	ل	300.	ش
3.	ج	40.	م	400.	ت
4.	د	50.	ن	500.	ث
5.	ه	60.	س	600.	خ
6.	و	70.	ع	700.	ذ
7.	ز	80.	ف	800.	ض
8.	ح	90.	ص	900.	ظ
9.	ط	100.	ق	1000.	غ
10.	ى				

This order is given in the following line:

أَبْجَدْ هَوَّزْ حُطِّي كَلَمَنْ سَعْفَصْ قُرِشَتْ ثَخَذْ ضَظِغْ

§ 13

EXERCISES IN READING

I

بِ تَ لِ وَ أَبٌ بَلْ قُلْ حَمٌ قُمْ كُلْ طِبْ

ṭib kul qum ḥamun qul bal ʾabun wa li ta bi

سِرْ لَا مَا لَمْ عَنْ خُذْ ذُو نَمْ فِي دُمْ كَيْ يَدٌ

yadun kai dum fī nam dhū khudh ʿan lam mā lā sir

وَيْ لُبٌّ مَدَّ طِبٌّ دَلَّ كُلٌّ

kullun dalla ṭibbun madda lubbun wai

II

فَرَحٌ قَتْلٌ شَرِبَ حَسُنَ فَرِحَ قَتَلَ كَتَبَ

farahun qatlun shariba hasuna fariha qatala kataba

إِبِلٌ حَبْلٌ ضَرْبٌ خَافَ طَالَ حُسْنٌ حَسَنٌ

'ibilun hablun darbun khāfa tāla husnun hasanun

رَأْسٌ خِفْتِ قُمْتَ مَوْتٌ جَارٌ بَيْتٌ فِيلٌ نُورٌ

ra'sun khifti qumta mautun jārun baitun fīlun nūrun

جَرَى أَكَلَ بِكْرٍ نَهْرٍ بَحْرٍ بُخْلٌ ظَهْرٍ

jarā 'akala bikrin nahrin bahrin bukhlun zahrin

III

هَارِبٌ نَفْسًا قُلْنَا كَاتِبٌ كِتَابٌ كَتَبْتُ كَتَبَتْ

hāribun nafsan qulnā kātibun kitābun katabtu katabat

كَتَبْتُمْ أَسَاسٌ فَتِّشْ فَتَّشَ أَقْتُلُ تَضْرِبُ يَكْتُبُ

katabtum 'asāsun fattish fattasha 'aqtulu tadribu yaktubu

مَكْتُوبٌ شُغْلُكُمْ كِتَابُهُ تَخْرُجُ بَعَثُوا فَرِحْنَا

maktūbun shughlukum kitābuhu takhruju baعathū farihnā

تَخْتَلِفُوا طَرِيقُكُمْ تَعْبَانُ سَرَطَانٌ جَالِسًا مِفْتَاحٌ

takhtalifū tarīqukum taعbānu saratānun jālisan miftāhun

تَدَارَكَ اِحْمَرَّتْ اِتَّخَذْتُمْ اِجْتَمَعْنَا اِخْتِلَافٌ

tadāraka ihmarrat ittakhadhtum ijtamaعnā ikhtilāfun

إِلَى عَلَى آخِذٌ آكِلٌ مُؤْمِنٌ تَتَذَكَّرُ اِضْطَرَبَتْ

عalā 'ilā 'ākhidhun 'ākilun mu'minun tatadhakkaru idtarabat

مُوسَى اِسْتِئْنَاسٌ اِسْتَحْلِفِنِي مُؤَاخَذَةٌ مُؤَلِّفُونَ

mu'allifūna mu'ā<u>kh</u>a<u>dh</u>atun istaḥlifīnī isti'nāsun mūsā

تَأْلِيفًا

ta'līfan

IV

اَلْقُطْرُ ٱلْمِصْرِيُّ يُكَوِّنُ ٱلزَّاوِيَةَ ٱلشَّمَالِيَّةَ ٱلشَّرْقِيَّةَ مِنْ أَفْرِيقِيَةَ وَيُقَالُ لَهُ أَيْضًا وَادِي ٱلنِّيلِ لِأَنَّ قِسْمَهُ ٱلْجَنُوبِيَّ وَاقِعٌ بَيْنَ سِلْسِلَتَيْ جِبَالٍ وَيَخْتَرِقُهُ نَهْرُ ٱلنِّيلِ ٱلْعَظِيمِ مُسَاحَتُهُ جُغْرَافِيًّا أَرْبَعُمِائَةِ أَلْفِ مِيلٍ مُرَبَّعٍ وَأَمَّا مُسَاحَتُهُ ٱلْمُقَاسَةُ فَهِيَ ٦٥ أَلْفَ مِيلٍ مُرَبَّعٍ مِنْهَا ٥٧٣٦ ... فَدَّانٍ أَرْضًا زِرَاعِيَّةً.

وَيَحُدُّ هٰذَا ٱلْقُطْرَ مِنَ ٱلشَّمَالِ ٱلْبَحْرُ ٱلْمُتَوَسِّطُ وَمِنَ ٱلشَّرْقِ خَطٌّ يَمْتَدُّ مِنْ خَانِ يُونُسَ عَلَى ٱلْبَحْرِ ٱلْمُتَوَسِّطِ إِلَى ٱلسُّوَيْسِ عَلَى ٱلْبَحْرِ ٱلْأَحْمَرِ وَٱلْبَحْرُ ٱلْأَحْمَرُ وَمِنَ ٱلْجَنُوبِ بِلَادُ ٱلنُّوبَةِ وَمِنَ ٱلْغَرْبِ بِلَادُ بَرْقَةَ.

وَٱلنِّيلُ نَهْرٌ يَخْتَرِقُ ٱلْقُطْرَ ٱلْمِصْرِيَّ مِنَ ٱلْجَنُوبِ إِلَى ٱلشَّمَالِ فَإِذَا وَصَلَ إِلَى قُرْبِ ٱلْقَاهِرَةِ ٱنْقَسَمَ إِلَى فَرْعَيْنِ يَسِيرُ أَحَدُهُمَا مَائِلًا إِلَى ٱلشَّرْقِ حَتَّى يَصُبَّ إِلَى ٱلْبَحْرِ ٱلْمُتَوَسِّطِ عِنْدَ مَدِينَةِ دِمْيَاطَ وَٱلْآخَرُ يَسِيرُ مَائِلًا إِلَى ٱلْغَرْبِ حَتَّى يَصُبَّ إِلَى ذٰلِكَ ٱلْبَحْرِ عِنْدَ ثَغْرِ رَشِيدَ.

وَيَنْقَسِمُ ٱلْقُطْرُ ٱلْمِصْرِيُّ بِهٰذَا ٱلِاعْتِبَارِ إِلَى قِسْمَيْنِ جَنُوبِيٍّ وَشَمَالِيٍّ أَوْ قِبْلِيٍّ وَبَحْرِيٍّ فَالْقِسْمُ ٱلْقِبْلِيُّ وَيُقَالُ لَهُ ٱلصَّعِيدُ أَوْ مِصْرُ ٱلْعُلْيَا يَمْتَدُّ

مِنْ آخِرِ حُدُودِ مِصْرَ جَنُوباً إِلَى نُقْطَةِ تَفَرُّعِ ٱلنِّيلِ وَٱلْبَحْرِيُّ وَيُقَالُ لَهُ مِصْرُ ٱلسُّفْلَى يَمْتَدُّ مِنْ نُقْطَةِ تَفَرُّعِ ٱلنِّيلِ إِلَى ٱلْبَحْرِ ٱلْمُتَوَسِّطِ.

وَيَنْقَسِمُ ٱلْوَجْهُ ٱلْبَحْرِيُّ إِلَى ثَلَاثَةِ أَقْسَامٍ مُتَوَسِّطٍ وَهُوَ ٱلْوَاقِعُ بَيْنَ فَرْعَيِ ٱلنِّيلِ وَقَدْ سُمِّيَ لِذٰلِكَ رَوْضَةَ ٱلْبَحْرَيْنِ وَيُقَالُ لَهُ أَيْضاً ٱلدَّلْتَا لِمُشَابَهَتِهِ بِحَرْفِ ٱلدَّالِ عِنْدَ ٱلْيُونَانِيِّينَ وَشَرْقِيٍّ وَهُوَ ٱلْوَاقِعُ إِلَى شَرْقِيِّ ٱلدَّلْتَا وَيُقَالُ لَهُ ٱلْحَوْفُ ٱلشَّرْقِيُّ وَغَرْبِيٍّ وَهُوَ ٱلْوَاقِعُ إِلَى غَرْبِيِّهَا وَيُقَالُ لَهُ ٱلْحَوْفُ ٱلْغَرْبِيُّ هٰذِهِ هِيَ أَقْسَامُ ٱلْقُطْرِ ٱلْمِصْرِيِّ ٱلطَّبِيعِيَّةُ أَمَّا أَقْسَامُهُ ٱلْإِدَارِيَّةُ فَتَخْتَلِفُ بِٱخْتِلَافِ ٱلْأَزْمَانِ.

TRANSCRIPTION AND LITERAL TRANSLATION

al-quṭru	l-miṣrīyu	yukawwinu	z-zāwiyata
The land	the Egyptian	forms	the angle

sh-shamālīyata	sh-sharqīyata	min	afrīqiyata	wa yuqālu
the northern	the eastern	of	Africa	and it is

lahu	aiḍan	wādia n-nīli	li'anna	qismahu
called	also	valley of the Nile	because	its part

l-janūbīya	wāqiعun	baina	silsilatai	jibālin
the southern	lies	between	two chains of mountains,	

wa	yakhtariquhu	nahru n-nīli	l-عaẓīmu.
and	cuts through it	the river of Nile	the mighty.

masāḥatuhu	jighrāfīyan	'arbaعu mi'ati 'alfi	mīlin
Its area (is)	geographically	400,000	miles

murabbaعin	wa	'ammā	masāḥatuhu	l-muqāsatu
square	and	as for	its area	the measured,

fa hiya	65 'alfa	mīlin	murabbaعin	minhā	5,736,000
it (is)	65,000	square	miles,	of which	5,736,000

faddānin	'arḍan	zarāعīyatan.
faddans (are)	ground	agricultural.

wa yaḥuddu hādha l-qutra mina sh-shamāli l-baḥru
And bounds this land on the North the sea

l-mutawassiṭu wa mina sh-sharqi khaṭṭun yamtaddu
the Mediterranean and on the East a line which extends

min khāni yūnusa ʿala l-baḥri l-mutawassiṭi 'ila
from Khan Yunus on the sea the Mediterranean to

s-suwaisi ʿala l-baḥri l-'aḥmari, wa l-baḥru l-'aḥmaru
Suez on the sea the Red, and the sea the Red;

wa mina l-janūbi bilādu n-nūbati wa mina
and on the South the land of Nubia; and on

l-gharbi bilādu barqata.
the West the district of Barqa.

wa n-nīlu nahrun yakhtariqu
And the Nile (is) a river (which) cuts through

l-quṭra l-miṣrīya mina l-janūbi 'ila sh-shamāli
the land the Egyptian from the South to the North

fa 'idhā waṣala 'ilā qurbi l-qāhirati
and when it comes to the neighbourhood of Cairo,

nqasama 'ilā farʿaini yasīru aḥaduhuma mā'ilan
it divides into two branches, goes one of them tending

'ila sh-sharqi ḥatta yaṣubba 'ila l-baḥri l-mutawassiṭi
to the East until it flows into the sea the Mediterranean

ʿinda madīnati dimyāṭa wa l-'ākharu yasīru mā'ilan
at the city of Damietta and the other goes tending

'ila l-gharbi ḥattā yaṣubba 'ila dhālika l-baḥri ʿinda
to the West until it flows into that sea at

thaghri rashīda.
the frontier of Rosetta.

wa yanqasimu l-quṭru l-miṣrīyu bi hādha
And is divided the land the Egyptian in this

liʿtibāri 'ilā qismaini janūbīyin wa shamālīyin au
way into two parts, a southern and a northern, or

qiblīyin wa baḥrīyin fa l-qiṣmu l-qiblīyu
a southern and a sea-coast, and the part the southern,

wa yuqālu lahu ṣ-ṣaعīdu au miṣru l-عulyā yamtaddu
and it is called the Sa'id or Egypt the upper, extends

min ākhiri ḥudūdi miṣra janūban 'ilā
from the end of the limits of Egypt (on the) South to

nuqṭati tafarruعi n-nīli wa l-baḥrīyu
the point of the branching of the Nile; and the sea-coast,

wa yuqālu lahu miṣru s-suflā yamtaddu min nuqṭati
and it is called Egypt the lower, extends from the point

tafarruعi n-nīli 'ila l-baḥri l-mutawassiṭi.
of the branching of the Nile to the sea the Mediterranean.

wa yuqsamu l-wajhu l-baḥrīyu 'ila
And is divided the portion the sea-coastal into

thalāthati 'aqsāmin mutawassiṭin wahuwa l-wāqiعu baina
three divisions, a middle, and it lies between

farعayi n-nīli wa qad summiya
two branches of the Nile, and it has been named

li dhālika rauḍatu l-baḥraini
on account of that garden of the two rivers

wa yuqālu lahu aiḍani dh-dhaltā li mushā-
and it is called also the Delta on account of its

bahatihi bi ḥarfi dh-dhāli عinda l-yūnānīyīna
resemblance to the letter dhal among the Greeks,

wa sharqīyin wahuwa l-wāqiعu 'ila sharqīyi dh-dhaltā
and an eastern, and it lies to the East of the Delta

wa yuqālu lahu l-ḥaufu sh-sharqīyu wa gharbīyin
and is called the border the eastern, and a western

wa huwa l-wāqiعu 'ilā gharbīyiha wa yuqālu lahu
and it lies to the West of it, and is called

l-ḥaufu l-gharbīyu. hādhihi hiya 'aqsāmu
the border the western. These are the divisions

l-quṭri l-miṣrīyi ṭ-ṭabīعīyatu ʾammā ʾaqsāmuhu
of the land the Egyptian the natural. As for its divisions

l-ʾidārīyatu fa takhtalifu bi khtilāfi
the administrative, they differ with the differing

l-ʾazmāni.
of the times.

CHAPTER TWO

(اَلْبَابُ ٱلثَّانِى Al-bābu th-thānī)

The Article. The Simple Nominal Sentence

1. There is no *indefinite* article in Arabic, but the presence of nunation at the end of a noun (see Chap. One, Sect. 5) indicates indefinite-ness. Thus بَيْتٌ baitun means a house, رَجُلٌ rajulun, a man.

2. The *definite* article is أَلْ al, the, which is prefixed to, and attached to, its noun, e.g. أَلْبَيْتُ al-baitu the house, أَلْبَابُ al-bābu, the door. The noun, being definite, loses its nunation.

The hamza of the definite article is hamzatu l-waṣl (See Chap. One, Sect. 7). Consequently it disappears when it follows another word, and in pronunciation the ل "l" follows immediately after the final vowel of the preceding word, e.g. أَلْوَلَدُ وَٱلْبِنْتُ al-waladu wa l-bintu, the boy and the girl. (Note: وَ wa meaning "and" is written as part of the following word.)

3. When the word to which the article is attached begins with certain letters termed *Sun-letters* (أَلْحُرُوفُ ٱلشَّمْسِيَّةُ al-ḥurūfu sh-shamsīya), the "l" of the article changes to the initial letters in question. The fourteen Sun-letters are ت, ث, د, ذ, ر, ز, س, ش, ص, ض, ط, ظ, ل, ن, e.g. أَلشَّمْسُ al-shamsu (pronounced ash-shamsu), the sun; أَلرَّجُلُ al-rajulu (pronounced ar-rajulu) the man. In such a case, no sukūn is placed over the ل "l", but a tashdīd is written over the first letter of the word, as shown.

4. *Adjectives* as attributes are placed after the nouns they qualify. If the noun has the article, the adjective also must have it, e.g. بَيْتٌ صَغِيرٌ baitun ṣaghīrun, a small house, but اَلْبَيْتُ ٱلصَّغِيرُ al-baitu ṣ-ṣaghīru, the small house. Note that اَلْبَيْتُ صَغِيرٌ al-baitu ṣaghīrun can only mean "the house is small".

Where two or more adjectives qualify the same noun it is not necessary to put "and" between them.

e.g. بَيْتٌ جَمِيلٌ جَدِيدٌ baitun jamīlun jadīdun, a fine new house; اَلْبَيْتُ ٱلْجَمِيلُ ٱلْجَدِيدُ al-baitu l-jamīlu l-jadīdu, the fine new house. But if the two adjectives form the predicate (copula) of a nominal sentence it is usual to insert "and", e.g. اَلْبَيْتُ جَمِيلٌ وَجَدِيدٌ al-baitu jamīlun wa jadīdun, the house is fine and new.

5. The verb "to be" is omitted in Arabic when it has a present indicative meaning, as the English "is" or "are", e.g. اَلْبَيْتُ قَدِيمٌ al-baitu qadīmun, the house (is) old. Such a sentence is termed a nominal sentence as opposed to a verbal sentence.

6. The *personal pronouns* of the singular are:

أَنَا 'anā, I

أَنْتَ 'anta, you (thou) masculine

أَنْتِ 'anti, you (thou) feminine

هُوَ huwa, he, it

هِيَ hiya, she, it

These pronouns are indeclinable. هُوَ and هِيَ are used to mean "it", according to the gender of the thing to which they refer, there being no neuter in Arabic.

VOCABULARY

a door, chapter	بَابٌ	bābun
a house	بَيْتٌ	baitun
a man	رَجُلٌ	rajulun
a boy, son	وَلَدٌ	waladun
a river	نَهْرٌ	nahrun
a sea	بَحْرٌ	baḥrun
a book	كِتَابٌ	kitābun
a street	شَارِعٌ	shāriعun
a chair	كُرْسِيٌّ	kursīyun
tea	شَايٌ	shāyun
coffee	قَهْوَةٌ	qahwatun
a cup	فِنْجَانٌ	finjānun
the Nile	اَلنِّيلُ	an-Nīlu
big, great, old	كَبِيرٌ	kabīrun
small, young	صَغِيرٌ	ṣaghīrun
old	قَدِيمٌ	qadīmun
new	جَدِيدٌ	jadīdun
long, tall	طَوِيلٌ	ṭawīlun
short	قَصِيرٌ	qaṣīrun
beautiful, fine	جَمِيلٌ	jamīlun

handsome, good Hassan (pr. noun m.)	حَسَنٌ	ḥasanun, Ḥasanun
broken	مَكْسُورٌ	maksūrun
broad, wide	وَاسِعٌ	wāsiʿun
narrow	ضَيِّقٌ	ḍayyiqun

NOTE: In the English exercises words in parentheses ( ) indicate the rendering in Arabic. Words in square brackets [ ] are not translated. Exercises are for translation from Arabic to English or *vice versa*.

EXERCISE 1

١—أَنَا صَغِيرٌ وَأَنْتَ كَبِيرٌ. ٢—أَنْتَ رَجُلٌ طَوِيلٌ. ٣—اَلشَّارِعُ
وَاسِعٌ وَطَوِيلٌ. ٤—اَلنِّيلُ نَهْرٌ، هُوَ نَهْرٌ كَبِيرٌ. ٥—اَلْبَابُ قَدِيمٌ.
٦—اَلْبَيْتُ جَمِيلٌ. ٧—نَهْرٌ قَصِيرٌ. ٨—اَلْبَحْرُ ٱلضَّيِّقُ. ٩—وَلَدٌ حَسَنٌ.
١٠—شَايٌ وَقَهْوَةٌ. ١١—اَلشَّايُ وَٱلْقَهْوَةُ. ١٢—أَنَا رَجُلٌ وَأَنْتَ وَلَدٌ.
١٣ — اَلْكُرْسِيُّ صَغِيرٌ. ١٤ — اَلْفِنْجَانُ قَدِيمٌ، هُوَ مَكْسُورٌ. ١٥ —
اَلْكِتَابُ جَمِيلٌ، هُوَ جَدِيدٌ. ١٦—اَلْبَابُ مَكْسُورٌ. ١٧—رَجُلٌ وَوَلَدٌ
وَبِنْتٌ. ١٨—أَنَا وَهِيَ. ١٩—أَنْتَ وَهُوَ. ٢٠—اَلشَّارِعُ ٱلضَّيِّقُ.

TRANSCRIPTION

1. ʼAnā ṣaghīrun wa ʼanta kabīrun. 2. ʼAnta rajulun ṭawīlun. 3. Ash-shāriʿu wāsiʿun wa ṭawīlun. 4. An-nīlu nahrun, huwa nahrun kabīrun. 5. Al-bābu qadīmun. 6. Al-baitu jamīlun. 7. Nahrun qaṣīrun. 8. Al-baḥru ḍ-ḍayyiqu. 9. Waladun ḥasanun. 10. Shāyun wa qahwatun. 11. Ash-shāyu wa l-qahwatu. 12. ʼAnā rajulun wa ʼanta waladun. 13. Al-kursīyu ṣaghīrun. 14. Al-finjānu qadīmun, huwa

maksūrun. 15. Al-kītabu jamīlun, huwa jadīdun. 16. Al-bābu maksūrun. 17. Rajulun wa waladun wa bintun. 18. 'Anā wa hiya. 19. 'Anta wa huwa. 20. Ash-shāriعu ḍ-ḍayyiqu.

EXERCISE 2

1. The house is large. 2. A large house. 3. A tall man and a short boy. 4. Hassan is a young (small) boy. 5. The river is narrow. 6. A wide street. 7. He is a new boy. 8. An old broken door. 9. The Nile is a long wide river. 10. The book is new. 11. A new book. 12. The sea is beautiful. 13. An old chair. 14. Nice tea. 15. Old coffee. 16. The cup is small. 17. A man and a boy. 18. You are a tall man, and I am short. 19. A small new book. 20. The long street.

CHAPTER THREE

(اَلْبَابُ الثَّالِثُ Al-bābu th-thālithu)

Gender. The Feminine

1. There are only two *genders* in Arabic, *masculine* and *feminine*. Generally speaking, there is no special sign of the masculine, and words should be assumed to be masculine unless they belong to one of the following categories:

(a) Words feminine by meaning, female human beings or animals, e.g. أُمٌّ 'ummun, mother, بِنْتٌ bintun, daughter, عَرُوسٌ ʿarūsun, bride.

(b) Words feminine by form. The principal feminine form is the ṭā' marbūṭa ةٌ atun (see Chap. One, Sect. 2, note 2) which is the usual feminine ending. The ṭā' marbūṭa is added to masculine nouns and adjectives (though not invariably) to make them feminine, e.g.

خَادِمٌ khādimun, servant; خَادِمَةٌ khādimatun, female servant

اِبْنٌ ibnun, son; اِبْنَةٌ ibnatun, daughter

كَبِيرٌ kabīrun, big, old; fem. كَبِيرَةٌ kabīratun

جَدِيدٌ jadīdun, new; fem. جَدِيدَةٌ jadīdatun

Words ending in ṭā' marbūṭa should be assumed to be feminine, unless known to be otherwise, e.g. كِتَابَةٌ kitābatun, writing. But خَلِيفَةٌ khalīfatun, Caliph, is masculine, being a male human being.

There are a few other feminine word forms, besides the tā' marbūṭa, but these will be explained later (see Chapter Eleven).

(c) Words feminine by convention. The following categories apply:

(i) Geographical names, that is, towns, villages, countries, etc., e.g. مِصْرُ miṣru, Egypt; دِمَشْقُ dimashqu, Damascus.

(ii) Parts of the body which occur in pairs are almost all feminine, e.g. عَيْنٌ ɛainun, eye; يَدٌ yadun, hand; رِجْلٌ rijlun, foot.

(iii) Certain other nouns are feminine for no apparent reason. Among the common ones are:

أَرْضٌ 'arḍun, earth	دَارٌ dārun, house, home
شَمْسٌ shamsun, sun	نَارٌ nārun, fire
نَفْسٌ nafsun, soul, self.	

In this category are a few words which may be either feminine or masculine, though in Classical Arabic the feminine was preferred, e.g.

طَرِيقٌ ṭarīqun, road, way حَالٌ ḥālun, condition, or state.

The latter word also occurs with the feminine ending, حَالَةٌ ḥālatun, condition or state.

2. The adjective must agree with the noun which it qualifies, e.g. رِجْلٌ صَغِيرَةٌ rijlun ṣaghīratun, a small foot; اَلْبِنْتُ ٱلْكَبِيرَةُ al-bintu l-kabīratu, the big (old) daughter; اَلْخَلِيفَةُ ٱلْجَدِيدُ al-khalīfatu l-jadīdu, the new caliph; دَارٌ قَدِيمَةٌ dārun qadīmatun, an old house.

Similarly, the adjective must agree with the noun to which it is the predicate in the nominal sentence, e.g. اَلشَّمْسُ حَارَّةٌ

ash-shamsu ḥarratun, the sun is hot; أَنْتِ حَاضِرَةٌ 'anti ḥāḍiratun, you (fem.) are present, but أَنْتَ حَاضِرٌ 'anta ḥāḍirun, you (masc.) are present.

COLLECTIVE NOUNS

3. Many words have a collective meaning in their singular form. This applies especially to natural features and animals, e.g. حَجَرٌ ḥajarun, rocks; شَجَرٌ shajarun, trees; بَقَرٌ baqarun, cows. To indicate a single object or animal, the feminine tā' marbūṭa ending is added: حَجَرَةٌ ḥajaratun, a rock; شَجَرَةٌ shajaratun, a tree; بَقَرَةٌ baqaratun, a cow.

THE INTERROGATIVE PARTICLE *

4. In the written language, questions are introduced by either of the particles هَلْ hal, or أَ 'a. The latter is written as if it were part of the word which follows it, e.g. هَلْ مِصْرُ بَعِيدَةٌ ؟ hal miṣru baعīdatun, or أَمِصْرُ بَعِيدَةٌ ؟ 'a-miṣru baعīdatun, is Egypt distant, far? The European *interrogative* sign is written in modern Arabic either in its normal form or reversed (؟ or ?). In spoken Arabic, these interrogative particles are almost never used, the interrogation being indicated by the tone of voice.

VOCABULARY

mother	أُمٌّ	'ummun
girl, daughter	بِنْتٌ	bintun
daughter	اِبْنَةٌ	ibnatun
son	اِبْنٌ	ibnun

* See also Appendix C, §2.

bride	(*f.*) عَرُوسٌ	عarūsun
Caliph	(*m.*) خَلِيفَةٌ	Khalīfatun
Egypt (Cairo)	(*f.*) مِصْرُ	Miṣru
Damascus	(*f.*) دِمَشْقُ	Dimashqu
eye	(*f.*) عَيْنٌ	عainun
hand	(*f.*) يَدٌ	yadun
foot (anatomical)	(*f.*) رِجْلٌ	rijlun
home, homeland, house	(*f.*) دَارٌ	dārun
hot	حَارٌّ، حَرٌّ	ḥārrun, ḥarrun
earth, land	(*f.*) أَرْضٌ	ʾarḍun
sun	(*f.*) شَمْسٌ	shamsun
present, ready	حَاضِرٌ	ḥāḍirun
stone (s) (*coll.*)	حَجَرٌ	ḥajarun
tree(s) (*coll.*)	شَجَرٌ	shajarun
cow(s), oxen (*coll.*)	بَقَرٌ	baqarun
distant, far	بَعِيدٌ	ba عīdun
garden, orchard	بُسْتَانٌ	bustānun
king	مَلِكٌ	malikun
queen	مَلِكَةٌ	malikatun
a place	مَحَلٌّ	maḥallun
a man, human being	إِنْسَانٌ	insānun

yes!	نَعَمْ	na ع am
no!	لَا	lā
grandfather, grandmother	جَدٌّ، جَدَّةٌ	jaddun, jaddatun
servant	خَادِمٌ (*m.*)، خَادِمَةٌ (*f.*)	khādimun, khādimatun
ugly, nasty	قَبِيحٌ	qabīḥun
hour, watch, clock, time	سَاعَةٌ	sā ع atun
strong, violent	شَدِيدٌ	shadīdun
doctor, physician	طَبِيبٌ	ṭabībun
clean	نَظِيفٌ	naẓīfun
dead	مَيِّتٌ	mayyitun
fire	نَارٌ (*f.*)	nārun

EXERCISE 3

١ — اَلسَّاعَةُ ٱلْجَدِيدَةُ ٱلْجَمِيلَةُ مَكْسُورَةٌ. ٢ — أَهِيَ سَاعَةٌ كَبِيرَةٌ؟
٣ — لَا، هِيَ صَغِيرَةٌ. ٤ — اَلْأُمُّ حَاضِرَةٌ. ٥ — اَلْعَرُوسُ بِنْتٌ جَمِيلَةٌ.
٦ — كِتَابَةٌ قَبِيحَةٌ. ٧ — خَلِيفَةٌ جَدِيدٌ. ٨ — هَلِ ٱلْبِنْتُ جَمِيلَةٌ؟ نَعَمْ!
٩ — رِجْلٌ نَظِيفَةٌ. ١٠ — اَلْأَرْضُ وَاسِعَةٌ. ١١ — دِمَشْقُ مَحَلٌّ حَارٌّ.
١٢ — اَلدَّارُ بَعِيدَةٌ وَٱلشَّمْسُ شَدِيدَةٌ. ١٣ — اَلْجَدُّ مَيِّتٌ. ١٤ — اَلْخَادِمَةُ
حَاضِرَةٌ. ١٥ — شَجَرَةٌ طَوِيلَةٌ. ١٦ — حَسَنٌ إِنْسَانٌ جَمِيلٌ، هُوَ طَبِيبٌ.
١٧ — اَلْبُسْتَانُ بَعِيدٌ. ١٨ — مَلِكٌ كَبِيرٌ. ١٩ — مَلِكَةٌ جَمِيلَةٌ. ٢٠ —
اَلْمَلِكَةُ جَمِيلَةٌ.

TRANSCRIPTION

1. As-sāعatu l-jadīdatu l-jamīlatu maksūratun. 2. ’A-hiya sāعatun kabīratun? 3. Lā! hiya saghīratun. 4. Al-’ummu ḥāḍiratun. 5. Al-عarūsu bintun jamīlatun. 6. Kitābatun qabīḥatun. 7. Khalīfatun jadīdun. 8. Hali l-bintu jamīlatun? Naعam! 9. Rijlun naẓīfatun. 10. Al-’arḍu wāsiعatun. 11. Dimashqu maḥallun ḥārrun. 12. Ad-dāru baعīdatun wa sh-shamsu shadīdatun. 13. Al-jaddu mayyitun. 14. Al-khādimatu hāḍiratun. 15. Sharajatun ṭawīlatun. 16. Ḥasanun ’insānun jamīlun. Huwa ṭabībun. 17. Al-bustānu baعīdun. 18. Malikun kabīrun. 19. Malikatun jamīlatun. 20. Al-malikatu jamīlatun.

EXERCISE 4

1. You (fem. sing.) are beautiful. 2. The tall tree is dead. 3. The mother is present. 4. Is the bride ready? No! 5. The dead Caliph. 6. The Caliph is dead. 7. A long foot. 8. Extensive (wide) land. 9. Damascus is distant. 10. The old watch is broken. 11. She is an ugly girl. 12. You are the queen. 13. The king is a fine man. 14. Are you the grandmother? No, I am the mother. 15. Awful (ugly) handwriting. 16. A large foot. 17. Is the garden clean? Yes, it is clean. 18. He is a doctor. 19. A long wide road. 20. The new house is small.

CHAPTER FOUR

(اَلْبَابُ الرَّابِعُ Al-bābu r-rābiع u)

Declension of Nouns.
The Three Cases

1. There are *three cases* in Arabic, and these are indicated merely by changing the vowelling of the final consonant (except in the dual and sound masculine plural endings). The "n" sound of nunation occurs after the final vowel in all three cases where required. The cases are:

(a) رَفْعٌ rafع (*nominative*, vowelled with ḍamma)

e.g. بَيْتٌ baitun, a house; اَلْبَيْتُ al-baitu, the house.

(b) نَصْبٌ naṣb (*accusative*, vowelled with fatḥa)

e.g. بَيْتًا baitan, اَلْبَيْتَ al-baita.

(c) جَرٌّ jarr (*genitive*, vowelled with kasra)

e.g. فِي بَيْتٍ fī baitin, in a house; فِي الْبَيْتِ fī l-baiti, in the house.

Note that in the accusative, the letter ʾalif is added to the indefinite noun, but this does not lengthen the fatḥa; it is merely a convention of spelling.

2. The English translation of case names given above is sometimes misleading, and it would be a great mistake for students to assume that where, for instance, a word would be considered accusative in English, or any other language, naṣb should be employed in Arabic. As a rough guide, the student would do well, at this stage, to think of naṣb as adverbial as well as objective. For example, حَالًا ḥālan, at present, at once, is really the *accusative indefinite* of ḥālun, a state, or condition. Jarr, the genitive, is used for posses-

sion or after prepositions. While rafع, the nominative, is used as the subject of a sentence, we have also seen (Chap. Two) that it is used for the predicate of a nominal sentence.

3. The Arabs call *declension* إِعْرَاب iعrāb, and words fully declined are said to be مُنْصَرِف munṣarif. However, certain classes of noun are not fully declined, and are termed غَيْرُ مُنْصَرِف ghair munsarif (other than munṣarif). European grammarians sometimes call these diptotes as opposed to the regular triptotes. Diptotes are declined as follows:

	Indefinite	Definite
Nominative	زَعْلَانُ zaعlānu* angry	اَلزَّعْلَانُ az-zaعlānū
Acc.	زَعْلَانَ zaعlāna	اَلزَّعْلَانَ az-zaعlāna
Gen.	زَعْلَانَ zaعlāna	اَلزَّعْلَانِ az-zaعlāni

It will be noted from the above that diptotes are quite normal when definite. When indefinite, they differ from triptotes in two respects. *First*, there is no nunation; *second*, there are only two different vowel endings, the accusative and genitive both having fatḥa.

For the present, the student should find out from the vocabularies or from a dictionary which words are diptotes.

THE GENITIVE WITH PREPOSITIONS

4. Every Arabic preposition (ḥarf jarr حَرْفُ جَرٍّ) takes its following noun in the genitive, e.g.

فِي fī, in فِي بُسْتَانٍ fī bustānin, in a garden.

فِي الْبَيْتِ fi l-baiti, in the house.

فِي مِصْرَ fī Miṣra (diptote), in Egypt.

مِنْ min, from مِنْ وَلَدٍ min waladin, from a boy.

* Modern usage. In older Arabic it means "in agony".

مِنَ ٱلْوَلَدِ ٱلطَّيِّبِ mina l-waladi ṭ-ṭayyibi, from the nice boy.

مِنْ وَلَدٍ زَعْلَانَ min waladin zaعlāna, from an angry boy.

مِنَ ٱلْوَلَدِ ٱلزَّعْلَانِ mina l-waladi z-zaعlāni, from the angry boy.

*لِ li, to, for, belonging to لِرَجُلٍ li rajulin, to a man.

إِلَى ilā, to إِلَى ٱلسُّوقِ ila s-sūqi, to the market.

إِلَى مَكَّةَ ilā Makkata (diptote), to Mecca.

عَلَى عalā, on عَلَى ٱلْمَائِدَةِ عala l-mā'idati, on the table.

5. Where a nominal sentence has a prepositional phrase as its predicate, and the subject is indefinite, it is usual not to put the subject first, e.g.

فِي ٱلْبُسْتَانِ رَجُلٌ قَبِيحٌ fi l-bustāni rajulun qabīḥun, an ugly man is in the garden.

NOT

رَجُلٌ قَبِيحٌ فِي ٱلْبُسْتَانِ rajulun qabīḥun fi l-bustāni.

In such sentences the verb "to be" understood can be translated by the English impersonal verb, "there is" or "there are", e.g. the sentence above: "There is an ugly man in the garden."

THE GENITIVE OF POSSESSION

(إِضَافَةٌ 'iḍāfa)

6. A noun followed by another noun in the genitive auto-

* With the definite article it is written لِلْ , e.g., لِلرَّجُلِ to or for the man.

matically loses its nunation. Moreover, where – as in the majority of instances – the following genitive noun is definite, the first noun also is automatically definite. A NOUN FOLLOWED BY A GENITIVE MUST NOT TAKE THE ARTICLE.

Thus بَيْتُ ٱلرَّجُلِ baitu r-rajuli means *the* house of the man; بَيْتُ مُحَمَّدٍ baitu Muḥammadin means *the* house of Muhammad, or Muhammad's house.

In the first example, if it is intended that "house" should be indefinite, with the meaning *a* house of the man's, and implying that he has other houses also, then another idiom must be used, as بَيْتٌ لِلرَّجُلِ baitun li r-rajuli, literally, a house to or of the man. Similarly, بَيْتٌ لِمُحَمَّدٍ baitun li Muḥammadin, a house of Muhammad's.

7. It is a rule of ʾiḍāfa that nothing must interpose between the noun and its following genitive. Consequently, if the noun is to be qualified with an adjective, the latter must come AFTER the genitive, e.g.

بَيْتُ مُحَمَّدٍ ٱلْكَبِيرُ baitu Muḥammadini l-kabīru, Muhamman's big house.

بَيْتُ ٱلرَّجُلِ ٱلْقَدِيمُ baitu r-rajuli l-qadīmu, the man's old house.

Note that by altering the vowelling of the adjectives above, quite different meanings are given, e.g.

بَيْتُ مُحَمَّدٍ ٱلْكَبِيرِ baitu Muḥammadini l-kabīri, the house of the great Muhammad.

بَيْتُ ٱلرَّجُلِ ٱلْكَبِيرِ baitu r-rajuli l-kabīri, the house of the old man.

As will be seen, the adjective of the noun made definite by iḍāfa takes the article.

It is possible for a noun to form iḍāfa with a following *indefinite* genitive. In such cases, that noun still remains indefinite, even though it loses its nunation, as the following example shows:

(without a qualifying adjective)

فِنْجَانُ قَهْوَةٍ finjānu qahwatin, a cup of coffee.

(with a qualifying adjective)

فِنْجَانُ قَهْوَةٍ كَبِيرٌ finjānu qahwatin kabīrun, a large cup of coffee.

Such instances are less frequent than the definite iḍāfa, except, perhaps, in Classical poetry. In modern prose, for instance, one would not expect to encounter

بَيْتُ مُحَمَّدٍ كَبِيرٌ baitu Muḥammadin kabīrun

instead of بَيْتٌ كَبِيرٌ لِمُحَمَّدٍ baitun kabīrun li-Muḥammadin

with the meaning of "a large house of Muḥammad's".

VOCABULARY

angry (lit. in agony)	زَعْلَانُ	zaعlānu	bread	خُبْزٌ	khubzun
good, nice, satisfactory	طَيِّبٌ	ṭayyibun	meat	لَحْمٌ	laḥmun
just	عَادِلٌ	عādilun	butter	زُبْدَةٌ ، زُبْدٌ	zubdatun, zubdun
honest, upright	صَالِحٌ	ṣāliḥun	milk	حَلِيبٌ ، لَبَنٌ	ḥalībun, labanun
truthful, honest	صَادِقٌ	ṣādiqun	plate	صَحْنٌ	ṣaḥnun
Mecca	مَكَّةُ	Makkatu	knife	سِكِّينٌ	sikkīnun
market (*m.* or *f.*)	سُوقٌ	sūqun	fork	شَوْكَةٌ	shaukatun
table	مَائِدَةٌ	mā'idatun	spoon	مِلْعَقَةٌ	milعaqatun
			in	فِي	fī

from	مِنْ	min
to, for, belonging to	لِ	li
on, upon	عَلَى	ʿalā
with	مَعَ	maʿa
minister (political)	وَزِيرٌ	wazīrun
stale, old	بَائِتٌ	bā'itun

EXERCISE 5

١ — عَلَى ٱلْمَائِدَةِ صَحْنٌ وَسِكِّينٌ . ٢ — مِلْعَقَةُ ٱلْوَلَدِ ٱلنَّظِيفَةُ. ٣ — ٱلْحَلِيبُ طَيِّبٌ. ٤ — مِنَ ٱلسُّوقِ ٱلْقَدِيمِ. ٥ — لِسُوقِ مَكَّةَ. ٦ — ٱبْنُ حَسَنٍ وَلَدٌ صَالِحٌ. ٧ — ٱبْنَةُ مُحَمَّدٍ (هِيَ) فِى بُسْتَانِ حَسَنٍ ٱلصَّادِقِ. ٨ — مَلِكُ مِصْرَ مَلِكٌ عَادِلٌ. ٩ — هُوَ ٱبْنُ ٱلْمَلِكِ ٱلزَّعْلَانِ. ١٠ — أَنْتَ زَعْلَانُ مِنْ حَسَنٍ وَهُوَ وَلَدٌ طَيِّبٌ. ١١ — اَلْخُبْزُ بَائِتٌ وَٱللَّحْمُ شَدِيدٌ. ١٢ — اَلزُّبْدُ مِنْ حَلِيبِ (لَبَنِ) بَقَرَةِ مُحَمَّدٍ. ١٣ — شَوْكَةُ أُمِّ ٱلْخَلِيفَةِ عَلَى ٱلْمَائِدَةِ ٱلصَّغِيرَةِ. ١٤ — مَكَّةُ مَحَلُّ حَسَنٍ. ١٥ — أَنْتَ فِى بُسْتَانِ حَسَنٍ ٱلْجَمِيلِ. ١٦ — اَلْمَائِدَةُ فِى بَيْتٍ لِمُحَمَّدٍ. ١٧ — اَلْخُبْزُ عَلَى ٱلصَّحْنِ ٱلْجَدِيدِ، هُوَ مَعَ ٱلزُّبْدَةِ. ١٨ — هَلِ ٱللَّبَنُ جَدِيدٌ؟ لَا، هُوَ قَدِيمٌ. ١٩ — أَنْتِ فِى بُسْتَانِ ٱلْمَلِكِ. ٢٠ — شَايُ ٱلْوَلَدِ فِى ٱلْفِنْجَانِ ٱلْكَبِيرِ.

TRANSCRIPTION

1. ʿala l-mā'idati ṣaḥnun wa sikkīnun. 2. Milʿaqatu l-waladi n-naẓīfatu. 3. Al-ḥalību ṭayyibun. 4. Mina s-sūqi l-qadīmi. 5. Li-sūqi Makkata. 6. Ibnu Ḥasanin waladun

ṣāliḥun. 7. Ibnatu Muḥammadin (hiya) fī bustāni Ḥasanini ṣ-ṣādiqi. 8. Maliku Miṣra malikun ʿādilun. 9. Huwa bnu l-maliki z-zaʿlāni. 10. 'Anta zaʿlānu min Ḥasanin, wa huwa waladun ṭayyibun. 11. Al-khubzu qadīmun wa l-laḥmu shadīdun. 12. Az-zubdu min ḥalībi (labani) baqarati Muḥammadin. 13. Shaukatu 'ummi l-khalīfati ʿala l-mā'idati ṣ-ṣaghīrati. 14. Makkatu maḥallun ḥasanun. 15. 'Anta fī bustāni Ḥasanini l-jamīli. 16. Al-mā'idatu fī baitin li-Muḥammadin. 17. Al-khubzu ʿala ṣ-ṣaḥni l-jadīdi. Huwa maʿa z-zubdati. 18. Hali l-labanu jadīdun? Lā, huwa qadīmun. 19. 'Anti fī bustāni l-maliki. 20. Shāyu l-waladi fi l-finjāni l-kabīri.

EXERCISE 6

1. The king is angry with the new minister. 2. There is a beautiful new table in Hassan's house. 3. On the table are a knife, fork and spoon. 4. The milk is with the bread and butter. 5. The new market of Damascus is in a long, narrow street. 6. The meat is on the plate. 7. He is a good and just man from Mecca. 8. The king's young son is in one of the minister's houses (lit. a house to the minister). 9. The Caliph's grandmother is dead. 10. Hassan's beautiful mother is a doctor (fem.). 11. Is there a fire in the house? 12. Is there a strong chair in the man's house? 13. Is there fresh (new) coffee in the large cup? 14. The knife and fork belong to the minister. 15. I am a just man, and you are a reliable servant. 16. I am from Egypt. 17. Damascus is beautiful. 18. The King of Egypt is a just man. 19. Yes, he is a short man. 20. The doctor's old broken watch is with the book on the table.

CHAPTER FIVE

(اَلْبَابُ الْخَامِسُ Al-bābu l-khāmisu)

Number. The Sound Masculine and Feminine Plurals. Personal Pronouns. Some simple Verb Forms

1. There are *three numbers* in Arabic: Singular (مُفْرَدٌ mufrad), Dual (مُثَنًّى muthannan), and Plural (جَمْعٌ jamع).

The *Dual* is formed by adding the termination انِ āni in the Nominative and يْنِ aini in the other cases. (The latter, which we may term the oblique case, is the only form used in the colloquial, and becomes ain.)

e.g. مَلِكٌ malikun, a king; مَلِكَانِ مَلِكَيْنِ malikāni, malikaini, two kings.

اَلْمَلِكُ al-maliku, the king; اَلْمَلِكَانِ اَلْمَلِكَيْنِ al-malikāni, al-malikaini, the two kings.

When the noun ends in tā' marbūṭa, this changes to an ordinary tā' before any suffix is joined to it, consequently

مَلِكَةٌ malikatun, a queen, forms the dual مَلِكَتَانِ malikatāni, two queens.

اَلْمَلِكَةُ al-malikatu, the queen, اَلْمَلِكَتَانِ al-malikatāni, the two queens.

2. There are two types of plural in Arabic:

(i) The *Sound Plural* (اَلْجَمْعُ السَّالِمُ al-jamعu s-sālim) which has different masculine and feminine forms. This is formed by adding certain endings to nouns.

(ii) The *Broken Plural* (الجمع المكسر al-jamعu l-mukassar or جمع التكسير jamعu t-taksīr), formed by internal changes, sometimes with the addition of prefixes and suffixes (see Chaps. Six and Seven).

3. The Sound Masculine Plural of nouns and adjectives is formed by adding ون ūna to the Nominative, and ين īna to the Oblique, e.g. معلم muعallimun, a teacher, pl. معلمون، معلمين muعallimūna, muعallimīna. خياط khayyāṭun, a tailor, pl. خياطون ، خياطين khayyāṭūna, khayyāṭīnā. حسن ḥasanun, good, nice, pl. حسنون ḥasanūna. كثير kathīrun, much, many, pl. كثيرون kathīrūna.

4. Many nouns and adjectives cannot form the sound masculine plural, and for them the broken plural (see succeeding chapters) is used as the masculine plural. Similarly, some nouns and adjectives cannot form the broken plural, and must invariably take the sound plural.

When the dictionary does not give the plural of a noun or adjective, this usually means that it takes the sound masculine plural. Among the common types of noun to take the sound masculine plural are participles of verbs, and also nouns of profession or occupation like خياط, khayyāṭun, a tailor, and خباز khabbāzun, a baker. In these latter the middle radical consonant is doubled and is followed by an ʾalif of prolongation.

5. Apart from a very few exceptions, two of which are given below, the sound masculine plural can only be used of male human beings. Names of animals, inanimate objects, and abstract nouns which have no broken plural should take the sound feminine plural given below.

Exceptions:

سَنَةٌ sanatun, year, plural سِنُونَ sinūna or سَنَوَاتٌ sanawātun.

أَرْضٌ 'arḍun, earth, plural أَرَضُونَ 'araḍūna or أَرَاضٍ 'arāḍin.

Even these two exceptions have, it will be seen, alternative plural forms, and أَرَضُونَ is seldom encountered in prose.

6. The Sound Feminine Plural is formed by adding اتٌ ātun in the nominative, and اتٍ ātin in the oblique. The final "n" is treated as a nunation, and therefore disappears when the word is definite, e.g. حَيَوَانٌ ḥayawānun, animal; pl. حَيَوَانَاتٌ. اِجْتِمَاعٌ ijtimāعun, meeting; pl. اِجْتِمَاعَاتٌ

Where the noun in the singular has the tā' marbūṭa feminine ending, this is removed before the sound feminine plural ending is added, e.g. مَلِكَةٌ malikatun, queen, pl. مَلِكَاتٌ مَلِكَاتٍ malikātun, malikātin. كَثِيرَةٌ kat͟hīratun, much, many (feminine), pl. كَثِيرَاتٌ, kat͟hīrātun. خَادِمَةٌ k͟hādimatun, a maid-servant, pl. خَادِمَاتٌ k͟hādimātun. When definite, اَلْمَلِكَةُ al-malikatu; pl. اَلْمَلِكَاتُ ، اَلْمَلِكَاتِ al-malikātu, al-malikāti, the queens.

The sound feminine plural is not confined to female human beings, but is used with many abstract nouns, infinitives, and other forms. It does not follow, either, that a feminine noun ending in tā' marbūṭa will take the sound feminine plural. In fact, the whole question of the plural in Arabic is complicated to the beginner. He will ultimately learn to associate certain singular forms with certain plural forms, but there will be many instances when the dictionary is the only guide. It should be stressed that the plural of a word should be learned with its singular.

7. A few feminine nouns take the sound masculine plural. The commonest is سَنَةٌ sanatun, year, which has already been given. Conversely, some masculine nouns take the feminine plural, as حَيَوَانٌ ḥayawānun, animal, already noted.

AGREEMENT OF ADJECTIVES

8. Adjectives agree with their nouns in gender, case, and number, with certain exceptions:

(a) For the agreement of the broken plural see the next chapters.

(b) The sound feminine plural noun usually has its adjective in the feminine singular. This is occasionally so even when female human beings are concerned.

e.g. حَيَوَانَاتٌ وَحْشَةٌ ḥayawānātun waḥshatun, wild animals; خَادِمَاتٌ جَمِيلَةٌ khādimātun jamīlatun, beautiful maidservants (خَادِمَاتٌ جَمِيلَاتٌ khādimātun jamīlātun is preferable, especially in modern Arabic).

Examples of regular agreement:

خَادِمٌ غَائِبٌ khādimun ghā'ibun, an absent servant.

خَادِمَانِ غَائِبَانِ khādimāni ghā'ibāni, two absent servants.

خَادِمُونَ غَائِبُونَ khādimūna ghā'ibūna, absent servants.

خَادِمَةٌ غَائِبَةٌ khādimatun ghā'ibatun, an absent maidservant.

خَادِمَتَانِ غَائِبَتَانِ khādimatāni ghā'ibatāni, two absent maidservants.

خَادِمَاتٌ غَائِبَاتٌ khādimātun ghā'ibātun
or
خَادِمَاتٌ غَائِبَةٌ khādimātun ghā'ibatun } absent maidservants.

9. The personal pronouns are:

Singular	Dual	Plural
أَنَا ʼanā, I		نَحْنُ naḥnu, we
أَنْتَ ʼanta, thou (you) masc.	أَنْتُمَا ʼantumā, you (two) m. & f.	أَنْتُمْ ʼantum, you (masc.)
أَنْتِ ʼanti, thou (you) feminine		أَنْتُنَّ ʼantunna, you (fem.)
هُوَ huwa, he	هُمَا humā, they (two) m. & f.	هُمْ hum, they (masc.)
هِيَ hiya, she		هُنَّ hunna, they (fem.)

(Attached pronouns will be explained later.)

NOTE: Where only one form is shown above, there is no distinction between masculine and feminine forms. Where dual or plural pronouns refer to mixed sexes, the masculine predominates and the masculine form of the pronoun is used. Thus if the pronoun "they" refers to "men and women" previously mentioned in the passage concerned, the form هُمْ hum, not هُنَّ hunna, would be used. This would be the case even if the pronoun referred to "two women and one man".

SOME SIMPLE VERB FORMS

10. Verbs will be dealt with in detail from Chapter Twelve onwards. However, to make more realistic sentences possible for translation a few forms will be introduced here.

The simplest form of any Arabic verb is the third person masculine singular of the Perfect which usually has a past meaning.

e.g. وَصَلَ waṣala, he arrived, or he has arrived.

طَلَبَ ṭalaba, he demanded, requested, or he has demanded, etc.

كَانَ kāna, he was.

حَضَرَ ḥaḍara, he attended, was present, etc.

This part of the verb invariably ends with the vowel fatḥa.

We have already pointed out that the tā', in the form of the tā' marbūṭa, is a feminine ending. The third person Perfect of the verb may be made feminine merely by adding a tā', but in this case it is the ordinary tā', not the marbūṭa. Thus from وَصَلَ waṣala we have وَصَلَتْ waṣalat, she arrived. From كَانَ kāna we have كَانَتْ kānat, she was. From كَتَبَ kataba, he wrote, we have كَتَبَتْ katabat, she wrote.

We have noticed that the sound masculine plural is characterised by the wāw with a nūn added, thus مُعَلِّمٌ muعallimun, schoolmaster, plural مُعَلِّمُونَ muعallimūna. Similarly, with the Perfect of the verb we add the wāw to make it masculine plural. In this case, however, there is no nūn. Thus: كَتَبَ kataba, كَتَبُوا katabū, they (masc.) wrote. كَانَ kāna, كَانُوا kānū, they were. It should be pointed out that in the Arabic spelling an 'alif is written after the wāw; but this is merely a convention of orthography, and the 'alif is not pronounced. Its existence, in certain cases, prevents ambiguity, such as the wāw's being read at the beginning of the next word as "and".

The dual of parts of the verb in the Perfect are formed by adding the 'alif, which we have already seen in the dual noun ending, انِ āni, to the singular, e.g.

كَتَبَا katabā, they (two) wrote.

كَتَبَتَا katabatā, they (two) wrote (fem.).

11. The normal sentence order is: VERB – SUBJECT – OBJECT – ADVERBIALS.

e.g. حَضَرَ حَسَنٌ الْاجْتِمَاعَ أَمْسِ haḍara Ḥasanuni l-ijtimāعa 'amsi, Hassan attended the meeting yesterday.

12. When the verb in the third person comes first it is *always singular*, though it agrees with its subject in gender.

e.g. كَتَبَ ٱلْوَلَدَانِ kataba l-waladāni, the two boys wrote.

كَتَبَ ٱلْمُعَلِّمُونَ kataba l-muعallimūna, the teachers wrote.

كَتَبَتِ ٱلْمُعَلِّمَتَانِ katabati l-muعallimatāni, the two teachers (fem.) (or schoolmistresses) wrote.

كَتَبَتِ ٱلْمُعَلِّمَاتُ katabati l-muعallimātu, the teachers (fem.) wrote.

Should the subject have already been mentioned, however, in the previous sentence the verb agrees with it in number as well as in gender, e.g. حَضَرَ ٱلْمُعَلِّمُونَ وَطَلَبُوا خُبْزًا haḍara l-muعallimūna wa ṭalabū khubzan, the teachers arrived (were present) and demanded bread. Here the second verb (طَلَبُوا) is in the plural because the subject in the plural (ٱلْمُعَلِّمُونَ) has been mentioned in the previous sentence. The verb حَضَرَ is in the singular because it comes before its subject (ٱلْمُعَلِّمُونَ).

VOCABULARY

language	لُغَةٌ (pl. لُغَاتٌ)	lughatun pl. lughātun
world	عَالَمٌ	عālamun
word	كَلِمَةٌ (pl. كَلِمَاتٌ)	kalimatun, pl. kalimātun
window	شُبَّاكٌ ، نَافِذَةٌ	shubbākun, nāfidhatun
a Muslim	مُسْلِمٌ	Muslimun
a believer	مُؤْمِنٌ	mu'minun

food	أَكْلٌ	ʾaklun
a cook	طَبَّاخٌ	ṭabbākhun
a baker	خَبَّازٌ	khabbāzun
a tailor	خَيَّاطٌ	khayyāṭun
a teacher	مُعَلِّمٌ	muعallimun
animal	حَيَوَانٌ	ḥayawānun
year	سَنَةٌ	sanatun
a meeting	اِجْتِمَاعٌ	ijtimāعun
much, many	كَثِيرٌ	kathīrun
wild (beast)	وَحْشٌ	waḥshun
ill, sick	مَرِيضٌ	marīḍun
hard, difficult	صَعْبٌ	ṣaعbun
easy	سَهْلٌ	sahlun
weak	ضَعِيفٌ	ḍaعīfun
present, found	مَوْجُودٌ	maujūdun
absent	غَائِبٌ	ghāʾibun
day	يَوْمٌ	yaumun
today	اَلْيَوْمَ	al-yauma
yesterday	أَمْسِ	ʾamsi
to arrive (lit. "he arrived")	وَصَلَ	waṣala

to demand, request from	طَلَبَ	ṭalaba
to be (lit. "he was")	كَانَ	kāna
to attend, be present	حَضَرَ	ḥaḍara
to write (to)	كَتَبَ (لِ)	kataba (li)

EXERCISE 7

١ — فِى ٱلْعَالَمِ لُغَاتٌ كَثِيرَةٌ. ٢ — هُمَا خَيَّاطَانِ. ٣ — كَانَ خَبَّازَانِ
فِى ٱلْبَيْتِ. ٤ — ٱلْمُعَلِّمُونَ مَوْجُودُونَ. ٥ — فِى كِتَابِ حَسَنٍ كَلِمَاتٌ
كَثِيرَةٌ صَعْبَةٌ. ٦ — ٱلْمُؤْمِنُونَ غَائِبُونَ ٱلْيَوْمَ. ٧ — كَانُوا فِى ٱلشَّارِعِ
أَمْسِ، وَٱلْيَوْمَ هُمْ فِى ٱلْبَيْتِ. ٨ — وَصَلَتِ ٱلسَّنَةُ ٱلْجَدِيدَةُ. ٩ — فِى
ٱلْبَيْتِ شُبَّاكَانِ (نَافِذَتَانِ). ١٠ — طَلَبَ أَكْلاً مِنَ ٱلطَّبَّاخِينَ. ١١ —
كَتَبَ ٱلْخَلِيفَةُ لِلْمُؤْمِنِينَ فِى دِمَشْقَ. ١٢ — طَلَبَ حَيَوَاناً وَوَصَلَ رَجُلٌ.
١٣ — حَضَرَ ٱلْوَزِيرُ ٱلْمَرِيضُ ٱلْاِجْتِمَاعَ. ١٤ — ٱلْكِتَابُ سَهْلٌ لِلطَّبِيبِ.
١٥ — أَفِى بُسْتَانِ ٱلْمُعَلِّمِ حَيَوَانٌ وَحْشٌ؟ ١٦ — طَلَبْتُ مِنَ ٱلْخَادِمِينَ
خُبْزاً وَزُبْداً وَشَاياً وَحَلِيباً. ١٧ — فِى مِصْرَ مُسْلِمُونَ كَثِيرُونَ. ١٨ —
أَهُنَّ مُسْلِمَاتٌ؟ ١٩ — لِبُسْتَانِ ٱلْحَسَنَيْنِ بَابَانِ. ٢٠ — كَانَ ٱلْكِتَابَانِ
عَلَى ٱلْمَائِدَةِ أَمْسِ. ٱلْيَوْمَ هُمَا فِى بَيْتِ ٱلطَّبِيبِ.

TRANSCRIPTION

1. Fī l-عālami lughātun kathīratun. 2. Humā khayyāṭāni. 3. Kāna khabbāzāni fi l-baiti. 4. Al-muعallimūn maujūdūna. 5. Fī kitābi Ḥasanin kalimātun kathīratun ṣaعbatun. 6. Al-mu'minūna gha'ibūna l-yauma. 7. Kānū fi sh-shāriعi

'amsi, wa l-yauma hum fi l-baiti. 8. Waṣalati s-sanatu l-jadīdatu. 9. Fi l-baiti shubbākāni (nāfidhatāni). 10. Ṭalaba 'akalan min aṭ-ṭabbākhaini. 11. Kataba l-khalīfatu lil-mu'minīna fī Dimashqa. 12. Ṭalaba ḥayawānan wa waṣala rajulun. 13. Ḥaḍara l-wazīru l-marīḍu lijtimāعa. 14. Al-kitābu sahlun li ṭ-ṭabībi. 15. 'A-fī bustāni l-muعallimi ḥayawānun waḥshun? 16. Ṭalabat min al-khādimīna khubzan wa zubdan wa shāyan wa ḥalīban. 17. Fī Miṣra Muslimūna kathīrūna. 18. 'A-hunna Muslimātun? 19. Li-bustāni l-Ḥasanaini bābāni. 20. Kāna l-kitābāni عala l-mā'idati 'amsi. Al-yauma humā fī baiti ṭ-ṭabībi.

EXERCISE 8

1. Two difficult languages. 2. He wrote two easy books for the boy. 3. The bread arrived from the baker yesterday. 4. The food of the two cooks [who are] present (الحاضرين) today is beautiful. 5. The Muslim teachers are absent today. 6. It was a house belonging to (لِ) two believers. 7. Hassan's house has (لِ) two windows, two doors, and a large garden. 8. They (dual) are sick, weak men. 9. There are many wild animals in the world. 10. They attended many meetings. 11. They asked for (demanded) good tailors. 12. Two little words. 13. In the book are many difficult words. 14. They (dual) arrived from Egypt yesterday. 15. You (dual) are teachers. 16. We are upright Muslims. 17. They are schoolmistresses in Damascus. 18. Many years. 19. Two days. 20. You and I are good doctors. He is an animal doctor (a doctor of the animals).

CHAPTER SIX

(اَلْبَابُ السَّادِسُ Al-bābu s-sādisu)

The Broken Plural

1. Before dealing with broken plurals, it is necessary for the student to appreciate the importance of word forms, or patterns, in Arabic. The great majority of Arabic roots are *triliteral*, that is, they consist of three radical letters or consonants. The combination of these letters gives a basic meaning. By modifying the root, by the addition of prefixes and suffixes, and by changing the vowels, whether long or short, a large number of word patterns can be formed from each root. Many of these word patterns are associated with a meaning pattern. This is a great help in vocabulary acquisition.

The Arab grammarians expressed the various word patterns by using the root فَعَلَ faعala (to do). The ف represents the first radical, the ع the second, and the ل the third. Thus of words already given, حَسَنٌ ḥasanun is of the form فَعَلٌ faعalun; بَيْتٌ baitun (baytun) is of the form faعlun; كَبِيرٌ kabīrun of the form فَعِيلٌ faعīlun and so on.

2. For a large number of Arabic nouns the sound plural does not exist at all. The broken plural must be used.

Unfortunately, many different word patterns are used for the broken plural, and although certain of them are mostly associated with specific singular forms, this is not an invariable rule, and is of little help to the beginner. Consequently the plural of a new word should be learned from the dictionary at the same time as its singular. For this reason, the student should have an Arabic-English dictionary which gives plurals. Some dictionaries, being designed for Arabs learning English, do not give plurals.

3. The following are among the commoner patterns of the broken plural:

(a) أَفْعَالٌ ʼafʿālun, e.g. أَوْلَادٌ ʼaulādun (ʼawlādun) pl. of وَلَدٌ waladun; أَمْطَارٌ ʼamṭārun, pl. of maṭarun, مَطَرٌ rain; أَوْقَاتٌ ʼawqātun, pl. of وَقْتٌ waqtun, time.

(b) فُعُولٌ fuʿūlun, e.g. مُلُوكٌ mulūkun, pl. of مَلِكٌ malikun, king; حُرُوفٌ ḥurūfun, pl. of حَرْفٌ ḥarfun, letter; قُلُوبٌ qulūbun, pl. of قَلْبٌ qalbun, heart; سُيُوفٌ suyūfun, pl. of سَيْفٌ saifun, sword; عُلُومٌ ʿulūmun, pl. of عِلْمٌ ʿilmun, knowledge, science, study; دُرُوسٌ durūsun, pl. of دَرْسٌ darsun, lesson.

(c) فِعَالٌ fiʿālun, e.g. كِلَابٌ kilābun, pl. of كَلْبٌ kalbun, dog; رِجَالٌ rijālun, pl. of رَجُلٌ rajulun, man; جِبَالٌ jibālun, pl. of جَبَلٌ jabalun, mountain; among adjectives we find طِوَالٌ ṭiwalun, pl. of طَوِيلٌ ṭawīlun, tall; كِبَارٌ kibārun, pl. of كَبِيرٌ kabīrun, big, old; صِعَابٌ ṣiʿābun, pl. of صَعْبٌ ṣaʼbun, difficult.

(d) فُعُلٌ fuʿulun, e.g. كُتُبٌ kutubun, pl. of كِتَابٌ kitābun, book; مُدُنٌ mudunun, pl. of مَدِينَةٌ madīnatun, city; سُفُنٌ sufunun, pl. of سَفِينَةٌ safīnatun, a (large) ship; جُدُدٌ jududun, pl. of جَدِيدٌ jadīdun, new.

(e) أَفْعُلٌ afʿulun, e.g. أَنْهُرٌ ʼanhurun, pl. of نَهْرٌ nahrun, river; أَشْهُرٌ ashhurun, pl. of شَهْرٌ shahrun, month; أَرْجُلٌ ʼarjulun, pl. of رِجْلٌ rijlun, foot.

4. It will be noticed that adjectives as well as nouns may

have broken plurals. These plurals are used in place of the sound masculine plural, and normally refer to male human beings, e.g. رِجَالٌ طِوَالٌ rijālun ṭiwālun, tall men. Otherwise, broken plurals are usually considered to be feminine singular for the purpose of agreement: e.g. مُدُنٌ كَبِيرَةٌ mudunun kabīratun, large cities; دُرُوسٌ صَعْبَةٌ durūsun ṣaعbatun, difficult lessons. اَلْمُدُنُ كَبِيرَةٌ al-mudunu kabīratun, the cities are large.

However, in older Classical Arabic, especially poetry, as well as late Classical and Modern Prose of a rhetorical or studied nature, broken plural adjectives may be found with broken plural nouns even when these do not refer to male human beings.

e.g. عُلُومٌ صِعَابٌ عulūmun ṣiعābun, difficult sciences (instead of ṣaعbatun); سُفُنٌ طِوَالٌ sufunun ṭiwālun (for ṭawīlatun), long ships. The beginner is advised, nevertheless when writing Arabic, to treat broken plurals as feminine singular unless they refer to male human beings.

Broken plural adjectives are frequently used with nouns in the sound masculine plural, e.g. خَادِمُونَ كِبَارٌ khādimūna kibārun, old servants. The dictionary wili show us that the adjective كَبِيرٌ kabīrun does not form the sound masculine kabīrūna; consequently the broken plural, kibārun, has to do duty for it.

5. Some words have more than one broken plural; e.g. طَلَبَةٌ ṭalabatun and طُلَّابٌ ṭullābun, plurals of طَالِبٌ ṭālibun, student. In some cases, this involves difference of meaning, e.g., بَيْتٌ baitun means either a house or a verse of poetry. In the former, and commoner meaning, the plural is usually بُيُوتٌ buyūtun. In the latter meaning, the plural أَبْيَاتٌ

'abyātun is more common. Again, some words may take both the sound masculine plural and the broken plural, e.g. خَادِمُونَ khādimūna and خَدَمَةٌ khadamatun, plurals of خَادِمٌ khādimun, servant.

VOCABULARY

rain	مَطَرٌ (pl. أَمْطَارٌ)	maṭarun, *pl.* 'amṭārun
time	وَقْتٌ (pl. أَوْقَاتٌ)	waqtun, *pl.* 'auqātun
letter (of the alphabet)	حَرْفٌ (pl. حُرُوفٌ)	ḥarfun, *pl.* ḥurūfun
heart	قَلْبٌ (pl. قُلُوبٌ)	qalbun, *pl.* qulūbun
sword	سَيْفٌ (pl. سُيُوفٌ)	saifun, *pl.* suyūfun
knowledge, science, study	عِلْمٌ (pl. عُلُومٌ)	ʿilmun, *pl.* ʿulūmun
lesson	دَرْسٌ (pl. دُرُوسٌ)	darsun, *pl.* durūsun
dog	كَلْبٌ (pl. كِلَابٌ)	kalbun, *pl.* kilābun
mountain	جَبَلٌ (pl. جِبَالٌ)	jabalun, *pl.* jibālun
city, town	مَدِينَةٌ (pl. مُدُنٌ)	madīnatun, *pl.* mudunun
(large) ship	سَفِينَةٌ (pl. سُفُنٌ)	safīnatun, *pl.* sufunun
month	شَهْرٌ (pl. شُهُورٌ)	shahrun, *pl.* shuhūrun
student	طَالِبٌ (pl. طُلَّابٌ)	ṭālibun, *pl.* ṭullābun
to go (lit. he went)	ذَهَبَ	dhahaba
to go out (from)	خَرَجَ (مِنْ)	kharaja (min)
to kill	قَتَلَ	qatala
to find	وَجَدَ	wajada

before (*prep.* of time)	قَبْلَ	qabla
after (*prep.* of time)	بَعْدَ	baɛda
then	ثُمَّ	thumma
Arabic, Arabian, an Arab	عَرَبِىٌّ (*pl.* عَرَبٌ)	ɛarabīyun, *pl.* ɛarabun
English, Englishman	إِنْكِلِيزِىٌّ (*pl.* إِنْكِلِيزُ)	ʼinkilīzīyun, *pl.* ʼinkilīzun
profitable, useful	نَافِعٌ	nāfiɛun
watchful, guarding	حَارِسٌ	ḥārisun
fast, swift	سَرِيعٌ	sarīɛun
cutting	قَاطِعٌ	qāṭiɛun
a little, a few	قَلِيلٌ (pl. قَلِيلُونَ)	qalīlun, *pl.* qalīlūna
Alexandria (city)	ٱلْإِسْكَنْدَرِيَّةُ	Al-ʼiskandarīyatu
London	لُنْدُنُ	Lundunu

EXERCISE 9

١ — وَجَدُوا كِلَابًا كَثِيرَةً فِى ٱلسُّوقِ أَمْسِ. ٢ — كَتَبَتِ ٱلْبِنْتُ ٱلْعَرَبِيَّةُ حُرُوفًا إِنْكِلِيزِيَّةً جَمِيلَةً. ٣ — قَتَلْتَ (2nd pers. masc. sing.) رَجُلَيْنِ بِٱلسَّيْفِ قَبْلَ شَهْرَيْنِ. ٤ — خَرَجَتْ سُفُنٌ كَثِيرَةٌ طَوِيلَةٌ مِنَ ٱلسُّوَيْسِ (Suez). ٥ — ٱلدُّرُوسُ ٱلْعَرَبِيَّةُ نَافِعَةٌ لِلطُّلَّابِ. ٦ — ٱلْكَلْبُ حَيَوَانٌ حَارِسٌ. ٧ — كَانَ ٱلطُّلَّابُ فِى ٱلْقَاهِرَةِ قَبْلَ شُهُورٍ قَلِيلَةٍ. ٨ — ثُمَّ ذَهَبُوا إِلَى دِمَشْقَ. ٩ — لِلْوَزِيرِ خَادِمٌ سَرِيعٌ. ١٠ — أَوْقَاتُ ٱلْأَمْطَارِ طَوِيلَةٌ فِى

ٱلْهِنْدِ (India). ١١ — خَرَجَ ٱلطُّلَّابُ مِنَ ٱلدُّرُوسِ قَبْلَ سَاعَةٍ. ١٢ —
هِيَ عُلُومٌ صَعْبَةٌ. ١٣ — وَجَدَا جِبَالًا جَمِيلَةً بَعِيدَةً مِنَ ٱلْمَدِينَةِ. ١٤ — هَلِ
ٱلسُّيُوفُ نَافِعَةٌ؟ ١٥ — لَا، ٱلْكُتُبُ نَافِعَةٌ. ١٦ — لِمُحَمَّدٍ سَيْفٌ قَاطِعٌ
وَلِحَسَنٍ قَلْبٌ صَالِحٌ. ١٧ — هُمُ ٱلرِّجَالُ ٱلْكِبَارُ وَنَحْنُ ٱلْأَوْلَادُ ٱلصِّغَارُ.
١٨ — هُوَ نَهْرٌ صَعْبٌ لِلسُّفُنِ ٱلْكَبِيرَةِ. ١٩ — وَصَلَتْ بِنْتَانِ وَطَلَبَتَا
خُبْزًا وَلَبَنًا مِنَ ٱلْخَدَمَةِ. ٢٠ — نَحْنُ رِجَالٌ صِعَابٌ.

TRANSCRIPTION

1. Wajadū kilāban kat͟hīratan fī s-sūqi ʼamsi. 2. Katabati l-bintu l-ʿarabīyatu ḥurūfan inkilīzīyatan jamīlatan. 3. Qatalta rajulaini bi s-saifi qabla s͟hahraini. 4. K͟harajat sufunun kat͟hīratun ṭawīlatun mina s-suwaisi. 5. Ad-durūsu l-ʿarabīyatu nāfiʿatun li ṭ-ṭullābi. 6. Al-kalbu ḥayawānun ḥārisun. 7. Kāna ṭ-ṭullābu fi l-qāhirati qabla s͟huhūrin qalīlatin. 8. T͟humma d͟hahabū ʼilā Dimas͟hqa. 9. Li l-wazīri k͟hādimun sarīʿun. 10. ʼAuqātu l-ʼamṭāri ṭawīlatun fi l-Hindi. 11. K͟haraja ṭ-ṭullābu mina d-durūsi qabla sāʿatin. 12. Hiya ʿulūmun ṣaʿbatun. 13. Wajadā jibālan jamīlatan baʿīdatan mina l-madīnati. 14. Hali s-suyūfu nāfiʿatun? 15. Lā, al-kutubu nāfiʿatun. 16. Li Muḥammadin saifun qāṭiʿun wa li Ḥasanin qalbun ṣāliḥun. 17. Humu r-rijālu l-kibāru wa naḥnu l-ʼaulādu ṣ-ṣig͟hāru. 18. Huwa nahrun ṣaʿbun li s-sufuni l-kabīrati. 19. Waṣalat bintāni wa ṭalabatā k͟hubzan wa-labanan mina l-k͟hadamati. 20. Naḥnu rijālun ṣiʿābun.

EXERCISE 10

1. The students went to the teachers' houses. 2. They came out of the lessons two hours ago (lit. before two hours). 3. After a long time the new teachers arrived. 4. They (هِيَ)

are swift rivers. 5. A few English boys arrived today in the large ship. 6. They are from many cities. 7. The king killed the minister with (بِ) the sword, then went out to the mountain. 8. There is a watchful dog in Muhammad's house. 9. They found the Arab boy an hour ago (before one hour). 10. Hassan's books are easy. 11. The students attended the lessons yesterday. 12. Long months. 13. The cow has (لِ) a big heart. 14. The time of the rains has gone. 15. The boys' Arabic letters are ugly. 16. There was a cutting sword in the tall man's hand. 17. They sought learning in Egypt. 18. Cairo and Damascus are great cities. 19. They (هُمَا) are Arab cities. 20. The large new ships arrived in Alexandria from London two days ago.

CHAPTER SEVEN

(اَلْبَابُ اَلسَّابِعُ Al-bābu s-sābiعu)

The Broken Plural (*continued*)

1. Further forms of the broken plural are:

(f) فُعَلَاءُ fuعalā'u (diptote), e.g. وُزَرَاءُ wuzarā'u, pl. of وَزِيرٌ wazīrun, a minister (political); أُمَرَاءُ 'umarā'u, pl. of أَمِيرٌ 'amīrun, a prince, commander; سُفَرَاءُ sufarā'u, pl. of safīrun, سَفِيرٌ an ambassador.

(g) أَفْعِلَاءُ 'afعilā'u (diptote), e.g. أَصْدِقَاءُ 'aṣdiqā'u, pl. of صَدِيقٌ ṣadīqun, a friend; أَنْبِيَاءُ 'anbiyā'u, pl. of نَبِيٌّ nabīyun, نَبِيءٌ nabī'un a prophet; أَقْرِبَاءُ 'aqribā'u, pl. of قَرِيبٌ qarībun, a relative أَغْنِيَاءُ 'aghniyā'u, pl. of غَنِيٌّ ghanīyun, rich, rich man.

The above two plural forms are common for nouns and adjectives of the form فَعِيلٌ, when they denote human beings.

(h) فُعْلَانٌ fuعlānun, e.g. بُلْدَانٌ buldānun, pl. of بَلَدٌ baladun, a district, country, town; قُضْبَانٌ quḍbānun, pl. of قَضِيبٌ qaḍībun, a rod, sceptre, line (of railway track, modern usage). Care should be taken in identifying this form by checking that the final nūn is a letter of increase, not a radical. There must be three radical consonants before the ending انٌ ānun, otherwise the nūn is likely to be a radical letter.

2. While it is difficult, and often impossible, to guess the broken plural of a triliteral (three radical) noun and vice-versa, the case is otherwise with quadriliteral (four consonant) nouns. Here the plural can frequently be deduced from the singular and vice-versa. The following forms are encountered:

(i) فَعَالِلُ faعālilu (diptote), plural of فَعْلَلٌ faعlalun, فَعْلِلٌ faعlilun, فَعْلَلَةٌ faعlalatun, etc.

e.g. جَوَاهِرُ jawāhiru, pl. of جَوْهَرٌ jauharun, a jewel.

تَجَارِبُ tajāribu, pl. of تَجْرِبَةٌ tajribatun, an experiment, trial.

مَجَالِسُ majālisu, pl. of مَجْلِسٌ majlisun, a council.

مَنَازِلُ manāzilu, pl. of مَنْزِلٌ manzilun, a house, lodging, dwelling.

مَكَاتِبُ makātibu, pl. of { مَكْتَبٌ maktabun, an office; a school (obsolete meaning), and مَكْتَبَةٌ maktabatun, a library, a desk. }

(though in the latter word, the sound feminine plural, مَكْتَبَاتٌ maktabātun is also used.)

(j) فَعَالِيلُ fa'ālīlu (diptote), e.g.

سَلَاطِينُ salāṭīnu, pl. of سُلْطَانٌ sulṭānun, a sultan.

مَكَاتِيبُ makātību, pl. of مَكْتُوبٌ maktūbun, a letter.

صَنَادِيقُ ṣanādīqu, pl. of صُنْدُوقٌ ṣundūqun, a chest, case, box.

فَنَاجِينُ fanājīnu, pl. of فِنْجَانٌ finjānun, a cup.

مَنَادِيلُ manādīlu, pl. of مِنْدِيلٌ mandīlun, a napkin, veil, towel (handkerchief in modern Arabic).

NOTE: The student must be able to distinguish which of these two plural forms is apt for each four-consonant word. This depends on a very simple rule. In almost every case, plural form (i) فَعَالِلُ faع̣ālilu is used for nouns which have no long vowel in the singular, but merely short vowels after the first and third consonants. It does not matter what these short vowels are and there may be a feminine ending of tā' marbūṭa. On the other hand, where the singular has a long vowel after the third consonant in the singular, whether it be ā, ī or ū (see above examples), plural form (j) is usual.

(k) Certain nouns which would otherwise have form (j) take the plural فَعَالِلَةٌ faعālilatun, e.g.

تَلَامِذَةٌ talāmid͟hatun, pl. of تِلْمِيذٌ tilmīd͟hun, a scholar; (تَلَامِيذُ talāmīd͟hu (j) also occurs).

This form is used for a small number of Arabicised foreign words, of which tilmīd͟hun is one. Similarly أُسْتَاذٌ 'ustād͟hun (from the Persian), a teacher, professor, also a courtesy title, and it has the plural أَسَاتِذَةٌ 'asātid͟hatun as well as أَسَاتِيذُ 'asātīd͟hu. Sometimes the singular does not have the long vowel after the third consonant, e.g.

أَسَاقِفَةٌ 'asāqifatun, pl. of أُسْقُفٌ 'usqufun, a bishop, from the Greek *episkopos*.

صَيَادِلَةٌ ṣayādilatun, pl. of صَيْدَلِيٌّ ṣaidalīyun, a chemist.

3. The following words deserve special notice:

اِبْنٌ ibnun, a son, plural بَنُونَ بَنِينَ banūna, banīna (sound masc. pl.) or أَبْنَاءٌ 'abnā'un.

اِبْنَةٌ ibnatun or بِنْتٌ bintun, daughter, pl. بَنَاتٌ banātun.

أَخٌ ʼakhun, brother, pl. إِخْوَانٌ ʼikhwānun or إِخْوَةٌ ʼikhwatun.

أُخْتٌ ʼukhtun, sister, pl. أَخَوَاتٌ ʼakhawātun.

أَبٌ ʼabun, father, pl. آبَاءٌ ʼābāʼun.

أُمٌّ ʼummun, mother, pl. أُمَّهَاتٌ ʼummahātun, or أُمَّاتٌ ʼummātun (not commonly used).

When the word إِبْنٌ ibnun, son, forms part of a proper name, and has a name before it as well as after it, the initial *ʼalif* is not written; e.g. اَلْقَاسِمُ بْنُ سَلَّامٍ al-Qāsimu bnu Sallāmin, al-Qāsim son of Sallām. When, however, this man is merely referred to as "son of Sallam" it is written اِبْنُ سَلَّامٍ, Ibn Sallām (cf. ابن خلدون Ibn Khaldūn, etc.). This form is also used at the beginning of a line. The *ʼalif* in ابن has hamzatu l-waṣl.

VOCABULARY

near *adj.*	قَرِيبٌ	qarībun
school (مَدَارِسُ *pl.*)	مَدْرَسَةٌ	madrasatun, *pl.* madārisu
to take	أَخَذَ	ʼakhadha
to mention	ذَكَرَ	dhakara
to know	عَرَفَ	ʿarafa
to	إِلَى	ʼilā
about, concerning	عَنْ	ʿan
or	أَوْ	ʼau
Tanta (town in Egypt)	طَنْطَا	Ṭanṭā

(Other words in the accompanying chapter.)

EXERCISE 11

١ — كَانَ قَضِيبٌ فِى يَدِ ٱلْمَلِكِ قَبْلَ سَاعَةٍ. ٢ — ذَكَرَ ٱلسَّفِيرُ
ٱلْإِنْكِلِيزِىُّ ٱلْأَخْبَارَ ٱلطَّيِّبَةَ عَنِ ٱلسُّفُنِ. ٣ — أَصْدِقَاءُ حَسَنٍ ٱلْأَغْنِيَاءُ
مَوْجُودُونَ فِى ٱلْبَيْتِ مَعَ أَقْرِبَاءِ ٱلْأَمِيرِ ٱلْعَرَبِىِّ. ٤ — أَخَذَتِ ٱلْبِنْتُ
جَوَاهِرَ جَمِيلَةً مِنَ ٱلْوَزِيرِ. ٥ — مُحَمَّدٌ نَبِىُّ ٱلْعَرَبِ. ٦ — هُمْ فِى مَجْلِسِ
ٱلسُّلْطَانِ ٱلْيَوْمَ. ٧ — حَضَرُوا ٱلْمَجْلِسَ فِى مَنْزِلِ ٱلْأَمِيرِ. ٨ — وَجَدَتْ
كُتُبًا كَثِيرَةً جَمِيلَةً فِى صَنَادِيقَ قَدِيمَةٍ. ٩ — ٱلْقَاهِرَةُ وَٱلْإِسْكَنْدَرِيَّةُ
وَطَنْطَا بُلْدَانٌ كَبِيرَةٌ فِى مِصْرَ. ١٠ — أَخَذَ ٱلسَّفِيرُ فِنْجَانَ شَاىٍ فِى
مَكْتَبِ ٱلْوَزِيرِ. ١١ — وَجَدَ ٱلرَّجُلُ ٱلْمَكَاتِيبَ عَلَى ٱلْمَكْتَبَةِ ٱلْجَدِيدَةِ.
١٢ — بَلَغَتِ ٱلْأَخْبَارُ مِنَ ٱلْوَزِيرِ أَوْ مِنَ ٱلْمَلِكِ. ١٣ — وَصَلَ ٱلتَّلَامِذَةُ
إِلَى ٱلْمَدْرَسَةِ. ١٤ — مَنَادِيلُ ٱلتَّلَامِيذِ نَظِيفَةٌ ٱلْيَوْمَ. ١٥ — تَجَارِبُ
ٱلْأَسَاتِذَةِ نَافِعَةٌ. ١٦ — ٱبْنُ ٱلسَّفِيرِ وَأُخْتُ ٱلْأَمِيرِ صَدِيقَانِ. ١٧ —
هَلْ عَرَفَتْ أُمُّ ٱلسُّلْطَانِ أَخْبَارَ ٱلْيَوْمِ؟ ١٨ — لَا، هِىَ خَرَجَتْ مِنَ
ٱلْمَدِينَةِ قَبْلَ يَوْمَيْنِ. ١٩ — أَنْتُمُ ٱلْأَغْنِيَاءُ. ٢٠ — ذَكَرَ كُتُبَ ٱلْأَنْبِيَاءِ.

TRANSCRIPTION

1. Kāna qaḍībun fi yadi l-maliki qabla sāʿatin. 2. Dhakara s-safīru l-'inkilīzīyu l-'akhbāra ṭ-ṭayyiba ʿani s-sufuni. 3. 'Aṣdiqā'u Ḥasanini l-'aghniyā'u maujūdūna fi l-baiti, maʿa 'aqribā'i l-'amīri l-ʿarabīyi. 4. 'Akhadhati l-bintu jawāhira jamīlatan mina l-wazīri. 5. Muḥammadun nabīyu l-ʿarabi. 6. Hum fī majlisi s-sulṭāni l-yauma. 7. Ḥaḍarū l-majlisa fī manzili l-'amīri. 8. Wajadat kutuban kathīratan jamīlatan fī ṣanādīqa qadīmatin. 9. Al-Qāhiratu wa l-'Iskandarīyatu wa Ṭanṭā buldānun kabīratun fī Misra. 10. 'Akhadha s-safīru

finjāna shāyin fī maktabi l-wazīri. 11. Wajada r-rajulu l-makātība ʿala l-maktabati l-jadīdati. 12. Balaghati l-'akhbāru mina l-wazīri 'au mina l-maliki. 13. Waṣalū t-talāmidhatu 'ila l-madrasati. 14. Manādīlu t-talāmīdhi naẓīfatuni l-yauma. 15. Tajāribu l-'asātidhati nāfiʿatun. 16. Ibnu s-safīri wa 'ukhtu l-'amīri ṣadīqāni. 17. Hal ʿarafat 'ummu s-sulṭāni 'akhbāra l-yaumi? 18. Lā, hiya kharajat mina l-madīnati qabla yaumaini. 19. 'Antumu l-'aghniyā'u. 20. Dhakara kutuba l-'anbiyā'i.

EXERCISE 12

1. News about the experiments reached the council of ministers yesterday. 2. They are upright princes. 3. The new ambassador is the friend of (the) rich men. 4. He is near to (مِنْ) the town. 5. There were jewels in the old chests. 6. The king's son mentioned the good news in the council today. 7. The clean cups are in the big boxes. 8. The professor took the king's sons to (the) school. 9. The mothers of the pupils attended with the teachers. 10. They learned (بَلَغَتْهُمُ lit. "reached them") the news about the sultan's letters. 11. He is with Hassan's friend in the office. 12. They are in the garden of Muhammad's house. 13. They went to Cairo or Damascus two months ago. 14. She is the daughter of the king and the sister of the prince. 15. The relatives killed the ambassador and left the house. 16. She found old cups in the house. 17. They are old handkerchiefs. 18. He asked for tea in a clean cup. 19. The rich men are present. 20. Are you prophets?

CHAPTER EIGHT

(اَلْبَابُ ٱلثَّامِنُ)

The Genitive

('Iḍāfa إِضَافَةٌ)

1. Declension of nouns has been dealt with in Chapter Four. The purpose of this chapter is to explain the genitive further. We have already mentioned that the noun with a following *definite* genitive or iḍāfa is *ipso facto* definite, and that a noun with iḍāfa always loses its nūnation.

2. In the dual, and the sound masculine plural, the final nūn and its vowel are omitted. Thus انِ and يْنِ (āni and aini) become ا and يْ (ā and ai); ونَ and ينَ (ūna and īna) become و and ي (ū and ī).

e.g.

بَيْتَا ٱلرَّجُلِ baitā r-rajuli, the two houses of the man.

بَيْتَا مُحَمَّدٍ baitā Muḥammadin, the two houses of Muhammad.

بَابَا بَيْتَيِ ٱلرَّجُلِ bābā baitayi r-rajuli, the two doors of the two houses of the man.

اِبْنَتَا ٱلْوَزِيرِ ibnatā l-wazīri, the two daughters of the minister.

مُعَلِّمُو ٱلْوَلَدِ muعallimū l-waladi, the teachers of the boy (the boy's teachers).

كَتَبَ لِمُعَلِّمِي ٱلْمَدْرَسَةِ kataba li muعallimī l-madrasati, he wrote to the teachers of the school.

3. Certain words, *when followed by a genitive*, have long vowels as their case endings, viz.:

	father	father-in-law	brother	mouth
Nom. و -ū	أَبُو 'abū	حَمُو ḥamū	أَخُو 'akhū	فُو fū
Acc. ا -ā	أَبَا 'abā	حَمَا ḥamā	أَخَا 'akhā	فَا fā
Gen. ى -ī	أَبِي 'abī	حَمِي ḥamī	أَخِي 'akhī	فِي fī
Normal form without gen.	أَبٌ 'abun	حَمٌ ḥamun	أَخٌ 'akhun	فَمٌ famun

The last named is particularly irregular.

To these should be added the word ذُو dhū (possessor, master, of) which is only used with a following genitive:

Nom. dhū ذُو   Acc. ذَا dhā   Gen. ذِى dhī

e.g. وَصَلَ أَبُو مُحَمَّدٍ waṣala 'abū Muḥammadin, the father of Muhammad arrived.

قَتَلُوا أَبَا مُحَمَّدٍ qatalū 'abā Muḥammadin, they killed Muhammad's father.

كَتَبَتْ لِأَبِي مُحَمَّدٍ katabat li 'abī Muḥammadin, she wrote to Muhammad's father.

كَانَ رَجُلٌ ذُو مَالٍ كَثِيرٍ فِى قَصْرِ السُّلْطَانِ kāna rajulun dhū mālin kathīrin fī qaṣri s-sulṭāni, a rich man was in the sultan's palace (a man, possessor of much wealth).

4. It is a rule of 'iḍāfa that a noun cannot be separated from its following genitive. If, therefore, it is qualified by an adjective, the adjective must come after the genitive.

e.g. سَاعَةُ ٱلرَّجُلِ ٱلْقَدِيمَةُ sāʿatu r-rajuli l-qadīmatu, the man's old watch (clock).

بَيْتُ مُحَمَّدٍ ٱلْكَبِيرُ baitu Muḥammadini l-kabīru, Muhammad's large house.

فِى بَيْتِ مُحَمَّدٍ ٱلْكَبِيرِ fī baiti Muḥammadini l-kabīri, in Muhammad's large house.

It should be noted that here the adjective takes the definite article, because when a noun is qualified by a *definite* genitive it automatically becomes definite. بَيْتُ مُحَمَّدٍ كَبِيرٌ baitu Muḥammadin kabīrun could only mean "Muhammad's house is big". On the other hand the third sentence above is ambiguous, since it could mean "in old (big) Muhammad's house".

5. If the genitive refers to two nouns, it must follow the first, while the second takes the suffix of the personal pronoun (see Chapter Nine). بَيْتُ ٱلْوَزِيرِ وَبُسْتَانُهُ baitu l-wazīri wa bustānuhu, the minister's house and garden (literally "and his garden").

6. In the case of parts of the body of which there are two, the dual, not the plural, should be used, e.g.
عَيْنَا ٱلْبِنْتِ ʿainā l-binti, not عُيُونُ ٱلْبِنْتِ ʿuyūnu l-binti, the girl's (two) eyes.

7. Although the genitive is primarily for possession, it is also used partitively.

e.g. قِطْعَةُ لَحْمٍ qiṭʿatu laḥmin, a piece of meat or flesh.

فِنْجَانُ قَهْوَةٍ finjānu qahwatin, a cup of coffee.

In addition, it may be used to denote the material of which something is composed:

e.g. كُرْسِيُّ خَشَبٍ kursīyu khashabin, a chair (made) of wood, a wooden chair.

In such cases, the ʾiḍāfa may be replaced by the preposition مِنْ min, followed by a genitive. When this happens, of course, the noun, being indefinite, and having no iḍāfa retains its nunation.

e.g. قِطْعَةٌ مِنْ لَحْمٍ (اللَّحْمِ) qiṭʿatun min laḥmin (or better, qiṭʿatun mina l-laḥmi).

كُرْسِيٌّ مِنْ خَشَبٍ (الْخَشَبِ) kursīyun min khashabin (or al-khashabi).

The optional (but more usual) use of the article in the above examples with لحم and خشب should be noted. When a noun is used in a general sense, not to denote a single unit, the article is more often than not employed.

8. The genitive often occurs after an adjective to define or limit its application; e.g.

قَلِيلُ الْعَقْلِ qalīlu l-ʿaqli, little of understanding, stupid.

كَثِيرُ الْمَالِ kathīru l-māli, abundant of wealth, rich.

حَسَنُ الْوَجْهِ ḥasanu l-wajhi, handsome of face.*

9. Some nouns in Arabic are used with a following genitive noun to denote a quality which, in English, would normally be expressed simply by an adjective. These include:

ذُو dhū (already mentioned), dual masc. ذَوَا dhawā, plural dhawū ذَوُو, fem. sing. ذَاتُ dhātu, dual ذَاتَا dhātā, pl. ذَوَاتُ dhawātu. أَبُو ʾabū; أُمُّ ʾummu; اِبْنُ ibnu; صَاحِبُ ṣāḥibu.

These words are, of course, un-nunated because of the following genitive, and they all mean, in a loose sort of sense, master of, endowed with, possessor of. They are not so common in modern Arabic.

* See also Appendix C, §3.

e.g.

صَاحِبُ عِلْمٍ ṣāḥibu ʿilmin, "master of learning", learned.

ذَاتُ حُسْنٍ dhātu ḥusnin (fem.), "possessor of beauty", beautiful.

أَبُو لِسَانَيْنِ 'abū lisānaini, "father of two tongues", dissembling.

ابْنُ خَمْسِينَ سَنَةً ibnu khamsīna sanatan, "son of 50 years", 50 years old.

These expressions can nearly always be replaced by simple adjectives. For example, the adjective (fem.) جَمِيلَةٌ jamīlatun could replace ذَاتُ حُسْنٍ dhātu ḥusnin. The indiscriminate use of the above compound expressions in modern Arabic would be considered an affected mannerism.

VOCABULARY

father	أَبٌ (أَبُو) (pl. آبَاءٌ)	'abun ('abū), *pl.* 'ābā'un
father-in-law	حَمٌ (حَمُو) (pl. أَحْمَاءٌ)	ḥamun (ḥamū), *pl.* 'aḥmā'un
brother	أَخٌ (أَخُو) (pl. إِخْوَانٌ)	'akhun ('akhū), *pl.* 'ikhwānun
mouth	فَمٌ (فُو) (pl. أَفْوَاهٌ)	famun (fū), *pl.* 'afwāhun
possessor of	ذُو	dhū
palace, castle	قَصْرٌ (pl. قُصُورٌ)	qaṣrun, *pl.* quṣūrun
a piece	قِطْعَةٌ (pl. قِطَعٌ)	qiṭʿatun, *pl.* qiṭaʿun

meat		لَحْمٌ	laḥmun
wood		خَشَبٌ	khashabun
mind, intellect, intelligence	(عُقُولٌ *pl.*)	عَقْلٌ	ع‍aqlun, *pl.* ع‍uqūlun
wealth, property	(أَمْوَالٌ *pl.*)	مَالٌ	mālun, *pl.* 'amwālun
face	(وُجُوهٌ *pl.*)	وَجْهٌ	wajhun, *pl.* wujūhun
friend, companion, master	(أَصْحَابٌ *pl.*)	صَاحِبٌ	ṣāḥibun, *pl.* 'aṣḥābun
tongue	(أَلْسِنَةٌ *pl.*)	لِسَانٌ	lisānun, *pl.* 'alsinatun
tribe	(قَبَائِلُ *pl.*)	قَبِيلَةٌ	qabīlatun, *pl.* qabā'ilu
a morsel, bit	(لُقَمٌ *pl.*)	لُقْمَةٌ	luqmatun, *pl.* luqamun
iron		حَدِيدٌ	ḥadīdun
sheikh, old man, elder, tribal leader	(شُيُوخٌ *pl.*)	شَيْخٌ	shaikhun, *pl.* shuyūkhun
room	(حُجَرٌ *pl.*)	حُجْرَةٌ	ḥujratun, *pl.* ḥujarun
kitchen	(مَطَابِخُ *pl.*)	مَطْبَخٌ	maṭbakhun, *pl.* maṭābikhu
people, men		نَاسٌ	nāsun
women		نِسَاءٌ	nisā'un
merchant	(تُجَّارٌ *pl.*)	تَاجِرٌ	tājirun, *pl.* tujjārun

to fall, befall, happen	وَقَعَ	waqaʿa
to place, put	وَضَعَ	waḍaʿa
to carry, bear	حَمَلَ	ḥamala
to see	نَظَرَ	naẓara
to look at	نَظَرَ إِلَى	naẓara ʾilā
very (after *adj.*) (e.g. حَسَنٌ جِدًّا, very good)	جِدًّا	jiddan
Iraq	ٱلْعِرَاقُ	Al-ʿirāqu

EXERCISE 13

١ — وَقَعَ ٱبْنُ ٱلْمُعَلِّمِ ٱلصَّغِيرُ عَلَى ٱلْأَرْضِ. ٢ — حَمَلَ ٱلتَّاجِرُ ٱلْكُتُبَ ٱلْجَدِيدَةَ وَذَهَبَ لِلْمَدْرَسَةِ. ٣ — نَظَرَتِ ٱلنِّسَاءُ مُعَلِّمِي ٱلْأَبْنَاءِ فِى شَارِعِ ٱلْمَدِينَةِ. ٤ — هُوَ رَجُلٌ ذُو مَالٍ كَثِيرٍ وَهُوَ قَلِيلُ ٱلْعَقْلِ. ٥ — هُنَّ طَبَّاخَاتٌ فِى مَطْبَخِ ٱلْمَلِكِ. ٦ — وَضَعَتِ ٱلْأُمُّ لُقْمَةَ لَحْمٍ وَقِطْعَةَ خُبْزٍ عَلَى ٱلْمَائِدَةِ. ٧ — نَظَرُوا أَبَا مُحَمَّدٍ ٱلْكَثِيرَ ٱلْمَالِ. ٨ — وَجَدَ ٱلْأَمِيرُ وَلَدَيِ ٱلْوَزِيرِ فِى حُجْرَةٍ صَغِيرَةٍ فِى ٱلْقَصْرِ. ٩ — عَيْنَا ٱلْأَمِيرَةِ جَمِيلَتَانِ جِدًّا. ١٠ — خَيَّاطُو دِمَشْقَ طَيِّبُونَ. ١١ — كَانَ صُنْدُوقُ خَشَبٍ وَصُنْدُوقُ حَدِيدٍ فِى بَيْتِ ٱلشَّيْخِ. ١٢ — هِىَ مَعَ أَخِي حَسَنٍ. ١٣ — نَظَرَا وَجْهَ صَاحِبِ ٱلْبَيْتِ ثُمَّ ذَهَبَا. ١٤ — هُمَا قَبِيلَتَا ٱلْعِرَاقِ. ١٥ — مُعَلِّمُو ٱلْأَوْلَادِ نَاسٌ طَيِّبُونَ. ١٦ — قَتَلَ ٱلْوَزِيرُ ٱبْنَيِ ٱلْمَلِكِ أَمْسِ.

١٧ — هِيَ ذَاتُ فَمٍ كَبِيرٍ. ١٨ — نَظَرُوا شُبَّاكَيِ (نَافِذَتَيِ) ٱلْبَيْتِ مِنْ
بَعِيدٍ. ١٩ — ٱلنِّسَاءُ هُنَّ ٱلطَّبَّاخَاتُ فِي بُيُوتِ ٱلْعَرَبِ. ٢٠ — طَلَبَ
ٱلْمُعَلِّمُ سَاعَتَيْ وَلَدَيْنِ لِتَجْرِبَةٍ نَافِعَةٍ.

EXERCISE 14

1. There are many pieces of wood in the dirty garden of the Sheikh. 2. Two morsels of meat fell on the ground from the table. 3. The teachers of the big new school are good. 4. He is a man of wealth. 5. You are of small intelligence. 6. The Sheikhs of Cairo are learned (lit. "masters of learning"). 7. The woman demanded bread of the merchant. 8. There is an iron chest in the man's room. 9. He placed the Sultan's two old books on the large table. 10. He found a man of learning from Damascus in the market. 11. News of the two sons of the minister arrived yesterday from the city. 12. The two men wrote to the merchant and asked for wood for the kitchen. 13. The cow's tongue is long. 14. The boy saw Muhammad's father's face in the window of the house. 15. The master of the house arrived and killed the Sheikh's two dogs. 16. The bread of the Cairo bakers is beautiful. 17. They are beautiful women. 18. Hassan's teachers have arrived today. 19. The man wrote two long letters to the minister. 20. There were two useful experiments in the school today.

CHAPTER NINE
(اَلْبَابُ ٱلتَّاسِعُ)

The Attached Pronouns

1. In addition to the *detached pronouns* (ضَمَائِرُ مُنْفَصِلَةٌ ḍamā'ir munfaṣila) given in Chapters Two and Five, Arabic has also *attached pronouns* (ضَمَائِرُ مُتَّصِلَةٌ ḍamā'ir muttaṣila). They are:

	Singular	Dual	Plural
1st Person Masc. and Fem.	ـِى -ī (نِى -nī when attached to a verb)	(as plural)	نَا -nā
2nd Person Masc.	كَ -ka	كُمَا -kumā	كُمْ -kum
2nd Person Fem.	كِ -ki	كُمَا -kumā	كُنَّ -kunna
3rd Person Masc.	هُ -hu (هِ -hi)	هُمَا -humā (هِمَا -himā)	هُمْ -hum (هِمْ him)
3rd Person Fem.	هَا -hā	هُمَا -humā (هِمَا -himā)	هُنَّ -hunna (هِنَّ -hinna)

2. They are used in the following ways:

(a) Attached to the verb as direct object:

فَتَحَ ٱلْبَابَ fataḥa l-bāba, he opened the door.

فَتَحَهُ fataḥahu, he opened it.

قَفَلَتْ شُبَّاكًا qafalat shubbākan (modern usage), she closed a window.

قَفَلَتْهُ qafalathu, she closed it.

ضَرَبُونِي ḍarabūnī, they hit me.

(b) Attached to a preposition:

وَصَلُوا مِنْ بَغْدَادَ waṣalū min Baghdāda (diptote), they arrived from Baghdad.

وَصَلُوا مِنْهَا waṣalū minhā, they arrived from it (i.e. from there).

قَالَ ٱلْمَلِكُ لَكُمْ qāla l-maliku lakum, the king said to you.

Note that the preposition لِ li, to, changes its vowel to fatḥa (لَ la) before the attached pronouns, except with the 1st person, لِي lī, to me.

(c) Attached to a noun to indicate possession.

كِتَابِي kitābī, my book.

(Note that the final vowel disappears with this particular suffix, consequently there is no distinction of case.)

مِنْ بَيْتِي min baitī, from my house.

بَيْتُهُ baituhu, his house.

The attached pronoun is, in fact, a genitive of ʼiḍāfa, and therefore makes its noun definite. Thus, بَيْتُهُ baituhu tends to imply that he had only one house. If you wish to say "a house of his, one of his houses", you must use some such expression as بَيْتٌ لَهُ baitun lahu (lit. a house to him), or بَيْتٌ مِنْ بُيُوتِهِ baitun min buyūtihi, a house from his houses.

(d) After the particles إِنَّ ʼinna, أَنَّ ʼanna, etc. (See Chapter Eighteen).

3. The attached pronouns, هُ hu, هُمَا huma, هُمْ hum, هُنَّ hunna, take the kasra in place of the damma (as shown in

the above table) when preceded by a kasra or yā', whether long vowel or diphthong. Students should realise that this change of vowel is purely euphonic and has no connection with declension.

e.g. إِلَيْهِ ilaihi, to him, it, عَلَيْهِ ع alaihi, on him, it; لِكُرْسِيِّهِ li kursīyihi, to his chair, فِيهِمَا fīhimā, in them (dual); قَالَ لِخَادِمِهِ qāla li khādimihi, he said to his servant.

4. The suffixes كُمْ kum and هُمْ hum become كُمُ kumu and هُمُ humu, when followed by hamzatu l-waṣl, or in poetry, where the metre demands an extra syllable.

وَجَدَهُمُ الْيَوْمَ wajadahumu l-yauma, he found them today.

5. The following anomalies occur with the first person singular suffix:

(a) the final nūn of مِنْ min, from, is doubled: مِنِّي, minnī, from me.

(b) the pronoun becomes يَ -ya, instead of ي -ī, after an unvowelled ا, و, ى.

e.g. إِلَيَّ 'ilayya, to me; دُنْيَايَ dunyāya, my world.

6. As already stated, these pronouns form an 'iḍāfa, and when attached to a noun, they make it definite. For this reason, the final nūn of the sound masculine and the dual endings is removed.

مُعَلِّمُونَ mu ع allimūna, teachers.

الْمُعَلِّمُونَ al-mu ع allimūna, the teachers.

مُعَلِّمُوكَ mu ع allimūka, your teachers.

مِنَ الْمُعَلِّمِينَ mina-l-mu ع allimīna, from the teachers.

مِنْ مُعَلِّمِيَّ min mu ع allimīya, from my teachers.

الرِّجْلَانِ ar-rijlāni, الرِّجْلَيْنِ ar-rijlaini, the (two) feet.

رِجْلَايَ طَوِيلَتَانِ rijlāya ṭawīlatāni, my (two) feet are long.

ضَرَبُوا رِجْلَيَّ ḍarabū rijlayya, they struck my (two) feet.

Note: "my teachers" (*nom.*) is مُعَلِّمِيَّ instead of مُعَلِّمُوىَ, the و being replaced by ى which is then doubled ىّ.

7. When a pronoun is attached to the third person masculine plural of the perfect verb, the conventional and unpronounced final ʾalif of the verb is removed.

e.g. ضَرَبُوا الْعَدُوَّ ḍarabū, l-ʿadūwa, they struck the enemy,
but ضَرَبُوهُ ḍarabūhu, they struck him.

8. Certain forms of the *Perfect Verb* have been given in Chapter Five. Here are the remaining forms, with فَتَحَ fataḥa, to open:

فَتَحْتُ fataḥtu, I opened.

فَتَحْتَ fataḥta, you (masc. sing., thou) opened.

فَتَحْتِ fataḥti, you (fem. sing., thou) opened.

فَتَحْنَا fataḥnā, we opened (note this is the same ending as the attached pronoun).

فَتَحْتُمْ fataḥtum, you (masc. pl.) opened.

فَتَحْتُنَّ fataḥtunna, you (fem. pl.) opened.

فَتَحُوا fataḥū, they (masc.) opened.

فَتَحْنَ fataḥna, they (fem.) opened.

(For full tables see Chapter Twelve.)

Note: The practice in Classical Arabic verb tables is to begin with the 3rd person. This is followed in later chapters of this book.

9. Although Arabic has verbs meaning to possess, these are not usually used where in English the verb "to have" would be used. Instead, phrases introduced by the following prepositions are used: مَعَ maʿa, لِ li, and عِنْدَ ʿinda; e.g. لِزَيْدٍ (لَهُ) كُتُبٌ كَثِيرَةٌ li zaidin (or lahu) kutubun kat͟hīratun, Zaid (or he) has many books.

The sentence literally means: to Zaid many books ("are" being understood). It is thus a nominal sentence, "many books" being the subject, and "to Zaid" the predicate. Therefore كُتُبٌ كَثِيرَةٌ kutubun kat͟hīratun is in the nominative.

مَعَ ٱلْأَوْلَادِ جُنَيْهَانِ maʿa l-ʾaulādi junaihāni, the boys have two pounds (lit. "with the boys", etc.).

The preposition مَعَ usually implies not merely possession, but having the thing possessed actually with one.

عِنْدَ ٱلشَّيْخِ عَدَدٌ مِنَ ٱلْخَادِمِينَ ʿinda s͟h-s͟haik͟hi ʿadadun mina l-k͟hādimīna, the sheikh has a number of servants.

Although عِنْدَ ʿinda is used with the mere meaning of possession, and is particularly common with this implication in modern written and spoken Arabic, in Classical Arabic it frequently means "at or in the house of". Thus عِنْدِي حَسَنٌ ʿindī Ḥasanun means "Hassan is (staying) at my house".

Note also its use for time and place, as:

عِنْدَ ٱلْفَجْرِ ʿinda l-fajri, at dawn, daybreak.

عِنْدَ بَابِ ٱلْمَدِينَةِ ʿinda bābi l-madīnati, at the city gate.

VOCABULARY

here	هُنَا	hunā
there	هُنَاكَ (هُنَالِكَ)	hunāka (hunālika)

to open (*trans.*)		فَتَحَ	fataḥa
to close (*trans.*)		قَفَلَ	qafala
to strike, hit		ضَرَبَ	ḍaraba
to enter (with direct object or فِي)		دَخَلَ	da<u>kh</u>ala
to say		قَالَ	qāla
to ride		رَكِبَ	rakiba
to leave, abandon		تَرَكَ	taraka
enemy	(*pl.* أَعْدَاءٌ)	عَدُوٌّ	عadūwun, *pl.* ’aعdā’un
world	(*fem.*)	دُنْيَا	dunyā (indeclinable)
pound, guinea	(*pl.* جُنَيْهَاتٌ)	جُنَيْهٌ	junaihun, *pl.* junaihātun
by, with, in possession of, at		عِنْدَ	عinda
between		بَيْنَ	baina
paper	(*pl.* أَوْرَاقٌ)	وَرَقٌ	waraqun, *pl.* ’aurāqun
a piece of paper		وَرَقَةٌ	waraqatun
pen	(*pl.* أَقْلَامٌ)	قَلَمٌ	qalamun, *pl.* ’aqlamūn
ink		حِبْرٌ	ḥibrun
silver		فِضَّةٌ	fiḍḍatun
gold		ذَهَبٌ	<u>dh</u>ahabun
name	(*pl.* أَسْمَاءٌ)	اِسْمٌ	ismun, *pl.* ’asmā’un
donkey	(*pl.* حَمِيرٌ)	حِمَارٌ	ḥimārun, *pl.* ḥamīrun
horse	(*pl.* أَحْصِنَةٌ ، حُصُنٌ)	حِصَانٌ	ḥiṣānun, *pl.* ’aḥṣinatun, ḥuṣunun

slave	عَبْدٌ (*pl.* عَبِيدٌ)	عabdun, *pl.* عabīdun
noon, midday	ظُهْرٌ	ẓuhrun
head	رَأْسٌ (*pl.* رُؤُوسٌ)	ra'sun, *pl.* ru'ūsun
chest	صَدْرٌ (*pl.* صُدُورٌ)	ṣadrun, *pl.* ṣudūrun
shop	دُكَّانٌ (*pl.* دَكَاكِينُ)	dukkānun, *pl.* dakākīnu
roof, ceiling	سَقْفٌ (*pl.* سُقُوفٌ)	saqfun, *pl.* suqūfun
wall	حَائِطٌ (*pl.* حِيطَانٌ)	ḥā'iṭun, *pl.* ḥīṭānun
motor-car	سَيَّارَةٌ	sayyāratun
	عَرَبَةٌ	عarabatun
bicycle	عَجَلَةٌ	عajalatun
	دَرَّاجَةٌ	darrājatun
minute (of time)	دَقِيقَةٌ (*pl.* دَقَائِقُ)	daqīqatun, *pl.* daqā'iqu
what?	مَا ، مَاذَا	mā, mā<u>dh</u>ā
why?	لِمَاذَا	limā<u>dh</u>ā
soldier	جُنْدِيٌّ (*pl.* جُنْدٌ ، جُنُودٌ)	jundīyun, *pl.* jundun, junūdun
sad	حَزِينٌ	ḥazinun
in, at	فِي	fī
by, with, in	بِ	bi
Abu Bakr (*pr. n. masc.*)	أَبُو بَكْرٍ	'Abū Bakrin
Zaid (*pr. n. masc.*)	زَيْدٌ	Zaidun
dirty	وَسِخٌ	wasi<u>kh</u>un

EXERCISE 15

١ — أَفَتَحْتِ ٱلْأَبْوَابَ هُنَاكَ؟ ٢ — نَعَمْ، فَتَحْتُهَا قَبْلَ سَاعَاتٍ، ثُمَّ
قَفَلْتُهَا مِنْ جَدِيدٍ (afresh, again) قَبْلَ دَقِيقَتَيْنِ. ٣ — دَخَلَتِ ٱلنِّسَاءُ
وَوَجَدْنَ أَوْلَادَهُنَّ. ٤ — وَجَدْنَا كُتُبًا كَثِيرَةً جَدِيدَةً فِى دُكَّانِ أَبِى بَكْرٍ.
٥ — مَاذَا ٱسْمُكَ؟ اِسْمِى حَسَنٌ وَٱسْمُ أَبِى مُحَمَّدٌ. ٦ — رَكِبَتْ بَنَاتُ
ٱلْمَدْرَسَةِ عَجَلَاتِهِنَّ (دَرَّاجَاتِهِنَّ) مِنْ بُيُوتِهِنَّ إِلَى ٱلسُّوقِ. ٧ — وَصَلَ
ٱلْمَلِكُ مِنَ ٱلْقَصْرِ بِسَيَّارَتِهِ (بِعَرَبَتِهِ). ٨ — رَكِبَ ٱلشُّيُوخُ حَمِيرَهُمْ
وَحُصُنَهُمْ. ٩ — كَتَبَ ٱلْوَلَدُ مَكْتُوبًا طَوِيلًا بِقَلَمِهِ وَحِبْرِهِ عَلَى وَرَقِ
أَخِيهِ. ١٠ — وَجَدَ جُنُودُ ٱلْمَلِكِ ذَهَبًا وَفِضَّةً فِى بَيْتِ ٱلْوَزِيرِ وَقَتَلُوا
عَبْدَهُ. ١١ — وَجَدُونِى بَيْنَ عَدُوِّى وَصَدِيقِى. ١٢ — لِى جُنَيْهَاتٌ كَثِيرَةٌ
فِى ٱلْبَيْتِ. ١٣ — عِنْدِى خَادِمَانِ وَخَادِمَةٌ. ١٤ — ضَرَبْتُ رَأْسَهُ
أَمْسِ. ١٥ — لِمَاذَا تَرَكْتَ بَيْتَكَ؟ حِيطَانُهُ وَسِخَةٌ. ١٦ — أَنْتُمْ حَزِنُونَ.
مَاذَا فِى صُدُورِكُمْ؟ ١٧ — ضَرَبَ ٱلْأَوْلَادُ ٱلصِّغَارُ سَقْفَ ٱلْبَيْتِ بِٱلْحَجَرِ.
١٨ — ٱلدُّنْيَا صَعْبَةٌ ٱلْيَوْمَ. ١٩ — كَانَ زَيْدٌ هُنَا أَمْسِ مَعَ أَبْنَائِهِ.
٢٠ — قَفَلَ أَصْحَابُ ٱلدَّكَاكِينِ دَكَاكِينَهُمْ عِنْدَ ٱلظُّهْرِ.

EXERCISE 16

1. Your friend opened the windows and closed the door an hour ago (before an hour). 2. My teachers found me in the street with my father's horse. 3. He hit me on my head. 4. My car is very fast. 5. The room is small and its ceiling is old and dirty. 6. Why did you ride your bicycles to school today? 7. The news about (عَنْ) you reached me yesterday.

8. The enemy is there at the gate of the city. 9. I have two pounds with me today, and he has a pound. 10. The mother is present here, and her many sons are at school (lit. in the school). 11. The schoolmistresses went out of the school and closed its doors. 12. Why have you ridden your donkeys from your homes to the city? 13. What have you written with (بِ) your pen on the paper? 14. He said to the women: You arrived a moment ago (before a minute). 15. His head is big and his feet are small. 16. The wall and ceiling of the room are dirty. 17. The girls are in their father's shop in the market. 18. I entered her house and she struck me. 19. I left her in the street far (بَعِيدَةً) from her house. 20. There are many beautiful cities in Egypt. They have wide streets.

CHAPTER TEN

(اَلْبَابُ ٱلْعَاشِرُ)

Demonstrative Pronouns

1. The *Demonstrative Pronoun* (اِسْمُ ٱلْإِشَارَة ismu-l'ishāra) as normally used is as follows:

This, these.

	Masculine	Feminine
Singular, all cases	هٰذَا hādhā	هٰذِهِ hādhihi
Dual Nominative	هٰذَانِ hādhāni	هٰتَانِ hātāni
Accusative and Genitive	هٰذَيْنِ hādhaini	هٰتَيْنِ hātaini

Plural, all cases, masc. and fem. هٰؤُلَاءِ hā'ulā'i

It will be noted that the 'alif of the long ā after the initial ه of all these forms is written as a short vertical stroke above the letter. In unpointed Arabic, this 'alif is not normally shown. It is *incorrect* to write an ordinary 'alif, thus هَاذَا.

There are really two elements in the above forms, the ذَا which is the basis, and the preceding هَا, which reinforces it. Sometimes, though infrequently in modern *written* Arabic, the hā' is omitted, and the following forms result:

	Masc.	Fem.
Singular	ذَا dhā	ذِى *dhī (or ذِهِ dhihi)
Dual Nom.	ذَانِ dhāni	تَانِ tāni
Acc., Gen.	ذَيْنِ dhaini	تَيْنِ taini

Plural all cases, masc. and fem. أُولَى 'ūlā or أُولَاءِ 'ūlā'i

* NOTE: In the full form, هٰذِى hādhī sometimes occurs for هٰذِهِ hādhihi.

2. That, those.

These are based on the forms already given with the addition of the suffix كَ ka, which implies distance, but without the preliminary هَا. In some examples a ل is interpolated.

	Masc.	Fem.
Singular	ذَاكَ dhāka	تِلْكَ tilka
	or	
	ذٰلِكَ dhālika	تَاكَ tāka (very rarely)
	(more common)	تِيكَ tīka
Dual Nom.	ذَانِكَ dhānika	تَانِكَ tānika
Gen. and Acc.	ذَيْنِكَ dhainika	تَيْنِكَ tainika

Plural, all cases, أُولَائِكَ ʾūlāʾika masc. and fem.

(very rarely أُولَالِكَ ʾūlālika or أُولَاكَ ʾūlāka)

3. If the demonstrative qualifies a simple noun, it precedes it and the noun takes the article, e.g. هٰذَا ٱلْكِتَابُ hādhā l-kitābu, this book.

But if the noun is defined by a following genitive or a pronominal suffix the demonstrative is placed after these, e.g. إِبْنُ ٱلْمَلِكِ هٰذَا ibnu l-maliki hādhā this son of the king; كِتَابُكُمْ هٰذَا kitābukum hādhā, this book of yours. هٰذِهِ and تِلْكَ have the meaning of "these" and "those" respectively when used with broken plurals of inanimate objects, e.g. هٰذِهِ ٱلْكُتُبُ hādhihi l-kutubu, these books; تِلْكَ ٱلْأَيَّامُ tilka l-ʾayyāmu, those days.

4. If the demonstrative is used pronominally and as subject of a nominal sentence, then:

(a) If the predicate is an indefinite noun, no copula is necessary, e.g. هٰذَا كِتَابٌ hādhā kitābun, this is a book.

(b) If the predicate is defined by the article the 3rd pers. pron. is used as a copula to prevent the demonstrative from being taken adjectivally (as in 3), e.g. هٰذَا هُوَ ٱلْوَلَدُ hādhā huwa l-waladu, this is the boy.

(c) If the predicate is defined by a following genitive or a pronominal suffix, the demonstrative is put first and no copula is needed, e.g. هٰذَا كِتَابُكُمْ this is your book.

5. The Interrogative pronouns (اِسْمُ ٱلاِسْتِفْهَامِ ismu li -stifhām) are مَنْ man, who?; مَا mā, what? (sometimes مَاذَا mādhā); أَيٌّ ʼayyun, fem. أَيَّةٌ ʼayyatun, which?; كَمْ kam, how much? how many?

مَنْ is indeclinable (مَبْنِيٌّ mabnī). The genitive relation is expressed by placing it after a noun, e.g. كِتَابُ مَنْ kitābu man, whose book?

مَا is also indeclinable. After some prepositions it is sometimes written مَ as لِمَ lima, for what? why? (for لِمَا or لِمَاذَا).

أَيٌّ, fem. أَيَّةٌ is declinable and is treated as a noun, so takes a following noun in the genitive, e.g. أَيُّ رَجُلٍ ʼayyu rajulin, which man? أَيَّةُ بِنْتٍ ʼayyatu bintin, which girl?

كَمْ takes the following noun in the accusative singular, e.g. كَمْ وَلَدًا kam waladan, how many boys?

VOCABULARY

a person, individual (أَشْخَاصٌ *pl.*)	شَخْصٌ	shakhṣun, *pl.* ʼashkhāṣun
shade	ظِلٌّ	ẓillun
famous	مَشْهُورٌ	mashhūrun
not (with perfect of verb)	مَا	mā

to return (*intrans.*)		رَجَعَ	rajaعa
until, up to (with genitive)		حَتَّى	ḥattā
reason, cause	(*pl.* أَسْبَابٌ)	سَبَبٌ	sababun, *pl.* ʼasbābun
calamity, great misfortune	(*pl.* مَصَائِبُ)	مُصِيبَةٌ	muṣībatun, *pl.* maṣāʼibu
neglect, carelessness		غَفْلَةٌ	ghaflatun
woman		اِمْرَأَةٌ	imraʼatun
to study		دَرَسَ	darasa
agriculture		زِرَاعَةٌ	zirāعatun
mosque	(*pl.* جَوَامِعُ)	جَامِعٌ	jāmiعun, *pl.* jawāmiعu
university	(*pl.* جَامِعَاتٌ)	جَامِعَةٌ	jāmiعatun *pl.* jāmiعātun
each, all, everybody,		كُلٌّ	
e.g. every man		كُلُّ رَجُلٍ	
the East		اَلشَّرْقُ	ash-sharqu
the West		اَلْغَرْبُ	al-gharbu
inhabitant	(*pl.* سُكَّانٌ)	سَاكِنٌ	sākinun, *pl.* sukkānun
village	(*pl.* قُرًى)	قَرْيَةٌ	qaryatun, *pl.* quran
dirty		وَسِخٌ	wasikhun

and, so (implying a close connection or suggestion of cause and effect between the two sentences joined). It is written as part of the word it precedes.	فَ fa

EXERCISE 17

١ — مَا وَصَلَ هٰذَا ٱلْكِتَابُ ٱلنَّافِعُ حَتَّى ٱلسَّاعَةِ. ٢ — هٰذَا كِتَابٌ صَعْبٌ. ٣ — دَخَلَ ٱلْمُعَلِّمُ وَقَالَ لِتِلْمِيذٍ مِنَ ٱلتَّلَامِذَةِ: كُتُبُكَ هٰذِهِ وَسِخَةٌ جِدًّا. ٤ — وَجَدْتُ هَتَيْنِ ٱلْبِنْتَيْنِ فِي تِلْكَ ٱلدَّارِ. ٥ — أَحَضَرْتُمْ ذٰلِكَ ٱلْمَجْلِسَ أَمْسِ؟ ٦ — هٰؤُلَاءِ ٱلْأَشْخَاصُ قَتَلُوا أَوْلَادَهُ ٱلصِّغَارَ. ٧ — تِلْكَ ٱلشَّجَرَةُ ذَاتُ ظِلٍّ. ٨ — أُولَائِكَ ٱلرِّجَالُ ذَوُو عِلْمٍ. ٩ — خَرَجَ ذَاكَ ٱلرَّجُلُ ٱلْمَشْهُورُ مِنَ ٱلْمَدِينَةِ وَمَا رَجَعَ حَتَّى ٱلْيَوْمِ. ١٠ — عَرَفَ ٱلنَّاسُ سَبَبَ هٰذِهِ ٱلْمُصِيبَةِ فَقَفَلُوا أَبْوَابَهُمْ. ١١ — مُصِيبَتُكُمْ هٰذِهِ مِنْ سَبَبِ غَفْلَتِكُمْ. ١٢ — هٰذِهِ ٱلِامْرَأَةُ مَنْ؟ هِيَ مِنَ ٱلْغَائِبَاتِ. ١٣ — تَرَكَ ٱلْمُعَلِّمُونَ كَمْ وَلَدًا فِي ٱلْمَدْرَسَةِ بَعْدَ ٱلدُّرُوسِ؟ ١٤ — أَيَّةُ ٱمْرَأَةٍ مَوْجُودَةٌ فِي ذٰلِكَ ٱلدُّكَّانِ؟ ١٥ — مَنْ رَكِبَ حِصَانِي وَمَا قَفَلَ ٱلْبَابَ؟ ١٦ — دَرَسَ ٱلزِّرَاعَةَ فِي جَامِعَةِ ٱلْقَاهِرَةِ. ١٨ — هٰذَا ٱلْجَامِعُ مَشْهُورٌ فِي ٱلشَّرْقِ وَٱلْغَرْبِ. ١٩ — طَلَبَ سُكَّانُ هٰذِهِ ٱلْقَرْيَةِ بُيُوتًا جَدِيدَةً وَمَدْرَسَةً كَبِيرَةً. ٢ — لِمَا أَنْتُمْ حَاضِرُونَ وَهُمْ غَائِبُونَ؟

EXERCISE 18

1. Did you know that famous man? No, I knew his elder (big) brother. 2. This is a good man, and that (fem.) is a bad woman. 3. This tree has good shade. 4. These Arabs are nice persons. 5. Those men have not arrived so far (until the hour). 6. This woman returned from Cairo yesterday. 7. Which man did you find in that room? 8. Which woman killed the minister's father? 9. How many persons attended that meeting of the council yesterday? 10. What did you demand of (مِنْ) your students in the university? 11. This is the great (big) mosque of the city. 12. I found these books in Muhammad's shop in the little market. 13. This is a great calamity to the inhabitants of my village. 14. All this has two reasons, the sword of the foe and the neglect of the prince. 15. Whose son is Hassan? He is the minister's son. 16. These two men are friends, and those two are enemies. 17. That daughter of the sheikh is beautiful of face. 18. The two men mounted (rode) their horses and left (went out of) the city. 19. This is a new English car. 20. We have studied agriculture from these two new books.

CHAPTER ELEVEN

(اَلْبَابُ الْحَادِى عَشَرَ)

Adjectives

1. Some of the commonest forms of *adjectives* (اِسْمُ صِفَةٍ ism ṣifa) are given below. Of these, the first is the *active participle*; the rest are forms which give the meaning of the active participle, with, at any rate originally, some intensification in meaning. They are derived from what might be termed 'stative' verbs, that is, verbs which denote a state or condition rather than an act. They are not normally derived from transitive verbs.

(a) فَاعِلٌ fāعilun (properly the active participle) e.g. صَادِقٌ ṣādiqun, upright; عَادِلٌ عādilun, just, جَاهِلٌ jāhilun, ignorant.

(b) فَعِيلٌ faعīlun, e.g. سَعِيدٌ saعīdun, happy; كَبِيرٌ kabīrun, great; كَثِيرٌ kathīrun, much, many.

(c) فَعُولٌ faعūlun denoting intensity, e.g. جَهُولٌ jahūlun, very ignorant; كَسُولٌ kasūlun, very lazy.

(d) فَعْلَانُ faعlānu (without nunation), e.g. غَضْبَانُ ghaḍbānu, angry.

2. Another intensive form of the active participle is faععālun; but these words are nouns rather than adjectives. They are used to denote occupations, e.g.

خَبَّازٌ khabbāzun, baker. خَيَّاطٌ khayyāṭun, tailor.

طَبَّاخٌ ṭabbākhun, cook. جَزَّارٌ jazzārun, butcher.

بَقَّالٌ baqqālun, greengrocer.

Unlike the adjectives mentioned in paragraph 1, nouns of this form are usually derived from transitive, not stative, verbs. They form the sound masculine plural, e.g. طَبَّاخُونَ ṭabbākhūna, cooks. They add tā' marbūta to form the feminine, and also take the sound feminine plural, e.g. خَيَّاطَةٌ khayyāṭun, pl. خَيَّاطَاتٌ khayyāṭātun, tailoress, needlewoman.

3. Another common form of adjective expressing the meaning of the active participles of stative verbs is that used for colours or defects. They have the masculine singular in أَفْعَلُ 'afعalu, and the feminine singular in فَعْلَاءُ faعlā'u (both diptotes). The plural, فُعْلٌ fuعlun, is a triptote, and is used for both genders.

Here are typical examples.

Sing. Masc.	*Fem.*	*Plural*
أَسْوَدُ 'aswadu, black	سَوْدَاءُ saudā'u	سُودٌ sūdun
أَبْيَضُ 'abyaḍu, white	بَيْضَاءُ baiḍā'u	بِيضٌ bīḍun
أَحْمَرُ 'aḥmaru, red	حَمْرَاءُ ḥamrā'u	حُمْرٌ ḥumrun
أَزْرَقُ 'azraqu, blue	زَرْقَاءُ zarqā'u	زُرْقٌ zurqun
أَخْضَرُ 'akhḍaru, green	خَضْرَاءُ khaḍrā'u	خُضْرٌ khuḍrun
أَصْفَرُ 'aṣfaru, yellow	صَفْرَاءُ ṣafrā'u	صُفْرٌ ṣufrun
أَطْرَشُ 'aṭrashu, deaf	طَرْشَاءُ ṭarshā'u	طُرْشٌ ṭurshun
أَخْرَسُ 'akhrasu, dumb	خَرْسَاءُ kharsā'u	خُرْسٌ khursun
أَعْمَى 'aعmā, blind	عَمْيَاءُ عamyā'u	عُمْيٌ عumyun
أَعْرَجُ 'aعraju, lame	عَرْجَاءُ عarjā'u	عُرْجٌ عurjun

أَحْدَبُ {'aḥdabu, humpbacked حَدْبَاءُ ḥadbâ'u حُدْبٌ ḥudbun

NOTE: The fem. of the dual changes hamza into و e.g. سَوْدَاوَانِ saudāwāni.

4. For the *comparative* and *superlative* of adjectives, (اِسْمُ التَّفْضِيلِ ismu t-tafḍīl), sometimes termed the Elative, the same form as that for colours and defects, though only in the masculine singular, is employed: أَفْعَلُ 'afعalu.

The feminine is فُعْلَى fuعlā. But though the Arab grammarians imply that this form exists for all elatives, in practice it is only encountered with a few words, except in ancient poetry. The masculine plural is أَفَاعِلُ 'afāعilu, the feminine plural is فُعْلَيَاتٌ fuعlayātun and فُعَلٌ. But students will have little use for anything but the masculine singular, because this should always be used when the meaning is comparative. And even when the meaning is superlative, the masculine singular can be used except when the adjective has the definite article اَلْ (This will be dealt with in greater detail in Chapter 40).

e.g. أَكْبَرُ 'akbaru, greater, fem. كُبْرَى kubrā, from كَبِيرٌ kabīrun, big.

أَسْهَلُ 'ashalu, easier, fem. سُهْلَى suhlā, from سَهْلٌ sahlun, easy.

أَصْبَرُ 'aṣbaru, more patient, from صَبُورٌ ṣabūrun.

أَجْهَلُ 'ajhalu, more ignorant, from جَاهِلٌ jāhilun.

It will be seen that, to form the elative from any adjective, the three radical consonants only should be taken, then prefixed with a hamza. Long vowels must be removed, like the yā' in كَبِيرٌ and the wāw in صَبُورٌ.

5. If the root has a doubled consonant, as جَدِيدٌ jadīdun, new, the superlative form is أَجَدُّ ʼajaddu, instead of أَجْدَدُ ʼajdadu. From قَلِيلٌ qalīlun, little, few, comes أَقَلُّ ʼaqallu, less, fewer (instead of ʼaqlalu) and so on.

6. The Arabic preposition for "than" in such English phrases as "smaller than" is مِنْ min (from), e.g. أَصْغَرُ مِنْ ʼaṣgharu min.

e.g. حَسَنٌ أَصْغَرُ مِنْ أُخْتِهِ Ḥasanun ʼaṣgharu min ʼukhtihi, Hasan is smaller (younger) than his sister.

هِيَ أَكْبَرُ مِنْهُ hiya ʼakbaru minhu, she is bigger than him.

اَلتَّلَامِذَةُ أَجْهَلُ مِنْ إِخْوَانِهِمْ فِي مَدْرَسَةِ ٱلْقَاهِرَةِ at-talāmidhatu ajhalu min ikhwānihim fī madrasati l-Qāhirati, the pupils are more ignorant than their brethren (fellows) in the Cairo school.

Note the use of the plural of أَخٌ ʼakhun here.

اَلْمُعَلِّمَاتُ أَجَدُّ مِنَ ٱلْمُعَلِّمِينَ al-muعallimātu ʼajaddu mina l-muعallimīna, the schoolmistresses are newer than the schoolmasters.

7. In the Superlative, the Arabs prefer to use the Elative as a noun, followed by a genitive, rather than as an adjective;

e.g. هُوَ أَكْبَرُ رَجُلٍ فِي ٱلْمَدِينَةِ huwa ʼakbaru rajulin fi l-madīnati, he is the greatest man in the city,

instead of

هُوَ ٱلرَّجُلُ ٱلْأَكْبَرُ فِي ٱلْمَدِينَةِ huwa ar-rajulu l-ʼakbaru fi l-madīnati,

though the latter is permissible.*

* See Appendix C, §4 (a).

In this case, there is no need to put the Elative in the feminine or plural, e.g.

هِيَ أَصْبَرُ زَوْجَةٍ hiya ʼaṣbaru zaujatin, she is the most patient wife.

اَلنِّسَاءُ أَصْبَرُ سُكَّانٍ an-nisāʼu ʼaṣbaru sukkānin, the women are the most patient inhabitants.

8. The substantives خَيْرٌ khairun, good, and شَرٌّ sharrun, evil, are used as Elatives with the meanings "better" and "worse", e.g. هُوَ خَيْرٌ مِنْكَ huwa khairun minka, he is better than you.

VOCABULARY

colour	لَوْنٌ (pl. أَلْوَانٌ)	launun, *pl.* ʼalwānun
hair	شَعْرٌ	shaعrun
yesterday	اَلْبَارِحَ	al-bāriḥa
origin	أَصْلٌ (pl. أُصُولٌ)	ʼaṣlun, *pl.* ʼuṣūlun
boundary, limit	حَدٌّ (pl. حُدُودٌ)	ḥaddun, *pl.* ḥudūdun
a beggar	سَائِلٌ	sāʼilun
North	شَمَالٌ	shamālun
South	جَنُوبٌ	janūbun
army	جَيْشٌ (pl. جُيُوشٌ)	jaishun, *pl.* juyūshun
pleasant	لَطِيفٌ (pl. لُطَفَاءُ ، لِطَافٌ)	laṭīfun, *pl.* luṭafāʼu, liṭāfun
to stop, stand up	وَقَفَ	waqafa

history, date	تَأْرِيخٌ (pl. تَوَارِيخُ)	ta'rīkhun, *pl.* tawarīkhu
better, best	أَحْسَنُ	'aḥsanu
Syria (Damascus)	اَلشَّأْمُ ، اَلشَّامُ	ash-sha'mu, ash-shāmu
camel	جَمَلٌ (pl. جِمَالٌ)	jamalun, *pl.* jimālun
desert	صَحْرَاءُ (pl. صَحَارَى)	ṣaḥrā'u, *pl.* ṣaḥārā

EXERCISE 19

١ — هٰذِهِ ٱلْبِنْتُ ٱلْجَمِيلَةُ وَصَلَتْ مِنْ بَغْدَادَ قَبْلَ أَشْهُرٍ قَلِيلَةٍ. هِىَ أَجْمَلُ
بِنْتٍ فى تِلْكَ ٱلْمَدِينَةِ ٱلْمَشْهُورَةِ. ٢ — لَوْنُ وَجْهِهَا أَبْيَضُ. ٣ — كَانَ
ٱلْعَبْدُ ٱلْأَسْوَدُ فِى ٱلْحُجْرَةِ ٱلزَّرْقَاءِ. ٤ — قَالَ ٱلْمُعَلِّمُ لِتَلَامِذَتِهِ : لِمَاذَا
كَتَبْتُمْ دُرُوسَكُمْ بِٱلْحِبْرِ ٱلْأَخْضَرِ؟ ٥ — فى قُرَى ٱلشَّرْقِ وَجَدْتُ نِسَاءً
طُرْشًا وَرِجَالًا خُرْسًا ! ٦ — هٰذَا ٱلسَّائِلُ أَعْمَى وَأَعْرَجُ وَهُوَ أَصْفَرُ
ٱللَّوْنِ. ٧ — ٱلْمَلِكُ أَعْدَلُ ، فَٱلسُّكَّانُ أَسْعَدُ مِنْ آبَائِهِمْ. ٨ — هِىَ أَكْبَرُ
مُصِيبَةٍ فى تَأْرِيخِ ٱلْعَالَمِ حَتَّى ٱلْيَوْمِ. ٩ — ٱلْأَبُ ٱلصَّبُورُ أَحْسَنُ مِنَ ٱلْأَبِ
ٱلْغَضْبَانِ. ١٠ — خَرَجَ ٱلتِّلْمِيذُ ٱلتَّعْبَانُ مِنَ ٱلدَّرْسِ وَهُوَ أَجْهَلُ وَلَدٍ فى
ٱلْمَدْرَسَةِ. ١١ — تَرَكَ ٱلْمُعَلِّمُ ٱلْجَدِيدُ ٱلْوَلَدَ ٱلْكَسُولَ فى ٱلْمَدْرَسَةِ بَعْدَ
ٱلدُّرُوسِ. ١٢ — دَخَلَ جَيْشُ ٱلْأَمِيرِ ٱلْمَدِينَةَ مِنَ ٱلشَّمَالِ فَخَرَجَ جُنُودُ
ٱلْمَلِكِ مِنَ ٱلْجَنُوبِ ، وَتَرَكُوا ٱلسُّكَّانَ لِسُيُوفِ ٱلْأَعْدَاءِ. ١٣ — نَظَرَ ٱلرَّجُلُ
أَجْمَلَ بِنْتٍ فى أَطْوَلِ شَارِعٍ فى ٱلْمَدِينَةِ ، فَوَقَفَ حَالًا . ١٤ — شَعْرُ
هٰذَا ٱلرَّجُلِ ٱلْأَسْوَدُ أَجْمَلُ مِنْ شَعْرِكَ ٱلْأَبْيَضِ. ١٥ — هٰذَا ٱلطَّرِيقُ

أَصْعَبُ مِنْ ذٰلِكَ، هُوَ أَصْعَبُ طُرُقِ ٱلشَّأْمِ. ١٦ — ٱلنِّيلَانِ ٱلْأَبْيَضُ
وَٱلْأَزْرَقُ أَصْلَا ٱلنِّيلِ ٱلْكَبِيرِ وَهُوَ نَهْرُ مِصْرَ. ١٧ — ذَهَبَتِ ٱلنِّسَاءُ
لِحُدُودِ ٱلْبِلَادِ ٱلْبَعِيدَةِ. ١٨ — حَضَرَ أَكْثَرُ ٱلنَّاسِ ٱلْاِجْتِمَاعَ ٱلْبَارِحَ.
١٩ — عَيْنَا ٱلْاِمْرَأَةِ ٱلسَّوْدَاوَانِ كَبِيرَتَانِ جِدًّا. ٢٠ — ٱلْجَمَلُ خَيْرٌ مِنَ
ٱلْحِصَانِ لِسُكَّانِ ٱلصَّحْرَاءِ.

EXERCISE 20

1. He is worse than his father, and his grandfather is the worst man in the village. 2. My mother's eyes are blue, and mine (my eyes) are green. 3. The Red Sea is the boundary of Arabia in the West and the South. 4. I have found a book better than that in the city library. 5. My house is more spacious (wider) than yours (your house): it is the most spacious house in Baghdad. 6. The deaf (*plural*) stood up in the meeting, and said: "We are happier than you (*plural*)". 7. This boy is very ignorant, and that [one] is very lazy. Their teacher is angry with (مِنْ) them. 8. The blind hump-backed beggar demanded food of (مِنْ) the women. 9. He arrived from the far (most distant) South yesterday and entered Damascus. 10. I rode my brown (red) horse, and the sheikh rode a white camel. 11. The army of Egypt halted (stopped) in the North of the deserts of Arabia. 12. Men are stronger than women. 13. Hassan has the longest hair of the students. 14. My father hit the biggest boy and left the two smaller [ones]. 15. The students studied the easiest of the books about the origin of (the) animals, in the university. 16. Who closed the newest window in the house? 17. He opened the door, entered the room, and took

(use ذَهَبَ بِ) the newest plate and the best spoon from the table. 18. This milk is older than that. 19. The two tallest soldiers returned, and mounted the biggest horses. 20. These two ignoramuses have asked for the best books in the bookshop (lit. shop of the books).

CHAPTER TWELVE

(اَلْبَابُ ٱلثَّانِى عَشَرَ)

The Verb

(فِعْلٌ fiعl)

1. Arabic *verbs* are mostly *triliteral*, that is, they are based on roots of three consonants. Thus, the basic meaning of *writing* is given by the three consonants *k-t-b*. The basic meaning of *killing* is expressed by the consonants *q-t-l*. As has been stated, the simplest form of a verb is the third person masculine singular of the Perfect. For example, كَتَبَ kataba means, he wrote, he has written, and قَتَلَ qatala means, he killed. In an Arabic dictionary, all words derived from triliteral roots are entered under this part of the verb. Thus, مَكْتَبٌ maktabun, meaning an office, or the place where one writes, is derived from كَتَبَ kataba, and will be found in the dictionary under this root. There are also derived verb forms, in which additions to the triliteral root give different shades of meaning; these will be dealt with from Chapter Nineteen onwards.

2. In the simple triliteral verb, the first and third root consonants (or radicals) are vowelled with fatḥa; but the second radical may be vowelled with fatḥa, kasra, or damma.

e.g. فَتَحَ fataḥa, to open, conquer (literally, he opened, he has opened).

حَزِنَ ḥazina, to be sad (literally, he was or became sad).

كَبُرَ kabura, he was, or became, big or old.

Verbs having kasra or ḍamma generally denote a state, or the entering of a state: to be or become the basic meaning.

Kasra frequently denotes a temporary state, damma a more permanent one. But this can only be taken as a general guide.

3. Some verbs, though often classed as triliteral, have the same letter as the second and third radical. In this case, the second radical has shadda, and the verb has the appearance of being biliteral.

e.g. مَرَّ marra, for مَرَرَ marara, to pass (by, بِ bi),

جَرَّ jarra, for جَرَرَ jarara, to drag, draw.

حَجَّ ḥajja, for حَجَجَ ḥajaja, to make the pilgrimage.

فَكَّ fakka, for فَكَكَ fakaka, to loosen.

NOTE: Arab grammarians and lexicographers differed in their attitude to these roots, which Europeans call "doubled". Some considered them biliteral, others triliteral. Their place in dictionaries therefore varies. For example, مَرَّ marra may be placed before all other roots beginning with م and ر; or, it may occur among them, after مرد but before مرز. Doubled verbs will be dealt with in Chapter Twenty-four.

4. By reason of the presence of one of the semi-vowels among the three radicals, some roots may appear to be biliteral, e.g. قَالَ qāla, to say (he said); رَمَى ramā, to throw, he threw. But these are in reality triliteral, and will be explained among the irregular verbs in Chapters Twenty-seven to Twenty-nine.

5. There is a comparatively small number of quadriliteral verbs, with four radicals. Very few occur among the 5,000 commonest words in the language. They will be discussed in Chapter Thirty-one. An example is دَحْرَجَ daḥraja to roll (transitive). These also may have derived forms.

TENSES

6. Arabic, in common with other Semitic languages, is deficient in tenses, and this does make for ease in learning. Moreover, the tenses do not have accurate time-significances as

in Indo-European languages. There are two main tenses, the Perfect اَلْمَاضِي al-māḍī, denoting actions completed at the time to which reference is being made; and the Imperfect اَلْمُضَارِعُ al-muḍāriع, for incompleted actions. There is also an Imperative, اَلْأَمْرُ al-ʾamr, which may be considered a modification of the Imperfect.

7. The Perfect Stem is obtained by cutting off the last vowel of the 3rd singular masculine perfect, and the perfect is declined by adding to this stem the following endings:

Singular		*Dual*		*Plural*	
3. masc.	ـَ a	3. masc.	ـَا a	3. masc.	ـُوا ū
3. fem.	ـَتْ at	3. fem.	ـَتَا ata	3. fem.	ـْنَ na
2. masc.	ـْتَ ta	2. m.&f.	ـْتُمَا tumā	2. masc.	ـْتُمْ tum
2. fem.	ـْتِ ti			2. fem.	ـْتُنَّ tunna
1. m.&f.	ـْتُ tu			1. m.&f.	ـْنَا nā

e.g.

Sing. 3. masc.	كَتَبَ	kataba he has written, (or he wrote).
,, 3. fem.	كَتَبَتْ	katabat, she has written.
,, 2. masc.	كَتَبْتَ	katabta, you (man) have written.
,, 2. fem.	كَتَبْتِ	katabti, you (woman) have written.
,, 1. masc. & fem.	كَتَبْتُ	katabtu, I have written.
Dual 3. masc.	كَتَبَا	katabā, they two (men) have written.
,, 3. fem.	كَتَبَتَا	katabatā, they two (women) have written.

Dual 2. masc. & fem.	كَتَبْتُمَا	katabtumā, you two have written.
Plural 3. masc.	كَتَبُوا	katabū, they (men) have written.
,, 3. fem.	كَتَبْنَ	katabna, they (women) have written.
,, 2. masc.	كَتَبْتُمْ	katabtum you (men) have written.
,, 2. fem.	كَتَبْتُنَّ	katabtunna, you (women) have written.
,, 1. masc. & fem.	كَتَبْنَا	katabnā, we have written.

In the same way from verbs of the forms فَعِلَ faعila and فَعُلَ faعula we have: شَرِبَ shariba, he drank, شَرِبَتْ sharibat, she drank, etc.: from كَرُمَ karuma, he was noble, كَرُمْتُ karumtu, I was noble, etc.

AGREEMENT OF THE VERB WITH ITS SUBJECT

8. The normal order in an Arabic *verbal sentence* is *Verb – Subject – Direct Object – Adverbial and other matter.* Even if the subject is not mentioned separately, it is already implicit in the verb as a pronoun. For example, we may say وَصَلَ زَيْدٌ waṣala Zaidun, Zaid arrived. Here Zaid is the subject. But if we merely say وَصَلَ waṣala, this is still a complete sentence, meaning "he arrived". The final fatḥa of the verb is really a pronominal suffix meaning "he".

e.g. ضَرَبَ ٱلْأَبُ وَلَدَهُ حَالًا ḍaraba l-'abu waladahu ḥālan.

Verb Subj. Obj. Adverbial

The father beat his son at once.

When the verb in the 3rd person comes before the subject it is always in the singular.

e.g. كَتَبَ ٱلْمُعَلِّمُ kataba l-muعallimu, the teacher wrote.

كَتَبَ ٱلْمُعَلِّمَانِ kataba l-muعallimāni, the two teachers wrote.

كَتَبَ ٱلْمُعَلِّمُونَ kataba l-muعallimūna, the teachers wrote.

The verb preceding its subject, however, will agree with it in gender.

كَبُرَ ٱلْوَلَدُ kabura l-waladu, the boy grew.

كَبُرَتِ ٱلْبِنْتُ kaburati l-bintu, the girl grew.

كَبُرَتِ ٱلْبَنَاتُ kaburati l-banātu, the girls grew.

كَبُرَتِ ٱلْبِنْتَانِ kaburati-l-bintāni, the (two) girls grew.

NOTE: the kasra added to "kaburat" is due to the hamzatu l-waṣl which follows.

For this purpose, broken plurals are considered to be feminine, unless they refer to male human beings.

e.g. ظَهَرَتِ ٱلنُّجُومُ ẓaharati n-nujūmu, the stars appeared. (pl. of نَجْمٌ najmun.)

But

ظَهَرَ ٱلرِّجَالُ ẓahara r-rijālu, the men appeared.

However, in Classical Arabic, a feminine verb will often be found with a broken plural, even referring to male human beings, ظَهَرَتِ ٱلرِّجَالُ ẓaharati r-rijālu. The student is not recommended to imitate this which is unusual in modern Arabic, even in literature.

Note that it is the actual gender which counts, not the form of the word. Thus خَلِيفَةٌ khalīfatun, Caliph, is masculine, though it has a feminine ending.

قَتَلَ ٱلْخَلِيفَةُ ٱلْوَزِيرَ qatala l-khalīfatu l-wazīra
(*Not* قَتَلَتْ qatalat).

Similarly, سِنُونَ sinūna, one plural of سَنَةٌ sanatun, year, though in the form of the sound masculine plural, would count as a broken plural and take the feminine singular verb.

When the verb follows the subject it agrees with it in number and gender (the rule of the broken plural given above, however, still applies).

e.g. اَلْأَوْلَادُ فَتَحُوا ٱلْبَابَ al-'aulādu fataḥū l-bāba, the boys opened the door.

اَلْبَنَاتُ دَخَلْنَ al-banātu dakhalna, the girls entered.

When the sentence *begins* with a verb it is known as a verbal sentence (جُمْلَةٌ فِعْلِيَّةٌ jumla fiʿlīya), e.g. خَرَجَ ٱلْوَلَدُ kharaja l-waladu, the boy went out. A sentence introduced by *the subject* is called a nominal sentence (جُمْلَةٌ ٱسْمِيَّةٌ jumla ismīya) whether or not the subject is followed by a verb,

e.g. اَلْوَلَدُ صَغِيرٌ al-waladu ṣaghīrun, the boy is small.

اَلْوَلَدُ خَرَجَ al-waladu kharaja, the boy went out.

9. Since, as we have already noted, the normal sentence order in Arabic is for the verb (in the singular) to come first, the question of when the 3rd person plural verb is used arises. There are three situations in which it is required:

(a) The subject may not be mentioned by name, e.g.

ذَهَبُوا dhahabū, they went, have gone.

(b) The subject may be placed first for stress or emphasis,

e.g. لَمَّا وَصَلَتِ ٱلْبَنَاتُ ٱلْأَوْلَادُ خَرَجُوا lamma wasalati l-banātu l-'aulādu kharajū, when the girls arrived, the boys went out.

Here the juxtaposition of البنات and الاولاد gives stress to the latter.

(c) The subject may already have been mentioned in the preceding sentence,

e.g. وَصَلَتِ ٱلْبَنَاتُ وَجَلَسْنَ فِى ٱلْفَصْلِ waṣalati l-banātu wa jalasna fī l-faṣli, the girls arrived and sat down in the class(room).

10. The *Perfect* may be translated by the *Historic Past* or the *Past Perfect*, e.g. وَصَلَ waṣala, "he arrived" (at some time in the past) or he has arrived (in the recent past). When translating, the student will often only have the context and common-sense to guide him. However, the particle قَدْ qad is sometimes placed before the Perfect verb. It is a confirmatory particle, which may make the verb definitely Past Perfect,

e.g. قَدْ وَصَلَ qad waṣala, he has arrived (not "he arrived").

However, this particle may also make the verb Pluperfect, so that the verb given might also mean "he had arrived", according to the context.

VOCABULARY

فَهِمَ to understand

قَوْلٌ speech

طَلَعَ to rise (of the sun); ascend; go out

غَرَبَ to set (of the sun)

قَمَرٌ moon

قَصَدَ to intend, to travel towards

سَائِحٌ a traveller, tourist

نَزَلَ to descend, alight, stay (at a place)

مَاءٌ water

خَمْرٌ *fem.*, wine

حَوْشٌ courtyard, enclosure

نَهَارٌ day, daytime

صَيْدٌ hunt, hunting

قَبِلَ to accept, receive

ضَيْفٌ *pl.* ضُيُوفٌ guest

كَسَرَ to break

كُبَّايَةٌ *pl.* كُبَّايَاتٌ glass (drinking), tumbler

بَعَثَ to send

فَلَّاحٌ *pl.* فَلَّاحُونَ peasant, cultivator

حَاكِمٌ *pl.* حُكَّامٌ governor, ruler

بَعُدَ (عَنْ) to be distant (from)

نَحْوَ towards, in the direction of, about

نِصْفٌ a half

غَنِيٌّ *pl.* أَغْنِيَاءُ rich

فَرِحَ to rejoice

صَبِيٌّ *pl.* صِبْيَانٌ a youth

طَعَامٌ food

جَلَسَ to sit

ظَهَرَ to appear

شَرِبَ to drink

لَيْلٌ *pl.* لَيَالٍ night, night time

لَيْلَةٌ a (single) night

مَوْضُوعٌ *pl.* مَوَاضِيعُ، مَوْضُوعَاتٌ subject (matter)

EXERCISE 21

١ — أَكَتَبْتَ ٱلْمَكْتُوبَ؟ ٢ — لَا مَا كَتَبْتُ ٱلْمَكْتُوبَ. ٣ — هَلْ فَهِمْتُمْ
قَوْلَنَا. ٤ — نَعَمْ فَهِمْنَا قَوْلَكُمْ. ٥ — طَلَعَتِ ٱلشَّمْسُ. ٦ — غَرَبَ ٱلْقَمَرُ.
٧ — قَصَدَ ٱلشَّامَ ٱلسَّائِحُ وَخَادِمُهُ وَدَخَلَا ٱلْمَدِينَةَ. ٨ — خَرَجْنَا مِنْ بَابِ
ٱلْمَدِينَةِ. ٩ — طَلَعَ ٱلرِّجَالُ ٱلْجَبَلَ وَنَزَلُوا. ١٠ — هَلْ شَرِبْتُمُ ٱلْمَاءَ؟
١١ — لَا مَا شَرِبْنَا ٱلْمَاءَ شَرِبْنَا ٱلْخَمْرَ. ١٢ — أَكَسَرْتُمَا كُبَّايَةَ ٱلْمَاءِ
أَنْتِ وَأَخُوكِ؟ ١٣ — لَا مَا كَسَرْنَا كُبَّايَةَ ٱلْمَاءِ. ١٤ — بَعَثَتْ هٰؤُلَاءِ

ٱلْفَلَّاحِينَ إِلَى بَيْتِ ٱلْحَاكِمِ. ١٥ — رَجَعْتَ إِلَى بَيْتِ أَبِيكَ. ١٦ — بَعُدَتِ ٱلدَّارُ نَحْوَ نِصْفِ سَاعَةٍ. ١٧ — قَصَدتُّ (for قَصَدْتُ) هٰذِهِ ٱلدَّارَ وَوَجَدتُّ (for وَجَدْتُ) أَصْحَابَهَا مِنَ ٱلْأَغْنِيَاءِ. ١٨ — فَتَحَ لَهُ صَاحِبُ ٱلدَّارِ بَابَ ٱلْحَوْشِ. ١٩ — خَرَجْتُ فِي هٰذَا ٱلنَّهَارِ إِلَى ٱلصَّيْدِ. ٢٠ — قَبِلُوا ٱلضَّيْفَ عِنْدَهُمْ هٰذِهِ ٱللَّيْلَةَ. ٢١ — فَرِحَ ٱلصَّبِيُّ وَطَلَبَ مِنَ ٱلرَّجُلِ ٱلطَّعَامَ.

EXERCISE 22

1. Have you written your letters to your friends today? 2. Yes, we have written them (كَتَبْنَاهَا) and put them on that big table. 3. The beggar sought food from me. 4. The maid opened the door of the house, and they entered. 5. Have you been out hunting (to the hunt) today? No, I did not go out hunting, I went to the city, to the market. 6. The sun has set, and the moon has risen. 7. Muhammad and his son went into the city, and came out of it (use خَرَجَ) an hour later (lit., after an hour). 8. He struck me two minutes ago (lit. before two minutes). 9. The men sat down and drank tea with the sheikh. 10. We returned from the hunt with the minister, then attended the council meeting. 11. They drank (the) coffee with the women. 12. I received the guests at my house (عِنْدِي) and my wife received the female guests. 13. I stayed (use نَزَلَ) with (عِنْدَ) Hassan and his brother Muhammad. 14. Have you understood what I said (lit. my speech)? 15. He said this an hour ago, and you knew it from his books. 16. Why have you (fem. sing.) closed the door and opened the window? 17. The wind is from the North today. 18. You studied this subject months ago (lit. before months). 19. They mounted their horses and made for Damascus, and arrived there two days later. 20. The girls went to (the) school, and asked for the new books.

CHAPTER THIRTEEN

(اَلْبَابُ ٱلثَّالِثَ عَشَرَ)

The Verb with Pronominal Object
The Verb "To Be"

1. The use of the *attached pronouns* as direct object to the verb has been illustrated in Chapter Nine. Here it should again be stressed that, for the first person singular pronoun, the form نِي -nī is used, *not* ي, -ī.

e.g. ضَرَبَنِي ḍarabanī, he struck me.

2. In the third person masculine plural verb, such as وَجَدُوا wajadū, they found, from وَجَدَ wajada, the final 'alif is omitted when a pronoun is attached.

e.g. وَجَدُوهُ wajadūhu, they found him (it).

3. In the second person masculine plural, such as وَجَدْتُمْ wajadtum, you found, a wāw is added to the verb before the pronoun, e.g. وَجَدْتُمُوهَا wajadtumūhā, you found her (it), them (with broken plural non-human objects)

وَجَدْتُمُونِي wajadtumūnī, you have found me.

4. Some verbs in Arabic are doubly transitive, and take two direct objects where we would expect one direct and one indirect object. These will be dealt with in greater detail in Chapter 45, 3(a), and they include verbs of giving, seeing and thinking, e.g. حَسِبْتُهُ جَاهِلاً ḥasibtuhu jāhilan·

I considered him ignorant.

5. The verb "to be" كَانَ kāna (lit. he was) is a *weak* (مُعْتَلّ mu ع tall) *verb*, and will be treated in full in Chapter

Twenty-eight, where it is included among the hollow verbs. As it is used so often, however, its Perfect is given here.

Sing.	3. masc.	كَانَ	kāna, he was.
,,	3. fem.	كَانَتْ	kānat, she was.
,,	2. masc.	كُنْتَ	kunta, you (m.) were.
,,	2. fem.	كُنْتِ	kunti, you (f.) were.
,,	1. masc. & fem.	كُنْتُ	kuntu, I was.
Dual	3. masc.	كَانَا	kānā, they two (m.) were.
,,	3. fem.	كَانَتَا	kānatā, they two (f.) were.
,,	2. masc. & fem.	كُنْتُمَا	kuntumā, you two were.
Plur.	3. masc.	كَانُوا	kānū, they (m.) were.
,,	3. fem.	كُنَّ	kunna, they (f.) were.
,,	2. masc.	كُنْتُمْ	kuntum, you (m.) were.
,,	2. fem.	كُنْتُنَّ	kuntunna, you (f.) were.
,,	1. masc. & fem.	كُنَّا	kunnā, we were.

6. The Perfect كَانَ is used with the Perfect of another verb to express the Pluperfect, the subject being normally placed between the two verbs.

e.g. كَانَ زَيْدٌ كَتَبَ kāna Zaidun kataba, Zaid had written. Note that, where the subject is plural, referring to human beings, كَانَ will be in the singular, according to the rule of the preceding verb: but the second verb, its subject having been mentioned already, must agree with it in number.

e.g. كَانَ ٱلرِّجَالُ شَرِبُوا kāna r-rijālu sharibū, the men had drunk.

The interpolation of قَدْ qad also occurs,

e.g. كَانَ ٱلرِّجَالُ قَدْ شَرِبُوا kāna r-rijālu qad sharibū, with the same meaning.

7. When كَانَ is used as a copula, its predicate (خَبَرٌ khabar) is put in the accusative as if it were a direct object.

e.g. كَانَ زَيْدٌ وَلَدًا kāna Zaidun waladan, Zaid was a boy.

كَانَتْ فَاطِمَةُ ٱبْنَةَ ٱلْمَلِكِ kānat Fāṭimatu bnata l-maliki, Fatima was the King's daughter.

كَانَ ٱلْبُسْتَانُ كَبِيرًا kāna l-bustānu kabīran, the garden was large.

8. The verb "to be" cannot be used impersonally in Arabic, as in English, e.g. "there was a thief in the house". In Arabic, we say "a thief was in the house" (the verb, of course, usually being placed first). كَانَ لِصٌّ فِي ٱلْبَيْتِ kāna laṣṣun fi l-baiti. Consequently, in such sentences the verb كَانَ may be feminine, if the subject demands this,

e.g. كَانَتْ قَلْعَةٌ فَوْقَ ٱلْجَبَلِ kānat qalʿatun fauqa l-jabali. There was a fort on top of the hill.

Beginners tend to translate such sentences treating the subject of كَانَ as its object, as if the Arabic read "it was a fort on top of the hill"; putting قَلْعَةٌ in the accusative. They should carefully avoid this common error, which is made even by Arab schoolchildren.

ALL. EACH. EVERY.

9. كُلٌّ kullun is used to mean "all", "each", or "every". When followed by an indefinite noun in the genitive singular, it means "each" or "every",

e.g. وَصَلَ كُلُّ وَلَدٍ every, or each boy arrived.

When followed by a definite noun in the genitive plural, it means "all", e.g. حَضَرَ كُلُّ ٱلْوُزَرَاءِ all the ministers attended.

حَضَرَ كُلُّ وُزَرَاءِ ٱلْحُكُومَةِ ٱلاجْتِمَاعَ all the ministers of the government attended the meeting.

In the latter case, if it is the subject of a following verb, the verb will be in the plural, when referring to human beings,

e.g. وَصَلَ كُلُّ ٱلْوُزَرَاءِ وَجَلَسُوا all the ministers arrived and sat down.

جَمِيعٌ jamīʿun also is used to mean "all". Like كُلٌّ it is a noun and is followed by a genitive,

e.g. حَضَرَ جَمِيعُ ٱلْوُزَرَاءِ all the ministers attended.

Both these words may take a plural attached pronoun as their genitive,

e.g. كُلُّهُمْ all of them.

جَمِيعُكُمْ all of you.

They may occur in apposition to the nouns to which they refer,

e.g. وَصَلَ ٱلرِّجَالُ كُلُّهُمْ The men arrived, all of them.

ضَرَبْتُهُمْ جَمِيعَهُمْ I hit them, all of them.

(جَمِيعَ is in the accusative here).

VOCABULARY

حَزِنَ to be or become sad	عَلِيٌّ Ali *pr. n. masc.*
حُزْنٌ sadness	قَلْعَةٌ *pl.* قِلَاعٌ fortress, citadel
تَاجِرٌ *pl.* تُجَّارٌ merchant	سَمِعَ to hear
مُهِمٌّ important	أَسَرَ to take prisoner

بِضَاعَةٌ *pl.* بَضَائِعُ goods, merchandise

نُورٌ *pl.* أَنْوَارٌ light *n.*

سُكَّرٌ sugar

فَاكِهَةٌ *pl.* فَوَاكِهُ fruit

ثَوْبٌ *pl.* ثِيَابٌ garment

لَبِسَ to wear, put on

جُنَيْنَةٌ *pl.* جَنَائِنُ garden

قُمَاشٌ *pl.* أَقْمِشَةٌ cloth

خَيْلٌ *pl.* خُيُولٌ horses (*collective* and *plural*)

خَرُوفٌ *pl.* خِرْفَانٌ sheep, lamb

سَمَكٌ *pl.* أَسْمَاكٌ fish

رَئِيسٌ *pl.* رُؤَسَاءُ chairman, president, head

وِزَارَةٌ ministry, cabinet

أَخَذَ (ـُ) to take

رَئِيسُ ٱلْوُزَرَاءِ Prime Minister

حُكُومَةٌ *pl.* ـَاتٌ government

سِيَاسَةٌ *pl.* ـَاتٌ policy, politics

دَوْلَةٌ *pl.* دُوَلٌ state, power

مُنْذُ since *prep.*

اَلْآنَ now

أَيْضًا also

كَثِيرًا *adv.* greatly, much, a lot

تُفَّاحٌ apple, apples

تُفَّاحَةٌ an apple

تَمْرٌ (*collective*), dates

عَمِلَ to do

عَمَلٌ *pl.* أَعْمَالٌ work, deed, doing

إِيطَالِيَا Italy

EXERCISE 23

١ — سَمِعَتِ ٱلنِّسَاءُ ٱلْخَبَرَ عَنْ مَوْتِ رَئِيسِ ٱلْوُزَرَاءِ فَلَبِسْنَ ثِيَابَهُنَّ ٱلسَّوْدَاءَ وَحَزِنَّ (for حَزِنْنَ) كَثِيرًا . ٢ — وَكَانَ حُزْنُ ٱلتُّجَّارِ كَثِيرًا أَيْضًا . ٣ — كَانَ عَلَيَّ أَخْذِي لِلْمَدِينَةِ ، وَنَظَرْتُ نُورًا هُنَاكَ فِي قَلْعَةٍ مِنْ

قِلَاعِ ٱلْمَلِكِ. ٤ — قَدْ بَلَغَتْنَا أَخْبَارٌ مُهِمَّةٌ عَنْ سِيَاسَةِ ٱلْحُكُومَةِ ٱلْجَدِيدَةِ.
٥ — كَانَتْ إِيطَالِيَا مِنَ (among) ٱلدُّوَلِ ٱلْكُبْرَى. ٦ — كُنَّا حَزِينِينَ لَمَّا
أَسَرَ ٱلْأَعْدَاءُ كَثِيرِينَ مِنْ جُنُودِنَا قَبْلَ سَنَةٍ. ٧ — كَانَتْ عِنْدِي فَوَاكِهُ
كَثِيرَةٌ فِى جُنَيْنَتِي، مِنْهَا (among them, including) ٱلتُّفَّاحُ وَٱلتَّمْرُ.
٨ — ذَكَرَ أُسْتَاذُ ٱلْجَامِعَةِ ٱلْحَيَوَانَاتِ ٱلْمُهِمَّةَ، مِنْهَا ٱلْخَيْلَ وَٱلْخِرْفَانَ،
وَذَكَرَ ٱلْأَسْمَاكَ أَيْضًا. ٩ — قَالَ لَهُمْ: لِمَاذَا أَخَذْتُمُ ٱبْنِي وَضَرَبْتُمُوهُ؟
١٠ — وَجَدَ ٱلْأَوْلَادُ قُمَاشًا فِى ٱلشَّارِعِ وَأَخَذُوهُ. ١١ — وَضَعَتْ أُمِّي
ٱلسُّكَّرَ عَلَى ٱلْمَائِدَةِ. ١٢ — هٰذِهِ ٱلْوِزَارَةُ كَانَتْ قَدْ عَمِلَتْ ذٰلِكَ مُنْذُ
سِنِينَ كَثِيرَةٍ. ١٣ — وِزَارَتُكُمْ ضَعِيفَةٌ جِدًّا ٱلْآنَ. ١٤ — أَيَّةُ بَضَائِعَ عِنْدَ
ذٰلِكَ ٱلتَّاجِرِ ٱلْغَنِيِّ؟ ١٥ — عِنْدَهُ أَقْمِشَةٌ مِنْ جَمِيعِ ٱلْأَلْوَانِ. ١٦ —
ٱلسُّكَّرُ أَهَمُّ بَضَائِعِ بِلَادِنَا ٱلْيَوْمَ. ١٧ — وَصَلَ ٱلْوُزَرَاءُ كُلُّهُمْ
وَدَخَلُوا ٱلْقَصْرَ وَجَلَسُوا عَلَى كَرَاسِيهِمْ، ثُمَّ وَصَلَ ٱلرَّئِيسُ. ١٨ — كَانَ
ٱجْتِمَاعٌ مُهِمٌّ لِلْوِزَارَةِ ٱلْجَدِيدَةِ قَبْلَ يَوْمَيْنِ. ١٩ — طَلَبَ ٱلْعَرَبُ
جِمَالَهُمْ فَرَكِبُوهَا (them). ٢٠ — كَانَ جَمَلُ ٱلشَّيْخِ أَسْرَعَ مِنْ خَيْلِنَا
كُلِّهَا ٱلْبَارِحَ.

EXERCISE 24

1. Has this news reached you about the death of many of our soldiers? 2. No, and our sorrow is very great now. 3. The Prime Minister said: These merchants have many goods important to our country. 4. He also mentioned the new policy of the government. 5. Ali said: There were many fine fruits in my garden, but the boys of the village have

entered it in the night and taken them. 6. They became sad when they heard what he said (his speech). 7. The cloth of these garments is very old. It is my grandmother's cloth. 8. The soldiers found the enemy and took them prisoner. 9. The women wore their white clothes when the men returned. 10. Cairo is the largest city in the Arab East. 11. These sheep have been mine since the days of your father. 12. Each scholar took an apple and two dates from the fruits of the school garden. 13. What have you done to this fish? 14. The soldiers rode their horses to the fortress, (and) captured it, and took prisoner the inhabitants. 15. They killed the old and left the young, all of them. 16. There were lights from the windows of my friend's house. 17. That merchant has all the sugar in the market. 18. The wives had demanded a great deal of work from their servants, (fem.) so the latter (these) left the food on the table and went out. 19. We have attended every meeting of the council. 20. You were our friends, and now you are our enemies (أَعْدَاؤُنَا)*

* See pp. 114, 115 on the orthography of final *hamza*.

CHAPTER FOURTEEN

(اَلْبَابُ ٱلرَّابِعَ عَشَرَ)

The Imperfect

1. The *Imperfect tense* (اَلْمُضَارِعُ) expresses an action still unfinished at the time to which reference is being made. It is most frequently translated into English by the Present or the Future.

2. Whereas in the Perfect, as we have seen, the different persons were expressed by suffixes, the Imperfect has prefixes. It also has some suffixes to denote number and gender.

The prefixes and suffixes are as follows:

3. masc.	يَــْـــُ	3. masc.	يَــْـــَانِ	3. masc.	يَــْـــُونَ
3. fem.	تَــْـــُ	3. fem.	تَــْـــَانِ	3. fem.	يَــْـــْنَ
2. masc.	تَــْـــُ	2. m. & f.	تَــْـــَانِ	2. masc.	تَــْـــُونَ
2. fem.	تَــْـــِينَ			2. fem.	تَــْـــْنَ
1. m. & f.	أَــْـــُ			1. m. & f.	نَــْـــُ

Full form of Imperfect Indicative of كَتَبَ

Sing. 3. masc.	يَكْتُبُ	yaktubu, he writes (or will write)
„ 3. fem.	تَكْتُبُ	taktubu, she writes.
„ 2. masc.	تَكْتُبُ	taktubu, you (masc.) write.

Sing. 2. fem.	تَكْتُبِينَ	taktubīna, you (fem.) write.
„ 1. masc. & fem.	أَكْتُبُ	'aktubu, I write.
Dual 3. masc.	يَكْتُبَانِ	yaktubāni, they two (masc.) write.
„ 3. fem.	تَكْتُبَانِ	taktubāni, they two (fem.) write.
„ 2. masc. & fem.	تَكْتُبَانِ	taktubāni, you two write.
Plur. 3. masc.	يَكْتُبُونَ	yaktubūna, they (masc.) write.
„ 3. fem.	يَكْتُبْنَ	yaktubna, they (fem.) write.
„ 2. masc.	تَكْتُبُونَ	taktubūna, you (masc.) write.
„ 2. fem	تَكْتُبْنَ	taktubna, you (fem.) write.
„ 1. masc. & fem.	نَكْتُبُ	naktubu, we write.

3. It will be noted that after the pronominal prefix the first radical or consonant of the verb has sukūn (the كْ in this case). The second radical (ت) has ḍamma. But this is not always so, for the vowelling of the second radical in the Imperfect, no less than in the Perfect, may be fatḥa, ḍamma, or kasra, and in the majority of verbs only the dictionary will show which vowelling is used with any particular verb.

The following points may, however, give some guidance:

(a) Most verbs whose second or third radical is a guttural (i.e. ح خ ع غ ه) take a ـَ e.g. فَتَحَ to open, Imperfect يَفْتَحُ; مَنَعَ, to hinder, Imperfect يَمْنَعُ. There are, however, many exceptions as دَخَلَ to enter, Imperfect يَدْخُلُ; بَلَغَ, to reach, Imperfect يَبْلُغُ; رَجَعَ to return, Imperfect يَرْجِعُ.

(b) Verbs of the form فَعِلَ generally take َ— as شَرِبَ to drink; Imperfect يَشْرَبُ; exceptions, however, occur as حَسِبَ to esteem; Imperfect يَحْسِبُ (حَسَبَ to reckon, makes يَحْسُبُ).

(c) Verbs of the form فَعُلَ may only take ُ— as كَرُمَ to be noble, Imperfect يَكْرُمُ.

4. The Imperfect in itself denotes only unfinished action, but it may be made to indicate the future by putting the independent word سَوْفَ before it or prefixing the contraction سَ, e.g. سَوْفَ يَكْتُبُ or سَيَكْتُبُ he will write.

But where it is clear from the context that the Imperfect has a Future meaning, these particles need not be inserted.

e.g. ذَهَبَ ٱلْبَارِحَ وَيَذْهَبُ غَداً أَيْضاً He went yesterday and will go tomorrow also.

Here the use of the word "tomorrow" makes it clear that the verb refers to future time.

5. When used with a Present significance, the Imperfect may give the meaning of the *Continuous Present* or the *Habitual Present*, e.g.

(Continuous) يَذْهَبُ ٱلْآنَ He is (actually) going now.

(Habitual) يَذْهَبُ كُلَّ يَوْمٍ He goes every day.

(Note كُلَّ accus. here)

The Past Continuous and Habitual are expressed by the Perfect of كَانَ followed by the Imperfect of the verb concerned, e.g.

(Continuous) لَمَّا مَرَّ بِبَيْتِي كَانَ يَذْهَبُ لِلسُّوقِ When he passed by my house, he was going to the market.

(Habitual) كَانَ يَذْهَبُ لِلسُّوقِ كُلَّ صَبَاحٍ He used to go to the market every morning.

6. As we have seen, the verb "to be" is not used in Arabic to express the *Present Indicative.* A *Nominal Sentence* is used instead. Consequently, when the Imperfect of كَانَ is used, it must have some other meaning. The Imperfect of كَانَ is given below. (A fuller explanation of this type of verb will be given under the "Hollow Verb" in Chapter Twenty-eight.)

Sing. 3. masc.	يَكُونُ	yakūnu, he will be.
„ 3. fem.	تَكُونُ	takūnu, she will be.
Sing. 2. masc.	تَكُونُ	takūnu, you (m.) will be.
„ 2. fem.	تَكُونِينَ	takūnīna, you (f.) will be.
„ 1. masc & fem.	أَكُونُ	ʾakūnu, I shall be.
Dual 3. masc.	يَكُونَانِ	yakūnāni, they two (m.) will be.
„ 3. fem.	تَكُونَانِ	takūnāni, they two (f.) will be.
„ 2. masc. & fem.	تَكُونَانِ	takūnāni, you two will be.
Plur. 3. masc.	يَكُونُونَ	yakūnūna, they (m.) will be.
„ 3. fem.	يَكُنَّ	yakunna, they (f.) will be.
„ 2. masc.	تَكُونُونَ	takūnūna, you (m.) will be.

Plur. 2. fem. تَكُنَّ takunna, you (f.) will be.

„ 1. masc. & fem. نَكُونُ nakūnu, we shall be.

6. The *Future Perfect* is expressed by using the Imperfect of كَانَ with the Perfect of the verb concerned,

e.g. يَكُونُ زَيْدٌ كَتَبَ Zaid will have written.

Frequently, the particle قَدْ is inserted:

يَكُونُ زَيْدٌ قَدْ كَتَبَ

THE ORTHOGRAPHY OF FINAL HAMZA

7. In Chapter One no attempt was made to give exhaustive rules for writing the *hamza* in order to avoid confusing the beginner. However, the final hamza may have already caused some confusion, and a few rules will now be given. It should be mentioned, though, that they do not cover the writing of hamza as a final radical for a verb. First, the student should study the following table:

A.		*With pronominal suffix*
Nom.	جُزْءٌ (a part)	جُزْؤُهُ (his or its part)
Accus.	جُزْءًا	جُزْءَهُ
Gen.	جُزْءٍ	جُزْئِهِ

بَدْءٌ beginning, and عِبْءٌ burden, may be written in the same way (but the accusative of عِبْءٌ with attached pronoun is عِبْئَهُ, etc.). Note that final hamza, when preceded by an unvowelled letter, is written "on the line", as the Arabs put it; that is, alone. When, however, a pronominal suffix is added, the hamza is no longer final, and is written on the semi-vowel appropriate to its own vowelling (و for ḍamma, and ى, without dots, for kasra) except in the accusative, when it is written on ى if the previous letter is one which connects, or otherwise "on the line".

Similar rules apply when a long vowel or diphthong, with ا or و or ى precede the final hamza, since from the Arab viewpoint these, too, are unvowelled letters.

e.g.

B.		*With pronominal suffix*
Nom.	ضَوْءٌ light	ضَوْؤُهَا its (fem.) light
Acc.	ضَوْءًا	ضَوْءَهُ
Gen.	ضَوْءٍ	ضَوْئِهِ
C.		
Nom.	وُزَرَاءُ (diptote) ministers	وُزَرَاؤُهُمْ their ministers
Acc.	وُزَرَاءَ	وُزَرَاءَهُمْ
Gen.	وُزَرَاءَ	وُزَرَائِهِمْ (defined as triptote)

In the latter type, however, when 'alif precedes final hamza in a triptote the indefinite accusative is not written with 'alif (as in بَيْتًا a house), to avoid two 'alifs coming together.

e.g.

D.		
Nom.	بِنَاءٌ building	بِنَاؤُهُ his building
Acc.	بِنَاءً	بِنَاءَهُ
Gen.	بِنَاءٍ	بِنَائِهِ
E.		
Nom.	نَبِيءٌ a prophet	نَبِيؤُهُمْ their prophet
Acc.	نَبِيئًا	نَبِيئَهُمْ

Gen. نَبِيءٍ نَبِيئِهِمْ

The orthography of the *hamza* in شَيْءٌ, thing, is similar to that in نَبِيءٌ.

In table E, note the difference in the writing of hamza in the indefinite accusative.

VOCABULARY

NOTE: Verbs marked with an asterisk have been given before but are repeated here to show the vowelling of the Imperfect, indicated in brackets beside the verb in Arabic.

مَنَعَ (ـَ) (عَنْ) to hinder (from)

ذَهَبَ* (ـَ) to go

جَمَعَ (ـَ) to gather

قَطَعَ (ـَ) to cut

رَفَعَ (ـَ) to raise, lift

سَمِعَ* (ـَ) to hear

لَعِبَ (ـَ) to play

عَمِلَ* (ـَ) to work, do

حَمَلَ (ـِ) to carry

جَلَسَ* (ـِ) to sit

غَسَلَ (ـِ) to wash *trans.*

كَسَرَ* (ـِ) to break

حَسِبَ (ـِ) to estimate

بَلَغَ* (ـُ) to reach

حَضَرَ* (ـُ) to attend

دَخَلَ* (ـُ) to enter

دَرَسَ* (ـُ) to study

سَكَنَ (ـُ) to live, dwell, inhabit (with فِي or direct object)

طَلَبَ* (ـُ) to demand, request

كَرُمَ (ـُ) to be or become noble

كَبُرَ (ـُ) to be or become big, old

شَيْءٌ *pl.* أَشْيَاءُ thing

جُزْءٌ *pl.* أَجْزَاءٌ a part

عِبْءٌ *pl.* أَعْبَاءٌ a burden

حَمَّالٌ a porter

ضَوْءٌ *pl.* أَضْوَاءٌ light, brightness

حِمْلٌ *pl.* أَحْمَالٌ a load

بَدْءٌ beginning

بَعْدَ ٱلظُّهْرِ (in) the afternoon

بِنَاءً عَلَى in accordance with

صَبَاحًا ، فِي ٱلصَّبَاحِ in the morning

أَللّٰهُ (Allāhu) God

مَسَاءً ، فِي ٱلْمَسَاءِ in the evening

؟ . . . أَمْ . . . or (in a double question, the first of which is preceded by أَ or هَلْ)

لَيْلاً ، فِي ٱللَّيْلِ at night

أَمْ لَا؟ or not?

أُسْبُوعٌ *pl.* أَسَابِيعُ week

دُخَانٌ smoke, tobacco

عَامٌ *pl.* أَعْوَامٌ year

شَرِبَ دُخَانًا to smoke

حَبْلٌ *pl.* حِبَالٌ rope

غَدًا tomorrow

حِينَ , حِينَمَا when

حَقٌّ *pl.* حُقُوقٌ a right

لَمَّا (with perfect only), when

EXERCISE 25

١ — مَاذَا يَمْنَعُكَ عَنْ ذٰلِكَ بَعْدَ ٱلظُّهْرِ؟ ٢ — هَلْ تَحْمِلُ جُزْءًا مِنْ ذٰلِكَ أَمْ لَا؟ ٣ — قَالَتِ ٱلْأُمُّ لِٱبْنِهَا ٱلصَّغِيرِ : أَيُّ شَيْءٍ كَسَرْتَ ٱلْآنَ؟ ٤ — فَقَالَ ٱلْوَلَدُ : كُنْتُ أَلْعَبُ فِي ٱلْحُجْرَةِ وَوَقَعَ شَيْءٌ (something) مِنَ ٱلْمَائِدَةِ . ٥ — سَوْفَ يَجْلِسُ ٱلْوُزَرَاءُ أُسْبُوعًا (for a week) بِنَاءً عَلَى قَوْلِ ٱلرَّئِيسِ . ٦ — غَسَلَتِ ٱلْاِمْرَأَةُ ثِيَابَهَا فِي ٱلنَّهْرِ صَبَاحًا . ٧ — حَسِبْتُ ٱلْحَمَّالِينَ كَسَالَى (pl. of كَسْلَانُ) كُلَّهُمْ . ٨ — كَانَ مُحَمَّدٌ نَبِيًّا (نَبِيًّا) كَبِيرًا . ٩ — يَكُونُ ضَوْءُ ٱلشَّمْسِ شَدِيدًا بَعْدَ ٱلظُّهْرِ . ١٠ — كَانَ

ٱلتَّلَامِذَةُ يَشْرَبُونَ ٱلدُّخَانَ فِى ٱلْبَدْءِ وَكَانَ ذٰلِكَ عِبْئًا كَبِيرًا عَلَى
ٱلْمُعَلِّمِ. ١١ — جَمَعَ ٱلْجَيْشَ وَقَالَ لِلْجُنُودِ : ٱللّٰهُ أَكْبَرُ. ١٢ — أَتَعْمَلُ
هٰذَا ٱلْعَمَلَ فِى ٱللَّيْلِ أَمْ غَدًا؟ ١٣ — سَوْفَ نَسْمَعُ ٱلْأَخْبَارَ مِنْ مِصْرَ
فِى ٱلْمَسَاءِ. ١٤ — ٱلسُّكَّانُ طَيِّبُونَ وَوُزَرَاؤُهُمْ مِنْ أَحْسَنِ ٱلنَّاسِ.
١٥ — سَتَدْخُلُ ٱلنِّسَاءُ بُيُوتَهُنَّ وَيَسْكُنَّ (for يَسْكُنْنَ) فِيهَا حَتَّى بَدْءِ
ٱلْعَامِ ٱلْجَدِيدِ. ١٦ — حِينَ يَكْبُرُ هٰذَا ٱلْوَلَدُ يَكُونُ مِنْ أَطْيَبِ ٱلرِّجَالِ.
١٧ — قَطَعَ ٱلْحَمَّالُونَ حِبَالَ أَحْمَالِهِمْ وَرَفَعُوهَا مِنْ حَمِيرِهِمْ. ١٨ — بَعْدَ
هٰذِهِ ٱلْأَعْمَالِ سَوْفَ يَكْرُمُ ٱسْمُكَ بَيْنَ إِخْوَانِكَ وَأَخَوَاتِكَ. ١٩ — تَكُونُ
ٱبْنَتِى هٰذِهِ قَدْ حَضَرَتْ دُرُوسَ ٱلْمَدْرَسَةِ مُنْذُ بَدْءِ ٱلسَّنَةِ وَدَرَسَتِ
ٱلْمَوْضُوعَ كَثِيرًا فَلِمَاذَا لَا تَسْمَعُونَ قَوْلَهَا؟ ٢٠ — حِينَ تَبْلُغُ مَنْزِلَ
ٱلشَّيْخِ تَطْلُبُ مِنْهُ ٱلشَّاىَ.

EXERCISE 26

1. We are students, and we seek learning. 2. At the start (in the beginning) the women saw the light of the sun, and they will also see it in the afternoon. 3. The porters will carry all the loads from the house to the car. 4. Were you (plural) collecting the boxes in the morning or not? 5. The Prophet of God will have gone to Mecca tomorrow evening. 6. The people will hear the news and will kill their ministers. 7. Ali cut the rope from his friend's hands during the night (by night), and they broke a part of (مِنْ) the wall, and went out of the fortress. 8. This thing will be a big burden to (عَلَى) us. 9. She will be in Damascus in two weeks' time (after two weeks). 10. She used to smoke a lot, but her father prevented her a year ago. 11. We have many ancient (old) rights, and the government knows them. 12. My

father used to raise great stones from the ground and carry them from our garden to Hassan's (garden). 13. The clean boy washes his face and hands every day in the morning and evening. 14. What are you doing now? Are you studying your lessons? 15. He has broken everything in the room. 16. The Arabs were noble and used to live in the desert. 17. I considered (حَسِبَ) him better than me in this work. 18. In accordance with the president's speech, we attended the meeting. 19. The minister has grown old – he is the oldest minister in the Arab world today. 20. The news will reach you tomorrow when you are in the council.

CHAPTER FIFTEEN

(اَلْبَابُ ٱلْخَامِسَ عَشَرَ)

Moods of the Imperfect
The Subjunctive

1. So far we have given only the *Imperfect Indicative*, the Imperfect which makes a plain statement, whether applicable to the present or the future. But the Imperfect, by slight changes, may be in the *Subjunctive* or *Jussive moods*, the former implying wish, purpose (or command in indirect speech), and the latter command (or, with the negative, prohibition). The reader will have noted that in the Indicative the final vowel of the Imperfect is ḍamma in the singular number. Thus يَكْتُبُ yaktubu, he writes. For the subjunctive, this ḍamma is changed to fatḥa, يَكْتُبَ yaktuba; while, for the Jussive, it is replaced by sukūn, يَكْتُبْ yaktub. In addition, those parts which, in the indicative, end in a nūn following a long vowel lose the nūn in both Subjunctive and Jussive, which are then identical. e.g. يَكْتُبُونَ yaktubūna becomes يَكْتُبُوا yaktubū (as in the Perfect third person plural, the final ʾalif here is merely a spelling convention).

يَكْتُبَانِ yaktubāni becomes يَكْتُبَا yaktubā.

تَكْتُبِينَ taktubīna becomes تَكْتُبِي taktubī.

But those feminine plural forms which end in the suffix نَ na do not change, and are therefore the same for all three moods.

2. Here is the complete table for the Subjunctive (اَلْمُضَارِعُ اَلْمَنْصُوبُ) :

Singular			*Dual*		
3. masc.	يَكْتُبَ	yaktuba	3. masc.	يَكْتُبَا	yaktubā.
3. fem.	تَكْتُبَ	taktuba.	3. fem.	تَكْتُبَا	taktubā.
2. masc.	تَكْتُبَ	taktuba.	2. m. & f.	تَكْتُبَا	taktubā.
2. fem.	تَكْتُبِي	taktubī.			
1. m. & f.	أَكْتُبَ	aktuba.			

Plural

3. masc.	يَكْتُبُوا	yaktubū.
3. fem.	يَكْتُبْنَ	yaktubna.
2. masc.	تَكْتُبُوا	taktubū.
2. fem.	تَكْتُبْنَ	taktubna.
1. m. & f.	نَكْتُبَ	naktuba.

NOTE. The Imperfect Subjuctive of كَانَ is declined like the indicative subject to the same changes in the endings as in the verb above.

3. The Subjunctive can only be used after certain particles (conjunctions):

أَنْ 'an, that. أَلَّا 'allā (for 'an lā) that not.

لِ li, in order to. لِئَلَّا li'allā, in order not to.

كَيْ kai, in order to. كَيْلَا kailā, in order not to.

لِأَنْ li'an in order to.

حَتَّى ḥattā, so that.

لَنْ lan, shall not (used as a strong negation of the future).

e.g. قَالَ لَهُ أَنْ يَذْهَبَ حَالًا he told him to go at once.

أَمَرَهُ أَلَّا (أَنْ لَا) يَحْضُرَ he ordered him not to attend.

قَدِمَ مُحَمَّدٌ لِيَعْمَلَ وَاجِبَهُ (or لِأَنْ) Muhammad advanced to do his duty.

فَتَحَ ٱلْغَفِيرُ ٱلْبَابَ لِكَيْ يَنْظُرَ حَالَ ٱلْبَيْتِ the watchman opened the door to see (so that he could see) the state of the house.

تَرَكَ ٱلْوَزِيرُ ٱلْقَصْرَ كَيْلَا يَنْظُرَ ٱلْمَلِكَ the minister left the palace so that he should not see the king.

لَنْ أَفْعَلَ ذٰلِكَ I shall (certainly) not do that.

لَنْ تَهْرُبَ مِنَ ٱلْقِتَالِ you shall not flee from the fight.

It is not necessary to repeat the particle where two subjunctive sentences follow each other linked by a conjunction such as فَ, وَ, or أَوْ.

e.g.

فَتَحَ ٱلْغَفِيرُ ٱلْبَابَ لِيَدْخُلَ ٱلْبَيْتَ وَيَنْظُرَ حَالَ ٱلْأَثَاثِ The watchman opened the door to enter the house and see the condition of the furniture.

4. It is difficult to specify which of the above particles should be used in any given context. لَنْ is restricted to the denial of the future, and is a fairly strong particle, often carrying the force of 'you shall not', 'they shall not at all' and similar expressions in English. It is common in classical literature. The student who wishes to write modern Arabic should use it sparingly. حَتَّى has some sense of finality about it; it tends to mean the ultimate aim.

The rest are synonymous.* But it may be said that لِكَيْ and

* But see Appendix C, §5 for further details, which to some extent replace the following explanation.

كَيْ are the least frequently used.

5. The student should distinguish between the use of لِ as a preposition followed by a noun in the genitive and as a particle introducing the Subjunctive.

حَتَّى does not necessarily take the subjunctive. For example, it may take a genitive noun (but not a pronoun) with the meaning of "up to", "until", "as far as" or "even" ("including").

It may also take a Perfect verb, with the meaning of "until", e.g. ضَرَبَهُ حَتَّى صَرَخَ He beat him till he cried out.

VOCABULARY

أَمْرٌ *pl.* أَوَامِرُ command

أَمْرٌ *pl.* أُمُورٌ affair, matter

أَمَرَ (ـُ) to command (with *acc.* of the person and بِ of thing)

سَمَحَ (ـَ) to allow (with لِ for the person and بِ for the thing)

غُرْفَةٌ *pl.* غُرَفٌ room

صَرَفَ (ـِ) to spend

فِرَاشٌ bed, bedding

غَفِيرٌ *pl.* غُفَرَانٌ watchman, caretaker

أُورُبَّا Europe

قَيْدٌ *pl.* قُيُودٌ bond

رَقَدَ (ـُ) to sleep, lie down

عَاقِلٌ intelligent

أَمَامَ before (of place)

وَعَدَ to promise (with *acc.* of the person and بِ of thing)

سِرٌّ *pl.* أَسْرَارٌ a secret

مَطْلُوبٌ *pl.* مَطَالِيبُ demand, desire, requirement

وَاجِبٌ *pl.* ـَاتٌ — duty

قَدَمَ (ـُ) to advance *intrans.*, come forward

بَعَثَ (ـَ) to send

لَجْنَةٌ *pl.* لِجَانٌ committee, commission

سَأَلَ, *imperf.* يَسْأَلُ to ask

زِيَارَةٌ *pl.* ـَاتٌ — a visit

بِرِيطَانِيَا Britain

كِذْبٌ *pl.* أَكْذَابٌ a lie

حَقِيقَةٌ *pl.* حَقَائِقُ truth, reality

جَرِيدَةٌ *pl.* جَرَائِدُ newspaper

مُدِيرٌ *pl.* ـُونَ — director, governor

جِسْمٌ *pl.* أَجْسَامٌ body

دَمٌ *pl.* دِمَاءٌ blood

يَدَوِيٌّ manual

اَلْأَعْمَالُ ٱلْيَدَوِيَّةُ manual labour

عَامِلٌ *pl.* عُمَّالٌ a labourer, worker

حِزْبٌ *pl.* أَحْزَابٌ party (political)

EXERCISE 27

١ — طَلَبَ ٱلْمُدِيرُ مِنْكُمْ أَنْ تَحْضُرُوا عِنْدَهُ . ٢ — أَمَرْتُهُمَا أَنْ يَجْلِسَا . ٣ — حَضَرَ ٱلتَّاجِرُ عِنْدِى لِيَطْلُبَ ٱلْبَضَائِعَ . ٤ — هَلْ فَتَحْتَ لَهُمُ ٱلْبَابَ لِيَدْخُلُوا عِنْدَنَا؟ سَأَفْتَحُ ٱلْبَابَ لَهُمْ حَالاً . ٥ — خَرَجَ ٱلرِّجَالُ لِيَذْهَبُوا إِلَى ٱلصَّيْدِ . ٦ — طَلَبَ ٱلصَّبِىُّ مِنَ ٱلرَّجُلِ أَنْ يَسْمَحَ لَهُ بِغُرْفَةٍ نَظِيفَةٍ لِيَصْرِفَ لَيْلَتَهُ فِيهَا . ٧ — فَتَحْتُ ٱلْبَابَ حَتَّى أَدْخُلَ ٱلْغُرْفَةَ . ٨ — كَانَتْ أَوَامِرُ ٱلسُّلْطَانِ أَنْ يَرْجِعَ ٱلْحَاكِمُ مِنْ زِيَارَتِهِ لِبِرِيطَانِيَا لِيَعْمَلَ وَاجِبَهُ فِى بِلَادِهِ . ٩ — قَالَ ٱلرَّجُلُ هٰذِهِ ٱلْأَكْذَابَ لِيَكُونَ مَشْهُورًا فِى جَمِيعِ أُورُبَّا . ١٠ — أَمَرَ ٱلْمَلِكُ جُنُودَهُ أَنْ يَقْطَعُوا قُيُودَ ٱلْغَفِيرِ ٱلْكَسْلَانِ لِكَىْ يَرْجِعَ لِعَمَلِهِ ٱلْمُهِمِّ . ١١ — اَلْمَطْلُوبُ مِنَ ٱلْعُمَّالِ أَلَّا يَتْرُكُوا أَعْمَالَهُمُ ٱلْيَدَوِيَّةَ حَتَّى يَأْمُرَهُمُ ٱلْحِزْبُ بِذٰلِكَ .

١٢ — قَالَ ٱلرَّئِيسُ فِى ٱللَّجْنَةِ : مِنْ وَاجِبَاتِ ٱلْجَرَائِدِ أَنْ تَكْتُبَ ٱلْحَقِيقَةَ. ١٣ — لَنْ تَرْقُدَ عَلَى فِرَاشِكَ أَمَامَ عَيْنَىَّ! ١٤ — وَعَدَ ٱلْوَلَدُ ٱلْعَاقِلُ أَنْ يَعْمَلَ مَا (that which) فِى كِتَابِ ٱللّٰهِ وَقَوْلِ ٱلنَّبِىِّ. ١٥ — لِلنَّاسِ ٱلْبِيضِ وَٱلسُّودِ دَمٌ أَحْمَرُ فِى أَجْسَامِهِمْ. ١٦ — بَعَثَ ٱلشَّيْخُ ٱبْنَهُ ٱلْكَبِيرَ لِيَطْلُبَ ٱلْعِلْمَ هُنَاكَ. ١٧ — قَدِمَ ٱلضَّيْفُ حَتَّى وَصَلَ إِلَى بَابِ ٱلْقَصْرِ فَطَلَبَ مِنَ ٱلْجُنْدِىِّ أَنْ يَفْتَحَهُ. ١٨ — مَاذَا تَقْصِدُ مِنْ هٰذَا ٱلشَّرِّ؟ ١٩ — سَأَلْتُهُ عَنْ هٰذِهِ ٱلْأُمُورِ ٱلْبَارِحَ وَهُوَ طَلَبَ وَقْتًا لِيَدْرُسَهَا. ٢٠ — قَالَ لَهُ أَنْ يَأْخُذَ أَقْدَمَ كِتَابٍ مِنَ ٱلْمَكْتَبَةِ كَىْ يَنْظُرَهُ ذَوُو ٱلْعِلْمِ.

EXERCISE 28

1. I sent a boy with him to see what (مَا) he would do. 2. Muhammad and his servant intended to go to (إِلَى) the market. 3. I shall return to the house to see what you are (m.sing.) doing. 4. I have commanded the servant to appear (be present) before me. 5. I have promised him that that shall be a secret between me and (between) him. 6. Will (أ) you permit me to leave these things in front of you until the evening? 7. The teacher has ordered that you spend the day, all of it, in the classroom, to do what he asked (of) you yesterday. 8. It is required of the watchmen that they leave their work to attend a meeting of the Labour Party (the party of the workers) to hear the news of the chairman's visit to Britain and Italy. 9. The ambassador came from Europe two months ago, to ask about the truth of the matter. 10. It is for you to (لَكَ أَنْ or عَلَيْكَ أَنْ) do your duty. 11. The

intelligent man should (لِ . . . . أَنْ) know the truths from the lies in the newspapers. 12. The men asked their wives to be in their houses in the afternoon, and this was difficult for (عَلَى) them. 13. Why are you lying on your bed? Is your body weak, or are you lazy? 14. The governor and the Director of Works (أَشْغَال) attended the committee meeting to hear the government's orders. 15. These apples have the colour of blood; (هِيَ) they are among (from) the finest fruit in your garden. 16. They opened the windows of the room, so that their relatives should see the sun in the morning. 17. The moonlight (light of the moon) is beautiful tonight. 18. The governor ordered his men to cut Hassan's bonds, so that he could return to his mother. 19. They told the two boys to open the door so that the women could come in. 20. Thou shalt not break anything (a thing) in this house!

CHAPTER SIXTEEN

(اَلْبَابُ السَّادِسَ عَشَرَ)

The Moods of the Imperfect
The Jussive

1. The Jussive Mood (اَلْمُضَارِعُ الْمَجْزُومُ) has the same forms as the Subjunctive except that where the third radical is the last letter, it takes jazma (sukūn) e.g.

Singular			*Dual*		
3. masc.	يَكْتُبْ	yaktub.	3. masc.	يَكْتُبَا	yaktubā.
3. fem.	تَكْتُبْ	taktub.	3. fem.	تَكْتُبَا	taktubā.
2. masc.	تَكْتُبْ	taktub.	2. masc.	تَكْتُبَا	taktubā.
2. fem.	تَكْتُبِي	taktubī.			
1. m. & f.	أَكْتُبْ	aktub.			

Plural

3. masc.	يَكْتُبُوا	yaktubū.
3. fem.	يَكْتُبْنَ	yaktubna.
2. masc.	تَكْتُبُوا	taktubū.
2. fem.	تَكْتُبْنَ	taktubna.
1. m. & f.	نَكْتُبْ	naktub.

2. The verb كَانَ in the Jussive loses its و (see Chapter Twenty-eight) when the last radical is vowelless, e.g.

Singular			*Dual*		
3. masc.	يَكُنْ	yakun.	3. masc.	يَكُونَا	yakūnā.

3. fem.	تَكُنْ	takun.	3. fem.	تَكُونَا	takūnā.
2. masc.	تَكُنْ	takun.	2. m. & f.	تَكُونَا	takūnā.
2. fem.	تَكُونِي	takūnī.			
1. m. & f.	أَكُنْ	akun.			

Plural

3. masc.	يَكُونُوا	yakūnū.
3. fem.	يَكُنَّ	yakunna.
2. masc.	تَكُونُوا	takūnū.
2. fem.	تَكُنَّ	takunna.
1. m. & f.	نَكُنْ	nakun.

3. The Jussive may be used (a) alone; (b) after certain particles, and (c) in conditional sentences. (This last usage will be dealt with in Chapter 35).

(a) Used alone, its purpose is to express a command. In the second person it would have the same meaning as the Imperative (see Chapter Seventeen), and it is not so used, except, rarely, for the sake of politeness. تَكْتُبْ would resemble the English "you write!" instead of the peremptory command "write!". Used with the first and third persons, it can often be translated as "let me" or "let him". The first person is comparatively infrequent, e.g. أَذْهَبْ لِلسُّوقِ let me go to the market, a sort of command to oneself, implying certainty or definite intention.

It is commonly used with the third person, e.g.

حِينَ (عِنْدَمَا) يَحْضُرُ يَلْبَسْ ثِيَابًا نَظِيفَةً when he attends, let him (he must) wear clean clothes.

In this sense it is generally reinforced by the particle لِ

حِينَ (عِنْدَمَا) يَحْضُرُ لِيَلْبَسْ ثِيَابَهُ ٱلْبَيْضَاءَ when he attends, (then) let him wear his white clothes.

This لِ is preceded by the conjunction فَ when there is a close connection with the previous sentence. In this case, لِ loses its vowel, e.g.

حِينَ (عِنْدَمَا) يَحْضُرُ فَلْيَلْبَسْ ثِيَابًا جَدِيدَةً when he attends, then let him wear new clothes.

The sukūn of the Jussive is changed to kasra when followed by hamzatu l-waṣl; (for example, with the Definite Article).

فَلْيَلْبَسِ ٱلثِّيَابَ ٱلْجَدِيدَةَ then let him wear the new clothes.

(b) After certain particles.

(i) After لَا with prohibitions. There is no negative Imperative in Arabic. Consequently, لَا must be used with the Jussive in its place,

e.g. لَا تَكْتُبْ do not write.

لَا تَكُنْ كَذَّابًا don't be a liar.

(ii) After لَمْ to deny a statement. When so used it gives the verb the meaning of the Perfect,

e.g. لَمْ يَكْتُبْ = مَا كَتَبَ he did not write.

An extension of لَمْ, لَمَّا means "not yet".

e.g. أَمَرْتُهُ وَلَمَّا يَذْهَبْ I ordered him, and he has not yet gone.

4. The Jussive may be rendered more emphatic by adding نْ an or نَّ anna, thus forming the two Energetic Forms (Modus energicus).

	Modus energicus I	*Modus energicus II*
Sing. 3. masc.	يَكْتُبَنَّ yaktubanna he shall write	يَكْتُبَنْ yaktuban.

Sing.	3. fem.	تَكْتُبَنَّ	taktubanna	تَكْتُبَنْ	taktuban.
,,	2. masc.	تَكْتُبَنَّ	taktubanna	تَكْتُبَنْ	taktuban.
,,	2. fem.	يَكْتُبِنَّ	taktubinna	تَكْتُبِنْ	taktubin.
,,	1. m. & f.	أَكْتُبَنَّ	aktubanna	أَكْتُبَنْ	aktuban.
Dual	3. masc.	يَكْتُبَانِّ	yaktubānni.		
,,	3. fem.	تَكْتُبَانِّ	taktubānni.		
,,	2. m. & f.	تَكْتُبَانِّ	taktubānni.		
Plur.	3. masc.	يَكْتُبُنَّ	yaktubunna	يَكْتُبُنْ	yaktubun.
,,	3. fem.	يَكْتُبْنَانِّ	yaktubnānni.		
,,	2. masc.	تَكْتُبُنَّ	taktubunna	تَكْتُبُنْ	taktubun.
,,	2. fem.	تَكْتُبْنَانِّ	taktubnānni.		
,,	1. m. & f.	نَكْتُبَنَّ	naktubanna	نَكْتُبَنْ	naktuban.

Note that certain forms are missing in Energetic Form II. The Energetic Moods are not much used, especially in modern Arabic. In the Qur'ān, Sermons, and other rhetorical literature, they are employed for exhortation. They tend to give an antique flavour to the language.

They may be strengthened by prefixing the particle لَ

e.g. لَيَكْتُبَنَّ let him surely write.

With the negative particle لَا they give the meaning of "thou shalt not".

لَا تَقْتُلَنْ or لَا تَقْتُلَنَّ thou shalt not kill.

The beginner is advised not to spend too much time over the energetic moods in the earlier stages of his studies.

5. The commonest particle of the Vocative in Arabic is

يَا . Though sometimes translated by "O", "Oh" in modern idiomatic English, there is frequently no need to translate it at all. It is not used when the following noun has the definite article. It is followed by the nominative without nunation, when the noun is not followed by ʾiḍāfa (a genitive), or by any predicate, whether in the form of a prepositional phrase or a direct object. These latter eventualities will be dealt with in the following chapter.

e.g. يَاحَسَنُ O Hassan!

يَا وَلَدُ Oh! boy (in address).

VOCABULARY

جَانِبٌ *pl.* جَوَانِبُ side

غَرِيبٌ *pl.* غُرَبَاءُ strange, stranger

مَوْضِعٌ *pl.* مَوَاضِعُ place

مَكَانٌ *pl.* مَكَانَاتٌ ، أَمْكِنَةٌ ، أَمَاكِنُ place

قَدَرَ (ـِ) to be able, can

غَيْرُ un-, non-, another, other than (with *genitive*)

غَيْرُهُ another (other than he)

غَيْرُ طَيِّبٍ not good

كَذَبَ (ـِ) to lie, to tell lies

ضِيقٌ need

دُخُولٌ entering *n.*

ذَهَابٌ going *n.*

قَادِمٌ coming, next, approaching

عَالِمٌ *pl.* عُلَمَاءُ learned (man)

سَفَرٌ *pl.* أَسْفَارٌ journey, travel, travelling

سِفَارَةٌ *pl.* اتٌ — embassy

طَرِيقَةٌ *pl.* طَرَائِقُ manner, way

وَطَنٌ *pl.* أَوْطَانٌ home, homeland, country, fatherland

جَيِّدٌ excellent

جَزِيرَةٌ *pl.* جَزَائِرُ ، جُزُرٌ island

فَقِيرٌ *pl.* فُقَرَاءُ poor (man)

كَاتِبٌ *pl.* كَتَبَةٌ clerk

كَاتِبٌ *pl.* كُتَّابٌ writer

مَقَالَةٌ *pl.* ـَاتٌ — article, essay

بَحَثَ عَنْ (ـَ) to search for

بَحَثَ فِى (ـَ) to study, investigate, discuss

خِدْمَةٌ *pl.* خِدَمَاتٌ service

نَشَرَ (ـُ) to publish, spread

قَالَ to say, conjugated like كَانَ Followed by لِ with noun or pronoun, it means "to say to", "to tell".

لٰكِنْ (lākin), but

بَعْضٌ some, one of (with *genitive*)

تَحْتَ under

بِلَادُ ٱلْعَرَبِ Arabia

مَالِطَا, مَالِطَةُ Malta

EXERCISE 29

١ — لَمْ يَكُنْ يَسْمَحُ ٱلْوَزِيرُ أَنْ يَجْلِسَ رَجُلٌ فِى جَانِبِهِ. ٢ — لَا تَتْرُكْ صَدِيقَكَ فِى ٱلضِّيقِ. ٣ — عَرَفَهُ ٱلرِّجَالُ وَلَمْ يَمْنَعُوهُ مِنَ ٱلدُّخُولِ فَدَخَلَ. ٤ — قَلْبُهَا لَمْ يَكُنْ يَفْرَحُ لِشَيْءٍ. ٥ — يَا بِنْتُ لَا تَفْتَحِى ٱلْبَابَ لِلْغُرَبَاءِ. ٦ — لَا تَحْزَنُوا يَا أَوْلَادُ. ٧ — نَحْنُ تَعْبَانُونَ فَلْنَجْلِسْ دَقِيقَةً فِى هٰذَا ٱلْمَكَانِ. ٨ — لَمْ يَقْدِرُوا أَنْ يَرْجِعُوا إِلَى ٱلْمَدِينَةِ. ٩ — نَظَرَ ٱلْوَلَدُ دَارًا وَلَمْ يَكُنْ غَيْرُهَا فِى ذٰلِكَ ٱلْمَكَانِ. ١٠ — قَالَ ٱللّٰهُ لِيَكُنْ نُورٌ فَكَانَ نُورٌ. ١١ — لِيَكُنْ سَفَرُنَا لِوَطَنِنَا فِى ٱلشَّهْرِ ٱلْقَادِمِ لٰكِنْ لَا تَكْذِبْ بِهٰذِهِ ٱلطَّرِيقَةِ، يَا كَاتِبُ! ١٢ — بَحَثَ كَاتِبٌ مِنَ ٱلْكُتَّابِ ٱلْعَرَبِ عَنْ حَالَةِ بِلَادِ ٱلْعَرَبِ وَقَالَ فِى مَقَالَةٍ فِى جَرِيدَةِ ٱلْيَوْمِ: هُنَاكَ فُقَرَاءُ كَثِيرُونَ وَأَغْنِيَاءُ قَلِيلُونَ. ١٣ — قَدْ كَانَتْ خِدَمَاتُ هٰذَا ٱلْعَالِمِ جَيِّدَةً جِدًّا. ١٤ — اَلشَّمْسُ شَدِيدَةٌ هُنَا، فَلْنَنْزِلْ هُنَا فِى هٰذَا ٱلْمَوْضِعِ ٱلْكَثِيرِ ٱلظِّلِّ.

١٥ — نَشَرَ بَعْضُ ٱلْجَرَائِدِ تِلْكَ ٱلْأَخْبَارَ تَحْتَ ٱسْمِ رَئِيسِ ٱلْوِزَارَةِ.
١٦ — لَا تَدْخُلْ دَارَ سِفَارَةِ مِصْرَ بَعْدَ هٰذَا يَا كَذَّابُ. ١٧ — لِأَكُنْ
أَنَا صَدِيقَكَ. ١٨ — لَا تَنْشُرَنَّ هٰذِهِ ٱلْمَقَالَةَ. ١٩ — أَمَرَتْهُ ٱلْحُكُومَةُ أَنْ
يَنْشُرَ ٱلْحَقَائِقَ. ٢٠ — تَذْهَبِي لِلسُّوقِ، يَا ٱبْنَتِي.

EXERCISE 30

1. I did not (مَا) know the affair and did not (لَمْ) understand it. 2. O boys, do not open the door. O girl, do not lie. 3. The pupils were idle (كَسَالَى *pl.* of كَسْلَانُ) and did not do their duty. 4. They heard your speech and did not understand it. 5. Do not leave your friends in (the) anxiety. 6. Do not prevent me from going. 7. Let us drink (the) coffee. 8. The father and his son were not able to return to their house (. . . that they should return.) 9. Let me be (*jussive*) at your side among (بَيْنَ) these strange people in this strange place. 10. Oh Muhammad, I told Hassan to come in, but someone else (other than he) entered. 11. In the coming week a famous scholar will come to the embassy to discuss the state of the schools in our homeland. 12. The poor clerks shall not work every day in the service of this government. 13. Let the newspapers publish the good news, so that the people may know it at once. 14. I told him to go but he did not go. 15. Malta is a small island, and travelling to it is very nice. 16. One of the writers wrote an excellent article on this subject. 17. Do not work in this manner, workman! 18. Let Baghdad be the most beautiful city under the sun, workers; so you must do your duties. 19. He has left our country, so let him not return. 20. This is the truth; let her mention it in her speech!

CHAPTER SEVENTEEN

(اَلْبَابُ ٱلسَّابِعَ عَشَرَ)

The Imperative

1. The *Imperative* (فِعْلُ أَمْرٍ) is formed from the Jussive, of which it may be considered a modification, by taking away the pronominal prefix, and replacing it by an 'alif, e.g.

كَتَبَ to write; Jussive, يَكْتُبْ let him write.

Imperative, اُكْتُبْ write!

This 'alif may be vowelled with damma or kasra.

(a) Verbs having ḍamma on the middle radical in the Imperfect take ḍamma also on the 'alif of the Imperative, e.g.

(i) see كَتَبَ above.

(ii) بَعُدَ to be distant, Jussive, يَبْعُدْ let him keep at a distance, Imperative, اُبْعُدْ keep at a distance!

(b) All other verbs (i.e. those taking fatḥa or kasra on the middle radical of the Imperfect) take kasra with the initial 'alif of the Imperative, e.g.

(i) ضَرَبَ to strike; Jussive يَضْرِبْ let him strike.

Imperative, إِضْرِبْ strike! إِضْرِبْهُ strike him!

(ii) مَنَعَ to prevent; Jussive يَمْنَعْ let him prevent.

Imperative, إِمْنَعْ prevent! إِمْنَعْهُ prevent him!

Note that with a pronominal suffix as direct object, the verb still takes sukūn.

2. The 'alif of the Imperative, perhaps, originally served to prevent the word beginning with an unvowelled consonant, e.g. "ktub". This is borne out by the fact that the 'alif carries

hamzatu l-waṣl, and could be also written إ , أ. Consequently, the above vowellings only apply at the beginning of a statement, or of direct speech (in Modern Arabic usage). Otherwise, this 'alif takes the vowel of the end of the previous word, e.g.

إِذْهَبْ لِلْبَابِ وَٱفْتَحْهُ go to the door, and open it.

إِجْلِسْ وَٱكْتُبْ sit down and write.

But

ثُمَّ قَالَ ٱلْوَزِيرُ هٰذَا ٱلْقَوْلَ : أُكْتُبْ مَكْتُوبًا طَوِيلًا لِأَخِي Then the minister made this statement: "Write a long letter to my brother".

3. The parts of the Imperative, naturally all second person, are as follows:

Sing. 2. masc.	أُكْتُبْ	uktub
„ 2. fem.	أُكْتُبِي	uktubī
Dual 2. masc. & fem.	أُكْتُبَا	uktubā
Plur. 2. masc.	أُكْتُبُوا	uktubū
„ 2. fem.	أُكْتُبْنَ	uktubna.

The Imperative of كَانَ is:

Sing. 2. masc.	كُنْ	kun
„ 2. fem.	كُونِي	kūnī
Dual 2. masc. & fem.	كُونَا	kūnā
Plur. 2. masc.	كُونُوا	kūnū
„ 2. fem.	كُنَّ	kunna.

4. As stated in the previous chapter, the negative Imperative is expressed by the Jussive preceded by لا,

e.g. لَا تَكْتُبْ , do not write.

THE VOCATIVE

5. The use of the *Vocative* with يَا has been mentioned in the previous chapter. When the noun after يَا has a following Genitive it is in the Accusative instead of the Nominative. This commonly occurs in certain proper names which consist of أَبُو plus a Genitive or عَبْد followed by one of the ninety-nine names of God, e.g.

يَا أَبَا بَكْرٍ Oh Abu Bakr! يَا عَبْدَ ٱللّٰهِ Oh Abdullah!

يَا عَبْدَ ٱلْحَمِيدِ Oh Abdul Hamid!

But it may also occur with ordinary ʼiḍāfa, e.g.

يَا كَاتِبَ ٱلْمَحْكَمَةِ Oh clerk of the court!

Another vocative particle, أَيُّهَا fem. أَيَّتُهَا is used only when the following noun has the definite article.

أَيُّهَا ٱلتِّلْمِيذُ Oh scholar! أَيَّتُهَا ٱلْبِنْتُ Oh girl!

It may be preceded by يَا , e.g يَا أَيُّهَا ٱلْوَزِيرُ Oh minister!

Note that the noun after أَيُّهَا must be in the Nominative.

THE ACTIVE PARTICIPLE

6. *The Active Participle* (اِسْمُ ٱلْفَاعِلِ), which is better so called than by the European term "Present Participle", is of the form فَاعِلٌ for the simple triliteral verb, e.g.

كَاتِبٌ writing; طَالِبٌ demanding.

7. The Active Participle is also used as a noun with what might be termed a technical meaning. Thus, كَاتِبٌ writing, has come to mean a clerk; طَالِبٌ demanding, has come to mean a student (originally طَالِبُ عِلْمٍ "seeker of learning");

فَارِسٌ riding, a horseman or knight. In such instances, the participle takes one of several broken plural forms, e.g.

كَاتِبٌ clerk, pl. كَتَبَةٌ

كَاتِبٌ writer, pl. كُتَّابٌ

طَالِبٌ student, pl. طَلَبَةٌ or طُلَّابٌ

فَارِسٌ knight, pl. فَوَارِسُ

These plurals should not be employed when the participle has a verbal force, e.g.

هُمْ كَاتِبُو هٰذِهِ ٱلْمَكَاتِيبِ they are the writers of these letters.

أَنَا كَاتِبٌ مَكْتُوبًا I am writing a letter.

8. When used with كَانَ, the Active Participle gives the meaning of the Past or Future Continuous, and as such, may replace the Imperfect, e.g.

كَانَ خَارِجًا مِنْ بَيْتِهِ for كَانَ يَخْرُجُ مِنْ بَيْتِهِ he was going out of his house.

يَكُونُ نَازِلًا عِنْدِي for يَكُونُ يَنْزِلُ عِنْدِي he will be staying with me.

9. The Active Participle, when used verbally, may take a direct object, and in these circumstances it retains its nunations, as the object, being in the Accusative, is *not* an ʾiḍāfa, e.g.

هُوَ رَاكِبٌ حِصَانًا he is riding a horse.

كَانَ رَاكِبًا حِصَانًا he was riding a horse.

هُمْ قَاتِلُونَ أَعْدَاءَهُمْ they are killing their foes.

كَانُوا قَاتِلِينَ أَعْدَاءَهُمْ they were killing their foes.

THE VERBAL NOUN (INFINITIVE) OF THE SIMPLE TRILITERAL VERB

10. There is no set form for the *Infinitive* or, more properly, *Verbal Noun*, of the triliteral verb in its root form. Instead there is a large number of noun forms (three or four dozen), any one of which may be used for any particular verb. Indeed, only the dictionary will show what form of Verbal Noun is used with any particular verb. The Arabs call the Verbal Noun the مَصْدَرٌ, literally, "source".

Here are a few examples:

قَتَلَ to kill	v.n.	قَتْلٌ the act of killing
فَرِحَ to rejoice	,,	فَرَحٌ rejoicing
دَخَلَ to enter	,,	دُخُولٌ entering
خَرَجَ to go out	,,	خُرُوجٌ going out
نَزَلَ to descend, alight, stay (in a place)	,,	نُزُولٌ descending, staying.

The Verbal Noun is sometimes placed in the accusative after its own verb, as a sort of adverb or object, with little or no addition to the meaning.

قَتَلَهُ قَتْلًا, he killed him.

With some authors this may become a mannerism; though at times it may serve either to balance the sentence from the musical point of view, to add a sense of finality, or to give some stress. On the other hand, when the Verbal Noun so used is qualified by an adjective, it then describes the manner of the action. In this connection it must be remembered that Arabic has no adverbs.

e.g. ضَرَبْتُهُ ضَرْبًا شَدِيدًا I struck him hard (lit. a hard or strong striking).

This usage is termed the Absolute Object (اَلْمَفْعُولُ اَلْمُطْلَقُ).

VOCABULARY

صَدَقَ (ـُ) to tell the truth

سَكَتَ (ـُ) to be or remain silent

سَيِّدٌ *pl.* سَادَةٌ lord, master (term of respect), Mr. (*mod.*)

سَيِّدَةٌ *pl.* ـاتٌ lady, mistress (term of respect), Mrs. (*mod.*)

فَعَلَ (ـَ) to do

وَسْطٌ *pl.* أَوْسَاطٌ middle, centre

ظَرِيفٌ *pl.* ظُرَفَاءُ witty (witty person), amusing, agreeable

مَحْكَمَةٌ *pl.* مَحَاكِمُ court, law court

شَاهِدٌ *pl.* شُهُودٌ witness

كَافِرٌ *pl.* كُفَّارٌ unbeliever, infidel

دِينٌ *pl.* أَدْيَانٌ religion

اَلْإِسْلَامُ Islam (religion)

سَارِقٌ *pl.* سَرَقَةٌ a thief

بِئْرٌ (*f.*) *pl.* آبَارٌ a well

بَخِيلٌ *pl.* بُخَلَاءُ a miser, avaricious

بَدَنٌ *pl.* أَبْدَانٌ body

بَرْدٌ cold *n.*

بَارِدٌ cold *adj.*

بَرٌّ land (as opposed to بَحْرٌ sea)

بَرًّا by land, on land

بَيْرُوتُ Beirut

تَبِعَ (ـَ) to follow

تُرْكِيَّا Turkey

تُرْكِيٌّ *pl.* تُرْكٌ، أَتْرَاكٌ Turkish, a Turk

قِتَالٌ fighting, battle

EXERCISE 31

١ — إِفْتَحِي ٱلْبَابَ يَا أُمِّي. ٢ — يَا أَوْلَادُ لَا تَدْخُلُوا. ٣ — أُصْدُقُوا
يَا تَلَامِذَةُ وَلَا تَكْذِبُوا. ٤ — أُسْكُتْ يَا أَيُّهَا ٱلتِّلْمِيذُ وَٱجْلِسْ عَلَى مَكَانِكَ.
٥ — يَا عَبْدَ ٱللهِ ٱفْتَحْ بَابَ ٱلدَّارِ. ٦ — يَا أَيُّهَا ٱلرِّجَالُ ٱمْنَعُوهُمْ مِنَ
ٱلدُّخُولِ عَلَيْنَا. ٧ — أُنْظُرِي أَيَّتُهَا ٱلسَّيِّدَةُ مَا (what) فَعَلْتِ.

٨ — وَجَدُوا ٱمْرَأَةً جَالِسَةً فِي غُرْفَةٍ صَغِيرَةٍ. ٩ — إِتْبَعُوا دِينَ ٱلْإِسْلَامِ يا أَيُّهَا ٱلْكُفَّارُ. ١٠ — يا بِنْتُ، ٱسْمَعِي كَلَامَ ٱلشُّهُودِ فِي ٱلْمَحْكَمَةِ. ١١ — وَجَدتُّ (for وَجَدْتُ) ٱلسَّارِقَ قَرِيبًا مِنَ ٱلْبِئْرِ مَعَ قَبِيلَةٍ تُرْكِيَّةٍ. ١٢ — فِي جِبَالِ تُرْكِيَّا بَرْدٌ شَدِيدٌ. ١٣ — أَيَّتُهَا ٱلسَّيِّدَةُ، لَا تَفْعَلِي ذٰلِكَ. ١٤ — نَحْنُ فِي وَسْطِ ٱلْجُزْءِ ٱلْبَارِدِ مِنْ بِلَادِ تُرْكِيَّا. ١٥ — ذَهَبُوا لِبَيْرُوتَ عَلَى ٱلْبَرِّ وَنَحْنُ ذَهَبْنَا بِٱلْبَحْرِ. ١٦ — لَا تَكُنْ بَخِيلًا، يَا ٱبْنِي. ١٧ — نَظَرْنَا أَبْدَانَ ٱلْأَمْوَاتِ (pl. of مَيِّتٌ) فِي ٱلصَّحْرَاءِ لَمَّا ذَهَبْنَا لِدِمَشْقَ. ١٨ — كُنْ صَادِقًا يَا عَبْدَ ٱللّٰهِ، فَذٰلِكَ شَيْءٌ مُهِمٌّ فِي دِينِ ٱلْإِسْلَامِ. ١٩ — نَحْنُ تَابِعُونَ ٱلْجَيْشَ لِلْقِتَالِ. ٢٠ — لَا تَكُونُوا مِنَ ٱلْكَذَّابِينَ.

EXERCISE 32

1. See, O boys, what you have done. 2. O friend, enter and sit by my side. 3. O scholar, open the door of the room. 4. I was going to the city. 5. Where is Mr. (السَّيِّد) Hassan living? 6. He is living in the middle of the city. 7. I was writing a letter, when (فَ) our friend entered. 8. Do not prevent me from entrance to (عَلَى) you. 9. They are famous thieves. I have seen them in the court when I was a witness. 10. Lady, do not be one of (مِنْ) the unbelievers; follow the religion of Islam. 11. The miserly Turk returned to his fatherland by land. 12. The sultan said to the Arabs: "Be silent, you witty men!" 13. Tell the truth, women! Have the men of the village gone to the fight or not? 14. The dead man's

body was extremely cold. 15. The cold is extreme (شَدِيدٌ) in the mountains of Turkey. 16. The Arabs were riding their camels to the nearby well. 17. There are many clerks in the government offices in Cairo. 18. Go to school (the school), boys, and learn your lessons. 19. The students of Damascus University have arrived in Cairo for an important meeting with their Egyptian brethren (brothers.) 20. Leave this work to the women.

CHAPTER EIGHTEEN

(اَلْبَابُ ٱلثَّامِنَ عَشَرَ)

The Passive Verb

1. The Active voice of the verb is called in Arabic مَعْلُومٌ ("known"), whereas the *Passive* is termed مَجْهُولٌ ("unknown") The Passive is formed by merely changing the vowelling of the Active, and is standard for all verbs, irrespective of the varied vowelling of the Active. It is characterised by damma on the first syllable, so that in unvowelled Arabic, when it is desired to draw the reader's attention to the fact that a verb is passive, the placing of damma over the first syllable is usually considered sufficient to indicate this. However, after the initial ḍamma, kasra follows in the Perfect, and fatha in the Imperfect, e.g.

	ACTIVE		PASSIVE	
Perfect				
	كَتَبَ	he wrote.	كُتِبَ	it was written.
	كَتَبَ خِطَابًا	he wrote a letter.	كُتِبَ خِطَابٌ	a letter was written.
	ضَرَبَنِي	he struck me.	ضُرِبْتُ	I was struck.
Imperfect				
	يَكْتُبُ	he writes.	يُكْتَبُ	it is (being) written.
	يَضْرِبُكَ	he strikes (or will strike) you	تُضْرَبُ	you are (will be) struck

The following tables will illustrate the vowelling:

PERFECT

Sing. 3. masc.	ضُرِبَ	ḍuriba	he was struck.
,, 3. fem.	ضُرِبَتْ	ḍuribat	she was struck.
,, 2. masc.	ضُرِبْتَ	ḍuribta	you (m.) were struck.
,, 2. fem.	ضُرِبْتِ	ḍuribti	you (f.) were struck.
,, 1. m. & f.	ضُرِبْتُ	ḍuribtu	I was struck.

etc.

IMPERFECT

Sing. 3. masc.	يُضْرَبُ	yuḍrabu	he is struck.
,, 3. fem.	تُضْرَبُ	tuḍrabu	she is struck.
,, 2. masc.	تُضْرَبُ	tudrabu	you (m.) are struck.
,, 2. fem.	تُضْرَبِينَ	tuḍrabīna	you (f.) are struck.
,, 1. m. & f.	أُضْرَبُ	uḍrabu	I am struck.

etc.

Similarly, the Imperfect Subjunctive and Jussive may be made Passive by a change in the vowelling.

2. Unlike the practice in English and other Indo-European languages, it is not correct to use the Passive in Arabic when the doer of the act is mentioned particularly if a *human being* is mentioned in this capacity. Thus, "Hassan was struck by Zaid" must be turned into "Zaid struck Hassan", or "Zaid was the one who struck Hassan", e.g.

كَانَ زَيْدٌ ٱلَّذِى (who) ضَرَبَ حَسَنًا or ضَرَبَ زَيْدٌ حَسَنًا

This rule is not broken by such sentences as قُتِلَ بِالسَّيْفِ, "he was killed by the sword".

Here, بِ introduces the instrument, not the actual killer of the person concerned. At times in modern Arabic, especially journalese, the rule may appear to be circumvented, if not broken, and this is often due to the literal translation of European phraseology. The student will notice these instances in the course of his reading.

3. The Passive is sometimes used in what appears to be an impersonal manner, e.g. ذُكِرَ "it has been mentioned". (See below under أَنَّ). But in such cases, what follows the verb is really its subject, even though it may be a whole sentence.

4. The Arabs do not term the subject of a Passive Verb its فَاعِلٌ, as this means literally "doer"; they call it, instead, نَائِبُ ٱلْفَاعِلِ "the deputy or representative of the doer".

PASSIVE PARTICIPLE

5. *The Passive Participle* (the term "Past Participle" is not recommended) is formed on the measure مَفْعُولٌ for the simple triliteral verb, e.g. مَضْرُوبٌ struck; مَفْتُوحٌ opened. It is declined like other nouns, and takes the Sound Plural

6. But, as is the case with the Active Participle, it sometimes acquires a technical meaning and is used as a noun in its own right. It then usually takes a broken plural of the measure مَفَاعِيلُ e.g.

from	كَتَبَ	to write	مَكْتُوبٌ	written, a letter, pl. مَكَاتِيبُ
	سَجَنَ	to imprison	مَسْجُونٌ	imprisoned, a prisoner, pl. مَسَاجِينُ
	جَنَّ	to make mad	مَجْنُونٌ	mad, madman, pl. مَجَانِينُ

THE PARTICLE إِنَّ AND ITS SISTERS

7. There is a type of *nominal sentence* in Arabic which is introduced by one of certain particles, all of which are

characterised by a doubled final letter, usually nūn. They are as follows:

إِنَّ usually not translated, though old grammars translate it by the Biblical "verily".

أَنَّ that

لٰكِنَّ but, like لٰكِنْ but the latter should be followed by a verb.

لِأَنَّ because

لَعَلَّ perhaps – comparatively rare in modern Arabic.

All these participles resemble verbs, in that they must be followed either by a noun in the accusative, or by an attached pronoun which is grammatically considered to be in the accusative. After them the verb "to be" is understood, therefore a predicate may follow in the nominative.

e.g. إِنَّ حَسَنًا مَوْجُودٌ.
(verily) Hassan is present.

(It is not necessary for إِنَّ to be translated by "verily" except in ancient or religious literature.)

After إِنَّ the predicate is sometimes strengthened by لَ,

e.g. إِنَّكَ لَعَاقِلٌ you are intelligent.

This is more often the case when some phrase interposes between the subject and predicate, or when the subject after إِنَّ is a long sentence or phase, e.g.

إِنَّكَ ، يَا سُلَيْمَانُ ، لَرَجُلٌ عَظِيمٌ (verily) you, O Solomon, are a great man.

إِنَّ ٱلرَّجُلَ ٱلْمَوْجُودَ فِى بَيْتِى لَصَدِيقُ أَخِى The man present in my house is my brother's friend.

8. When the subject after these particles is an attached pronoun in the First Person Singular or Plural, there are alternative orthographical variants.

e.g. إِنَّنِي ʼinnanī or إِنِّي ʼinnī

إِنَّنَا ʼinnanā or إِنَّا ʼinnā

9. إِنَّ is used to introduce speech after the verb قَالَ to say, as well as to begin an ordinary nominal sentence.

e.g. قَالَ سُلَيْمَانُ إِنَّ دَاوُدَ حَاضِرٌ. Solomon said that David (was) present.

10. أَنَّ is used for indirect speech after verbs other than قَالَ, or in what resembles indirect speech or thought. It is also used to introduce a sentence which occupies the place of the subject or object of a sentence.

بَلَغَنِي أَنَّ زَيْدًا عَاقِلٌ lit. "that Zaid is intelligent has reached me" (I have heard that Zaid is intelligent, it has come to my notice that Zaid is intelligent).

Note that here the verb بَلَغَ is *not* impersonal; its subject is the whole clause introduced by أَنَّ.

ذُكِرَ أَنَّ ٱلْمَلِكَ مَرِيضٌ It has been mentioned (it is said) that the king is ill.

أَعْلَمُ أَنَّ زَيْدًا يَحْضُرُ I know that Zaid will be present.

لِأَنَّ, لَعَلَّ and لٰكِنَّ similarly introduce nominal sentences.

لٰكِنَّ is often prefixed with وَ, وَلٰكِنَّ.

11. All these particles may have a verb in their predicates, provided that their own accusative noun or pronoun comes first, e.g.

إِنَّ ٱلْخَوْفَ قَدْ غَلَبَهُ (verily) fear had overcome him.

غَضِبْتُ لِأَنَّ خَادِمِي لَمْ يَغْسِلْ ثِيَابِي I was angry because my servant did not wash my clothes.

لَعَلَّ ٱلسُّرُورَ قَتَلَهُ perhaps joy killed him.

حَضَرَ ٱلْيَهُودُ لٰكِنَّ ٱلْعَرَبَ غَابُوا the Jews attended, but the Arabs stayed away.

The only circumstance in which anything is allowed to interpose between these particles and their accusative is when that accusative is an indefinite noun, and the predicate is a prepositional phrase, or هُنَا "here" or هُنَاكَ "there". This prepositional phrase then comes after the particle, e.g.

إِنَّ فِى ٱلشَّارِعِ رَجُلًا in the street is a man.

Further details on the use of these particles will be found later in this grammar.

VOCABULARY

خِطَابٌ *pl.* ـَاتٌ letter (*mod.*), speech, discourse (*class.*)

نَائِبٌ *pl.* نُوَّابٌ deputy, representative, M.P.

مَرِيضٌ *pl.* مَرْضَى sick, ill

غَلَبَ (ـِ) to conquer, defeat, overcome (with direct obj. or with عَلَى)

خَوْفٌ fear *n.*

غَضِبَ (ـَ) to be, become, angry (with عَلَى)

يَهُودِيٌّ *pl.* يَهُودٌ a Jew, Jewish

مُؤَرِّخٌ *pl.* ـُونَ historian

تَارِيخٌ *pl.* تَوَارِيخُ history, date

شَجَاعَةٌ bravery, courage

مَشْغُولٌ busy, occupied

خَطَرٌ *pl.* أَخْطَارٌ danger

سِيرَةٌ *pl.* سِيَرٌ life, biography, manner of living

خَسَارَةٌ loss

نَجْمٌ *pl.* نُجُومٌ star

عَظِيمٌ *pl.* عِظَامٌ ، عُظَمَاءُ great, powerful

سُرُورٌ joy, pleasure

هَدِيَّةٌ *pl.* هَدَايَا gift, present

نَفِيسٌ precious, valuable

مَجْرُوحٌ *pl.* مَجَارِيحُ ، مَجْرُوحُونَ wounded, wounded man

مِفْتَاحٌ *pl.* مَفَاتِيحُ key

أُمَّةٌ *pl.* أُمَمٌ nation, people

عَبَرَ (ـُ) to cross, cross over

مُدَّةٌ *pl.* مُدَدٌ period (of time)

مَادَّةٌ *pl.* مَوَادُّ substance, matter

حَرْبٌ *f.* *pl.* حُرُوبٌ war

حَضْرَةٌ a term of respect, his honour, etc. (lit. presence)

فَقَدَ (ـِ) to lose, miss

سَمَاءٌ *pl.* سَمٰوَاتٌ sky, heaven

EXERCISE 33

١ — ذُكِرَ ٱسْمُ حَسَنٍ لِشَجَاعَتِهِ ، وَلِأَنَّهُ كَانَ مِنَ ٱلْمَجَارِيحِ . ٢ — إِنَّ زَيْداً ٱلضَّارِبُ وَعُمَرُ هُوَ ٱلْمَضْرُوبُ . ٣ — عَرَفْنَا مِنْ كُتُبِ ٱلتَّارِيخِ وَمِنْ سِيرَةِ ٱلنَّبِيِّ أَنَّ جَيْشَهُ غُلِبَ فِى هٰذَا ٱلْيَوْمِ ، لٰكِنَّهُ غَلَبَ عَلَى أَعْدَائِهِ بَعْدَ ذٰلِكَ . ٤ — وَصَلَنَا (reached us) ٱلْخَبَرُ مِنْ حَضْرَةِ ٱلنَّائِبِ أَنَّهُ مَشْغُولٌ . ٥ — كَتَبْنَا خِطَاباً لَهُ قَبْلَ شَهْرَيْنِ وَلَمْ نَسْمَعْ أَخْبَارَهُ . لَعَلَّهُ قَدْ غَضِبَ عَلَيْنَا . ٦ — إِنَّ فِى ٱلسَّمَاءِ ضَوْءًا عَظِيماً مِنْ تِلْكَ ٱلنُّجُومِ ٱللَّيْلَةَ . ٧ — قَالَ هٰذَا ٱلطَّبِيبُ ٱلْمَشْهُورُ إِنَّ خَوْفَ ٱلْمَوْتِ أَكْبَرُ خَطَرٍ لِلْمَرِيضِ . ٨ — أُمِرَ ٱلْيَهُودِىُّ أَنْ يَقْدَمَ لِلْوَزِيرِ وَأَنْ يَحْمِلَ مَعَهُ هَدَايَا نَفِيسَةً . ٩ — إِنَّا لِلّٰهِ وَإِنَّا إِلَيْهِ رَاجِعُونَ (Qur'ān, Sūra 2, 151) . ١٠ — إِنَّ هٰذَا ٱلْمُؤَرِّخَ مَعْرُوفٌ بَيْنَ ٱلْعُلَمَاءِ . ١١ — كُسِرَ سَيْفُ ٱلْجُنْدِىِّ .

فَكَبُرَ سُرُورُ ٱلْمَسَاجِينِ. ١٢ — بَلَغَنَا فِى أَخْبَارِ ٱلْجَرَائِدِ ٱلْيَوْمَ أَنَّ خَسَارَةَ
هٰذَا ٱلتَّاجِرِ ٱلْغَنِىِّ كَبِيرَةٌ جِدًّا. ١٣ — إِنَّ ٱلْخَشَبَ مَادَّةٌ مُهِمَّةٌ.
١٤ — لَمْ تَدْخُلِ ٱلْبِنْتُ ٱلْبَيْتَ لِأَنَّ ٱلْمِفْتَاحَ فُقِدَ. ١٥ — إِنَّ هٰذِهِ ٱلْمُدَّةَ
طَوِيلَةٌ لِعَمَلِكَ ٱلصَّغِيرِ. ١٦ — كُتِبَ فِى ٱلتَّارِيخِ أَنَّ ٱلْجَيْشَ عَبَرَ ٱلنَّهْرَ
وَوَصَلَ إِلَى بَغْدَادَ بَعْدَ سَاعَتَيْنِ. ١٧ — يَا أَحْمَدُ، مَاذَا دَرَسْتَ عَنْ أُمَمِ
ٱلدُّنْيَا ٱلْكَثِيرَةِ؟ إِنَّكَ جَاهِلٌ. ١٨ — إِرْجِعِي لِمَكَانِكِ، أَيَّتُهَا ٱلْبِنْتُ.
لَعَلَّكِ تَكُونِينَ عَاقِلَةً بَعْدَ هٰذَا. ١٩ — قَالَ لِلنِّسَاءِ ٱرْكَبْنَ فَرَكِبْنَ حَمِيرَهُنَّ.
٢٠ — أُقْتُلُوا أَعْدَاءَكُمْ يَا جُنُودُ. إِنَّ ذٰلِكَ مِنْ وَاجِبَاتِكُمْ.

EXERCISE 34

1. The doors of the house were opened, and the presents were received with (ب) joy. 2. I did not know that you were (are) busy today. 3. I know that the Arabs are the conquerors and the enemies the conquered. 4. The men mentioned are [some] of (من) my friends. 5. His courage has been mentioned in the history books. 6. He was killed with the sword because the madmen were angry with him. 7. You have been here a long time (period), perhaps you will go now. 8. The sick M.P.s attended this meeting, because the nation demanded that of them. 9. (إِنَّ) Courage is better than fear. 10. He said that all the wood had been put on the fire. 11. Look at the lives of (the) great men in the books of the historians. 12. Many soldiers crossed the river, but (لٰكِنَّ) the wounded were not able to leave their positions (places), so they were killed. 13. There are (begin with (إِنَّ) many valuable substances in the stars. 14. His honour the M.P. lost the key of

his car, so he returned home (to his house) in his friend's old car. 15. I heard that (أَنَّ) the merchants' losses have been very great this year. 16. The reason for that is the danger of war. 17. (إِنَّ) The Jews are a very old nation in the history of the world. 18. Verily the fear of God is in your hearts. Let it open the gates of heaven to you! 19. Oh Hassan, you are a great man today. A year ago you were [one] of (مِنْ) the poor. 20. The teacher said that Solomon was king of the Jews.

CHAPTER NINETEEN

(اَلْبَابُ التَّاسِعَ عَشَرَ)

Derived Forms of the Triliteral Verb
General Introduction

1. Although Arabic is poor in verb tenses, it is rich in *derived* verb forms which extend or modify the meaning of the root form of the verb, giving many exact shades of meaning. This is a common feature of Semitic languages, though it perhaps reaches its greatest extent in Arabic. The simple or root form of the verb is called اَلْفِعْلُ الْمُجَرَّدُ (the "stripped" or "naked" verb), while the derived forms are said to be مَزِيدٌ ("increased"). Derived forms are made by adding letters before or between the three radicals. Thus كَتَبَ means "to write"; كَاتَبَ "to write to", "correspond with"; and تَكَاتَبَ "to write to each other", "to correspond with each other". قَتَلَ means "to kill"; قَتَّلَ "to massacre". كَسَرَ "to break" (trans.); تَكَسَّرَ and اِنْكَسَرَ "to be broken", "to break" (intrans.).

2. Beginners often consider these forms a bugbear. But once their peculiarities are grasped, and it is realised that each derived form is associated with certain meaning patterns, they become a great help to the speedy acquisition of vocabulary. As we have said, the acquisition of an understanding of word patterns is of prime importance in learning Arabic.

3. The derived forms are generally numbered by Europeans from II upwards, I being the root form. The exact number of derived forms is open to dispute: fourteen (Nos.II–XV) could be given, but this number would increase if one took into account a number of quasi-quadriliteral

Form No.	Perfect	Imperfect
	(3rd pers. sing. m.)	(3rd pers. sing. m.)
II	فَعَّلَ faعّala (e.g. عَلِمَ to know; عَلَّمَ to teach)	يُفَعِّلُ yufaعّilu
III	فَاعَلَ fāعala (e.g. كَتَبَ to write; كَاتَبَ to write to)	يُفَاعِلُ yufāعilu
IV	أَفْعَلَ 'afعala (e.g. عَلِمَ to know; أَعْلَمَ to inform)	يُفْعِلُ yufعilu
V	تَفَعَّلَ tafaعّala (e.g. كَسَرَ to break; تَكَسَّرَ to be broken)	يَتَفَعَّلُ yatafaعّalu
VI	تَفَاعَلَ tafāعala (e.g. تَكَاتَبَ to write to one another)	يَتَفَاعَلُ yatafāعalu
VII	اِنْفَعَلَ infaعala (e.g. اِنْكَسَرَ to break *intrans.*)	يَنْفَعِلُ yanfaعilu
VIII	اِفْتَعَلَ iftaعala (e.g. نَفَعَ to profit, benefit *trans.*; اِنْتَفَعَ بِ to profit by)	يَفْتَعِلُ yaftaعilu (note insertion of ت after first radical)
IX	اِفْعَلَّ ifعalla (e.g. اِحْمَرَّ to become red)	يَفْعَلُّ yafعallu
X	اِسْتَفْعَلَ istafعala (e.g. حَسُنَ to be good; اِسْتَحْسَنَ to think good, admire)	يَسْتَفْعِلُ yastafعilu
XI	اِفْعَالَّ ifعālla	يَفْعَالُّ yafعāllu
XII	اِفْعَوْعَلَ ifعauعala	يَفْعَوْعَلُ yafعauعalu
XIII	اِفْعَوَّلَ ifعawwala	يَفْعَوِّلُ yafعawwilu
XIV	اِفْعَنْلَلَ ifعanlala	يَفْعَنْلِلُ yafعanlilu
XV	اِفْعَنْلَى ifعanlā	يَفْعَنْلَى yafعanlā

Verbal Noun	Meaning Patterns
تَفْعِيلٌ tafعīlun تَفْعِلَةٌ tafعilatun تَفْعَالٌ tafعālun (rare)	Strengthening or intensifying of meaning. Applying act to a more general object. Causative. Transitive of intransitive roots.
فِعَالٌ fiعālun مُفَاعَلَةٌ mufāعalatun	Relation of the action to another person. Attempting the act.
إِفْعَالٌ ifعālun	Transitive of intransitive verbs. Causative of transitive verbs. Also for "stative verbs" derived from nouns.
تَفَعُّلٌ tafaععulun	Reflexive of II (or sometimes of I). Verbs derived from nouns of quality or status. To consider or represent oneself as having a quality expressed in the root meaning.
تَفَاعُلٌ tafāعulun	Reflexive of III, often implying the mutual application of the action.
اِنْفِعَالٌ infiعālun	Passive sense (perhaps originally reflexive).
اِفْتِعَالٌ iftiعālun	Reflexive of I, but used for varied twists of meanings from the root idea.
اِفْعِلَالٌ ifعilālun	The possession or acquisition of colours or defects.
اِسْتِفْعَالٌ istifعālun	Asking for the act or quality of the root. Esteeming or thinking someone or thing to have the quality of the root. Originally, perhaps, a reflexive of IV.
اِفْعِيلَالٌ ifعīlālun	Similar to IX, perhaps intensive.
اِفْعِيعَالٌ ifعīعālun	Very rare, with specialised meanings.
اِفْعِوَّالٌ ifعīwwālun	
اِفْعِنْلَالٌ ifعinlālun	
اِفْعِنْلَاءٌ ifعinlā'un	

forms listed by Lane on page xxviii of Vol. One of his "Arabic Lexicon". However, the beginner will only be concerned with forms II to X: the remaining rare forms, if ever encountered at all, will be easily understood by the more experienced scholar.

(There are also three derived forms of the quadriliteral verb which will be dealt with in their appropriate place.)

4. Even leaving out of account the very rare derived forms from number XI upwards, very few verb roots have all the other derived forms from II to X; some have only one or two, while four or five is a good average. Despite this, there is often a good deal of overlapping of meaning between the forms. On the other hand, we sometimes find that the root form is no longer in use, whereas the derived forms are. It is the presence of available, but neglected, derived forms which makes Arabic potentially one of the very richest of languages, able to coin new words to meet modern requirements without necessarily adopting foreign words. This fact has been exploited by linguistic academies in centres like Cairo and Damascus in their efforts to abolish non-Arabic words.

5. In this chapter the common derived forms will be listed, together with their meaning patterns, for reference only. (They should not be learned by heart at this stage.) The various forms will be dealt with in detail in later chapters.

6. It may be noticed that, in respect of their vowelling (in the Imperfect), the derived forms II to X fall into three classes:

(a) II, III and IV, which have ḍamma followed by kasra.

(b) V and VI which have fatḥa throughout.

(c) VII, VIII and X which have kasra on the middle radical (or ع ain), but fathas on preceding *vowelled* letters.

(NOTE: IX may be considered to have had this form, yafعalilu, originally, but to have lost the kasra when the two lāms were written together with tashdīd.)

7. The verbal nouns of all the forms except II, V, VI and sometimes III, have a long ā between the last two radicals.

8. Verbal nouns regularly take the sound feminine plural, e.g. اِنْتَخَبَ (نَخَبَ VIII), to choose, elect.

v.n. اِنْتِخَابٌ pl. اِنْتِخَابَاتٌ elections.

Some verbal nouns of form II also take a broken plural (in addition to the sound feminine) of the pattern تَفَاعِيلُ .

9. The Participles are easily grasped, as for all forms they are prefixed with mīm vowelled with ḍamma (مُ). The middle radical (or ع ain) is vowelled with kasra for the Active and fatḥa for the Passive, except for form IX where, in any case, there is only an active participle.

No. of Form	Perfect	Participles	
		Active	Passive
II	فَعَّلَ faعّala	مُفَعِّلٌ mufaععilun	مُفَعَّلٌ mufaععalun
III	فَاعَلَ fāعala	مُفَاعِلٌ mufāعilun	مُفَاعَلٌ mufāعalun
IV	أَفْعَلَ 'afعala	مُفْعِلٌ mufعilun	مُفْعَلٌ mufعalun
V	تَفَعَّلَ tafaععala	مُتَفَعِّلٌ mutafaععilun	مُتَفَعَّلٌ mutafaععalun
VI	تَفَاعَلَ tafāعala	مُتَفَاعِلٌ mutafāعilun	مُتَفَاعَلٌ mutafāعalun
VII	اِنْفَعَلَ infaعala	مُنْفَعِلٌ munfaعilun	مُنْفَعَلٌ munfaعalun
VIII	اِفْتَعَلَ iftaعala	مُفْتَعِلٌ muftaعilun	مُفْتَعَلٌ muftaعalun
IX	اِفْعَلَّ ifعalla	مُفْعَلٌّ mufعallun	—
X	اِسْتَفْعَلَ istafعala	مُسْتَفْعِلٌ mustafعilun	مُسْتَفْعَلٌ mustafعalun

VOCABULARY

NOTE: The following additional vocabulary is not based specifically on the preceding chapter. The two exercises which follow it may be regarded as partly for grammatical revision.

ثَابِتٌ fixed, firm

ثَقِيلٌ heavy

خَفِيفٌ light (in weight)

جَبِينٌ *pl.* جُبُنٌ forehead

وَجَعٌ *pl.* أَوْجَاعٌ pain *n.*

جَلْسَةٌ *pl.* جَلَسَاتٌ session, sitting

جَمَالٌ beauty

أَجْنَبِيٌّ *pl.* أَجَانِبُ foreign(er)

مَجْهُولٌ unknown

جَوَابٌ *pl.* أَجْوِبَةٌ reply, answer

جَارٌ *pl.* جِيرَانٌ neighbour

حُرِّيَّةٌ liberty, freedom

حَارِسٌ *pl.* حُرَّاسٌ guard, sentry

حُسَيْنٌ Hussein (pr. n. masc.)

فَصْلُ ٱلرَّبِيعِ or اَلرَّبِيعُ spring

اَلصَّيْفُ summer

اَلْخَرِيفُ autumn

اَلشِّتَاءُ winter

خُصُوصِيٌّ private

خُصُوصًا especially

دِرْهَمٌ *pl.* دَرَاهِمُ dirhem (coin or weight) (in the plural, also money)

دَفَعَ (ـَ) to push, pay

دُوَلِيٌّ international

اِنْتِخَابَاتٌ elections (political, etc.)

بِدُونِ ، بِلَا without (with genitive)

جِسْمٌ *pl.* أَجْسَامٌ body (anatomical)

فَصْلٌ *pl.* فُصُولٌ season

لُبْنَانُ Lebanon

EXERCISE 35

١ — هٰذِهِ ٱلْحَجَرَةُ ثَابِتَةٌ فِى ٱلْحَائِطِ وَهِيَ ثَقِيلَةٌ جِدًّا. ٢ — لِي وَجَعٌ شَدِيدٌ فِى جَبِينِي يَا وَلَدُ. ٣ — سَتَكُونُ ٱلْجَلْسَةُ ٱلْجَدِيدَةُ لِلَّجْنَةِ ٱلدُّوَلِيَّةِ فِى مِصْرَ. ٤ — وَسَوْفَ يَحْضُرُهَا بَعْضُ ٱلْأَجَانِبِ. ٥ — وَإِنَّ سَبَبَ ٱلِٱجْتِمَاعِ وَمَوْضُوعَهُ ٱلْحُرِّيَّةُ. ٦ — كَتَبْتُ لِحُسَيْنٍ فِى ٱلرَّبِيعِ وَوَصَلَنِي جَوَابُهُ فِى ٱلْخَرِيفِ. ٧ — وُجِدَ جِسْمُهُ فِى بَيْتِ جَارِهِ، وَهُوَ مَيِّتٌ، وَقَاتِلُهُ مَجْهُولٌ. ٨ — تَرَكُوا أَبْوَابَ ٱلْمَدِينَةِ بِدُونِ حَارِسٍ لِأَنَّهُمْ قَدْ ذَهَبُوا كُلُّهُمْ لِلِٱنْتِخَابِ. ٩ — إِنَّ جَمَالَ لُبْنَانَ فِى ٱلصَّيْفِ مَشْهُورٌ بَيْنَ ٱلْأَجَانِبِ، لٰكِنَّهَا أَجْمَلُ بِكَثِيرٍ فِى ٱلشِّتَاءِ. ١٠ — كَانَ ٱلْمَطَرُ خَفِيفًا وَخُصُوصًا فِى ٱلرَّبِيعِ. ١١ — قَدْ دَفَعْتَ ٱلْجُنَيْهَيْنِ مِنْ دَرَاهِمِي ٱلْخُصُوصِيَّةِ. ١٢ — فَلِذٰلِكَ إِنِّي غَضِبْتُ عَلَيْكَ. ١٣ — أَيْنَ كِتَابَا هٰذَا ٱلْكَاتِبِ ٱلْكَبِيرِ، فِى ٱلْمَكْتَبَةِ؟ ١٤ — قَفَلْتُ ٱلشَّبَابِيكَ (ٱلنَّوَافِذَ) قُفُولًا وَجَلَسْتُ بِجَانِبِ ٱلنَّارِ ٱلْخَفِيفَةِ. ١٥ — تُرِكَ ٱلْوَلَدُ ٱلصَّغِيرُ بِلَا أَبٍ وَلَا أُمٍّ. ١٦ — كَمْ دِرْهَمًا مَعَكَ؟ ١٧ — لَا تَكُنْ مِنَ ٱلْكَاذِبِينَ. كُنْ صَالِحًا. ١٨ — إِنَّ كِتَابَ سِيرَةِ ٱلنَّبِيِّ نَافِعٌ جِدًّا لِلْمُسْلِمِينَ. ١٩ — أُطْلُبْ مِنْ صَدِيقِكَ أَنْ يَعْبُرَ ٱلشَّارِعَ وَيَذْهَبَ لِدُكَّانِ ٱلْخَبَّازِ فِى ٱلسُّوقِ ٱلْقَدِيمِ. ٢٠ — إِنَّ ٱلْوَاجِبَ عَلَيْكَ أَنْ تَسْمَعَ قَوْلَ ٱلْأَقْرِبَاءِ.

EXERCISE 36

1. The elections are near and I am without my car. 2. Pay the two dirhems and go back to your house, you thief! 3. This is my private book, so do not take it away (use ذَهَبَ بِ).

4. International meetings are important, especially in this period of danger. 5. Hussein is the father of Hassan and the brother of Muhammad. He is the tallest man in the room, and the newest M.P. in the Lebanon. 6. I have heard that you have a pain in the head. 7. Why don't you ask for the doctor? 8. The foreigner said to the girl that he had heard about her beauty from his neighbour. 9. This is a heavy book – that light one is better for a small boy. 10. Liberty (the liberty) was unknown among the Egyptians before the days of Islam. 11. What is your reply to the sentry's words? 12. I saw Hussein in the spring, then I did not see him until the new year. 13. Summer is better than winter in our country, but autumn is the best season. 14. This session is very important to the Arabs. 15. Will you be at school (in the school) this evening after lessons? 16. I asked you not to return without your sister. So where is she? 17. Let her go to her grandmother's (house). 18. You are worse than him. 19. The minister has been struck in the streets, and his assailants (strikers) are unknown. 20. Ask of the prisoners, perhaps they know.

CHAPTER TWENTY

(اَلْبَابُ ٱلْعِشْرُونَ)

Derived Forms of the Triliteral Verb: II, III and IV

1. It will help the student to consider Derived Forms II, III and IV as one group, since they all have the vowel pattern of ḍamma for the prefix and kasra for the middle radical in the Imperfect.

e.g. from عَلِمَ ع alima, to know.

II عَلَّمَ ع allama, to teach; يُعَلِّمُ YU-ع al-LI-mu

III عَالَمَ* ع ālama, to vie in learning with; يُعَالِمُ YU-ع ā-LI-mu.

IV أَعْلَمَ 'aع lama, to inform; يُعْلِمُ YUع-LI-mu.

FORM II فَعَّلَ

2. Conjugation of كَسَرَ II, كَسَّرَ to break in pieces, smash.

Perf.	Imperf. Indic.	Imperf. Subj.	Imperf. Juss.
كَسَّرَ	يُكَسِّرُ	يُكَسِّرَ	يُكَسِّرْ
كَسَّرَتْ	تُكَسِّرُ	تُكَسِّرَ	تُكَسِّرْ
كَسَّرْتَ	تُكَسِّرُ	تُكَسِّرَ	تُكَسِّرْ
كَسَّرْتِ	تُكَسِّرِينَ	تُكَسِّرِى	تُكَسِّرِى
كَسَّرْتُ	أُكَسِّرُ	أُكَسِّرَ	أُكَسِّرْ
etc.	etc.	etc.	etc.

* NOTE: This is not a very common verb, but is used so as to show the three forms from a single root. This illustrates the difficulty of finding a root with *commonly used* verbs from a number of derived forms.

It will be seen that the prefixes and suffixes used to specify person, gender and number are exactly the same as in the root form of the verb. There are no different conjugations in Arabic in the sense in which they are encountered in languages like Greek, Latin and French. Consequently, in explaining derived forms, the conjugation table or paradigm will only be shown for the singular: the student will be able to work out the dual and plural for himself.

3. The Imperative does not have the prefixed ʼalif, and is as follows:

masc. sing.	كَسِّرْ
fem. sing.	كَسِّرِي
dual	كَسِّرَا
masc. pl.	كَسِّرُوا
fem. pl.	كَسِّرْنَ

4. The participles are as follows: Active, مُكَسِّرٌ
Passive, مُكَسَّرٌ

5. The normal form for the Verbal Noun is تَفْعِيلٌ, e.g. تَكْسِيرٌ. An alternative form occasionally met with is تَفْعِلَةٌ, e.g. تَجْرِبَةٌ from جَرَّبَ to try, experiment. This form will be found to be usual with irregular verbs with wāw, yāʼ or hamza as final radical (see Chapters Twenty-six and Twenty-nine). Even rarer is تَفْعَالٌ, e.g. تَرْحَابٌ from رَحَّبَ to welcome.

6. The Passive is:

Perfect	Imperfect
كُسِّرَ	يُكَسَّرُ
etc.	etc.

MEANING PATTERNS

7. (a) *Stative* or *intransitive* verbs are made *transitive*, e.g.

قَرُبَ to be near.

قَرَّبَ to make near, bring someone or something near.

كَثُرَ to be numerous.

كَثَّرَ to make numerous.

(b) *Transitive* verbs are made *causative* or *doubly transitive*, e.g. عَلِمَ to know or learn; عَلَّمَ to teach.

ذَكَرَ to mention, remember; ذَكَّرَ to remind.

(c) The meaning of the root form is strengthened, either by making the act more final, or making it more intense and wider in application, e.g.

كَسَرَ to break; كَسَّرَ to smash, break in pieces.

قَطَعَ to cut; قَطَّعَ to cut in pieces.

قَتَلَ to kill; قَتَّلَ to massacre.

(d) Sometimes it has an *estimative* meaning, where the root verb is intransitive, e.g.

صَدَقَ to be sincere; صَدَّقَ to believe, consider sincere.

كَذَبَ to lie; كَذَّبَ to consider a liar, accuse of lying.

(e) This form is also found in *denominal* verbs, that is, verbs derived from nouns, giving the meaning of making, dealing with, or collecting, e.g.

from نَوْعٌ type, kind; نَوَّعَ to compose, assort.

جِلْدٌ skin, leather; volume. جَلَّدَ to skin, bind.

جُنْدٌ soldiers, army; جَنَّدَ to levy troops.

FORM III فَاعَلَ

8. Conjugation of كَاتَبَ to write to, correspond with.

	Imperf.		
Perf.	Indic.	Subj.	Juss.
كَاتَبَ	يُكَاتِبُ	يُكَاتِبَ	يُكَاتِبْ
كَاتَبْتَ	تُكَاتِبُ	تُكَاتِبَ	تُكَاتِبْ
كَاتَبَتْ	تُكَاتِبُ	تُكَاتِبَ	تُكَاتِبْ
كَاتَبْتِ	تُكَاتِبِينَ	تُكَاتِبِي	تُكَاتِبِي
كَاتَبْتُ	أُكَاتِبُ	أُكَاتِبَ	أُكَاتِبْ
etc.	etc.	etc.	etc.

Imperative

كَاتِبْ

كَاتِبِي etc.

Part. Active مُكَاتِبٌ

Part. Passive مُكَاتَبٌ

Verbal noun كِتَابٌ, more usually مُكَاتَبَةٌ

Passive, Perf. كُوتِبَ Imperf. Indic. يُكَاتَبُ

9. The Verbal Noun has two alternative forms. The dictionary will show which one is normally used, though often both are possible. Where this is so, there may be different shades of meaning. Thus, in the verb given above, مُكَاتَبَةٌ is the usual Verbal Noun, signifying the act of writing to, or corresponding with, anyone. Its plural, مُكَاتَبَاتٌ means "correspondence". The other form, كِتَابٌ, is used as a simple noun to mean "a book", though in older Arabic it may mean "a letter".

MEANING PATTERNS

10. (a) Normally this form expresses the relation or application of the act of the root form to another person, e.g.

كَتَبَ to write; كَاتَبَ to write to.

جَلَسَ to sit; جَالَسَ to sit with.

شَرِبَ to drink; شَارَبَ to drink with.

Note also:

عَمِلَ to do; عَامَلَ to treat anyone, to behave to someone, deal with.

Verbal Noun, مُعَامَلَةٌ treatment, dealing.

(b) It also often expresses the meaning of attempting to do something, e.g.

قَتَلَ to kill; قَاتَلَ to try to kill (therefore, normally) to fight against.

سَبَقَ to precede; سَابَقَ to try to precede, (therefore, normally) to compete with, race against (سِبَاقٌ, a race).

Note that the verb حَاوَلَ to try, attempt, is of this form. (The wāw is radical; see Chapter Twenty-eight on the Hollow Verb.)

11. This verbal form is, of course, transitive, and it takes the accusative of the person, e.g.

كَانَ ٱلشَّاعِرُ يُجَالِسُ ٱلسُّلْطَانَ the poet used to sit with the sultan.

كَاتَبَهُ he wrote to him.

قَاتَلَ ٱلْعَرَبُ أَعْدَاءَهُمْ قِتَالًا شَدِيدًا the Arabs fought their foes fiercely.

FORM IV أَفْعَلَ

12. Conjugation of أَجْلَسَ to make to sit, seat.

	Imperf.		
Perf.	Indic.	Subj.	Juss.
أَجْلَسَ	يُجْلِسُ	يُجْلِسَ	يُجْلِسْ
أَجْلَسَتْ	تُجْلِسُ	تُجْلِسَ	تُجْلِسْ
أَجْلَسْتَ	تُجْلِسُ	تُجْلِسَ	تُجْلِسْ
أَجْلَسْتِ	تُجْلِسِينَ	تُجْلِسِي	تُجْلِسِي
أَجْلَسْتُ	أُجْلِسُ	أُجْلِسَ	أُجْلِسْ
etc.	etc.	etc.	etc.

Imperative

أَجْلِسْ

أَجْلِسِي etc.

Part. Active مُجْلِسٌ

Part. Passive مُجْلَسٌ

Verbal noun إِجْلَاسٌ

Passive, Perf. أُجْلِسَ Imperf. Indic. يُجْلَسُ

MEANING PATTERNS

13. (a) The Fourth Form is Causative. It makes intransitive verbs transitive, and transitive verbs doubly transitive, e.g.

حَضَرَ to be present; أَحْضَرَ to cause to be present, bring.

جَلَسَ to sit; أَجْلَسَ to seat.

(b) Often forms II and IV have the same meaning, with perhaps a slight difference, e.g.

خَبَّرَ and أَخْبَرَ both mean to inform, give news.

صَلَّحَ to repair; أَصْلَحَ to rectify, reform.

عَلَّمَ to teach; أَعْلَمَ to inform.

As a doubly transitive verb, a Form IV Verb may have two direct objects in the accusative, e.g.

أَخْبَرْتُ حَسَنًا الْخَبَرَ I informed Hassan of the news.

(more often بِٱلْخَبَرِ).

(c) More rarely, Form IV verbs may be formed from nouns, e.g.

أَصْبَحَ to do in the morning

from صَبَاحٌ morning. This verb is commonly used meaning "to become".

(d) There are a few intransitive verbs of this form, e.g.

أَسْلَمَ to become a Muslim.

أَقْبَلَ to approach.

VOCABULARY

كَ like, as (preposition attached to nouns only, not pronouns)

سَلَامٌ (عَلَى) peace, greeting (to, upon).

لُطْفٌ friendliness, kindness

بَدْوٌ، بَادِيَةٌ desert

بَدَوِيٌّ *pl.* بَدْوٌ Bedouin

حَوْلَ around *prep.*

أُفْقٌ *pl.* آفَاقٌ horizon

بُعْدٌ distance

عَنْ from, concerning

وَالِدٌ father } (lit. begetter)

وَالِدَةٌ mother }

أَثْنَاءَ، فِي أَثْنَاءِ during

مَرَّةٌ *pl.* ـَاتٌ time (occasion)

VERBS OF FORM II

سَلَّمَ to deliver

سَلَّمَ عَلى to greet

كَلَّمَ to speak to, address; to tell (+ subjunctive)

قَبَّلَ to kiss

قَدَّمَ to bring

بَلَّغَ to convey, inform

فَتَّشَ to inspect

فَتَّشَ عَنْ to search for

مُفَتِّشٌ inspector

بَشَّرَ to take good news to

دَبَّرَ to propose, manage

قَدَّرَ to determine, estimate value,

صَدَّقَ to believe

VERES OF FORM III

خالَفَ to disobey, go against, contravene

شاوَرَ to consult, ask advice of

شاهَدَ to witness, see

دافَعَ عَنْ to defend

قاطَعَ to interrupt

هاجَمَ to attack

راقَبَ to watch, supervise, oversee

خالَطَ to mix with, have intercourse with

سافَرَ to travel

جاوَرَ to be neighbour to, adjacent to

جِوارٌ neighbourhood

VERBS OF FORM IV

أَرْسَلَ to send

أَصْبَحَ to become

أَخْبَرَ to inform (with acc. of person and بِ of thing)

أَعْلَمَ to inform

أَظْلَمَ to be or become dark

أَحْضَرَ to bring forward, present

أُغْرِمَ بِ to be fond of

أَحْسَنَ to treat anyone kindly, to do anything well

EXERCISE 37

١ — كَلَّمْتُهُ أَنْ يُرْسِلَ مُفَتِّشًا لِيُشَاوِرَ ٱلْبَدْوَ. ٢ — قَتِّلُوا ٱلْأَعْدَاءَ، يَا جُنُودُ. ٣ — قَالَ ٱلْأَبُ لِٱبْنَتِهِ ٱلصَّغِيرَةِ: قَبِّلِي أُمَّكِ. ٤ — شَاهَدَ مُفَتِّشُو ٱلْوِزَارَةِ أَعْمَالَ ٱلْأَوْلَادِ عَنْ بُعْدٍ. ٥ — إِنَّ ٱلرِّجَالَ فَتَّشُوا ذٰلِكَ ٱلْجِوَارَ وَبَعْدَ ٱلتَّفْتِيشِ رَجَعُوا. ٦ — أَمَرَهُمُ ٱلشَّيْخُ أَنْ يَذْهَبُوا حَالًا لِتَبْشِيرِ ٱلْأَمِيرِ. ٧ — طَلَبَ زَيْدٌ أَنْ يُخْبِرُوا أَبَاهُ أَنَّهُ وَجَدَ ٱبْنَهُ وَأَنَّهُ سَيَكُونُ عِنْدَهُ غَدًا. ٨ — عَرَفَ ٱلشَّيْخُ أَنَّ ضَيْفَهُ خَالَطَ ٱلْبَدْوَ. ٩ — ٱلْإِنْسَانُ يُدَبِّرُ وَٱللّٰهُ يُقَدِّرُ (proverb). ١٠ — نُرْسِلُ لَهُ مَنْ يُخْبِرُهُ بِذٰلِكَ. ١١ — أَخْبِرْنَا عَنِ ٱسْمِكَ. ١٢ — سَلَّمْتُ عَلَى وَالِدِى بِٱلطَّرِيقَةِ ٱلْعَرَبِيَّةِ، وَهِىَ: «ٱلسَّلَامُ عَلَيْكَ». ١٣ — إِنَّ وَاجِبَكَ أَنْ تُصَدِّقَ أَصْدِقَاءَكَ وَأَنْ تُدَافِعَ عَنْهُمْ. ١٤ — يُحْسِنُ هٰذَا ٱلْكَاتِبُ عَمَلَهُ فِى ٱلْمَكْتَبِ، وَيُعَامِلُ إِخْوَانَهُ بِلُطْفٍ، فَأَصْبَحَ أَطْيَبَ رَجُلٍ فِى ٱلْمَكْتَبِ وَمَكَانُهُ هُنَاكَ كَمَكَانِ ٱلْأَبِ فِى ٱلْبَيْتِ أَوِ ٱلْمَلِكِ فِى ٱلْبِلَادِ. ١٥ — سَافَرْتُمْ إِلَى أَبْعَدِ آفَاقِ ٱلدُّنْيَا، لِأَنَّكُمْ مُغْرَمُونَ بِٱلسَّفَرِ. ١٦ — نَظَرْتُ جَيْشَ ٱلْعَدُوِّ حَوْلَ ٱلْمَدِينَةِ، فَدَخَلْتُ قَلْعَةَ ٱلْحَاكِمِ وَأَعْلَمْتُهُ بِذٰلِكَ، لٰكِنَّهُ قَاطَعَنِى فِى كَلَامِى. ١٧ — ثُمَّ هَاجَمَ ٱلْأَعْدَاءُ ٱلْمَدِينَةَ أَثْنَاءَ ٱللَّيْلِ، وَفَتَحُوهَا بِدُونِ قِتَالٍ. ١٨ — فِى ذٰلِكَ ٱلْيَوْمِ ٱلْمُظْلِمِ، أَحْضَرَ ٱلْحَارِسُ جُنْدِيًّا، وَبَلَّغَ هٰذَا (the latter) ٱلْمَلِكَ أَنَّ وَالِدَتَهُ قَدْ قُتِلَتْ فِى ٱلْمَدِينَةِ ٱلْمُجَاوِرَةِ. ١٩ — قَدِّمْنَ ٱلْقَهْوَةَ يَا نِسَاءُ. ٢٠ — طَلَبَ ٱلرَّجُلُ مِنْ صَاحِبِ ٱلدُّكَّانِ أَنْ يُجَلِّدَ ٱلْكِتَابَ.

EXERCISE 38

1. Servant, bring us fresh (new) coffee at once from the kitchen. 2. The minister commanded them to bring forward the robber. 3. I ordered them to tell their friends about this affair, but they did not believe me. 4. Man proposes, but God disposes. 5. Send that man to me, so that I may supervise his work. He has disobeyed my orders many times. 6. Bring in the doctor so that we can consult him about the prince's condition. 7. God brings you good news about a son, whose name is (his name is) Jesus (يَسُوعُ). 8. Attack (the attack) is the best way of defence. 9. Do not mix with the people next door (lit. in the neighbouring house). 10. The government inspectors travelled to the village, greeted the sheikh, and witnessed the horse races. Then they inspected the new houses. 11. We saw the bedouins round the well, from a distance, during the journey. 12. He kissed her hands and informed her that he (أَنَّهُ) had become prime minister. 13. They are fond of travel. 14. I will inform you during the coming (مُقْبِل) month. 15. He was big like his father, but his sister was small like her mother. 16. He was speaking to his wife, but she cut him short. 17. The horizon was dark, but the bedouin mounted his camel and left the village. 18. My son did his studies well, and his teacher treated him kindly (use بِلُطْف). 19. Where is peace in this world of ours? 20. They are the new inspectors of agriculture.

CHAPTER TWENTY-ONE

(اَلْبَابُ ٱلْحَادِى وَٱلْعِشْرُونَ)

Derived Forms of the Triliteral Verb: Forms V and VI

1. Derived Forms V and VI form a pair. They tend to be Reflexives of Forms II and III, from which they are formed by prefixing تَ. Moreover, they are both vowelled entirely by fatḥa in the imperfect, but take damma on the middle radical in the verbal noun.

FORM V تَفَعَّلَ

2. Conjugation of تَسَلَّمَ to take over, receive:

	Imperf.		
Perf.	Indic.	Subj.	Juss.
تَسَلَّمَ	يَتَسَلَّمُ	يَتَسَلَّمَ	يَتَسَلَّمْ
تَسَلَّمَتْ	تَتَسَلَّمُ	تَتَسَلَّمَ	تَتَسَلَّمْ
تَسَلَّمْتَ	تَتَسَلَّمُ	تَتَسَلَّمَ	تَتَسَلَّمْ
تَسَلَّمْتِ	تَتَسَلَّمِينَ	تَتَسَلَّمِى	تَتَسَلَّمِى
تَسَلَّمْتُ	أَتَسَلَّمُ	أَتَسَلَّمَ	أَتَسَلَّمْ
etc.	etc.	etc.	etc.

Imperative

تَسَلَّمْ — Part. Active مُتَسَلِّمٌ

تَسَلَّمِى etc. — Part. Passive مُتَسَلَّمٌ

Verbal noun تَسَلُّمٌ

Passive, Perf. تُسُلِّمَ — Imperf. Indic. يُتَسَلَّمُ

MEANING PATTERNS

3. (a) This is most frequently the reflexive of II.

فَرَّقَ to separate; تَفَرَّقَ (to separate oneself), to scatter.

عَلَّمَ to teach; تَعَلَّمَ (to teach oneself), to learn.

ذَكَّرَ to remind; تَذَكَّرَ (to be reminded), to remember.

(b) It is also used to form verbs from nouns, especially nouns of quality or status, e.g.

from نَصْرَانِيٌّ a Christian; تَنَصَّرَ to become a Christian.

يَهُودِيٌّ a Jew; تَهَوَّدَ to become a Jew.

(c) Closely related to meaning (b) is that of thinking or representing oneself to have a certain quality or status, e.g.

كَبِيرٌ great; تَكَبَّرَ to think oneself great, to be proud.

نَبِيٌّ prophet; تَنَبَّأَ to represent oneself to be a prophet.

FORM VI تَفَاعَلَ

4. This only differs from V in having the ʾalif after the first radical. It is conjugated as follows:

Conjugation of تَقَاتَلَ to fight with one another:

	Imperf.		
Perf.	Indic.	Subj.	Juss.
تَقَاتَلَ	يَتَقَاتَلُ	يَتَقَاتَلَ	يَتَقَاتَلْ
تَقَاتَلَتْ	تَتَقَاتَلُ	تَتَقَاتَلَ	تَتَقَاتَلْ
تَقَاتَلْتَ	تَتَقَاتَلُ	تَتَقَاتَلَ	تَتَقَاتَلْ
تَقَاتَلْتِ	تَتَقَاتَلِينَ	تَتَقَاتَلِي	تَتَقَاتَلِي
تَقَاتَلْتُ	أَتَقَاتَلُ	أَتَقَاتَلَ	أَتَقَاتَلْ
etc.	etc.	etc.	etc.

Imperative

تَقَاتَلْ		Part. Active	مُتَقَاتِلٌ
تَقَاتَلِي etc.		Part. Passive	مُتَقَاتَلٌ
Verbal noun	تَقَاتُلٌ		
Passive, Perf.	تُقُوتِلَ	Imperf. Indic.	يَتَقَاتَلُ

MEANING PATTERNS

5. (a) The reflexive of III, e.g.

قَاتَلَ to fight; تَقَاتَلَ to fight each other.

حَارَبَ to fight; تَحَارَبَ to fight each other.

عَاوَنَ to co-operate with; تَعَاوَنَ to co-operate together.

وَافَقَ to agree with; تَوَافَقَ to agree together.

In this sense, this form of verb must always have a dual or plural subject, though, of course, when the *third person* verb comes first it will always be in the singular.

تَوَافَقَ ٱلْحِزْبَانِ the two parties agreed with each other.

تَقَاتَلَ ٱلْجَيْشَانِ the two armies fought each other.

But the subject is sometimes a collective word such as نَاسٌ or قَوْمٌ people.

تَعَاوَنَ ٱلْقَوْمُ the people co-operated (together).

(b) Even more than Form V, Form VI is used with the meaning of simulating a state or status, or representing oneself to have it, e.g.

جَاهِلٌ ignorant; تَجَاهَلَ to affect ignorance.

مَشْغُولٌ busy; تَشَاغَلَ to pretend to be busy.

ظَاهِرٌ clear (from ظَهَرَ to appear); تَظَاهَرَ to feign.

VOCABULARY

أَثَرٌ *pl.* آثَارٌ trace, footstep (in *pl.* also means "antiquities")

شُجَاعٌ *pl.* شُجْعَانٌ brave

جِهَةٌ *pl.* اتٌ — side, point of view

كَذٰلِكَ in the same way likewise, moreover

شِدَّةٌ strength, severity, violence

بِشِدَّةٍ violently, strongly

طِفْلٌ *pl.* أَطْفَالٌ child, baby

ضَحِكَ (ـَ) to laugh (at عَلَى)

نَصْرَانِيٌّ *pl.* نَصَارَى Christian

قَوِيٌّ *pl.* أَقْوِيَاءُ strong

قُوَّةٌ *pl.* قُوَّاتٌ ، قُوًى power, strength, force

ذِرَاعٌ (*f.*) *pl.* أَذْرُعٌ arm, forearm

سِلَاحٌ *pl.* أَسْلِحَةٌ weapon, arm

VERBS OF FORM V

تَكَلَّمَ to speak (may be *transitive*)

تَتَبَّعَ to follow

تَقَدَّمَ to come forward

تَفَرَّقَ to separate, one from another

تَشَكَّرَ to be grateful

تَذَكَّرَ to remember

تَمَهَّلَ to go slowly, to be slow

تَعَجَّبَ to wonder, be astonished

تَعَلَّمَ to learn

تَشَرَّفَ to have the honour, be honoured

تَوَقَّعَ to expect

VERBS OF FORM VI

تَحَادَثَ to converse together

تَفَارَقَ to disperse

تَقَابَلَ to meet each other

تَعَاوَنَ to co-operate together

تَقَاتَلَ to fight each other

تَوَافَقَ to agree together

تَظَاهَرَ to feign, show, demonstrate

EXERCISE 39

١ — هَلْ تَتَكَلَّمُ ٱللُّغَةَ ٱلْعَرَبِيَّةَ؟ نَعَمْ، يَا سَيِّدِى، أَتَكَلَّمُهَا قَلِيلًا.

٢ — ٱلْأَمِيرُ وَأَخُوهُ جَلَسَا يَتَحَادَثَانِ فِى (about) تِلْكَ ٱلْأُمُورِ. ٣ — لَمَّا سَمِعَ ٱلرِّجَالُ ذٰلِكَ، تَقَدَّمُوا جَمِيعًا إِلَى جِهَتِهِ. ٤ — هَلْ تَتَذَكَّرِينَ مَا أَمَرْتُكِ يَا خَادِمَةُ؟ ٥ — تَعَجَّبْنَا مِنْ قُوَّةِ ٱلْعَدُوِّ وَشِدَّةِ ٱلْقِتَالِ فِى ذٰلِكَ ٱلْيَوْمِ ٱلْمَشْهُورِ. ٦ — ضَحِكَ ٱلطِّفْلُ عَلَى جَدِّهِ لِتَمَهُّلِهِ لَمَّا عَبَرَ ٱلشَّارِعَ. ٧ — إِنَّ ٱلتَّعَاوُنَ مَعَكُمْ شَيْءٌ مُهِمٌّ وَنَتَشَرَّفُ بِهِ. ٨ — لَا تَتَقَاتَلُوا يَا أَصْدِقَاءُ، بَلْ (but) تَظَاهَرُوا ٱلتَّوَافُقَ. ٩ — تَفَارَقَ ٱلْعَرَبِيُّ وَٱلْإِنْكِلِيزِيُّ وَلَمْ يَتَقَابَلَا حَتَّى هٰذَا ٱلْوَقْتِ. ١٠ — إِنِّى مُتَشَكِّرٌ لَكَ لِأَنَّكَ عَلَّمْتَنِي كَثِيرًا مِنْ لُغَتِكَ ٱلصَّعْبَةِ. ١١ — ٱلذِّرَاعُ ٱلطَّوِيلَةُ أَهَمُّ (more important) مِنَ ٱلسِّلَاحِ ٱلْجَمِيلِ لِلْجُنْدِيِّ ٱلْقَوِيِّ.

١٢ — تَتَبَّعُوا آثَارَ أَعْدَائِهِمِ ٱلشُّجْعَانِ، ثُمَّ تَفَرَّقُوا بَعْدَ ذٰلِكَ. ١٣ — قَالَ أَبِي: ٱلْأَمْرُ كَذٰلِكَ، فَلَا تَتَوَقَّعْ حُضُورِى بَيْنَ مُوَافِقِيكَ. ١٤ — تَرَكْنَاهُمْ يَتَحَادَثُونَ. ١٥ — هَلْ مِنْ وَاجِبِي أَنْ أَتَنَصَّرَ لِأَنَّكِ زَوْجَتِي وَقَدْ تَنَصَّرْتِ أَنْتِ؟ ١٦ — ذَكَّرْتُهُ لٰكِنَّهُ لَمْ يَتَذَكَّرْ. ١٧ — لَا تُعَاوِنْ ذَاكَ ٱلرَّجُلَ ٱلْمُتَكَبِّرَ. ١٨ — نَتَوَقَّعُ كَمْ ضَيْفًا ٱللَّيْلَةَ؟ ١٩ — إِنَّهُ مِنَ ٱلْمُتَوَقَّعِ أَنْ يَذْهَبَ ٱلْمَلِكُ لِمَكَّةَ. ٢٠ — نَتَسَلَّمُ ٱلْبَضَائِعَ غَدًا.

EXERCISE 40

1. We conversed about this affair yesterday morning, but did not agree. 2. The Muslims and Christians fought each other a long time (use مُدَّة) ago, but they agree today in

many things. 3. The learned men were talking together about the antiquities of Egypt. 4. We expect the enemies' advance from this side. 5. The children were grateful to their grandmother, and kissed her; she was astonished at this. 6. She remembered that they (أنّهم) used to laugh at her. 7. Let us agree and co-operate; let us learn our new and important work, and be strong in everything. 8. Moreover, let us follow the road of duty. 9. Hassan and Zaid fought violently, but Hassan's arm broke, and his sword fell to the ground. 10. Strength is more important than weapons to the brave. 11. The travellers separated in the desert and were killed by the Bedouins. 12. I do not understand you. Speak Arabic! 13. I am a foreigner. Can you go slowly in your speech; then perhaps I will understand you? 14. You are feigning ignorance, sir. You know our language. 15. We met in Damascus two years ago. 16. The king was astonished at the bravery of his young soldiers. 17. I am going to the university to meet a professor. 18. We co-operated during the war, then separated after it. 19. The learned man used to feign ignorance, and the people did not hear his words. 20. It was anticipated (مِنَ الْمُتَوَقَّعِ) that the session would be long, because the subject was difficult and important.

CHAPTER TWENTY-TWO

(اَلْبَابُ ٱلثَّانِى وَٱلْعِشْرُونَ)

Derived Forms of the Triliteral Verb: Forms VII and VIII

1. Derived forms VII, VIII, IX and X, as already stated, really form a group. They all begin with ʾalif, which has hamzatu l-waṣl, but which takes kasra when beginning a statement. (They should be distinguished in this respect from Form IV, in which the additional ʾalif has the proper hamza, or hamzatu l-qaṭʿ). Moreover, in the Imperfect, all except IX take a kasra on the Middle Radical, after previous fatḥas. In Form IX we may imagine that there was originally a kasra but with the telescoping of the doubled final radical, it disappeared.

FORM VII إِنْفَعَلَ

2. Conjugation of إِنْكَسَرَ to break (intransitive):

Perf.	Imperf. Indic.	Imperf. Subj.	Imperf. Juss.
إِنْكَسَرَ	يَنْكَسِرُ	يَنْكَسِرَ	يَنْكَسِرْ
إِنْكَسَرَتْ	تَنْكَسِرُ	تَنْكَسِرَ	تَنْكَسِرْ
إِنْكَسَرْتَ	تَنْكَسِرُ	تَنْكَسِرَ	تَنْكَسِرْ
إِنْكَسَرْتِ	تَنْكَسِرِينَ	تَنْكَسِرِى	تَنْكَسِرِى
إِنْكَسَرْتُ	أَنْكَسِرُ	أَنْكَسِرَ	أَنْكَسِرْ
etc.	etc.	etc.	etc.

Imperative

إِنْكَسِرْ　　Part. Active مُنْكَسِرٌ

إِنْكَسِرِي etc.　　Part. Passive مُنْكَسَرٌ

Verbal noun إِنْكِسَارٌ

(Passive, Perf. اُنْكُسِرَ (rare) Imperf. Indic. يُنْكَسَرُ)

MEANING PATTERN

3. Though originally the Reflexive of the root form, it is, to all intents and purposes, a Passive now, e.g.

كَشَفَ to uncover; إِنْكَشَفَ to be uncovered.

كَسَرَ to break (tr.); إِنْكَسَرَ to break (intr.).

عقد to hold (*mod.*, of meetings, conferences); إنعقد to be held.

قَلَبَ to overturn; إِنْقَلَبَ to be overturned or reversed.

Note, however, إِنْصَرَفَ to go off, depart.

The use of this form as a pure Passive has become very widespread in colloquial language. In Classical Arabic it might be argued that there is a subtle difference between the Passive of Form I and Form VII. If one says كُسِرَ ٱلشُّبَّاكُ the window was broken, one ought to imply, theoretically at any rate, that the agent is discoverable; whereas if one uses the VII form and says إِنْكَسَرَ ٱلشُّبَّاكُ one ought, again theoretically, to suggest that the human agency, if any, is undiscoverable!

4. Form VII is not found in verbs beginning with hamza, yā', rā', lām, and nūn. (See below, Form VIII).

FORM VIII اِفْتَعَلَ

5. This may present some difficulty at first, because a tā' is inserted between the first and second radicals, in addition to the prefixing of 'alif with hamzatu l-waṣl.

Conjugation of اِجْتَمَعَ to assemble.

Perf.	Imperf. Indic.	Imperf. Subj.	Imperf. Juss.
اِجْتَمَعَ	يَجْتَمِعُ	يَجْتَمِعَ	يَجْتَمِعْ
اِجْتَمَعَتْ	تَجْتَمِعُ	تَجْتَمِعَ	تَجْتَمِعْ
اِجْتَمَعْتَ	تَجْتَمِعُ	تَجْتَمِعَ	تَجْتَمِعْ
اِجْتَمَعْتِ	تَجْتَمِعِينَ	تَجْتَمِعِي	تَجْتَمِعِي
اِجْتَمَعْتُ	أَجْتَمِعُ	أَجْتَمِعَ	أَجْتَمِعْ
etc.	etc.	etc.	etc.

Imperative

اِجْتَمِعْ Part. Active مُجْتَمِعٌ

اِجْتَمِعِي etc. Part. Passive مُجْتَمَعٌ

Verbal noun اِجْتِمَاعٌ

Passive, Perf. أُجْتُمِعَ Imperf. Indic. يُجْتَمَعُ

6. The tā' introduced after the first radical undergoes certain changes:

(a) If the first radical is one of the emphatic letters ص, ض, ط, ظ, the tā' is changed into a ط; this is assimilated to a ط or ظ which is then written with tashdīd e.g. صَنَعَ "to make" forms اِصْطَنَعَ; ضَرَبَ "to strike" forms اِضْطَرَبَ; طَلَعَ "to rise" forms اِطَّلَعَ; ظَلَمَ "to be dark" forms اِظَّلَمَ and اِطَّلَمَ.

(b) If the first radical is د, ذ or ز, the tā' is softened to د; this is assimilated to a ذ, which is then written with tashdīd e.g. دَرَكَ forms اِدَّرَكَ; زَحَمَ forms اِزْدَحَمَ; ذَخَرَ forms اِذَّخَرَ and اِدَّخَرَ.

(c) If the first radical is ث, it sometimes assimilates the ت e.g. ثَبَتَ forms اِثَّبَتَ or اِتَّبَتَ.

MEANING PATTERNS

7. (a) Form VIII is the most elusive from this point of view, and is difficult to pin-point. Indeed, it seems to be reserved for odd by-ways of meaning, e.g.

ضَرَبَ to strike; اِضْطَرَبَ to be disturbed, shaken.

حَمَلَ to carry; اِحْتَمَلَ to bear, in the sense of endure, to be probable.

حَرَمَ to forbid; اِحْتَرَمَ to respect.

It often has the same meaning as the root form, e.g.

بَسِمَ to smile; اِبْتَسَمَ (same meaning).

(b) Like VII, it can be the reflexive of the Simple Verb,

e.g. جَمَعَ to collect; اِجْتَمَعَ to collect themselves, assemble. (hence اِجْتِمَاعٌ meeting)

سَمِعَ to hear; (لِ) اِسْتَمَعَ to listen (to).

شَغَلَ to occupy, keep busy; اِشْتَغَلَ to be busy, to work.

(c) It also has the sense of doing something for oneself:

كَسَبَ to acquire; اِكْتَسَبَ to gain.

كَشَفَ to uncover; اِكْتَشَفَ to discover.

بَدَعَ to initiate; اِبْتَدَعَ to invent.

(d) There is occasionally a reflexive meaning such as one might expect of Form VI, خصم to strive; اِخْتَصَمَ to strive with one another; III شارك to take part with; اِشْتَرَكَ to contribute towards, participate.

(شَرِكَة = a commercial firm or company)

8. Some triliteral verbs have ت as final radical. In the Perfect, where the pronominal suffix of the person has vowelled ت, the two letters are assimilated, and may be written as one, with tashdīd, e.g. لفت VIII, اِلْتَفَتَ to turn towards, pay attention to.

اِلْتَفَتُّ I turned towards.

اِلْتَفَتَّ you (masc. sing.) turned towards.

اِلْتَفَتِّ you (fem. sing.) turned towards.

اِلْتَفَتُّمْ you (masc. pl.) turned towards.

Similar assimilation may take place where the final radical is د and ط, and even ذ, ض, ظ and ث. In these instances, however, the two letters are written separately, but the ت of the suffix may have tashdīd, e.g.

عَقَدَ to tie, hold (a meeting);

عَقَدتُّ I tied.

(مِن) اِنْبَسَطَ to be pleased, VII of بَسَطَ to spread out:

اِنْبَسَطتَّ you (masc. sing.) were pleased.

بَعَثَ to send; بَعَثتُّ I sent.

قَبَضَ to grasp, arrest (with direct object or على)

قَبَضتُّ I grasped.

VOCABULARY

قَسَمَ (ـِ) to divide

قِسْمٌ *pl.* أَقْسَامٌ division, part

إِذَا ، إِذَا بِ behold! see!

إِذَنْ ، إِذًا therefore, then

قَدَمٌ *pl.* أَقْدَامٌ foot (part of body, or measurement)

شَابٌّ *pl.* شُبَّانٌ youth, young man

مِثْلٌ *pl.* أَمْثَالٌ like (this word is a noun and takes a following *genitive*; it does not change for the *feminine*)

أَخِيرٌ last, recent

أَخِيرًا recently, finally

سِيَاسِيٌّ (*pl. of noun* سَاسَةٌ and *sound plural*); political politician

فَرَنْسَا France

فَرَنْسِيٌّ ، فَرَنْسَاوِيٌّ French

بِرِيطَانِيَا Britain

أَلْمَانِيَا Germany

مُمْكِنٌ possible (*Act. Part.* of أَمْكَنَ)

رَاكِبٌ *pl.* رُكَّابٌ passenger (rider)

عَدَدٌ *pl.* أَعْدَادٌ number, amount

عَدَمٌ lack

عَامِلٌ *pl.* عُمَّالٌ labourer, worker

مُسْتَشْفًى hospital

VERBS OF FORM VII

اِنْبَسَطَ (مِنْ) to be pleased (with)

اِنْصَرَفَ to depart, go away

اِنْكَسَرَ to be broken

اِنْكَشَفَ to be disclosed

اِنْهَزَمَ to be defeated

اِنْعَقَدَ to be tied, to be held (meeting)

اِنْقَلَبَ to be overturned, reversed

VERBS OF FORM VIII

اِفْتَكَرَ to think

Note: (فَكَّرَ فِي Form II, to think about)

اِقْتَرَبَ to approach (with مِنْ)

اِلْتَفَتَ (إِلَى) to turn (to), pay attention (to)

اِضْطَرَبَ to be disturbed, excited

اِنْتَظَرَ to await, expect

اِعْتَرَفَ (بِ) to recognize, confess

اِنْتَصَرَ (عَلَى) to be victorious (over) (lit. to be helped)

اِحْتَرَمَ to respect

اِشْتَغَلَ to be busy, occupied, to work

اِجْتَمَعَ to gather together, assemble (hence ٱلْمُجْتَمَعُ, society in the general sense)

EXERCISE 41

١ — قَدِ ٱنْبَسَطْنَا مِنَ ٱنْكِشَافِ هٰذِهِ ٱلدَّرَاهِمِ فِى ٱلْجُنَيْنَةِ. ٢ — اِنْقَلَبَتْ سَيَّارَةٌ فِى شَارِعٍ رَئِيسِيٍّ وَأَفْتَكِرُ أَنَّ رَاكِبَيْنِ مِنَ ٱلرُّكَّابِ حُمِلَا إِلَى ٱلْمُسْتَشْفَى. ٣ — لِمَاذَا ٱنْهَزَمْتُمْ؟ إِنَّكُمْ كَثِيرُونَ وَٱلْأَعْدَاءُ قَلِيلُو ٱلْعَدَدِ.

٤ — قَالَتِ ٱلْخَادِمَةُ: يَا سَيِّدِى، ٱنْكَسَرَ ٱلْفِنْجَانُ، وَمَا كَسَرْتُهُ أَنَا.

٥ — اِنْعَقَدَ أَمْسِ ٱجْتِمَاعٌ بَيْنَ سُفَرَاءِ بِرِيطَانِيَا وَفَرَنْسَا وَأَلْمَانِيَا، وَبَعْدَ سَاعَةٍ ٱنْصَرَفَ ٱلسَّفِيرُ ٱلْفَرَنْسِيُّ. ٦ — فَكِّرْ فِى هٰذَا ٱلْأَمْرِ مُدَّةً طَوِيلَةً.

٧ — أَفْتَكِرُ أَنَّ ٱلِاضْطِرَابَ ٱلسِّيَاسِيَّ سَبَبُهُ عَدَمُ ٱلْحُرِّيَّةِ. ٨ — أَيْنَ ٱحْتِرَامُ ٱلْآبَاءِ وَٱلْأُمَّهَاتِ فِى ٱلْمُجْتَمَعِ ٱلْيَوْمَ؟ ٩ — اِلْتَفِتْ إِلَيَّ يَا وَلَدُ، كَيْفَ تَشْتَغِلُ؟ ١٠ — مِثْلُ هٰذَا ٱلْعَمَلِ غَيْرُ مُمْكِنٍ فِى ٱلْمُجْتَمَعِ ٱلْعَرَبِيِّ. ١١ — لَمَّا ٱقْتَرَبَ مِنَّا كُنَّا فِى ٱنْتِظَارِهِ. ١٢ — اِعْتَرَفَتِ ٱلْحُكُومَةُ أَخِيرًا بِحُقُوقِ ٱلشُّبَّانِ. ١٣ — اِقْسِمِ ٱلتُّفَّاحَ قِسْمَيْنِ.

١٤ — اِنْتَصَرَتْ بِرِيطَانِيَا عَلَى أَلْمَانِيَا وَإِيطَالِيَا فِى ٱلْحَرْبِ ٱلْأَخِيرَةِ.

١٥ — اِنْتَظَرْنَا وَإِذَا بِجُنْدِيٍّ مِصْرِيٍّ يُقْبِلُ عَلَيْنَا. ١٦ — لَنَا سُيُوفٌ

قَاطِعَةٌ ، إِذاً لَا تَقْتَرِبُوا مِنَّا . ١٧ — ذَهَبْتُ عَلَى قَدَمَيَّ وَزَوْجَتِي
رَكِبَتْ جَمَلِي . ١٨ — أُكْتُبْ هٰذَا ٱلْخِطَابَ بِكُلِّ ٱحْتِرَامٍ . ١٩ — ٱلْأَوْلَادُ
غَائِبُونَ . إِذَنْ نَنْصَرِفُ وَنَرْجِعُ بَعْدَ ٱلظُّهْرِ . ٢٠ — ٱلتَّفْكِيرَ قَبْلَ
ٱلْعَمَلِ !

EXERCISE 42

1. The Labour Party (lit. party of the workers) was victorious in the recent elections. 2. How many hours have you been waiting for us? 3. I turned to him respectfully (with respect), greeted him, then went off. 4. You will be pleased with your large shares. 5. I told the politicians recently to recognize the rights of the Arabs. 6. They said that is not possible now. 7. Do you think that Germany was not defeated in the recent war? Then who was victorious? 8. A meeting was held between the Prime Ministers, and it was attended by (use *Active*) a number of Arab ministers. 9. The state of the world has become disturbed, and we do not know the reasons. 10. Why do you not think about the matter? Perhaps the truth will be revealed to you. 11. The vehicle turned over and the merchandise was broken. 12. Lo and behold [there was] a man riding a white horse. 13. The young men divided everything (translate literally). 14. Men like these (the likes of these men) do not recognize the truth, even (حَتَّى) when they hear it. 15. Go away, girl, and occupy yourself in the kitchen. That is your duty. 16. I told you to approach me. Why do you not do so (that)? 17. There is a political disturbance in the streets today. 18. I was angry at the breaking of the two plates. 19. My grandmother thinks that the youth of today are lazy. 20. She is not pleased with them.

CHAPTER TWENTY-THREE

(اَلْبَابُ ٱلثَّالِثُ وَٱلْعِشْرُونَ)

Derived Forms of the Triliteral Verb: Forms IX, X, and XI

1. Form IX, اِفْعَلَّ is characterised by a prefixed ʾalif with hamzatu l-waṣl and the doubling of the final radical. In certain parts, however, the doubled letter is written as two separate letters; in which case, the first of these two has kasra in some instances, thus bringing it into line, as regards vowelling, with forms VII, VIII and X. In this connection note especially the Jussive aud Imperative in the following table.

Conjugation of اِحْمَرَّ to be or become red:

Perfect

	Sing.	Dual	Plur.
3. p. m.	اِحْمَرَّ	اِحْمَرَّا	اِحْمَرُّوا
3. ,, f.	اِحْمَرَّتْ	اِحْمَرَّتَا	اِحْمَرَرْنَ
2. ,, m.	اِحْمَرَرْتَ	اِحْمَرَرْتُمَا	اِحْمَرَرْتُمْ
2. ,, f.	اِحْمَرَرْتِ		اِحْمَرَرْتُنَّ
1. ,,	اِحْمَرَرْتُ		اِحْمَرَرْنَا

	Imperfect Indic.	Subj.	Juss.
Sing. 3. p. m.	يَحْمَرُّ	يَحْمَرَّ	يَحْمَرِرْ
,, 3. ,, f.	تَحْمَرُّ	تَحْمَرَّ	تَحْمَرِرْ
,, 2. ,, m.	تَحْمَرُّ	تَحْمَرَّ	تَحْمَرِرْ

	Imperfect Indic.	Subj.	Juss.
Sing. 2. ,, f.	تَحْمَرِّينَ	تَحْمَرِّي	تَحْمَرِّي
,, 1. ,,	أَحْمَرُّ	أَحْمَرَّ	أَحْمَرِرْ
Dual 3. ,, m.	يَحْمَرَّانِ	يَحْمَرَّا	يَحْمَرَّا
,, 3. ,, f.	تَحْمَرَّانِ	تَحْمَرَّا	تَحْمَرَّا
,, 2. ,,	تَحْمَرَّانِ	تَحْمَرَّا	تَحْمَرَّا
Plur. 3. ,, m.	يَحْمَرُّونَ	يَحْمَرُّوا	يَحْمَرُّوا
,, 3. ,, f.	يَحْمَرِرْنَ	يَحْمَرِرْنَ	يَحْمَرِرْنَ
Plur. 2. ,, m.	تَحْمَرُّونَ	تَحْمَرُّوا	تَحْمَرُّوا
,, 2. ,, f.	تَحْمَرِرْنَ	تَحْمَرِرْنَ	تَحْمَرِرْنَ
,, 1. ,,	نَحْمَرُّ	نَحْمَرَّ	نَحْمَرِرْ

Imperative

Sing. 2. m. اِحْمَرِرْ Dual. 2. اِحْمَرَّا Plur. 2. m. اِحْمَرُّوا

,, 2. f. اِخْمَرِّي ,, 2. f. اِحْمَرِرْنَ

Part. Active مُحْمَرٌّ
Part. Passive not used.

Verbal noun اِحْمِرَارٌ
Passive tenses not in use.

2. The rule as to when the final doubled radical is to be written as one letter with tashdīd, and when as two separate letters, is the same as the rule that will be given in the next chapter for the Doubled Verb. It is quite simple:

(a) When the final letter has sukūn, either because of the suffix, or because it is Jussive or Imperative, the two letters must be written separately, e.g.

اِحْمَرَّ iḥmarra, he became red. BUT

اِحْمَرَرْنَا iḥmararnā, we became red.

اِحْمَرِرْ iḥmarir, become red! (Imperative masc. sing.)
BUT

اِحْمَرِّي iḥmarrī, become red! (Imperative fem. sing.)

(b) When the final letter is vowelled, the two are coalesced. This does not, of course, apply to the verbal noun, where the long ʾalif interposes between the two final letters.

3. Form IX is only used for colours and defects, and therefore the corresponding adjectives will also be found of the measure أَفْعَلُ (see Chapter Eleven).

e.g. أَسْوَدُ black. اِسْوَدَّ to be or become black.

4. Form XI, اِفْعَالَّ is rarely found except in poetry. Some Arab grammarians describe it as stronger, others as weaker than IX. But the truth may well be that it is used, either for the exigencies of metre, or for the musical effect. It is conjugated exactly the same, save that the ʾalif comes before the last (doubled) radical. See the table in Chapter Nineteen.

FORM X اِسْتَفْعَلَ

5. This is an extremely common form.

Conjugation of اِسْتَحْسَنَ to think beautiful, and, more commonly, to consider preferable or desirable, to admire.

Perfect	Imperfect Indic.	Imperfect Subj.	Imperfect Juss.
اِسْتَحْسَنَ	يَسْتَحْسِنُ	يَسْتَحْسِنَ	يَسْتَحْسِنْ
اِسْتَحْسَنَتْ	تَسْتَحْسِنُ	تَسْتَحْسِنَ	تَسْتَحْسِنْ
اِسْتَحْسَنْتَ	تَسْتَحْسِنُ	تَسْتَحْسِنَ	تَسْتَحْسِنْ

Perfect	Indic.	Subj.	Juss.
اِسْتَحْسَنْتِ	تَسْتَحْسِنِينَ	تَسْتَحْسِنِي	تَسْتَحْسِنِي
اِسْتَحْسَنْتُ	أَسْتَحْسِنُ	أَسْتَحْسِنَ	أَسْتَحْسِنْ
etc.	etc.	etc.	etc.

Imperative

اِسْتَحْسِنْ Part. Active مُسْتَحْسِنٌ

اِسْتَحْسِنِي etc. Part. Passive مُسْتَحْسَنٌ

Verbal noun اِسْتِحْسَانٌ

Passive, Perf. اُسْتُحْسِنَ Imperf. Indic. يُسْتَحْسَنُ

MEANING PATTERNS OF FORM X

6. (a) There are two common meanings. The first is to desire or ask for oneself the action or state of the root verb.

e.g. حَضَرَ to attend; اِسْتَحْضَرَ to summon (to ask for the attendance of).

عَلِمَ to know; اِسْتَعْلَمَ to ask for information, to inquire about.

أَذِنَ to permit; اِسْتَأْذَنَ to ask for permission (to ask leave to depart).

غَفَرَ to forgive; اِسْتَغْفَرَ to ask forgiveness.

(b) Equally common is the estimative significance. This is usually from intransitive verbs.

e.g. حَسُنَ to be beautiful; اِسْتَحْسَنَ to find beautiful, to consider preferable.

قَبُحَ to be ugly; اِسْتَقْبَحَ to loathe, find ugly.

(c) Causative.

خَدَمَ to serve; اِسْتَخْدَمَ to employ (cause to serve).

شَهِدَ to witness; اِسْتَشْهَدَ to call to witness (cause to witness).

(d) This form is particularly rich in various extensions of meaning from the root, which cannot be classified.

e.g. عَمِلَ to do; اِسْتَعْمَلَ to use.

حَقَّ to be or become true or certain; اِسْتَحَقَّ to deserve, merit.

قَبِلَ to receive, accept; اِسْتَقْبَلَ to welcome or receive a person.

VOCABULARY

اَلْمُسْتَقْبَلُ the future

رَأْىٌ *pl.* آرَاءٌ opinion

وَاقِعَةٌ *pl.* وَقَائِعُ event

قَلَمُ رَصَاصٍ pencil

وَطَنِيٌّ national, nationalist *mod.*

رَسَمَ (ـُ) to draw, sketch

رَسْمٌ *pl.* رُسُومٌ sketch, drawing

رَسْمِيٌّ *adj.* official

عُضْوٌ *pl.* أَعْضَاءٌ member

قُنْبُلَةٌ *pl.* قَنَابِلُ bomb

ذَرِّيٌّ atomic

اَلْيَابَانُ Japan

يَابَانِيٌّ Japanese

رُوسِيَّا Russia

رُوسِيٌّ *pl.* رُوسٌ Russian

إِنْكِلْتَرَا England

أَمْرِيكَا ، أَمِيرِكَا America

أَمْرِيكِيٌّ American

ضِدَّ *prep.* against

أُورُبَّا ، أُورُوبَّا Europe

قَانُونٌ *pl.* قَوَانِينُ law (cf. canon)

شَأْنٌ *pl.* شُؤُونٌ matter, affair

رِئَاسَةٌ leadership, chairmanship, presidency

فَارِسٌ *pl.* فَوَارِسُ ، فُرْسَانٌ horseman, knight

قِصَّةٌ *pl.* قِصَصٌ story

صُورَةٌ *pl.* صُوَرٌ picture

اَلصِّحَافَةُ the press (newspapers)

أَمَّا . . . فَ . . . as for . . .

ضَرُورِيٌّ necessary, essential

VERBS OF FORM X

اِسْتَفْهَمَ to enquire

اِسْتَقْبَلَ to receive, entertain

اِسْتَخْدَمَ to employ

اِسْتَعْمَلَ to use

اِسْتَحْسَنَ to approve, think best, admire

اِسْتَكْبَرَ to consider great

اِسْتَعْجَلَ to hasten, be in a hurry

اِسْتَعْلَمَ to ask anyone for information about something

EXERCISE 43

١ — نَظَرَ ٱلْمَلِكُ ٱحْمِرَارَ ٱبْنَتِهِ حِينَمَا قَابَلَتِ ٱلْأَمِيرَ ٱلْأَجْنَبِيَّ . ٢ — اِبْيَضَّ وَجْهُ ٱلْفَارِسِ لَمَّا أَقْبَلَ ٱلْأَعْدَاءُ عَلَيْهِ . ٣ — لَا تَحْمَرَّ يَا وَلَدُ ، إِنِّي لَا أُكَلِّمُ أَبَاكَ عَمَّا (عَنْ مَا for) فَعَلْتَ ٱلْبَارِحَ . ٤ — اِسْتَعْمِلْ قَلَمَ رَصَاصٍ لِرَسْمِكَ . ٥ — نَسْتَحْسِنُ أَنْ يَحْضُرَ كُلُّ ٱلْأَعْضَاءِ ٱلْجُدُدِ لِيَسْمَعُوا كَلَامَ ٱلرُّوسِيِّ وَٱلْأَمْرِيكِيِّ عَنْ (فِي) هٰذِهِ ٱلشُّؤُونِ ٱلْمُهِمَّةِ . ٦ — كَانَ ٱلِاسْتِعْجَالُ سَبَبَ تِلْكَ ٱلْوَاقِعَةِ . ٧ — اِسْتَخْدَمَتِ ٱلشَّرِكَةُ عُمَّالًا أَجَانِبَ كَثِيرِينَ قَبْلَ ٱلْقَانُونِ ٱلْأَخِيرِ . ٨ — اِسْتَعْمَلَتْ أَمْرِيكَا ٱلْقُنْبُلَةَ ٱلذَّرِّيَّةَ ضِدَّ

ٱلْيَابَانَ فِى ٱلْحَرْبِ. ٩ — سَوْفَ لا نَسْمَعُ إِلَى آرَائِكُمْ فِى ٱلْمُسْتَقْبَلِ.
١٠ — اِسْتَقْبَلَ رَئِيسُ ٱلْوُزَرَاءِ ٱلْيَابَانِيُّ سُفَرَاءَ دُوَلِ أُورُبَّا ٱسْتِقْبَالاً رَسْمِيًّا
وَتَكَلَّمُوا عَنْ سِيَاسَةِ رُوسِيَّا. ١١ — جَلَسُوا تَحْتَ رِئَاسَةِ رَئِيسِ وُزَرَاءِ
إِنْكِلْتَرَّا. ١٢ — يَا بَنَاتُ، ٱرْسُمْنَ صُوَراً لِهٰذِهِ ٱلْقِصَّةِ ٱلْعَرَبِيَّةِ ٱلْقَدِيمَةِ
ٱلْمَشْهُورَةِ. ١٣ — «هَلْ» حَرْفُ (particle) ٱسْتِفْهَامٍ فِى ٱللُّغَةِ ٱلْعَرَبِيَّةِ.
١٤ — لا نَعْرِفُ شَيْئاً عَنْ ذٰلِكَ، فَلْنَسْتَفْهِمِ ٱلْأُسْتَاذَ. ١٥ — إِنَّ
ٱلصَّحَافَةَ ٱلْعَرَبِيَّةَ ضَعِيفَةٌ جِدًّا. أَمَّا ٱلصَّحَافَةُ ٱلْإِنْكِلِيزِيَّةُ فَنَسْتَكْبِرُهَا.
١٦ — لا يَسْتَحْسِنُونَ سِيَاسَةَ ٱلْحِزْبِ ٱلْوَطَنِيِّ. ١٧ — اِسْتَعْجَلَ ٱلْفَارِسُ
فَوَقَعَ مِنْ حِصَانِهِ. ١٨ — ٱسْتُعْمِلَتِ ٱلْقَنَابِلُ فِى ٱلْحُرُوبِ مُنْذُ سِنِينَ
كَثِيرَةٍ جِدًّا. ١٩ — اِخْضَرَّ ٱلْبَحْرُ وَكَبُرَ خَوْفُ رُكَّابِ ٱلسَّفِينَةِ. ٢٠ —
يَزْرَقُّ ٱلنِّيلُ (Nile) ٱلْأَبْيَضُ، فَمَا هُوَ سَبَبُ ٱسْمِهِ ٱلْغَرِيبِ؟ ٢١ —
إِنِّى لَمْ أَسْمَعْ تِلْكَ ٱلْقِصَّةَ.

EXERCISE 44

1. What have you done girl? Why did you blush (become red)? 2. The garden will become green in the summer after the rains of spring. 3. I do not think much of (use اِسْتَحْسَنَ) the English press today. 4. We expect reform in the future; for that is the reason for the new law. 5. The official view is that haste is necessary to these two states, because the enemy have used these weapons for (since) many years. 6. Enquire of the inspector about the employment of Japanese workers in agriculture. 7. I fought against the enemy in Europe. 8. The king received the members of the council in his palace. 9. That was the work of the nationalists. 10. They

are under the leadership of Hassan Abdullah. 11. (إِنَّ) His story is very strange. 12. He used to be (كَانَ) a teacher in Cairo University. 13. My friend was employed in a foreign embassy for a long period. 14. But he was not happy there, so he thought best to leave his work (use أَنْ with the subjunctive). 15. A bomb fell on the Minister's car and killed him. 16. They used (the) atomic power. 17. Two atomic bombs fell on Japan during the late war. 18. Do not think much of the small; but do not also belittle (إِسْتَصْغَرَ) the great. Remember the story of David (دَاوُد). 19. I drew a sketch of this picture, but people thought it ugly. 20. What is your opinion of (فِي) these Italian pictures? Do you find them good or not?

CHAPTER TWENTY-FOUR

(اَلْبَابُ ٱلرَّابِعُ وَٱلْعِشْرُونَ)

Irregular Verbs. The Doubled Verb

1. The term "*irregular*" is, perhaps, inaccurate with regard to Arabic Verbs, if by "irregular" we mean isolated idiosyncrasies. Yet there are whole classes of verbs in which certain changes or deviations take place owing to the laws of contraction and assimilation. There are three causes:

(a) Where one of the three radicals is a weak letter, that is, a wāw or a yā'.

(b) Where one of the three radicals is a hamza. Early Arab philologers classed the hamza as a weak letter with the و and ى, but in fact the main trouble is in rules of orthography, rather than in actual changes.

(c) Where the second and third radical are identical, i.e. the doubled verb. We have already encountered nouns and adjectives from these verbs, e.g.

جَدٌّ a grandfather; جَدِيدٌ new.

The Arabs divide verbs into two classes:

(a) *Sound* (فِعْلٌ سَالِمٌ).

(b) *Unsound* (فِعْلٌ غَيْرُ سَالِمٍ).

These latter are further divided into:

(i) فِعْلٌ صَحِيحٌ, comprising

(1) *The doubled verb.* (2) *The hamzated verb.*

(ii) The weak verb فِعْلٌ مُعْتَلٌّ in which one of the radicals is wāw or yā'.

Note: مُعْتَلٌّ = sick

THE DOUBLED VERB فِعْلٌ مُضَاعَفٌ

2. It has been argued that the Semitic languages were originally bi-literal rather than triliteral, thus bringing them into line with, and postulating common ancestry with, Hamitic languages. However this may be, we do find a large number of roots in Arabic in which there are only two radicals, but (except in a few particles), the second radical has been doubled, thus moulding the root into triliteral form.* Apart from this, the three radicals of a root are practically always different. We have odd cases of the first and third radical being identical, e.g.

بَابٌ door (from *b.w.b.*), and قَلِقَ to be restless, disturbed.

But it is almost unknown for the first and second radicals to be the same. An exception is بَبْغَاءُ parrot.

3. The rules affecting the doubled verb have already been touched upon in explaining form IX of the triliteral verb.

(a) *Assimilation* (إِدْغَامٌ) takes place, and the two identical radicals are written as one with tashdīd, when the third radical carries a vowel.

e.g. (عَلَى) رَدَّ to restore, to reply (to); رَدَّ he replied; رَدُّوا they replied.

In the Imperfect, this necessitates shifting the vowel forward from the second radical:

يَرُدُّ yaruddu, he restores, for يَرْدُدُ yardudu.

Exception: the Passive Perfect of III is رُودِدَ rūdida.

(b) Assimilation does not take place where the third

* When we discuss quadriliteral roots, we shall find that sometimes the biliteral root is doubled, e.g. سَلْسَلَ from سَلَّ.

radical has sukūn. This, of course, applies especially to the Imperative and Jussive, as well as certain other forms.

e.g. رَدَدْنَا we restored.

رَدَدْنَ they (fem.) restored.

يَرْدُدْنَ they (fem.) restore.

نَرْدُدْ we restore (Jussive).

اُرْدُدْ restore! (Imperative).

NOTE: Thus verbs of the form فَعِلَ and فَعُلَ are only distinguished from those of فَعَلَ in the uncontracted forms, e.g. مَلَّ to be bored with; مَلِلْتُ I was bored.

(c) Where the second radical is separated from the third by a long vowel no assimilation can take place.

e.g. مَرْدُودٌ Passive Participle, I.

إِرْدَادٌ Verbal Noun, IV.

4. Conjugation of دَلَّ to show:

Perfect

Sing. 3. m.	دَلَّ	Dual	دَلَّا	Plur.	دَلُّوا
,, 3. f.	دَلَّتْ	,,	دَلَّتَا	,,	دَلَلْنَ
,, 2. m.	دَلَلْتَ	,,	دَلَلْتُمَا	,,	دَلَلْتُمْ
,, 2. f.	دَلَلْتِ			,,	دَلَلْتُنَّ
,, 1.	دَلَلْتُ			,,	دَلَلْنَا

Imperfect Indic.	Subj.	Juss.
يَدُلُّ	يَدُلَّ	يَدْلُلْ, also يَدُلَّ or يَدُلِّ
تَدُلُّ	تَدُلَّ	تَدْلُلْ or يَدُلُّ

Imperfect Indic.	Subj.	Juss.
تَدُلُّ	تَدُلَّ	تَدْلُلْ
تَدُلِّينَ	تَدُلِّي	تَدُلِّي
أَدُلُّ	أَدُلَّ	أَدْلُلْ
يَدُلَّانِ	يَدُلَّا	يَدُلَّا
تَدُلَّانِ	تَدُلَّا	تَدُلَّا
تَدُلَّانِ	تَدُلَّا	تَدُلَّا
يَدُلُّونَ	يَدُلُّوا	يَدُلُّوا
يَدْلُلْنَ	يَدْلُلْنَ	يَدْلُلْنَ
تَدُلُّونَ	تَدُلُّوا	تَدُلُّوا
تَدْلُلْنَ	تَدْلُلْنَ	تَدْلُلْنَ
نَدُلُّ	نَدُلَّ	نَدْلُلْ

Imperative

أُدْلُلْ or دُلَّ دُلِّ دُلُّ

أُدْلُلِي or دُلِّي

أُدْلُلَا or دُلَّا

أُدْلُلُوا or دُلُّوا

أُدْلُلْنَ

Part. Active دَالٌّ Part. Passive مَدْلُولٌ

It will be noted that in the Imperative and Jussive the rule may be broken and the two repeated radicals may be written with ta<u>sh</u>dīd. In this case, the third radical is vowelled, usually with fatḥa, but occasionally with ḍamma or kasra.

5. **Passive.**

Perf.	Imperf. Indic.	Juss.
دُلَّ	يُدَلُّ	يُدْلَلْ
دُلَّتْ	تُدَلُّ	تُدْلَلْ
دُلِلْتَ	تُدَلُّ	تُدْلَلْ
دُلِلْتِ	تُدَلِّينَ	تُدَلِّي
دُلِلْتُ	أُدَلُّ	أُدْلَلْ
etc.	etc.	etc.

DERIVED FORMS

6.	Perf.	Imperf.	Imper.	Part. Act.	Verbal Noun
II	دَلَّلَ	يُدَلِّلُ	دَلِّلْ	مُدَلِّلٌ	تَدْلِيلٌ
III	دَالَّ	يُدَالُّ	دَالِلْ	مُدَالٌّ	دِلَالٌ
(Passive	دُولِلَ	يُدَالُّ)			
IV	أَدَلَّ	يُدِلُّ	أَدْلِلْ	مُدِلٌّ	إِدْلَالٌ
V	تَدَلَّلَ	يَتَدَلَّلُ	تَدَلَّلْ	مُتَدَلِّلٌ	تَدَلُّلٌ
VI	تَدَالَّ	يَتَدَالُّ	تَدَالَلْ	مُتَدَالٌّ	تَدَالٌّ
VII	اِنْدَلَّ	يَنْدَلُّ	اِنْدَلِلْ	مُنْدَلٌّ	اِنْدِلَالٌ
VIII	اِمْتَدَّ	يَمْتَدُّ	اِمْتَدِدْ	مُمْتَدٌّ	اِمْتِدَادٌ

(The VIII form of مَدَّ to stretch out, is given here, because in the VIII form of دَلَّ there is assimilation = اِدَّلَّ).

IX Seldom occurs.

X	اِسْتَدَلَّ	يَسْتَدِلُّ	اِسْتَدْلِلْ	مُسْتَدِلٌّ	اِسْتِدْلَالٌ

VOCABULARY

عَادَةٌ *pl.* ـَاتٌ custom, habit

مَسْأَلَةٌ *pl.* مَسَائِلُ problem, question, matter

مُوَظَّفٌ *pl.* ـُونَ official *n.*

سُورِيَّا Syria

سُورِيٌّ Syrian

مَشْرُوعٌ *pl.* ـَاتٌ ، مَشَارِيعُ scheme, project

أَهْلٌ *pl.* أَهَالٍ people

أَمَلٌ *pl.* آمَالٌ hope

حَرٌّ ، حَرَارَةٌ heat

حَارٌّ hot

حِكَايَةٌ *pl.* ـَاتٌ story

بِسُرْعَةٍ quickly, with speed

أَفْضَلُ (مِنْ) better (than), preferable (to)

DOUBLED VERBS

مَدَّ (ـُ) to stretch out *tr.*

أَمَدَّ IV to help

اِمْتَدَّ VIII to stretch *intr.*

قَصَّ (ـُ) to narrate, recount, tell

ضَمَّ (ـُ) to collect *tr.*

اِنْضَمَّ مَعَ ، إِلَى VII to join, adhere

عَدَّ (ـُ) to count, consider

أَعَدَّ IV to prepare *tr.*

اِسْتَعَدَّ X to prepare oneself, be prepared

قَرَّ (ـِ) to be settled

قَرَّرَ II to lay down, ordain, decide

تَقْرِيرٌ *pl.* تَقَارِيرُ report

قَرَارٌ decision, determination

عَمٌّ uncle (paternal)

عَمَّةٌ aunt (paternal)

اِهْتَمَّ بِ VIII to be concerned about, bother about, be interested in

ظَنَّ (ـُ) to think, consider

أَحَبَّ IV to love, like

ضَرَّ (ـُ) to injure

اِضْطَرَّ VIII to compel

سَرَّ (ـُـ) to rejoice *tr.*, make glad

جَدَّ (ـُـ) to be new

تَجَدَّدَ V to be renewed

أَحَسَّ بِ IV to feel, be aware of

جُنَّ (ـُـ) to be or go mad

مَرَّ بِ، عَلَى (ـُـ) to pass (by)

تَمَّ (ـِـ) to be completed

أَتَمَّ IV to complete

اِسْتَحَقَّ X to deserve, merit

EXERCISE 45

١ — مَدَّتِ ٱلْأَمِيرَةُ يَدَهَا إِلَى ٱلْأَمِيرِ ٱلسُّورِيِّ كَعَادَتِهَا فَقَبَّلَهَا. ٢ — كَانَتِ ٱلطَّرِيقُ ٱلطَّوِيلَةُ تَمْتَدُّ أَمَامَنَا فَٱسْتَعْدَدْنَا لِلسَّفَرِ، وَأَحْسَسْنَا بِسُرُورٍ فِى قُلُوبِنَا. ٣ — إِنَّ ٱلنِّسَاءَ جُنِنَّ حِينَمَا نَظَرْنَ هٰذَا ٱلْمَشْرُوعَ، لٰكِنَّ رِجَالَهُنَّ لَمْ يَهْتَمُّوا بِهِ. ٤ — كَانَ عَمِّى رَجُلًا ظَانًّا يُحِبُّ ٱلْكُتُبَ وَٱلدُّرُوسَ. ٥ — قَدْ قُرِّرَ هٰذَا ٱلْكِتَابُ لِلْمَدَارِسِ ٱلْمِصْرِيَّةِ كُلِّهَا. ٦ — مَا هِىَ حِكَايَةُ ذٰلِكَ ٱلْمُوَظَّفِ؟ اُقْصُصْهَا عَلَىَّ مِنْ فَضْلِكَ (please). ٧ — أَعَدَّ ٱلْمُسَافِرُونَ ٱلْخَيْلَ لِسَفَرِهِمْ لِسُورِيَّا. ٨ — لِلشَّرِكَاتِ ٱلدَّوْلِيَّةِ أَنْ تُتِمَّ ٱلْمَشْرُوعَ. ٩ — عَلَى كُلِّ حَالٍ (in any case) هِىَ ٱضْطُرَّتْ إِلَى ٱلتَّعَاوُنِ مَعَ ٱلْحُكُومَةِ. ١٠ — كَتَبَ ٱلرَّئِيسُ فِى (concerning) ٱلْمَسْأَلَةِ فِى جَرِيدَةٍ مِنَ ٱلْجَرَائِدِ. ١١ — سَرَّنِى أَنَّ ٱسْتِحْقَاقَاتِكَ مَذْكُورَةٌ فِى ٱلتَّقْرِيرِ. ١٢ — اِنْضَمَّ جَيْشُ سُورِيَّا مَعَ جَيْشِ مِصْرَ لِيُمِدَّهُ فِى تِلْكَ ٱلْأَيَّامِ ٱلصَّعْبَةِ. ١٣ — تَجَدَّدَ تَجْلِيدُ ٱلْكِتَابِ. ١٤ — أَمَرَرْتُمْ بِأَهْلِ ٱلْقَرْيَةِ بِٱلْقُرْبِ مِنَ ٱلْبِئْرِ؟ ١٥ — ضُمَّ ٱلْجُنُودَ وَعُدَّهُمْ حَالًا. ١٦ — إِنَّ هٰذَا ٱلْقَرَارَ صَعْبٌ جِدًّا فِى أَوْقَاتِ ٱلْبَرْدِ ٱلشَّدِيدِ. ١٧ — تَظُنُّ عَمَّتِى ٱلْحَرَّ

أفضل من البرد. ١٨ — الأمل يسر الإنسان. ١٩ — حائط البيت
بارد جدا وكان حارا قبل ساعات. ٢٠ — تم سرورنا لما أمرنا الملك
أن ننسحب.

EXERCISE 46

1. The minister has written long reports on this matter, so the government has been compelled to do something (literally: a thing) for the deserving officials. 2. Syria asks for an international scheme for the renewal of the people's hopes, and the completion of their happiness. 3. Help your friends in times of anxiety, as is (like) the custom of the Christians, Muslims and Jews. 4. I realized that he (بأنه) had gone mad through (from) the heat. 5. I passed many fine buildings during my visit to the West. 6. Affairs have settled down in the foreign companies. 7. The government has laid it down that the people should be ready to fight, all of them, and to join the army at all times. 8. Tell me (على) the story, for I like it greatly. 9. The English like horse racing in the cold season. 10. Do you think he is pleased? (translate: do you think him pleased?) 11. He is angry at the government's decision. 12. I am not bothered about the Syrian question. 13. Hope is preferable to fear. 14. The cultivation (agriculture) stretches from here to Damascus. 15. My work will be complete in a week's time. 16. Go quickly, and tell that passing man to wait a minute. 17. May you deserve what I have done for you and your brother. 18. Work does not harm. 19. Be ready in front of the door and wait for me. 20. It is your duty to be concerned with the future of your country.

CHAPTER TWENTY-FIVE

(أَلْبَابُ الْخَامِسُ وَالْعِشْرُونَ)

Hamzated Verbs. Hamza as Initial Radical

1. The main trouble with hamzated verbs is orthography, since the hamza may be written on the 'alif (أ a, or أ u), under the 'alif (إ i), on the wāw (ؤ) or on the yā (ئ) which then loses its two dots – or even unsupported by another letter (except at the beginning of a word). In addition, there is some irregularity in Form VIII of the verb.

2. The hamza is a consonant, and, as such, may be the initial or first radical, as in أَكَلَ to eat, and أَخَذَ to take; the middle or second radical, as in سَأَلَ to ask; بَؤُسَ to be brave; سَئِمَ to be disgusted at; and the final or third radical as in قَرَأَ to read; خَطِئَ to transgress; and بَطُؤَ to be slow.

3. The whole question of the orthography of hamza, especially with verbs, is very confused, and, in some cases, alternative usages will be encountered. The following rules are only general guides, and should be taken in conjunction with the verb tables in this chapter and the next:

(a) At the beginning of a word hamza is invariably written over or under 'alif (except in certain Quranic usages),

e.g. أَخَذَ he took; أُخِذَ he or it was taken;

إِسْحَاقُ Isḥāq (Isaac); إِنْذَارٌ a warning.

(b) When this initial hamza is followed by an 'alif of prolongation (long vowel ā), the latter is replaced by a madda over the initial 'alif.

e.g. آخِذٌ 'ākhidhun, for أَاخِذٌ, Active Participle of أَخَذَ.

(c) Otherwise, the hamza tends to be written over the semi-consonant corresponding to the vowel of the preceding letter.

e.g. يَأْخُذُ ya'khudhu, he takes.

يُؤْخَذُ yu'khadhu, he or it is taken.

سُؤَالٌ su'ālun, a question.

اِسْتِئْنَافٌ isti'nāfun, Verbal Noun of اِسْتَأْنَفَ X, to appeal.

(d) Where the previous consonant has sukūn, the hamza tends to be written over the semi-consonant coinciding with its own vowel.

e.g. مَسْؤُولٌ mas'ūlun, asked, responsible, passive participle of سَأَلَ to ask.

أَسْئِلَةٌ 'as'ilatun, questions, pl. of سُؤَالٌ

يَيْأَسُ yay'asu, he despairs, Imperf. of يَئِسَ

In the Perfect of verbs with medial hamza, this rule is applied instead of (c) above, even though the previous radical is vowelled, because otherwise there would be no visible difference between the varied vowellings of the middle radical. Thus, ba'usa, to be brave, is written بَؤُسَ; sa'ima min, to be disgusted with, is written سَئِمَ مِنْ.

In the Perfect of the Passive Verb, the hamza of the middle radical is always written on kasra, سَأَلَ he asked; سُئِلَ he was asked.

(e) In Form VIII of the verb, however, two variations occur. For اِئْتَلَفَ بِ to be familiar with (أَلِفَ VIII), in addition to the regular form, we find اِيتَلَفَ, the yā' replacing the hamza. Moreover, in some verbs instead of this hamza we find the tā' of Form VIII doubled,

e.g. from أَخَذَ ، اِتَّخَذَ for اِئْتَخَذَ to take, adopt.

4. The reader may find books printed in France and North Africa, as well as in India, Pakistan and Persia – especially older editions – in which hamza is not shown, and the hamza over yā' will therefore appear merely as a proper yā' with the two dots, e.g.

جرايد for جَرَائِدُ, pl. of جَرِيدَةٌ newspaper.

This calls to mind the fact that in Classical Spoken Arabic only certain tribes actually pronounced non-initial hamza. Indeed, such hamzas are almost unknown even in modern spoken Arabic. In the recension of the Quran, the hamza was introduced into the standard dialect of Arabic – the literary language – and the orthography was such that, if the hamza were not pronounced but replaced by the weak letters 'alif, wāw or yā', the written form would still be correct. Thus مُؤَلِّفٌ with the hamza would be pronounced mu'allifun; without the hamza, it would be muwallifun. يَأْخُذُ with hamza would be ya'khudhu, without hamza, yākhudhu; جَرَائِدُ with hamza jarā'idu, without hamza, jarāyidu, and so on. This fact may help the student to write the hamza correctly.

5. The following idiosyncrasies of individual verbs may be noted here.

(a) In certain verbs: أَخَذَ to take; أَمَرَ to command; أَكَلَ to eat, the initial hamza is dropped in the Imperative, and we have:

Verb	Imperative		
	m. sing.	f. sing.	dual, etc.
أَخَذَ	خُذْ	خُذِي	خُذَا
أَمَرَ	مُرْ	مُرِي	مُرَا
أَكَلَ	كُلْ	كُلِي	كُلَا

(b) The verb سَأَلَ to ask, is sometimes written in the Imperfect as if there were no hamza, and it were a biliteral verb.

أَسَلُ I ask. تَسَلُ you ask (m.s.) etc.

In the Imperative, we also find سَلْ for اِسْأَلْ etc.

6. Conjugation of أَلِفَ to get, be, accustomed to:

Perf.	Imperf. Indic.	Subj.	Juss.
أَلِفَ	يَأْلَفُ	يَأْلَفَ	يَأْلَفْ
أَلِفَتْ	تَأْلَفُ	تَأْلَفَ	تَأْلَفْ
أَلِفْتَ	تَأْلَفُ	تَأْلَفَ	تَأْلَفْ
أَلِفْتِ	تَأْلَفِينَ	تَأْلَفِي	تَأْلَفِي
أَلِفْتُ	آلَفُ	آلَفَ	آلَفْ
etc.	etc.	etc.	etc.

Imperative		
إِيلَفْ	Part. Active	آلِفٌ
إِيلَفِي etc.	Part Passive	مَأْلُوفٌ
Passive Perf. أُلِفَ	Imperf. Indic.	يُؤْلَفُ

أَمَلَ to hope: Imperf. Indic. يَأْمُلُ Imper. أُومُلْ

أَثَرَ to quote: Imperf. Indic. يَأْثِرُ Imper. إِيثِرْ

DERIVED FORMS

7.

	Perf.	Imperf. Indic.	Imper.	Part. Act.	Verbal Noun
II	أَلَّفَ	يُؤَلِّفُ	أَلِّفْ	مُؤَلِّفٌ	تَأْلِيفٌ
III	آلَفَ	يُؤَالِفُ	آلِفْ	مُؤَالِفٌ	إِلَافٌ or مُؤَالَفَةٌ

IV	آلَفَ	يُؤْلِفُ	آلِفْ	مُؤْلِفٌ	إِيلَافٌ
V	تَأَلَّفَ	يَتَأَلَّفُ	تَأَلَّفْ	مُتَأَلِّفٌ	تَأَلُّفٌ
VI	تَآلَفَ	يَتَآلَفُ	تَآلَفْ	مُتَآلِفٌ	تَآلُفٌ

VII Wanting in all verbs beginning with hamza wāw, yā', rā', lām, nūn.

VIII	إِيتَلَفَ	يَأْتَلِفُ	إِيتَلِفْ	مُؤْتَلِفٌ	إِيتِلَافٌ

IX Wanting.

X	اِسْتَأْلَفَ	يَسْتَأْلِفُ	اِسْتَأْلِفْ	مُسْتَأْلِفٌ	اِسْتِئْلَافٌ

VOCABULARY

أَظْهَرَ IV to show

مَلَاكٌ ، مَلَكٌ *pl.* مَلَائِكَةٌ angel

رَسُولٌ *pl.* رُسُلٌ apostle

قِيَامَةٌ Resurrection

دِينِيٌّ religious

حَرَكَةٌ *pl.* ـَاتٌ movement

دَعْوَةٌ invitation

كَلِمَةٌ *pl.* ـَاتٌ word

قَامُوسٌ *pl.* قَوَامِيسُ dictionary

قَتْلٌ murder, killing

مَمْنُوعٌ forbidden

قِرْشٌ ، غِرْشٌ *pl.* قُرُوشٌ ، غُرُوشٌ piastre

مُضِرٌّ (بِ) harmful (to)

خِنْزِيرٌ *pl.* خَنَازِيرُ pig, pork

لَقَّبَ II to name, nickname

لَقَبٌ *pl.* أَلْقَابٌ name, title, nickname

حَيَاةٌ life

HAMZATED VERBS AND THEIR DERIVATIVES

أَمِنَ (ـَ) to be secure

آمَنَ بِ IV to believe in (religious)

آخَذَ III to blame

اِتَّخَذَ VIII to take to oneself, adopt

أَمَلَ (ـُ) to hope

تَأَمَّلَ (فِي) V to observe, look at

أَثَّرَ (فى ، على) II to make an impression (on), influence

تَأَثَّرَ V to be influenced, impressed

تَأَخَّرَ V to be late

أَذِنَ بِ (ـَ) to allow

اِسْتَأْذَنَ X to ask permission (beg leave)

أَكَّدَ II to assure, confirm

تَأَكَّدَ V to be sure (of)

آجَرَ IV to let (for hire)

اِسْتَأْجَرَ X to hire, rent

آلَفَ III to be intimate with

أَلَّفَ II to compile, write, compose

مُؤَلِّف compiler, writer, author

أَدَّبَ II to discipline

أَدَب *pl.* آدَاب courtesy; literature

EXERCISE 47

١ — لُقِّبَ ٱلْخَلِيفَةُ بِلَقَبِ «أَمِيرِ ٱلْمُؤْمِنِينَ» لِرِئَاسَتِهِ ٱلدِّينِيَّةِ.
٢ — يُؤْمِنُ ٱلْمُسْلِمُ بِٱللّٰهِ وَمَلَائِكَتِهِ وَرُسُلِهِ وَكُتُبِهِ وَيَوْمِ ٱلْقِيَامَةِ.
٣ — إِنَّ فِى ٱلْقَوَامِيسِ ٱلْعَرَبِيَّةِ كَلِمَاتٍ كَثِيرَةً دِينِيَّةً. ٤ — إِنَّ دِينَنَا
لَا يَأْذَنُ بِٱلْقَتْلِ. ٥ — اِسْتَأْذَنَ ٱلضُّيُوفُ فَٱنْصَرَفُوا فِى عَرَبَةٍ مُسْتَأْجَرَةٍ.
وَكَانَتِ ٱلْأُجْرَةُ غِرْشَيْنِ (قِرْشَيْنِ) مِصْرِيَّيْنِ. ٦ — كُلُّ ٱلْأَجَانِبِ يَتَّخِذُونَ
هٰذِهِ ٱلْعَادَةَ ٱلْقَبِيحَةَ، وَآمُلُ أَلَّا تَتَّخِذَهَا أَنْتَ يَا ٱبْنِى. ٧ — أَثَّرَتْ
حَيَاةُ رَسُولِ ٱللّٰهِ فِى ٱلْمُسْلِمِينَ جَمِيعِهِمْ. ٨ — أَنْتَ مُسْلِمٌ فَلَا تَأْكُلْ
لَحْمَ ٱلْخِنْزِيرِ: إِنَّ ذٰلِكَ مَمْنُوعٌ فِى دِينِنَا. ٩ — لَا تَتَأَخَّرْ لِدَعْوَتِى.
١٠ — أَنَا مُتَأَكِّدٌ مِنْ أَنَّ حَرَكَاتِ ٱلْمُدُنِ مُضِرَّةٌ بِٱلْإِنْسَانِ. ١١ —
يَظْهَرُ أَنَّ تَآلِيفَ ٱلْكُتُبِ غَيْرُ نَافِعٍ فِى هٰذِهِ ٱلْأَيَّامِ. ١٢ — ذَهَبَ مَالُهُ
كُلُّهُ، لِذٰلِكَ يُؤَاخِذُهُ أَبُوهُ. ١٣ — تَأَمَّلْ تِلْكَ ٱلْبِنْتَ ٱلْمُحْمَرَّةَ. ١٤ — إِنَّ

ٱلتَّأْكِيدَ غَيْرُ مُمْكِنٍ لِمُؤَلِّفِي كُتُبِ ٱلتَّأْرِيخِ. ١٥ — أَظْهِرْ أَدَبَكَ لِلضُّيُوفِ، يَا وَلَدُ. ١٦ — إِنَّنَا نَتَأَثَّرُ مِنْ أَعْمَالِ أَجْدَادِنَا (ancestors). ١٧ — أَفِي ٱلشَّارِعِ سَيَّارَةٌ لِلْإِيجَارِ؟ ١٨ — كَانَتْ ظُنُونُهُمْ كَظُنُونِ ٱلْجَمِيعِ. ١٩ — إِنَّ ٱلْمُعَلِّمَ ٱلطَّيِّبَ يُؤَدِّبُ ٱلتَّلَامِذَةَ وَلَا يُؤَالِفُهُمْ. ٢٠ — إِنَّ حَرَارَةَ ٱلشَّمْسِ مُضِرَّةٌ فِى ٱلشَّرْقِ.

EXERCISE 48

1. The pig was eaten in the Christian's house. 2. How did the Muslims name their Caliph? 3. They named him with the title of "Prince of the Faithful". 4. The affairs of the state became secure after the murder of the author of that harmful book. 5. Look at the influence of religious opinions on the history of the world. 6. Religion is an important matter, more important than wealth. 7. I accept your kind invitation, and I will try not to be late. 8. But I am very busy, so I will hire a car. 9. Arab thought and literature deserve long study. 10. Muhammad blamed the Christians and the Jews because they went against his religion. 11. Yet they believed in the Day of Resurrection. 12. Wine drinking is forbidden to the Muslim. 13. This author has many famous compilations. 14. It appears that you have disciplined your sons, yet they blame you. 15. The angels and the apostles are servants of God. 16. I am certain that this word is [to be] found in the dictionary. 17. Show your two piastres to the owner of the horse, perhaps he will hire it to you. 18. There is much traffic (movement) in the streets of Baghdad. 19. The heat was the cause of his sickness. 20. Do not be influenced by my opinions. Think about the matter.

CHAPTER TWENTY-SIX

(اَلْبَابُ ٱلسَّادِسُ وَٱلْعِشْرُونَ)

Hamzated Verbs. Hamza as Middle and Final Radical

1. The Verb with Hamza as Middle Radical:

The Middle Radical may be vowelled with fatḥa, ḍamma, or kasra. As explained in rule (d) of Hamza orthography in the previous chapter, this means that the hamza may be written over 'alif, wāw, or yā'.

2. Conjugation of سَأَلَ to ask:

Perf.	Imperf. Indic.		Subj.	
سَأَلَ	يَسْأَلُ	(also written يَسْـَٔلُ)	يَسْأَلَ	(يَسْـَٔلَ)
سَأَلَتْ	تَسْأَلُ		تَسْأَلَ	
سَأَلْتَ	تَسْأَلُ		تَسْأَلَ	
سَأَلْتِ	تَسْأَلِينَ		تَسْأَلِي	
سَأَلْتُ	أَسْأَلُ		أَسْأَلَ	
etc.	etc.		etc.	

Jussive

يَسْأَلْ	(يَسْـَٔلْ)	or	يَسَلْ
تَسْأَلْ		,,	تَسَلْ
تَسْأَلْ		,,	تَسَلْ
تَسْأَلِي		,,	تَسَلِي
أَسْأَلْ		,,	أَسَلْ
etc.			etc.

Imperative

اِسْأَلْ (also written اِسَلْ) or سَلْ

اِسْأَلِي (,, ,, اِسَلِي) ,, سَلِي

etc. etc.

Part. Act. سَائِلٌ

Part. Pass. مَسْؤُولٌ (also written مَسْئُولٌ or مَسْءُولٌ)

Passive Perf. سُئِلَ, Imperf. Indic. يَسْأَلُ (also written يَسَلُ).

3. Example of the form فَعَلَ : كَأَبَ to be cast down.

Imperf. Indic. يَكْأَبُ (also written يَكَبُ).

Imper. اِكْأَبْ (,, ,, اِكَبْ).

4. Example of the form فَعُلَ : بَؤُسَ to be brave.

Imperf. Indic. يَبْؤُسُ

Imper. اُبْؤُسْ

DERIVED FORMS

5.	Perf.	Imperf. Indic.	Imper.	Part. Act.	Part. Pass.
II.	سَأَّلَ	يُسَئِّلُ	سَئِّلْ	مُسَئِّلٌ	مُسَأَّلٌ
III.	سَاءَلَ	يُسَائِلُ	سَائِلْ	مُسَائِلٌ	مُسَاءَلٌ
IV.	أَسْأَلَ	يُسْئِلُ	أَسْئِلْ	مُسْئِلٌ	مُسْأَلٌ
V.	تَسَأَّلَ	يَتَسَأَّلُ	تَسَأَّلْ	مُتَسَئِّلٌ	مُتَسَأَّلٌ
VI.	تَسَاءَلَ	يَتَسَاءَلُ	تَسَاءَلْ	مُتَسَائِلٌ	مُتَسَاءَلٌ
VII.	اِنْسَأَلَ	يَنْسَئِلُ	اِنْسَئِلْ	مُنْسَئِلٌ	مُنْسَأَلٌ

	Perf.	Imperf. Indic.	Imper.	Part. Act.	Part. Pass.
VIII.	اِلْتَأَمَ	يَلْتَئِمُ	اِلْتَئِمْ	مُلْتَئِمٌ	مُلْتَأَمٌ

(from لَأَمَ to bind up a wound, as this form of سَأَلَ does not occur).

IX. does not occur.

X.	اِسْتَلْأَمَ	يَسْتَلْئِمُ	اِسْتَلْئِمْ	مُسْتَلْئِمٌ	مُسْتَلْأَمٌ

Verbal Noun

II.	تَسْئِيلٌ	IV.	إِسْآلٌ	VI.	تَسَاؤُلٌ	VIII.	اِلْتِئَامٌ
III.	مُسَاءَلَةٌ	V.	تَسَؤُّلٌ	VII.	اِنْسِئَالٌ	X.	اِسْتِلْآمٌ

6. Example of verb, whose third radical is hamza:
قَرَأَ to read.

Perf.	Imperf. Indic.	Subj.	Juss.
قَرَأَ	يَقْرَأُ	يَقْرَأَ	يَقْرَأْ
قَرَأَتْ	تَقْرَأُ	تَقْرَأَ	تَقْرَأْ
قَرَأْتَ	تَقْرَأُ	تَقْرَأَ	تَقْرَأْ
قَرَأْتِ	تَقْرَئِينَ	تَقْرَئِي	تَقْرَئِي
قَرَأْتُ	أَقْرَأُ	أَقْرَأَ	أَقْرَأْ
etc.	etc.	etc.	etc.

Imperative

اِقْرَأْ

اِقْرَئِي etc.

Part. Active قَارِئٌ

Part. Passive مَقْرُوءٌ

Pass. Perf. قُرِئَ

قُرِئْتُ etc.

Imperf. Indic. يُقْرَأُ

Note the orthography of the hamza in the following examples. They represent the usual modern practice, though the student should not be surprised if he encounter other minor variants from time to time.

3 Masc. Pl. Perf.	قَرَأُوا , قَرَؤُوا , قَرَؤُا they read, have read
,, ,, Imperf. Indic.	يَقْرَأُونَ , يَقْرَؤُونَ , يَقْرَؤُنَ they read
3 Masc. Sing. Imperf. Indic. with Pronominal suffix	يَقْرَؤُهُ } he reads it
,, ,, Subjunctive	يَقْرَأَهُ } he reads it
3 Masc. Dual Perf.	قَرَآ they (two) read, have read
,, ,, Imperf. Indic.	يَقْرَآنِ they (two) read

7. Conjugation of verbs which take kasra in the Imperf.: هَنَأَ to be healthy, Imperf. Indic. يَهْنِئُ Imperative اِهْنِئْ.

8. Conjugation of verbs of the form فَعِلَ : خَطِئَ to sin.

Perf.	Imperf. Indic.	Imper.
خَطِئَ	يَخْطَأُ	اِخْطَأْ
خَطِئْتَ	تَخْطَأُ	اِخْطَئِي
خَطِئْتِ	تَخْطَأُ	etc.
خَطِئْتَ	تَخْطَئِينَ	
خَطِئْتُ	أَخْطَأُ	
etc.	etc.	

9. Conjugation of verbs of the form فَعُلَ : بَطُؤَ to be slow.

Perf.	Imperf. Indic.	Imper.
بَطُؤَ	يَبْطُؤُ	اُبْطُؤْ
بَطُؤْتُ	تَبْطُؤُ	اُبْطُؤِي
بَطُؤْتَ	تَبْطُؤُ	etc.
etc.	etc.	

DERIVED FORMS

10.	Perf.	Imperf. Indic.	Imper.	Part. Act.	Part. Pass.
II.	قَرَّأَ	يُقَرِّئُ	قَرِّئْ	مُقَرِّئٌ	مُقَرَّأٌ
III.	قَارَأَ	يُقَارِئُ	قَارِئْ	مُقَارِئٌ	مُقَارَأٌ
IV.	أَقْرَأَ	يُقْرِئُ	أَقْرِئْ	مُقْرِئٌ	مُقْرَأٌ
V.	تَقَرَّأَ	يَتَقَرَّأُ	تَقَرَّأْ	مُتَقَرِّئٌ	مُتَقَرَّأٌ
VI.	تَقَارَأَ	يَتَقَارَأُ	تَقَارَأْ	مُتَقَارِئٌ	مُتَقَارَأٌ
VII.	اِنْقَرَأَ	يَنْقَرِئُ	اِنْقَرِئْ	مُنْقَرِئٌ	مُنْقَرَأٌ
VIII.	اِقْتَرَأَ	يَقْتَرِئُ	اِقْتَرِئْ	مُقْتَرِئٌ	مُقْتَرَأٌ
IX.	Does not occur.				
X.	اِسْتَقْرَأَ	يَسْتَقْرِئُ	اِسْتَقْرِئْ	مُسْتَقْرِئٌ	مُسْتَقْرَأٌ

Verbal Noun

II. تَقْرِئَةٌ	IV. إِقْرَاءٌ	VI. تَقَارُؤٌ	VIII. اِقْتِرَاءٌ
III. مُقَارَأَةٌ	V. تَقَرُّؤٌ	VII. اِنْقِرَاءٌ	X. اِسْتِقْرَاءٌ

VOCABULARY

وَفْدٌ *pl.* وُفُودٌ delegation

صَرَّحَ II to declare, permit *mod.*

حَادِثٌ *pl.* حَوَادِثُ event *mod.*

نَفَّذَ II to carry out, execute

تَنْفِيذٌ execution

تَنْفِيذِىٌّ executive *adj.*

سَبِيلٌ *pl.* سُبُلٌ path, road, method

فِى سَبِيلِ (with following *gen.*) in the way of, in aid of, towards

عَلَاقَةٌ *pl.* ـَاتٌ relationship(s), relation(s)

نِظَامٌ *pl.* أَنْظِمَةٌ arrangement, system, discipline

إِدَارَةٌ administration, management

شَعْبٌ *pl.* شُعُوبٌ people, nation

اِسْتِقْلَالٌ independence

حُلْمٌ *pl.* أَحْلَامٌ dream

رُجُوعٌ return

ثَمَنٌ *pl.* أَثْمَانٌ price

جِدَارٌ *pl.* جُدْرَانٌ wall

حَاجَةٌ *pl.* ـَاتٌ, ... إِلَى ... فِى need, in ... of ...

مُرُورٌ passing *n.*

بِرْمِيلٌ *pl.* بَرَامِيلُ barrel, cask, vat, drum

نَفْطٌ ، نِفْطٌ oil, naphtha, tar

زَيْتٌ oil

زَيْتُونٌ olive (زَيْتُونَةٌ an olive)

صَنَعَ (ـَ) to make, do, manufacture

صِنَاعَةٌ *pl.* صَنَائِعُ craft, industry

مَصْنَعٌ *pl.* مَصَانِعُ factory, workshop

اِرْتَفَعَ VIII to rise, to be raised

سِجْنٌ *pl.* سُجُونٌ prison

نَتِيجَةٌ *pl.* نَتَائِجُ result

اِمْتِحَانٌ *pl.* ـَاتٌ examination

نَجَاحٌ success

زَمَنٌ ، زَمَانٌ *pl.* أَزْمِنَةٌ time

فَأْسٌ (*f.*) *pl.* فُؤُوسٌ axe

VERBS WITH MEDIAL HAMZA

سَئِمَ (َ) (مِنْ) to loathe, be disgusted with

شَأَمَ (َ) (with عَلَى) to draw ill luck upon, bode ill for

تَفَأَّلَ V, تَفَاءَلَ VI, اِفْتَأَلَ VIII بِ to draw a good omen from, bode well of

VERBS WITH FINAL HAMZA

بَدَأَ (َ) to begin *trans.*	هَنَّأَ II to congratulate
اِبْتَدَأَ VIII to begin *intrans.*	مَلَأَ (َ) to fill
قَرَأَ (َ) to read	نَشَأَ (َ) to grow *intrans.*
اَلْقُرْآنُ the Qur'ān (Koran)	أَنْشَأَ IV to establish, set up
نَبَّأَ II (with *acc.*) بِ to inform ... of ...	جَرُؤَ (ُ) to dare, be brave
اِلْتَجَأَ إِلَى VIII to take refuge (with)	جَرِىءٌ *pl.* أَجْرِاءُ bold, brave

EXERCISE 49

١ — سَئِمَ ٱلْوَفْدُ ٱلْمِصْرِىُّ مِنَ ٱلْحَوَادِثِ ٱلْأَخِيرَةِ. ٢ — نَسْأَلُ ٱللّٰهَ أَنْ يُمِدَّنَا فِى تَنْفِيذِ ٱلْمَشْرُوعِ. ٣ — لِمَاذَا تَتَفَأَّلُونَ بِرُجُوعِ ٱلْمَلِكِ وَقَدْ صَرَّحَ مُتَكَلِّمٌ بِٱسْمِ ٱلْحُكُومَةِ أَنَّ ٱلْمُشْكِلَةَ ٱنْحَلَّتْ؟ ٤ — اِفْتَأَلَتْ زَوْجَةُ قَيْصَرَ (Caesar) مِنْ حُلْمِهِ فِى شَهْرِ مَارِسَ (March)[1]. ٥ — اِبْتَدَأْتُ فِى قِرَاءَةِ ٱلْقُرْآنِ قَبْلَ شَهْرَيْنِ وَأَتْمَمْتُهَا أَثْنَاءَ شَهْرٍ كَامِلٍ. ٦ — نَفَّذَتِ ٱلسُّلْطَةُ ٱلتَّنْفِيذِيَّةُ هٰذَا ٱلْقَانُونَ فِى سَبِيلِ ٱلْإِصْلَاحِ. ٧ — نَبَّأَتْ شَرِكَةُ نَفْطِ

---

[1] Also آذَارُ (see Chapter 36)

ٱلْعِرَاقِ ٱلْحُكُومَةَ ٱلْعِرَاقِيَّةَ بِأَنَّ ثَمَنَ ٱلزَّيْتِ سَوْفَ يَرْتَفِعُ إِلَى جُنَيْهَيْنِ لِلْبِرْمِيلِ فِى ٱلسَّنَةِ ٱلْجَدِيدَةِ. ٨ — أَنْشَأَتِ ٱلْحُكُومَةُ صِنَاعَاتٍ خَفِيفَةً. ٩ — اِتْبَعِ ٱلنِّظَامَ ٱلْمَعْرُوفَ وَٱمْلَأْ بِرْمِيلَكَ بِٱلزَّيْتُونِ. ١٠ — أُهَنِّئُ هٰذِهِ ٱلشَّرِكَةَ لِأَنَّ عَلَاقَاتِ ٱلْإِدَارَةِ مَعَ ٱلْعُمَّالِ حَسَنَةٌ جِدًّا. ١١ — نَحْنُ فِى حَاجَةٍ كَبِيرَةٍ إِلَى ٱلِٱسْتِقْلَالِ، فَلْنَدْفَعْ ثَمَنَهُ. ١٢ — هَرَبَ ٱلْقَاتِلُ مِنَ ٱلسِّجْنِ وَٱلْتَجَأَ فِى بَيْتٍ مِنْ بُيُوتِ ٱلْقَرْيَةِ. ١٣ — وَجَدَ فَأْسًا هُنَاكَ لٰكِنَّهُ لَمْ يَجْرُؤْ عَلَى أَنْ يَسْتَعْمِلَهَا. ١٤ — نَشَأَ فِى بَيْتٍ صَغِيرٍ قَرِيبٍ مِنْ بَابِ ٱلْمَدِينَةِ. ١٥ — اِبْدَأُوا تَصْلِيحَ ٱلْجِدَارِ يَا عُمَّالُ. ١٦ — صَنَعَ سُيُوفًا لِلرِّجَالِ ٱلْأُجَرَاءِ فِى مَصْنَعٍ لَهُ. ١٧ — بَعْدَ مُرُورِ ٱلزَّمَانِ رَجَعَ ٱلْمُسَافِرُ لِوَطَنِهِ وَٱسْتَقَرَّ هُنَاكَ. ١٨ — لَا تَقْرَئِى هٰذَا ٱلْكِتَابَ يَا ٱبْنَتِى. ١٩ — سَلُوا مُعَلِّمِيكُمْ عَنْ نَتَائِجِ ٱمْتِحَانَاتِكُمْ. ٢٠ — إِنَّ وَاجِبَ ٱلشَّعْبِ أَنْ يُهَنِّئَ رَئِيسَ ٱلْوُزَرَاءِ عَلَى نَجَاحِ ٱلْمَشْرُوعِ.

EXERCISE 50

1. The government congratulated the delegation on their success in the way of improving the relations between the people and the administration. 2. A government spokesman announced the return of the price of oil to what it was before the war. 3. Life is our prison, and we take refuge in dreams. 4. Events have deprived (use منع) us of liberty since the war, and we are in need of it. 5. The wall of this room has become dirty with the passage of time. 6. This executive arrangement began a week ago. 7. A cask of olives reached me yesterday. 8. The servants cut the wood with their axes, then

informed their master of the completion of the work. 10. I have read the whole of the Quran. 11. Do you draw a good omen from the establishment of these factories? 12. No, it bodes ill to me (lit. I draw a bad omen from it). 13. I filled the guests' cups with coffee, and they drank it. 14. This writer grew up in the city of Baghdad (بَغْدَادُ). 15. He was ill, yet he began his examination. 16. The result is not known, because it is in God's hands. 17. Ask the scholars about that great man. He became disgusted with city life (the life of cities). 18. What have you made today? 19. Don't ask me about that. It is my secret. 20. Market prices have gone up in recent days.

CHAPTER TWENTY-SEVEN

(اَلْبَابُ ٱلسَّابِعُ وَٱلْعِشْرُونَ)

Weak Verbs. The Assimilated Verb

1. The *Weak Verbs* (أَفْعَالٌ مُعْتَلَّةٌ) are those in which one radical is one of the two semi-vowels or semi-consonants, wāw and yā'. They are of three classes:

A. Those with a weak *Initial Radical* (فِعْلٌ مِثَالٌ), sometimes called in English the Assimilated Verb.

B. Those with weak *Middle Radical*, the Hollow Verb (فِعْلٌ أَجْوَفُ).

C. Those with weak *Final Radical* (فِعْلٌ نَاقِصٌ), sometimes called the Defective Verb in English.

2. The weak radical in these verbs may undergo, according to certain rules, any one of the following changes:

(a) It may change to a long "ā" or 'alif,

e.g. Root Q-W-L. قَالَ he said, for قَوَلَ.

(b) It may change to a long "ū" (wāw) or "ī" (yā'),

e.g. يَقُولُ he says, for يَقْوُلُ.

قِيلَ it was said, for قُوِلَ.

(c) It may disappear entirely,

e.g. يَقُلْ let him say (Jussive) for يَقْوُلْ.

قِفْ stop! Imperative of وَقَفَ.

يَصِلُ he arrives, for يَوْصِلُ.

(d) In some cases, in disappearing the weak letter leaves some vestige in the shape of a short vowel (see the first example in (c) above).

(e) In certain parts it may be replaced by hamza, which early Arabic lexicographers therefore classed as a weak letter, e.g. قَائِل for قَاوِل, Active Participle of قَالَ to say. لِقَاءٌ for لِقَايٌ, Verbal Noun of لَاقَى, to meet. (لَقِيَ III).

(f) In compensation for the change of the weak radical to 'alif, we sometimes find the feminine ending ة added, e.g. إِقَامَةٌ and اِسْتِقَامَةٌ Verbal Nouns of قَامَ IV and X respectively. Similarly, certain Verbal Nouns with the feminine ending occur in the assimilated verb, the weak initial radical being omitted, e.g. صِفَةٌ quality, a verbal noun of وَصَفَ to describe.

A grasp of the above principles will assist the student to recognise weak verbs when he encounters them in reading.

The Assimilated Verb. A. With yā'

3. The initial may be wāw or yā', but the latter, being easier—and also rarer—will be dealt with first. Such verbs are regular, the yā' always appearing like any other radical, except in the following isolated parts:

(a) In the Imperfect Passive, yā' turns to wāw.

(b) A similar change occurs in the Imperfect and the Participles of Form IV.

(c) The yā' is changed to a tā' in Form VIII.

See the following tables where the above are underlined.

Conjugation of the verbs, whose first radical is ى: يَبِسَ to be dry.

Perf.	Imperf. Indic.	Subj.	Juss.
يَبِسَ	يَيْبَسُ	يَيْبَسَ	يَيْبَسْ
يَبِسَتْ	تَيْبَسُ	تَيْبَسَ	تَيْبَسْ
يَبِسْتَ	تَيْبَسُ	تَيْبَسَ	تَيْبَسْ

Perf.	Imperf. Indic.	Subj.	Juss.
يَبِسْتَ	تَيْبَسِينَ	تَيْبَسِي	تَيْبَسِي
يَبِسْتُ	أَيْبَسُ	أَيْبَسَ	أَيْبَسْ
etc.	etc.	etc.	etc.

Imperative

اِيبَسْ

اِيبَسِي etc.

Part. Act. يَابِسٌ

Part. Pass. مَيْبُوسٌ

Verbal Noun يَبْسٌ

Pass. Perf. يُبِسَ

Imperf. Indic. يُوبَسُ

DERIVED FORMS

	Perf.	Imperf. Indic.	Imper.	Part Act.	Part. Pass.
II.	يَبَّسَ	يُيَبِّسُ	يَبِّسْ	مُيَبِّسٌ	مُيَبَّسٌ
III.	يَابَسَ	يُيَابِسُ	يَابِسْ	مُيَابِسٌ	مُيَابَسٌ
IV.	أَيْبَسَ	يُوبِسُ	أَيْبِسْ	مُوبِسٌ	مُوبَسٌ
V.	تَيَبَّسَ	يَتَيَبَّسُ	تَيَبَّسْ	مُتَيَبِّسٌ	مُتَيَبَّسٌ
VI.	تَيَابَسَ	يَتَيَابَسُ	تَيَابَسْ	مُتَيَابِسٌ	مُتَيَابَسٌ
VII.	اِنْيَبَسَ	يَنْيَبِسُ	اِنْيَبِسْ	مُنْيَبِسٌ	مُنْيَبَسٌ
VIII.	اِتَّبَسَ	يَتَّبِسُ	اِتَّبِسْ	مُتَّبِسٌ	مُتَّبَسٌ
IX.	Does not occur.				
X.	اِسْتَيْبَسَ	يَسْتَيْبِسُ	اِسْتَيْبِسْ	مُسْتَيْبِسٌ	مُسْتَيْبَسٌ

Verbal Noun

II.	تَيْبِيسٌ	IV.	إِيبَاسٌ	VI.	تَيَابُسٌ	VIII.	اِتِّبَاسٌ
III.	مُيَابَسَةٌ	V.	تَيَبُّسٌ	VII.	اِنْيِبَاسٌ	X.	اِسْتِيبَاسٌ

Although there are few very common verbs beginning with yā', whether root or derived, there are a few which deserve mention.

e.g. (مِنْ) يَئِسَ (ـَـ) to despair (of).

أَيْأَسَ IV to drive anyone to despair.

يَبِسَ (ـَـ) to become dry, wither (given above).

يَبَّسَ II to dry anything.

يَسِرَ (ـَـ) to be or become easy.

يَسَّرَ II to facilitate.

يَقِظَ (ـَـ) to wake up.

يَقَّظَ II, أَيْقَظَ IV to awaken (trans.)

تَيَقَّظَ V, إِسْتَيْقَظَ X same meaning as root form.

The Assimilated Verb. B. With wāw

4. In the root form practically all these verbs except the doubled ones, and all the commonly-used ones:

(a) Lose the wāw in the Imperfect,

e.g. وَصَلَ to arrive, to link; Imperfect, يَصِلُ

but it is reinstated in the Passive, يُوصَلُ.

(b) Lose both this wāw and the preceding 'alif (which would normally be found) in the Imperative.

وَصَفَ to describe; صِفْ describe!

وَضَعَ to place, put; ضَعْ put!

Conjugation of وَصَلَ.

Perf.	Imperf. Indic.	Subj.	Juss.
وَصَلَ	يَصِلُ	يَصِلَ	يَصِلْ
وَصَلَتْ	تَصِلُ	تَصِلَ	تَصِلْ
وَصَلْتَ	تَصِلُ	تَصِلَ	تَصِلْ
وَصَلْتِ	تَصِلِينَ	تَصِلِي	تَصِلِي
وَصَلْتُ	أَصِلُ	أَصِلَ	أَصِلْ
etc.	etc.	etc.	etc.

Imperative

صِلْ — Part. Act. وَاصِلٌ

صِلِي etc. — Part. Pass. مَوْصُولٌ

Verbal Noun وَصْلٌ or وُصُولٌ or صِلَةٌ

Pass. Perf. وُصِلَ — Imperf. Indic. يُوصَلُ

5. We pointed out in Chapter Fourteen that verbs of the form فَعِلَ, يَفْعَلُ are rare in Arabic. Many of them have initial wāw, e.g.

وَثِقَ (ب), to trust; Imperf. يَثِقُ; Imperative ثِقْ

وَرِثَ, to inherit; Imperf. يَرِثُ; Imperative رِثْ

وَرِمَ, to swell; Imperf. يَرِمُ; Imperative رِمْ

6. Of those few verbs which retain the wāw in the Imperfect, the least uncommon is وَجِلَ to be afraid.

يَوْجَلُ Imperf. اِيجَلْ Imperative (for اِوْجَلْ)

7. Doubled verbs having initial wāw retain it in the Imperfect, and merely follow the rules already given for the Doubled Verb, e.g. وَدَّ to love.

Imperfect يَوَدُّ; Imperative وَدَّ.

8. Derived Forms. These are regular, except for the following points:

(a) In VIII, the wāw changes to tā' and appears in the doubling of the tā' of increase,

e.g. from وَضَحَ to be clear اِتَّضَحَ (same meaning).

(b) Where the wāw has sukūn and is preceded by kasra, it changes to yā',

e.g. Verbal Nouns of IV and X.

وَجَدَ to find IV أَوْجَدَ to create, v.n. إِيجَادٌ.

وَدَعَ to let, allow; X اِسْتَوْدَعَ to let, deposit; v.n. اِسْتِيدَاعٌ.

Table of Derived Forms

	Perf.	Imperf. Indic.	Imper.	Part. Act.	Part. Pass.
II.	وَصَّلَ	يُوَصِّلُ	وَصِّلْ	مُوَصِّلٌ	مُوَصَّلٌ
III.	وَاصَلَ	يُوَاصِلُ	وَاصِلْ	مُوَاصِلٌ	مُوَاصَلٌ
IV.	أَوْصَلَ	يُوصِلُ	أَوْصِلْ	مُوصِلٌ	مُوصَلٌ
V.	تَوَصَّلَ	يَتَوَصَّلُ	تَوَصَّلْ	مُتَوَصِّلٌ	مُتَوَصَّلٌ
VI.	تَوَاصَلَ	يَتَوَاصَلُ	تَوَاصَلْ	مُتَوَاصِلٌ	مُتَوَاصَلٌ
VIII.	اِتَّصَلَ	يَتَّصِلُ	اِتَّصِلْ	مُتَّصِلٌ	مُتَّصَلٌ
X.	اِسْتَوْصَلَ	يَسْتَوْصِلُ	اِسْتَوْصِلْ	مُسْتَوْصِلٌ	مُسْتَوْصَلٌ

Verbal Noun

II. تَوْصِيلٌ IV. إِيصَالٌ VI. تَوَاصُلٌ VIII. اِتِّصَالٌ

III. وِصَالٌ or مُوَاصَلَةٌ V. تَوَصُّلٌ X. اِسْتِيصَالٌ

Forms VII and IX do not occur.

VOCABULARY

يَئِسَ (ـَ) (مِنْ) to despair (of)

أَيْأَسَ IV to drive to despair

يَبِسَ (ـَ) to be, become, dry

يَبَّسَ II to dry

يَسُرَ (ـُ) to be, become, easy

يَسَّرَ II to facilitate

اِسْتَيْقَظَ X to wake up, awaken

أَيْقَظَ IV to wake anyone up

وَاجَهَ III to face, stand up to, encounter

اِتَّجَهَ VIII to turn towards

وَجَبَ عَلَى (ـِ) to be incumbent on, the duty of

وَافَقَ III to agree with

اِتَّفَقَ VIII to agree together; to happen

وَرَدَ (ـِ) to arrive; to come to water (of animal)

وَصَفَ (ـِ) to describe

سَرِيرٌ pl. أَسِرَّةٌ bed

عَسُرَ (ـُ) to be difficult

عَسَّرَ II to make difficult

سَاعَدَ III to help

غَضَبٌ anger

يَأْسٌ despair

رِسَالَةٌ pl. رَسَائِلُ essay, letter, message

خَطِرٌ، مُخْطِرٌ dangerous

تَقْوَى piety, fear of God

حَبِيبٌ pl. أَحِبَّاءُ، أَحْبَابٌ loved one, friend

عَجِيبَةٌ pl. عَجَائِبُ marvel, wonder

عَجِيبٌ wonderful

حَرَّكَ II to move *trans.*

تَحَرَّكَ V to move *intrans.*

يَسِيرٌ easy

مَوْقِفٌ pl. مَوَاقِفُ situation; park for vehicles *mod.*

وُصُولٌ arrival

صِلَةٌ link, connection

اِتِّفَاقٌ، اِتِّفَاقِيَّةٌ agreement (political, commercial, and otherwise)

وَارِدَاتٌ imports

صَادِرَاتٌ exports

وَعْدٌ *pl.* وُعُودٌ promise

وَصْفٌ *pl.* أَوْصَافٌ description

صِفَةٌ quality

عَسِيرٌ difficult

فَشِلَ (ـَ) to fail

دِقَّةٌ exactitude, accuracy

بِدِقَّةٍ exactly

اَلَّذِى which (*masc.* relative pronoun) (see Ch. 34)

نَشَّفَ to dry

EXERCISE 51

١ — حَتَّى وُصُولِ ٱلْمُسَاعَدَةِ بَئِسَ ٱلْجُنُودُ مِنْ نَتِيجَةِ ٱلْقِتَالِ، لِأَنَّ مَوْقِفَهُمْ قَدْ عَسَرَ. ٢ — وَصَلْنَا إِلَى مَوْقِفِ ٱلْعَرَبَاتِ، وَتَرَكْنَا سَيَّارَتَنَا فِيهِ. ٣ — بَشَّرَتِ ٱلْحُكُومَةُ بِٱلِٱتِّفَاقِيَّةِ ٱلْإِنْكِلِيزِيَّةِ ٱلْمِصْرِيَّةِ ٱلْجَدِيدَةِ. ٤ — أَصْبَحَتِ ٱلْأَرْضُ يَابِسَةً، وَفَشِلَتِ ٱلزِّرَاعَةُ فَكَانَتِ ٱلْوَارِدَاتُ أَكْثَرَ مِنَ ٱلصَّادِرَاتِ. ٥ — عَلَى ٱلْمَسَاجِينِ أَنْ يَسْتَيْقِظُوا حَالًا وَيَقِفُوا فِى حُجَرِهِمْ لِتَفْتِيشِ ٱلْمُدِيرِ. ٦ — لَا تَضَعْ يَدَيْكَ عَلَى ٱلْمَائِدَةِ. ٧ — وَاجَهَ حَسَنٌ عَدُوَّهُ وَفِى قَلْبِهِ غَضَبٌ وَيَأْسٌ. ٨ — وَرَدَتْ رِسَالَةٌ مُهِمَّةٌ مِنْهُ فِيهَا وَعْدُ ٱلْمُسَاعَدَةِ. ٩ — وَصَفَ ٱلْمُؤَلِّفُ عَجَائِبَ ٱلدُّنْيَا فِى كِتَابٍ عَجِيبٍ. ١٠ — إِنَّ ٱلتَّقْوَى مِنْ صِفَاتِ ٱلْمُؤْمِنِ. ١١ — يَا طَبَّاخَاتُ، لَا تُعَسِّرْنَ ٱلْيَسِيرَ، بَلِ ٱعْمَلْنَ أَعْمَالَكُنَّ حَتَّى يَيْسَرَ ٱلْعَسِيرُ. ١٢ — لَا تَتَحَرَّكْ يَا أَسِيرُ وَصِفْ لِى صِلَتَكَ بِهٰؤُلَاءِ ٱلرِّجَالِ. ١٣ — يَجِبُ عَلَيْكُمْ

أَنْ تَتَوَافَقُوا فِى هٰذِهِ ٱلْأُمُورِ. ١٤ — وَبَيْنَمَا كَانَ رَاقِدًا عَلَى سَرِيرِهِ،
ٱتَّفَقَ أَنَّ رَجُلًا غَيْرَ مَعْرُوفٍ أَيْقَظَهُ. ١٥ — نَشَّفَتِ ٱلنِّسَاءُ مَلَابِسَهُنَّ
وَلَبِسْنَهَا وَٱتَّجَهْنَ إِلَى ٱلْجُنُودِ. ١٦ — مَاذَا وَعَدتَّ؟ أَوَافَقْتَهُمْ؟ إِذَنْ
أَيْأَسْتَنِي. ١٧ — حَرِّكُوا أَيْدِيَكُمْ. ١٨ — نَحْنُ مُوَافِقُونَ لِذٰلِكَ فِى أَوْقَاتِ
ٱلشِّدَّةِ هٰذِهِ. ١٩ — ضَعُوا أَقْلَامَكُمْ عَلَى مَوَائِدِكُمْ. ٢٠ — وَرَدَ ٱلْجَمَلُ
ٱلْمَاءَ وَشَرِبَ كَثِيرًا وَلَمْ يَقِفْ حَتَّى وُصُولِى.

EXERCISE 52

1. Quickness to anger is a bad quality. 2. How many apples have you promised? It is your duty to bring more than that. 3. We have described all these events to you so that you may know that piety is preferable to despair, and we have put our ideas in our many letters to you during a period of two years. 4. The situation of our loved ones is perilous. They face difficulties from every side. 5. He had despaired of life before your arrival. 6. My wife drives me to despair, as she wakes me up every day in the morning. 7. We stopped in the car park and alighted (نزل) from our vehicles. 8. This agreement between two enemies is remarkable. It is [one] of (use مِنْ) the wonders of the world. 9. Speech is easy, but deeds are hard. 10. He has described the qualities of the Arabs exactly. 11. Dry that book which has fallen into the water, so that you can use it again for your lessons. 12. The pupil turned towards his teacher and his tongue became dry from fear. 13. By chance (ٱتِّفَاقًا) the animal came to the water, and the trees moved. 14. I attempted a description of that animal, but failed because of its quickness. 15. Let us agree together and facilitate matters. 16. Your anger has made them difficult. 17. We will arrive in two hours time, since the road has become hard. 18. Wake up, women, and do your duty in the kitchen. 19. My work has become easy. 20. I don't agree with you.

CHAPTER TWENTY-EIGHT

(اَلْبَابُ ٱلثَّامِنُ وَٱلْعِشْرُونَ)

The Hollow Verb

1. *Hollow verbs* (فِعْلٌ أَجْوَفُ) are those in which the middle radical is و or ى. They are conjugated according to the following rules:

(a) In the Perfect if the final radical is vowelled, the weak letter (i.e. و or ى) changes to the long vowel *'alif*.

e.g. كَانَ for كَوَنَ, he was.

قَامَتْ for قَوَمَتْ she stood up.

بَاعُوا for بَيَعُوا they sold.

(b) In the Imperfect if the final radical is vowelled, the weak middle radical is changed to و, ى or ا, in accordance with the vowelling of the particular verb, as shown in the dictionary.

خَافَ to fear; أَخَافُ I fear.

قَامَ to stand up; نَقُومُ we stand up.

بَاعَ to sell; تَبِيعُونَ you (*pl.*) sell.

(c) If the final radical is unvowelled (e.g. in the Jussive, Imperative, or other parts in which the final radical regularly has *sukūn* before its pronominal suffix) the weak middle radical disappears, but the preceding initial radical takes the short vowel appropriate to the vowelling of the particular verb.

كَانَ (ـُ) to be; كُنْتُ I was.

قَامَ (ـُ) to stand up; قُمْنَ they (*f. pl.*) stood up.

بَاعَ (ـِ) to sell; نَبِعْ let us sell (Jussive). بِعْتُ I sold.

نَامَ (ـَ) to sleep; يَنَمْنَ they (*f. pl.*) sleep.

NOTE: In applying the above three rules the beginner is advised to compare with some simple regular verb. For example, if he has to write "I was", he may take "I opened" as a model. This is فَتَحْتُ and the final radical, ح has *sukūn*. According to rule (c), therefore, the middle radical, the *wāw* of كَانَ must be removed, and we have كُنْتُ. Most verbs of the form كَانَ، يَكُونُ have a *ḍamma* in the Perfect when the middle radical is elided, e.g.

صَامَ (ـُ) to fast; صُمْتُ I fasted

Most having the form بَاعَ، يَبِيعُ also take *kasra* in the Perfect when there is no middle radical. بِعْتُ I sold. The common exceptions are:

نَالَ to obtain, نِلْتُ I obtained; with Imperfect يَنَالُ.

نَامَ to sleep, نِمْتُ I slept; with Imperfect يَنَامُ.

(d) In the Imperative, not only does the middle radical disappear when the final radical is unvowelled (as in the Jussive), but in addition, the prefixed *'alif* of the regular Imperative is omitted, e.g.

قَالَ to say; Imperative قُلْ (*m. s.*)

but قُولِي (*f. s.*)

بَاعَ to sell; Imperative بِعْنَ (*f. pl.*)

.but بِيعُوا (*m. pl.*)

(e) In the root form the weak medial is changed to *hamza* in the Active Participle:

قَالَ قَائِلٌ   بَاعَ بَائِعٌ

(f) For verbs with *kasra* in the Imperfect, the Passive Participle is of the pattern مَبِيعٌ, sold. Otherwise, it is as مَقُولٌ, said; مَخُوفٌ, feared.

2. Conjugation of قَامَ (ـُ) (for قَوَمَ), to rise, set out; (with بِ) to carry out, undertake.

Perfect

Sing.	قَامَ	Dual	قَامَا	Plural	قَامُوا
,,	قَامَتْ	,,	قَامَتَا	,,	قُمْنَ
,,	قُمْتَ	,,	قُمْتُمَا	,,	قُمْتُمْ
,,	قُمْتِ			,,	قُمْتُنَّ
,,	قُمْتُ			,,	قُمْنَا

Imperfect

		Indic.	Subj.	Juss.
Sing.	3. m.	يَقُومُ	يَقُومَ	يَقُمْ
,,	3. f.	تَقُومُ	تَقُومَ	تَقُمْ
,,	2. m.	تَقُومُ	تَقُومَ	تَقُمْ
,,	2. f.	تَقُومِينَ	تَقُومِى	تَقُومِى
,,	1.	أَقُومُ	أَقُومَ	أَقُمْ
Dual	3. m.	يَقُومَانِ	يَقُومَا	يَقُومَا
,,	3. f.	تَقُومَانِ	تَقُومَا	تَقُومَا
,,	2.	تَقُومَانِ	تَقُومَا	تَقُومَا
Plur.	3. m.	يَقُومُونَ	يَقُومُوا	يَقُومُوا
,,	3. f.	يَقُمْنَ	يَقُمْنَ	يَقُمْنَ
Plur.	2. m.	تَقُومُونَ	تَقُومُوا	تَقُومُوا
,,	2. f.	تَقُمْنَ	تَقُمْنَ	تَقُمْنَ
,,	1.	نَقُومُ	نَقُومَ	نَقُمْ

Imperative

S. 2. m.	قُمْ		
,, 2. f.	قُومِى	Part. Act.	قَائِمٌ
D. 2.	قُومَا	Part. Pass.	مَقُومٌ
Pl. 2. m.	قُومُوا		
,, 2. f.	قُمْنَ		

Passive

Perf.	Imperf. Indic.	Subj.	Juss.
قِيمَ	يُقَامُ	يُقَامَ	يُقَمْ
قِيمَتْ	تُقَامُ	تُقَامَ	تُقَمْ
قِمْتَ	تُقَامُ	تُقَامَ	تُقَمْ
قِمْتِ	تُقَامِينَ	تُقَامِى	تُقَامِى
قِمْتُ	أُقَامُ	أُقَامَ	أُقَمْ
etc.	etc.	etc.	etc.

3. Conjugation of verb, whose middle radical is ى : صَارَ (for صَيَرَ) to become.

Perfect

Sing. 3. m.	صَارَ	Dual	صَارَا	Plural	صَارُوا
,, 3. f.	صَارَتْ	,,	صَارَتَا	,,	صِرْنَ
,, 2. m.	صِرْتَ	,,	صِرْتُمَا	,,	صِرْتُمْ
,, 2. f.	صِرْتِ			,,	صِرْتُنَّ
,, 1.	صِرْتُ			,,	صِرْنَا

Imperfect

		Indic.	Subj.	Juss.
Sing.	3. m.	يَصِيرُ	يَصِيرَ	يَصِرْ
,,	3. f.	تَصِيرُ	تَصِيرَ	تَصِرْ
,,	2. m.	تَصِيرُ	تَصِيرَ	تَصِرْ
,,	2. f.	تَصِيرِينَ	تَصِيرِى	تَصِيرِى
,,	1.	أَصِيرُ	أَصِيرَ	أَصِرْ
Dual	3. m.	يَصِيرَانِ	يَصِيرَا	يَصِيرَا
,,	3. f.	تَصِيرَانِ	تَصِيرَا	تَصِيرَا
,,	2.	تَصِيرَانِ	تَصِيرَا	تَصِيرَا
Plur.	3. m.	يَصِيرُونَ	يَصِيرُوا	يَصِيرُوا
,,	3. f.	يَصِرْنَ	يَصِرْنَ	يَصِرْنَ
,,	2. m.	تَصِيرُونَ	تَصِيرُوا	تَصِيرُوا
,,	2. f.	تَصِرْنَ	تَصِرْنَ	تَصِرْنَ
,,	1.	نَصِيرُ	نَصِيرَ	نَصِرْ

Imperative

صِرْ

صِيرِى

صِيرَا

صِيرُوا

صِرْنَ

Part. Act. صَائِرٌ

Part. Pass. مَصِيرٌ

Passive

Perf.	Imperf. Indic.	Subj.	Juss.
صِيرَ	يُصَارُ	يُصَارَ	يُصَرْ
صِيرَتْ	تُصَارُ	تُصَارَ	تُصَرْ
صِرْتَ	تُصَارُ	تُصَارَ	تُصَرْ
etc.	etc.	etc.	etc.

4. Conjugation of the form فَعِلَ.

خَافَ (for خَوِفَ) to fear

Perf.	Imperf. Indic.	Subj.	Juss.
خَافَ	يَخَافُ	يَخَافَ	يَخَفْ
خَافَتْ	تَخَافُ	تَخَافَ	تَخَفْ
خِفْتَ	تَخَافُ	تَخَافَ	تَخَفْ
خِفْتِ	تَخَافِينَ	تَخَافِي	تَخَافِي
خِفْتُ	أَخَافُ	أَخَافَ	أَخَفْ
etc.	etc.	etc.	

Imperative

خَفْ	Part. Act. خَائِفٌ
خَافِي etc.	Part. Pass. مَخُوفٌ

Passive

Perf.	Imperf. Indic.	Subj.	Juss.
خِيفَ	يُخَافُ	يُخَافَ	يُخَفْ
خِيفَتْ	تُخَافُ	تُخَافَ	تُخَفْ
خِفْتَ etc.	etc.	etc.	etc.

DERIVED FORMS

5. In forms II, III, V, VI, and IX, the weak medial is treated as if it were a normal sound letter, and therefore irregularity does not occur. In the following tables, therefore, students should observe carefully forms IV, VII, VIII and X, where the hollowness still remains. They should also note that in these forms there is no distinction of vowelling between verbs like قَالَ with *wāw* and those like بَاعَ with *yā'*. Note the compensatory feminine ending of the verbal nouns in IV and X. Note that the weak radical becomes *'alif* in both Perfect and Imperfect in VII and VIII. Special attention should be paid to IV, which is tricky to the beginner.

6. Derived Forms of the Hollow Verb with Medial *wāw*:

	Perf.	Imperf. Indic.	Imper.	Part. Act.	Part. Pass.
II.	قَوَّمَ	يُقَوِّمُ	قَوِّمْ	مُقَوِّمٌ	مُقَوَّمٌ
III.	قَاوَمَ	يُقَاوِمُ	قَاوِمْ	مُقَاوِمٌ	مُقَاوَمٌ
IV.	أَقَامَ	يُقِيمُ	أَقِمْ	مُقِيمٌ	مُقَامٌ
V.	تَقَوَّمَ	يَتَقَوَّمُ	تَقَوَّمْ	مُتَقَوِّمٌ	مُتَقَوَّمٌ
VI.	تَقَاوَمَ	يَتَقَاوَمُ	تَقَاوَمْ	مُتَقَاوِمٌ	مُتَقَاوَمٌ
VII.	اِنْقَامَ	يَنْقَامُ	اِنْقَمْ	مُنْقَامٌ	مُنْقَامٌ
VIII.	اِقْتَامَ	يَقْتَامُ	اِقْتَمْ	مُقْتَامٌ	مُقْتَامٌ
IX.	اِسْوَدَّ	يَسْوَدُّ	اِسْوَدِدْ	مُسْوَدٌّ	wanting.
X.	اِسْتَقَامَ	يَسْتَقِيمُ	اِسْتَقِمْ	مُسْتَقِيمٌ	مُسْتَقَامٌ

Verbal Noun

II.	تَقْوِيمٌ	V.	تَقَوُّمٌ	VIII.	اِقْتِيَامٌ
III.	مُقَاوَمَةٌ	VI.	تَقَاوُمٌ	IX.	اِسْوِدَادٌ
IV.	إِقَامَةٌ	VII.	اِنْقِيَامٌ	X.	اِسْتِقَامَةٌ

7. Derived forms of the Hollow Verb with Medial *yā'*:

	Perf.	Imperf. Indic.	Imper.	Part. Act.	Part. Pass.
II.	صَيَّرَ	يُصَيِّرُ	صَيِّرْ	مُصَيِّرٌ	مُصَيَّرٌ
III.	صَايَرَ	يُصَايِرُ	صَايِرْ	مُصَايِرٌ	مُصَايَرٌ
IV.	أَصَارَ	يُصِيرُ	أَصِرْ	مُصِيرٌ	مُصَارٌ
V.	تَصَيَّرَ	يَتَصَيَّرُ	تَصَيَّرْ	مُتَصَيِّرٌ	مُتَصَيَّرٌ
VI.	تَصَايَرَ	يَتَصَايَرُ	تَصَايَرْ	مُتَصَايِرٌ	مُتَصَايَرٌ
VII.	إِنْصَارَ	يَنْصَارُ	إِنْصَرْ	مُنْصَارٌ	مُنْصَارٌ
VIII.	إِصْطَارَ	يَصْطَارُ	إِصْطَرْ	مُصْطَارٌ	مُصْطَارٌ
IX.	إِبْيَضَّ	يَبْيَضُّ	إِبْيَضِضْ	مُبْيَضٌّ	wanting.
X.	إِسْتَصَارَ	يَسْتَصِيرُ	إِسْتَصِرْ	مُسْتَصِيرٌ	مُسْتَصَارٌ

Verbal Noun.

II.	تَصْيِيرٌ	V.	تَصَيُّرٌ	VIII.	إِصْطِيَارٌ
III.	مُصَايَرَةٌ	VI.	تَصَايُرٌ	IX.	إِبْيِضَاضٌ
IV.	إِصَارَةٌ	VII.	إِنْصِيَارٌ	X.	إِسْتِصَارَةٌ

VOCABULARY

أَقَامَ IV to set, set up, place; (with فِى) to settle, stay (in a place)

خَوَّفَ II ; أَخَافَ IV to terrify

إِسْتَرَاحَ X to rest

رَاحَةٌ rest, ease

إِسْتِرَاحَةٌ rest-house

مَاتَ (ـُ) to die

قَالَ (ـِ) to take a siesta

طَالَ (ـُ) to be long

طَوَّلَ II to make long; to take a long time

أَطَالَ IV to lengthen

سَارَ (ـِ) to go, journey

عَادَ (ـُ) to return

أَعَادَ IV to repeat, bring back

اِعْتَادَ VIII to be accustomed to

أَصَابَ IV to hit the mark, afflict, attack

نَاوَلَ III to hand over (with double *accusative*)

سُلْطَةٌ authority, rule, control

اَلسُّلُطَاتُ the authorities

سُهُولَةٌ ease, easiness

صِحَّةٌ health, soundness

أَرَادَ IV to wish, want

زَارَ (ـُ) to visit

اِزْدَادَ VIII to increase *intrans.*

أَطَاعَ IV to obey

اِسْتَطَاعَ X to be able (with object in *accus.*, or *subjunctive* preceded by أَنْ)

بَحَثَ (ـَ) to investigate

صَانَ (ـُ) to protect

صِيَانَةٌ protection, conservation

تُرَابٌ soil, earth

فَرَّ (ـِ) to flee, run away

جَعَلَ (a) with *object*: to make
(b) with *imperfect* verb: to begin doing anything

زَوْجٌ *pl.* أَزْوَاجٌ husband, one of a pair

رَصَاصَةٌ bullet

بُنْدُقِيَّةٌ *pl.* بَنَادِقُ rifle, gun

صَاحَ (ـِ) to cry out

نَوْمٌ sleep

طَارَ (ـِ) to fly

طَائِرَةٌ *pl.* ـَاتٌ aeroplane

طَيَّارٌ aviator, pilot

مَطَارٌ *pl.* ـَاتٌ airfield, airport

مَصْلَحَةٌ *pl.* مَصَالِحُ department (of government), interest (e.g. in his interests)

EXERCISE 53

١ — أَقَامَ ٱلْعَرَبُ فِى بَعْضِ مُدُنِ سُورِيَا لٰكِنَّهُمْ لَمْ يَفْرَحُوا فِيهَا.
٢ — طِرْنَا لِمَحَلٍّ بَعِيدٍ فِى الصَّحْرَاءِ، وَنَزَلْنَا فِى الاِسْتِرَاحَةِ الحُكُومِيَّةِ.
٣ — كَانَ الْمَطَارُ هُنَاكَ صَغِيرًا جِدًّا، وَلٰكِنَّ الطَّيَّارَ يَعْرِفُهُ مِنْ زَمَانٍ
(for some time). ٤ — كُنَّا فِى طَائِرَةٍ إِنْكِلِيزِيَّةٍ، وَنِمْتُ أَنَا فِيهَا أَثْنَاءَ
السَّفَرِ كَعَادَتِى فِى البَيْتِ. ٥ — لٰكِنْ صَحِبَنَا سَائِحَانِ فَرَنْسِيَّانِ لَمْ يَزُورَا
البِلَادَ مِنْ قَبْلُ. فَلَمْ يَسْتَطِيعَا النَّوْمَ. ٦ — أَصْبَحَتْ صِيَانَةُ التُّرَابِ
مِنْ أَهَمِّ الحَاجَاتِ فِى الشَّرْقِ. ٧ — أَصَابَتْ حُسَيْنًا رَصَاصَةٌ مِنْ
بُنْدُقِيَّةٍ، وَالفَاعِلُ مَجْهُولٌ، وَالمُصَابُ (victim) زَوْجُ أُخْتِى. ٨ — لَا
تَصِحْ حِينَمَا تَفِرُّ، حَتَّى لَا يَعْرِفَ العَدُوُّ شَيْئًا (anything) عَنْ
حَرَكَاتِكَ. ٩ — أَرَدْتُ أَنْ أَزُورَ البِلَادَ الشَّمَالِيَّ، لٰكِنِّى ٱنْتَظَرْتُ وُصُولَ
الرَّبِيعِ لِشِدَّةِ الشِّتَاءِ هُنَاكَ وَٱزْدِيَادِ البَرْدِ فِى ذٰلِكَ الفَصْلِ. ١٠ — يَا
سَيِّدِى المُحْتَرَمُ، أُخْبِرُكَ بِأَنِّى أَسْتَطِيعُ أَنْ أَسِيرَ لِدِمَشْقَ وَأَنْ أَعُودَ مِنْهَا
بَعْدَ يَوْمَىْ رَاحَةٍ، كَمَا (as) قُلْتَ لِى. خَادِمُكَ المُطِيعُ، حَسَنٌ.
١١ — الدُّنْيَا (here, meaning 'weather') حَارَّةٌ ٱلْآنَ، فَلْنَسْتَرِحْ هُنَا
سَاعَةً حَتَّى نُعِيدَ قُوَّتَنَا وَنَصُونَ صِحَّتَنَا. ١٢ — لِمَاذَا طَوَّلْتِ فِى السُّوقِ،
يَا زَوْجَتِى لَعَلَّ التُّجَّارَ قَدْ بَاعُوا جَمِيعَ بَضَائِعِهِمْ لَكِ. ١٣ — أَنْتَ أَصْبَحْتَ
ضَعِيفًا مِنْ ذٰلِكَ العَمَلِ، أَمَّا أَنَا فَإِنِّى أَعْتَادُهُ. ١٤ — نَاوِلْنِى فِنْجَانَ
شَاىٍ جَدِيدٍ. ١٥ — أَخُوكَ خَائِفٌ. هَلْ خَوَّفْتَهُ؟ ١٦ — لَا، هُوَ
يُخَافُ بِسُهُولَةٍ. ١٧ — أَطَالَ (may . . . prolong) ٱللّٰهُ حَيَاتَكَ

(*Perfect* used for pious wish). ١٨ — طَالَ مَرَضُ النِّسَاءِ لٰكِنَّهُنَّ
مُتْنَ أَخِيرًا (in the end). ١٩ — ابْعُدْ مِنِّي، (عَنِّي) لَعَلَّكَ تُصَابُ
بِهٰذَا المَرَضِ الخَطِرِ. ٢٠ — صُنْ سِرَّكَ وَعَلَى أَيِّ حَالٍ لَا تَتَكَلَّمْ
عَنْهُ لِلنِّسَاءِ وَالأَطْفَالِ.

EXERCISE 54

1. An inspector of the Soil Conservation Department flew from the city to investigate the problem. 2. He returned and handed over his report to the Minister. 3. The latter put it on his desk, but was unable to do anything (شَيْءٌ) because his wife began to visit him in his office every afternoon (every day after noon), and he left most of his work to a clerk. 4. We wish to write about this because difficulties have increased in the government recently. 5. Every official must do his duty and obey orders. 6. The sentry's sleeping was the cause of his being hit by a bullet. 7. Preserve your rifles, soldiers, and do not flee before the enemy. 8. How many times have I said that to you, but you have not listened. 9. We must not take the siesta in times of war. 10. They arrived by aeroplane and settled in a place near the airfield. 11. Their habit was to emerge every evening and terrify the inhabitants. 12. I think it best that you travel by air like the other tourists. 13. Hassan was a brave airman and died in his plane. 14. Take your ease (*translate literally*) in the rest house. 15. I am glad that the authorities have extended your stay here. 16. Take it easy, and have another look (lit. return the look) at these papers. 17. Perhaps you will find in them something which (مَا) will not please you. 18. Your visit has lasted a long time. I think it best that you set out at once, and return to your people, your relations, and your country. 19. Are you accustomed to my ideas or not (أَمْ لَا)? 20. Our relations with his government frightened his enemies greatly.

CHAPTER TWENTY-NINE

(اَلْبَابُ التَّاسِعُ وَالْعِشْرُونَ)

The Verb with Weak Final Radical

(*Defective Verb*)

1. The verb with weak final radical is called فِعْلٌ نَاقِصٌ in Arabic, and, sometimes, in English, by the somewhat ambiguous term *Defective*. The weak radical may be considered to have been originally either *wāw* or *yā'*, but it may be written also as *'alif*, according to the following rules:

(a) When the Perfect has ا, the Imperfect ***must*** have و.

e.g. دَعَا to call; Imperfect يَدْعُو

(b) When the Perfect has *yā'*, the Imperfect also ***must*** have *yā'*. This occurs in the following types:

(i) faعala, yafعilu رَمَى، يَرْمِي to throw.

(ii) faعila, yafعalu لَقِيَ، يَلْقَى to meet.

(iii) ***The passive of all forms.***

e.g. دُعِيَ يُدْعَى to be called.

رُمِيَ يُرْمَى to be thrown.

لُقِيَ يُلْقَى to be met.

Note that the final *yā'* in some instances is ***'alif maqṣūra***, and is pronounced like *'alif*.

(c) There is also a rare form which has *wāw* in Perfect and Imperfect. These are verbs of the form faعula, yafعulu. An example is سَرُوَ يَسْرُو to be noble; but the beginner is unlikely to encounter this type.

(d) In the derived forms the weak final is always written as *yā'* in both tenses, whatever the root form may be, e.g.

إِلْتَقَى to meet (لَقِيَ VIII),

تَدَاعَى, to call one another (دَعَا VI).

2. Rules for the elision of the weak radical.

(a) Complicated rules will not be given. It is better to see from the tables. Nevertheless, it is important to note that in the verb when the weak radical is the last letter of the word it is removed in those parts where it should be unvowelled. This applies to the Jussive and Imperative.

e.g. from رَمَى	إِرْمِ	throw!
دَعَا	أُدْعُ	call!
لَقِيَ	إِلْقَ	meet! (I).
إِلْتَقَى	إِلْتَقِ	meet! (VIII)

(b) In the Verbal Noun of derived forms III (type فِعَالٌ), IV, VII, VIII, IX and X, the weak radical, when occurring after *'alif*, is changed to *hamza*:

From	لَاقَى III	v.n.	لِقَاءٌ
,,	أَلْقَى IV	,,	إِلْقَاءٌ
,,	إِنْلَقَى VII	,,	إِنْلِقَاءٌ
,,	إِلْتَقَى VIII	,,	إِلْتِقَاءٌ
,,	إِعْمَايَ IX	,,	إِعْمِيَاءٌ
,,	إِسْتَلْقَى X	,,	إِسْتِلْقَاءٌ

3. Conjugation of دَعَا to call (of the form فَعَلَ).

Perfect

Singular		Dual		Plural	
3. masc.	دَعَا	3. masc.	دَعَوَا	3. masc.	دَعَوْا
3. fem.	دَعَتْ	3. fem.	دَعَتَا	3. fem.	دَعَوْنَ
2. masc.	دَعَوْتَ	2.	دَعَوْتُمَا	2. masc.	دَعَوْتُمْ
2. fem.	دَعَوْتِ			2. fem.	دَعَوْتُنَّ
1.	دَعَوْتُ			1.	دَعَوْنَا

Imperfect

	Indic.	Subj.	Juss.
Sing. 3. masc	يَدْعُو	يَدْعُوَ	يَدْعُ
,, 3. fem.	تَدْعُو	تَدْعُوَ	تَدْعُ
,, 2. masc.	تَدْعُو	تَدْعُوَ	تَدْعُ
,, 2. fem.	تَدْعِينَ	تَدْعِي	تَدْعِي
,, 1.	أَدْعُو	أَدْعُوَ	أَدْعُ
Dual 3. masc.	يَدْعُوَانِ	يَدْعُوَا	يَدْعُوَا
,, 3. fem.	تَدْعُوَانِ	تَدْعُوَا	تَدْعُوَا
,, 2.	تَدْعُوَانِ	تَدْعُوَا	تَدْعُوَا
Plur. 3. masc.	يَدْعُونَ	يَدْعُوا	يَدْعُوا
,, 3. fem.	يَدْعُونَ	يَدْعُونَ	يَدْعُونَ
,, 2. masc.	تَدْعُونَ	تَدْعُوا	تَدْعُوا
,, 2. fem.	تَدْعُونَ	تَدْعُونَ	تَدْعُونَ
,, 1.	نَدْعُو	نَدْعُوَ	نَدْعُ

Imperative

Sing. masc.	اُدْعُ	Dual	اُدْعُوَا	Plur. masc.	اُدْعُوا
,, fem.	اُدْعِي			,, fem.	اُدْعُونَ

Part. Active

Sing. nom. masc.	دَاعٍ	(with Art.	اَلدَّاعِي)	fem.	دَاعِيَةٌ
,, accus. ,,	دَاعِيًا	(,, ,,	اَلدَّاعِيَ)	,,	دَاعِيَةً
,, gen. ,,	دَاعٍ	(,, ,,	اَلدَّاعِي)	,,	دَاعِيَةٍ

Dual nom. masc.	دَاعِيَانِ	fem.	دَاعِيَتَانِ
,, gen. accus. ,,	دَاعِيَيْنِ	,,	دَاعِيَتَيْنِ
Plur. nom. ,,	دَاعُونَ	,,	دَاعِيَاتٌ
,, gen. accus. ,,	دَاعِينَ	,,	دَاعِيَاتٍ

Part. Pass. مَدْعُوٌّ

Passive Perfect

Sing. 3. masc.	دُعِيَ	Dual	دُعِيَا	Plur.	دُعُوا
,, 3. fem.	دُعِيَتْ	,,	دُعِيَتَا	,,	دُعِينَ
,, 2. masc.	دُعِيتَ	,,	دُعِيتُمَا	,,	دُعِيتُمْ
,, 2. fem.	دُعِيتِ			,,	دُعِيتُنَّ
,, 1.	دُعِيتُ			,,	دُعِينَا

	Pass. Imperf. Indic.	Subj.	Juss.
Sing. 3. masc.	يُدْعَى	يُدْعَى	يُدْعَ
„ 3. fem.	تُدْعَى	تُدْعَى	تُدْعَ
„ 2. masc.	تُدْعَى	تُدْعَى	تُدْعَ
„ 2. fem.	تُدْعَيْنَ	تُدْعَيْ	تُدْعَيْ
„ 1.	أُدْعَى	أُدْعَى	أُدْعَ
Dual 3. masc.	يُدْعَيَانِ	يُدْعَيَا	يُدْعَيَا
„ 3. fem.	تُدْعَيَانِ	تُدْعَيَا	تُدْعَيَا
„ 2.	تُدْعَيَانِ	تُدْعَيَا	تُدْعَيَا
Plur. 3. masc.	يُدْعَوْنَ	يُدْعَوْا	يُدْعَوْا
„ 3. fem.	يُدْعَيْنَ	يُدْعَيْنَ	يُدْعَيْنَ
„ 2. masc.	تُدْعَوْنَ	تُدْعَوْا	تُدْعَوْا
„ 2. fem.	تُدْعَيْنَ	تُدْعَيْنَ	تُدْعَيْنَ
„ 1.	نُدْعَى	نُدْعَى	نُدْعَ

The following points should be particularly noted in the above tables:

(a) Active Perfect: The final radical disappears in the 3rd Person Fem. Sing. and Dual. In the 3rd Pers. Masc. Plural also it disappears, but the previous radical has a diphthong to compensate it:

دَعَوْا *daʿaw*, for دَعَوُوا *daʿawū*.

(b) Active Imperfect: Note the elision of the weak *wāw* in the 2nd P. Fem. Sing., and the 2nd and 3rd P. Masc. Plur. in both Indicative and Subjunctive. In the Jussive it also disappears in all parts in which it would otherwise be the final letter. The same applies to the Imperative.

(c) The complicated forms of the Active Participle should be especially noted, as some of these participles are of frequent use as nouns, e.g. قَاضٍ a judge; دَاعٍ muezzin. Used thus, with technical meanings, these Active Participles take broken plurals of the form قُضَاةٌ, دُعَاةٌ when applied to human beings.

(d) The Passive table above can be taken as a model for all *Defective Verbs* whatever the vowelling of the Active may be.

4. Conjugation of the verb رَضِيَ (عَنْ) to be pleased (with)

(Of the form فَعِلَ)

Perfect

Sing. 3. masc.	رَضِيَ	Dual	رَضِيَا	Plur.	رَضُوا
,, 3. fem.	رَضِيَتْ	,,	رَضِيَتَا	,,	رَضِينَ
,, 2. masc.	رَضِيتَ	,,	رَضِيتُمَا	,,	رَضِيتُمْ
,, 2. fem.	رَضِيتِ			,,	رَضِيتُنَّ
,, 1.	رَضِيتُ			,,	رَضِينَا

	Imperf. Indic.	Subj.	Juss.
Sing. 3. masc.	يَرْضَى	يَرْضَى	يَرْضَ
,, 3. fem.	تَرْضَى	تَرْضَى	تَرْضَ
,, 2. masc.	تَرْضَى	تَرْضَى	تَرْضَ
,, 2. fem.	تَرْضَيْنَ	تَرْضَيْ	تَرْضَيْ
,, 1.	أَرْضَى	أَرْضَى	أَرْضَ

	Imperf. Indic.	Subj.	Juss.
Dual 3. masc.	يَرْضَيَانِ	يَرْضَيَا	يَرْضَيَا
„ 3. fem.	تَرْضَيَانِ	تَرْضَيَا	تَرْضَيَا
„ 2.	تَرْضَيَانِ	تَرْضَيَا	تَرْضَيَا
Plur. 3. masc.	يَرْضَوْنَ	يَرْضَوْا	يَرْضَوْا
„ 3. fem.	يَرْضَيْنَ	يَرْضَيْنَ	يَرْضَيْنَ
„ 2. masc.	تَرْضَوْنَ	تَرْضَوْا	تَرْضَوْا
„ 2. fem.	تَرْضَيْنَ	تَرْضَيْنَ	تَرْضَيْنَ
„ 1.	نَرْضَى	نَرْضَى	نَرْضَ

Imperative

Sing. masc.	اِرْضَ	Dual	اِرْضَيَا	Plur. masc.	اِرْضَوْا
„ fem.	اِرْضَيْ			„ fem.	اِرْضَيْنَ

Part. Act. رَاضٍ (with article اَلرَّاضِي) Part. Pass. مَرْضِيٌّ

Pass. Perf. رُضِيَ (see دُعِيَ) Imperf. Indic. يُرْضَى (see يُدْعَى)

The Passive of this measure is exactly the same as the Active, but for the change of the vowelling of the initial radical.

5. Conjugation of رَمَى to throw (of the form فَعَلَ).

Perfect

Sing. 3. masc.	رَمَى	Dual	رَمَيَا	Plur.	رَمَوْا
„ 3. fem.	رَمَتْ	„	رَمَتَا	„	رَمَيْنَ
„ 2. masc.	رَمَيْتَ	„	رَمَيْتُمَا	„	رَمَيْتُمْ
„ 2. fem.	رَمَيْتِ			„	رَمَيْتُنَّ
„ 1.	رَمَيْتُ			„	رَمَيْنَا

	Imperf. Indic.	Subj.	Juss.
Sing. 3. masc.	يَرْمِى	يَرْمِىَ	يَرْمِ
,, 3. fem.	تَرْمِى	تَرْمِىَ	تَرْمِ
,, 2. masc.	تَرْمِى	تَرْمِىَ	تَرْمِ
,, 2. fem.	تَرْمِينَ	تَرْمِى	تَرْمِى
,, 1.	أَرْمِى	أَرْمِىَ	أَرْمِ
Dual 3. masc.	يَرْمِيَانِ	يَرْمِيَا	يَرْمِيَا
,, 3. fem.	تَرْمِيَانِ	تَرْمِيَا	تَرْمِيَا
,, 2.	تَرْمِيَانِ	تَرْمِيَا	تَرْمِيَا
Plur. 3. masc.	يَرْمُونَ	يَرْمُوا	يَرْمُوا
,, 3. fem.	يَرْمِينَ	يَرْمِينَ	يَرْمِينَ
,, 2. masc.	تَرْمُونَ	تَرْمُوا	تَرْمُوا
,, 2. fem.	تَرْمِينَ	تَرْمِينَ	تَرْمِينَ
,, 1.	نَرْمِى	نَرْمِىَ	نَرْمِ

Imperative

Sing. masc.	اِرْمِ	Dual	اِرْمِيَا	Plur. masc.	اِرْمُوا
,, fem.	اِرْمِى			,, fem.	اِرْمِينَ

Verbal Noun رَمْىٌ

Part. Act. رَامٍ (with article اَلرَّامِى)   Part. Pass. مَرْمِىٌّ

Pass. Perf. رُمِىَ   Imperf. Indic. يُرْمَى

رُمِيتُ etc.   تُرْمَى etc.

6. Derived Forms are standard, whatever the vowelling of the root, and the final radical invariably appears as *yā'*.

Conjugation of the Derived forms of all Defective verbs.

	Perf.	Imperf. Indic.	Imper.	Part. Act.	Part. Pass.
II	لَقَّى	يُلَقِّي	لَقِّ	مُلَقٍّ	مُلَقًّى
III	لَاقَى	يُلَاقِي	لَاقِ	مُلَاقٍ	مُلَاقًى
IV	أَلْقَى	يُلْقِي	أَلْقِ	مُلْقٍ	مُلْقًى
V	تَلَقَّى	يَتَلَقَّى	تَلَقَّ	مُتَلَقٍّ	مُتَلَقًّى
VI	تَلَاقَى	يَتَلَاقَى	تَلَاقَ	مُتَلَاقٍ	مُتَلَاقًى
VII	اِنْلَقَى	يَنْلَقِي	اِنْلَقِ	مُنْلَقٍ	مُنْلَقًى
VIII	اِلْتَقَى	يَلْتَقِي	اِلْتَقِ	مُلْتَقٍ	مُلْتَقًى
IX	Very rare				
X	اِسْتَلْقَى	يَسْتَلْقِي	اِسْتَلْقِ	مُسْتَلْقٍ	مُسْتَلْقًى

Verbal Noun

II تَلْقِيَةٌ	V تَلَقٍّ	VIII اِلْتِقَاءٌ
III مُلَاقَاةٌ and لِقَاءٌ	VI تَلَاقٍ	IX Very rare
IV إِلْقَاءٌ	VII اِنْلِقَاءٌ	X اِسْتِلْقَاءٌ

The following points should be noted:

(a) The elision of the final radical in the Active Participle of the simple verb. These words are declined like دَاعٍ, already given in full.

(b) The nunation (with *kasra*) of the Active Participle in the derived forms of the verb is changed to ـًى in the definite, e.g. مرمٍ throwing, a thrower (from أرمى IV); المرمِي, the thrower; مرمِي الحجرة, the thrower of the stone.

(c) The *'alif maqṣūra* of the Passive Participle in the derived forms loses its nunation when the word is definite, e.g. ملقًى, الملقى. The feminine is ملقاة, الملقاة.

(d) Verbal Nouns: Note that in Form II these verbs always have the form تفعلة, not تفعيل. In III the first form of the verbal noun has an *'alif* in place of the weak radical, before the feminine ending. Forms V and VI elide the final radical when indefinite and they change the *ḍamma* of the middle radical of the regular verb to *kasra*. The *yā'* reappears when the word is definite. Finally, the verbal nouns in forms III (second type), IV, VII, VIII, IX and X have a final *hamza* in place of the weak radical.

(e) Form IX is extremely rare in this type of verb, but when it occurs, the doubled final radical appears as an 'alif followed by a *yā'*. From عمِي to be or become blind, we also have اعمايَ with the same meaning. The XIth Form also occurs, and in it the *yā'* is doubled, as it should be, e.g. اعمايّ, also with the same meaning.

7. When an attached pronoun is added to any word ending in *'alif maqṣūra*, the latter is written as an *'alif*, according to its actual sound. This applies to pronominal objects of defective verbs.

e.g. رمى he threw; رماه he threw him or it.

يلقى he meets; يلقاهم he meets them.

لاقى he encountered; لاقاك he encountered you.

But note that the *yā'*, if preceded by *kasra*, is no longer an *'alif maqṣūra*.

e.g. لَقِيَ he met; لَقِيَهُ he met him.

يَرْمِي he throws; يَرْمِيهِ he throws it.

The same change to *ʾalif* occurs also in nouns.

e.g. رِضًى consent; رِضَاهَا her consent. بِدُونِ رِضَاهَا without her consent.

This rule does not apply to the prepositions عَلَى "on" and إِلَى "to", which, as already shown, become diphthongs when a pronoun is attached, e.g. عَلَيْهَا on her, it; إِلَيْهِمْ to them, etc.

8. The Defective and Hollow Verbs can cause much difficulty for the beginner in one way or another. This is particularly so when he encounters certain forms of these verbs in unvowelled Arabic. Let us take as an example the phrase لم يقل. Here it would be difficult to tell whether the verb is:

from a hollow verb (ـُ) قَالَ

" " " " (ـِ) قَالَ

" " doubled " قَلَّ

" " defective " قَلَا ، قَلَى

The root of the verb in the phrase لم يجد could be either وَجَدَ or جَادَ or جَدَّ. In most cases, of course, the context should prove a guide to the correct root. Where there is doubt the student may have to check several possible roots before finding the correct one.

VOCABULARY

رَجَا (ـُ) to hope for, request (*acc.* of person or thing)

رَجَاءٌ hope

تَلَا (ـُ) to read, recite

دَعَا (ـُ) to call, pray for, invite

اِدَّعَى VIII to claim

اِسْتَدْعَى X to summon

دَنَا مِنْ (ـُ) to approach

شَكَا (ـُ) (مِنْ ، عَنْ) to complain (about)

شَكْوَى *pl.* شَكَاوٍ complaint

نَادَى III to call

نَجَا (ـُ) to escape

عَفَا (ـُ) (عن) to forgive

صَفَا (ـُ) to be pure, clear

صَافٍ pure, clear

سَمَّى II to name, call (doubly *trans.*; or second object with ب)

بَكَى (ـِ) to weep

جَرَى (ـِ) to run, flow, happen

مَشَى (ـِ) to walk, go

مُشَاةٌ infantry (*pl.* of Act. Part.)

مَوَاشٍ cattle *pl.* of مَاشِيَةٌ

تَغَدَّى V to lunch, have lunch

تَعَشَّى V to dine, have dinner, supper

أَعْطَى IV to give (doubly *trans.*)

مَضَى (ـِ) to pass, go away

مَاضٍ (*with article* المَاضِى) **past**, last

قَضَى (ـِ) to decide, judge

اِقْتَضَى VIII to demand, require

قَاضٍ *pl.* قُضَاةٌ judge (Cadi)

بَنَى (ـِ) to build

سَقَى (ـِ) to water

غُشِيَ عَلَيْهِ *Pass.* he fainted

غُشِيَ عَلَيْهَا *Pass.* she fainted

تَمَنَّى V to wish, hope, **beg**

رَبَّى II to train, bring up, breed

تَرْبِيَةٌ education, upbringing

مَعْهَدٌ *pl.* مَعَاهِدُ institute

تُوُفِّيَ V *Pass.* to die

هَدَى (ـِ) to guide

صِرَاطٌ road, path (Quranic)

مُسْتَقِيمٌ straight

رَضِيَ عَنْ (ـَ) to be contented with, approve of

نَسِيَ (ـَ) to forget

نِسْيَانٌ forgetfulness, forgetting

بَقِيَ (ـَ) to remain

بَقَاءٌ remaining *n.*, existence

دَارُ الْبَقَاءِ the Hereafter, Heaven (lit. the House of Eternity)

لَقِيَ (ـَ) to meet someone

لَاقَى III ,, ,, ,,

أَلْقَى IV to throw

اِلْتَقَى VIII to meet one another

مُرٌّ bitter

امْرُؤٌ, مَرْءٌ man

عَاقَبَ (III) to punish

جَوٌّ sky, air, atmosphere

جَوِّيٌّ air- *adj.*

بَرِيدٌ post, mail

خَلَقَ (ـُ) to create

شَيْطَانٌ *pl.* شَيَاطِينُ Satan, devil

سَائِرٌ rest, remainder (with following *genitive*)

بَدَلًا عَنْ ، مِنْ instead of

عَالٍ *with article* العَالِي high

أَغْلَبِيَّةٌ majority

بَاصٌ ، بَصٌّ *pl.* بَاصَاتٌ bus

عِيدُ الْمِيلَادِ Christmas

EXERCISE 55

١ — أَرْجُوكَ أَنْ لَا (أَلَّا) تَدْعُوَ ذٰلِكَ الرَّجُلَ لِأَنَّهُ يَدَّعِي أَنَّهُ أَشْجَعُ جُنْدِيٍّ فِي جَيْشِ أَمِيرِ الْمُؤْمِنِينَ. ٢ — اِسْتَدْعِ صَاحِبَ الطَّائِرَةِ وَاسْأَلْهُ مِمَّا (مِنْ مَا for) يَشْكُو. ٣ — لِنُنَادِ التَّاجِرَ الْمَسْجُونَ وَنَقُلْ لَهُ إِنَّنَا قَدْ عَفَوْنَا عَنْهُ. ٤ — دَنَا الْجَمَاعَةُ وَتَلَوْا الْقُرْآنَ بِصَوْتٍ عَالٍ. ٥ — فَلْيَكُنِ الرَّجَاءُ فِي قَوْلِكَ بَدَلًا مِنَ الشَّكْوَى. ٦ — بَكَتْ زَوْجَةُ الْخَلِيفَةِ الْمُتَوَفَّى ثُمَّ قَبِلَتْ دَعْوَتَهُمْ. ٧ — نَجَا أَغْلَبِيَّةُ الْمُشَاةِ بِحَيَاتِهِمْ وَهُدُوا إِلَى مَحَلٍّ فِيهِ (in which) مَاءٌ وَأَكْلٌ. ٨ — تَغَدَّيْنَا فِي بَيْتِكَ ، فَاسْتَحْسِنْ أَنْ تَتَعَشَّى عِنْدِي. ٩ — أَعْطِنِي خُبْزًا وَزُبْدًا حَتَّى لَا أَمُوتَ.

١٠ — أَتَمَنَّى أَنْ يَكُونَ القَاضِى قَدْ لاَقَى عَمَّهُ فِى أَثْنَاءِ زِيَارَتِهِ لِعَدَن.
١١ — مَشَتِ البِنْتُ لِتَزُورَ عَمَّتَهَا لٰكِنَّهَا رَجَعَتْ بِالْبَاصِ. ١٢ — لاَ
تَشُكَّ لِمَا مَضَى : فَكِّرْ فِى المُسْتَقْبَلِ. ١٣ — بَنَى القَاضِى بَيْتًا جَدِيدًا
فِى حَيِّ العَرَبِ، وَسَكَنَهُ فِى الشَّهْرِ المَاضِى. ١٤ — اِهْدِنَا الصِّرَاطَ
المُسْتَقِيمَ (Quran, sura I). ١٥ — بَقُوا وَاقِفِينَ مُدَّةً طَوِيلَةً، ثُمَّ غُشِىَ
عَلَى رَجُلَيْنِ مِنْهُمْ وَغَلَبَهُمَا النِّسْيَانُ. ١٦ — يَا خَادِمُ، أَلْقِ هٰذَا
الخِطَابَ فِى الصُّنْدُوقِ الخَاصِّ بِالْبَرِيدِ الجَوِّىِّ لَعَلَّهُ يَصِلُ أَخِى فِى
إِنْكِلْتَرَّا قَبْلَ عِيدِ المِيلَادِ. ١٧ — كَانَتِ الأَحْوَالُ تَقْتَضِى أَنْ نُرَبِّى
أَوْلَادَنَا فِى مَعْهَدِ التَّرْبِيَةِ. ١٨ — خَلَقَنَا اللّٰهُ لِأَنْ نَرْجِعَ إِلَيْهِ بَعْدَ
المَوْتِ. وَنَسْكُنَ دَارَ البَقَاءِ. ١٩ — هٰذَا المَرْءُ مِثْلُ شَيْطَانٍ لَا يَرْضَى
عَنِ الصَّالِحَاتِ (righteous deeds). ٢٠ — تَذَكَّرَ زَيْدٌ مَا جَرَى لٰكِنْ
نَسِيَهُ سَائِرُ الرِّجَالِ. ٢١ — سَقَيَا بُسْتَانَيْهِمَا بِالمَاءِ الصَّافِى. أَمَّا
مَوَاشِيهِمَا فَأَشْرَبَاهَا مَاءً مُرًّا. ٢٢ — لَقِيتُ كَلْبًا فِى شَارِعِ « غُرْدُونَ »
(Gordon) فَحَمَلْتُهُ إِلَى بَيْتِى وَسَمَّيْتُهُ بِغُرْدُونَ بَعْدَ ذٰلِكَ. ٢٣ —
فَلْنَلْتَقِ فِى الجُنَيْنَةِ لِأَنَّ الجَوَّ جَمِيلٌ اليَوْمَ. ٢٤ — حَضَرَ السَّارِقُونَ
المَحْكَمَةَ وَقُضِىَ (حُكِمَ or) عَلَيْهِمْ بِالسِّجْنِ.

EXERCISE 56

1. Abu Bakr (may God be pleased with him!) (Use Perfect, "God has been pleased with him", for a pious wish) was the first Caliph in the history of the Islamic State. 2. We read in the opening sura (سُورَةٌ) of the Quran: "Lead us in the straight path". 3. The foreign traveller mounted a swift

camel and escaped. For two months he drank camels' milk, and found it very bitter, because he was used to cow's milk. 4. They met in an elevated place, and the atmosphere was pure there. They had become disgusted with the smoke of cities. 5. Hassan will remain here instead of his father. As for the rest of those present, let them lunch with us, then we will give them the presents, and they can leave. 6. I used to meet him in the bus every day when I was studying in the Institute of Education. 7. We hope that the judge will treat these men as (كَمَا) they deserve when they appear before him. They stole many letters from the air mail, and opened them. Then, when they found no money in them, they threw them in the river. 8. Indeed, they are devils, and the majority of the inhabitants of this city fear them. 9. In the past many people complained about your friend's doings, but we forgave him. Now we shall weep, but we shall also punish him. 10. The teacher said to the girls: "Run", and to the boys, "Walk!". 11. Have you forgotten that your father died last week? 12. God created us that we might go to heaven. 13. I have called you, so approach me and tell me about your complaint. 14. The foreign commander did not know correct Arabic, so he called the infantry "cattle"! 15. Summon the man who (ٱلَّذِى) claims that his son is a prophet. 16. You two have built a beautiful house, you have watered a beautiful garden, but you have not brought up your children; and this is the most important of your duties as parents and Muslims. 17. We hope that you will reçite the Quran in the mosque tomorrow. You are the best reciter in the village. 18. Our hearts have become pure. 19. The ministers have invited me to dine with them. 20. This invitation was unexpected, and I cannot go as I am busy that night. 21. He greeted her, and passed on to his uncle's house, and remained there until sunset.

CHAPTER THIRTY

(اَلْبَابُ ٱلثَّلَاثُونَ)

The Doubly and Trebly Weak Verb

1. Taking the hamza as a weak consonant, it is possible for two, or even three, radicals of a triliteral verb to be weak. Such verbs were termed لَفِيف (*complicated, tangled*) by the philologers. They are, obviously, of rare occurrence, but they do include some common verbs, and, in any case, they must be given for completeness. The following types may be encountered:

2. Verbs with *wāw* and *yā'* as 2nd and 3rd radicals respectively. These must be conjugated as Deficient verbs, the Medial *wāw* remaining in all parts. Consequently there is no need to give any tables, e.g.

رَوَى يَرْوِي to recount, transmit,

(hence رِوَايَة a story or play).

Imperative, اِرْوِ

The derived forms present no problems.

3. Doubled verbs with *yā'* as Medial and Final Radicals. Conjugation of حَيِيَ also written حَيَّ (for حَيِوَ) to live.

Perf.	Imperf. Indic.
حَيِيَ	يَحْيَى (also written يَحْيَا)
حَيِيتُ	
حَيِيتَ etc.	

In the derived forms, the second *yā'* is changed to *'alif*, e.g. in Form IV أَحْيَا (to resuscitate, revive)

In X the forms إِسْتَحْيَا , إِسْتَحَى and إِسْتَحَى (to spare alive, to feel ashamed) are encountered. The second *yā'* of this root appears to have been originally a *wāw*, as is seen in the word حَيَوَانٌ animal.

4. Verbs in which the first and third radicals are weak letters. These follow the rules that govern the conjugation of the Assimilated and the Defective verbs; e.g.

Perf. وَقَى to guard: Imperf. Indic. يَقِي; Juss. يَقِ.

Imper. Masc. Sing. قِ; Fem. Sing. قِي; Plur. قُوا.

Part. Act. وَاقٍ (with Article الْوَاقِي).

VIII. form إِتَّقَى to fear (God).

Perf. وَفَى to be complete, fulfil (a promise).

IV. form أَوْفَى to fulfil a vow; Imperf. Indic. يُوفِي; Imper. أَوْفِ; Verbal Noun إِيفَاءٌ.

Perf. وَلِيَ to be near, follow; Imperf. Indic. يَلِي; Juss. يَلِ; Imper. لِ.

5. Verbs with *wāw* or *yā'* for all three radicals. Only يَيِيَ is encountered, and that only in II يَيَّا , to write, a beautiful *yā'*.

	Perfect	Imperfect	Jussive
3. m.	يَيَّا	يُيَيِّي	يُيَيِّ
3. f.	يَيَّتْ	etc.	
2. m.	يَيَّيْتَ	etc.	
	etc.		

6. Doubled Verbs with Initial *hamza*, e.g.

(ـُـ) أَجَّ to burn (ـُـ) أَمَّ to direct one's steps towards.

Such verbs must follow the rules of the doubled verb, and those of the Verb with initial *hamza*. Needless to say, the *hamza* cannot be removed (e.g. as the Imperative of أَخَذَ).

Conjugation أَجَّ	Perfect	Imperfect Indicative	Jussive
Sing. 3. m.	أَجَّ	يَؤُجُّ	يَأْجُجْ or يَؤُجَّ
„ 3. f.	أَجَّتْ	تَؤُجُّ	etc. etc.
„ 2. m.	أَجَجْتَ	تَؤُجُّ	
„ 2. f.	أَجَجْتِ	تَؤُجِّينَ	
„ 1.	أَجَجْتُ	أَؤُجُّ	

7. Verbs with Initial *hamza* and Medial *wāw* or *yā'*:

These are conjugated like hollow verbs, save that the rules of orthography for the *hamza* must be followed:

e.g. آبَ for أَوَبَ to return.

Perf.	Imperf. Indic.	Juss.
آبَ	يَؤُوبُ (also written يَؤُبُ)	يَؤُبْ
آبَتْ	تَؤُوبُ	تَؤُبْ
أُبْتَ etc.	تَؤُوبُ etc.	تَؤُبْ etc.

Imper.		
أُبْ	Part. Active	آئِبٌ
أُوبِي	Pass. Perf.	إِيبَ

So too the rarer verbs:

آفَ (for أَوَفَ), to injure.

آلَ (for أَوَلَ), to come, return.

آدَ (for أَيَدَ), to be strong. II أَيَّدَ to strengthen.

8. Verbs with Medial *hamza* and Initial *wāw* or *yā'*. These are very rare, but the following are the most common.

(ـَـ) يَئِسَ, to despair. As is usual with verbs with Initial *yā'* that letter is not elided. With *wāw* we find وَأَلَ ، يَئِلُ, to seek refuge; and the Quranic وَأَدَ ، يَئِدُ, to bury (a female child) alive. In these the *wāw* is elided according to the rules for the Assimilated Verb, and the orthography of the *hamza* follows the normal rules.

In the unlikely event of derived forms being encountered, they follow the normal rules; e.g. from وَأَدَ VIII إِتَّأَدَ to act slowly, Imperfect يَتَّئِدُ, Imperative اِتَّئِدْ. It should be noted that the *hamza* is a normal consonant, and may therefore be doubled; e.g. تَوَأَّدَ V; Imperfect يَتَوَأَّدُ; with the same meaning as VIII.

9. The Hollow Verb with final *hamza*. This is an extremely common class, and in many parts, the *hamza* is written, as the Arabs say, "on the line", that is, to our way of thinking, suspended in mid-air,

e.g. سَاءَ for سَوَأَ to be bad.

جَاءَ for جَيَأَ to come.

Conjugation of جَاءَ to come.

Perf.	Imperf. Indic.	Juss.
جَاءَ	يَجِيءُ	يَجِئْ
جَاءَتْ	تَجِيءُ	تَجِئْ
جِئْتَ etc.	تَجِيءُ etc.	تَجِئْ etc.

Imper.

جِئْ	Verbal Noun مَجِيءٌ
جِيئِي etc.	Part. Active جَاءٍ (with Article اَلْجَائِي)
	Pass. Perf. جِيءَ Imperf. يُجَاءُ

The student may wonder how such a verb can have a Passive. But verbs in Arabic may be transitive through a preposition, and this especially applies to verbs of motion which, with بِ, mean to bring or take;

e.g. جَاءَ بِ to bring. ذَهَبَ to go; ذَهَبَ بِ to take (away).

سَاءَ (for سَوَأَ) to be bad.

Perf.	Imperf. Indic.	Juss.
سَاءَ	يَسُوءُ	يَسُؤْ
سَاءَتْ	تَسُوءُ	تَسُؤْ
سُؤْتَ	تَسُوءُ	تَسُؤْ
etc.	etc.	etc.

Imper.

سُؤْ Verbal Noun سُوْءٌ

سُوئِي Part. Active سَاءٍ (with Article اَلسَّائِي)

Pass. Perf. سِيءَ Imperf. Indic. يُسَاءُ

Of the Derived forms is IV أَسَاءَ to make bad; Imperf. Indic. يُسِيءُ; Imper. أَسِئْ; Verbal Noun إِسَاءَةٌ; Part. Act. مُسِيءٌ.

Conjugation of شَاءَ (for شَيِءَ) to wish.

Perf.	Imperf. Indic.	Juss.
شَاءَ	يَشَاءُ	يَشَأْ
شَاءَتْ	تَشَاءُ	تَشَأْ
شِئْتَ etc.	تَشَاءُ etc.	تَشَأْ etc.

Imper. شَأْ Verbal Noun شَيْءٌ and مَشِيئَةٌ

Pass. Perf. شِيءَ Part. Act. شَاءٍ (with Article اَلشَّائِي).

10. Verbs with Medial *hamza* and Final *yā'*. These include the common verb رَأَى to see, which also has certain irregularities of its own, in that the *hamza* is dropped in the Imperfect and Imperative, and in Form IV.

Perfect.

Sing.	3. masc.	رَأَى	Dual	رَأَيَا	Plur.	رَأَوْا
,,	3. fem.	رَأَتْ	,,	رَأَتَا	,,	رَأَيْنَ
,,	2. masc.	رَأَيْتَ	,,	رَأَيْتُمَا	,,	رَأَيْتُمْ
,,	2. fem.	رَأَيْتِ			,,	رَأَيْتُنَّ
,,	1.	رَأَيْتُ			,,	رَأَيْنَا

		Imperfect Indic.	Subj.	Juss.
Sing.	3. masc.	يَرَى	يَرَى	يَرَ
,,	3. fem.	تَرَى	تَرَى	تَرَ
,,	2. masc.	تَرَى	تَرَى	تَرَ
,,	2. fem.	تَرَيْنَ	تَرَيْ	تَرَيْ
,,	1.	أَرَى	أَرَى	أَرَ
Dual	3. masc.	يَرَيَانِ	يَرَيَا	يَرَيَا
,,	3. fem.	تَرَيَانِ	تَرَيَا	تَرَيَا
,,	2.	تَرَيَانِ	تَرَيَا	تَرَيَا
Plur.	3. masc.	يَرَوْنَ	يَرَوْا	يَرَوْا
,,	3. fem.	يَرَيْنَ	يَرَيْنَ	يَرَيْنَ
,,	2. masc.	تَرَوْنَ	تَرَوْا	تَرَوْا
,,	2 fem.	تَرَيْنَ	تَرَيْنَ	تَرَيْنَ
,,	1.	نَرَى	نَرَى	نَرَ

Imperative

Sing. رَ	Dual رَيَا	Plur. رَوْا
„ رَىْ		„ رَيْنَ

Verbal Noun رَأْى

Part. Active رَاءٍ (with Article اَلرَّائِى)

Part. Pass. مَرْئِىّ

Pass. Perf. رُئِىَ Imperf. Indic. يُرَى

When united with a suffix the forms used are رَآهُ he saw him; يَرَاهَا he sees her, etc.

Of the Derived Forms the following occur:

III. رَاءَى, to dissemble; Imperf. Indic. يُرَائِى; Verbal Noun مُرَاءَاةٌ or رِئَاءٌ.

IV. أَرَى to show; Imperf. Indic. يُرِى; Juss. يُرِ; Imper. أَرِ; Verbal Noun إِرَاءٌ or إِرَاءَةٌ.

VI. تَرَاءَى to look at one another.

VIII. اِرْتَأَى to think.

11. Verbs with Initial *hamza* and Final *yā'* or, rarely, *wāw*. These include the extremely common verb (ـِـ) أَتَى, to come; (also, with or without بِ) to bring. (ـِـ) أَبَى to deny, refuse. These verbs are conjugated as Defective Verbs, the *hamza* being always retained.

Perf.	Imperf. Indic.	Subj.	Juss.
أَتَى	يَأْتِى	يَأْتِىَ	يَأْتِ
أَتَتْ	تَأْتِى	تَأْتِىَ	تَأْتِ
أَتَيْتَ etc.	تَأْتِى etc.	تَأْتِىَ etc.	تَأْتِ etc.

Imper. { اِيتِ (from اِئْتِ) also shortened تِ
اِيتِي etc.

Part. Active آتٍ (with Article اَلْآتِي)

Pass. Perf. أُتِيَ Imperf. Indic. يُؤْتَى.

Of this verb the IV form is آتَى "to bring"; Imperf. Indic. يُؤْتِي; Juss. يُؤْتِ; Imper. آتِ; Pass. Perf أُوتِيَ.

12. Verbs with Final *hamza* and Initial *wāw* (or *yā'*). These may occur with different vowellings. For example, there is وَدَأَ, يَدَأُ to level; but the only verb likely to be encountered is وَطِئَ, يَطَأُ to tread. It is conjugated according to the rules of the verb with final *hamza* and the assimilated verb, e.g. Imperative, طَأْ tread.

13. Trebly weak verbs. The doubled verb with initial *hamza* has already been mentioned. There are also وَأَى, يَئِي, to promise, threaten; and أَوَى يَأْوِي (إِلَى) to take refuge (with), the second named being quite common.

The student can work the first out for himself, with the aid of the dictionary, noting that the Imperative masculine singular is just إِ "i"! fem sing. إِي; masc. pl. إُوا.

The few derived forms which may be encountered can be easily worked out by the student himself.

VOCABULARY

رَوَى (ـِ) to recount, tell	أَحْيَا IV to resuscitate, revive
رَاوٍ *pl.* رُوَاةٌ a recounter, transmitter	تَأَجَّجَ V to burn, be aflame
حَيِيَ (ـَ) to live	آبَ (ـُ) to return

سُوءٌ ، سُوءٌ *n.*, evil (badness)

سَيِّئٌ evil *adj.*

أَتَى (ـِ) to come

بِ — to bring

جَاءَ (ـِ) to come

شَاءَ (ـَ) to wish

رَأَى (يَرَى) to see

رِوَايَةٌ *pl.* اتٌ — story, account, play

وَطِئَ (ـَ) to tread

أَوَى (ـِ) إِلَى to take refuge with

آوَى IV to harbour, provide refuge, shelter, lodging

عُمْرٌ life, age

عَيَّنَ II to appoint

زَوَّجَ II to marry (someone to somebody)

تَزَوَّجَ V to marry (someone)

اِخْتَارَ VIII to choose

أَجَابَ عَلَى IV to reply to

ضَابِطٌ *pl.* ضُبَّاطٌ officer

نَفَرٌ *pl.* أَنْفَارٌ private (mil.)

شَاوِيشٌ ، جَاوِيشٌ (*Turk.*) sergeant

سَاقَ (ـُ) to drive

سَائِقٌ ، سَوَّاقٌ driver

اِحْتَاجَ إِلَى VIII to need

عَاشَ (ـِ) to live

أَضَاعَ IV to lose

أَفَادَ IV to benefit *trans.*

فَائِدَةٌ *pl.* فَوَائِدُ benefit, profit, interest

اِسْتَفَادَ مِنْ X to benefit from

نَحْوَ in the direction of, towards *prep.*

غَابَ (ـِ) to be absent, go absent

بَيْضٌ *un.* بَيْضَةٌ eggs

عَامٌّ general *adj.*, public

أَمْكَنَ IV to be possible (for)

خَاصٌّ special

قَضِيَّةٌ *pl.* قَضَايَا case (legal)

قَادَ (ـُ) to lead

قَائِدٌ leader, general

أَنْقَذَ IV to save, deliver

EXERCISE 57

١ — يَرْوِى رَاوٍ مِنَ الرُّوَاةِ أَنَّ سُكَّانَ مَرْوَ (Merv) ٱجْتَمَعُوا حَوْلَ وَالِيهِمْ وصَاحُوا : يَحْيَ حَاكِمُنَا الكَرِيمُ. ٢ — أَيُمْكِنُنِي أَنْ أُحْضِرَ هٰذِهِ القَضِيَّةَ الخَاصَّةَ؟ ٣ — لَمْ تَسْتَفِدْ مِنْ زِيَارَتِكَ لِلسُّوقِ، لِأَنَّكَ بِعْتَ البَيْضَ ثُمَّ أَضَعْتَ الدَّرَاهِمَ. ٤ — زَوَّجَ تَاجِرٌ غَنِيٌّ بِنْتَهُ الجَمِيلَةَ بِضَابِطٍ مِنْ ضُبَّاطِ الجَيْشِ العِرَاقِىِّ. ٥ — وقَبْلَ هٰذَا كَانَ سَائِقُ ذٰلِكَ الضَّابِطِ — وهُوَ نَفَرٌ فى الجَيْشِ — يُرِيدُ أَنْ يَتَزَوَّجَهَا لٰكِنَّ أَبَاهَا أَبَى. ٦ — أُخْتِيرَ حَسَنٌ مُسَاعِدًا لِلْمُدِيرِ العَامِّ. ٧ — رَأَوْا مَدِينَةً كَبِيرَةً فى البُعْدِ فَمَشَوْا نَحْوَ بَابِهَا ودَخَلُوهَا وأَوَوْا إِلَى حَاكِمِهَا. ٨ — كَانَ شَاوِيشٌ يَسُوقُ سَيَّارَةَ القَائِدِ. ٩ — عُمْرُكَ كَمْ سَنَةً؟ ١٠ — عُيِّنَ شَابٌّ وَزِيرًا، ونَحْنُ مُحْتَاجُونَ إِلَى رَجُلٍ قَوِيٍّ. فَمَا فَائِدَةُ تَعْيِينِهِ؟ ١١ — عِشْتَ مَعَنَا سَنَةً ولَمْ تُفِدْنَا شَيْئًا. ١٢ — نَادَى المُعَلِّمُ اسْمَ زَيْدٍ وأَجَابَ صَدِيقُهُ : «غَائِبٌ». ١٣ — كَانَ يَتَأَجَّجُ بِحُبِّ اللّٰهِ ولِذٰلِكَ كَادَ يَحْيَا لِلدِّينِ. ١٤ — لَمَّا أَتَانَا أَوْلَادُنَا بَعْدَ غِيَابٍ (*v.n.*) طَوِيلٍ حَزِنَّا (حَزِنَّا for) مِنْ سُوءِ حَالِهِمْ. ١٦ — قُلْ لَنَا مَا تَشَاءُ. ١٧ — وَطِئْتُ تِلْكَ الأَرْضَ الغَرِيبَةَ ولَمْ أَجِدْ مَنْ (anyone who) يُؤْوِينِى. ١٨ — آبَ وَلَدِى مِنَ المَدْرَسَةِ وجَاءَ بِرِوَايَةٍ سَيِّئَةٍ. ١٩ — سَوْفَ تَجِيءُ بَعْدَ يَوْمَيْنِ وتَرَى سَبَبَ كُلِّ شَيْءٍ. ٢٠ — لَمْ نَرَ مِثْلَ هٰذَا المَشْهُورِ فى الحَرْبِ العَالَمِيَّةِ الكُبْرَى.

EXERCISE 58

1. It is recounted that the general led his army in[to] the inferno of the fighting, and returned defeated (*accusative*), and took refuge with the inhabitants of Merv. 2. We cannot attend this case in the court, because the victim is our friend. 3. The officer appointed an army private as my special driver. 4. The transmitters have brought back to life the history of Islam, and we see the past in their stories. 5. Long live the king. (lit. may the king live). 6. I have chosen a sergeant because the officers have gone absent, all of them. 7. The servant lost the food, so I took advantage of the food of his neighbour's cook. 8. I have long lived in the desert, so I don't need anything. 9. They have not trodden on the soil of their native land for (since) two years, but they will return to it in a month's time. 10. I came, I saw, I conquered. 11. I complained of the badness of my condition, so I got married. 12. My father married me (بِ) to an ugly woman; her name was Hind (هِنْدُ). 13. She provided shelter for me, but did not benefit me. 14. Do not drive my car, you are a bad driver. 15. Bring me those eggs and put them on the table. 16. I said to the beggar: What do you want of (from) me? He replied: I don't want anything of a man like you. 17. The benefits of this good government are known to all (عِنْدَ ٱلْجَمِيعِ). 18. Go towards the city, and stop at the bridge. 19. Bring me flesh and bring me wine! 20. There is (يُوجَدُ) a green hill far away, and they recount that Our Lord (سَيِّدُ) died there to save us all.

CHAPTER THIRTY-ONE

(اَلْبَابُ ٱلْحَادِى وَٱلثَّلَاثُونَ)

The Quadriliteral Verb

1. As far back as the 9th century, Arabic grammarians and philologers had classified Arabic roots as:

(a) *Biliteral,* ثُنَائِىٌّ, including, in their pure form, particles like قَدْ and عَنْ; but also, the doubled verb, though the latter was moulded into triliteral form.

(b) *Triliteral,* ثُلَاثِىٌّ, by far the largest part of the language.

(c) *Quadriliteral,* رُبَاعِىٌّ, comprising many roots, but few derivations and comparatively few common words. Among the nouns are words like عَقْرَبٌ scorpion; بُسْتَانٌ garden; بُرْهَانٌ proof.

(d) *Quinquiliteral,* خُمَاسِىٌّ, a very small section of the vocabulary, and confined to nouns. No verb can have more than four radicals, when the letters of increase are stripped away. Among common quinquiliteral words are عَنْكَبُوتٌ a spider, and عَنْدَلِيبٌ nightingale.

2. Here we are concerned with the quadriliteral; more particularly, its verbs. It has a root form and three derived forms.

The Root Form corresponds in form and vowelling to Form II of the triliteral, e.g. دَحْرَجَ to roll (transitive), compared with عَلِمَ II, عَلَّمَ to teach.

		دَحْرَجَ	عَلَّمَ
Perfect	3. m.	دَحْرَجَ	عَلَّمَ
	3. f.	دَحْرَجَتْ	عَلَّمَتْ
	2. m.	دَحْرَجْتَ	عَلَّمْتَ
	2. f.	دَحْرَجْتِ	عَلَّمْتِ
		etc.	etc.
Imperfect (Indicative)			
	3. m.	يُدَحْرِجُ	يُعَلِّمُ
		etc.	etc.
Imperative			
	m.s.	دَحْرِجْ	عَلِّمْ
		etc.	etc.
Participles			
Active		مُدَحْرِجٌ	مُعَلِّمٌ
Passive		مُدَحْرَجٌ	مُعَلَّمٌ
Verbal Noun			
		دِحْرَاجٌ or دَحْرَجَةٌ	no comparison.
Passive			
Perf.	3 m.	دُحْرِجَ	عُلِّمَ
Imperf.	3 m.	يُدَحْرَجُ	يُعَلَّمُ

Note that the doubled ل of عَلَّمَ corresponds to the unvowelled ح followed by the ر in دَحْرَجَ.

3. Quadriliteral verbal roots are of three types:

(a) Those of genuine four-radical origin, or at least thought to be, e.g. دَحْرَجَ. Sometimes these were of foreign origin, as تَلْمَذَ to make a disciple; and تَرْجَمَ to translate; in both of which the *tā'* is a radical; and عَسْكَرَ to camp, or levy troops.

The Arab philologers noted the frequent presence of the letters ل and ر in quadriliteral and quinquiliteral roots. The term "genuine four-radical" is open to suspicion in many cases, but those wishing to pursue the subject may check Lane's lists of *Quasi-quadriliteral* measures in page xxviii of Vol. I of his Lexicon.

(b) Verbs formed by the doubling of a biliteral root, sometimes with a suggestion of onomatopoeia, e.g. تَمْتَمَ to stammer; غَرْغَرَ to gargle; سَلْسَلَ to form a chain or sequence.

(c) Composite roots taken from a familiar phrase or combination of roots. These are rare, but we may note حَمْدَلَ to say الحَمْدُ لِلّٰهِ; بَسْمَلَ to say بِسْمِ اللّٰهِ.

DERIVED FORMS

4. The root form is expressed in Arabic as فَعْلَلَ, with the derived forms:

II تَفَعْلَلَ; III إِفْعَنْلَلَ; IV إِفْعَلَلَّ.

The following are examples:

II. تَدَحْرَجَ to roll (intrans.)

Imperf. Indic.	يَتَدَحْرَجُ	Imperative	تَدَحْرَجْ
Active Participle	مُتَدَحْرِجٌ	Verbal Noun	تَدَحْرُجٌ

Other verbs of this form are: تَزَلْزَلَ to be shaken; تَمَذْهَبَ to follow a sect.

III. اِخْرَنْطَمَ to raise the nose, be proud.

Imperf. Indic.	يَخْرَنْطِمُ	Imperative	اِخْرَنْطِمْ
Active Participle	مُخْرَنْطِمٌ	Verbal Noun	اِخْرِنْطَامٌ

IV. اِطْمَأَنَّ to be tranquil.

Imperf. Indic.	يَطْمَئِنُّ	Imperative	اِطْمَأْنِنْ
Active Participle	مُطْمَئِنٌّ	Verbal Noun	اِطْمِئْنَانٌ

Other verbs of this form are: اِضْمَحَلَّ to dwindle away; اِقْشَعَرَّ to shudder.

5. Of these only II is fairly common, and it is often passive or stative where I is active or causative. It is also customary to form verbs of this sort from nouns, as in the example given تَمَذْهَبَ; from مَذْهَبٌ a noun from ذَهَبَ to go, which has the specialized meaning of a religious way or sect. Other examples are تَمَسْلَمَ to become a Muslim; تَفَلْسَفَ to philosophize from فَيْلَسُوفٌ a philosopher. Many such verbs are to be found in Modern Arabic such as تَسَوْدَنَ to become (like a) Sudanese; تَأَمْرَكَ to be like (or become) an American.

VOCABULARY

زَخْرَفَ to adorn, embellish

زَخْرَفَةٌ *pl.* زَخَارِفُ adornment

زَلْزَلَ to shake *tr.*, frighten

تَزَلْزَلَ II to shake *intr.*, tremble, quake

غَرْغَرَ to gargle

حَلْقٌ throat

عُنُقٌ ، عُنْقٌ neck

تَرْجَمَ to translate, interpret

مُتَرْجِمٌ translator

تُرْجُمَانٌ interpreter, dragoman, guide

تَمْتَمَ to stammer

دَحْرَجَ to roll *tr.*

تَدَحْرَجَ II to roll *intr.*

هَنْدَسَ to sketch, make a plan

مُهَنْدِسٌ engineer

وَسْوَسَ to whisper, suggest evil (of Satan)

تَفَلْسَفَ II to philosophize

فَلْسَفَةٌ philosophy

فَيْلَسُوفٌ *pl.* فَلَاسِفَةٌ philosopher

تَقَهْقَرَ II to be repulsed, driven back

تَمَذْهَبَ II to follow a sect (مَذْهَبٌ)

صُوفِىٌّ *pl.* صُوفِيَّةٌ Sufi

صُوفٌ wool

اِخْرَنْطَمَ III to be proud

الخَرْطُومُ Khartoum

خُرْطُومٌ elephant's trunk; hose

فِيلٌ *pl.* أَفْيَالٌ elephant

اِضْمَحَلَّ IV to fade away, dwindle

اِطْمَأَنَّ IV to be tranquil, calm

اِقْشَعَرَّ IV to shudder with horror

بَيْطَرَ to practise veterinary surgery

بَيْطَارٌ *pl.* بَيَاطِرَةٌ veterinary surgeon

اِمْتِيَازٌ *pl.* — اتٌ privilege, concession (*modern commercial*)

مَرْكَزٌ centre, headquarters

مَرْكَزِىٌّ central

مَحَلِّىٌّ local

أَشَارَ إِلَى IV to point at, refer to

أَذَاعَ IV to broadcast

مَبْلَغٌ extent; sum (of money)

عَاصِمَةٌ *pl.* عَوَاصِمُ capital (city)

أُذُنٌ *pl.* آذَانٌ ear

عِيدٌ *pl.* أَعْيَادٌ festival, holiday

EXERCISE 59

١ — تَمَذْهَبُوا مَذْهَبَ الصُّوفِيَّةِ فَلَبِسُوا مَلَابِسَ مِنَ الصُّوفِ.

٢ — سَمِعْنَا مِن إِذَاعَةِ الخُرْطُومِ أَنَّ عَدَدًا كَبِيرًا مِنَ الأَفْيَالِ نُظِرَتْ فى جَنُوبِ السُّودَانِ. ٣ — لِذٰلِكَ سَافَرَ رَئِيسُ بَيَاطِرَةِ الحُكُومَةِ المَرْكَزِيَّةِ مِنَ العَاصِمَةِ لِيَرَى حَالَ الحَيَوَانَاتِ. ٤ — كَانَ ذٰلِكَ الرَّجُلُ فَيْلَسُوفًا، وفى فَلْسَفَتِهِ أَنَّ زَخَارِفَ الدُّنْيَا مِن وَسَاوِسِ شَيْطَانٍ. ٥ — لِلْمُهَنْدِسِينَ

اِمْتِيَازَاتٍ خَاصَّةٍ فى البِلادِ الشَّرْقِيَّةِ. ٦ — شَعَرْتُ بِأَلَمٍ فى العُنُقِ
والحَلْقِ فَغَرْغَرْتُ. ٧ — هذا المُتَرْجِمُ يُتَمْتِمُ دائمًا فى قَوْلِهِ لٰكِنَّ
تَرْجَمَتَهُ جَمِيلَةٌ جِدًّا. ٨ — إِنَّهُ قَدْ تَرْجَمَ القُرْآنَ إلى اللُّغَةِ الفارِسِيَّةِ
(Persian). ٩ — يا مُخْرَنْطِمُ إِنَّ شَأْنَكَ سَوْفَ يَضْمَحِلُّ فى المُسْتَقْبَلِ.
١٠ — دَحْرَجَ وَلَدٌ حَجَرَةً مِن سَقْفِ البيتِ فَوَقَعَتْ على رأْسِ عَمِّهِ.
١١ — زَلْزَلَ الولدُ شَجَرَةَ التُّفَّاحِ وَوَقَعَ تُفَّاحٌ كَثيرٌ مِنها. ١٢ — تَقَهْقَرَ
جَيْشُ العَدُوِّ، فَسَوْفَ يَطْمَئِنُّ أَمْرُنَا. ١٣ — لَمَّا أَشَارَ الحَاكِمُ إِلَيْنَا
اِقْشَعْرَرْنَا وَتَزَلْزَلْنَا. ١٤ — إِنَّ مَرْكَزَ الادَارَةِ هو الخُرْطُومُ. ١٥ —
دَفَعَتِ الحُكُومَةُ المَحَلِّيَّةُ مَبْلَغًا كَبِيرًا لإِصْلاحِ الإِدَارَةِ. ١٦ — أَرانى
التُّرْجُمانُ مَنَاظِرَ القَاهِرَةِ المَشْهُورَةَ. ١٧ — زَخْرِفُوا قُلُوبَكُمْ بِالتَّقْوَى،
يا مُؤْمِنُونَ. ١٨ — هذا الرَّجُلُ يَتَفَلْسَفُ، لٰكِنَّهُ لا يَعْرِفُ شَيْئًا عن
الفَلْسَفَةِ. ١٩ — تَكَلَّمْ كَلامًا وَاضِحًا ولا تُتَمْتِمْ. ٢٠ — كانَ الرِّجالُ
يُشِيرُونَ إلى رَئِيسِ الإِدَارَةِ.

EXERCISE 60

1. It has been broadcast in the capital that the sum needed is two pounds per (for each) inhabitant. 2. I refer to the local order about the appointment of veterinary surgeons. 3. This is a matter for the central government. 4. The government has given special privileges to the wool merchants. 5. Why do you follow the Christian way, and you a philosopher? 6. Religion is better than philosophy, for the latter (هذه) will dwindle away. 7. We shuddered with horror when we saw the elephants' trunks. 8. Be tranquil, and do not think about worldly adornments (the adornments of the world).

9. Satan has whispered these thoughts in your ears. 10. The earth trembled, the rocks were rolled from the mountains and the people stammered in their speech. 11. My throat was constricted (closed), I had a pain in my neck, so I gargled with hot water. 12. We have translated this book that you might know and believe. 13. He used to practise veterinary surgery, but now he is a translator in a government office. 14. The women adorned their faces for the holiday. 15. The engineer became famous, so he became proud. 16. Roll that big stone from the door. 17. Why do you always philosophize in times of trouble? 18. They attacked the frontiers but were driven back and defeated. 19. What do you think about the Sufis? 20. I don't know anything (a thing) about them.

CHAPTER THIRTY-TWO

(اَلْبَابُ ٱلثَّانِى وَٱلثَّلَاثُونَ)

Various Unorthodox Verbs

1. The Verb لَيْسَ not to be.

Perfect

Sing. 3. masc.	لَيْسَ	Dual	لَيْسَا	Plur.	لَيْسُوا
,, 3. fem.	لَيْسَتْ	,,	لَيْسَتَا	,,	لَسْنَ
,, 2. masc.	لَسْتَ	,,	لَسْتُمَا	,,	لَسْتُمْ
,, 2. fem.	لَسْتِ			,,	لَسْتُنَّ
,, 1.	لَسْتُ			,,	لَسْنَا

This is all that exists of the verb. Only the Perfect occurs, and when used *it has the meaning of the Imperfect*. Like كَانَ it may take a predicate in the accusative: لَسْتُ عَرَبِيًّا I am not an Arab. It is also used with ب: لَسْتُ بِعَرَبِيٍّ. Note that, unlike other hollow verbs its middle radical does not change to *'alif*.

2. The Verbs نِعْمَ and بِئْسَ are Verbs of *Praise* and *Blame* (أَفْعَالُ ٱلْمَدْحِ وَٱلذَّمِّ). These, like لَيْسَ, only occur in the Perfect, and have the Imperfect meaning. They are only found in the 3rd Person, e.g. نِعْمَ fem. نِعْمَتْ.

Examples of use:

نِعْمَ زَيْدٌ Zaid is good.

نِعْمَ زَيْدٌ مُعَلِّمًا ,, ,, ,, as a teacher.

نَعْمَتْ فَاطِمَةُ Fatima is good.

نَعْمَتْ فَاطِمَةُ زَوْجَةً „ „ „ as a wife.

Or نَعْمَ فَاطِمَةُ, since the verb is sometimes put in the masculine even with a feminine subject, because the Arabs were not certain that these were verbs at all.

THE VERB عَسَى

3. This is one way of saying "perhaps" or "it may be" in Arabic. It is almost never used except in the 3rd Person of the Perfect, and it gives a *Present* or *Future* meaning. It is followed by a sentence in the *Subjunctive* introduced by أَنْ the subject of which is also the subject of عَسَى:

عَسَى زَيْدٌ أَنْ يَقُومَ عَسَى أَنْ يَقُومَ زَيْدٌ	perhaps Zaid is standing, or will stand (difference of emphasis in the two forms). The first sentence suggests "perhaps it is Zaid who will stand".

This verb gives the sense of nearness, and in the rare instances in which it occurs in 1st or 2nd Persons it means "nearly".

عَسَيْتُ أَنْ أَفْعَلَ ذٰلِكَ I am nearly doing that.

THE VERB OF WONDER (أَفْعَالُ التَّعَجُّبِ)

4. The verb of Wonder is formed on the measure of Derived Form IV (with a prefixed *hamza*) from any adjective.

From	حَسَنٌ	good	أَحْسَنَ
	طَيِّبٌ	good	أَطْيَبَ
	سَهْلٌ	easy	أَسْهَلَ

From	كَرِيم	noble	أَكْرَمَ
	جَدِيد	new	أَجَدَّ
	جَيِّد	excellent	أَجْوَدَ

Note that in hollow roots the correct radical appears. In the doubled root, the doubled radical is written with *tashdīd*. They are used as follows:

(a) مَا أَحْسَنَ زَيْدًا how good is Zaid!

مَا أَحْسَنَ فَاطِمَةَ ,, ,, ,, Fatima!

مَا أَحْسَنَ بَيْتَنَا ,, ,, ,, our house!

مَا أَكْرَمَ الرِّجَالَ ,, noble are the men!

مَا أَطْيَبَ الْمُعَلِّمَاتِ ,, good are the teachers (fem.)!

Note that we have here a *verb*, not an adjective. It must always have *fatḥa* at the end, and the noun at which wonder is expressed is its object, and is therefore in the accusative. The verb itself is always masculine singular, and we may, perhaps, imagine مَا to be its subject; "what has made Zaid good?" or "that which . . .!"

(b) A much rarer form, found in the Qur'ān and early poetry in particular, uses the Singular Masculine Imperative of Form IV, and prefixes the Preposition بِ to the object (thing or person).

e.g. أَحْسِنْ بِزَيْدٍ how good is Zaid!

أَحْسِنْ بِفَاطِمَةَ ,, ,, ,, Fatima, etc.

A pronominal object may be used with either form.

مَا أَحْسَنَهُ or أَحْسِنْ بِهِ how good he is!

If two such verbs apply to one object, the second one must take a pronominal termination referring to the object already mentioned.

مَا أَجْمَلَ فَاطِمَةَ وَمَا أَطْوَلَهَا how beautiful is Fatima and how tall.

WISHES (THE OPTATIVE)

5. In Classical Arabic it was customary to express wishes, especially pious wishes in which the name of God was mentioned, in the *Perfect*, as if the wish had already been fulfilled, e.g.

رَحِمَهُ اللّٰهُ May God have mercy on him (literally, God has had mercy on him)

Certain formulae of this kind are used in old literature whenever the name of the Prophet Muhammad or the early saints of Islam are mentioned.

e.g. For the Prophet صَلَّى اللّٰهُ عَلَيْهِ وَسَلَّمَ May God bless him and save him (abbreviated to صلعم).

For the early Khalifas, Companions of the Prophet, etc., رَضِيَ اللّٰهُ عَنْهُ may God be pleased with him (abbreviated to رضه).

This Perfect may be preceded by the negative لا,

e.g. لا شَلَّتْ يَدَاكَ, May thy hands not grow dry!

Later, especially in speech and popular language, the *Imperfect* came to be used in this context, e.g. اللّٰهُ يَرْحَمُهُ or يرحمه الله God have mercy on him! (of the dead).

THE VERB زَالَ

6. The verb زَالَ Imperf. يَزَالُ to cease is used preceded by the negative particles ما, لا, or لَمْ, and followed either by an Imperfect Verb, or a participle or other adjective in the accusative, to mean that the action is still continuing.

ما زال / لم يزل حسن ذاهباً / يذهب — Hassan is still going. (lit. did not cease to go).

ما زالوا يقاتلون / لم يزالوا مقاتلين — they still fought.

لا يزال حيًّا — he is still alive.

Sometimes the *Predicate* after زال may take the form of a *prepositional* phrase:

ما زالت / لم يزل الأمور على تلك الحال — matters were still in that condition.

THE VERB عاد

7. The verb عاد, Imperfect يعود, which is used in the normal manner to mean "to return", has also a special usage in which it means "to do again". Like the previous verb, it may be followed by an Imperfect Verb or an accusative. It occurs sometimes in the *positive*, as well as the *negative*.

ما عاد يرجع — he did not return again.

لم نعد نرجع — we did not return again.

لا تعد تفعل كذلك — do not do so again.

لا أعود أفعله — I will not do it again.

لم يعد المسير ممكنا — the journey was no longer possible.

ضربه وعاد يضربه — he hit him again, went on hitting him.

ضربه ثم عاد — he hit him, then did it again.

THE VERB كَادَ

8. The Verb كَادَ means literally "to be on the point of", but it is used to mean "nearly" or "almost", followed by the Imperfect Indicative, or, occasionally, by أَنْ plus the Subjunctive:

كَادَ أَنْ يَفْعَلَ ذٰلِكَ or كَادَ يَفْعَلُ ذٰلِكَ he nearly did that.

كِدْتُ أَمُوتُ I almost died.

When used in the negative it means "scarcely".

مَا كَادَ يَنْظُرُ إِلَيَّ he scarcely looked at me.

لَمْ يَكَدِ الْعَرَبُ يَقِفُونَ فِى تَقَدُّمِهِمْ the Arabs scarcely halted in their advance.

THE VERB دَامَ

9. The Verb دَامَ, to continue, preceded by the *Conjunction* مَا "as long as" and followed by a verb in the Imperfect, or an Accusative is used to express "as long as, while", e.g.

مَا دَامَ يَقُومُ / مَا دَامَ قَائِمًا } as long as he stands.

مَا دُمْتُ أَقُومُ / مَا دُمْتُ قَائِمًا } as long as I stand.

THE VERBS قَلَّ AND طَالَ

10. The Verb قَلَّ, to be little or rare, is used in the phrase قَلَّ مَا (also written قَلَّمَا) to express "seldom",

e.g. قَلَّ مَا جِئْتَنَا (قَلَّمَا) you have seldom come to us.

The verb طَالَ, Imperf. يَطُولُ, to be long, is used in the phrase طَالَ مَا (also generally written طَالَمَا) to express "for a long time".

e.g. طَالَمَا (طَالَ مَا) شَرَّفْتَنَا long have you honoured us.

THE VERB كَانَ AND ITS SISTERS

11. As already stated, كَانَ may take a *predicate* in the Accusative, e.g. كَانَ مُحَمَّدٌ تَاجِرًا Muhammad was a merchant.

Certain other verbs, termed its "sisters" (أَخَوَاتُ كَانَ) do the same. لَيْسَ has been referred to earlier.

The following are the principal verbs of this group:

بَقِيَ	to remain.
دَامَ	to last, continue (see para. 9).
زَالَ	to cease (see para. 6).
صَارَ (ِ)	to become.
أَصْبَحَ IV	to become; also, to enter upon the morning, or to do in the morning.
أَمْسَى IV	to become; also, to do in the evening, etc.
بَاتَ (ِ)	to become; also, to spend the night.

e.g. بَقِيتُ وَاقِفًا I remained standing.

أَصْبَحَ الْجُنُودُ تَعْبَانِينَ the soldiers became tired.

12. The verbs صَارَ to become; أَخَذَ to take; جَعَلَ to make or do or put, also mean "to begin" when followed by a verb in the Imperfect:

{صَارُوا / أَخَذُوا / جَعَلُوا} يَبْكُونَ they began to weep.

Note also use with Verbal Noun with فِي or بِ,

e.g. أَخَذْنَا بِالْمَسِيرِ we began to travel.

VOCABULARY

اِقْتِصَادٌ economy, economics

اِقْتِصَادِيٌّ economic

مِنْطَقَةٌ *pl.* مَنَاطِقُ region, zone

حَدَثَ (ـُ) to happen; to be new, young

حَدِيثٌ *pl.* أَحَادِيثُ Hadith, tradition of the Prophet

مُحَدِّثٌ a recounter of Hadith

لَدَى with, at

حَلَّ مَحَلَّ . . . (ـِ) to take the place of, fill the position of

أَسَاسٌ *pl.* أُسُسٌ basis, foundation

أَسَّسَ II to found, establish

ثَارَ (ـُ) to rebel

دِعَايَةٌ propaganda

اِنْتَهَى VIII to come to an end

أَدَّى II to perform

أَدَّى إِلَى II to lead to

مَحَطَّةٌ *pl.* ـَاتٌ station

قِطَارٌ *pl.* ـَاتٌ train

بُولِيسٌ ، شُرْطَةٌ police

مُسْتَعْمَرَةٌ colony

اَلاِسْتِعْمَارُ colonisation; imperialism

سَقَطَ (ـُ) to fall

هَبَطَ (ـُ) to fall, descend, land

أَعْلَنَ IV to notify, advertise, announce

إِعْلَانٌ *pl.* ـَاتٌ advertisement, announcement

عَسْكَرِيٌّ *pl.* عَسَاكِرُ soldier, policeman

مُعَسْكَرٌ *pl.* ـَاتٌ camp

حَفْلَةٌ *pl.* ـَاتٌ celebration, party

دَائِرَةٌ *pl.* دَوَائِرُ circle; office

عِنْدَمَا when (*relative*)

عَرَضَ (ـِ) to display, show

مَعْرِضٌ *pl.* مَعَارِضُ show, exhibition

اِتَّصَلَ بِ VIII to link with, get in touch with

خِلَالَ during

تَذْكِرَةٌ *pl.* تَذَاكِرُ ticket

اِشْتَرَى VIII to buy

صَوْتٌ *pl.* أَصْوَاتٌ voice

ضَعُفَ (ـُ) to become weak

تَوَّجَ II to crown

تَاجٌ *pl.* تِيجَانٌ crown

EXERCISE 61

١ — حَدَثَ ذلك خِلَالَ يومِ العيدِ. ٢ — صارَ الناسُ يَبْكُونَ عِنْدَمَا
أُعْلِنَ ٱنْتِهَاءُ المَعْرِضِ. ٣ — أَخَذَتِ النساءُ يَصِحْنَ : فَلْيَسْقُطِ
الاسْتِعْمَارُ، وعُدْنَ يَصِحْنَ حَتَّى ضَعُفَتْ أَصْوَاتُهُنَّ. ٤ — هَبَطَتِ الطائرةُ
على المَطَارِ وخَرَجَ الرُّكَّابُ منها، وجَعَلُوا يَجْرُونَ إلى مَكْتَبِ المُدِيرِ.
٥ — رَأَيْتُ صُورَةَ أَخِي الغَائِبِ فى جَرِيدَةِ البُولِيسِ (الشُّرْطَةِ).
٦ — إِنَّ رَأْىَ الدَّوَائِرِ الرَّسْمِيَّةِ أَنَّ حالَةَ مِنْطَقَتِنَا الاقْتِصَادِيَّةَ ما كَادَتْ
تَتَحَسَّنُ مُنْذُ ٱبْتِدَاءِ السَّنَةِ، ولَيْسَ ذلك بِدِعَايَةٍ. ٧ — ذَهَبَ حسنٌ
إلى المَحَطَّةِ وٱشْتَرَى تَذْكِرَةً لِلْخُرْطُومِ، ثُمَّ رَكِبَ القِطَارَ. ٨ — عَسَى
حسنٌ أَلَّا يَرْجِعَ إِلَيْنَا. ٩ — نِعْمَ البُخَارِيُّ (Al-Bukhārī) مُحَدِّثًا :
إِنَّهُ أَحْسَنُ كَاتِبِ الأَحَادِيثِ : رَحِمَهُ ٱللّٰهُ. ١٠ — ما أَفْضَلَ المَلِكَةَ
وما أَجْمَلَهَا : إِنَّنَا لَمْ نَزَلْ نَحْتَرِمُهَا مُنْذُ يومِ تَتْوِيجِهَا. ١١ — بَدَأَ
التُّجَّارُ يَعْرِضُونَ بَضَائِعَهُمْ لِلْبَيْعِ. ١٢ — دَخَلْتُ بيتَهُ، وهو يَبْقَى
جالسًا لا يَسْتَطِيعُ أَنْ يقومَ لأَنَّهُ ما كان أَكَلَ شيئًا مُدَّةَ أُسْبُوعٍ، ولَيْسَ
لَدَيْهِ دَرَاهِمُ يَشْتَرِى بها (with it) طَعَامًا. ١٣ — مَنْ يَحُلُّ مَحَلَّ
مُؤَسِّسِ هذه المَدْرَسَةِ؟ ١٤ — حَضَرْنَا حَفْلَةَ شَاىٍ فى المُعَسْكَرِ وقَابَلْنَا
عَسَاكِرَ كَثِيرِينَ هُنَاكَ. ١٥ — اِتَّصَلَ الوَزِيرُ بِأَصْحَابِ الجَرَائِدِ، فَأَدَّى

ذلك إلى تحسين العلاقات بين الصحافة والحكومة. ١٦ — قلّما ثار الإنكليز أثناء تاريخهم الطويل. ١٧ — طالما غبت، فأصبحت كغريب أو أجنبيّ. ١٨ — افتتح النادى على أساس جديد، وهو دفع جنيه للسنة. ١٩ — كان محمّد (صلّى الله عليه وسلّم) رسول الله وأبو بكر (رضى الله عنه) خليفته.

EXERCISE 62

1. How excellent is this exhibition; the club will benefit greatly from it. 2. When I attended the party of the circle of authors, a strange thing happened to me. 3. A police ʿaskari came in searching for the revolutionaries. 4. That station used to broadcast a great deal of propaganda under the name of "Voice of Freedom". 5. The science of the *hadith* is very important for the believers. 6. The war had scarcely ended when a new war began, so the great powers fought again. 7. The basis of the new economic policy is not sound. 8. Hassan is still filling the place of the governor of the region. 9. Muhammad (may God bless him and save him!) was a good prophet. 10. Rarely have I read an advertisement like that during my whole life. 11. My father got in touch with his brother, and they began a policy of strict economy. 12. He told the merchants to display their wares in the camp, so that the soldiers would buy them. 13. Down with colonization, for it is not the basis of sound government. 14. The times of trains are advertised in the daily papers. 15. So long as the tickets are dear, I shall travel by donkey. 16. He began to weaken after his coronation; God rest his soul! He is in a better place now! 17. Two stones fell from the wall, but I did not think about them. Then a month later the whole wall broke and fell. 18. The crown became important. 19. He read the whole of the Quran, then read it again. 20. That is the duty of every Muslim.

CHAPTER THIRTY-THREE

(اَلْبَابُ ٱلثَّالِثُ وَٱلثَّلَاثُونَ)

How To Use an Arabic Dictionary

1. It is unfortunately true that only when one has a grasp of the structure of the language, and, in particular, when one knows the various derived forms of the verbs, both strong and weak, is one competent to use an Arabic dictionary with ease. There are two reasons for this. First, practically all Arabic dictionaries enter words under their *roots*. Only the roots are in alphabetical order. Secondly, unless one is familiar with the changes which take place in irregular verbs one has difficulty in deciding under which root to look up many words.

2. Taking the first point, the following words would all appear under عَلِمَ *to know* or *get to know:* عَلَّمَ *to teach;* أَعْلَمَ *to inform;* تَعَلَّمَ *to learn;* إِسْتَعْلَمَ *to ask information;* عَلَّامٌ *a learned person;* عَالَمٌ *world;* مُعَلِّمٌ *teacher;* عَلَمٌ *a sign, token, flag, or milestone.* Therefore, on encountering a strange word the student must first sort out the root letters (usually three) from the letters of increase. He must note, for example, that the ***mīm*** of مجلس *council* is a letter of increase, and that the root is جلس *to sit.* Once the root has been found in the dictionary the student will be faced with a whole series of derivations, often numbering between 30 and 50. The problem is how to find the required derivation quickly. In modern dictionaries the root form of the verb comes first, followed by the various derived forms in numerical order, as given in this grammar. After the verbs come the nouns (and adjectives), beginning with the simplest, that is, those with no letter of increase; then those merely increased by a long vowel; and so on to the derived nouns with the prefixed ***mīm.***

3. The second point, however, concerns "*irregular*" roots, where the beginner may have difficulty in deciding which the root letters are. The following points should be noted, but even so the beginner must be prepared to spend some time looking up a given word under alternative possible roots:

(a) Letters of increase, even those used in pronominal prefixes and suffixes, may also be radicals. For example, the student may think that the verb تَرَكَ (if it is unvowelled in the text) *to leave*, is a doubled verb, and the *tā'* the pronominal prefix of the second person. Again, اِلْتَفَتَ *he glanced* might be اِلْتَفَّتْ *she wrapped herself* from لَفَّ VIII. An initial *'alif* with *hamza* may be a letter of increase, or it may be a radical. أَسَرَ *he imprisoned* might be أَسَرَّ (سَرَّ IV).

(b) Care must be taken in recognizing those verbs which lose a weak radical in certain parts: the Hollow and Defective Verbs in particular, and also the Assimilated Verb. It must be mentioned that the weak letter may be *wāw* or *yā'*, and this will affect the position of the root in the dictionary. True, in many cases the two alternatives do not occur; but we have, for example, both قَالَ (ـُ) *to say*, and قَالَ (ـِ) *to spend the heat of the day in siesta*. The following phrase ما قال, unvowelled, might therefore mean either *he did not say*, or *he did not spend the heat of the day in sleep*.

(c) Certain derivations which are formed in regular manner are not shown in dictionaries. For example, the participles are not given unless they also have a technical nominal meaning. We do not find, for instance, ذَاهِبٌ *going;* but we find مُعَلِّمٌ *a teacher*, Active Participle of عَلَّمَ ; كَاتِبٌ *a clerk;* مَكْتُوبٌ *a letter*, respectively Active and Passive Participles of كَتَبَ. In such cases these nouns are entered among the nouns, not with the verbs. The ***verb of wonder*** is not given, and the comparative-superlative is rarely shown. Noun entries are given under their singular, but good dictionaries designed for Europeans add the plural(s) afterwards, often with the Arabic letter ج meaning جَمْعٌ *plural.* When no broken plural is given, the word must be assumed to have the sound plural, masculine or feminine as the case may be.

4. The student requires a dictionary which shows the following:

(i) Broken plurals, where applicable.

(ii) Full vowelling of the Verb, including the vital vowelling of the Imperfect.

(iii) Verbal Nouns, which are generally given in the accusative (as if they were absolute objects) after their verbs. But with derived forms, where there is only one form of Verbal Noun, it is not given. Where a Verbal Noun has a technical meaning and takes a broken plural, it is entered separately under the noun also, e.g. تَجْرِبَةٌ pl. تَجَارِبُ *experiment*, Verbal Noun of جَرَّبَ *to try, test.*

Unfortunately certain dictionaries, although otherwise good, do not provide this information because they are designed for Arabs learning English, not vice-versa. The reader is assumed, not always correctly, to know these details. Some words have more than one meaning, especially verbs, and these should be noted. Again, certain verbs take a preposition instead of, or even as an alternative to, a direct object. This is given after the verb in the dictionary. Thus رَغِبَ فِي *to love.* This must be used with all parts of the verb where the action is carried on, e.g. الْمَرْغُوبُ فِيهَا *beloved (girl.)* Where a verb takes a direct object this is often indicated by the letters ه or هـ, the former being used for animate beings and the latter for inanimate objects.

5. In order to illustrate the use of a dictionary, the following passage from Ibn Baṭṭūṭa (إبن بطوطة) will be explained:

كُنْتُ اردت الدخول الى ارض الظلمة والدخول اليها من بُلْغار (Bulgaria). وبينهما مسيرة اربعين يوماً. ثم أُضربت عن ذلك لعظم المؤونة فيه وقلة الجدوى. والسفر اليها لا يكون إلا فى عجلات صغار تجرها كلاب كبار. فإن تلك المفازة فيها الجليد. فلا تثبت قدم الآدمى ولا حافر الدابة فيها. والكلاب لها الأظفار فتثبت اقدامها فى الجليد. ولا يدخلها إلا الأقوياء من التجار الذين يكون لأحدهم مائة عجلة أو نحوها موقرة بطعامه وشرابه وحطبه. فإنها لا شجر فيها ولا حجر ولا مدر. والدليل بتلك الأرض هو الكلب الذى قد سار فيها مراراً كثيرة وتنتهى قيمته إلى الف دينار ونحوها. وتربط العربة إلى عنقه. ويُقرن معه ثلاثة من الكلاب ويكون هو المقدَّم. وتتبعه سائر الكلاب بالعربات فإذا وقف وقفت.

أَرَدْتُّ I formed the desire or wish (رود IV).

مَسِيرَةٌ journey, from سَارَ, يَسِيرُ to go, journey.

مَؤُونَةٌ trouble, from مَأَنَ to supply. (مَؤُونَةٌ also means "provisions")

جَدْوَى gift; advantage, profit, from جَدَا, يَجْدُو to make a gift.

تَجُرُّهَا draw them, from جَرَّ to draw, drag.

مَفَازَةٌ desert steppe, from root فَازَ (مِن), يَفُوزُ escape (from).

دَابَّةٌ beast of burden, Act. Part. (*f*). of دَبَّ to walk slowly (of an animal).

تُجَّارٌ merchants, pl. of تَاجِرٌ

مَدَرٌ villages, towns. The root here is مَدَرَ

VOCABULARY

ظُلْمَةٌ darkness

مَسِيرَةٌ journey (distance)

أَرْبَعِينَ يَوْمًا forty days

قِلَّةٌ lack, smallness

عَجَلَةٌ *pl.* ـَاتٌ — wheel (sledge)

جَرَّ (ـُـ) to draw, drag

جَلِيدٌ snow, ice

مَفَازَةٌ desert

ثَبُتَ (ـُـ) to be firm, to grip

آدَمِيٌّ man (from آدَمُ Adam)

حَافِرٌ *pl.* حَوَافِرُ hoof

دَابَّةٌ *pl.* دَوَابُّ beast (of burden)

أَحَدٌ one (of + *gen.*)

ظُفْرٌ *pl.* أَظْفَارٌ claw, talon; finger-nail

مِائَةٌ ، مِئَةٌ a hundred

أَلْفٌ a thousand

أَوْقَرَ IV to load

حَطَبٌ wood, firewood

دَلِيلٌ *pl.* أَدِلَّاءُ guide

اَلَّذِي *pl.* اَلَّذِينَ *m.*, which, who (*relative*)

قِيمَةٌ *pl.* قِيَمٌ price, value

رَبَطَ (ـُـ) to tie, connect, link

ثَلَاثَةٌ three

إِذَا if, when

قَرَنَ (ـِـ) to join, couple

قَرْنٌ *pl.* قُرُونٌ horn; century

ثَوْرٌ *pl.* ثِيرَانٌ bull

أَضْرَبَ عَنْ to leave, forsake a thing, desist from

إِلَّا except, if not

مَرَّةٌ *pl.* ـَاتٌ ، مِرَارٌ — time, turn

مُقَدَّمٌ chief

عُظْمٌ magnitude, greatness

دِينَارٌ Dinar (a coin)

EXERCISE 63

Translate the passage from Ibn Battuta given above in this chapter.

EXERCISE 64

1. I entered the house, and was afraid of the darkness in it. 2. London (لَنْدَن) is a distance of 40 miles (مِيل) from my house; consequently I go there to buy most of my requirements. 3. A car (the car) has four wheels (أَرْبَع عَجَلَات). 4. Do not drag these things in the snow. 5. I was afraid of the lack of provisions in the desert. 6. We need wood for the fire, for winter has begun. 7. The donkey is a useful beast of burden. 8. Load two camels with water. 9. Hassan was one of our guides. 10. The claws of wild animals grip (lit. are firm in) the ground. 11. The price of meat has become high (great) since the war. 12. Tie your horse to that tree. 13. This animal has two long horns. 14. This is the century of progress. 15. We have many bulls, but we need more cows. 16. The hooves of the camel are firm in the desert. 17. In the severe English winter there is much snow, especially in the North. 18. What is the value of this gold? 19. It is worth two pounds. 20. You are few, and we are a hundred.

CHAPTER THIRTY-FOUR

(اَلْبَابُ ٱلرَّابِعُ وَٱلثَّلَاثُونَ)

Relative Sentences

1. The *Relative Pronoun* (اَلاِسْمُ ٱلْمَوْصُولُ) is expressed by:

(a) اَلَّذِى, which is declined as follows:

		Sing.	Dual	Plural
Masc.	Nom.	اَلَّذِى	اَللَّذَانِ	اَلَّذِينَ
	Acc., Gen.	اَلَّذِى	اَللَّذَيْنِ	اَلَّذِينَ
Fem.	Nom.	اَلَّتِى	اَللَّتَانِ	اَللَّاتِى or اَللَّوَاتِى
	Acc., Gen.	اَلَّتِى	اَللَّتَيْنِ	اَللَّاتِى or اَللَّوَاتِى

This pronoun is a combination of the definite article أَلْ (hence the *'alif* has *hamzatu l-waṣl*), the particle, لَ and the demonstrative ذا , ذى . Note those parts in which two *lāms* are written, namely the dual, and also the feminine plural.

(b) مَنْ he who, whomsoever; and مَا that which, whatsoever.

(c) أَىٌّ fem: أَيَّةٌ, which is followed by a Genitive, with the meanings, whichever and whatever. It is compounded as أَيُّمَنْ, whosoever; and أَيُّمَا whatsoever.

2. The words مَنْ and مَا are always treated as nouns, whereas اَلَّذِى is usually treated as an adjective governing a noun which has already been mentioned. It is, however, sometimes used as a noun, in which case it is synonymous with مَنْ and مَا.

3. The Relative Pronoun is called اَلْاِسْمُ ٱلْمَوْصُولُ, and the Relative sentence which follows اَلصِّلَةُ. When the relative pronoun refers to any part of the relative sentence which follows except the subject, it must be repeated by an attached pronoun, known as the عَائِدٌ or رَاجِعٌ, *returner*, e.g.

اَلرَّجُلُ ٱلَّذِى ذَهَبَ	the man who went.
اَلرَّجُلُ ٱلَّذِى رَأَيْتُهُ	the man whom I saw (lit. the man who I saw him).
اَلرَّجُلُ ٱلَّذِى مَرَرْتُ بِهِ فِى ٱلشَّارِعِ	the man whom I passed in the street.
اَلرَّجُلُ ٱلَّذِى كَتَبْتُ لَهُ خِطَابًا	the man to whom I wrote a letter (lit. the man who I wrote to him a letter).
اَلرَّجُلُ ٱلَّذِى قَابَلْتُ ٱبْنَهُ	the man whose son I met (lit. the man who I met his son).

The عَائِدٌ may be omitted, especially in modern Arabic, where the meaning is clear. In Classical Arabic it is frequently omitted after مَنْ and مَا, e.g.

عَجِبْتُ مِمَّا (مِنْ مَا) رَأَيْتُ	I was astonished at what I saw.
أَحْبَبْتُ مَنْ رَأَيْتُ	I loved the man (lit. whom) I saw.

4. *The relative pronoun is always omitted when it refers to an indefinite noun.* This is especially difficult for Europeans to appreciate: e.g.

رَأَيْتُ ٱلْوَلَدَ ٱلَّذِى تَرَكَ أَبَاهُ	I saw the boy who had left his father; *but*
رَأَيْتُ وَلَدًا قَدْ تَرَكَ أَبَاهُ	I saw a boy who had left his father.

In such cases the relative sentence is itself called a صِفَةٌ, or adjective; e.g.

دِمَشْقُ مَدِينَةٌ فِيهَا عَجَائِبُ كَثِيرَةٌ. Damascus is a city in which are many marvels.

5. Certain constructions with the Passive Participle may be construed as shortened Relative Sentences.

اَلشُّهُودُ ٱلْمَذْكُورَةُ أَسْمَاؤُهُمْ أَدْنَاهُ the witnesses, whose names are mentioned below.

The Article here may be regarded as a shortened Relative pronoun, the following clause as a whole depending on it; e.g. "The witnesses, who (mentioned are their names)". The following phrases of a similar nature are much used:

اَلْمُومَأُ إِلَيْهِ or اَلْمُشَارُ إِلَيْهِ the above-mentioned.

اَلرَّجُلُ ٱلْمُشَارُ إِلَيْهِ
اَلرَّجُلُ ٱلْمُومَأُ إِلَيْهِ } the man above-mentioned.

اَلْمَرْأَةُ ٱلْمُشَارُ (ٱلْمُومَأُ) إِلَيْهَا the woman above-mentioned.

اَلرِّجَالُ ٱلْمُشَارُ (ٱلْمُومَأُ) إِلَيْهِمْ the men above-mentioned.

VOCABULARY

اِسْتَمَعَ (إِلَى) VIII to listen (to)

كَمَا like, as

كَأَنَّ as, as if

عَزَمَ (ـِ) (عَلَى) to determine (on)

زَيَّنَ II to adorn

لُؤْلُؤٌ *pl.* لَآلِئُ pearl

غِنَاءٌ song

غَنَّى II to sing

أَطْلَقَ ٱلرَّصَاصَ (ٱلنَّارَ) (عَلَى) IV to shoot (at)

كَمِّيَّةٌ quantity

أَوَّلُ أَمْسِ the day before yesterday

مَعْرَكَةٌ *pl.* مَعَارِكُ battle

دَمٌ *pl.* دِمَاءٌ blood

سَالَ (ـِ) to flow

عَائِلَةٌ family

زَهْرَةٌ ، زَهْرٌ *pl.* زُهُورٌ flower, flowers

وَرْدَةٌ ، وَرْدٌ *pl.* وُرُودٌ rose, roses

تَمَتَّعَ بِ V to enjoy

اَلْبَحْرُ ٱلْأَبْيَضُ ٱلْمُتَوَسِّطُ the Mediterranean Sea

اَلْبَحْرُ ٱلْأَحْمَرُ the Red Sea

اَلْخَلِيجُ ٱلْفَارِسِيُّ the Persian Gulf

أَعْلَى higher, highest (*compar.-superl.*)

بَيَانٌ declaration, statement, announcement

آخَرُ *f.* أُخْرَى another

أَلْغَى IV to cancel, annul

تَسَلَّحَ V to arm oneself

رَغِبَ فِى (ـَ) to desire, love

رَغْبَةٌ love, desire

تَدَابِيرُ measures, steps

لَازِمٌ necessary

خُطْبَةٌ *pl.* خُطَبٌ sermon (in the mosque)

حُكْمٌ rule

ذَاتِىٌّ self- (*adj.*)

وَزِيرُ ٱلْخَارِجِيَّةِ foreign minister, foreign secretary

إِمْبَرَاطُورٌ *pl.* أَبَاطِرَةٌ emperor

إِمْبَرَاطُورِيَّةٌ empire

شَكٌّ *pl.* شُكُوكٌ doubt

شَكَّ (ـُ) (فِى) to doubt

جَلَالَةٌ majesty (term of respect)

جَلِيلٌ exalted

مَجِيدٌ glorious

مَجْدٌ glory

مُشْكِلَةٌ *pl.* مَشَاكِلُ difficulty, problem

إِفْرِيقِيَا Africa

أَثَارَ IV to arouse, incite

عَاطِفَةٌ *pl.* عَوَاطِفُ emotion, feeling

فِلَسْطِينُ Palestine

عُثْمَانِىٌّ Ottoman

عَصْرٌ *pl.* عُصُورٌ age, era, epoch, afternoon

EXERCISE 65

١ — اِسْتَمِعْ إلى قَوْلٍ يَجِيءُ مِن القَلْبِ. ٢ — الجَوَابُ لهذا السُؤَالِ
« لا » كَمَا قُلْتُ لكَ قَبْلًا. ٣ — عَزَمَ الرِجَالُ على ذلك السَبِيلِ
كَأَنَّ الشَيَاطِينَ قد أَقَامُوا فى قُلُوبِهِم. ٤ — لَمْ أَرَ المُغَنِّينَ ٱلَّذِينَ
غَنَّوْا ذلك الغِنَاءَ. ٥ — كَانَتِ المَعْرِكَةُ ٱلَّتِي تَحَارَبَ فيها العَرَبُ
والنَصَارَى مِن أَهَمّ مَعَارِكِ العُصُورِ الوُسْطَى. ٦ — نَحْنُ المُسَافِرَانِ
ٱللَّذَانِ سَافَرَا فى البَحْرِ الأَبْيَضِ المُتَوَسِّطِ والبَحْرِ الأَحْمَرِ والخَلِيجِ الفَارِسِيِّ.
٧ — هذا جَبَلٌ عَالٍ، أَعْلَى مِن الجَبَلِ ٱلَّذِى وُصِفَ فى بَيَانِكَ.
٨ — إِنَّ شُعُوبَ إِفْرِيقِيَّا تَرْغَبُ فى الاِسْتِقْلَالِ والحُكْمِ الذَاتِيِّ. ٩ —
خُذِ التَدَابِيرَ اللَازِمَةَ. ١٠ — كَانَتْ مع اللِصِّ ٱلَّذِى اطلق الرصاصة
عَلَيْنَا أَوَّلَ أَمْسِ كَمِّيَّةٌ مِن اللَآلِئِ. ١١ — قَالَ الخَلِيفَةُ فى خُطْبَتِهِ :
لا تُزَيِّنُوا أَجْسَامَكُم بِالأَشْيَاءِ ٱلَّتِي لا يَتَمَتَّعُ بِهَا الفُقَرَاءُ. ١٢ — تَسَلَّحَ
عَائِلَتُنَا فَسَالَ دَمُهُم فى تلك الحَرْبِ. ١٣ — فى بُسْتَانِي زُهُورُ الوَرْدِ
تُثِيرُ عَوَاطِفَنَا. ١٤ — رَغْبَتُنَا فى ذلك مَعْرُوفٌ عِنْدَ كُلِّكُم. ١٥ — لا
نَشُكُّ فى أَنَّ خِطَابَ (speech) جَلَالَةِ المَلِكِ خِطَابٌ مَجِيدٌ يَسْتَحِقُّ الذِكْرَ.
١٦ — تَرْجِعُ مَشَاكِلُ وَزِيرِ الخَارِجِيَّةِ إلى أَيَّامِ الإِمْبِرَاطُورِيَّةِ العُثْمَانِيَّةِ.
١٧ — كَانَ لَدَيْنَا شَكٌّ كَبِيرٌ فى أَمْرِ الإِمْبِرَاطُورِ، مع أَنَّ مَجْدَهُ أَثَّرَ فى
تَأْرِيخِ الشَرْقِ والغَرْبِ. ١٨ — هو مَلِكٌ جَلِيلٌ لا يُنْسَى ٱسْمُهُ فى
المُسْتَقْبَلِ. ١٩ — البِنْتَانِ ٱللَّتَانِ وَصَلَتَا مِن بَغْدَادَ فَقَدَتَا صُنْدُوقَيْهِمَا فى
القِطَارِ. ٢٠ — لا تَسْتَمِعْ إلى دِعَايَةِ الأَجَانِبِ.

EXERCISE 66

1. The reply which you sent yesterday does not require (demand) any thought. 2. The sermon which we heard in the mosque was glorious, but it did not mention the blood which flowed in the Arabs' battles. 3. He determined to shoot my family, but did not succeed. 4. Hassan had a quantity of pearls which had been sent to him from Africa. 5. As you said the day before yesterday, the song of this singer referred to self-government. 6. Don't listen to those who adorn their houses with flowers. 7. We enjoy the benefits which the foreign minister mentioned, nevertheless (مع أن) we doubt the solving of the problem. 8. Our emotions have been aroused, but our doubts have increased since the departure of his majesty the king to visit the emperor. 9. Their empire has come to an end, but its glory remains. 10. Our doubt remains, as if we were still in times of darkness. 11. We have taken the necessary measures for the annulment of the new law. 12. Mount Sanin (جَبَل صَنِّين) is higher than the mountains you have visited. It is the highest mountain in Lebanon. 13. Another statement has been broadcast. 14. We have crossed the Mediterranean twice. 15. The soldier whose name we have mentioned crossed the Persian gulf and visited Arabia. 16. The Red Sea is famous in the history of the Jews. 17. It is the sea which they crossed when they departed from Egypt and made for Palestine. 18. It is a high mountain. 19. The Egyptians armed themselves. 20. Our love for independence is what led to our departure from Egypt and our travelling to Palestine, for self government is better than good government.

CHAPTER THIRTY-FIVE

(اَلْبَابُ ٱلْخَامِسُ وَٱلثَّلَاثُونَ)

Conditional Sentences

1. *Conditional sentences* consist of a *Protasis*, that is, a sentence containing the condition (شَرْطٌ), and an *Apodosis* (جَزَاءُ ٱلشَّرْطِ or جَوَابُ ٱلشَّرْطِ answer of the condition), which is the main sentence expressing what will result from the condition. In Arabic the Protasis usually, and the Apodosis frequently, in a Verbal Sentence, have the verb in the Perfect or Jussive, with no particular inherent temporal significance.

2. There are two types of condition, the *Likely* and the *Unlikely*. The Unlikely condition is introduced by the conjunction لَوْ with the Perfect (or, very occasionally, Imperfect Indicative).

e.g. لَوْ كُنْتُ مَلِكًا حَكَمْتُ بِعَدَالَةٍ if I were king (but I am not, and am not likely to be) I would rule with justice.

The unlikely nature of the لَوْ condition may be illustrated by the reversed condition, وَدِدْتُ لَوْ كَانَ ٱلْمَوْقِفُ كَذٰلِكَ would that the situation were so! (lit. I wished that the situation were like that).

A more usual type is: لَوْ شَاءَ رَبُّكَ لَجَعَلَ ٱلنَّاسَ أُمَّةً وَاحِدَةً if thy Lord had wished, He would have made men one people. (Qur'ān 11, 120.)

An unlikely negative condition is often expressed by لَوْ لَا with a nominal sentence, giving the sense of the English "were it not for" or "if it were not for", e.g. لَوْ لَا ٱلْعَرَبُ ٱنْطَفَأَ نُورُ ٱلْحَضَارَةِ فِى ٱلْعُصُورِ ٱلْوُسْطَى if it were not for the Arabs, the light of civilization would have been extinguished in the Middle Ages. Note the noun after لَوْ لَا goes in the Nominative.

3. Sometimes we meet لَوْ أَنَّ, e.g.

لَوْ أَنَّكَ بَقِيتَ لَمَا جُرِحْتَ if only you had remained you would not have been wounded.

4. The Apodosis of the لَوْ condition may be introduced by the attached particle لَ, which adds nothing to the meaning. While this particle may occasionally be construed as giving stress, its function is really to warn the reader that the Apodosis is beginning; it is therefore almost compulsory where the Protasis is so complicated as to give a risk that the opening of the Apodosis may pass unnoticed.

لَوْ أَخَذْتَ ٱلْكِتَابَ ٱلَّذِى تَرَكْتُهُ عَلَى ٱلطَّاوِلَةِ وَقَرَأْتَهُ ، لَفَهِمْتَ آرَائِى فَهْمًا تَامًّا if you had taken the book which I left on the table, and read it, you would have understood my ideas fully (lit. a complete understanding).

Nevertheless, with some writers the use of لَ almost becomes a mannerism.

5. The Likely (or possible) Condition is usually introduced by إِنْ or إِذَا. As stated, the Perfect or Jussive may be used in both Protasis and Apodosis. There are four possibilities:

(a) The perfect is used in both parts:

إِنْ ذَهَبَ زَيْدٌ ذَهَبْتُ مَعَهُ if Zaid goes I shall go with him.

(b) The Jussive is used in the Protasis, the Perfect in the Apodosis:

إِنْ يَذْهَبْ زَيْدٌ ذَهَبْتُ مَعَهُ

(c) The Perfect is used in the Protasis, the Jussive in the Apodosis:

إِنْ ذَهَبَ زَيْدٌ أَذْهَبْ مَعَهُ

(d) The Jussive is used in both parts:

إِنْ يَذْهَبْ زَيْدٌ أَذْهَبْ مَعَهُ

NOTE: The Jussive is fairly rare after إِذَا.

6. As explained, there is no particular temporal significance in the verbs of conditional sentences, and often the context is the only guide:

e.g.

لِكُلِّ قَافِلَةٍ قَائِدٌ ، إِذَا وَقَفَ وَقَفَ كُلُّ تُبَّاعِهِ	*either*, each caravan had a leader, and when (if) he stopped, all his followers stopped. *or*, each caravan has a leader, and if (when) he stops, all his followers stop.

However, the sentence may be made definitely Perfect or Pluperfect, by prefacing either كَانَ or قَدْ to the verb:

إِنْ كَانَ قَامَ فَادْخُلْ بَيْتَهُ	if he has departed, then enter his house.
إِنْ كَانَ قَدْ قَامَ دَخَلُوا بَيْتَهُ	if he had departed, they entered his house.

Sometimes, the use of لَمْ with the Jussive gives a past significance, as in this passage from Ibn Baṭṭūṭa.

إِنْ لَمْ يُرْضِهِ تَرَكَهُ	if it has not pleased him, he leaves it.

On the other hand, لَمْ is synonymous with لَا in most conditional propositions in Classical Arabic literature, implying no time definition.

7. If the Protasis begins with إِنْ, the Apodosis *must* be introduced by the attached particle فَ in certain circumstances. (This usage should be clearly distinguished from

that of لَ with Unlikely Conditions, which is purely optional.) These circumstances may really be summarized by the statement that *when the Apodosis is anything but a straightforward positive verbal sentence, without any introductory particle, then* فَ *must be used.* Here are the chief circumstances in which فَ is obligatory, with examples:

(a) When the Apodosis is a nominal sentence:

إِنْ أَرَادَ ذٰلِكَ فَالْأَمْرُ لَهُ if he wishes that, it is his concern (lit. the matter is his).

(b) When the Apodosis is an Imperative.

إِنْ رَأَيْتَهُ فَأَخْبِرْهُ عَنْ حَالِي if you see him, (then) acquaint him of my condition.

(c) When the Apodosis is negative.

إِنْ رَفَضُوا فَلَا يَنْجَحُونَ if they refuse, they will not succeed.

(d) When the Apodosis is a future, expressed by the Imperfect Indicative with سَ or سَوْفَ.

إِنْ قَرَأْتَ ٱلْقُرْآنَ فَسَوْفَ تَتَعَلَّمُ أَسْبَابَ ٱنْتِشَارِ ٱلْإِسْلَامِ if you read the Qur'ān, you will learn the reasons for the spread of Islam.

Note that after سَ or سَوْفَ the *Indicative* is used.

(e) When the Apodosis is introduced by قَدْ.

إِنْ يَسْرِقْ فَقَدْ سَرَقَ أَخٌ لَهُ مِنْ قَبْلُ if he steals, one of his brothers has already stolen before him (Qur'ān 12, 77).

(f) When the Apodosis is introduced by لَنْ.

إِنْ خُنْتَنِي فَلَنْ تَنْجُوَ بِرَأْسِكَ if you betray me, you shall not escape with your life (head).

Note that لَنْ must take the Subjunctive, in accordance with its rule.

(g) When the Apodosis is a nominal sentence beginning with إِنَّ:

إِنْ عَبَدَ ٱلْأَصْنَامَ فَإِنَّهُ كَافِرٌ	if he worships idols, he is surely an infidel.
إِنْ فَعَلَ ذٰلِكَ فَإِنَّهُ قَدْ عَيَّبَ نَفْسَهُ أَيْضًا	if he has done that, then he has (surely) shamed himself also.

(h) When the Apodosis is introduced by an incomplete verb; لَيْسَ or the verb of Wonder or Admiration:

إِنْ يَقُلْ ذٰلِكَ فَلَيْسَ لَهُ بُرْهَانٌ	if he says that, there is no proof for it.
إِنْ حَضَرَتِ ٱلْاِجْتِمَاعَ فَمَا أَكْرَمَهَا !	if she attends the meeting, it is very kind of her (lit. then how kind she is!).

8. "If not" is expressed by إِلَّا (for إِنْ لَا), إِنْ لَمْ, لَوْلَا, لَوْلَمْ.

9. Conditional sentences may also be introduced by the following:

مَنْ he who, if anyone,	حَيْثُمَا wherever
أَيٌّ which, if any	مَهْمَا whatever
أَيُّمَنْ whoever	مَتَى when
مَا what, if anything	مَتَامَا (مَتَى مَا) whenever
كُلُّمَنْ everyone who	أَيْنَ where
كُلَّمَا whenever	أَيْنَمَا wherever
حَيْثُ where	كَيْفَ how
	كَيْفَمَا however

e.g.	مَنْ حَاوَلَ نَجَحَ	Whosoever tries succeeds.
	مَنْ قَالَ ذٰلِكَ كَذَبَ	Whoever (says / said) that lied.
	مَا تَزْرَعْ تَحْصُدْهُ	What you sow you will reap.
	مَتَى مَا رَأَيْتَهُ وَجَدْتَهُ يَلْبَسُ ٱلْبَيَاضَ	Whenever you see him, you will find him wearing white clothes.
	حَيْثُمَا ذَهَبْتَ رَافَقْتُكَ	Wherever you go, I will accompany you.
	كَيْفَمَا ٱجْتَهَدْتَ لَنْ تَنْجَحَ	However you strive, you will not succeed.
	كُلُّ مَنْ يَقْرَأْ هٰذَا يَمُتْ	Everyone who reads this will die.
	كُلَّمَا وَصَلُوا إِلَى نَهْرٍ صَنَعُوا مَرَاكِبَ وَعَبَرُوهُ	Whenever they reached a river, they built (made) boats and crossed it.
	أَيُّمَنْ جَاءَ قَاتِلْهُ	Whoever comes, fight him.
	أَيَّ وَاعِظٍ تَسْتَمِعْ إِلَيْهِ تَسْمَعْ نَفْسَ ٱلْكَلِمَاتِ.	Whichever preacher you listen to, you hear the same words.

With all these particles, the Perfect or Jussive (occasionally Imperative) is normal for both Protasis and Apodosis; the meaning is usually present or future. Note, however, the use of كُلَّمَا as illustrated above. This often appears, to our way of thinking, to be followed by a plain fact; yet the conditional element is present, none the less.

10. Sometimes the Apodosis is omitted, and must be supplied from the context. إِنْ رَجَعْتَ عَنْ قَوْلِكَ وَإِلَّا أَمَرْتُ بِقَتْلِكَ if you go back on your word, (good); otherwise I command that you shall be killed.

11. The Imperative, being related to the Jussive, may be used in the Protasis, and in this case, the Jussive is normally in the Apodosis:

عِشْ قَنِعًا لَا تَشْعُرْ بِعَدَمِ ٱلثَّرْوَةِ . live contented (if you live contented), you will not feel the lack of riches.

12. "Whatever the case may be" is used as a Protasis and is expressed by sentences such as مَهْمَا يَكُنْ مِنْ أَمْرٍ or مَهْمَا يَكُنِ ٱلْحَالُ. But مَهْمَا is also used to introduce an ordinary Protasis:

مَهْمَا حَصَلَ فَشِلْتَ whatever happens, you will fail.

13. We often meet what may be described as an "afterthought condition". A statement is made as if it were a fact, then a condition is added with the Jussive or Perfect; e.g.:

أَنَا رَئِيسُ ٱلْوُزَرَاءِ شِئْتُمْ أَمْ لَا I am Prime Minister, whether you wish or not.

قَالُوا إِنَّهُمْ نُبَالٌ وَإِنْ كَانُوا كُفَّارًا They said that they were noble, although they were infidels.

وَإِنْ is used where in English we would say "even though".

سَوْفَ أَسْتَمِرُّ وَإِنْ سَقَطَتِ ٱلسَّمَاءُ I will continue, even though the heavens were to fall.

14. The above may be considered as reversed conditions in which the Apodosis comes first, and these are not at all unusual in Arabic, e.g.

سَوْفَ أَجِدُكَ أَيْنَمَا تَكُنْ I will find you wherever you may be

for

أَيْنَمَا تَكُنْ سَوْفَ أَجِدُكَ wherever you may be, I will find you.

If this occurs, the rule about فَ with the Apodosis is not applied, e.g.

إِنْ مُتَّ فَسَوْفَ أَدْفِنُ جِسْمَكَ تَحْتَ كَرْمٍ	if you die, I will bury your body under a vine.
سَوْفَ أَدْفِنُ جِسْمَكَ تَحْتَ كَرْمٍ إِنْ مُتَّ	I will bury your body under a vine, if you die.

VOCABULARY

حَرِيقٌ *pl.* حَرْقَى fire, conflagration

طَفِئَ, (ـَ) اِنْطَفَأَ VII to go out, be extinguished

أَطْفَأَ IV to extinguish, put out

فِرْقَةُ ٱلْمَطَافِئِ fire brigade

صَلَّى II to pray

صَلَاةٌ prayer, praying

جَرِيحٌ *pl.* جَرْحَى wounded (man)

طَاوِلَةٌ *pl.* ـَاتٌ table (*Syr.* from *Ital.* "tavola"); backgammon

قَافِلَةٌ *pl.* قَوَافِلُ caravan

أَرْضَى IV to please (anyone)

خَانَ (ـُ) خِيَانَةٌ *v.n.* to betray

خَائِنٌ *pl.* خَوَنَةٌ ، خَانَةٌ ، خُوَّانٌ treacherous, traitor

صَنَمٌ *pl.* أَصْنَامٌ idol

عَبَدَ (ـُ) to worship

بُرْهَانٌ *pl.* بَرَاهِينُ proof

رَافَقَ III to accompany

رَفِيقٌ *pl.* رُفَقَاءُ companion

اِجْتَهَدَ VIII to strive, be diligent

نَجَحَ (ـَ) to succeed

زَرَعَ (ـَ) to sow (seeds)

حَصَدَ (ـِ) to reap

حَصَلَ (ـُ) to happen

حَصَلَ عَلَى to obtain

مَحْصُولٌ *pl.* ـَاتٌ ، مَحَاصِيلُ produce, crops, harvest

مَرْكَبٌ *pl.* مَرَاكِبُ small ship or boat (*mod.*)

وَعَظَ (يَعِظُ) to preach

وَاعِظٌ *pl.* وُعَّاظٌ preacher

دَفَنَ (ـِ) to bury

قَنِعَ بِ (ـَ) اِقْتَنَعَ بِ VIII to be contented with

قَنَّعَ II, أَقْنَعَ IV to satisfy, convince

قَنِعٌ *pl.* ـُونَ contented, satisfied

فِيمَا بَعْدُ later, in future

عَقْدٌ *pl.* عُقُودٌ knot, tie, contract

مُتَعَقِّدٌ contractor

بَالٌ mind, state

فَرِيقٌ *pl.* فُرُوقٌ party of men, group, section

دُولَابٌ *pl.* دَوَالِيبُ cupboard

رَدِيءٌ *pl.* أَرْدِئَاءُ ، أَرْدِيَاءُ bad, evil, wicked

بَلِيغٌ *pl.* بُلَغَاءُ eloquent

بِوَاسِطَةِ through, by means of

بَاطِلٌ vain, useless

دَفَّقَ II to pour *trans.*

اِنْدَفَقَ VII to pour *intr.*, to be poured

غَلَطٌ *pl.* أَغْلَاطٌ error, fault, mistake

EXERCISE 67

١ — لَوْ وَصَلَتْ فِرْقَةُ المَطَافِئِ قَبْلَ سَاعَةٍ لَمَا ٱنْتَشَرَ الحَرِيقُ لِلمَبَانِي المُجَاوِرَةِ . ٢ — لَوْ أَنَّكُم قد صَلَّيْتُم صَلَاةَ العَصْرِ كان يُمْكِنُنَا أَنْ نَقُومَ حَالًا . ٣ — لَوْ لا هذا التَاجِرُ ٱنْطَفَأَ الحَرِيقُ . ٤ — إِنْ مَاتَ الجَرْحَى فَأَنْتَ المَسْؤُولُ يا طَبِيبُ . ٥ — إِذَا تَضَعِ الزَوْجَةُ لَحْمًا على الطَاوِلَةِ أَكَلَهُ الكَلْبُ : لِهذا السَبَبِ إِنَّهَا كَانَتْ دَائِمًا تَضَعُهُ فى الدُولَابِ . ٦ — كَان هو المُقَدَّمَ ، إِذَا وَقَفَ وَقَفَ البَاقُونَ كَالعَادَةِ فى نِظَامِ القَوَافِلِ . ٧ — إِنْ كان خَانَ مَلِكَهُ كان أَرْدَأَ خَائِنٍ فى تَأْرِيخِ بِلَادِنَا ، وإِنْ لَمْ يَخُنْهُ ، كَذَبَ المُؤَرِّخُونَ . ٨ — إِنْ يَعْبُدِ الأَصْنَامَ

فَهُوَ مِنَ ٱلْكُفَّارِ. ٩ — إِنْ طَلَبَ ٱلْوَزِيرُ بُرْهَانًا فَأَرِهِ (رَأَى IV) هٰذَا
ٱلْمَكْتُوبَ ٱلَّذِى فِيهِ ٱسْمُ رَفِيقِكَ، وَقُلْ لَهُ : هَا هُوَ (here is, this is)
ٱسْمُ مَنْ رَافَقَنِى فِى سَفَرِى ٱلطَّوِيلِ، فَٱسْتَشِرْهُ، إِنْ شِئْتَ. ١٠ — إِنْ
وَعَظَهُمْ وَاعِظٌ بَلِيغٌ فَمَا ٱسْتَمَعُوا إِلَى خُطْبَتِهِ. ١١ — إِنْ قُمْتَ بِهٰذَا
ٱلْعَمَلِ بِوَاسِطَةِ مُتَعَهِّدٍ فَسَوْفَ تَنْجَحُ فِيمَا بَعْدُ، وَإِلَّا (if not,
otherwise) فَسَتَرَى ٱجْتِهَادَكَ بَاطِلًا. ١٢ — إِنْ دَفَنْتُ ٱبْنِى فَقَدْ دَفَنْتُ
آمَالِى مَعَهُ. ١٣ — إِنْ أَعْطَيْتُكَ ٱلشَّمْسَ وَٱلْقَمَرَ فَلَنْ تَقْتَنِعَ بِهِمَا!
١٤ — إِنْ وَجَدَا مَرْكَبًا فَإِنَّهُمَا عَبَرَا ٱلنَّهْرَ، هُمَا وَفَرِيقُهُمَا. ١٥ — إِنْ
لَمْ تَزْرَعْ فَلَيْسَ لَكَ مَحْصُولٌ تَحْصُدُهُ. ١٦ — كُلَّمَا وَجَدَ ٱلْجُنُودُ
أَعْدَاءَهُمْ قَتَلُوهُمْ. ١٧ — مَهْمَا حَصَلَ مِنْ شَرٍّ عِشْ قَنِعًا. ١٨ — مَنْ
يَنْسَ عُقُودَ ٱلصَّدَاقَةِ لَيْسَ بِصَدِيقٍ. ١٩ — أَرْضِ أُمَّكَ تُرْضِ أَبَاكَ،
لِأَنَّهُ يُحِبُّهَا. ٢٠ — سَوْفَ تُطْفِئُ نَارَ مَحَبَّتِنَا إِنْ دَفَقْتَ عَلَيْهَا مَاءَ
ٱلشَّكِّ.

EXERCISE 68

1. If hot water pours into the cupboards, all the contractor's work will be [in] vain. 2. Were it not for this wicked and eloquent preacher the inhabitants of the village would have been contented with what they had. 3. If only (use لَوْ أَنَّ) you had helped the wounded they would not have fallen into the hands of that treacherous enemy. 4. If you had witnessed what happened to the unbelievers who worshipped idols, you would have buried your doubts and the words of the Prophet would have satisfied you. 5. If you say the

afternoon prayer at once we can leave with the Mecca (مَكَّة) caravan. 6. When you open the window the wind comes into the room; when you open the door the rain comes in. 7. If my daughter had asked for a proof, I would have told her what was preached in the sermon in the mosque yesterday. 8. If what was on the table has not pleased him he takes what is in the cupboards also. 9. If he acts (use عَمِلَ) through this group, the result is in their hands because he has no authority over them. 10. If you see a fire, call the fire brigade; they will come and put it out quickly. 11. If he has a companion he will not be afraid of the dangers. 12. If you don't work hard (strive) you will certainly not succeed. 13. Whatever the case may be, the crops are bad this year; the reason is the lack of water. 14. If you are absent from the house a long time the fires will go out. 15. What you sow you reap. 16. If you don't find a boat on the river, that is not (use لَيْسَ) my fault. 17. Whoever betrays his country deserves death. 18. Wherever you go, I will accompany you. 19. Whenever I see you I remember my mother. 20. Live contented in the future, [and] you will find the ties of friendship a great help, and you will obtain what is more valuable than wealth -- a tranquil mind.

CHAPTER THIRTY-SIX

(أَلْبَابُ ٱلسَّادِسُ وَٱلثَّلَاثُونَ)

The Cardinal Numbers. Time. Dates

1. Although it is easy to learn the Arabic numerals for colloquial use, as they follow a simple general pattern, they are one of the trickiest features of written Arabic, particularly when fully vowelled, and the Arabs themselves frequently make errors in their use. It might be best to deal with them here in groups beginning with the numbers "one" and "two".

2. "One" masc. وَاحِدٌ } أَحَدٌ } fem. وَاحِدَةٌ } إِحْدَى } إِحْدَا with attached pronoun. Arabic sign ١

The first form is participal (Active Participle I), and is usually employed as an adjective after the noun:

وَصَلَ رَجُلٌ وَاحِدٌ one man (only) arrived.

قَرَأَ ٱلْكِتَابَ مَرَّةً وَاحِدَةً he read the book once (one time).

It may also be used (and declined) as a noun, e.g. جَاءَ كَثِيرُونَ لٰكِنْ بَقِيَ وَاحِدٌ فَقَطْ many came but only one remained; أَخَذْتُ وَاحِدًا, I took one. But it may not take an *'iḍāfa*. The meaning of the *'iḍāfa* may, however, be given by adding مِنْ, e.g. وَصَلَ وَاحِدٌ مِنْهُمْ one of them arrived.

The second form, أَحَدٌ, is usually used either with a negative, meaning no-one or none, or with a following ***genitive*** or *'iḍāfa* whether noun or pronoun, e.g.

لَمْ أَرَ أَحَدًا I did not see anyone.

وَصَلَتْ كُتُبٌ كَثِيرَةٌ لٰكِنِّي أَخَذْتُ أَحَدَهَا فَقَطْ	many books arrived but I took one of them only.
كَلَّمْنَا إِحْدَى ٱلنِّسَاءِ	we spoke to one of the women.
طَلَبْنَا جَرِيدَتَيْنِ لٰكِنَّ إِحْدَاهُمَا لَمْ تَصِلْ	we ordered two papers but one of them did not arrive.

Note: The singular noun in Arabic, when indefinite, means "one" or "a", so that the word for "one" is used much less frequently than in English, e.g. رَأَيْتُهُ مَرَّةً I saw him once.

أَعْطِنِي مِسْمَاراً، سَآخُذُ آخَراً فِيمَا بَعْدُ give me one nail; I will take another later.

3. "Two" masc. إِثْنَانِ; fem. إِثْنَتَانِ (nom.) ٢

إِثْنَيْنِ; fem. إِثْنَتَيْنِ (acc., gen.)

This number on the whole is seldom used, since the dual ending gives its meaning. Thus, بَيْتَانِ means "two houses"; if we write بَيْتَانِ ٱثْنَانِ, then some emphasis is implied on the word "two".

e.g. رَأَيْتُ رَاعِيَيْنِ ٱثْنَيْنِ فَقَطْ I saw two shepherds only (implying that I expected to see more).

قِيلَ لِي إِنَّ هُنَاكَ رُعَاةً كَثِيرِينَ لٰكِنِّي لَاقَيْتُ رَجُلَيْنِ مُسِنَّيْنِ ٱثْنَيْنِ فَقَطْ I was told that there were many shepherds there, but I met two old men only.

إِثْنَانِ is also used as a noun:

دَعَوْتُ جَمِيعَ أَقْرِبَائِي لٰكِنَّ ٱثْنَيْنِ غَابَا I invited all my relatives but two (of them) stayed away.

4. 3 to 10.

3 masc.	ثَلَاثَةٌ (also written ثَلٰثَةٌ)	fem. ثَلَاثٌ (also written ثَلٰثٌ)	٣
4 ,,	أَرْبَعَةٌ	,, أَرْبَعٌ	٤

5	masc.	خَمْسَةٌ	fem.	خَمْسٌ	٥
6	,,	سِتَّةٌ	,,	سِتٌّ	٦
7	,,	سَبْعَةٌ	,,	سَبْعٌ	٧
8	,,	ثَمَانِيَةٌ (also written ثَمَنِيَةٌ)	,,	ثَمَانٍ (also written ثَمَنٍ)	٨
9	,,	تِسْعَةٌ	,,	تِسْعٌ	٩
10	,,	عَشَرَةٌ	,,	عَشْرٌ	١٠

(i) It will be noted that these numbers reverse the genders, adding the *tā' marbūṭa* for the *masculine* form.

(ii) ثَمَانٍ 8 is declined like قَاضٍ.

(iii) They are all nouns, and, when not standing alone, take the nouns to which they refer as genitive plurals in *'iḍāfa*.

أُعْلِنَتْ ثَلَاثُ ثَلَّاجَاتٍ (بَرَّادَاتٍ) لِلْبَيْعِ فِي جَرِيدَةِ ٱلْيَوْمِ	three refrigerators were advertised for sale in today's paper.
عَدَدُ ٱلْغَائِبِينَ ثَمَانِيَةٌ	the number of absentees is eight.
لِي ثَمَانِيَةُ كُتُبٍ جَدِيدَةٍ	I have eight new books.
خُذْ عَشَرَةً مِنْ هٰذِهِ ٱلْكَرَاسِي وَٱتْرُكْ أَرْبَعَةً	take ten of these chairs, and leave four.

NOTE: The gender of the numeral depends on the singular of the noun, not its plural. For example, بَابٌ is masculine but its broken plural أَبْوَابٌ is, grammatically, feminine singular. Nevertheless, one writes أَرْبَعَةُ أَبْوَابٍ four doors, treating the noun as masculine. In the case of a broken plural of a feminine noun the numeral is put into the *feminine*.

5. 11 to 19.

11	masc.	أَحَدَ عَشَرَ	fem.	إِحْدَى عَشْرَةَ	١١
12	„	اِثْنَا عَشَرَ	„	اِثْنَتَا عَشْرَةَ	١٢
13	„	ثَلَاثَةَ عَشَرَ	„	ثَلَاثَ عَشْرَةَ	١٣
14	„	أَرْبَعَةَ عَشَرَ	„	أَرْبَعَ عَشْرَةَ	١٤
15	„	خَمْسَةَ عَشَرَ	„	خَمْسَ عَشْرَةَ	١٥
16	„	سِتَّةَ عَشَرَ	„	سِتَّ عَشْرَةَ	١٦
17	„	سَبْعَةَ عَشَرَ	„	سَبْعَ عَشْرَةَ	١٧
18	„	ثَمَانِيَةَ عَشَرَ	„	ثَمَانِيَ عَشْرَةَ	١٨
19	„	تِسْعَةَ عَشَرَ	„	تِسْعَ عَشْرَةَ	١٩

(i) All these are *indeclinable*, except Twelve.

(ii) They are followed by a *Singular* noun in the *Accusative*,

e.g. وَصَلَ سِتَّةَ عَشَرَ تِلْمِيذًا 16 pupils arrived.

مَرَرْتُ بِسَبْعَ عَشْرَةَ اِمْرَأَةً I passed 17 women.

أُرِيدُ تِسْعَةَ عَشَرَ I want nineteen.

لَكَ اِثْنَا عَشَرَ جُنَيْهًا you have twelve pounds (guineas).

قَدْ أَرْسَلَ لِي عَمِّي اِثْنَيْ عَشَرَ كِتَابًا فِي أَثْنَاءِ ٱلسَّنَةِ ٱلْمَاضِيَةِ. my uncle has sent me twelve letters during the last year.

6. 20 to 99.

20	عِشْرُونَ	masc. and fem.			٢٠
21 masc.	أَحَدٌ وَعِشْرُونَ		fem.	إِحْدَى وَعِشْرُونَ	٢١
22 „	اِثْنَانِ وَعِشْرُونَ		„	اِثْنَتَانِ وَعِشْرُونَ	٢٢

etc.

30	ثَلَاثُونَ	masc. and fem.	٣٠
40	أَرْبَعُونَ	„ „ „	٤٠
50	خَمْسُونَ	„ „ „	٥٠
60	سِتُّونَ	„ „ „	٦٠
70	سَبْعُونَ	„ „ „	٧٠
80	ثَمَانُونَ	„ „ „	٨٠
90	تِسْعُونَ	„ „ „	٩٠

(i) The tens from 20 to 90 are declined as nouns in the sound plural:

فِى هٰذَا ٱلشَّهْرِ ثَلٰثُونَ يَوْمًا there are 30 days in this month.

قَضَيْتُ أَرْبَعِينَ يَوْمًا فِى ٱلصَّحْرَاءِ I spent 40 days in the desert.

(ii) All these numbers from 20 to 99, like those from 11 to 19, are followed by a noun in the *Accusative Singular*. See the examples above.

7. From 100 upwards.

100	مِئَةٌ	(also frequently written مِائَةٌ, but the *'alif* is not pronounced)	١٠٠

From 200 upwards.

200	مِئَتَان (مِائَتَان)		٢٠٠
300	ثَلَاثُ مِئَةٍ	(also written ثَلَاثُمِئَةٍ or ثَلَاثُمِائَةٍ)	٣٠٠
400	أَرْبَعُ مِئَةٍ		٤٠٠
500	خَمْسُ مِئَةٍ		٥٠٠
600	سِتُّ مِئَةٍ		٦٠٠
700	سَبْعُ مِئَةٍ		٧٠٠

800	ثَمَانِى مِئَةٍ	٨٠٠
900	تِسْعُ مِئَةٍ	٩٠٠
1000	أَلْفٌ	١٠٠٠
2000	أَلْفَانِ	٢٠٠٠
3000	ثَلاَثَةُ آلاَفٍ	٣٠٠٠
	etc. to 10000.	
11000	أَحَدَ عَشَرَ أَلْفًا etc.	١١٠٠٠
100000	مِئَةُ أَلْفٍ	١٠٠٠٠٠
1000000	أَلْفُ أَلْفٍ or مَلْيُونٌ Plur. مَلاَيِينُ	١٠٠٠٠٠٠

0 Zero, Nil صِفْرٌ (hence "cypher").

(i) These numerals from 100 are nouns and take their following noun in the *Genitive Singular*. Note that as the word مِائَةٌ 100 is feminine the "three" in 300 has no *tā' marbūṭa*. As أَلْفٌ 1,000 is masculine the 3 of 3,000 has the *tā' marbūṭa* in accordance with the rule governing numbers 3 to 10.

(ii) In compound numerals over 100 the noun follows the rule governing its relation to the last element in the number. Thus in "103 men", the rule for 3 must be followed; therefore, the noun must be in the *Genitive Plural*.

e.g. مِائَةٌ وَثَلاَثَةُ أَوْلاَدٍ a hundred and three boys.

In "123 men" the last element, 23, has an *Accusative Singular* noun, e.g. مِائَةٌ وَثَلاَثَةٌ وَعِشْرُونَ رَجُلاً

In "2,300 men" the last element, 300, takes the *Genitive Singular*, e.g. أَلْفَانِ وَثَلاَثُ مِائَةِ رَجُلٍ

(iii) Note the order of the various elements in the following: أَلْفٌ وَتِسْعُ مِائَةٍ وَتِسْعٌ وَثَلَاثُونَ سَنَةً 1939 years. An older form is تِسْعٌ وَثَلَاثُونَ وَتِسْعُ مِائَةٍ وَأَلْفُ سَنَةٍ which, however, is not used in modern Arabic. Note that each element is connected by وَ.

8. "Some" is expressed by بَعْضٌ. It is also used in Classical Arabic to mean "one of", "a certain", e.g. قَالَ بَعْضُ ٱلشُّعَرَاءِ one of the poets said (but this may also mean "some of").

"A few" is expressed by بِضْعٌ or بِضْعَةٌ, followed by the Genitive, e.g. بِضْعُ أَيَّامٍ a few days (presumed to be between three and ten).

An undefined number over ten is expressed by نَيِّفٌ, e.g. مِائَةٌ وَنَيِّفُ نَفْسٍ, مِائَةُ نَفْسٍ وَنَيِّفٌ a hundred or more souls, a hundred or so souls.

"Approximately, in the region of" is expressed by نَحْوٌ, literally "towards". It is a noun with the following word in the Genitive, e.g.

حَمَلَ عَلَيْنَا نَحْوُ أَلْفِ فَارِسٍ about 1,000 cavalry attacked us.

رَأَيْنَا نَحْوَ مِائَةِ جَمَلٍ we saw about 100 camels.

This word is also used as preposition in the sense of "direction", as: رَكِبْتُ نَحْوَ ٱلْمَدِينَةِ I rode towards the city.

9. When a number is required to be *definite*, e.g. "the nine books", it is placed *after* the noun to which it refers in apposition with the definite article, e.g.

رَجِّعْ لِي ٱلْكُتُبَ ٱلْعَشَرَةَ ٱلَّتِي ٱسْتَلَفْتَهَا return me the ten books which you borrowed.

أَعْطِنِي كُتُبَ حَسَنٍ ٱلتِّسْعَةَ give me Hassan's nine books.

In the first example, however, the reader may encounter اَلْعَشَرَةُ كُتُبٍ in modern Arabic; this is the colloquial usage also.

TIME

10. Among the words used for *time* are وَقْتٌ pl. أَوْقَاتٌ used in the general sense (but not in asking and telling the time); زَمَنٌ or زَمَانٌ, pl. أَزْمِنَةٌ; عَصْرٌ pl. عُصُورٌ meaning "an age" or "era" (e.g. اَلْعُصُورُ الْوُسْطَى the Middle Ages), also "afternoon". قَرْنٌ pl. قُرُونٌ, "century"; سَنَةٌ or عَامٌ, pls. سِنُونَ سَنَوَاتٌ, أَعْوَامٌ, "year"; شَهْرٌ pl. شُهُورٌ, "month"; أُسْبُوعٌ, pl. أَسَابِيعُ, "week"; يَوْمٌ pl. أَيَّامٌ, "day"; سَاعَةٌ, pl. سَاعَاتٌ, "hour"; دَقِيقَةٌ, pl. دَقَائِقُ, "minute"; لَحْظَةٌ pl. لَحَظَاتٌ, "moment"; ثَانِيَةٌ, pl. ثَوَانٍ, "second". سَاعَةٌ also means a "watch" or "clock" and is used in telling the time:

اَلسَّاعَةُ كَمْ؟ what time is it?

اَلسَّاعَةُ ثَلَاثَةُ it is 3 o'clock.*

(Note the use of the masculine here)

The *Ordinals* (see Ch. Thirty-seven) are also used for expressing the time of day, as: اَلسَّاعَةُ ٱلرَّابِعَةُ four o'clock (the fourth hour).

11. The periods of the day are expressed by فِى, sometimes by عِنْدَ, or more commonly by the *Adverbial Accusative*, e.g.

فِى ٱلصَّبَاحِ or صَبَاحًا in the morning.

عِنْدَ ٱلظُّهْرِ at noon.

فِى ٱلْعَصْرِ in the afternoon.

فِى ٱلْمَسَاءِ or مَسَاءً in the evening.

* Numerals used in this way as abstract numbers are *diptote*.

فِى ٱللَّيْلِ or لَيْلًا at night.

فِى ٱلنَّهَارِ or نَهَارًا during the day.

نَهَارٌ means the daytime, whereas يَوْمٌ means the whole 24 hours. When a single night is specified, we say لَيْلَةٌ, e.g. لَيْلَةَ أَمْسِ last night.

12. The days of the week are:

يَوْمُ (نَهَارُ) ٱلْأَحَدِ	Sunday.
يَوْمُ (نَهَارُ) ٱلْاِثْنَيْنِ	Monday.
يَوْمُ (نَهَارُ) ٱلثَّلَاثَاءِ (ٱلثَّلٰثَاءِ)	Tuesday.
يَوْمُ (نَهَارُ) ٱلْأَرْبِعَاءِ	Wednesday.
يَوْمُ (نَهَارُ) ٱلْخَمِيسِ	Thursday.
يَوْمُ (نَهَارُ) ٱلْجُمْعَةِ	Friday.
يَوْمُ (نَهَارُ) ٱلسَّبْتِ	Saturday.

The word يَوْمٌ or نَهَارٌ is often omitted, e.g. اَلثَّلَاثَاءُ. Tuesday. "The week" is اَلْجُمْعَةُ or اَلْأُسْبُوعُ (usually the latter).

MONTHS OF THE CHRISTIAN YEAR

13. The Christian year is called اَلسَّنَةُ ٱلْمِيلَادِيَّةُ the birth year, or اَلسَّنَةُ ٱلْمَسِيحِيَّةُ the Messiah year, or, occasionally, اَلسَّنَةُ ٱلشَّمْسِيَّةُ, the sun year. Dates B.C. are called قَبْلَ ٱلْمِيلَادِ (abbreviated ق م); and A.D., بَعْدَ ٱلْمِيلَادِ (abbreviated ب م or just م).

The names of the months have two alternative forms, the first being used primarily in Egypt and the Sudan, the second in the Levant and Iraq.

	(1)	(2)
January	يَنَايِرُ	كَانُونُ ٱلثَّانِي
February	فِبْرَايِرُ	شُبَاطُ
March	مَارِسُ	آذَارُ
April	أَبْرِيلُ	نِيسَانُ
May	مَايُو	أَيَّارُ، نُوَّارُ
June	يُونِيُو	حَزِيرَانُ
July	يُولِيُو	تَمُّوزُ
August	أُغُسْطُسُ	آبُ
September	سِبْتَمْبِرُ	أَيْلُولُ
October	أُكْتُوبِرُ	تِشْرِينُ ٱلْأَوَّلُ
November	نُوفَمْبِرُ	تِشْرِينُ ٱلثَّانِي
December	دِسَمْبِرُ	كَانُونُ ٱلْأَوَّلُ

THE MUSLIM YEAR

14. This is called ٱلسَّنَةُ ٱلْهِجْرِيَّةُ after the هِجْرَةٌ (Hegira) or Flight (properly, Emigration) of the Prophet from Mecca to Medina on 16th July, 622 A.D. Dates have the word هِجْرِيَّةٌ in brackets after them, or simply هـ . As the year has only 354 days, the Muslim year progressively outstrips the Christian year. A.H. (the European form of هـ) 1381 began on 4th June, 1961. Comparative calendars of the Muslim and Christian years are available.* In the modern Islamic world

* Wustenfeld: Vergleichungs-Tabellen der muhammedischen und christlichen Zeitrechnung, Leipzig, 1854, and later editions.

M. O. Jimenez, Tablas de Conversion de Datas Islamicas a Cristianas y Viceversa, Granada, 1946.

one seldom sees the Hijrīya date alone. Newspapers, for instance, always show the Christian date, which is also operative in commerce and official pronouncements.

The following are the Islamic months:

1.	اَلْمُحَرَّمُ	7.	رَجَبٌ
2.	صَفَرٌ	8.	شَعْبَانُ
3.	رَبِيعُ ٱلْأَوَّلُ	9.	رَمَضَانُ (the month of fasting).
4.	رَبِيعُ ٱلثَّانِى	10.	شَوَّالٌ
5.	جُمَادَى ٱلْأُولَى	11.	ذُو ٱلْقَعْدَةِ
6.	جُمَادَى ٱلْآخِرَةُ	12.	ذُو ٱلْحِجَّةِ (month of the حَجّ).

Some names of these months are often used with special attributives, e.g.

مُحَرَّمُ ٱلْحَرَامِ　　صَفَرُ ٱلْخَيْرِ

رَجَبُ ٱلْفَرْدُ　　شَعْبَانُ ٱلْمُعَظَّمُ

رَمَضَانُ ٱلْمُكَرَّمُ etc.

MUSLIM FEASTS (HOLIDAYS)

15. The general term for a festival is عِيدٌ pl. أَعْيَادٌ. The chief ones are:

(a) أَوَّلُ ٱلسَّنَةِ or رَأْسُ ٱلسَّنَةِ New Year's day of the Islamic Calendar.

(b) اَلْمَوْلِدُ ٱلنَّبَوِىُّ The Birth of the Prophet.

(c) اَلْعِيدُ ٱلصَّغِيرُ "the small festival", at the beginning of the month of شَوَّالٌ after the end of the fast of the month of رَمَضَانُ.

(d) اَلْعِيدُ ٱلْكَبِيرُ "the great festival", also called عِيدُ ٱلْأَضْحَى "the sacrificial festival", on the 10th of the month of ذُو ٱلْحِجَّةِ when the pilgrims offer sacrifice in Mecca.

The commonest festival greeting is اَلْعِيدُ مُبَارَكٌ عَلَيْكَ the feast (is, or may be) blessed on you.

INDICATING DATES

16. To indicate the date, the Ordinal numbers are usually employed (see the following chapter). After the ordinal is put the name of the month, with or without the word شَهْر before it, and after that the number of the year, with or without the word سَنَة in the genitive or accusative.

e.g. فِي سَابِعِ (شَهْرِ) يَنَايِرَ (سَنَةَ) ١٩٥٦
(اَلْيَوْمُ) ٱلسَّابِعُ مِنْ (شَهْرِ) يَنَايِرَ فِي سَنَةِ ١٩٥٦
(On) the 7th January 1956

INDICATION OF AGE

17. How old are you? is expressed by عُمْرُكَ كَمْ سَنَةً (lit. your life is how many years?). An older form is اِبْنُ كَمْ سَنَةً أَنْتَ (lit. the son of how many years are you?) but this is rarely used now.

The answer to the above questions would be:

عُمْرِي عِشْرُونَ سَنَهْ
أَنَا ٱبْنُ عِشْرِينَ سَنَةً
I am twenty years old.

VOCABULARY

فَقَطْ ، فَقَطُّ only (at the end of the sentence or that part of the sentence to which it applies)

مِسْمَارٌ *pl.* مَسَامِيرُ nail

رَاعٍ *pl.* رُعَاةٌ shepherd

رَعِيَّةٌ *pl.* رَعَايَا flock, subjects (of a ruler)

مُسِنٌّ old, aged

بَرَّادَةٌ refrigerator (*mod.*) (Syria, Lebanon)

ثَلَّاجَةٌ refrigerator (Egypt, Sudan)

ضَأْنٌ (*m.s.* ضَائِنٌ, *f.* ضَائِنَةٌ) sheep

غَنَمٌ sheep

مَعْزٌ (*sing.* مَاعِزٌ) goats

شَاةٌ *pl.* شَاءٌ ، شِيَاهٌ a single sheep

إِبْلٌ ، إِبِلٌ camels (*collective* no *singular*)

نَاقَةٌ *pl.* نُوقٌ she-camel

حَدِيقَةُ ٱلْحَيَوَانَاتِ zoo, zoological gardens

حَمْلَةٌ attack

فِلَسْطِينِيٌّ Palestinian

لَاجِئٌ refugee

صَدَّرَ II to export

اِسْتَوْرَدَ X to import

تَصْرِيحٌ declaration (*mod.* permit, permission)

مُنَاسِبٌ suitable

مُنَاسَبَةٌ suitability

بِمُنَاسَبَةِ with reference to, on the occasion of (+*gen.*) (*mod.*)

اِسْتَقَالَ X to resign

زَادَ (ـِ) to increase (*intrans.*)

زَيَّدَ II to increase (*trans.*)

زِيَادَةٌ increase, more, surplus

عَلَّقَ II to hang (*trans.*), suspend

تَعَلَّقَ بِ V to hang from, depend on, be attached to, appertain to

اَلْمُعَلَّقَاتُ Muʿallaqāt, the name given to 7 pre-Islamic odes said to have been hung from the Kaʿba in Mecca

قَصِيدَةٌ *pl.* قَصَائِدُ ode, poem

دُكْتُورٌ *pl.* دَكَاتِرَةٌ doctor (*mod.*)

آتٍ coming, next

مِينَاءٌ *pl.* مَوَانٍ, مَوَانِئُ port, harbour

أَلْمَانِيَا Germany

أَلْمَانِيٌّ German (اَلْأَلْمَانُ the Germans)

جُمْهُورٌ *pl.* جَمَاهِيرُ public, crowd, masses

جُمْهُورِيَّةٌ republic

مُتَكَلِّمٌ بِٱسْمِ spokesman for

جُمْهُورِيٌّ republican

شِعْرٌ *pl.* أَشْعَارٌ poetry

سَعَادَةٌ happiness, good fortune

اَلصَّحْرَاءُ ٱلْكُبْرَى the Sahara (desert)

EXERCISE 69

١ — صَرَّحَ أَمْسِ مُتَكَلِّمٌ بِٱسْمِ الْحُكُومَةِ بِأَنَّ أَحَدَ الْوُزَرَاءِ قَدِ ٱسْتَقَالَ وَمِمَّا (مِنْ‌مَا) يَزِيدُ فِى صُعُوبَةِ رَئِيسِ الوِزَارَةِ أَنَّ سَبَبَ الاِسْتِقَالَةِ مَجْهُولٌ. ٢ — دَخَلَتِ الْمُعَلِّمَةُ الْجَدِيدَةُ الفَصْلَ لِتُعَلِّمَ البَنَاتِ التَّأْرِيخَ لٰكِنَّهَا وَجَدَتْ إِحْدَاهُنَّ فَقَطْ وَهِىَ لَاجِئَةٌ. ٣ — أَعْطِنِى مِسْمَارَيْنِ ٱثْنَيْنِ وَضَعِ الْمَسَامِيرَ البَاقِيَةَ فِى ذٰلِكَ الصُّنْدُوقِ الكَبِيرِ. ٤ — خَرَجَ ثَلَاثَةُ رُعَاةٍ وَمَعَهُمْ تِسْعُ ضَأْنٍ وَخَمْسٌ وَعِشْرُونَ نَاقَةً وَجَمَلَانِ. ٥ — أَزُرْتُمْ حَدِيقَةَ الْحَيَوَانَاتِ بِبَيْرُوتَ؟ هُنَاكَ أَرْبَعَةُ أَفْيَالٍ صَغِيرَةٍ وَإِبِلٌ كَثِيرٌ. ٦ — اَلْمُعَلَّقَاتُ السَّبْعُ مِنْ أَشْهَرِ قَصَائِدِ الشِّعْرِ العَرَبِىِّ. ٧ — فِى قَرْيَتِنَا دُكْتُورٌ وَاحِدٌ ٱلْآنَ: كَانَ ٱثْنَانِ قَبْلَ الْحَرْبِ. ٨ — قَدِمَتْ ثَمَانِى نِسَاءٍ مِنْ بَابِ الْمَدِينَةِ بَعْدَ حَمْلَةِ ٱلْأَلْمَانِ وَكُنَّ يَحْمِلْنَ أَطْفَالَهُنَّ. ٩ — حَلِيبُ البَقَرِ أَحْسَنُ مِنْ حَلِيبِ المَعْزِ، خُصُوصًا إِذَا بَقِىَ بَارِدًا فِى الثَّلَّاجَةِ: إِنِّى قُلْتُ لَكَ ذٰلِكَ أَلْفَ مَرَّةٍ، فَلِمَاذَا تَشْتَرِى لَبَنَ المَعْزِ وَتَتْرُكُهُ فِى الشَّمْسِ؟ اِرْجِعْ لِعَقْلِكَ يَا خَادِمُ! ١٠ — نَتَعَلَّمُ كَثِيرًا عَنْ أَفْكَارِ رَعَايَا خُلَفَاءِ بَغْدَادَ مِنْ كِتَابِ «أَلْفِ لَيْلَةٍ وَلَيْلَةٌ»، لٰكِنَّ هٰذِهِ القِصَصَ غَيْرُ مُنَاسِبَةٍ لِلصِّبْيَانِ فِى بَعْضِ الأَمَاكِنِ. ١١ — حِينَمَا كُنْتُ أَعْبُرُ الصَّحْرَاءَ

الكُبْرَى سَنَةَ أَلْفٍ وتِسْعِ مِائَةٍ وخَمْسٍ وعِشْرِينَ لَقِيتُ سِتَّةَ شُيُوخٍ مُسِنِّينَ لَمْ يَرَوْا أَجْنَبِيًّا قَبْلَ ذلك اليومِ، فَحَمَلُوا عَلَّ. ١٢ — ثُمَّ أَرَيْتُهُمْ تَصْرِيحِي مِنَ الحاكِمِ، لٰكِنْ زَيَّدَ ذلك شَكَّهُمْ فى أَمْرِى وخَوْفَهُمْ مِنِّي. ١٣ — اِسْتَوْرَدَتْ لُبْنَانُ أَلْفَ بَرَّادَةٍ ونَيِّفًا فى السَنَةِ الماضِيَةِ وسَوْفَ تَسْتَوْرِدُ أَكْثَرَ من هذا المِقْدارِ (amount) فى السَنَةِ الآتِيَةِ. ١٤ — وصَدَّرَتْ فَوَاكِهَ كَثِيرَةً فى تِلْكَ المُدَّةِ مِن مِيناءِ بَيْرُوتَ. ١٥ — مَضَى تِسْعَةَ عَشَرَ قَرْنًا مُنْذُ مِيلادِ المَسِيحِ. ١٦ — كان حَسَنٌ يَسْتَيْقِظُ صَبَاحًا ويَسُوقُ غَنَمَ أَبِيهِ إلى مَحَلٍّ بَعِيدٍ مِن البيتِ، ولَمْ يَكُنْ معهُ ساعَةٌ، فَفِي المَسَاءِ كان يَسْأَلُ كُلَّ مارٍّ: الساعةُ كَمْ يا سَيِّدِى؟ ١٧ — إِنَّ هذه البِلَادَ جُمْهُورِيَّةٌ مُنْذُ ثَلٰثَةِ أَعْوامٍ وتُسِرُّ سِياسَةُ الحُكُومَةِ الجُمْهُورَ. ١٨ — وُلِدْتُ بِلُنْدُنَ (London) سَنَةَ ١٩١٤ م. ١٩ — عَلَّقَ الزَّائِرُ مَلَابِسَهُ ٱلوَسِخَةَ بالشَجَرَةِ الكبيرةِ يومَ الأَحَدِ وقَامَ يومَ الأَرْبِعاءِ، واليومَ يومُ السَبْتِ ومَلَابِسُهُ لا تَزالُ تَتَعَلَّقُ مِن الشَجَرَةِ. ٢٠ — تَكَلَّمْتُ مع أَغْلَبِيَّةِ سُكَّانِ القَرْيَةِ بِمُنَاسَبَةِ إِضاعَةِ شاةِ الشَيْخِ.

EXERCISE 70

Note: Numbers given in words should be translated in words. 1. My sister opened one of the boxes only; there are many long nails in the other, and she has not opened it since she came from Palestine with the refugees. 2. Why have you three refrigerators in your house, and you say that you are a poor shepherd? 3. One came, and one stayed away because he wanted to visit the zoo. There were two this year. I invited three last year, but one died in February. God have mercy on his soul (use *Perfect*). 4. I am an old man now, but I cannot say that my happiness has increased since my youth. I have eight sons and three daughters, but all of them have got married and left home. 5. The minister explained in his statement with regard to the economic state of the republic that imports were more than exports. 6. The country had exported seventeen thousand cars in the previous year, but had imported commodities whose value was greater than that. 7. The future of this country depends on trade, and there are a hundred reasons for the present difficulties. "Still", he said, "I am the one responsible, and so I resign". 8. We read in the history of the Arabs that the seven poems known as the "Muʿallaqāt" were hung in Mecca. Some scholars say that there were ten (they were ten). 9. He is a Palestinian, but he studied in a university in Germany and became a doctor in Nineteen hundred and thirty-five. 10. Our country will have a new port in the coming year, and it will be suitable for the biggest ships. 11. September has thirty days, but October has thirty-one. February has only 28 or 29. 12. I worked with sheep and goats for a week (use the accusative) and then resigned. Now I am working with camels. But I really want to work with elephants. 13. This tribe attacked a caravan a few days ago, and killed about 100 men. This attack has increased the public's fear of the Arabs. 14. I do not know what time it is because I have no watch. 15. I lost it on Sunday night when I was going from my house to my friend's house. 16. I looked for it on Monday morning. 17. Those two boys were born in 1931 A.D. 18. I met him in Ramaḍān, 1370 A.H. 19. How old is your eldest daughter? She is seventeen, and my youngest son is three. 20. I spent the holiday in my garden. There are twelve apple trees in it, but my neighbour's sons have taken much of the fruit. 21. I heard that you have 50 or so cows. Why, then, do you buy milk in the market?

CHAPTER THIRTY-SEVEN

(اَلْبَابُ ٱلسَّابِعُ وَٱلثَّلاثُونَ)

The Ordinal Numbers. Fractions

1. The *Ordinals* from 1 to 10 are generally formed on the measure of the Active Participle, فَاعِلٌ, more or less from the Cardinals

اَلْأَوَّلُ	fem.	اَلْأُولَى	the first.
اَلثَّانِى	,,	اَلثَّانِيَةُ	the second.
(without article ثَانٍ)			
اَلثَّالِثُ	,,	اَلثَّالِثَةُ	the third.
اَلرَّابِعُ	,,	اَلرَّابِعَةُ	the fourth.
اَلْخَامِسُ	,,	اَلْخَامِسَةُ	the fifth.
اَلسَّادِسُ	,,	اَلسَّادِسَةُ	the sixth.
اَلسَّابِعُ	,,	اَلسَّابِعَةُ	the seventh.
اَلثَّامِنُ	,,	اَلثَّامِنَةُ	the eighth.
اَلتَّاسِعُ	,,	اَلتَّاسِعَةُ	the ninth.
اَلْعَاشِرُ	,,	اَلْعَاشِرَةُ	the tenth.

All the above are declined fully.

2. After 10, the *Cardinal* Numbers are used as Ordinals, save in so far as the above numbers are included in them. Those from 11 to 19 are indeclinable.

اَلْحَادِى عَشَرَ	fem.	اَلْحَادِيَةَ عَشْرَةَ	the eleventh.
اَلثَّانِى عَشَرَ	„	اَلثَّانِيَةَ عَشْرَةَ	the twelfth.
اَلثَّالِثَ عَشَرَ	„	اَلثَّالِثَةَ عَشْرَةَ	the thirteenth.
اَلرَّابِعَ عَشَرَ	„	اَلرَّابِعَةَ عَشْرَةَ	the fourteenth.

etc.

Higher numbers run as follows:

Masc. and Fem.

twentieth اَلْعِشْرُونَ

اَلْحَادِى وَٱلْعِشْرُونَ	fem.	اَلْحَادِيَةُ وَٱلْعِشْرُونَ	the twenty-first.
اَلثَّانِى وَٱلْعِشْرُونَ	„	اَلثَّانِيَةُ وَٱلْعِشْرُونَ	the twenty-second.
اَلثَّالِثُ وَٱلْعِشْرُونَ	„	اَلثَّالِثَةُ وَٱلْعِشْرُونَ	the twenty-third.

etc.

اَلْمِئَةُ masc. and fem. the hundredth.

اَلْآخِرُ	fem.	اَلْآخِرَةُ	the last.
اَلْأَخِيرُ	„	اَلْأَخِيرَةُ	

The Ordinals have the Sound Plurals, e.g.

اَلْأَوَّلُونَ	fem.	اَلْأَوَّلَاتُ
اَلثَّالِثُونَ	„	اَلثَّالِثَاتُ

Note the following plurals:

اَلْأَوَّلُ the first;	أَوَائِلُ the early part;
اَلْأَوْسَطُ the middle;	أَوَاسِطُ the middle part;
اَلْآخِرُ the last;	أَوَاخِرُ the last part.

فِى أَوَائِلِ ٱلْقَرْنِ ٱلتَّاسِعَ عَشَرَ in the early 19th century.

فِى أَوَاسِطِ ٱلسَّنَةِ in the middle of the year.

نَحْوَ أَوَاخِرِ ٱلْأَمْرِ towards the end of the affair.

3. The *Numerical Adverbs*, "first", "secondly", "thirdly", may be expressed by the *Accusative Indefinite* of the Ordinal.

e.g. أَوَّلًا ، ثَانِيًا ، ثَالِثًا first, secondly, thirdly.

4. The Numerical Adverbs "once", "twice", "several times", may be expressed by the use of the noun مَرَّةٌ in the accusative,

e.g. مَرَّةً once

مَرَّتَيْنِ twice

مَرَّاتٍ or مِرَارًا several times.

Note مَرَّتَيْنِ أَوْ ثَلَاثَ, "two or three times".

"Thrice" (three times), "four times", etc. are expressed by the use of مَرَّةٌ as a genitive of *'iḍāfa* following the Cardinal Number in the Accusative,

e.g. ثَلَاثَ مَرَّاتٍ thrice; أَرْبَعَ مَرَّاتٍ four times.

قَدْ قَابَلْتُهُ خَمْسَ مَرَّاتٍ أَثْنَاءَ ٱلشَّهْرِ ٱلْمَاضِى I have met him five times during the past month.

"Once" used historically, "once upon a time", may be expressed in any of the following ways:

(a) يَوْمًا; (b) يَوْمًا مَا (on a certain day); (c) فِى يَوْمٍ مِنَ ٱلْأَيَّامِ
(d) فِى ذَاتِ يَوْمٍ ، ذَاتَ يَوْمٍ

The occurrence of an action once or more times with the verb is often expressed by the Verbal Noun, with the feminine ending added, known as the اِسْمُ ٱلْمَرَّةِ. This is always of the measure فَعْلَةٌ with the root form of the verb. With derived forms the *tāʾ marbūṭa* is simply appended to the Verbal Noun:

نَظَرَ إِلَيَّ نَظْرَةً غَرِيبَةً	he gave me a strange glance.
اُفْتُتِحَتِ ٱلْمَدْرَسَةُ ٱلْجَدِيدَةُ اِفْتِتَاحَتَيْنِ رَسْمِيَّتَيْنِ	the new school was opened officially twice.
ضَرَبَهُ ثَلَاثَ ضَرَبَاتٍ	he hit him three times (lit. three blows).

5. The *Fractions* (with the exception of "a half") are of the type فُعْلٌ or فُعُلٌ with the Plural أَفْعَالٌ:

$\frac{1}{2}$	نِصْفٌ			Plur.	أَنْصَافٌ	١/٢
$\frac{1}{3}$	ثُلْثٌ	or	ثُلُثٌ	,,	أَثْلَاثٌ	١/٣
$\frac{1}{4}$	رُبْعٌ	,,	رُبُعٌ	,,	أَرْبَاعٌ	١/٤
$\frac{1}{5}$	خُمْسٌ	,,	خُمُسٌ	,,	أَخْمَاسٌ	١/٥
$\frac{1}{6}$	سُدْسٌ	,,	سُدُسٌ	,,	أَسْدَاسٌ	١/٦
$\frac{1}{7}$	سُبْعٌ	,,	سُبُعٌ	,,	أَسْبَاعٌ	١/٧
$\frac{1}{8}$	ثُمْنٌ	,,	ثُمُنٌ	,,	أَثْمَانٌ	١/٨
$\frac{1}{9}$	تُسْعٌ	,,	تُسُعٌ	,,	أَتْسَاعٌ	١/٩
$\frac{1}{10}$	عُشْرٌ	,,	عُشُرٌ	,,	أَعْشَارٌ	١/١٠

e.g. $\frac{2}{3}$ ثُلْثَانِ, $\frac{3}{4}$ ثَلَاثَةُ أَرْبَاعٍ

If a whole and a fraction are united, they must be joined by وَ; e.g.

$4\frac{5}{6}$ = أَرْبَعَةٌ وَخَمْسَةُ أَسْدَاسٍ ; ٤ ٥/٦

% (per cent) = بِٱلْمِائَةِ ، فِى ٱلْمِائَةِ ٪

e.g. 20% عِشْرُونَ فِى ٱلْمِائَةِ ; ٪٢٠

percentage = مِئَوِيَّةٌ

6. The *Multiplicative Adjectives* are of the form مُفَعَّلٌ,

e.g. مُثَنًّى two-fold,

مُثَلَّثٌ three-fold (also means a triangle) pl. مُثَلَّثَاتٌ

مُرَبَّعٌ four-fold (also means a square) pl. مُرَبَّعَاتٌ

Single, simple, singular, is مُفْرَدٌ.

7. The *Distributive Adjectives*, 2 by 2, 3 by 3, etc., are expressed:

(a) By repeating the ordinal in the accusative.

دَخَلُوا ثَلَاثَةً ثَلَاثَةً they entered three by three, in threes.

(b) By the forms فُعَالُ or مَفْعَلُ;

e.g. جَاءُوا مَثْنَى or جَاءُوا ٱثْنَيْنِ ٱثْنَيْنِ they come two by two.

مَرَرْتُ بِقَوْمٍ مَثْنَى وَثُلَاثَ I passed by people (walking) in twos and threes.

8. The *Numerical Adjectives* expressing the composition of anything are of the measure فُعَالِىٌّ

e.g. ثُنَائِىٌّ twofold, biliteral.

ثُلَاثِىٌّ threefold, triliteral.

رُبَاعِىٌّ fourfold, quadriliteral or a quatrain in poetry, hence the "Rubāعiyyāt" (رُبَاعِيَّاتٌ) of عUmar Khayyām.

VOCABULARY

قَوْمِيّ national, nationalist

بَحْث *pl.* أَبْحَاث research, investigation

شَرْقِيّ Eastern, Oriental

قَابَلَ III to meet, to correspond to, be equivalent to

أَطْلَقَ IV to fire, throw

أَطْلَقَ ٱلنَّارَ عَلَى to fire at

أَطْلَقَ كَلِمَةً عَلَى to use a word with a certain meaning

وَكِيل *pl.* وُكَلَاء agent

وَكَالَة agency

تَوَكَّلَ عَلَى V to entrust oneself to, rely on

سَابِق former

سَابِقاً formerly

أَمْن security

أَزْمَة *pl.* إِزَم dearth, scarcity; crisis (*mod.*)

مُنَاقَشَة discussion (*mod.*)

بَرْلَمَان *pl.* ـَات Parliament (*Fr.*)

بَرْنَامِج *pl.* بَرَامِج scheme, programme

فَرْد *pl.* أَفْرَاد individual *n.*

لِوَاء *pl.* أَلْوِيَة standard, flag; Brigade, major-general

مُرَاسِل correspondent

أَسَاسِيّ fundamental(ist)

أَيْ that is to say, namely

قُنْصُل *pl.* قَنَاصِل consul

شَرِيف *pl.* أَشْرَاف noble (*n.* and *adj.*)

شَرَّفَ II to honour

إِشْتَمَلَ عَلَى VIII to comprise, include

فَرْع *pl.* فُرُوع branch

اَلْمَغْرِب N.W. Africa, the Maghrib (also used for Morocco) (lit. the West)

اَلْجَزَائِر Algeria, Algiers

مَرَّاكُش Morocco, Marrakesh

إِحْتَوَى عَلَى VIII to contain, comprise

حَوَى (ـِ) to comprise, contain

مُحْتَوَيَات contents (of a book, etc.)

قَارَّةٌ *pl.* اتٌ — continent

سُنَّةٌ (سُنَنٌ) Sunna, religious law in Islam

أَهْلُ ٱلسُّنَّةِ *sing.* سُنِّيٌّ the Sunnites

اَلشِّيعَةُ *sing.* شِيعِيٌّ the Shi'ites

أَشَاعَ IV to spread *trans.*, make known

شُيُوعِيٌّ Communist

اَلشُّيُوعِيَّةُ Communism

اِشْتِرَاكِيٌّ Socialist

اَلْاِشْتِرَاكِيَّةُ Socialism

حِزْبُ ٱلْعُمَّالِ the Labour Party

إِثْرَ ، أَثَرَ following on, immediately after

أَثَرَ or فِى ، عَلَى إِثْرِ (*same meaning*)

وَفَّقَ II to help, give success to (usually used of God)

تَوْفِيقٌ success (due to God); proper name masc.

حَلَّ (ـُ) to resolve, solve

حَلٌّ solution, resolving *v.n.*

مَثَّلَ II to represent

صَلَحَ لِ (ـُ) to be suitable for

اِخْتَلَفَ عَنْ VIII to differ from

تَقْرِيبًا almost, approximately

شَكْلٌ *pl.* أَشْكَالٌ shape, kind

EXERCISE 71

١ — يَقُولُ رَئِيسُ ٱلْحِزْبِ ٱلْقَوْمِيِّ ٱلسَّابِقُ إِنَّ أَبْحَاثَ ٱلْعُلَمَاءِ أَكَّدَتْ أَنَّ
هذه السَّنَةَ هِيَ السنةُ السَّابِعَةُ والثَّمَانُونَ فى تَأْرِيخِ الحِزْبِ ، وهو
أَقْدَمُ حِزْبٍ فى بِلَادِنَا : هو أَقْدَمُ مِن الحِزْبِ الاِشْتِرَاكِيِّ — أَىْ حِزْبِ
العُمَّالِ — والحِزْبِ الشُّيُوعِيِّ بِكَثِيرٍ. ٢ — اِسْمُ هذا الشَّهْرِ ذُو القَعْدَةِ ،
وهو الشَّهْرُ الحَادِىَ عَشَرَ. ٣ — نَرْجُوكُم أَنْ تُشَرِّفُونَا بِحُضُورِكُم عِنْدَنَا
فى اليومِ الأَوَّلِ مِن شَهْرِ يَنَايِرَ. ٤ — تَنْعَقِدُ الحَفْلَةُ فى بَيْتِي ٱلَّذِى

كان سَابِقًا بيتَ وَكِيلِ القُنْصُلِ فى مَرَّاكُش. ٥ — إِنَّنِي ٱشْتَرَيْتُهُ مِنهُ حِينَمَا ٱسْتَقَالَ إِثْرَ ٱبْتِدَاء الأَزْمَةِ وسَافَرَ إلى المَغْرِبِ. ٦ — نَتَوَكَّلُ على اللّٰهِ ٱلَّذِى وَفَّقَ المُسْلِمِينَ الأَوَّلِينَ فى أَوَائِلِ القَرْنِ السَابِعِ، فَإِنَّهُ سَوْفَ يُوَفِّقُ المُؤْمِنِينَ فى المُسْتَقْبَلِ، لأَنَّ التَوْفِيقَ مِن اللّٰهِ، ولا مِن غَيْرِهِ. ٧ — تُطْلَقُ كَلِمَةُ «مَجْلِسٍ» عَلَى البَرْلَمَانِ فى بَعْضِ الدُوَلِ الشَرْقِيَّةِ. ٨ — جَرَتْ مُنَاقَشَةٌ طَوِيلَةٌ فى مَجْلِسِ الأَمْنِ مِن هَيْئَةِ الأُمَمِ المُتَّحِدَةِ عَن مَشَاكِلِ القَارَّةِ الإِفْرِيقِيَّةِ. وتَقَدَّمَ مُمَثِّلُو آسِيَا بِبَرْنَامِجٍ جديدٍ لِحَلِّ تِلْكَ المَشَاكِلِ بِأَسْرَعِ مَا أَمْكَنَ (as quickly as possible). ٩ — طَلَبَ مِن الأُمَّةِ أَنْ تُحَارِبَ كَمَا حَارَبَتْ فى الماضى. ١٠ — تَعَلَّمْنَا هذا مِن مُرَاسِلِي الجَرَائِدِ الكُبْرَى الغَرْبِيَّةِ. ١١ — إِنَّ فى هذا الكِتَابِ مُحْتَوَيَاتٍ ذَاتَ فَائِدَةٍ كبيرةٍ لِأَهْلِ السُنَّةِ ولِلشِيعَةِ أَيْضًا. ١٢ — قد شَرَّفْتُمُونِى بِزِيَارَتِكُم وأَرْجُوكُم أَنْ تَجِيئُوا مَرَّةً ثَانِيَةً فى يومٍ مِن الأَيَّامِ. ١٣ — يَشْتَمِلُ قَصْرُ المَلِكِ على أَجْزَاءٍ مُخْتَلِفَةٍ فالخُمْسُ مِنهُ تَقْرِيبًا بيتٌ خُصُوصِيٌّ لِلمَلِكِ وأَقَارِبِهِ، وخُمْسٌ آخَرُ مَسَاكِنُ لِلخَدَمَةِ، والأَخْمَاسُ الثَلَاثَةُ البَاقِيَةُ تُسْتَعْمَلُ كَمَكَاتِبَ لِلوُزَرَاءِ وأَعْضَاءِ الحُكُومَةِ. ١٤ — كان الأَشْرَافُ ثَلَاثَةً فى المائَةِ مِن الرَعَايَا، لَكِنْ مع ذلك كانوا يَمْلِكُونَ نِصْفَ الأَرَاضِى. ١٥ — فى اللُغَةِ العَرَبِيَّةِ تُوجَدُ أَفْعَالٌ ثُنَائِيَّةٌ وثُلَاثِيَّةٌ ورُبَاعِيَّةٌ. ١٦ — بُنِيَتِ القَلْعَةُ فى شَكْلٍ مُرَبَّعٍ

كبير. ١٧ — خرج المساجين اثنين اثنين. ١٨ — لماذا رسمت
مثلثا وقلت: ارسم مسدسا؟ ١٩ — كنت في الجزائر السنة
الماضية وقابلت ابن عمي (cousin) ست مرات. ٢٠ — زرت
بيروت للمرة الثالثة في اواسط شهر ايلول.

EXERCISE 72

1. He founded the first national newspaper to appear (which appeared) in the Eastern world; it corresponds to *The Times* (التايمس) in Britain. 2. He fired at the former agent for (ل) the thirteenth time and wounded him. 3. The twenty-first chapter contains fundamental knowledge about the *sunna* and the views of the Shiʿites about it. 4. In the early part of the twentieth century the majority of people thought Socialism a branch of Communism, and this was one of the reasons for the Labour Party's lack of success in the elections for Parliament. 5. It is the duty of every individual first to believe as the Muslims believed formerly, secondly to say his prayers five times a day, and thirdly to trust in God, for success is from Him. 6. What is the use of long discussion in this crisis? You have seen the programme which was made known in the Security Council of the United Nations. 7. You are nobles, and we have been honoured by your visit. Indeed, you have paid us three honours: by your coming, your precious gifts, and your kind words. 8. The flag of independence was raised here yesterday for the first time since the middle of the century. 9. The women looked at the presents they had received from their husbands with the look of happy children. 10. The consul claims that this correspondent only sends half the news; but my view is that he sends no more than a quarter of it. 11. The reason is that he spends forty per cent of his time in private investigations,

and does not think about the contents of the paper for which he works. 12 *Shape* is a singular noun. 13. The solution to this problem is threefold. 14. I read my thousandth book following my admission (دُخُولٌ) to hospital. It was a book not suitable for children. 15. I scarcely noticed the difference in his appearance when he returned after an absence of 25 years. 16. He is about seventy now, but if you saw him you would think he was 50, no more. 17. A third of the representatives have resigned following the receipt of the recent petition. 18. But the real reason is the company's lack of capital. 19. They have been told five times so far that there is (هُنَاكَ) hope of an improvement in the situation, but they have despaired since the resignation of the director. 20. Once upon a time there rose a great man from among the people.

CHAPTER THIRTY-EIGHT

(اَلْبَابُ ٱلثَّامِنُ وَٱلثَّلاثُونَ)

The Structure of Arabic Noun Forms

1. There are *three parts of speech* in Arabic:

(a) Verb فِعْل, pl. أَفْعَال

(b) Noun اِسْم pl. أَسْمَاء. This includes what we would call adjectives.

(c) Particles حَرْف pl. حُرُوف. That is, prepositions, conjunctions and interjections.

2. We have seen that, although the Verbal Noun is termed the مَصْدَر or source, it would seem that the actual root in Arabic consists usually of three consonants – occasionally two, the second being doubled; and, more rarely, four or even five consonants.

Arabic roots can be seen most clearly in the third person masculine singular of the Perfect of the simple verb; whereas the verbal noun not infrequently includes a letter of increase. For example, جُلُوس is the Verbal Noun of جَلَسَ to sit. In such cases it might appear that the verb is the source of the noun, not vice versa. On the other hand, some roots appear to have been originally nouns, not verbs. When we look up the word رَأْس head, in the dictionary, the first entry under the root is the simple verb رَأَسَ, Imperf. يَرْأَسُ يَرْؤُسُ, Verbal Noun رِئَاسَة "to be chief (of a tribe)". But common sense tells us that really the noun رَأْس is a primitive noun, and the verb was formed from that noun. The Medieval Arabic lexicographer would usually put the noun رأس first under this root, and the verb later. Modern dictionaries put the verb first in order to standardize the sequence of entries under all roots.

3. We find, then, that there are three types of nouns, having regard for their possible derivation:

(i) *Primitive Nouns*, such as أُذْنٌ ear; بَيْتٌ house (originally, tent), ثَوْرٌ ox; in fact, those simple nouns which describe everyday objects familiar in primitive society. With these we may also class nouns adopted from foreign languages, e.g. جِنْسٌ species, race, from the Greek *genos*; from which Verbs جَنَّسَ (II) to specify; جَانَسَ (III) to be of the same type as.

(ii) *De-verbal Nouns*. We have already seen numerous noun forms derived from verbs, e.g. قَتْلٌ killing, from قَتَلَ; مَجْلِسٌ session, council, from جَلَسَ to sit; كَبِيرٌ great, from كَبُرَ to be great.

(iii) *De-nominal Nouns*, that is, nouns derived from other nouns, e.g. وَطَنِيَّةٌ patriotism, from وَطَنٌ homeland جِنْسِيَّةٌ (mod.), nationality, from جِنْسٌ race. In modern Arabic we also have compound nouns such as الرَّأْسَمَالُ, or, more correctly, رَأْسُ ٱلْمَالِ capital (head of wealth); عَرْضَحَالٌ (عَرْضُ ٱلْحَالِ) petition (showing of state). We may mention also مَأْسَدَةٌ (pl. مَآسِدُ) a place abounding in lions, from أَسَدٌ lion.

DE-VERBAL NOUNS. THE مَصْدَرٌ.

4. The Verbal Noun properly expresses the verbal idea in the form of a noun, but it sometimes has a remoter meaning and is then known as اِسْمُ مَصْدَرٍ. Some grammars attempt to associate various measures of the Verbal Noun with specific root verb vowellings. This is not, on the whole,

very helpful, and the student had best learn the Verbal Noun of any new verb from the dictionary.

It may be mentioned here, however, that we often encounter what is called the مَصْدَرٌ مِيمِيٌّ, the Verbal Noun beginning with the letter *mīm*, existing side by side with some other form of noun.

Such words are often identical with the *Noun of Place and Time* (see Chapter Thirty-nine); e.g. مَقْصِدٌ and قَصْدٌ from قَصَدَ, to intend; مَقْتَلٌ and قَتْلٌ, murder, from قَتَلَ. It must be pointed out also that some verbs have several Verbal Nouns, though often there is a distinction in meaning, e.g. وَصْفٌ description, صِفَةٌ quality, from وَصَفَ to describe.

5. The Verbal Nouns of Derived forms have already been given, although there are some alternative forms, particularly in II and III. Verbal Nouns of II sometimes take a broken plural when used technically, e.g. تَجْرِبَةٌ an experiment, pl. تَجَارِبُ or occasionally تَجْرِبَاتٌ, from جَرَّبَ to test, try; تَرْكِيبٌ v.n. of رَكَّبَ to set up, compose, may take the plural تَرَاكِيبُ when it has the meaning "a construction". But all Verbal Nouns may take the sound feminine plural:

تَصْلِيحٌ repair, v.n. of صَلَّحَ, pl. تَصْلِيحَاتٌ repairs.

تَنَقُّلٌ v.n. of تَنَقَّلَ to be transferred, transported, pl. تَنَقُّلَاتٌ transfers, postings.

The Passive Participle is sometimes used as an alternative Verbal Noun from Derived forms, e.g. مُقْتَضًى necessity, for اِقْتِضَاءٌ, from اِقْتَضَى, to demand, necessitate.

6. We may distinguish broadly two uses of the Verbal Noun, although there is much overlapping: (a) as a Noun, (b) as a Verb. To these should be added as a third usage the absolute object. While (a) is grammatically obvious, (b) is

not, at least to the beginner, because an Arabic verbal noun, used verbally, may have its own subject and object.

(a) As a Noun. In its most extreme form, this takes the form of the complete divorcing of any action from the meaning. Thus, كِتَابٌ a book, is really a verbal noun of كَتَبَ III. In modern Arabic we may speak about اِقْتِصَادٌ, economy or economics, but it is really the verbal noun of قَصَدَ VIII.

But there is also an in-between stage, in which the *maṣdar* acts grammatically exactly as a noun, although the verbal force is not absent:

اَلْقَتْلُ جَرِيمَةٌ عَظِيمَةٌ murder is a serious crime.

(Note the use of the article, because we are thinking of murder in general, not of any particular act of murder.)

Here, قَتْلٌ the Verbal Noun, is merely the subject of a Nominal Sentence of which جَرِيمَةٌ عَظِيمَةٌ is the Predicate.

عَجِبْتُ مِنْ قَتْلِ زَيْدٍ I was astounded at the murder of Zaid.

Here, قَتْلٌ has a verbal force. Indeed, we could say instead, عَجِبْتُ مِنْ أَنْ زَيْدًا قُتِلَ. Zaid is, in effect, the object of قَتْلٌ, yet he appears as an ordinary *'iḍāfa* following a noun. In fact, apart from the context, or commonsense in some passages, we have no guarantee that the *'iḍāfa* after the Verbal Noun is its object: it *could* be its subject, and the sentence given might mean "I was astounded at Zaid's committing murder!"

(b) As a Verb. If we add another noun, and say:

عَجِبْتُ مِنْ قَتْلِ زَيْدٍ أَبَاهُ I was astounded at Zaid's killing his father.

the Verbal Noun now has both a subject زَيْدٌ and an object, أَبَاهُ. While the subject remains as an *'iḍāfa* in the Genitive, the object goes into the Accusative.

Thus we have a rule: ***When the verbal noun is used with verbal force, and only the subject or the object is mentioned***, not both, ***then that subject or object is treated as an*** ʾidāfa. ***If, however, both the subject and the object are mentioned, the subject remains in the Genitive, but the object is put in the Accusative.***

The subject may be a pronoun, as in

عَجِبْتُ مِنْ ضَرْبِهِ مُحَمَّدًا I was astounded at his beating Muhammad.

If the object is a Pronoun, it must be appended to the word إِيَّا. Thus عَجِبْتُ مِنْ ضَرْبِ مُحَمَّدٍ إِيَّاهُمْ I was astounded at Muhammad's beating them.

The object may be replaced by a Genitive with لِ, e.g. مَحَبَّتِي لِبَلَدِي my love for my country, instead of مَحَبَّتِي بَلَدِي.

كَرِهَ لَوْمَ أَبِيهِ لَهُ he hated his father's blaming him.

The Preposition لِ is also used when the Verbal Noun is employed indefinitely with an adverbial meaning.

قُمْتُ إِكْرَامًا لَهُ I rose in honour of him.

The Arabs call this usage اَلْمَفْعُولُ لَهُ, as it gives the reason for لِ the action of the main Verb. In fact the Verbal Noun replaces the Subjunctive.

(c) As the Absolute Object (اَلْمَفْعُولُ الْمُطْلَقُ). This has already been touched on in Chapter Seventeen. The following methods of use may be distinguished:

(i) The Verbal Noun alone. فَرِحَ فَرْحًا he rejoiced. Here the Verbal Noun adds nothing, except possibly a little stress or a sense of finality.

(ii) Qualified with an Adjective, thus specifying the type of action (called in Arabic لِلتَّمْيِيزِ "for distinguishing"):

فَرِحَ فَرَحًا عَظِيمًا he rejoiced greatly.

This may also be used with the Passive, e.g.

ضُرِبَ زَيْدٌ ضَرْبًا شَدِيدًا Zaid was struck violently.

(iii) Qualified otherwise, e.g. by an *'iḍāfa*:

حَارَبَ مُحَارَبَةَ ٱلْجُنُونِ (ٱلْمَجْنُونِ or) he fought like a madman (the fighting of madness, or of a madman).

By a sentence: فَرِحَ فَرْحًا كَادَ يَسْتَطِيرُ بِهِ he rejoiced with a rejoicing which nearly made him fly.

By the demonstrative: ضَرَبْتُهُ هٰذَا ٱلضَّرْبَ I struck him thus (this striking).

(iv) To describe the type of act. Here the Verbal Noun of the Simple Verb may take the form فِعْلَةٌ, and is called اِسْمُ ٱلنَّوْعِ (the noun of kind).

هَرَبَ هِرْبَةَ ٱلْجَبَانِ he fled like a coward (lit. the fleeing of the coward).

(v) To specify the number of times the act is committed. Here, the measure فَعْلَةٌ is used for the single act, and it takes the dual and the sound feminine plural. The name of this is اِسْمُ ٱلْمَرَّةِ (the noun of times).

ضَرَبْتُهُ ضَرْبَةً I struck him one blow.

ضَرَبْتُهُ ضَرْبَتَيْنِ I struck him twice.

ضَرَبْتُهُ ثَلَاثَ ضَرَبَاتٍ I struck him three blows.

Note: (a) Sometimes the Verbal Noun is omitted but its Adjective retained.

ضَرَبْتُهُ شَدِيدًا he hit him hard, for ضَرَبْتُهُ ضَرْبًا شَدِيدًا

This is more common in modern Arabic.

(b) The Verbal Noun of a different verb, but with a similar meaning, may be used:

قَعَدُوا جُلوسًا they sat down.

where قَعَدَ and جَلَسَ both mean "to sit".

THE ACTIVE PARTICIPLE اِسْمُ ٱلْفَاعِلِ

7. Like the verbal noun, it may be used with greater or less verbal force.

(a) As a Noun. At one extreme, we find the noun acquiring a technical meaning as a noun. Thus, كَاتِبٌ a clerk, مُعَلِّمٌ a teacher. As we have pointed out, when this occurs with the Active Participle of the Simple Triliteral verb, it usually takes a broken plural, as كَتَبَةٌ and كُتَّابٌ, plurals of كَاتِبٌ. These broken plurals, however, are not used when the participle has an ordinary verbal sense, save in poetry.

(b) As a noun with vestiges of verbal force, as in expressions like ذَابِحُ ٱلْأَطْفَالِ a massacrer of children. Although grammarians do mention the possibility of putting الأطفال in the accusative as an object thus, ذَابِحُ ٱلْأَطْفَالَ, this is rare and not to be recommended. However, if it is made definite, and we say اَلذَّابِحُ ٱلْأَطْفَالَ he who kills children, اَلْأَطْفَالَ must be in the accusative. Again, we may replace the object by ل + the Genitive. He who strives after knowledge, e.g. اَلطَّالِبُ لِلْعِلْمِ.

(c) As a Verb, capable of taking its own object:

هُوَ رَاكِبٌ he is riding.

هُوَ رَاكِبٌ حِصَانًا he is riding a horse.

هُمْ رَاكِبُونَ they are riding.

كَانُوا رَاكِبِينَ حُصُنًا they were riding horses.

Note that there is no *'iḍāfa* here, consequently رَاكِبٌ retains its nunation. In all these sentences, the Active Participle could be replaced by the Imperfect Verb.

e.g. (هُوَ) يَرْكَبُ he is riding.

Sometimes the Active Participle is used with the meaning of the future, e.g. أَمَامَهُ أَجَلٌ لَا يَعْلَمُ مَا ٱللّٰهُ فَاعِلٌ بِهِ, Before him is a period with which he does not know what God will do. This is common in modern colloquial.

VOCABULARY

وَحِيدٌ sole, only

أَضْرَبَ عَنْ IV to quit; to go on strike (*mod.*)

إِضْرَابٌ strike (*mod.*)

اِشْتَرَكَ فِي VIII to take part in, subscribe to

شَرْطٌ *pl.* شُرُوطٌ condition (laid down)

بِشَرْطِ أَنْ + *subj.* on condition that

اِتَّهَمَ . . . بِ VIII to accuse anyone of . . .

تُهْمَةٌ charge, accusation

أُسْطُولٌ *pl.* أَسَاطِيلُ fleet

خَطٌّ handwriting

خُطَّةٌ policy, linc

عِدَّةٌ *pl.* عِدَدٌ a number, several (+*gen.*)

قِيَادَةٌ leadership

نَشَاطٌ energy, zeal, activity

بَذَلَ (ـُ) to give generously, squander

بَذَلَ جُهْدَهُ to do one's utmost

رَأْسٌ cape, headland

تَنَقَّلَ V اِنْتَقَلَ VIII to be moved transferred, posted

جِنْسٌ *pl.* أَجْنَاسٌ species, type, kind, class

جِنْسِيَّةٌ nationality (*mod.*)

زَادَ عَلَى (ـِ) to exceed, increase, add to

تَرْكِيبٌ composition, structure, syntax

جَرِيمَةٌ *pl.* جَرَائِمُ crime

عَجِبَ مِنْ (ـَ) to wonder at, be surprised at

عَجَزَ عَنْ (ـِ) to be incapable of
كَرِهَ (ـَ) to hate
كَرَاهِيَةٌ hatred
لَامَ (ـُ) to blame
جَبَانٌ coward
هَرَبَ (ـُ) to flee, run away
مَتَى when?
نَوْعٌ *pl.* أَنْوَاعٌ sort, type, kind
رَأْسَمَالِيٌّ capitalist (*mod.*)

بَحَّارٌ sailor
سَائِلٌ *pl.* سَوَائِلُ liquid
فَاتِرٌ luke-warm
صَفْحَةٌ *pl.* صَفَحَاتٌ page (of book)
خُلْقٌ *pl.* أَخْلَاقٌ moral character
عَنْوَنَ to address a letter
عُنْوَانٌ address *pl.* عَنَاوِينُ
وَاضِحٌ clear
أَمَّا ... فَ as for, as to

EXERCISE 73

١ — يَرْجِعُ تَأْرِيخُ الشِّيعَةِ إِلَى مَقْتَلِ عَلِيٍّ ٱلَّذِى كَانَ الْخَلِيفَةَ الرَّابِعَ ، فَكَانَ أَصْدِقَاؤُهُ وَمُسَاعِدُوهُ يَكْرَهُونَ النَّاسَ الْمَسْؤُولِينَ عَنْ هٰذِهِ الْجَرِيمَةِ الْعَظِيمَةِ. ٢ — أَنْتَ الرَّجُلُ الْوَحِيدُ ٱلَّذِى يَسْتَطِيعُ أَنْ يَقُومَ بِالتَّصْلِيحَاتِ اللَّازِمَةِ لِعَرَبَتِي لِطُولِ تَجَارِبِكَ فِى الْأَعْمَالِ مِنْ هٰذَا النَّوْعِ. ٣ — زِدْ عَلَى ذٰلِكَ أَنَّ سَائِرَ الْعُمَّالِ قَدْ أَضْرَبُوا كَرَاهِيَةً لِلتَّنَقُّلَاتِ الْأَخِيرَةِ. ٤ — وَلَا يَرْجِعُونَ لِعَمَلِهِمْ إِلَّا بِشَرْطِ* أَنْ يَشْتَرِكُوا فِى تَدْبِيرِ الشَّرِكَةِ. ٥ — كَانَ الْبُؤْسُ يَمْلَأُ قُلُوبَ الْبَحَّارِينَ فِى الْأَسَاطِيلِ الثَّلَاثَةِ لَمَّا جَاءَهُمُ الْخَبَرُ عَنِ الْخُطَّةِ الْأَخِيرَةِ ٱلَّتِى أَدَّتْ إِلَى ٱسْتِقَالَةِ وَزِيرِ الْحَرْبِيَّةِ (war minister). ٦ — أَعْجَبُ مِنْ قِرَاءَتِكَ هٰذَا الْكِتَابَ

* Note that the whole sentence beginning with أَنْ takes the place of an iḍāfa, and بشرط , therefore loses its nunation.

الطويل بتلك السرعة. إنك بذلت جهدك. ٧ — أما أنا فإني عاجز
عن أن أقرأ كذلك مهما كانت مقتضيات الأحوال، فلا تلمني.
٨ — لماذا تهرب يا جبان؟ متى تعترف بأن الأمل خير من
اليأس؟ ٩ — تعجبت الجرائد هنا من اتخاذ رأسماليين أجانب
جنسية الجمهورية الجديدة. ١٠ — متى عزمت على قيادة الجيش
لمقاتلة العدو؟ ١١ — ألم تسمع أن معظم (أغلب=) الأسطول
خرج من الميناء أمس وانكسر على رأس صخري قريب من العاصمة؟
١٢ — قلت: سأقدم لك الشاى تقديما، وأرى أن كلمة «الشاى»
وإن دخلت فى تركيب كلامك لم تدخل قط (at all) فى تركيب
هذا السائل الضعيف الفاتر! ١٣ — إن خطك سيئ. ألا تعرف
أشكال الحروف العربية المختلفة؟ من فضلك اكتب هذه الصفحة
كتابة جيدة من جديد، وإلا فلن تنتقل إلى فصل أعلى! ١٤ — مات
ممات (موت=) الفقر بعد نشاطه المستمر. ١٥ — قام المتهم فقال
للقاضى: يا حضرتك، إن تهمتى من نوع لا يسمع عنه حتى اليوم.
١٦ — حصل ثلاثة إضرابات فى هذا العام. ١٧ — زرته وهو
مريض، يرقد على سريره رقدة المائت. ١٨ — قال الضيف: أنت
مناد خادمك، ألا تتذكر أنك أرسلته للسوق قبل ساعة ليشترى
احتياجات الحفلة؟ ١٩ — انظر هذين! الزوج راكب جمله، وزوجته
ماشية على جنبه! ٢٠ — إنا من الله وإنا إليه راجعون.

EXERCISE 74

1. Necessity is the sole teacher of the man who squanders his money. 2. We know that special instructions (تَعْلِيمَات) arrived a number of days before the recent strike. 3. The moving of the capital will necessitate also a number of postings of officials from one place to another. 4. Your hatred of that man is a question of race, and I blame you for it. Nevertheless I agree with you that he is a man of bad character. 5. I was sorry for his death because I knew that the accusation was not true. 6. When will the capitalists realize that the payment of high rents is among the most important causes of lack of confidence among the workers? 7. His crime was the opening of letters, addressed to his uncle in clear handwriting. 8. I wondered at his leadership of the fleet and his energy in everything he did during the war. 9. Your giving him this sum was one of the conditions of your appointment. 10. Quit your work for a short period and take part in our festival out of respect for our customs. 11. You have constructed the sentence well (*use absolute object*). 12. What sort of man is this? He fled like a coward, and then returned as if he were a victorious sailor. 13. When will you realize that we are incapable of hating anybody properly? (*absolute obj.*). 14. The (female) servants came quickly to my table and placed on it three glasses of a green lukewarm liquid. 15. It was of a type which scarcely anyone drinks here except ignorant foreigners. 16. I will accept this line on condition that you make three announcements of it; one today, another tomorrow, and a third in a week's time 17. He walked like an old man. 18. I am going out because I don't like your talk. 19. I am telling you this so that you won't blame me later. 20. I saw your children throwing stones and breaking the windows of my neighbour's house.

CHAPTER THIRTY-NINE

(أَلْبَابُ ٱلتَّاسِعُ وَٱلثَّلَاثُونَ)

Noun Forms. The Noun of Place and Time. The Noun of Instrument. The Diminutive

1. Students will have noticed in previous chapters a number of nouns formed by the prefixing of *mīm* to the triliteral root, e.g. مَكْتَبٌ an office, from كَتَبَ ; مَجْلِسٌ council from جَلَسَ. These two nouns belong to the category known as the *Noun of Place and Time* (اِسْمُ ٱلْمَكَانِ وَٱلزَّمَانِ). It expresses the place where the action of the verb is committed, or the time or occasion of that action. Such nouns are nearly always of the measure مَفْعَلٌ or مَفْعِلٌ, e.g.

مَنْزِلٌ a house or lodging; from نَزَلَ to alight.

مَجْلِسٌ a council; from جَلَسَ to sit.

مَشْرِقٌ East; from شَرَقَ to rise.

مَغْرِبٌ West; from غَرَبَ to set.

مَسْجِدٌ mosque; from سَجَدَ to prostrate oneself.

مَخْزَنٌ a store; from خَزَنَ to store.

مَأْوًى a lodging, refuge; from أَوَى إِلَى to resort to.

مَوْعِدٌ an appointment; from وَعَدَ to promise.

مَرْعًى pasture; from رَعَى to tend cattle.

مَوْضِعٌ place; from وَضَعَ to place.

مَوْقِفٌ a situation; from وَقَفَ to stop, stand.

The plural form is مَفَاعِل as مَنَازِل, مَجَالِس

Sometimes the feminine ending is added to the singular:

مَكْتَبَة desk, library, bookshop; from كَتَبَ to write.

مَدْفَنَة a cemetery; from دَفَنَ to bury.

مَهْلَك
مَهْلِك
مَهْلَكَة
مَهْلِكَة
مَهْلُكَة

a desert; place of destruction; from هَلَكَ to perish.

Note from the above last form that the Middle Radical sometimes has *ḍamma*.

Very occasionally, especially from roots with initial *wāw* or *yā'*, we find the form مِفْعَال, which, as we shall see, is the form of the *Noun of Instrument*, e.g.

مِيعَاد (for مِوْعَاد) an appointment; from وَعَدَ to promise.

مِيلَاد (for مِوْلَاد) birth; from وَلَدَ to give birth to.

For the *Derived Verbs*, the Passive Participle takes the place of the Noun of Place and Time:

e.g. مُصَلًّى place of prayer; from صَلَّى (II) to pray.

مُلْتَقًى a meeting place; from اِلْتَقَى (VIII) to meet.

2. Note the following modifications from the various classes of *Weak verb*.

(i) Doubled verb.

مَقَرّ abode; from قَرَّ to settle.

مَحَلّ place and مَحَلَّة city-quarter } from حَلَّ to alight.

(ii) Hollow verb.

مَقَامٌ place; from قَامَ to rise.

مَغَارَةٌ cave; from غَارَ to sink in the earth

مَقَالَةٌ an article, essay; from قَالَ to say.

Here the correct forms would be مَقْوَمٌ, مَغْوَرَةٌ, مَقْوَلَةٌ.

THE NOUN OF INSTRUMENT (اِسْمُ ٱلْآلَةِ)

3. This describes the *instrument* with which the action of the verb is carried out. It resembles the Noun of Place and Time, beginning with the *mīm*, but this letter is vowelled with *kasra* instead of *fatḥa*. The commonest form is مِفْعَالٌ:

e.g. مِفْتَاحٌ a key; from فَتَحَ to open.

مِيزَانٌ balance, scales; from وَزَنَ to weigh.

The second form is مِفْعَلَةٌ,

e.g. مِكْنَسَةٌ broom; from كَنَسَ to sweep.

مِرْوَحَةٌ fan; from رَاحَ to blow.

Thirdly, we find مِفْعَلٌ,

e.g. مِبْرَدٌ a file; from بَرَدَ to file.

مِقَصٌّ scissors; from قَصَّ to cut.

مِكْوًى iron; from كَوَى to iron.

Occasionally, we find *ḍamma*, as in مُدُقٌّ a hammer; from دَقَّ to pound (also مِدَقٌّ and مِدَقَّةٌ).

For the first form, we have the plural مَفَاعِيلُ as مَفَاتِيحُ and مَوَازِينُ. For the rest, we have مَفَاعِلُ, as مَكَانِسُ, مَبَارِدُ, مَقَاصٌّ (for مَقَاصِصُ).

THE DIMINUTIVE

4. *The Diminutive* (اِسْمُ ٱلتَّصْغِيرِ) can be formed from any noun. If there are three consonants in the noun, the Diminutive is فُعَيْلٌ. If there are four or more, the form is فُعَيْلِلٌ.

(a) Three consonants.

بَحْرٌ sea, becomes بُحَيْرَةٌ (note fem. ending) lake

كَلْبٌ dog, becomes كُلَيْبٌ

بَابٌ door, becomes بُوَيْبٌ

ظِلٌّ shadow, becomes ظُلَيْلٌ

شَابٌّ youth, becomes شُبَيْبٌ

The *dim.* of كِتَابٌ a book, is كُتَيِّبٌ

Note that the full form returns in the doubled verb, as in the last two examples above. Where there are weak radicals which have changed, they must be reinstated, as in بُوَيْبٌ, the *wāw* having been changed to ʾ*alif* in باب.

The feminine ending is retained in words like قَلْعَةٌ fort, from which the diminutive is قُلَيْعَةٌ; شَجَرَةٌ a tree, from which we have شُجَيْرَةٌ a bush; مُدَيْدَةٌ from مُدَّةٌ a period.

In feminine nouns which have not the feminine ending, this occurs in the diminutive:

شُمَيْسَةٌ from شَمْسٌ (f.) sun.

دُوَيْرَةٌ from دَارٌ (f.) house.

حُوَيْلَةٌ from حَالٌ (f.) state, condition.

(b) Four consonants: here the form is فُعَيْلِلٌ.

e.g. عَقْرَبٌ a scorpion عُقَيْرِبٌ

مُسْلِمٌ Muslim. مُسَيْلِمٌ

مُسْلِمَةٌ ,, (fem.) مُسَيْلِمَةٌ

Note the following:

عُصْفُورٌ a sparrow, عُصَيْفِيرٌ

سُلْطَانٌ a sultan, سُلَيْطِينٌ

حَمْرَاءُ red (fem.) حُمَيْرَاءُ

(c) Five consonants: here one consonant, usually the last, must be removed to form the Diminutive:

e.g. عَنْدَلِيبٌ nightingale, *dim.* عُنَيْدِلٌ

سَفَرْجَلٌ quince, سُفَيْرِجٌ

إِمْبَرَاطُورٌ Emperor, أُبَيْطِرٌ

(note the broken plural: أَبَاطِرَةٌ)

But where the fifth consonant is the *nūn* of the suffix انٌ this may be retained, as زَعْفَرَانٌ saffron; the diminutive being زُعَيْفِرَانٌ.

5. Note the following forms:

أَبٌ father; *dim.* أُبَيٌّ

أَخٌ brother أُخَيٌّ

أُخْتٌ sister أُخَيَّةٌ

اِبْنٌ son بُنَيٌّ

بِنْتٌ ، اِبْنَةٌ daughter بُنَيَّةٌ

شَيْءٌ thing شُوَيَّةٌ ، شُوَيٌّ (used in colloquial to mean "a little", "slightly").

USE OF THE DIMINUTIVE

6. The student will probably have little cause to use these forms; the important thing is for him to recognise them. They are used as follows:

(a) In proper names,

e.g. حُسَيْنٌ Ḥusain, *dim.* of حَسَنٌ
عُبَيْدٌ ؏Ubaid, *dim.* of عَبْدٌ
in عُبَيْدُ ٱللّٰهِ ؏Ubaidullāh.

(b) With a specialised meaning,

e.g. بُحَيْرَةٌ lake, from بَحْرٌ
كُتَيِّبٌ booklet, from كِتَابٌ
كُلَيْبٌ puppy, from كَلْبٌ

(c) For endearment,

e.g. يَا بُنَيَّ, regularly used by a father to his son.

(d) To express contempt,

e.g. if a grown man were termed رُجَيْلٌ.

7. The Diminutive is sometimes used also with triliteral prepositions,

e.g. قَبْلَ ٱلْفَجْرِ before dawn.
قُبَيْلَ ٱلْفَجْرِ a little before dawn.
بُعَيْدَ ٱلظُّهْرِ a little after noon.

An even rarer usage is with the Verb of Wonder:

e.g. مَا أُحَيْسِنَهُ from مَا أَحْسَنَهُ how handsome he is!
مَا أُمَيْلِحَهُ from مَا أَمْلَحَهُ with the same meaning.

VOCABULARY

(excluding words occurring in the body of the chapter)

بَيْتُ لَحْمَ (*diptote*) Bethlehem

بَيْتُ ٱلْمَقْدِسِ Jerusalem

قَدُسَ (ـُ) to be holy

قَدَّسَ II to make holy, sanctify

عَيْنُ سَلْوَانَ Ain Sulwan (place-name) (سُلْوَانٌ = solace, comfort)

عَيْنٌ *pl.* عُيُونٌ ، أَعْيُنٌ spring,* stream

أَبْرَأَ IV to cure

ضَرِيرٌ *pl.* أَضِرَّاءُ blind

نَقَرَ (ـُ) to hollow out, pierce, peck

مِنْقَارٌ *pl.* مَنَاقِيرُ beak, bill (of bird)

حَبَسَ (ـِ) to imprison, shut up

نَفْسٌ *pl.* أَنْفُسٌ self, same

نَفْسُهُ ، نَفْسُهَا himself, herself, etc.

عِبَادَةٌ worship, piety

وَلَدَ (يَلِدُ) to bear a child, beget

مِيلٌ *pl.* أَمْيَالٌ mile

قَبْرٌ *pl.* قُبُورٌ tomb, grave

يَعْقُوبُ (*diptote*) Jacob

قُبَّةٌ *pl.* قُبَبٌ dome

مَعْقُودٌ arched, vaulted (in this context)

كَنِيسَةٌ *pl.* كَنَائِسُ church

غَايَةٌ limit, extreme

أَبْصَرَ IV to see

وِطَاءٌ depression (of land)

عَمُودٌ *pl.* أَعْمِدَةٌ pillar, column

رُخَامٌ marble

مَلِيحَةٌ beautiful thing, attractive thing

رُكْنٌ *pl.* أَرْكَانٌ ، رُكُونٌ corner

هَيْكَلٌ *pl.* هَيَاكِلُ temple, shrine, statue, altar

دَاخِلَ inside *prep.*

خَارِجَ outside *prep.*

مِذْوَدٌ *pl.* مَذَاوِدُ manger

طَيْرٌ *pl.* طُيُورٌ bird

مَسَافَةٌ *pl.* ـَاتٌ distance

قِطٌّ *pl.* قُطُوطٌ cat

عُشٌّ *pl.* عِشَاشٌ nest (of bird)

عَضَّ (ـَ) to bite

---

* NOTE: A little later in the following extract عَيْنٌ is also used with the common meaning of "eye".

EXERCISE 75

Notes:

(a) This exercise is not intended to test the accompanying chapter which is largely concerned with word structure rather than syntax or grammar.

(b) The student will have observed that in previous exercises some vowel points from common words and particles have been gradually dropped. From now onwards non-essential vowels will be omitted. The same applies to orthographical signs.

From a description of the Holy Land by the geographer al-Idrīsī (12th century A.D.)

(بَيْتُ لَحْمٌ) سِرْتُ من بيتِ المَقْدِسِ إلى مدينة بَيْتَ لَحْمَ فوجدتُ على
طريقى عَيْنَ سُلْوَانَ. وهى العين التى أَبْرَأَ فيها السيدُ المَسيح
(Christ) الضَرِيرَ الأَعْمَى. ولَمْ تَكُنْ له قَبْلَ ذلك عينان. وبِقُرْبِهَا
بُيُوتٌ كثيرة مَنْقُورَةٌ فى الصخر. وفيها رجالٌ حَبَسُوا أَنْفُسَهُمْ فيها
عِبَادَةً. وأَمَّا بيت لحم — وهو الموضعُ الذى وُلِدَ فيه السيدُ المسيحُ —
فَبَيْنَهُ وبَيْنَ المَقْدِسِ ستةُ أَمْيَالٍ. وفى وَسَطِ الطريق قَبْرٌ ولَدَى يَعْقُوبَ.
وهو قَبْرٌ عَلَيْهِ اثنا عشر حَجَرًا. وفوقَهُ قُبَّةٌ مَعْقُودَةٌ بِالصخر وبيت لحم
هُنَاكَ. وفيها كَنِيسَةٌ حسنة البِنَاء مُزَيَّنَةٌ الى أَبْعَدِ غَايَةٍ حتى أَنَّهُ*
ما أُبْصِرَ فى جميع الكنائس مِثْلُهَا بِنَاءً. وهى فى وَطَاءٍ مِنَ الأَرْض،

---

* The student should notice this use of the vague attached pronoun هُ, which refers back to nothing in particular. The particles أَنَّ and إِنَّ etc. *must* be followed by an accusative, and if no noun is available, a pronoun must be used. This pronoun normally refers back to some noun in the previous sentence which also plays a part in the sentence after أَنَّ etc. When, however, no such noun is available, the neutral pronoun هُ is used merely to satisfy grammatical requirements. It is not, of course, translated.

وَلَهَا بابٌ من جِهَةِ المغربِ ، وبها من اعمدة الرُخَامِ كُلٌّ مَليحَةٍ وفى
رُكْنِ الهَيْكَلِ فى جهة الشمالِ المغارةُ التى وُلِدَ بها السيدُ المسيح ، وهى
تَحْتَ الهيكل ودَاخِلَ المغارة المِذْوَدُ الذى وُجِدَ بِهِ. وإذا خَرَجْتَ من
بيت لحم نَظَرْتَ فى الشرق كَنِيسَةَ المَلَائِكَةِ الذين بَشَّرُوا الرُعاةَ
بِمَوْلِدِ السيدِ المسيحِ.

EXERCISE 76

1. My brother was accused of worshipping idols outside the Mosque of Omar (عُمَر). 2. These birds have long beaks. 3. We saw a spring of pure flowing (running) water outside the cave. 4. The tomb of these men is at (على) a distance of four miles from the place in which they were imprisoned. 5. If you ask the director of stores, he will issue you with three files, one [pair of] scissors, and two hammers; one big, one small. 6. My black cat gave birth to seven kittens, one of them black, three grey, two white and one brown. 7. In one of the corners of this consecrated temple (use *pass. part.* pf قدس II) are three marble pillars. 8. The women saw a vaulted dome in the middle (وَسَطَ) of the pasture-land, near the lake, and they realised that it was the tomb of Jacob. 9. I was extremely afraid of the situation (lit. I feared the extremity of fear). 10. His name will become holy a little after his death. 11. My house is a place of prayer, and you have made it (use جَعَلَ) a market in which merchandise is bought and sold. 12. You have swept the room with a new broom, and you have ironed my clothes with a new iron, yet all your work is bad. 13. Our appointment was for five o'clock. Why did you not arrive until seven o'clock? 14. London (لُنْدُنْ) is a meeting place for students from every nation. 15. Outside my office is a bush in which there is a nightingale's nest.

16. Shortly after mid-day, my son, we will meet in Husain's garden. In it are many different kinds of fruit, including (منها) quince and apple, and I prefer quince. 17. I opened his desk with the key, and found his new article on Arab independence in it and it was in excellent handwriting. 18. The sparrow is a small bird [well-]known in England. 19. A little scorpion bit him while he was repairing the fan in my brother's room. 20. Weigh everything on the official scales in the market; I have no confidence in the merchants' scales.

CHAPTER FORTY

(اَلْبَابُ ٱلْأَرْبَعُونَ)

The Relative Noun and Adjective
Various Adjectival Forms

1. The *Relative Adjective* (اِسْمُ ٱلنِّسْبَةِ) is formed by adding ـِيٌّ to a Noun, and denotes that the person or thing governed is related to or connected with the original noun. It is most frequently formed from geographical and other proper names, names of occupation, tribe, land, city, and the like. If the noun has the feminine ending ةَ this must be dropped before adding ىّ.

عَرَبٌ Arabs (collective);	عَرَبِيٌّ Arabic, Arab.
مِصْرُ Egypt;	مِصْرِيٌّ Egyptian, an Egyptian.
مَكَّةُ Mecca;	مَكِّيٌّ Meccan.
طَبِيعَةٌ nature;	طَبِيعِيٌّ natural.
عِلْمٌ science;	عِلْمِيٌّ scientific.
ثَقَافَةٌ culture;	ثَقَافِيٌّ cultural.
صِنَاعَةٌ art, craft, industry;	صِنَاعِيٌّ artificial, industrial.
حَدِيدٌ iron;	حَدِيدِيٌّ iron.
يَوْمٌ day;	يَوْمِيٌّ daily.

Non-radical letters in the noun, particularly long vowels

or diphthongs, are sometimes dropped, as in the following examples:

مَدِينَة city;	مَدَنِيّ civil, civilian.
قُرَيْش Quraish (a tribe);	قُرَشِيّ Quraishi, Quraishite.
ثَقِيف Thaqīf (a tribe);	ثَقَفِيّ Thaqifite.

2. Sometimes the final *'alif* occurring in a foreign name is retained with a following *wāw* added, or replaced by a *wāw*, although this is frowned upon by purists, e.g.:

فَرَنْسَاوِيّ or فَرَنْسَوِيّ for فَرَنْسِيّ, from فَرَنْسَا France.

دُنْقُلَاوِيّ for دُنْقُلِيّ, of or from Dongola (a Sudanese province).

Note also the following:

إِنْكِلْتَرَا England;	إِنْكِلِيزِيّ English.
بِرِيطَانِيَا Britain;	بِرِيطَانِيّ British.
إِيطَالِيَا Italy;	إِيطَالِيّ Italian.
اَلْيَمَن Yemen;	يَمَنِيّ (يَمَانٍ *antiq.*) Yemeni, Yemenite.
هَرَاة Herat;	هَرَوِيّ of Herat.
مَرْو Merv;	مَرْوَزِيّ of Merv.
اَلرَّيّ Rai;	رَازِيّ of Rai.

3. The words أَبٌ father, and أَخٌ brother, take back their original *wāw* and form أَبَوِيّ fatherly; أَخَوِيّ brotherly.

If a noun ends in ا, ًا, ى, ًى, this is changed to *wāw* before the ending, e.g. مَعْنَوِيّ abstract, from مَعْنًى meaning; دُنْيَوِيّ worldly, from دُنْيَا world.

Note also نَبَوِيٌّ, from نَبِيءٌ or نَبِيٌّ prophet; ثَانَوِيٌّ secondary, from ثَانٍ (مَدْرَسَةٌ ثَانَوِيَّةٌ secondary school); سَنَوِيٌّ annual, from سَنَةٌ a year.

The same is the case with the *hamza* in the ending اءٌ, اءُ, e.g. سَمَاءٌ heaven, سَمَاوِيٌّ heavenly. But شِتَاءٌ winter, becomes شَتَوِيٌّ wintry (without the *'alif*). Note also that the word قَرْيَةٌ village, forms قَرَوِيٌّ villager.

. These adjectives usually take the sound plural, e.g. مِصْرِيٌّ Egyptian; pl. مِصْرِيُّونَ. There are some exceptions to this rule, such as: عَرَبِيٌّ pl. عَرَبٌ, e.g. كَاتِبٌ عَرَبِيٌّ an Arab writer; كُتَّابٌ عَرَبٌ Arab writers; بَغْدَادِيٌّ pl. بَغَادِدَةٌ Baghdadi.

It must be remembered that in Arabic many of these adjectives are also used as nouns.

THE RELATIVE NOUN

5. The Feminine Singular of the Relative Adjective forms the *Relative Noun* which frequently has a specialised meaning, abstract or concrete, e.g.

إِنْسَانٌ man;	إِنْسَانِيٌّ human;	إِنْسَانِيَّةٌ humanity.
إِلٰهٌ God;	إِلٰهِيٌّ divine;	إِلٰهِيَّةٌ divinity.
شَهْرٌ month;	شَهْرِيٌّ monthly;	شَهْرِيَّةٌ monthly salary.
يَوْمٌ day;	يَوْمِيٌّ daily;	يَوْمِيَّةٌ diary, journal.

In some cases this form exists where the Relative Adjective does not, or is seldom seen. Thus, for example, the Relative Adjective is rarely formed from the so-called Elative form but we find أَقَلِّيَّةٌ with the meaning "minority", from أَقَلُّ less, least; and أَكْثَرِيَّةٌ "majority", from أَكْثَرُ more, most.

All these nouns have the Feminine Sound Plural.

Some Verbal Nouns form the Relative Noun with a special meaning, e.g. اِتِّفَاقٌ, v.n. of وفق VIII, with the meaning "agreement" forms اِتِّفَاقِيَّةٌ which is used today to mean an agreement of an official, political, commercial, or international nature, or a treaty. This is typical of the great extension in the use of the Relative Noun and Adjective in modern Arabic, so much so, that it is almost permissible to make them up for oneself. Such phrases as اَلسَّنَةُ ٱلْمَدْرَسِيَّةُ "the school year", the Relative Adjective being formed from the Noun of Place and Time of دَرَسَ "to study", are characteristic of the modern idiom.

6. A rare form of Relative Adjective ends in ـَانِيٌّ. From رُوحٌ spirit, we have رُوحَانِيٌّ spiritual, and رُوحَانِيَّةٌ spirituality. From جِسْمٌ body; جِسْمَانِيٌّ bodily, corporeal.

Note also إِسْكَنْدَرَانِيٌّ Alexandrian, from اَلْإِسْكَنْدَرِيَّةُ Alexandria (in Egypt); لَاذَقَانِيٌّ of or from اَللَّاذِقِيَّةُ Latakia (a town in Syria).

ADJECTIVAL FORMS

7. The student has now encountered nearly all the Adjectival forms (اِسْمُ صِفَةٍ). Most of them resemble in meaning the Active Participle of the Simple Verb and are termed in Arabic اَلْأَسْمَاءُ ٱلْمُشَابِهَةُ لِٱسْمِ ٱلْفَاعِلِ. They include the following:

(i) فَاعِلٌ, the Active Participle itself.

(ii) فَعِيلٌ, e.g. كَبِيرٌ, from كَبُرَ; etc. This form sometimes has the meaning of the Passive Participle, in which case the Plural is usually of the measure فَعْلَى, e.g. جَرِيحٌ pl. جَرْحَى wounded, from جَرَحَ; قَتِيلٌ, murdered, pl. قَتْلَى from قَتَلَ.

(iii) فَعُولٌ, e.g. صَبُورٌ patient, from صَبَرَ.

(iv) فَعْلَانُ, e.g. كَسْلَانُ lazy, from كَسِلَ.

(v) فَعْلَانٌ, e.g. فَرْحَانٌ glad, joyful; from فَرِحَ.

(vi) أَفْعَلُ, for Colours and Defects.

(vii) فَعْلٌ, e.g. صَعْبٌ difficult, from صَعُبَ.

(viii) فَعَلٌ, e.g. حَسَنٌ good, beautiful, from حَسُنَ.

(ix) فَعِلٌ, e.g. فَرِحٌ joyful, from فَرِحَ.

The following have intensive meanings:

(x) فَعَّالٌ, e.g. كَذَّابٌ a liar, addicted to lying; from كَذَبَ. عَلَّامٌ, a savant, learned man; from عَلِمَ.

This form is also used for professions and occupations, etc., e.g. نَجَّارٌ a carpenter; خَيَّاطٌ a tailor.

(xi) فِعِّيلٌ, e.g. صِدِّيقٌ righteous, very trustworthy.

(xii) مِفْعِيلٌ, e.g. مِسْكِينٌ poor, unfortunate, wretched.

(xiii) مِفْعَالٌ, e.g. مِقْدَامٌ brave.

Some of these forms may be given an even more intensive meaning by the addition of the Feminine ending, even when referring to males, e.g. عَلَّامَةٌ very learned, a very learned man; مِقْدَامَةٌ very brave.

FURTHER NOTES ON THE ELATIVE (اِسْمُ ٱلتَّفْضِيلِ)

8. The *Elative* (see Chapter Eleven) is always formed from the three radicals. Thus from حَبِيبٌ beloved, is formed أَحَبُّ (for أَحْبَبُ) more beloved, dearer. In the case of Participles of the Derived forms, words with more than three consonants, and words of the form أَفْعَلُ, the Elative is formed by using either أَكْثَرُ or أَشَدُّ followed by a noun in the accusative (a Verbal Noun, as a rule), e.g. مُجْتَهِدٌ diligent; أَكْثَرُ ٱجْتِهَادًا more diligent (lit. "more as to diligence"). أَسْوَدُ black; أَشَدُّ سَوَادًا blacker (lit. "stronger as to blackness").*

9. If the second part of the comparison is not a noun but a whole sentence or an adverbial determination, it is preceded by مِمَّا (for مِنْ مَا) with a Verb or the Preposition مِنْ with an attached Pronoun, e.g.

اَلْهَوَاءُ (الطَّقْسُ or) أَلْطَفُ ٱلْيَوْمَ مِنْهُ أَمْسِ. the weather is pleasanter today than it was yesterday (lit. "than it yesterday").

OR

اَلْهَوَاءُ أَلْطَفُ ٱلْيَوْمَ مِمَّا كَانَ أَمْسِ. (lit. "than it *was* yesterday")

Metaphorical expressions such as "as quick as lightning", "as sweet as sugar" are usually put into the comparative in Arabic, as a literal translation is not possible, e.g.

أَسْرَعُ مِنَ ٱلْبَرْقِ lit. "quicker than lightning".

أَحْلَى مِنَ ٱلسُّكَّرِ lit. "sweeter than sugar".

---

* See Appendix C, §4 (c).

Another method of rendering it would be سَرِيعٌ كَالْبَرْقِ lit. "quick like lightning".

(كَ "like as" is an attached Preposition taking, of course, the Genitive.)

VOCABULARY

(*excluding words occurring in the body of the chapter*)

عَوْنٌ *pl.* أَعْوَانٌ helper, attendant

يُقَالُ لَهُ he is called

بَيْنَ يَدَيْهِ in front of him

لِ belonging to, to

أَزَالَ IV to put an end to, remove

سَمْعًا وَطَاعَةً I hear and obey (lit. hearing and obeying)

هَلَكَ (ـَ) هَلِكَ (ـِ) to perish

أَهْلَكَ IV to ruin, destroy

تَعَلُّقَاتٌ property

مَلَكَ (ـِ) to possess

غَالٍ expensive

رَخِيصٌ cheap

حِيلَةٌ *pl.* حِيَلٌ stratagem, trick

خَلَّصَ II to save

تَخَلَّصَ V to be saved

مِنْ فَضْلِكَ please! (lit. from your kindness)

وَدَّعَ II to take leave of, say goodbye to

أَوْصَى بِ IV to make recommendation, recommend

ضَجِيجٌ clamour

عَلَا (ـُ) to rise, be or become high

صِيَاحٌ shouting

اسْتَغَاثَ بِ X to ask help of

تَعَالَى may He (God) be exalted (lit. He has become exalted)

أَخْطَأَ IV to make a mistake, err

غَفَرَ لِ (ـِ) to forgive

فَحْمٌ charcoal, coal

خَلٌّ vinegar

أَمَّمَ II to nationalise (from أُمَّةٌ nation)

وَاللّٰهِ oath on the name of God

عَبْقَرِيَّةٌ genius

EXERCISE 77

Note: The following exercise is not specially connected with the contents of the chapter.

حُكِى أنَّ هارونَ الرشيدَ استدعى رجلاً من اعوانه يُقالُ لَهُ صَالِحْ ، فلمّا حضر بين يَدَيْهِ قال له : « يا صالح سِرْ الى منصور وقُلْ له : إنَّ لنا عندك أَلْفَ أَلْفِ دِرْهَمٍ ، والرأى قد اقتضى انك تحمل ذلك المبلغ لنا فى هذه الساعة ، وقد امرتُك يا صالح أنَّهُ إنْ لَمْ يَحْصُلْ لك ذلك المبلغ من هذه الساعةِ الى قبل المغرب أنْ تُزِيلَ رأْسَهُ عن جسدِهِ و تَأْتِيَنا به ». فقال صالح : سَمْعًا وطاعةً.

ثم سار الى منصور وأَخْبَرَهُ بما ذَكَرَ اميرُ المؤمنين . فقال منصور : « قد هلكتُ ، واللّهِ إنَّ تَعَلُّقَاتى وما تَمْلِكُهُ يدى اذا بيعَتْ بأَغْلَى قيمةٍ لا يزيدُ ثَمَنَها على مائةِ الف ، فمِن أَيْنَ أَقْدِرُ يا صالح على التسعمائة أَلْفِ دِرْهَمٍ الباقِيَة؟ » فقال له صالح : « دَبِّرْ لك حِيلَةً تَتَخَلَّصُ بِها عاجلاً وإلّا هلكتَ ، فإنّى لا أَقْدِرُ أنْ أَتَمَهَّلَ عليك لحظةً بعد المدة التى عَيَّنَها لى الخليفةُ فَأَسْرِعْ بحيلةٍ ». فقال المنصور : « يا صالح ، أَسْأَلُك أنْ تحملَنى ، من فَضْلِكَ ، الى بيتى لِأُوَدِّعَ أولادى ، وأهلى ، وأُوصِىَ لأقاربى ». قال صالح : « فَمضيتُ معه الى بيته فجعل يودّع اهلَه ، وارتفعَ الضجيجُ فى منزله وعَلا البُكاءُ والصِياحُ والاِسْتِغَاثَةُ باللّه تَعَالَى ».

(From الف ليلة وليلة, *The Thousand and One Nights*).

EXERCISE 78

1. Among his helpers were an Egyptian, two Italians and three old Meccans whom he had met on the pilgrimage a year previously. 2. This region is called the light industries region: it was established by the government after the war had put an end to the former industries of our country. 3. I read in his diary how he saved himself and all he possessed by a stratagem. 4. Please show me the way to the civil airport. 5. Everything was expensive in England after the war. 6. Education is cheap in the French government secondary schools. 7. The majority recommended the nationalisation of all foreign commercial companies, so a cry and clamour arose from the minority. 8. My husband has said farewell to me for the last time, so I ask help of God most high in my difficult problems. 9. To err is human, to forgive is divine. 10. The workers' monthly pay was increased by an agreement between them and the employers. 11. Spiritual health is more important than bodily health. 12. I am a patient man and am not quick to anger. 13. I met a beggar in the streets – and he had been a carpenter formerly: "I am a poor unfortunate", he said, "give me something" (a thing). 14. "I have no money with me", I said, "ask help of God most high". 15. He was a very learned man, and was more diligent than other scholars. 16. Your face is blacker than coal, my son. Where have you been? 17. The university is bigger today than it was formerly. 18. They are better in work than they are in words. 19. Her words were as sweet as sugar, but her thoughts were as bitter as vinegar. 20. You are very worldly men. 21. The genius of Omar is famous in the history of the caliphs.

CHAPTER FORTY-ONE

(اَلْبَابُ ٱلْحَادِى وَٱلْأَرْبَعُونَ)

Abstract Nouns. Proper Names

1. Nouns may be classified according to their meanings as

(a) Names of *Classes* or *Species*, (اِسْمُ ٱلْجِنْسِ)

(b) *Proper Names* (اِسْمُ عَلَمٍ).

2. The first type may be subdivided into:

(a) *Concrete* اِسْمُ عَيْنٍ whether Nouns such as رَجُلٌ man; فَرَسٌ horse, or Adjectives such as رَاكِبٌ riding; جَالِسٌ sitting.

(b) *Abstract* اِسْمُ مَعْنًى, whether nouns such as عِلْمٌ science, learning, جَهْلٌ ignorance; or adjectives such as مَفْهُومٌ understood.

3. When *Abstract Nouns* are used in a general sense and without further determination they always take the Article,

e.g. اَلشَّجَاعَةُ فَضِيلَةٌ bravery is a virtue.

But the same rule applies to all nouns used in a general or generalizing sense, as in the names of materials,

e.g. اَلذَّهَبُ وَٱلْفِضَّةُ مَعْدَنَانِ gold and silver are (two) metals.

We do, however, have such renderings as: صُنْدُوقُ ذَهَبٍ, gold box; صُنْدُوقٌ مِنْ ذَهَبٍ, (lit. a box from gold) instead of صُنْدُوقٌ مِنَ ٱلذَّهَبِ.

The same rule is applied to people and animals, as in the following examples: لَنْ يَدْخُلَ ٱلْكَذَّابُونَ ٱلْجَنَّةَ liars shall not enter heaven; اَلْحِصَانُ حَيَوَانٌ كَرِيمٌ would translate "horses are noble animals" as well as, "the horse is a noble animal".

In a sentence like هٰذَا ٱلْبَيْتُ غَيْرُ مُلَائِمٍ لِلْأَثَاثَاتِ ٱلثَّقِيلَةِ, this house is not suitable for heavy furniture, the indefinite can also be used, as لِأَثَاثَاتٍ ثَقِيلَةٍ.

4. Proper names are always definite and so can be the subject of a Nominal Sentence,

e.g. حُسَيْنٌ مُعَلِّمٌ Hussein is a teacher.

بَغْدَادُ مَدِينَةٌ جَمِيلَةٌ Baghdad is a beautiful city.

Note, however, that some proper names include the article,

e.g. Khartoum is اَلْخُرْطُومُ; Cairo is اَلْقَاهِرَةُ.

5. Many names take the form of a noun followed by a Genitive in *ʾiḍāfa*,

e.g. عَبْدُ ٱللّٰهِ Abdullah (or Abdullahi)

أَبُو بَكْرٍ Abu Bakr.

In such names, the first part is declined, but the genitive naturally cannot change,

e.g. جَاءَ أَبُو بَكْرٍ Abu Bakr came.

رَأَيْتُ أَبَا بَكْرٍ I saw Abu Bakr.

مَرَرْنَا بِأَبِي بَكْرٍ We passed Abu Bakr.

أَيْنَ عَبْدُ ٱللّٰهِ Where is Abdullah?

نَادِ عَبْدَ ٱللّٰهِ Call Abdullah!

Note: In modern Arabic place names consisting of أَبُو plus

a Genitive, sometimes the nominative form is used in all cases in unvowelled writing or print,

e.g. أَبُو حَمَد Abu Hamad (a town in the Sudan)

نَزَلَ بِأَبُو حَمَد He alighted at Abu Hamad.

for بِأَبِى حَمَد

زار أبو حمد He visited Abu Hamad.

for زار أبا حمد

6. Classical Arabic proper names are a difficult subject, and often a source of trouble when one tries to look them up in the index of a book. They include these elements:

(a) The Name Proper, e.g. زَيْد Zaid; جَعْفَر Ja'far; سُلَيْمَان Sulaimān (Solomon) اَلْخَلِيل al-Khalīl.

(b) The *Kunya* (كُنْيَة), containing a term of relationship such as "father", "mother", "brother", "son", "sister",

e.g. ابن بطّوطة Ibn Baṭṭūṭa.

ابن احمد Ibn Aḥmad.

أُمّ كُلثوم Umm Kulthūm.

أخو هرون Akhū Hārūn.

(c) The *Nickname* (لَقَب), usually given to a grown man, referring to some quality for which he is famous (أبو بكر الصّدّيق Abū Bakr aṣ-Ṣiddīq i.e. "the righteous"), to some event with which he is associated (تَأَبَّطَ شَرًّا Ta'abbaṭa Sharran, given to the poet who, as the name signifies, carried evil, in his case a ghoul, under his arm!) or to a place of origin or residence, or a tribe, e.g. الخَلِيلُ بْنُ أَحْمَدَ الفَرَاهِيدِىّ al-Khalīl ibn Aḥmad al-Farāhīdī (tribe); أَبُو عَمْرو الشَّيْبَانِىّ, Abū 'Amr ash-Shaibānī (tribe); الهَرَوِىّ, al-Harawī (of the town of Herat); الأَنْدَلُسِىّ al-Andalusī (the Andalusian); البَغْدَادِىّ, al-Baghdādī (of Baghdad).

Note that some compound names are indeclinable, e.g تَأَبَّطَ شَرًّا given above, which is really a verb with its object, in fact, a complete sentence.

In the case of authors and other famous historical characters, the name by which a man is popularly known may be any one of the above three elements, e.g. (a) الخليل بن احمد is known as الخليل; (b) أبو الحُسَيْن محمد بن جُبَيْر is known as إبن جُبَيْر; (c) محمد بن جرير الطَبَرِىّ is known as الطبرى from Tabaristan, his place of birth.

Older writers in giving a person's proper name will often include a whole pedigree after the Kunya and two or more names and أَلْقَابٌ (pl. of لَقَبٌ).

7. The two names ع‍Umar (Omar) and ع‍Amr (Amr). عُمَرُ is a diptote. عَمْرٌو is a triptote and is declined as follows: Nom. عَمْرٌو ع‍amrun; Acc. عَمْرًا ع‍amran; Gen. عَمْرٍو ع‍amrin. This is purely a convention of spelling and does not affect the pronunciation. The otiose و distinguishes the two names in unvowelled script.

8. For the rule of when بن is used for إبن ibn, see Chapter Seven, sec. 3.

VOCABULARY

ثِقَةٌ confidence, trust (in passage (A) Ex. 79 a reliable scholar, authority)

نَحَوِىٌّ grammarian

مَعْرُوفٌ بِ known as

أَخَذَ عَنْ to study under, learn from (*antique usage*)

خِلَافَةٌ caliphate (office; or period of reign)

مَعْنًى *pl.* مَعَانٍ meaning

بُخْلٌ greed, avarice, stinginess

رَذِيلَةٌ *pl.* رَذَائِلُ vice, a vice

فَضِيلَةٌ *pl.* فَضَائِلُ virtue, a virtue

مَعْدِنٌ *pl.* مَعَادِنُ mine, metal

إِبْطٌ *m.* or *f.*, *pl.* آبَاطٌ armpit

غُولٌ *pl.* أَغْوَالٌ ، غِيلَانٌ demon (ghoul)

شَبَحٌ *pl.* أَشْبَاحٌ phantom, ghost

أُسْطُورَةٌ *pl.* أَسَاطِيرُ legend

حَيْثُ where, since

فَاوَضَ III to negotiate with

مُفَاوَضَاتٌ negotiations

بَلَاغٌ *pl.* ـَاتٌ — message, announcement; communiqué (*mod.*)

قَارِئٌ *pl.* قُرَّاءٌ reader

فَنٌّ *pl.* فُنُونٌ art *n.*

فَنِّيٌّ artistic, technical

فَنَّانٌ artist

بَرْقِيَّةٌ / تِلِغْرَافٌ } telegram

إِجْرَاءَاتٌ measures, steps

نُفُوذٌ influence

نَافِذَةٌ *pl.* نَوَافِذُ window

فُرْصَةٌ *pl.* فُرَصٌ chance, opportunity

بَخْتٌ fortune, good luck

بَخِيتٌ fortunate, lucky

كَفَى (ـِ) to suffice, be sufficient for

كِفَايَةٌ a sufficiency, enough (*mod.*)

وُجْهَةُ نَظَرٍ point of view (*mod.*)

زَعَمَ (ـُ) to claim, assert

زَعِيمٌ *pl.* زُعَمَاءُ leader, spokesman

تَضَمَّنَ V to include, contain

أَهَمِّيَّةٌ importance

مَبْدَأٌ *pl.* مَبَادِئُ principle, element

تَوَلَّى V to take upon oneself, be entrusted with

وِلَايَةٌ *pl.* ـَاتٌ — province

مُبَاحَثَةٌ discussion

عُلُوٌّ height

عَكْسٌ the opposite of anything

بِٱلْعَكْسِ on the contrary

عَلَى ٱلسَّوَاءِ equally, alike

بَشَرٌ man, mankind

EXERCISE 79

A

(From Ibn al-Anbārī, 13th century A.D., نُزْهَةُ ٱلْأَلِبَّاءِ, a collection of biographies of Lexicographers. The following piece is about al-Qirmīsīnī who was so called because he came from Qirmīsīn, a village in N. Iraq.)

وأمّا (as for) «أبو الحسن بن هارون بن نَصْر» المعروف
«بالقِرْمِيسِينِيّ» النَحَوِيّ، فإنَّهُ أخذ عن «عَلِي بن سليمان الأَخْفَشِيّ»
وأخَذَ عنهُ عبدُ السَلام بن حُسَيْن البَصْرِيّ قال «ابْنُ أَبِي
الفَوَارِس»: تُوُفِّيَ عَلِي بن هارون القرميسيني النحوى فى جمادى
الآخرة سَنَةَ إِحْدَى وسبعين وثلاثمائة فى خلافة «الطائِع» قال:
وكَانَ عِنْدَهُ[1] من أبى حسن الأخفشى أشياءُ كثيرةٌ وسمعتُ منه يقولُ:
كَانَ ثقةً جَمِيلَ الأَمْرِ[2] وكان مولدُهُ سنةَ تسعين ومائتين.

B

١ — ما هو معنى البخل والكرم؟ إنَّ الأوّلَ عكسُ الثانى، فذاك
(the former) رَذيلةٌ وهذا فضيلةٌ، حَيْثُ أنَّ دِينَيِ الاسلامِ والمَسِيحِيّةِ
يَطْلُبَانِ مِن الانسان الإِعْطاءَ. وللبخيتِ الذى له اكثرُ مِمَّا يكفيهِ
أنْ يَهْتَمَّ بالمَساكِينِ وأنْ يُعْطِيهم ما (that which) يَعيشون به.
هذا مَبْدَأٌ فى كِلا الدِينَيْن ذو اهمية كبيرة ولهذا المبدإ الأساسى نفوذٌ

[1] عند is used in the sense "to have".

[2] جميل الأمر: The word أمر adds nothing to the meaning here.

عَظِيمٌ فى تأريخ البَشَر. ٢ — فى اثناء تلك المباحثة زَعَمَ أحدُ الاعضاء
أنَّ البرقيةَ تَتَضَمَّنُ خبراً مهماً عن المفاوضات الأخيرة. ٣ — لُقِّبَ
هذا الشاعرُ بتأبَّطَ شرًّا لأنَّهُ كان يحمل غولاً تحت إبطه فى يومٍ من
الايام. أمّا أنا، فاعتبرُ هذه القصَّةَ أُسْطُورَةً كاذبةً لا تَسْتَحِقُّ اهتمامَ
القارئ. ٤ — إنَّ الشِعْرَ فَنٌّ والشاعرَ فَنَّانٌ بالكلمات، والشعر فى رأى
العرب اكبر فنٍّ ادبىٍّ. ٥ — ما هى وجهةُ نظرِ الزعيمِ فى الإجراءات
اللازمة؟ أَلَمْ يُجِبْ على التلغراف؟ مَتَى يصدر بلاغٌ عن المسألة؟
٦ — كان لى اكبرُ بختٍ حَيْثُ أنّى اكتشفتُ فضَّةً ومعادنَ اخرى فى
الولاية الجنوبية. ٧ — تكونُ لك فرصةُ نظرِ البنتِ مِن جديدٍ من تلك
النافذة العالية، وذلك كفايةٌ لشابٍّ مِثْلِكَ.

EXERCISE 80

A

The meaning of greed is that a man (the man) wants to take everything for himself, and does not like to give to others (use غيره). It is one of the greatest vices in Islam and Christianity alike. Its opposite is generosity, which was the greatest virtue of the desert Arabs in the Days of Ignorance. There is a famous Arabic book about greed called كتاب البخلاء. It is by al-Jāḥiẓ, who lived in the Ninth Century. I hope that you will have the chance to read it, as it is a book of considerable importance in the history of Arabic literature. It is a great book even from the Europeans' point of view, and those who do not know Arabic can read it in a good French translation. It contains stories of many mean men in the various provinces of the Islamic Empire.

B

Perhaps, reader (use يا), you are among those lucky students who are concerned with Arabic poetry. Now poetry is the oldest art of the Arabs, and its principles have scarcely changed during a period of thirteen hundred years. The ancient Arabs told many stories about their poets. There is a remarkable legend about Ta'abbaṭa Sharran, the famous poet. It is said that one day he went out into the desert, where he met a ghoul – that is, a species of ghost. The poet carried it home under his arm(pit), and scared his relations. After this incident, he was nicknamed Ta'abbaṭa Sharran.

C

1. Gold and silver are precious metals. Much of our gold comes from South Africa. 2. An announcement has been heard that the negotiations between the two sides have succeeded. 3. I replied to him by telegram that I would take the necessary steps. 4. During the discussions he mentioned that two windows were not enough even (حتى) for the smallest room in the house. 5. Their leader complained of the height of the chair on which the president was sitting. "He sits like an oriental prince", he said. 6. This is a matter of (ذو) great importance to the government.

CHAPTER FORTY-TWO

(اَلْبَابُ ٱلثَّانِى وَٱلْأَرْبَعُونَ)

The Feminine

1. The *Feminine* has been dealt with briefly in Chapter Three. The commonest Feminine ending is, of course, the *tā' marbūṭa*. Two other Feminine forms were described in Chapter Eleven: the Feminine of the Colour and Defect Adjectives, and the Feminine of the Elative.

2. There are a number of nouns which are of the form of the Colour-Defect Adjectives, and they too are Feminine. In many cases they may originally have been Feminine adjectives, but were so often used with some common Feminine nouns, such as أَرْضٌ "earth", that the noun was omitted, and the Adjective used alone as a Noun, e.g.

صَحْرَاءُ desert, pl. صَحْرَاوَاتٌ ، صَحَارَى

بَطْحَاءُ a wide river bed, pl. بَطْحَاوَاتٌ بِطَاحٌ

Some Feminine Nouns of this type diverge from the normal measure, e.g. كِبْرِيَاءُ pride.

The *'alif mamdūda* is recognized by the Arab grammarians as being a Feminine ending. But there are many words with this ending which are Masculine. The student must be guided by the dictionary in this matter.

3. Similarly there are many nouns of the Feminine Elative measure which are Feminine, though here again, the dictionary should be consulted. We may say that the *'alif maqṣūra* MAY BE a Feminine ending, e.g. دُنْيَا "world" (Feminine of أَدْنَى "lower", Elative of دَنِيٌّ "low".). The regular spelling would be دُنْيَى but the *'alif maqṣūra* is

written as *'alif* instead of *yā'* to avoid possible confusion with two successive *yā*'s. The "present world", or the "lower world", was originally termed اَلدَّارُ (الحياة or) الدُّنْيا, دارٌ being Feminine. Then the noun was omitted. In contrast, the "future world" (or hereafter) is termed اَلدَّارُ ٱلْآخِرَةُ or الأُخْرَى. So we may speak of الأُخْرَى or الآخِرَةُ omitting دار.

In some words there is a modification of vowelling, as in ذِكْرَى (fem.) "remembrance".

4. Some words may be spelt with final *'alif maqṣūra* or *mamdūda* at will, e.g. فَوْضَى, فَوْضَاءُ "anarchy", used classically in the expression قَوْمٌ فَوْضَاءُ (people without a chief); and ضَوْضًى, ضَوْضَاءُ "clamour, uproar"; used today by schoolmasters of an unruly class! Note that the latter has *nunation* when *maqṣūra*. Both words are, however, Masculine.

5. The addition of *tā' marbūṭa* to a Collective Noun to form the Noun of Unity has been noted in Chapter Three. Such collectives may be Masculine or Feminine, e.g. نَحْلَةٌ "a bee"; نَحْلٌ كَثِيرٌ or نَحلٌ كَثِيرَةٌ "many bees".

6. There are some Collectives, however, from which no Noun of Unity, or Singular, can be formed:

e.g. خَيْلٌ horses. إِبْلٌ camels.

قَوْمٌ people (or a people). نِسَاءٌ women.

نَاسٌ people (the form أُنَاسٌ also exists).

The last two are of disputed derivation, but may be considered broken plurals. Note إِنْسَانٌ "human being", generally shown in dictionaries under أَنِسَ as well as (نسو) نَسَا.

We may divide such words, as to gender, into two groups.

(a) Those referring to irrational beings are usually Feminine: e.g.

خَيْلٌ كَرِيمَةٌ fine (noble) horses.

إِبْلٌ كَثِيرَةٌ many camels.

(b) Those referring to human beings are usually considered to be Plurals, and are Masculine or Feminine according to significance, e.g.:

نَاسٌ كِرَامٌ noble people.

نساء كَرِيمَةٌ or نساء كَرِيمَاتٌ noble women.

جَاءَ نَاسٌ كَثِيرُونَ وَحَضَرُوا ٱلْمَعْرِضَ many people came and attended the exhibition.

7. The following should be noted:

Masc. الأَوَّلُ ; Fem. الأُولَى the first

Masc. الآخَرُ ; Fem. الأُخْرَى the other.

No Masc. Fem. حُبْلَى pregnant.

8. Some words which cannot, for obvious reasons, refer to the male, retain a Masculine form:

e.g. حَامِلٌ pregnant (lit. carrying).

عَاقِرٌ barren, sterile (woman).

عَجُوزٌ senile woman (uncomplimentary when applied to a man).

8. Certain adjectives have no separate form for the feminine.

(a) Those of the form فَعِيلٌ when they have the meaning of the Passive Participle, e.g.:

قَتِيلٌ slain; *synonym* مَقْتُولٌ killed.

كَانَتِ ٱلْقَتِيلُ جَمِيلَةً the slain girl was beautiful.

(b) Those of the form فَعُولٌ with the meaning of the Active Participle, e.g. صَبُورٌ patient. كَانَتْ بِنْتًا صَبُورًا she was a patient girl.

9. Adjectives of the form فَعْلَانُ, without *nunation*, take their feminine form in فَعْلَى, e.g. غَضْبَانُ angry; fem. غَضْبَى. Note, however, with *nunation*, the *tā' marbūṭa* is added, e.g. نَدْمَانٌ repentant; fem. نَدْمَانَةٌ.

10. In Chapter Three we pointed out that some words were feminine for no apparent reason, while others could be of either gender, again with no apparent explanation. Some dictionaries list these, as Hava's Arabic-English Dictionary (in the explanatory remarks of the preface). The following feminine words should be added to those given in Chapter Three; they are only the commoner ones:

بِئْرٌ well.	حَرْبٌ war.	رِيحٌ wind.
عَصًا staff, stick.	فَأْسٌ axe.	كَأْسٌ cup, glass.
نَعْلٌ sandal, horseshoe.	قَوْسٌ bow (weapon).	

11. The following should be added to the words given in Chapter Three which may be masculine or feminine at will; the letters of the alphabet, e.g. أَلِفٌ مَقْصُورٌ or مَقْصُورَةٌ (although they are usually feminine),

إِصْبَعٌ finger.	سُلَّمٌ ladder.
جَنَاحٌ wing (usually masc.).	سَمَاءٌ heaven.
حَانُوتٌ shop, stall.	فِرْدَوْسٌ paradise, garden.
خَمْرٌ wine (usually fem.).	فَرَسٌ horse.
رُوحٌ spirit.	قَفًا neck.

سِكِّينٌ knife. كَبِدٌ liver.

سِلْمٌ peace. لِسَانٌ tongue.

مُوسَى razor.

VOCABULARY

صَيَّرَ II to put, place (in Ex. 81), lit. to cause to become

عَجَلَةٌ carriage (in Ex. 81)

مُؤَخَّرٌ ، مُؤَخَّرَةٌ the rear of anything

اِسْتَلْقَى X to lie down, throw oneself down

ظَهْرٌ *pl.* ظُهُورٌ the back (anatomical)

حَثَا (ـُ) to pour dust (upon)

نَفَذَ (ـُ) to pierce, penetrate, be effective

اِغْتَرَّ VIII to be deceived, beguiled

غَرَّ (ـُ) to deceive, beguile

صَنْدَلٌ sandalwood

كَافُورٌ camphor

رَمَادٌ ashes

اَلْهِنْدُ India, or the Indians

مَنْظَرٌ *pl.* مَنَاظِرُ sight, view

هِنْدِيٌّ *pl.* هُنُودٌ Indian

رُبَّمَا perhaps, sometimes, it may be

أَحْرَقَ IV to burn *tr.*

اِحْتَرَقَ VIII to be burned, to burn *intr.*

كِبْرِيَاءُ *f.* pride

فَوْضَاءُ ، فَوْضَى anarchy

ضَوْضَاءُ ، ضَوْضَى noise, clamour

عَمَّ (ـُ) to be, or become, general or widespread

كَسَبَ (ـِ) to win, gain

اَلطِّبُّ ، عِلْمُ ٱلطِّبِّ medicine (the study, science or profession)

دَاءٌ *pl.* أَدْوَاءٌ sickness, disease

دَوَاءٌ *pl.* أَدْوِيَةٌ medicine

اَلدُّوَلِيَّةُ internationalism

EXERCISE 81

(From the Travels of Ibn Baṭṭūṭa, 14th Cent., A.D.)

مَوْتُ مُلوكِ سَرَنْدِيبَ (Ceylon)

اذا مات المَلِكُ بِبِلادِ سَرَنْدِيبَ، صُيِّرَ عَلَى عَجَلَةٍ قَرِيباً من الأرض
وعُلِّقَ فى مُؤَخَّرِها مُسْتَلْقِياً على ظَهْرِهِ يَجُرُّ شَعَرَ رَأْسِهِ التُّرابَ عن
الأرض. وٱمْرَأَةٌ بِيَدِها مكنسةٌ تحثو الترابَ على رأسه وتُنَادِى : أيها
الناس، هذا مَلِكُكُم بِالْأَمْسِ قد مَلَكَكُم وكان أَمْرُهُ نَافِذاً فيكم.
وقد صار إلى ما تَرَوْنَ من تَرْكِ الدُنيا. وأَخَذَ روحَه مَلْأَكُ الموتِ.
فلا تَغْتَرُّوا بالحياة بَعْدَهُ. وكلامٌ نَحْوُ هذا[1] ثلاثةَ أيامٍ. ثُمَّ يُهَيَّأُ له
الصَنْدَلُ والكَافُورُ والزَعْفَرانُ فيُحْرَقُ بِهِ ثُمَّ يُرْمَى بِرَمادِهِ فى الرِيحِ.
والهِنْدُ كُلُّهم يُحْرِقُونَ مَوْتَاهُمْ[2] بالنارِ. وسرنديبُ آخِرُ الجَزَائِرِ وهى من بلاد
الهِنْد ورُبَّما أُحْرِقَ الملكُ فتَدْخُلُ نِسَاؤُهُ النارَ فتَحْتَرِقْنَ معه :

EXERCISE 82

A

The people have been deceived by pride, so anarchy has become general. Every day we hear a clamour in the streets of the capital. The youth drink wine, get drunk, then run from shop to shop. They have already burnt more than a hundred shops. One boy, perhaps his age was about ten, broke the windows of a number of shops with a small axe. If this is the new spirit of nationalism, then I prefer internationalism.

---

[1] "is" or "there is" understood here.

[2] ى of مَوْتَى becomes ا with pron. suffix.

B

India beguiled me during the late World War. I served in the Indian Army with Indian troops, but I also saw many of the remarkable sights (مَنَاظِر) of that beautiful country. Some parts of it are like paradise to whomsoever loves colour and brightness. But it has too many inhabitants, many of whom are very poor. The new national government is fighting poverty with great energy, and I hope that it will succeed.

C

The Prime Minister's house caught fire this afternoon, and the fire brigade did not arrive until four hours later. This was because their vehicles were in a bad condition. Two of them had broken down (use كسر VII) and were awaiting repair. Among those who died in the fire were the Prime Minister's old mother, and his pregnant second wife.

D

I found a thief in the house during the night. I had no rifle or other weapon with me, so I hit him on the neck with a silver cup which I had won when I rode in horse races. When the doctor saw the thief, he said that he had become unhappy because his wife was barren, and that was the reason for his resorting to a life of crime. My wife is a very patient woman, but she does not believe all these new ideas which have come into medicine. "This man is not sick", she says, "he is a criminal. But that is a nasty word, and people don't like nasty words these days, even when they are the truth. This man's sickness is thieving, and the suitable medicine is prison."

CHAPTER FORTY-THREE

(أَلْبَابُ ٱلثَّالِثُ وَٱلْأَرْبَعُونَ)

Number

1. For the three numbers: Singular (مُفْرَدٌ), Dual (مُثَنًّى) and Plural (جَمْعٌ), see Chapters Five, Six and Seven.

2. The Sound Masculine Plural is used for:

(a) *Masculine Proper Names*, except those which end in ة,

e.g. زَيْدٌ Zaid; pl. زَيْدُونَ ; مُحَمَّدٌ Muhammad; pl. مُحَمَّدُونَ

قَرَأْتُ سَبْعَةَ مُحَمَّدِينَ فِي كَشْفِ ٱلطَّلَبَةِ I read seven Muhammads among the list of students.

(b) *Diminutives* of *Proper Names* and of *Class Names* which indicate rational beings, e.g.

عُمَيْرٌ dim. of عُمَرُ 'Umar; pl. عُمَيْرُونَ.

رُجَيْلٌ little man, pl. رُجَيْلُونَ.

(c) *Participles*, when they refer to male human beings, e.g. مُؤْمِنٌ believer; pl. مُؤْمِنُونَ.

But note the use of broken plural outlined in Chapter Seventeen, when the *Active Participle* has acquired a technical nominal significance, e.g.

كَاتِبٌ writing, clerk, writer; pl. كُتَّابٌ ، كَتَبَةٌ

The sound masculine plural may, however, often also be used: كَاتِبُونَ writers.

(d) Nouns of the form فَعَّالٌ which denote occupations and professions: نَجَّارٌ carpenter; pl. نَجَّارُونَ.

(e) Relative adjectives: مِصْرِىٌّ Egyptian; pl. مِصْرِيُّونَ.

Note, however, such exceptions as:

عَرَبِىٌّ Arab, pl. عَرَبٌ ; أَجْنَبِىٌّ, foreign, pl. أَجَانِبُ.

يَهُودِىٌّ Jew, Jewish, pl. يَهُودٌ.

(f) Adjectives of the form أَفْعَلُ denoting Elatives, e.g. أَكْثَرُ; pl. اَلْأَكْثَرُونَ. (Note also the Broken Plural, e.g. اَلْأَكْبَرُ, "the greatest" pl. اَلْأَكَابِرُ; اَلْأَعْظَمُ; pl. اَلْأَعَاظِمُ).

(g) The following sound masculine plurals should be noted:

اِبْنٌ son (for بَنَوٌ);	Plur.	بَنُونَ	(also أَبْنَاءٌ)
عَالَمٌ world;	,,	عَالَمُونَ	
أَرْضٌ earth;	,,	أَرَضُونَ*	(also أَرَاضٍ)
أَهْلٌ family;	,,	أَهْلُونَ	(also أَهَالٍ)
إِوَزٌّ goose;	,,	إِوَزُّونَ	
ذُو master;	,,	ذَوُونَ	

Also the Fem. سَنَةٌ "year"; Plur. سِنُونَ (as well as سَنَوَاتٌ).

3. The Sound Feminine Plural is used for:

(a) Feminine proper names, e.g. هِنْدٌ Hind; pl. هِنْدَاتٌ.

(b) Masculine proper names ending in ة; طَرَفَةُ; pl. طَرَفَاتٌ.

(c) Many class names ending in ة, e.g. حَارَةٌ city quarter; pl. حَارَاتٌ.

*Rare

(d) The Feminines of adjectives whose Masculine take the Sound Masculine Plurals,

e.g. كَاتِبَاتٌ female writers.

خَيَّاطَاتٌ tailoresses.

مِصْرِيَّاتٌ Egyptian women.

(e) The Feminine adjectives which end in ى — *'alif maqṣūra* or اءُ — *'alif mamdūda*:

e.g. كُبْرَى greatest (f.); pl. كُبْرَيَاتٌ (rare).

حَمْرَاءُ red (f.); pl. حَمْرَاوَاتٌ.

(f) Such words sometimes take the sound feminine plural when they are used as nouns,

e.g. خَضْرَاوَاتٌ vegetables (lit. "greens"), صَحْرَاوَاتٌ deserts (alternative pls. صَحَارَى, etc.).

(g) Names of the letters of the Alphabet and the months:

e.g. كَتَبْتُ ثَلَاثَ طَاءَاتٍ I wrote three *tā*'s.

قَضَيْتُ مُحَرَّمَاتِ ٱلثَّلَاثِ سَنَوَاتِ ٱلْمَاضِيَةِ فِي ٱلْقَاهِرَةِ. I have spent the Muharrams of the last three years in Cairo.

(h) Verbal nouns of the derived forms:

e.g. تَصَرُّفٌ disposal; pl. تَصَرُّفَاتٌ

إِسْتِعْمَالٌ use; pl. إِسْتِعْمَالَاتٌ

Note, however, that Verbal Nouns of II and IV sometimes also have broken plurals:

II تَصْوِيرٌ picture; pl. تَصَاوِيرُ or تَصْوِيرَاتٌ

تَجْرِبَةٌ experiment; pl. تَجَارِبُ or تَجْرِبَاتٌ

IV إِرْجَافٌ false news, pl. أَرَاجِيفُ or إِرْجَافَاتٌ

(i) Diminutives of words denoting things and irrational beings:

كُلَيْبٌ little dog, pup; pl. كُلَيْبَاتٌ

شُمَيْسَةٌ little sun; pl. شُمَيْسَاتٌ

كُتَيِّبٌ booklet; pl. كُتَيِّبَاتٌ

Note also وُلَيْدَاتٌ meaning "children" irrespective of sex.

(j) Foreign words, unless properly Arabicized,

e.g. بَارَاشُوط parachute; pl. بَارَاشُوطَاتٌ

This applies to some words which denote male human beings, especially titles.

e.g. بَاشَا (Turkish) Pasha; pl. بَاشَوَاتٌ

آغَا (Turkish) Aga; pl. آغَوَاتٌ, آغَاوَاتٌ

خَوَاجَةٌ, خَوَاجَا (Persian) Sir, Mr; pl. خَوَاجَاتٌ

بَكْ, بَيك (Turkish) Bey, Beg; pl. بَكَوَاتٌ

*We may note here that there has been a move in the modern Arab world against the use of foreign words, and language academies have busied themselves substituting words from old Arabic roots:

e.g. اَلْأَشِعَّةُ ٱلنَّافِذَةُ (lit. the piercing rays) for إِكْسَرَاى

pl. إِكْسَرَايَاتٌ X-rays.

Nevertheless, foreign words continue to be used, especially in common speech. Often, a broken plural is formed, where the foreign words lend themselves to this,

e.g. سِيكَارَةٌ (سِيجَارَةٌ), cigarette; pl. سَكَائِرُ, سَكَايِرُ; دُونْكِى (Sudan) donkey engine, and, by extension, deep bore well with pumping engine; pl. دَوَانِكُ.

The sound Feminine plural دُونْكِيَاتٌ would be more orthodox.

* See also Appendix C, §7.

FURTHER MEASURES OF THE BROKEN PLURAL

4. A number of measures have been included in Chapters Six and Seven of the Broken Plural; again when referring to the Colour Defect Adjectives and the Elative (Chapter Eleven), and the Active Participle (Chapter Seventeen). A few further measures are given here, but a more complete list will be found in Wright's Arabic Grammar, Part I, paras. 304/5.

(a) فِعَلٌ pl. of فِعْلَةٌ, e.g. قِطْعَةٌ a piece; pl. قِطَعٌ;

سِيرَةٌ life, biography; pl. سِيَرٌ.

(b) فُعَلٌ often pl. of فُعْلَةٌ

e.g. قُبَّةٌ dome; pl. قُبَبٌ;

صُورَةٌ form, picture; pl. صُوَرٌ

This is also an alternative plural to the Feminine Elative,

e.g. الْكُبْرَى the greatest, fem; pl. الْكُبَرُ '

(c) فَعِيلٌ e.g. عَبْدٌ slave; pl. عَبِيدٌ; حِمَارٌ donkey, ass; pl. حَمِيرٌ

(d) فُعَّلٌ an alternative to فُعَّالٌ, when used as the plural of the Active Participle. Its use is largely poetical, and is not recommended to students:

e.g. حَاضِرٌ present, attendant; pl. حُضَّرٌ or حُضَّارٌ

(e) فُعَلَةٌ. This is commonly found as the plural of the technically used Active Participle of Simple Verbs endings in و or ى,

e.g. قَاضٍ (Act. Part. of قَضَى) judge; pl. قُضَاةٌ

وَالٍ (,, ,, ,, وَلِيَ) governor; pl. وُلَاةٌ

(f) فَعْلَى This is fairly often met as the plural of فَعِيلٌ with a Passive sense:

e.g. قَتْلَى (from قَتِيلٌ), slain, victim;

مَوْتَى (from مَيِّتٌ for مَوِيتٌ) dead.

(g) فُعْلَانٌ

بَلَدٌ district, country; pl. بُلْدَانٌ

فَارِسٌ rider; pl. فُرْسَانٌ

شَابٌّ (for شَابِبٌ) youth; pl. شُبَّانٌ

شُجَاعٌ brave; pl. شُجْعَانٌ

(h) فَعَائِلُ

جَزِيرَةٌ island; pl. جَزَائِرُ (also جُزُرٌ)

جَرِيدَةٌ newspaper; pl. جَرَائِدُ

رِسَالَةٌ letter; pl. رَسَائِلُ

عَجِيبَةٌ wonder; pl. عَجَائِبُ

عَجُوزٌ old woman; pl. عَجَائِزُ

ضَمِيرٌ pronoun, conscience; pl. ضَمَائِرُ

(i) فَعَالٍ, (فَعَالِى when definite).

عَذْرَاءُ virgin; pl. عَذَارٍ

فَتْوَى Mufti's legal decision; pl. فَتَاوٍ

Note also لَيْلٌ night; pl. لَيَالٍ

أَهْلٌ people, family; pl. أَهَالٍ

أَرْضٌ land, earth; pl. أَرَاضٍ

(j) فَعَالَى as an alternative to (i), e.g. عَذَارَى virgins; from فُعْلَى when *not* Superlative (fem.), e.g. حُبْلَى pregnant; pl. حَبَالَى.

From فَعْلَانُ, e.g. كَسْلَانُ lazy; pl. كَسَالَى.

From فَعِيلَةٌ with Weak final radical:

e.g. هَدِيَّةٌ present, gift; pl. هَدَايَا.

رَعِيَّةٌ flock; pl. رَعَايَا. مَنِيَّةٌ fate, death; pl. مَنَايَا.

5. Where a Noun has more than four radicals their number must be reduced to four to form a Broken Plural:

e.g. عَنْكَبُوتٌ spider; pl. عَنَاكِبُ

إِمْبَرَاطُورٌ emperor; pl. أَبَاطِرَةٌ.

عَنْدَلِيبٌ nightingale; pl. عَنَادِلُ

This rule may be ignored in colloquial speech:

e.g. عَنْقَرِيب wooden bed (Egypt); pl. عَنَاقِرِب

تَرْجُمَانٌ dragoman, guide, interpreter; pl. تَرَاجِمَان

But no purist would allow these plurals in print.

6. Where a Noun has two or more Plurals, these may be used for different meanings:

e.g. عَيْنٌ eye; pl. عُيُونٌ etc.

عَيْنٌ notable; pl. أَعْيَانٌ

عَبْدٌ slave; pl. عَبِيدٌ

عَبْدٌ worshipper (of God); pl. عِبَادٌ

7. Sometimes a further Plural may be formed from a Plural. It may be Sound Fem. or Broken, and is used to give a more extensive meaning:

حَرْبٌ war; pl. حُرُوبٌ pl.pl. حُرُوبَاتٌ campaigns.

فَتْحٌ conquest; pl. فُتُوحٌ pl.pl. فُتُوحَاتٌ

طَرِيقٌ road, way; pl. طُرُقٌ pl.pl. طُرُقَاتٌ

يَدٌ hand; pl. أَيْدٍ pl.pl. أَيَادٍ

إِنَاءٌ vessel; pl. آنِيَةٌ pl.pl. أَوَانٍ

8. The Feminine ending ة may be used as a kind of Collective Plural for the following two categories of nouns:

(a) فَعَّالٌ

e.g. قَوَّاسٌ bowman; pl. قَوَّاسَةٌ

(b) The relative adjective:

e.g. سُودَانِيٌّ Sudanese; pl. سُودَانِيَّةٌ (or سُودَانِيُّونَ)

صُوفِيٌّ Sufi (mystic); pl. صُوفِيَّةٌ (or صُوفِيُّونَ)

9. The following irregular plurals should be noted:

أُمٌّ mother; Plur. أُمَّهَاتٌ and أُمَّاتٌ

فَمٌ mouth; Plur. أَفْوَاهٌ

مَاءٌ water (for مَاهٌ for مَوَهٌ); Plur. أَمْوَاهٌ and مِيَاهٌ (for مِوَاهٌ)

شَفَةٌ lip (for شَفْهَةٌ); Plur. شِفَاهٌ (also شَفَوَاتٌ and شَفَهَاتٌ)

شَاةٌ sheep (for شَوْهَةٌ); Plur. شَاهٌ and شِيَاهٌ

أَمَةٌ maid-servant; Plur. إِمَاءٌ and أَمَوَاتٌ.

اِمْرَأَةٌ woman; Plur. نِسَاءٌ and نِسْوَةٌ and نِسْوَانٌ

إِنْسَانٌ man; Plur. أُنَاسٌ usually نَاسٌ

قَوْسٌ bow; Plur. قِسِيٌّ and قُسِيٌّ

VOCABULARY

اِقْتَرَفَ VIII to commit (a sin or crime)

نَدِمَ عَلَى (ـَ) to repent, regret

قَصَّرَ II to fall short, be remiss

تَلَهَّفَ V to regret something missed

اَلْمَصِيرُ the future, result, issue

تَقْرِيرُ ٱلْمَصِيرِ self-determination (*mod.*)

بَصَّرَ II to open anyone's eyes, enlighten

هَجَرَ (ـُ) to forsake, abandon

إِنَّمَا a strong affirmative particle; indeed, in truth, only

بَادَرَ III to hasten

نَهَبَ (ـَ) to plunder, carry off

اِغْتَنَمَ VIII to seize (plunder, or opportunity)

فَاتَ (ـُ) to elapse (of time); to pass (*intr.*)

فَاتَ to escape, miss (*tr.*)

فَوْتٌ *v.n.* of فَاتَ

هُدًى guidance

شَفَةٌ *pl.* شَفَهَاتٌ ، شَفَوَاتٌ ، شِفَاهٌ lip

إِنَاءٌ *pl.* آنِيَةٌ vessel, pot

مَسَكَ (ـِ) to seize, hold

قَبَضَ (ـِ) to seize, grasp

قَبَضَ عَلَى to seize, arrest

سِنٌّ *pl.* أَسْنَانٌ tooth, age

نَوَى (ـِ) to intend

نِيَّةٌ *pl.* ـَاتٌ intention

رِحْلَةٌ *pl.* رِحَالٌ journey

سَعَى (ـَ) to exert oneself, make an effort

مَسْعًى *pl.* مَسَاعٍ effort

مُسْتَوًى *pl.* مُسْتَوَيَاتٌ standard

دَرَجَةٌ *pl.* ـَاتٌ degree, step

آلَةٌ *pl.* ـَاتٌ tool, instrument

فَضْلًا عَنْ apart from, not to mention, in addition to

وُضُوحٌ clarity

قَصْدًا intentionally, deliberately, on purpose

EXERCISE 83

A

(Extract from a sermon by Ibn al-Jauzi, 12th cent. A.D.)

إِخْوانى[1]، ٱعلموا أنَّ مَنْ عَمِلَ فى الأيام خيراً حُمِدَ أَمْرُهُ. ومَن ٱقْتَرَفَ فيها شرًّا أَضاعَ عُمْرَهُ. سَيَنْدَمُ غداً مَنْ قَصَّرَ، على تَقْصيرِهِ. ويَتَلَهَّفُ مَنْ تَرَكَ العَمَلَ لِمَصيرِهِ. ويَبْكِى هاجِرُ الهُدَى بعد تَبْصيرِهِ. إِنَّمَا هِيَ[2] أَوْقاتٌ مُبادِرَةٌ تَذْهَبُ، وٱغْتِنامُ أيامٍ تُنْهَبُ، فَبادِرْ بِعُمْرِكَ قَبْلَ الفَوْتِ. وٱغْتَنِمْ حياتَكَ قبل المَوْتِ.

B

أولائك الناسُ لا تكفيهم حكومةٌ عادلةٌ، إنَّمَا يُبادِرُونَ الى تقديرِ المصيرِ والحُكْمِ الذاتِى كَمَا فَعَلَ سائرُ أُمَمِ هذه القارةِ ونِيَّتُهُم ألَّا تَفُوتَهُمُ الفُرْصَةُ. نَعَمْ، إنّهم يَغْتَنِمُونَ الفُرصةَ ويَسْعَوْنَ لِيَسْتَحِقُّوا الاسْتِقْلالَ.

C

١ — اِفتح شَفَتَيْكَ كَيْ أرى أسنانَكَ. ٢ — كَيْفَ ٱنكَسَرَ الإناء وكان فى يَدَيْكَ قبل دقيقة؟ امْسِكْ هذه الآنيةَ مَسْكًا قويًا لعلَّها لا تَقَعُ من يَدِكَ. ٣ — رِحْلَةُ ٱبْنِ بَطُّوطَةَ من الهند للصينِ مَشْهُورَةٌ. فَفي أَوائلِها قَبَضَهُ الكُفَّارُ ولكنه نَجَا منهم. واخيرًا وَصَلَ الى الصين بعد مَساعٍ شديدةٍ. ٤ — رُفِعَ مُسْتَوَى الحياةِ (العيشة) فى أوربا لدرجةٍ غيرِ

---

[1] يا is here omitted.

[2] "they", i.e. the days of one's life.

متوقعةٍ. ٥ — الحَمْدُ لِلّٰهِ رَبِّ العٰلَمِينَ (Qur’ān, I). ٦ — لِى صعوبةٌ
كبيرةٌ مع أسماء المسلمين، فأَجِدُ نِصْفَهم مُحَمَّدِينَ! ٧ — لاقوا
أَرْبَعَ نِسَاءٍ بَيْضَاوَاتٍ ذوات حُسْنٍ وجَمَالٍ. ٨ — لهذه الآلةِ استعمالاتٌ
كثيرة مختلفة. ٩ — أَخَذَتِ المَنِيَّةُ وَالِيَ الولايةِ الشمالية، وتَرَكَ
ثلاثة أولاد وأربع بنات. ١٠ — رَأَيْتُ عَنَاكِبَ كثيرة فى حَجَرَات
الباشوات والبكوات، فأكنسى كلَّ الحجرات مِن جديد.

EXERCISE 84

A

The three Muhammads co-operated in the committing of this crime; then the first two repented of it. I forgave them, but as for the third, I don't know what the outcome will be. He is not the son of poor parents: indeed, his father and his uncle are wealthy, and give him everything he asks for. But it seems that he reads the crime stories of modern European authors, and takes every opportunity to thieve and fight. The whole town is afraid of him, and his father can do nothing with him. The police have arrested him seven times during the last seven months. I hope that in the future we will find good uses for his exertions and that he will become a useful member of (the) society.

B

These girls scarcely open their mouths when they speak. Has it escaped them that clarity is the most important thing in speech? They are all Hinds, and they all want to be writers; they are exerting themselves a great deal to reach a high level in their studies. Apart from their speech, they have been very successful in their work.

C

1. What is your intention in this long and difficult journey? There is not (لَيْسَ) a place in the world which some traveller has not visited, and you are old (كَبِيرُ ٱلسِّنِّ). I think it best for you to remain at home and leave all these exertions to someone else. 2. He seized the vessels and placed them all on the floor, then broke them deliberately with a strange, heavy instrument. 3. You are all Aghas and Beys in the view of the republicans; whatever you were formerly, peasant or princes.

CHAPTER FORTY-FOUR

(اَلْبَابُ ٱلرَّابِعُ وَٱلْأَرْبَعُونَ)

Declension of the Noun

1. *Declension* was dealt with briefly in Chapter Four. The Arabic for declining a word is إِعْرَابٌ, v.n. of عَرَبَ IV. A Noun declined is said to be مُعْرَبٌ (Passive Part.). But this term is also used of conjugating a verb, especially with reference to the Imperfect, whose three moods are considered to correspond roughly to the three cases, with their change of final vowels. A word whose final vowel is static is said to be مَبْنِيٌّ *indeclineable*, but this term is used almost solely of unchanging verbal forms (e.g. the Perfect) and of Particles like قَدْ, مِنْ. A few isolated Nouns may be considered مَبْنِيٌّ, such as حَذَارِ "caution"; and قَطَامِ, a woman's name.

2. Words ending in the *'alif maqṣūra* are not مَبْنِيٌّ, but declined by تَقْدِيرٌ, that is, notionally, e.g.

(i) كُبْرَى fem. Elative of كَبِيرٌ

(ii) دُنْيَا world.

(iii) ذِكْرَى remembrance.

(iv) هُدًى guidance.

(v) مُصْطَفًى Mustafa (proper name).

(vi) عَصًا a stick.

Of the above, nos. (i) to (iii) have no Nunation. They are therefore Diptotes, or غَيْرُ مُنْصَرِفٍ (see Chapter Four). They are the same for all cases. However, (i) and (iii) would change to *'alif* if a Pronoun were attached:

e.g. لِي ذِكْرَى حَزِينَةٌ I have a sad remembrance (nom. indef.)

ذِكْرَى ٱلْمَاضِي بَاطِلَةٌ Remembrance of the past is vain (nom.def.).

ذِكْرَاهُ بَاطِلَةٌ Its remembrance is vain (nom. with attached pronoun).

حَزِنْتُ مِنْ ذِكْرَى ٱلْمَاضِي I became sad at the remembrance of the past (gen. def.).

حَزِنْتُ مِنْ ذِكْرَاهُ I became sad at the remembrance of it (gen. with attached pronoun).

اَلدُّنْيَا مَكَانٌ حَزِنٌ The world is a sad place (nom. def.).

تَرَكَ ٱلدُّنْيَا He left the world (acc.def.).

تَعِبْتُ مِنْ هٰذِهِ ٱلدُّنْيَا I tired of this world (gen. def.).

3. Nouns (iv), (v) and (vi) are Triptotes or مُنْصَرِفٌ. They have *Nunation*, but this is removed when they are Definite. Again final *yā'* changes to *'alif*, when a Pronoun is attached:

e.g. لَيْسَ لِي هُدًى I have no guidance (nom.indef.).

لِي عَصًا طَوِيلَةٌ I have a long stick (nom.indef.).

اَلْهُدَى ضَرُورِيٌّ Guidance is necessary (nom.def.).

اَلْعَصَا مَكْسُورَةٌ The stick is broken (nom.def.).

عَصَا أَبِي مَكْسُورَةٌ My father's stick is broken (nom.def. with *'iḍāfa*).

عَصَاهُ ٱنْكَسَرَتْ His stick broke (nom.def. with attached pronoun).

أَعْطِنِي هُدًى بَيِّنًا	Give me clear guidance (acc.indef.).
أَعْطِنِي عَصًا جَدِيدَةً	Give me a new stick (acc.indef.).
أَعْطِنِي عَصَا أَبِي	Give me my father's stick (acc.def. with *'iḍāfa*).
أَعْطِنِي عَصَاهُ	Give me his stick (acc.def. with attached pronoun).
خِفْتُ مِنَ ٱلْعَصَا	I was afraid of the stick (gen.def.).
خِفْتُ مِنْ عَصَا أَبِي	I was afraid of my father's stick (gen. def. with *'iḍāfa*).
خِفْتُ مِنْ عَصَاهُ	I was afraid of his stick (gen.def. with attached pronoun).

4. The following types of Noun are Diptotes:

(a) Broken Plurals of the following forms:

e.g.	فُعَلَاءُ	وُزَرَاءُ	ministers; pl. of	وَزِيرٌ
	فَعْلَى	مَرْضَى	sick people; pl. of	مَرِيضٌ
	فَعَائِلُ	مَدَائِنُ	cities; pl. of	مَدِينَةٌ
	فَعَالَى	يَتَامَى	orphans; pl. of	يَتِيمٌ
	فَعَالِلُ	دَرَاهِمُ	dirhems (silver coins); money; pl. of	دِرْهَمٌ
	فَعَالِيلُ	خَنَازِيرُ	pigs; pl. of	خِنْزِيرٌ

Also the following plurals:

أُوَلُ (from أَوَّلُ first)

أُخَرُ (from آخَرُ other)

أَشْيَاءُ (from شَيْءٌ thing)

(b) The following feminine forms:

e.g. سَوْدَاءُ black

غَضْبَى angry

ذِكْرَى remembrance

كُبْرَى greatest

(c) The Masculine Singular Elative and Colour-Defect Nouns of the form أَفْعَلُ,

e.g. أَطْوَلُ longer, longest.

أَشْهَبُ grey.

Among the rare exceptions is أَرْمَلٌ widower, whose fem. is أَرْمَلَةٌ.

(d) Adjectives of the form فَعْلَانُ whose fem. is فَعْلَى.

(Note, however, نَدْمَانٌ boon companion; fem. نَدْمَانَةٌ).

(e) The numerals which end in ة when they stand alone as pure numbers, e.g. ثَلَاثَةُ نِصْفُ سِتَّةَ three is half of six.

(f) Most proper names, whether personal or geographical,

e.g. طَرَفَةُ Ṭarafa (masc.)

سُلَيْمَانُ Sulaimān (Solomon)

فَارِسُ Persia (Fars province)

أَحْمَدُ Aḥmad (as an Elative this is bound to be diptote)

يَحْيَى Yaḥyā, يَزِيدُ Yazīd } Names beginning with a *yā' of increase*, resembling the 3rd Person Sing. of the Imperfect must be Diptotes.

It may be mentioned that names of foreign origin are almost invariably Diptotes, e.g. لُنْدُنُ London; بَارِيسُ Paris.

On the other hand, there are many Triptote Personal Names. The chief guide here is the dictionary, e.g. زَيْدٌ Zaid. عَمْرٌو ʿAmr. هِنْدٌ Hind (a woman's name, sometimes a Diptote). جَعْفَرٌ Jaʿfar. They include many names either of participal form, e.g. مُحَمَّدٌ Muḥammad; مَحْمُودٌ Maḥmūd, or from the class of Adjectives resembling the Active Participle in meaning, e.g. حَسَنٌ Ḥasan (lit. "beautiful"), سَعِيدٌ Saʿīd (lit. "happy").

5. As already stated, Diptotes are treated as Triptotes when they are made *definite* in any way, e.g. by the Article, by an attached Pronoun or an *ʾiḍāfa*:

e.g. Nom.	مَدَائِنُ	cities;	اَلْمَدَائِنُ	the cities.
Acc.	مَدَائِنَ	cities;	مَدَائِنَهُمْ	their cities.
Gen.	مَدَائِنَ	cities;	مِنْ مَدَائِنِ بِلَادِ ٱلْعَرَبِ	from the cities of Arabia.

6. Nouns ending in ـٍ *in* have been dealt with when occuring as Active Participles of the Defective Verb, e.g. قَاضٍ, نَادٍ (see Chapter Twenty-nine). A similar phenomenon takes place in the case of some Broken Plurals derived from triliteral roots with the third radical *wāw* or *yā*ʾ,

e.g. جَارِيَةٌ slave-girl; فَتْوَى mufti's ruling.

Nom. and Gen. فَتَاوٍ ;جَوَارٍ

Accus. فَتَاوِيَ ;جَوَارِيَ

With Article, Nom. and Gen. اَلْفَتَاوِي ;اَلْجَوَارِي

With Article, Accus. اَلْفَتَاوِيَ ;اَلْجَوَارِيَ

The *yā*ʾ is similarly written when such words are made definite by *iḍāfa*.

VOCABULARY

يَتِيمٌ *pl.* أَيْتَامٌ ، يَتَامَى orphan

خِنْزِيرٌ *pl.* خَنَازِيرُ pig

جَارِيَةٌ *pl.* جَوَارٍ slave-girl, servant-girl

أَرْمَلٌ widower

مِيزَانِيَّةٌ budget

اَلْبُرْتُغَالُ ، اَلْبُرْتُقَالُ Portugal

بُرْتُقَالٌ oranges

جَبْهَةٌ *pl.* جَبَهَاتٌ forehead, front

اِسْتَعْمَرَ X to colonize

رُوسِيَا Russia

إِذْنٌ permission

اِقْتَرَحَ (بِـ) VIII to recommend, suggest

حِمَايَةٌ protection

غَادَرَ III to desert, leave

تَلَا (ـُ) to follow

وَسِيلَةٌ *pl.* وَسَائِلُ mean

اِعْتَقَلَ VIII to intern, arrest

أَعْدَمَ IV to execute (put to death)

رَمْلٌ sand

عَرَقٌ perspiration, sweat

فَجْأَةً suddenly

تَوَقَّفَ V to hesitate, stop

آسِيَا Asia

EXERCISE 85

A

كان العَرَقُ يسيل على جَبهَةِ الرجل حِينَما رأى الخِنْزِيرَ الوَحْشِيَّ. فما كان له أَيَّةُ حِمايةٍ. وفى تلك اللحظة فكَّر فى ولده الصغير الذى يصير يتيماً إن مات هو، وفى زوجته التى تُصْبِح أرملةً باكيةً. وفَجْأَةً تَوَقَّفَ الخنزيرُ، فأَخذَ الرجلُ يَجْرِى عبْرَ الرملِ ، فَغَادَرَ المكانَ باسرع ما أَمْكَنَ حَتَّى وصل إلى بيتٍ ودَخَلَهُ.

B

١ — إِسْتَعْمَرَتْ روسيا مُعْظَمَ آسِيا الشماليةَ أَثْناء القَرن التاسع عشر.

٢ — وَجَدتُ جَارِيَتِي قد أَكَلَتْ جَمِيعَ البُرْتُقَالِ ولَمْ أَر وسيلةً إلى شِراءِ فَواكِهَ أُخرى. ٣ — قَرَأَ الوزيرُ ميزانيةَ السنة التالية ولم يَرْضَ عنها. ٤ — أُعتقل المجرمُ واقترح الناسُ كُلُّهم بِاعدامه.

EXERCISE 86

1. My world came to an end when I became a widow, for, when I was eleven, my father died, and my mother had died three years previously. 2. We see in Russia's budget large sums for the defence of her borders. 3. The helping and guidance of widows is among the duties recommended to believers. 4. He had many pigs, apart from his cows and sheep. 5. He met a black girl, so he took her into employment [as] a servant girl in his house in Baghdad. But she deserted him suddenly without permission two days later. 6. They followed the enemy and found them hesitating in the sand, so they destroyed them straight away. 7. Portugal had many colonies in the past, and her sailors were famous. 8. I knew from the perspiration flowing on his forehead that his endeavours had tired him, but this was my only means of finishing the work at the appointed time. 9. I saw Muḥammad on my right and Aḥmad on my left. As for the boastful Ṭarafa, I did not see him at all. He had deserted me in my time of difficulty. 10. I met a lame man and a tall negro (black) in the street, and I did not know whence they had come.

CHAPTER FORTY-FIVE

(أَلْبَابُ ٱلْخَامِسُ وَٱلْأَرْبَعُونَ)

- The Use of the Cases

1. As already stated, the Arab grammarians used case terminology for the Verb in the Imperfect as well as for Nouns:

Noun	Nominative	ـُ	Imperfect	Indicative	ـُ
	Accusative	ـَ		Subjunctive	ـَ
	Genitive	ـِ		Jussive	ـْ

The Jussive may be approximated to the Genitive since the *sukūn* changes to *kasra* when *hamzatu l-waṣl* follows, e.g.

إِنْ يَتَكَلَّمْ if he speak; إِنْ يَتَكَلَّمِ ٱلْحَقَّ if he speak the truth.

Here, however, we are only concerned with *Noun* cases, and the English grammatical terms, though inadequate as will be seen, must be used.

2. The *Nominative* (رَفْعٌ) is used:

(a) For the *Subject* (فَاعِلٌ) of a *Verbal* sentence, e.g.

وَصَلَتِ ٱلْجَرَائِدُ ٱلْيَوْمَ صَبَاحًا the newspapers arrived this morning.

(b) For the *Subject* (termed مُبْتَدَأٌ "beginning") of a *Nominal* sentence, e.g. اَلْوَلَدُ مَجْرُوحٌ the boy is wounded.

(c) As the *Predicate* (خَبَرٌ "information") of a *Nominal* sentence. مَجْرُوحٌ is the *Predicate* of the above sentence.

(d) As the *Predicate* of إِنَّ, أَنَّ, etc., e.g.

إِنَّ رَبَّكُمْ رَحِيمٌ verily your Lord is merciful.

غَضِبْتُ مِنْ أَنَّ ٱلْبَيْضَةَ مَكْسُورَةٌ I was angry that the egg (was) broken.

(e) After the *Vocative* Particle أَيُّهَا (always used with the

Article), e.g. أَيُّهَا ٱلْمُسْلِمُونَ O Muslims! Also after يَا, in the Singular without *nunation*, e.g. يَا وَلَدُ O boy! يَا مُحَمَّدُ O Muhammad!

(f) For the *Adjective of*, or a *Noun in apposition to*, another *Nominative*, e.g.

جَاءَ ٱلرَّجُلُ ٱلنَّبِيلُ the noble man came;

قَامَ ٱلرَّجُلُ وَأَبُوهُ the man and his father rose.

3. The *Accusative* (نَصْبٌ) is used:

(a) As the *Object* (مَفْعُولٌ بِهِ) of a Verb, e.g.

قَابَلْتُ خَدَّامَةً فِي بَيْتِهِ I met a servant-girl in his house.

Some Verbs take *two* Objects, e.g. *

أَعْطَيْتُ حَسَنًا كِتَابًا I gave Hassan a book.

حَسِبْتُ مُحَمَّدًا كَذَّابًا I considered Muhammad a liar.

Occasionally there may be *three* Objects, e.g.

أَخْبَرْتُ حَسَنًا مُحَمَّدًا كَاذِبًا I informed Hassan that Muhammad was lying.

Some Verbs which in English take direct Objects are said in Arabic to be transitive by means of a Preposition. A good dictionary will always give the appropriate Preposition. Below are some examples:

فَازَ عَلَى to surpass, beat (someone); مَرَّ بِ to pass (someone);

رَغِبَ فِي to desire.

Some Verbs may take either a direct Object or a Preposition. This is especially true of *Verbs of Motion*, thus we have:

ذَهَبَ ٱلسُّوقَ he went to the market; or ذَهَبَ لِلسُّوقِ.

The second version is the more usual.

جَاءَ لِي or جَاءَنِي he came to me.

* See Appendix C, §6 for further notes on Doubly Transitive Verbs, with special reference to VERBS OF THE HEART (أَفْعَالُ ٱلْقَلْبِ).

Here the first version is more customary in writing.

When used with ب such Verbs mean "to bring" or "take away", e.g.

ذَهَبَ بِدَرَاهِمِي he went off with my money;

جَاءَ بِمُجَلَّدَيْنِ he brought two volumes;

أَتَانِي بِمُجَلَّدَيْنِ he brought me two volumes.

The *Transitive Verb* is termed مُتَعَدٍّ and the Intransitive (غَيْرُ مُتَعَدٍّ or لَازِمٌ).

(b) As the *Absolute Object* (اَلْمَفْعُولُ ٱلْمُطْلَقُ) (see pp. 331 *ff*)

e.g. قَلِقْتُ قَلَقًا I was disturbed, upset.

(c) *Adverbially* for *Time and Place* (ظَرْفٌ; اَلْمَفْعُولُ فِيهِ), e.g.

لَبِثْتُ عِنْدَهُمْ سَنَةً كَامِلَةً I stayed with them a whole year.

تَنَبَّهْتُ صَبَاحًا I awoke in the morning.

اِلْتَفَتَ يَمِينًا وَيَسَارًا he looked right and left.

سَافَرَ بَرًّا وَبَحْرًا he travelled by land and sea.

Such Accusatives may be replaced by Prepositional phrases, often with فى, hence the grammatical term المفعول فيه.

تَنَبَّهْتُ فِى ٱلصَّبَاحِ I awoke in the morning.

اِلْتَفَتَ إِلَى ٱلْيَمِينِ وَٱلْيَسَارِ he looked to the right and left.

قَامَ عِنْدَ ٱلْفَجْرِ he arose (or, set out) at dawn.

Many so-called Particles or Prepositions are really *Adverbial Accusatives* of Nouns, at least in origin, e.g.

خَلْفَ behind; فَوْقَ above; تَحْتَ beneath, under; نَحْوَ towards; قَبْلَ before; بَعْدَ after.

All these words will be found under their triliteral roots in the dictionary.

(d) To express *Aim or Purpose* (اَلْمَفْعُولُ لَهُ) This is expressed by a Verbal Noun in the Accusative, e.g.

قُمْتُ إِكْرَامًا لَهُ I rose to honour him.

صَمَتُّ اْحْتِرَامًا لَهُ I kept silent out of respect for him.

The Arabic terminology indicates that this Accusative could be replaced by a *Subjunctive* Verb or a Verbal Noun introduced by لِ. Thus the above two examples might be rendered as قُمْتُ لِأُكْرِمَهُ and صَمَتُّ لِأَحْتَرِمَهُ.

(e) To determine *Ḥāl.* This is a peculiarly Arabic construction which is used to describe the *Condition* or *Circumstance* obtaining at the time when the action of the main Verb takes place. The term "condition" may lead to confusion since the sort of condition in a conditional sentence is termed شَرْطٌ, and the sentence جُمْلَةٌ شَرْطِيَّةٌ *Ḥāl*, however, is ***condition*** in the sense of ***state***. It may be expressed by an Accusative or by a Finite verb, e.g.

جَاءَ حَسَنٌ رَاكِبًا or جَاءَ حَسَنٌ يَرْكَبُ Hassan came riding.

Such a ***Ḥāl*** Accusative may take its own direct object, e.g.

جَاءَ رَاكِبًا حِمَارًا أَبْيَضَ he came riding a white donkey.

وَصَلُوا رَاكِبِينَ حَمِيرًا they arrived riding donkeys.

The ***Ḥāl*** usually refers to the subject of the sentence, as to Hassan in the first example; but it could refer to the object or even to some Genitive, e.g.

رَأَيْتُ حَسَنًا رَاكِبًا or رَأَيْتُ حَسَنًا يَرْكَبُ I saw Hassan riding.

مَرَرْنَا بِالنِّسَاءِ مَاشِيَاتٍ (يَمْشِينَ) جَنْبَ جِمَالِهِنَّ we passed the women walking beside their camels.

The Accusative *Ḥāl* is nearly always an Active Participle. It may also be a Passive Participle, e.g.

رَأَيْتُ حَسَنًا مَقْتُولًا I saw Hassan slain.

تَرَكَ ٱلْبِلَادَ مَنْفِيًا he left the country, exiled.

Occasionally, a Verbal Noun may replace the Active Participle:

اِسْتَقْبَلُوهُ جُلُوسًا they received him seated.

for جَالِسِينَ

The verbal *Ḥāl* occasionally refers not to any specific part of the previous sentence (i.e. Subject, Object, etc.), but to the whole statement.

شَتَمَهُمْ وَٱلْقَاضِى يَبْقَى صَامِتًا he insulted them, while the judge remained (*lit.* remains) silent.

Even a nominal sentence could be used here وَٱلْقَاضِى صَامِتٌ.
In such sentences the و which introduces the *Ḥāl* might be translated "while".

(f) For *Specification* (تَمْيِيز), with the meaning of "in regard to", e.g.

زَيْدٌ أَكْثَرُ عِلْمًا مِنْ حَسَنٍ Zaid is greater in knowledge than Hassan.

طِبْ نَفْسًا be good in regard to soul (i.e. rejoice heartily).

Such is the construction after كَمْ how much, how many, e.g.

كَمْ تُفَّاحًا فِى ٱلْمَطْبَخِ how many apples are there in the kitchen?: (as also after the numbers 11 to 99).

(g) The *Predicate* of كَانَ and its sisters (Chapter Thirty-two), e.g.

كَانَتْ مَدِينَةُ بَغْدَادَ مَشْهُورَةً فِي ٱلْعُصُورِ ٱلْوُسْطَى the city of Baghdad was famous in the Middle Ages.

(h) For the *Subject of* إِنَّ *and its sisters,* e.g.

إِنَّ زَيْدًا قَائِمٌ (truly) Zaid is standing.

Note that nothing should interpose between such Particles and their Accusative, the only normal exception being the Predicate, when it consists of a prepositional phrase, e.g.

قَالَ إِنَّ فِي ٱلْبُسْتَانِ رَجُلاً غَرِيباً he said that in the garden (was) a strange man.

This is most likely to happen when the Accusative after the Particle is indefinite, and the sentence can be translated as "there is, are", "there was, were", e.g. the example above "he said that there was a strange man in the garden". هُنَاكَ "there" is sometimes interposed.

(i) In the construction of لَا لِنَفْيِ ٱلْجِنْسِ, that is, after the لا which denies absolutely the class or species in the place or circumstances defined in the sentence. This Accusative has no nunation, e.g.

لَا رَجُلَ فِي ٱلْبَيْتِ there is not a man in the house.

Note the following expressions:

لَا مَفَرَّ مِنْ ذٰلِكَ there is no escape from that.

لَا شَكَّ مِنْ (أَنْ ، أَنَّ) there is no doubt.

لَا بُدَّ مِنْ (أَنْ ، أَنَّ) it is inevitable (stronger than the above).

The following sentences illustrate the use of the last two:

لا شَكَّ مِنْ أَنَّ الْعَرَبَ غَلَبُوا	There is no doubt that the Arabs won.
لا شَكَّ مِنْ ذٰلِكَ	There is no doubt about that.
وُصُولُ الْعَرَبِ ، ولا شَكَّ ، أَنْقَذَ الْمُحَاصَرِينَ	The arrival of the Arabs without doubt saved the besieged.
لا بُدَّ مِنْ أَنْ نُقَاوِمَهُمْ (— مِنْ مُقَاوَمَتِهِمْ)	We must definitely resist them.
اِنْتِشَارُ ٱلتَّعْلِيمِ ، ولا بُدَّ ، سَوْفَ يُؤَدِّى إِلَى رَفْعِ مُسْتَوَى ٱلْعِيشَةِ فِى الشَّرْقِ الأَوْسَطِ.	The spread of education will lead, inevitably, to the raising of the standard of life in the Middle East.

(j) After إِلَّا (see Chapter Fifty-one).

(k) When the Noun after the *Vocative Particle* (يَا) is defined by a *Genitive*, e.g.

يَا أَبَا بَكْرٍ O Abu Bakr!; يَا أَمِيرَ الْمُؤْمِنِينَ O Prince of the Believers (Caliph)!

(l) With الْمَفْعُولُ مَعَهُ, a comparatively rare construction in which the Accusative is used to mean "with", "by", or "during", e.g.

سِرْتُ وَالنِّيلَ I travelled along the Nile.

سَافَرْتُ وَاللَّيْلَ I travelled during the night.

سَافَرَ زَيْدٌ وَأَخَاهُ Zaid travelled along with his brother.

This usage is rather antique, it is found in poetry and the Quran, and is not recommended to the student for general use.

(m) For any *Adjective governing an Accusative Noun*, or any *Noun in apposition to another Accusative Noun*, e.g.

رَأَيْتُ مَنْظَرًا جَمِيلًا I saw a beautiful scene.

رَأَيْتُ أَسَدًا وَفِيلًا I saw a lion and elephant.

(n) In certain *Exclamations*, the usual explanation being that there is a suppressed verb (فِعْلٌ مَحْذُوفٌ), e.g.

مَرْحَبًا بِكَ welcome to you (أُرَحِّبُ بِكَ understood).

مَهْلًا slowly! (أَمْهِلْ understood).

وَالنَّجَاةَ النَّجَاةَ escape! escape!

The و here, sometimes written with *'alif* وا introduces several such expressions. Sometimes اه is added to the noun: وَاحَسْرَتَاهْ woe! alas! (lit. sigh). Note also وَيْبَكَ ، وَيْحَكَ ، وَيْلَكَ woe to you!

4. The *Genitive* (جَرٌّ) is used:

(a) For إِضَافَةٌ, that is, after a Noun (see Chapters Seven and Eight).

(b) *After a Preposition* (حَرْفُ جَرٍّ see Chapter Four) Arabic grammarians say that the إضافة has the force of one of the Prepositions, and indeed it may be replaced by this construction, e.g. ثَوْبُ حَرِيرٍ or ثَوْبٌ مِنْ حَرِيرٍ a garment of silk; صَلَاةُ ٱلْمَغْرِبِ or الصَّلَاةُ عِنْدَ الْمَغْرِبِ the prayer of sunset; قَصْرُ دِمَشْقَ ٱلْمَلَكِيُّ or القصرُ الملكيُّ بِدِمَشْقَ the royal palace in Damascus.

(c) For *Adjectives agreeing with*, or *Nouns in apposition to*, other Genitive Nouns.

(d) In the following common constructions:

(i) After كُلٌّ, each, every, all. كُلَّ يَوْمٍ every day; كُلُّ واحدٍ every one; كُلُّ المدينةِ the whole city; كُلُّ الناسِ (or النّاسُ كُلُّهُمْ) all the people.

(ii) جَمِيعٌ and كَافَّةٌ which may replace كل; e.g. جَمِيعُ المُسْلِمِينَ or كَافَّةُ المسلمين all the Muslims.

(iii) بَعْضٌ some, or one of, e.g. بَعْضُ الشُّعَرَاءِ one of the poets, a certain poet, some poets; قَالَ بَعْضٌ someone said; أَكَلْتُ بَعْضَ الطَّعَامِ وتَرَكْتُ البَاقِيَ I ate some of the food and left the rest.

(iv) مِثْلٌ likeness. This is used where the English would have "like" or "as", but is a noun, e.g. حَسَنٌ مِثْلُ زَيْدٍ Hassan is like Zaid; كَانَ حسنٌ مِثْلَ زَيْدٍ Hassan was like Zaid; أَعْطَى جُنَيْهًا وأَعْطَيْتُ مِثْلَهُ he gave a pound and I gave the same.

مِثْلٌ forms the Plural أَمْثَالٌ, but it has no Feminine, e.g.

لا تَسْتَمِعْ إِلَى أَمْثَالِهِمْ	do not listen to men like them (lit. "their likenesses").
لا تَزُرْ نِسَاءً أَمْثَالَهُنَّ	do not visit women like them.
بِنْتٌ مِثْلُهَا لاتَسْتَحِقُّ آحْتِرَامَنَا	a girl like her does not merit our respect.

(v) سِوًى properly "another", means also "except". It is a noun, e.g.

مَرَرْتُ بِرَجُلٍ سِوَاكَ	I passed by a man other than you.
كُنْتُ أَنْتَظِرُكَ لٰكِنْ جَاءَ سِوَاكَ	I expected you but someone else came.
كُنْتُ بَارِعًا فِي كُلِّ مَوْضُوعٍ سِوَى ٱلْعُلُومِ	I was expert in every subject except science.

(vi) غَيْرٌ, also a Noun, means "another", but often corresponds to the prefixes non-, un-, im-, etc., e.g. غَيْرُ مُمْكِنٍ "impossible". It cannot form the Feminine or Plural, e.g.

هٰذَا ٱلْكِتَابُ غَيْرُ صَالِحٍ لِلْأَطْفَالِ	this book is unsuitable for children.
دَعَوْتُ أُخْتَهُ لٰكِنْ جَاءَتْ غَيْرُهَا	I invited his sister but someone else came (fem.).
رَأَيْتُ نَاسًا غَيْرَ سُكَّانِ مَكَّةَ	I saw people who were not the inhabitants of Mecca.

(vii) كِلَانِ "both", normally used without *nunation* with a following Genitive, e.g. جَاءَ كِلَا ٱلرَّجُلَيْنِ both men came; رَأَيْتُ كِلَا ٱلرَّجُلَيْنِ I saw both the men; مَرَرْتُ بِكِلَا ٱلرَّجُلَيْنِ I passed by both the men. Its Feminine is كِلْتَانِ, e.g.

تَكَلَّمَتْ كِلْتَا ٱلْبِنْتَيْنِ both the girls spoke;

لَقِينَا كِلْتَا ٱلْبِنْتَيْنِ we met both the girls.

When the following Genitive is an attached Pronoun, ***and only then***, the forms كِلَيْ masc. and كِلْتَيْ fem. are used in the Accusative and Genitive, e.g. جَاءَ كِلَاهُمَا both of them came; رَأَيْتُ كِلَيْهِمَا I saw both of them; مَرَرْتُ بِكِلَيْهِمَا I passed both of them.

(viii) رُبَّ "many a" is followed by an Indefinite Noun, e.g.

رُبَّ رَجُلٍ كَرِيمٍ قَابَلْتُ many a noble man have I met.

رُبَّ جُنْدِيٍّ مَاتَ فِى تِلْكَ ٱلْمَعْرَكَةِ many a soldier died in that battle.

Note that رُبَّمَا means "perhaps" and is followed by a verbal sentence, e.g. رُبَّمَا يَجِيءُ perhaps he will come.

VOCABULARY

طَافَ (ـُ) to wander, go round

خَرَاجٌ poll-tax

نَقَّاشٌ engraver, painter, sculptor

حَدَّادٌ blacksmith, ironworker

رَحًى *f.*, *pl.* أَرْحَاءٌ mill

طَحَنَ (ـَ) to grind, mill

آنِفًا previously (in a document ="above", "aforesaid")

كَعْبُ ٱلْأَحْبَارِ Ka'b al-'Aḥbār, name of a Jewish divine (Ex. 87)

حَبْرٌ *pl.* أَحْبَارٌ a Jewish divine

دَرَى (ـِ) to know

أَدْرَى IV to inform

اَلتَّوْرَاةُ the Pentateuch, Torah (loosely, the Old Testament)

فَنِيَ (ـَ) to perish, come to an end

أَجَلٌ the (fixed) term of one's life

نِصَابٌ *pl.* نُصُبٌ handle

سُرَّةٌ the navel

طَرِيحٌ (= مَطْرُوحٌ) prostrate, thrown on the ground, lying on the ground

تَوَعَّدَ V to threaten, warn

خَنْجَرٌ *pl.* خَنَاجِرُ dagger

أَيْشٍ what (Ex. 87)

EXERCISE 87

The Death of the Second Caliph, ʿUmar ibn al-Khaṭṭāb. (From the Annals of aṭ-Ṭabarī, 838–923 A.D.)

خَرَجَ عمرُ بن الخطاب يَوْماً يطُوفُ فى السوقِ فَلَقِيَهُ أبو لُؤْلُؤَةٍ ، وكان نَصْرانيًّا ، فقال : يا أميرَ المؤمنين إنّ عَلَيَّ خَرَاجاً كثيراً . قال : وكم خراجك؟ قال : درهمان فى كل يوم ، وقال : أَيْش (أَيُّ شَيْءٍ) صِنَاعَتُكَ؟ قال : نَجّارٌ ونَقّاشٌ وحَدّادٌ . قال (عمر) : فما أُرى خراجَك بكثيرٍ على (according to) ما تَصْنَعُ من الأعمال . قد بَلَغَنِي أنّك تقول : لو أردتُ ان اعمل رَحًى تَطْحَنُ بالريح فَعَلْتُ . قال : نعم . قال : فاعملْ لى رحًى . قال : لَئِنْ سَلِمْتَ لأَعْمَلَنَّ لك رحًى يَتَحَدَّثُ بها (عَنْها =) مَن بالمشرق والمغرب . ثُمَّ انصرفَ عنه . فقال عمر : لَقَدْ تَوَعَّدَنِى العبدُ آنفاً . ثم انصرف عمر إلى منزله ، فلما كان من الغدِ (لما كان الغدُ =) جَاءَهُ كَعْبُ الأحبار فقال : يا امير المؤمنين إنّك مَيِّتٌ فى ثلاثة أيام . قال : وما يُدْرِيكَ؟ قال : أَجِدُهُ فى كتابِ الله التَّوْراةِ . قال عمر : اللّهَ (fear God!) إنّك لَتجِدُ عمر بن الخطاب فى التوراة ؟ قال : لا ولكنّى أجدُ صِفَتَكَ وانّه قد فنى أَجَلُكَ . وعمر لا يُحِسُّ وجعاً ولا ألمًا . فلما كان الغَدُ جَاءَهُ كَعْبٌ فقال : يا امير المؤمنين ، ذهب يومٌ وبقى يومان . ثم جاءه مِن غدِ الغد ، فقال : ذهب يومان وبقى يومٌ وليلةٌ فلما كان الصُبْحُ خَرَجَ عمر الى الصلاة ودخل أبو لؤلؤة فى الناس ، فى يَده خنجرٌ لَهُ رَأْسانِ ، نِصَابُهُ فى

وَسْطِهِ ، فضربَ عمرَ ستَّ ضَرَبَات ، إِحْدَاهُنَّ تحت سُرَّتِهِ وهى التى قتلْته وقتل معه كُلَيْب بن ابى أَلبُكَيْر اللَّيْثِىّ وكان خَلْفَهُ ، فلمّا وجد عمر حَرَّ السلاح سَقَطَ وقال : أَفى الناس عَبْدُ الرَّحْمَانِ بن عَوْف؟ قالوا : نعم يا امير المؤمنين، هو ذا (there he is, that is he). قال : تَقَدَّمْ فَصَلِّ بالناس. فصلَّى عبدُ الرحمان بن عوف ، وعمرُ طَرِيحٌ ثم أُدْخِلَ دارَه.

EXERCISE 88

No translation from English to Arabic is given here. Instead, it is recommended that the student re-read the passage in the previous exercise, noting the various grammatical and syntactical features, and then REWRITE THE WHOLE PASSAGE WITH FULL VOWELLING AND ORTHOGRAPHICAL SIGNS.

The following points should help the student:

كَم خراجك Grammatically كَم is the Predicate, and is said to be مُقَدَّمٌ "brought forward". خراجك is the subject of this nominal sentence.

ما أرى خراجك بكثير Verbs of thought and estimation are doubly transitive. The first object of ارى here is خراجك. The second, which should have been كثيراً, is replaced by a genitive after a preposition (ب).

لئن سلمت فاعملنّ The لَ before إن adds nothing to the meaning. This is a conditional, and the apodosis has the Energetic form of the Jussive for stress.

إنّك ميّتٌ Here ميت which resembles the Active Participle مَائِتٌ "dying", in meaning, is used with a future sense.

وإنّه قد فنى أجلك The pronoun ه after إنّ refers to nothing previously mentioned, as would normally be the case. It is a Neutral Pronoun, not translated, which merely serves to satisfy the grammatical requirement of an Accusative after إنّ. The Arab grammarians call this ضمير ٱلشّأن (pronoun of circumstance).

من غد الغد On the day after the following day, i.e. two days later.

في يده خنجر A nominal *Ḥāl* sentence referring to ابو لؤلؤة.

إحداهنّ The Feminine إحدى refers to ضربة "a blow". هنّ is Feminine Plural, according to antique usage, referring to ضربات. Modern Arabic would normally have إحداها.

أدخل داره The Verb أدخل is doubly transitive, e.g. أدخل عمر داره "he took 'Umar into his house". When the Verb is Passive the first Object takes the place of the Subject, but the second Object دار still remains in the Accusative. In either case we could write في داره as an alternative.

CHAPTER FORTY-SIX

(اَلْبَابُ ٱلسَّادِسُ وَٱلْأَرْبَعُونَ)

The Permutative

(اَلْبَدَلُ the substitution)

1. The Permutative must follow immediately the word for which it is substituted (اَلْمُبْدَلُ مِنْهُ).

There are four kinds of substitution:

(a) The substitution of the whole for the whole (بَدَلُ ٱلْكُلِّ مِنَ ٱلْكُلِّ) i.e. where the Permutative is exactly equivalent to the word for which it is substituted, e.g.

جَاءَ زَيْدٌ أَخُوكَ Zaid, thy brother came.

جَاءَنِي قَوْمُ ٱلْمَدِينَةِ كُبَرَاؤُهُمْ وَصُغَرَاؤُهُمْ the people of the city, the great and the small, came to me.

(b) The part is substituted for the whole (بَدَلُ ٱلْبَعْضِ مِنَ ٱلْكُلِّ) e.g.

قَبِّلْهُ ٱلْيَدَ kiss him the hand, i.e. kiss his hand; أَكَلَ ٱلرَّغِيفَ نِصْفَهُ he ate the loaf, half of it, i.e. he ate the half of the loaf.

(c) A possession or quality is substituted for the name (بَدَلُ ٱلْاِشْتِمَالِ i.e. Permutative of inclusion), e.g. أَعْجَبَنِي زَيْدٌ ثَوْبُهُ Zaid, his garment pleased me, i.e. Zaid's garment pleased me; مَدَحْتُ زَيْدًا حُسْنَهُ I praised Zaid, his beauty, i.e. I praised Zaid's beauty.

(d) A word is used to correct the previous one (بَدَلُ ٱلْغَلَطِ the Permutative of error), e.g. مَرَرْتُ بِكَلْبٍ فَرَسٍ I passed by a dog (no, I mean) a horse. This usage is very rare.

PRONOUNS. EMPHASIS

2. The *Personal Pronoun* (ضَمِير) may be either *Separate* or *Attached.*

The Separate Pronoun is always Nominative, except when used for stress in apposition to a Noun or an Attached Pronoun, e.g. ضَرَبَنِي أَنَا he struck *me* (accus.).

مَرَرْتُ بِكَ أَنْتَ I passed by you (gen.).

But the *Emphasis* is more often achieved by the use of نَفْس pl. أَنْفُس meaning "myself", "yourself", etc., e.g.

كَتَبَ ٱلْمُعَلِّمُ الكِتَابَ نَفْسَهُ the teacher wrote the book himself.

كَلَّمْتُهُمْ أَنْفُسَهُمْ I spoke to them themselves.

Occasionally, this word is placed in the Genitive after بِ, e.g.

زَيْدٌ نَفْسُهُ or زَيْدٌ بِنَفْسِهِ Zaid himself.

Used similarly, though less frequently, and for things rather than people generally, is عَيْن (pl. أَعْيُن) e.g. اَلْأَمْرُ عَيْنُهُ the matter itself.

The *Reflexive Pronoun* in the Accusative is also expressed by these three words with pronominal suffixes, e.g.

قَتَلَ نَفْسَهُ he killed himself.

If the Pronoun depends on a Preposition, it is enough to use the pronominal suffix, e.g.

أَخَذْتُ لِي شَيْئًا I took something for myself. (NOT لِي نَفْسِي)

It should be noted that نفس and عين may be used as independent Nouns with a following Genitive, e.g. قَابَلْتُ نَفْسَ الرَّجُلِ I met the same man (for الرَّجُلَ نَفْسَهُ or الرَّجُلَ بِنَفْسِهِ). أَعْطَانِي عَيْنَ هَدِيَّةِ أَبِي She gave me the self-same present as my father.

NOTE: When نَفْس means "soul", it takes the Plural نُفُوس and is Feminine.

3. The Attached Pronoun may be either Accusative or Genitive, but not Nominative. It may be attached to the form إِيَّا to form a Detached Accusative Pronoun as follows:

3. Masc.	إِيَّاهُ him.	إِيَّاهُمَا them both	إِيَّاهُمْ them.
3. Fem.	إِيَّاهَا her.		إِيَّاهُنَّ ,,
2. Masc.	إِيَّاكَ you.	إِيَّاكُمَا you both	إِيَّاكُمْ you.
2. Fem.	إِيَّاكِ ,,		إِيَّاكُنَّ ,,
1.	إِيَّايَ me.		إِيَّانَا us.

It is used as follows:

(a) To carry the Object of a singly transitive Verb. In this case, stress is implied, and this may be further heightened by reversing the sentence order and putting the Object first, e.g. إِيَّاكَ نَعْبُدُ وَإِيَّاكَ نَسْتَعِينُ Thee do we worship and Thee do we ask for help (Qur'ān I).

(b) To carry the second Object of a doubly transitive Verb, when that Object is a Pronoun, e.g.

أَعْطَانِي إِيَّاهُ (إِيَّاهَا) he gave me it.

But أَعْطَانِيهِ is equally common. Nevertheless, when a doubly transitive Verb has a Noun as first Object and a Pronoun as the second, the second must have إِيَّا, e.g. أَعْطَى حَسَنًا إِيَّاهُ he gave it to Hassan. Again, if both Objects are Pronouns, the second must have إِيَّا if it is not of a later person than the first:

i.e. أَعْطَانِيكَ he gave me you.

أَعْطَانِيهِ he gave me it.

أَعْطَاكَهُ he gave you it.

but أَعْطَاكَ إِيَّاىَ he gave you me.

أَعْطَاهُ إِيَّاكَ he gave him you.

أَعْطَاهُ إِيَّاهُ he gave him it.

(c) It is also used independently as a warning, e.g.

إِيَّاكَ take care!; إِيَّاكَ وَٱلنَّارَ be careful of the fire.

4. If the Conjunctions وَ, فَ, "and", "so" and لَ "verily" are prefixed to the Pronouns هُوَ and هِيَ, the ه usually loses its vowel, e.g. وَهْوَ for وَهُوَ; فَهْيَ for فَهِيَ.

5. The first Person Singular attached Pronoun ى is often omitted and replaced by a *kasra* in cries and commands, chiefly in the Quran, e.g. رَبِّ for رَبِّي my Lord!

اِتَّقِنِ for اِتَّقِنِي fear me!

6. The attached Pronoun هُ is often used after إِنَّ and its sisters in a vague general sense, referring to a whole sentence or the general situation. This is merely a device to provide an Accusative after the Particle, since the Arabs like to use this particle. It is termed ضَمِيرُ ٱلشَّأْنِ, e.g.

ظَهَرَ لِلْقَائِدِ أَنَّهُ لَا مَفَرَّ مِنَ الْمُحَارَبَةِ it appeared to the general that there was no escape from fighting.

Here the sentence after أَنَّ is introduced by the لا of *Denial of the Species*, which does not therefore provide a Noun to serve as Accusative after أَنَّ. An alternative way of writing this, though less idiomatic, would be ... أَنْ لَا مَفَرَّ ...

7. The *Reciprocal Pronoun* "one another" is expressed by the use of بَعْضٌ "one, some", e.g. قَدْ سَاعَدْنَا بَعْضُنَا بَعْضًا we have helped one another (or بَعْضُنَا الْبَعْضَ)

With Prepositions the بعض is often not repeated, e.g. دَنَا العَسَاكِرُ مِنْ بَعْضِهِمْ the soldiers approached one another.

VOCABULARY

رَغِمَ (ـُ) to dislike	اِسْتَلَفَ VIII to borrow
رَغَّمَ, أَرْغَمَ IV to compel	اِنْتَبَهَ VIII to pay attention
عَلَى ٱلرَّغْمِ مِنْ (أن);	طَقْسٌ climate, weather
بِٱلرَّغْمِ من (أن) despite, in spite of (the fact that)	رَفَضَ (ـُ) to refuse, reject
حِرْفَةٌ *pl.* حِرَفٌ profession, trade	دَهَّشَ II to surprise
شَبَابٌ youth (*abstract*)	أَدْهَشَ IV ,, ,,
لَهَا (يَلْهُو) to play	دَهِشَ (ـَ), دُهِشَ (*pass.*) مِنْ to be surprised by
سَكْرَانُ *pl.* سَكَارَى drunk	طُفُولِيَّةٌ childhood
فَشَلٌ sluggishness; failure (*mod.*)	مُفْلِسٌ bankrupt
مُؤَهِّلَاتٌ qualifications (*mod.*)	أَفْلَسَ IV to go bankrupt
نَصِيحَةٌ advice	إِفْلَاسٌ bankruptcy

EXERCISE 89

A

قد اتخذ حَسَنٌ حِرْفَةَ الكِتَابَةِ منذ شبابه حينما خرج من المدرسة المُتوسّطة (Intermediate) لكنه لا مُؤَلَّفَات له بالمَعْنَى الصحيح ، وهو بلغ الستين من عمْره الآن وسببُ ذلك كسله لانه بذل وقته شارباً وآكلاً ولاهياً. فقد ألّف عدداً من الكُتَيِّبَات ومقالات الجرائد اليومية ، وقال لى بِنَفْسه ، وهو سكران ، اِنّه لم يُحقّقْ آمالَ أَبَوَيْهِ

ومعلميه ، وانه حَزِنَ كثيرًا مِن فشلِه أوّلَ الأمر ، ثُمَّ اعتاد اليه . وجميعنا قد رَأَيْنَا رجالاً امثالَه فَشلوا فى أعمالهم على الرغم من مُؤَهّلاتِهِم البالغةِ ، بل رُبَّمَا أعطيناهم نصيحة صالحة مُفيدة ولم يَستمعوا إليها .

B

١ — اذهبْ لحجرتى وآتِنى بالكتاب الذى استلفتُهُ من المكتبة أوّلَ أمسِ . ٢ — قِفْ خَلْفَهُ وَٱنْتَبِهْ اكرامًا للواعظ ! ٣ — إنّ الطقسَ فى البَحْرَيْنِ (Bahrain) أشدُّ حَرًّا منه فى سوريا ، وذلك ، ولا شكّ ، يزيدُ صعوبة الحياة فى تلك الجزيرة . ٤ — إنّ حياتَنا قصيرة ولا بُدَّ من الموت فى النهاية ، فَلْنَقُمْ باعمال يرضى عنها الله لنستحقَّ البقاء فى الحياة الآخرة . ٥ — نَظَرْتُ كِلَيْهِما قادمَين وقد ناديتُ خادمَين غَيْرَهما .

C

١ — كان زيدٌ أخوك نفسُهُ الذى انصرف عند وصول الأمير . ٢ — طَلَبوا أكلاً فأعْطَيْتُهُم إيّاهُ ، ثم رَجَعوا فى اليوم التالى بعين الطلبِ فَرَفضتُ . ٣ — رأيتُ ولداً عابراً الشارع وفيه حَرَكَاتٌ (traffic) كثيرة ، فَصِحْتُ : إيّاكَ والعرباتِ ! فهو جَعَلَ يجرى حتى وصل الى الجنب الآخر . ٤ — دُهِشْتُ من أنّهُ لا بُدّ من ٱلالتجاء إلى عرب الصحراء . ٥ — تَكَاتَبْنا بَعْضُنَا البعضَ مُدَّةَ خمسين سنة . ٦ — مررت بحيوانات جِمالٍ وهن من قافلةٍ واقفة تحت الأشجار .

EXERCISE 90

1. Despite what the unbelievers say, the souls of the righteous are in the hands of God. 2. I was surprised that there was nothing in the cupboard after the party. There is no doubt that the servants have eaten all that remained. But what can I do? This is a general custom among the servants of government officials, and it is inevitable (لا بُدّ ..). 3. If I go to the palace to present my petition in the morning, they say "The king is still sleeping"; if I go in the afternoon, they say he is out hunting; and if I go in the evening, they say he is receiving guests from among the ambassadors and other important foreigners. There is no benefit from this type of rule. 4. He surprised me, because he was reading weighty volumes, and he was still in his youth. 5. *Him* I praise, but *you* I ask for help, because you have been my friend since childhood. 6. I refused to visit him, saying that the weather was bad, but he was too intelligent to believe me. The real reason was that he had refused to take *my* advice. 7. His qualifications were not adequate (sufficient) for a profession of this sort (*use* مثل). We were both in the same class in school, and the teacher expected great things of both of us. But he used to play while I worked, and he rarely paid attention to what the teacher said in lessons. You may (قد) say: "Many a man has succeeded in life without great qualifications". But how many have succeeded without work? 8. How much money did you lend him? I saw him drunk five minutes ago, yet he is bankrupt. 9. They spoke to one another, and after a short time had elapsed they were fighting each other. 10. I passed you walking with my sister last night. Does my father know, and is it your intention to propose to her? I fear very much that there is no hope for you. My father will certainly refuse to marry her to you, because a poor man like you cannot give her the things she is used to. My advice to you is to work hard to become rich, perhaps you will then gain my father's consent (موافقة) to the marriage.

CHAPTER FORTY-SEVEN

(اَلْبَابُ ٱلسَّابِعُ وَٱلأَرْبَعُونَ)

Particles. Prepositions

1. The Arab grammarians call the *Particle* حَرْفٌ pl. حُرُوفٌ (which also means "letter"). They are used in place of what we should call *Prepositions*, *Conjunctions* and *Interjections*, and, sometimes, *Adverbs*.

2. The Preposition is called حَرْفُ ٱلْجَرِّ, the word governed by a preposition is مَجْرُورٌ, and the preposition with its noun is اَلْجَارُّ وَٱلْمَجْرُورُ.

3. Prepositions are: A. *Inseparable*, consisting of one letter always attached to the following word; B. *Separate*, which stand alone and are either true particles or nouns in the Accusative.

A. INSEPARABLE PREPOSITIONS

(1) بِ "in, by, with" etc.

Verbs denoting "to adhere", "attach", "seize", "begin", are construed with بِ e.g. عَلِقَ "to hang on", بَدَأَ "to begin with".

"To believe in" is آمَنَ بِ, e.g. آمَنْتُ بِٱللّٰهِ I believe in God.

"To swear by" is أَقْسَمَ بِ, e.g. أَقْسَمْتُ بِرَأْسِي I swear by my head. Sometimes the verb is omitted.

After إِذَا "See! Behold!" بِ is used (but the noun alone in the Nom. may be used), e.g. إِذَا بِرَجُلٍ قَدْ أَتَى Behold a man came (or إِذَا رَجُلٌ).

In negative sentences if the predicate is a noun, بِ is often, prefixed to it, e.g.

لَيْسَ هُوَ بِفَارِسٍ he is not a rider (or لَيْسَ فَارِسًا)

مَا هُمْ بِعَالِمِينَ they are not aware (or مَا هُمْ عَالِمُونَ)

Many intransitive verbs of motion become transitive when they are followed by بِ, e.g. أَتَى بِشَيْءٍ he came with a thing, i.e. he brought it. (This بِ is called بَاءُ ٱلتَّعْدِيَةِ).

NOTE: The expression بِأَبِي أَنْتَ means "at the price of my father thou art to be redeemed", i.e. "thou art so dear to me, that I would redeem thee at the price of my father". (This is called بَاءُ ٱلتَّفْدِيَةِ, the *bā'* of redemption.)

Prepositions are sometimes described by the Arabs as being interchangeable (مُتَبَادِلَةٌ) and this is true in some instances. Thus, while geographically we more often use بِ of a town or village (بِلُنْدُنَ "in London") and فِى of an area or country (فِى فَرَنْسَا "in France"); we also find فِى لندن and بفرنسا.

(2) and (3) تَ and وَ "by" in an oath, e.g. تَٱللهِ and وَٱللهِ "by God". (تَ occurs only in this expression, and is rare and antique – not to be used by students.) If, however, a verb is used in the oath, بِ must be used.

(4) لِ "for, to, because of".

لِ is used to express the Dative and denotes possession (= "have").

As a Conjunction (with the Subjunctive of the verb) it denotes "in order that, so that".

It denotes the English "of", when it follows an indeterminate noun, e.g. كِتَابٌ لِزَيْدٍ a book of (belonging to) Zaid; صَاحِبٌ لِي a friend of me, i.e. one of my friends.

It is used especially for the editor of a book, e.g.

قَصَصُ ٱلْأَنْبِيَاءِ لِلثَّعْلَبِيِّ The Stories of the Prophets of (i.e. written by) Thaعlabī.

لِ also denotes "for the benefit of" (opposite of عَلَى) and so denotes a creditor (عَلَى the debtor), e.g.

لِي عَلَيْكَ أَلْفُ دِرْهَمٍ you owe me a thousand dirhams.

It is also used to denote the Purpose and the Cause, e.g.

قُمْتُ لِمُعَاوَنَتِهِ I rose to help him.

لِهٰذَا / لِذٰلِكَ } for this reason, therefore

NOTE 1: قَالَ لِ "to say to" often means, especially in the Passive, "to call, name", e.g. قِيلَ (يُقَالُ) لَهُ he was (is) called.

NOTE 2: لِ is changed to لَ before Pronominal suffixes (except with the 1st Person), e.g. لَهُ, لَهَا etc. It is also changed to لَ after the particle of address يَا, e.g. يَا لَلْعَجَبِ "O wonder", يَا لَزَيْدٍ "O Zaid!" (i.e. come and help O Zaid!).

(5) كَ "as, like" is usually counted among the prepositions, although it is really a noun meaning "similarity", e.g. كَزَيْدٍ like Zaid.

It is *not* used with Pronominal suffixes.

B. SEPARATE PREPOSITIONS

(1) إِلَى "to, unto, until".

Is nearly related in meaning to لِ and serves to express motion towards a place, e.g.

جَاءَ إِلَى ٱلْمَدِينَةِ he came to the city.

In relation to time it expresses continuance up to a certain point of time, e.g.

مِنَ ٱلْاِبْتِدَاءِ إِلَى ٱلْاِنْتِهَاءِ from beginning to end.

Notice specially إِلَى آخِرِهِ (abbreviated اِلَخ) "and so forth", "et cetera".

With suffixes: إِلَيْهِ "to him", إِلَيَّ "to me", etc.

(2) حَتَّى "up to, as far as".

Is not used with suffixes.

It is sometimes used to mean "even" and then exercises no influence on the case of the following word, e.g.

أَكَلْتُ ٱلسَّمَكَةَ حَتَّى رَأْسَهَا I ate the fish, even its head.

(3) عَلَى "over, on, against".

With suffixes: عَلَيْهِ "on him"; عَلَيَّ "on me" etc.

Used of place. عَلَى ٱلطَّرِيقِ on the way.

جَلَسَ عَلَى ٱلْمَائِدَةِ he sat at table.

مَدِينَةٌ عَلَى نَهْرٍ a city on a river.

Notice specially:

تَفَرَّجَ عَلَى شَيْءٍ to look (with pleasure) at a thing.

اِطَّلَعَ عَلَى شَيْءٍ / وَقَفَ عَلَى شَيْءٍ } to examine into a thing.

غُشِيَ (or أُغْمِيَ) عَلَيْهِ he fainted (lit. it was made dark upon him).

اَلسَّلَامُ عَلَيْكُمْ Peace be on you! (the greeting of Moslems to one another, the answer being وَعَلَيْكُمُ ٱلسَّلَامُ).

رَحْمَةُ ٱللّٰهِ عَلَيْهِ God's mercy be upon him.

صَلَّى ٱللّٰهُ عَلَيْهِ وَسَلَّمَ God give him blessing and peace.

Used in a hostile sense:

خَرَجَ عَلَيْهِ he went out (to war) against him.

So with verbs denoting anger:

غَضِبْتُ عَلَيْكَ I was angry with thee.

Used with Adjectives:

ذٰلِكَ صَعْبٌ (سَهْلٌ) عَلَيَّ that is too hard (easy) for me.

"To incite to" حَثَّ عَلَى; "to induce to" حَمَلَ عَلَى, e.g.

حَمَلْتُهُ عَلَى شَيْءٍ I have induced him to (do) something.

عَلَى is also used to indicate that a burden, duty or debt lies on one, e.g.

فَرْضٌ عَلَى إِنْسَانٍ a duty incumbent on a man.

يَجِبُ عَلَى فُلَانٍ it is the duty of such and such a one.

هٰذَا لِي عَلَيْكَ you owe me this (see A, 4).

فَضْلٌ عَلَى a preference over.

Common expressions with على are:

بِنَاءً عَلَى according to.

عَلَى أَنْ on the supposition that.

عَلَى قَدْرِ ٱلْإِمْكَانِ so far as possible.

عَلَيَّ بِهِ bring him here to me.

عَلَى ٱلرَّأْسِ وَٱلْعَيْنِ (lit. on the head and eye) willingly, with pleasure.

بِٱللّٰهِ عَلَيْكَ I conjure thee by God.

(4) عَنْ "from, about, concerning".

With suffixes: عَنْهُ "from him", عَنِّي "from me", عَنَّا "from us", etc.

Used of place=away from, and so is used with verbs denoting "to flee", "avoid", "restrain oneself", "forbid", "hinder", "defend" (with many of these verbs مِنْ can be used), e.g.

مَنَعَ عَنْ (or مِنْ) to prevent from . . .

اِجْتَنَبَ عَنْ (or مِنْ) to avoid . . .

دَافَعَ عَنْ شَخْصٍ أَوْ شَيْءٍ to defend someone or something.

It is also used with verbs meaning to "uncover", "reveal", "open" and "ask", e.g.

كَشَفَ عَنْ شَيْءٍ to uncover something.

سَأَلَ عَنْ شَخْصٍ أَوْ شَيْءٍ to ask about someone or something.

In the sense of the Latin *de* "concerning", e.g.

حُكِيَ عَنْ سُلَيْمَانَ it is told concerning Solomon.

To indicate the source of information, e.g.

حُكِيَ عَنِ ٱلشَّافِعِيِّ it is told on the authority of ash-Shāfiʿī.

It is sometimes used of time, e.g. عَنْ قَرِيبٍ "shortly, soon".

Notice specially:

رَضِيَ ٱللّٰهُ عَنْهُ May God be pleased with him.

فَضْلًا عَنْ apart from.

The following usages should also be noted:

(a) In signing a letter, عَنْ means "for", "on behalf of", e.g. عَنْ مُدِيرِ ٱلْأَعْمَالِ for the Director of Works.

(b) In asking leave of a host, one may say عَنْ إِذْنِكَ "by your leave", "by your permission".

(5) فِى "in".

With suffixes: فِيهِ in him, فِىَّ in me, etc.

It expresses rest in place or time and answers the questions "where?" and "when?", e.g. فِى ٱلدَّارِ in the house, فِى هٰذِهِ ٱلسَّنَةِ in this year.

Sometimes it expresses motion to a place, e.g. وَقَعَ فِى ٱلْجُبِّ he fell into the cistern.

It also denotes "among", e.g. مَنْ فِينَا who among us.

It is used with verbs of speaking and thinking:

تَكَلَّمَ فِى to speak about . . .

إِفْتَكَرَ فِى to think over . . .

تَأَمَّلَ فِى شَيْءٍ to consider something.

Also after the verbs of desiring: رَغِبَ فِى to wish for something; طَمِعَ فِى to yearn after.

"To multiply by" is ضَرَبَ فِى e.g.

اِضْرِبْ ثَلَاثَةً فِى سَبْعَةٍ multiply three by seven.

(6) لَدَى, لَدُنْ, لَدَا "with" (Latin "apud").

With suffixes لَدُنْهُ with him, لَدُنِّى with me etc.; لَدَيْهِ with him, لَدَىَّ with me. Rarer than عِنْدَ.

(7) مَعَ (rarely مَعْ) "with".

With suffixes مَعَهُ with him, مَعِى with me, etc.

It denotes association in place or connection in time, e.g.

سَارَ مَعِي he travelled with me.

جِئْتُكَ مَعَ طُلُوعِ ٱلشَّمْسِ I came to you at sunrise.

It often means "to have something with one", e.g.

مَعِي سَاعَةٌ I have a watch with me.

It also translates the English "besides", e.g.

مَعَ كَوْنِهِ غَرِيبًا besides his being a stranger.

Notice specially:

مَعَ ذٰلِكَ in spite of that.

مَعَ أَنْ (or أَنَّ) in spite of the fact that, although.

(8) مِنْ "from".

With suffixes مِنْهُ from him, مِنَّا from us, etc.

Used of place (often interchangeable with عَنْ):

خَرَجَ مِنَ ٱلْخَيْمَةِ he went out from the tent.

It is used with verbs denoting "to go out", "to free", "to forbid":

أَعُوذُ بِٱللّٰهِ مِنَ ٱلشَّرِّ I take refuge in God (to free me) from evil.

Used of time:

مِنَ ٱلصَّبَاحِ إِلَى ٱلْمَسَاءِ from morning to evening.

Sometimes used (like مُنْذُ) to mean "since".

مِنْ سَنَتَيْنِ i.e. two years ago.

It is also employed with verbs and nouns denoting nearness, as قَرُبَ, دَنَا e.g.

دَنَوْتُ مِنَ ٱلْعَدُوِّ I approached the enemy.

قَرِيبٌ مِنَّا near us.

Notice specially:

عَجِبَ (تَعَجَّبَ) مِنْ شَيْءٍ to wonder at something;

so with other verbs of feeling:

فَرِحَ مِنْ to rejoice at . . .

مَبْسُوطٌ مِنْ pleased at . . .

The word "than" after a Comparative is expressed by مِنْ,

e.g. أَسْرَعُ مِنَ ٱلْكَلْبِ swifter than the dog.

"A certain" is often expressed by مِنْ preceded by a word indefinite in the Sing. and followed by the same word definite in the Plur., e.g.

تَاجِرٌ مِنَ ٱلتُّجَّارِ a certain merchant.

It is also used partitively (لِلتَّبْعِيضِ) followed by a definite noun in the Plur. to indicate an indefinite number or quantity, e.g.

قَدْ أَرَاكُمْ مِنْ آيَاتِهِ he has already shown you some of his signs; and to indicate material, e.g.

كُرْسِيٌّ مِنْ خَشَبٍ a chair of wood.

It is very often used after مَا to explain (لِلتَّبْيِينِ) what is intended by the particle, e.g.

مَا كَانَ عِنْدِي مِنَ ٱلْمَالِ what was with me in the way of wealth, i.e. the wealth, which I had.

مَا عَمِلْتُمُوهُ بِنَا مِنَ ٱلْمَعْرُوفِ what you have done to us in the way of kindness, i.e. the kindness, which you have done us.

(9) مُنْذُ, مُذْ "since" (for مِنْ ذُو).

Is not used with suffixes.

It is sometimes followed by the Nominative, e.g.

مَا رَأَيْتُكَ مُنْذُ (مُذْ) يَوْمَ ٱلْأَحَدِ
مَا رَأَيْتُكَ مُنْذُ (مُذْ) يَوْمُ ٱلْأَحَدِ } I have not seen you since Sunday.

NOUNS USED AS PREPOSITIONS

4. Of the Prepositions which are really nouns in the Accusative (ظَرْفٌ) the following are the most common:

(1) أَمَامَ "before, opposite" (of place):

أَمَامَ ٱلْقَصْرِ before, opposite the castle.

أَمَامَ ٱلْقَاضِي before the judge.

(2) بَعْدَ "after" of time or rank (opposite of قَبْلَ):

بَعْدَ ٱلْمِيلَادِ after the birth (of Christ).

(3) بَيْنَ "between".

When two words are dependent on بَيْنَ, then if both are substantives the بَيْنَ need not be repeated, but if one (or both) is a pronoun it is always repeated, e.g.

بَيْنَ زَيْدٍ وَعَمْرٍو between Zaid and ʻAmr.

بَيْنَكَ وَبَيْنَ أَخِيكَ between thee and thy brother.

بَيْنِي وَبَيْنَكَ between me and thee.

مَا بَيْنَ and فِيمَا بَيْنَ are often used with the same meaning as بَيْنَ.

مَا بَيْنَ and بَيْنَ sometimes mean "both – and" or "partly – partly":

جَاءَنَا مَا بَيْنَ فَقِيرٍ وَغَنِيٍّ both poor and rich came to us.

(4) تَجَاهَ, تُجَاهَ
(5) تِلْقَاءَ } "opposite" (= حِذَاءَ).

(6) تَحْتَ "under, below" of place or rank (opposite to فَوْقَ).

تَحْتَ شَجَرَةٍ under a tree.

تَحْتَ ٱلْمَلِكِ below the king (in rank).

(7) حِذَاءَ "opposite":

حِذَاءَ ٱلدَّارِ opposite the house.

(8) حَوْلَ "round about".

حَوْلَ ٱلْمَدِينَةِ round about the city.

(9) خَلْفَ "behind":

خَلْفَ ظَهْرِى behind my back.

(10) دُونَ "on this side of, under, without":

دُونَ ٱلنَّهْرِ on this side of the river.

دُونَ قَدَمِكَ خَدُّ عَدُوِّكَ may the cheek of the enemy be under thy feet.

With the meaning "without" بِدُونِ or مِنْ دُونِ may be used instead of دُونَ:

دُونَ (بِدُونِ or مِنْ دُونِ) ذٰلِكَ without that.

(11) عِنْدَ "with, at":

Used of place:

جَلَسْتُ عِنْدَهُ I sat with (beside) him.

Used of time:

جَاءَ عِنْدَ طُلُوعِ ٱلشَّمْسِ he came at sunrise.

It is often used with the meaning "to have".

مَالٌ (or مَعِي or لِي) عِنْدِي I have wealth.

NOTE. عِنْدِي كَذَا means "according to my opinion it is so".

(12) عِوَضَ (or عِوَضًا عَنْ) "instead of, in place of":

أَخَذْتُ هٰذَا عِوَضَ ذٰلِكَ I took this in place of that.

(13) فَوْقَ "on, over, above": of place and rank (opposite of تَحْتَ):

فَوْقَ ٱلشَّجَرَةِ on (or above) the tree.

فَوْقَ ٱلْمَلِكِ above the king (in rank).

(14) قَبْلَ "before" of time (opposite of بَعْدَ):

قَبْلَ ٱلْمِيلَادِ before the birth (of Christ).

(15) قُدَّامَ "before" of place (more often أَمَامَ):

قُدَّامَ ٱلدَّارِ before the house.

(16) نَحْوَ "towards":

نَحْوَ ٱلْغَرْبِ towards the West.

(17) وَرَاءَ "behind, on the far side of":

وَرَاءَهُمْ behind them.

وَرَاءَ ٱلْجِبَالِ behind (on the far side of) the mountains.

5. Two prepositions often occur together. In this case, if the second was originally a noun, it must be put in the Genitive, e.g.

مِنْ بَيْنِهِمْ from between them, i.e. from the midst of them.

مِنْ فَوْقِ from over, i.e. above.

مِنْ تَحْتِ from under, i.e. underneath.

مِنْ عِنْدِ from with.

مِنْ عَلَى from on i.e. down from.

مِنْ دُونِ or بِدُونِ without

مِنْ قَبْلِ before.

مِنْ بَعْدِ after.

VOCABULARY

طَبَقٌ *pl.* أَطْبَاقٌ large meat tray or dish; plate

حَيْرَةٌ perplexity

زُقَاقٌ *pl.* أَزِقَّةٌ lane, side street

رِبْحٌ *pl.* أَرْبَاحٌ gain, profit

بِٱلْكُلِّيَّةِ altogether

إِخْتَفَى VIII to hide, disappear

EXERCISE 91

Note: This exercise is not specifically concerned with the grammatical matter in this chapter. It is partly a test in reading unvowelled Arabic.

قيلَ إنَّ لصَّين سرقا حماراً ومضى احدهما ليبيعه. فقَابَلَهُ رجل معه طبقٌ فيه سمك فقال له : أتبيع هذا الحمار؟ قال : نعم، قال : امسك هذا الطبق حتى أركبه واجربه، فإن اعجبني اشتريته بثمن

يعجبك. فأمسك اللص الطبق وركب الرجل الحمار وأخذ يُجْرِيه ذهاباً وأياباً حتى ابتعد عن اللص كثيرا. فدخل بعض الأزقة واختفى عنه بِالْكُلِّيَّةِ. وأخذت اللص الحيرة من ذلك وعرف أخيراً أنّها حيلة عليه. فرجع بالطبق فالتقاه رفيقه. فقال: ما فعلت بالحمار؟ هل بعته؟ قال: نعم. قال: بِكم؟ قال: برأس ماله. وهذا الطبق ربح!

EXERCISE 92

Rewrite the above passage with full vowelling and other orthographical signs.

The following notes may help:

قال In old Arabic, where two people are conversing, frequently the words of both speakers are introduced by "he said", where we might write: "the first said . . . the second said", or "the former said . . . then the latter replied". The sense of the passage shows who is speaking.

حتّى This introduces the Subjunctive of purpose. Note later in this passage we have a different use of this particle introducing a statement of fact in the Perfect.

اعجبنى Literally, "it aroused my admiration": here it means simply "if I like it". This is a Conditional.

إيَاباً Verbal Noun of آبَ, يؤوبُ to return.

برأس ماله، وهذا الطبق رِبْحٌ "For its capital, i.e. what we paid for it (=nothing!) and this tray (is) profit." A joke, of course, as the thieves paid nothing for the donkey!

CHAPTER FORTY-EIGHT

(أَلْبَابُ ٱلثَّامِنُ وَٱلأَرْبَعُونَ)

Adverbial Usages. Including Miscellaneous Quasi-adverbial Particles

1. Arabic has no *Adverbs*, properly speaking, but this lack is hardly felt owing to the inherent flexibility and expressiveness of the language. Only occasionally, in translating, does one feel a certain awkwardness which is unusual in a language potentially so succinct (and almost telegraphic) as Arabic. There are a number of ways of expressing what would necessitate Adverbs in English, and they could be summarized as follows:

(a) By *Prepositional* Phrases, e.g.

جَاءَ بِسُرْعَةٍ he came *quickly* (with speed).

(b) By the use of certain *Verbs*, e.g.

كَادَ : مَا كِدْتُ أَرَاهُ I *scarcely* saw him.

أَحْسَنَ to do *well*: أَحْسَنَ كِتَابَتَهُ he wrote *well*.

(c) By a number of uses of the *Accusative*. Indeed, this is the chief means employed; so much so that the Accusative in Arabic may also be described as an Adverbial case. The simplest use of the Accusative Noun is in words such as:

أَحْيَانًا "sometimes"; تَقْرِيبًا "approximately";

فَجْأَةً "suddenly".

(d) Into the above category should really go numerous *Prepositions* which end in the *un-nunated* Accusative; *un-nunated* because they have a following Genitive, e.g. بَعْدَ

"after"; بَعْدَ يَوْمَيْنِ "after two days". Of course we have أَيْنَ "where" and ثَمَّ "then", which are *un-nunated* though no Genitive follows.

(e) An extension of the above is found in such expressions as قَلِيلاً مَا "little"; كَثِيرًا مَا "often"; سَرْعَانَ مَا "quickly".

(f) The *Absolute Object* also comes under this heading, especially when qualified, e.g. ضَرَبْتُهُ ضَرْبًا شَدِيدًا I hit him *hard*.

(g) The *Ḥāl* construction also takes the place of Adverbs, e.g. جَاءَ مُسْرِعًا He came quickly.

(h) There are a few particles ending in the *un-nunated Nominative*, which, though obviously Nouns in origin, are the nearest approach to the true Adverb in Arabic, e.g. قَبْلُ "before", "previously"; بَعْدُ "after", "later".

(i) Finally, there are some particles ending in *sukūn* which play the part of Adverbs, e.g. فَقَطْ "only".

The following is a fairly comprehensive list of various Adverbial or Quasi-adverbial usages. Many have already been mentioned in this grammar, and are given again for completeness.

INSEPARABLE PARTICLES

2. (a) أَ a particle used to indicate a question (= هَلْ see Chapter Three, 4) (called the حَرْفُ ٱلْاِسْتِفْهَامِ); but only when no Interrogative pronoun occurs in the sentence, e.g.

أَفَعَلْتَ هٰذَا (or هَلْ فَعَلْتَ هٰذَا) have you done this?

but مَنْ فَعَلَ هٰذَا who has done this?

أَ — أَمْ in a double question; see أَمْ.

(b) سَ a particle used to give a Future meaning to the Imperfect. It is a shortened form of سَوْفَ "at the end."

سَأَفْعَلُهُ (سَوْفَ أَفْعَلُهُ) I shall do it.

(c) لَ a particle used for Emphasis, "certainly, truly", often omitted in translation, e.g.

لَفَعَلْتُهُ truly, I have done it.

Especially with the Modus Energicus:

لَأَضْرِبَنَّكَ I shall certainly strike thee.

Also in an Oath:

لَعَمْرُكَ by thy life.

لَ is often used before the Predicate of a Nominal sentence, which begins with إِنَّ (see below 3e).

It is often used to introduce the apodosis of a conditional sentence beginning with لَوْ.

SEPARATE ADVERBIAL PARTICLES

3. The most important separate particles are:

(a) إِذَنْ and إِذًا (related to إِذَا) "in that case, then", e.g.:

نَرُوحُ إِذًا let us go then.

(b) أَلَا (for أَ and لَا) "not" in an Interrogative sentence:

أَلَا أَفْعَلُهُ shall I not do it?

So أَلَمْ for أَ and لَمْ.

(c) أَمْ "or" in a double question:

أَأَفْعَلُهُ أَمْ لَا shall I do it or not?

(d) أَمَا (for أ and مَا) "not" in an Interrogative sentence:

أَمَا فَعَلْتَهُ have you not done it?

(e) إِنَّ "truly, certainly".

إِنَّ introduces Nominal sentences, the subject following in the Accusative, the Predicate often strengthened by لَ (see above 2c) following in the Noun, e.g.:

إِنَّ زَيْدًا عَاقِلٌ
إِنَّ زَيْدًا لَعَاقِلٌ } verily, Zaid is intelligent.

It may be used with Pronominal suffixes, the pronoun then being a subject, e.g. إِنَّهُ verily he, إِنِّي and إِنَّنِي verily I, إِنَّا and إِنَّنَا verily we.

(f) إِنَّمَا (for إِنَّ and مَا) is always at the beginning of a sentence and limits the word or clause at the end of it by its meaning "only", e.g.:

إِنَّمَا ٱلصَّدَقَاتُ لِلْفُقَرَاءِ the alms are for the poor only.

(g) أَىْ "i.e., that is" (= يَعْنِى).

(h) أَيْنَ "where?"

مِنْ أَيْنَ "whence?"

إِلَى أَيْنَ "whither?"

أَيْنَمَا "wherever".

(i) بَلْ "but rather, no on the contrary, but, but indeed".

(j) بَلَى "yes certainly" as answer to negative sentences.

(k) ثَمَّ "there".

(l) قَدْ before the Perfect expresses the completion or certainty of the action and can sometimes be translated "already", but is often to be left untranslated. It may also change the meaning of the Perfect to the Pluperfect.

With the Imperfect it means "sometimes", "may".

(m) فَقَطْ "only", always placed after the word it modifies.

(n) قَطُّ "never", follows a verb in the Perfect with a negative, e.g.:

مَا رَأَيْتُهُ قَطُّ I have never seen him.

(o) كَلَّا "not at all, by no means".

(p) لَا "not, no".

(1) As particle of Denial (لَا لِلنَّفْيِ) before the Imperf. Indic. with Present and Future meaning:

لَا أَفْعَلُهُ I do it not (or I shall not do it).

(2) As particle of Prohibition (لَا لِلنَّهْيِ) followed by the Jussive with the meaning of the Imperative:

لَا تَفْعَلْهُ do it not.

(3) As particle of Complete Denial (لَا لِنَفْيِ ٱلْجِنْسِ) (see Chapter Forty-five, 3 i)

(r) لَمَّا followed by the Jussive means "not yet".

(s) لَنْ "not" is followed by the Subjunctive, which then has the meaning of a Future:

لَنْ أَفْعَلَهُ I shall not do it.

(t) مَا "not" is followed by either Perfect or Imperfect, usually the former.

NOTE: For إِنْ as particle of Denial see Chapter Forty-Nine 3 (c) Note.

(u) مَتَى "when", also used as a Conjunction.

(v) نَعَمْ (rarely نَعِمْ) "yes", derived from نَعِمَ "(what you say) is agreeable".

(w) هَلْ Particle of Interrogation.

هَلْ فَعَلْتَهُ have you done it?

In an indirect question it denotes "whether", e.g.:

أَخْبِرْنِي هَلِ انْتَظَرْتَنِي tell me whether you have expected me.

هَلَّا (for هَلْ and لَا) "not" in an Interrogative sentence.

(x) هُنَا "here", or in a strengthened form هَاهُنَا (sometimes written هٰهُنَا).

(y) هُنَاكَ and هُنَالِكَ "there".

NOUNS USED AS ADVERBS

4. Several nouns are used as adverbs in the un-nunated *nominative*, and are, of course, indeclinable. Some of these words (those in the left-hand column below) are also used as prepositions, in which instance, as has been seen, they end in un-nunated fatḥa, e.g.:

بَعْدُ or مِنْ بَعْدُ "afterwards".	حَيْثُ "where".
مَا — بَعْدُ "not yet".	مِنْ حَيْثُ "whence".
قَبْلُ or مِنْ قَبْلُ "before".	إِلَى حَيْثُ "whither".
فَوْقُ ,, مِنْ فَوْقُ "above".	حَيْثُمَا "wherever".
تَحْتُ ,, مِنْ تَحْتُ "below".	غَيْرُ in the expression لَا غَيْرُ "nothing else, only this".

5. Most nouns used as Adverbs are employed in the Accusative:

قَلِيلًا "little".

قَلِيلًا مَا "seldom", followed by verb.

كَثِيرًا "much, very".

كَثِيرًا مَا "often", followed by verb.

جِدًّا "very".

يَوْمًا
يَوْمًا مَا } "one day, once".
ذَاتَ يَوْمٍ

اَلْيَوْمَ "today".

غَدًا "tomorrow".

دَائِمًا "always".

لَيْلًا "by night".

دَاخِلًا "inside".

خَارِجًا "outside".

مَعًا "together".

جَمِيعًا "altogether".

أَبَدًا "for ever" (with neg. "never").

نَهَارًا "by day".

يَمِينًا "on the right hand".

شِمَالًا 'on the left hand".

سَوْفَ (sign of Future tense).

كَيْفَ "how".

رُبَّمَا "often". (later "perhaps").

لَا سِيَّمَا (for لَا سِيَّ مَا "there is nothing like") "especially".

حِينَ (from the noun حِينٌ "time") in حِينَئِذٍ "then, at that time", so also وَقْتَئِذٍ "at that time".

اَلْبَتَّةَ "altogether", "decidedly".

تَارَةً — وَتَارَةً
تَارَةً — وَطَوْرًا } at one time – at another time.
تَارَةً — وَأَحْيَانًا

وَحْدَ "alone" is used with suffixes, e.g. وَحْدِى I alone, وَحْدَهُ he alone, etc.

عَلَّ and لَعَلَّ "perhaps" are often used with suffixes, e.g. لَعَلَّهُ perhaps he, لَعَلِّى (rarely لَعَلَّنِى) perhaps I.

لَيْتَ "would that" with suffixes لَيْتَهُ would that he, لَيْتَنِى (rarely لَيْتِى) would that I.

VOCABULARY

شَهِىّ appetising

مَلِيحٌ *pl.* مِلَاحٌ pretty, tasty; good

غِنًى sufficiency, wealth

سَاحِلٌ *pl.* سَوَاحِلُ sea shore, coast

شَاطِئٌ *pl.* شَوَاطِئُ river bank

بُطْءٌ slowness

بِبُطْءٍ slowly

بَطِىءٌ slow

خُطْوَةٌ *pl.* خُطُوَاتٌ step, pace

كَتِفٌ *pl.* أَكْتَافٌ shoulder

اِنْتَحَرَ VIII to commit suicide

عَبَسَ (ـِ) to frown

فُنْدُقٌ *pl.* فَنَادِقُ inn, hotel

لُوكَنْدَةٌ *pl.* ـَاتٌ — (*Syr. Eg.*) inn, hotel

اِذْهَبْ فِى حَالِكَ mind your own business!

غَرِقَ (ـَ) to drown *intr.*

نَطَّ (ـُ) to jump

نَطٌّ jumping (*v.n.* of above)

EXERCISE 93

From the *Kitāb al-Bukhalā'* of al-Jāḥiẓ

This is the story of a rich miser who would not invite his relatives to his house because of the cost of entertaining them. Finally, however, they prevail upon him to invite them and the following tells what happened:

فاتخذ لهم طعاما خفيفا شهيّا مليحا ، لا ثَمَنَ له ، فلما أكلوا وغسلوا
أيديهم اقبل عليهم فقال : أَسْأَلُكم بالله الذى لا شئَ اعظم منه ، أنا

السَّاعةَ أَيْسَرُ وأغنى أو قبل أَنْ تاكلوا طعامى؟ قالوا : ما نشكّ انك حين كان الطعام فى ملكك أغنى وايسر. قال : فأنَا الساعةَ أَقْرَبُ الى الفقر أَمْ تلك الساعة؟ قالوا : بَلْ انت الساعةَ اقربُ الى الفقر. قال : فَمَنْ يلومُنى على تَرْكِ دعوة قوم قَرَّبُونِى مِن الفقر، وبَاعَدُونى من الغِنَى؟ وكُلّما دعوتهم اكثَرَ كنتُ من الفقر اقربَ ومن الغنى ابعدَ.

NOTES:

الساعةَ "now" (Adverbial Acc.)

أو قبل أن تأكلوا "or (was I) before you ate?"

كنت اقرب من الفقر = كنتُ من الفقر اقربَ

EXERCISE 94

I met him walking slowly by the river bank, taking short paces. Where has this strange man come from, I thought, and why does he walk sadly as if (كَأَنَّ) the cares of the whole world were on his shoulders? I will invite him to my house, as I am a rich man, and I will give him tasty appetizing food. Perhaps when he leaves my house he will be happier than he was previously!

I called him, but he did not hear me and made no reply. It seemed that his private thoughts were too important for him (مِنْ أَنْ with *subjunctive*) to heed a passer-by. I called him again in a loud voice, and he turned towards me frowning.

He hesitated a little, then said angrily: "Have I met you before? Do you know me?".

"No", I said, "but I thought that you were perhaps in some difficulty, and I wanted to help you. Will you come to my house, and stay a little while and eat and drink something with me?"

"They say that an Englishman's home is his castle", he replied, "but you want to make yours an hotel, poorhouse, or orphan's home. Do you think that a stranger like you can help me? Allow me to give you some advice; and even if you won't allow me, I will give it: mind your own business!"

Then he went off, and I continued on my way.

On the following day I read in the local paper that the body of an unknown man had been found in the river, that he had drowned, and that there was no apparent cause for that. And even now I do not know whether (أَ) it was the man whom I had met who had drowned, or (أَمْ) someone else. But I always imagine that the troubles of that poor unfortunate frowning man became too great for him to bear, and so he committed suicide by jumping into the river. And I still ask myself occasionally: Could I have saved him?

CHAPTER FORTY-NINE

(اَلْبَابُ التَّاسِعُ وَالْأَرْبَعُونَ)

Particles. Conjunctions

1. Whereas in English it is considered bad style to commence a sentence with "and", in Arabic it is the rule rather than the exception to do so. Sentences are continually linked by وَ, فَ and less frequently, by ثُمَّ "then". Only at the end of a paragraph, or where there is a definite change of topic, is the *Conjunction* omitted. It is true that under Western influence the Conjunction is more frequently omitted in modern literary Arabic; but even so the Western reader will at first be struck by the ubiquitous و. It is by far the commonest conjunction; ف, as we have seen, has special implications. Doubtless, ثُمَّ, having the Accusative *un-nunated* ending, ought properly to be considered adverbial. As it often introduces sentences without a preliminary و or ف, however, it may properly be mentioned here.

There are, of course, many other Particles which may be described more or less as Conjunctions. Some of them have already been discussed, but they are mentioned again here for completeness.

Conjunctions may be either *Inseparable* (that is, joined to the first word of the sentence they introduce) or *Separate.*

2. The Inseparables are:

(a) وَ. This may join Sentences or Nouns, e.g.

(i) دَخَلَ زَيْدٌ وَجَلَسَ عَلَى كُرْسِيٍّ Zaid entered and sat on a chair.

(ii) جَاءَ زَيْدٌ وَحَسَنٌ Zaid and Hassan came.

It is not usually used in Arabic to link two Adjectives governing the same Noun. Thus the sentence "a large and beautiful city" would be مَدِينَةٌ كَبِيرَةٌ جَمِيلَةٌ rather than مَدِينَةٌ كَبِيرَةٌ وَجَمِيلَةٌ, though the latter is not grammatically incorrect, and may occasionally be encountered.

وَ between two sentences, of which the second is a Nominal sentence, often means "while". Such a sentence introduced by وَ is called a جُمْلَةٌ حَالِيَّةٌ "sentence of condition", e.g.:

قَامَ زَيْدٌ وَهُوَ بَاكٍ قَامَ زَيْدٌ وَهُوَ يَبْكِي	Zaid stood up, while he wept (Zaid stood up weeping).

also with change of Subject:

ذَهَبَ زَيْدٌ وَعَمْرٌو بَاقٍ ذَهَبَ زَيْدٌ وَعَمْرٌو يَبْقَى	Zaid went away and ʿAmr remained (while ʿAmr remained).

The وَ is usually dropped, when a Verbal *Ḥāl* sentence follows:

جَاءَ زَيْدٌ يَضْحَكُ Zaid came, while he laughed (laughing).

The *wāw* of *Ḥāl* (وَاوُ ٱلْحَالِ) is sometimes used before a Nominal sentence which has no Participle or Imperfect:

جَاءَ زَيْدٌ وَبِيَدِهِ سَيْفٌ Zaid came, and in his hand a sword (with a sword in his hand).

(b) فَ differs essentially from وَ, although there are many contexts in which either would be acceptable. It implies a close connection between the sentences before and after it. This connection may be either definite *Cause* and *Effect*, or a natural sequence of event

(i) Cause and effect:

قَامَ ٱلْوَزِيرُ فَقُمْتُ أَنَا أَيْضًا	the minister stood up, so I stood up also.
تَقَدَّمَ ٱلْعَدُوُّ نَحْوَهُمْ فَوَلَّوْا وَفَرُّوا مُسْرِعِينَ	the enemy advanced towards them; so they turned and fled hurriedly.

Conditionals, already dealt with, come under this category. But, as has been seen, in the Conditional with إِنْ the Apodosis is introduced by فَ only in certain given circumstances.

(ii) Natural sequence:

قَامَ فَاسْتَلَّ سَيْفَهُ فَانْتَظَرَ ٱلْعَدُوَّ He stood up, drew his sword, and waited for the enemy.

Here, both فَ's could be replaced by وَ. فَ is rarely used to join single words, but it may be so used when a closely connected sequence is intended, e.g.

أَدْخِلْ حَسَنًا فَمُحَمَّدًا فَزَيْدًا bring in Hassan, then Muhammad, then Zaid.

(here ثُمَّ could be used, or وَبَعْدَ ذٰلِكَ or وَبَعْدَهُ)

كَانَتْ حَيَاتُهُ دَائِرَةً مُسْتَمِرَّةً ٱلذَّهَابُ لِلْخَانِ فَشُرْبٌ فَسُكْرٌ فَنَوْمٌ فَٱلذَّهَابُ لِلْخَانِ his life was a constant round: going to the inn, drinking, getting drunk, sleeping, then going to the inn.

By its very nature, فَ is precluded from joining two Adjectives governing the same Noun. Such a usage, if encountered, would be most unusual.

(c) لِ "so that" with following Subjunctive:

جَاءَنِي لِيَطْلُبَ ٱلْمَالَ he came to me so that he might demand the wealth (to demand the wealth).

With the same meaning are used لِأَنْ, لِكَيْ; and negatively لِكَيْلَا, لِئَلَّا "so that not".

لِ with the Jussive (nearly always in the 3rd Person) expresses a demand:

لِيَكْتُبْ let him write!

3. The usual Separable Conjunctions are:

(a) إِذْ "when, since, after, because" with following Nominal or Verbal sentence.

(b) إِذَا "when, if" originally used of time, but often of condition. In direct questions = "whether".

إِذْ and إِذَا also mean "behold!", in which case the former is always followed by a Verbal sentence, the latter by a Nominal sentence in which the Subject is either in the Nominative or takes بِ:

إِذْ أَتَى رَجُلٌ
إِذَا رَجُلٌ (بِرَجُلٍ) قَدْ أَتَى } behold, a man came!

إِذَا مَا means "whenever".

(c) إِنْ "if, whether" introduces Conditional sentences or indirect Questions.

وَإِنْ means "and if, even if, although". لَئِنْ = "verily if".

NOTE: There is also a particle of Denial إِنْ e.g.:
إِنْ رَأَيْتُ مِنْهَا أَمْرًا أَغْمِصُهُ I have not seen anything of her, that I despise.

This usage, though common in the Quran, is rare elsewhere, and should not be used by students.

(d) إِلَّا used for Exception, see Chapter Fifty-one. Note, however, the following uses of this particle as a conjunction:

(i) إِلَّا أَنَّ; كُنْتُ أُحِبُّهُ إِلَّا أَنَّهُ كَانَ دَائِمًا يَتَكَلَّمُ بِصَوْتٍ عَالٍ I liked him, save that he always spoke in a loud voice.

(ii) وَإِلَّا; قُمْ وَإِلَّا ضَرَبْتُكَ Stand up, otherwise I will beat you. (Quasi-condition, or after-thought condition).

(e) أَمَّا "as for" with a following Nominative, the Predicate being always strengthened with a فَ, e.g.:

أَمَّا جَبَلُ ٱلشَّيْخِ فَهُوَ جَبَلٌ شَامِخٌ as for Mt. Hermon, it is a lofty mountain.

أَمَّا ٱلْكَلْبُ فَلَقِيتُهُ فِي ٱلطَّرِيقِ as for the dog, I met him on the road.

(According to Arabian grammarians أَلْكَلْبُ is the Subject, all the rest is Predicate.)

(f) أَنْ "that" with following Verbal sentence, the verb being occasionally in the Perf., nearly always in the Imperf. Subjunctive.

كَأَنْ = "as though"; لِأَنْ = "because".

With Negative: أَلَّا (for أَنْ and لَا) "that not"; لِئَلَّا "so that not".

(g) أَنَّ "that" with a Nominal sentence.

In compounds:

كَأَنَّ / كَأَنَّمَا "just as if", "it is as if".

لِأَنَّ "because".

إِلَّا أَنَّ, غَيْرَ أَنَّ "except that, yet".

(h) أَوْ "or"; إِمَّا — أَوْ "either – or".

With the Subjunctive أَوْ means "unless that, until that".

(i) بَيْنَمَا (more rarely بَيْنَا) "while".

(j) ثُمَّ "then, thereupon" often followed by إِنَّ.

(k) حَتَّى "until" (= إِلَى أَنْ); with a Nominal sentence often حَتَّى أَنَّ.

(l) كَيْ or لِكَيْ "in order that" with following Subjunctive.

With Negative كَيْلَا and لِكَيْلَا "in order that not".

(m) لٰكِنْ and لٰكِنَّ "but", the former being followed by a verb, the latter only by nouns in the Accusative, or Pronominal suffixes: لٰكِنَّهُ "but he".

(n) لَمَّا "when, after" with following Perfect to be translated usually by the Pluperfect.

(o) لَوْ "if" in Conditional sentences referring to a mere supposition.

(p) مَا "so long as" (مَا ٱلدَّيْمُومَةِ "the مَا of continuance"), is often used in compound Conjunctions:

بَعْدَ مَا "after".

بَيْنَمَا and فِيمَا "while".

قَبْلَ مَا "before" (always with the Imperf.).

It is often used also to generalize, e.g.:

إِذْمَا } "whenever". مَتَى مَا "whenever".
إِذَامَا } "if ever". كُلَّمَا "as often as".

In these cases it is followed by the Perf. or the Juss. in the sense of the Present.

(q) مَتَى "when", مَتَى مَا "whenever".

(r) مُنْذُ or مُذْ "since".

VOCABULARY

وَلَّى II to turn round, back *intr.*

اِسْتَلَّ سَيْفًا VIII to draw a sword

خَانٌ *pl.* ـَاتٌ — inn, khan

اِسْتَدَارَ X to be round

لَجَّ (ـِ) to persevere, continue

اَلشَّرِيعَةُ the Shariʿa, Muslim law

سَحَابٌ cloud (*collective*)

شَرْعِيٌّ a legalist, lawyer, expert on the Shariʿa; legal *adj.*

شَامِخٌ *pl.* شَوَامِخُ lofty

مُتَقَدِّمٌ ancient, an ancient (of historical personages)

حَكِيمٌ *pl.* حُكَمَاءُ wise, wise man; doctor (popular)

حِكْمَةٌ *pl.* حِكَمٌ wisdom, aphorism

اَلْيُونَانُ Greece, the Greeks

يُونَانِيٌّ Greek, a Greek

اِسْتَدَلَّ على . . . بـ X to prove . . . by . . .

ذَبَلَ (ـُ) to wither, fade

بُرْجٌ *pl.* بُرُوجٌ tower

مِعْمَارٌ architect

EXERCISE 95

The geographer, al-Masʿūdī, writes about the roundness of the earth.

قد تُنُوزِعَ فى شكل البِحَارِ. فذهب الأكثرُ من الفلاسفة المتقدمين من الهند وحكماء اليونانيين ، الّا مَنْ خالفهم وذهب الى قول الشرعيين ، أنّ البحرَ مستديرٌ على مواضع من الأرض واستدلوا على صِحّة ذلك بدلائل كثيرة ، منها (among them, including) اذا لَجَجْتَ فيه (i.e. the sea) غابت عنك الارضُ والجبال شيئًا بعدَ شيءٍ حتى يغيب

ذلك كله ، ولا ترى شيئًا من شوامخ الجبال ، واذا اقبلتَ أيضًا نحو الساحل ، ظهرتْ تلك الجبالُ شيئًا بعد شيء ، وظهرت الاشجارُ والارضُ.

NOTE: تُنُوزِعَ (Pass. Perf. of نزع VI) "was disputed".

EXERCISE 96

NOTE: It is not intended to test and practise by exercises the whole content of this chapter and similar chapters largely of a revisional nature. In any case, it is assumed that by this stage the student will already have commenced reading literature or magazines or newspapers, if rather laboriously.

1. Turn round and face me, for I have drawn my sword and do not wish to strike a man in the back. 2. He persevered in his study of the religious law in order to take it (use Form VIII) as a profession. 3. Give me a clean glass, otherwise I will go and drink in another inn. 4. I have a little round picture (use diminutive) of my mother, and it resembles her, save that the colours have faded. 5. The ancients used to build their palaces and castles with lofty towers, then after the passage of time, the custom changed; so that we rarely see towers in the buildings of modern architects. 6. Uneducated people today call the doctor "Hakim", since they consider wisdom one of his qualities. 7. As for the science of medicine, it began, perhaps, in Greece, a number of centuries before Christ. 8. Caesar (قَيْصَرُ) said: I came, I saw, I conquered – and that was when he returned to Italy from France with his army. 9. I used to eat at his house frequently, until he moved to another town; then I did not see him after that until the day of his death. 10. While we were watching, he was raised up to heaven in a cloud.

CHAPTER FIFTY

(اَلْبَابُ ٱلْخَمْسُونَ)

Particles. Interjections.

1. The Vocative (حَرْفُ ٱلنِّدَاءِ) is expressed by the particles يَا and أَيُّهَا Fem. أَيَّتُهَا (but the Masc. is often used for the Fem.) or يَا أَيُّهَا.

أَيُّهَا and يَا أَيُّهَا are followed by the noun in the Nominative with the Article:

يَا أَيُّهَا ٱلتِّلْمِيذُ O scholar!

يَا is followed by the noun in the Nominative without Article (and without Nunation in the Sing.) if the person addressed is present and the noun is not determined by any following words, e.g.

يَا وَلَدُ O boy! يَا مُحَمَّدُ O Mohammed!

يَا أَوْلَادُ O boys!

If the person addressed is absent or the noun is determined by some word or words after it, then the noun is put in the Accusative, e.g.:

يَا غَافِلاً O careless! (not addressed to any one particular person).

هَا See there!

هُوَ ذَا See there he is!

يَا طَالِعًا ٱلْجَبَلَ O thou, who climbest the mountain!

يَا عَبْدَ ٱللّٰهِ O Abdullah!

NOTE 1: يَا is sometimes written without *'alif* when the following word begins with an *'alif*, e.g.:

يَأَخِي O my brother! يَأَهْلاً welcome!

Notice specially:

يَا أَبَتِ O my father! يَا أُمَّاهْ O mother!

يَا رَبِّ O my Lord!

NOTE 2: The noun that follows يَا often takes the Vocative ending ـَاهْ (see below on وَا).

2. Some of the commonest Interjections are:

أَوَّاهْ, أَهْ, آهْ, آهِ, أَوْهْ, آ, أَ Ah!

وَا Oh! The following noun often has the ending ـَا or ـَاهْ in pause, e.g.

وَا أَسَفَا or وَا أَسَفَاهْ O sorrow!

وَا حَسْرَتَا O grief!

وَيْ Alas! also with suffixes: وَيْكَ Alas for thee!

Also وَيْلَكَ, وَيْحَكَ. The most common is وَيْلَكَ.

هَيَّا Come! with the Preposition بِ: هَيَّا بِنَا Come, let us go!

هَيْهَاتَ Far from it!

أُفِّ, أُفْ Fie!

بَخْ and بَخْ بَخْ Bravo!

طُوبَى (Fem. of the Elative أَطْيَبُ "best") Hail!

طُوبَاكَ or طُوبَى لَكَ Hail to thee!

هَلُمَّ, in the Plural هَلُمُّوا "Hither!"

هَاتِ (properly the Imper. IV of أَتَى "to come") "give, bring here!" also used in the Fem.

دُونَكَ and دُونَكُمْ "Beware!".

إِيَّاكَ and إِيَّاكُمْ "Beware!".

3. Certain nouns are used in the Accusative as Interjections.

أَهْلًا وَسَهْلًا Welcome!

عَجَبًا Strange!

مَهْلًا Slowly!

مَرْحَبًا Welcome!

مَرْحَبًا بِكَ Welcome to thee!

سَمْعًا وَطَاعَةً (lit. "hearing and obeying".) At your service!

تَبًّا لَكَ Alas for thee!

4. Many religious expressions are used interjectionally: e.g.

اَللّٰهْ or يَا اَللّٰهْ or very commonly اَللّٰهُمَّ O God!

وَٱللّٰهِ بِٱللّٰهِ تَٱللّٰهِ By God!

اَلْحَمْدُ لِلّٰهِ Thanks to God!

إِنْ شَاءَ ٱللّٰهُ If God will!

بِسْمِ ٱللّٰهِ ٱلرَّحْمٰنِ ٱلرَّحِيمِ In the name of God the Compassionate, the Merciful!

مَعَاذَ ٱللّٰهِ or أَعُوذُ بِٱللّٰهِ God forbid it! (lit. "I take refuge in God").

لَا حَوْلَ وَلَا قُوَّةَ إِلَّا بِٱللّٰهِ ٱلْعَظِيمِ	There is no might and no power, save in God the Mighty! (Expression of astonishment and alarm.)
مَا شَاءَ ٱللّٰهُ	What God will! (Astonishment.)
أَسْتَغْفِرُ ٱللّٰهَ	I ask pardon of God! (Used to decline a compliment.)

Praises constantly appended to the name of God:

تَعَالَى (Perf. IV of عَلَا)	He is exalted!
عَزَّ وَجَلَّ	He is powerful and glorified!
سُبْحَانَهُ	Praised be He!

There are no vocabulary or exercises for this chapter.

CHAPTER FIFTY-ONE

(اَلْبَابُ اَلْحَادِى وَالْخَمْسُونَ)

Exception

1. The commonest way of expressing *Exception* (إِسْتِثْنَاءٌ) is by the Particle إِلَّا (a modification of إِنْ لَا "if not"). This Particle takes the Accusative in its following Noun in most, but not all, circumstances. The following rules apply. For the purpose of explanation, we consider the situation of the two important elements involved, i.e. the thing (or person) *Excepted*, and the *Generality*. Thus, if I say: "The teachers came, apart from George", George is the Exception, and the teachers are the Generality. The following situations may occur in Arabic:

(a) The Generality *may not be mentioned at all.*

e.g.

مَا بَقِيَ إِلَّا حَسَنٌ only Hassan remained (lit. did not remain except Hassan).

مَا رَأَيْتُ إِلَّا حَسَنًا I saw only Hassan.

مَا رَضِيتُ إِلَّا عَنْ حَسَنٍ I was pleased only with Hassan.

Here, it will be noted that "Hassan", the Noun after إِلَّا, changes its case as if إِلَّا were not there,

e.g. بَقِيَ حَسَنٌ Hassan remained.

رَأَيْتُ حَسَنًا I saw Hassan, etc.

To put it another way, the noun after إِلَّا goes into the case in which the generality would have been, had it been mentioned. Note that this situation can only occur in a negative sentence. The following are the rules, when the generality is mentioned:

(b) In *Positive Sentences* إِلَّا invariably takes the *Accusative*, e.g.

إِلَّا ٱلْمَلِكَ قَامَ كُلُّ ٱلْحَاضِرِينَ except the King, all present stood up (the *Excepted* coming first).

قَامَ ٱلْجَمِيعُ إِلَّا ٱلْمَلِكَ all stood up except the King.

(c) In *Negative Sentences* the Accusative may be used, but there are alternative usages as under:

(i) Where the Excepted comes *first*, it may be in the *Nominative*

إِلَّا حَسَنًا (or حَسَنٌ) مَا حَضَرَ التَّلَامِذَةُ except Hassan, the pupils did not attend.

(ii) Where the Generality comes *first*, the Excepted may be put in the same case as the Generality.

مَا حَضَرَ التَّلَامِذَةُ إِلَّا حَسَنًا (or حَسَنٌ) the pupils did not attend, except Hassan.

لَمْ يَمُرَّ بِالْجُنُودِ إِلَّا قَائِدَهُمْ (or بِقَائِدِهِمْ) he did not pass the soldiers, except their leader.

كَانَ يَكْرَهُ كُلَّ النَّاسِ إِلَّا أَبَاهُ he hated everybody except his father.

Note that in this eventuality, the Generality may be expressed by أَحَدٌ "one", e.g.

مَا جَاءَ أَحَدٌ إِلَّا حَسَنٌ (حَسَنًا) no one came except Hassan.

مَا ضَرَبْتُ أَحَدًا إِلَّا حَسَنًا I struck no one except Hassan.

مَا مَرَرْتُ بِأَحَدٍ إِلَّا حَسَنٍ (or حَسَنًا) I passed no one but Hassan.

2. The above rules may seem complicated, but it is best for the novice to use the Accusative in all circumstances where the Generality is mentioned. The following table, however, summarizes what has been said:

Table to show the cases to be used after إِلَّا:

Position of the Generality	*Positive Sentence*	*Negative Sentence*
Not mentioned	—	In the case in which the generality would have been, had it been mentioned.
First	Accusative	Accusative (or in the Case of the generality).
Last	Accusative	Accusative (or Nominative).

3. Other Exceptive Constructions are:

(a) غَيْر This is a Noun, as explained in Chapter Forty-five, 4 d (vi), and takes *'iḍāfa*. It is placed in the case in which the Noun after إِلَّا would have been placed, according to the above table, e.g.

مَا بَقِيَ غَيْرُ حَسَنٍ only Hassan remained.

مَا ضَرَبْتُ غَيْرَ حَسَنٍ I struck no one except Hassan.

غَيْرَ is also used in the *un-nunated* Accusative followed by a sentence with أَنَّ, e.g.

كَانَ مَسْرُورًا غَيْرَ أَنَّهُ يَخَافُ مِنْ غَضَبِ الْمَلِكِ	he was happy, except that he feared the King's wrath.

Here إِلَّا could replace غَيْرَ.

(b) مَا عَدَا and مَا خَلَا. These act as Verbs, and take an Accusative, e.g.

جَاءَ الْقَوْمُ مَا عَدَا (مَا خَلَا) حَسَنًا	The people came, apart from Hassan.

(c) These two words occasionally occur without مَا, and then take the Genitive, as Prepositions. The above sentence would then read:

جَاءَ الْقَوْمُ عَدَا (خَلَا) حَسَنٍ

But the use of خَلَا in this way was disputed by the grammarians.

4. Related to *Exception* is the use of لَا سِيَّمَا, "especially". It invariably takes the Nominative.

كَانُوا كُفَّارًا لَاسِيَّمَا كِبَارُهُمْ	they were infidels, especially their old men.
رَأَيْتُهُمْ كُلَّهُمْ لَا سِيَّمَا حَسَنٌ ٱلَّذِى كَانَ فِى مُقَدِّمَتِهِمْ	I saw them all, especially Hassan, who was in their forefront.
غَضِبْتُ مِنْهُمْ لَا سِيَّمَا قَائِدُهُمْ	I was angry with them, especially their leader.

Note: For إِلَّا أَنَّ and وَإِلَّا see Chapter Forty-Nine, 3 (d).

VOCABULARY

عِيَادَةٌ (from عَادَ) doctor's surgery (*mod.*); out-patients' department (*mod.*)

نُسْخَةٌ *pl.* نُسَخٌ copy (of book, etc.)

مَاهِرٌ *pl.* مَهَرَةٌ clever, skilful, skilled

بَارِعٌ clever, accomplished

ذُو خِبْرَةٍ experienced

وَافِرٌ plentiful, abundant

اِحْتَضَرَ VIII to be on the point of death

بُرْهَةٌ *pl.* ـَاتٌ —، بُرَهٌ a space of time (with or without مِنَ الزَّمَانِ)

فِئَةٌ *pl.* ـَاتٌ — company, group, faction

نَتَجَ عَنْ (ـَ) to result from

تَقْلِيدٌ *pl.* تَقَالِيدُ tradition (lit. imitation)

اَلصِّينُ China, the Chinese

صِينِيٌّ Chinese

ثَائِرٌ *pl.* ثُوَّارٌ a revolutionary, rebel

اَلْعَامَّةُ، عَامَّةُ النَّاسِ the common people, the masses

EXERCISE 97

A

لٰكِنَّ هناك فى الشرق الأوسط فئةً يكرهون تأثير الغرب ، فيقولون : ما أعطانا هذا التأثيرُ الا عدم الايمان ، وما نَتَجَ عنه الا إنكارُ تقاليدنا وعاداتنا وتأريخنا . وهذا ما يعتقدُهُ الكثير من سكان تلك البلاد . لكنهم ينسون حديث النبى (صلعم) : « أُطلبِ العلم ولو من الصين » .

B

استقال جميع اعضاء الحكومة ما عدا اثنين منهم ، وهما وزير الخارجية ووزير الاقتصادية والتجارة : وهذان وغيرهما من المفكرين من بين سكان البلاد ، يَرَوْنَ خَطَرًا كبيرًا فى مَطَالِبِ الثُوّار ؛ فهى ، ولا شك ، تضرّ باقتصاد الدولة الا انها تُثِيرُ عواطف العامّة .

C

الا الأولاد والبنات، خرج جميع ناس القرية للمزارع ، فهذا فصل الخريف ومحصولات هذه السنة وافرة جدًّا، والسبب كثرة الامطار التى سقطت فى جميع الشهور تقريبا الا شهر آذار (مارس).

EXERCISE 98

Rewrite the whole of Exercise 97, with full vowelling and orthographical signs.

NOTE: In translating, the student is advised to follow the order of the English where possible, putting the Generality before the Exception, and vice versa, in the Arabic, according to the order in the English.

Further, الا, by far the commonest exceptive particle, should be used wherever admissible. ما عدا and ما خلا are not so common, and should be sparingly introduced.

EXERCISE 99

A

All the patients (the sick) waited for the doctor in his out-patients' department several hours, except one, and this man knew the doctor's habits. The reason for the doctor's delay was that, while returning from visiting a patient in his house, he stopped on his way home at an inn to have a drink (to drink something). He frequently did this, especially in the winter. Consequently, he had lost many patients. And he might have lost more, except that he was clever and experienced.

B

When I entered my friend's house, I only saw a ghost. I was only a youth, and that sight terrified me. Apart from my father, I had never seen a dying man before. No-one was with my friend, except his neglectful inexperienced servant, so I decided to remain with him for a time.

C

Hassan had wanted to read al-Jahiz's "Book of Misers", and told his father that. When his birthday arrived, he was expecting his father to give him a copy, but he gave him another book instead. He was very angry, for a time, but when he read the book, he liked it very much.

D

No strangers have ever entered our city except ten travellers who had lost the way. All of them were killed, except two. We allowed them to survive because one of them was a blacksmith and the other a carpenter.

CHAPTER FIFTY-TWO

(اَلْبَابُ ٱلثَّانِي وَٱلْخَمْسُونَ)

The Rules of Arabic Versification

NOTE: For a more complete account, Wright's Arabic Grammar should be consulted (Part IV. Prosody).

1. Whereas in most languages there are two genres or classes of writing, *Prose* and *Poetry*, in Arabic there are three:

(a) Prose (نَثْرٌ)

(b) Poetry (شِعْرٌ; نَظْمٌ)

(c) *Rhymed Prose* (سَجْعٌ). This third genre is common in what might be termed "art prose", – that type of studied prose literature which used the devices of rhetoric (or بَلَاغَةٌ) to a considerable degree. The language of the Qur'ān, however, is not allowed by Muslims to belong to any genre, although the early chapters or *sūras* (that is, early chronologically) do contain rhyme. Rhymed prose has not, of course, any regular metre, while poetry has both rhyme and metre.

2. Classical Arabic is a language of *syllable length* rather than *stress*; it is quantitative rather than qualitative: and this must be realized to understand the rules of Arabic poetry. The metres were codified in the 8th century by al-Khalīl ibn Aḥmad, and his codification has remained substantially unchanged.

Scanning Arabic poetry necessitates recognizing the *length* of syllable, which may be either *short* or *long*.

(a) The *short syllable* consists of a consonant with a short vowel, e.g. all three syllables in كَتَبَ *ka-ta-ba*, "he wrote".

(b) Long syllables consist of a vowelled letter followed by an unvowelled letter. The unvowelled letter may be

(i) A long vowel, as كَا kā, in كَاتَبَ *kā-ta-ba.*

(ii) A consonant with *sukūn*, as مَكْ *mak* in مَكْتَبٌ *mak-ta-bun.* Note that it is the ACTUAL SOUND which counts. Thus the third syllable مَكْتَبٌ is long (*bun*), because, although written as a single letter with nunation, it sounds as if the word were spelled مَكْتَبُنْ. Similarly, مَكْتَبًا, which is really مَكْتَبَنْ. Consequently an *'alif* with *hamzatu l-waṣl* does not count. Thus the words كَانَ اسْمُهُ حَسَنًا would be scanned as follows: *Kā nas mu hu ḥa sa nan.*

— — ⏑ ⏑ ⏑ ⏑ —

NOTE: The Pronominal suffix ه and the second syllable in أَنَا may be either long or short.

Two short syllables are considered equal to one long one, which often replaces them.

3. Arabic verse has both Rhyme (قَافِيَةٌ pl. قَوَافٍ) and Metre (وَزْنٌ or بَحْرٌ).

Every Verse or Line (بَيْتٌ pl. أَبْيَاتٌ) consists of two Half-Verses (شَطْرٌ or مِصْرَاعٌ)

At the end of the Verse i.e. in Pause (وَقْفٌ) the Nunation is dropped and sometimes the vowel is omitted altogether.

The vowel of the rhyme letter is usually considered long, as the metres almost always end with a long syllable.

In most older poetry, and much modern poetry, all lines are of the same length, and the same rhyme persists throughout the poem, which may contain up to 100 or more lines or verses. But later in the Medieval period varied rhyme schemes were introduced. For example, the two halves of each verse might rhyme together, especially in Rajaz metre (see below), and in didactic poetry. Again, complicated rhyme schemes were evolved such as: a a a a a, b b b b a, c c c c a, d d d d a, etc., the unit concerned being the half-verse. The poem with the uniform rhyme and metre is the

قَصِيدَةٌ or ode *par excellence*. It is found in the famous pre-Islamic Seven Odes known as the Muعallaqāt (اَلْمُعَلَّقَاتُ).

4. Al-Khalīl codified the Metres by expressing the various feet with the root فعل. He discovered the following different types of foot (تَفْعِيلٌ pl. تَفَاعِيلُ).

(a) فَعُولُنْ ⏑ ⏓ —

(b) فَاعِلُنْ ⏓ ⏑ ⏓

(c) مُسْتَفْعِلُنْ — ⏓ ⏑ ⏓

(d) مَفَاعِيلُنْ ⏑ ⏓ — ⏓

(e) فَاعِلَاتُنْ ⏓ ⏑ ⏓ —

(f) مَفْعُولَاتُ ⏓ — ⏓ ⏑

(g) مُفَاعَلَتُنْ ⏑ ⏓ ⏑ ⏑ —

(h) مُتَفَاعِلُنْ ⏑ ⏑ ⏓ ⏑ —

These Feet are subject to certain changes, e.g.:

(a) فَعُولُنْ ⏑ — — becomes فَعُولُ ⏑ — ⏑

(b) فَاعِلُنْ — ⏑ — ,, فَعِلُنْ ⏑ ⏑ —

(c) مُسْتَفْعِلُنْ — — ⏑ — becomes
- مُتَفْعِلُنْ ⏑ — ⏑ —
- مُفْتَعِلُنْ — ⏑ ⏑ —
- مُتَعِلُنْ ⏑ ⏑ ⏑ —

(d) مَفَاعِيلُنْ ⏑ — — — ,,
- مَفَاعِلُنْ ⏑ — ⏑ —
- مَفَاعِيلُ ⏑ — — ⏑

(e) فَاعِلَاتُنْ — ⏑ — — becomes { فَاعِلَاتُ — ⏑ — ⏑ ; فَعِلَاتُنْ ⏑ ⏑ — — ; فَعِلَاتُ ⏑ ⏑ — ⏑ }

(f) مَفْعُولَاتُ — — — ⏑ " { مَفْعُلَاتُ — ⏑ — ⏑ ; فَعُولَاتُ ⏑ — — ⏑ }

(g) مُفَاعَلَتُنْ ⏑ — ⏑ ⏑ — " { مُفَاعَلْتُنْ ⏑ — — — ; مُفَاعَتُنْ ⏑ — ⏑ — (rare) }

(h) مُتَفَاعِلُنْ ⏑ ⏑ — ⏑ — " مُتْفَاعِلُنْ — — ⏑ —

Such changes may occur spasmodically within a single poem, save that the final (rhyme-) foot of each verse must be of the same pattern throughout a poem.

If Catalexis (rejection of the last syllable) occurs at the end of a verse, then ⏑ — — is changed to ⏑ —; — ⏑ — to — — etc.

5. The principal metres are as follows:

(a) Ṭawīl اَلطَّوِيلُ:

فَعُولُنْ مَفَاعِيلُنْ فَعُولُنْ مَفَاعِيلُنْ

فَعُولُنْ مَفَاعِيلُنْ فَعُولُنْ مَفَاعِيلُنْ

مَفَاعِيلُنْ is frequently changed to مَفَاعِلُنْ, especially in the rhyme foot.

(b) Kāmil اَلْكَامِلُ

مُتَفَاعِلُنْ مُتَفَاعِلُنْ مُتَفَاعِلُنْ

مُتَفَاعِلُنْ مُتَفَاعِلُنْ مُتَفَاعِلُنْ

The two short syllables of each foot are often combined to form one long syllable in which case the foot might be scanned as مُتْفَاعِلٌ (or مُسْتَفْعِلٌ). The rhyme is frequently shortened to مُتَفَاعِلْ ⏑⏑ — — or مُتَفَا ⏑⏑ —.

(c) Wāfir اَلْوَافِرُ

مُفَاعَلَتُنْ مُفَاعَلَتُنْ فَعُولُنْ

مُفَاعَلَتُنْ مُفَاعَلَتُنْ فَعُولُنْ

مُفَاعَلَتُنْ often changes to مُفَاعَلْتُنْ or مَفَاعِيلُنْ.

(d) Rajaz اَلرَّجَزُ (especially in didactic poems; such a poem being called أُرْجُوزَةٌ):

مُسْتَفْعِلُنْ مُسْتَفْعِلُنْ مُسْتَفْعِلُنْ

مُسْتَفْعِلُنْ مُسْتَفْعِلُنْ مُسْتَفْعِلُنْ

e.g.

قَالَ مُحَمَّدٌ هُوَ ٱبْنُ مَالِكِ

أَحْمَدُ رَبِّى ٱللّٰهَ خَيْرَ مَالِكِ

"Said Muḥammad ibn Mālik: I praise my Lord God, the best Ruler."

(Beginning of the 'Alfīyā of Ibn Mālik.)

In this metre Catalexis of the last foot (change ⏓ ⏓ ⏑ — to ⏓ ⏓ —) is very common.

(e) Hazaj اَلْهَزَجُ common in Persian and Urdu also in Rubāɛīyāt رُبَاعِيَّاتٌ (e.g. the Rubāɛīyāt of ɛUmar-i-Khayyām).

مَفَاعِيلُنْ مَفَاعِيلُنْ

مَفَاعِيلُنْ مَفَاعِيلُنْ

(f) Basīṭ اَلْبَسِيطُ

مُسْتَفْعِلُنْ فَاعِلُنْ مُسْتَفْعِلُنْ فَاعِلُنْ

مُسْتَفْعِلُنْ فَاعِلُنْ مُسْتَفْعِلُنْ فَاعِلُنْ

مُسْتَفْعِلُنْ may change to مُتَفْعِلُنْ and فَاعِلُنْ to فَعِلُنْ and even فَعْلُنْ (⏑ ⏑ — or — —) especially in the rhyme foot.

(g) Khafīf اَلْخَفِيفُ

فَاعِلَاتُنْ مُسْتَفْعِلُنْ فَاعِلَاتُنْ

فَاعِلَاتُنْ مُسْتَفْعِلُنْ فَاعِلَاتُنْ

فَاعِلَاتُنْ may change to فَعِلَاتُنْ or فَعْلَاتُنْ (⏑ ⏑ — — or — — —) especially in the rhyme foot.

(h) Sarīع اَلسَّرِيعُ

مُسْتَفْعِلُنْ مُسْتَفْعِلُنْ فَاعِلُنْ

مُسْتَفْعِلُنْ مُسْتَفْعِلُنْ فَاعِلُنْ

مُسْتَفْعِلُنْ may change to مُتَفْعِلُنْ (⏑ — ⏑ —) and فَاعِلُنْ to فَعِلُنْ or فَعْلُنْ (⏑ ⏑ — or — —).

The other metres are much less frequently encountered in Classical Arabic.

RHYME

6. Rhyme in Arabic poetry consists essentially of a *Consonant*. This consonant may have *sukūn*, whether real or imposed, e.g. the poem by ʼAbū l-عAtāhīya:

مَا لَنَا لَا نَتَفَكَّرْ أَيْنَ كِسْرَى أَيْنَ قَيْصَرْ

What is (wrong) with us, that we do not think?
Where is Chosroes, where is Caesar?

Usually, however, the rhyme consonant has a vowel, which should be constant throughout the poem, or at least, with that rhyme. Thus كَتَبَ rhymes with عَرَبَ, the rhyme letter (رَوِيّ) having *fatḥa*. As already stated, the rhyme vowel is usually considered long, the above two words being considered "katabā" ʿarabā. كَلَّمُوا rhymes with سَلَّمْ. The nūnation is always removed for rhyme purposes. Sometimes a *kasra* rhyme may be varied with *ḍamma* or vice versa, but *fatḥa* must not be varied. *Kasra* and *ḍamma* are considered related sounds. If a long vowel occurs in the syllable previous to the rhyme, or the syllable before that, it should be constant, e.g. سَلَامُ and كَلَامُ; كَبِيرُ and جَدِيرُ; صَبُورُ and شُهُورُ; كَامِلَا and قَابِلَا.

In this connection, the long vowel ـُو is always considered equivalent to ـِي; but *'alif* (ـَا) cannot be varied (e.g. صَبُورُ rhymes with كَبِيرُ but not with كِبَارُ).

7. Arabs tend to recognize the metres of their poetry rather by an innate sense of the rhythm of the language than by identifying the precise metre concerned. They have their own particular method of reciting poetry; and Arabic poetry needs to be declaimed to be appreciated. Only by listening to an Arab reading Arabic poetry can one acquire a feeling for it. Only then can a non-Arab appreciate the outstanding genius of Arabic poets such as al-Mutanabbī.

SUPPLEMENT

SELECTIONS

FROM THE QUR'ĀN

Sūra 1

سُورَةُ ٱلْفَاتِحَةِ

بِسْمِ ٱللَّهِ ٱلرَّحْمٰنِ ٱلرَّحِيمِ

ٱلْحَمْدُ لِلّٰهِ رَبِّ ٱلْعَالَمِينَ . ٱلرَّحْمٰنِ الرَّحِيمِ. مَالِكِ يَوْمِ ٱلدِّينِ .
إِيَّاكَ نَعْبُدُ وَإِيَّاكَ نَسْتَعِينُ . ٱهْدِنَا ٱلصِّرَاطَ ٱلْمُسْتَقِيمَ. صِرَاطَ ٱلَّذِينَ
أَنْعَمْتَ عَلَيْهِمْ. غَيْرِ ٱلْمَغْضُوبِ عَلَيْهِمْ وَلَا ٱلضَّالِّينَ —

Sūra 112

سُورَةُ ٱلْإِخْلَاصِ

قُلْ هُوَ ٱللّٰهُ أَحَدٌ. ٱللّٰهُ ٱلصَّمَدُ. لَمْ يَلِدْ وَلَمْ يُولَدْ. وَلَمْ يَكُنْ
لَهُ كُفُوًا أَحَدٌ —

Sūra 113

سُورَةُ ٱلْفَلَقِ

قُلْ أَعُوذُ بِرَبِّ ٱلْفَلَقِ. مِنْ شَرِّ مَا خَلَقَ. وَمِنْ شَرِّ غَاسِقٍ إِذَا
وَقَبَ. وَمِنْ شَرِّ ٱلنَّفَّاثَاتِ فِى ٱلْعُقَدِ. وَمِنْ شَرِّ حَاسِدٍ إِذَا حَسَدَ —

Sūra 114

سُورَةُ ٱلنَّاسِ

قُلْ أَعُوذُ بِرَبِّ ٱلنَّاسِ. مَلِكِ ٱلنَّاسِ. إِلٰهِ ٱلنَّاسِ. مِنْ شَرِّ ٱلْوَسْوَاسِ ٱلْخَنَّاسِ. ٱلَّذِى يُوَسْوِسُ فِى صُدُورِ ٱلنَّاسِ. مِنَ ٱلْجِنَّةِ وَٱلنَّاسِ —

Fables

From مجانى الأدب by لويس شَيْخو (A.D 1859 – A.D. 1927)

اَلنُّمُوسُ وَٱلدَّجَاجُ

بَلَغَ ٱلنُّمُوسَ أَنَّ ٱلدَّجَاجَ قَدْ مَرِضُوا فَلَبِسُوا جُلُودَ طَوَاوِيسَ وَأَتَوْا لِيَزُورُوهُم فقالوا لهم السَلَامُ عليكم أَيَّها الدَجاجُ كَيْفَ أَنْتُمْ وكَيْف أَحْوالُكم فقالوا إنّا بِخَيْرٍ يَوْمَ لا نَرَى وُجُوهَكم (مَغْزاهُ) أَنَّ كَثِيرًا يُظْهِرُونَ المَحَبَّةَ ويُبْطِنُونَ البَغْضاءَ

قِطَّتَانِ وَقِرْدٌ

قِطَّتانِ ٱخْتَطَفَتَا جُبْنَةً وذَهَبَتَا بها إلى القِرْدِ لكَيْ يَقْسِمَها بينهما فَقَسَمَها إلى قِسْمَيْنِ أَحَدُهما أَكْبَرُ من الثانِي ووَضَعَهما فى مِيزانِه فرَجَحَ الأَكْبَرُ فأَخَذَ منه شَيْئًا بأَسْنانِه وهو يُظْهِرُ أَنَّهُ يُرِيدُ مُساواتَهُ بالأَصْغَرِ ولكن إذْ كان ما أَخَذَهُ منه هو أَكْثَرُ من اللازِمِ رَجَحَ الأَصْغَرُ فَفَعَلَ بهذا ما فَعَلَه بذاكَ ثُمَّ فَعَلَ بذاك ما فعله بهذا وهٰكَذا حَتَّى كادَ يَذْهَبُ بالجُبْنَةِ فقالت له القِطَّتانِ نَحْنُ رَضِينا بهذه القِسْمَةِ فأَعْطنا

الجُبْنَةَ فقال إذا كُنْتُمَا أَنْتُمَا رَضِيتُمَا فإنَّ العَدْلَ لا يَرْضَى وما زالَ يَقْضَمُ القِسْمَ الراجِحَ منها كَذٰلِكَ حتَّى أَتَى عليهما جميعًا فَرَجَعَتِ القطّتانِ بِحُزْنٍ وخَيْبَةٍ وهما يقولانِ

وَمَا مِنْ يَدٍ إِلَّا يَدُ ٱللّٰهِ فَوْقَهَا وَلَا ظَالِمٌ إِلَّا سَيُبْلَى بِأَظْلَمِ

صَائِدٌ وَعُصْفُورٌ

كان صائِدٌ يَصِيدُ العَصافِيرَ فى يَوْمٍ بارِدٍ فكان يَذْبَحُها والدُّمُوعُ تَسِيلُ فقال عُصْفُورٌ لِصاحِبِهِ لا بَأْسَ عليك من الرَجُلِ أَمَا تَراه يبْكى فقال له الآخَرُ لا تَنْظُرْ دُمُوعَهُ وَٱنْظُرْ ما تَصْنَعُ يَداهُ —

أَسْوَدُ

أَسْوَدُ فى فَصْلِ الشتاءِ أَقْبَلَ يَأْخُذُ الثَلْجَ وَيَفْرُكُ به بَدَنَهُ فقيلَ له لِماذا ذلك فقال لَعَلِّى أَبْيَضُّ فقال له حَكِيمٌ يا هذا لا تُتْعِبْ نَفْسَكَ فَرُبَّمَا ٱسْوَدَّ الثَلْجُ من جِسْمِكَ وهو باقٍ على حالِهِ (مَغْزاهُ) أَنَّ الشَرِيرَ يَقْدِرُ أَنْ يُفْسِدَ الخَيْرَ وقَلِيلًا ما يُصْلِحُهُ الخَيْرُ

أَسَدٌ وَثَعْلَبٌ وَذِئْبٌ

وَهُوَ مَثَلُ مَنِ ٱتَّعَظَ بِغَيْرِهِ وَٱعْتَبَرَ بِهِ

أَسَدٌ وَثَعْلَبٌ وذِئْبٌ ٱصْطَحَبُوا فَخَرَجُوا يَتَصَيَّدُونَ فصادوا حِمارًا وأَرْنَبًا وظَبْيًا فقال الأسدُ للذئبِ ٱقْسِمْ بيننا فقال الأَمْرُ بَيِّنٌ الحمارُ للأسدِ والأَرْنَبُ للثعلبِ والظبىُ لى فخَبَطَهُ الأسدُ فأَطارَ رَأْسَهُ ثُمَّ أَقْبَلَ على الثَّعْلَبِ وقال ما كان أَجْهَلَ صاحِبَك بالغَنِيمَةِ هاتِ أَنتَ

فقال يا أَبا الحارِثِ الأَمْرُ واضِحٌ الحِمارُ لِغَدائِك والظَبْىُ لِعَشائك تَتَخَلَّلْ بِالأَرْنَبِ فيما بين ذلك فقال له الأسدُ ما أَقْضاك من عَلَّمك هذا الفِقْهَ فقال رَأْسُ الذِئْبِ الطائِرُ من جُثَّتِهِ —

ثَعلَبٌ وَضَبُعٌ

حُكِىَ أَنَّ الثَعْلَبَ ٱطَّلَعَ فى بِئْرٍ وهو عاطِشٌ وعليها رِشاءٌ فى طَرَفَيْهِ دَلْوانِ فقَعَدَ فى الدَلْوِ العُلْيا فٱنْحَدَرَتْ فشَرِبَ فجاءتِ الضَبُعُ فٱطَّلَعَتْ فى البِئْرِ فأَبْصَرَتِ القَمَرَ فى الماء مُنْتَصِفاً والثعلبُ قاعدٌ فى قَعْرِ البئرِ فقالت له ما تَصْنَعُ هُنا فقال لها إِنّى أَكَلْتُ نِصفَ هذه الجُبْنَةِ وبَقِىَ نِصْفُهَا لَكِ فٱنْزِلى فكُلِيها فقالت وكيف أَنْزِلُ قال تَقْعُدِينَ فى الدَلْوِ فقَعَدَتْ فيها فٱنْحَدَرَتْ وٱرْتَفَعَ الثعلبُ فى الدَلْوِ الأُخْرَى فلمَّا ٱلْتَقَيَا فى وَسَطِ البئرِ قالت له ما هذا قال كذا التُجَّارُ تَخْتَلِفُ فضَرَبَتْ بهما العَرَبُ المَثَلَ فى المُخْتَلِفِينَ —

حِكايَةُ ٱلْحِمارِ وَٱلثَّوْرِ مَعَ صَاحِبِ ٱلزَّرْعِ

From ألف ليلة وليلة ("The Thousand and One Nights". Authors Unknown)

قال انه كان لبعض التجار أَموال ومواشٍ وكان له زوجة وأولاد وكان الله تعالى أَعطاه معرفة أَلسن الحيوانات والطير وكان مسكن ذلك التاجر الأرياف وكان عنده فى داره حمار وثور فأتى يومًا الثور الى مكان الحمار فوجده مكنوسًا مرشوشًا وفى معلفه شعير مغربل وتبن مغربل وهو راقد مستريح وفى بعض الأوقات يركبه صاحبه

لحاجة تعرض له ويرجع على حاله فلمّا كان فى بعض الأيام سمع التاجر الثور وهو يقول للحمار هَنيئًا لك ذلك أنا تعبان وأنت مستريح تأكل الشعير مُغربلًا ويخدمونك وفى بعضِ الأوقات يركبك صاحبك ويرجع وأنا دائما للحرث والطحن فقال له الحمار إذا خرجت إلى الغيط ووضعوا على رقبتك الناف فارقد ولا تقم ولو ضربوك فإن قمت فارقد ثانيًا فإذا رجعوا بك ووضعوا لك الفول فلا تأكله كأنّك ضعيف وامتنع من الأكل والشرب يومًا أو يومين أو ثلاثة فإنّك تستريح من التعب والجهد وكان التاجر يسمع كلامهما فلمّا جاء السوّاق إلى الثور يعلفه أكل منه شيئًا يسيرًا فأصبح السوّاق يأخذ الثور إلى الحرث فوجده ضعيفا فقال له التاجر خذ الحمار وأَحرثه مكانه اليوم كله فرجع الرجل وأخذ الحمار مكان الثور وأَحرثه مكانه اليوم كله فلمّا رجع آخر النهار شكره الثور على تفضّلاته حيث أراحه من التعب فى ذلك اليوم فلم يرد عليه الحمار جوابًا وندم أشدّ الندامة فلمّا كان ثانى يوم جاء الزرّاع وأخذ الحمار وأَحرثه إلى آخر النهار فلم يرجع الحمار إلّا مسلوخ الرقبة شديد الضعف فتأمّله الثور وشكره ومجّده فقال له الحمار كنت مقيمًا مستريحًا فما ضرّنى إلّا فضولى ثم قال اعلم أنّى لك ناصح وقد سمعت صاحبنا يقول إن لم يقم الثور من موضعه فأعطوه للجزّار ليذبحه ويعمل جلده نطعًا وأنا خائف عليك ونصحتك والسلام فلمّا سمع الثور كلام الحمار شكره وقال غد اسرح معهم ثم إن الثور أكل علفه بتمامه حتى لحس المذود بلسانه كل ذلك

وصاحبهما يسمع كلامهما فلمّا طلع النهار خرج التاجر وزوجته إلى دار البقر وجلسا لجاء السوّاق وأخذ الثور وخرج فلما رأى الثور صاحبه حرّك ذنبه وضرط وبرطع فضحك التاجر حتّى استلقى على قفاه فقالت له زوجته من أىّ شىء تضحك فقال لها شىء رأيته وسمعته ولا أقدر أن ابوح به فأموت فقالت له لا بدّ أن تخبرنى بذلك وما سبب ضحكك ولو كنت تموت فقال لها ما أقدر أن أبوح به خوفًا من الموت فقالت له أنت لم تضحك إلّا علىّ ثم إنّها لم تزل تلحّ عليه وتلج فى الكلام إلى أن غلبت عليه وتحيّر فأحضر أولاده وأرسل أحضر القاضى والشهود وأراد أن يوصى ثم يبوح لها بالسرّ ويموت لأنّه كان يحبّها محبّة عظيمة لأنّها بنت عمّه وأمّ أولاده وكان قد عمر من العمر مائة وعشرين سنة ثم إنّه ارسل أحضر جميع أهلها وأهل حارته وقال لهم حكايته وأنّه متى قال لأحد على سرّه مات فقال لها جميع الناس ممّن حضرها بالله عليك اتركى هذا الأمر لئلا يموت زوجك أبو أولادك فقالت لهم لا أرجع عنه حتى يقول لى ولو يموت فسكتوا عنها ثم إنّ التاجر قام من عندهم وتوجه إلى دار الدواب ليتوضّأ ثم يرجع يقول لهم ويموت وكان عنده ديك تحته خمسون دجاجة وكان عنده كلب فسمع التاجر الكلب وهو ينادى الديك ويسمّيه ويقول له أنت فرحان وصاحبنا رائح يموت فقال الديك للكلب وكيف ذلك الأمر فأعاد الكلب عليه القصة فقال له الديك والله إن صاحبنا قليل العقل أنا لى خمسون زوجة أرضى هذه واغضب هذه وهو ما له الّا زوجة واحدة

ولا يعرف صلاح أمره معها فما له لا يأخذ لها بعضًا من عيدان
التوت ثم يدخل إلى حجرتها ويضربها حتّى تموت أو تتوب ولا تعود
تسأله عن شيء قال فلمّا سمع التاجر كلام الديك وهو يخاطب
الكلب رجع إلى عقله وعزم على ضربها ودخل عليها الحجرة بعد أن
قطع لها عيدان التوت وخبأها داخل الحجرة وقال لها تعالى[1] داخل
الحجرة حتّى أقول لك ولا ينظرنى أحد ثم أموت فدخلت معه ثم إنّه
قفل باب الحجرة عليهما ونزل عليها بالضرب إلى أن أُغمى عليها
فقالت له تبت ثم إنّها قَبَّلَتْ يديه ورجليه وتابت وخرجت هى واياه
وفرح الجماعة وأهلها وقعدوا فى أسرّ الأحوال إلى الممات.

From the Prolegomena (المُقَدِّمَة) of ابن خَلْدُون
(A.D. 1332 – A.D. 1406)

فى وجوه المعاش وأصنافه ومذاهبه

اِعْلَمْ أنّ المعاش هو عبارةٌ عن ابتغاء الرزق والسعى فى تحصيله وهو
مفعل من العيش كأنه لما كان العيش الذى هو الحياة لا يحصل
الا بهذه جعلت موضوعًا له على طريق المبالغة ثم ان تحصيل الرزق
وكسبهُ إما أن يكون بأخذه من يد الغير وانتزاعه بالاقتدار عليه
على قانون متعارف ويسمّى مغرمًا وجباية وإما ان يكون من الحيوان
الوحشى بافتراسه وأخذه برميه من البر أو البحر ويسمّى اصطيادًا
وإما أن يكون من الحيوان الداجن باستخراج فضوله المنصرفة بين
الناس فى منافعهم كاللبن من الانعام والحرير من دوده والعسل من
نحله أو يكون من النبات فى الزرع والشجر بالقيام عليه واعداده

[1] Come!

لاستخراج ثمرته ويسمّى هذا كله فلحًا واما ان يكون الكسب من الاعمال الانسانية إما فى مواد معينة وتسمى الصنائع من كِتابة ونجارة وخياطة وحياكة وفروسية وامثال ذلك أو فى مواد غير معينة وهى جميع الامتهانات والتصُّرفات واما ان يكون الكسب من البضائع واعدادها للاعواض اما بالتقلُّب بها فى البلاد واحتكارها وارتقاب حوالة الاسواق فيها ويسمى هذا تجارة فهذه وجوه المعاش وأصنافه وهى معنى ما ذكره المحقِّقون من اهل الأدب والحكمة كالحريرى وغيره فانهم قالوا المعاش امارة وتجارة وفلاحة وصناعة فأما الامارة فليست بمذهب طبيعى للمعاش فلا حاجة بنا الى ذكرها وقد تقدم شىء من احوال الجبايات السلطانية فى الفصل الثانى وأما الفلاحة و الصناعة والتجارة فهى وجوه طبيعية للمعاش أما الفلاحة فهى متقدمة عليها كلها بالذات إذ هى بسيطة وطبيعية فطرية لا تحتاج الى نظر ولا علم ولهذا تنسب فى الخليقة الى آدم ابى البشر وانه معلّمها والقائم عليها اشارةً الى أنها أقدمُ وجوه المعاش وأنسبُها الى الطبيعة وأما الصنائع فهى ثانيتها ومتأخرة عنها لأنها مركّبة وعلمية تصرف فيها الأفكار والأنظار ولهذا لا يوجد غالباً الا فى أهل الحضر الذى هو متأخر عن البدو وثانٍ عنه ومن هذا المعنى نسبت الى إدريس الأب الثانى للخليقة فانه مستنبطها لِمَن بعده من البشر بالوحى من اللّه تعالى واما التجارة وإن كانت طبيعية فى الكسب فالأكثر من طرقها ومذاهبها انما هى تحيُّلات فى الحصول على ما بين القيمتين فى الشراء والبيع لتحصل فائدة الكسب من تلك الفضلة ولذلك اباح الشرع فيه المكاسبة لما انه من باب المقامرة إلّا انه ليس أخذًا لمال الغير مجانًا فلهذا اختص بالمشروعية.

From the Cosmography of القَزْوِينى **(A.D. 1203–A.D. 1283)**

البصرة

البصرة هى المدينة المشهورة التى بناها المسلمون. قال الشعبى مصرت البصرة قبل الكوفة بسنة ونصف، وهى مدينة على قرب البحر، كثيرة النخيل والأشجار سَبِخة التربة، ملحة الماء لأن المدّ يأتى من البحر يمشى الى ما فوق البصرة بثلثة أيام. وماءُ دِجلة والفُرات اذا انتهى الى البصرة خالطه ماءُ البحر يصير ملحا، وامّا نخيلها فكثير جدًّا. قال الأصمعى*: سمعت الرشيد يقول: نظرنا فاذا كلّ ذهب وفضّة على وجه الأرض لا يبلغ ثمن نخل البصرة. ومن عجائبها أمور ثلاثة، احدها انّ دجلة والفرات يجتمعان قربَ البصرة ويصيران نهرًا عظيماً يجرى من ناحية الشمال الى الجنوب، فهذا يسمّونه جزرًا، ثم يرجع من الجنوب الى الشمال ويسمّونه مدًّا. يفعل ذلك فى كل يوم وليلة مرّتين، فاذا جزر، نقص نقصا كثيرا بحيث لو قِيس لكان الذى ذهب مقدار ما بقى أو اكثر، وينتهى كل اول شهر فى الزيادة الى غايته، ويسقى المواضع العالية والأراضى القاصية. ثم يشرع فى الانتقاص، فهذا كل يوم وليلة انقص من الذى كان قبله الى آخر الاسبوع الاول من الشهر. ثم يشرع فى الزيادة فهذا كل يوم وليلة اكثر من الذى قبله الى نصف الشهر. ثم يأخذ فى النقص الى آخر الاسبوع، ثم فى الزيادة الى آخر الشهر، وهكذا أبدًا لاينحلّ هذا القانون ولا يتغير. وثانيها انك لو التمست ذبابة على رطبها على النخل او فى جواخينها او معاصرها ما وجدت الّا

* famous Arab philologist, eighth century A.D.

فى الفرط ولو ان معصرة دون الفيض او تمرة منبوذة دون المسناة لما استبنتها من كثرة الذبّان وذكروا ان ذلك لطلسم. وثالثها ان الغربان القواطع فى الخريف تسوّد جميع نخل البصرة واشجارها حتى لا يرى غصن الّا وعليه منها ولم يوجد فى جميع الدهر غراب ساقط على نخلة غير مصرومة ولو بقى عليها عذق واحد، ومناقير الغربان كالمعاول، والتمر فى ذلك الوقت على الأعذاق غير متماسك، فلو لا لطف الله تعالى لتساقطت كلها بنقر الغربان، ثم تنتظر صرامها فاذا تمّ الصرام رأيتَها تخلّلت اصول الكرب فلا تدع حشفة الّا استخرجتها، فسبحان من قدر ذلك لطفاً بعباده.

From إرشاد الأرِيب الى معرفة الأديب (Dictionary of Learned Men) of ياقوت (A.D. 1179 – A.D. 1229)

إسحاق بن ابراهيم المَوْصِلى[1]

كنيته أبو محمد وكان الرشيد إذا أراد ان يولع به كناه أبا صُفيان، وموضوعه من العلم ومكانه من الأدب والشعر لو أردنا استيعابه طال الكتاب، وخرجنا من غرضنا من الاختصار ومن وقف على الأخبار وتتبع الآثار علم موضعه واما الغناء فكان اصغر علومه وادنى ما يوصف به، وان كان الغالب عليه لأنه كان له فى سائر علومه نظراء، ولم يكن له فى هذا نظير لحق فيه من مضى وسبق من بقى فهو إمام هذه الصناعة على أنه اكره الناس للغناء والتسمّى به ويقول: وددت انّى أُضْرب كلما أراد منى من يندبنى ان اغنّى وكلما قال قائل اسحاق الموصلى المغنّى عشر مقارع (لا أطيق اكثر من هذا) وأُعفَى من الغناء والنسبة اليه. وكان المأمون[2] يقول: لولا ما سبق

[1] Celebrated musician at the court of Hārūn ar-Rashīd.
[2] Son of Hārūn.

لإسحاق على السنة الناس وشهر به من الغناء عندهم ، لولّيته القضاء بحضرتى ، فانه أولى به واحقّ واعفّ واصدق تديّناً وامانةً من هؤلاء القضاة. قال : بقيت زمانًا من دهرى اغلّس الى هُشَيْم،[1] فاسمع منه الحديث ، ثم اصير الى الكسائى[1] فأقرأ عليه جزءًا من القرآن ، وآتى الفرّاء[1] فأقرأ عليه جزءًا ، ثم آتى منصور زلزل[2] فيضاربنى طريقين أو ثلاثة ، ثم عاتكة[1] بنت شهدة ، فآخذ منها صوتًا أو صوتين ، ثم آتى الأصمعى فأناشده ، وآتى أبا عُبَيدة[1] فأذاكره ، ثم الى أبى فاعلمه ما صنعت ومن لقيت وما اخذت ، واتغدى معه ، واذا كان العشاء رُحْت الى الرشيد. وقال الأصمعى : خرجت مع الرشيد فلقيت اسحاق الموصلى بها فقلت له : هل حملتَ شيئًا من كتابك؟ فقال : حملتُ ما خفّ. فقلت : كم مقداره؟ فقال : ثمانية عشر صندوقاً. فعجبتُ ، وقلت : اذا كان ما خفّ فكم يكون ما ثقل؟ فقال : اضعاف ذلك.

From كتاب البخلاء of الجاحظ (d. *circa* A.D. 872)

كذب بكذب

ومثل هذا الحديث ما حدّثنى به محمد بن يَسير عن والٍ كان بفارِس ، إما ان يكون خالداً[3] أخا مَهْرَوَيْه[3]، أو غيره. قال : بينا[4] هو يومًا فى مجلس ، وهو مشغول بحسابه وأمره ، وقد احتجب جهده[5] ،

[1] A contemporary of al-Mauṣilī.
[2] al-Mauṣilī's uncle.
[3] Name of person.
[4] = بينَمَا.
[5] إِحْتَجَبَ جُهْدَه, he concealed himself (from people) as much as he could.

اذ نجم شاعر من بين يديه، فأنشده شعرا مدحه فيه وقرّظه ومجّده. فلما فرغ قال: قد احسنت. ثم اقبل على كاتبه، فقال: أعطه عشرة آلاف درهم. ففرح الشاعر فرحا قد يستطار له.[1] فلمّا رأى حاله قال: وإنى لأرى هذا القول قد وقع منك هذا الموقع![2] اجعلها عشرين الف درهم. وكاد الشاعر يخرج من جلده. فلما رأى فرحه قد تضاعف، قال: وإنّ فرحك ليتضاعف على قدر تضاعُف القول! أعطه يا فلان اربعين الفاً. فكاد الفرح يقتله. فلما رجعتْ اليه نفسه، قال له: انت، جُعِلتُ فداك، رجل كريم: وأنا اعلم انك كلما رأيتَنى قد ازددت فرحا، زدتَنى فى الجائزة. وقبول هذا منك لا يكون الّا من قلّة الشكرِ له. ثم دعا له وخرج.

قال:[3] فأقبل عليه كاتبه، فقال: سبحانَ اللّٰه! هذا كان يرضى منك باربعين درهما، تأمر له باربعين الف درهم! قال: ويلك! وتريد ان تعطيه شيئًا؟ قال: ومن انفاذ امرك بدّ؟ قال: يا احمق، انما هذا رجل سرّنا بكلام، وسررناه بكلام! هو حين زعم أنى احسن من القمر واشدّ من الاسد، وأن لسانى اقطع من السيف، وأن امرى انفذُ من السِنان، جعل فى يدى من هذا شَيْئًا ارجع به الى شيءٍ؟ ألسنا نعلم انه قد كذب؟ ولكنه قد سرّنا حين كذب لنا.[4] فنحن ايضا نسرّه بالقول، ونأمر له بالجوائز، وإن كان كذبًا: فيكون كذبٌ بكذب، وقولٌ بقول. فأمّا أن يكون كذب بصدق، وقول بفعل، فهذا هو الخُسرانُ الذى ما سمعتُ به!

---

[1] قَدْ يُسْتَطَارُ لَهُ could have taken flight on account of it.

[2] This speech has moved you!

[3] I.e. the narrator.

[4] For us, for our sake.

From تُحفة النُظّار فى غرائب الامصار وعجائب الاسفار (Book of Travels) of ابن بطّوطة (A.D. 1304 – A.D. 1377)

I

ولما كان عند الظهر، سمعنا كلامًا عند الحوض، فظنوا انهم اصحابهم. فأشاروا إلىّ بالنزول معهم فنزلنا ووجدْنا قومًا آخرين فاشاروا عليهم ان يذهبوا فى صحبتهم فأبوا. وجلس ثلاثتهم أمامى، وأنا مواجه لهم. ووضعوا حبل قنّب كان معهم بالارض. وأنا انظر اليهم واقول فى نفسى : بهذا الحبل يربطوننى عند القتل. واقمت كذلك ساعة. ثم جاء ثلاثة من اصحابهم الذين أخذونى، فتكلموا معهم، وفهمت انهم قالوا لهم : لأى شىء ما قتلتموه؟ فاشار الشيخ الى الأسود كأنه اعتذر بمرضه. وكان احد هؤلاء الثلاثة شابًا حسن الوجه فقال لى : أتُريد ان اسرّحك؟ فقلت : نعم. فقال : اذهب ! فأخذت الجبّة التى كانت علىّ فاعطيته اياها، واعطانى مُنَيَّرة[1] بالية عنده. وأرانى الطريق فذهبت. وخفت ان يبدو لهم فيدركونى، فدخلت غيضة قصب واختفيت فيها الى أن غابت الشمس ثم خرجت وسلكت الطريق التى أرانيها[2] الشاب فأفضَتْ بى الى ماء فشربت منه. وسرت الى ثلث الليل فوصلت الى جبل فنمت تحته. فلما أصبحت سلكت الطريق فوصلت ضحًى الى جبل من الصخر عالٍ، فيه شجر أُمّ غِيلانَ والسِدْر. فكنت اجنى النَبْق فآكله حتى أثر الشوك فى ذراعى آثارًا هى باقية به حتى الآن.

II

فاذا تلك الطريق تفضى الى قرى الكفّار. فأتبعتُ طريقا أخرى فأفضت بى الى قرية خربة، ورأيت بها أسودَيْن عريانين فخفتهما،

---

[1] A blue cloak.

[2] = ارانى إياها

واقمت تحت اشجار هنالك. فلما كان الليل دخلت القرية ووجدت داراً، في بيت من بيوتها شبه خابية كبيرة يصنعونها لاختزان الزرع، وفي اسفلها نقب يسع الرجل. فدخلتها ووجدت داخلها مفروشاً بالتبن، وفيه حجر جعلت رأسي عليه ونمت. وكان فوقها طائر يرفرف بجناحيه اكثر الليل، واظنه كان يخاف، فاجتمعنا خائفين. واقمت على تلك الحال سبعة أيام، من يوم أُسرت وهو يوم السبت.

From فتح الأندلس **by** جرجي زيدان **(A.D. 1861 – A.D. 1914)**

الأَنْدَلُس والقُوط[1] وطُلَيْطُلَة[2]

الأندلس إحدى مقاطعات اسبانيا واسمها في الأصل وندلوسيا نسبةً الى الوندال[3] أو الفندال وكانوا قد استوطنوها بعد الرومان فلما فتحها العرب سموها الاندلس ثم اطلقوا هذا الاسم على اسبانيا كلها.

وكانت اسبانيا في جملة مملكة الرومان الغربية الى القرن الخامس للميلاد فسطا عليها القوط وهم من القبائل الجرمانية[4] الذين رحلوا من أعالي الهند الى أوربا طلباً للمرعى والمعاش وأقاموا في بوادي اوربا كما أقام العرب في بوادي الشام والعراق. ثم سطا القوط على مملكة الرومان الغربية قبل سطو العرب على المملكة الشرقية ببضعة القرون وأنشأوا الممالك في فرنسا والمانيا وانكلترا وغيرها وهي الدول الباقية في اوربا الى الآن.

وكان في جملة تلك القبائل قبيلة القوط الغربيين « ڤيسيقوط »[5] سطوا على اسبانيا في القرن الخامس واستخرجوها من الرومانيين

---

[1] The Goths. [2] Toledo.
[3] The Vandals.
[4] Germanic.
[5] Visigoths.

وأنشأوا فيها دولة قوطية انتهت بالفتح الاسلامى سنة ٩٢هـ (٧١١م) على يد طارق بن زياد القائد البربرى الشهير.

و كانت عاصمة مملكة القوط فى اسبانيا عامئذ مدينة طليطلة على ضفاف نهر التاج[1] فى أواسط اسبانيا. وكانت طليطلة فى ذلك العهد مدينة عامرة فيها الحصون والقلاع والقصور والكنائس والديور. وكانت مركز الدين والسياسة وفيها يجتمع مجمع الاساقفة كل عام ينظر فى الامور العامة.

وكان ملك الاسبان عام الفتح الملك رودريك[2] والعرب يسمونه « لذريق » وهو قوطى الأصل تولى الملك سنة ٧٠٩ م ولم يكن من العائلة المالكة ولكنه اختلس الملك اختلاساً وترك أبناء الملك السابق ناقمين عليه. وكانت اسبانيا تنقسم يومئذ الى ولايات أو دوقيات[3] يتولى كل دوقية منها حاكم يُسمَّى الدوق أو الكونت ويرجعون فى أحكامهم جميعًا الى الملك المقيم فى طليطلة.

وطليطلة واقعة على أكمة مؤلفة من أكمات يحيط بها نهر التاج من كل جهاتها إلا الشمال بما يشبه حدوة الفرس تمامًا. ووراء النهر من الشرق والغرب والجنوب جبال متسلسلة تحجب الأفق عن أهل المدينة وفيها مغارس الزيتون وكروم العنب وغابات السنديان والصنوبر. وفى منتصف المدينة الكنيسة الكبرى التى جعلها المسلمون بعد الفتح جامعاً وهى من الفخامة والمناعة على جانب عظيم.[4] وكان الناظر إذا ألقى نظره على أبنية طليطلة من شاهق تبين فيها من ضروب الأبنية مزيجاً من الطرز الرومانية والطرز القوطية وحول

---

[1] River Tagus.
[2] Roderic.
[3] Dukedoms.
[4] To a great extent.

المدينة من الشمال ووراء النهر من الجهات الأخرى مغارس الفاكهة والأثمار وسائر أصناف الأشجار إذا أطل الواقف من إحدى نوافذ منازلها أشرف عليها كلها.

From الأيام **(Autobiography) by** طه حسين **(A.D. 1891 –)**

I

لقد رأيتك (يا بنتى) ذات يوم جالسة على حِجْر ابيك وهو يقصّ عليك قصة اديپ ملكا[1] وقد خرج من قصْره بعد أن فَقَأَ عينيه لا يدرى كيف يسير. واقبلت ابنته أنتيجون[2] فقادتْه وأرشدته. رأيتك ذلك اليوم تسمعين هذه القصة مبتهجة من أولها ثم أخذ لونك يتغير قليلاً قليلاً واخذتْ جبهتك السمْحة تربدّ شيئًا فشيئا وما هى إلّا ان اجهشتِ بالبكاء، وانكببْت على ابيك لثْمًا وتقبيلا. واقبلت أمك فانتزعتْك من بين ذراعيه، وما زالت بك حتى هدأ روعُك. وفهمتْ امك وفهم ابوك وفهمتُ أنا ايضاً انك إنما بكيت لانك رأيت اديپ الملك كأبيك مكفوفاً لا يبصر ولا يستطيع أن يهتدى وحْدَه. فبكيت لابيك كما بكيت لاديپ.

II

والنساء فى قرى مصر لا يحببن الصمت ولا يملن اليه، فاذا خلت إحداهن الى نفسها ولم تجد من تتحدث اليه، تحدثت الى نفسها ألوانًا من الحديث، فغنّت إن كانت فرحة، وعددت إن كانت محزونة، وكل امرأة فى مصر محزونة حين تريد، وأحبّ شىء الى نساء القرى إذا خلون الى انفسهن أن يذكرن آلامهن وموتاهن فيعددن،

[1] Oedipus Rex.
[2] Antigone.

وكثيرًا ما ينتهى هذا التعديد الى البكاء حقاً. وكان صاحبنا أسعد الناس بالاستماع الى أخواته وهن يتغنين والى امه وهى تعدد.

وكان غناء أخواته يغيظه ولا يترك فى نفسه أثراً، لانه كان يجده سخيفا لا يدل على شيء، بينما كان تعديد أمه يهزه هزاً عنيفاً وكثيراً ما كان يبكيه. وعلى هذا النحو حفظ صاحبنا كثيراً من الأغانى وكثيراً من التعديد وكثيرا من جد القصص وهزلها.

From يوميات نائب فى الأرياف **by** توفيق الحكيم **(A.D. 1898 –)**

أبصرتُ سائق السيارة مختفياً خلف جِذْع السَنْط شاحب الوجه، بارز العينين، يشاهد هذا المنظر ولا يملك نفسه:

– لا حَوْلَ ولا قوةَ الّا بالله! إنّا لله وانّا إليه راجعون! ولمحه الطبيب فانتهره وأمره بالابتعاد. وصحتُ أنا كذلك فى السائق صيحة انصرف بعدها الى سيارة وقبع فيها. ما الذى روّعه؟ أهو منظر العظام فى ذاتها، أم فكرة الموت الممثَّلة فيها، ام المصير الآدمى وقد رآه أمامه رأىَ العين؟ ولماذا لم يَعُدْ منظر الجثث أو العظام يؤثّر فى مثلى وفى مثل الطبيب، وحتى فى مثل اللحّاد والحرّاس هذا التأثير؟ يخيَّل إلىَّ ان هذه الجثث والعظام قد فقدتْ لدينا ما فيها من رموز. فهى لا تعدو فى نظرنا قِطع الأخشاب وعيدان الحطب وقوالب الطين والآجر. إنها اشياء تتداولها أيدينا فى عملنا اليومى. لقد انفصل عنها ذلك «الرمز» الذى هو كل قوتنا. نعم، وما يبقى من كل تلك الأشياء العظيمة المقدَّسة التى لها فى حياتنا البشرية كل الخطر لو نزعنا عنها ذلك «الرمز» أيبقى منها أمام أبصارنا اللاهية، غير المكترِثة، غير جسم مادى: حجر أو عَظْم، لا يساوى شيئًا ولا يعنى

شيئا. ما مصير البشرية وما قيمتها لو ذهب عنها « الرمز »؟ هو فى ذاته كائن لا وجود له. هو لا شئ، وهو مع ذلك كل شئ فى حياتنا الآدمية. هذا « اللاشيء » الذى نشيّد عليه حياتنا هو كل ما نملك من سموّ نختال به ونمتاز على غيرنا من المخلوقات. هنا كل الفرق بين الحيوانات العليا والحيوانات الدنيا.

قطع الطبيب سلسلة تفكيرى بمقصّ طبّى فى يده ذات القُفّاز الجلدى الشفّاف يفحص به العظام...

From the novel سَارَةُ[1] by عباس محمود العقّاد (A.D. 1889 – A.D. 1964)

اللقاء

ألفى همّام نفسه، وهو عائد الى منزله، على مقربة من مسكن صاحبه الأستاذ زاهر، وهو رجل ظريف طيب النحيزة. وكان يومئذ يسكن فى بيت من بيوت الحجرات المفروشة تُديره خائطة فرنسية كان اسمها ماريانا... فدلف هام الى المنزل يزور صاحبه ويقضى معه فترة يقفزان فيها بين معارض الحديث التى لا وصلة بينها، ويضحكان ضحكاً كثيرا، إن لم تكن فيه فكاهة عالية ففيه ولا شك تمرين نافع للرئتين.

ووجد ماريانا فى فناء الدار تُطعم الديكة الرومية التى لها صفحة من المكرونة البائتة، وعندها فتاة مليحة يصعب تقدير سنها، لأنها تصلح[2] للعشرين كما تصلح للخامسة والعشرين، وتُسمّى[3] آنسة كما تسمى سيدة، وهى مشغولة بكساء تقلّبه وتُمعن النظر فيه.

---

[1] Sarah.
[2] might be; *lit.* suitable for.
[3] might well be called.

قال همام : أسعد الله الصباح ، اين زاهر يا مدام؟[1] فردت التحية بمثلها ، وقالت : أوَلا نراك إلا زائراً لزاهر؟ إنه خرج منذ هنيهة على أن يعود بعد قليل.

والتفت همام الى صفحة المكرونة قائلاً : أرى ان الديكة اليوم ايطالية وليست رومية ! فلم تجب ماريانا بغير ابتسامة عريضة ، وانما اجابت الفتاة قائلة : إن كان الجنس بالطعام فالديكة هنا عالمية لا تدين[2] بجنس من الاجناس : مصرية إن اكلت الفول المُدَمَّس[3] ، وانجليزية ان اكلت البطاطس ، وهندية إن صبرت على الصيام الطويل.

فنظرت اليها ماريانا نظرة العتب المصطنع ، واستظرف همام جوابها واستغرب مشاركتها فى الحديث فى وقت واحد[4] ، ورحب مع ذلك بهذه المشاركة التى احسّ لتَوّها[5] انها وافقت هواه ، وانه كان يسوق الحديث اليها إن أبطأ المساق[6]. قال همام : إن الآنسة تعرف كل شيء عن ديكة البيت وتذبْذُبها فى الوطنية ، ولكنى لا اذكر انى رأيتك هنا يا آنسة قبل الآن.

ماذا يقول؟ أيقول لا أذكر انى رأيتك؟ أكان من الجائز إذن ان يراها ويهملها وينسى انه رآها؟

أحس همام أيضاً ان الكلمة لم توافق هواها ، وسمعها تجيب بشيء من الامتعاض المكتوم كأنها تخاطب نفسها : ولماذا تدعونى يا آنسة ! أتستصغرنى؟ انى ربة بيت ، وأم !

---

[1] Madame.

[2] دان ب belong to. [3] boiled (Egypt).

[4] at the same time.

[5] at once (تَوّ).

[6] a *v.n.* of سَاقَ.

From تونس تأريخ خلاصة **by** حسن حُسْنى عبد الوهّاب الصُمادحى
(A.D. 1883 –)

افتكّ النصارى غَرْناطَة[1] سنه ٨٩٧ هجرية من ملوكها بنى الأحمر[2] على يد فَرْدِند الكاثوليكى[3] صاحب قشتالة[4]. فهاجر عندئذ خَلْق عظيم من مسلمى الأندلس الى المغرب والمشرق. وبقى كثير من ضعفاءهم بمواطنهم مُسهانين فى اعتقادهم مضطهدين فى حقوقهم الى اوائل القرن الحادى عشر للهجرة إذ تكالب عليهم الاسْبان بتوحّش وأخرجوهم من ديارهم جميعاً بعد ان ساموهم سوء العذاب وشرّدوهم كلّ مُشرَّدٍ. فنزل بعضهم بعد مشاقّ لا تُحصى بالمغرب الاقصى لقربه من بلادهم وقصد آخرون القطر التونسى لِما كان يبلغهم عن كرم اهله وخِصْب تُرْبته. فوفدوا ملتجئين برقابهم ودينهم الى هذه الديار سنة ١٠١٦ وما بعدها وكان اول وُرودهم على عهد عثمان داى[5]. فآستبشر بقدوم هؤلاء المنكوبين وأنس غربتهم[6] وحثّ أهل الحاضرة على إكرامهم حتى أنساهم فَقْدَ وطنهم.

ثم إن هذا الداى أقطع مهاجرى الأندلس ما اختاروا من الاراضى ووزّع على محتاجيهم الاموال والنفقات فآنتشروا فى اكناف البلاد يشيّدون القُرى ويُنشئون المزارع والبساتين حتى استأنف القُطرُ عُمرانَه المفقود وثروته الغابرة. فمِن التى أسّسوها: سُلَيْمَان[7] وقُرُنْبَالِيَة والجُدَيْدَة وزَغْوَان وطِبُرْبة ومجَاز الباب وتَسْتُور وقلعة الاندلس وغيرها.

---

[1] Granada. [2] بنو الأحمر last Muslim dynasty which ruled Granada A.D. 1239 to A.D. 1492.
[3] Ferdinand the Catholic. [4] Castile.
[5] ʿUthmān (Otman) Dey, Governor of Tunis, A.D. 1595 to A.D. 1610.
[6] Softened their exile.
[7] *et seq.* names of towns.

وعلاوةً على ذلك فقد استوطن منهم جانبٌ وافرٌ[1] حاضرةَ تونس واتخذوا بها حاراتٍ عُرفتْ بهم واسواقاً للصناعات التى جلبوها معهم كصناعة الشاشية[2] ونسْج الحرير ونقْش الرخام والجبْس والزلّيج. وقد نقل اهل البلاد عنهم اصول تلك الحِرَف حتى اتقنوها. وبالجملة فقد حصل للقطر من هجرة الأندلسيين اليه ثروة واسعة وعمران دافق.

From الغربال by ميخائيل نُعَيْمَة (A.D. 1894 –)

الرواية التمثيلية ومسألة اللغات

اكبر عقبة صادفتها فى تأليف « الآباء والبنين »[3] هى اللغة العامية والمقام الذى يجب ان تُعطاه فى مثل هذه الروايات. فى عُرْفى — واظن الكثيرين يوافقونى على ذلك — ان اشخاص الرواية يجب ان يخاطبونا باللغة التى تعوّدوا ان يعبّروا بها عن عواطفهم وافكارهم، وإن الكاتب الذى يحاول ان يجعل فلاحاً اميا يتكلم بلغة الدواوين الشعرية والمؤلفات اللغوية يظلم فلاحه ونفسه وقارئه وسامعه، لا بل يظهر اشخاصه فى مظهر الهزل حيث لا يقصد الهزل ويقترف جرماً ضد فن جماله فى تصوير الانسان حسبما نراه فى مشاهد الحياة الحقيقية.

هناك أمر آخر جدير بالاهتمام متعلق باللغة العامية — وهو أن هذه اللغة تستر تحت ثوبها الخشن كثيراً من فلسفة الشعب واختباراته فى الحياة وامثاله واعتقاداته التى لو حاولتَ ان تؤديها بلغة فصيحة

[1] جانب وافر a sufficient number.

[2] Sheshiya; red felt cap (similar to the tarbush) worn in North Africa.

[3] الآباء والبنون, a previous work of the author.

لكننَ كمن يترجم اشعاراً وامثالاً عن لغة اعجمية. وربما خالفنا فى ذلك بعض الذين تأبطوا القواميس وتسلّحوا بكتب الصرف والنحو كلها قائلين إن «كل الصيد فى جوف الفرإ» وأن لا بلاغة أو فصاحة أو طلاوة فى اللغة العامية لا تستطيع أن تأتى بمثلها بلغة فصحى. فلهؤلاء ننصح أن يدرسوا حياة الشعب ولغته بامعان وتدقيق.

الرواية التمثيلية، من بين كل الأساليب الأدبية، لا تستطيع ان يستغنى عن اللغة العامية. انما العقدة هى أننا لو اتبعنا هذه القاعدة لوجب أن نكتب كل رواياتنا باللغة العامية، إذ ليس بيننا من يتكلم عربية الجاهلية أو العصور الاسلامية الأولى، وذاك يعنى انقراض لغتنا الفصحى. ونحن بعيدون عن أن نبتغى هذه الملمة القومية فأين المخرج؟

عبثاً بحثت عن حل لهذا المشكل فهو اكبر من ان يحله عقل واحد. وجُلّ ما توصلت اليه بعد التفكير هو أن أجعل المتعلمين من اشخاص روايتى يتكلمون لغة معربة، والاميين اللغة العامية. لكنى اعترف باخلاص أن هذا الأسلوب لا يحل العقدة الأساسية. فالمسألة لا تزال بحاجة الى اعتناء اكبر رجال اللغة وكُتّابها.

From دمعة وابتسامة **by** جبْران خليل جبران

صوت الشاعر **(A.D. 1883 – A.D. 1931)**

احنُّ الى بلادي لجمالها واحب سكان بلادى لتعاستهم، ولكن اذا ما هبَّ قومي مدفوعين بما يدعونهُ وطنية وزحفوا عَلَى وطن قريبي وسلبوا امواله وقتلوا رجاله ويتموا اطفاله ورملوا نساءه وسقوا

ارضه دماء بنيه واشبعوا ضواريه لحوم فتيانه كرهت اذ ذاك بلادي وسكان بلادي.

اتشببُ بذكر مسقط رأسي واشتاق الى بيت ربيت فيهِ، ولكن اذا مرّ عابر طريق وطلب مأوى في ذلك البيت وقوتاً من سكانه ومُنع مطروداً استبدلت تشبيبي بالرثاء وشوقي بالسلو وقلت بذاتي: ان البيت الذي يضن بالخبز عَلَى محتاجه، وبالفراش على طالبه لهو احق البيوت بالهدم والخراب.

احب مسقط رأسي ببعض محبتي لبلادي. واحب بلادي بقسم من محبتي للارض وطني. واحب الارض بكليتي لانها مرتع الانسانية روح الالوهية على الارض. الانسانية المقدسة روح الالوهية على الارض. تلك الانسانية الواقفة بين الخرائب، الساترة قامتها العارية بالاطار البالية، الذارفة الدموع السخية على وجنتيها الذابلتين، المنادية ابناءَها بصوت يملأ الاثير أنةً و عويلاً وابناؤُها مشغولون عن ندائها باغاني العصبية، منصرفون عن دموعها بصقل السيوف. تلك الانسانية الجالسة وحدها تستغيث بالقوم وهم لا يسمعون، وان سمعها فرد واقترب منها ومسح دموعها و عزّاها في شدائدها قال القوم: اتركوه فالدموع لاتؤثر بغير الضعيف.

الانسانية روح الالوهية على الارض. تلك الالوهية السائرة بين الامم المتكلمة بالمحبة المشيرة الى سبل الحياة والناس يضحكون مستهزئين باقوالها وتعاليمها. تلك التي سمعها بالامس الناصري[1] فصلبوه، وسقراط[2] فسمموه، والتي سمعها اليوم القائلون بالناصري و سقراط

[1] The Nazarene.
[2] Socrates.

وجاهروا باسمها امام الناس والناس لايقدرون على قتلهم ، لكنهم يسخرون بهم قائلين : السخرية اقسى من القتل وامرّ.

ولم تقوَ اورشليم[1] عَلَى قتل الناصرى ، فهو حيٌّ الى الابد. ولا آثينا[2] على اعدام سقراط ، فهو حيٌّ الى الابد. ولن تقوى السخرية على سامعي الانسانية وتابعي اقدام الالوهية ، فسيحيون الى الابد — الى الابد.

Specimen of modern Arabic verse from الجداول of إيليا أبو ماضى (A.D. 1889 – A.D. 1957)

لستُ أدرى

جئتُ لا أعلم من أين ولكنّى أتيتُ
ولقدْ أبصرتُ قُدّامى طريقًا فمشيتُ
وسأبقى سائرًا إن شئتُ هذا أم أبيتُ
كيف جئتُ؟ كيف أبصرتُ طريقى؟ . . .
لستُ أدرى

أجديد أم قديم أنا فى هذا الوجود
هل أنا حُرٌّ طليق أم أسير فى قيود
هل أنا قائد نفسى فى حياتى ام مَقُود
أتمنّى أنّنى أدرى ولكن . . . . . .
لستُ أدرى

[1] Jerusalem.
[2] Athens.

Proverbs and Aphorisms

(حِكَمٌ وَأَمْثَالٌ)

اَلْأَمْثَالُ مَصَابِيحُ ٱلْأَقْوَالِ

اَلْعَجَلَةُ مِنَ ٱلشَّيْطَانِ وَٱلتَّأَنِّي مِنَ ٱلرَّحْمٰنِ

فِي ٱلْإِعَادَةِ إِفَادَةٌ

قَدْ يَسُوءُ ٱلصَّالِحُ

إِنَّ ٱلْكَذُوبَ قَدْ يَصْدُقُ

رِسَالَةُ ٱلسَّكْرَانِ تُقْرَأُ فِي ٱلْخَمَّارَةِ

أَرْبَعُ نِسَاءٍ وَٱلْقِرْبَةُ يَابِسَةٌ !

اَلشَّبَابُ مَطِيَّةُ ٱلْجَهْلِ

قَوْلُ ٱلْحَقِّ لَمْ يَدَعْ لِي صَدِيقًا

كُلُّ فَتَاةٍ بِأَبِيهَا مُعْجَبَةٌ

كَلِّمِ ٱلنَّاسَ عَلَى قَدْرِ عُقُولِهِمْ

كُلُّ غَرِيبٍ لِلْغَرِيبِ نَسِيبٌ

اَلْوَعْدُ سَحَابٌ وَٱلْفِعْلُ مَطَرٌ

اَلْعُذْرُ أَقْبَحُ مِنَ ٱلذَّنْبِ

اَلْأَدَبُ يُزَيِّنُ ٱلْغَنِيَّ وَيَسْتُرُ فَقْرَ ٱلْفَقِيرِ

اَلْقُبْحُ حَارِسُ ٱلْمَرْأَةِ

اَلرِّجَالُ قَوَالِبُ ٱلْأَحْوَالِ

كُلُّ شَيْءٍ عَادَةٌ حَتَّى ٱلْعِبَادَةُ

اَلشَّرُّ قَدِيمْ

غَابَ عَنَّا فَفَرِحْنَا ، جَاءَنَا أَثْقَلُ مِنْهُ

لَا تَأْمَنِ ٱلْأَمِيرَ إِذَا غَشَّكَ ٱلْوَزِيرُ

عِشْ تَرَ

كَمْ قُبَّةٍ تُزَارُ وَصَاحِبُهَا فِي ٱلنَّارِ

إِنَّ ٱلْبَطَالَةَ وَٱلْكَسَلَ أَحْلَى مَذَاقًا مِنَ ٱلْعَسَلِ

اِحْفَظْ لِسَانَكَ ، إِنْ صُنْتَهُ صَانَكَ ، إِنْ خُنْتَهُ خَانَكَ

لَوْ لَا مُرَبِّى مَا عَرَفْتُ رَبِّى.

SELECTIONS FROM THE ARABIC PRESS

From الأهرام, daily newspaper, Cairo

فوزى يطير الى اكرا[1] لتنفيذ الميثاق الافريقى

v خبراء يطيرون لتأليف الجهاز الدائم لمؤتمر القمة

** تقرر ان يطير الدكتود محمود فوزى وزير الخارجية الى اكرا لحضور اجتماع وزراء الخارجية خلال هذا الاجتماع الذى سيعقد فى منتصف الشهر القادم ، تأليف الجهاز الدائم للميثاق الافريقى ، الذى وقعه الرئيس جمال عبد الناصر فى الدار البيضاء مع اقطاب الدولة الافريقية فى يناير الماضى.

سيطير خبراء من الدول الافريقية السبع التى اشتركت فى مؤتمر الدار البيضاء فى اوائل الشهر القادم الى اكرا لعقد اجتماع تحضيرى لوزراء الخارجية للاتفاق على تفاصيل تأليف اللجان السياسية والعسكرية والاقتصادية والثقافية والسكرتيرية الدائمة للميثاق

سيمثل الجمهورية العربية فى هذا الاجتماع سبعة من الخبراء العرب فى النواحى السياسية والعسكرية والاقتصادية والثقافية.

---

[1] Accra.

برئاسة الاستاذ محمود رياض مستشار رئيس الجمهورية. سيعقد هذا الاجتماع التحضيرى فى الاسبوع الاول من الشهر القادم ثم ينقلب فى نهايته الى مؤتمر على مستوى وزراء الخارجية.

التنظيم الجديد لوزارة الادارة المحلية

ه مديرين عامين يرأسون الادارات الفنية

** تم وضع مشروع تنظيم وزارة الادارة المحلية ستتكون الوزارة من خمس ادارات، هى ادارات الشئون المالية والادارية والقانونية والعلاقات العامة والتفتيش الفنى. سيرأس هذه الادارات مدير عام او موظف من الدرجة الاولى. ستضم الوزارة اقساما فنية تختص ببحث المسائل التى يحيلها الى الوزارة مجلس الامة او الاتحاد القومى او الوزارات المختلفة.

لن تضم الوزارة ادارات تمثل المراقبات الفنية فى المحافظات. اذ سيبقى اشراف الوزارات التنفيذية المختلفة على النواحى الفنية فى المجالس المحلية بحيث يكون المحافظ فى حكم نائب الوزير لكل وزير يشرف فنيا على النواحى المتصلة بعمل الوزارة. ستزود الادارات والاقسام الفنية بحاجتها من الموظفين عن طريق موظفى الوحدات المجمعة وادارة البلديات وادارة المديريات التى ضمت لوزارة الادارة المحلية من الوزارات الاخرى.

From, أخبار اليوم, Cairo

سياسة التخطيط

هذا من ناحية، ومن ناحية أخرى فان الدولة التزمت سياسة التخطيط الاقتصادى والاجتماعى، ولم تعد الميزانية العامة فى ظل هذه السياسة الا مرحلة من مراحل الخطة الشاملة التى وضعتها الحكومة بكافة أجهزتها وناقشتها على مختلف المستويات واستصدرت قرارا جمهوريا باعتمادها، وأصبحت محددة فى دقة تامة وتفصيل دقيق، بحيث يصبح أى تعديل فى الميزانية خارج عنها، منافيا لمبدأ التخطيط ومتعارضا معه. وقد يكون معرقلا لسير الخطة التى تقوم على تفضيل الأهم على المهم وعلى توفير الامكانيات اللازمة

للتنفيذ على التوقيت الزمنى المتسلسل وذلك كله وفقا لمقتضيات التناسق بين المشروعات والاعمال وبين جوانب السياسة العامة للدولة ، وبين مختلف القطاعات.

ان هذه السياسة الجديدة التى يتبعها القيسونى[1] فى اعداد ميزانية الدولة تمنع الانحراف الذى حدث فى الماضى عندما كان مجلس النواب يزيد فى اعتمادات الميزانية دون طلب الحكومة.

ولكنها — السياسة الجديدة — لن تمنع مجلس الامة من مناقشة الحكومة فيما يرى ادخاله من تعديل. فاذا وافقت عليه — فى نطاق الخطة الشاملة طبعا — امكن اجراؤه فى حدود الدستور.

ومن شأن هذا كله أن يجعل المناقشة فى مجلس الامة ايجابية ومجدية.[2]

From الحياة, daily newspaper, Beirut

لجنة الادارة تجتمع ظهر السبت للشروع فى درس مشروع الايجارات

لمندوب « الحياة » الخاص :

كان من المنتظر ان تجتمع لجنة الادارة والعدل ظهر هذا النهار الخميس للشروع فى درس مشروع قانون الايجارات الجديد ، غير ان هذا الاجتماع ارجىء الى ظهر يوم السبت المقبل.

وبرر الشيخ بهيج تقى الدين[1] رئيس اللجنة هذا التأجيل بقوله : ان الرغبة فى دعوة جميع ممثلى لجنة المستأجرين والنقابات والهيئات المعنية بهذه القضية ، والملاكين ، كل هذا اوجب تأجيل الموعد الى يوم السبت حتى يتسنى دعوتهم الى حضور الجلسة والوقوف على ارائهم.

وفى الواقع ، فأن قلم المجلس تولى امس توجيه الدعوة الى هؤلاء الممثلين مذكرا اياهم بوجوب اعداد ملاحظاتهم بشأن المطالب التى ينادون بها.

وقد اشرنا فى عدد امس الى ان النقابات العمالية اجتمعت وقررت بالاجماع رفض المشروع من اساسه.

---

[1] Name of person.

[2] أَجْدَى (جدو IV) to be useful.

اشتباك فى بعلبك[1] واعتقال الفاعلين

لخلاف على ضمان ارض فى حلبتا[2] (قضاء بعلبك) اقدم دعاس طعان دندش[3] وولده نوفل[4] وخليل سعيد علاء الدين[5] جميعهم من زبود على ضرب نايف ديب سيف الدين[6] الذى ادعى انهم اشهروا عليه اسلحة كانوا يحملونها. وبنفس اليوم وثأرا لنسيبهم نايف[7] المذكور تصدى محمد ديب سيف الدين[8] وعلى مهدى سيف الدين لدعاس[9] وولده، وقد قام درك بعلبك بالتحقيق واوقف خليل علاء الدين ومحمد سيف الدين ومهدى سيف الدين وفتشوا منازلهم فلم يعثر على شيء ممنوع، والتحريات ناشطة لتوقيف دعاس.

From العَلَم, daily newspaper, Rabat (Morocco)

سفير المغرب فى بغداد يشكر
الشعب العراق والحكومة العراقية

أصدر سعادة سفير المغرب فى بغداد يوم امس البيان التالى : يتقدم سفير المملكة المغربية فى العراق الى الشعب العراق النبيل والى صاحب السيادة رئيس مجلس السيادة العراق والى السادة الوزراء واعضاء الهيئات الديبلوماسية المنتدبة بالعراق واصحاب الفضيلة العلماء ورجال الدين وممثلى الهيئات والاحزاب السياسية وممثلى النقابات والمنظمات الاجتماعية ورجال الصحافة والمنظمات النسوية وكافة المعوزين بوفاة المغفور له الملك الراحل محمد الخامس سواء من تفضل منهم بزيارة دار السفارة أيام قراءة الفاتحة أو من عبروا عن مشاعرهم بالبرقيات والرسائل يتقدم اليهم جميعا بعميق شكره وبالغ تأثره لما عبروا عنه من العواطف ومشاعر الحزن على فقيد المغرب الراحل والتى كانت له ولاعضاء السفارة المغربية أكبر مواساة لهذا الخطب الجلل الذى حل بالشعب المغربى داعيا الى الله تعالى أن يحفظهم وان لايريهم بأسا ولا مكروها.

[1] Baalbek.
[2] Locality.
[3] *Et seq.*, names of persons.

From البرق, Arabic weekly, Paris

الاصلاح الزراعى فى الجزائر

دخل الإصلاح الزراعي في دوره الانشائي وذلك بعد احداث صندوق يساعد على امتلاك الأراضي الفلاحية. وتم تحويل ما يزيد عن الف هكتار كانت تابعة إما لأملاك الدولة وإما للشركات. فانتزع من الشركة الجزائرية ٦٦ الف هكتار ومن الشركة السويسرية بجنيف[1] ١٦ الف هكتار بحيث بلغ المجموع مائة الف هكتار ستوزع فى قطع ذات مساحات تتراوح بين ١٠ و ٢٥ هكتار.

وفى المناطق المتمتعة بالري سيجري الانتزاع على الاراضي التي تزيد مساحتها عن ٥٠ هكتاراً او فى حالة وجود اطفال لا تتجاوز ١٥٠ هكتاراً. اما العشرون الف هكتار المتحصل عليها فستوزع على قطع ذات خمسة هكتارات. وينخرط المحرزون على تلك القطع. فى تعاضدية وشركة فلاحية احتياطية. وليس من الضرورى ان يكونوا مسلمين .

ADVERTISEMENTS AND ANNOUNCEMENTS

مصانع « العلوية » لصاحبها محمد حسين العلوى

ان مصانع « العلوية » على استعداد لتقديم أية مساعدة تتعلق باجهزة « العلوية ». ان كان لديك أية مشكلة أو أية فكرة أو شكاية عن هذا النتاج الذى اشتريته أو أى استعلام عن امور أخرى تتعلق بهذا النتاج الرجاء إعلامنا.

ضمان

نشهد بأن صناعة جهاز العلوية مكفولة من أى خلل أو عيب، وتعتبر هذه الكفالة ملغاة عند وقوع أى خلل بها وذلك فى حالة سوء استعمال الجهاز أو عدم الاعتناء به أو فى حالة تصليحه من قبل أى شخص ليس وكيلا لجهاز العلوية. ان هذه الشهادة تعتبر الكفالة الوحيدة ويجب ان تعاد مع الجهاز فى حالة طلب خدمة مكفولة له والا فان أيِ تصليح لا يعتبر مجانا.

---

[1] Geneva.

إن التحسين الذى طرأ على إنتاج بطاريات « فيدور » يمهد الطريق إلى استئناف التجارة مع السوق العالمية. وفى إمكان هذه الشركة المشهورة أن تنتج بطاريات جافة تصلح لجميع الأغراض، وهى تنتج أنواعاً كثيرة من أحدث أجهزة الراديو، ومجموعة كبيرة من المعدات الكهربائية المنزلية. ويسر شركة « فيدور » أن تمد عملاءها فيما وراء البحار بتفاصيل منتجاتها والشروط التجارية

مكتبة محمد على
لطبع وبيع الكتب الشرقية

لدينا مجموعة كبيرة من الكتب (جديدة ومستعملة) عن مصر وبلاد العرب وتركيا وايران والهند والصين الخ بكل اللغات.
سترسل الكتالوجات عند الطلب.
إلى المؤلفين والناشرين: الرجاء إعلامنا بمطبوعاتكم.
اخصائيون[1] فى الرسوم الدقيقة والمخطوطات والفخار وغيرها من منتجات الهند وايران.

شركة ذات شهرة عالمية

بحاجة الى مهندسين وكيماويين قديرين لهم رغبة فى اتخاذ الصناعة مهنة لهم. على الراغبين ان يكونوا مستعدين للعمل فى بيروت او فى جدة (المملكة العربية السعودية). يتلقى الفائزون التدريب اللازم براتب كامل قبل تسلمهم مهام العمل.
ترسل الطلبات الى صندوق البريد رقم ١٠٠١ بيروت قبل ١٥ آذار.

المملكة المغربية
وزارة الاقتصاد الوطنى
المكتب المغربى للمراقبة والتصدير
اعلان عن عرض اثمان

يتسلم المكتب المغربى للمراقبة والتصدير ٧٢ نهج محمد سميحة بالدار البيضاء حتى نهاية ١٨ مارس ١٩٦١ عروضا بشأن امداده ببذلات صالحة لشواش المكتب.
ويمكن الحصول على دفتر التكاليف وعلى المزيد من الارشادات لدى مصلحة الادوات التابعة للمكتب بالعنوان المذكور اعلاه.

[1] Specialists.

وينبغي ان ترسل العروض الى ادارة المكتب م. م. ت فى ظرف مزدوج مختوم بالشمع مع البريد الموصى عليه وان يكتب على الظرف الخارجي الاسم التجارى لصاحب العرض مع عبارة « اعلان عن عرض اثمان بشان اللباس ».

اعلان

مطلوب لوزارة الداخلية — مصلحة تسجيل السيارات والآليات — سيارتان جيب[1] من صنع ١٩٦٠ او ١٩٦١.
تعينت الساعة العاشرة من يوم السبت فى ٢٥ اذار سنة ١٩٦١ موعدا للتلزيم بطريقة المناقصة.
تقدم العروض الى مكتب ادارة المناقصات — بناية منصور سلامه — شارع شاتوبريان — قبل الساعة ١٢ من يوم الجمعة ٢٤ اذار سنة ١٩٦١.
يمكن الاطلاع على دفتر الشروط فى محاسبة الداخلية.

اعلان

مطروح مجددا للبيع بالمزاد العلنى كامل عقار الدولة رقم ٥٣٩ من منطقة برج الشمالى — صور،[2] المحتوى على ارض[3] بعل سليخ تزرع حبوب مساحته ٣٢٨٥ مترا مربعا.
تجرى المزايدة فى صور لدى الحاكم المنفرد من الساعة التاسعة حتى الحادية عشرة من يوم الخميس الواقع فى ٣٠ اذار سنة ١٩٦١.
يمكن الاطلاع على دفتر الشروط فى مديرية الشؤون العقارية فى بيروت دائرة املاك الدولة — بناية البرلمان — وفى امانة السجل العقارى فى صيدا[4] وفى المكتب العقارى المعاون فى صور خلال الدوام الرسمى.
فعلى الراغبين بالشراء الحضور فى الوقت المعين مصحوبين بالتأمين المحدد فى دفتر الشروط.

---

[1] Jeep.
[2] Tyre.
[3] "treeless watered (by natural sources)"
[4] Sidon.

عطاءات ومناقصات

مراقبة الشئون البلدية والقروية بمحافظة البحيرة[1] — تقبل عطاءات لغاية ظهر يوم الاثنين الموافق ١٩٦١/٣/٢٧ لعملية انشاء الوحدة الزراعية بناحية رشيد[1]— وتطلب المستندات من المراقبة بدمنهور[1] على ورقة دمغة فئة الخمسين مليما[2] نظير دفع مبلغ ٥٠٠، ٨٠ج.م[3] يضاف اليها مبلغ ثلاثمائة مليم فى حالة طلب المستندات بالبريد — وكل عطاء غير مصحوب بتأمين موقت قدره ٢٪ (اثنان فى المائة) من قيمته او مخالف لنصوص المواصفات والشروط العمومية لن يلتفت اليه — ٥٢٦١.

CORRESPONDENCE

أيها الأخ المخلص السيد فلان

بعد السؤال عن خاطركم الأمل أن تكون بما يُرام من صحة وعافية على الدوام. ثم اننا نتقدم اليك بالتهنئة بمناسبة قدوم السنة الجديدة. هذا واننا مشتاقون كثيراً لرؤياك ومشاهدة عاصمة بلادكم الجميلة فى هذه الايام، أيام عيد الميلاد. وسأكتب لك خطاباً مطوّلا فى بحر هذا الأسبوع وسلّم لنا على جميع الاصدقاء، ومنى اليكم الف سلام.

المخلص لكم
فلان

حضرة الأخ الفاضل السيد فلان دام بقاؤه

بعد التحية والسلام والأمل ان تكونوا بغاية الصحة والسلامة لقد تشرفنا بورود تحريركم المؤرخ فى ١٤ الجارى ونشكر حضرتكم جزيل الشكر وما شرحتم به صار لدينا معلوماً. اما بخصوص البضائع التى توجد عندكم فى الوقت الحالى فكما سبق وعرّفناكم ان جميع الأصناف تهمنا وفى استطاعتنا عرضها على أسواق سوريا واستيرادها،

[1] In Egypt. [2] Egyptian coin. [3] جنيه مصرى

خاصّةً الاشياء التى تمّ اختراعها فى الآونة الأخيرة. وهنا نرجوكم ان كان فى استطاعتكم ان ترسلوا لنا عن طريق البريد هذه الطلبية الصغيرة، المبينة أدناه، فنرجوكم ان تعرّفونا عن السعر حتى نقدم لكم قيمتها على أحد مصارف طرفكم.

أخى سيحرر لكم اليوم وهو بصحة جيدة وجميعنا هنا نذكر حضرتكم بالثناء ونهديكم عاطر التحية. وختامًا تفضلوا بقبول ازكى سلامنا وشكرنا.

كاتبه
مخلصكم
فلان الفلانى

الى حضرة ابن عمنا العزيز السيد فلان المحترم

تحيةً وسلامًا، والرجاء ان تكونوا بكمال الصحة والسلامة. لقد ورد الينا بأحسن وقت كتابكم الكريم المؤرخ فى ٦ من الشهر الماضى وشكرناكم مزيد الشكر، أما الجرائد الانكليزية التى وعدتمونى بارسالها فلم تصل بعد فلا اعرف سبب التأخير. انى ذهبت اليوم الى دائرة البريد وهناك موظّف قال لى ان الطائرة من انكلترا متأخرة لسبب ضباب على مطار روما وليس لديهم خبر عن وصولها. وقد زارنا البارح صاحب الطرفين[1] محمود سليم على طريقه الى نيو يورك حيث سيحل محل أخيه فى القنصلية هناك، بقى عندنا حوالى ساعتين وسرّنا حضوره غاية السرور إذ لم نره من مدة طويلة ويعزّ علينا. رافقناه جميعاً الى المطار خارج المدينة.

هذا والرجاء ان تبقوا جميعًا على احسن حال واقبلوا منا أزكى السلام والتحية ودمتم.

مخلصكم
فلان

[1] Mutual friend.

APPENDIX A

Colloquial Arabic Dialects

1. A comprehensive and practical guide to spoken Arabic is well beyond the scope of this Grammar. The following notes are intended merely as a preliminary guide, a statement of broad principles in fact, with only sketchy details.

2. Whereas Latin developed into different languages, such as Italian, French, and Castilian (Spanish) in the course of the centuries, Arabic did not split up into separate languages over the same period and in a comparable geographical area. The reason was that Arabic was the language of a religion, Islam, as well as of government. This meant that in the first place the written language was shielded from the usual linguistic decay; and secondly, that the colloquial speech did not diverge as widely as might otherwise have been the case. As a consequence the spoken Arabic of countries as mutually remote as Iraq, the Sudan, Morocco, can be described as dialects rather than separate languages.

Colloquial Arabic is, for convenience, divided into geographical areas, each with its own general characteristics and peculiarities; but within each area there is considerable diversity in sub-dialects. Nevertheless, the main dialects all have certain features and tendencies in common and are seldom mutually completely unintelligible. In fact a person who is familiar with, say, the spoken Arabic of Egypt will soon understand a Lebanese or an Iraqi. Indeed, in some cases the difference between the colloquial as a whole and written Arabic is much greater than that between one colloquial dialect and another.

The main dialect areas are:

Egypt (Lower Egypt, the Cairene dialect). The Sudan

(and Upper Egypt). The Maghrib (Tunisia, Algeria, Morocco). The Levant Coast (Syria and Lebanon). Iraq. The Arabian Peninsula.

3. The differences between Classical and Colloquial Arabic may be analysed under three headings: Phonology, Grammar, and Vocabulary.

4. *Phonology*

In most of the dialects the pronunciation of certain letters of the alphabet differs to some extent from that of recognised classical usage. Generally speaking we may say that consonants difficult to pronounce (in the mouths of certain groups of peoples) are simplified. This simplification can often be parallelled in other Semitic languages such as Hebrew and Syriac.

The *hamza* goes frequently unpronounced except at the beginning of a word. Thus the word مَسْؤُول "responsible" becomes something like *masūl*. سَأَلَ "he asked" becomes *sāl* as though written سَال; قَرَأَ "he read" becomes *qara*.

The consonant ث becomes either *tā'* or *sīn*. For example we have *talāta* for ثلاثة "three". For مَثَلاً we have both *masalan* and *matalan*, the latter being heard in some parts of the Levant. There seems to be no guiding rule in this matter. In Iraq and the Arabian Peninsula, however, the true pronunciation of ث is used.

ج becomes a hard *g* in Egyptian Arabic. Thus جَرْدَل "bucket" becomes *gardal*. Although this pronunciation of the ج can be heard elsewhere it is particularly associated with Egyptian Arabic.

ذ becomes *d* or *z* except in Iraq and the Arabian Peninsula. Thus we have *hāda* for هذا, and *kazālik* for كذلك.

ض is usually considered a peculiarly Arabic sound, hence the appellation لغة الضاد for the Arabic language. Yet it is frequently confused with ظ. In Iraq and areas in the

Arabian Peninsula both these letters have a sound similar to that of ذ. In Egypt and the Levant ظ is sometimes pronounced as a ض in addition to its own sound as *ẓ*. In both these areas, however, the word ضَابِط "officer" is pronounced *ẓābiṭ*. In Syria and Lebanon مَضْبُوط "correct" is heard as both *maẓbūṭ* and *maḍbūṭ*.

ق becomes a *hamza* in the dialects of Lower Egypt and the towns of Syria, Lebanon, Israel, and the western area of Jordan. Thus the word قَالَ "he said" becomes *'āl*. In other regions, particularly the Sudan, parts of Iraq and the Arabian Peninsula and the Maghrib the ق becomes a hard *g*, thus *gāl* for قال. This *g* pronunciation was recognised in Classical times as an alternative pronunciation; for example, in Ibn Duraid's introduction to his famous dictionary, the "Jamhara" (9th–10th Century). This pronunciation is that of the Persian گ *gāf*.

In the vowel sounds there is considerable divergence in the colloquials from the Classical. For example, *ḍamma* often becomes *kasra*. Thus the proper name حُسَيْن may be heard as *Ḥisain*. It is often omitted altogether in words like مُنَوَّر and مُبَارَك which are heard as *mnawwar* and *mbārak* (or even *embārak*). The *fatḥa* in words of the فَعِيل form is often not sounded and we have *kbīr* for كَبِير. Diphthongs may become long vowels, and vice versa. In the Syrian dialect شَيْء "thing" is heard as *shī* and كَيْفَ "how" as *kīf*.

Verb vowellings are also frequently varied. يَكْتُبُ "he writes" may be heard as *yiktob*, *yiktib*, or *yaktib*. كَبُرَ "he grew" as *kibir*.

5. *Grammar*

In grammar all the dialects resemble one another in that practically all final vowels disappear. This applies especially to those vowels indicating the cases of nouns and the moods of verbs. Nunation disappears altogether except in a few isolated adverbial usages such as *ḥālan* "at once", *aḥyānan* "sometimes", and *taqrīban* "approximately".

بَيْتٌ "house" is *bait* in all cases. كَتَبَ "he wrote" is pronounced as *katab*; يَكْتُبُ as *yaktub* (or one of the variations shown in Section 4). A final vowel may be used if the following word begins with a *hamzatu l-waṣl*, and this will be either *fatḥa* or *ḍamma* or *kasra*, e.g.

mā yaعrifa l-walad, "he does not know the boy". *Iqlibi l-waraqa*, "turn the piece of paper over".

Even when the following word begins with a consonant vestiges of a final vowel are sometimes heard. Thus in Egypt *katabă gawāb* "he wrote a letter" is heard as well as *katab gawāb*.

The Demonstrative Pronouns are often simplified, shortened or otherwise modified in the different dialects. Thus the rendering for "this book" may be *il-kitáb-da* (or *ik-kitáb-da*) in Egypt and the Sudan, or *hal-kitāb*, *hel-kitāb* in Syria and the Lebanon and Iraq.

Conjunctive Particles are largely omitted. Thus the sentence أُرِيدُ أَنْ أَكْتُبَ لِأَخِي "I wish to write to my brother" would be rendered in colloquial speech as *'arīd 'aktub li-'akhī*. The "doubled" Particles إِنَّ, أَنَّ, فَإِنَّ etc. are scarcely ever heard. فَ is even rarer.

In the Dual and the sound Masculine Plural, only the oblique forms are used. Thus رَجُلَانِ, oblique رَجُلَيْنِ, "two men" is *rajulain* in all cases (with the final *kasra* unpronounced). مُعَلِّمُونَ, oblique مُعَلِّمِينَ, "teachers", is *muعallimīn* in all cases (with the *fatḥa* over the *nūn* unpronounced).

The verbal suffixes undergo some simplification. For example يَكْتُبُونَ "they write" becomes يَكْتُبُوا in most of the dialects, but not in Iraq and the Arabian Peninsula as a rule.

The Dual forms of the Perfect and Imperfect are not used in colloquial speech. One can hear يكتبون and يكتبوا for the Feminine, يَكْتُبْنَ; and even sometimes يَكْتُبْ for تَكْتُبْ (fem.).

In the dialects of Egypt and the Levant *b* or *be* is prefixed to the persons of the Imperfect to make it a Present Indicative. Thus *byiktub* means "he writes"; *betimshi* "she walks"; *baعrif* "I know".

Various means are employed to indicate the Future tense of the Imperfect. In Egypt we may hear (*huwa*) *ḥa yimshi* for سَوْفَ يَمْشِي which in Syria (and Lebanon) would be expressed by *raḥ yimshi.* In Iraq *da* is placed before the Imperfect. Occasionally also the Active Participle will be used with a future meaning, e.g. *anā māshi as-sūq*, "I shall go to the market". A frequent use of the Active Participle, found in some areas, is to give it a meaning of the Perfect. Thus the phrase آخِذ بِنْت فُلَان can mean "he took (in marriage) the daughter of such-and-such a one".

To express possession the plain *'iḍāfa* is not exclusively used; instead, several words with the meaning of "property" are employed. In Egypt *betāع* (for *matāع*) is used; in the Maghrib *mtaع*; in Syria *tabaع*; in Iraq *māl. Ḥaqq* may also be heard. Thus كِتَابِي, "my book", is expressed by *al-kitāb betāعi* or *mtaعi* or *tabaعi* or *māli* or *ḥaqqi* according to the dialect area.

In the negative, لا tends to be replaced by ما. In Egypt and parts of the Levant the word "not" is expressed by *mush*; in Iraq by *mū*, and in parts of Syria by *mo* and *mau.* These variations, however, are not usually used with the Perfect or Imperfect; *mā* is used in these cases. In Egypt and parts of the Levant the verb in the negative has *sh* as a suffix. Thus "he did not strike" would be *mā ḍarabsh*. "I did not see him" as *ma shuftūsh* (colloquial شَاف "to see"). This final *sh* is presumably شَيْء "thing" in origin and appears in these cases as *shī* in the Maghrib. In colloquial Arabic لا tends to mean merely "no", though it is used in prohibition with the verb in some areas. Thus "do not go" may be *lā tamshī* (*timshi*) or *mā tamshī* (*sh*). In popular intercourse the word نَعَمْ "yes" is less common than such expressions as *eh*, *ay*, and *aiwa*. The last is used extensively in Egypt and the Levant.

The Relative Pronoun الّذى is rare. Instead we hear simplifications like *al* (the Article), *alli*, *illi*, *elli*, *halli* or *yalli*. Thus الكتاب الذى قرأته becomes *al-kitāb al*, *elli*, *halli*, etc. *qarētuh* (*garētuh*, etc.) *ē* or *ai* takes the place of the *hamza*.

The above are only a few of the grammatical variations of colloquial Arabic dialects and are not intended to be exhaustive for any dialect.

6. *Vocabulary*

Uniformity of vocabulary is, according to the philologists, the least important prerequisite for linguistic homogeneity. Languages of the same family and dialects of the same language may differ considerably in vocabulary. So it is with the various dialects of Arabic. We must not be surprised to find that a refrigerator is *barrāda* in the Lebanon and *tallāja* in the Sudan; or that a bedsheet is *sharshaf* in one country and *milāya* in another. Strangely enough, the commoner the word the more likely it is to differ from area to area. شِعْر "poetry" is the same everywhere. It is the everyday things, especially modern or foreign importations, which show most variety.

Dialectical variations may be due to three causes: loan words, corruption of classical words, or selection from classical synonyms.

(*a*) *Loan words*. These are numerous and are employed to describe modern machines and techniques. Various learned academies such as the Egyptian Academy have tried to discourage the use of these by inventing suitable words from Arabic roots, a perfectly feasible procedure. But such fabrications do not easily gain ground among the masses. Thus we can hear *ōtō* or *ōtombīl* for a car, or *ɛarabīya* (Egypt) or *sayyāra*; the two latter are Arabic. A truck may be *lūrī* (i.e. "lorry") or *sayyārat naql*. Similarly, use of the word "telephone" (written in Arabic تلفون) is discouraged by the language reformers in favour of the word هاتِف which might be translated as "an unseen man whose voice is heard".

To list the foreign vocabulary in Arabic would require a book. Some of this vocabulary is Turkish (dating back to the Ottoman Empire or even earlier) and Persian. Titles such as *bey* and *pasha* are Turkish. *Bāsh*, Turkish for "head" is used in compounds for "chief", as *bāshmufattish* "chief inspector", *bāshkātib* "chief clerk", *bāshmuhandis* "chief engineer". The Turkish word *ḍughri* is used for "straight on" or "straight ahead". The adoption of foreign words in Arabic goes back to pre-Islamic times. The Quran itself contains words of Persian, Greek, and Aramaic origin.

In adopting foreign words the Arabs try to give them Broken Plurals (or, in many cases, sound Feminine Plurals) wherever possible. Thus the plural of *tāks* or *tāksi*, "taxi" can be *tawākis* or *tawāks*; the plural of *lūrī* "lorry" *lawāri* or *lūrīyāt*. The plural of *film* "a film" is *'aflām*.

Foreign words may undergo considerable corruption. From the French "vapeur" we have *wābūr* or *bābūr* used in Egypt and the Sudan for a steamer or pumping engine. In Syria it has the former meaning.

(*b*) *Corruptions of Classical words*. The following are a few examples:

Zay, meaning "like" (مِثْل or كَ), from the classical زِيّ "a manner" or "fashion".

baṭṭāl "bad" from بَطَلَ "to be useless or corrupted".

badal safarīya "travelling allowance", from بَدَلَ "to change" and سَفَرٌ "travelling".

itɛashsha "to dine", for تَعَشَّى.

Such corruptions may affect either the actual form of the word or its meaning.

(*c*) *Selection from Classical synonyms.*

The Medieval Arabs boasted of the richness of their language and of the large number of مُتَرَادِفَاتٌ or synonyms. The student of this grammar will have encountered four words for "garden": بُسْتَانٌ, حَدِيقَةٌ, جُنَيْنَةٌ, جَنَّةٌ. The first three are all common in colloquial Arabic. There are also many words for animals, and natural phenomena such as clouds. The various names for the camel are legion. The student must not be surprised to find the word بَعِيرٌ *baɛīr* used in some localities almost exclusively for "camel" instead of the commoner جَمَلٌ. He may also find هُدُومٌ instead of مَلَابِسُ for "clothes". He will rarely hear the classical ذَهَبَ "to go"; instead it will be رَاحَ *rāḥ* or *masha* (مَشَى lit. "to walk").

7. It is advisable for the student to begin by learning one single dialect, presumably one for which he has a practical need. He can later turn to other dialects and learn the various principles governing them and the characteristic differences which distinguish one from the other.

The following preliminary bibliography can be taken as a guide:

Egypt: W. H. T. Gairdner: *Egyptian Colloquial Arabic*, Cairo, 1944.

T. F. Mitchell: *An Introduction to Egyptian Colloquial Arabic*, Oxford, 1956.

Iraq: Van Ess: *The Spoken Arabic of Iraq*, 2nd edition, Oxford, 1938.

Haim Blanc: *Communal Dialects in Baghdad*, Harvard U.P., 1964.

Syria, Lebanon, Palestine:

R. Nakhla: *Grammaire du Dialecte Libano-Syrien.* Beirut, 1937/8.

G. R. Driver: *A Grammar of the Colloquial Arabic of Syria and Palestine*, Probsthain & Co., London (Printed in Vienna), 1925.

A. Barthélemy: *Dictionnaire Arabe-Français* (5 fascicules), Paris, 1934–1954.

Rice and Sa'īd: *Eastern Arabic*, Beirut, 1961.

Cantineau and Helbaoui: *Arabe Orientale* (*Parler de Damas*), Paris, 1953.

M. Piamenta: *Tenses, Aspects, Moods in the Arabic dialect of Jerusalem*, Jerusalem, 1964.

South Arabia (Ḥaḍramawt):

R. B. Serjeant, *Prose and Poetry from Ḥaḍramawt*, London, 1951.

Sudan:

J. S. Trimingham: *Sudan Colloquial Arabic*, Second edition, Oxford, 1946.

The Maghrib:

Gaudefroy-Demombynes & Mercier: *Manuel d'Arabe Marocain*, Paris, 1925.

Louis Brunot: *Introduction à l'arabe marocain*, Paris 1950.

J. Jourdain: *Cours pratique d'arabe dialectal* (Tunisian), 7th ed., Tunis, 1956.

Central and West Africa:

G. J. Lethem: *Colloquial Arabic, Nigeria and Lake Chad*, London, 1920.

Arabic Phonetics:

W. H. T. Gairdner: *The Phonetics of Arabic*, London, 1925.

Jean Cantineau: *Etudes de Linguistique Arabe*, Paris, 1960.

C. Rabin: *Ancient West Arabian*, London, 1951.

This list does not include popular primers for travellers.

APPENDIX B

Guide to Further Study

1. Many students will doubtless have used this grammar under a teacher's guidance; for them these notes will not be necessary. For those, however, who are studying without the aid of a teacher these brief remarks, we hope, will be of some assistance.

2. *Works of Reference. Dictionaries*

While this grammar contains a substantial vocabulary of over 4,000 words the student wishing to proceed further will certainly require dictionaries. Those by **Elias E. Elias,** *Arabic-English and English-Arabic*, published in Cairo in several editions, range from pocket dictionaries to larger volumes comprising over 60,000 words each. They suffer from the fact that they are compiled primarily for Arabs studying English. Consequently, they do not give broken plurals of nouns, the vowelling of verbs in the imperfect, or their verbal nouns. Moreover, the English-Arabic dictionaries do not always indicate sufficiently clearly which words under any given reference are commonest, which are antiquated rather than modern, nor what fine shades of meaning distinguish them. In spite of their manifold drawbacks, however, these dictionaries represent no mean achievement. In the field of Arabic-English dictionaries, that of **Hava** published by the Catholic Press of Beirut (in several editions) is an excellent short work. It gives the plurals, verb-vowelling, and verbal nouns. At the same time, for those engaged in a profound study of modern Arabic literature it has some gaps. The best modern Arabic-English dictionary is undoubtedly that of **Wehr** (translated by Cowan), *A Dictionary of Modern Written Arabic*, Wiesbaden, 1961.

In the field of large-scale dictionaries nothing complete and satisfactory exists. **Lane's** *Arabic-English Lexicon* (8 vols), recently reprinted, is a classic work, but it was never completed and ceases to be more than rough notes from the middle of the letter *qāf* onwards. This work is, however, being completed in **Jorg Kraemer's** *Wörterbuch der Klassischen Arabischen Sprache* (Wiesbaden, Harrassowitz, 1957 onwards).

Of Arabic-Arabic dictionaries the 15th century *Qāmūs* of al-Fīrūzābādī is the most comprehensive short work (4 vols.). Of the larger works Ibn Manẓūr's *Lisān al-ع Arab* (13th century) and Murtaḍā az-Zabīdī's *Tāj al-ع Arūs* (18th century) are the most famous. All these works, however, will be beyond the great majority of students at this stage. They have the disadvantage that they are arranged in the "rhyme order", that is, according to the last radical of the root.

A number of handy modern Arabic-Arabic dictionaries also exists, the most popular perhaps being the *al-Munjid* of **Louis Ma'luf** (New Edition, Beirut, 1956). There are also some specialised vocabularies such as *Dictionary of Sentences, English-Arabic* by **Ismail Mazhar** (Cairo, 1957), *Word-count of modern Arabic prose* by **J. M. Landau** (New York, 1959) with word frequencies but no translations, and *Manual of Diplomatic and Political Arabic* by **Bernard Lewis** (Luzac, London, 1947).

3. *Advanced Grammars*

The best advanced reference grammar is that by **William Wright,** first published in 1862 and recently reprinted (2 vols.). It uses the Latin grammatical terminology which may make difficulties for a large number of students who have no knowledge of Latin. Another excellent grammar is one by **Howell** published in Allahabad, India, 1883–1911, in seven volumes and based on the works of Arab grammarians. It is extremely full and prolix, and probably of less practical use for that reason. Good grammars have also been compiled in France and Germany notably the *Grammaire de l'arabe* *classique* by **Gaudefroy-Demombynes** and **Blachère,** published in Paris, 1952.

4. *Further Prose Composition* (translation from English to Arabic).

Unfortunately there is no satisfactory material readily available for Arabic in the shape of selected passages for translation.

5. *Further Reading. Anthologies*

There is a number of literary anthologies which may be read by those students not wishing to embark on whole works. On the modern side **Chaim Rabin's** *Arabic Reader,** published by Lund Humphries, London, 1962, is a useful collection. It enables the reader to find the vowelling, translation, and grammatical explanation of every word in the accompanying text without turning over the page. The extracts are all short but include well-known authors like Ṭāhā Ḥusain, Taufīq al-Ḥakīm, al-ʻAqqād.

On the classical side mention must be made of **Thornton and Nicholson's** *Elementary Arabic*, Vols. II, III, and IV (1st, 2nd and 3rd Reading Books), published in Cambridge, 1907–11, which have full vocabularies. Of works published in the Near East, **Cheikho's** *Majānī l-'Adab* in six volumes, published in Beirut during the last century, may still be found. **Fu'ād Afrām al-Bustānī's** *al-Majānī l-Ḥadīṯha* is, however, superior, having full footnotes explaining difficult words and sentences. This work is in five volumes published in Beirut in 1946. There is also **M. C. Lyons'** *An Elementary Classical Reader*, Cambridge, 1962.

Those students specialising in modern Arabic will wish to read the newspapers. A selection would be invidious, but *al-Ahram* (الأهرام) of Cairo and *al-Jarida* (الجَرِيدة) and *al-Hayat* (الحَيَاة) of Beirut may be recommended. There are also numerous journals and magazines, both learned and popular. The Iraq Petroleum Company and the Kuwait Oil Company publish excellent illustrated magazines, أَهْلُ النِّفْطِ

* 2nd Revised Edition.

and اَلْكُوَيْتِىّ respectively. Reading the captions of the illustrations is a useful aid to learning one type of modern Arabic.

For modern newspaper Arabic the publications of the Middle East Centre for Arabic Studies, Shemlan, Lebanon, deserve special mention. These include a reader, *The Way Prepared*, and *A Selected Word List of Modern Literary Arabic*.

6. *Modern Literature*

Some very good modern Arabic literature exists, its chief sources being the Lebanon and Egypt. There is also a new school of writers in Iraq which is showing much promise. Perhaps the best of the modern works to begin with is the autobiographical work (in novel form) الأيام of **Ṭāhā Ḥusain** (طه حسين). Another is the satirical and amusing novel يَوْمِيَّاتُ نَائِبٍ فِى ٱلْأَرْيَافِ by **Taufīq al-Ḥakīm** (توفيق الحكيم) which depicts Egyptian rural officialdom of a generation ago. This author has written a number of fine plays of which أَهْلُ ٱلْكَهْفِ and سُلَيْمَانُ ٱلْحَكِيمِ, of the phantasy type, and رَصَاصَةٌ فِى ٱلْقَلْبِ, with a modern environment, may be mentioned. Al-Ḥakīm has also many one-act plays which make interesting reading. For the short story **Maḥmūd Taimūr** (محمود تيمور) can be recommended both for his excellent style of writing and his art of story-telling.

Arabic poetry, whether modern or classical, is not an easy subject for study. For the student interested in modern Arabic poetry **Arberry's** *Modern Arabic Poetry* (Cambridge, 1950) can be recommended as an anthology, containing among other things some fine examples of verse by the modern Lebanese-American (or Syrian-American, as it is usually called) school, of whom an outstanding figure is Eliya Abū Māḍī (إيليا أبو ماضى). Of an older period are the Egyptians Ḥāfiẓ Ibrāhīm (حافظ إبراهيم), and Shauqī (شوقى), whose poems are not easy for Europeans. Shauqi's poetical dramas are good but may not have a ready appeal. Perhaps his مصرع كليوباترا (the Death of Cleopatra) may be of interest to those acquainted with the works of Shakespeare.

During the last few years a number of younger writers have achieved prominence. Among those deserving mention are the Egyptians Nagīb Maḥfūẓ, Yaḥyā Ḥaqqi and Al-Sharqāwi; the Lebanese woman writer, Laila Ba'labakki, and the young Iraqi poetess, Nāzik al-Malā'ika. A brief account of some of the chief writers of the older generation may be found in Khemiri and Kampffmeyer, *Leaders in Contemporary Arabic Literature*; Berlin-Dahlem, 1930.

7. *Classical Literature*

Classical Arabic literature is tremendously copious and covers a wide field in style and subject. Much of it is difficult and it is not easy to advise the student where to begin. All should read the Quran, however. Its language is by no means simple but many translations exist which will assist in its study. **Arberry's** *The Quran Interpreted* (London, 1955) may be recommended. Among older translations there is one by **Rodwell** (Everyman Edition) and an earlier translation by **Sale.** There is, of course, a very extensive literature on the Quran and the religion of Islam. In the latter field **Gibb's** *Muhammadanism* (Home University Library) is a good primer (4th impression, revised edition, 1928). For the *ḥadīth*, or Traditions of the Prophet Muhammad, there is a selection of the *Ṣaḥīḥ of al-Bukhārī* in the Semitic Study Series (Leyden, 1906). **Guillaume's** book *The Traditions of Islam* (Oxford, 1924) is still a classic. Books on Sufiism have been written by **Nicholson** (*The Mystics of Islam*, London, 1914) and **Arberry** (*Sufiism*, London, 1950). For works on *tafsīr* *Baiḍāwī's Commentary on Sūrah 12 of the Qur'ān* by **A. F. L. Beeston** (Oxford and New York, 1963) can be recommended.

The study of classical Arabic poetry necessitates commentaries and preferably a teacher. A few lines of classical verse may take an hour or two to elucidate. Of all the poets perhaps **'Abu l-ʿatāhiya** (أبو العتاهية) is the easiest. Readers may, however, find that his theme – the vanity of the world and the reality and imminence of death – palls after a time. Of the later poets **'Abu Nuwas** (أبو نُواس) may have a greater appeal. But the student will ultimately have to face pre-Islamic and early Islamic poetry. The short poems of chivalry in **'Abū Tammām's** (أبو تمّام) collection known as the *Ḥamāsa* (الحماسة) make a suitable beginning for study. Some of these poems were fairly effectively translated by **Lyall** in his *Translations of Ancient Arabic Poetry*, published in 1885. In the poetical sense, however, these poems are really untranslatable. The poems in the celebrated *Muعallaqāt* (المُعلَّقات) are an essential study, even though they may not at first have the same appeal as the *Ḥamāsa* to the non-Arab.

Of the later poets **'Abū Firās** (أبو فراس) will be enjoyed. His poems written during his captivity in Byzantium have a charm all their own, largely because of the genuineness of their emotions. **Al-Mutanabbi** (المتنبي), who has been called the Shakespeare of the Arabs, may at first repel Western readers, but the student is advised to persevere with him. In time a non-Arab may at least be able to appreciate why he is so admired in the East. Once the excessive pride of al-Mutanabbi is accepted, his real genius may be descried, however dimly.

Arabic prose ranges from the comparatively simple writing of biographers and historians to the poetical, artificial and brilliant and excessively difficult (even for Arabs) prose of the *Maqāmāt* (مَقامات) of **al-Ḥarīrī** (الحريرى) and **al-Hamadhānī** (الهمذاني). Probably the historical and geographical writers are the best to begin with. Among the best known of works in this category are the *Travels of Ibn Baṭṭūṭa* (ابن بطوطة). **Sir Hamilton Gibb** has already translated a selection of Ibn Baṭṭūṭa for the Broadway Travellers series (Routledge, London, 1929), and the first volume of his full translation appeared in 1958. Another travel author is **Ibn Jubair** (ابن جبير), whose works have been published in the Gibb Memorial series (ed. William Wright, 1907). The *Annals of Ṭabarī* (الطبرى) are the obvious choice for historical reading, while at a later stage the student will be ready to apply himself to the celebrated *Muqaddima*, or Prolegomena, of **Ibn Khaldūn's** *History*, now available also in **Rosenthal's** excellent translation (3 vols., London, 1958). There is also **W. J. Fischel's** *Ibn Khaldun and Tamerlane* (Berkeley, 1952).

There is a large literature of collected biographies, the most famous work being the *Biographical Dictionary of Ibn Khallikān* (ابن خلّكان). There is a translation of this by **De Slane** (Paris, 1883, 6 vols.). Another work is **Yāqūt's** (ياقوت) *Dictionary of Learned Men.*

For literature of a less classifiable type the *ʿUyūn al-'akhbār* (عيون الأخبار) of **Ibn Qutaiba** (ابن قتيبة) deserves mention. His section on "sermons" contains examples of early preaching in Islam and will repay study.

The Medieval Arabs had a fine sense of humour. **Al-Jāḥiẓ's** (الجاحظ) *Book of Misers* (كتاب البخلاء), also available in French translation, is an outstanding collection of witty and satirical tales.

The celebrated **Alf Laila wa Laila** (ألف ليلة وليلة), *Thousand and One Nights*, contains a rich store of legend, story, and anecdote in the original Arabic. This work is of interest also for its language, and the student will encounter in it occasional grammatical errors and colloquialisms.

An important development in prose literature was the cultivation of rhymed prose (سَجْعٌ) and other artificial devices collectively known as بَلَاغَةٌ (rhetoric). This led to the use by authors of a *recherché* vocabulary, demanded partly by the exigencies of rhyme, but also out of a desire to display erudition. This culminated in the tenth century (A.D.) in the devising of the "maqāma" form in which an anecdote or a situation is used as an excuse for a linguistic *tour de force.* The leading writers of *Maqāmāt* were **Badīʿ az-zamān al-Hamadhānī** (d. 1008 A.D.) and **al-Ḥarīrī** (d. 1122 A.D.). These works will be beyond the grasp of the student for some time to come. They are, however, available in various translations.

APPENDIX C

Supplementary Grammatical Notes

§ 1

The Phonology of Arabic

(see pages 6 ff.)

1. At first sight, the lack of a scientific account of the phonology of Arabic in the body of this grammar might seem surprising. This omission has, however, been deliberate, and is based on the following considerations:

(a) We are concerned here only with the written language, not the spoken language.[1] As to how classical Arabic was spoken it is not possible, even now, to dogmatise in detail despite extensive Mediaeval grammatical and lexicographical Arabic literature, and accounts of the dialects of Arabia and of the various methods of Quranic reading.

(b) Written Arabic is only heard in reciting the Quran, verse, rhetorical utterances, oratory and the like, and also in broadcasts from the Arabic radio stations. This being so, one can hardly speak of the phonology of written Arabic in the same way as one could of a spoken dialect.

(c) Nevertheless, written Arabic must not be treated as a dead language, as if the written words were mere hieroglyphics. While to teach the beginner a scientific phonology of the language would be, in the opinion of the authors, of doubtful value and might only create an additional hurdle to the student, he certainly needs a rough guide to the sounds of the language. This is what has been provided in Chapter One, sections 3 and 4.

---

[1] See Appendix A.

(d) There are few students of Arabic today who will not wish sooner or later to visit an Arab country and perhaps pass from the classical to the colloquial language with a minimum of difficulty. Even for them – particularly in the early stages – a detailed study of phonology is of secondary consideration: a rough guide to pronunciation is their prime need.

Despite all these arguments, however, the authors of this grammar realise that further phonological notes may be desired by some students. To this end the following brief notes are intended to fill the gap in a very rudimentary way. To those who wish to undertake a more thorough study of the phonetics of Arabic the following two works can be consulted:

W. H. T. Gairdner, *The Phonetics of Arabic*, Oxford, 1925.
Jean Cantineau, *Etudes de Linguistique Arabe*, Paris, 1960.

The Consonants

2. ب b; م m; و w; ف f. These are pronounced more or less as their English equivalents. It should be observed, however, that و, when having a *sukūn* and ending a syllable, should still be pronounced as a consonant, with the lips rounded and protruding. (See reference to diphthongs, page 9.)

ت t and د d. These consonants are closer in pronunciation to the Italian dentals *t* and *d* than the English sound. They are uttered with the tip of the tongue against the upper teeth.

ل l. See Gairdner, pp. 17–19 for the two types of *l* sound.

ث th and ذ dh. As in the words think and that respectively. It should be noted that the Arabic pronunciation is more emphatic than the English. (See also Appendix A, page 497.)

س s and ز z. These are more sibilant than in English. In the former the "hiss" and in the latter the "buzz" are stronger and clearer in Arabic.

ص ṣ; ض ḍ; ط ṭ; ظ ẓ. These are pronounced by the point of the tongue with the teeth-ridge, while the back of the tongue is raised towards the soft palate. More than one pronunciation of ظ (ẓ) is heard. In sound it is related rather to ذ (dh) than to ز (z). In Iraq and the Arabian Peninsula the three consonants ذ, ض, ظ, are pronounced practically the same, that is with a dh sound. (See also Appendix A, pp. 497–498).

ر r. The ر is rolled, similar to the Scottish *r* but not as emphatic or as prolonged. In some of the dialects there is more than one sound. Among most Jews and Christians of Baghdad and the people of Mosul district, for example, it has a sound rather like the French *r grasseye* (or like the غ).

ج j. The accepted sound of this consonant is the *j* in the word John. It is also pronounced as the hard *g*, as in the English word *gag*, and the French *j*, as in the word *jour*, over a large area of the Arabic-speaking world. The hard *g* is used all over Lower Egypt. Although this pronunciation can be heard elsewhere it is particularly associated with Egyptian usage. The French *j* pronunciation is used in the Lebanon, in Palestinian urban dialects (i.e. in Israel and Jordan on the Western Bank), and large areas of Syria. (In North Syria, however, it has the English sound.) Rarer dialectal pronunciations of ج are *gy*, *dy*, *dz*, *d* and *y*.

ى y. As with the و, care should be taken to retain the consonantal sound in diphthongs.

ق q. The student must take great care in distinguishing this sound from that of ك k. It can cause confusion in meaning if not properly pronounced. Thus قَلْبٌ heart; كَلْبٌ dog. (See also Appendix A, page 498.)

ح ḥ. Students tend to pronounce this consonant either as ه h or like خ kh. Care should be taken to avoid particularly the latter sound by eliminating any suspicion of what Gairdner calls "scrape".

For notes on the ع see Gairdner, pp. 28–29.

The Vowels and Diphthongs

3. (a) The Classical Arab philologists unfortunately give us little guidance on the correct pronunciation of the vowels.

They usually content themselves with explaining the meanings of the words *fatḥa*, *ḍamma*, and *kasra*. They do, however, refer to a feature called *'imāla* (*v.n.* of the 4th form verb, أَمَالَ to cause to incline) whereby the ا َ (*ā*) in certain localities inclines from *ā* to *ē* (just as *fatḥa* does from *a* to *e*). This is heard in the Maghribi dialects, in the Lebanon and parts of Syria. Thus the word سَاكِن sākin (dwelling, inhabitant) is heard as sēkin. It has the sound of the *ai* in the French word *aigu*.

(b) The six vowels (three short and three long) and two diphthongs of written Arabic do not represent all the sounds heard in the colloquial – or even in Quranic reading. As stated on page 8 the proximity of certain consonants affects the vowel sounds. To appreciate this one need only note the difference in the sound of the *fatḥa* in دَرْبٌ (road, way) and ضَرْبٌ (striking, blow). Likewise, the difference in the sound of the long *ā* in اَلْحِسَابُ (the account) and اَلْمَاضِي (the past). The *ā* in the latter word is a "back vowel" and is heard almost as the *a* in the word father as pronounced in London and South-East England.

Reading aloud

4. There are basically two methods of reading aloud:

(a) As in Quranic reading, all the final vowel points being pronounced, except in pause, i.e. at the end of a sentence (in the English sense of that word).

(b) Omitting the final vowels of inflection. For example the following sentence – قَالَ لِي اَلْحَقِيقَةَ وَ مَا كَذَبْ would be read:

(a) qāla lī l-ḥaqīqata wa mā ka<u>dh</u>ab.

(b) qāl lī l-ḥaqīqa wa mā ka<u>dh</u>ab.

Note the disappearance of the tā 'marbūṭa in (b).

§ 2

The Interrogative Particle

(see Chapter 3, para. 4, page 29)

Students are at times in doubt as to which of the two particles أَ and هَلْ to use. In many instances there is a free choice. The following points, however, should be noted:

(a) أَ is the first word in a sentence and cannot be preceded even by the conjunction. Thus, while we can write وَهَلْ كَتَبْتَ, with أَ the وَ must follow, as, أَوَكَتَبْتَ.

(b) أَ may be followed by a word beginning with *hamza*, e.g. أَأَنْتَ فِي ٱلْبَيْتِ, are you in the house? The purists, however, insisted in such cases the interrogative particle have *madda*, as . . . آنْتَ. In writing modern Arabic it is recommended by some that هَلْ be used when a word beginning with a *hamza* follows the interrogative particle.

(c) It is better not to interpose the attached sign of the future, سَ, between أَ and the verb. Thus, هَلْ سَتَكْتُبُ being preferable to أَسَتَكْتُبُ.

(d) Wright (*A Grammar of the Arabic Language*, *Vol. II*, *para.* 167) says that هَلْ "introduces questions of a more lively sort". This statement is plausible, though perhaps of dubious practical value.

§ 3

Improper Annexation

(see Chapter 8, on *'iḍāfa*, especially para. 8, pages 65–66)

The examples given in paragraph 8 are, contrary to the rules applied to "proper annexation", indefinite. In order to define these expressions the article is added to the adjective, e.g. كَثِيرُ ٱلْمَالِ, rich (*lit.* much of wealth) اَلرَّجُلُ ٱلْكَثِيرُ ٱلْمَالِ, *the* rich man.

§ 4

The Comparative and Superlative (Elative)

(see Chapter 11, para. 7, page 89)

(a) As stated in Chapter 11 it is preferable to use the Elative as the first element in an *'iḍāfa* construction, i.e. followed by a noun in the indefinite genitive, e.g. هُوَ أَطْوَلُ وَلَدٍ فِى ٱلْغُرْفَةِ, he is the tallest boy in the room. Note that this genitive noun is also commonly used in the definite plural as follows:—

هُوَ أَطْوَلُ ٱلْأَوْلَادِ, he is the tallest boy. The form هُوَ ٱلْوَلَدُ ٱلْأَطْوَلُ is rare.

(b) The Elative may be preceded by مِنْ to mean "one of the . . . est", "one of the most . . .", "among the most . . .", "among the . . . est", e.g.

هُوَ مِنْ أَكْرَمِ ٱلنَّاسِ he is one of the most generous people.

(c) (see Chapter 40, para. 8)

The student should note the frequent use of أَقَلّ, elative of قَلِيل, in modern politico-economic expressions such as أَقَلُّ تَقَدُّمًا with the meaning "under-developed" (*lit.* less advanced), e.g.

اَلدُّوَلُ ٱلْأَقَلُّ تَقَدُّمًا the under-developed countries.

§ 5

Subjunctive Particles

(see Chapter 15, para. 4, page 122)

The remarks made in Chapter 15 on the choice of subjunctive particles require some amplifications and amendment.

(a) أَنْ follows verbs expressing desire, dislike, command, prohibition, duty, fear, necessity, and kindred notions, e.g.

أُرِيدُ أَنْ أَنْتَظِرَ I want to wait.

مِنْ وَاجِبِي أَنْ أَنْتَظِرَ it is my duty to wait.

خَافَ مِنْ أَنْ يَنْتَظِرَ he was afraid to wait.

(b) كَيْ ، لِكَيْ ، لِأَنْ ، لِ indicate purpose, intention, object, and the like, e.g. اِنْتَظَرُوا لِيَرَوْهُ they waited to see him. Their negatives are كَيْلَا ، لِكَيْلَا ، لِئَلَّا.

(c) Some beginners tend to circumvent the subjunctive by using إِنَّ or أَنَّ instead of a subjunctive particle, e.g. قَالَ لَهُمْ أَنْ يَنْتَظِرُوا in error for قَالَ لَهُمْ إِنَّهُمْ يَنْتَظِرُونَ he told them to wait. خَشِيَ أَنَّهُمْ يَمُوتُونَ in error for خَشِيَ أَنْ يَمُوتُوا he was afraid that they would die. This mistake should be avoided.

(d) The use of the subjunctive may, however, often be avoided by the substitution of a verbal noun with the definite article, or in a prepositional phrase, or with the *mafعūl lahu* expression in the accusative, e.g.

خَرَجُوا لِيَسْتَقْبِلُوا ٱلْأَمِيرَ for خَرَجُوا لِٱسْتِقْبَالِ ٱلْأَمِيرِ

They went out to receive the prince.

قُمْتُ لِأُكْرِمَ ٱلْوَزِيرَ for قُمْتُ إِكْرَامًا لِلْوَزِيرِ

I rose out of respect for the minister.

§ 6

Doubly Transitive Verbs

(see Chapter 45, para. 3, page 392)

Doubly transitive verbs are of three main types:

(a) Causative verbs, mostly of the second or fourth derived forms, where the root verb is transitive, e.g. عَلَّمَ II to teach, from عَلِمَ to know or learn.

(b) Verbs implying giving, or some similar notion, as filling, satisfying, allowing, appointing: also the reverse meanings of forbidding and depriving. To these should be added verbs of asking, entreating and the like; e.g.

أَعْطَى حَسَنٌ مُحَمَّدًا كِتَابَيْنِ Hasan gave Muhammad two books

مَلَأَ ٱلدَّلْوَ مَاءً he filled the bucket with water.

(modern Arabic usually replaces the second object مَاءً by a prepositional phrase بِمَاءٍ or بِالْمَاءِ).

أَنْشَدَ ٱلشَّاعِرُ ٱلنَّاسَ قَصِيدَةً the poet recited an ode to the people.

حَرَمَهُ ٱللّٰهُ بَرَكَةً God has deprived him of a blessing.

أَسْأَلُ ٱللّٰهَ ٱلْعَفْوَ I ask pardon of God.

(c) What the Arabs call "Verbs of the Heart" (أَفْعَالُ ٱلْقَلْبِ). These are sometimes called also verbs of certainty and doubt (أَفْعَالُ ٱلْيَقِينِ وَ ٱلشَّكِّ). These are at times what might be called "estimative" verbs, such as حَسِبَ to think, reckon. They include verbs of thinking, knowing, finding, and imagining, e.g.

أَظُنُّ حَسَنًا عَاقِلًا I think Hasan (is) intelligent.

وَجَدْتُ زَيْدًا قَائِدًا عَظِيمًا I found Zaid (to be) a great commander.

§ 7

Composite Words

Composite words in Arabic fall into three categories.

1. A word compounded of two foreign words, e.g. سِرْدَابٌ pl. سَرَادِيبُ, underground vault, cellar. From two Persian words *sard* cold and *āb* water (because kept cool by means of cold water).

2. A word made up of one Arabic and one foreign word, e.g. بَاشْمُهَنْدِس *pl.* باشمهندسون chief engineer. From Arabic مهندس engineer, and Turkish *bāsh* head. كُتُبْخَانَة *pl.* كُتُبْخَانَات bookshop or library. From Arabic كُتُب books, and Persian *khāneh* house.

3. A compound of two Arabic words, e.g. from رَأْسُ ٱلْمَالِ, capital (finan.), we have, اَلرَّأْسَمَالِيَّةُ capitalism, الرأسماليون capitalists. بَرْمَائِيٌّ amphibious; from بَرٌّ land, and مَاءٌ water.

Some of the Arabic–Turkish compounds are tending to disappear gradually, being replaced by wholly Arabic words. While on the other hand new compound words are being introduced to meet the needs of science and technology, like تربو نفّاث turbo-jet; مُحَرِّكٌ تربومروحي turbo-prop engine.

VOCABULARY

(1) The unvowelled words shown in brackets indicate the root letters. Some non-Arabic words (place names, etc.) are given under a root form whenever the construction of the word allows of this; otherwise they are placed in alphabetical order according to the initial letter of the word.

(2) A few words may be written with alternative vowelling. These are shown thus: لِصّ which means that this particular word may be spelled لَصّ, لُصّ, or لِصّ. Where this happens in the case of the vowelling of the second radical of the Imperfect it is indicated as follows: (ـُـِ), e.g. يَنْفُرُ or يَنْفِرُ.

ا

أَ *interrogation particle* (attached)

(ابد)

أَبَدًا ever (with *negative* = never)

إِلَى ٱلْأَبَدِ for ever

(ابط)

تَأَبَّطَ V to carry under the arm

إِبْطٌ *pl.* آبَاطٌ armpit

(ابل)

إِبْلٌ إِبِلٌ camels (*coll.*)

(ابو)

أَبٌ *pl.* آبَاءٌ father (*pl.* also, ancestors)

أَبُو . . . father of, possessor, owner of

أَبَوَانِ (*dual*) parents

(ابى)

أَبَى (ـَـ) to refuse, reject

(اتى)

أَتَى (ـِـ) to come

بِ — to bring

آتٍ coming, following

(اثث)

أَثَاثٌ *pl.* ـَاتٌ — furniture

(اثر)

أَثَّرَ II (*with* عَلَى or فِى) to influence, impress

تَأَثَّرَ V to be affected, influenced

أَثَرٌ *pl.* آثَارٌ trace, footstep (in *pl.* also antiquities)

أَثَرَ, إِثْرَ, فِى أَثَرِ, فِى إِثْرِ following on, immediately after

أَثِيرٌ ethereal atmosphere

تَأْثِيرٌ influence, impression

(اجج)

تَأَجَّجَ V to burn, be aflame

(اجر)

آجَرَ IV to rent, hire (to someone)

اِسْتَأْجَرَ X to rent, hire

أُجْرَةٌ *pl.* أُجَرٌ rent, reward, fee

آجُرٌّ baked bricks

(اجل)

أَجَّلَ II to postpone, delay (something)

أَجَلٌ *pl.* آجَالٌ the (fixed) term of one's life

لِأَجْلِ for the sake of, for

(اخذ)

أَخَذَ (ـُ) *v.n.* أَخْذٌ to take; (+ *imperf.* to begin); to learn from, study under (*antiq.*)

آخَذَ III *v.n.* مُؤَاخَذَةٌ to blame

اِتَّخَذَ VIII to take for oneself, adopt

(اخر)

أَخَّرَ II to delay (someone, anything)

تَأَخَّرَ V to be late, delayed, behind

أَخِيرٌ last, recent

أَخِيرًا last, finally, recently

آخَرُ *f.* أُخْرَى *pl.* أُخَرُ, آخَرُونَ another, other

آخِرٌ *pl.* أَوَاخِرُ last, end (*pl.* = latter part)

(الْحَيَاةُ) الْآخِرَةُ; (الدَّارُ) الْأُخْرَى the world to come, the Hereafter

مُؤَخَّرًا lately, recently

(اخو)

أَخٌ, أَخُو (with following *gen.*), *pl.* إِخْوَةٌ, إِخْوَانٌ brother

أُخْتٌ *pl.* أَخَوَاتٌ sister

(ادب)

أَدَّبَ II to discipline

أَدَبٌ *pl.* آدَابٌ literature, arts, politeness

أَدِيبٌ *pl.* أُدَبَاءُ cultured, educated man, literary figure

(ادم)

آدَم; بَنُو آدَمَ Adam; mankind

آدَمِىّ man

(ادو)

أَدَاة pl. أَدَوَات tool, implement, instrument

(ادى)

أَدَّى II to perform; to lead to (*with* إِلَى)

(اذ)

إِذْ since

إِذَا if, when; behold (*with* بِ)

إِذًا, إِذَنْ therefore, so, then

(اذن)

أَذِنَ (ـَ) to permit

اِسْتَأْذَنَ X to ask permission

إِذْن permission

أُذُن pl. آذَان ear

أَذَان Moslem call to prayer

مُؤَذِّن Muezzin (caller to prayer)

مَأْذَنَة, مِئْذَنَة pl. مَآذِن minaret

(ارب)

أَرِيب clever, able

(ارخ)

أَرَّخَ II to date; write history

تَارِيخ, تَأْرِيخ pl. تَوَارِيخ date; history

مُؤَرِّخ historian

(ارض)

أَرْض (*f.*) pl. أَرَاضٍ, أَرَضُون earth, land

(ارنب)

أَرْنَب pl. أَرَانِب rabbit, hare

(ازل)

أَزَلِيَّة, أَزَل eternity

(ازم)

أَزْمَة pl. إِزَم dearth, scarcity; crisis (*mod.*)

(اسس)

أَسَّسَ II to found, establish, build

أَسَاس pl. أُسُس foundation

أَسَاسِىّ fundamental(ist)

اَلْإِسْبَان; إِسْبَانِىّ, إِسْبَانِيَا Spain; Spanish, the Spaniards

(استذ)

أُسْتَاذ pl. أَسَاتِذَة, أَسَاتِيذ professor, teacher

(اسد)

أَسَد pl. أُسْد, أُسُود lion

(اسر)

أَسَرَ (ـِ) to take prisoner, captive

أَسِيرٌ *pl.* أُسَرَاءُ captive, prisoner of war

أُسْطُولٌ *pl.* أَسَاطِيلُ fleet, flotilla

(اسو)

مُؤَاسَاةٌ consolation; help

(أصل)

أَصْلٌ *pl.* أُصُولٌ origin, root, principle

إِفْرِيقِيَةُ, إِفْرِيقِيَا Africa

(افق)

أُفُقٌ *pl.* آفَاقٌ horizon

(اكد)

أَكَّدَ II to assure, confirm

تَأَكَّدَ (مِنْ) V to be assured (of)

أَكِيدٌ firm, certain

(اكل)

أَكَلَ (ـُ) *v.n.* أَكْلٌ to eat

أُكْلٌ food

(اكم)

أَكَمَةٌ *pl.* ـَاتٌ, آكَامٌ summit, hillock, rising ground

(ال)

أَلْ, اَلْ *definite article*

(الف)

أَلَّفَ II to compose, write, compile (a book, etc.)

آلَفَ III to be intimate with

أَلْفٌ *pl.* أُلُوفٌ, آلَافٌ thousand (1,000)

مَأْلُوفٌ customary, usual

مُؤَلِّفٌ composer, author

مُؤَلَّفَاتٌ (*pl.*) compositions, compilations

(الم)

آلَمَ III to pain

تَأَلَّمَ (مِنْ) VIII to suffer (from), be pained (by)

أَلَمٌ *pl.* آلَامٌ pain, grief

مُؤْلِمٌ painful

أَلْمَانِيَا Germany

أَلْمَانِيٌّ; اَلْأَلْمَانُ German, a German; the Germans

(اله)

إِلٰهٌ *pl.* آلِهَةٌ a god, divinity

اَللّٰهُ God

أُلُوهِيَّة divineness

(الى)

إِلَى to

أَنْ — (*with verb*) until

(امم)

أَمَّمَ II to nationalise (*mod.*)

أُمّ *pl.* أُمَّات, أُمَّهَات mother

أَمَامَ in front of, before

إِمَام *pl.* أَئِمَّة, أَيِمَّة Imam, religious leader, leader of prayer, leader

أُمَّة *pl.* أُمَم nation

أُمِّيّ illiterate

أَمْ or

أَمَّا . . . فَ as for . . .

إِمَّا . . . وَإِمَّا; إِمَّا . . . أَوْ either . . . or

إِمْبَرَاطُور *pl.* أَبَاطِرَة Emperor

إِمْبَرَاطُورِيَّة empire

(امر)

أَمَرَ (ـُ) to command, order

أَمْر *pl.* أَوَامِر command, order

أَمْر *pl.* أُمُور thing, affair

إِمَارَة rule, power; princedom

أَمِير *pl.* أُمَرَاء prince, ruler, Emir

مَأْمُور *pl.* مَأْمُورُون, مَآمِير official, functionary; district officer (in some Arab countries)

مُؤْتَمَر *pl.* ات — conference

أَمِيرِكَا, إِمْرِيكَا America

إِمْرِيكِيّ American

(امل)

أَمَلَ (ـُ) to hope, hope for

تَأَمَّلَ V (also with فِي) to look at, observe, study

أَمَل *pl.* آمَال hope

(امن)

أَمُنَ (ـُ) to be secure

أَمَّنَ II to insure (*mod.*), assure

آمَنَ (ب) IV to believe (in)

أَمَانَة faithfulness; security; a trust, secretariat.

أَمْن, أَمَان safety, protection, security

مَجْلِس الأَمْن Security Council

إِيمَان belief, faith

أَمِينٌ *pl.* أُمَنَاءُ faithful, trustworthy; pr. n. masc.

مُؤْمِنٌ believer, faithful (in religious sense), Moslem

(ان)

إِنْ if

إِلَّا (إِنْ لَا) if not; except

أَنْ (+*verb*) that *conj.*

أَنَّ (with *n.* or *pron.*) that *conj.*

إِنَّ verily, truly; that (after قَالَ)

إِنَّمَا indeed, in truth, only (*strong affirmative particle*)

(انن)

أَنَّةٌ moaning, lamenting *n.*

(انا)

أَنَا I

(انت)

أَنْتَ *m.* أَنْتِ *f.* أَنْتُمَا *dual* you

أَنْتُمْ *m.pl.* أَنْتُنَّ *f.pl.* you

اَلْأَنْدَلُسُ Andalusia, Spain

(انس)

أَنَّسَ II to render agreeable, to make friendly

إِنْسَانٌ man (human being)

إِنْسَانِيٌّ human *adj.*

أُنَاسٌ, نَاسٌ people, men (*pl.* of إِنْسَانٌ?)

نِسَاءٌ women

آنِسَةٌ young lady, miss (*mod.*)

(انف)

اِسْتَأْنَفَ X to appeal; begin anew

أَنْفٌ *pl.* أُنُوفٌ, آنَافٌ nose, forepart, point

آنِفًا formerly, before, above, aforesaid

إِنْجِلْتَرَّا, إِنْكِلْتَرَّا England

إِنْكِلِيزِيٌّ *pl.* إِنْكِلِيزٌ English(man)

(انى)

تَأَنَّى II to procrastinate, delay

(اهل)

أَهْلٌ *pl.* أَهَالٍ, أَهْلُونَ (*rare*) people, family

أَهْلًا وَسَهْلًا welcome!

مُؤَهِّلَاتٌ qualifications (*mod.*)

(او)

أَوْ or

(اوب)

آبَ (يَؤُوبُ) to return

أُورُبَّا Europe

أُورُبِّىّ European

(اول)

آلَةٌ pl. ـَاتٌ — instrument, tool, machine

آلِىٌّ mechanic(al)

آلِيَّاتٌ machines, mechanical things

أَوَّلُ fem. أُولَى pl. أَوَّلُونَ, أَوَائِلُ first

أَوَّلاً first adv.

(اون)

آنٌ, أَوَانٌ pl. آوِنَةٌ time, moment, season

اَلآنَ now

(اوى)

أَوَى (يَأْوِى) (إِلَى) to take refuge (with)

آوَى (يُؤْوِى) IV to harbour, shelter

مَأْوًى shelter, refuge

(اى)

أَىْ that is to say, i.e.

أَىٌّ f. أَيَّةٌ which? whichever, any

أَيُّهَا f. أَيَّتُهَا vocative particle, O, Oh

(ايا)

إِيَّاهُ, إِيَّاهَا him, her

(ايض)

أَيْضًا also

(اين)

أَيْنَ where?

مِنْ أَيْنَ whence?

ب

بِ (attached) in, by, with

(بأر)

بِئْرٌ pl. (f.) آبَارٌ well n.

(بأس)

بَئِسَ (ـَ) to be afflicted

بِئْسَ to be bad

بَؤُسَ (ـُ) to be brave

بَأْسٌ misfortune

لا — (مِنْ) never mind (about), no matter!

(بحث)

بَحَثَ (ـَ) (عَنْ) to investigate, examine, search for

بَاحَثَ III to discuss with, hold a discussion with

بَحْثٌ pl. أَبْحَاثٌ examination, enquiry, research

مُبَاحَثَة discussion

(بحر)

بَحْر *pl.* بُحُور, أَبْحُر, بِحَار sea; course (of a week, etc.)

بُحَيْرَة *pl.* — اتٌ lake

بَحَّار sailor

(بخت)

بَخْت luck, good fortune

بَخِيت *pl.* — ونَ lucky, fortunate

(بخر)

بَاخِرَة *pl.* بَوَاخِر steam-ship (*mod.*)

(بخل)

بُخْل greed, avarice

بَخِيل *pl.* بُخَلَاء greedy, avaricious

(بدد)

بُدّ escape

لَا بُدَّ; — مِنْ (+ أَنْ before *verb*) no doubt; it is inevitable

(بدأ)

بَدَأَ (ـَ) *v.n.* بَدْء to begin

اِبْتَدَأَ VIII to begin

اِبْتِدَاءً مِنْ beginning from

اِبْتِدَائِيّ elementary, primary

مَبْدَأ *pl.* مَبَادِئ principle, basis

(بدر)

بَادَرَ III to hasten

(بدل)

بَدَلَ (ـُ) to change, exchange *trans.*

اِسْتَبْدَلَ X to take in exchange

بَدَل, بَدِيل substitute

بَدَلًا عَنْ instead of

بَدْلَة suit of clothes (*mod.*)

(بدن)

بَدَن *pl.* أَبْدَان body

(بدو)

بَدَا (ـُ) to appear

بَادِيَة *pl.* بَوَادٍ desert

بَدْو Bedouin, Bedu (*coll.*)

بَدَوِيّ (a) Bedouin, nomad

(بذل)

بَذَلَ (ـُ) to give generously, squander

بَذَلَ جُهْدَهُ to do one's best, utmost

بِذْلَة *pl.* بِذَلَات everyday clothes

(برر)

بَرّ (*opp.* بَحْر) land

بَرًّا وَبَحْرًا by land and sea

بَرْبَرٌ Berbers

(برأ)

أَبْرَأَ IV to cure, make whole

بَرِيءٌ *pl.* أَبْرِيَاءُ innocent, not guilty

اَلْبُرْتُغَالُ, اَلْبُرْتُقَالُ; بُرْتُقَالٌ orange; Portugal

(برج)

بُرْجٌ *pl.* بُرُوجٌ tower, castle

(برح)

اَلْبَارِحَ yesterday

(برد)

بَرْدٌ cold *n.*

بَرَّادَةٌ refrigerator (*mod.*)

بَرِيدٌ *pl.* بُرُدٌ post, courier

بَارِدٌ cold *adj.*

بَرْدَانُ cold *adj.* (used of human beings)

مِبْرَدٌ *pl.* مَبَارِدُ file (instrument)

(برز)

بَارِزٌ prominent, outstanding

(برطع)

بَرْطَعَ *quad.* to move about, be restless

(برع)

بَارِعٌ excellent, distinguished, clever

(برق)

بَرْقٌ *pl.* بُرُوقٌ lightning

بَرْقِيَّةٌ telegram, telegraph (*mod.*)

إِبْرِيقٌ *pl.* أَبَارِيقُ pot, ewer

(برك)

بَارَكَ (فِي) III to bless

بَرَكَةٌ *pl.* ـَاتٌ — blessing

بِرْكَةٌ *pl.* بِرَكٌ pool, pond, tank

مُبَارَكٌ blessed; pr. n. masc.

بَرْلَمَانٌ *pl.* ـَاتٌ — Parliament (*mod.*)

(برمج)

بَرْنَامَجٌ *pl.* بَرَامِجُ scheme, programme

(برمل)

بِرْمِيلٌ *pl.* بَرَامِيلُ barrel, vat, cask

(بره)

بُرْهَةٌ *pl.* بُرُهَاتٌ, بُرَهٌ a period of time

(برهن)

بُرْهَانٌ *pl.* بَرَاهِينُ proof

(بستن)

بُسْتَانٌ *pl.* بَسَاتِينُ garden

(بسط)

بَسَطَ (ـُ) to spread out *trans.*; to please

اِنْبَسَطَ (مِنْ) VII to be pleased (at)

بِسَاطٌ *pl.* بُسُطٌ, أَبْسِطَةٌ carpet, rug

بَسِيطٌ *pl.* بُسَطَاءُ simple

مَبْسُوطٌ contented, happy, cheerful (*Syr.* and *Eg.*)

(بسل)

بَسَالَةٌ bravery, heroism

بَاسِلٌ *pl.* بُسَلَاءُ bold, brave, gallant

(بسم)

اِبْتَسَمَ VIII to smile

اِبْتِسَامٌ smile; pr. n.

بَاشَا *pl.* بَاشَوَاتٌ, بَاشَاوَاتٌ Pasha (title) (*Turk.*)

(بشر)

بَشَّرَ . . بِ II to give (anyone) good news about (something)

بَاشَرَ III to be busy with, manage, direct, do directly (as opposed to indirectly)

اِسْتَبْشَرَ (بِ) X to rejoice at (good news)

بُشْرٌ good news

بَشَرٌ, بَشَرِيَّةٌ mankind, humanity

مُبَاشِرٌ direct

(بشع)

بَشِعٌ ugly, repulsive, deformed

(بصص)

بَصٌّ, بَاصٌّ *pl.* ـَاتٌ (*Eur.*) bus

(بصر)

بَصَّرَ II to open the eyes, enlighten anyone

أَبْصَرَ IV to see

اَلْبَصْرَةُ Basra

(بصق)

بَصَقَ (ـُ) to spit

(بصل)

بَصَلٌ onion, bulb

(بضع)

بِضْعٌ, بِضْعَةٌ some (number between 3 and 10)

بِضَاعَةٌ *pl.* بَضَائِعُ goods, wares

(بطط)

بَطَّةٌ *pl.* بَطٌّ duck

بَطَاطَا, بَطَاطِسُ potatoes

(بطأ)

بَطُؤَ (ـُ), أَبْطَأَ IV to be slow, go slowly

بُطْءٌ slowness

بَطِيءٌ slow, tardy

(بطح)

بَطْحَاءُ, بَطْحَةٌ *pl.* بِطَاحٌ, بَطْحَاوَاتٌ a wide valley; dry bed of torrent

(بطر)

بَيْطَرَ to practice veterinary surgery

بَيْطَارٌ *pl.* بَيَاطِرَةٌ veterinary surgeon

بَطَّارِيَّةٌ (*Eur.*) battery

(بطل)

بَطَالَةٌ idleness, uselessness

بَاطِلٌ vain, useless

بَطَلٌ *pl.* أَبْطَالٌ hero

(بطن)

بَطْنٌ *pl.* بُطُونٌ belly, abdomen

بَاطِنٌ *pl.* بَوَاطِنُ interior, hidden

(بعث)

بَعَثَ (ـَ) to send

بَاعِثٌ *pl.* بَوَاعِثُ cause, motive, reason

مَبْعُوثٌ envoy, delegate

(بعد)

بَعُدَ (ـُ) (عَنْ) to be far (from)

بَعَّدَ II to make distant

بَاعَدَ III to keep anybody away

أَبْعَدَ IV to remove *trans.*

اِبْتَعَدَ VIII to go far (from); part; quit

بُعْدٌ distance

بَعْدَ after *prep.*

بَعْدُ afterwards

بَعْدُ yet (with *neg.* = not yet)

بَعِيدٌ far, distant, remote

(بعض)

بَعْض one of, some

بَغْدَادُ Baghdad

(بغض)

بُغْضَاء hatred, detestation

(بغل)

بَغْل pl. أَبْغَال, بِغَال mule

(بغى)

اِبْتَغَى VIII to desire, wish for

(بقر)

بَقَر pl. أَبْقَار oxen, ox

(بقع)

بُقْعَة pl. بُقَع, بِقَاع depression; plain in hilly country; valley

(بقل)

بَقْل pl. بُقُول vegetable, green

بَقَّال greengrocer

(بقى)

بَقِيَ (َ) to remain, stay

بَقَاء remaining, existence v.n.

دَارُ ٱلْبَقَاءِ Heaven

بَاقٍ, بَاقِيَة remainder, rest

(بكر)

بَاكِرًا early, in the morning, tomorrow

(بكم)

أَبْكَمُ pl. بُكْم dumb, mute

(بكى)

بَكَى (ِ) to weep

أَبْكَى IV to cause to weep

بُكَاء weeping, v.n.

(بل)

بَلْ but, nay rather

(بلل)

مَبْلُول wet, moistened

(بلح)

بَلَح dates (coll.)

(بلد)

بِلَاد pl. بُلْدَان country

بَلَد, بَلْدَة pl. بِلَاد, بُلْدَان town, district (also country)

بَلَدِيَّة municipality

(بلس)

إِبْلِيس pl. أَبَالِسَة devil, Satan, Iblis

بُولِيس police

(بلع)

بَلَعَ (ـَ) to swallow

(بلغ)

بَلَغَ (ـُ) to reach

بَلَّغَ II to convey, inform

بَالَغَ III to exaggerate, over-reach

بَلَاغ *pl.* ـَاتٌ — message, announcement, communiqué

بَلَاغَةٌ rhetoric

بَلِيغٌ *pl.* بُلَغَاءُ eloqu nt

مَبْلَغٌ *pl.* مَبَالِغُ sum (of money), amount

(بلو)

بَلَا (ـُ) to test, try, afflict

(بلى)

بَالٍ decayed, rotten, tattered

(بنن)

بُنٌّ coffee, coffee berries

بُنِّيٌّ coffee-coloured, brown

(بندق)

بُنْدُقِيَّةٌ rifle, gun

(بنى)

بَنَى (ـِ) to build

بِنَاءٌ *pl.* أَبْنِيَةٌ building, *n.*

بِنَاءً عَلَى in accordance with

بِنَايَةٌ *pl.* ـَاتٌ — edifice, building

اِبْنٌ *pl.* أَبْنَاءٌ, بَنُونَ son

بِنْتٌ, اِبْنَةٌ *pl.* بَنَاتٌ girl, daughter

بَنَّاءٌ *pl.* بَنَّاؤُونَ mason, builder

مَبْنًى *pl.* مَبَانٍ building, edifice

(بهج)

اِبْتَهَجَ VIII to rejoice

(بوب)

بَابٌ *pl.* أَبْوَابٌ door, gate; chapter; class

بَوَّابٌ doorkeeper

(بوح)

بَاحَ (ـُ) to reveal

أَبَاحَ IV to permit

(بون)

بَوْنٌ interval; difference

(بيت)

بَاتَ (ـِ) to pass the night, sojourn

بَيْتٌ *pl.* بُيُوتٌ house, tent

بَيْتٌ *pl.* أَبْيَاتٌ verse

بَائِتٌ stale, dry (bread, food)

بَيْرُوت Beirut

(بيض)

اِبْيَضَّ IX to be, or become white

بَيْضَة، بَيْض egg, eggs

أَبْيَض *f.* بَيْضَاء *pl.* بِيض white

الدَّارُ ٱلْبَيْضَاء Casablanca (in Morocco)

(بيع)

بَاعَ (ـِ) to sell

بَائِع *pl.* بَاعَة seller

بَيْع، مَبِيع sale

(بين)

بَيَّنَ II to make clear, explain

اِسْتَبَانَ X to be clear; recognize as evident

بَيْنَ between, among

بَيْنَا، بَيْنَمَا while, during

بَيَان *pl.* ـات declaration, announcement, statement, explanation

ت

(تبن)

تِبْن straw

(تبع)

تَبِعَ (ـَ) to follow, belong to

تَتَبَّعَ V, اِتَّبَعَ VIII to follow

(تبغ)

تِبْغ tobacco

(تجر)

تَاجِر *pl.* تُجَّار merchant

تِجَارَة commerce, trade

(تحت)

تَحْتَ under, below

(تحف)

تُحْفَة *pl.* تُحَف precious article, gift, masterpiece

مَتْحَف *pl.* مَتَاحِف museum

(ترب)

تُرَاب *pl.* أَتْرِبَة earth, dust

تُرْبَة *pl.* تُرَب soil, cemetery, tomb

(ترجم)

تَرْجَمَ to translate, interpret

تَرْجَمَة *pl.* تَرَاجِم translation

مُتَرْجِم translator, interpreter

مُتَرْجَم translated

تُرْجُمَان *pl.* تَرَاجِمَة guide, dragoman

(ترع)

تُرْعَةٌ *pl.* تُرَعٌ channel, canal

(ترك)

تَرَكَ (ـُ) to leave, abandon

تُرْكِيَّا Turkey

تُرْكِيٌّ *pl.* تُرْكٌ *pl. pl.* أَتْرَاكٌ Turk, Turkish

(تسع)

تِسْعٌ *f.* تِسْعَةٌ nine

تِسْعُونَ ninety

تَاسِعٌ ninth

تُسْعٌ *pl.* أَتْسَاعٌ a ninth (fraction)

(تعب)

أَتْعَبَ IV to make tired, tire

تَعَبٌ tiredness

تَعْبَانُ tired

(تعس)

تَعَاسَةٌ misfortune

(تفح)

تُفَّاحٌ apples (*coll.*)

تُفَّاحَةٌ single apple

(تقن)

مُتْقَنٌ solid, strong, well-made

(تلل)

تَلٌّ *pl.* تِلَالٌ small hill, hillock

تِلِغْرَافٌ telegram, telegraph

(تلمذ)

تِلْمِيذٌ *pl.* تَلَامِيذُ، تَلَامِذَةٌ pupil, disciple

(تلو)

تَلَا (ـُ) to read, recite; follow

(تمم)

تَمَّ (ـِ) to be complete, completed, finished

أَتَمَّ IV to complete *trans.*

تَمَامٌ completion, end, perfection

تَمَامًا completely, exactly

تَامٌّ perfect, complete

تَمْتَمَ to stammer

(تمر)

تَمْرٌ dried dates

(توّ)

تَوٌّ single, sole (*antiq.*); تَوًّا now, immediately

(توب)

تَابَ (ـُ) to repent

(توت)

تُوتٌ mulberry

(توج)

تَوَّجَ II to crown

تَاجٌ *pl.* تِيجَانٌ crown

(تور)

اَلتَّوْرَاةُ The Torah, Pentateuch (loosely, the Old Testament)

تُونُسُ Tunisia

(تين)

تِينٌ figs

ث

(ثأر)

ثَأْرٌ vengeance (bloodfeud)

(ثبت)

ثَبُتَ (ُ) to be firm, sure

ثَابِتٌ firm, sure, established

(ثخن)

ثَخِينٌ thick, fat

(ثرو)

ثَرَاءٌ, ثَرْوَةٌ wealth, riches

مُثْرٍ wealthy, rich man

(ثعلب)

ثَعْلَبٌ *pl.* ثَعَالِبُ fox

(ثغر)

ثَغْرٌ *pl.* ثُغُورٌ frontier, mouth, boundary

(ثقف)

ثَقَافَةٌ education, culture

مُثَقَّفٌ educated, cultured

(ثقل)

ثَقُلَ (ُ) to be heavy

ثَقِيلٌ heavy

(ثلث)

ثَلٰثٌ, ثَلَاثٌ *f.* ثَلٰثَةٌ, ثَلَاثَةٌ three

ثَلٰثُونَ, ثَلَاثُونَ thirty

ثَالِثٌ third (ordinal)

ثُلْثٌ a third (fraction)

مُثَلَّثٌ *pl.* — اتٌ triangle

يَوْمُ الثَّلَاثَاءِ Tuesday

(ثلج)

ثَلْجٌ *pl.* ثُلُوجٌ snow, ice

ثَلَّاجَةٌ refrigerator (*mod.*)

(ثمم)

ثُمَّ then, moreover, thereupon

ثَمَّ there, yonder

(ثمر)

ثَمَرٌ ثَمَرَةٌ *pl.* أَثْمَارٌ fruit, fruits

مُثْمِرٌ fruitful, productive

(ثمن)

ثَمَنٌ *pl.* أَثْمَانٌ price

ثَمِينٌ expensive, valuable

ثَمَانٍ *f.* ثَمَانِيَةٌ eight

ثَمَانُونَ eighty

ثَامِنٌ eighth (ordinal)

ثُمْنٌ *pl.* أَثْمَانٌ an eighth (fraction)

(ثنى)

اِسْتَثْنَى X to except, set aside, exclude

ثَنَاءٌ praise

فِى أَثْنَاءِ, أَثْنَاءَ during

اِثْنَانِ *f.* اِثْنَتَانِ two

يَوْمُ الاِثْنَيْنِ Monday

ثَانٍ *f.* ثَانِيَةٌ second (ordinal)

ثَانِيًا secondly

ثَانِيَةٌ *pl.* ثَوَانٍ second (unit of time)

(ثوب)

ثَوْبٌ *pl.* ثِيَابٌ garment

(ثور)

ثَارَ (ـُ) to rise up, break out; revolt, rebel

أَثَارَ IV to arouse, incite

ثَائِرٌ *pl.* ثُوَّارٌ rebel, rebellious

ثَوْرَةٌ revolt, insurrection

ثَوْرٌ *pl.* ثِيرَانٌ, أَثْوَارٌ bull

(ثوم)

ثُومٌ garlic

ج

(جبب)

جُبَّةٌ *pl.* جُبَبٌ top-coat, long cloak

(جبر)

جَبَرَ (ـُ), أَجْبَرَ IV (*with* على) to compel, oblige, force

إِجْبَارِيٌّ compulsory

جَبَّارٌ *pl.* جَبَابِرَةٌ mighty, powerful, giant

(جبس)

جِبْسٌ lime, gypsum, plaster

(جبل)

جَبَلٌ *pl.* جِبَالٌ mountain

(جبن)

جَبِينٌ *pl.* جُبُنٌ forehead, brow

جَبَانٌ *pl.* جُبَنَاءُ coward

جُبْنٌ, جُبْنَةٌ cheese

(جبه)

جَبْهَةٌ *pl.* جَبَهَاتٌ brow, forehead, front

(جبى)

جِبَايَةٌ tax, tribute

جَابٍ tax-collector

(جثث)

جُثَّةٌ *pl.* جُثَثٌ corpse, body

(جدد)

جَدَّ (ـِـ) to be new; to be serious

جَدَّدَ II to renew

تَجَدَّدَ V to be renewed

جِدٌّ seriousness

جِدًّا very

جَدٌّ *pl.* أَجْدَادٌ grandfather, ancestor

جَدَّةٌ grandmother

جُدَّةٌ Jidda (town in Arabia)

جَدِيدٌ *pl.* جُدُدٌ new

(جدر)

جَدِيرٌ (بِ) worthy (of)

جِدَارٌ *pl.* جُدُرٌ, جُدْرَانٌ wall

(جدل)

جَدْوَلٌ *pl.* جَدَاوِلُ brook; list, table

(جذب)

جَذَبَ (ـِـ) to attract, draw

(جذع)

جِذْعٌ *pl.* جُذُوعٌ trunk (of tree, body); beam

(جرر)

جَرَّ (ـُـ) to drag, draw

جَرَّةٌ *pl.* جِرَارٌ jar

(جرأ)

جَرُؤَ (ـُـ) to be brave, dare

جَرِيءٌ *pl.* أَجْرِاءُ brave

(جرب)

جَرَّبَ II to try, put to test, tempt

تَجْرِبَةٌ *pl.* تَجَارِبُ trial, temptation, experiment

جَوْرَبٌ *pl.* ـَـاتٌ, أَجْرِبَةٌ sock, stocking

(جرح)

جَرَحَ (ـَـ) to wound, hurt, injure

جَرْحٌ *pl.* جُرُوحٌ wound, cut, injury

جِرَاحَةٌ surgery (art of)

جَرَّاحٌ surgeon

جَرِيحٌ *m.* and *f.*, *pl.* جَرْحَى wounded man, or woman

مَجْرُوحٌ *pl.* مَجَارِيحُ wounded (man)

(جرد)

جَرِيدَةٌ *pl.* جَرَائِدُ newspaper, journal (*mod.*)

(جرم)

أَجْرَمَ IV to commit a crime

جُرْمٌ *pl.* أَجْرَامٌ crime, sin

جَرِيمَةٌ *pl.* جَرَائِمُ crime

مُجْرِمٌ criminal

(جرى)

جَرَى (ـِ) to run, flow, happen

أَجْرَى IV to carry out, execute

جَارٍ running, current

جَارِيَةٌ *pl.* جَوَارٍ slave-girl, servant-girl

إِجْرَاءَاتٌ steps, measures (*mod.*)

لَازِمَةٌ — necessary steps

(جزأ)

جُزْءٌ *pl.* أَجْزَاءٌ part, portion

أَجْزَائِيٌّ chemist, druggist, apothecary

(جزر)

جَزَرَ (ـُ) to ebb (sea)

جَزْرٌ ebb

جَزَّارٌ butcher, slaughterer

جَزِيرَةٌ *pl.* جُزُرٌ, جَزَائِرُ island

شِبْهُ جَزِيرَةٍ peninsula

اَلْجَزَائِرُ Algeria, Algiers

(جزل)

جَزِيلٌ abundant, much

(جزى)

جَازَى III to reward, requite, punish

جَزَاءٌ, مُجَازَاةٌ requittal, reward

جِزْيَةٌ poll tax

(جسس)

جَاسُوسٌ *pl.* جَوَاسِيسُ spy

(جسد)

جَسَدٌ *pl.* أَجْسَادٌ body

(جسر)

جِسْر *pl.* جُسُور bridge

جَسَارَة courage, audacity

جَسُور bold, courageous

(جسم)

جِسْم *pl.* أَجْسَام body

(جعل)

جَعَلَ (ـَ) to place, put, make (+ *imperf.*, to begin to)

(جفف)

جَافّ dry, withered

(جفن)

جَفْن *pl.* أَجْفَان, جُفُون eye-lid

(جلل)

جُلّ main part of a thing; gist

جَلَالَة majesty

جَلَل serious, momentous

جَلِيل *pl.* أَجِلَّاء exalted, great; pr. n. masc.

اَلْجَلِيل Galilee

مَجَلَّة magazine, book, review (*mod.*)

(جلب)

جَلَبَ (ـُ) to gather, bring, import

(جلد)

جَلَّدَ II to bind (book); skin

جِلْد *pl.* جُلُود skin, hide, leather

مُجَلَّد *pl.* ات — volume, tome

جَلِيد snow, ice

(جلس)

جَلَسَ (ـِ) to sit

جَالَسَ III to sit with

أَجْلَسَ IV to seat, make one sit

جَلْسَة *pl.* جَلَسَات session, sitting

مَجْلِس *pl.* مَجَالِس council, assembly, parliament

(جمع)

جَمَعَ (ـَ) to gather, add

اِجْتَمَعَ VIII to gather together, assemble

ب — to meet (anyone)

يَوْمُ الْجُمْعَة Friday

جَمَاعَة party, community, group

جَمْعِيَّة society, league, association, (trade-) union

اِجْتِمَاع *pl.* ات — meeting, gathering, social life

اِجْتِمَاعِيٌّ social

جَامِعٌ comprehensive

جَامِعٌ *pl.* جَوَامِعُ mosque

جَامِعَةٌ university; league

جَمِيعٌ all

جَمِيعًا all together, *adv.*

أَجْمَعُ *pl.* ـُونَ whole, all

إِجْمَاعٌ unanimity, agreement on a matter

مَجْمُوعٌ *pl.* مَجَامِيعُ total; united

مَجْمُوعَةٌ collection

مَجْمَعٌ *pl.* مَجَامِعُ assembly, learned body

اَلْمُجْتَمَعُ society (as a whole)

(جمل)

جَمَلٌ *pl.* جِمَالٌ camel

جَمَالٌ beauty

جُمْلَةٌ *pl.* جُمَلٌ sum, total; sentence, phrase

بِالْجُمْلَةِ in the aggregate; wholesale (commerce)

إِجْمَالًا generally speaking, in general

جَمِيلٌ beautiful, handsome; good deed, kindness; pr. n. masc.

(جمهر)

جُمْهُورٌ *pl.* جَمَاهِيرُ public, crowd; the masses

جُمْهُورِيَّةٌ *pl.* ـَاتٌ republic

جُمْهُورِيٌّ republican

(جنن)

جَنَّ (ـُ) to go mad

جُنُونٌ madness

جِنَّةٌ, جِنٌّ jinn, genii, demon

جَنَّةٌ garden, Paradise

جُنَيْنَةٌ *pl.* ـَاتٌ, جَنَائِنُ (small) garden

مَجْنُونٌ *pl.* مَجَانِينُ madman, mad

(جنب)

جَانِبٌ *pl.* جَوَانِبُ side

بِجَانِبِ, بِجَنْبِ beside

جَنُوبٌ the south

جَنَابٌ polite form of address

أَجْنَبِيٌّ *pl.* أَجَانِبُ foreign, foreigner, strange, stranger

(جنح)

جَنَاحٌ *pl.* أَجْنِحَةٌ wing

(جند)

جَنَّدَ II to levy troops, conscript

جُنْدٌ *pl.* جُنُودٌ; جُنْدِيٌّ troop, army; soldier

(جنس)

جِنْسٌ *pl.* أَجْنَاسٌ kind, class, sex, species, genus

جِنْسِيَّةٌ nationality (*mod.*)

(جنى)

جَنَى (ـِ) to gather (fruit, etc.)

جُنَيْهٌ *pl.* ـَاتٌ — pound, guinea

(جهد)

اِجْتَهَدَ VIII to strive, work hard, be diligent

جُهْدٌ *pl.* جُهُودٌ striving, zeal, effort

جِهَادٌ Jihad, holy war

مَجْهُودٌ *pl.* ـَاتٌ — effort

(جهر)

جَاهَرَ III to declare openly

(جهز)

جَهَّزَ II to equip, get ready, fit out, furnish

جِهَازٌ *pl.* أَجْهِزَةٌ apparatus, set, machine, outfit

جَاهِزٌ ready-made, fitted

(جهش)

أَجْهَشَ IV to burst into tears

(جهل)

جَهِلَ (ـَ) to be ignorant, not to know

تَجَاهَلَ VI to feign ignorance

اَلْجَاهِلِيَّةُ the Days of Ignorance (period before Islam)

جَاهِلٌ *pl.* جُهَّالٌ ignorant

جَهُولٌ (very) ignorant

مَجْهُولٌ unknown

(جهنم)

جَهَنَّمُ hell

(جوّ)

جَوٌّ sky, atmosphere, air

جَوِّيٌّ air, *adj.*

(جوب)

أَجَابَ (عَلَى) IV to answer, reply to

جَوَابٌ *pl.* أَجْوِبَةٌ answer, reply

(جوخ)

جَوْخَانٌ *pl.* جَوَاخِينُ hearth, place for drying dates

(جود)

جَادَ (ـُ) to excel in, be good at

جَوْدَةٌ goodness, excellence

جَوَادٌ generous

جَوَادٌ *pl.* جِيَادٌ swift horse, steed

جَيِّدٌ good, excellent

جَيِّدًا well, *adj.*

(جور)

جَاوَرَ III to adjoin, be neighbour to

جِوَارٌ; بِجِوَارِ neighbourhood; in the neighbourhood of, near, by

جَارٌ *pl.* جِيرَانٌ neighbour

مُجَاوِرٌ neighbouring, next-door

(جوز)

جَازَ (ـُ) to pass, be allowable, be permitted

تَجَاوَزَ VI to exceed, go beyond

جَوْزٌ nut

جَوَازُ سَفَرٍ *pl.* — جَوَازَاتُ passport

إِجَازَةٌ permission, licence, leave

جَائِزٌ passing, lawful, permitted

جَائِزَةٌ *pl.* جَوَائِزُ prize

(جول)

جَالَ (ـُ) to travel, roam

تَجَوَّلَ V to wander

(جوع)

جَائِعٌ hungry

(جوف)

جَوْفٌ *pl.* أَجْوَافٌ hollow *n.*, belly

(جوهر)

جَوْهَرٌ *pl.* جَوَاهِرُ jewel, essence, nature

(جيأ)

جَاءَ (ـِ) to come

— بِ to bring

(جيب)

جَيْبٌ *pl.* جُيُوبٌ pocket

(جيش)

جَيْشٌ *pl.* جُيُوشٌ army

(جيل)

جِيلٌ *pl.* أَجْيَالٌ generation, age

ح

(حبب)

أَحَبَّ IV to love, like

حُبٌّ, مَحَبَّةٌ love

حَبِيبٌ *pl.* أَحْبَابٌ, أَحِبَّاءُ friend, beloved

مَحْبُوبٌ beloved

حَبٌّ *pl.* حُبُوبٌ grain, seed, pill, berry

(حبر)

حَبْرٌ *pl.* أَحْبَارٌ learned man, doctor, rabbi (*antiq.*)

حِبْرٌ ink

(حبس)

حَبَسَ (ـِ) to imprison, shut up

(حبل)

حَبْلٌ *pl.* حِبَالٌ rope

حُبْلَى *pl.* حَبَالَى pregnant

(حتى)

حَتَّى until, even, so that

(حثو)

حَثَا (ـُ) to pour (dust)

(حجج)

حَجَّ (ـُ) to perform the pilgrimage (to Mecca)

حِجٌّ pilgrimage (to Mecca)

حَاجٌّ *pl.* حُجَّاجٌ pilgrim, Haji

(حجب)

حَجَبَ (ـُ) to conceal, hide veil

اِحْتَجَبَ VIII to conceal oneself

حَاجِبٌ *pl.* حَوَاجِبُ eyebrow

— *pl.* حُجَّابٌ door-keeper, chamberlain

مَحْجُوبٌ concealed, veiled

(حجر)

حَجَرٌ *pl.* أَحْجَارٌ, حِجَارَةٌ, حِجَرٌ stone

حُجْرَةٌ *pl.* حُجَرٌ, حُجُرَاتٌ room, chamber, quarter

حِجْرٌ lap, knees (*Eg.*)

(حدد)

حَدَّ (ـُ) to limit

حَدَّدَ II to limit, confine; define; sharpen

حَدٌّ *pl.* حُدُودٌ boundary, limit, frontier

حَدِيدٌ *n.* iron

حَدَّادٌ blacksmith

(حدب)

أَحْدَبُ hunch-backed, hump-backed

(حدث)

حَدَثَ (ـُ) to happen, occur

حَدَّثَ II to narrate to

أَحْدَثَ IV to cause to happen, bring into being

تَحَدَّثَ V to relate a thing, speak, converse

تَحَادَثَ VI to converse (with one another)

حَادِثٌ, حَادِثَةٌ *pl.* حَوَادِثُ event, accident; news

حَدِيثٌ *pl.* حِدَاثٌ new, recent

حَدِيثٌ *pl.* أَحَادِيثُ story, Hadith (tradition of the Prophet); talk, conversation

مُحَدِّثٌ relater of Tradition

(حدر)

إِنْحَدَرَ VII to come or go down, descend

(حدق)

حَدِيقَةٌ *pl.* حَدَائِقُ park, large garden

(حدو)

حِدْوَةٌ horseshoe

(حرر)

حَرَّرَ II to write, edit; liberate

حَرٌّ, حَرَارَةٌ heat

حُرِّيَّةٌ freedom, liberty

حَرِيرٌ *pl.* حَرَائِرُ silk

حُرٌّ *pl.* أَحْرَارٌ free, freeman

حَارٌّ hot

تَحْرِيرٌ *pl.* تَحَارِيرُ writing, editing letter; freedom, liberty

مُحَرِّرٌ editor

(حرب)

حَارَبَ III to go to war with, fight with

تَحَارَبَ VI to fight each other

حَرْبٌ (*f.*) *pl.* حُرُوبٌ war

مِحْرَابٌ *pl.* مَحَارِيبُ niche in mosque, direction of Mecca

(حرث)

حَرَثَ (ـُـ) *v.n.* حَرْثٌ to till the soil, plough

أَحْرَثَ IV to cause to plough

حَارِثٌ ploughman

أَبُو ٱلْحَارِثِ name for a lion

مِحْرَاثٌ *pl.* مَحَارِيثُ plough

(حرز)

أَحْرَزَ IV to guard, look after, preserve; obtain

(حرس)

حَرَسَ (ـُـ) to guard, watch

حَارِسٌ *pl.* حُرَّاسٌ watchful, guard, sentry

(حرف)

اِنْحَرَفَ (عَنْ) VII to swerve, deviate (from)

حَرْفٌ (*m.* or *f.*) *pl.* حُرُوفٌ, أَحْرُفٌ letter (of alphabet); particle (gram.)

حِرْفَةٌ *pl.* حِرَفٌ trade, craft

(حرق)

حَرَقَ (ـِ), أَحْرَقَ IV to burn *trans.*

اِحْتَرَقَ VIII to be burned

حَرِيقٌ fire, conflagration

(حرك)

حَرَّكَ II to move *trans.*

تَحَرَّكَ V to move *intrans.*

حَرَكَةٌ movement; vowel point; traffic (*mod.*)

مُحَرِّكٌ *pl.* ـاتٌ engine (*mod.*)

(حرم)

حَرَمَ (ـِ) to refuse, forbid

حَرَّمَ II to forbid (in religion)

اِحْتَرَمَ VIII to venerate, honour, respect

حُرْمَةٌ *pl.* حُرَمٌ woman, wife (Moslem)

حَرَامٌ unlawful (in religion); sacred

حَرَامِيٌّ *pl.* حَرَامِيَّةٌ thief

(حرى)

تَحَرَّى V to inquire into, investigate

تَحَرٍّ *pl.* تَحَرِّيَاتٌ inquiry, investigation

(حزب)

حِزْبٌ *pl.* أَحْزَابٌ party (political, etc.)

(حزن)

حَزِنَ (ـَ) to be sad

حُزْنٌ *pl.* أَحْزَانٌ sadness

حَزِينٌ, حَزِنٌ, مَحْزُونٌ sad

(حسس)

أَحَسَّ بِ IV to feel; be concerned, aware of

(حسب)

حَسَبَ (ـُ); حَسِبَ (ـِ) to count, reckon, calculate; think, esteem

عَلَى حَسَبِ, حَسَبَ in accordance with

حِسَابٌ *pl.* ـاتٌ account, reckoning; regard, esteem

(حسد)

حَسَدَ (ـُـ) to envy, grudge

(حسن)

أَحْسَنَ IV to be good to, charitable towards; know a subject well, excel in, make well

إِسْتَحْسَنَ X to approve, admire, esteem good, think best, recommend

حُسْنٌ beauty

حَسَنٌ good, handsome; pr. n. m.

حُسَيْنٌ Hussein

أَحْسَنُ better, best

(حشف)

حَشَفٌ (*coll.*) bad dates

(حصص)

حِصَّةٌ *pl.* حِصَصٌ part, share, portion

(حصد)

حَصَدَ (ـُـ) to mow, reap

حَصَادٌ harvest, harvest-time

(حصل)

حَصَلَ (ـُـ) *v.n.* حُصُولٌ to happen; to acquire, obtain (*with* عَلَى)

حَصَّلَ II to attain, acquire, realise

تَحَصَّلَ V to result, be obtained, realised

حَاصِلٌ *pl.* حَوَاصِلُ, ـَاتٌ — result, product

مَحْصُولٌ *pl.* مَحَاصِيلُ, ـَاتٌ — produce

(حصن)

حِصْنٌ *pl.* حُصُونٌ fortress

حِصَانٌ *pl.* حُصُنٌ, أَحْصِنَةٌ horse

(حصو)

أَحْصَى IV to number, count, take census

(حضر)

حَضَرَ (ـُـ) to be present, attend

أَحْضَرَ IV to bring (a person, thing); to cause to attend

إِحْتَضَرَ VIII to be on the point of death

إِسْتَحْضَرَ X to summon; to get ready, prepare

حَضْرَةٌ *pl.* حَضَرَاتٌ presence, polite form of address

حُضُورٌ presence

حَاضِرٌ ready, present

حَاضِرَةٌ capital city

تَحْضِيرِيّ preparatory

(حطط)

حَطَّ (ـُ) to put, put down

مَحَطَّةٌ station (railway, etc.)

(حطب)

حَطَبٌ wood, firewood

(حظظ)

حَظٌّ *pl.* حُظُوظٌ happiness, luck

مَحْظُوظٌ happy, lucky

(حفد)

حَفِيدٌ *pl.* أَحْفَادٌ grandchild

(حفر)

حَفَرَ (ـُ) to dig

حَافِرٌ *pl.* حَوَافِرُ hoof

(حفظ)

حَفِظَ (ـَ) *v.n.* حِفْظٌ to keep, preserve, guard, retain; commit to memory, learn by heart

حَافِظٌ one who has learnt the Qur'ān by heart

مُحَافِظٌ guardian, keeper; governor (in some Arab countries)

مُحَافَظَةٌ governorate, district

(حفل)

حَفَلَ (ـِ) to gather, assemble, *intrans.*

بِـ — to celebrate (feast, etc.)

اِحْتَفَلَ لِ VIII to receive with honour

حَفْلَةٌ crowd of people, celebration

اِحْتِفَالٌ *pl.* ـَاتٌ — celebration, festivity, pomp

حَافِلٌ (بِ) full (of, with)

مَحْفِلٌ *pl.* مَحَافِلُ celebration, party, gathering

(حقق)

حَقَّ (ـِ) to be true, right

حَقَّقَ II to verify, confirm

اِسْتَحَقَّ X to deserve, merit; to fall due (payment)

حَقٌّ *pl.* حُقُوقٌ right, truth, worth, law

حَقٌّ right, true, *adj.*; worthy of (*with* بِ)

حَقًّا in reality, truly

حَقِيقَةٌ *pl.* حَقَائِقُ truth, reality

فِي ٱلْحَقِيقَةِ, حَقِيقَةً truly, really

(حقر)

حَقِير humble, despised

(حقل)

حَقْل *pl.* حُقُول field

(حكر)

إِحْتَكَرَ VIII to buy up (especially grain); to withhold stocks against high price; to corner the market

(حكم)

حَكَمَ (ـُ) to rule; govern, judge

حُكْم *pl.* أَحْكَام rule, order, authority, law; sentence (judgement)

حِكْمَة *pl.* حِكَم wisdom, aphorism, witticism

حُكُومَة government

حَاكِم *pl.* حُكَّام ruler, governor

حَكِيم *pl.* حُكَمَاء wise (man), doctor

مَحْكَمَة *pl.* مَحَاكِم tribunal, court of law

(حكى)

حَكَى (ـِ) to relate, speak

حِكَايَة story

(حلل)

حَلَّ (ـُ) to solve (a problem); dissolve (a solid), loosen

— (ـُ) to alight, abide, settle

. . . مَحَلَّ — to fill the place of

حَلَّ (ـِ) to be lawful (in religion)

حَلَّلَ II to analyse

إِنْحَلَّ VII to be loosened, solved, cease

إِحْتَلَّ VIII to occupy (of a country)

حَلّ solving, dissolving, solution

حُلُول coming (of time); alighting

حَلَال (*opp.* حَرَام) lawful, right, allowed (relig.)

مَحَلّ *pl.* ـَات, مَحَالّ place

مَحَلَّة quarter of a town

مَحَلِّيّ local

(حلب)

حَلِيب milk

حَلَب Aleppo (in Syria)

(حلف)

حَلَفَ (ـِ) *v.n.* حَلْف to swear (an oath)

إِسْتَحْلَفَ X to make swear, give an oath

حِلْفٌ *pl.* أَحْلَافٌ pact, alliance,

حَلِيفٌ *pl.* حُلَفَاءُ ally, confederate

(حلق)

حَلَقَ (ـِ) *v.n.* حِلَاقَةٌ to shave

حَلْقٌ *pl.* أَحْلَاقٌ throat

حَلْقَةٌ *pl.* حَلَقَاتٌ link, ring, circle

حَلَّاقٌ barber

(حلك)

حَالِكٌ dark, black

(حلم)

حَلَمَ (ـُ) to dream

حُلْمٌ *pl.* أَحْلَامٌ dream

حَلِيمٌ *pl.* حُلَمَاءُ gentle, forbearing, mild; pr. n. m.

(حلو)

حَلَاوَةٌ sweetness, sweetmeat

حَلْوَى, حَلَاوَى sweetmeat, halva

حُلْوٌ sweet, agreeable

(حمم)

حَمَّامٌ *pl.* ـَاتٌ — bath

(حمد)

حَمِدَ (ـَ) *v.n.* حَمْدٌ to praise

مُحَمَّدٌ, أَحْمَدُ, مَحْمُودٌ Muhammad, Ahmad, Mahmud

(حمر)

إِحْمَرَّ IX to be, become, red

أَحْمَرُ *f.* حَمْرَاءُ *pl.* حُمْرٌ red

حِمَارٌ *pl.* حَمِيرٌ ass, donkey

(حمض)

حَامِضٌ sour, acid, *adj.*

(حمص)

حِمْصُ Homs (in Syria)

(حمق)

حُمْقٌ stupidity

أَحْمَقُ *pl.* حُمْقٌ stupid, a fool

(حمل)

حَمَلَ (ـِ) to carry, bear; to attack, charge (*with* عَلَى); to induce to (*with* عَلَى)

إِحْتَمَلَ VIII to bear, suffer, endure; be probable or possible

حِمْلٌ *pl.* أَحْمَالٌ load, burden

حَمْلَةٌ attack, charge in battle

حَمَّالٌ porter, carrier

حَامِلٌ (*f.*) pregnant

مُحْتَمَلٌ probable, possible, bearable

(حمو)

حَمٌ *pl.* أَحْمَاءٌ father-in-law (with following *gen.* حَمُو)

حَمَاةٌ *pl.* حَمَوَاتٌ mother-in-law; Hama (in Syria)

(حمى)

حَمَى (ـِ) to defend, protect

حِمَايَةٌ protection, protegé

حَامٍ *pl.* حُمَاةٌ protector

حَامِيَةٌ guard, garrison

مُحَامٍ *pl.* مُحَامُونَ lawyer, solicitor

(حنن)

حَنَّ (ـِ) إِلَى to yearn towards, have a longing for

(حنبل)

حَنْبَلِيٌّ Hanbalite, follower of the rite of Ḥanbal

(حنت)

حَانُوتٌ *pl.* حَوَانِيتُ shop, wine-shop

(حنط)

حِنْطَةٌ wheat

(حنف)

حَنَفِيٌّ Hanafite, follower of the rite of Abū Ḥanīfa

حَنَفِيَّةٌ water-tap (*mod.*)

(حوج)

اِحْتَاجَ إِلَى VIII to need

حَاجَةٌ *pl.* ـَاتٌ, حَوَائِجُ need, necessity; object, thing

فِى حَاجَةٍ إِلَى, بِحَاجَةٍ إِلَى in need of

مُحْتَاجٌ needy one, needful

(حور)

مُحَاوَرَةٌ conversation, debate

(حوز)

حَازَ (ـُ) to get, acquire, possess, win

حِيَازَةٌ possession

(حوش)

حَوْشٌ *pl.* أَحْوَاشٌ courtyard, enclosure

(حوض)

حَوْضٌ *pl.* حِيَاضٌ, أَحْوَاضٌ tank, pool

(حوط)

أَحَاطَ (بِ) IV to surround

حَائِطٌ *pl.* حِيطَانٌ wall

اِحْتِيَاطٌ investment, security, reserve (commercial and financial)

(حوك)

حَاكَ (ـُـ) *v.n.* حِيَاكَةٌ to weave

حَائِكٌ *pl.* حَاكَةٌ weaver

(حول)

حَوَّلَ II to change, alter, transfer

حَاوَلَ III to attempt, try

أَحَالَ IV to transmit, transfer

تَحَيَّلَ V to exercise cunning

حَالٌ (*m.* or *f.*) *pl.* أَحْوَالٌ, حَالَةٌ *pl.* اتٌ — condition, state, case

حَالًا at once, immediately

حَالِيٌّ actual, present (time)

حَوْلٌ power, might

حَوَالَى, حَوْلَ about, approximately, around

حَوَالَةٌ draft, transfer document, bill (comm.)

آلأَسْوَاقِ — fluctuation of markets

حِيلَةٌ *pl.* حِيَلٌ trick, stratagem

تَحْوِيلٌ transfer, exchange (comm.)

مُحَالٌ impossible, absurd

مُحْتَالٌ cunning, sly, artful

(حوى)

حَوَى (ـِـ) to contain

اِحْتَوَى عَلَى VIII to comprise, contain

مُحْتَوَيَاتٌ (*pl.*) contents

(حيى)

حَيِيَ (يَحْيَا, يَحْيَى) to live

حَيَّا II to greet, salute

أَحْيَا IV to bring to life, make to live

حَيَاةٌ life

حَيٌّ *pl.* أَحْيَاءٌ alive; quarter of a town; settlement; section of tribe

حَيَّةٌ snake, viper

حَيَوَانٌ *pl.* اتٌ — animal

تَحِيَّةٌ greeting, salutation

(حيث)

حَيْثُ where, since

حَيْثُمَا wherever

مِنْ حَيْثُ, in respect of, whence,

بِحَيْثُ so that

(حير)

حَيَّرَ II to confuse

تَحَيَّرَ V to be confused

حَيْرَةٌ perplexity

حَارَةٌ quarter of a city

(حين)

حِينٌ *pl.* أَحْيَانٌ time

أَحْيَانًا at times, sometimes, from time to time

حِينَئِذٍ then, at that time

حِينَ, حِينَمَا when, whenever

خ

(خبأ)

خَبَأَ (ـَ) to conceal, hide

خَابِئَةٌ *pl.* خَوَابِئُ large jar, vat

(خبر)

خَبَّرَ II, أَخْبَرَ IV to inform

خَابَرَ III to negotiate with, get news from

اِسْتَخْبَرَ X to seek information, get to know

خِبْرَةٌ experience, knowledge, expertness

خَبَرٌ *pl.* أَخْبَارٌ news

خَبِيرٌ *pl.* خُبَرَاءُ expert, well-informed

مُخْتَبِرٌ experienced, expert

(خبز)

خُبْزٌ bread

خَبَّازٌ baker

(خبط)

خَبَطَ (ـِ) to strike, trample on

(خبى)

خَابِيَةٌ *pl.* خَوَابٍ large jar, vat

(ختم)

خَتَمَ (ـِ) to seal, close, conclude, stamp

خَتْمٌ *pl.* خُتُومٌ, أَخْتَامٌ seal

خَاتَمٌ *pl.* خَوَاتِمُ seal-ring, signet

خُتُمٌ *pl.* خِتَامٌ; خَوَاتِمُ *pl.* خَاتِمَةٌ end, conclusion

خِتَامًا finally, in conclusion

(خدد)

خَدٌّ *pl.* خُدُودٌ cheek

مِخَدَّةٌ cushion, pillow

(خدع)

خَدَعَ (ـُ) to deceive

(خدم)

خَدَمَ (ـُـ) to serve

إِسْتَخْدَمَ X to employ

مُسْتَخْدِمٌ employer

مُسْتَخْدَمٌ employee, employed person

خِدْمَةٌ *pl.* خِدَمَاتٌ service

خَادِمٌ *pl.* ـُونَ, خُدَّامٌ, خَدَمٌ

خَادِمَةٌ servant

(خرب)

خَرَبَ (ـَـ) to ruin, demolish

خَرِبَ (ـَـ) to be ruined

خَرَّبَ II to lay waste, destroy, raze

خِرْبَةٌ *pl.* خِرَبٌ a ruin, waste

خَرَابٌ ruin, destruction

خَرِبٌ wasted, ruined

(خرج)

خَرَجَ (ـُـ) *v.n.* خُرُوجٌ to go out

أَخْرَجَ IV to expel, take out

إِسْتَخْرَجَ X to extract, take or draw out

خَارِجٌ exterior, outside *n.*

خَارِجَ outside *prep.*

وَزِيرُ ٱلْخَارِجِيَّةِ Minister of Foreign Affairs

خَرَاجٌ poll tax levied on non-Muslims

مَخْرَجٌ outlet, issue, exit

(خردل)

خَرْدَلٌ mustard

(خرس)

أَخْرَسُ *f.* خَرْسَاءُ *pl.* خُرْسٌ dumb

(خرط)

إِنْخَرَطَ (فِى) VII to join, associate with

(خرطم)

إِخْرَنْطَمَ (*quad.*) III to be proud

خُرْطُومٌ *pl.* خَرَاطِيمُ elephant trunk

اَلْخُرْطُومُ Khartum (in the Sudan)

(خرع)

إِخْتَرَعَ VIII to invent

إِخْتِرَاعٌ *pl.* ـَاتٌ invention

(خرف)

خَرُوفٌ *pl.* خِرْفَانٌ lamb

خَرِيفٌ autumn

(خزن)

إِخْتَزَنَ VIII to store, lay up

مَخْزَنٌ *pl.* مَخَازِنُ; store, shop

اَلْمَخْزَنُ the Government (in Morocco)

(خسس)

خَسٌّ lettuce

(خسر)

خَسِرَ (ــَ) *v.n.* خُسْرٌ to lose, suffer loss or damage

خُسْرَانٌ, خَسَارَةٌ loss, damage

(خشب)

خَشَبٌ wood

(خشن)

خَشِنٌ *pl.* خِشَانٌ rough, coarse, gross

(خشى)

خَشِيَ (ــَ) to fear, dread

(خصص)

خَصَّ (ــُ) to concern

اِخْتَصَّ VIII (*with* ب) to be one's property; be special, peculiar, proper to

خَاصٌّ, خُصُوصِيٌّ special, private

فِي خُصُوصِ, بِخُصُوصِ with reference to, concerning

خَاصَّةً, خُصُوصًا especially, particularly

(خصب)

خِصْبٌ fertility

خَصِبٌ, خَصِيبٌ fertile

(خصر)

اِخْتَصَرَ VIII to shorten, abridge

مُخْتَصَرٌ shortened, abridged; summary, compendium (with *fem. pl.*)

(خصم)

خَصْمٌ *pl.* خُصُومٌ adversary, antagonist

خَصْمٌ discount, rebate (comm.)

(خضب)

خَضَّبَ II to dye

(خضر)

اِخْضَرَّ IX to be, become, green

أَخْضَرُ *f.* خَضْرَاءُ *pl.* خُضْرٌ green

خُضَارٌ vegetation, vegetables, greens

(خضع)

خَضَعَ (ــَ) to submit (to), obey

(خطط)

خَطَّطَ II to plan

خَطٌّ *pl.* خُطُوطٌ line, handwriting

خُطَّةٌ *pl.* خُطَطٌ policy, line

(خطأ)

خَطِئَ (ـَ) to err, sin

أَخْطَأَ IV to err, make a mistake; miss (the way, etc.)

خَطَأٌ *pl.* أَخْطَاءٌ error, sin, mistake

مُخْطِئٌ wrong, mistaken

(خطب)

خَطَبَ (ـُ) to make a speech; to betroth, ask in marriage

خَاطَبَ III to address anyone, converse with

خَطْبٌ *pl.* خُطُوبٌ affair, matter, cause of an affair

خِطَابٌ *pl.* ـَاتٌ — letter, speech, address

خُطْبَةٌ *pl.* خُطَبٌ sermon

(خطر)

خَطَرٌ *pl.* أَخْطَارٌ danger, risk

خَطِرٌ, مُخْطِرٌ dangerous

خَطِيرٌ great, important, momentous

خَاطِرٌ *pl.* خَوَاطِرُ thought, idea; heart (*fig.*), sake, mind

(خطف)

اِخْتَطَفَ VIII to snatch, grab for oneself

(خطو)

خَطَا (ـُ) to step, walk

خَطْوَةٌ *pl.* خَطَوَاتٌ خُطْوَةٌ *pl.* خُطُوَاتٌ step, pace

(خفف)

خَفَّ (ـِ) *v.n.* خِفَّةٌ to be light (in weight)

خَفِيفٌ *pl.* خِفَافٌ light

(خفى)

خَفِيَ (عَلَى) (ـَ) to be hidden (from)

اِخْتَفَى VIII to disappear, hide

مَخْفِيٌّ hidden concealed

(خلل)

تَخَلَّلَ V to mix in; penetrate, be pierced; use a toothpick

خَلٌّ vinegar

خِلَالَ during

خَلِيلٌ *pl.* أَخِلَّاءُ, خُلَّانٌ friend, companion; pr. n. m.

(خلج)

خَلِيجٌ *pl.* خُلُجٌ gulf, canal

(خلس)

اِخْتَلَسَ VIII to steal, cheat, swindle, seize by trickery, usurp

(خلص)

خَلَّصَ II to save

تَخَلَّصَ V to be saved

إِخْلَاصٌ sincerity, devotedness

خَالِصٌ pure, unmixed, free of

مُخْلِصٌ sincere, devoted

(خلط)

خَلَطَ (ـِ) to mix, *trans.*

خَالَطَ III to mix with, have intercourse with

تَخَالَطَ VI to mix, mingle with one another

مُخْتَلِطٌ mixed

(خلف)

خَلَفَ (ـُ) to succeed, replace

خَالَفَ III to oppose, disagree with, contravene

إِخْتَلَفَ (عَنْ) VIII to differ (from)

خَلْفَ behind, at the back of

خِلَافٌ disagreement, contravention; other than

خِلَافَةٌ succession, caliphate

خَلِيفَةٌ *pl.* خُلَفَاءُ successor, caliph

إِخْتِلَافٌ difference

مُخْتَلِفٌ varied, different

(خلق)

خَلَقَ (ـُ) to create

خَلْقٌ creation, creatures, mankind, people

خُلْقٌ *pl.* أَخْلَاقٌ moral character

الْمَخْلُوقَاتُ created things

(خلو)

خَلَا (ـُ) to be empty, vacant, alone

خَالٍ empty, vacant

(خمر)

خَمْرٌ *f.* wine

خَمَّارَةٌ tavern, inn

(خمس)

خَمْسَةٌ *f.* خَمْسٌ five

خُمْسٌ *pl.* أَخْمَاسٌ a fifth (fraction)

خَمْسُونَ fifty

خَامِسٌ fifth (ordinal)

يَوْمُ الْخَمِيسِ Thursday

(خنجر)

خَنْجَرٌ *pl.* خَنَاجِرُ dagger

(خنزر)

خِنْزِيرٌ *pl.* خَنَازِيرُ pig, pork

(خنس)

اَلْخَنَّاسُ Satan (*lit.* he who holds back or hides)

(خوف)

خَافَ (ـَ) to fear

خَوَّفَ II to terrify, cause to fear

أَخَافَ IV to frighten, terrify

خَوْفٌ *pl.* أَخْوَافٌ fear, fright

مَخَافَةٌ fear

(خول)

خَالٌ *pl.* أَخْوَالٌ maternal uncle

خَالَةٌ *pl.* ـَاتٌ maternal aunt

(خون)

خَانَ (ـُ) to betray, act treacherously

خِيَانَةٌ treachery, betrayal

خَائِنٌ *pl.* خُوَّانٌ, خَانَةٌ, خَوَنَةٌ traitor, treacherous

خَانٌ *pl.* ـَاتٌ inn, shop, caravanserai

(خيب)

خَيْبَةٌ disappointment

(خير)

اِخْتَارَ VIII to choose, select

خَيْرٌ good, *n.* and *adj.*; prosperity

خَيْرٌ مِنْ better than

مُخْتَارٌ selection (with *fem. pl.*); mukhtar (village headman); pr. n. m.

اِخْتِيَارِيٌّ voluntary

(خيط)

خَاطَ (ـِ) to sew

خَيْطٌ *pl.* خُيُوطٌ, خِيطَانٌ thread, string

خِيَاطَةٌ tailoring, sewing

خَيَّاطٌ tailor

خَائِطَةٌ needlewoman, seamstress

(خيل)

خُيِّلَ II *pass.* (with لِ or إِلَى) to seem to anyone, imagine a thing

تَخَيَّلَ V to imagine, fancy

اِخْتَالَ VIII to be haughty, conceited

خَيْلٌ *pl.* خُيُولٌ (*coll.*) horses

(خيم)

خَيْمَةٌ *pl.* خِيَامٌ tent

د

(دبب)

دُبٌّ *pl.* أَدْبَابٌ bear

دَابَّةٌ *pl.* دَوَابُّ animal, beast, beast of burden

(دبر)

دَبَّرَ II to arrange, plan, manage

تَدْبِيرٌ *pl.* تَدَابِيرُ arrangement, measure, step

(دجج)

دَجَاجَةٌ, دَجَاجٌ hen

(دجل)

دِجْلَةُ Tigris (river)

(دجن)

دَاجِنٌ *pl.* دَوَاجِنُ tame (animal)

(دحرج)

دَحْرَجَ (*quad.*) to roll, *trans.*

تَدَحْرَجَ II to roll, *intrans.*, be rolled

(دخل)

دَخَلَ (ـُ) *v.n.* دُخُولٌ to enter

دَخْلٌ income, revenue

دَاخِلٌ inside, *n.*

دَاخِلَ inside, *prep.*

وِزَارَةُ الدَّاخِلِيَّةِ Ministry of Interior

دَخِيلٌ *pl.* دُخَلَاءُ guest, intruder

(دخن)

دُخَانٌ; شَرِبَ دُخَانًا smoke; to smoke (tobacco)

(درب)

دَرَّبَ II to train, exercise, drill

دَرْبٌ *pl.* دُرُوبٌ path, way, road

(درج)

دَرَجَةٌ *pl.* ـَاتٌ — degree, step

دَارِجٌ common, current, in general use

لُغَةٌ دَارِجَةٌ common language, vulgar tongue

دَرَّاجَةٌ bicycle

(درس)

دَرَسَ (ـُ) to study

دَرَّسَ II to teach, lecture

دَرْسٌ *pl.* دُرُوسٌ lesson, study

مَدْرَسَةٌ *pl.* مَدَارِسُ school

مُدَرِّسٌ teacher, lecturer

إِدْرِيسُ Idris, Enoch

(درك)

أَدْرَكَ IV to overtake, know, understand, grasp

دَرَكٌ police (*Syr.*, *Leb.*)

(درهم)

دِرْهَمٌ *pl.* دَرَاهِمُ dirham (coin or weight), drachma; (in *pl.*, money)

(درى)

دَرَى (ـِ) to know

أَدْرَى IV to inform, teach

(دستر)

دُسْتُورٌ *pl.* دَسَاتِيرُ rule, regulation; political constitution (*mod.*)

(دعو)

دَعَا (ـُ) to call, name, pray; pray for (*with* لِ)

اِدَّعَى VIII to claim

اِسْتَدْعَى X to summon

دُعَاءٌ *pl.* أَدْعِيَةٌ call, prayer

دَعْوَةٌ invitation

دَعْوَى *pl.* دَعَاوٍ claim, lawsuit

دِعَايَةٌ propaganda

دَاعٍ *pl.* دُعَاةٌ calling, one who prays

دَاعٍ, دَاعِيَةٌ *pl.* دَوَاعٍ cause, motive, reason

(دفتر)

دَفْتَرٌ *pl.* دَفَاتِرُ register, account book, note-book

(دفع)

دَفَعَ (ـَ) to pay, push

دَافَعَ عَنْ III to defend

دِفَاعٌ defence

(دفق)

دَفَّقَ II to pour *trans.*; bestow profusely

اِنْدَفَقَ VII to be poured

دَافِقٌ profuse

(دفن)

دَفَنَ (ـِ) to bury

(دقق)

دَقَّ (ـُ) to knock; crush

دَقَّقَ II to examine minutely, in detail

دِقَّةٌ, تَدْقِيقٌ exactness, preciseness, minuteness

بِدِقَّةٍ in detail, exactly

دَقِيقٌ *pl.* أَدِقَّةٌ, دِقَاقٌ fine, thin, minute, exact; fine flour

دَقِيقَةٌ *pl.* دَقَائِقُ minute (of time)

مِدَقٌّ, مُدُقٌّ *pl.* مَدَاقُّ hammer, mallet, pestle

(دكتر)

دُكْتُورٌ *pl.* دَكَاتِرَةٌ doctor (*mod.*)

(دكن)

دُكَّانٌ *pl.* دَكَاكِينُ shop

(دلل)

دَلَّ (ـُ) (عَلَى) to guide, show, prove, lead (to)

إِسْتَدَلَّ عَلَى . . . بِ X to prove . . . by . . .

دَلَّالٌ broker, auctioneer

دَلَالَةٌ pl. دَلَائِلُ guidance, guiding, indication, proof

دَلِيلٌ *pl.* أَدِلَّاءُ guide

(دلب)

دُولَابٌ *pl.* دَوَالِيبُ cupboard; wheel

(دلف)

دَلَفَ (ـَ) to saunter along, move slowly

(دلو)

دَلْوٌ *pl.* دِلَاءٌ bucket

(دمر)

دَمَّرَ II to destroy, lay waste

(دمشق)

دِمَشْقُ Damascus

(دمع)

دَمْعٌ, دَمْعَةٌ *pl.* دُمُوعٌ tear

(دمغ)

دَمْغَةٌ stamp, seal

دِمَاغٌ *pl.* أَدْمِغَةٌ brain

(دمى)

دَمٌ *pl.* دِمَاءٌ blood

(دنر)

دِينَارٌ *pl.* دَنَانِيرُ dinar (gold coin); currency unit used in some modern Arab countries

(دنو)

دَنَا (ـُ) (مِنْ) to approach, be near

دَنِيٌّ *pl.* أَدْنِيَاءُ bad, base, low; near

دُنْيَا *f.* world; lowest; nearest (*elat. f.*)

(دهر)

دَهْرٌ *pl.* دُهُورٌ time, fate, destiny

(دهش)

دَهَشَ (ـَ) to amaze, surprise

دُهِشَ مِنْ to be surprised by (*pass.*)

أَدْهَشَ IV to surprise, astonish

(دوأ)

دَاءٌ *pl.* أَدْوَاءٌ sickness, disease

(دود)

دُودَةٌ *pl.* دُودٌ, دِيدَانٌ worm

(دور)

دَارَ (ـُ) to revolve, turn, go round, circulate

أَدَارَ IV to direct, administer, manage

اِسْتَدَارَ X to be round

دَارٌ (*f.*) *pl.* دُورٌ, دِيَارٌ house, home, homeland, seat

دِيَارٌ country (*pl.* of دَارٌ)

دَوْرٌ *pl.* أَدْوَارٌ turn, age, period

دَائِرَةٌ *pl.* دَوَائِرُ circle; office

دَيْرٌ *pl.* أَدْيِرَةٌ, دُيُورٌ monastery

إِدَارَةٌ administration, management

مُدِيرٌ director, manager, governor

مُسْتَدِيرٌ round, circular

(دول)

تَدَاوَلَ VI to do by turns, negotiate with one another

دَوْلَةٌ *pl.* دُوَلٌ state, power, country

دُوَلِيٌّ international (*mod.*)

(دوم)

دَامَ (ـُ) to last, endure, continue

مَا دَامَ so long as, as long as

عَلَى ٱلدَّوَامِ continually

دَائِمٌ continuing, lasting, permanent

دَائِمًا always

(دون)

دُونَ before; without, short of, beyond

بِدُونِ without

دِيوَانٌ *pl.* دَوَاوِينُ diwan, collection of poetry; council of state

(دوى)

دَوَاءٌ *pl.* أَدْوِيَةٌ medicine

دَوَاةٌ *pl.* دَوًى inkstand

(ديك)

دِيكٌ cock

— رُومِيٌّ turkey

(دين)

دَانَ لِ (ـِ) to submit, yield to

تَدَيَّنَ بِ V to profess or follow a religion

دَيْنٌ pl. دُيُونٌ debt, loan

دِينٌ pl. أَدْيَانٌ; دِيَانَةٌ pl. ـَاتٌ religion

يَوْمُ الدِّينِ Day of Judgement

دِينِيٌّ religious, pertaining to religion

ذ

(ذا)

هٰذَا (ذَا) f. هٰذِهِ (هٰذِى) this

ذَاكَ, ذٰلِكَ f. تِلْكَ that

كَذٰلِكَ, كَذَا, هٰكَذَا likewise, thus

لِهٰذَا therefore

(ذأب)

ذِئْبٌ pl. ذِئَابٌ wolf

(ذبب)

ذُبَابٌ pl. ذِبَّانٌ flies

تَذَبْذُبٌ fickleness, wavering

(ذبح)

ذَبَحَ (ـَ) to slay, slaughter

(ذبل)

ذَبَلَ (ـُ) to wither, dry up, fade

(ذرر)

ذَرِّيٌّ atomic

(ذرع)

ذِرَاعٌ pl. أَذْرُعٌ arm

(ذرف)

ذَرَفَ (ـِ) to flow, shed tears

(ذقن)

ذَقَنٌ pl. ذُقُونٌ beard, chin

(ذكر)

ذَكَرَ (ـُ) v.n. ذِكْرٌ to mention, record, remember

ذَكَّرَ II, أَذْكَرَ IV to remind

ذَاكَرَ III to confer with

تَذَكَّرَ V to remember, recollect

ذِكْرٌ, ذِكْرَى pl. ذِكْرَيَاتٌ remembrance, recollection

ذَكَرٌ pl. ذُكُورٌ male, masculine

ذَاكِرَةٌ memory (faculty)

تَذْكِرَةٌ *pl.* تَذَاكِرُ ticket, note

مُذَكَّرٌ masculine

مُذَكِّرَةٌ note, memorandum, memoir

(ذكى)

ذَكَاءٌ intelligence, perception

ذَكِيٌّ *pl.* أَذْكِيَاءُ perceptive, intelligent, quick of understanding

(ذلل)

ذَلِيلٌ *pl.* أَذِلَّاءُ low, abject, wretched

(ذمم)

ذَمَّ (ـُ) to blame, rebuke, censure

ذِمَّةٌ conscience, moral sense, honour

ذِمَّةٌ *pl.* ذِمَمٌ covenant, security, protection

أَهْلُ الذِّمَّةِ protected community, tributaries; Jews and Christians in Islam

(ذنب)

ذَنْبٌ *pl.* ذُنُوبٌ sin, fault, guilt

ذَنَبٌ *pl.* أَذْنَابٌ tail

مُذْنِبٌ guilty

(ذهب)

ذَهَبَ (ـَ) *v.n.* ذَهَابٌ to go

ب — to take away

ذَهَبٌ gold *n.*

مَذْهَبٌ *pl.* مَذَاهِبُ sect, rite, tenet, school, way

تَمَذْهَبَ *quad.* II to follow a sect, rite; hold a belief

(ذهن)

ذِهْنٌ *pl.* أَذْهَانٌ mind, intellect

(ذو)

ذُو *f.* ذَاتُ master of, possessor of

ذَاتٌ self, person, self-same, essence

ذَاتَ يَوْمٍ one day

ذَاتِيٌّ *adj.* self-

(ذوب)

ذَابَ (ـُ) to melt, dissolve *intrans.*

(ذود)

مِذْوَدٌ *pl.* مَذَاوِدُ manger

(ذوق)

ذَاقَ (ـُ) to taste *trans.*

ذَوْقٌ *pl.* أَذْوَاقٌ; مَذَاقٌ taste

(ذيع)

أَذَاعَ IV to make public (news); broadcast (*mod.*)

إِذَاعَة publication (news), broadcast

مُذِيع broadcaster, announcer

مِذْيَاع *pl.* مَذَايِيعُ, — ات micro-phone

(ذيل)

ذَيْل *pl.* ذُيُول tail, appendix

ر

(رأس)

رَأَسَ (ـَ); رَؤُسَ (ـُ) to be chief of a tribe; be head of

رَأْس *pl.* رُؤُوس head (part of body); cape (*geog.*)

رَئِيس *pl.* رُؤَسَاء head (chief, president, etc.), chairman

رِئَاسَة leadership, headship, chairmanship, presidency

رَأْسُ المَالِ, الرَّأْسَمَالُ capital (*mod.*)

رَأْسَمَالِيّ capitalist (*mod.*)

(رأى)

رَأَى (يَرَى) to see

أَرَى IV to show

رَأْي *pl.* آرَاء opinion

رُؤْيَة vision, seeing, sight

رُؤْيَا vision, dream

مِرْآة *pl.* مَرَايَا mirror

(ربب)

رَبّ *pl.* أَرْبَاب lord, master

رَبَّةُ بَيْت housewife

رُبَّ + *gen.* many a

رُبَّمَا perhaps

(ربح)

رَبِحَ (ـَ) to gain, win

رِبْح *pl.* أَرْبَاح gain, profit

(ربد)

إِرْبَدَّ IX to alter (expression of face); be ash-coloured, pale

(ربط)

رَبَطَ (ـُ) to tie, bind

رَابِطَة *pl.* رَوَابِطُ connection, bond, league (body binding together people)

(ربع)

رُبْع *pl.* أَرْبَاع a quarter (¼)

رَابِع fourth (ordinal)

رَبِيعٌ spring, spring season

رَبِيعُ ٱلأَوَّلِ Rabi' I (3rd month in Islamic Calendar)

رَبِيعُ ٱلثَّانِى (ٱلآخَرُ) Rabi' II (4th month in Islamic Calendar)

أَرْبَعٌ f. أَرْبَعَةٌ four

أَرْبَعُونَ forty

يَوْمُ ٱلأَرْبِعَاءِ Wednesday

مُرَبَّعٌ pl. اتٌ — a square, four-sided

(ربو)

رَبَّى II to educate, bring up, breed

تَرْبِيَةٌ education, training

مُرَبٍّ educator, one who brings up

(رتب)

رَتَّبَ II to arrange, plan

رُتْبَةٌ pl. رُتَبٌ rank, position

رَاتِبٌ pl. رَوَاتِبُ salary, pension

(رتع)

مَرْتَعٌ pl. مَرَاتِعُ pasture ground

(رثو)

رِثَاءٌ elegy, lament for the dead

(رجأ)

أَرْجَأَ IV to put off, postpone

(رجب)

رَجَبُ Rajab (7th month of Islamic Calendar)

(رجح)

رَجَحَ (ـَ) to outweigh, weigh more than

(رجع)

رَجَعَ (ـِ) v.n. رُجُوعٌ to return *intrans.*

رَجَّعَ II to return *trans.*

رَاجَعَ III to consult, review, revise

(رجف)

اِرْتَجَفَ VIII to tremble, shake *intrans.*

(رجل)

رِجْلٌ (*f.*) *pl.* أَرْجُلٌ foot

رَجُلٌ *pl.* رِجَالٌ man

(رجو)

رَجَا (ـُ) to beg, hope, request

رَجَاءٌ hope, request

(رحب)

رَحَّبَ بِ II to welcome

ترحاب welcome

مرحبا (ب) welcome (to)!

(رحل)

رحل (ـَ), إرتحل VIII to depart, migrate, travel, journey

رحلة *pl.* رحال journey

راحل *pl.* رحل traveller; late, departed (deceased)

رحال, رحالة great or eminent traveller

مرحلة pl. مراحل stage, day's journey

(رحم)

الرحمن, الرحيم the Merciful, the Compassionate (attributes of God)

(رحى)

رحى *pl.* أرحاء mill

(رخص)

رخصة permit, licence (*mod.*)

رخيص cheap

(رخم)

رخام marble

(رخو)

رخو lax, soft, loose

(ردد)

رد (ـُ) to give back, answer, retort

رد repulse, return, reply (to على)

(ردأ)

ردىء *pl.* أردياء, أردئاء bad, *adj.*

(ردى)

إرتدى VIII to wear, put on (coat, etc.)

رداء *pl.* أردية cloak, coat

(رذل)

رذيلة *pl.* رذائل vice

(رزق)

رزق (ـُ) to grant, bestow (of God), sustain

رزق *pl.* أرزاق sustinence, means of livelihood

(رزم)

رزم (ـُ) to pack up, wrap

رزمة *pl.* رزم package, bale, ream

(رزن)

رزين weighty, grave, calm

(رسل)

أرسل IV to send

رِسَالَةٌ *pl.* ـَاتٌ, رَسَائِلُ letter, essay, message

رَسُولٌ *pl.* رُسُلٌ messenger, apostle

مُرَاسِلٌ (newspaper) correspondent (*mod.*)

(رسم)

رَسَمَ (ـُ) to trace, design, draw, sketch

رَسْمٌ *pl.* رُسُومٌ tracing, drawing, sketch; tax, duty, custom

رَسْمِيٌّ official, authoritative

(رشش)

رَشَّ (ـُ) to sprinkle

(رشد)

أَرْشَدَ IV to direct, guide

رُشْدٌ rectitude, maturity

سِنُّ الرُّشْدِ age of discretion, majority

رَشِيدٌ upright, righteous; pr. n. m.

(رشق)

رَشِيقٌ fine, elegant

(رشو)

رَشَا (ـُ) to bribe

رِشْوَةٌ *pl.* رِشًى bribe

رِشَاءٌ rope

(رصص)

رَصَاصٌ; قَلَمُ رَصَاصٍ lead; pencil

رَصَاصَةٌ *pl.* ـَاتٌ bullet

(رضو)

رَضِيَ (ـَ) (*with* عَنْ, بِ or مِنْ) to be content, pleased, satisfied (with)

أَرْضَى IV to please

رَاضٍ *pl.* رَاضُونَ pleased, content, satisfied

مُرْضٍ satisfactory, pleasing

(رطب)

رَطْبٌ damp, moist

رُطَبٌ *pl.* أَرْطَابٌ ripe, fresh dates

رُطُوبَةٌ humidity, moisture, damp, *n.*

مُرَطِّبٌ cool, fresh, moist

(رعد)

رَعَدَ (ـُ) to thunder

رَعْدٌ *pl.* رُعُودٌ thunder

(رعى)

رَعَى (ـَ) to pasture, graze, tend (cattle)

رَعِيَّةٌ *pl.* رَعَايَا flock, subjects (of a ruler)

رَاعٍ *pl.* رُعَاةٌ shepherd

مَرْعًى *pl.* مَرَاعٍ pasturage, pasture

(رغب)

رَغِبَ (ـَ) (*with* فِى) to wish (for), desire, like

رَغْبَةٌ wish, desire

(رغف)

رَغِيفٌ *pl.* أَرْغِفَةٌ loaf

(رغم)

رَغَمَ (ـُ) to compel; dislike

أَرْغَمَ IV to compel

عَلَى الرَّغْمِ مِنْ, رَغْمًا عَنْ, بِالرَّغْمِ عَنْ despite (the fact that)

(رفف)

رَفْرَفَ to flutter

(رفأ)

مَرْفَأٌ *pl.* مَرَافِئُ harbour (for ships)

(رفض)

رَفَضَ (ـُ) to refuse, reject

(رفع)

رَفَعَ (ـَ) to raise, lift

اِرْتَفَعَ VIII to be raised, to rise

(رفق)

رَافَقَ III to accompany

رَفِيقٌ *pl.* رُفَقَاءُ companion

(رقق)

رِقٌّ slavery

رَقِيقٌ *pl.* رُقَاقٌ slave

(رقب)

رَاقَبَ III to observe, watch, guard, oversee, supervise, control; to fear (God)

اِرْتَقَبَ VIII to wait for

رَقَبَةٌ *pl.* رِقَابٌ neck

مُرَاقَبَةٌ watching over, observation, surveillance, supervision

رَقِيبٌ *pl.* رُقَبَاءُ guardian, censor

مُرَاقِبٌ supervisor, foreman, controller

(رقد)

رَقَدَ (ـُ) to sleep, lie down

رُقَادٌ sleep

(رقص)

رَقَصَ (ـُ) to dance

(رقم)

رَقَمٌ *pl.* أَرْقَامٌ figure, number

(ركب)

رَكِبَ (ـَ) *v.n.* رُكُوبٌ to ride

رَكَّبَ II to compose, form, construct

رُكْبَةٌ *pl.* رُكَبٌ knee

رَاكِبٌ *pl.* رُكَّابٌ rider, passenger

تَرْكِيبٌ composition, construction, structure

مَرْكَبٌ *pl.* مَرَاكِبُ small ship, boat

(ركز)

مَرْكَزٌ *pl.* مَرَاكِزُ centre

مَرْكَزِيٌّ central

(ركش)

مَرَّاكُشُ Morocco, Marrakesh

(ركض)

رَكَضَ (ـُ) to run

(ركن)

رُكْنٌ *pl.* أَرْكَانٌ, رُكُونٌ corner; support

(رمد)

رَمَادِيٌّ grey (*lit.* ash coloured)

(رمز)

رَمْزٌ *pl.* رُمُوزٌ sign, symbol, allegory, type

(رمض)

رَمَضَانُ Ramadan (9th month in Islamic Calendar; month of fasting)

(رمل)

رَمَّلَ II to widow, make widowed

رَمْلٌ, رَمْلَةٌ sand, sandy ground

أَرْمَلٌ *f.* أَرْمَلَةٌ *pl.* أَرَامِلُ widower, widow

(رمن)

رُمَّانٌ pomegranate (*coll.*)

(رمى)

رَمَى (ـِ) *v.n.* رَمْيٌ to throw; subdue; accuse

(رهن)

رَهْنٌ pledge, mortgage

(روح)

رَاحَ (ـُ) to depart, go

أَرَاحَ IV to permit, or cause, to rest

تَرَاوَحَ VI to alternate

اِرْتَاحَ VIII to rest, be comfortable, at ease

اِسْتَرَاحَ X to rest, sit down

رَاحَةٌ rest, ease, comfort

رُوحٌ (*f.*) *pl.* أَرْوَاحٌ soul, spirit, breath

طَوِيلُ الرُّوحِ long-suffering, patient

رِيحٌ (*f.*) *pl.* أَرْيَاحٌ wind

رَائِحَةٌ *pl.* رَوَائِحُ smell, odour

اِسْتِرَاحَةٌ a rest-house

مِرْوَحَةٌ *pl.* مَرَاوِحُ fan

(رود)

أَرَادَ IV to wish, want

إِرَادَةٌ will, wish

(روس)

رُوسِيَّا Russia

رُوسِيٌّ Russian

اَلرُّوسُ Russia, the Russians

(روض)

رَوْضَةٌ *pl.* رِيَاضٌ meadow, garden

اَلرِّيَاضُ Riyad (city in Arabia)

رِيَاضَةٌ exercise, sport

اَلْعُلُومُ الرِّيَاضِيَّةُ mathematics

(روع)

رَوَّعَ II to frighten, terrify

رَوْعٌ fear, fright

(روم)

رَامَ (ـُ) to desire

رُومِيٌّ Greek, Byzantine

اَلرُّومَانُ the Romans

(روى)

رَوَى (ـِ) to quote, narrate, report, relate a tradition

رَوِيَ (ـَ) to be watered, irrigated

أَرْوَى IV to irrigate

اِرْتَوَى VIII to be watered, irrigated

رِيٌّ irrigation

رِوَايَةٌ narrative, narration, tale, play (theatre)

رَاوٍ, رَاوِيَةٌ *pl.* رُوَاةٌ narrator, story-teller, transmitter

(ريف)

رِيفٌ *pl.* أَرْيَافٌ cultivated land, land by river; countryside

ز

(زبن)

زَبُونٌ *pl.* زَبَائِنُ customer

(زبد)

زُبْدٌ, زُبْدَةٌ butter, cream

(زجج)

زُجَاجٌ; زُجَاجَةٌ glass, glass vessels; a glass vessel

(زحف)

زَحَفَ عَلَى (ـَ) to march against

(زحم)

زَاحَمَ III to crowd, press

تَزَاحَمَ VI to crowd together

اِزْدَحَمَ VIII to be crowded

زَحْمَةٌ pressure, throng; trouble

اِزْدِحَامٌ *pl.* ـَاتٌ crowding, a crowd

(زخرف)

زَخْرَفَ (*quad.*) to adorn

زَخْرَفَةٌ *pl.* زَخَارِفُ adornment

(زرر)

زِرٌّ *pl.* أَزْرَارٌ button

(زرع)

زَرَعَ (ـَ) to sow, plant, till the soil

زَرْعٌ plantation, farming, produce

زِرَاعَةٌ cultivation, agriculture

زَارِعٌ *pl.* زُرَّاعٌ cultivator

مُزَارِعٌ, زَرَّاعٌ cultivator

مَزْرَعَةٌ *pl.* مَزَارِعُ (sown) field

(زرق)

اِزْرَقَّ IX to be(come) blue

أَزْرَقُ *f.* زَرْقَاءُ *pl.* زُرْقٌ blue

(زرى)

اِزْدَرَى VIII to scorn, despise

(زعج)

أَزْعَجَ IV to disturb, agitate

اِنْزَعَجَ VII to be disturbed, troubled, upset

زَعَجٌ agitation, disturbance

مُزْعِجٌ disturbing, upsetting

(زعل)

زَعِلَ (ـَ) to be angry, sorry

زَعْلَانُ in agony; angry (*mod.*)

(زعم)

زَعَمَ (ـُ) to claim, assert

زَعَامَةٌ leadership, authority

زَعِيمٌ *pl.* زُعَمَاءُ leader, spokesman

(زقق)

زُقَاقٌ *pl.* أَزِقَّةٌ lane, side-street, bye-way

(زكو)

زَكَاةٌ alms (in Islam)

زَكِيٌّ *pl.* أَزْكِيَاءُ pure, just

(زلل)

زَلْزَلَ to shake, *trans.*

تَزَلْزَلَ II to shake, *intrans.*, be shaken

زَلْزَلَةٌ earthquake

(زلج)

زُلَّيْجٌ coloured tiles and pottery (*Magh.*)

(زمل)

زَمِيلٌ *pl.* زُمَلَاءُ colleague, companion

(زمن)

زَمَانٌ, زَمَنٌ *pl.* أَزْمِنَةٌ, أَزْمَانٌ time

(زنج)

زِنْجٌ black, negro races

زِنْجِيٌّ *pl.* زُنُوجٌ negro, black

زَنْجِبَارُ Zanzibar

زَنْجَبِيلٌ ginger

(زهد)

زُهْدٌ abstinence; indifference (to worldly things)

زَاهِدٌ *pl.* زُهَّادٌ ascetic, abstainer, abstaining

زَهِيدٌ little, insignificant

(زهر)

زَهَرَ (ـَ) to shine

اِزْدَهَرَ VIII to flourish

زَهْرٌ *pl.* أَزْهَارٌ, زُهُورٌ flower, blossom

زَاهِرٌ shining, flourishing; pr. n. m.

الْجَامِعُ الْأَزْهَرُ the Azhar University and Mosque (in Cairo)

مُزْدَهِرٌ flourishing

(زهى)

زُهَاءَ about (quantity, number)

(زوج)

زَوَّجَ II (*with* بِ or لِ) to marry (anyone to)

تَزَوَّجَ V to be married (to)

اِزْدَوَجَ VIII to be doubled

زَوْجٌ *pl.* أَزْوَاجٌ husband, couple, pair

زَوْجَةٌ *pl.* ـَاتٌ — wife

(زود)

زَوَّدَ II to provide, supply, equip

زَادٌ provisions

(زور)

زَارَ (ـُ) to visit

زَوَّرَ II to falsify, counterfeit

زِيَارَةٌ a visit

زَائِرٌ *pl.* زُوَّارٌ visitor

اَلزَّوْرَاءُ a name of Baghdad

(زول)

زَالَ (ـُ) to cease

أَزَالَ IV to abolish, remove

(زيت)

زَيْتٌ *pl.* زُيُوتٌ oil

زَيْتُونٌ (*coll.*) olive, olives

(زيد)

زَادَ (ـِ) to add, increase (*with* فِي, عَلَى)

زَيَّدَ II to increase (a thing), *trans.*

زَايَدَ III to outbid one another (in an auction)

أَزَادَ IV to increase, *trans.*

اِزْدَادَ VIII to be increased

زَيْدٌ Zaid (pr. n. m.)

زِيَادٌ Ziyād (pr. n. m.)

زِيَادَةٌ increase

زَائِدٌ exceeding, excessive

مَزَادٌ auction

مَزِيدٌ excess, extra

(زين)

زَيَّنَ II to adorn, beautify

مُزَيِّنٌ hairdresser

س

سَوْفَ see سَ

(سأر)

سَائِرٌ remainder, rest (see also سير)

(سأل)

سَأَلَ (ـَ) to ask

سُؤَالٌ *pl.* أَسْئِلَةٌ question

سَائِلٌ beggar (*lit.* asker)

مَسْأَلَةٌ *pl.* مَسَائِلُ matter, question, subject, problem

مَسْؤُولٌ responsible, in charge (for, of عَنْ)

(سأم)

سَئِمَ (مِنْ) to loathe, be disgusted (with)

(سبب)

سَبَّبَ II to cause

سَبَبٌ *pl.* أَسْبَابٌ cause, reason, occasion

(سبت)

سَبْتٌ *pl.* سُبُوتٌ Sabbath, Saturday

(سبح)

سَبَحَ (َ) to swim, float

سَبَّحَ II to praise, magnify (God)

سُبْحَانَهُ (سُبْحَانَ ٱللّٰهِ) Praised be He (God)

(سبخ)

سَبِخٌ saline (of soil)

(سبع)

سَبْعَةٌ *f.* سَبْعٌ seven

سُبْعٌ *pl.* أَسْبَاعٌ a seventh (fraction)

سَبْعُونَ seventy

سَابِعٌ seventh (ordinal)

أُسْبُوعٌ *pl.* أَسَابِيعُ week

(سبق)

سَبَقَ (ُ) to precede, go before

سَابَقَ III to vie with, compete with, try to precede

سَابِقٌ former, previous, forerunner

سَابِقًا formerly, earlier

مُسَابَقَةٌ ;—َاتٌ *pl.* سِبَاقٌ race, contest

(سبل)

سَبِيلٌ *pl.* سُبُلٌ path, way, course

(ستت)

سِتَّةٌ *f.* سِتٌّ (see also سدس) six

سِتُّونَ sixty

سِتٌّ *pl.* سِتَّاتٌ (see also سود) lady, mistress

(ستر)

سَتَرَ (ُ) to cover, veil

سِتَارٌ *pl.* سَتَائِرُ, سُتُرٌ curtain

(سجد)

سَجَّادَةٌ *pl.* ;—َاتٌ سَجَاجِيدُ prayer-carpet; carpet

مَسْجِدٌ *pl.* مَسَاجِدُ mosque

(سجع)

سَجْعٌ rhymed prose

(سجل)

سَجَّلَ II to register, record

(سجن)

سَجَنَ (ـُ) to imprison

سِجْنٌ *pl.* سُجُونٌ prison

سَجِينٌ *pl.* سُجَنَاءُ prisoner

مَسْجُونٌ *pl.* مَسَاجِينُ prisoner

(سحب)

سَحَبَ (ـَ) to drag, draw, withdraw

اِنْسَحَبَ VII to go off, withdraw, be withdrawn

سَحَابٌ cloud (*coll.*)

(سحق)

إِسْحٰقُ, إِسْحَاقُ Isaac

(سحل)

سَاحِلٌ *pl.* سَوَاحِلُ bank, coast, shore

(سخر)

سَخِرَ (ـَ) to mock, laugh at (*with* بِ or مِنْ)

سُخْرِيَّةٌ ridicule, derision

(سخف)

سَخِيفٌ silly

(سخن)

سُخُونَةٌ heat, fever

سُخْنٌ hot

(سخو)

سَخِيٌّ bountiful

(سدد)

سَدَّ (ـُ) to close, stop (up), dam

سَدَّ حَاجَةً to fulfil a need

سَدٌّ *pl.* أَسْدَادٌ dam

(سدر)

سِدْرٌ species of lotus

(سدس)

سُدْسٌ *pl.* أَسْدَاسٌ (see also ستت) a sixth (fraction)

سَادِسٌ sixth (ordinal)

(سرر)

سَرَّ (ـُ) to rejoice, *trans.*

سِرٌّ *pl.* أَسْرَارٌ secret *n.*

كَاتِمُ ٱلسِّرِّ (الأَسْرَارِ) secretary

سِرِّيّ secret *adj.*

سُرَّة the navel

سُرُور pleasure, joy

سَرِير *pl.* أَسِرَّة bed

مَسْرُور glad, pleased

(سرح)

سَرَحَ (َ) to pasture in the morning

سَرَّحَ II to send away, set free

أَطْلَقَ سَرَاحَهُ he set him free, let him go

(سرع)

سُرْعَة speed

سَرِيع *pl.* سِرَاعٌ speedy, fast

سَرِيعاً quickly

(سرق)

سَرَقَ (ِ) to steal

سَرِقَة theft, robbery

سَارِق *pl.* سُرَّاق, سَرَقَة thief, robber

(سرول)

سِرْوَال *pl.* سَرَاوِيلُ trousers, pantaloons

(سطح)

سَطْح *pl.* سُطُوح roof, surface

(سطر)

سَطْر *pl.* سُطُور line

أُسْطُورَة *pl.* أَسَاطِيرُ fable, legend

(سطل)

سَطْل *pl.* سُطُول pail, bucket

أُسْطُول navy, fleet

(سطو)

سَطَا عَلَى (ُ) to assault, overpower

(سعد)

سَاعَدَ III to help, assist

أَسْعَدَ IV to make happy, fortunate

سَعَادَة happiness

سَاعِد *pl.* سَوَاعِدُ fore-arm

اَلْمَمْلَكَةُ ٱلْعَرَبِيَّةُ ٱلسُّعُودِيَّة kingdom of Saudi Arabia

سَعِيد *pl.* سُعَدَاءُ happy, fortunate; pr. n. m.

مُسَاعَدَة help, assistance

مُسَاعِد assistant

(سعر)

سِعْر *pl.* أَسْعَار price, rate, current price

(سعف)

أَسْعَفَ بِ IV to help, aid

إِسْعَافٌ أَوَّلِيٌّ first aid (*mod.*)

(سعل)

سَعَلَ (ـُ) to cough

سُعَالٌ cough

(سعى)

سَعَى (ـَ) *v.n.* سَعْيٌ to exert oneself, make an effort

مَسْعًى *pl.* مَسَاعٍ effort, enterprise, endeavour

(سفر)

سَافَرَ III to travel

سَفَرٌ *pl.* أَسْفَارٌ journey, travel

سُفْرَةٌ dining table, table cloth (dining room)

سَفِيرٌ *pl.* سُفَرَاءُ ambassador

سِفَارَةٌ embassy

(سفرجل)

سَفَرْجَلٌ *pl.* سَفَارِجُ quince (fruit)

(سفل)

أَسْفَلُ low, lower, bottom

(سفن)

سَفِينَةٌ *pl.* سُفُنٌ ship, vessel

(سقط)

سَقَطَ (ـُ) *v.n.* سُقُوطٌ to fall

تَسَاقَطَ VI to fall one after another

مَسْقَطٌ Muscat (in Arabia)

مَسْقَطُ ٱلرَّأْسِ birthplace

(سقف)

سَقْفٌ *pl.* سُقُوفٌ roof, ceiling

أُسْقُفٌ *pl.* أَسَاقِفَةٌ bishop

(سقى)

سَقَى (ـِ) to water, give to drink

سَاقٍ cup-bearer (*class.*); waiter (*mod.*)

سَاقِيَةٌ *pl.* سَوَاقٍ water wheel, irrigation canal

(سكك)

سِكَّةٌ *pl.* سِكَكٌ coin; way, route, road

سِكَّةٌ حَدِيدِيَّةٌ, سِكَّةُ ٱلْحَدِيدِ railway

(سكت)

سَكَتَ (ـُ) *v.n.* سُكُوتٌ to be silent

سَاكِتٌ silent

(سكر)

سَكِرَ (ـَ) to be drunk

سُكَّرٌ sugar

سَكْرَانُ *pl.* سَكَارَى drunk

سِيكَارَةٌ *pl.* سَكَائِرُ cigarette

سِكْرِتِيرٌ (*Fr.*) secretary

(سكن)

سَكَنَ (ـُ) to dwell, live, inhabit; be still, quiescent

سَاكِنٌ *pl.* سُكَّانٌ inhabitant; still, quiet

سِكِّينٌ *pl.* سَكَاكِينُ knife

اَلْمَسْكُونَةُ the world

مَسْكَنٌ *pl.* مَسَاكِنُ dwelling place

مِسْكِينٌ *pl.* مَسَاكِينُ poor, lowly, wretched

اَلْإِسْكَنْدَرِيَّةُ Alexandria

(سلل)

اِسْتَلَّ (سَيْفًا) VIII to draw (a sword)

دَاءُ ٱلسِّلِّ consumption (disease), T.B.

سَلَّةٌ *pl.* سِلَالٌ basket

مَسْلُولٌ consumptive

سَلْسَلَ to chain, connect a thing with

سِلْسِلَةٌ *pl.* سَلَاسِلُ chain, series

مُتَسَلْسِلٌ consecutive, serial

(سلب)

سَلَبَ (ـُ) to rob, seize, plunder

أُسْلُوبٌ *pl.* أَسَالِيبُ style, method

(سلح)

سَلَّحَ II to arm, *trans.*

تَسَلَّحَ V to arm oneself, be armed

سِلَاحٌ *pl.* أَسْلِحَةٌ weapon, arm(s)

(سلخ)

سَلَخَ (ـُ or ـَ) to flay, skin

(سلط)

تَسَلَّطَ (عَلَى) V to exercise power (over)

سُلْطَةٌ power, authority, rule

سُلْطَانٌ *pl.* سَلَاطِينُ sultan, ruler, authority

(سلع)

سِلْعَةٌ *pl.* سِلَعٌ article for sale, goods, belongings

(سلف)

اِسْتَلَفَ VIII to borrow

سَلَفٌ payment in advance

سَلَفٌ *pl.* أَسْلَافٌ predecessor, ancestor

سَالِفٌ predecessor, former

سَالِفُ ٱلذِّكْرِ aforementioned, previously said

(سلق)

سَلَقَ (ـُ) to boil (of an egg, meat, etc.)

(سلك)

سَلَكَ (ـُ) *v.n.* سُلُوكٌ to take a road, course; to behave

سِلْكٌ *pl.* أَسْلَاكٌ wire

لَا سِلْكِيَّةٌ wireless

سُلُوكٌ conduct, behaviour, manner

حُسْنُ السلوك good behaviour

حَسَنُ السلوك well-behaved, mannerly

(سلم)

سَلِمَ (ـَ) to be safe, unharmed

سَلَّمَ ... إِلَى II to deliver something to

سَلَّمَ عَلَى II to greet

أَسْلَمَ IV to turn Muslim

تَسَلَّمَ V to take over, receive

سُلَّمٌ (*m.* or *f.*) *pl.* سَلَالِمُ ladder, steps

سَلَامٌ peace, greeting

اَلسَّلَامُ عَلَيْكُمْ (عَلَيْكَ) a greeting (*lit.* peace be upon you)

سَلَامَةٌ safety, health, well-being

اَلْإِسْلَامُ Islam

سُلَيْمَانُ Solomon

سَالِمٌ safe, sound, whole; pr. n. m.

سَلِيمٌ *pl.* سُلَمَاءُ sound, safe; pr. n. m.

مُسْلِمٌ a Muslim

(سلو)

سَلَّى II to divert, amuse, console, cheer

تَسَلَّى V to be diverted, cheered, amused

سَلْوٌ consolation, diversion

تَسْلِيَةٌ diversion, amusement

(سمم)

سَمَّ (ـُ), سَمَّمَ II to poison

سُمٌّ *pl.* سُمُومٌ poison

سَامّ poisonous

(سمح)

سَمَحَ (َ) to permit, allow (*with* لِ for person, and بِ for thing)

سَامَحَ III to pardon, excuse

سَمْحٌ smooth, compliant

تَسَامُحٌ tolerance

(سمر)

سَامَرَ III to converse with, entertain

مِسْمَارٌ *pl.* مَسَامِيرُ nail

(سمط)

سِمَاطٌ *pl.* أَسْمِطَةٌ tablecloth

(سمع)

سَمِعَ (َ) to hear

اِسْتَمَعَ إِلَى VIII to listen to

سُمْعَةٌ fame, reputation, report

(سمك)

سَمَكٌ *pl.* أَسْمَاكٌ fish

(سمن)

سَمْنٌ fat, butter, rancid butter

سَمِينٌ *pl.* سِمَانٌ fat, *adj.*

(سمو)

سَمَّى II to name, call

سَامَى III to vie in glory with

تَسَمَّى V to be called, named; (*with* إِلَى or بِ) to claim relationship to, with

سُمُوٌّ height, highness; title given to ruler, prince

سَمَاءٌ *pl.* سَمَوَاتٌ sky, heavens

اِسْمٌ *pl.* أَسْمَاءٌ, أَسَامٍ, أَسَامِيُّ name

سَامٍ high, exalted

(سنن)

سِنٌّ *pl.* أَسْنَانٌ tooth, age

سُنَّةٌ *pl.* سُنَنٌ Sunna (in Islam), law, usage, tradition

سُنِّيٌّ Sunni, Sunnite (orthodox Muslim)

سِنَانٌ *pl.* أَسِنَّةٌ spear, spear-head

مُسِنٌّ old, of advanced age

(سند)

سَنَدَ إِلَى (ُ) to lean upon

أَسْنَدَ إِلَى IV to ascribe to (a tradition, etc.)

اِسْتَنَدَ إلى VIII to lean upon; have recourse to (God)

سَنَد *pl.* أَسْنَاد document, bill, deed (legal or comm.), support

إِسْنَاد ascribing of a tradition; isnād

مِسْنَد *pl.* مَسَانِد cushion, pillow

سِنْدِيَان evergreen oak, ilex

(سنط)

سَنْط acacia tree

(سنو)

سَنَة *pl.* سِنُون, سَنَوَات year

مُسَنَّاة *pl.* مُسَنَّوَات, مُسَنَّيَات dam, dyke

(سنى)

تَسَنَّى V to be facilitated, made possible

(سهل)

سُهُولَة; بِسُهُولَة ease; easily

سَهْل easy

سَهْل *pl.* سُهُول plain (*geog.*)

(سهم)

سَهْم *pl.* سِهَام arrow

سَهْم *pl.* أَسْهُم lot, share; share (in a company)

(سوأ)

سَاءَ (ـُ) to be bad, evil

سُوء, سَوْء *pl.* أَسْوَاء bad, evil *n.*

سُوءُ الْحَظّ misfortune

سُوءُ التَّفَاهُم misunderstanding

سَيِّئ bad, evil, *adj.*

(سوح)

سَاحَة square, place (piazza), court

(سود)

سَادَ (ـُ) to rule, have dominion over

سَوَّدَ II to make black

اِسْوَدَّ IX to be, become, black

أَسْوَد *f.* سَوْدَاء *pl.* سُود black

اَلسُّودَان the Sudan

سَيِّد *pl.* سَادَة Mr., gentleman, sir; descendant of the Prophet

سَيِّدَة lady, mistress, Mrs., madam

سِيَادَة authority, sovereignty, title

(سور)

سُورَة *pl.* سُوَر Sūra, verse of Qur'ān

سُورِيَّا Syria

سُورِيٌّ Syrian

(سوس)

سِيَاسَةٌ politics (*mod.*); government, administration (*class.*)

سِيَاسِيٌّ *pl.* (of *noun*) سَاسَةٌ political, politician

(سوع)

سَاعَةٌ hour, clock, watch, time

(سوف)

سَوْفَ (also سَـ) *future particle* (before *imperf.*)

مَسَافَةٌ distance

(سوق)

سَاقَ (ـُ) *v.n.* مَسَاقٌ to drive, lead

سَاقٌ *pl.* سِيقَانٌ leg, stem (of a plant)

سُوقٌ (*m.* or *f.*) *pl.* أَسْوَاقٌ market

سَائِقٌ *pl.* سُوَّاقٌ; سَوَّاقٌ *pl.* ـُونَ driver, chauffeur

(سوى)

سَوِىَ (ـَ) to be worth

سَاوَى III to be equal, be equivalent to

سِوَى except, save

سَوَاءٌ equity, like, sameness

خَطُّ ٱلْاِسْتِوَاءِ Equator

مُسَاوَاةٌ equality

مُسَاوٍ equal

مُسْتَوًى *pl.* مُسْتَوَيَاتٌ standard, level *n.*

(سيح)

سَاحَ (ـِ) to travel, tour

سِيَاحَةٌ (long) journey; tourism (*mod.*)

سَائِحٌ *pl.* سُيَّاحٌ, سُوَّاحٌ traveller, tourist

مَسَاحَةٌ area, extent

(سير)

سَارَ (ـِ) to travel, go

سَيْرٌ, مَسِيرٌ way, journey

سِيرَةٌ manner, way of life, biography

مَسِيرَةٌ distance

سَائِرٌ remainder, rest (see also (سأر)

سَيَّارَةٌ motor car

(سيطر)

سَيْطَرَ (على) to rule (over)

سَيْطَرَةٌ rule, domination

(سيف)

سَيْفٌ *pl.* سُيُوفٌ sword

(سيل)

سَالَ (ـِ) to flow, become liquid

سَائِلٌ *pl.* سَوَائِلُ liquid

سَيَلَانٌ flowing, flood

ش

(شأم)

شَأَمَ (ـُ) (with *accus.* or عَلَى) to draw ill-luck upon; bode ill for

شُؤْمٌ bad omen, ill luck

تَشَاؤُمٌ pessimism

مُتَشَائِمٌ pessimist

اَلشَّامُ, اَلشَّأْمُ Syria, Damascus

(شأن)

شَأْنٌ *pl.* شُؤُونٌ matter, affair, condition, thing, state, dignity

فِى شَأْنِ concerning

(شبب)

شَبَّبَ II to laud; rejuvenate

تَشَبَّبَ V to be rejuvenated

شَبِيبَةٌ, شَبَابٌ youth, the time of youth

(in his youth فِى شَبَابِهِ)

شَابٌّ *pl.* شُبَّانٌ, شَبَابٌ young man

(شبح)

شَبْحٌ *pl.* أَشْبَاحٌ ghost, apparition

(شبع)

شَبِعَ (ـَ) to be satisfied, satiated

أَشْبَعَ IV to satisfy

شَبْعَانُ satisfied, satiated

(شبك)

اِشْتَبَكَ VIII to be entangled confused, ambushed

شُبَّاكٌ *pl.* شَبَابِيكُ window

(شبه)

شَابَهَ III, أَشْبَهَ IV to resemble

شِبْهٌ similarity, likeness

شِبْهُ جَزِيرَةٍ peninsula

(شتم)

شَتَمَ (ـُ) to abuse

(شتو)

شِتَاءٌ winter

(شجر)

شَجَرَةٌ, شَجَرٌ (*coll.*), *pl.* أَشْجَارٌ tree

شُجَيْرَةٌ (*dim.*) bush

(شجع)

شَجَّعَ II to encourage

شَجَاعَةٌ courage

شُجَاعٌ *pl.* شُجْعَانٌ courageous, brave

(شحب)

شَاحِبٌ ghastly, drawn (of face)

(شخص)

شَخْصٌ *pl.* أَشْخَاصٌ person

(شدد)

شِدَّةٌ; بِشِدَّةٍ force, violence, strength; violently, strongly

شَدِيدٌ strong, violent, tough

(شذذ)

شَاذٌّ *pl.* شَوَاذٌّ odd, strange, eccentric, rare

(شرر)

شَرٌّ badness, evil, *n.*

شَرٌّ bad, worse, worst, *elative*

شِرِّيرٌ evil, bad, wicked

شَرَرٌ, شِرَارٌ, شَرَارَةٌ spark(s)

(شرب)

شَرِبَ (ـَ) *v.n.* شُرْبٌ to drink

شَرِبَ دُخَانًا — to smoke

شَارَبَ III to drink with

(شرح)

شَرَحَ (ـَ) to explain

شَرْحٌ *pl.* شُرُوحٌ explanation, commentary

اِنْشِرَاحٌ joy, happiness (*lit.* expansion)

(شرد)

شَرَّدَ II to drive into exile, disperse, *trans.*

(شرط)

شَرْطٌ *pl.* شُرُوطٌ condition, term, stipulation

بِشَرْطِ أَنْ on condition that

شُرْطَةٌ police

شُرْطِيٌّ policeman

(شرع)

شَرَعَ (ـَ) to begin

شَرْعٌ divine, religious law (Islam)

شَرِيعَةٌ Shari'a, Moslem law, code

شَارِعٌ *pl.* شَوَارِعُ street

مَشْرُوعٌ *pl.* مَشْرُوعَاتٌ, مَشَارِيعُ scheme, project

مَشْرُوعِيَّةٌ undertaking

(شرف)

شَرَّفَ II to honour (anyone)

أَشْرَفَ IV to overlook, supervise (*with* عَلَى)

تَشَرَّفَ V to have the honour (to), be honoured (by) (*with* بِ)

شَرِيفٌ *pl.* أَشْرَافٌ noble, *n.* and *adj.*, exalted, Sherif (title)

(شرق)

شَرْقٌ east, *n.*, orient

شَرْقِيٌّ eastern, oriental

شُرُوقٌ sunrise

مَشْرِقٌ (the) east (place and time of sunrise)

(شرك)

شَارَكَ III to share with, participate

اِشْتَرَكَ فِى VIII to participate in; subscribe to

شَرِكَةٌ *pl.* اتٌ — company (commercial)

شَرَاكَة partnership

اِشْتِرَاكٌ *pl.* اتٌ — participation, subscription

اِشْتِرَاكِيَّةٌ socialism

اِشْتِرَاكِيٌّ Socialist

شَرِيكٌ *pl.* شُرَكَاءُ partner

مُشْرِكٌ idolator, polytheist

مُشْتَرِكٌ joint, common; subscriber

(شرى)

شَرَى (ـِ) *v.n.* شِرَاءٌ to buy

اِشْتَرَى VIII (*more commonly used*) to buy

شَارٍ ;مُشْتَرٍ *pl.* شُرَاةٌ buyer

(شسع)

شَاسِعٌ extensive, remote

(شطط)

شَطٌّ *pl.* شُطُوطٌ shore, bank

(شطأ)

شَاطِئٌ *pl.* شَوَاطِئُ river bank, coast

(شطن)

شَيْطَانٌ *pl.* شَيَاطِينُ Devil, Satan

(شعب)

شَعْبٌ *pl.* شُعُوبٌ people, tribe

شَعْبَانُ 8th month in Islamic calendar

(شعر)

شَعَرَ (ــُـ) *v.n.* شُعُورٌ to know; feel, perceive (*with* بِ)

شَعْرٌ hair

شِعْرٌ *pl.* أَشْعَارٌ poetry; feeling, knowledge, perception

لَيْتَ شِعْرِى would that I knew!

شَعِيرٌ barley

شَاعِرٌ *pl.* شُعَرَاءُ poet

مَشْعَرٌ *pl.* مَشَاعِرُ feeling, sense

(شعل)

شَعَلَ (ــُـ) to kindle

(شغل)

تَشَاغَلَ VI to pretend to be busy

اِشْتَغَلَ VIII to be occupied, work

شُغْلٌ *pl.* أَشْغَالٌ work, business

مَشْغُولٌ busy, occupied

(شفف)

شَفَّافٌ transparent, very fine

(شفق)

شَفَقَ (ــَـ) (*with* عَلَى) to pity

شَفَقَةٌ compassion, pity

(شفه)

شَفَةٌ *pl.* شِفَاهٌ, شَفَةٌ, شَفَهَاتٌ, شَفَوَاتٌ lip

(شفى)

شَفَى (ــِـ) to heal, cure

شِفَاءٌ cure, recovery

مُسْتَشْفًى *pl.* مُسْتَشْفَيَاتٌ hospital

(شقق)

شَقَّ (ــُـ) to split, cleave

شَاقٌّ hard, severe, troublesome

أَعْمَالٌ شَاقَّةٌ penal servitude

شَقِيقٌ *pl.* أَشِقَّاءُ blood brother

مَشَقَّةٌ *pl.* مَشَاقُّ misfortune, hardship

مُشْتَقٌّ derived (a word)

(شقر)

أَشْقَرُ *f.* شَقْرَاءُ *pl.* شُقْرٌ reddish-coloured

(شقو)

شَقَاءٌ misery, destitution

شَقِيٌّ *pl.* أَشْقِيَاءُ miserable, abject

(شكك)

شَكَّ (ـُ) (*with* فى) to doubt

شَكٌّ *pl.* شُكُوكٌ doubt

(شكر)

شَكَرَ (ـُ) *v.n.* شُكْرٌ to thank

تَشَكَّرَ V to be grateful, thankful

شَاكِرٌ thankful

(شكل)

شَكَّلَ II to form, fashion; to mark with vowel points

شَاكَلَ III to bear resemblance to, be like

شَكْلٌ *pl.* أَشْكَالٌ shape, form kind, sort; vowel point

مُشْكِلَةٌ *pl.* مَشَاكِلُ difficult matter, problem

(شكو)

شَكَا (ـُ) (مِنْ ,عَنْ) to complain (of)

شَكْوَةٌ, شَكْوَى *pl.* شَكَاوٍ complaint

(شلح)

شَلَحَ (ـَ) to strip, undress, *intrans.*

شَلَّحَ II to rob, plunder, strip

(شمم)

شَمَّ (ـُ) to smell, *trans.*

(شمخ)

شَامِخٌ high, lofty

(شمس)

شَمْسٌ (*f.*) *pl.* شُمُوسٌ sun

(شمع)

شَمْعَةٌ wax candle

(شمل)

شَمَلَ (ـُ) to include, embrace

اِشْتَمَلَ عَلَى VIII to contain, comprise

شَمَالٌ north

شِمَالٌ left hand

شَامِلٌ comprehensive

(شنع)

شَنِيعٌ ugly, foul

(شهب)

أَشْهَبُ *f.* شَهْبَاءُ *pl.* شُهْبٌ grey

اَلشَّهْبَاءُ a name of Aleppo

(شهد)

شَهِدَ (ـَ) to witness, testify

شَاهَدَ III to see, witness

اِسْتَشْهَدَ X to call to witness

شَهَادَةٌ evidence, testimony; certificate, diploma; martyrdom

شَاهِدٌ witness

شَهِيدٌ *pl.* شُهَدَاءُ martyr

مَشْهَدٌ scene; place of martyrdom; town in Persia

(شهر)

شَهَرَ (َ) (*with* ب) to make public, divulge

أَشْهَرَ (عَلَى) IV to draw a weapon (against)

شَهْرٌ *pl.* شُهُورٌ, أَشْهُرٌ month

مَشْهُورٌ, شَهِيرٌ famous

(شهق)

شَاهِقٌ *pl.* شَوَاهِقُ high, lofty

(شهى)

اِشْتَهَى VIII to desire eagerly, covet

شَهْوَةٌ *pl.* شَهَوَاتٌ pleasure, indulgence

شَهِيٌّ longing for; appetising

(شور)

شَاوَرَ III to seek advice, consult

اشَارَ إِلَى IV to indicate, refer to

أَشَارَ عَلَى IV to advise

اِسْتَشَارَ X see شَاوَرَ

(مَجْلِسُ) الشُّورَى council

إِشَارَةٌ indication, sign, signal, hint

إِشَارَةً إِلَى (لِ) with reference to

مُشَارٌ إِلَيْهِ (إِلَيْهَا etc.) aforesaid, referred to

مَشُورَةٌ advice, consultation, counsel

مُسْتَشَارٌ advisor

(شوش)

شَاوُوشٌ, شَاوُشٌ *pl.* شُوَّاشٌ commissionaire, messenger (*Magh.*)

شَاوِيشٌ *pl.* ـَاتٌ — sergeant

(شوق)

اِشْتَاقَ إِلَى VIII to long for

شَوْقٌ *pl.* أَشْوَاقٌ longing, desire

(شوك)

شَوْكٌ *pl.* أَشْوَاكٌ thorn

شَوْكَةٌ fork, thorn

(شول)

شَوَّال 10th month of Islamic calendar

(شوه)

شَاة *pl.* شَاء, شِيَاه ewe, sheep

(شوى)

شَوَى (ـِ) to roast, *trans.*

شَاى tea

(شيأ)

شَاءَ (ـَ) to wish, will

إِنْ شَاءَ ٱللهُ (also written إِنْشَاء . . .) if God wills! (D.V.)

شَيْء *pl.* أَشْيَاء thing (with *neg.* = nothing)

مَشِيئَة wish, will

(شيب)

مَشِيب old age

شَائِب old, white-haired

(شيخ)

شَيْخ *pl.* شُيُوخ, مَشَائِخ sheikh, old man, tribal leader, title of respect

مَشِيخَة sheikhdom

(شيد)

شَيَّدَ II to build up

(شيع)

شَاعَ (ـِ) to be spread abroad, published

أَشَاعَ IV to publish, disseminate news, make public

إِشَاعَة widespread report, rumour

شَائِع widespread, prevalent

شِيعَة Shīʿa sect of Islam; of the followers of Ali

شِيعِيّ Shīʿite, Shīʿi, follower of the shīʿa

شُيُوعِيَّة communism

شُيُوعِيّ Communist

(شيل)

شَالَ (ـِ) to lift up, take away

ص

(صبب)

صَبَّ (ـُ) to pour out

(صبح)

أَصْبَحَ IV to become; (*lit.* to do in the morning; to enter upon the morning)

صَبَاحٌ, صُبْحٌ *pl.* أَصْبَاحٌ morning

صَبَاحَ ٱلْخَيْرِ Good morning!

صَبِيحٌ beautiful, comely

مِصْبَاحٌ *pl.* مَصَابِيحُ lamp, torch

(صبر)

صَبَرَ (ـِ) to be patient; to persevere in, bear patiently (with عَلَى)

صَبْرٌ patience

صَابِرٌ patient, *adj.*

صَبُورٌ (very) patient

(صبع)

إِصْبَعٌ, أُصْبُعٌ *pl.* أَصَابِعُ finger

(صبغ)

صَبَغَ (ـُ) to dye, colour

صَبَّاغٌ dyer

(صبن)

صَابُونٌ soap

(صبو)

صَبِيٌّ *pl.* صِبْيَانٌ youth, boy

صَبِيَّةٌ *pl.* صَبَايَا young girl

(صحح)

صَحَّ (ـِ) to be sound, true, correct; recover from an illness

يَصِحُّ ٱلْقَوْلُ it is true to say

صَحَّحَ II to correct, make sound, valid

صِحَّةٌ health, validity, correctness

صَحِيحٌ correct, right, valid

إِصْحَاحٌ *pl.* ـَاتٌ — chapter of a book (of Holy Scripture)

(صحب)

صَحِبَ (ـَ), صَاحَبَ III to accompany, be the friend of

اِصْطَحَبَ VIII to keep company with one another

صُحْبَةٌ company (of friends)

صَاحِبٌ *pl.* أَصْحَابٌ, صَحْبٌ friend, companion; owner, possessor, master

اَلصَّحَابَةُ the companions of Muhammad

(صحر)

صَحْرَاءُ *pl.* صَحَارَى, صَحْرَاوَاتٌ desert

(صحف)

صَحِيفَةٌ *pl.* صُحُفٌ, صَحَائِفُ page (of a book)

صُحُفِيٌّ, صَحَافِيٌّ journalist (*mod.*)

صَحَافَةٌ journalism, the press (*mod.*)

مُصْحَف *pl.* مَصَاحِف Qur'ān, prayer-book

(صحن)

صَحْن *pl.* صُحُون plate

صَحْنُ ٱلدَّار courtyard of a house

(صحو)

صَحَا (ـُ) to be clear, bright (of sky, weather, etc.); to awake from sleep

صَاحٍ clear (day, sky, weather etc.); awake, conscious

(صخر)

صَخْر rock

(صدد)

صَدَد subject matter

بِصَدَد concerning, in the matter of

(صدأ)

صَدَأ rust

(صدر)

صَدَر (ـُ) to go out, issue *intrans.*

صَدَّر II to export (*mod.*)

أَصْدَر IV to issue, send forth

اِسْتَصْدَر X to issue

صَدْر *pl.* صُدُور chest (part of body)

صَادِرَات exports (*mod.*)

(صدع)

صُدَاع headache

(صدغ)

صُدْغ *pl.* أَصْدَاغ temple (of forehead)

(صدف)

صَادَف III to encounter, come across, happen on

مُصَادَفَة encounter, meeting

صُدْفَة *pl.* صُدَف chance, occurrence

صُدْفَةً, بِالصُّدْفَةِ by chance, coincidence

(صدق)

صَدَق (ـُ) to be true, right, sincere, tell the truth

صَدَّق II to believe, confirm

صِدْق truth, veracity

صَدَقَة *pl.* اتٌ — alms, charity

صَدَاقَة friendship, sincerity

صِدِّيق trustworthy, faithful (title of the second Caliph, Abu Bakr)

صَدِيق *pl.* أَصْدِقَاءُ, صِدْقَان friend

(صدل)

صَيْدَلَةٌ pharmacy

صَيْدَلِيٌّ *pl.* صَيَادِلَةٌ chemist, druggist, pharmacist

(صدى)

تَصَدَّى لِ V to apply oneself to anything; to oppose

صَدًى *pl.* أَصْدَاءٌ sound, voice, echo

(صرر)

أَصَرَّ عَلَى IV to persist in

(صرح)

صَرَّحَ II to declare clearly; announce; permit

صَرَاحَةٌ clarity

صَرِيحٌ obvious, clear

تَصْرِيحٌ *pl.* ـــ اتٌ declaration, permit

(صرخ)

صَرَخَ (ـُ) to cry out

صُرَاخٌ, صَرْخَةٌ a cry

صَارُوخٌ *pl.* صَوَارِيخُ rocket, meteor

(صرط)

صِرَاطٌ way, path (relig.)

(صرع)

صَارَعَ III to struggle, contend with; wrestle

(صرف)

صَرَفَ (ـِ) to spend, use (time), change (money)

تَصَرَّفَ V to carry out, dispose of

اِنْصَرَفَ VII to be removed; depart, go; be changed; be used

صَرْفٌ accidence (*grammar*)

صِرْفٌ pure, unmixed

صَرَّافٌ money-changer, banker, cashier

مَصْرِفٌ *pl.* مَصَارِفُ bank

مَصْرُوفٌ *pl.* مَصْرُوفَاتٌ, مَصَارِيفُ expense, expenditure

مُتَصَرِّفٌ Mutasarrif (governor in some Arab countries)

(صرم)

صَرَمَ (ـِ) to pluck

صِرَامٌ time of trimming palm trees

صَارِمٌ sharp, severe

(صعب)

صُعُوبَةٌ difficulty

صَعْبٌ *pl.* صِعَابٌ difficult, hard

(صعد)

صَعِدَ (ـَ) *v.n.* صُعُودٌ to ascend

مِنَ ٱلْآنَ فَصَاعِدًا from now onwards

اَلصَّعِيدُ Upper Egypt

(صغر)

صَغُرَ (ـُ) to be, become, small

اِسْتَصْغَرَ X to belittle, think little of

صِغْرٌ smallness, youth

صَغِيرٌ *pl.* صِغَارٌ small, young

(صغو)

أَصْغَى IV to hearken, listen

(صفف)

صَفٌّ *pl.* صُفُوفٌ line, class, row

(صفح)

صَافَحَ III to shake hands (in greeting)

صَفْحَةٌ *pl.* صَفَحَاتٌ page (of a book); plate

(صفر)

اِصْفَرَّ IX to become yellow, pale

صِفْرٌ *pl.* أَصْفَارٌ zero

صَفَرٌ 2nd month of Islamic calendar

أَصْفَرُ *f.* صَفْرَاءُ *pl.* صُفْرٌ yellow, pale

(صفو)

صَفَا (ـُ) to be clear, pure

اِصْطَفَى VIII to choose

صَفَاءٌ clearness, purity

صَافٍ pure, clear; net (weight etc.)

مُصْطَفًى Mustafa (*lit.* chosen), pr.n.m.

(صقر)

صَقْرٌ *pl.* صُقُورٌ, أَصْقُرٌ hawk

(صقع)

صَقِيعٌ frost

(صقل)

صَقَلَ (ـُ) to polish

(صلب)

صَلَبَ (ـِ) to crucify

صَلِيبٌ crucifix

صَلِيبِيٌّ crusader

(صلح)

صَلُحَ (ـُ) to be sound, honest; to be suitable, good, fit for (*with* لِ)

صَلَّحَ II to repair

صَالَحَ III to make peace with, reconcile

أَصْلَحَ IV to improve, reform, repair

تَصَالَحَ VI to be reconciled, make peace one with the other

صُلْحٌ peace, reconciliation

صَلَاحٌ goodness; adjustment

إِصْلَاحٌ *pl.* ـَاتٌ — reform, improvement

إِصْطِلَاحٌ *pl.* ـَات — technical use, idiom

صَالِحٌ good, proper, honest; self-interest (*mod.*); pr. n. m.

مَصْلَحَةٌ *pl.* مَصَالِحُ interest, advantage, good; administrative department

مُصْطَلَحٌ *pl.* ـَاتٌ — (see إِصْطِلَاحٌ)

(صلد)

صَلْدٌ hard, solid

(صلع)

أَصْلَعُ bald

(صلو)

صَلَّى II to pray

صَلَاةٌ, صَلٰوةٌ (*antiq.*) *pl.* صَلَوَاتٌ prayer

مُصَلًّى place of prayer

(صمم)

صَمَّمَ II to plan, design; (*with* عَلَى) to determine upon

تَصْمِيمٌ plan, design

صَمِيمٌ sincere, true

(صمت)

صَمَتَ (ـُ) to be silent

صَمْتٌ silence

صَامِتٌ silent

(صمد)

اَلصَّمَدُ the eternal (God)

(صنبر)

صَنَوْبَرٌ pine (tree)

(صندق)

صُنْدُوقٌ *pl.* صَنَادِيقُ box, chest; fund

(صنع)

صَنَعَ (ـَ) to make, do; manufacture (*mod.*)

اِصْطَنَعَ VIII to be artificial, contrived

صِنَاعَةٌ *pl.* ـَاتٌ —, صَنَائِعُ art; industry (*mod.*)

مَصْنَعٌ *pl.* مَصَانِعُ factory

(صنف)

صِنْفٌ *pl.* أَصْنَافٌ, صُنُوفٌ class, category, brand

(صنم)

صَنَمٌ *pl.* أَصْنَامٌ idol

(صوب)

أَصَابَ IV to hit, afflict

مُصِيبَةٌ *pl.* مَصَائِبُ misfortune, calamity

(صوت)

صَوْتٌ *pl.* أَصْوَاتٌ voice, sound; vote (*mod.*)

(صور)

صَوَّرَ II to depict, make a picture

تَصَوَّرَ V to imagine

صُورَةٌ *pl.* صُوَرٌ picture, form, copy; manner

تَصْوِيرٌ *pl.* تَصَاوِيرُ picture

صُورُ Tyre (in Lebanon)

(صوف)

صُوفٌ *pl.* أَصْوَافٌ wool

صُوفِيٌّ Sufi, mystic

(صوم)

صَامَ (ـُ) to fast

صِيَامٌ, صَوْمٌ fasting, fast

صَائِمٌ *pl.* صُوَّمٌ one who fasts; fasting, *adj.*

(صون)

صَانَ (ـُ) to protect, preserve

صِيَانَةٌ preservation, protection, conservation

(صيح)

صَاحَ (ـِ) to cry out

صِيَاحٌ, صَيْحَةٌ cry, shout, shouting

(صيد)

صَادَ (ـِ), تَصَيَّدَ V, اِصْطَادَ VIII to hunt

صَيْدٌ hunt, hunting, *n.*

صَيَّادٌ, صَائِدٌ hunter

صَيْدَا Sidon (in Lebanon)

(صير)

صَارَ (ـِ) to become; (with *imperf.*) begin to, to go

مَصِيرٌ the future, result, outcome

تَقْرِيرُ ٱلْمَصِيرِ self-determination (*mod.*)

(صيف)

صَيْفٌ *pl.* أَصْيَافٌ summer

(صين)

اَلصِّينُ China

صِينِيَّةٌ *pl.* صَوَانِى tray

ض

(ضأل)

ضَئِيلٌ *pl.* ضُؤَلَاءُ thin, small, insignificant

(ضأن)

ضَأْنٌ (*sing.* ضَائِنٌ) sheep (*coll.*)

(ضبب)

ضَبَابَةٌ *pl.* ضَبَابٌ mist (thin cloud)

(ضبط)

ضَبَطَ (ـِ) to put right, correct, do a thing well, regulate

ضَبْطٌ exactness, correctness

بِالضَّبْطِ exactly

ضَابِطٌ *pl.* ضُبَّاطٌ officer (military)

مَضْبُوطٌ correct, right, well-regulated

(ضبع)

ضَبُعٌ *pl.* ضِبَاعٌ hyena

(ضجج)

ضَجِيجٌ, ضَجَّةٌ tumult, cry

(ضجر)

ضَجَرٌ unrest, disquiet

(ضجع)

ضَجَعَ (ـَ) to lie, recline

مَضْجَعٌ *pl.* مَضَاجِعُ couch

(ضحك)

ضَحِكَ (ـَ) *v.n.* ضِحْكٌ to laugh

مُضْحِكٌ funny, comic, laughable

(ضحو)

ضُحًى, ضَحَاءٌ forenoon

ضَحِيَّةٌ *pl.* ضَحَايَا sacrifice, victim

عِيدُ ٱلْأَضْحَى Sacrificial Festival (Moslem Festival)

ضَاحِيَةٌ *pl.* ضَوَاحٍ outskirts, suburb of a town

(ضخخ)

مِضَخَّةٌ pump

(ضخم)

ضَخْمٌ *pl.* ضِخَامٌ large, heavy, bulky

(ضدد)

ضَادَّ III to oppose, go against

ضِدّ against, opposite, contrary to *prep.*

(ضرر)

ضَرَّ (ـُ) to injure, harm

أَضَرَّ بِ IV to injure, harm

اِضْطَرَّ VIII to compel

ضَرَّاء adversity

ضَرَر harm, injury

ضَرِير *pl.* أَضْرَار, أَضِرَّاء blind

ضَرُورِيّ necessary, essential

مُضِرّ harmful, injurious

(ضرب)

ضَرَبَ (ـِ) *v.n.* ضَرْبٌ, ضَرْبَةٌ (a blow) to beat; strike a coin; play (a musical instrument)

ضَرَبَ مَثَلاً to quote a proverb, give a parable, example

ضَارَبَ III to fight; have traffic with; compete with

أَضْرَبَ عَن IV to quit, cease (work, etc.); to go on strike (*mod.*)

اِضْطَرَبَ VIII to be agitated, troubled, unsettled

ضَرْبٌ pl. ضُرُوبٌ kind, manner

إِضْرَابٌ *pl.* ـَاتٌ — strike (*mod.*)

ضَرِيبَةٌ *pl.* ضَرَائِبُ tax, impost

اِضْطِرَابٌ *pl.* ـَاتٌ — trouble, agitation (often used in political sense)

(ضرط)

ضَرَطَ (ـِ) to fart, break wind

(ضرع)

ضَارَعَ III to resemble

تَضَرَّعَ (إِلَى) V to beseech

(ضرو)

ضَارٍ *f.* ضَارِيَةٌ *pl.* ضَوَارٍ voracious, carnivorous (beast)

(ضعف)

ضَعُفَ (ـُ) to be, become, weak

تَضَاعَفَ VI to be doubled

ضُعْفٌ weakness

ضِعْفٌ *pl.* أَضْعَافٌ double

ضَعِيفٌ *pl.* ضُعَفَاءُ weak

(ضغط)

ضَغَطَ (ـَ) to press, squeeze

ضَغْطٌ pressure, compulsion

(ضفف)

ضِفَّةٌ *pl.* ضِفَافٌ bank, side, of a river

(ضلل)

ضَلَّ (ـِ) to err, wander; stray from path (relig.)

ضَالٌّ *pl.* ضَالُّونَ strayed, erring

(ضلع)

ضِلْعٌ *pl.* ضُلُوعٌ rib

(ضمم)

ضَمَّ (ـُ) to collect, gather, amalgamate

اِنْضَمَّ (إِلَى, مَعَ) VII to join

(ضمحل)

اِضْمَحَلَّ (*quad.*) IV to vanish, disappear, grow faint, dwindle away

(ضمر)

ضَمِيرٌ *pl.* ضَمَائِرُ conscience; pronoun

(ضمن)

ضَمِنَ (ـَ) to include, guarantee

تَضَمَّنَ V to include, comprise

ضِمْنَ (with following *gen.*) within, inside, enclosed (*prep.*)

ضَمَانٌ guarantee

مَضْمُونٌ guaranteed

مَضْمُونٌ *pl.* ـَاتٌ contents (of a letter)

(ضنن)

ضَنَّ بِ (ـَ) to withhold, keep back

(ضهد)

اِضْطَهَدَ VIII to persecute, maltreat

(ضهى)

ضَاهَى III to resemble (a person or thing)

(ضوأ)

أَضَاءَ IV to light, *trans.*

ضَوْءٌ *pl.* أَضْوَاءٌ light

(ضوض)

ضَوْضَاءُ, ضَوْضَى noise, uproar, clamour

(ضيع)

ضَاعَ (ـِ) to be lost

أَضَاعَ IV to lose

ضَيْعَةٌ *pl.* ضِيَاعٌ village

(ضيف)

أَضَافَ IV to treat with hospitality

أَضَافَ (إِلَى) IV to add, join (to)

ضَيْفٌ *pl.* ضُيُوفٌ guest

إِضَافَةٌ addition, annexation, joining

إِضَافِيٌّ additional, auxiliary

(ضيق)

ضَايَقَ III to annoy, oppress

ضِيقٌ need, anxiety

ضَيِّقٌ narrow

ط

(طبب)

طِبٌّ medicine (the art of)

طَبِيبٌ *pl.* أَطِبَّاءُ physician

(طبخ)

طَبَخَ (ـُ) *v.n.* طَبْخٌ to cook, *trans.*

طَبِيخٌ cooked food

طَبَّاخٌ a cook

مَطْبَخٌ *pl.* مَطَابِخُ kitchen

(طبع)

طَبَعَ (ـَ) *v.n.* طَبَاعَةٌ, طَبْعٌ to print, stamp

طَبْعًا naturally

طَبِيعَةٌ *pl.* طَبَائِعُ nature

طَابِعٌ *pl.* طَوَابِعُ stamp, seal, signet

طَابِعُ بَرِيدٍ postage stamp

اِنْطِبَاعٌ *pl.* ـَاتٌ — impression

مَطْبَعَةٌ *pl.* مَطَابِعُ printing press

(طبق)

طَابَقَ III to agree, conform with

طِبْقًا لِ in accordance with, conformance with

طَبَقٌ *pl.* أَطْبَاقٌ plate, tray

طَبَقَةٌ *pl.* ـَاتٌ — grade, layer, stratum, class

طَابِقٌ pl. طَوَابِقُ floor, storey

(طحن)

طَحَنَ (ـُ) *v.n.* طَحْنٌ to mill, grind (flour)

طَاحُونٌ *pl.* طَوَاحِينُ mill

(طرأ)

طَرَأَ عَلَى (ـُ) to happen to, befall one suddenly

أَطْرَأَ IV to praise highly, overwhelm with praise

طَارِئَةٌ *pl.* طَوَارِئُ emergency, accident, mishap

(طرب)

طَرَّبَ II to sing, chant, trill

(طرح)

طَرَحَ (ـَ) to throw, cast down; subtract (math.)

مَطْرَحٌ *pl.* مَطَارِحُ place (*Syr.* and *Eg.*)

طَرِيحٌ *pl.* طَرْحَى prostrate, thrown on the ground

(طرد)

طَرَدَ (ـُ) to expel, drive away

إِسْتَطْرَدَ X to digress

طَرْدٌ *pl.* طُرُودٌ parcel, bale

طَرِيدٌ expelled, outcast

(طرز)

طَرْزٌ form, shape, manner, style

طِرَازٌ *pl.* طُرُزٌ model, style; embroidery

(طرش)

أَطْرَشُ *f.* طَرْشَاءُ, *pl.* طُرْشٌ deaf

(طرف)

طَرَفٌ *pl.* أَطْرَافٌ side, end, part

(طرق)

طَرَقَ (ـُ) to strike, knock at

طَرِيقٌ (*m.* or *f.*) *pl.* طُرُقٌ road, way

طَرِيقَةٌ *pl.* طَرَائِقُ path, manner, fashion, method; order (relig.)

(طرو)

طَرِيٌّ fresh, tender, moist

(طعم)

طَعَّمَ II to graft; vaccinate

أَطْعَمَ IV to feed, *trans.*

طَعْمٌ taste, flavour

طَعَامٌ *pl.* أَطْعِمَةٌ food

مَطْعَمٌ *pl.* مَطَاعِمُ restaurant

(طفأ)

طَفِئَ (ـَ) to go out, be extinguished

أَطْفَأَ IV to extinguish

إِنْطَفَأَ VII to be extinguished, go out

فِرْقَةُ ٱلْمَطَافِئِ fire brigade (*mod.*)

(طفل)

طِفْلٌ *pl.* أَطْفَالٌ child, baby

طُفُولَةٌ, طُفُولِيَّةٌ childhood

(طقس)

طَقْسٌ *pl.* طُقُوسٌ climate, weather; rite, liturgy

(طقم)

طَقْمٌ uniform (dress)

(طلب)

طَلَبَ (ـُ) *v.n.* طَلَبٌ to seek, ask

طَلَبِيَّةٌ order, demand, request

طَالِبٌ *pl.* طُلَّابٌ, طَلَبَةٌ student

مَطْلُوبٌ *pl.* مَطَالِيبُ demand, requirement

(طلسم)

طِلَسْمٌ *pl.* طَلَاسِمُ talisman

(طلع)

طَلَعَ (ـُ) طُلُوعٌ to ascend, go up; rise (of sun)

اِطَّلَعَ VIII to examine (*with* عَلَى)

(طلق)

طَلَّقَ II to divorce

أَطْلَقَ IV to set free, throw, cast

أَطْلَقَ . . . عَلَى to use a word to mean

أَطْلَقَ سَرَاحَهُ to set (him) free

أَطْلَقَ نَارًا ، رَصَاصًا to shoot, fire at (*with* على)

اِنْطَلَقَ VII to go, depart

طَلِيقٌ free, unfettered

طَلْقُ ٱللِّسَانِ eloquent of speech

— ٱلْيَدَيْنِ — liberal, open-handed

اَلْهَوَاءُ ٱلطَّلْقُ the open air

طَلَاقٌ divorce

طَلَاقَةٌ fluency, volubility; openness

مُطْلَقًا, عَلَى ٱلْإِطْلَاقِ absolutely

مُطْلَقٌ absolute, free, unrestricted

(طلو)

طَلَاوَةٌ beauty, elegance

(طمر)

طِمْرٌ *pl.* أَطْمَارٌ tatters, rags

(طمع)

طَمِعَ (ـَ) to covet, desire

طَمَعٌ greed, avidity

(طمن)

اِطْمَأَنَّ (*quad.*) IV to feel secure, tranquil, calm oneself

طُمَأْنِينَةٌ, اِطْمِئْنَانٌ tranquillity, reassurance, feeling of security

مُطْمَئِنٌّ tranquil, at ease

(طهر)

طَهُرَ (ـُ) to be clean, pure

طَهَّرَ II to purify, cleanse, circumcize

طُهُورٌ purity

طَاهِرٌ pure, clean

(طهو)

طَهَا (ـُ) to cook

طَاهٍ *pl.* طُهَاةٌ cook

(طور)

تَطَوَّرَ V to be developed, evolve through time, by stages

طَوْرٌ *pl.* أَطْوَارٌ stage, time, state

طَوْرًا بَعْدَ طَوْرٍ time after time

طُورٌ mountain; Mount Sinai

تَطَوُّرٌ *pl.* ـَاتٌ transition, development, evolving

(طوس)

طَاوُوسٌ *pl.* طَوَاوِيسُ peacock

(طوع)

أَطَاعَ IV to obey

تَطَوَّعَ V to do voluntarily, volunteer

إِسْتَطَاعَ X to be able

طَاعَةٌ obedience

طَاعَةً, طَوْعًا voluntarily, willingly

سَمْعًا وَطَاعَةً at your service (*lit.* hearing and obeying)

تَطَوُّعًا voluntarily

إِسْتِطَاعَةٌ ability, power

مُطِيعٌ obedient

مُتَطَوِّعٌ volunteer

مُسْتَطَاعٌ possible

(طوف)

طَافَ (ـُ) to go round, circumambulate

طَوَافٌ Circumambulation ceremony (Pilgrimage to Mecca)

طُوفَانٌ flood, deluge

طَائِفَةٌ party, sect, community, denomination

مُطَوِّفٌ Mecca pilgrimage guide

(طوق)

أَطَاقَ IV to be able, bear, support

طَاقَةٌ ability, power; window

(طول)

طَالَ (ـُ) to be long

طَالَمَا . . . (followed by *verb*) for a long time

طَوَّلَ II to make long; take a long time in (*with* فى)

أَطَالَ IV to make long, lengthen, extend

طُولٌ length

طَائِلٌ advantage, benefit

طَاوِلَةٌ *pl.* ـَاتٌ — table (*Syr.*); the game of backgammon

طَوِيلٌ *pl.* طِوَالٌ long, tall

(طوى)

طَوَى (ـِ) to fold, fold up

فى طَيِّه herewith, enclosed

(طيب)

طَابَ (ـِ) to be good, calm oneself

طَابَتْ نَفْسُهُ to be cheerful

طَيَّبَ II to spice, perfume

طِيبٌ *pl.* أَطْيَابٌ spice, perfume

طَيِّبٌ good *adj.*

طَيِّبَةٌ *pl.* ـَاتٌ — good thing

طُوبَى blessedness

(طير)

طَارَ (ـِ) to fly

أَطَارَ IV to cause to fly

طَائِرٌ, طَيْرٌ *pl.* طُيُورٌ bird

طَيَرَانٌ flying, *n.*, flight of a bird; aviation (*mod.*)

طِيَرَةٌ portent, evil omen

طَيَّارٌ air pilot

طَائِرَةٌ, طَيَّارَةٌ aeroplane, aircraft

مَطَارٌ aerodrome, airport

(طين)

طِينٌ clay, mud, mortar

ظ

(ظبى)

ظَبْيٌ gazelle

(ظرف)

اِسْتَظْرَفَ X to find or consider clever or agreeable

ظَرْفٌ *pl.* ظُرُوفٌ vessel, receptacle, envelope; circumstance, space of time

ظَرْفُ فِنْجَانٍ saucer

ظَرِيفٌ *pl.* ظُرَفَاءُ witty person agreeable; pr. n. m.

(ظفر)

ظَفِرَ بِ (ـَ) to conquer, overcome

ظَفَرٌ success, victory

ظُفْرٌ pl. أَظْفَارٌ, أَظَافِيرُ finger nail, claw

(ظلل)

ظَلَّ (ـَ) to continue, remain

ظَلَّ يَفْعَلُ to continue to do, act

ظِلٌّ shade

مُظِلٌّ shady

(ظلم)

ظَلَمَ (ـِ) to oppress, wrong, harm

أَظْلَمَ IV to be, become, dark

ظُلْمٌ oppression, ill-treatment

ظُلْمَةٌ, ظَلَامٌ dark, *n.* darkness

ظَالِمٌ pl. ـُونَ, ظَلَمَةٌ oppresser

مُظْلِمٌ dark, *adj.*

مَظْلُومٌ oppressed; having a grievance (*mod.*)

(ظمأ)

ظَمِئَ (ـَ) to be thirsty

ظَمْءٌ thirst

ظَمْآنُ, ظَمِيءٌ thirsty

(ظنن)

ظَنَّ (ـُ) to think

ظَنٌّ pl. ظُنُونٌ thought, supposition

(ظهر)

ظَهَرَ (ـَ) v.n. ظُهُورٌ to appear, seem

أَظْهَرَ IV to show

تَظَاهَرَ VI to feign, make a show of, demonstrate

ظَهْرٌ pl. ظُهُورٌ back (anatomical), reverse side

ظُهْرٌ; بَعْدَ ٱلظُّهْرِ noon; afternoon

ظَاهِرٌ manifest, external

مَظْهَرٌ pl. مَظَاهِرُ appearance

مُظَاهَرَةٌ demonstration (*political, etc.*)

ع

(عبأ)

عِبْءٌ pl. أَعْبَاءٌ burden, load

عَبَاءٌ, عَبَاءَةٌ pl. أَعْبِئَةٌ, عُبِيٌّ camel-hair cloak of Bedouin

(عبث)

عَبَثًا to no purpose, in vain

(عبد)

عَبَدَ (ـُ) *v.n.* عِبَادَةٌ to worship

عَبَّدَ II to build, construct a road

اِسْتَعْبَدَ X to enslave

عِبَادَةٌ religious service, worship

عُبُودِيَّةٌ bondage, slavery

عَبْدٌ *pl.* عَبِيدٌ؛ عَبْدُ ٱللهِ servant, slave; Abdullah, Abdullahi, pr. n. m.

عَبْدٌ *pl.* عِبَادٌ worshipper

عَابِدٌ *pl.* ـُونَ, عَبَدَةٌ, عُبَّادٌ worshipper

مَعْبَدٌ *pl.* مَعَابِدُ temple, place of worship

(عبر)

عَبَرَ (ـُ) *v.n.* عُبُورٌ to pass, cross, cross over

عَبَّرَ (عَنْ) II to explain, express

اِعْتَبَرَ VIII to consider, esteem, reckon

عَبْرَ over, across (on the other side)

عَبْرَةٌ *pl.* ـَاتٌ — tear

عِبْرَانِيٌّ, عِبْرِيٌّ Hebrew

عِبَارَةٌ expression, style, diction

هٰذَا عِبَارَةٌ عَنْ . . . that means

اِعْتِبَارًا مِنْ . . . effective from . . . . , in effect from . . . (*mod.*)

عَابِرُ ٱلسَّبِيلِ wayfarer

(عبس)

عَبَسَ (ـِ) to frown

عَبَّاسٌ Abbas, pr. n. m. (*lit.* lion)

بَنُو ٱلْعَبَّاسِ the Abbasids

(عبو)

عَبَّى II to fill

عَبَّى جَيْشًا to mobilise army

(عتب)

عَاتَبَ III to blame, censure, reproach, reprove

عَتَبَةٌ *pl.* ـَاتٌ — threshold

(عتق)

أَعْتَقَ IV to free, emancipate

عَاتِقٌ *pl.* عَوَاتِقُ shoulder

عَتِيقٌ *pl.* عُتُقٌ old, antiquated

(عتل)

عَتَّالٌ porter

(عتم)

عَتَمَ (ـِ) to become dark

عَتْمَةٌ darkness

(عثر)

عَثَرَ على (ـُ) to stumble (upon)

(عثم)

عُثْمَانُ Othman, Uthman, pr. n. m.

عُثْمَانِيٌّ Ottoman, *n.* and *adj.*

اَلْعُثْمَانِيُّونَ the Ottoman Turks

(عجب)

عَجِبَ (ـَ) to wonder

أَعْجَبَ ب IV to admire, be pleased with

تَعَجَّبَ (مِنْ) V to wonder, be surprised (at)

عَجِيبٌ wonderful, strange

عَجِيبَةٌ *pl.* عَجَائِبُ a wonder

(عجز)

عَجَزَ (عَنْ) (ـِ) to be unable (to), helpless

عَاجِزٌ helpless, unable, impotent

عَجُوزٌ *pl.* عَجَائِزُ old (woman)

مُعْجِزَةٌ *pl.* ـَاتٌ miracle

(عجل)

عَجِلَ (ـَ), اِسْتَعْجَلَ X to hurry, hasten, be quick

عَجَلٌ, عَجَلَةٌ haste, hurry

عِجْلٌ *pl.* عُجُولٌ calf

عَجَلَةٌ cart-wheel; bicycle (*mod.*)

تَعْجِيلٌ (see عَجَّلَ)

عَاجِلًا soon, quickly

عَاجِلًا أَمْ آجِلًا sooner or later

(عجم)

بِلَادُ العجم, اَلْعَجَمُ name given to Persia by Arabs

أَعْجَمِيٌّ foreign, non-Arab, Persian; obscure in language

(عجن)

عَجَنَ (ـُ) to knead

(عدد)

عَدَّ (ـُ) to number, count, regard

عَدَّدَ II to keen, recount the praises of the dead

أَعَدَّ IV to prepare, make ready

تَعَدَّدَ V to be multiplied, numerous

إِسْتَعَدَّ X to be ready, prepare oneself

عَدَدٌ *pl.* أَعْدَادٌ number, *n.*

عِدَّةٌ *pl.* عِدَدٌ a number, several

تَعْدَادٌ enumeration

إِسْتِعْدَادٌ preparedness, readiness, ability, aptitude

عَدِيدٌ، مُتَعَدِّدٌ numerous

مُعَدَّاتٌ (*sing.* مُعَدٌّ) equipment

مُسْتَعِدٌّ ready, prepared (of a person)

(عدس)

عَدَسٌ lentils

(عدل)

عَدَلَ (ـِ) to act justly

عَدَّلَ II to modify, adjust, straighten, make equal

عَادَلَ III to be equivalent to

إِعْتَدَلَ VIII to be straight, moderate

عَدْلٌ، عَدَالَةٌ justice

إِعْتِدَالٌ moderation, equality, equinox

عَادِلٌ just, upright, *n.* and *adj.*

مُعَدَّلٌ average

مُعْتَدِلٌ temperate, moderate

(عدم)

عَدِمَ (ـَ) to lack, want, cease to exist

أَعْدَمَ IV to deprive of, annihilate, execute

عَدَمٌ lack of, non-existence

عَدِيمٌ lacking, *adj.*

(عدن)

عَدَنُ Aden

جَنَّاتُ عَدْنٍ Paradise, Garden of Eden

مَعْدِنٌ *pl.* مَعَادِنُ mineral, metal, mine

(عدو)

عَدَا (ـُ) to run; infect

عَادَى III to treat as an enemy

أَعْدَى IV to infect (with a disease)

إِعْتَدَى عَلَى VIII to be hostile towards

عَدَاوَةٌ hostility, enmity

عَدَا، عَنْ، مَا عَدَا save, except, beside

عَدُوٌّ *pl.* أَعْدَاءٌ enemy

(عذب)

عَذَّبَ II to torment, torture, make suffer

تَعَذَّبَ V to suffer, be punished

عَذَابٌ punishment, torment

عُذُوبَةٌ sweetness, agreeableness

عَذْبٌ sweet (water)

(عذر)

عَذَرَ (ـِ) to excuse

تَعَذَّرَ V, اِعْتَذَرَ IV to apologise; be effaced

تَعَذَّرَ عَلَى V to be impossible

عُذْرٌ *pl.* أَعْذَارٌ excuse, apology, plea

عَذْرَاءُ *pl.* عَذَارَى virgin

(عذق)

عَذْقٌ *pl.* أَعْذَاقٌ palm tree

(عرب)

عَرَّبَ II to Arabize (of a foreign word), translate, render, into Arabic

أَعْرَبَ IV to express clearly, parse, speak a good Arabic style

تَعَرَّبَ V, اِسْتَعْرَبَ X to become an Arab, adopt customs, etc. of the Arabs

عَرَبِيٌّ *pl.* عَرَبٌ, *pl. pl.* أَعْرَابٌ Arab, Arabic

أَعْرَابِيٌّ desert Arab, Bedouin

اَلْعَرَبُ ٱلْعَرْبَاءُ the pure Arabs

تَعْرِيبٌ Arabicizing, rendering into Arabic

إِعْرَابٌ syntax, parsing

عَرَبَةٌ *pl.* اتٌ — cart, carriage, cab; motor car (Egypt and Sudan)

عُرُوبَةٌ quality or state of being an Arab; "Arabdom", Arabism (*mod.*)

عُرْبُونٌ *pl.* عَرَابِينُ pledge, earnest

مُعْرَبٌ declinable (word)

(عرج)

أَعْرَجُ *f.* عَرْجَاءُ *pl.* عُرْجٌ lame

(عرس)

عَرُوسٌ *pl.* عَرَائِسُ bride

عَرِيسٌ *pl.* عُرْسٌ bridegroom

(عرش)

عَرْشٌ *pl.* عُرُوشٌ throne

(عرض)

عَرَضَ (ـِ) to offer, present, happen to, befall, expose

عَرَّضَ II to widen; expose to (*with* لِ)

عَارَضَ III to oppose, contradict

تَعَرَّضَ لِ V to interfere in

اِعْتَرَضَ VIII to review (army, troop, etc.); (*with* عَلَى) to oppose, object to

عَرْضٌ *pl.* عُرُوضٌ breadth, width; exhibition, review; submission, presentation

يَوْمُ ٱلْعَرْضِ Day of Judgment

عَرْضَحَال *pl.* ـَات (*mod.*) petition

عِرْضٌ honour, good repute

عَرَضًا by chance, accidentally

عَارِضٌ *pl.* عَوَارِضُ accident

عَرِيضٌ *pl.* عِرَاضٌ wide, broad

عَرِيضَةٌ petition

مَعْرِضٌ *pl.* مَعَارِضُ exhibition, exposition; topics of conversation (in *pl.*)

مَعْرُوضٌ petition, offered, presented

مُعَارَضَةٌ opposition

(عرف)

عَرَفَ (ـِ) to know, get to know

عَرَّفَ II to inform, make known, introduce (one person to another)

تَعَارَفَ VI to know each other

اِعْتَرَفَ (بِ) VIII to acknowledge, admit, confess

عُرْفٌ acknowledgment; common language, custom

فِى عُرْفِى in my opinion

مَعْرِفَةٌ *pl.* مَعَارِفُ knowledge, acquaintance

مَعْرُوفٌ favour, good deed (*lit.* known)

(عرق)

عَرِقَ (ـَ) to sweat, perspire

عَرَقٌ perspiration

عَرَقٌ arak, distilled spirit (dates, raisins, etc.)

عِرْقٌ *pl.* عُرُوقٌ vein, artery, root

عَرِيقٌ noble, rooted

اَلْعِرَاقُ Iraq

(عرقل)

تَعَرْقَلَ (*quad.*) II to be confused, entangled, complicated

عَرَاقِيلُ difficulties, complications

(عرك)

عَارَكَ III to fight

مَعْرَكَةٌ *pl.* مَعَارِكُ battle

(عرى)

عَارٍ *pl.* عُرَاةٌ naked, free (from)

عُرْيَانٌ *pl.* ـُونَ — naked

(عزز)

عَزَّ (ـِ) to be mighty, noble, dear

(اللّٰهُ) عَزَّ وَجَلَّ God, exalted and magnified (be his name)!

عِزَّةٌ power, might

عَزِيزٌ dear, powerful

(عزب)

أَعْزَبُ *f.* عَزْبَاءُ *pl.* عُزْبٌ unmarried, celibate

(عزف)

(على) عَزَفَ (ـِ) to play upon a musical instrument

(عزل)

عَزَلَ (ـِ) to remove, set apart, discharge, depose (from office); insulate (*mod.*)

اِعْتَزَلَ VIII to retire from, abdicate, isolate oneself

عَازِلٌ insulator (*mod.*)

مُعْتَزِلٌ Mu'tazilite, seceder (in Islam), dissenter

(عزم)

عَزَمَ (ـِ) to invite; make a spell, recite charms

عَزَمَ عَلَى to determine upon, resolve to do

عَزْمٌ resolution, purpose

عَازِمٌ firm, resolute, determined

عَزِيمَةٌ invitation

(عزى)

عَزَّى II to comfort

(عسر)

(على) عَسُرَ (ـُ) to be difficult (for)

عَسَّرَ II to make difficult

عُسْرٌ difficulty

عَسِيرٌ difficult

(عسكر)

عَسْكَرٌ pl. عَسَاكِرُ army, troops, soldiery

عَسْكَرِىٌّ soldier, military

عَسْكَرِيَّةٌ military service, the military

مُعَسْكَرٌ pl. ـَات — army camp

(عسل)

عَسَلٌ honey

(عسى)

عَسَى it may be, perhaps

(عشش)

عُشٌّ pl. عِشَاشٌ nest (of bird)

(عشب)

عُشْبٌ pl. أَعْشَابٌ green herb, grass, pasturage, herbiage

(عشر)

عَاشَرَ III to associate with, be in company with

عُشْرٌ pl. أَعْشَارٌ tenth, tithe

عَشَرَةٌ f. عَشْرٌ ten

عِشْرُونَ twenty

عَاشِرٌ tenth (ordinal)

عَاشُورَاءُ 10th day of Muharram

عَشِيرَةٌ pl. عَشَائِرُ tribe, kinsfolk

مُعَاشَرَةٌ social intercourse

(عشق)

عَشِقَ (ـَ) to love, have passion for

عِشْقٌ love, passion

عَاشِقٌ pl. عُشَّاقٌ lover

مَعْشُوقٌ beloved one

(عشو)

تَعَشَّى V to sup, eat in the evening

عَشَاءٌ evening meal (time)

عَشِيَّةٌ pl. عَشَايَا evening

(عصب)

عَصَبٌ pl. أَعْصَابٌ nerve, sinew

عَصَبِىٌّ nervous, sinewy

عُصْبَةٌ pl. عُصَبٌ troop, band, group

عَصَبِيَّةٌ, تَعَصُّبٌ obstinacy, fanaticism, extremism, bigotry (in religion, politics, etc.)

مُتَعَصِّبٌ fanatical, fanatic, extremist

(عصر)

عَاصَرَ III to be contemporary with

عَصْرٌ *pl.* عُصُورٌ time, age, epoch, afternoon

صَلاَةُ ٱلْعَصْرِ afternoon prayer (Muslim)

مُعَاصِرٌ contemporary

مَعْصَرٌ, مَعْصَرَةٌ *pl.* مَعَاصِرُ place where one presses fruit

(عصف)

عَاصِفَةٌ *pl.* عَوَاصِفُ hurricane, storm, tempest

(عصفر)

عُصْفُورٌ *pl.* عَصَافِيرُ sparrow, small bird

(عصم)

عَاصِمَةٌ *pl.* عَوَاصِمُ capital city

مِعْصَمٌ *pl.* مَعَاصِمُ wrist

(عصى)

عَصَى (ـِ) to rebel

عَصاً *pl.* عِصِيٌّ stick, cane

عِصْيَانٌ disobedience

عَاصٍ *pl.* عُصَاةٌ rebel, rebellious

(عضض)

عَضَّ (ـُ) to bite

(عضد)

عَضَدَ (ـُ) to aid, assist

تَعَاضُدٌ co-operation

(عضل)

عَضَلَةٌ *pl.* ـَاتٌ, عَضَلٌ muscle

(عضو)

عُضْوٌ *pl.* أَعْضَاءٌ member, limb

(عطر)

عَطَّرَ II to scent, perfume

عِطْرٌ *pl.* أَعْطَارٌ perfume, scent

عَاطِرٌ sweet-smelling

عَطَّارٌ grocer

(عطس)

عَطَسَ (ـُ) to sneeze

(عطش)

عَطْشَانُ *pl.* عَطْشَى, عَطَاشَى thirsty

عَاطِشٌ thirsty

(عطف)

عَطَفَ كَلِمَةً (ـِ) to join one word to another by a conjunction

عَطَفَ عَلَى to be kind to, have feeling, or pity, for

اِنْعَطَفَ VII to be bent, inclined

عَطْفَةٌ lane, side street, turning

عَاطِفَةٌ *pl.* عَوَاطِفُ kindness, pity, feeling, emotion

(عطل)

عَطَلَ (ـُ) to be idle, workless, spoiled; to be devoid of (*with* عَنْ)

عَطَّلَ II to delay, hinder

عُطْلَةٌ vacant time, holiday

عَاطِلٌ idle, void, devoid

مُعَطَّلٌ unemployed

(عطو)

أَعْطَى IV (with *accus.* of person and thing) to give

تَعَاطَى VI to engage in (business, commerce)

اِسْتَعْطَى X to beg

عَطَاءٌ *pl.* عَطَاءَاتٌ gift; offer, tender

(عظم)

عَظْمٌ *pl.* عِظَامٌ bone

عَظَمَةٌ greatness

عَظِيمٌ *pl.* عِظَامٌ, عُظَمَاءُ great, excellent

(عفف)

عَفِيفٌ *pl.* أَعِفَّاءُ virtuous, chaste

(عفر)

عَفَرٌ dust

(عفرت)

عِفْرِيتٌ *pl.* عَفَارِيتُ demon, devil

(عفش)

عَفْشٌ luggage, baggage (*mod. Eg.* and *Syr.*)

(عفن)

عَفِنٌ decayed, rotten

(عفو)

عَفَا (ـُ) (عَنْ) to pardon, forgive

عَافَى III to restore to health

أَعْفَى (عَنْ) IV to exempt, excuse

عَفْوٌ pardon, amnesty

عَافِيَةٌ *pl.* عَافِيَاتٌ, عَوَافٍ good health

(عقب)

عَقَّبَ II to follow on behind

عَاقَبَ III to punish

عَقِبٌ *pl.* أَعْقَابٌ heel of foot

عَقَبَةٌ *pl.* عِقَابٌ mountain road or pass, obstacle

عُقْبَةٌ difficulty, obstacle

عِقَابٌ, مُعَاقَبَةٌ punishment

عُقَابٌ *pl.* عِقْبَانٌ eagle

عُقُوبَةٌ penalty, punishment

عَاقِبَةٌ *pl.* عَوَاقِبُ end, result

يَعْقُوبُ Jacob

(عقد)

عَقَدَ (ِ) to tie, knot, bind, conclude, ratify; summon

عَاقَدَ III to make a contract with, enter into a compact with

إِنْعَقَدَ VII to be convened, gather (a meeting)

إِعْتَقَدَ VIII to believe, have a belief

عَقْدٌ *pl.* عُقُودٌ binding, contract; knot; decade

عِقْدٌ *pl.* عُقُودٌ necklace

عُقْدَةٌ *pl.* عُقَدٌ knot, joint; dilemma

عَقِيدَةٌ *pl.* عَقَائِدُ article of faith, belief

مُتَعَهِّدٌ contractor

(عقر)

عَقَارٌ *pl.* ـَاتٌ — real estate, landed property

عَقَّارٌ *pl.* عَقَاقِيرُ drug, aromatic

عَاقِرٌ (*f.*) *pl.* عَوَاقِرُ barren (woman), unfruitful (land)

(عقرب)

عَقْرَبٌ *pl.* عَقَارِبُ scorpion, hand of clock

(عقل)

عَقَلَ (ُ) to bind, tie

إِعْتَقَلَ VIII to restrain, intern; confine (as a prisoner)

عَقْلٌ *pl.* عُقُولٌ intelligence, intellect, sense

إِعْتِقَالٌ interment

عِقَالٌ *pl.* عُقُلٌ rope, cord (of bedouin headcloth), tether

عَاقِلٌ *pl.* عُقَلَاءُ intelligent

عَاقِلٌ *pl.* عُقَّالٌ an initiate (among the Druzes)

عَقِيلَةٌ *pl.* ـَاتٌ —, عَقَائِلُ lady, wife

مَعْقِلٌ *pl.* مَعَاقِلُ stronghold, fortress

مُعْتَقَلٌ *pl.* ات — place of interment, concentration camp

مَعْقُولٌ intelligible, reasonable

(عقم)

عَقَمَ (ـِ) to sterilise, disinfect, render barren

عَقِيمٌ sterile, barren, futile

(عكر)

عَكَّرَ II, أَعْكَرَ IV to make turbid, muddle, confuse

(عكس)

عَكَسَ (ـِ) to reverse, invert

عَاكَسَ III to oppose, contradict

اِنْعَكَسَ VII to reflect, be inverted

عَكْسٌ *pl.* أَعْكَاسٌ the opposite or contrary of anything

بِٱلْعَكْسِ on the contrary

(علل)

عَلَّ (see لَعَلَّ)

عِلَّةٌ *pl.* عِلَلٌ weakness, sickness, disease; cause, reason

عَلِيلٌ sick, weak, diseased, ill

(علب)

عُلْبَةٌ *pl.* عُلَبٌ small box

(علج)

عَالَجَ III to treat (an ill person), treat of (an affair), work at, exercise skill at

عِلَاجٌ, مُعَالَجَةٌ treatment, remedy

(علف)

عَلَفَ (ـِ) to feed (a beast)

عَلَفٌ fodder

مَعْلَفٌ *pl.* مَعَالِفُ manger

(علق)

عَلَّقَ II to hang (up), attach, suspend (on, to بِ, عَلَى)

عَلَّقَ فِي II to note down, comment on

تَعَلَّقَ بِ V to be attached to, appertain to, hang from, depend on

عَلَاقَةٌ *pl.* ـَاتٌ, عَلَائِقُ connection, relation, attachment, liaison

تَعْلِيقٌ news commentary (*mod.*)

تَعَلُّقَاتٌ possessions, properties

مِعْلَقَةٌ *pl.* مَعَالِقُ (for مِلْعَقَةٌ which see) spoon

اَلْمُعَلَّقَاتُ the Muʿallaqat (famous pre-Islamic odes suspended in the Kaʿba in Mecca)

مُعَلِّق news commentator (*mod.*)

(علك)

عَلَكَ (ـُـ) to chew

(علم)

عَلِمَ (ـَـ) to know, get to know

عَلَّمَ II to teach

أَعْلَمَ IV to inform (doubly or trebly transitive)

تَعَلَّمَ V to learn

اِسْتَعْلَمَ X to ask for information

عِلْمٌ *pl.* عُلُومٌ knowledge, science

تَعْلِيمٌ *pl.* ـَـاتٌ, تَعَالِيمُ education, instruction

عَالَمٌ *pl.* عَالَمُونَ world, universe

عَالِمٌ *pl.* عُلَمَاءُ wise, learned man

مُعَلِّمٌ teacher

مُتَعَلِّمٌ educated, educated person

(علن)

عَلَنَ (ـَـ) to be open, manifest, public

أَعْلَنَ IV to publish, advertise, inform, declare

عَلَانِيَةً, عَلَنًا publicly, openly

عَلَنِيٌّ public, open

إِعْلَانٌ *pl.* ـَـاتٌ — advertisement, announcement

(علو)

عَلَا (ـُـ) to rise, be or become high

تَعَالَى VI to be exalted

عُلُوٌّ height

عَلَاوَةً عَلَى in addition to

عَلِيٌّ Ali (pr. n. m.)

عَالٍ high

أَعْلَى *f.* عُلْيَا *pl.* أَعَالٍ higher, highest, nobler; upper part

عَلَى on, upon, against

عَلَى أَنْ provided that; with the intention of

عَلَى يَدِ... through, by, at the hands of

(علون)

عُنْوَانٌ (see also عُنْوَانٌ) address, title

(عمم)

عَمَّ (ـُـ) to be universal, widespread

عَمّ *pl.* عُمُومَة, أَعْمَام paternal uncle

عُمُوم (the) public

عُمُومًا, عَامَّةً generally

عُمُومِيّ, عَامّ public, general, *adj.*

عَامَّة *pl.* عَوَامّ the generality, the masses

لُغَة عَامِّيَّة colloquial language

(عمد)

عَمَّدَ II to baptise

اِعْتَمَدَ عَلَى VIII to depend upon, rely on

عَمُود *pl.* أَعْمِدَة column, pillar

اِعْتِمَاد trust, confidence; credit (commercial)

(عمر)

عَمِرَ (ـِ) to live long

عَمَرَ (ـُ) to inhabit, be inhabited (by بِ)

عَمَّرَ II to build, construct

أَعْمَرَ IV to develop (a country, etc.)

اِسْتَعْمَرَ X to colonize

عُمْر *pl.* أَعْمَار life, age

عُمَر ‘Umar, Omar (pr. n. m.)

عَمْرو ‘Amr (pr. n. m.)

عِمَارَة *pl.* ـَات, عَمَائِر edifice, building; fleet

عَامِر inhabited, flourishing

عُمْرَان prosperity of a land, civilisation

مِعْمَار *pl.* مِعْمَارِيَّة, مِعْمَارِيّ mason

مَعْمُور inhabited

اَلْمَعْمُورَة the world

مُسْتَعْمَرَة colony

(عمش)

أَعْمَش weak-sighted, half blind

(عمق)

عُمْق *pl.* أَعْمَاق depth

عَمِيق *pl.* عُمُق deep

(عمل)

عَمِلَ (ـَ) to do, make, work

عَامَلَ III to treat, act towards, deal with

اِسْتَعْمَلَ X to use

عَمَل *pl.* أَعْمَال action, deed, work

عُمْلَة currency, money

عَامِل *pl.* عُمَّال worker, labourer; provincial governor (*antiq.*)

عَمِيلٌ *pl.* عُمَلَاءُ agent, representative (comm.)

حِزْبُ ٱلْعُمَّالِ the Labour Party (*mod.*)

مُعَامَلَةٌ treatment, dealings towards (in *pl.* business)

(عمى)

أَعْمَى *f.* عَمْيَاءُ *pl.* عُمْيٌ blind

(عن)

عَنْ from, away from, about, concerning

(عنب)

عِنَبٌ *pl.* أَعْنَابٌ grape, vine

(عند)

عِنْدَ with, by, at, in possession of (to have)

عِنْدَئِذٍ then, at that time

عَنِيدٌ *pl.* عُنُدٌ stubborn, obstinate

(عندلب)

عَنْدَلِيبٌ *pl.* عَنَادِلُ nightingale

(عنز)

عَنْزٌ, عَنْزَةٌ she-goat

(عنصر)

عُنْصُرٌ *pl.* عَنَاصِرُ element, origin, race

(عنف)

عُنْفٌ harshness, severity

عُنْفُوَانُ ٱلشَّبَابِ prime of youth

عَنِيفٌ harsh, severe

(عنق)

عَانَقَ III to embrace

تَعَانَقَ VI to embrace one another

عُنْقٌ *pl.* أَعْنَاقٌ neck

(عنقد)

عُنْقُودٌ *pl.* عَنَاقِيدُ bunch of grapes

(عنكب)

عَنْكَبُوتٌ *pl.* عَنَاكِبُ spider

(عنون)

عَنْوَنَ to address a letter

عُنْوَانٌ *pl.* عَنَاوِينُ title, address

(عنى)

عَنَى (ـِ) to mean, intend, concern

يَعْنِي that is to say, that means, *i.e.*

عَانَى III to suffer, sustain

اِعْتَنَى بِ VIII to manage, take care of, pay attention to

عَنَاءٌ toil, difficulty, trouble

عِنَايَةٌ, اِعْتِنَاءٌ care, solicitude, anxiety

مَعْنًى *pl.* مَعَانٍ meaning, sense

مَعْنَوِيٌّ ideal, mental, abstract

(عهد)

عَهِدَ (ـَ) to fulfil (a promise)

عَهِدَ (إِلَى) to impose a condition; enjoin; know; enter an agreement with

عَاهَدَ III to make a covenant or agreement (with anyone)

تَعَهَّدَ (بِ) V to contract, undertake, agree, pledge; look after, take care of

تَعَاهَدَ VI to contract together, make mutual agreement

عَهْدٌ *pl.* عُهُودٌ covenant, agreement; time, epoch

وَلِيُّ عَهْدٍ heir apparent

مُعَاهَدَةٌ agreement, treaty

مَعْهَدٌ *pl.* مَعَاهِدُ institute

(عوج)

أَعْوَجُ *f.* عَوْجَاءُ *pl.* عُوجٌ crooked

(عود)

عَادَ (ـُ) to return, to do again

عَيَّدَ II to feast, keep a feast (day)

أَعَادَ IV to restore, repeat

تَعَوَّدَ (بِ) V, اِعْتَادَ VIII to be accustomed (to)

عُودٌ *pl.* عِيدَانٌ lute, stick

عِيَادَةٌ surgery, doctor's out-patients' department

عِيدٌ *pl.* أَعْيَادٌ festival, feast day

عَادَةٌ *pl.* —َاتٌ, عَوَائِدُ custom, habit

عَادِيٌّ, اِعْتِيَادِيٌّ, مُعْتَادٌ habitual, customary

عَائِدَةٌ *pl.* عَوَائِدُ benefit, avail, use, return

(عوذ)

عَاذَ بِ (ـُ) to seek, take refuge in, with

مَعَاذٌ, مَعَاذَةٌ asylum, refuge

مَعَاذَ ٱللّٰهِ God forbid!

(عور)

أَعَارَ IV to lend

اِسْتَعَارَ X to borrow; use an expression metaphorically

اِسْتِعَارَةٌ borrowing, metaphor

أَعْوَرُ *f.* عَوْرَاءُ *pl.* عُورٌ one-eyed

مُسْتَعَارٌ borrowed, metaphorical

(عوز)

عَازَ (ـُ) to need, want, lack

عَائِزٌ needy, wanting

مُعْوِزٌ destitute, bereaved

(عوض)

عَوَّضَ II to give in exchange, compensate

عِوَضٌ *pl.* أَعْوَاضٌ exchange, compensation, instead (of)

عِوَضًا عَنْ، مِنْ instead of

تَعْوِيضٌ compensation

(عوق)

عَوَّقَ II to hinder, delay

(عول)

عَالَ (ـُ) to support, nourish

أَعَالَ IV to sustain a family

عَائِلَةٌ family

عَوِيلٌ wailing, lamenting

مِعْوَلٌ *pl.* مَعَاوِلُ pickaxe

(عوم)

عَامَ (ـُ) to swim, float

عَامٌ *f.* ـَاتٌ، أَعْوَامٌ year

عَامَئِذٍ (in) that year

(عون)

عَاوَنَ III, أَعَانَ IV to help

تَعَاوَنَ VI to give mutual aid, co-operate

اِسْتَعَانَ X to ask help of

إِعَانَةٌ، مَعُونَةٌ، عَوْنٌ aid, assistance

عَوْنٌ *pl.* أَعْوَانٌ aider, assister, helper

تَعَاوُنٌ mutual assistance, co-operation

مُعَاوِنٌ assistant

(عوه)

عَاهَةٌ bane, pest, blight

(عيب)

عَابَ (ـِ) to be faulty

عَيْبٌ *pl.* عُيُوبٌ blemish, fault, shame

(عير)

عَارٌ disgrace, shame

عِيَارٌ standard, measure

(عيش)

عَاشَ (ـِ) to live

تَعَيَّشَ V to earn a living

عَيْش ;عِيشَة life, living; bread (*Eg.*)

مَعَاش ,مَعَاشَة livelihood, means of living, wage

(عيط)

عَيَّطَ II to cry out, shout

(عين)

عَيَّنَ II to appoint, specify

عَايَنَ III to survey, see

عَيْن (*f.*) *pl.* عُيُون ,أَعْيُن eye, self; spring, well, fountain

عَيْن *pl.* أَعْيَان notable man

عَيْنًا in kind

(عيى)

عَيَّان ill, sick

غ

(غبب)

غِبَّ after

(غبر)

غُبَار dust

غَابِر going, passing away, remaining, past

(غبط)

غِبْطَة happiness, beatitude

(غبو)

غَبَاوَة heedlessness, ignorance, stupidity

غَبِيّ *pl.* أَغْبِيَاء ignorant, stupid

(غثث)

غَثّ lean, meagre

(غدر)

غَدَرَ (ـِ) to deceive

غَادَرَ III to forsake, depart, leave, quit (a place)

غَدِير *pl.* غُدْرَان pool of water

(غدو)

تَغَدَّى V to take a morning meal, lunch

غَد the day after

غَدًا tomorrow

غَدَاء morning meal, lunch

غَدَاة ,غُدُوّ early morning

(غذى)

غَذَّى II to nourish (of food)

غِذَاء nutriment, food, aliment

مُغَذٍّ nourishing, *adj.*

(غرر)

غَرْغَرَ (*quad.*) to gargle

(غرب)

غَرَبَ (ـُ) to set (of sun)

اِغْتَرَبَ VIII to emigrate, live in a strange land

اِسْتَغْرَبَ X to regard as strange, a stranger

غَرْبٌ West, *n.*

غُرْبَةٌ, اِغْتِرَابٌ state of exile, strange land, strangeness

غُرَابٌ *pl.* غِرْبَانٌ raven

غُرُوبٌ sunset

غَرِيبٌ *pl.* غُرَبَاءُ strange, stranger

غَرِيبَةٌ *pl.* غَرَائِبُ a strange thing, a wonder

مَغْرِبٌ *pl.* مَغَارِبُ West, the Maghrib (North Africa)

اَلْمَغْرِبُ اَلْأَقْصَى ;اَلْمَغْرِبُ Morocco

(غربل)

غَرْبَلَ (*quad.*) to sift, sieve

غِرْبَالٌ *pl.* غَرَابِيلُ sieve

(غرد)

غَرَّدَ II to warble, sing (of a bird)

(غرس)

غَرَسَ (ـِ) to plant

اِنْغَرَسَ VII to be planted

مَغْرِسٌ *pl.* مَغَارِسُ plantation, grove (olive, etc,)

(غرش)

غِرْشٌ *pl.* غُرُوشٌ piastre

(غرض)

غَرَضٌ *pl.* أَغْرَاضٌ aim, object, wish

(غرف)

غُرْفَةٌ *pl.* غُرَفٌ room

(غرق)

غَرِقَ (ـَ) to sink, be drowned

اِسْتَغْرَقَ X to absorb, take in, fill, comprise

(غرم)

غَرِمَ (ـَ) to pay a fine, tax

أَغْرَمَ IV to impose tax, fine

أُغْرِمَ بِ to be very fond of, in love with

غَرَامٌ love, passion, fondness

غَرَامَةٌ fine, indemnity, loss

مَغْرَمٌ *pl.* مَغَارِمُ debt, obligation

(غرو)

أَغْرَى IV to incite, urge

لَا غَرْوَ no wonder!

(غزر)

غَزُرَ (ـُ) to be copious, abundant

غَزَارَةٌ abundance

غَزِيرٌ *pl.* غِزَارٌ abundant, copious

(غزل)

غَزَلَ to spin (wool, etc.)

تَغَزَّلَ بِ V to sing praises of, court (a woman)

غَزْلٌ spun thread, yarn

غَزَلٌ amorous talk, erotic verses, love poetry

غَزَالٌ *pl.* غِزْلَانٌ gazelle

(غزو)

غَزَا (ـُ) to raid, invade enemy country

غَزْوٌ raid, invasion

غَزْوَةٌ *pl.* غَزَوَاتٌ incursion

غَازٍ *pl.* غُزَاةٌ warrior, invader, victorious

مَغْزًى (ٱلْكَلَامِ) sense, moral, meaning (of a story, discourse)

(غسق)

غَسَقَ (ـِ) to become dark

(غسل)

غَسَلَ (ـِ) *v.n.* غَسْلٌ to wash, *intrans.*

غَسَّالٌ laundryman

(غشش)

غَشَّ (ـُ) to falsify, cheat, deceive

(غشى)

غَشِيَ (ـَ) to cover, conceal

غُشِيَ عَلَيْهِ he fainted, swooned

(غصب)

غَصَبَ, اِغْتَصَبَ VIII to take by violence, violate, usurp

غَصَبَ عَلَى (ـِ) to force, compel

غَصْبٌ force, compulsion

غَصْبًا by force, forcibly

غَصْبًا عَنْ in spite of

(غصن)

غُصْنٌ *pl.* غُصُونٌ branch, twig

(غضض)

غَضٌّ fresh, tender

(غضب)

غَضِبَ (ـَ) to be or become angry

أَغْضَبَ IV to make angry

غَضَبٌ anger

غَضْبَانُ angry

مَغْضُوبٌ عَلَيْهِ object of anger

(غطى)

غَطَّى II to cover up, conceal

تَغَطَّى V to be covered up, concealed

غِطَاءٌ *pl.* أَغْطِيَةٌ, غِطْيَانٌ cover, covering, lid

(غفر)

غَفَرَ لِ (ـِ) to forgive, pardon

اِسْتَغْفَرَ X to ask pardon, forgiveness

غَفِيرٌ *pl.* غُفَرَانٌ watchman

جَمٌّ غَفِيرٌ a large crowd

مَغْفِرَةٌ forgiveness, pardon

(غفل)

غَفَلَ عَنْ (ـُ) to be heedless of, neglect, disregard

غَفْلَةٌ heedlessness, carelessness, disregard

غَفْلَانُ careless, neglectful

(غلل)

غَلَّ (ـُ) to fetter, shackle

أَغَلَّ, غَلَّ IV to yield a crop, income

اِسْتَغَلَّ X to exploit, take the proceeds of

اِسْتَغَلَّ مَالاً X to invest money

غَلَّةٌ *pl.* ـَاتٌ, غِلَالٌ revenue from land; crops, yield

اِسْتِغْلَالٌ exploitation

(غلب)

غَلَبَ (ـِ) to conquer, subdue

تَغَلَّبَ عَلَى V to prevail over, overcome

اِنْغَلَبَ VII to be overcome, defeated

غَلَبَةٌ victory, conquest

غَالِبٌ *pl.* غَلَبَةٌ victor, conqueror

فِى ٱلْغَالِبِ, غَالِبًا generally, usually

أَغْلَبِيَّةٌ majority

(غلس)

غَلَّسَ II to journey, or do a thing before dawn

(غلط)

غَلِطَ (ـَ) to make a mistake, be mistaken

غَلَطٌ، غَلْطَةٌ *pl.* أَغْلاطٌ mistake, error

غَالِطٌ، غَلْطَانُ wrong, mistaken

(غلظ)

غَلِيظٌ *pl.* غِلاظٌ thick, rough, coarse

(غلف)

غِلافٌ cover (of a book); envelope

مُغَلَّفٌ *pl.* مُغَلَّفاتٌ envelope, wrapper

(غلق)

أَغْلَقَ IV to close, bolt (a door)

(غلم)

غُلامٌ *pl.* غِلْمانٌ (a) youth

(غلو)

غَالَى III to exaggerate (in speech), overreach

غَالٍ expensive

مُغَالاةٌ exaggeration

(غلى)

غَلَى (ـِ) to boil (of pot, kettle, etc.)

غَلَّى II, أَغْلَى IV to boil, *trans.*

(غمم)

غَمَّ (ـُ) to grieve

غَمٌّ *pl.* غُمُومٌ anxiety, grief, sorrow

مَغْمُومٌ anxious, troubled, grieved

(غمد)

غَمَدَ (ـِ)، أَغْمَدَ IV to sheathe (sword)

(غمر)

غَمَرَ (ـُ) to submerge, overtake, cover; be abundant

(غمض)

غَمَّضَ II, أَغْمَضَ IV to shut (the eyes)

غَامِضٌ obscure

(غمى)

غُمِيَ عَلَيْهِ he fainted, swooned

(غنم)

غَنِمَ (ـَ) to plunder, obtain

اِغْتَنَمَ VIII to sieze as spoils

اِسْتَغْنَمَ، اغْتَنَمَ X (followed by الْفُرْصَةَ) to sieze the opportunity

غَنَمٌ (*coll.*) sheep

غَنِيمَةٌ *pl.* غَنَائِمُ plunder, booty

(غنى)

غَنِيَ بِ (ـَ) to be content with

غَنَّى II, تَغَنَّى V to sing, chant

إِسْتَغْنَى عَن to dispense with, be in no need of

غِنًى, غَنَاءٌ sufficiency, wealth, riches

أُغْنِيَّةٌ pl. أَغَانٍ, أَغَانِيُّ song, غِنَاءٌ

غَنِيٌّ pl. أَغْنِيَاءُ rich, rich man, wealthy

مُغَنٍّ singer

(غوث)

غَاثَ (ـُ) أَغَاثَ IV to aid, succour

إِسْتَغَاثَ بِ X to seek aid, call for help

غَوْثٌ pl. إِغَاثَةٌ aid, succour

(غور)

أَغَارَ عَلَى IV attack, raid

غَارَةٌ pl. ـَاتٌ raid, incursion

مَغَارَةٌ pl. ـَاتٌ cave

(غوص)

غَاصَ (ـُ) to plunge, dive

غَوَّاصٌ diver

غَوَّاصَةٌ submarine (*mod.*)

(غول)

إِغْتَالَ VIII to destroy, assassinate (kill secretly)

إِغْتِيَالٌ assassination, murder

غُولٌ ghoul (see exercises 79–80)

(غيى)

غَايَةٌ pl. ـَاتٌ extremity, term, ultimate object, end, highest degree

(غيب)

غَابَ (ـِ) to be absent, absent oneself, disappear

غِيَابٌ absence

غَيْبٌ pl. غُيُوبٌ distant, hidden things

غَائِبٌ absent

غَابَةٌ pl. ـَاتٌ, غَابٌ forest

(غير)

غَارَ (ـِ) to be jealous

غَيَّرَ II to change, *trans.*

تَغَيَّرَ V to change, *intrans.*, be changed

غَيْرٌ other, another

غَيْرُ (+*gen.*) not, another, other than

غَيْرُ مُمْكِنٍ impossible

مِنْ غَيْرِ without

غَيْرَةٌ jealousy, zeal

غَيُورٌ jealous

(غيض)

غَيْضَةٌ *pl.* غِيَاضٌ thicket

(غيط)

غَيْطٌ garden, field

غَيَّظَ II to annoy, anger

(غيظ)

اِغْتَاظَ VIII to become angry

غَيْظٌ anger, rage, wrath

(غيل)

أُمُّ غَيْلَانَ (or غِيلَانَ) sweet lote-tree

(غيم)

غَامَ (ـِ) to be cloudy

غَيْمٌ *pl.* غُيُومٌ cloud

ف

(ف)

فَ and, then

(فأد)

فُؤَادٌ *pl.* أَفْئِدَةٌ heart, soul, mind

(فأر)

فَأْرٌ *pl.* فِئْرَانٌ mouse

(فأس)

فَأْسٌ (*f.*) *pl.* فُؤُوسٌ axe, hatchet; Fez (city in Morocco)

(فأل)

تَفَاءَلَ IV, تَفَأَّلَ V to draw a good omen (from) (بِ)

فَأْلٌ, تَفَاؤُلٌ (good) omen, augury

تَفَاؤُلٌ optimism

مُتَفَائِلٌ an optimist

(فأى)

فِئَةٌ *pl.* فِئَاتٌ company, party, faction, group, band; rate, price

(فتت)

فَتَّتَ II to break, crush

(فتح)

فَتَحَ (ـَ) *v.n.* فَتْحٌ to open, conquer

اِنْفَتَحَ VII to be opened, open, *intrans.*

اِفْتَتَحَ VIII to open, inaugurate, commence, introduce

فُتُوحٌ *pl.* ـَاتٌ opening, *n.*, capture, conquest

اَلْفَاتِحَةُ the opening Sūra of the Qur'ān

اِفْتَتاحِيٌّ opening, *adj.*, introductory, leading (of a newspaper article)

مِفْتاحٌ pl. مَفاتِيحُ key

مَفْتُوحٌ open, *adj.*, conquered (country)

(فتر)

فاتِرٌ lukewarm

(فتش)

فَتَّشَ II to examine, investigate, inspect; (*with* عَلَى, عَنْ) to seek, look for

تَفْتِيشٌ search, inspection, examination

مُفَتِّشٌ inspector, investigator

(فتك)

فَتَكَ (ـُ) to act violently, assault

فَتْكٌ violence

(فتن)

فَتَنَ (ـِ) to rouse to rebellion, incite; infatuate, charm

فِتْنَةٌ seduction, sedition

(فتو)

أَفْتَى IV to give a legal decision or opinion (in Islamic law)

فُتُوَّةٌ youth, manliness, generosity

فَتًى *pl.* فِتْيانٌ young man, youth

فَتاةٌ *pl.* فَتَياتٌ young woman, girl

فَتْوَى *pl.* فَتاوٍ Fatwa, edict, decision in sacred law

مُفْتٍ Mufti, doctor, expounder of sacred law

(فجأ)

فاجَأَ III to surprise anyone, fall upon anyone suddenly

فَجْأَةً suddenly, unawares

(فجر)

اِنْفَجَرَ VII to burst forth, explode

فَجْرٌ dawn, daybreak

(فجع)

فَجِيعَةٌ *pl.* فَجائِعُ calamity, misfortune, loss (of property or family)

فاجِعٌ calamitous

(فحش)

فَحُشَ (ـُ) to be excessive, immoderate, foul (in manner, language, etc.)

فَاحِش excessive, indecent, venal; exhorbitant (price); foul (language)

(فحص)

فَحَصَ (ـَ) v.n. فَحْص to examine, inspect, scrutinise

(فحم)

فَحْم charcoal

فَحْم حَجَر coal

(فخذ)

فَخِذ pl. أَفْخَاذ thigh

(فخر)

فَخَرَ (ـُ), اِفْتَخَرَ VIII to be proud, glory, boast (of, in ب)

فَخْر glory, excellence, honour

فَخْرِيّ honorary

فَاخِر, مُفْتَخِر excellent, splendid, illustrious

فَخَّار pottery, earthenware

فَاخُورِيّ potter

(فخم)

فَخَّمَ II to show honour to

فَخَامَة honour, excellence (used in certain titles)

فَخِيم honoured

(فدن)

فَدَّان pl. فَدَادِين Feddan (field measure used in some Arab countries); yoke of oxen

(فدى)

فَدَى (ـِ) to redeem, ransom

فِدًى, فِدَاء ransom, redemption

(فرر)

فَرَّ (ـِ) to flee, escape

فِرَار flight, escape

مَفَرّ pl. مَفَارّ escape, place of escape

(فرأ)

فَرَأ pl. أَفْرَاء wild ass

(فرت)

اَلْفُرَات the river Euphrates

(فرج)

تَفَرَّجَ (عَلَى) V to look (with pleasure) at; "sight-see"

فَرَج joy, comfort, relief

(فرح)

فَرِحَ (ـَ) to rejoice, be glad

فَرَح pl. أَفْرَاح joy, rejoicing

فَرِح, فَرْحَان glad

(فرخ)

أَفْرَاخٌ, فَرْخَةٌ chicken

(فرد)

أَفْرَدَ IV to make single, set apart

اِنْفَرَدَ VII to be single, alone, isolated

فَرْدٌ *pl.* أَفْرَادٌ one, one of a pair, individual

فَرْدَةٌ, فَرْدٌ parcel, bale

فَرِيدٌ unique; pr. n. m.

اِنْفِرَادٌ solitude, isolation, aloneness

مُفْرَدٌ singular, single

مُنْفَرِدٌ (عَنْ) alone, isolated (from)

(فردس)

فِرْدَوْسٌ *pl.* فَرَادِيسُ Paradise, garden

(فرس)

اِفْتَرَسَ VIII to kill, as a wild animal its prey

بِلَادُ ٱلْفُرْسِ, بِلَادُ فَارِسَ Persia

فَارِسِيٌّ Persian, *n.* and *adj.*

اَلْفَارِسِيَّةُ the Persian language

فَرَسٌ (*m.* and *f.*) *pl.* أَفْرَاسٌ horse, mare

فُرُوسِيَّةٌ horsemanship

فَارِسٌ *pl.* فُرْسَانٌ, فَوَارِسُ horseman, knight

(فرش)

فَرَشَ (ـُ) to spread out, *trans.*; furnish (a house)

مَفْرُوشٌ, فَرْشٌ *pl.* مَفْرُوشَاتٌ house furniture

فُرْشَةٌ *pl.* فُرَشٌ brush

فَرْشَةٌ, فِرَاشٌ *pl.* فُرُشٌ, أَفْرِشَةٌ bed, bedding

(فرص)

فُرْصَةٌ *pl.* فُرَصٌ opportunity, chance, good occasion

(فرض)

فَرَضَ (ـِ) to suppose, presume; (*with* عَلَى) to impose upon, make obligatory

أَفْرَضَ IV, اِفْتَرَضَ VIII (see فرض على)

فَرْضٌ *pl.* فُرُوضٌ supposition; duty

فَرِيضَةٌ *pl.* فَرَائِضُ duty, obligation, ordinance

مَفْرُوضٌ supposed; obligatory

(فرط)

فَرْطٌ excess

(فرع)

فَرْعٌ *pl.* فُرُوعٌ branch, tributary (of river, stream)

(فرغ)

فَرَغَ (ـَ) to be vacant, empty; (*with* مِنْ) finish

فَرَاغٌ emptiness, vacuum

وَقْتُ الْفَرَاغِ leisure time

فَارِغٌ empty, vacant

(فرق)

فَرَّقَ II to scatter, disperse, separate, grade, *trans.*

فَارَقَ III to leave, part from, separate from

تَفَرَّقَ V, اِفْتَرَقَ VIII to be separated

تَفَارَقَ VI to separate (from each other)

فَرْقٌ difference, distinction

اَلْفُرْقَانُ the Qur'ān

فِرْقَةٌ *pl.* فِرَقٌ party, group, company (military), team

فَرِيقٌ *pl.* أَفْرِقَاءُ, فُرُوقٌ party, division, general (military)

(فرك)

فَرَكَ (ـُ) to rub

(فرن)

فُرْنٌ *pl.* أَفْرَانٌ oven

(فرنج)

إِفْرَنْجِيٌّ *coll.* إِفْرَنْجٌ European (Frank)

فَرَنْسَا France

فَرَنْسَاوِيٌّ, فَرَنْسَوِيٌّ, فَرَنْسِيٌّ French, *adj.* and *n.*

(فزع)

فَزِعَ (ـَ) to fear, be afraid

فَزْعٌ fear, fright

(فسح)

فَسِيحٌ spacious, roomy, ample

(فسخ)

فَسَخَ (ـَ) to annul, abrogate

(فسد)

أَفْسَدَ IV to corrupt

فَسَادٌ corruption, decomposition, invalidity

فَاسِدٌ corrupt, bad, invalid

(فسر)

فَسَّرَ II to explain, interpret, make plain

اِسْتَفْسَرَ X to enquire, seek explanation

تَفْسِيرٌ *pl.* تَفَاسِيرُ explanation, interpretation, commentary

(فشل)

فَشَلَ (ـَ) to fail, lose heart

فَشَلٌ failure

(فصح)

فِصْحٌ Passover, Easter

فَصَاحَةٌ eloquence, lucidity, literary style

فَصِيحٌ clear, eloquent, literary, classical (of language)

(فصل)

فَصَلَ (ـِ) to separate, divide, sever

فَصَّلَ II to cut into parts, cut out (of cloth); isolate; detail

اِنْفَصَلَ (عَنْ) VII to be separate, detached (from)

فَصْلٌ *pl.* فُصُولٌ season, chapter, classroom, division

تَفْصِيلٌ *pl.* تَفَاصِيلُ detail, detailed statement

فَيْصَلٌ *pl.* فَيَاصِلُ judge, arbiter, referee; pr. n. m.

(فضض)

فِضَّةٌ silver, *n.*

(فضل)

فَضَّلَ II to prefer

أَفْضَلَ IV to favour, make excellent

تَفَضَّلَ V to show kindness, do a favour

تَفَضَّلْ (*Imperative* of V) please! welcome!

فَضْلٌ *pl.* فُضُولٌ excellence, virtue, merit, kindness

مِنْ فَضْلِكَ please!

فَضْلًا عَنْ besides, apart from, *a fortiori*

فَضْلَةٌ remainder, surplus, redundancy

فُضُولٌ intrusion, inquisitiveness, meddlesomeness

فَضِيلَةٌ *pl.* فَضَائِلُ virtue; a title of respect

تَفَضُّلٌ *pl.* ـَاتٌ kindness

فَاضِلٌ virtuous, superior; pr. n. m.

أَفْضَلُ preferable, better (than مِنْ)

اَلْأَفْضَلُ the best

(فضو)

أَفْضَى IV to lead anyone to a place (with بِ of person and عَلَى of object)

فَضَاءٌ open, wide, space

فَاضٍ empty; free, idle (of time)

(فطر)

فَطَرَ (ـُـ) to break, breakfast

عِيدُ ٱلْفِطْرِ Muslim festival at the end of Ramadan

فِطْرَةٌ pl. فِطَرٌ innate quality, religious feeling

فُطُورٌ breakfast

(فظع)

فَظِيعٌ hideous, repulsive, ugly, abominable

(فعل)

فَعَلَ (ـَـ) to do, make

فِعْلٌ pl. أَفْعَالٌ deed, verb

مَفْعَلٌ noun of place

(فعى)

أَفْعًى pl. أَفَاعٍ viper

(فقأ)

فَقَأَ (ـَـ) to put out an eye

(فقد)

فَقَدَ (ـِـ) v.n. فَقْدٌ, فُقْدَانٌ to lose, miss

فَقِيدٌ lost, missed; lamented; deceased

(فقر)

فُقْرٌ, فَقْرٌ poverty

فَقِيرٌ pl. فُقَرَاءُ poor, needy, poor man

(فقه)

فِقْهٌ Fiqh, jurisprudence

فَقِيهٌ pl. فُقَهَاءُ Faqih, jurisprudent

(فكك)

فَكَّ (ـُـ) to loosen, untie, open, separate

اِفْتَكَّ VIII to recover, *trans.*, set free

فَكٌّ pl. فُكُوكٌ jaw, jawbone

(فكر)

فَكَّرَ (فِي) II to think (about)

اِفْتَكَرَ VIII to think

فِكْرٌ, فِكْرَةٌ pl. أَفْكَارٌ thought, *n.*

(فكه)

فُكَاهَةٌ jesting, joking, merriment

فُكَاهِيٌّ humorous, funny

فَاكِهَةٌ *pl.* فَوَاكِهُ fruit

(فلل)

فُلْفُلٌ, فِلْفِلٌ pepper

(فلح)

فَلَاحَةٌ, فَلْحٌ agriculture, husbandry

فَلَّاحٌ peasant, farmer

(فلذ)

فُولَاذٌ steel

(فلس)

أَفْلَسَ IV to become bankrupt

فَلْسٌ *pl.* فُلُوسٌ fils (small coin used in some Arab countries)

إِفْلَاسٌ bankruptcy, insolvency

مُفْلِسٌ bankrupt, insolvent

فِلَسْطِينُ Palestine

فِلَسْطِينِيٌّ Palestinian

(فلسف)

تَفَلْسَفَ II (*quad.*) to philosophise, become a philosopher

فَلْسَفَةٌ philosophy

فَيْلَسُوفٌ *pl.* فَلَاسِفَةٌ philosopher

(فلق)

فَلَقٌ dawn

(فلك)

فَلَكٌ *pl.* أَفْلَاكٌ celestial sphere, orbit, sky, heavens

عِلْمُ ٱلْفَلَكِ astronomy

فَلَكِيٌّ astronomer

(فلن)

فُلَانٌ a certain (person), so-and-so

(فم)

فَمٌ see under (فوه)

(فنن)

فَنٌّ *pl.* فُنُونٌ art

فَنِّيٌّ technical, artistic

(فنجن)

فِنْجَانٌ *pl.* فَنَاجِينُ cup, coffee cup

(فندق)

فُنْدُقٌ *pl.* فَنَادِقُ inn, hotel

(فنر)

فَنَارٌ *pl.* ـَاتٌ — lighthouse

(فنس)

فَانُوسٌ *pl.* فَوَانِيسُ lamp, lantern

(فنى)

فَنِيَ (ـَ) to perish, be transitory

فِنَاءٌ courtyard (of a house)

(فهم)

فَهِمَ (ـَ) to understand

اِسْتَفْهَمَ X to enquire

(فوت)

فَاتَ (ـُ) *v.n.* فَوْتٌ to elapse, pass by, enter, escape

(فور)

فَوْرًا, عَلَى ٱلْفَوْرِ immediately, at once

(فوز)

فَازَ (ب) (ـُ) *v.n.* فَوْزٌ to acquire, win, succeed; (*with* عَلَى) defeat

مَفَازَةٌ *pl.* ـَاتٌ desert

(فوض)

فَوَّضَ II to authorize

فَاوَضَ III to discuss, converse, negotiate with

فَوْضَى, فَوْضَاءُ anarchy

قَوْمٌ فَوْضَى tribe, people, without a leader

مُفَاوَضَةٌ discussion, talk, negotiation

(فوق)

اِسْتَفَاقَ X to awake

فَاقَةٌ poverty, want, need

فَوْقَ above, on

(فول)

فُولٌ beans (veg.)

(فوه)

فَمٌ *pl.* أَفْوَاهٌ mouth

فُوهَةٌ opening, mouth

(فى)

فِي in, by, at, concerning

(فيد)

أَفَادَ IV to benefit anyone, acquaint a. o. with

اِسْتَفَادَ مِنْ X to benefit from

فَائِدَةٌ *pl.* فَوَائِدُ profit, benefit

مُفِيدٌ useful

(فيض)

فَاضَ (ـِ) to overflow, be abundant

أَفَاضَ IV to pour (water, etc.), fill

فَيْضٌ abundance

فَيَضَانٌ flood, innundation

فَائِضٌ interest (on money)

(فيل)

فِيلٌ *pl.* أَفْيَالٌ elephant

ق

(قبب)

قَبَّةٌ collar (of shirt, etc.)

قُبَّةٌ *pl.* قِبَبٌ cupola, dome, vault, alcove, saint's tomb

(قبح)

اِسْتَقْبَحَ X to find, consider, ugly or bad

قُبْحٌ ugliness

قَبِيحٌ *pl.* قِبَاحٌ bad, ugly

(قبر)

قَبَرَ (ـُ) to bury

قَبْرٌ *pl.* قُبُورٌ grave

مَقْبَرَةٌ *pl.* مَقَابِرُ cemetery

(قبرس)

قُبْرُصُ, قُبْرُسُ Cyprus

(قبس)

اِقْتَبَسَ (مِنْ) VIII to quote, cite (from an author, book)

(قبض)

قَبَضَ (ـِ) to seize, grasp; (*with* على) to arrest; receive money

اِنْقَبَضَ VII to shrink, contract, *intrans.*

قَبْضٌ seizure; receiving of money

قَبْضَةٌ handle, hilt

مَقْبَضٌ *pl.* مَقَابِضُ handle, hilt

(قبط)

قُبْطِيٌّ *coll.* قُبْطٌ *pl.* أَقْبَاطٌ Copt, Coptic

(قبع)

قَبَعَ (ـَ) to conceal oneself

قُبَعٌ, قُبَّعَةٌ hat (*mod.*)

(قبل)

قَبِلَ (ـَ) to accept, receive

قَبَّلَ II to kiss

قَابَلَ III to meet, correspond to

أَقْبَلَ IV to approach (+ عَلَى with object)

تَقَابَلَ VI to meet one another

اِسْتَقْبَلَ X to receive (a person), welcome

قَبْلُ before, *adv.*, formerly

قَبْلًا before, *adv.*, formerly

قَبْلَ before (of time) ***prep.***

مِنْ قِبَلِ from, by, on the part of

قِبْلَةٌ south, Qibla, direction of Mecca

قِبْلِيٌّ southern

اَلْوَجْهُ ٱلْقِبْلِيُّ Upper Egypt

قَبُولٌ receiving *n.*, acceptance

قَبِيلَةٌ *pl.* قَبَائِلُ tribe

قَابِلٌ لِ capable of, subject to

اَلْمُسْتَقْبَلُ the future

(قتل)

قَتَلَ (ـُ) *v.n.* قَتْلٌ to kill, murder

قَتَّلَ II to massacre

قَاتَلَ III to fight

تَقَاتَلَ VI to fight one another

قَتْلٌ murder, killing

قِتَالٌ (*v.n.*, III) battle, fighting

قَتِيلٌ killed, victim

(قتم)

قَاتِمٌ dark coloured

(قحط)

قَحْطٌ drought, famine

(قد)

قَدْ, (لَقَدْ with *Perfect* only) (*particle* of strengthening with *Perfect*, often making the *Perfect Pluperfect*) already; (with *Imperfect*) sometimes, may, might, probably

(قدر)

قَدَرَ (ـِ) to be able

قَدَّرَ II to value, estimate, assess, determine

اِقْتَدَرَ عَلَى VIII to be able to do something

قَادِرٌ (عَلَى) able (to do a thing)

قَدْرٌ *pl.* أَقْدَارٌ quantity, amount; degree, value; power, ability

قَدَرٌ fate, destiny; power

قُدْرَةٌ power, might

مِقْدَارٌ *pl.* مَقَادِيرُ amount, quantity

(قدس)

قَدُسَ (ـُ) to be or become holy

قَدَّسَ II to hallow, sanctify

بَيْتُ ٱلْمَقْدِسِ, اَلْقُدْسُ (ٱلشَّرِيفُ) Jerusalem

(قدم)

قَدِمَ (ـَ) *v.n.* قُدُومٌ to arrive, come, advance, approach

قَدَّمَ II to present, bring, offer

تَقَدَّمَ V to come forward, approach

قَدَمٌ *pl.* أَقْدَامٌ foot (anatomical or measure)

قُدَّامَ in front of

قَادِمٌ approaching, coming, next

فِى ٱلْأُسْبُوعِ ٱلْقَادِمِ in the coming week, next week

قَدِيمٌ *pl.* قُدَمَاءُ old, ancient

مُقَدَّمٌ chief, head

مُتَقَدِّمٌ ancient (of an historical character)

(قذر)

قَذِرٌ dirty, filthy, unclean

(قرر)

قَرَّ (ـِ) to stay, dwell, be rested, refreshed; (*with* عَلَى) to persist, persevere in

قَرَّ عَيْنًا to be refreshed, consoled, content

قَرَّرَ II to settle, fix, establish, decide, prescribe

أَقَرَّ بِ IV to acknowledge, admit, confess

اِسْتَقَرَّ X to be at rest, settle; (*with* فِى) to dwell, inhabit

قَرَارٌ decision, determination

تَقْرِيرٌ *pl.* تَقَارِيرُ report

قَارَّةٌ continent

مَقَرٌّ *pl.* مَقَارُّ residence, site, seat (of government or administration)

(قرأ)

قَرَأَ (ـَ) *v.n.* قِرَاءَةٌ to read, recite

اَلْقُرْآنُ the Qur'ān, Koran

(قرب)

قَرُبَ (ـُ) (مِنْ) to be near (to)

اِقْتَرَبَ (مِنْ) VIII to approach

قُرْبٌ nearness, proximity

قِرْبَةٌ water-skin

قَرِيبٌ (مِنْ) near (to)

قَرِيبٌ *pl.* أَقْرِبَاءُ, أَقَارِبُ relation, relative

تَقْرِيبًا approximately, about, almost

عَلَى مَقْرَبَةٍ مِنْ near, in the neighbourhood of

(قرح)

اِقْتَرَحَ VIII to suggest, propose

(قرد)

قِرْدٌ *pl.* قُرُودٌ ape

(قرش)

قُرَيْشٌ (tribe of) Quraish

قُرَشِيٌّ Quraishite

قِرْشٌ *pl.* قُرُوشٌ (see also غرش) piastre

(قرض)

اِنْقَرَضَ VII to disappear, be cut off, become extinct

اِسْتَقْرَضَ X to borrow

قَرْضٌ *pl.* قُرُوضٌ loan

(قرطب)

قُرْطُبَةُ Cordova (in Spain)

(قرطس)

قِرْطَاسٌ *pl.* قَرَاطِيسُ paper

(قرظ)

قَرَّظَ II to laud, eulogize

(قرع)

قَرَعَ (ـَ) to knock, rap (on a door)

أَقْرَعُ bald, baldheaded

مِقْرَعَةٌ *pl.* مَقَارِعُ knocker, baton

(قرف)

اِقْتَرَفَ VIII to commit (crime, sin)

(قرن)

قَرَنَ (ـِ) to join, couple

قَارَنَ (بَيْنَ) III to compare (one thing with another)

اِقْتَرَنَ VIII to marry, be joined (to بِ)

قَرْنٌ *pl.* قُرُونٌ century, horn

قَرِينٌ *f.* قَرِينَةٌ spouse

(قرى)

قَرْيَةٌ *pl.* قُرًى village

قَرَوِيٌّ villager, village *adj.*

(قزز)

قَزَازٌ (*mod.* corruption of زُجَاجٌ) glass, glassware

(قسط)

قَسَّطَ II to pay by instalments

قِسْطٌ *pl.* أَقْسَاطٌ payment (in part) by instalment

(قسم)

قَسَمَ (ـِ) to divide, share

اِنْقَسَمَ VII to be divided

قِسْمٌ *pl.* أَقْسَامٌ part, department

قَسَمٌ *pl.* أَقْسَامٌ oath

قِسْمَةٌ part, share, lot, portion, Kismet

تَقْسِيمٌ (*v.n.*, II) partition

(قسو)

قَاسَى III to endure, suffer

قَسَاوَةٌ harshness, severity

قَاسٍ *pl.* قُسَاةٌ harsh, hard, severe

(قشعر)

اِقْشَعَرَّ (*quad.*) IV to shake with fear, have the hair standing on end, shudder

قَشْعَرِيرَةٌ shaking with fear, *n.*, gooseflesh

(قصص)

قَصَّ (ـُ) to narrate, tell a tale (to عَلَى)

قَصَّ (ـُ) to cut

قِصَّةٌ *pl.* قِصَصٌ story, tale

مِقَصٌّ *pl.* مَقَاصُّ scissors

(قصب)

قَصَبٌ cane, sugar cane

(قصد)

قَصَدَ (ـِ) to intend, propose, make for, travel towards

قَصْدٌ purpose, aim

قَصْدًا intentionally

قَصِيدَةٌ *pl.* قَصِيدٌ, قَصَائِدُ ode, poem, qasida

اِقْتِصَادٌ economy, economics

اِقْتِصَادِيٌّ economic

مَقْصَدٌ, مَقْصُودٌ purpose, aim, intention

(قصر)

قَصَّرَ II to fall short

قَصْرٌ *pl.* قُصُورٌ palace, castle

قَصِيرٌ *pl.* قِصَارٌ short

(قصو)

اِسْتَقْصَى X *v.n.* اِسْتِقْصَاءٌ to investigate, explore, examine thoroughly

قَاصٍ far-off, distant

أَقْصَى *f.* قُصْوَى *pl.* أَقَاصٍ more distant, extreme

أَقَاصِي ٱلْأَرْضِ uttermost ends of the earth

(قضب)

قَضِيبٌ *pl.* قُضْبَانٌ wand, sceptre

(قضم)

قَضِمَ (ـَ) to crunch, nibble, gnaw

(قضى)

قَضَى (ـِ) to decide, be judge; spend (time), complete, accomplish

اِنْقَضَى VII to pass away, cease, end

اِقْتَضَى VIII to desire, be required, necessitate

قَضَاءٌ decision, judgment, end, settlement, accomplishment; district (admin.)

قَضِيَّةٌ *pl.* قَضَايَا affair, case, matter

قَاضٍ *pl.* ـُونَ, قُضَاةٌ judge

قَضَّاءٌ arbitrator

مُقْتَضًى *pl.* مُقْتَضَيَاتٌ necessity, necessitated, requirement

بِمُقْتَضَى according to (*mod.*)

(قطط)

قَطُّ not at all, never (after the *Perfect*)

فَقَطْ, فَقَطُّ only

قِطٌّ *pl.* قِطَاطٌ cat

(قطب)

قُطْبٌ *pl.* أَقْطَابٌ axis, pivot; distinguished person

(قطر)

قُطْرٌ *pl.* أَقْطَارٌ country

قِطَارٌ *pl.* ـَاتٌ — (railway) train

(قطع)

قَطَعَ (ـَ) to cut

قَطَّعَ II to smash, cut into small pieces

قَاطَعَ III to cut anyone short, interrupt; boycott (*mod.*)

أَقْطَعَ IV to assign land as fee

قِطْعَةٌ *pl.* قِطَعٌ piece

قِطَاعٌ *pl.* ـَاتٌ — sector

قَطِيعٌ *pl.* قُطْعَانٌ flock, herd

قَاطِعَةٌ *pl.* قَوَاطِعُ bird of passage

تَقَاطُعٌ junction (on road or railway)

مُقَاطَعَةٌ province, county

(قطن)

قَطَنَ (ـُ) to inhabit a place

قُطْنٌ *pl.* أَقْطَانٌ cotton

(قعد)

قَعَدَ (ـُ) to sit, reside, stay

ذُو ٱلْقَعْدَةِ 11th month of Islamic Calendar

قَاعِدَةٌ *pl.* قَوَاعِدُ rule, foundation, base

(قعر)

قَعْرٌ bottom (of sea, well)

(قفر)

قَفْرٌ *pl.* قِفَارٌ desert

(قفز)

قَفَزَ (ـِ) to jump, leap

قُفَّازٌ gloves

(قفل)

قَفَلَ (ـِ), أَقْفَلَ IV to shut, close, lock

قَافِلَةٌ *pl.* قَوَافِلُ caravan; convoy (*mod.*)

(قفو)

اِقْتَفَى VIII to follow, imitate

قَفًا *f.* back of head, neck

(قلل)

قَلَّ (ـِ) to be few, small, less

قَلَّمَا rarely

اِسْتَقَلَّ X to be independent

قِلَّةٌ smallness, paucity, lack

قَلِيلٌ *pl.* قَلِيلُونَ few, little

قَلِيلاً (a) little, *adv.*

اِسْتِقْلَالٌ independence

(قلب)

قَلَبَ (ـِ) to change, overturn, overthrow

تَقَلَّبَ V to be fickle, inconsistant, inconstant

اِنْقَلَبَ VII to revolve, be overturned; (*with* إِلَى) turn into

قَلْبٌ *pl.* قُلُوبٌ heart

تَقَلُّبَاتٌ vicissitudes

اِنْقِلَابٌ *pl.* ـَاتٌ — revolution

قَالِبٌ *pl.* قَوَالِبُ mould, cast

(قلد)

قَلَّدَ II to imitate; gird

تَقْلِيدٌ *pl.* تَقَالِيدُ tradition, imitation

(قلع)

قَلْعَةٌ *pl.* قِلَاعٌ fortress, citadel

(قلق)

قَلِقَ (ـَ) to be disturbed, agitated

أَقْلَقَ IV to disturb, agitate

قَلَقٌ trouble, unrest

(قلم)

قَلَمٌ *pl.* أَقْلَامٌ pen; office

قَلَمُ رَصَاصٍ lead pencil

إِقْلِيمٌ *pl.* أَقَالِيمُ zone, province (of a country)

(قمم)

قِمَّةٌ *pl.* قِمَمٌ summit

(قمح)

قَمْحٌ wheat, grain

(قمر)

قَمَرٌ (*f.*) *pl.* أَقْمَارٌ moon

مُقَامَرَةٌ game of chance

(قمس)

قَامُوسٌ *pl.* قَوَامِيسُ dictionary

(قمش)

قُمَاشٌ *pl.* أَقْمِشَةٌ cloth, woven material

(قمص)

قَمِيصٌ *pl.* قُمْصَانٌ shirt

(قنن)

قَانُونٌ *pl.* قَوَانِينُ rule, canon, law; stringed musical instrument

(قنب)

قِنَّبٌ hemp, flax

(قنبل)

قُنْبُلَةٌ *pl.* قَنَابِلُ bomb, shell

(قندل)

قِنْدِيلٌ *pl.* قَنَادِيلُ lamp

(قنصل)

قُنْصُلٌ *pl.* قَنَاصِلُ Consul

قُنْصُلِيَّةٌ Consulate

(قنع)

قَنِعَ (ـَ) (بِ) to be content (with)

قَنَّعَ II, أَقْنَعَ IV to convince, persuade, satisfy

اِقْتَنَعَ (بِ) VIII to be contented, satisfied (with)

قَنَاعَةٌ contentment

قَنِعٌ *pl.* ـُونَ satisfied

(قنو)

قَنَاةٌ *pl.* قَنَوَاتٌ canal, conduit

(قهر)

قَهَرَ (ـَ) to conquer, subdue

اَلْقَاهِرَةُ Cairo

(قهقر)

تَقَهْقَرَ (*quad.*) II to retreat, withdraw, go backwards

(قهو)

قَهْوَةٌ coffee

(قوت)

قُوتٌ *pl.* أَقْوَاتٌ provisions, food, victuals, sustinence

(قود)

قَادَ (ـُ) to lead, guide

قِيَادَةٌ guidance, leadership

قَائِدٌ *pl.* قُوَّادٌ, قَادَةٌ guide, leader; commander (military)

(قول)

قَالَ (ـُ) *v.n.* قَوْلٌ, مَقَالٌ to say

اِسْتَقَالَ X to resign

قَوْلٌ *pl.* أَقْوَالٌ speech

مَقَالَةٌ *pl.* ـَاتٌ article (in newspaper, etc.)

(قوم)

قَامَ (ـُ) *v.n.* قِيَامٌ to rise, stand up, set out

قَامَ بِ to undertake, carry out

قَامَ عَلَى to rise against, revolt; carry out, manage

قَاوَمَ III to resist

أَقَامَ IV to set up, place, establish; stay, settle in (فِي) a place

اِسْتَقَامَ X to be straight, straightforward

قَامَةٌ figure, stature

قَوْمٌ *pl.* أَقْوَامٌ people, nation, tribe

قِيَامَةٌ Resurrection

قِيمَةٌ *pl.* قِيَمٌ price, value

مَقَامٌ *pl.* ـَاتٌ rank, place

(قوى)

قَوِيَ (ـَ) to be, become, strong; (*with* عَلَى) prevail against

قُوَّةٌ *pl.* ـَاتٌ, قُوًى power, strength

قَوِيٌّ *pl.* أَقْوِيَاءُ strong, powerful

(قيد)

قَيَّدَ II to bind, limit, restrict; register

قَيْدٌ *pl.* قُيُودٌ fetter, chain, limit, stipulation, bond

عَلَى قَيْدِ ٱلْحَيَاةِ alive, living

(قيس)

قَاسَ (ـِ) to measure, compare

قَايَسَ III to measure; (*with* بَيْنَ) to compare a thing with another

قِيَاسٌ *pl.* ـَاتٌ, أَقْيِسَةٌ measure, rule, analogy

مِقْيَاسٌ *pl.* مَقَايِيسُ measuring instrument, scale (of map)

(قيظ)

قَيْظٌ heat of summer, summer (drought)

(قيل)

قَالَ (ـِ) to take a siesta, rest in the afternoon

ك

(كَ)

كَ like (attached preposition)

كَأَنَّمَا, كَأَنَّ, كَأَنْ as though, just as if

كَذَا (*see also* ذا) thus, so

كَذٰلِكَ (*see also* ذا) likewise, thus

كَمَا as, even as

(كأب)

كَئِبَ to grieve, be sad, cast down

كَآبَةٌ grief, sorrow, sadness

كَئِيبٌ sad, grieved

(كأس)

كَأْسٌ (*f.*) *pl.* كُؤُوسٌ cup

(كبب)

اِنْكَبَّ VII to fall prostrate

(كبد)

كَابَدَ III تَكَبَّدَ V to suffer, endure

كَبِدٌ *pl.* أَكْبَادٌ liver, interior; heart (poet.)

(كبر)

كَبُرَ (ـُ) to grow big, old

تَكَبَّرَ V to be proud, arrogant

اِسْتَكْبَرَ X to esteem great, important

كِبْرِيَاءُ, كِبْرٌ pride

كَبِيرٌ *pl.* كِبَارٌ big, great, old (of a person)

(كبرت)

كِبْرِيتٌ sulphur, matches

(كبس)

كَبَسَ (ـِ) to press, squeeze

(كبو)

كَبَا (ـُ) to stumble, fall on face

كُبَّايَةٌ pl. ـَاتٌ tumbler, glass (for drinking)

(كتب)

كَتَبَ (ـُ) v.n. كِتَابَةٌ to write

كَاتَبَ III to write to, correspond with

تَكَاتَبَ VI to write to each other, correspond

كِتَابٌ pl. كُتُبٌ book; letter (in older language)

كِتَابَةٌ writing, handwriting

كَاتِبٌ pl. كُتَّابٌ, كَتَبَةٌ clerk, writer

مَكْتَبٌ pl. مَكَاتِبُ office; school (*antiq.*)

مَكْتَبَةٌ pl. ـَاتٌ library, desk

مُكَاتَبَاتٌ correspondence

مَكْتُوبٌ pl. مَكَاتِيبُ letter

(كتف)

كَتِفٌ, كِتْفٌ pl. أَكْتَافٌ shoulder

(كتل)

كُتْلَةٌ pl. كُتَلٌ bloc (pol.)

(كتم)

كَتَمَ (ـُ) to hide, conceal, *trans.*

كَاتِمُ السِّرِّ, ٱلْأَسْرَارِ secretary

(كثر)

كَثُرَ (ـُ) to be much, many, numerous

كَثَّرَ II to make numerous, increase

كَثْرَةٌ, كِثْرَةٌ abundance, great number

كَثِيرٌ pl. ـُونَ, كِثَارٌ much, many

كَثِيراً very, much, greatly, a lot

كَثِيراً مَا (before a *verb*) often, oft-times

(كثف)

كَثِيفٌ thick, dense, compact

(كدر)

كَدَّرَ II to vex, trouble, grieve, upset

كَدَرٌ trouble, vexation

(كذب)

كَذَبَ (ـِ) to lie, tell falsehood

كِذْبٌ pl. أَكْذَابٌ a lie

كَذَّابٌ ,كَاذِبٌ liar

كَذُوبٌ great liar

(كرر)

كَرَّرَ II to repeat; purify, refine

كُرَّةٌ (for كُرَةٌ) see under كرو

تَكْرَارًا repeatedly

(كرب)

كَرْبٌ grief, sorrow

كَرَبٌ stump of a palm branch

(كرث)

اِكْتَرَثَ VIII to mind, look after; heed

(كرد).

كُرْدِيٌّ *coll.* كُرْدٌ *pl.* أَكْرَادٌ Kurd, Kurdish

(كرس)

كُرَّاسَةٌ *pl.* كَرَارِيسُ pamphlet, exercise book

كُرْسِيٌّ *pl.* كَرَاسٍ, كَرَاسِيُّ throne, chair

(كرم)

كَرُمَ (ـُ) to be noble, generous

أَكْرَمَ IV to honour

تَكَرَّمَ V to do a kindness, act generously

كَرَمٌ generosity, honour, nobleness

كَرْمٌ *pl.* كُرُومٌ vineyard

كَرِيمٌ *pl.* كِرَامٌ generous, noble, honourable

(كره)

كَرِهَ (ـَ) to hate, loathe

أَكْرَهَ IV to force, compel

كَرَاهِيَةٌ hatred, aversion

أَكْرَهُ ٱلنَّاسِ most unwilling, disapproving, of people

مَكْرُوهٌ adversity, misfortune

(كرو)

كُرَةٌ *pl.* ـَاتٌ sphere, ball, globe

(كسب)

كَسَبَ (ـِ) to earn, acquire, gain

كَاسَبَ III to seek to gain, acquire for oneself

كَسْبٌ earnings, gain

مَكْسَبٌ gain, profit

(كسر)

كَسَرَ (ـِ) to break, *trans.*

كَسَّرَ II to smash

تَكَسَّرَ V to break, *intrans.* be broken

اِنْكَسَرَ VII to break *intrans.*

(كسل)

كَسَلٌ idleness

كَسْلَانُ *pl.* كَسَالَى lazy, idle

كَسُولٌ (very) lazy

(كسو)

اِكْتَسَى VIII to be dressed, clothed, wear

كِسَاءٌ *pl.* أَكْسِيَةٌ garment, dress

(كشف)

كَشَفَ (ـِ) *v.n.* كَشْفٌ to uncover, examine, reveal

اِنْكَشَفَ VII to be uncovered, revealed

اِكْتَشَفَ VIII to discover, find out

اِكْتِشَافٌ *pl.* ـَاتٌ — discovery

(كعب)

كَعْبٌ *pl.* كُعُوبٌ ankle

(كفف)

كَفَّ (ـُ) (عَنْ) to cease (from)

كَفٌّ *pl.* كُفُوفٌ palm of the hand

كَافَّةٌ (followed by *gen.*) all

كَافَّةً all *adv.*

مَكْفُوفٌ blind

(كفأ)

كَافَأَ III to reward, recompense, remunerate, repay

كَفَاءَةٌ equality, likeness; competence, fitness, efficiency

كُفُوءٌ equal, like, *n.*

(كفح)

كَافَحَ III to struggle against

مُكَافَحَةٌ, كِفَاحٌ struggle, combat

(كفر)

كَفَرَ (ـُ) to become an infidel; (*with* بِ) to renounce, deny (God)

كَافِرٌ *pl.* كُفَّارٌ infidel, unbeliever

(كفل)

كَفَلَ (ـِ) to guarantee, be responsible for, stand security

كَفَالَةٌ bail, security, guarantee

(كفى)

كَفَى (ـِ) to suffice, satisfy

كِفَايَةٌ satisfaction, sufficiency

كَافٍ sufficient, enough

(كلل)

كُلٌّ (followed by *gen.*) each, every, all, the whole

كِلَانِ *f.* كِلْتَانِ both

كُلَّمَا whenever, as often as

كُلِّيَّةٌ *pl.* ـَاتٌ college

(كلب)

تَكَالَبَ VI to attack as a mob

كَلْبٌ *pl.* كِلَابٌ dog

(كلف)

كَلَّفَ II to cost; (*with* بِ) to charge one with an affair or matter

تَكْلِيفٌ *pl.* تَكَالِيفُ trouble, ceremony, formality

(كلم)

كَلَّمَ II to speak to, tell

كَالَمَ III to converse with, address

تَكَلَّمَ V to speak

كَلِمَةٌ *pl.* ـَاتٌ word

كَلَامٌ speech

(كم)

كَمْ how much? how many?

كَمِّيَّةٌ quantity

(كمل)

كَمَلَ (ـُ), اِكْتَمَلَ VIII to be complete, finished

كَمَّلَ II, أَكْمَلَ IV to finish, complete

كَمَالٌ perfection, completeness; pr. n. m.

كَامِلٌ perfect, complete, entire; pr. n. m.

(كمن)

كَمَنَ (ـُ) to hide, conceal, secrete

(كنن)

كَنَّ (ـُ) to keep a secret, conceal

(كنس)

كَنَسَ (ـِ) to sweep

كَنِيسٌ *pl.* كَنَائِسُ synagogue

كَنِيسَةٌ *pl.* كَنَائِسُ church

مِكْنَسَةٌ *pl.* مَكَانِسُ broom, besom

(كنز)

كَنْزٌ *pl.* كُنُوزٌ treasure

(كنف)

أَكْنَفَ IV to help anyone

كَنَفٌ *pl.* أَكْنَافٌ refuge, shelter, protection

(كنه)

كُنْهٌ substance, essence

(كنى)

كَنَى (ـِ), كَنَّى ب II to give a surname

كُنْيَةٌ surname, epithet

(كهرب)

كَهْرَبَاءُ, كَهْرَبَائِيَّةٌ electricity

(كهف)

كَهْفٌ *pl.* كُهُوفٌ cavern, cave

(كوخ)

كُوخٌ *pl.* أَكْوَاخٌ hut, cottage

(كود)

كَادَ (ـَ) to be on the point of, almost to do; (with *neg.*) hardly did

(كوع)

كُوعٌ *pl.* أَكْوَاعٌ elbow

(كوف)

اَلْكُوفَةُ Kufa (ancient city of Iraq)

(كون)

كَانَ (ـُ) to be

كَوَّنَ II to form, create

كَوْنٌ, كِيَانٌ existence, presence, nature, being

كَائِنٌ *pl.* كَائِنَاتٌ (a) being

مَكَانٌ *pl.* أَمَاكِنُ place

(كوى)

كَوَى (ـِ) to iron

مِكْوًى *pl.* مَكَاوٍ iron (for ironing)

(كى)

كَىْ, لِكَىْ so that, in order to (+ *subj.*)

(كيس)

كِيسٌ *pl.* أَكْيَاسٌ bag, purse, wallet

(كيف)

كَيْفَ how, how?

(كيل)

كَالَ (ـِ), كَيَّلَ II to measure, weigh

كَيْلٌ *pl.* أَكْيَالٌ measure

(كيم)

كِيمِيَاءُ, كِيمِيَا chemistry

كِيمَاوِيٌّ, كِيمِيٌّ chemical

ل

(ل)

لِ to, for, *prep.*; (+ *subj.*) so that, in order to

لَا no, not

بِلَا without (+ *gen.*)

لِأَنَّ because (+*accus.*)

لِكَيْ (see also كَيْ) so that (+ *subj.*)

لِمَ, لِمَا, لِمَاذَا why

(لأل)

لُؤْلُؤٌ, لُؤْلُؤَةٌ *pl.* لَآلِئُ pearl, pearls; pr. n. fem.

(لأم)

لَاءَمَ III to suit, agree with, be appropriate

مُلَائِمٌ convenient, suitable, fit

(لبث)

لَبِثَ (ـَ) to delay, tarry, stay

مَا لَبِثَ أَنْ فَعَلَ he did not delay to do, lost no time in doing

(لبس)

لَبِسَ (ـَ) *v.n.* لُبْسٌ to wear, dress

لِبَاسٌ *pl.* أَلْبِسَةٌ clothes; trousers, shorts, underpants (*mod.*)

مَلَابِسُ (*pl* of مَلْبَسٌ) clothes

(لبن)

لَبَنٌ milk, sour milk

لُبْنَانُ Lebanon

(لبى)

لَبَّى II to respond, answer (in the affirmative), obey

(لجج)

لَجَّ (ـِ) to persevere in, persist

لُجَّةٌ *pl.* لُجَجٌ depth (of sea)

(لجأ)

لَجَأَ (ـَ), اِلْتَجَأَ VIII to flee, take flight, take refuge (with, at إِلَى)

لَاجِئٌ *pl.* لَاجِئُونَ, مُلْتَجِئٌ *pl.* مُلْتَجِئُونَ refugee

(لجن)

لَجْنَةٌ *pl.* لِجَانٌ committee

(لحح)

أَلَحَّ عَلَى IV to press, insist, urge, oppress

(لحد)

لَاحِدٌ *pl.* لُحَّادٌ grave-digger

(لحس)

لَحَسَ (ـَ) to lick

(لحظ)

لَاحَظَ III to regard, observe, remark

لَحْظٌ glance

لَحْظَةٌ glance, moment

مُلاحَظَةٌ observation, remark

(لحق)

لَحِقَ (ـَ) to follow, overtake; concern

أَلْحَقَ بِ IV to annexe, join to, attach to

اِلْتَحَقَ بِ VIII to be annexed, joined to; reach

لَاحِقَةٌ *pl.* لَوَاحِقُ appurtenance

مُلْحَقٌ *pl.* ـَاتٌ appendix, supplement; dependency (of a country)

مُلْحَقٌ attaché (dipl.)

(لحم)

لَحْمٌ *pl.* لُحُومٌ meat

(لحن)

لَحْنٌ *pl.* أَلْحَانٌ melody, air, tone, chant

(لحى)

لِحْيَةٌ *pl.* لِحًى beard

(لخص)

لَخَّصَ II to extract, summarize sum up

مُلَخَّصٌ *pl.* ـَاتٌ summary, abstract

(لدى)

لَدُنْ, لَدَى at, by, with, near

(لذذ)

أَلَذَّ IV to make pleasant, sweet, agreeable

لَذَّةٌ pleasure, delight

لَذِيذٌ sweet, pleasant, delightful (to the senses)

(لزم)

لَزِمَ (ـَ) *v.n.* لُزُومٌ to be necessary

اِلْتَزَمَ VIII to be obliged; undertake; monopolize; be held responsible for

لَازِمٌ necessary

لَازِمَةٌ *pl.* لَوَازِمُ need, necessity

(لسن)

لِسَانٌ (*m. and f.*) *pl.* أَلْسُنٌ, أَلْسِنَةٌ tongue, language

(لصص)

لِصٌّ *pl.* لُصُوصٌ robber

(لطف)

لَاطَفَ III to treat with kindness, be friendly to

لُطْفٌ kindness, friendliness

لَطِيفٌ *pl.* لِطَافٌ friendly, pleasant, kind; pr. n. m.

(لعب)

لَعِبَ (ـَ) to play

(لعل)

لَعَلَّ perhaps (+ *accus.*)

(لعق)

مِلْعَقَةٌ *pl.* مَلَاعِقُ spoon

(لعن)

لَعَنَ (ـَ) to curse

لَعْنَةٌ curse, imprecation

(لغز)

لُغْزٌ *pl.* أَلْغَازٌ riddle, enigma

(لغو)

لُغَةٌ *pl.* ـَاتٌ — language

لُغَوِيٌّ linguistic, appertaining to language

(لغى)

أَلْغَى IV to abolish, render invalid, cancel, exclude

(لفف)

لَفَّ (ـُ) to wrap, fold, roll up

لِفًّا included, within

(لفت)

اِلْتَفَتَ إِلَى VIII to turn to, consider, pay attention to

(لفظ)

لَفَظَ (ـِ) to pronounce, utter (a word)

لَفْظٌ *pl.* أَلْفَاظٌ utterance, word, pronunciation

(لفى)

أَلْفَى IV to find, notice

(لقب)

لَقَّبَ II to name, nickname, entitle, ***doubly transitive, or, more commonly, the second object with*** ب

لَقَبٌ *pl.* أَلْقَابٌ surname, title, epithet

(لقط)

اِلْتَقَطَ VIII to pick up, catch, glean

(لقم)

لُقْمَةٌ *pl.* لُقَمٌ a morsel, bite

(لقى)

لَقِيَ (ـَ), لَاقَى III to meet, find

أَلْقَى IV to throw, cast; to deliver (a speech, talk, etc.)

تَلَقَّى V to receive, encounter

تَلَاقَى VI, اِلْتَقَى VIII to meet one another

اِلْتَقَى بِ VIII to meet with

اِسْتَلْقَى X to fall, lie on one's back

لِقَاءٌ, مُلَاقَاةٌ meeting, encounter

مُلْتَقًى meeting place

(لكك)

لَكٌّ gum, lac

(لكن)

لٰكِنْ, وَلٰكِنَّ but

لُوكَنْدَةٌ *pl.* —َاتٌ hotel (*mod. Eg.* and *Syr.*)

(لم)

لَمْ not (+ *juss.* negation of *perf.*)

لَمَّا not yet (+ *jussive*)

لَمَّا when

(لمم)

لَمَّ (ـُ) to collect, gather, amass

أَلَمَّ بِ IV to be well acquainted with (a subject), know, experience

إِلْمَامٌ knowledge, experience

مُلِمٌّ (بِ) knowledgeable, experienced, expert (in)

مُلِمَّةٌ disaster, accident, stroke of misfortune

(لمح)

لَمَحَ (ـَ) to glance at

لَمْحَةٌ glance, brief glimpse

(لمس)

لَمَسَ (ـِ) to feel, touch

اِلْتَمَسَ (مِنْ) VIII to beseech, entreat, desire, request

(لمع)

لَمَعَ (ـَ) to flash, shine, *intrans.*

أَلْمَعَ IV to cause to shine; deal with, allude to (*with* إِلى)

لَامِعٌ shining, flashing, brilliant

(لن)

لَنْ negation of *future* (+ *subj.*)

(لهب)

اِلْتَهَبَ VIII to flame, blaze, be inflamed

لَهِيبٌ flame

(لهت)

لَاهُوتٌ divinity

إِلَاهِيٌّ divine

أُلُوهِيَّةٌ divinity, divineness

(لهج)

لَهْجَةٌ tone, accent; dialect speech

(لهف)

تَلَهَّفَ V to regret having missed something

(لهو)

لَهَا (ـُ) to play, divert oneself

لَهْوٌ amusement, diversion

لَاهٍ *f.* لَاهِيَةٌ heedless, indifferent, forgetful

(لو)

لَوْ if (a supposition)

وَلَوْ although

لَوْلَا were it not for

لَوْ لَمْ unless, if not

(لوح)

لَاحَ (ـُ) to glimmer, appear, seem

لَوْحٌ *pl.* أَلْوَاحٌ board, tablet, plate, plank

لَائِحَةٌ *pl.* لَوَائِحُ appearance; regulation; schedule

(لوز)

لَوْزٌ almond (tree and fruit)

(لوم)

لَامَ (ـُ) to censure, blame

لَوْمٌ blame, censure

(لون)

لَوْنٌ *pl.* أَلْوَانٌ colour; kind, sort

(لوى)

لِوَاءٌ *pl.* أَلْوِيَةٌ flag, district; (*mod.*) brigade, major-general

(ليت)

لَيْتَ would that!

(ليس)

لَيْسَ not, not to be

(ليق)

لَاقَ (ـِ) to be fitting, worthy, suitable

(ليل)

لَيْلٌ *pl.* لَيَالٍ; لَيْلَةٌ night; a night

لَيْلًا by night

(لين)

لَيَّنَ II to soften

لَيِّنٌ soft, tender, flexible, pliable

م

(ما)

مَا, مَاذَا, مَ what

مَا not

(مأن)

مَؤُونَة *pl.* مُؤَن provisions

(مأى)

مِائَة, مِئَة a hundred

(متر)

مِتْر *pl.* أَمْتَار metre (measure)

(متع)

تَمَتَّعَ بِ V, اِسْتَمْتَعَ X to enjoy

مَتَاع *pl.* أَمْتِعَة goods, effects, property

(متن)

مَتْن text of a book

مَتِين solid, strong, firm

(متى)

مَتَى when? when

(مثل)

مَثَّلَ II to represent, act

تَمَثَّلَ V to appear, make an appearance (before someone)

اِمْتَثَلَ VIII to obey

مَثَل *pl.* أَمْثَال parable, proverb

مِثْل *pl.* أَمْثَال as, like, likeness

مِثَال *pl.* أَمْثِلَة pattern, model

تِمْثَال *pl.* تَمَاثِيل statue, figure, image

تَمْثِيلِيّ dramatic

(مجد)

مَجَّدَ II to praise, glorify, honour

مَجْد glory

مَاجِد, مَجِيد noble, glorious; pr. n. m.

(مجن)

مَجَّانًا free, gratis

(محن)

اِمْتِحَان *pl.* — َات examination

(محو)

مَحَا (ـُ) to erase, blot out, efface

(مخخ)

مُخّ *pl.* مِخَاخ brain

(مدد)

مَدَّ (ـُ) to stretch, lengthen, spread, extend

أَمَدَّ IV to help, aid, reinforce

تَمَدَّدَ V to stretch oneself, be extended; rest

اِمْتَدَّ VIII to be stretched, prolonged; reach

مَدٌّ *pl.* مُدُودٌ tide, flux, flow

مُدَّةٌ period (of time)

مَادَّةٌ *pl.* مَوَادُّ material, matter, element; item, article

مَادِّيٌّ material, *adj.*

مَدِيدٌ long, prolonged, extended

(مدح)

مَدَحَ (ـَ) to praise, extol, commend

(مدن)

مَدِينَةٌ *pl.* مُدُنٌ , مَدَائِنُ city

اَلْمَدِينَةُ Medina (city of Arabia)

مَدَنِيٌّ civil *adj.*

(مُذْ) see (مُنْذُ)

(مرر)

مَرَّ (بِ ، عَلَى) to pass (by)

أَمَرَّ IV to make bitter, embitter

اِسْتَمَرَّ X to continue, last

مُرٌّ bitter

مُرُورٌ passing, passing by, passage; traffic (*mod.*)

مَرَّةٌ *pl.* ـَاتٌ , مِرَارٌ a time, once

مِرَارًا several times, often

مُسْتَمِرٌّ continuous, continual

تَمَرْمَرَ II (*quad.*) to murmur

(مرأ)

اِمْرُؤٌ , مَرْءٌ man

اِمْرَأَةٌ , مَرْأَةٌ *pl.* نِسْوَةٌ , نِسَاءٌ woman

(مرج)

مَرْجٌ *pl.* مُرُوجٌ meadow

(مرد)

تَمَرَّدَ V to rebel, revolt

(مرس)

مَارَسَ III to practise, exercise (a profession, calling)

(مرض)

مَرِضَ (ـَ) to be or fall sick, ill

مَرَضٌ *pl.* أَمْرَاضٌ illness

مَرِيضٌ *pl.* مَرْضَى ill, sick

(مركش)

مَرَّاكُشُ Marrakesh, Morocco

(مرن)

مَرَّنَ II to practise, exercise

مَارُونِيٌّ *pl.* مَوَارِنَةٌ Maronite

(مزج)

مَزَجَ (ـُ) to mix, *trans.*

(مزح)

مَزَحَ (ـَ) to joke, jest

(مزق)

مَزَّقَ II to tear, *trans.*

(مسح)

مَسَحَ (ـَ) to wipe, clean, rub off; annoint; measure (a piece of land)

مَسَاحَةٌ area, surface, survey of land

مَسِيحِيٌّ Christian

(مسك)

مَسَكَ (ـِ)، تَمَاسَكَ VI to seize, hold, comprehend

أَمْسَكَ IV to hold back, restrain; abstain from (عَنْ)

تَمَسَّكَ بِ V to cling to, adhere to, hold fast to (a religion, faith, opinion, belief, etc.)

(مسى)

مَسَاءٌ evening, *n.*

أَمْسِ yesterday, last night

أَوَّلُ أَمْسِ the day before yesterday

(مشى)

مَشَى (ـِ) *v.n.* مَشْيَةٌ to walk, go

مُشَاةٌ (*pl.* of مَاشٍ) infantry

مَاشِيَةٌ *pl.* مَوَاشٍ cattle

(مصر)

مَصَّرَ II to build (a town)

مِصْرٌ *pl.* أَمْصَارٌ chief town of a country, boundaries of two countries

مِصْرُ Egypt, Cairo

(مضى)

مَضَى (ـِ) *v.n.* مُضِيٌّ to pass, go, depart

أَمْضَى IV to sign; execute, accomplish

مُضِيٌّ course of time

إِمْضَاءٌ signature; execution, accomplishment

مَاضٍ past, last

(مطر)

مَطَرٌ *pl.* أَمْطَارٌ rain

(مطو)

مَطِيَّةٌ riding-beast

(مع)

مَعَ، مَعْ with

مَعًا together, simultaneously

مَعَ أَنَّ although, in spite of

(معز)

مَعَزٌ, مَعْزٌ (*sing.* مَاعِزٌ) goats

(معض)

اِمْتِعَاضٌ anger, vexation, exasperation

(معن)

أَمْعَنَ IV to act rigorously, be zealous, consider

أَمْعَنَ النَّظَرَ to consider closely, think over

(مكك)

مَكَّةُ Mecca (city of Arabia)

(مكث)

مَكَثَ (ـُ) to stay, abide, dwell, tarry

(مكر)

مَكَرَ (ـُ)to deceive, trick

(مكس)

مَكْسٌ *pl.* مُكُوسٌ excise duty

(مكن)

أَمْكَنَ IV to enable, be possible

تَمَكَّنَ V to be enabled

مَكَانٌ (see كون)

مَكَانَةٌ place, rank; influence, power

مَكِينَةٌ machine

مُمْكِنٌ possible

(ملأ)

مَلَأَ (ـَ) to fill, *trans.*

(ملح)

مِلْحٌ salt, salty

مِلَاحَةٌ navigation

مَلَّاحٌ sailor

مَلِيحٌ *pl.* مِلَاحٌ good, handsome, pleasant, pretty

مَلِيحَةٌ *pl.* مَلَائِحُ a pleasant thing

(ملك)

مَلَكَ (ـِ), اِمْتَلَكَ VIII to possess, own

مَلَّكَ II to give a. o. possession of

مِلْكٌ *pl.* أَمْلَاكٌ possession, property

مُلْكٌ sovereignty, ownership

مُلْكِيٌّ royal; civilian (opp. military)

مَلَكٌ, مَلْأَكٌ, مَلْآكٌ *pl.* مَلَائِكَةٌ angel

مَلِكٌ *pl.* مُلُوكٌ king

مَلَكَةٌ *pl.* ـَاتٌ queen

مَالِكٌ ruling, ruler, possessor, owner

مَلَّاكٌ owner of property

مَلَكِيٌّ, مُلُوكِيٌّ royal

مَمْلَكَةٌ *pl.* مَمَالِكُ kingdom

اَلْمَمْلَكَةُ الْمُتَّحِدَةُ the United Kingdom

مَمْلُوكٌ *pl.* مَمَالِيكُ Mamluke, slave

مِلْيُونٌ *pl.* مَلَايِينُ million

(من)

مَنْ who?, who

مِنْ from, than

(منن)

مَنٌّ favour

مَنُونٌ death

(منذ)

مُنْذُ, مُذْ since, *prep.*

(منع)

مَنَعَ (ـَ) to prevent, forbid

اِمْتَنَعَ VIII to refuse

مَنَاعَةٌ strength of a position

مَمْنُوعَاتٌ forbidden things

(منى)

تَمَنَّى V to wish

مَنِيَّةٌ fate, death, destiny

(مهد)

مَهَّدَ II to level, prepare, make easy

مَهْدٌ *pl.* مُهُودٌ cradle

(مهر)

مَهْرٌ *pl.* مُهُورٌ dowry

مُهْرٌ seal, signet

مَاهِرٌ *pl.* مَهَرَةٌ skilful, skilled

(مهل)

تَمَهَّلَ V to be slow

(مهن)

مِهْنَةٌ *pl.* مِهَنٌ profession, trade

اِمْتِهَانٌ service

(موت)

مَاتَ (ـُ) to die

مَوْتٌ, مَمَاتٌ death

مَيِّتٌ *pl.* أَمْوَاتٌ, مَوْتَى dead

(موج)

مَوْجٌ *pl.* أَمْوَاجٌ wave (sea, air)

(موز)

مَوْزٌ banana (tree and fruit)

(موس)

مُوسَى Moses

مُوسِيقَى music

(مول)

مَالٌ *pl.* أَمْوَالٌ wealth, property, goods, capital

(موه)

مَاءٌ *pl.* مِيَاهٌ water

(ميد)

مَائِدَةٌ *pl.* ـَاتٌ —, مَوَائِدُ table

مَيْدَانٌ *pl.* مَيَادِينُ arena, square, field; sphere; course (for racing)

(ميز)

مَيَّزَ II to distinguish, differentiate; prefer

إِمْتَازَ VIII to be distinguished, distinct

إِمْتِيَازٌ *pl.* ـَاتٌ — distinction, privilege, preference

مُمْتَازٌ distinguished, distinct, select

(ميل)

مَالَ (ـِ) to incline, bend

مَيْلٌ *pl.* مُيُولٌ inclination

مِيلٌ *pl.* أَمْيَالٌ mile

(مين)

مِينَاءٌ *pl.* (*fem.*) مَوَانِئُ port (sea)

ن

(نبب)

أُنْبُوبٌ *pl.* أَنَابِيبُ pipe, tube

(نبأ)

نَبَّأَ II to inform (anyone) of (a thing)

تَنَبَّأَ V to make oneself out to be a prophet

نَبَأٌ *pl.* أَنْبَاءٌ news, information

نُبُوءَةٌ, نُبُوَّةٌ prophecy

نَبِيءٌ, نَبِيٌّ *pl.* أَنْبِيَاءُ, ـُونَ prophet

نَبَوِيٌّ prophetic, pertaining to the prophet

(نبت)

نَبَتَ (ـُ) to grow, sprout (of plant)

نَبَاتٌ *pl.* ـَاتٌ — plant, vegetation

(نبح)

نَبَحَ (ـَ) to bark (of dog)

(نبذ)

نَبَذَ (ـِ) to produce (date-) wine

نَبِيذٌ *pl.* أَنْبِذَةٌ wine

نُبْذَةٌ *pl.* نُبَذٌ section, part; article (in newspaper), treatise

(نبر)

مِنْبَرٌ *pl.* مَنَابِرُ pulpit, tribune; stage

(نبط)

اِسْتَنْبَطَ X to find out, contrive

(نبع)

نَبَعَ (ـُ) to spring, gush (of water)

نَبْعٌ spring (of water)

مَنْبَعٌ *pl.* مَنَابِعُ source, origin

يَنْبُوعٌ *pl.* يَنَابِيعُ fountain

(نبغ)

نَبَغَ (ـُ) to rise, appear, excel

نَابِغَةٌ *pl.* نَوَابِغُ distinguished (person)

(نبق)

نَبْقٌ lote tree and its fruit; wild apple, crab apple; mealy matter of palm pith

(نبل)

نَبِيلٌ *pl.* نُبَلَاءُ، نِبَالٌ noble, sagacious; pr. n. m.

(نبه)

نَبَّهَ II to warn, inform

تَنَبَّهَ V to wake up, be alert

اِنْتَبَهَ VIII to pay attention, notice

تَنْبِيهٌ warning, notice

نَبِيهٌ awake, clever; pr.n. m.

(نتج)

نَتَجَ (ـُ) أَنْتَجَ IV to produce, bring forth

نَتَجَ (ـِ) عَنْ to arise, result from

نِتَاجٌ product

نَتِيجَةٌ *pl.* نَتَائِجُ result, conclusion, consequence

إِنْتَاجٌ production, producing

مُنْتَجَاتٌ, مَنْتُوجَاتٌ products

مُنْتِجٌ producer

(نثر)

نَثَرَ (ـُ) to scatter, disperse, sprinkle, *trans.*

نَثْرٌ, مَنْثُورٌ prose

(نجب)

نَجِيبٌ noble, excellent; pr. n. m.

(نجح)
نَجَحَ (ـَ) to succeed, prosper
نَجَاحٌ success, prosperity
نَاجِحٌ successful, prosperous, thriving

(نجد)
نَجَدَ (ـُ), أَنْجَدَ IV to help, aid

(نجر)
نِجَارَةٌ carpentry
نَجَّارٌ carpenter, joiner

(نجز)
أَنْجَزَ IV to complete, accomplish, achieve

(نجل)
نَجْلٌ *pl.* أَنْجَالٌ son, offspring
اَلْإِنْجِيلُ The Gospel
مِنْجَلٌ *pl.* مَنَاجِلُ sickle

(نجم)
نَجَمَ (ـُ), أَنْجَمَ IV to appear, rise
نَجْمٌ *pl.* نُجُومٌ star
نَاجِمٌ clear
مَنْجَمٌ *pl.* مَنَاجِمُ mine; source
مُنَجِّمٌ astrologer

(نجو)
نَجَا (ـُ) to escape, be delivered, saved
نَجَاةٌ escape, deliverance

(نحب)
نَحْبٌ death
قَضَى نَحْبَهُ he died

(نحر)
اِنْتَحَرَ VIII to commit suicide

(نحز)
نَحِيزَةٌ nature (of a person)

(نحس)
نُحَاسٌ copper
نَحَّاسٌ coppersmith

(نحل)
نَحْلٌ bees (*coll.*)
نَحِيلٌ thin, emaciated

(نحن)
نَحْنُ we

(نحو)
نَحْوَ towards, near, like, about
نَحْوٌ *pl.* أَنْحَاءٌ method, way; region; approximation
عِلْمُ ٱلنَّحْوِ grammar (esp. syntax)

نَحْوِيٌّ *pl.* ـُونَ, نُحَاةٌ grammarian

نَاحِيَةٌ *pl.* نَوَاحٍ side, direction; district; point of view; sphere

(نخب)

نَخَبَ (ـَ), اِنْتَخَبَ VIII to choose, elect

اِنْتِخَابٌ *pl.* ـَاتٌ — election

نَاخِبٌ, مُنْتَخِبٌ elector

(نخل)

نَخْلَةٌ, نَخِيلٌ, نُخَيْلَةٌ palm tree

(ندب)

نَدَبَ (ـُ) to weep, bewail, lament

نَدَبَ (ـَ), اِنْتَدَبَ VIII to call, appoint, delegate, depute; invite or urge

اِنْتِدَابٌ mandate (*mod; pol.*)

مَنْدُوبٌ delegated, commissioner

(ندر)

نَدَرَ (ـُ) to be rare, infrequent scarce

نَادِرٌ *pl.* نَوَادِرُ rare, rare thing, rarity

نَادِرًا seldom, rarely

(ندل)

مَنْدِيلٌ *pl.* مَنَادِيلُ kerchief, handkerchief

(ندم)

نَدِمَ (ـَ) to repent, regret

نَدَامَةٌ repentance

نَدِيمٌ *pl.* نُدَمَاءُ associate, friend, confidant, boon companion; pr. n. m.

(ندو)

نَادَى III to call, summon, proclaim

نِدَاءٌ, مُنَادَاةٌ call

نَادٍ *pl.* أَنْدِيَةٌ club, place of assembly

نَدْوَةٌ assembly, forum

مُنْتَدًى assembly-hall

(نذر)

نَذَرَ (ـُ) to make a vow

أَنْذَرَ بِ IV to warn

نَذْرٌ *pl.* نُذُورٌ vow

إِنْذَارٌ warning

(نذل)

نَذْلٌ *pl.* أَنْذَالٌ vile, mean; simpleton

نَذِيلٌ abject

(نزع)

نَزَعَ (ـَ) to remove, take away; to spoil

نَازَعَ III to dispute with, fight

تَنَازَعَ VI to contend among themselves

اِنْتَزَعَ VIII to remove, take away, pull from, be snatched, pulled; be spoilt

(نزل)

نَزَلَ (ـِ) *v.n.* نُزُولٌ to alight, descend, lodge

أَنْزَلَ IV to cause to descend

نَزِيلٌ *pl.* نُزَلَاءُ guest

مَنْزِلٌ *pl.* مَنَازِلُ dwelling house

(نزه)

نُزْهَةٌ amusement, pleasure; pr. n. f.

(نسب)

نَسَبَ (ـُ) إِلَى to attribute to, ascribe (something) to

نَاسَبَ III to resemble; be appropriate, fit, suitable

تَنَاسَبَ VI to correspond with (each other)

نَسَبٌ *pl.* أَنْسَابٌ lineage

نِسْبَةٌ relation, affinity

نِسْبَةٌ, تَنَاسُبٌ proportion

نِسْبَةً إِلَى alluding to, referring to

بِالنِّسْبَةِ إِلَى in comparison with; in relation to

نَسِيبٌ *pl.* أَنْسِبَاءُ kinsman

أَنْسَبُ more fitted or suitable

مُنَاسِبٌ suitable, convenient, proper, fit

مُنَاسَبَةٌ suitability, appropriateness; connection

بِمُنَاسَبَةِ (+ *gen.*) in connection with; on the occasion of

(نسج)

نَسَجَ (ـُ) to weave

نَسِيجٌ *pl.* أَنْسِجَةٌ, نَسَائِجُ textile, fabric, tissue

مَنْسُوجَاتٌ textiles

(نسخ)

نَسَخَ (ـُ) to copy, transcribe; abrogate, abolish

نُسْخَةٌ *pl.* نُسَخٌ copy, manuscript

(نسر)

نَسْرٌ *pl.* نُسُورٌ eagle, vulture

(نسق)

نَسَّقَ II to place in order, arrange symmetrically

تَنَاسُقٌ arrangement, order

(نسك)

نَاسِكٌ *pl.* نُسَّاكٌ hermit, ascetic, recluse

(نسل)

نَسَلَ (ـُ) to beget

تَنَاسَلَ VI to multiply by generation, procreate

نَسْلٌ posterity, progeny

تَنَاسُلٌ descent by generation; procreation

(نسم)

نَسَمَةٌ *pl.* ـَاتٌ — soul, person, breath of life

(نسو)

نِسَاءٌ, نِسْوَةٌ women

(نسى)

نَسِيَ (ـَ) to forget

أَنْسَى IV to cause to forget

تَنَاسَى VI to pretend to forget; feign forgetfulness

نِسْيَانٌ forgetfulness, forgetting

(نشأ)

نَشَأَ (ـَ) to grow up (child); originate, rise

أَنْشَأَ IV to found, create, originate, establish

إِنْشَاءٌ originating, founding, establishment; composition, style

مَنْشَأٌ (place of) origin; source

(نشب)

نَشِبَ (ـَ) to break out (war)

(نشد)

نَاشَدَ III to recite to anyone; to cause to swear, ask one to swear by (بِ) God

أَنْشَدَ IV to quote, recite (verses, etc.)

(نشر)

نَشَرَ (ـُ) *v.n.* نَشْرٌ to publish, spread abroad

إِنْتَشَرَ VIII to be published; spread abroad

نَشْرَةٌ announcement, publication, bulletin

إِنْتِشَارٌ dissemination, spreading; circulation

نَاشِرٌ publisher

(نشط)

نَشَطَ (ـَ) to be active, energetic

نَشَاطٌ energy, zeal, activity, liveliness

نَشِيطٌ *pl.* نِشَاطٌ active, energetic, lively

(نشف)

نَشَفَ (ـَ) to be or become dry

نَاشِفٌ dry

مِنْشَفَةٌ *pl.* مَنَاشِفُ towel

(نشل)

نَشَلَ (ـُ) to take away, snatch, steal

(نصص)

نَصٌّ *pl.* نُصُوصٌ text (of a book); definition; wording; stipulation

(نصب)

نِصَابٌ *pl.* نُصُبٌ handle (of weapon)

نَصِيبٌ fortune, lot

(نصت)

نَصَتَ إِلَى (ـِ) to listen to

(نصح)

نَصَحَ (ـَ) to advise, counsel

نَصِيحَةٌ *pl.* نَصَائِحُ advice

نَاصِحٌ adviser

(نصر)

نَصَرَ (ـُ) to assist, aid (give victory)

تَنَصَّرَ V to become a Christian

اِنْتَصَرَ عَلَى VIII to conquer, vanquish a.o.

نَصْرٌ aid, victory

نَصْرَانِيٌّ *pl.* نَصَارَى Christian (*lit.* Nazarene)

اِنْتِصَارٌ victory, triumph

نَاصِرٌ *pl.* أَنْصَارٌ helper

مَنْصُورٌ conqueror (lit. the assisted of God); pr.n. m.

(نصف)

نَاصَفَ III to divide into halves

أَنْصَفَ IV to act impartially

اِنْتَصَفَ VIII to be divided into halves

نِصْفٌ *pl.* أَنْصَافٌ a half, half

نِصْفُ ٱللَّيْلِ midnight

إِنْصَافٌ equity, justice, impartiality

مُنْتَصَف middle

(نصو)

نَاصِيَة *pl.* نَوَاصٍ forelock

(نضج)

نَاضِج cooked well, ripe, mature

(نضل)

نِضَال struggle

(نطط)

نَطَّ (ـُ) *v.n.* نَطّ to leap, jump

(نطر)

نَاطُور *pl.* نَوَاطِير guard, keeper, overseer (esp. of garden, vineyard, etc.)

(نطع)

نَطْع leather mat

(نطق)

نَطَقَ (ـِ) to speak, express

اِسْتَنْطَقَ X to question, examine, interrogate (by a judge, etc.)

نِطَاق limit, boundary; zone, sphere

نَاطِق spokesman, speaker

مَنْطِق logic

مِنْطَقَة *pl.* مَنَاطِق zone

مُسْتَنْطِق examining judge; interrogator

(نظر)

نَظَرَ (ـُ) *v.n.* نَظَر to look (at إِلَى), see, oversee

اِنْتَظَرَ VIII to await, expect

نَظَر *pl.* أَنْظَار regard; theory

نَظَرًا إِلَى in regard to; in view of

نَظْرَة glance, look

نَاظِر *pl.* نُظَّار inspector, overseer, minister; seer, beholder

نَظَّارَات glasses, spectacles

نَظِير *pl.* نُظَرَاء peer, corresponding to, equal, *n.*

مَنْظَر *pl.* مَنَاظِر view, scene, scene of play

(نظف)

نَظَّفَ II to clean, *trans.*

نَظَافَة cleanliness

نَظِيف *pl.* نُظَفَاء clean, *adj.*

(نظم)

نَظَمَ (ـِ) *v.n.* نَظْم to arrange; compose (verse)

نَظَّمَ II to put in order, arrange, regulate, organize

تَنَظَّمَ V, اِنْتَظَمَ VIII to be arranged, regulated

نِظَامٌ *pl.* أَنْظِمَةٌ system, method, order; regulation, law

تَنْظِيمٌ *pl.* ـَاتٌ regulation; arrangement, compilation, poetry writing

اِنْتِظَامٌ regularity, order

(نعج)

نَعْجَةٌ *pl.* نِعَاجٌ sheep

(نعر)

نَاعُورَةٌ *pl.* نَوَاعِيرُ irrigating wheel, water wheel

(نعس)

نَعَسَ (ـَ) to be or become sleepy

(نعش)

مُنْعِشٌ refreshing

(نعم)

نَعِمَ (ـَ) *v.n.* نَعْمَةٌ to live in ease

نِعْمَ to be good, excellent

أَنْعَمَ عَلَى IV to show favour to; be kind to

نَعَمْ yes

نَعَمٌ, أَنْعَامٌ cattle, cloven-hoofed

نِعْمَةٌ *pl.* نِعَمٌ favour, benefit

نَاعِمٌ soft, tender

نَعِيمٌ pleasant; pr. n. m.

(نغم)

نَغْمَةٌ *pl.* نَغَمَاتٌ melody, tune

(نفث)

نَفَّاثٌ *pl.* ـَاتٌ blower

طَائِرَةٌ نَفَّاثَةٌ jet aircraft

(نفخ)

نَفَخَ (ـُ) to blow

(نفد)

نَفِدَ (ـَ) to be exhausted, consumed; be out of print (book, etc.)

(نفذ)

نَفَذَ (ـُ) to pierce, penetrate, be effective

نَفَّذَ II to execute, fulfil

أَنْفَذَ IV to carry out, execute

نُفُوذٌ penetration; influence

ذُو نُفُوذٍ influential; person of influence

تَنْفِيذٌ execution; fulfilment

تَنْفِيذِيٌّ executive *adj.* (*mod.*)

نَفِيذٌ effective (of an order or command)

نَافِذَةٌ *pl.* نَوَافِذُ window

(نفر)

نَفَرَ (ـِـ) to turn away, flee, avoid

نُفُورٌ flight, aversion

نَفَرٌ *pl.* أَنْفَارٌ person; a number of people; private (in armed forces)

(نفس)

تَنَفَّسَ V to breathe

نَفْسٌ (*m.* and *f.*) *pl.* نُفُوسٌ, أَنْفُسٌ soul, self; self-same

نَفَسٌ *pl.* أَنْفَاسٌ breath

نَفِيسٌ precious

(نفط)

نَفْطٌ oil, petroleum

(نفع)

نَفَعَ (ـَـ) to be useful, profitable

اِنْتَفَعَ (بِ، مِنْ) VIII to use, benefit (from, by)

نَفْعٌ ; مَنْفَعَةٌ *pl.* مَنَافِعُ use, benefit

نَافِعٌ useful, profitable

(نفق)

نَفَقَةٌ *pl.* ـَاتٌ expense, cost, expenditure, maintenance

مُنَافِقٌ hypocrite; deceiver

(نفى)

نَفَى (ـِـ) to expel, banish, exile; deny, exclude

نَافَى III to contradict, be inconsistent with

نَفْيٌ exile, expulsion, banishment; denial

مَنْفِيٌّ exiled, an exile

(نقب)

نَقْبٌ *pl.* أَنْقَابٌ hole in a wall, breach, tunnel

نِقَابٌ *pl.* نُقُبٌ veil

نِقَابَةٌ *pl.* ـَاتٌ syndicate, corporation

نِقَابَةُ ٱلْعُمَّالِ trade union (*mod.*)

نَقِيبٌ *pl.* نُقَبَاءُ chief, head

(نقح)

نَقَّحَ II to revise, correct (book)

(نقد)

نَقَدَ (ـُ), إِنْتَقَدَ VIII to criticize

نَقْدٌ, إِنْتِقَادٌ criticism

نَقْدٌ *pl.* نُقُودٌ cash, ready money

نَاقِدٌ critic

(نقذ)

أَنْقَذَ IV to rescue, deliver, save

(نقر)

نَقَرَ (ـُ) *v.n.* نَقْرٌ to hollow out, pierce, peck (of a bird)

مِنْقَارٌ *pl.* مَنَاقِيرُ beak, bill (of bird)

(نقش)

نَقَشَ (ـُ) to paint, sculpture

نَاقَشَ III to argue with

مُنَاقَشَةٌ discussion, argument

نَقَّاشٌ painter, sculptor, engraver

(نقص)

نَقَصَ (ـُ) *v.n.* نَقْصٌ to decrease, diminish, fall short

نَاقَصَ III to reduce (price, etc.)

إِنْتَقَصَ VIII to abate, diminish

مُنَاقَصَةٌ tender (in commerce), public auction

نَاقِصٌ defective, diminished, deficient, imperfect, wanting, lacking

(نقض)

نَاقَضَ III to contradict

نَقْضٌ *pl.* أَنْقَاضٌ ruins

(نقط)

نُقْطَةٌ *pl.* نُقَطٌ point, dot, spot; drop

(نقع)

نَاقِعٌ penetrating, pervading; deadly (poison)

مُسْتَنْقَعٌ *pl.* ـَاتٌ marsh, swamp

(نقل)

نَقَلَ (ـُ) *v.n.* نَقْلٌ to move, remove, transport, transfer; copy, translate, quote

تَنَقَّلَ V to be transferred, moved, posted

إِنْتَقَلَ VIII to move, *intrans.*, be transferred, removed, transported

— إِلَى رَحْمَةِ ٱللهِ he died

(نقم)

إِنْتَقَمَ (مِنْ) VIII to take revenge (on)

إِنْتِقَامٌ, نِقْمَةٌ vengeance

(نقى)

نَقِيَ (ـَ) to be pure

إِنْتَقَى VIII to choose, select

نَقَاوَةٌ, نَقَاءٌ purity, innocence

نَقِيٌّ pure, clean, innocent

(نكب)

نَكَبَ (ـُ) to afflict

مَنْكُوبٌ victim

(نكت)

نُكْتَةٌ pl. نُكَتٌ witticism; speck, spot

(نكح)

نَكَحَ (ـَ) to marry

(نكد)

مَنْكُودُ ٱلْحَظِّ unhappy, unfortunate

(نكر)

أَنْكَرَ IV to deny

(نمذج)

نَمُوذَجٌ pl. ـَاتٌ sample, example

(نمر)

نَمِرٌ pl. نُمُورٌ, نُمُورَةٌ leopard, panther, tiger

نُمْرَةٌ pl. نُمَرٌ (*Eur.*) number

(نمس)

نِمْسٌ pl. نُمُوسٌ ichneumon, weasel

نَامُوسٌ pl. نَوَامِيسُ law, moral law; mosquito

(نمط)

نَمَطٌ pl. نِمَاطٌ fashion, way, manner

(نمل)

نَمْلَةٌ pl. نَمَلٌ ant

(نمو)

نَمَا (ـُ) to grow, develop, *intrans.*

نُمُوٌّ growth, development

(نمى)

إِنْتَمَى إِلَى VIII to trace one's origin to, go back to

(نهب)

نَهَبَ (ـَ) v.n. نَهْبٌ to plunder, pillage

(نهج)

نَهْجٌ way, road, street (current in Maghribi usage)

مَنْهَجٌ, مِنْهَاجٌ pl. مَنَاهِجُ way, method

(نهد)

تَنَهَّدَ V to sigh, groan

(نهر)

اِنْتَهَرَ VIII to drive, drive away roughly, upbraid, chide

نَهْرٌ *pl.* أَنْهَارٌ, أَنْهُرٌ river

نَهَارٌ day, daylight

نَهَارًا by day

(نهز)

اِنْتَهَزَ ٱلْفُرْصَةَ VIII to seize the opportunity

(نهض)

نَهَضَ (َ) *v.n.* نُهُوضٌ to rise

اِسْتَنْهَضَ X to urge, incite, stir up

نَهْضَةٌ awakening, arising, revival, emancipation

(نهك)

أَنْهَكَ IV to weaken, enfeeble, overcome

(نهى)

اِنْتَهَى VIII to finish, conclude, end, *intrans.*

نِهَايَةٌ end, utmost, extremity

اِنْتِهَاءٌ end, termination, limit

مُنْتَهًى end

(نوب)

نَوْبَةٌ a time, turn, occasion; suite (in music)

بِٱلنِّيَابَةِ عَنْ on behalf of

نَائِبٌ *pl.* نُوَّابٌ deputy, representative, substitute

مَجْلِسُ ٱلنُّوَّابِ Parliament

(نوت)

نُوتِيٌّ sailor

(نوخ)

مُنَاخٌ *pl.* ـَاتٌ — climate

(نور)

نَارٌ (*f.*) *pl.* نِيرَانٌ fire, *n.*

نُورٌ *pl.* أَنْوَارٌ light, *n.*

(نوع)

نَوَّعَ II to assort, classify, compose

نَوْعٌ *pl.* أَنْوَاعٌ sort, kind

(نوف)

نَافَ (ُ) (عَلَى) to be above, or more than

نَيِّفٌ more, upwards of

(نوق)

نَاقَةٌ *pl.* نُوقٌ she-camel

(نول)

نَالَ (َ) to attain, obtain

نَاوَلَ III to give, hand to

تَنَاوَلَ VI to obtain, receive, take, partake

نَوَالٌ attainment, attaining; pr. n. f.

نَوْلٌ *pl.* أَنْوَالٌ loom

نَيْلٌ obtaining, attaining, *n.*

مِنْوَالٌ mode, manner, fashion

(نوم)

نَامَ (ـَ) (نِمْتُ etc.) to sleep

نَوْمٌ, مَنَامٌ sleep

(نوى)

نَوَى (ـِ) to resolve, intend

نِيَّةٌ *pl.* ـَاتٌ — intention

(نيف)

نَافٌ yoke

(نيل)

اَلنِّيلُ the (river) Nile

(ه)

ـهُ — (attached *pron.*) his, its, him, it

(ها)

هَا behold! here! here you are! take!

ـهَا — (attached *pron.*) her, its, it

(هات)

هَاتِ come! bring!

(هب)

هَبَّ (ـُ) *v.n.* هُبُوبٌ to blow (of wind)

هَبَّ (ـُ) to awake (from sleep); begin, start (to do)

(هبط)

هَبَطَ (ـُ) to fall, descend, land (aircraft)

هُبُوطٌ fall, abatement

(هتف)

هَتَفَ (ـِ) to call, shout

هَاتِفٌ telephone (a lately introduced word and in use in some Arab countries. See also Appendix A, Sec. 6 (a)

(هجر)

هَجَرَ (ـُ) to forsake, abandon

هَاجَرَ III to emigrate

هِجْرَةٌ flight, emigration, migration

اَلْهِجْرَةُ The Hegira (emigration of the Prophet Muhammad from Mecca in 622 A.D.) Beginning of Muslim era.

مُهاجِر emigrant, immigrant

مَهْجَر term used for settlement of Arabic-speaking communities abroad (partic. the Americas in modern times)

(هجس)

هاجِس *pl.* هَواجِس unrest, disturbance, troubled thought

(هجم)

هَجَمَ (ـِ) (عَلَى) to attack, assault

هاجَمَ III to attack

هُجُوم attack, assault

(هدد)

هَدَّدَ II to threaten, menace

(هدأ)

هَدَأَ (ـَ) *v.n.* هُدُوء to be calm, quiet, tranquil

هادِئ quiet, calm, tranquil

(هدر)

هَدِير murmur (of water), roaring (of sea and waves)

(هدف)

هَدَف *pl.* أَهْداف aim, target

(هدم)

هَدَمَ (ـِ) *v.n.* هَدْم to destroy, raze

هُدُوم (*pl.*) clothes, garments

(هدن)

هُدْنَة armistice, truce

(هدى)

هَدَى (ـِ) to guide

أَهْدَى IV to present, bestow (with double *accus.*)

اِهْتَدَى VIII to guide oneself; be rightly guided

هُدًى guidance, way of salvation

هَدِيَّة *pl.* هَدايا a present, gift

(هذب)

مُهَذَّب educated, refined, polished

(هرر)

هِرّ cat

(هرب)

هَرَبَ (ـُ) *v.n.* هُرُوب to flee, escape

هَرَّبَ II to smuggle; put to flight

(هرم)

هَرَم *pl.* أَهْرام pyramid

(هرن)

هَارُونُ Harun, Aaron

(هزز)

هَزَّ (ـُ) *v.n.* هَزٌّ to shake, stir, brandish

(هزأ)

هَزَأَ بِ, إِسْتَهْزَأَ X to mock, scoff at, deride

(هزع)

هَزِيعٌ watch or division of the night

(هزل)

هَزَلَ (ـِ) *v.n.* هَزْلٌ to joke, jest

هُزَالٌ thinness

هَزِيلٌ thin, meagre, emaciated

(هزم)

إِنْهَزَمَ VII to be defeated, put to flight (of an army)

(هطل)

هَطَلَ (ـِ) to rain, send rain

(هكذا)

see under (ذا)

(هكل)

هَيْكَلٌ *pl.* هَيَاكِلُ temple, altar, statue, skeleton

(هل)

هَلْ *particle* of interrogation

(هلل)

إِسْتَهَلَّ X to appear first (of moon); begin

هِلَالٌ crescent, new moon

(هلك)

هَلَكَ (ـِ) to perish

أَهْلَكَ IV to ruin, destroy, lay waste

إِسْتَهْلَكَ X to consume, spend, exhaust

هَلَاكٌ destruction

إِسْتِهْلَاكٌ consumption

مَهْلَكٌ, مَهْلَكَةٌ place of destruction, desert

مُسْتَهْلِكٌ consumer

(هلم)

هَلُمَّ come here!

هَلُمَّ جَرًّا and so on; etcetera

(همم)

هَمَّ (ـُ) to be important, to concern; (*with* بِ) to intend; (*with* إِلَى) to be anxious about

إهتمّ ب VIII to take pains in; to be interested in

همّ *pl.* هموم care, anxiety

همّة *pl.* همم concern; energy

أهمّيّة importance

ذو أهمّيّة important, of importance

إهتمام care, effort, interest

هامّ important

همام pr.n.m.

مهمّ *pl.* مهامّ important

مهامّ important duties

مهموم anxious

(همك)

إنهمك (فى) VII to be engrossed (in), absorbed (in)

(همل)

أهمل IV to neglect, ignore

إهمال neglect

(هنا)

هنا, ههنا here

هنالك, هناك there

(هنأ)

هنئ (ـَ) to be pleasant, enjoyable (food, etc.)

هنّأ II to congratulate, felicitate

هناء pleasure, happiness, delight

هنيئًا good wish!

تهنئة *pl.* تهانئ congratulation

هنيّة, هنيهة, هنيئة a little while, a moment

(هند)

الهند India

هندىّ *pl.* هنود, هند Indian, an Indian

(هندس)

هندس to sketch (in engineering, etc.), plan

هندسة engineering, architecture, geometry

مهندس engineer

(هو)

هو; هما, هم he, it; they (*dual*), they (*pl.*)

هو ذا see! behold!

(هود)

تهوّد V to become a Jew

يهودىّ *pl.* يهود Jew, Jewish

(هون)

هَانَ (ـُ) to be or become easy

أَهَانَ IV to offend, insult, despise

هَيِّنٌ easy

(هوى)

هَوَاءٌ pl. أَهْوِيَةٌ air, atmosphere, weather

هَوًى passion

(هى)

هِىَ; هُمَا, هُنَّ she, it; they (*dual*), they (*pl.*)

(هيأ)

هَيَّأَ II to prepare (*trans.*)

تَهَيَّأَ لِ V to be prepared for

هَيْئَةٌ pl. ـَاتٌ — form, aspect; body (*i.e.* aggregate of persons or things), corporation

(هيب)

هَابَ (ـَ) to fear, hold in awe

هَيْبَةٌ respect, awe, veneration

(هيج)

هَاجَ (ـِ) to stir up

(هيم)

هَامَ (ـِ) to love passionately

(هيى)

هَيَّا up!

هَيَّا بِنَا come, let us go!

و

(و)

وَ and; by (in an oath); with

(وا)

وَا oh! ah! alas!

(وبأ)

وَبَاءٌ pl. أَوْبِئَةٌ plague

(وبخ)

وَبَّخَ II to censure, rebuke, reprimand

(وبل)

وَبَالٌ misfortune, evil consequences

(وتر)

تَوَتُّرٌ tension, strain

(وثق)

وَثِقَ (يَثِقُ) بِ to trust, have confidence in

وَثَّقَ II to make firm

ثِقَةٌ pl. ـَاتٌ — trust, confidence, reliable, authority

وُثُوقٌ trust, confidence

وَثِيقَةٌ *pl.* وَثَائِقُ document, deed, certificate

مِيثَاقٌ covenant

(وجب)

وَجَبَ (يَجِبُ) to be, make, necessary; (*with* عَلَى) to be incumbent upon

أَوْجَبَ IV to cause; to make binding

اِسْتَوْجَبَ X to deserve, be worthy of

وُجُوبٌ (a) necessity

إِيجَابٌ affirmation

إِيجَابِيٌّ affirmative, positive

وَاجِبٌ *pl.* ـَاتٌ a duty; (*with* عَلَى) incumbent on

بِمُوجِبِ according to

(وجد)

وَجَدَ (يَجِدُ) to find

وُجُودٌ (*v.n.*) existence

مَوْجُودٌ existing, present, found

(وجز)

وَجِيزٌ small, brief

(وجع)

وَجَعٌ *pl.* أَوْجَاعٌ pain

(وجن)

وَجْنَةٌ *pl.* وَجَنَاتٌ cheek

(وجه)

وَجَّهَ II to direct, *trans.*, turn (thing, person) towards

وَاجَهَ III to meet, confront

تَوَجَّهَ V to go, make for, repair to

اِتَّجَهَ VIII to turn, *intrans.*

وَجْهٌ *pl.* وُجُوهٌ face, manner, surface, aspect

جِهَةٌ *pl.* ـَاتٌ side, direction, point of view, dimension, district

مِنْ جِهَةِ (with following *gen.*) concerning

وُجْهَةُ نَظَرٍ point of view (*mod.*)

اِتِّجَاهٌ direction, way

تُجَاهَ opposite, in front, towards

وَجِيهٌ *pl.* وُجَهَاءُ respected, distinguished person, chief, notable

(وحد)

وَحَّدَ II to unify, unite

اِتَّحَدَ VIII to be united

وَحْدَهُ by himself, alone

وَحْدَةٌ unity, oneness; solitude; unit

أَحَدٌ *f.* إِحْدَى *pl.* آحَادٌ one, anyone (with *neg.* no-one)

يَوْمُ ٱلْأَحَدِ Monday

وَاحِدٌ *f.* وَاحِدَةٌ one, single

وَحِيدٌ alone, single, unique, only; sole

(وحش)

وَحْشٌ *pl.* وُحُوشٌ wild (animal)

(وحى)

وَحْيٌ (divine) inspiration

(ودد)

وَدَّ (ـَ) to love, wish for

وِدَادٌ friendship, love; pr.n.f.

(ودع)

وَدَعَ (يَدَعُ) to lay down, leave, let (only in *imperf.* and *imper.*)

دَعْهُ يَذْهَبُ let him go

وَدَّعَ II, أَوْدَعَ IV to take leave of, bid farewell to

أَوْدَعَ IV, اِسْتَوْدَعَ X to deposit, store

وَدَاعٌ departure, bidding farewell

(ودى)

وَادٍ *pl.* أَوْدِيَةٌ valley

(ورأ)

وَرَاءَ behind, beyond

(مَا) وَرَاءَ ٱلْبِحَارِ overseas

(ورث)

وَرِثَ (يَرِثُ) to inherit

وَرَّثَ II, أَوْرَثَ IV to bequeath

إِرْثٌ, وِرَاثَةٌ inheritance

تُرَاثٌ legacy, heritage

تُرَاثُ ٱلْإِسْلَامِ legacy of Islam

وَارِثٌ *pl.* وَرَثَةٌ heir

(ورد)

وَرَدَ (يَرِدُ) to arrive (lit. go down to water)

أَوْرَدَ IV to bring

اِسْتَوْرَدَ X to import

وَرْدٌ, وَرْدَةٌ *pl.* وُرُودٌ rose, blossom

وُرُودٌ arrival

وَارِدَاتٌ imports

إِيرَادَاتٌ revenues

(ورق)

وَرَقٌ *pl.* أَوْرَاقٌ paper, foliage

وَرَقَةٌ leaf (of a tree), piece of paper, note, etc.

(وزر)

وِزَارَةٌ ministry, office of a vizier

وَزِيرٌ *pl.* وُزَرَاءُ minister (political), vizier

وَزِيرُ ٱلْخَارِجِيَّةِ Foreign minister

رَئِيسُ ٱلْوُزَرَاءِ Prime Minister

هَيْئَةُ ٱلْوُزَرَاءِ Cabinet

(وزع)

وَزَّعَ II to distribute, share out, allot

(وزن)

وَزَنَ (يَزِنُ) to weigh *trans.*

وَزْنٌ *pl.* أَوْزَانٌ weight, measure; measure of a verse

مِيزَانٌ *pl.* مَوَازِينُ scales, balance

مِيزَانِيَّةٌ budget

(وزى)

وَازَى III to correspond to, be parallel with

(وسس)

وَسْوَسَ to whisper, suggest

وَسْوَاسٌ *pl.* وَسَاوِسُ whisperer, suggester (Satan)

(وسخ)

وَسِخٌ dirty

(وسط)

وَسْطٌ (*m.* and *f.*) *pl.* أَوْسَاطٌ middle, centre

وَاسِطَةٌ *pl.* وَسَائِطُ means, instrument

بِوَاسِطَةِ (followed by *gen.*) by means of, through

وَسِيطٌ *pl.* وُسَطَاءُ mediator, intermediary

أَوْسَطُ *f.* وُسْطَى *pl.* أَوَاسِطُ mean, middle, middle part

اَلشَّرْقُ ٱلْأَوْسَطُ the Middle East

مُتَوَسِّطٌ middle, medium

(وسع)

وَسِعَ (يَسَعُ) to hold, have capacity, be wide

سَعَةٌ width, extent, capacity; comfort

وَاسِعٌ wide, spacious, extensive

(وسل)

تَوَسَّلَ إِلَى V to get the means to; to implore, seek

وَسِيلَةٌ *pl.* وَسَائِلُ means

(وشك)

أَوْشَكَ أَنْ IV to be on the point of

(وصف)

وَصَفَ (يَصِفُ) to describe

صِفَةٌ *pl.* ـاتٌ — attribute, quality

وَصْفٌ *pl.* أَوْصَافٌ description

مُوَاصَفَاتٌ specifications

(وصل)

وَصَلَ (يَصِلُ) *v.n.* وُصُولٌ to arrive, reach (with *direct obj.* or إِلَى); link, join

وَصَّلَ II, أَوْصَلَ IV to bring, conduct, deliver, cause to arrive

وَاصَلَ III enter into relation with, be contiguous to, continue, persevere in

تَوَصَّلَ V to reach

اِتَّصَلَ VIII (*with* إِلَى) to arrive at, reach; (*with* بِ) to be in touch with, connected with

صِلَةٌ union, connection

وُصُولٌ arrival

وَصْلٌ receipt

وُصْلَةٌ connection

وَاصِلٌ joining, joint

مُوَاصَلَةٌ union, continuity, communication

اَلْمَوْصِلُ Mosul (in Iraq)

(وصى)

وَصَّى II to make a will, recommend, order

أَوْصَى IV to charge, commend

وَصِيَّةٌ *pl.* وَصَايَا charge, will, command

تَوْصِيَةٌ order, recommendation

وَصِيٌّ *pl.* أَوْصِيَاءُ testator, guardian, trustee

(وضأ)

تَوَضَّأَ V to perform religious ablutions

(وضح)

وُضُوحٌ clarity

وَاضِحٌ clear, obvious

(وضع)

وَضَعَ (يَضَعُ) to put, place, set down

وَضْعٌ *pl.* أَوْضَاعٌ situation, state of affairs, place

مَوْضِعٌ *pl.* مَوَاضِعُ place, site, spot

مَوْضُوعٌ *pl.* ـَاتٌ , مَوَاضِيعُ subject, subject-matter

(وطأ)

وَطِئَ (يَطَأُ) to tread on, step on

وَطَاءٌ depression (of land)

تَوْطِئَةٌ foreword, preface (of book, etc.)

(وطن)

اِسْتَوْطَنَ X to live or settle in a place

وَطَنٌ *pl.* أَوْطَانٌ home, homeland, native place

وَطَنِيٌّ *n.* and *adj.* indigenous native; national, nationalist, patriot(ic) (*mod.*)

وَطَنِيَّةٌ nationalism, patriotism (*mod.*)

مَوْطِنٌ *pl.* مَوَاطِنُ native land

مُوَاطِنٌ compatriot, fellow-countryman, citizen

مُوَاطِنِيَّةٌ citizenship (*mod.*)

(وظف)

وَظَّفَ II to give office to, appoint

تَوَظَّفَ V to be employed, appointed

وَظِيفَةٌ *pl.* وَظَائِفُ office, appointment, function

مُوَظَّفٌ official, functionary

(وعد)

وَعَدَ (يَعِدُ) to promise (with *acc.* of person and بِ of thing)

أَوْعَدَ IV to threaten, promise

تَوَعَّدَ V to threaten

وَعْدٌ *pl.* وُعُودٌ promise

مِيعَادٌ *pl.* مَوَاعِيدُ appointed time, appointment

(وعب)

اِسْتَوْعَبَ X to absorb, study, exhaust (a subject)

(وعظ)

وَعَظَ (يَعِظُ) to exhort, warn, preach

اِتَّعَظَ VIII to be exhorted

(وفد)

وَفَدَ (يَفِدُ) to reach, arrive, come to (إِلَى)

أوفد IV to send

وفد *pl.* وفود deputation, delegation

(وفر)

وفر II to economise, save

وافر abundant

(وفق)

وفق II to help, give success (of God); to conciliate (two parties); to match (two things)

وافق III to be suitable, correspond to, suit, agree with; (*with* على) to agree to

توافق VI to agree with each other

اتفق VIII to agree; happen

توفيق success (from God); pr.n.m.

اتفاق agreement

اتفاقية agreement (political or commercial)

(وفى)

وفى ب (يفى) to fulfil

توفى V (*pass.*) to die

وفاء fulfilment (of a promise); payment (of a debt)

وفاة *pl.* وفيات death

وفى perfect, complete

(وقب)

وقب (يقب) to be eclipsed (of the moon)

(وقت)

وقت II to fix, appoint, determine a time

وقت *pl.* أوقات time

موقت temporary; fixed (time)

(وقد)

أوقد IV to kindle (fire)

وقود fuel

(وقر)

وقر II to honour, respect, venerate

أوقر IV to load

وقور venerable

(وقع)

وقع (يقع) *v.n.* وقوع to fall, happen

وقع II to sign (name)

توقع V to expect

واقع situated; happening, actuality

وَاقِعَةٌ *pl.* وَقَائِعُ event, catastrophe

وَاقِعَةُ ٱلْحَالِ state of affairs

مَوْقِعٌ *pl.* مَوَاقِعُ place; event

مَوْقِعَةٌ battle

(وقف)

وَقَفَ (يَقِفُ) *v.n.* وُقُوفٌ to stop, stand up; (*with* عَلَى) to ascertain, be acquainted with

وَقَّفَ II أَوْقَفَ IV to sieze, arrest, stop *trans.*

تَوَقَّفَ V to hesitate

وَقْفٌ *pl.* أَوْقَافٌ wakf, religious foundation (Muslim)

مَوْقِفٌ *pl.* مَوَاقِفُ situation, place, stand, attitude; stopping place; car-park (*mod.*)

(وقى)

وَقَى (يَقِي) to guard, protect, preserve

اِتَّقَى (يَتَّقِي) VIII to fear (God)

وِقَايَةٌ protection, preservation

تَقْوَى fear of God, piety

تَقِيٌّ *pl.* أَتْقِيَاءُ God-fearing, pious

(وكأ)

اِتَّكَأَ VIII to support oneself

(وكب)

مَوْكِبٌ *pl.* مَوَاكِبُ procession

(وكل)

وَكَّلَ II to appoint as an agent, represent

تَوَكَّلَ (عَلَى) V, اِتَّكَلَ VIII to trust in, rely on

وَكَالَةٌ representation, agency

وَكِيلٌ *pl.* وُكَلَاءُ agent

(ولل)

وَلْوَلَ to howl, wail

(ولد)

وَلَدَ (يَلِدُ) to beget, bear

وَلَّدَ II to generate; act as midwife

وَلَدٌ *pl.* أَوْلَادٌ boy, son, child

وِلَادَةٌ birth

وَالِدٌ father

وَالِدَةٌ mother

مَوْلِدٌ birthplace, birthday

مِيلَادٌ time of birth, birth

عِيدُ الْمِيلَادِ Christmas

اَلسَّنَةُ المِيلَادِيَّةُ (*abbr.* before dates م) Christian year (calendar)

مُوَلَّدٌ of mixed origin (properly: of an Arab father and foreign mother)

مُوَلَّدَةٌ post-classical (of Arabic words)

(ولع)

وَلِعَ ب (يَوْلَعُ) to be attached to, be fond of, show affection for

(ولى)

وَلِيَ (يَلِي) to be near, follow

وَلَّى II to appoint (as governor), to set anyone over, entrust any one with an affair; to flee, turn one's back

تَوَلَّى V to take charge of, take in hand

تَوَالَى VI to follow one after another

اِسْتَوْلَى عَلَى X to master, control, overcome

وِلَايَةٌ province, state

اَلْوِلَايَاتُ ٱلْمُتَّحِدَةُ the U.S.A.

وَلِيٌّ *pl.* أَوْلِيَاءُ master, saint (Muslim), lord, patron, guardian

وَالٍ *pl.* وُلَاةٌ Governor

أَوْلَى better, more suitable, fitter

مَوْلًى master, lord; ally, follower, client; freed slave

(ومأ)

مُومَأٌ إِلَيْهِ above-mentioned, aforesaid

(ونى)

مِينَاءٌ ,مِينَا *pl.* مَوَانِئُ ,مَوَانٍ port (sea)

(وهب)

وَهَبَ (يَهَبُ) to present, give, grant

وَهَّابِيٌّ Wahhabite, Wahhabi

(وهم)

تَوَهَّمَ V to imagine, fancy

اِتَّهَمَ (. . . ب . . .) VIII to accuse (anyone of something)

وَهْمٌ *pl.* أَوْهَامٌ imagination, prejudice

تُهْمَةٌ accusation

(ويب)

وَيْبَكَ woe to you!

(ويح)

وَاحَةٌ *pl.* اتٌ — oasis

وَيْحَكَ woe to you!

(ويل)

وَيْلَكَ woe to you!

وَيْلاه alas!

ى

(يا)

. . . يا O, Oh (*voc.*)

(يأس)

يَئِسَ (يَيْأَسُ) (مِنْ) to despair (of)

أَيْأَسَ IV to drive to despair

يَأْسٌ despair

يَافَا Jaffa (port town in Israel)

(يبس)

يَبِسَ (ـَ) to be dry

يَبَّسَ II to dry (*trans.*)

يَبْسٌ dry (land, etc.)

(يبن)

اَلْيَابَانُ Japan, the Japanese

يَابَانِيٌّ Japanese, *n.* and *adj.*

(يتم)

يَتَّمَ II to bereave a child of its parents, orphan

يَتِيمٌ *pl.* أَيْتَامٌ, يَتَامَى orphan

(يدو)

يَدٌ (*f.*) *pl.* أَيْدٍ, أَيَادٍ hand

بَيْنَ يَدَيْهِ before him, in his presence

. . . عَلَى يَدِ by, at the hands of

يَدَوِيٌّ manual, hand- *adj.*

(يسر)

يَسُرَ (ـُ) to be easy

يَسَّرَ II to make easy

تَيَسَّرَ V to be made easy, possible

يَسَارٌ the left hand

يَسِيرٌ easy, small

(يقظ)

أَيْقَظَ IV to waken *trans.*

تَيَقَّظَ V to be awakened

اِسْتَيْقَظَ X to wake up

يَقْظَةٌ awakening, wakefulness, watchfulness, attention

يَقْظَانُ awake, watchful

(يقن)

يَقِنَ (ـَ) to be certain

تَيَقَّنَ V to convince oneself

يَقِينٌ certain belief, conviction

(يمن)

اَلْيَمَنُ the Yemen (S.W. Arabia), *Arabia Felix*

يَمَنِىٌّ, يَمَانٍ Yemenite, Yemeni

يَمِينٌ (*f.*) right hand, oath

(ينع)

يَانِعٌ ripe

يُوسُفُ Yusuf, Joseph

(يوم)

يَوْمٌ *pl.* أَيَّامٌ day

اَلْيَوْمَ today

ذَاتَ يَوْمٍ one day

يَوْمًا by day, one day

يَوْمًا فَيَوْمًا day by day

يَوْمِىٌّ daily, *adj.*

يَوْمِيًّا daily, *adv.*

يَوْمَئِذٍ then, at that time, on that day

يَوْمُ ٱلدِّينِ Day of Judgement

(يون)

اَلْيُونَانُ Greece, the Greek nation

يُونَانِىٌّ Greek, a Greek

GRAMMATICAL INDEX

NOTE The main references to major points of grammar are indicated in the chapter titles, as listed in the "Table of Contents". This index is, however, more exhaustive. In general, English grammatical terminology is its basis, but some important Arabic grammatical terms are also given in transliteration, followed by the Arabic form in brackets.

A

B

C

D

E

F

G

H

I

J

K

L

M

N

Q

R

S

T

Post-Alpha

FOLLOW-UP GUIDE

Dr Ilana Ibberson

First Printing, 2023

ISBN: 9798388074522

After my skin has decayed,

yet in my flesh I will see God;

I will see him for myself.

Yes, I will see him with my own eyes.

I am overwhelmed at the thought!

- Job 19:26-27; NLT -

Acknowledgement

In preparing 'Post-Alpha: Follow-up Guide' I wish to acknowledge indebtedness to Alpha International for permission to quote their excellent resources.

My sincere and special thanks are also due to the Alpha team and Head of Pastoral Integration and e-Learning at KingsGate Community Church for allowing me to play a significant role together in helping many to encounter Jesus who is the Author and the Finisher of our life.

Hana Obberson
Spalding, England

Contents

Preface

I used to have a life-long question to think over and looked for the answer: 'what should I live for?' Haven't you ever thought of it or a similar question before?

The famous Russian writer, Leo Tolstoy once had a philosophical thinking and wrote 'What Men Live By.' In his book, an angel of God had to find three truths when he was punished by God for disobeying and not following orders. He was forbidden to go back to heaven until he found the three truths: 'what dwells in a man?', 'what is not given to man?' and 'what men live by?

Apparently, the answer for 'what men live by' is quite different from the answer for 'what I should live for' because the former is self-centred whereas the latter is God-centred. Nonetheless, the bottom line of these questions implies that most of us are searching for a fundamental and ultimate purpose of life.

If anyone is searching for the answer of 'what I should live for,' I believe that the Alpha course lays stepping stones to the ultimate answer for the life-long question. The Alpha course is organised as a series of interactive sessions that explore the basics of the Christian faith over 10 weeks, including a day or weekend away as known 'Holy Spirit

Day.' Each session begins with a meal (or refreshments) followed by a video (used to be a talk) and then discussion in small groups. In April 2016, the Alpha course introduced its film series, where traditional Alpha content is shown in a series of films, stories and interviews.

While being involved in the Alpha course over the years, I have sensed that there is need for a follow-up after completion of the course. Certainly, it may not be a big problem for those who are with the church community and have spiritual mentors and good resources available to grow for the next step in their faith journey. Nevertheless, the reality is that not all of the Alpha participants are in such situations. Basically, my heart's desire for meeting the need has driven me to write this book. By now you understand why the book has been brought forth. I have tried to make it simple and practical so that anyone can easily take it all in and benefit from it.

Let Your Faith Journey Begin

'What does *alpha* mean?' This is one of the common questions that we as table/group leaders are frequently asked from the attendees whenever the course was on. It is not surprising to have such question because it is not an English word but a Greek word, precisely the first letter of the Greek alphabet (uppercase A; lowercase α). Apparently, the Greek alphabet is the ancestor of modern languages, derived from the Phoenician alphabet. Etymologically, *alpha* came from *aleph* (א, the first letter of the Hebrew alphabet), meaning 'ox' in Phoenician.

In the Greek numeral system, the letter was taken as the symbol of 1 (one), presenting the first or the beginning. In this respect, the name of the Alpha course is very appropriate and significant because the attendee can taste and see the basic beliefs of the Christian faith for the first time if they come to the course as a non-believer. On the other hand, when the Alpha course ends and if he or she had an encounter of Jesus during the course, then his or her true faith journey begins from the moment when the course is over. It is just like this: when a baby is born, it is not an end of his or her life journey but his or her new life has just begun.

If you are reading the book after you have recently completed the Alpha course, I would say, 'Congratulations on your achievement so far! Now your faith journey has begun.'

Are you excited for your new faith journey? Or are you afraid of the unknown things ahead? Don't worry and relax! You will grow as long as you are spiritually well-nourished just like a baby grows with a balanced and nutritious diet along with good care. I hope that you can find a way to grow well while reading.

If you are reading the book as a table/group leader, I hope that you can get some nuggets which benefit you as a better helper to those who are looking for their ultimate life question during the Alpha course.

Bon voyage!'

How Was Your Alpha

Welcome to an Alpha revisit!

If you took the Alpha course some time ago, then let me take your memory back to the past for a while. Was it fun? Was it challenging? Was it life-transforming? Was it unforgettable? Was it overwhelming? I don't know about you but definitely I can say that I had remarkably exciting and unforgettable occasions during the course.

No matter what experiences you had with the Alpha course, most of us would agree that we were able to interact well with others and to knit a very unique and special bonding together over 10 weeks, dealing with a series of sessions. The reason is that its main target attendees are so-called non-believers. So, the course is intentionally designed for them and run in an informal, fun and friendly atmosphere even though we had to talk about fundament and important topics. Of course, there is no doubt that some might receive its benefits more than others depending on their own expectations and enthusiasm for the Alpha course. One thing I have discovered with various groups of people over the years is that individuals differ from one another and have different understanding of and experiences with 'faith' to some degree.

To refresh our memory and perhaps broaden our perspectives or benefit from others' experiences, let us recap briefly each session herein below. I do hope that you may find many interesting things.

Is There More To Life Than This?

On the very first day, some possible questions that you might be asked were 'How did you end up coming here today?' or 'If it turned out there was a God after all, and you could ask one question what would it be?' or 'What's your expectation during the Alpha?', etc.

Can you think about this for a moment, please? John Wimber who was Founder of Vineyard Church said that 'people come to church for a variety of reasons, but they stay for only one - friendship.' Alpha pioneer Nicky Gumbel said that 'Alpha is about sharing God's love through friendship.' I could not agree more on those statements.

How was your Alpha group back then? Did you feel that you were loved and cared by others? I hope so. If not, you could not complete it, could you? I strongly believe that building a good rapport among a group of people and making a friendship within the group are the essential factors of the Alpha course. Who was the jokester in your group? If you had one(s), then you were fortunate. I assume that you guys laughed a lot during the course.

As a matter of fact, I have found one of the icebreaker questions interesting to know people's mindset: 'which person from history would you like to be stuck in a lift with and why?' To this question, quite a lot of people mentioned the names of celebrity believers worldwide. I reckon that both celebrities and their beliefs are undoubtedly powerful and influential in people's belief system.

Okay. Let us go back to the question again: *is there more to life than this?* What was your answer ***back then***? What is your answer ***now***? One thing I can assure you is that by the grace of God you are who you are now.

Checkpoint #1

Jesus said,
'I am the way and the truth and the life.'

(John 14:6; NIV)

Now do you truly believe this from your heart? Do you remember what Jesus did for you? He gave you his life so that you have *the everlasting life* through him. He made a way to Father God. He taught you the truth which sets you free.

Who Is Jesus?

Let us assume that someone comes to you and asks, 'Who are you?' What would be your response to that person? Would you ignore him or her? Or would you kindly tell him or her about you? If so, how would you describe yourself? I guess that it totally depends on who that person is and what intention he or she has.

Do you remember what your response or answer was on the second week of your Alpha course when you were asked 'who Jesus is' or 'what you would say to Jesus if you had a chance to meet him'?

Not surprisingly, many people are not sure of the existence of Jesus in history. On top of it, the traditional Judaism (the religion of the Jewish people) has absolutely rejected Jesus as the Messiah (the anointed one by God to save the people of the world) although it is widely believed that he was truly a man who lived in Israel 2,000 plus years ago. Yes, many simply consider Jesus as either a prophet or a good teacher or a godly man.

Do you still remember what you learnt about him during the Alpha? What was your conclusion about him?

Is it true that Jesus had a human body like us? As we look at the scriptures, indeed he was tired (John 4:6) and hungry (Matthew 4:2). He had human emotions like anger (Mark 11:15-17), love (Mark 10:21), and sadness (John

11:32-36). Also, he had human experiences like temptation (Mark 1:13), learning (Luke 2:48-52), work (Mark 6:3) and obedience (Luke 2:51). Nevertheless, we understand that he was more than a man, a great human and a religious teacher.

One day Jesus asked his disciples, 'Who do you say I am?' (Matthew 16:15; NIV). One of them, Simon Peter, answered, 'You are the Messiah, the Son of the living God.' Take notice what Jesus told him here. 'Blessed are you … for this was not revealed to you by flesh and blood, but by my Father in heaven' (Matthew 16:17; NIV). It implies that we *only can* know that Jesus is the Messiah with *a grace of* our heavenly Father. Do you truly know how much you are blessed in this sense? *Only* Father enables us to know and believe that Jesus is the Messiah.

Do you fully understand that Jesus is the incarnated God, meaning that the deity become flesh? He as a human being came to the world in order to dwell among us. It is called 'Immanuel' (עמנואל in Hebrew) meaning that *God is with us*. That is why we celebrate Christmas to commemorate his birth. How exciting news it is indeed! Perhaps someone might wonder why he did that. This leads to another important point to consider.

He came to the world with a specific mission - showing us the way which leads to the place where we came and should go back after this earthly life. A metaphor below might help us understand this.

> Suppose you are an ant lover and see a colony of ants on a road where you are standing and then notice a huge convoy of lorries coming towards the colony. The ants have no idea that they are doomed sooner or later. What can you do? If a

chance of becoming an ant would be given to you, would you take it in order to warn the ants about the coming danger ahead and save their lives? Perhaps the ants won't know the fact that you love them and then gave up humanity to save them. Furthermore, they won't appreciate you and even would reject you and hate you. Yet, this is the only way that you can save them even if it looks lunatic. Will you do that?

Well…this is exactly what 'Immanuel' means.

This is God who loved us so much and gave up his deity and then came to us and lived among us and completed his mission. The incarnated God Jesus' mission looks crazy, doesn't it? He became a human being to show us the way and also taught us the truth which sets us free and gave us the most precious gift, *the everlasting life* by means of his death on the cross.

Checkpoint #2

In the beginning was the Word, and the Word was with God, and the Word was God. He was with God in the beginning… The Word became a human being … No one has ever seen God. The only Son, who is the same as God and is at the Father's side, has made him known.

(John 1:1-2, 14a, 18; NIV)

For God so loved the world that he gave his one and only Son, that whoever believes in him shall not perish but have eternal life.

(John 3:16; NIV)

Slowly read the scriptures above again and ask the Holy Spirit to help you truly believe them. Write them down on a separate piece of paper and memorise them if you can. We will talk about power of memorising scriptures later. Remember the Word of God is a powerful weapon to defeat the enemy.

Why Did Jesus Die?

Earlier you were told that Jesus came to us for his wild mission and ultimately paid the price of his death on the cross. Do you remember why he had to die? I do hope that you know it by now?

The prophet Isaiah clearly said that Jesus was put to death for the sins of the people of God (Isaiah 53:8).

What is sin(s)? Perhaps we most often think of it as wrongdoing or transgression of God's law. Sin(s) includes a failure to do what is right. It also offends people. It is violence and lovelessness towards other people, and ultimately, rebellion against God. Someone says that sin has an 'I' in the middle. Have you noticed that our selfish nature causes us to fall into sinful ways?

As we look at the origin of sin, it is tragic because it represents a fall from the high original status of humankind. The very first human beings, Adam and Eve, were without faults in the beginning but the old serpent (Satan, שטן in Hebrew) made them to rebel against God. Here we see the tendency of sin to begin with a subtle appeal to something attractive and good in itself, to an act that is somehow plausible and directed towards some good end. However, its consequence is irreversible unless we pay for it so that we become a slave of sin.

We could not solve the issue of sin all by ourselves. The reason is that '... for all have sinned and fall short of the glory of God' (Romans 3:23; NIV).

Can we find any solution for our sin? We cannot. Here is the good news: *Jesus can.*

Yes, God made Jesus who had no sin to be sin for us (2 Corinthians 5:21). It means that he became sin for us and carried it into the cross. Then he had to die with the sin so that we can be free from the sin and are no longer slaves of the sin.

What a blessing to know such profound meaning of Jesus' death on the cross!

Have you noticed that some Christians wear a cross necklace as an indication of commitment to their faith? Actually, I am happy to see a cross without a crucified Jesus' image on it. The reason is that Jesus was no longer bound to death but raised from the dead.

Wait! Have you prepared your response to those who argue about Jesus' resurrection? Or are you sure of it? At least, we can be sure about it as we see what his disciples did *before* and *after* Jesus' death. They were cowards and ran away when Jesus was arrested and then crucified. Nonetheless, they became brave, and even most of them were martyred after they saw the resurrected Jesus with their own eyes. As far as eyewitness testimony is concerned, it is a prominent and compelling form of evidence in court.

Let us think about this for a moment: why a multitude of people under religious persecution died for the sake of their Christian faith? Can you die for something which is false and lies? Certainly not! Again, I say that we *only can* believe Jesus' resurrection by *the grace of* our heavenly Father.

If you wish to study about Jesus' resurrection in greater detail, I suggest you to read *Who Moved the Stone?* by Frank Morison. This book is considered by many to be a classic apologetic on the resurrection. Frank Morison set out to prove that the story of Christ's resurrection was only a myth. Nevertheless, his probing eventually led him to discover the validity of the biblical record in a moving and personal way.

So far we have talked about Jesus' crucifixion and resurrection. Remember that both of them are very important in Christian faith because they are his ultimate mission to complete for the sake of the world.

One of the last sayings of Jesus on the cross was *tetelestai* (τετέλεσται in Greek) meaning 'it is finished.' He truly knew that he had completed all the prophecies here on earth. Hence, he said 'it's finished.' On top of it, he was *the first* to be resurrected of many who will be resurrected in the future. Does this really excite you? It does to me. Imagine that he guarantees the resurrection of all those who belong to him by showing his resurrection as the first fruit.

Blessed and holy are those who share in the first resurrection (Revelation 20:6).

To conclude, let me cite the scriptures in order to sum up Jesus' mission in a nutshell.

The Spirit of the Lord is on me,
because he has anointed me
to proclaim good news to the poor.
He has sent me to proclaim freedom for the prisoners
and recovery of sight for the blind,
to set the oppressed free,
to proclaim the year of the Lord's favour

Luke 4: 18-19; NIV

Checkpoint #3

Jesus said, 'I am the resurrection and the life. The one who believes in me will live, even though they die; and whoever lives by believing in me will never die. Do you believe this?'

(John 11:25-26; NIV)

Can you say that I do believe this? If so, praise and thank God for that.

How Can I Have Faith?

In our Alpha group, two questions have usually been asked for this topic: 'what is faith?' and 'what does faith mean to you personally?' Most people in our group generally answered something like this: faith is belief and trust in and loyalty to God/supreme deity. They defined it very well, didn't they? It implies that most people know what faith means. However, when it comes to the personal level, seemingly it's more than we know and say.

Can you tell me 'what' is the important point to consider when we play 'trust games'? All players must depend on each other. Can you trust someone who is a stranger? Can you trust a liar or a robber or a deceiver, etc.? Do you agree that trust can only be built and earned through a mutual relationship over the time? Obviously, we only trust someone based on our honest and positive experiences with him or her over the time.

Is faith a blind leap or something more? For this, Nicky Gumbel stated that faith is not a blind leap but a step based on evidence. Interestingly, someone in our group raised a possibility of taking the blind leap, saying that if someone who is trustworthy would say so, then she would do it even if she won't know its consequence. What do you think about this?

Perhaps these can be two sides of the same coin. We can take a step of faith with either evidence or proven statements of the person whom we truly trust. I'll leave that to your own decision.

Here is an important question concerning faith. Are you sure that you are saved by the blood/work of Jesus? If so, you have known it by faith. For this, the Bible clearly says that faith is the assurance about what we do not see (Hebrew 11:1). It is a gift from God (Ephesians 2:8).

If you are not sure of it and then would ask me, 'how can I have faith?' The Bible gives you an answer to that. Faith comes from hearing of God's word (Romans 10:17). *Hearing* here requires not only the physical act of hearing with your ears but also *receiving* what you heard. For instance, when you read the gospel message, you should receive it by faith.

Do you remember what St. Augustine said, 'I believe, in order to understand; and I understand, the better to believe'?

Do you have faith now? Thank God and cherish it because it is the gift from him.

Checkpoint #4

I write these things to you who believe in the name of the Son of God so that you may know that you have eternal life.

(1John 5:13; NIV)

Faith comes from hearing of God's word.

(Romans 10:17: NIV)

Have you set apart or spare a particular time during the day to hear God's word? In order to have faith and remain strong in faith, taking the Word of God (the Bible) is a vital and essential activity every day.

Why And How Do I Pray?

What is a Christian prayer? Some says that for a believer, prayer is, or should be, like spiritual breathing. Without praying we can't have faith living in us. Certainly, many believers know that the prayer is the most important and vital activity of our Christian lives and deepens our intimacy with God.

If you would ask other Christians why they pray, they would say that they do it with several reasons such as God's help, protection, guidance, blessings, healing, salvation, forgiveness, thanking/praising, decision-making, plans, etc. Whatever reasons we pray, one thing we should remember is this: we pray to the *Father* through *Jesus* by *the Holy Spirit* (Ephesians 2:18).

Yes, we pray *through* Jesus because he is our high priest in heaven who has given us direct access to Father God by his sacrifice. Also, he is now interceding (praying) on our behalf before the Father. Yes, we pray to the Father in the name of or by the authority of Jesus and in the power of the Holy Spirit.

Jesus knew the importance of prayers when he lived here as a human being. Here are examples of his prayerful life. 'Very early in the morning, while it was still dark, Jesus got up, left the house and went off to a solitary place, where he prayed' (Mark 1:35; NIV). After feeding the

5,000 men plus women and children, he sent away the people and then went up into a mountain to pray alone (Matthew 14:23). Before he chose the twelve disciples, he went out to a mountainside to pray and spent the whole night praying to Father (Luke 6: 12).

How busy life he had! It shows a contrast to people whom I asked, 'why you don't pray.' They usually said that they were either busy or tired. No matter how busy or tired we are, we still can pray, can't we? I believe that it's all about our attitude and awareness of the importance of prayer. Supposedly, when you are dating someone, are you not making time to see her or him despite your busyness or tiredness? Perhaps I can share my experience of 'how much God loves our prayer despite circumstances we are in.'

My daughter wasn't a sleeping baby at all. She awakened me almost every two hours throughout the night. Every day I was extremely exhausted physically and tried to sleep whenever I was able to do so. I was very tired so that I couldn't have set apart a proper prayer time either. And then God was merciful to restore my dry spirit by challenging me to take an hour prayer slot once a month for the nation as a part of the national prayer campaign in 2009. I simply told God, 'I will take an hour slot at 5 a.m. if you let her sleep through while praying.' I boldly took that challenge but was half in doubt by wondering whether she would sleep through for an hour. To my surprise, she wasn't awake at all whenever I did the prayer slot for six months. Wow! I told God that I would carry on praying not only every month but every day if he would continuously let her sleep around that time. Certainly, I learnt how much God loves our prayer no matter what. As long as we are determined to do so, God enables us to do that. It is all about our attitude and determination.

Now we are ready to move to the next point, 'how to' pray. As a practical tip, three things were mentioned during the Alpha course. Do you remember them? TSP!

- **T**hank God for the blessings you received;
- **S**orry for your sins; and
- **P**lease give us our daily need.

Some people pray by following the elements of the Lord's Prayer which Jesus taught his disciples as the way to pray. If you want to deepen your knowledge of the Lord' Prayer, I suggest you reading my book, *My Book For You, Friend.* It is mainly written for spiritual seekers by elaborating each element of the Lord's Prayer along with simple explanations and real life stories.

Another point I'd like to draw your attention to is 'does God always answer our prayers?' Yes, he does *always* just like traffic lights.

- **Green light**: it means 'Go.' When God answers yes, it is to give us confidence.
- **Red light**: it means 'Stop.' When God answers no, it is to prevent errors.
- **Amber light**: it means 'Get ready to stop/go.' When God withholds an answer, it is for us to grow through faith. Simply remember that we are waiting in expectation to receive it in his time.

Let me close this topic with what Jesus said about prayer. He told his disciples a parable to show them that they should *always* pray and not give up. In his parable the evil and unrighteous judge eventually gave in to get a complaining and persistent but powerless woman off his back (Luke 18:1-7). Thus, we should keep praying because we can surely count on God who hears us and responds in ways that are for our best good.

Also, Jesus said, 'Ask and it will be given to you' (Matthew 7:7; NIV).

Do you believe this? Why not pray then?

Checkpoint #5

Jesus said, 'Ask and it will be given to you.'

(Matthew 7:7; NIV)

Remember this scripture whenever you pray to Father. It gives power to your prayer.

Why And How Should I Read the Bible?

The Word of God is *spiritual food* just like prayer is spiritual breathing. Our spirit needs to grow. What is the spiritual food to make our spirit grow? The spoken words of Jesus are spirit and life which can feed us (John 6:63).

Jesus said that people do not live by *bread alone* but by every word that comes from the mouth of God (Matthew 4:4). He said that our spirit needs food just like our body does. The God's words (personification) here invite us to eat and drink for living of our spirit:

Come, everyone who thirsts, come to the waters;
and he who has no money, come, buy and eat!
Come, buy wine and milk
without money and without price.
Why do you spend your money for that which is not bread,
and your labour for that which does not satisfy?
Listen diligently to me, and eat what is good,
and delight yourselves in rich food.

Isaiah 55:1-2; ESV

One of the great things about reading the Bible is that it helps us increase intimacy with God. The more we hear his voice through Bible reading regularly, the more we want to read it and long to get to know him.

Have you ever experienced certain scriptures come alive while reading the Bible or hearing the audio Bible? What I mean here is that the written/recorded words became very personal so that they seem to be God's personal message for you.

Nicky Gumbel in the Alpha video shared his experience. Do you remember it? He wondered whether his father was in heaven because his father had never shown a glimpse of his faith before his passing away. While pondering, the scripture, 'for everyone who calls on the name of the Lord will be saved' (Romans 10:13; NIV) was repeated in four different occasions. In the very last time the scripture was on the big billboard. I guess God's voice was very loud and clear by then!

I don't know about you but I experienced living and personal words in many occasions. Here is one of the occasions.

Many years ago, I was invited to join a mission trip to Myanmar also known as Burma in Southeast Asia. A relatively large group was formed with a dental care team along with a discipleship training team. I as a translator joined the group in a very last minute. This meant that I didn't have enough time to apply for a visa to Myanmar. Apparently, the group leader suggested that I could get the visa from the Myanmar embassy in Thailand when we would stop by for the transit on the following day afternoon.

As scheduled, we first flew to Thailand and arrived at Suvarnabhumi Airport (BKK) at night. When I passed through customs, the officer asked me whether I had a visa to Myanmar. I said to him that I would get it from the Myanmar embassy on the following day's morning. Then he chuckled and then told me that I would need 'black money (bribery)' to get it. I said in my heart, 'Nope. I would never do that.'

The airport was extremely well air-conditioned despite the tropical climate outside. We were all half awake half asleep, shivering with such cold air throughout the night. In the morning I went to the restroom after dozing off and was ready for the day after washing. As soon as I sat on a seat at the airport lounge, I opened my Bible. In fact, wherever I went, I always took that Bible with me although it was quite heavy and big. The reason was that I didn't want to cut the flow from my daily reading. Anyway, I was reading the book of Matthew around that time. On that morning I was reading chapter 11. Whether you believe or not, it didn't take me long to read this,

I will send **my messenger** ahead of you,
who will prepare your way before you

Matthew 11:10; NIV

Wow! I knew immediately what God was telling me at that time. I was happy to go to the embassy. You can guess the rest of my story. I was on board with my visa to Myanmar on that day afternoon.

There are many ways that God can speak to us. There is no doubt that God speaks to us personally while reading the Bible. How do we hear God speak through the Bible?'

Obviously, we need to read the Bible regularly. In order to do this, first get a Bible if you don't have one. Then make a plan like finding a good time and a (solitary) place to read it regularly. Before reading, first of all ask God to speak to you:

> Dear God, open my eyes now so that I may see beautiful, marvellous and wonderful things in your words in Jesus' name. Amen.

I would like to draw your attention to the scriptures talking about how blessed we can be when we take the Word of God every day.

> Blessed is the one ... whose delight is in the law of the Lord, and who meditates on his law day and night. That person is like a tree planted by streams of water, which yields its fruit in season and whose leaf does not wither - whatever they do prosper.
>
> Psalm 1:1-3; NIV

The Psalmist (song composer) mentions here that a Bible lover who reads the Word of God constantly and chews or think over what he or she has read is like a tree planted by streams of water. The tree never withers but bears its fruit in season abundantly. For instance, as we learn what the Bible teaches us and how to conduct our business in an ethical, God-intended manner, we will become more successful and more prosperous. Even we can learn the importance of tithing (giving 10 percent of our income back to God) and how that directly impacts our prosperity.

Checkpoint #6

Open my eyes that I may see wonderful things in your law.

(Psalm 119:18; NIV)

Memorise this scripture and pray with it before reading/hearing the Bible every day.

How Does God Guide Us?

How do you feel when you hear that God has a special plan for your life? The plan is very unique just like our finger prints/marks. Yours are different from others and mine. I truly praise God because I am fearfully and wonderfully made according to his perfect will (Palms 139:14).

During the Alpha course, I usually illustrate this with jigsaw puzzles.

> God has a huge jigsaw puzzle. Its pieces fit into its own places to complete the whole. You have a piece of the jigsaw puzzle which is unique although it looks similar to your neighbours' pieces. However, your neighbours' cannot fit into your place. When we will stand before King Jesus later, he would ask us whether we find our piece and fit it into the right place to complete the whole. Imagine the complete picture of the jigsaw puzzle with a missing piece which is yours. Ouch! It won't be pretty at all.

In this respect, it perfectly makes sense why we should be guided by God. Certainly, he knows us and wants us to find our piece and fit that into his big picture after all.

Make me know Your ways, O Lord;
Teach me Your paths.
Lead me in Your truth and teach me.

Psalm 25:4-5; ESV

Do you remember how God guides us for his will during the Alpha course? 5Cs!

- Commanding scriptures
- Compelling spirit
- Counsel of the saints
- Common sense
- Circumstantial signs

Have you experienced God's guidance through the 5Cs yet? A good example of the 5Cs in the Bible is so-called *Macedonian Call.*

It happened when Apostle Paul and his companions took on Paul's second missionary journey. Paul's plan was to visit and strengthen the congregations/churches he had planted in the Asian province of Galatia during his first journey. They had plans to head directly west, but they were kept by *the Holy Spirit* from preaching the word in the province of Asia. When they came to the seaport city of Troas, they were waiting for the guidance of the Holy Spirit.

In the night, Paul received *a vision* of a man of Macedonia (the northern and central parts of modern-day Greece), begging him, 'Come over to Macedonia and help us' (Acts 16:9; NIV). 'After Paul had seen the vision, we got ready at once to leave for Macedonia, concluding that God had called us to preach the gospel to them' (Acts 16:10; NIV).

As a consequence of Paul's obedience to the vision, many things happened in Macedonia: Lydia's conversion (Acts 16:14-15), the deliverance of a fortune-telling slave girl (Acts 16:16-18), Paul and Silas' imprisonment in Philippi (Acts 16:16-28), the conversion of the jailer and his whole household (Acts 16:29-34) and Paul's preaching in the Areopagus in Athens (Acts 17:16-34). Areopagus is a small hill covered in stone seats in Northwest of the city of Athens, Greece. This place was once used as a forum for the rulers of Athens to hold trials, debate, and discuss important matters.

Perhaps I can share my personal experience here. I am a dreamer of dreams. I had a series of dreams in the past. Whenever I woke up from the dreams, I felt strange. Of course, I didn't know where I was but vividly remembered the places. Some years later, my family had opportunities to do several missions overseas. One of the places where we had to go was the Golan Heights which are located to the east of the Sea of Galilee in the far north of Israel. There is the famous Nimrod Fortress/Castle, situated on the southern slopes of Mount Hermon. The Fortress has two towers which overlook the Golan Heights and were built with the purpose of guarding a major access route to Damascus against armies coming from the west. It is a strategically important military place in Israeli history.

Certainly, it was my first visit to that site; nevertheless, I noticed that I had been there before in my dream. You can find the full story of the mission in *Shofar-blowing: Sounds From Heaven To Earth*.

Before closing, one thing we need to remember is this: when God guides us through the 5Cs, we should *obey* it. Certainly, it requires our faith, yet it is worth it. The more we obey, the more we receive his guidance! I do pray that you will experience God's guidance through the 5Cs more often so that you become mature (Ephesians 4:13-15).

Checkpoint #7

The LORD says,

'I will guide you along the best pathway for your life. I will advise you and watch over you.'

(Psalm 32:8: NLT)

Be ready to be lead by the Holy Spirit all the time and remember 5Cs - commanding scriptures, compelling spirit, counsel of the saints, common sense, and circumstantial signs.

Who Is The Holy Spirit?

I was born in a Christian family and grown up with a conservative church background. I had never known 'Holy Spirit' until I heard of *Pentecost Sunday* for the first time in my early twenties. I wondered about it and read the second chapter of Acts in the New Testament as below:

When the day of Pentecost came,
they were all together in one place.
Suddenly a sound like the blowing of
a violent wind came from heaven
and filled the whole house where they were sitting.
They saw what seemed to be tongues of fire
that separated and came to rest on each of them.
All of them were filled with the Holy Spirit
and began to speak in other tongues
as the Spirit enabled them.

Acts 2:1-4; NIV

To me, it was remarkable, fascinating and eye-opening. I was really curious about what 120 believers experienced at that time. Thankfully, I had praying friends round. We gathered and prayed together every night for more than a year. On the night before the Pentecost Sunday, I had prepared myself by means of cleansing not only spiritually but also physically for the Holy Spirit encounter. Frankly speaking, I didn't know properly who the Holy Spirit was by then but simply longed to experience what 120 believers had. By God's favour and mercy, I saw and tasted it while waiting for the Holy Spirit in our prayer time. I do not have right words to describe such supernaturally phenomenon, yet there is no doubt that it was a wonderful and unforgettable experience.

Surprisingly, it is true that many misunderstand 'Holy Spirit' is an impersonal force. However, 'Holy Spirit' is indeed a divine person because he possesses a mind, emotions, and a will. He thinks and knows (1 Corinthians 2:10). He also grieves (Ephesians 4:30). He intercedes for us (Romans 8:26-27). He makes decisions according to his will (1 Corinthians 12:7-11).

Ruach (רוּח in Hebrew) means spirit, breath, or wind. The first mention of *Ruach* in the Bible is the first chapter of Genesis. What the Spirit of the Lord did was hovering over the waters in the midst of chaos before creation.

And the earth was a formless and desolate emptiness,
and darkness was over the surface of the deep,
and the Spirit (Ruach) of God
was hovering over the surface of the waters.

Genesis 1:2; NIV

From the Bible, we can clearly see that the Holy Spirit -the Spirit of God- was involved in creation. He brought order out of chaos (Genesis 1:2) and gave life to mankind (Genesis 2:7).

He empowered people to do the works such as Artisan Bezalel (Exodus 31:1-5), Judge Samson (Judges 15:14), Prophet Isaiah (Isaiah 61:1-3), etc. Here I would like to introduce a concept of 'anointing' to understand the Holy Spirit's empowering. I won't go into details but in modern days, it is widely understood as an outpouring of God's power to accomplish divine assignments. A person can use his or her spiritual gift to a 'higher degree' by anointing. For further study on this, I recommend you to read an excellent book, *Claim Your Anointing* by Julia C. Loren.

When Jesus was baptised by John in the Jordan River, Holy Spirit came upon him like a dove.

As soon as Jesus was baptised,
he went up out of the water.
At that moment heaven was opened,
and he saw the Spirit of God descending
like a dove and alighting on him.

Matthew 3:16; NIV

Jesus himself described 'Holy Spirit' as the comforter (John 14:26), the guider (John 16:13) and the advocate or the teacher (John 14:26). Furthermore, he told his disciples to wait for the gift promised by the Father (Luke 24:49).

I assume that you have heard enough of him. Now is your turn to taste him. The more you get close to him, the more you know him. The more you know him, the more you love him.

Checkpoint #8

'...you will receive power when the Holy Spirit comes on you'

(Acts 1:8a)

Why don't you diligently study on the Holy Spirit who imparts spiritual life to us?

What Does The Holy Spirit Do?

The Holy Spirit does everything. Yes! He gives us power (Acts 1:8). He convicts us of sin, righteousness, and judgement (John 16:8-11). He is our intercessor and helps in our weakness and helps us pray (Romans 8:26-27). He seals in the lives of believers and enables us to understand God's word (Ephesians 1:13). He makes us new and grants us the eternal life (Romans 8:10-11).

He comforts us and counsels us to bear the fruit of the Spirit: love, joy, peace, forbearance, kindness, goodness, faithfulness, gentleness and self-control (Galatians 5:22-23).

He teaches and reminds us (John 14:26). He dwells in us and fills us (1 Corinthians 3:16). He guides to all truth and knowledge of what is to come (John 16:13-15).

He is the source of revelation, wisdom and power (1 Corinthians 2:10-11). He empowers and enables us to manifest various gifts: healing, prophecy, speaking tongues and interpretation, the word of knowledge, the word of wisdom, working of miracles, discerning of spirits, etc. He works these gifts in us for the profit of all (1 Corinthians 12:4-11).

Above all, the Holy Spirit makes us more like Jesus (2 Corinthians 3:18).

Checkpoint #9

The Spirit and the bride say, ‘Come!’

And let the one who hears say, ‘Come!’

Let the one who is thirsty come; and let the one who wishes take the free gift of the water of life.

(Revelation 22:17)

Father God, teach us always to have the thirst and hunger for the Holy Spirit.

How Can I Be Filled With The Holy Spirit?

The Bible commands us to be filled with the Holy Spirit (Ephesians 5:18). Being filled with the Holy Spirit is not optional but a command. It is not just one-time phenomenon but we must *continually* be filled with the Spirit.

Perhaps you may ask, 'why I must be filled with the Spirit?' The obvious reason is that when we walk in the Spirit, we will not fulfil the desires of the flesh such as sexual immorality, impurity, passion, evil desire, and covetousness, idolatry, etc. We can truly be lead by the Spirit in every situation. Also, we can be pure and holy by the Spirit. What God says in Leviticus 19:2 -you shall be holy, for I, the Lord your God, am holy- can be possible *only* by the Spirit. As we are lead by the Spirit, we can surrender to God's will without much difficulty. Also, we can walk not by sight but the power of the Spirit (Zechariah 4:6).

Let us think about 'how we can *continually* be filled with the Holy Spirit.'

I had opportunities to help many be filled with the Holy Spirit in the past. From my experiences, I definitely can say that the main hindrance blocking persons to be filled with the Holy Spirit was sin. It is just like this metaphor.

Imagine a cook has prepared a tasty food for you and is ready to serve. However, an issue he or she cannot give you the food is the unclean plate you offer. He or she would tell you that he or she cannot give you the food until you have a clean dish to take it. In this respect, knowing power of repentance is the first step to be filled with the Holy Spirit.

Another hindrance is lack of faith. As mentioned earlier, faith comes by hearing (Romans 10:17). It is a blessing to simply believe what you heard about the Spirit. There is no need to doubt or fear of the Spirit and what he does for us. Do you remember one of his attributes is to comfort (John 16:7)? In time of distresses, who can you turn to for comfort? Who comforts a crying baby? It will be a mother-like person who has a warm heart and a deep trust. I personally believe that the Spirit is just like that.

Here are four practical suggestions to stay *continually* filled with the Holy Spirit:

1. You can decide to walk in obedience to God every day. The Bible says that God freely gives the Holy Spirit to those who hear and obey Him (Acts 5:32). As a matter of fact, whether you obey or not depends on your attitude and determination. You can offer your life to God as a living sacrifice every day (Romans 12:1).

2. When you get up in the morning and later throughout your day, you can make a daily habit to ask the Father to fill you afresh with the Holy Spirit. As Luke 11:13 says, if imperfect parents know how to lovingly take care of their children and give them what they need, how much more the perfect Father in heaven will give the Holy Spirit's fullness when his children ask him. In

faith ask the Father to fill you, and by faith receive that infilling.

3. Wait on the Holy Spirit! It is quite challenging for an impatient culture to wait. Nevertheless, the Bible says we are to wait until we are empowered by the Holy Spirit (Luke 24:49). In *Waiting On God,* Andrew Murray describes why we need to wait on the Spirit. 'As you wait before God in holy silence, he sees it as a confession that you have nothing, no wisdom to pray aright, no strength to work aright. Waiting is the expression of need, of emptiness.'

4. Finally, receiving impartation from others who are full of the Holy Spirit is a good way. They may be people in your environment like your pastors or anointed, godly individuals in the church community where a move of God is taking place. 'Impartation' is a way by which God uses to transfer mantles of the anointing from one person to another. For instance, Prophet Elisha picked up the mantle and gained his master Elijah's power/anointing of miracle and prophecy. He immediately used the mantle to part the waters of the Jordan River and cross back over. The company of prophets recognized that Elisha was Elijah's successor as the Lord's leading prophet in the land (2 Kings 2:1-15).

All of us are made to manifest the glory of God and usher his presence. As we continue to desire more of God, honour the Holy Spirit, and surrender our hearts to him, there is no doubt that staying *continually* filled and overflowing in the Spirit will be a natural and everyday occurrence for us.

Checkpoint #10

'Do not get drunk on wine, which leads to debauchery. Instead, be filled with the Spirit.'

(Ephesians 5:18; NIV)

The more we live life to be filled by the Holy Spirit, the more we will hunger for God.

'O Holy Spirit, you are welcome here right now.

Come flood this place and fill the atmosphere with your glory.

O Holy Spirit, you are the one my heart longs for.

Come and overcome me by your mighty presence.'

How Can I Make The Most Of The Rest Of My Life?

> This means that anyone who belongs to Christ has become a new person. The old life is gone; a new life has begun!
>
> 2 Corinthians 5:17; NLT

I like springtime in the UK when the temperature starts to rise, and the daylight gets longer. The garden begins to burst forth with the spring flowers, and the tender green shoots appear on the trees and in the ground. I can feel the power of life after a severely cold and frosty winter season.

While looking out of the window at all the indications of new life, I am reminded of the miracle of being born-again through Jesus Christ. We have been born again into the Kingdom of God by his death. We also have received the gift of new life through his resurrection. Does your life, or mine, look as different from the old as spring does to winter?

Look at a daffodil and see its colourful bloom. Does it look anything like the bulb which it came from? Nope. We only can see its' transformed beauty. How about a yellow brimstone butterfly in early spring? Does it look anything like its' bluish-green caterpillar? Of course not! We only see its' utterly transformed beauty.

What do people see when they look at Christians?

We, *Christians* don't live in the past any more. The Holy Spirit dwells in us when we are born again. Therefore, we no longer live the life that we used to live in. We have the gift of the new life through Jesus Christ.

Nevertheless, we cannot deny our daily struggling as Apostle Paul experienced (Romans 7:13-20). Our perfect and transformed life won't happen overnight but it is continuously happening by the Holy Spirit. Have you heard that you look different after the born-again experience? It is a good sign of your new life. Yet, we still can see our old nature, which is the nature that we were born with, inclines towards sin in our daily life. In this regard, the scripture says about spiritual transformation by the renewing of our mind (Romans 12:2). What we feed our mind greatly affects us just like what we feed our bodies. So, when we feed our mind with the Holy Spirit, our thinking will be guided and determined by him so that we can live a transformed life.

This gives us a real comfort: the Holy Spirit works to fulfil God's destiny in us. For this, the scripture says, 'He has created us anew in Christ Jesus, so we can do the good things he planned for us long ago' (Ephesians 2:10; NLT). It implies that we became his children for fulfilling such destiny (Romans 8:14). On one hand it is obviously great news, yet we should remember that it can be done *only* by the Holy Spirit. If we are in the Holy Spirit, we are blessed because we know that we can fulfil our unique destiny with a help of the Holy Spirit. What a blessing to know the Holy Spirit personally and cooperate with him!

Checkpoint #11

'Behold I make all things new.'

(Revelation 21:5)

Declare this with me from your heart:

'I am no longer bound by sin. Indeed, I become a new creation in Christ and am able to please God and live in His ways. Fill me O God with your spirit and fill me again till I will find your heart. Make me new every day till I become more like you, Jesus.'

How Can I Resist Evil?

Most people agree that evil exists because of bad things happening around them and around the world. Interestingly, many atheists believe that too. In fact, nobody doubts that spiritual forces of evil that are at work in the world as we see wicked and terrible things are happening and bear pains and suffering as results.

One of my Alpha attendees raised a question: if God exists, then why does he allow evil? This is a common question raised when we hear disturbing instances in the news like child-rape, terrorist bombing and other alarming activities, etc. Wait, let us think in reverse: God doesn't exist; therefore, evil doesn't exist, does it? Apparently, Isaiah 45:7 says that the creator God allows both good and evil exist. Furthermore, Proverbs 16:4 says, 'The Lord has made everything for his own purposes, even the wicked for a day of disaster.' Seemingly, to the Creator there is an obvious reason for the existence of evil.

As a part of Religious Education assignment at school, my teenage daughter asked me to help her debate on 'God doesn't exist if he allows evil and suffering in the world.' I believe that her argument was pretty good. It goes something like this: first of all, evil shows us that we are but beasts without God. Secondly, we witness how terrible evil is so that we can see God's love on the other hand. Thirdly, we don't see God visually but when we love others, then people can see him through us. Ironically, people would have a harder time understanding the love of God without the obvious evil and hatred of his enemy.

The Bible clearly tells us that the ultimate goal of the devil is to destroy us (John 10:10) because we are created in the image of God whom he hates. In order to fulfil his goal, he uses his tactics of *doubt*, *temptation*, *deception* and *condemnation* as we learnt during the Alpha course.

Have you noticed that sin always begins with a small thing?

In the Garden of Eden, the ancient serpent (Satan, שטן) came to the first man and woman Adam and Eve whom God created. He tempted them to rebel against the creator. Both of them fell into temptation. They ate from the tree of the knowledge of good and evil, which God told them not to eat from. Thus, sin came into the world legally. 'Therefore, just as sin came into the world through one man, and death through sin, and so death spread to all men because all sinned' (Romans 5:12; ESV).

Who could imagine that eating the forbidden fruit caused *death* to come into the world and passed down from generations to generations?

Do you remember what sins the King David of Israel committed?

> One evening in Jerusalem, David was walking on his house rooftop after taking a nap. He spotted a beautiful woman bathing nearby. He asked his servants about her and was told she was Bathsheba, the wife of Uriah the Hittite, one of his mighty men. Despite her marital status, David

> summoned her to the palace, and then they slept together. Bathsheba later discovered that she was pregnant, and informed David about it.

Take a note of what David's immediate reaction was here: he was to attempt to hide his sin.

> He commanded Uriah to report back to him from the battlefield. He answered David's summons. David sent him home, hoping that he would sleep with his wife and thus provide a cover for the pregnancy. Instead of obeying David's orders, Uriah slept in the quarters of the palace servants. He did the same thing the next night as well. Finally, David commanded his military general, Joab, to place Uriah on the front lines of battle and then purposefully to fall back from him, leaving Uriah exposed to enemy's attack. Joab followed the king's directive, and Uriah was killed in battle.

Apparently, King David committed all sins above not during his wartime. David should have kept on his toes, shouldn't he? 'Stay alert! Watch out for your great enemy, the devil. He prowls around like a roaring lion, looking for someone to devour' (1 Peter 5:8; NIV).

The Bible tells us that we can overcome evil. 'Do not be overcome by evil, but overcome evil with good' (Romans 12:21; NIV).

Let us look at two outstanding characters in the Bible who triumphantly overcame evil.

Jesus was tempted by the devil in the three areas where *all* human beings can easily fall into. The first temptation concerns *the lust of the flesh* (Matthew 4:3-4). Jesus was very hungry after 40 days' fasting in the wilderness. The devil tempted him to convert stones into bread, but Jesus overcame with the Word of God. '*It is written*, man does not live on bread alone but on every word that comes from the mouth of the Lord.' (Italics mine, Deuteronomy 8:3; NIV)

The second concerns *the pride of life* (Matthew 4:5-7). Here the cunning devil also quoted scriptures in the Bible, 'For he will give his angels charge concerning you to guard you in all your ways. They will bear you up in their hands, that you do not strike your foot against a stone' (Psalm 91:11-12; NIV). Jesus again replied with the word of God, '*It is also written*. Do not put the Lord your God to the test' (Italics mine, Deuteronomy 6:16; NIV).

The third concerns *the lust of the eyes*. The devil took Jesus to a very high mountain and showed him all the kingdoms of the world and their glory. He said to Jesus, 'All these things I will give you, if you fall down and worship me' (Matthew 4:8-10; NIV). For this, Jesus replied, 'Go, Satan! For *it is written* you shall worship the Lord your God and serve him only.' (Italics mine, Deuteronomy 6:13; NIV)

Jesus was tempted but overcame. How did he do that? He resisted every temptation with every word of God. Remember the beginning of his statements - *it is written!*

Do you remember how Joseph, the second-in-command in the land of Egypt resisted the coercive temptation?

The wife of his master Potiphar tried to seduce him to have sex with her twice. Yet, he refused to become a victim of sexual assault. How could he do that? *His attitude* is the answer. 'No one is greater in this house than I am. My master has withheld nothing from me except you, because you are his wife. How then could I do such a wicked thing and *sin against God*?' (Italics mine, Genesis 39:9; NIV)

Think about this honestly: what would you do when no one else is looking at you in your workplace? What would you do when you are sexually tempted but no one else is around you?, etc.

Well…your responses depend on your attitude in such situations, don't they? Perhaps a Latin phrase, *Coram Deo* will help you out in this respect. It literally means 'before the face of God' or 'in the presence of God.' Whenever you are tempted or are in such situations, remember that God is watching you and you are in his presence. *Coram Deo* defiantly helps you out not to sin against God like what Joseph did.

Checkpoint #12

O Lord, you have examined my heart and know everything about me. You know when I sit down or stand up. You know my thoughts even when I'm far away. You see me when I travel and when I rest at home. You know everything I do. You know what I am going to say even before I say it, Lord.

(Psalm 139:1-4)

Remember *Coram Deo* and practice it all the time and in all your ways so that you can resist evil.

Why And How Should I Tell Others?

> All authority in heaven and on earth has been given to me. Therefore go and make disciples of all nations, baptizing them in the name of the Father and of the Son and of the Holy Spirit, and teaching them to obey everything I have commanded you. And surely I am with you always, to the very end of the age.
>
> Matthew 28:18-20; NIV

The scriptures above are known as the Great Commission. Our Lord Jesus gave his final instructions to his followers: *going* to all nations and *making* his disciples afterwards. Why? God loved the world and gave his one and only Son Jesus so that *everyone* who believes in him will not perish but have the eternal life (John 3:16). It is good news for everyone, isn't it? We heard it first from someone else; therefore, we should tell others about the good news, shouldn't we? That's fair enough!

I met a lady who was serving as a table/group leader. She told me her story of 'how she came to the church.' Her neighbour constantly invited her to a Christmas carol service five times but she declined the invitation five times.

She couldn't refuse her sixth invitation and finally came to the church. She genuinely appreciated her neighbour's persistence over the years. I couldn't agree more!

In 2022, I conducted a small scale survey from groups of people who completed the Alpha course and/or continuously serve the Alpha course afterwards for a purpose of writing this book. The majority said that they heard about the Alpha course either from a friend or from the church's advertisement. I am not surprised that quite a lot of people came to the church because of their friends' invitation.

Now we know why, and then let us move to 'how can we tell others?' The best way to do this is to start with the group of people who you are very close to such as family, relatives and a circle of friends. They are the ones who know you very well. When they notice that you have changed, and then they might be curious about it and perhaps will ask you, 'what happened to you?' Of course, you need courage to speak out and also know 'what and how to say.'

The following is a practical way to share your faith with others.

- **Prepare yourself always**.

  First of all, consider praying for someone whom you are going to talk to and preparing yourself for a day of talking about your faith if you have planned it in advance. Especially, pray for a change. Prayer has power to change lives. Believe the power of prayer.

- **Prepare your story**.

Here is an example of Nicky Gumbel. Keep it short (about 3 minutes). Make it personal. Tell three things: (1) briefly *describing* your former life, (2) *talking* about how you could have a relationship with Jesus and (3) *mentioning* something of what it has meant since then. Write it out in full because it helps you structure your thoughts in order.

- **Prepare some probing questions to ask.**

It is helpful to transition from simple conversation into a discussion of faith with probing questions if you are confident. The following are good questions you may ask:

- Do you believe in an afterlife?
- What will happen when you die?
- If you die right now, are you sure that you'd go to heaven? Why?
- Do you feel that you fulfil your life goal?
- Do you ever feel like something is missing in your life?, etc.

- **Prepare Bible verses.**

- Jesus said to him, 'I am the way, and the truth, and the life. No one comes to the Father except through me.'
(John 14:6; ESV)

- Jesus said to them, 'I am the bread of life; whoever comes to me shall not hunger, and whoever believes in me shall never thirst.'
  (John 6:35; ESV)

- For the wages of sin is death, but the free gift of God is eternal life in Christ Jesus our Lord.
  (Romans 6:23; ESV)

- And this is the promise that he made to us eternal life.
  (1 John 2:25; ESV)

- I write these things to you who believe in the name of the Son of God, that you may know that you have eternal life.
  (1 John 5:13; ESV)

Here I have cited some scriptures related to the eternal life. Yet, you can ask the Holy Spirit for a specific verse(s) for the one whom you are going to talk about your faith on that day if you will have planned in advance. When you do this, you might experience something special which God would have for that person.

Finally, be a good listener so that you might have an opportunity to share your faith with others with a help of the Holy Spirit. While listening, we can ask the Holy Spirit about 'what specific things to do for them.' It depends on the situations which they hold on to, you can pray with them. Pray a simple but genuine prayer for them!

Checkpoint #13

Therefore go and make disciples of all nations.

(Matthew 28:19)

It is not optional but a command to obey. Get started to pray for the person who needs to hear the good news.

Does God Heal Today?

God never changes because he is the same yesterday and today and forever (Hebrews 13:8). He healed the sick in the past, so does he today. Exodus 15:26 says, 'I am the Lord who heals you.' This statement is true because he never lies. To heal or fix the creature is the creator's nature, isn't it? It is just like a potter who has the authority to break and mould the clay. God is a potter and we are the clay. Does it make sense?

When Jesus came to the world, what he mainly did was three things as below: (1) teaching at the synagogues, (2) proclaiming the good news of the kingdom, and (3) healing every disease and sickness among the people (Matthew 4:23).

Not only Jesus himself but also his twelve disciples cast out all demons and healed all diseases (Matthew 10:8). Of course, Jesus gave them power and authority before sending them out. In obedience they went out and then witnessed many healings.

I believe that God's desire for healing the sick is to use us as a channel to release his power. Imagine that when we turn on the switch, the light is on. We simply release the electricity to the bulb by touching the switch with our finger. We are not the one who generates the electricity but releases it to light. Remember our stance: God is the one who heals, and we are the ones who release his healing power. How simple it is!

How can we see healing? Please remember four things: pray, fast, believe and persevere.

How should we pray for healing? 'Your kingdom come, your will be done, on earth as it is in heaven' (Matthew 6:10; NIV). It is perfectly fine to pray like this because there is no pain in heaven (Revelation 21:4). Therefore, believe that healing is very natural when his kingdom comes and his will is done in the person's body as it is in heaven. Do it in faith!

I do have many stories to tell about healing the sick. This one is really nice to share:

> Mr D took the Alpha course a few years back. Obviously, his Alpha journey became his faith journey. He was a good man but sceptical in Christian faith in the beginning. Nevertheless, he kept coming along week by week. To my surprise, when we arrived at the session of faith, he was sure of being a Christian. During the week just before the session of healing, his elbow bone was broken when he and his wife were moving the sofa. His wife accidentally pushed the sofa while his arm was trapped between the sofa and the wall. I saw his fractured bones from the X-ray picture. Our Alpha team was running the online course at that time. This means that we had to trust 100 percent the Holy Spirit in terms of physical healing because we could not lay our hands on him. I instructed Mr D step by step. He simply but

> seriously followed all instructions given. Finally, he put his hand on his fractured elbow, and I prayed for healing at the end. When we finished the healing prayer, he was very hot and dripping in sweat. Of course the pain was gone!

Healing plays a powerful role in having an individual faith and in sharing the message of good news of the kingdom with unbelievers. I witnessed many occasions that when people got healed by prayer, they couldn't deny God's supernatural power but accepted him as their author and saviour of life.

If you haven't prayed for the sick yet, why don't you try to do that? The following is Nicky Gumbel's simple healing ministry model:

1. Ask where it hurts.
2. Lay hands on the person.
3. Ask the Holy Spirit to come.
4. Ask how are they doing/if they can feel anything different.
5. Sometimes you need to pray more than once.

The more you pray for the sick, the more confident you become. Once you build some degree of confidence in healing prayer, you can exercise 'words of knowledge.' It is a gift of the Holy Spirit which provides information to someone about the condition of another person by supernatural knowledge (1 Corinthians 12:8). In many ways it is an excellent God-given ability to build up the body of Christ. Particularly, it is very powerful in healing ministry because it increases your faith by knowing that God definitely heals that person whom you are going to pray for.

Also, it touches the person's heart by knowing that God personally cares for him or her.

Here I can share my experience related to 'words of knowledge.'

> I met Mr A some years ago. At that time he had an issue of DDD (Degenerative Disc Disease) and constantly suffered from back pain caused by worn-down vertebral discs. He couldn't lift up things and even his young son for many years. While listening to his background story, the Holy Spirit gave me the words of knowledge to stop certain ages on his life timeline. To my surprise, all the ages mentioned were significant in dealing with his life issues in the past. You can guess that once all his life issues were dealt with, and then he got healed afterwards.

In general, 'words of knowledge' can be manifested by a vision, pictures, dreams, impressions, sympathy pain (feeling pain in particular part of your body even though you haven't had the pain before) and hearing or seeing words.

Checkpoint #14

'God sent out his word and healed them, snatching them from the door of death.'

(Psalm 107:20; NLT)

God promises us to heal the sick because of his mercy and compassion. When you pray for the sick, remember that you are partnering with the Holy Spirit who gives us power/anointing for healing.

What About The Church?

According to sociologists, human beings are social by nature. Thus, individuals tend to live in communities with other people related by ethnicity, nationality, religion, or some other cultural element.

In a Christian circle, you often hear the word 'church.' To understand its broad meaning is very important because it is more than just a building for Christian services as many usually misunderstand.

A Greek word, *ecclesia* (ἐκκλησία in Greek, gathering of those summoned) means 'church' in modern times. It was originally applied in the classical period to an official assembly of citizens. In the Old Testament, *ecclesia* was used for the general assembly of the Jewish people, especially when they gathered for hearing the Torah (תורה, the substance of divine revelations from God for the Jewish people which is often restricted to signify the first five books of the Hebrew Bible).

In the New Testament, it was used for the entire body of believers throughout the world or the believers in particular areas or the congregational meeting in a 'house-church.'

Apparently, the institution of church is originally God's idea. 'I will build my church, and the gates of hell shall not prevail against it' (Matthew 16:18; ESV). Not only the New Testament time but also in the Old Testament time,

God instructed Moses to build a *tabernacle* - a portable tent representing the presence of God in the middle of his people. The tabernacle was the place where God commanded the people of Israel to carry out the animal sacrifices and to celebrate the appointed festivals throughout the year. In the tabernacle, the people of Israel made joyful noises and sounds of worship and praises.

From time to time I met some folks who were hurt and disappointed by others in the church community. They gave up connecting with 'church' due to the hurts and disappointments they got in the past. Have you heard of 'forgiven sinners'? The church is a gathering of a bunch of people who are forgiven sinners by God's mercy. It means that nobody in the church community is perfect and free from sinning. By God's grace we become what we are.

In fact, we should connect with 'church' because we are the body of Jesus Christ (1 Corinthians 12:27). Like a branch that grows because of its connection to the tree, we can thrive when we stay connected to the church and also bear the fruit of the Holy Spirit.

Moreover, there are many things we can do together in and with the church. For instances, we are to love one another (Romans 13:8), forgive one another (Ephesians 4:32), encourage one another (1 Thessalonians 4:18), and pray for one another (James 5:16). We can also find older, godly mentors (Titus 2:1-8), and have fellowship (dynamic relationship) with one another (1 John 1:7). The church is the place for effective evangelism, outreach, and global missions to take place which only we can do *together*.

One of powerful examples of the 'church together' can be found in the book of Joshua.

> Joshua led the people of Israel to the land of Canaan God promised. They first crossed the Jordan River and were instructed to conquer the land by God. Jericho was the first city to take down. It was a great city with false gods. Joshua was instructed to silently march around the walled city once a day for six days. On the seventh day the people of Israel marched around the city seven times. The Ark of the Covenant went first followed by seven priests, holding seven shofars (שופרות in Hebrew; ram's horns). As they marched, the priests were to blow the shofars. On the seventh around, they were to blow one long blast in unison, and the people were to give a great shout for God. The great walls of Jericho fell down to the ground at the sounds of shofars and shouts.

God instructed this 'Jericho mission' to fulfil his plan. It obviously shows that only the whole congregation could do it together.

> … We will grow to become in every respect the mature body of him who is the head, that is, Christ. From him the whole body, joined and held together by every supporting ligament, grows and builds itself up in love, as each part does its work.
>
> Ephesians 4:15-16; NIV

The church is often called the ‘body of Christ’ because Christ is the head of the church, and we are called to do the work of Christ, each like members of a body. ‘Body of Christ’ is a significant term to understand the church. We have different skills, purposes, and spiritual gifts, yet every believer is equally important to fulfil the great commission together. Take note: this term acknowledges diversity within the body of Christ. Certainly, the body needs many parts to function properly. Each of us can contribute to God’s missions with our various gifts.

Checkpoint #15

Suppose the foot says, 'I am not a hand. So I don't belong to the body.' By saying this, it cannot stop being part of the body.

And suppose the ear says, 'I am not an eye. So I don't belong to the body.' By saying this, it cannot stop being part of the body.

If the whole body were an eye, how could it hear? If the whole body were an ear, how could it smell? God has placed each part in the body just as he wanted it to be. If all the parts were the same, how could there be a body? As it is, there are many parts. But there is only one body.

The eye can't say to the hand, 'I don't need you!' The head can't say to the feet, 'I don't need you!'

...You are the body of Christ. Each one of you is a part of it.

(1 Corinthians 12:15-21 and 27; NIV)

Recommended Reading

During the Alpha course, you might be occupied with many things so that perhaps you could not have enough time to look at good resources available. Now is the time for you to relax, focus, and explore particular themes.

Most of the books listed below are mainly recommended by *Alpha International* and by me depending on themes. They are listed by theme so that you can easily choose books to explore more of what you would like to know further.

The survey mentioned earlier shows that reading Christian books is one element to grow and stay strong in their Christian faith after the Alpha course. For instance, you can deepen and widen your knowledge on 'grace' by reading Philip Yancey's book, *What's So Amazing About Grace?* In order to tell others about Jesus' resurrection in great detail, read Frank Morison's book, *Who Moved the Stone?* To be continuously filled with the Holy Spirit, read Andrew Murray's *Waiting On God*, and so on.

Try to keep feeding yourself continuously with the Word of God and good Christian books and audio books recommended by godly people. I do hope that you can benefit from the books below and stay strong in faith and grow in faith.

- **Is there more to life than this?**
  What's So Amazing About Grace? Philip Yancey

- **Who is Jesus?**
  Mere Christianity. C.S. Lewis
  Jesus Is. Judah Smith

- **Why did Jesus die?**
  The Cross of Christ. John Stott
  Searching Issues. Nicky Gumbel
  Mud, Sweat and Tears. Bear Grylls
  Who Moved the Stone? Frank Morison

- **How can I have faith?**
  The Reasons for God. Tim Keller
  Life Change. Mark Elsdon-Dew

- **Why and how do I pray?**
  God on Mute. Peter Greig
  Prayer. Philip Yancey
  My Book For You, Friend. Hana Ibberson

- **Why and how should I read the Bible?**
  Why Trust the Bible? Amy Orr-Ewing
  30 Days. Nicky Gumbel

- **How does God guide us?**
  Chasing the Dragon. Jackie Pullinger
  The Hiding Place. Corrie ten Boom

- **Who is the Holy Spirit?**
  Come, Creator Spirit. Raniero Cantalamessa

Claim Your Anointing. Julia C. Loren.

- **What does the Holy Spirit do?**
  The God Who Changes Lives. Vol.1, 2, 3 & 4 ed. M. Elsdon-Dew

- **How can I be filled with the Holy Spirit?**
  The Mystery of Pentecost. Raniero Cantalamessa
  Sober Intoxication of the Spirit: Filled With the Fullness of God. Raniero Cantalamessa
  Waiting On God. Andrew Murray

- **How can I make the most of the rest of my life?**
  The Jesus Lifestyle. Nicky Gumbel
  Life in Christ. Raniero Cantalamessa

- **How can I resist evil?**
  The Screwtape Letters. C.S. Lewis
  Café Theology. Mike Lloyd

- **Why and how should I tell others?**
  Searching Issues. Nicky Gumbel
  Lord...Help My Unbelief. John Young and David Wilkinson

- **Does God heal today?**
  Power Evangelism. John Wimber
  Dirty Glory. Peter Greig

- **What about the church?**
  Questions of Life. Nicky Gumbel

To The Table/Group Leader

This part has been designated for those who are serving or potentially will serve others in the future on the Alpha course. Yes, freely you have received so that it is right freely to give to others (Matthew 10:8).

Have you heard of 'teaching someone else is the best way to learn?' Research shows that children can teach younger kids even though they are still learning themselves. For instance, first-born children are more intelligent than their later-born siblings because they spend more time to show their younger siblings the ropes.

I met a beautiful couple who had served the Alpha course over the decades since they had their own Alpha for the first time. Needless to say, they once encountered Jesus during the course and since then their life was absolutely transformed, even quitting smoking. I believe that this is a true beauty of the Alpha course because its main purpose is to help others encounter Jesus.

> After my skin has been destroyed, yet in my flesh I will see God; I will see him for myself. Yes, I will see him with my own eyes. I am overwhelmed at the thought!

Job 19:26-27; NIV

Carefully look at what Job declared here. After he came out from all afflictions he had gone through, he became to *know God* rather than what he *knew about God* before. In other words, his head knowledge of God became his experiential knowledge of him. During the Alpha, your role as a table/group leader is to help the attendees experience this.

Let us recall your experiences with the Alpha course. Do you remember 'what and who' helped you finish your Alpha journey? What made your life change? To whom did you owe a great deal for that change? All of these questions enable you to be who you are now. Now is your turn to do the same for others.

Jesus walked beside the Sea of Galilee and saw Simon Peter and his brother Andrew casting a net into the lake. They were once his disciples but went back to their own occupation, *fishermen* after Jesus' death. When Jesus saw them again, he reassured them that he will make them fishers of men rather than fishers of the fish. The reason Jesus said so is that they knew how to catch the fish. In the same way they could catch men as well.

According to fish mania, selecting a fishing spot (where) and choosing fishing gear (how) are important to catch the fish. In the same way, you need to know 'where' and 'how' to fish if you are happy to be a fisher of men. In this sense,

I believe that the Alpha course is a good place to fish. While serving on Alpha, you can learn how to fish.

The following are some helpful advices which you can take in and consider using them in the near future:

1. Remember the Holy Spirit is the source of your ability and power to serve.

2. Attitude is not behaviour; it is the thinking that creates behaviour.

3. Have a humble servanthood. Not only did Jesus serve others, but he told us to do the same.

4. Put yourself in someone's shoes. Think everything from their perspective by humbling yourself and putting his or her needs before your own.

5. When the Alpha course is on, pray for everyone in your table/group. For instance, set a reminder alarm notification to pray for them every day. Ask the Holy Spirit about specific words for anyone in your table/group.

6. Ask intercessors in your life/cell/house group to pray for the Alpha course regularly while it is on.

7. Show everyone (in your table/group) you care. For instance, text them personal messages or your concerns for them. Ask them about any prayer requests. Pray with them if needed, etc.

8. Be ready to go the extra mile. For instance, if someone struggles with money, try connecting him or her with financial experts and professional service (e.g. CAP-Christians Against Poverty). If someone begins to speak in tongues during the Alpha, help him or her out until he or she becomes confident in speaking tongues alone.

9. Be accountable to everyone in your table/group. For instance, check on their Bible reading, prayer time, etc. Talk about the next step or follow-up courses or resources continually to grow after the Alpha.

Let me close this part by talking about a humble servanthood a bit more. Jesus said that he came to the world not to be served but to serve others and to give his life as a ransom for many (Matthew 20:28). He was the perfect example of a humble servant whom we should follow. An incident shows his humble servanthood.

In the first century, people who lived in Israel must wash their feet before a communal meal since they walked in sandals on the filthy roads and had to recline at a low table. When Jesus rose from the table and began to wash the feet of the disciples, he was doing the work of the lowliest of servants of houses. After washing their feet, he told his disciples, 'I have given you an example to follow. Do as I have done to you' (John 13:15; NLT).

He as their lord and teacher served his disciple because he wanted to teach them to wash one another's feet by demonstrating his act of loving and serving them. Bearing in mind of importance of the humble servanthood, here are some practical things you can think and do:

- Be prayerful all the time.
- Be ready to keep learning.
- Be ready to seek accountability.
- Be open-minded to divergent views.
- Stop criticising others' weaknesses.
- Be an effective communicator by building rapport.
- Be more vulnerable by allowing others to see your authentic self. This often enables you to connect deeply with them.
- Be sensitive to others' needs.
- Help others discover God's plan for their lives.

Participants' Comments

It is quite good to reflect on people's thoughts about the Alpha course. On the one hand if we would hear their positive words, then we could be greatly encouraged, but on the other hand we could be challenged by taking their constructive criticisms for improvement after all.

According to the survey mentioned earlier, more than half of the people responded that the course met their expectations. Nevertheless, there are a couple of reasons that some were not fully satisfied with the course. One of them is its length. Seemingly, it is relatively long for non-believers so that they were overwhelmed when they missed one or two fundamental sessions. The other is a language barrier of people whose English is not the first language. So, they could neither actively engage in discussion nor fully understood all the things.

To my knowledge, *Alpha International* has worked hard to improve its course over the decades in relation to the language barrier by producing both multi-lingual subtitled films and brand new (contextualised) film in the vernacular (e.g. Alpha Next Gen series in Cantonese, targeting at students, young adults and the digital generation).

Here is what *The Guardian* mentioned about the Alpha course: ‘what Alpha offers, and what is attracting thousands of people, is permission, rare in secular culture, to discuss the big questions: life and death and their meaning.’

Time Magazine wrote, ‘The miracle formula church leaders are hoping will reverse this religious decline… many claim Alpha has changed their lives and appear genuinely happier for the experience.’

An evangelical Christian magazine, *Christianity Today* also stated, ‘Alpha has succeeded in many cases in turning faithful churchgoers from an inward focus on church work to an outward focus on evangelistic outreach.’

In addition, there are many amazing and life transforming stories which we can hear from different parts of the world. I have just picked up three stories (from Alpha International website at www.alpha.org).

Jayson as a young Catholic missionary in the Philippines has been serving communities in the remote areas of Barili, Cebu. He has to walk over two hours to reach this remote village to share the Gospel with those who need it most.

Tammy came to faith through an Alpha course in Canada and then led her husband, sister and brother-in-law to Jesus. She ended up pastoring the church where she first encountered Jesus and now is Pastor of Groundswell in Canada.

A lady called Red was invited by her friend to Redeemer King Church just before lockdown began in the UK. The church decided to run Alpha online despite the unpleasant situation at the time. Red was able to join the course from home. After the first week, she gave her life to Jesus. After the course, she said, 'I've been reading the Bible loads. I've never read it before. There's a lot of hope in there and I think I'm going to be all right.'

Here are some positive words from people's experiences at KingsGate Alpha (in Peterborough) as below:

'It's been a beautiful, great and wonderful experience.'

'I felt welcome and felt part of a family.'

'I have felt the love of Jesus and the dawning of a new realisation.'

'I felt really connected.'

'I loved hearing about peoples stories.'

'It was a positive experience to learn more about God.'

'I feel closer to God. I pray more and read the word of God more.'

'Now I have a better relationship with God.'

'It helped me to understand God a lot.'

'I experienced new feeling of the Holy Spirit.'

'It's been humbling and enriching.'

‘It helped me to have more faith in Jesus Christ.’

‘It's been a revelation.’

‘It is an eye-opening.’

‘It is informative, friendly, and encouraging.’

‘I loved to see all the miracles (healing session).’

‘I was most interested in learning more about the evidence of it all. It is revealing, but maybe not life-changing.’

‘We loved every session!’

‘It was good to meet new people.’

‘What a fun evening with our group, learning and sharing our thoughts! It has been great.’

‘I really enjoyed it.’

‘It was very practical. A must!’

‘It is a great experience whether new to faith or not.’

‘It is refreshing.’

‘Amazing, super enlightening and spirit filled experience.’

‘Informative, welcoming, enjoyable and thoughtful.’

‘Passing on knowledge, love, friendship and caring.’

‘Good and positive experience.’

‘Holy Spirit has been breathed into me.’

‘Good answers to my questions.’

‘Friendly, interesting, everyone so nice!’

‘My expectation for the course was to have a better relationship with God. I feel closer to him than before.’

‘The course ran well. I thoroughly enjoyed it.’

‘Great course! I highly recommend it.’

Postface

Someone says, 'if you want to walk fast, walk alone, but if you want to walk far, walk together.' We need each other for a long journey, don't we? -especially, it is a faith journey. Sometimes we as friends walk side by side, other times one behind the other, taking turns with the lead as one gets tired - being together to help each other. 'A person standing alone can be attacked and defeated, but two can stand back-to-back and conquer. Three are even better, for a triple-braided cord is not easily broken' (Ecclesiastes 4:12; NLT). Do you agree that we are meant to walk together and to give each other the strength and motivation to carry on our life (and faith) journey if needed?

One day a Pharisee (so-called an expert in the law) asked Jesus, 'what is the greatest commandment?' For that question, Jesus answered, 'Love the Lord your God with all your heart, with all your soul, and with all your mind. This is the greatest and most important commandment. The second is like it: Love your neighbour as yourself. On these two commandments depend all the Law and the Prophets' (Matthew 22:37-40; ESV).

In the beginning of the book, I mentioned the life-long question, 'what should I live for? Our life is meant to love God as well as our neighbour with our whole being as the scriptures above say. I often made a tongue-in-cheek remark, ‘When do I go to the heavenly home? Well…it will be the time when I will have finished learning to love God and my neighbour here on the earth.’ From my experiences I assure you that the Alpha is a really good place to practice loving your neighbour.

About The Author

Hana has lived in various countries and was involved in several missions in the past. She has a husband and a 14 year-old daughter. She studied in a wide range of academic disciplines in Pharmacy, Healing Ministry, Christian Counselling, Anthropology, Missiology, English Language Teaching, Linguistics, and Applied Linguistics. She and her family participated in *Celebration for the Nations* in Wales (2007-2014) and in Israel (2016-2017), and founded and ran *Celebration Colchester* for two years until they went to Mozambique to be part of 'Harvest School' (*Iris Global*) in June-October, 2015. From 2016 she and her husband are the co-founders of *Nehemiah 9.3 Mission* (www.nehemiah93.com) and also are actively involved in the Alpha course to help people encounter Jesus. She wrote other books, *Shofar-blowing: Sounds From Heaven To Earth*, *My Book For You, Friend* and *Celebration for the Nations and Beyond* (forthcoming book).

Printed in Great Britain
by Amazon

21838285R00056